It's amazing what you can use for a ramp, given the right motivation.

Someone's collapsed fence was blocking half the road, jutting up at an angle, and I hit it at about fifty miles an hour. The handlebars shuddered in my hands like the horns of a mechanical bull, and the shocks weren't doing much better. I didn't even have to check the road in front of us because the moaning started as soon as we came into view. They'd blocked our exit fairly well while Shaun played with his little friend, and mindless plague carriers or not, they had a better grasp of the local geography than we did. We still had one advantage: Zombies aren't good at predicting suicide charges. And if there's a better term for driving up the side of a hill at fifty miles an hour with the goal of actually achieving flight when you run out of "up," I don't think I want to hear it.

The front wheel rose smoothly and the back followed, sending us into the air with a jerk that looked effortless and was actually scarier than hell. I was screaming. Shaun was whooping with gleeful understanding. And then everything was in the hands of gravity, which has never had much love for the terminally stupid. We hung in the air for a heart-stopping moment, still shooting forward. At least I was fairly sure the impact would kill us.

Praise for
The Newsflesh Trilogy

Feed

"Gripping, thrilling, and brutal...A masterpiece of suspense with engaging, appealing characters who conduct a soul-shredding examination of what's true and what's reported." —*Publishers Weekly* (starred review)

"Intelligent and intense, a thinking-person's post-apocalyptic zombie thriller set in a fully realized future that is both fascinating and horrifying to behold." —John Joseph Adams

"I can't wait for the next book." —N. K. Jemisin

Deadline

"Intelligent and exciting...raises the bar for the genre." —*Telegraph*

"Campy and yet smart, horror with heart, a summer beach read that will stay in your head." —*RT Book Reviews*

"Deft cultural touches, intriguing science, and amped-up action will delight Grant's numerous fans." —*Publishers Weekly* (starred review)

Blackout

"Wry and entertaining." —*NPR Books*

"Brilliant...powerfully addictive." —*SFFWorld*

THE
RISING

By Mira Grant

Parasitology

Parasite

Symbiont

Chimera

Newsflesh

Feed

Deadline

Blackout

Feedback

Rise: A Newsflesh Collection

The Rising: The Complete Newsflesh Trilogy

Apocalypse Scenario #683: The Box (ebook novella)

Into the Drowning Deep

Writing as Seanan McGuire

Rosemary and Rue

A Local Habitation

An Artificial Night

Late Eclipses

One Salt Sea

Ashes of Honor

Chimes at Midnight

The Winter Long

Once Broken Faith

The Brightest Fell

Discount Armageddon

Midnight Blue-Light Special

Half-Off Ragnarok

Pocket Apocalypse

Chaos Choreography

Magic for Nothing

Tricks for Free

Sparrow Hill Road

Every Heart a Doorway

Down Among the Sticks and Bones

Beneath the Sugar Sky

THE
RISING

THE NEWSFLESH TRILOGY

MIRA
GRANT

www.orbitbooks.net

Omnibus copyright © 2019 by Seanan McGuire

Feed copyright © 2010 by Seanan McGuire; *Deadline* copyright © 2011 by Seanan McGuire; *Blackout* copyright © 2012 by Seanan McGuire
Excerpt from *Into the Drowning Deep* copyright © 2017 by Seanan McGuire

Author photograph by Beckett Gladney
Cover design by Lisa Marie Pompilio
Cover art by Arcangel and Crystal Ben
Cover copyright © 2019 by Hachette Book Group, Inc.

Orbit
Hachette Book Group
1290 Avenue of the Americas
New York, NY 10104
orbitbooks.net

First Omnibus Edition: February 2019

Orbit is an imprint of Hachette Book Group.
The Orbit name and logo are trademarks of Little, Brown Book Group Limited.

The publisher is not responsible for websites (or their content) that are not owned by the publisher.

The Hachette Speakers Bureau provides a wide range of authors for speaking events. To find out more, go to www.hachettespeakersbureau.com or call (866) 376-6591.

Library of Congress Control Number: 2018962103

ISBNs: 978-0-316-45145-1 (trade paperback), 978-0-316-45147-5 (ebook)

Printed in the United States of America

LSC-C

10 9 8 7 6 5 4 3 2 1

Contents

FEED

This book is gratefully dedicated to
Gian-Paolo Musumeci
and
Michael Ellis.

They each asked me a question.
This is my answer.

BOOK I

The Rising

You can't kill the truth.

—Georgia Mason

Nothing is impossible to kill. It's just that sometimes after you kill something, you have to keep shooting it until it stops moving. And that's really sort of neat when you stop to think about it.

—Shaun Mason

Everyone has someone on the Wall.

No matter how remote you may think you are from the events that changed the world during the brutal summer of 2014, you have some-one on the Wall. Maybe they're a cousin, maybe they're an old family friend, or maybe they're just somebody you saw on TV once, but they're yours. They belong to you. They died to make sure that you could sit in your safe little house behind your safe little walls, watching the words of one jaded twenty-two-year-old journalist go scrolling across your computer screen. Think about that for a moment. They *died* for you.

Now take a good look at the life you're living and tell me: Did they do the right thing?

—**From *Images May Disturb You*,
the blog of Georgia Mason, May 16, 2039**

One

Our story opens where countless stories have ended in the last twenty-six years: with an idiot—in this case, my brother Shaun—deciding it would be a good idea to go out and poke a zombie with a stick to see what happens. As if we didn't already know what happens when you mess with a zombie: The zombie turns around and bites you, and you become the thing you poked. This isn't a surprise. It hasn't been a surprise for more than twenty years, and if you want to get technical, it wasn't a surprise *then*.

When the infected first appeared—heralded by screams that the dead were rising and judgment day was at hand—they behaved just like the horror movies had been telling us for decades that they would behave. The only surprise was that this time, it was really happening.

There was no warning before the outbreaks began. One day, things were normal; the next, people who were supposedly dead were getting up and attacking anything that came into range. This was upsetting for everyone involved, except for the infected, who were past being upset about that sort of thing. The initial shock was followed by running and screaming, which eventually devolved into more infection and attacking, that being the way of things. So what do we have now, in this enlightened age twenty-six years after the Rising? We have idiots prodding zombies with sticks, which brings us full circle to my brother and why he probably won't live a long and fulfilling life.

"Hey, George, check this out!" he shouted, giving the zombie another poke in the chest with his hockey stick. The zombie gave a low moan, swiping at him ineffectually. It had obviously been in a state of full viral amplification for some time and didn't have the strength or physical dexterity left to knock the stick out of Shaun's hands. I'll give Shaun this much: He knows not to bother the fresh ones at close range. "We're playing patty-cake!"

"Stop antagonizing the locals and get back on the bike," I said, glaring from behind my sunglasses. His current buddy might be sick enough to be nearing its second, final death, but that didn't mean there wasn't a healthier pack roaming the area. Santa Cruz is zombie territory. You don't go there unless you're suicidal, stupid, or both. There are times when even I can't guess which of those options applies to Shaun.

"Can't talk right now! I'm busy making friends with the locals!"

"Shaun Phillip Mason, you get back on this bike *right now*, or I swear to God, I am going to drive away and leave you here."

Shaun looked around, eyes bright with sudden interest as he planted the end of his hockey stick at the center of the zombie's chest to keep it at a safe distance. "Really? You'd do that for me? Because 'My Sister Abandoned Me in Zombie Country Without a Vehicle' would make a great article."

"A posthumous one, maybe," I snapped. "Get back on the goddamn *bike!*"

"In a minute!" he said, laughing, and turned back toward his moaning friend.

In retrospect, that's when everything started going wrong.

The pack had probably been stalking us since before we hit the city limits, gathering reinforcements from all over the county as they approached. Packs of infected get smarter and more dangerous the larger they become. Groups of four or less are barely a threat unless they can corner you, but a pack of twenty or more stands a good chance of breaching any barrier the uninfected try to put up. You get enough of the infected together and they'll start displaying pack hunting techniques; they'll start using actual tactics. It's like the virus that's taken them over starts to reason when it gets enough hosts in the same place. It's scary as hell, and it's just about the worst nightmare of anyone who regularly goes into zombie territory— getting cornered by a large group that knows the land better than you do.

These zombies knew the land better than we did, and even the most malnourished and virus-ridden pack knows how to lay an ambush. A low moan echoed from all sides, and then they were shambling into the open, some moving with the slow lurch of the long infected, others moving at something close to a run. The runners led the pack, cutting off three of the remaining methods of escape before there was time to do more than stare. I looked at them and shuddered.

Fresh infected—really fresh ones—still look almost like the people that they used to be. Their faces show emotion, and they move with a jerkiness that could just mean they slept wrong the night before. It's harder to kill something that still looks like a person, and worst of all, the bastards are fast. The only thing more dangerous than a fresh zombie is a pack of them, and I counted at least eighteen before I realized that it didn't matter, and stopped bothering.

I grabbed my helmet and shoved it on without fastening the strap. If the bike went down, dying because my helmet didn't stay on would be one of the better options. I'd reanimate, but at least I wouldn't be aware of it. "Shaun!"

Shaun whipped around, staring at the emerging zombies. "Whoa."

Unfortunately for Shaun, the addition of that many zombies had turned his buddy from a stupid solo into part of a thinking mob. The zombie grabbed the hockey stick as soon as Shaun's attention was focused elsewhere, yanking it out of his hands. Shaun staggered forward and the zombie latched onto his cardigan, withered fingers locking down with deceptive strength. It hissed. I screamed, images of my inevitable future as an only child filling my mind.

"*Shaun!*" One bite and things would get a lot worse. There's not much worse than being cornered by a pack of zombies in downtown Santa Cruz. Losing Shaun would qualify.

The fact that my brother convinced me to take a dirt bike into zombie territory doesn't make me an idiot. I was wearing full off-road body armor, including a leather jacket with steel armor joints attached at the elbows and shoulders, a Kevlar vest, motorcycling pants with hip and knee protectors, and calf-high riding boots. It's bulky as hell, and I don't care, because once you factor in my gloves, my throat's the only target I present in the field.

Shaun, on the other hand, is a moron and had gone zombie baiting in nothing more defensive than a cardigan, a Kevlar vest, and cargo pants. He won't even wear goggles—he says they "spoil the effect." Unprotected mucous membranes can spoil a hell of a lot more than that, but I practically have to blackmail him to get him into the Kevlar. Goggles are a nonstarter.

There's one advantage to wearing a sweater in the field, no matter how idiotic I think it is: wool tears. Shaun ripped himself free and turned, running for the motorcycle with great speed, which is really the only effective weapon we have against the infected. Not even the fresh ones can keep up with an uninfected human over a short sprint. We have speed, and we have bullets. Everything else about this fight is in their favor.

"Shit, George, we've got company!" There was a perverse mixture of horror and delight in his tone. "Look at 'em all!"

"I'm *looking*! Now get on!"

I kicked us free as soon as he had his leg over the back of the bike and his arm around my waist. The bike leapt forward, tires bouncing and shuddering across the broken ground as I steered us into a wide curve. We needed to get out of there, or all the protective gear in the world wouldn't do us a damn bit of good. I might live if the zombies caught up with us, but my brother would be dragged into the mob. I gunned the throttle, praying that God had time to preserve the life of the clinically suicidal.

We hit the last open route out of the square at twenty miles an hour, still gathering speed. Whooping, Shaun locked one arm around my waist and twisted to face the zombies, waving and blowing kisses in their direction. If it were possible to enrage a mob of the infected, he'd have managed it. As it was, they just moaned and kept following, arms extended toward the promise of fresh meat.

The road was pitted from years of weather damage without maintenance. I fought to keep control as we bounced from pothole to pothole. *"Hold on, you idiot!"*

"I'm holding on!" Shaun called back, seeming happy as a clam and oblivious to the fact that people who don't follow proper safety procedures around zombies—like not winding up around zombies in the first place—tend to wind up in the obituaries.

"Hold on with both arms!" The moaning was only coming from three sides now, but it didn't mean anything; a pack this size was almost certainly smart enough to establish an ambush. I could be driving straight to the site of greatest concentration. They'd moan in the end, once we were right on top of them. No zombie can resist a good moan when dinner's at hand. The fact that I could hear them over the engine meant that there were too many, too close. If we were lucky, it wasn't already too late to get away.

Of course, if we were lucky, we wouldn't be getting chased by an army of zombies through the quarantine area that used to be downtown Santa Cruz. We'd be somewhere safer, like Bikini Atoll just before the bomb testing kicked off. Once you decide to ignore the hazard rating and the signs saying *Danger: Infection*, you're on your own.

Shaun grudgingly slid his other arm around my waist and linked his hands at the pit of my stomach, shouting, "Spoilsport," as he settled.

I snorted and hit the gas again, aiming for a nearby hill. When you're being chased by zombies, hills are either your best friends or your burial ground. The slope slows them down, which is great, unless you hit the peak and find out that you're surrounded, with nowhere left to run to.

Idiot or not, Shaun knows the rules about zombies and hills. He's not as dumb as he pretends to be, and he knows more about surviving zombie encounters than I do. His grip on my waist tightened, and for the first time, there was actual concern in his voice as he shouted, "George? What do you think you're doing?"

"Hold, on," I said. Then we were rolling up the hill, bringing more zombies stumbling out of their hiding places behind trash cans and in the spaces between the once-elegant beachfront houses that were now settling into a state of neglected decay.

Most of California was reclaimed after the Rising, but no one has ever managed to take back Santa Cruz. The geographical isolation that once made the town so desirable as a vacation spot pretty much damned it when the virus hit. Kellis-Amberlee may be unique in the way it interacts with the human body, but it behaves just like every other communicable disease known to man in at least one way: Put it on a school campus and it spreads like wildfire. U.C. Santa Cruz was a perfect breeding ground, and once all those perky co-eds became the shuffling infected, it was all over but the evacuation notices.

"Georgia, this is a hill!" he said with increasing urgency as the locals lunged toward the speeding bike. He was using my proper name; that was how I could tell he was worried. I'm only "Georgia" when he's unhappy.

"I got that." I hunched over to decrease wind resistance a few more precious degrees. Shaun mimicked the motion automatically, hunching down behind me.

"Why are we going *up* a hill?" he demanded. There was no way he'd be able to hear my answer over the combined roaring of the engine and the wind, but that's my brother, always willing to question that which won't talk back.

"Ever wonder how the Wright brothers felt?" I asked. The crest of the hill was in view. From the way the street vanished on the other side, it was probably a pretty steep drop. The moaning was coming from all sides now, so distorted by the wind that I had no real idea what we were driving into. Maybe it was a trap; maybe it wasn't. Either way, it was too late to find another path. We were committed, and for once, Shaun was the one sweating.

"Georgia!"

"Hold on!" Ten yards. The zombies kept closing, single-minded in their pursuit of what might be the first fresh meat some had seen in years. From the looks of most of them, the zombie problem in Santa Cruz was decaying faster than it was rebuilding itself. Sure, there were plenty of fresh ones—there are always fresh ones because there are always idiots who wander into quarantined zones, either willingly or by mistake, and the average hitchhiker doesn't get lucky where zombies are concerned—but we'll take the city back in another three generations. Just not today.

Five yards.

Zombies hunt by moving toward the sound of other zombies hunting. It's recursive, and that meant our friends at the base of the hill started for the peak when they heard the commotion. I was hoping so many of the locals had been cutting us off at ground level that they wouldn't have many bodies left to mount an offensive on the hill's far side. We weren't supposed to make it that far, after all; the only thing keeping us alive was the fact that we had a motorcycle and the zombies didn't.

I glimpsed the mob waiting for us as we reached the top. They were standing no more than three deep. Fifteen feet would see us clear.

Liftoff.

It's amazing what you can use for a ramp, given the right motivation. Someone's collapsed fence was blocking half the road, jutting up at an angle, and I hit it at about fifty miles an hour. The handlebars shuddered in my hands like the horns of a mechanical bull, and the shocks weren't doing much better. I didn't even have to check the road in front of us because the moaning started as soon as we came into view. They'd blocked our exit fairly well while Shaun played with his little friend, and mindless plague carriers or not, they had a better grasp of the local geography than we did. We still had one advantage: Zombies aren't good at predicting suicide charges. And if there's a better term for driving up the side of a hill at fifty miles an hour with the goal of actually achieving flight when you run out of "up," I don't think I want to hear it.

The front wheel rose smoothly and the back followed, sending us into the air with a jerk that looked effortless and was actually scarier than hell. I was screaming. Shaun was whooping with gleeful understanding. And then everything was in the hands of gravity, which has never had much love for the terminally stupid. We hung in the air for a heart-stopping moment, still shooting forward. At least I was fairly sure the impact would kill us.

The laws of physics and the hours of work I've put into constructing and maintaining my bike combined to let the universe, for once, show mercy. We soared over the zombies, coming down on one of the few remaining stretches of smooth road with a bone-bruising jerk that nearly ripped the handlebars out of my grip. The front wheel went light on impact, trying to rise up, and I screamed, half terrified, half furious with Shaun for getting us into this situation in the first place. The handlebars shuddered harder, almost wrenching my arms out of their sockets before I hit the gas and forced the wheel back down. I'd pay for this in the morning, and not just with the repair bills.

Not that it mattered. We were on level ground, we were upright, and there was no moaning ahead. I hit the gas harder as we sped toward the outskirts of town, with Shaun whooping and cheering behind me like a big suicidal freak.

"Asshole," I muttered, and drove on.

News is news and spin is spin, and when you introduce the second to the first, what you have isn't news anymore. Hey, presto, you've created opinion.

Don't get me wrong, opinion is powerful. Being able to be presented with differing opinions on the same issue is one of the glories of a free media, and it should make people stop and think. But a lot of people don't *want* to. They don't want to admit that whatever line being touted by their idol of the moment might not be unbiased and without ulterior motive. We've got people who claim Kellis-Amberlee was a plot by the Jews, the gays, the Middle East, even a branch of the Aryan Nation trying to achieve racial purity by killing the rest of us. Whoever orchestrated the creation and release of the virus masked their involvement with a conspiracy of Machiavellian proportions, and now they and their followers are sitting it out, peacefully immunized, waiting for the end of the world.

Pardon the expression, but I can smell the bullshit from here. Conspiracy? Cover up? I'm sure there are groups out there crazy enough to think killing thirty-two percent of the world's population in a single summer is a good idea—and remember, that's a conservative estimate, since we've never gotten accurate death tolls out of Africa, Asia, or parts of South America—but are any of them nuts enough to do it by turning what used to be Grandma loose to chew on people at random? Zombies don't respect conspiracy. Conspiracy is for the living.

This piece is opinion. Take it as you will. But get your opinions the hell away from my news.

—From *Images May Disturb You,*
the blog of Georgia Mason, September 3, 2039

———

Zombies are pretty harmless as long as you treat them with respect. Some people say you should pity the zombie, empathize with the zombie, but I think they? Are likely to *become* the zombie, if you get my meaning. Don't feel sorry for the zombie. The zombie's not going to feel sorry for you when he starts gnawing on your head. Sorry, dude, but not even my sister gets to know me that well.

If you want to deal with zombies, stay away from the teeth, don't let them scratch you, keep your hair short, and don't wear loose clothes. It's that simple. Making it more complicated would be boring, and who wants that? We have what basically amounts to walking corpses, dude.

Don't suck all the fun out of it.

—From *Hail to the King*,
the blog of Shaun Mason, January 2, 2039

Two

Neither of us spoke as we drove through the remains of Santa Cruz. There were no signs of movement, and the buildings were getting widely spaced enough that visual tracking was at least partially reliable. I started to relax as I took the first exit onto Highway 1, heading south. From there, we could cut over to Highway 152, which would take us into Watsonville, where we'd left the van.

Watsonville is another of Northern California's "lost towns." It was surrendered to the infected after the summer of 2014, but it's safer than Santa Cruz, largely due to its geographical proximity to Gilroy, which is still a protected farming community. This means that while no one's willing to live in Watsonville for fear that the zombies will shamble down from Santa Cruz in the middle of the night, the good people of Gilroy aren't willing to let the infected have it either. They go in three times a year with flamethrowers and machine guns and clean the place out. That keeps Watsonville deserted, and lets the California farmers continue to feed the population.

I pulled off to the side of the road outside the ruins of a small town called Aptos, near the Highway 1 onramp. There was flat ground in all directions, giving us an adequate line of sight on anything that might be looking for a snack. My bike was running rough enough that I wanted to get a good look at it, and adding more gas probably wouldn't hurt. Dirt bikes have small tanks, and we'd covered a lot of miles already.

Shaun turned toward me as he dismounted, grinning from ear to ear. The wind had raked his hair into a series of irregular spikes and snarls, making him look like he'd been possessed. "That," he said, with almost religious fervor, "was the coolest thing you have ever done. In fact, that may have been the coolest thing you ever *will* do. Your entire existence has been moving toward one shining moment, George, and that was the moment when you thought, 'Hey, why don't I just go *over* the zombies?'" He paused for effect. "You are possibly cooler than God."

"Yet another chance to be free of you, down the drain." I hopped off the bike and pulled off my helmet, starting to assess the most obvious problems. They looked minor, but I still intended to get them looked at as soon as possible. Some damage was beyond my admittedly limited mechanical capabilities, and I was sure I'd managed to cause most of it.

"You'll get another one."

"That's the hope that keeps me going." I balanced my helmet against the windscreen before unzipping the right saddlebag and removing the gas can. Setting the can on the ground, I pulled out the first-aid kit. "Blood test time."

"George—"

"You know the rules. We've been in the field, and we don't go back to base until we've checked our virus levels." I extracted two small handheld testing units, holding one out to him. "No levels, no van. No van, no coffee. No coffee, no joy. Do you want the joy, Shaun, or would you rather stand out here and argue with me about whether you're going to let me test your blood?"

"You're burning cool by the minute here," he grumbled, and took the unit.

"I'm okay with that," I said. "Now let's see if I'll live."

Moving with synchronicity born of long practice, we broke the biohazard seals and popped the plastic lids off our testing units, exposing the sterile metal pressure pads. Basic field test units only work once, but they're cheap and necessary. You need to know if someone's gone into viral amplification—preferably before they start chewing on your tasty flesh.

I unsnapped my right glove and peeled it off, shoving it into my pocket. "On three?"

"On three," Shaun agreed.

"One."

"Two."

We both reached out and slid our index fingers into the unit in the other's hand. Call it a quirk. Also call it an early-warning system. If either of us ever waits for "three," something's very wrong.

The metal was cool against my finger as I depressed the pressure pad, a soothing sensation followed by the sting of the test's embedded needle breaking my skin. Diabetes tests don't hurt; they want you to keep using them, and comfort makes a difference. Kellis-Amberlee blood testing units hurt on purpose. Lack of sensitivity to pain is an early sign of viral amplification.

The LEDs on top of the box turned on, one red, one green, beginning to flash in an alternating pattern. The flashing slowed and finally stopped as the red light went out, leaving the green. Still clean. I glanced at the test I was holding and let out a slow breath as I saw that Shaun's unit had also stabilized on green.

"Guess I don't get to clean your room out just yet," I said.

"Maybe next time," he said. I passed him back his test, letting him handle the storage while I refilled the gas tank. He did so with admirable efficiency, snapping the plastic covers back onto the testing units and triggering the internal bleach dispensers before pulling a biohazard bag out of the first-aid kit and dropping the units in. The top of the bag turned red when he sealed it, the plastic melting itself closed. That bag was triple-reinforced, and it would take a Herculean effort to open it now that it was shut. Even so, he checked the seal and the seams of the bag before securing it in the saddlebag's biohazardous materials compartment.

While he was busy with containment, I tipped the contents of the gas can into the tank. I'd been running close enough to empty that the can drained completely, which was scary. If we'd run out of gas during the chase…

Best not to think about it. I put the gas cap back on and shoved the empty can into the saddlebag. Shaun was starting to climb onto the back of the bike. I turned toward him, raising a warning finger. "What are we forgetting?"

He paused. "Uh…to go back to Santa Cruz for postcards?"

"Helmet."

"We're on a flat stretch of road in the middle of nowhere. We're not going to have an accident."

"Helmet."

"You didn't make me wear a helmet before."

"We were being chased by zombies before. Since there are no zombies now, you'll wear a helmet. Or you'll walk the rest of the way to Watsonville."

Rolling his eyes, Shaun unstrapped his helmet from the left-hand saddlebag and crammed it over his head. "Happy now?" he asked, voice muffled by the face shield.

"Ecstatic." I put my own helmet back on. "Let's go."

The roads were clean the rest of the way to Watsonville. We didn't see any other vehicles, which wasn't surprising. More important, we didn't see any of the infected. Call me dull, but I'd seen enough zombies for one day.

Our van was parked at the edge of town, a good twenty yards from any standing structures. Standard safety precautions; lack of cover makes it harder for things to sneak up on you. I pulled up in front of it and cut the engine. Shaun didn't wait for the bike to come to a complete stop before he was leaping down and bounding for the door, yanking his helmet off as he shouted, "Buffy! How's the footage?"

Ah, the enthusiasm of the young. Not that I'm much older than he is—neither of us came with an original birth certificate when we were adopted, but the doctors estimated me as being at least three weeks ahead of him. From the way he acts sometimes, you'd think it was a matter of years, not just an accident of birth order. I removed my helmet and gloves and slung them over the handlebars, before following at a more sedate pace.

The inside of our van is a testament to what you can do with a lot of time, a reasonable amount of money, and three years of night classes in electronics. And help from the Internet, of course; we'd never have figured out the wiring without people chiming in from places ranging from Oregon to Australia. Mom did the structural reinforcements and security upgrades, supposedly as a favor, but really to give her an excuse to try building back doors into our systems. Buffy disabled them all as quickly as they were installed. That hasn't stopped Mom from trying.

After five years of work, we've managed to convert a mostly gutted Channel 7 news van into a state-of-the-art traveling blog center, with camera feeds, its own wireless tower, a self-sustaining homing device, and so many backup storage arrays that it makes my head hurt when I think about them too hard. So I don't think about them at all. That's Buffy's job, along with being the perkiest, blondest, outwardly flakiest member of the team. And she does all four parts of her job very, very well.

Buffy herself was cross-legged in one of the three chairs crammed into the van's remaining floor space, looking thoughtful as she held a headset up to one ear. Shaun was standing behind her, nearly jigging up and down in his excitement.

She didn't seem to register my presence as I stepped into the van, but spoke as soon as the door was closed, saying, "Hey, Georgia," in a dreamy, detached tone.

"Hey, Buffy," I said, heading for the minifridge and pulling out a can of Coke. Shaun takes his caffeine hot, and I take mine cold. Call it our way of rebelling against similarity. "How're we looking?"

Buffy flashed a quick thumbs-up, actually animated for a moment. "We're looking good."

"That's what I like to hear," I said.

Buffy's real name is Georgette Meissonier. Like Shaun and me, she was born after the zombies became a fact of life, during the period when Georgia, Georgette, and Barbara were the three most common girl's names in America. We are the Jennifers of our generation. Most of us just rolled over and took it. After all, George Romero *is* considered one of the accidental saviors of the human race, and it's not like being named after him is uncool. It's just, well, common. And Buffy has never been willing to be common when she can help it.

She was all cool professionalism when Shaun and I found her at an online job fair. That lasted about five minutes after we met in person. She introduced herself, then grinned and said, "I'm cute, blonde, and living in a world full of zombies. What do *you* think I should call myself?"

We looked at her blankly. She muttered something about a pre-Rising TV show and let it drop. Not that it matters, since as far as I'm concerned, as long as she keeps our equipment in working order, she can call herself whatever she damn well wants. Plus, having her on the team grants us an air of the exotic: She was born in Alaska, the last, lost frontier. Her family moved after the government declared the state impossible to secure and ceded it to the infected.

"Got it," she announced, disconnecting the headset and leaning over to flick on the nearest video feedback screen. The image of Shaun holding back his decaying pal with the hockey stick flickered into view. No sound came from the van's main speakers. A single moan can attract zombies from a mile away if you're unlucky with your acoustics, and it's not safe to soundproof in the field. Soundproofing works both ways, and zombies tend to surround structures on the off chance they might contain things to eat or infect. Opening the van doors to find ourselves surrounded by a pack we didn't hear coming didn't particularly appeal to any of us.

"The image is a little fuzzy, but I've filtered out most of the visual artifacts, and I can clean it further once I've had the chance to hit the source files. Georgia, thanks for remembering to put your helmet on before you started driving. The front-mount camera worked like a charm."

To be honest, I hadn't remembered that the camera was there. I'd been too focused on not cracking my skull open. Still, I nodded agreeably, taking a long drink of Coke before saying, "No problem. How many of the cameras kept feeding through the chase?"

"Three of the four. Shaun's helmet didn't come on until you were almost here."

"Shaun didn't have time to put on his helmet, or he would have ceased to have a head," Shaun protested.

"Shaun needs to stop talking about himself in the third person," Buffy said, and hit a button on her keyboard. The image was replaced by a close-up shot of the flickering lights on our blood tests. "I want to screen-shot this for the main site. What do you think?"

"Whatever you say," I said. The screen broadcasting our main external security camera was showing an abandoned, undisturbed landscape. Nothing moved in Watsonville. "You know I don't care about the graphics."

"And that's why your ratings aren't higher, George," said Shaun. "I like the lights. Use them as a slow fade in tonight's teaser, too—tack on something about, I don't know, how close is too close, that whole old saw."

"'Close Encounters on the Edge of the Grave,'" I murmured, moving toward the screen. It was a little too unmoving out there. Maybe I was being paranoid, but I've learned to pay attention to my instincts. God knows Shaun and Buffy weren't paying attention to anything but tomorrow's headlines.

Shaun grinned. "I like it. Grayscale the image except for the lights and use that."

"On it." Buffy typed a quick note before shutting down the screen. "Have we got any more big plans for the afternoon, folks?"

"Getting out of here," I said, turning back to the others. "I'm on the bike. I'll take point, but we need to get back to civilization."

Buffy blinked at me, looking baffled. She's a Fictional; her style of blogging is totally self-contained, and she only sees the field when Shaun and I haul her out to work our equipment. Even then, she pretty much never leaves the van. It's not her job to pay attention to anything that doesn't live on a computer screen.

Shaun, on the other hand, sobered immediately. "Why?"

"There's nothing moving out there." I opened the back door, scanning the land more closely. It had taken me a few minutes—maybe too long—to realize what was wrong, but now that I'd seen it, it was obvious.

There should always be something moving in a town the size of Watsonville. Feral cats, rabbits, even herds of wild deer looking for the overgrown remains of what used to be gardens. We've seen everything from goats to somebody's abandoned Shetland pony wandering through the remains of the old towns, living off the land. So where were they? There wasn't as much as a squirrel in sight.

Shaun grimaced. "Crap."

"Crap," I agreed. "Buffy, grab your gear."

"I'll drive," Shaun said, and started for the front of the van.

Buffy was looking between us with wide-eyed bafflement. "Okay, does somebody want to tell me what's causing the evacuation?" she demanded.

"There aren't any animals," Shaun said, dropping into the driver's seat.

I paused while yanking my gloves back on, taking pity, and replied, "Nothing clears the wildlife like the infected. We need to get out of here before we have—"

As if on cue, a low, distant moan came through the van's back door, carried by the prevailing winds. I grimaced.

"—company," Shaun and I finished, in unison.

"Race you home," I called, and ducked out the door. Buffy slammed it behind me, and I heard all three bolts click home. Even if I screamed, they'd never let me back inside. That's the protocol when you're in the field. No matter how loudly you yell, they never let you in.

Not if they want to live, anyway.

There were no zombies in sight, but the moaning from the north and east was getting louder. I tightened the straps on my gloves, grabbed my helmet, and slung my leg over the bike's still-warm seat. Inside the van, I knew Buffy would be checking her cameras, fastening her seatbelt, and trying to figure out why we were reacting so badly to zombies that probably weren't even in range. If there's really a God, she's never going to know the answer to that one.

The van pulled out, bumping and shaking as it made its way onto the freeway. I gunned the bike's engine and followed, pulling up alongside the van before moving out about ten feet ahead, where Shaun could see me and we could both watch the road for obstructions. It's a simple safety formation, but it's saved a lot of asses in the last twenty years. We rode like that, separated by a thin ribbon of broken road, all the way out of the valley, through the South Bay, and into the cool, welcoming air of Berkeley, California.

Home sweet zombie-free home.

...as he pressed his hand to her cheek, Marie could feel his flesh burning up from within, changing as the virus that slept in all of us awoke in her lover. She blinked back tears, licking suddenly dry lips before she managed to whisper, "I'm so sorry, Vincent. I never thought that it would end this way."

"It doesn't have to end this way for you," he replied, and smiled, sorrow written in his still-bright eyes. "Get the hell out of here, Marie.

There's nothing in this wasteland but the dead. Go home. Live, and be happy."

"It's too late for that. It's too late for me." She held up the blood testing kit and watched his eyes widen as he took in the meaning of the single red light burning at the top. "It's been too late since the attack." Her own smile was as weak as his. "You called me the hyacinth girl. I guess I belong in the wasteland."

"At least we're damned together," he said, and kissed her.

—From *Love as a Metaphor*,
**originally published in *By the Sounding Sea*,
the blog of Buffy Meissonier, August 3, 2039**

Shaun and I never met our parents' biological son. He was a kindergarten student during the Rising, and he survived the initial wave thanks to our parents, who pulled him out of class as soon as the data started pointing to public schools as amplification flash points. They did everything they could to protect him from the threat of infection. Everyone assumed he'd be one of the lucky ones.

The people next door had two golden retrievers, each weighing well over forty pounds, putting them in the range where amplification becomes possible. One of them was bitten—it was never determined by what—and began conversion. No one saw it coming because it had never happened before. Phillip Anthony Mason was the first confirmed case of human Kellis-Amberlee conversion initiated by an animal.

This honor does not help my parents sleep at night.

I am aware that my stance on pet ownership legislation is not popular. People love dogs, people love horses, and they want to continue to keep them in private homes. I understand this. I also understand that animals want to be free, and that sick animals are twice as likely to slip their restraints and go looking for comfort. Eventually, "comfort" becomes "something to bite." I support the Biological Mass Pet Ownership Restrictions, as do my parents. Were my brother alive today, he might feel different. But he's not.

—From *Images May Disturb You*,
the blog of Georgia Mason, November 3, 2039

Three

Buffy's neighborhood doesn't allow nonresident vehicles to enter without running blood tests on all passengers, so we dropped her at the gate where she could get tested and head inside on foot. I don't like pricking my fingers, and we were already looking at a second blood test when we reached the house. We live in an open neighborhood—one of the last in Alameda County—but our parents have to meet certain requirements if they want to keep their homeowner's insurance, and until we can afford to move out on our own, we have to play along.

"I'll upload the footage as soon as I finish cleaning it up," Buffy promised. "Drop me a text when you hit the house, let me know you made it okay?"

"Sure, Buff," I said. "Whatever you say."

Buffy's a great techie and a decent friend, but her ideas about safety are a little skewed, probably thanks to growing up in a high-security zone. She's less worried in the field than she is in supposedly protected urban environments. While there *are* more attacks on an annual basis in cities than in rural areas, there are also a lot more large men with guns once you get away from the creeks and the cornfields. Given a choice between the two, I'm going to take the city every time.

"See you tomorrow!" she said, and waved to Shaun through the van's front window before she turned to head for the guard station where she'd spend the next five minutes being checked for contamination. Shaun waved back and restarted the engine, backing the van away from the gate. That was my cue. I flashed a thumbs-up to show that I was good to go as I kicked my bike into a turn, leading the way back to Telegraph Avenue and into the tangled warren of suburban streets surrounding our house.

Like Santa Cruz, Berkeley is a college town, and we got swarmed during the Rising. Kellis-Amberlee hit the dorms, incubated, and exploded outward in an epidemic pattern that took practically everyone by surprise. "Practically" is the important word there. By the time the infection hit Berkeley, the first posts about activity in schools across the country were starting to show up online, and we had an advantage most college towns didn't: We started with more than our fair share of crazy people.

See, Berkeley has always drawn the nuts and flakes of the academic world. That's what happens when you have a university that offers degrees in both computer science and parapsychology. It was a city primed to believe any weird thing that came across the wire, and when all those arguably crazy people started hearing rumors about the dead rising from their graves, they didn't dismiss them. They began gathering weapons, watching the streets for strange behavior and signs of sickness, and generally behaving like folks who'd actually seen a George Romero movie. Not everyone believed what they heard...but some did, and that turned out to be enough.

That doesn't mean we didn't suffer when the first major waves of infection hit. More than half the population of Berkeley died over the course of six long days and nights, including the biological son of our adoptive parents, Phillip Mason, who was barely six years old. The things that happened here weren't nice, and they weren't pretty, but unlike many towns that started out with similar conditions—a large homeless population, a major school, a lot of dark, narrow, one-way streets—Berkeley survived.

Shaun and I grew up in a house that used to belong to the university. It's located in an area that was judged "impossible to secure" when the government inspectors started getting their act together, and as a result, it was sold off to help fund the rebuilding of the main campus. The Masons didn't want to live in the house where their son had died, and the security rating of the neighborhood meant they were able to get the property for a song. They finalized the adoptions for the two of us the day before they moved in, an "everything is normal" ratings stunt that eventually left them with a big house in the scary suburbs, two kids, and no idea what to do. So they did what came naturally: They gave more interviews, they wrote more articles, and they chased the numbers.

From the outside, they looked devoted to giving us the sort of "normal" childhood they remembered having. They never moved us to a gated neighborhood, they let us have pets that lacked sufficient mass for reanimation, and when public schools started requiring mandatory blood tests three times a day, they had us enrolled in a private school before the end of the week. There's a semifamous interview Dad gave right after that transfer, where he said they were doing their best to make us "citizens of the world instead of citizens of fear." Pretty words, especially coming from a man who regarded his kids as a convenient way to stay on top of the news feeds. Numbers start slipping? Go for a field trip to a zoo. That'll get you right back to the top.

There were a few changes they couldn't avoid, thanks to the government's anti-infection legislation—blood tests and psych tests and all that fun stuff—but they did their best, and I'll give them this much: A lot of the things they did for us weren't cheap. They paid for the right to raise us the way that they did. Entertainment equipment, internal security, even home medical centers can be bought for practically nothing. Anything that lets you outside, from vehicles to gasoline to gear that doesn't cut you off completely from the natural world...that's where things get expensive. The Masons paid in everything but blood to keep us in a place where there were blue skies and open spaces, and I'm thankful, even if it was always about ratings and a boy we never knew.

The garage door slid open as we pulled into the driveway, registering the sensors Shaun and I wear around our neck. In case of viral amplification, the garage becomes the zombie equivalent of a roach motel: Our sensors get us in, but only a clean blood test and a successful voice check gets us out. If we ever fail those tests, we'll be incinerated by the house defense system before we can do any further damage.

Mom's armored minivan and the old Jeep Dad insists on driving to his job on campus were parked in their normal spots. I pulled over and killed the bike's engine, removing my helmet as I started a basic postfield check of the machinery. I needed to see a mechanic; the ride through Santa Cruz had seriously damaged my shocks. Buffy's cameras were still attached to the helmet and back of the bike. I pulled them off and shoved them into my left saddlebag, unsnapping it and slinging it over my shoulder as Shaun pulled in behind me.

Shaun got out of the van and reached the back door three steps before I did. "We made good time," he said, positioning himself in front of the right-hand sensors.

"Sure did," I said, and positioned myself on the left.

"Please identify yourselves," said the bland voice of the house security system.

Most of the newer systems sound more like people than ours does. They'll even make jokes with their owners, to keep them at ease. Psychological studies have shown that closing the gap between man and machine increases comfort and acceptance and prevents nervous breakdowns stemming from isolation anxiety—in short, people don't get cabin fever as much when they think they have more people they can safely talk to. I think that's bullshit. If you want to avoid cabin fever, *go outside*. Our machines have stayed mechanical, at least so far.

"Georgia Carolyn Mason," said Shaun.

I smirked. "Shaun Phillip Mason."

The light above the door blinked as the house checked our vocal intonations. We must have passed muster, because it spoke again: "Voice prints confirmed. Please read the phrase appearing on your display screen."

Words appeared on my screen. I squinted to make them out through my sunglasses, and read, "Mares eat oats, and does eat oats, and little lambs eat ivy. A kid will eat ivy, too. Wouldn't you?"

The words blinked out. I glanced at Shaun, but couldn't quite see the words appearing on his screen before he was reciting them: "Oranges and lemons, say the bells of St. Clemens. You owe me five farthings, say the bells of St. Martins. When will you pay me, say the bells of Old Bailey."

The light over the door changed from red to yellow.

"Place your right hands on the testing pads," commanded the security system. Shaun and I did as requested, pressing our hands against the metal panels set into the wall. The metal chilled beneath my palm a split second before there was a stinging sensation in my index finger. The light above the door began to flash, alternating red and yellow.

"Think we're clean?" Shaun asked.

"If not, it's been nice knowing you," I said. Coming in together means that if one of us ever tests positive, that's all she wrote; they won't let anybody out of the garage until a cleanup crew arrives, and the chances of whoever comes up clean making it to the van before something happens aren't good. Our next-door neighbor used to call Child Protective Services every six months because our folks wouldn't stop us from coming in together. But what's the point of life if you can't take risks now and then, like coming into the damn house with your brother?

The light started flashing green instead of red, continuing to alternate with yellow for a few more seconds before yellow bowed out, leaving green to flash alone. The door unlocked, and the bland voice of the house said, "Welcome, Shaun and Georgia."

"S'up, the house?" Shaun replied, removing his shoes and tossing them into the outdoor cleaning unit before he walked inside, hollering, "Hey, 'rents! We're home!" Our parents hate being called " 'rents." I'm pretty sure that's why he does it.

"And we survived!" I added, copying the gesture and following him through the garage door. It swung closed and locked itself behind me. The kitchen smelled like spaghetti sauce and garlic bread.

"Failure to die is always appreciated," Mom said, entering the kitchen and putting an empty laundry basket on the counter. "You know the drill. Both of you, upstairs, and strip for sterilization."

"Yes, Mom," I said, picking up the basket. "Come, Shaun. The insurance bill calls us."

"Yes, master," he drawled. Ignoring Mom entirely, he turned and followed me up the stairs.

The house was a duplex before Mom and Dad had it converted back into a single-family home. Our bedrooms literally adjoin; there's an inside door between them. It makes life easier when it's time for editing and prep work, and it's been like that all our lives. On the few occasions when I've had to try sleeping without Shaun in the next room, well, let's just say I can go a long way on a six-pack of Coke.

I dropped the laundry basket in the hallway between our doors before going into my room and flicking the switch to turn on the overheads. We use low-wattage bulbs in the entire house, but I've abandoned white light entirely in my private space, preferring to live by the gleam of computer monitors and the comforting nonlight of black-light UV lamps. They can cause premature wrinkling if used extensively; what they can't do is cause corneal damage, and I appreciate that.

"Shaun! Inside door!"

"Got it," Shaun called. The connecting door slammed shut, and the band of light beneath it was cut off a second later as he slid the damper into place. Sighing with relief, I removed my sunglasses, forcing my eyes to open all the way. I'd been out in the sun for too long; even the UV lamps stung for a few seconds before my eyes adjusted and the room snapped into the sort of detailed focus most people only get in direct light.

"Retinal Kellis-Amberlee," as it's popularly called, is more properly referred to as "Acquired Kellis-Amberlee Optic Neuropathic Reservoir Condition." I've never heard anyone call it that outside a hospital, and even there, it's usually just "retinal KA." Those good old reservoir conditions: One more way for the virus to make life more interesting for everybody. My pupils are permanently dilated and don't contract in response to light, retinal scans are impossible, testing my vitreous and aqueous humors will always register a live infection, and best of all, my condition is advanced enough that my eyes don't even water. The virus produces a protective film and keeps the eyes from drying out. My tear ducts are atrophied. The only upside? Absolutely stellar low-light vision.

I tossed my sunglasses into the biohazard disposal canister and started across the room. My living space shares a lot of features with the van, including the part where Buffy maintains about ninety percent of the equipment and I understand less than half of it. Flat-screen monitors take up most of the walls, and we moved the group servers into my wardrobe last year when Shaun decided he needed more space for his weapons. Whatever. It's not like I was using it; I don't wear anything that actually needs to be hung up. I belong to the Hunter S. Thompson School of Journalistic Fashion: If I have to think about it, I have no business wearing it.

When you get right down to it, about the only similarity between my room and the room of your stereotypical twentysomething woman is the full-length mirror next to the bed. There's a wall dispenser mounted next to the mirror. I ripped loose a sheet of tear-away plastic and spread it on the floor, stepping onto it as I turned to face my reflection.

Hello, Georgia. Nice to see you're not dead yet.

Slicking my sweat-soaked hair back from my face, I started studying my clothes for the telltale fluorescence that under the black lights would indicate traces of blood.

Shaun and I operate under Class A-15 blogging licenses: We're cleared to report on events both inside and outside city limits, although we're still not permitted to enter any zones with a hazard rating at or above Level 3. The zones start at Level 10, the code for any area with resident mammals of sufficient body mass to undergo Kellis-Amberlee amplification and reanimation. Humans count. Level 9 means those mammals are not entirely kept in confinement. Buffy's neighborhood is considered a Level 10 hazard zone, which means it's safe to let your children play outside, except for the part where it would instantly convert the zone to a Level 9. Our house is classified as a Level 7 hazard, possessing free-range mammals of sufficient body mass for full viral amplification, local wildlife capable of carrying blood or other bodily wastes onto the property, insufficiently secured borders, and windows more than a foot and a half in diameter. There's legislation currently under review that would make it a federal offense to raise any child in a hazard zone above Level 8. I don't expect it to pass. It frightens me that it exists at all.

It requires an A-10 blogging license to enter a Level 3 hazard zone with any prayer of being allowed to exit it. We can't get those licenses or anything above until we turn twenty-five and pass a series of government-mandated tests, most of which center on the ability to make accurate headshots with a variety of firearms. That means no Yosemite for at least another two years. I'm fine with that. There's plenty of news to be found in more populated areas.

Shaun feels different, but he's an Irwin, and they thrive on wandering blindly into danger. All I've ever wanted to be is what I am—a Newsie. I'm happy this way. Danger is a side effect of what I do, not the reason behind it. That doesn't mean danger throws up its hands and says "oh, sorry, Georgia, I won't mess with you." Contamination is always a risk when dealing with zombies, especially when you have the recently infected involved. The older infected are usually too concerned with keeping themselves from dissolving to worry about smearing you with their precious bodily fluids, but new ones are fresh enough to have fluid to spare. They'll splatter you if they can manage it, and then count on the viral bricks filling their bloodstream to do the hard part for them. It's not great as a hunting strategy, but as a way of spreading the infection it works better than any uninfected person wants it to.

Not that anyone left in the world is actually uninfected—that's part of the problem. We call people who have succumbed to viral amplification "the infected," like it changes the fact that the virus is inside every one of us, patiently waiting for the day it gets invited to take over. The Kellis-Amberlee virus can remain in its dormant state for decades, if not forever; unlike the people it infects, it can wait. One day you're fine. The next day, your personal stockpile of virus wakes up, and you're on the road to amplification, the death of the part of you that's a thinking, feeling human being, and the birth of your zombie future. Calling zombies "the infected" creates an artificial feeling of security, like we can somehow avoid joining them. Well, guess what? We can't.

Viral amplification primarily occurs under one of two conditions: the initial death of the host causing a disruption of the body's nervous system and activating the virus already there, or contact with virus that has already switched over from "dormant" to "live." Hence the real risk of engaging the zombies, because any hand-to-hand conflict is going to result in a minimum casualty rate of sixty percent. Maybe thirty percent of those casualties are going to occur in the actual combat, if you're talking about people who know what they're doing. I've seen videos of martial arts clubs and idiots with swords going up against the zombies in the Rising, and I'll be among the first to admit that they're damned impressive to watch. There's this amazing contrast between the grace and speed of a healthy person and the shambling slowness of the zombie that just…It's like seeing poetry come alive. It's heartbreaking, and it's sad, and it's beautiful as hell.

And then the survivors go home, laughing and elated and mourning for their dead. They take off their armor, and they clean their weapons, and maybe one of them nicks his thumb on the edge of an arm guard or wipes his eyes with a hand that got a little too close to a leaking zombie. Live viral particles hit the bloodstream, the cascade kicks off, and amplification begins. In an average-sized human adult, full conversion happens inside of an hour and the whole thing starts again, without warning, without reprieve. The question "Johnny, is that you?" went from horror movie cliché to real-world crisis damn fast when people started facing the infected hand-to-hand.

The closest call I've ever had came when a zombie managed to spit a mouthful of blood in my face. If I hadn't been wearing safety goggles over my sunglasses, I'd be dead. Shaun's come closer than I have; I try not to ask anymore. I don't really want to know.

My armor and pants were clean. I removed them and tossed them onto the plastic sheeting, performing the same check on my sweatshirt and thermal pants before stripping them off and adding them to the pile. A quick examination of my arms and legs revealed no unexpected smears or streaks of blood. I already knew I wasn't wounded; I'd cleared two blood tests since the field. If I'd been so much as scratched, I'd have started amplification before we had hit Watsonville. My socks, bra, and underwear joined the rest. They hadn't been exposed to the outside air. That didn't matter; they went into a hazard zone. They were getting sterilized. There are a lot of folks who advocate for sterilization outside the home. They get shouted down by the people who want to keep it internal, since field sterilization— or even "front-yard chemical shower" sterilization—leaves the risk of recontamination before you reach a secure zone. So far, the groups have been able to keep things deadlocked and we've been able to keep doing our self-examinations in relative peace.

I stepped off the plastic sheet, folded it around my clothes, scooped it up, and carried it to the bedroom door, which I opened long enough to toss the whole bundle into the hamper. It would go through an industrial-grade bleaching guaranteed to neutralize any viral bodies clinging to the fabric, and the clothes would be ready to wear again by morning.

Even that brief blast of white light was enough to make my eyes burn. I scrubbed at them with the back of my hand as I turned toward the bathroom. Shaun's door was still closed. I called, "Showering now!" A thump on the wall answered me.

Shaun and I share a private bathroom with its own fully modernized and airtight shower system. Another little requirement of the household insurance—since we leave safe zones all the time in order to do our jobs, we have to be able to prove we've been properly sterilized, and that means logged computer verification of our sterilizations. The bathroom started life as the closets of our respective bedrooms. Personally, I consider this a much better use of the space.

The bathroom lights switched to UV when my door opened. I walked over and pressed my hand to the shower's keypad, saying, "Georgia Carolyn Mason."

"Accessing travel records," the shower replied. We don't screw with the shower the way we screw with the house system. House security is kept at an absolute minimum, but the shower is governmentally required for journalist use, and we could get in serious trouble if the records don't match up. The fines for posing a contamination risk are more than I could afford in six years of freelancing.

The shower door unsealed. "You have been exposed to a Level 4 hazard zone. Please enter the stall for decontamination and sterilization."

"Don't mind if I do," I said, and stepped in. The door shut behind me, locking with an audible hiss as the air lock seal engaged.

A stinging compound of antiseptic and bleach squirted from the bottommost nozzle on the wall, coating me with icy spray. I held my breath and closed my eyes, counting the seconds before it would stop. They can only legally bathe you in bleach for half a minute unless you've been in a Level 2 zone. At that point, they can keep dunking you until they're sure the viral blocks are clean. Everyone knows it doesn't do any good beyond the first thirty seconds, but that doesn't stop people from being afraid.

Travel in a Level 1 zone means they're not legally obligated to do anything but shoot you.

The bleach stopped. The upper nozzle came on, spraying out water almost hot enough to burn. I cringed but turned my face toward it, reaching for the soap.

"Clean," I said, once the shampoo was out of my hair. I keep it short for a variety of reasons. Most have to do with making myself harder to grab, but showering faster is also a definite motivation. If I wanted it to get any longer, I'd have to start using conditioner and a variety of other hair-care chemicals to make up for the damage the bleach does every day. My one true concession to vanity is dyeing it back to the color nature gave me every few weeks. I look terrible blonde.

"Acknowledged," said the shower, and the water turned off, replaced by jets of air from all four sides. The one good part of our shower system. I was dry in a matter of minutes, leaving only a little residual dampness in my hair. The door unsealed, and I stepped out into the bathroom, grabbing for my bottle of lotion.

Bleach and human skin aren't good buddies. The solution: acid-based lotion, usually formulated around some sort of citrus, to help repair the damage the bleaching does. Professional swimmers did it pre-Rising, and everybody does it now. It also helps to lend a standardized scent tag to people who have scrubbed themselves recently. My lotion was as close to scentless as possible, and it still carried a faint, irritating hint of lemon, like floor cleanser.

I worked the lotion into my skin and retreated to my own room, shouting, "Shaun, it's all yours!" I got the door closed as his was opening, spilling white light into the room. That's not uncommon. We're pretty good about our timing.

I grabbed my robe from the back of the door and shrugged it on as I walked to the main desk. The monitor detected my proximity and switched on, displaying the default menu screen. Our main system never goes offline. That's where group mail is routed, sorted according to which byline and category it's meant for—news to me, action to Shaun, or fiction, which goes straight to Buffy—and delivered to the appropriate in-boxes. I get the administrative junk that Shaun's too much of a jerk and Buffy's too much of a flake to deal with. Technically, we're a collective, but functionally? It's all me.

Not that I object to the responsibility, except when it fills my in-box to the point of inspiring nightmares. It's nice to know that our licenses are paid up, we're in good with the umbrella network that supports our accreditation, and nobody's suing us for libel. We make pretty consistent ratings, with Shaun and Buffy hitting top ten percent for the Bay Area at least twice a month and me holding steady in the thirteen to seventeen percent bracket, which isn't bad for a strict Newsie. I could increase my numbers if I went multi-media and started giving my reports naked, but unlike some people, I'm still in this for the news.

Shaun, Buffy, and I all publish under our own blogs and bylines, which is why I get so damn much mail, but those blogs are published under the umbrella of Bridge Supporters, the second-largest aggregator site in Northern California. We get readers and click-through traffic by dint of being listed on their front page, and they get a cut of our profits from all secondary-market and merchandise sales. We've been trying to strike out on our own for a while now, to go from being beta bloggers in an alpha world to baby alphas with a domain to defend. It's not easy. You need some story or feature that's big enough and unique enough to guarantee you'll take your readership with you, and our numbers haven't been sustainably high enough to interest any sponsors.

My in-box finished loading. I began picking through the messages, moving with a speed that was half long practice and half the desire to get downstairs to dinner. Spam; misrouted critique of Buffy's latest poem cycle, "Decay of the Human Soul: I through XII"; a threatened lawsuit if we didn't stop uploading a picture of someone's infected and shambling uncle—all the usual crap. I reached for my mouse, intending to minimize the program and get up, when a message toward the bottom of the screen caught my eye.

URGENT—PLEASE REPLY—YOU HAVE BEEN SELECTED.

I would have dismissed that as spam, except for the first word: urgent. People stopped flinging that word around like confetti after the Rising. Somehow, the potential for missing the message that zombies just ate your mom made offering to give people a bigger dick seem less important. Intrigued, I clicked the title.

I was still sitting there staring at the screen five minutes later when Shaun opened the door to my room and casually stepped inside. A flood of white light accompanied him, stinging my eyes. I barely flinched. "George, Mom says if you don't get downstairs, she'll...George?" There was a note of real concern in his voice as he took in my posture, my missing sunglasses, and the fact that I wasn't dressed. "Is everything okay? Buffy's okay, isn't she?"

Wordless, I gestured to the screen. He stepped up behind me and fell silent, reading over my shoulder. Another five minutes passed before he said, in a careful, subdued tone, "Georgia, is that what I think it is?"

"Uh-huh."

"They really...It's not a joke?"

"That's the federal seal. The registered letter should be here in the morning." I turned to face him, grinning so broadly that it felt like I was going to pull something. "They picked our application. They picked *us*. We're going to do it.

"We're going to cover the presidential campaign."

—————

My profession owes a lot to Dr. Alexander Kellis, inventor of the misnamed "Kellis flu," and Amanda Amberlee, the first individual successfully infected with the modified filovirus that researchers dubbed "Marburg Amberlee." Before them, blogging was something people thought should be done by bored teenagers talking about how depressed they were. Some folks used it to report on politics and the news, but that application was widely viewed as reserved for conspiracy nuts and people whose opinions were too vitriolic for the mainstream. The blogosphere wasn't threatening the traditional news media, not even as it started having a real place on the world stage. They thought of us as "quaint." Then the zombies came, and everything changed.

The "real" media was bound by rules and regulations, while the bloggers were bound by nothing more than the speed of their typing. We were the first to report that people who'd been pronounced dead were getting up and noshing on their relatives. We were the ones who stood up and said "yes, there are zombies, and yes, they're killing people" while the rest of the world was still buzzing about the amazing act of ecoterrorism that released a half-tested "cure for the common cold" into the atmosphere. We were giving tips on self-defense when everybody else was barely beginning to admit that there might be a problem.

The early network reports are preserved online, over the protests of the media conglomerates. They sue from time to time and get the reports taken down, but someone always puts them up again. We're never going to forget how badly we were betrayed. People died in the streets while news anchors made jokes about people taking their zombie movies too seriously and showed footage they claimed depicted teenagers "horsing around" in latex and bad stage makeup. According to the time stamps on those reports, the first one aired the day Dr. Matras from the CDC violated national security to post details on the infection on his eleven-year-old daughter's blog. Twenty-five years after the fact his words—simple, bleak, and unforgiving against their background of happy teddy bears—still send shivers down my spine. There was a war on, and the ones whose responsibility it was to inform us wouldn't even admit that we were fighting it.

But some people knew and screamed everything they understood across the Internet. Yes, the dead were rising, said the bloggers; yes, they were attacking people; yes, it was a virus; and yes, there was a chance we might lose because by the time we understood what was going on, the whole damn world was infected. The moment Dr. Kellis's cure hit the air, we had no choice but to fight.

We fought as hard as we could. That's when the Wall began. Every blogger who died during the summer of '14 is preserved there, from the politicos to the soccer moms. We've taken their last entries and collected them in one place, to honor them, and to remember what they paid for the truth. We still add people to the Wall. Someday, I'll probably post Shaun's name there, along with some lighthearted last entry that ends with "See you later."

Every method of killing a zombie was tested somewhere. A lot of the time, the people who tested it died shortly afterward, but they posted their results first. We learned what worked, what to do, and what to watch for in the people around us. It was a grassroots revolution based on two simple precepts: survive however you could, and report back whatever you learned because it might keep somebody else alive. They say that everything you ever needed to know, you learned in kindergarten. What the world learned that summer was "share."

Things were different when the dust cleared. Some people might find it petty to say "especially where the news was concerned," but if you ask me, that's where the real change happened. People didn't trust regulated news anymore. They were confused and scared, and they turned to the bloggers, who might be unfiltered and full of shit, but were fast, prolific, and allowed you to triangulate on the truth. Get your news from six or nine sources and you can usually tell the bullshit from the reality. If that's too much work, you can find a blogger who does your triangulation for you. You don't have to worry about another zombie invasion going unreported because someone, somewhere, is putting it online.

The blogging community divided into its current branches within a few years of the Rising, reacting to swelling ranks and a changing society. You've got Newsies, who report fact as untainted by opinion as we can manage, and our cousins, the Stewarts, who report opinion informed by fact. The Irwins go out and harass danger to give the relatively housebound general populace a little thrill, while their more sedate counterparts, the Aunties, share stories of their lives, recipes, and other snippets to keep people happy and relaxed. And, of course, the Fictionals, who fill the online world with poetry, stories, and fantasy. They have a thousand branches, all with their own names and customs, none of them meaning a damn thing to anyone who isn't a Fictional. We're the all-purpose opiate of the new millennium: We report the news, we make the news, and we give you a way to escape when the news becomes too much to handle.

—From *Images May Disturb You*,
the blog of Georgia Mason, August 6, 2039

Four

Presidential campaigns have traditionally been attended by "pet journalists" selected to follow the campaign and report on everything from the bright beginning to the sometimes-bitter end. The Rising didn't change that. Candidates announce their runs for the big chair, pick up their little flock of television, radio, and print reporters, and hit the road.

This year's presidential election is different, largely because one of the lead candidates, Senator Peter Ryman—born, raised, and elected in Wisconsin—is the first man to run for office who was under eighteen during the summer of '14. He remembers the feeling of being betrayed by the news, of watching people die because they trusted the media to tell them the truth. So when he announced his candidacy, he made it a point that he wouldn't just be inviting the usual crew to follow his campaign; he'd also invite a group of bloggers to walk the campaign trail with him from before the first primary all the way to the election, assuming he made it that far.

It was a bold move. It was a huge strike for the legitimacy of Internet news. Maybe we're licensed journalists now, with all the insurance costs and restrictions that implies, but we're still sneered at by certain organizations, and we can have trouble getting to information from a lot of the "mainstream" agencies. Having a presidential candidate acknowledge us was an amazing step forward. Of course, he was only going to allow three bloggers to come along. All of them had to have their Class A-15 licenses before they could even apply; if you were in the process of qualifying, your application would be thrown out without any sort of review.

Most of the bloggers we know applied, either singly or in groups, and we wanted that posting so bad that we could taste it. It was our ticket to the big leagues. Buffy had been operating under a Class B-20 license for years; as a Fictional, she didn't need the clearance for field work, political reporting, or biohazard zones, and so she'd never seen the point in paying the license fees or taking the tests. Shaun and I rushed her through her A-level tests and classifications so fast that she just looked sort of stunned when they handed her the upgraded license. We sent in our application the next day.

Shaun was sure we'd get it. I was sure we wouldn't. Now, still staring at my monitor, Shaun said, "George?"

"Yeah?"

"You owe me twenty bucks."

"Yeah," I agreed, before standing and throwing my arms around his neck. Shaun responded by whooping, putting his arms around my waist, and lifting me off the ground in order to whirl me around the room.

"We got the job!" he shouted.

"We got the job!" I shouted back.

After that, we devolved to shouting the words together, Shaun still swinging me in a circle, until the bedroom intercom crackled on and Dad's voice demanded, "Are you two making that racket for a reason?"

"We got the job!" we shouted, in unison.

"Which job?"

"The *big* job!" Shaun said, putting me down and grinning at the intercom like he thought it could see him. "The biggest big job in the history of big jobs!"

"The campaign," I said, aware that the grin on my face was probably just as big and stupid as the grin on Shaun's. "We got the posting for the presidential campaign."

There was a long pause before the intercom crackled again and Dad said, "You kids get dressed. I'll get your mother. We're going out."

"But dinner—"

"Can go into the fridge. If you two are going to go stalk politicians all over the country, we're going out for dinner first. Call Buffy and see if she wants to come. And that's an order."

"Yes, sir," said Shaun, saluting the intercom. It clicked off and he turned on me, holding out his right hand. "Pay up."

I pointed to the door. "Get out. There's about to be nudity, and you'll just complicate things."

"Finally, adult content! Should I turn the webcams on? We can have a front-page feed in less than five—" I grabbed my pocket recorder and flung it at his head. He ducked, grinning again. "—minutes. I'll go get some nicer clothes on. *You* can call the Buff one."

"Out," I said again, lips twitching as I fought a smile.

He walked back to the door between our rooms, stepping through before he shot back, "Wear a skirt, and I'll release you from your debts."

He managed to close the door before I found anything else to throw.

Shaking my head, I moved to the dresser, saying, "Phone, dial Buffy Meissonier, home line. Keep dialing until she picks up." Buffy has a tendency to leave her phone on vibrate and ignore it while she "follows her muse," which is basically a fancy way of saying "screws around online, writes a really depressing poem or short story, posts it, and makes three times what I do in click-through revenue and T-shirt sales." Not that I'm bitter or anything. The truth will make you free, but it won't make you particularly wealthy. I knew that when I chose my profession.

Playing with dead things is a little more lucrative, but Shaun doesn't make enough to support us both—not yet, anyway—and he isn't willing to move out without me. A lifetime spent within arm's reach and counting primarily on each other has left us a little dependent on one another's company. In an earlier, zombie-free era, this would have been dubbed "co-dependence" and resulted in years of therapy, culminating in us hating each other's guts. Adoptive siblings aren't supposed to treat each other like they're the center of the world.

Fortunately, or unfortunately, depending on your point of view, that was an attitude for a different world. Here and now, sticking with the people who know you best is the most guaranteed way of staying alive. Shaun won't leave the house until I do, and when we go, we'll be going together.

By the time Buffy picked up her phone, I had actually managed to find a dark gray tweed skirt that not only fit, but that I was willing to wear in a public place. I was digging for a top when the line clicked, and she said, peevishly, "I was writing."

"You're always writing, unless you're reading, screwing with something mechanical, or masturbating," I replied. "Are you wearing clothes?"

"Currently," she said, irritation fading into confusion. "Georgia, is that you?"

"It ain't Shaun." I pulled on a white button-down shirt, jamming the hem under the waistband of my skirt. "We'll be there to pick you up in fifteen. 'We' being me, Shaun, and the 'rents. They're taking the whole crew to dinner. It's just them trying to piggyback on our publicity for some rating points, but right now, failing to care."

Buffy isn't as slow on the uptake as she sometimes seems. Her voice suddenly tight with suppressed excitement, she asked, "Did we get it?"

"We got it," I confirmed. Her ear-splitting shriek of joy was enough to make me wince, even after it had been reduced by the phone's volume filters. Smiling, I pulled a crumpled black blazer out of my drawer and shrugged it on before grabbing a fresh pair of sunglasses from the stack on the dresser. "So we're picking you up in fifteen. Deal?"

"Yes! Yes, yes, deal, hallelujah, yes!" she babbled. "I have to change! And tell my roommates! And change! And see you! Bye!"

There was another click. My phone announced, "The call has been terminated. Would you like to place another call?"

"No, I'm good," I said.

"The call has been terminated," the phone repeated. "Would you like—"

I sighed. "No, thank you. Disconnect." The phone beeped and turned itself off. With the strides they've been making in voice-recognition software, you'd think they could teach the stuff to acknowledge colloquial English. One step at a time, I suppose.

Mom, Dad, and Shaun were in the living room when I came breezing down the stairs, shoving my handheld MP3 recorder into the loop at my belt. The backup recorder in my watch has a recording capacity of only thirty megabytes, and that's barely enough for a good interview. My handheld can hold up to five terabytes. If I need more than that before I can get to a server to dump the contents, I'd better be bucking for a Pulitzer.

Mom was wearing her best green dress, the one that appears in all her publicity shots, and Dad was in his usual professorial ensemble—tweed jacket, white shirt, khaki slacks. Put them next to Shaun, who was wearing a button-down shirt with his customary cargo pants, and they looked just like the last family publicity picture, even down to Mom's overstuffed handbag with all the guns inside it. She takes advantage of her A-5 blogging license in ways that boggle the mind, but it's the government's fault for leaving the loopholes there. If they want to give anybody with a journalist's license ranked Class A-7 or above the right to carry concealed weapons when entering any zone that's had a breakout within the last ten years, that's their problem. At least Mom's responsible about it. She always secures the safety on any gun that she's planning to take into a restaurant.

"Buffy's going to be ready in fifteen," I said, pushing my sunglasses more solidly up the bridge of my nose. Some of the newer models have magnetic clamps instead of earpieces. They won't come off without someone intentionally disengaging them. I would have been tempted to invest in a pair if they weren't expensive enough to require decontamination and reuse.

"The sun's going down; you could wear your contacts," Dad said, sounding amused. He's good at sounding amused. He's been sounding professionally amused since before the Rising, back when he used his campus webcast to keep biology students around the Berkeley area paying attention and doing their homework. Eventually, that same webcast let him coordinate pockets of survivors, moving them from place to place while reporting on the movement of the local zombie mobs. A lot of people owe their lives to that warm, professional-sounding voice. He could've become a news anchor with any network in the world after the dust cleared. He stayed at Berkeley instead, and became one of the pioneers of the evolving blogger society.

"I could also stick a fork in my eye, but where would be the fun in that?" I walked over to Shaun, offering a thin smile. He studied my skirt and then flashed me a thumbs-up sign. I had passed the all-judging court of my brother's fashion sense, which, cargo pants aside, is more advanced than mine will ever be.

"I called Bronson's. They have a table for us on the patio," Mom said, smiling beatifically. "It's a beautiful night. We should be able to see the entire city."

Shaun glanced at me, murmuring, "We let Mom pick the restaurant."

I smirked. "I can see that."

Bronson's is the last open-air restaurant in Berkeley. More, they're the last open-air restaurant in the entire Bay Area to be located on a hillside and surrounded by trees. Eating there is what I imagine it was like to go out to dinner before the constant threat of the infected drove most people away from the wilderness. The entire place is considered a Level 6 hazard zone. You can't even get in without a basic field license, and they require blood tests before they let you leave. Not that there's any real danger: It's surrounded by an electric fence too high for the local deer to jump over, and floodlights click on if anything larger than a rabbit moves in the woods. The only serious threat comes from the chance that an abnormally large raccoon might go into conversion, make it over the fence before it lost the coordination to climb trees, and drop down inside. That's never happened.

Not that this stops Mom from hoping to be there when it near-inevitably does. She was one of the first true Irwins, and old habits die hard, when they die at all. Shouldering her purse, she gave me a disapproving look. "Could you at least pretend to comb your hair?" she asked. "It looks like you have a hedgehog nesting on your head."

"That's the look I was going for," I said. Mom is blessed with sleek, well-behaved ash blonde hair that started silvering gracefully when Shaun and I were ten. Dad has practically no hair left, but when he had it, it was a muted Irish red. I, on the other hand, have thick, dark brown hair that comes in two settings: long enough to tangle, and short enough to look like I haven't brushed it in years. I prefer the short version.

Shaun's hair is a little lighter than mine, but still brown, and when he keeps it short, no one can tell that his is straight and mine wants to curl. It helps us get away with just saying we're twins, rather than going into the whole messy explanation.

Mom sighed. "You two realize the odds are good that someone already knows you got the assignment, and you're going to get swarmed tonight, yes?"

"Mmm-hmmm," I said. "Someone" probably received a quick phone call from one or both of our parents, and "someone" was probably already waiting at the restaurant. We grew up with the ratings game.

"Looking forward to it," said Shaun. He's better at playing nice with our parents than I am. "Every site that runs my picture tonight is five more foxy ladies around the country realizing that they want to hit the road with me."

"Pig," I said, and punched him in the arm.

"Oink," he said. "It's all right, we know the drill. Smile pretty for the cameras, show off my scars, let George and Dad look wise and trustworthy, pose for anyone who asks, and don't try to answer any questions with actual content."

"Whereas I don't smile unless forced, stay behind my sunglasses, and make a point of how incisive and hard-hitting every report I approve for release is going to be," I said, dryly. "We let Buffy babble to her heart's content about the poetic potential of traveling around the country with a bunch of political yahoos who think we're idiots."

"And we make the front page of every alpha site in the country, and our ratings go up nine points overnight," Shaun said.

"Thus allowing us to announce the formation of our own site early next week, just before heading out on the campaign trail." I slid my sunglasses down my nose, ignoring the way the light stung as I offered a brief smile. "We've thought about this as much as you have."

"Maybe more," Shaun added.

Dad laughed. "Face it, Stacy, they've got it covered. Kids, just in case there isn't another chance for me to tell you this, your mother and I are very proud of you. Very proud of you, indeed."

Liar. "We're pretty proud of us, too," I said.

"Well, then," Shaun said, clapping his hands together. "This is touching and all, but come on—let's go eat."

Getting out of the house is easier with our parents in tow, largely because Mom's minivan is kept ready at all times. Food, water, a CDC-certified biohazard containment unit for temperature-sensitive medications, a coffeemaker, steel-reinforced windows...We could be trapped inside that thing for a week, and we'd be fine. Except for the part where we'd go crazy from stress and confinement and kill each other before rescue came. When Shaun and I go into the field, we need to check our gear, sometimes twice, to make sure it's not going to let us down. Mom just grabs her keys.

Buffy was waiting at her neighborhood guard station, dressed in an eye-popping combination of tie-dyed leggings and knee-length glitter tunic, with star-and-moon hologram clips in her hair. Anyone who didn't know her would have thought she was completely devoid of sense, fashion *or* common. That's what she was aiming for. Buffy travels with more hidden cameras than Shaun and I combined. As long as people are busy staring at her hair, they don't wonder why she's so careful about pointing the tiny jewels she has pasted to her nails in their direction.

She waved and grabbed her duffel bag when the van pulled up. Then she ran to hop into the back with Shaun and me. The footage of that moment would be on the site within the hour.

"Hey, Georgia. Hey, Shaun—good evening, Mr. and Mrs. Mason," she chirped, buckling herself in while Shaun slammed the door. "I just finished watching your trip to Colma, Mrs. Mason. Really great stuff. I would never have thought to elude a bunch of zombies by climbing a high-dive platform."

"Why, thank you, Georgette," said Mom.

"Thrill as Buffy kisses ass," Shaun said, deadpan. Buffy shot him a poisonous look, and he just laughed.

Content that all was right with the world, I settled back in my seat, folded my arms across my chest, and closed my eyes, letting the chatter in the van wash over me without registering it. It had been a long day, and it was nowhere near over.

When blogging first emerged as a major societal trend, it was news rendered anonymous. Rather than trusting something because Dan Rather looked good on camera, you trusted things because they sounded true. The same went for reports of personal adventures, or people writing poetry, or whatever else folks felt like putting out there for the world to see; you got no context on who created it, and so you judged the work on the basis of what it actually was. That changed when the zombies came, at least for the people who went professional. These days, bloggers don't just report the news; they create it, and sometimes, they *become* it. Landing the position of pet bloggers for Senator Ryman's presidential campaign? That definitely counts as becoming the news.

That's part of why Shaun and Buffy keep me around. My journalistic integrity is unquestioned by our peers, and when we make the jump to alpha—the suddenly feasible jump to alpha—that's going to cement our credibility. Shaun and Buffy will bring in the readers. I'll make it okay for them to trust us. They just have to deal with my depressed personal ratings because part of what makes me so credible is the fact that my news is free from passion, opinion, and spin. I do op-ed, but for the most part, what you'll get from me is the truth, the whole truth, and nothing but the truth.

So help me God.

Shaun elbowed me when we reached Bronson's. I slid my sunglasses back into position and opened my eyes.

"Status?" I asked.

"A least four visible cameras. Probably twelve to fifteen, all told."

"Leaks?"

"That many cameras, at least six sites already know."

"Got it. Buffy?"

"Taking point," she said, and straightened, putting on her best camera-ready smile. My parents exchanged amused looks in the front seat.

"It's all uphill from here," I said.

Shaun leaned over and opened the van door.

Before the Rising, crowds of paparazzi were pretty much confined to the known haunts of celebrities and politicians—the people whose faces could be used to sell a few more magazines. The rise of reality television and the Internet media changed all that. Suddenly, anybody could be a star if they were willing to embarrass themselves in the right ways. People got famous for wanting to get laid, a stunt men have been trying to achieve since the day we discovered puberty. People got famous for having useless talents, memorizing trivia, or just being willing to get filmed twenty-four hours a day while living in a house full of strangers. The world was a weird place before the Rising.

After the Rising, with an estimated eighty-seven percent of the populace living in fear of infection and unwilling to leave their homes, a new breed of reality star was born: the reporter. While you can be an aggregator or a Stewart without risking yourself in the real world, it's hard to be an Irwin, a Newsie, or even a really good Fictional if you cut yourself off that way. So we're the ones who eat in restaurants and go to theme parks, the ones who visit national parks even though we'd really rather not, the ones who take the risks the rest of the country has decided to avoid. And when we're not taking those risks ourselves, we report on the people who are. We're like a snake devouring its own tail, over and over again, forever. Shaun and I have done paparazzi duty when the stories were thin on the ground and we needed to make a few bucks fast. I'd rather go for another filming session in Santa Cruz. Something about playing vulture just makes me feel dirty.

Buffy was the first to flounce into the crowd, looking like a little glittering ball of sunshine and happiness before they closed ranks around her, flashbulbs going off in all directions. Her giggle could cut through steel. I could hear it even after she'd made it halfway to the restaurant doors, distracting the worst of the paparazzi in the process. Buffy's cute, photogenic, a hell of a lot friendlier than I am, and, best of all, she's been known to drop hints about her personal life that can be turned into valuable rating points when the stories go live. Once, she even brought out a boyfriend. He didn't last long, but when she had him, Shaun and I could practically have danced naked on the van without getting harassed. Good times.

Shaun stepped out of the van already smiling. That smile's made him a lot of friends in the female portion of the blogosphere—something about him looking like he'd be just as happy to explore the dangerous wilderness of the bedroom as he is to explore the mysteries of things that want to make him die. They should know by now it's a gimmick, given his continuing lack of a social life that doesn't include the infected, but they keep falling for it. Half the cameras swung around to face him, and several of the chirpy little "anchorwomen"—because every twit who knows how to post an interview on the vid sites is an anchorwoman these days; just ask them—shoved their microphones into his face. Shaun immediately started giving them what they wanted, chattering merrily about our latest reports, offering coy, meaningless come-ons, and basically talking about anything and everything other than our new assignment.

Shaun's smoke screen gave me the opportunity I needed to slip out of the car and start worming my way toward the restaurant doors. Paparazzi gatherings are one of the few times you'll see a crowd in public. I spotted nervous-looking Berkeley Police in riot gear around the edge of the crowd as I made my way toward the thinner concentration of bodies. They were waiting for something to go wrong. They'd just have to keep waiting. There's only been one incident where an outbreak started from a gathering of licensed reporters, and it happened when a nervous celebrity—the real sort, a TV sitcom star, not one of the ones who built themselves celebrity out of boredom—freaked out, pulled a gun out of her purse, and started shooting. The jury found the TV star, not the paparazzi, at fault for the outbreak that followed.

One of the Newsies near the police offered me a sidelong nod, making no move to draw attention to my position. I nodded back, relieved by his discretion. He was just crowd-surfing, but it was a nice thing to do. I made a note of his face: If his site put in for an interview, I'd grant it.

Irwins get crowd-comfortable the easy way: When you live in the hope that an outbreak will happen where you can observe it, you don't worry about avoiding them the way a sane person might. Fictionals go one of two directions: Some avoid crowds like everybody else. Others refuse to acknowledge that they could possibly get infected when they haven't put it in the script and they go gaily bouncing hither and yon, ignoring the danger. Newsies tend to be more cautious because we know what could happen if we're not. Unfortunately, the demands of our job make it hard for us to be total hermits, and so even those of us who don't need the additional income or exposure from the paparazzi flocks join up with them from time to time, getting accustomed to the feeling of being surrounded by other bodies. The paparazzi flocks are our version of the obstacle course. Stand in them without freaking out and you might be ready for real field work.

My "skirt the crowd and keep your eyes on the door" technique seemed to be working. With Shaun and Buffy providing louder, more visible targets, no one was going for me. Besides, I have a well-established—and well-deserved—reputation for being the sort of interviewee who walks away leaving you with nothing you can use as a front-page quote or saleable sound byte. It's hard to interview someone who refuses to talk to you.

Ten feet to the door. Nine. Eight. Seven...

"—and this is my gorgeous daughter, Georgia, who's going to be the head of Senator Ryman's hand-selected blogging team!" Mom's hand caught my elbow just as the gushing, ebullient tone of her voice caught my ears. Trapped. She swung me around to face the crowd of paparazzi, fingers digging into my arm. More quietly, through gritted teeth, she said, "You owe me this."

"Got it," I said, out of the corner of my mouth, and let myself be turned.

Shaun and I figured out early what our purpose was in our parents' lives. When your classmates aren't allowed to go to the movies because they might be exposed to unknown individuals, while your parents are constantly proposing wild adventures in the outside world, you get the idea that maybe something's going on. Shaun was the first to realize how they were using us; it's about the only place where he grew up before I did. I got over Santa. He got over our parents.

Mom kept an iron grip on my arm as she mugged and preened, recreating her favorite photo opportunity, version five hundred and eleven:

the flamboyant Irwin poses with her stoic daughter, polar opposites united by a passion for the news. I once sat down with the news aggregators and compared a public-image search to the collection of private pictures on the house database. Eighty-two percent of the physical affection I've received from my mother has been in public, in careful view of one or more cameras. If that seems cynical, answer this: Why has she reliably, for my entire life, waited to touch me until there was someone with a visible camera in shooting range?

People wonder why I'm not physically affectionate. The number of times I've been a rating-boosting photo opportunity for my parents should be sufficient answer. The only person who's ever hugged me without thinking about the shooting angles and light saturation is my brother, and he's the only one whose hugs I've ever given a damn about.

My glasses filtered camera flashes, although it wasn't long before I had to close my eyes anyway. Some of the newer cameras have lights on them strong enough to take photographs in total darkness that seem to have been taken at noon, and there's not an intelligence check associated with buying that sort of equipment. One of those suckers goes off in your face, you know you've been photographed. I was going to have a migraine for days thanks to Mom's forced photo opportunity. There was no way I could have avoided it; it was give in before dinner or spend the entire meal being harangued about my duties as a good daughter, leading to a much longer photo session afterward. I'd rather kiss a zombie raccoon.

Buffy came to my rescue, slinking through the crowd with the sort of grace that only comes from the kind of practice most of our generation has avoided. Reaching out, she caught hold of my other arm and chirped, all dizzy good cheer, "Ms. Mason, Georgia, Mr. Mason says our table's ready! Only if you don't come now, they may release it, and then we'll have to wait at least a half an hour for another table." She paused before delivering the coup de grace. "An *inside* table."

That was the perfect thing to say. Sitting outside added to the family's mystique, making us look brave and adventurous. Parental opinion, not mine. I think eating outside when you don't have to makes you look like a suicidal idiot dying to get munched by a zombie deer. Shaun sides with everybody on this one—he'd rather eat outside when we have to eat with the parents in public, since that way there's the chance a zombie deer will come along and rescue him. He just agrees that it's a stupid thing to do. Mom doesn't see the stupidity. If it was a choice between an outdoor table where the photographers could get some decent shots and an indoor table where people might gossip about the fearless Stacy Mason losing her nerve, well... her answer was obvious.

Flashing her award-winning—literally—smile at the crowd, Mom pulled me into an "impulsive" hug and announced, "Well, folks, our table's ready." Noises of displeasure greeted her statement. Her smile widened. "But we'll be back after food, so if you guys want to grab a burger, we might be able to coax a few wise statements out of my girl." She gave me a squeeze and let go, to the sound of general applause.

I sometimes wonder why none of these news site cluster bombs ever catch the way her smile dies when she's not facing the cameras. They run solemn pictures of her once in a while, but they're as posed as the rest; they show her looking mournfully at abandoned playgrounds or locked cemetery gates, and once—when her ratings dipped to an all-time low during the summer Shaun and I turned thirteen and locked ourselves in our rooms—at the school Phillip had attended. That's our Mom, selling the death of her only biological child for a few points in the ratings game.

Shaun says I shouldn't judge her so harshly, since we make our living doing the same thing. I say it's different when we do it. We don't have kids. The only things we're selling are ourselves, and I guess we have a right to that.

Dad and Shaun were standing outside the restaurant doors, turned just far enough that none of the microphones capable of withstanding the crowd noise without shorting out would be able to make out what they were saying. As I drew closer, I heard Shaun saying, in an entirely pleasant tone, "...I really don't care what you consider 'reasonable.' You're not part of our team; you're not getting any exclusives."

"Now, Shaun—"

"Dinnertime," I said, snagging Shaun's arm as I walked past. He came with me as gratefully as I'd gone with Buffy a few moments before. Shaun, Buffy, and I walked into the restaurant practically arm-in-arm, with our parents trailing behind us, both struggling to conceal their irritation. Tough. If they didn't want us embarrassing them in public, they shouldn't have made us go out.

Our table proved to be nice enough to suit Mom's idea of propriety; it was located in the far corner of the yard, close to both the fence keeping out the woods and the fence isolating us from the street. Several enterprising paparazzi had drifted over to that portion of the sidewalk and were snapping candid shots through the bars. Mom flashed them a dimpled grin. Dad looked knowing and wise. I fought the urge to gag.

My handheld vibrated, signaling an incoming text message. I unclipped it from my belt, tilting it to show the screen.

"*Think this'll die down when we're on the road? —S*"

I smirked, tapping out, "*Once the media machine (aka 'Mom') has been left here? Absolutely. We'll be small potatoes next to the main course.*"

He tapped back: "*I love it when you compare people to food.*"

"*Practicing for the inevitable.*"

Shaun snorted laughter, nearly dropping his phone into the basket of breadsticks. Dad shot him a sharp look, and he put his phone down next to his silverware, saying angelically, "I was checking my ratings."

Dad's scowl melted instantly. "How's it looking?"

"Not bad. The footage the Buffster managed to clean before we hauled her away from her computer is getting a really good download rate." Shaun flashed a grin at Buffy, who preened. If you want her to like you, compliment her poetry. If you want her to love you, compliment her tech. "I figure once I do the parallel reports and record my commentary, my share's going to jump another eight points. I may break my own top stats this month."

"Show-off," I said, and smacked him on the arm with my fork.

"Slacker," he replied, still grinning.

"Children," said Mom, but there was no heat behind it. She loved it when we goofed around. It made us look more like a real family.

"I'm going to have the teriyaki soy burger," said Buffy. She leaned forward and said conspiratorially, "I heard from a guy who knows a girl whose boyfriend's best friend is in biotech that he—the best friend, I mean—ate some beef that was cloned in a clean room and didn't have a viral colony, and it tasted *just like* teriyaki soy."

"Would that it were true," said Dad, with the weird sort of mournfulness reserved for people who grew up before the Rising and were now confronted with something that's been lost forever. Like red meat.

That's another nasty side effect of the KA infection that no one thought about until they were forced to deal with it firsthand: Everything mammalian harbors a virus colony, and the death of the organism causes the virus to transmute into its live state. Hot dogs, hamburgers, steaks, and pork chops are things of the past. Eat them, and you're eating live viral particles. Are you sure there aren't any sores in your mouth? In your esophagus? Can you be one hundred percent certain that no part of your digestive tract has been compromised in any way? All it takes is the smallest break in the body's defenses and your slumbering infection wakes up. Cooking the meat enough to kill the infection also kills the flavor, and it's still a form of Russian roulette.

The most well-done steak in the world may have one tiny speck of rare meat somewhere inside it, and that's all that it takes. My brother wrestles with the infected, gives speeches while standing on cars in designated disaster zones, never wears sufficient armor, and generally goes through life giving the impression that he's a suicide waiting to happen. Even he won't eat red meat.

Poultry and fish are safe, but a lot of people avoid them anyway. Something about the act of eating flesh makes them uncomfortable. Maybe it's the fact that suddenly, after centuries of ruling the farmyard, mankind has reason to empathize with the chicken. We always had turkeys at Thanksgiving and geese at Christmas. Just another ratings stunt on the part of our increasingly media-savvy parents, but at least this one had some useful side effects. Shaun and I are some of the only people I know in our generation who don't have any unreasonable dietary hang-ups.

"I'm going to have the chicken salad and a cup of today's soup," I said.

"And a Coke," prompted Shaun.

"And a carafe," I corrected him.

He was still teasing me about my caffeine intake when the waiter appeared, accompanied by the beaming manager. No surprise there. As a family, we've been excellent customers for as long as I can remember. Every time a local outbreak has closed down outside gathering areas, Mom's been at Bronson's, eating in the enclosed dining area and making a point of being the first one outside when they're allowed to reopen it. They'd be stupid not to appreciate what we've done for their business.

The waiter was carrying a tray laden with our usual assortment of drinks: coffee for Mom and Dad, a virgin daiquiri for Buffy, a bottle of sparkling apple cider for Shaun—it looks like beer from any sort of a distance—and a pitcher of Coke for me.

"Compliments of the house," the manager declared, turning his smile on me and Shaun. "We're so proud of you. Going off to be media superstars! It runs in the family."

"It definitely does," simpered Mom, doing her best to look like a giggling schoolgirl. She was only succeeding at looking like an idiot, but I wasn't going to tell her that. We were almost on the campaign trail. It wasn't worth the fight.

"Be sure to sign a menu before you leave?" the manager pressed. "We'll put it on the wall. When you're too big to come to places like this, we'll be able to say, 'They ate here, they ate fries right there, right at that table, while they did their math homework.'"

"It was physics," protested Shaun, laughing.

"Whatever you say," said the manager.

The waiter passed drinks around as we placed our orders. He finished by pouring the first cup of Coke from my pitcher with a flourish of his wrist. I smiled at that, and he winked at me, clearly pleased. I let my smile die, spiking an eyebrow upward. Hours of practice with my mirror have shown me that particular expression's success in conveying disdain. It's one of the few facial expressions that's helped by my sunglasses, rather than being hindered by them. His pleasure faded, and he hustled through the rest of his duties without looking at me.

Shaun caught my eye, mouthing "That wasn't nice" at me.

I shrugged, mouthing "He should have known better" back at him. I don't flirt. Not with waiters, not with other reporters, not with anybody.

Finally, the staff retreated, and Mom raised her glass, clearly signaling for a toast. Choosing the path of least resistance, the rest of us did the same.

"To ratings!" she said.

"To ratings," we agreed and clinked our glasses around the table in doleful adherence to the ritual.

We were on the road to those ratings now. All we had to do was hope that we were good enough to keep them. Whatever it might take.

My friend Buffy likes to say love is what keeps us together. The old pop songs had it right, and it's all about love, full stop, no room for arguing. Mahir says loyalty is what matters—doesn't matter what kind of person you were, as long as you were loyal. George, she says it's the truth that matters. We live and die for the chance to maybe tell a little bit of the truth, maybe shame the Devil just a little bit before we go.

Me, I say those are all great things to live for, if they're what happens to float your boat, but at the end of the day, there's got to be somebody you're doing it for. Just one person you're thinking of every time you make a decision, every time you tell the truth, or tell a lie, or anything.

I've got mine. Do you?

**—From *Hail to the King*,
the blog of Shaun Mason, September 19, 2039**

Five

I D?"

"Georgia Carolyn Mason, licensed online news representative, After the End Times." I handed my license and photo identification to the man in black, turning my left wrist over to reveal the blue-and-red ID tattoo I had done when I tested for my first Class B license. Tattooing isn't legally required—yet—but it gives them something to identify your body by. Every little bit helps. "Registered with the North American Association of Internet Journalists; dental records, skin sample, and identifying markings on file."

"Remove the sunglasses."

That was a request I was all too familiar with. "If you'll check my file, you'll see that I have a filed notation of retinal Kellis-Amberlee syndrome. If there's another test we can perform, I'd be happy to—"

"Remove the sunglasses."

"You realize I won't display a normal retinal pattern?"

The man in black offered me the ghost of a smile. "Well, ma'am, if your eyes check normal, we'll know you've been making all this fuss because you weren't who you claimed to be, now, won't we?"

Damn. "Right," I muttered, and removed my glasses. Forcing myself to keep my eyes open despite the pain, I turned to press my face into the retinal scanner being held by the second member of Senator Ryman's private security team. They would compare the scan results to the ocular patterns in my file, checking for signs of degradation or decay that could signify a recent viral flare. Not that they'd get any useful results from me; retinal KA means my eyes *always* register as if I were harboring a live infection.

Buffy and Shaun were going through the standard version of the same process with their own detachments of black-suited security representatives just a few feet away from me. I was willing to bet theirs hurt less.

The light at the top of the retinal scanner went from red to green, and the man pulled it away, nodding to his companion. "Hand," said the first man.

I took a few precious seconds to slide my sunglasses back into place before holding out my right hand, and managed not to grimace as it was grabbed and thrust into a closed-case blood testing unit. Clinical interest took over, wiping away my distaste for the process as I studied the unit's casing.

"Is that an Apple unit?" I asked.

"Apple XH-224," he replied.

"Wow." I'd seen the top-of-the-line units before, but I'd never had the opportunity to use one. They're more sophisticated than our standard field units, capable of detecting a live infection at something like ten times the speed. One of those babies can tell you that you're dead before you even realize that you've been bitten. Which didn't make the process of getting tested any more enjoyable, but it definitely made it more interesting to observe. It was almost worth the pain. Almost.

Five red lights came on along the top of the box, beginning to blink as needles pricked the skin between my thumb and forefinger, at my wrist, and at the tip of my pinkie. Each time, the bite of the needle was followed by a cool blast of antiseptic foam. When all five lights had gone from red to green, the agent pulled the box away and smiled genuinely for the first time.

"Thank you for your cooperation, Miss Mason. You're free to proceed."

"Thanks," I said, and pushed my sunglasses farther up the bridge of my nose. My headache settled back into its previous grumble. "Mind if I wait for the rest of my crew?" Buffy was sticking her hand into the box, and they were waiting for Shaun's retinal check to complete. He has retinal scarring in his left eye from a stupid incident with some crappy Chinatown fireworks when we were fifteen, and that makes his scans take longer than they should. Mine may be weird, but they're a standard weird. His confuse just about every scanner we've ever met.

"Not at all," the agent said. "Just don't cross the quarantine line, or we'll have to start over."

"Got it." I stepped back and studied the area, careful to keep my feet well away from the red line marking the edge of the defined "safe" zone.

We'd been expecting increased security around the campaign, but this was more than I'd been bargaining for. They picked us up from Buffy's house; the senator's security dispatch wasn't even willing to let us near their cars unless they were collecting us from a secured location, which took our place out of the running. Given that they gave us blood tests before they said hello, I don't quite get the reasoning. Maybe they didn't want to deal with a zombie attack before lunch. Or maybe they were avoiding our parents, who were practically panting at the idea of a photo opportunity with the senator's men.

Once in the cars, we were transported to the Oakland Airport, where we had to take another blood test before they loaded us and our portable gear onto a private helicopter. We flew to what was supposedly an undisclosed location but I was pretty sure was the city of Clayton, near the foothills of Mount Diablo. Most of that area was purchased by the government after the original residents evacuated, and it's been rumored for years that they were using some of the old ranches as short-term housing. It's a nice place, assuming you don't mind the occasional threat of zombie coyotes, wild dogs, and bobcats. Rural areas offer a lot where privacy is concerned, but not so much if what you're looking for is safety.

Judging by the stables around the perimeter, our destination started life as a working farm. Now it was clearly a private residence, with electric fences spanning the spaces between buildings and barbed wire strung as far as the eye could see. Factor in the helipad and it didn't take any great leap of logic to conclude that this place confirmed the rumors about the government setting up hidey-holes out in the abandoned boonies. Nice digs, if you can get them. I smiled as I continued looking around. Our first day, and we already had a scoop: Government Use of Abandoned Land in Northern California Confirmed. Read all about it.

Buffy picked up her bags and walked over to me, looking flustered. "I don't think I've ever been poked that many times," she complained.

"At least now you know you're clean," I said. "Cameras rolling?"

"There was a minor EMP band at the entrance that took two and five off-line, but I anticipated for that and built in redundancies. One, three, and four, and six through eight, are all transmitting live and have been since pickup."

I looked at her flatly. "I didn't understand a word of that, so I'm just going to assume you said 'yes' and move on with my life, all right?"

"Works for me," she said, waving at Shaun as he joined us. "You're done?"

"They know Shaun can't be a zombie," I said, adjusting my sunglasses. "You need a brain to reanimate."

He elbowed me amiably and shook his head. "Dude, I'm amazed

they didn't strip search us. They should've bought us dinner first, or something."

"Will lunch do?" asked a jocular voice. All three of us turned, finding ourselves facing a tall, generically handsome man whose carefully cropped brown hair was starting to gray but had been left just long enough in the front to fall across his forehead and create the illusion of boyishness. His skin was tan but relatively unlined, and his eyes were very blue. He was casually dressed in tan slacks and a white shirt, with the sleeves rolled up around his elbows.

"Senator Ryman," I said, and offered him my hand. "I'm Georgia Mason. These are my associates, Shaun Mason—"

"Hey," interjected Shaun.

"—and Georgette Meissonier."

"You can call me Buffy," said Buffy.

"Of course," the senator said, taking my hand and shaking it. He had a good grip, solid without being overwhelming, and the teeth he revealed when he smiled were straight and white. "It's a pleasure to meet all three of you. I've been watching your precampaign preparations with interest." He released my hand.

"We had a lot to accomplish and not much time to accomplish it in," I said.

"A lot to accomplish" verged on understatement. We had seven baby bloggers contact us before we finished eating dinner, all wanting to know if we were planning to schism. Once people knew the size of the story we'd landed, there was no way striking out on our own would have been a surprise, so we didn't try to make it one. The folks at Bridge Supporters were sorry to see us go and pleased by our severance offer: We took exclusive rights to all campaign-trail stories to our new site, but we allowed them to keep running two of Buffy's ongoing poetry series, gave them first rights on any continuations to Shaun's series on exploring the ruins of Yreka, and guaranteed two op-ed pieces from me per month for the next year. They'd get click-through reads from the folks following us on campaign, and we'd get the same in return as existing Bridge Support readers found their way to our new site through the shared material. My friend Mahir had been looking to move on to new challenges, and he was glad to sign on to help me moderate the Newsies. Shaun and Buffy had their own hiring to do, and I left it to them.

Finding a host for our new site was disturbingly easy. One of Buffy's biggest fans runs a small ISP, and he was willing to put us up and online in exchange for a minimal fee and a lifetime membership to our exclusive features, once we had some to offer. Less than twenty minutes after calling him, we had a URL, a place to put our files, and our very first subscriber. The baby bloggers who contacted us the first night were quickly joined by two dozen others, and that gave us the liberty to pick and choose, looking for people who fit a profile other than "available." We wound up with twelve supporting betas, four in each major category, already producing content for a site that hadn't even officially launched yet. Never in my wildest dreams did I believe it could be that easy to get everything you'd ever wanted...but it was.

After the End Times went live six days after we got the notice that we had been chosen to accompany Senator Ryman's campaign, with my name on the masthead as senior editor, Buffy listed as our graphic designer and technical expert, and Shaun responsible for hiring and marketing. Whether we sank or swam, there was no going back; once you make alpha, you can never be a beta again. Blogging is a territorial world, and the other betas would eat you alive if you tried.

I hadn't slept more than four hours a night in two weeks. Sleep was a luxury reserved for people who weren't trying to design their futures around a meal ticket that might still prove to be a rotten apple. I just had to hope the dirt we found on the campaign trail would be enough to support us, or our careers would be short, sour, and too interesting by far.

"Still, you seem to have done all right," Senator Ryman said. His Wisconsin accent was stronger than it sounded on the newscasts; either he didn't realize we were filming, or he figured there was no point in playing fake around the people who were going to be sharing his quarters over the next year. "If you'll come with me, Emily has a nice lunch going, and she's been looking forward to meeting you."

"Is your wife coming with you for the whole campaign?" I asked. He started to walk toward a nearby door, and I followed, gesturing for the others to do the same. We knew the answer already—Emily Ryman was going to be staying on the family ranch in Parrish, Wisconsin, during most of the year, taking care of the kids while her husband did the moving and shaking—but I wanted him to say it for our pickup recordings. The best sound clips are the ones you gather for yourself.

"Em? I couldn't make her come the whole way if I used a tractor pull," the senator said, and opened the door. "Wipe your feet, all three of you. There's no point to making you go through another damned blood test— if you're this far past the gate and you're not clean, we're dead already. May as well be friendly about it." Then he was inside, bellowing, "Emily! The bloggers are here!"

Shaun gave me a look, mouthing "I like him." I nodded. We'd just met the man, and he was probably a master of political bullshit, but I was starting to like him, too. There was something about him that said "I know how pointless all of these political circuses are. Let's see how it long it takes for them to realize that I'm just playing along, shall we?" I had to respect that.

He might be playing us for a bunch of saps, but if he was, he'd slip eventually, and we'd take him apart. That would be almost as much fun as getting along with him, and definitely better for our market share.

The interior of the house was decorated with a distinctly Southwestern flare, all bright, solid colors and geometric patterns. Southwestern art has shifted in the last twenty years; before the Rising, any house with that many potted cacti and Native American–style throw rugs would have boasted a coyote statue or two and possibly a polished steer's skull, complete with horns. I've seen pictures—it was pretty morbid stuff. These days, representations of any animal that weighs more than forty pounds have a tendency to make people uncomfortable, so coyotes and steers are both out of fashion, unless you're dealing with a serious nihilist or some kid playing "creature of the night." Only the painted deserts remain. An enormous picture window took up half of one wall, marking the house as having been put up before the Rising. No one builds windows like that anymore. They're an invitation to attack.

The kitchen was defined by raised counters rather than walls, spilling tile flooring into the hall and attached dining room in an almost organic fashion. Senator Ryman was standing by the big butcher's block at the center when we entered, arms around the waist of a woman in blue jeans and a flannel lumberjack's shirt. Her brown hair was pulled back in a high, girlish ponytail. He was murmuring something in her ear, looking a good ten years younger than he had when we met outside.

Shaun and I exchanged a glance, debating the merits of retreating and allowing them this private time. My journalistic instincts said "stay," and I certainly wasn't turning off the cameras, but my sense of ethics told me that people deserve a chance to unwind before starting on something as huge as a full-on political campaign.

Luckily, Buffy saved us from the conundrum by barreling straight ahead, sniffing the air appreciatively, and asking, "What's for lunch? Wow, I'm starving. That smells like shrimp and mahimahi—am I close? Can I do anything to help?"

Senator Ryman stepped away from his wife, exchanging an amused look with her before turning a grin on Buffy, and said, "I think things are pretty much in hand. Besides which, Emily's too territorial to share her kitchen with another woman. Even if it's a borrowed kitchen."

"Quiet, you," said Emily, jabbing him in the ribs with a wooden spoon. He winced theatrically, and she laughed. The laugh was bright, perfectly in keeping with the practical, elegantly simple kitchen. "Now, let me see if I can guess which of you is which. I know you have two Georges and a Shaun—how is that fair?" She put on an exaggerated pout, not looking a bit like a senator's wife. "Three boys' names for two girls and a boy. It puts me at a disadvantage."

"We didn't get to choose our own names, ma'am," I said, fighting a smile. Shaun and I don't even know what names we were born with. We were orphaned in the Rising, and when the Masons adopted us, we were both listed under "Baby Doe."

"Oh, but one of you did," she said. "One of the Georges is also a Buffy, and if I remember my pop culture right, it should be the blonde one." She turned, extending a hand toward Buffy. "Georgette Meissonier, correct?"

"Absolutely," Buffy said, taking her hand. "You can call me Buffy. Everyone else does."

"It's a pleasure to meet you," Emily replied, and released her hand, turning toward Shaun and me. "That must make you the Masons. Shaun and Georgia. Yes?"

"Got it," Shaun said, saluting her. Somehow, he kept the gesture from looking like he was making fun. I've never understood how he does that.

I stepped forward, offering her a hand. "George is fine by me, or Georgia. Whichever is easier for you, Mrs. Ryman."

"Call me Emily," she said. Her grip was cool, and the glance she cast toward my sunglasses was understanding. "Are the lights too bright for you? They're all soft bulbs, but I can dim the window a bit more if you need me to."

"No, thank you," I said, eyebrows rising as I studied her face more closely. Her eyes weren't dark, as I had first assumed; what I had taken to be deep brown irises were actually her pupils, so dilated that they pushed the natural muddy hazel of her eyes into a thin ring around the edges. "Wouldn't you know if the lights were a problem?"

She smiled, wryly. "My eyes aren't as sensitive as they used to be. I was an early case, and there was some nerve damage by the time they figured out what was going on. You'll tell me if the lights get to be too much?"

I nodded. "Sure will."

"Wonderful. You three make yourselves comfortable. Lunch will be up in a few minutes. We're having fish tacos with mango salsa and virgin mimosas." She raised a finger to the senator, adding playfully, "I don't want to hear a word of complaint from you, Mister. We're not getting these nice reporters drunk before things even get started."

"Don't worry, ma'am," Shaun said. "Some of us can hold our liquor."

"And some of us can't," I said dryly. Buffy weighs ninety-five pounds, soaking wet. The one time we took her out drinking, she wound up climbing onto a table and reciting half of *Night of the Living Dead* before Shaun and I could pull her down. "Thank you, Mrs. . . . Emily."

Her smile was approving. "You can be taught. Now all of you, go sit down while I finish taking care of business. Peter, that means you, too."

"Yes, dear," said the senator, kissing her on the cheek before moving to take a seat at the dining room table. The three of us followed him in an obedient, slightly ragged line. I'll challenge senators and kings for the right to know the truth, but far be it from me to challenge a woman in her own kitchen.

Watching the places everyone took around the table was interesting in a purely sociological sense. Shaun settled with his back to the wall, affording him the best view of the room. He may seem like an idiot, but in some ways, he's the most careful of us all. You can't be an Irwin and not learn some things about keeping your exits open. If the zombies ever mob en masse again, he'll be ready. And filming.

Buffy took the seat nearest the light, where the cameras studded through her jewelry would get the best pickup shots. Her portables work on the principles defined during the big pre-Rising wireless boom; they transmit data to the server on a constant basis, allowing her to come back later and edit it at her leisure. I once tried to figure out how many transmitters she actually had on her, but wound up giving up and wandering off to do something more productive, like answering Shaun's fan mail. He gets more marriage proposals a week than he likes to think about, and he lets me handle them all.

The senator took the seat closest to the kitchen and his wife, thus conveniently leaving me the chair with the highest degree of shadow. So he was a family man *and* someone who understood that consideration was a virtue. Nice. I settled, asking, "You provide home-cooked meals for all your news staff?"

"Just the controversial ones," he replied, his tone easy and assured. "I'm not going to beat around the bush. I read your public reports, your op-ed pieces, everything, before I agreed to your application. I know you're smart and won't forgive bullshit. That doesn't," he held up a finger, "mean I'm going to be one hundred percent straight with you, because there are some things no reporter ever gets to be privy to. Mostly having to do with my home life and my family, but still, there are no-go zones."

"We respect that," I said. Shaun and Buffy were nodding.

Senator Ryman seemed to approve, because he nodded in turn, looking satisfied. "Nobody wanted me to bring blog folks on this campaign," he said, without preamble. I sat up a little straighter. The entire online community knew that the senator's handlers had been recommending against including bloggers in the official campaign press corps, but I'd never expected to hear it put so baldly. "They have this idea that you three will report whatever you damn well want to and not what's good for the campaign."

"So you're saying they're pretty smart, then?" Shaun asked, in a bland surfer-boy drawl that might almost have been believable, if he hadn't been smirking as he said it.

The senator roared with laughter, and Emily looked up from the stove, clearly amused. "That's what I pay them for, so I certainly hope so, Shaun. Yeah, they're pretty smart. They've got you pegged for exactly what you are."

"And what's that, Senator?" I asked.

Sobering, he leaned forward. "The children of the Rising. Biggest revolution that our generations—yours, mine, and at least two more besides—are ever going to see. The world changed overnight, and sometimes I'm sorry I was born too early to be in on the ground level of what it's turned into. You kids, you're the ones who get to shape the real tomorrow, the one that's going to matter. Not me, not my lovely wife, and certainly not a bunch of talking heads who get paid to be smart enough to realize that a bunch of Bay Area blogger kids are going to tell the truth as they see it, and damn the political consequences."

Eyebrows rising again, I said, "That does very little to explain why you felt it was important that we be here."

"You're here because of what you represent: the truth." The senator smiled, boyish once more. "People are going to believe whatever you say. Your careers depend on how many dead folks your brother can prod with a stick, how many poems your friend can write, and how much truth you can tell."

"So what if the things we say don't paint you in a good enough light?" Buffy frowned, tilting her head. It would have looked like a natural gesture if I hadn't known the silver moon-and-star earring dangling from her left ear was a camera that responded to head gestures. She was zooming in on the senator to catch his answer.

"If they don't paint me in a good enough light, I suppose I wasn't meant to be the President of the United States of America," he said. "You want to dig for scandals, I'm sure my opponents have road maps for you to follow. You want to report on this campaign, you report what you see, and don't worry about whether or not I'm going to like it. Because that doesn't matter a bit."

We were still staring at him, trying to frame responses to something that seemed about as realistic coming from a politician's mouth as sonnets coming out of a zombie's, when Emily Ryman walked over and started setting plates onto the table. I was grateful for the interruption. After the way the day had been going, I was running out of "surprised" and moving rapidly into the region of "mild shock," and this was enough to give me a chance to regroup.

Emily sat once she'd finished putting the plates down, reaching for Senator Ryman's hand. "Peter, will you say grace?"

"Of course," he said. Shaun and I exchanged glances before joining hands with each other and the Rymans, closing the circle around the table. Senator Ryman bowed his head, closing his eyes. "Dear Lord, we ask that You bless this table and those who have come to gather around it. Thank You for the good gifts that You have given us. For the health of ourselves and our families, for the company and food we are about to enjoy, and for the future that You have seen fit to set before us. Thank You, oh Lord, for Your generosity, and for the trials by which we may come to know You better."

Shaun and I left our eyes open, watching the senator as he spoke. We're atheists. It's hard to be anything else in a world where zombies can attack your elementary school talent show. Much of the country has turned back toward faith, however, acting under the vague supposition that it can't hurt anything to have God on your side. I glanced at Buffy, who was nodding along with the senator's words, eyes tightly closed. She's a lot more religious than most people would guess. Her family is French Catholic. She's been saying grace at any sort of large gathering since she was born, and she still attends a nonvirtual church on Sundays.

"Amen," said the senator. We all echoed it with varying degrees of certainty.

Emily Ryman smiled. "Everybody, eat up. There's more if you're still hungry, but I want to eat too, so you're going to have to serve yourselves after this round." The senator got a kiss on the cheek to go with his fish tacos; the rest of us just got fed.

Not that Shaun was going to let lunch pass without a little light conversation. Of the two of us, he's the gregarious one. Someone had to be. "Will you be coming along on the whole campaign, ma'am, or just this leg of it?" he asked, with uncharacteristic politeness. Then again, he's always had a healthy respect for women with food.

"You couldn't pay me enough to accompany this dog and pony show," Emily said, dryly. "I think you kids are totally insane. Entertaining as all heck, and I love your site, but insane."

"I'll take that as a 'no,'" I said.

"Uh-uh. For one thing, I am *not* taking the kids out on the road. No way. The tutors they hire for these things are never the sort I approve of." She smiled at the senator, who patted her knee in an unconsciously companionable fashion. "And they wind up seeing way too many reporters and politicians. Not the sort you want keeping company with a bunch of impressionable young kids."

"Look how it's warped us," said Shaun.

"Exactly," she said, unflustered. "Besides which, the ranch doesn't run itself."

I nodded. "Your family still manages an actual horse ranch, don't they?"

"You know the answer to that, Georgia," said the senator. "Been in Emily's family since the late eighteen hundreds."

"If you think the risk of zombie palominos is enough to make me give up my horses, you've never met a real horse nut," she said, grinning. "Now, don't get your back up. I know where you stand on the animal mass restrictions. You're a big supporter of Mason's Law, aren't you?"

"In all recreational and nonessential capacities, yes," I said.

Thanks to the Masons' biological son, Shaun and I have often found ourselves with an element of unasked-for name recognition when dealing with people who work with animals. Before Phillip, no one realized that *all* mammals with a body mass of forty pounds or more could become carriers of the live-state virus, or that Kellis-Amberlee was happy to cross species, going from man to beast and back again. Mom put a bullet through her only son's head, back when that was still something new enough to break you forever—when it felt like murder, not mercy. So yeah, I guess you could say I support Mason's Law.

"I would, too, in your position," Emily said. Her tone carried none of the accusations I'm used to hearing from animal rights activists; she was speaking the truth, and I could deal, or not, as I so chose. "Now, if everyone wants to tuck in, it's the start of a long day—and a longer month."

"Eat up, everybody, before your lunch gets cold," added the senator, and reached for the mimosas. Shaun and I exchanged a look, shrugged in near-unison, and reached for our forks.

One way or another, we were on our way.

———————————

My sister has retinal KA syndrome. That's where the filovirus does this massive replication thing in the ocular fluid—there's some more advanced technical term for it, but personally, I like to call it "eye goo," because it pisses George off—and the pupils dilate as wide as they can and never close down like they do in a normal person. Mostly only girls get it, which is a relief, since I look stupid in sunglasses. Her eyes are supposed to be brown, but everyone thinks they're black, because of her pupils being broken.

She was diagnosed when we were five, so I don't really remember her without her sunglasses. And when we were nine, we got this really *dumb* babysitter who took George's glasses, said, "You don't need these," and threw them into the backyard, thinking we were spoiled little suburban brats too afraid of the outdoors to go out after them. So it's pretty plain that she was about as bright as a box of zombies.

Next thing you know, there's me and George digging through the high grass looking for her sunglasses, when suddenly she freezes, eyes getting all wide, and says, "Shaun?" And I'm like, "What?" And she's all, "There's somebody else in the yard." And then I turn around, and wham, zombie, *right there*! I hadn't seen it because I don't see as well in low light as she does. So there are some advantages to having your pupils permanently dilated. Besides the part where they can't tell if you're stoned or not without a blood test when you're at school.

But anyway, zombie, in our backyard. So. Fucking. Cool.

You know, it's been more than a decade since that evening, and that is *still* probably the best present that she's ever gotten for me.

—From *Hail to the King*,
the blog of Shaun Mason, April 7, 2037

Six

Getting our equipment past the security screening offered by Senator Ryman's staff took six and a half hours. Shaun spent the first two hours getting underfoot as he tried to guard his gear and finally got all of us banished inside. Now he was sulking on the parlor couch, chin almost level with his chest. "What are they doing, taking the van apart to make sure we didn't stuff any zombies inside the paneling?" he grumbled. "Because, gee, *that* would work really well as an assassination tool."

"It's been tried," Buffy said. "Do you remember the guy who tried to kill George Romero with the zombie pit bulls?"

"That's an urban myth, Buffy. It's been disproven about ninety times," I said, continuing to pace. "George Romero died peacefully in his bed."

"And now he's a happy shambler at a government research facility," said Shaun, abandoning his sulk in order to make "zombie" motions with his arms. The ASL for "zombie" has joined the raised middle finger as one of the few truly universal hand gestures. Some points just need to be made quickly.

"It's sort of sad, thinking about him shuffling around out there, all decayed and mindless and not remembering the classics of his heyday," said Buffy.

I eyed her. "He's a government zombie. He eats better than we do."

"It's the principle of the thing," she said.

It took a while for the first Kellis-Amberlee outbreaks to be confirmed as anything but hoaxes, and even after that was accomplished, it took time for the various governmental agencies to finish fighting over whose problem it was. The CDC got sick of the arguing about three days in, jumped into things with both feet, and never looked back. They had squads in the field by the end of week two, capturing zombies for study. It was quickly apparent that there's no curing a zombie; you can't undo the amount of brain damage the virus does with anything gentler than a bullet to the brainpan. But you can work on ways to neutralize Kellis-Amberlee itself, and since all a zombie really does is convert flesh into virus, a few captive shamblers provided the best possible test subjects.

After twenty years of testing and the derailment of almost every technical field that didn't feed directly into the medical profession, we've managed little more than absolutely nothing. At this point, they can completely remove Kellis-Amberlee from a living body, using a combination of chemotherapy, blood replacement, and a nasty strain of Ebola that's been modified to search and destroy its cousin. There are just a few downsides, like the part where it costs upward of ten thousand dollars for a treatment, none of the test subjects has survived, and oh, right, the constant fear the modified virus will mutate like Marburg Amberlee did and leave us with something even worse to deal with. Where the living dead are concerned, we pretty much exist on square one.

It didn't take long for researchers to connect the health of their "pet" zombies to the amount of protein—specifically living or recently killed flesh; soybeans and legumes won't cut it—they consumed. Kellis-Amberlee converts tissue into viral blocks. The more tissue it can find, the less of the original zombie it converts. So if you feed a zombie constantly, it won't wither to the point of becoming useless. Most of the nation's remaining cattle ranches are there to feed the living dead. A beautiful irony, when you consider that cows break the forty-pound threshold, and thus reanimate upon death. Zombies eating zombies. Good work if you can get it.

A lot of folks leave their bodies to science. Your family skips funeral expenses, the government pays a nice settlement so they won't sue if your image winds up on television one of these days, and if you belong to one of those religious sects that believes the body has to remain intact in order to eventually get carried up to Heaven, you don't run the risk of offending God. You just risk eating the research scientists if containment fails, and some people don't see that as being as much of an abomination as cremation.

George Romero didn't mean to save the world any more than Dr. Alexander Kellis meant to almost destroy it, but you can't always choose your lot in life. Most people wouldn't have had the first idea of how to deal with the zombies if it weren't for the lessons they'd learned from Romero's movies. Go for the brain; fire works, but only if you don't let the burning zombie touch you; once you're bitten, you're dead. Fans of Romero's films applied the lessons of a thousand zombie movies to the reality of what had happened. They traded details of the attacks and their results over a thousand blogs from a thousand places, and humanity survived.

In interviews, Mr. Romero always seemed baffled and a little delighted by the power his movies had proven to have. "Always knew there was a reason people didn't like seeing the zombies win," he'd said. If anyone was surprised when he left his body to the government, they didn't say anything. It seemed like a fitting end for a man who went from king of bad horror to national hero practically overnight.

"They better not damage any of my equipment," Shaun said, snapping me back to the present. He was scowling at the window again. "Some of that stuff took serious barter to get."

"They're not going to damage your equipment, dumb ass. They're the government, we're journalists, and they know we'd tell everyone in the whole damn world, starting with our insurance agency." I leaned over to hit him in the back of the head. "They just need to make sure we're not carrying any bombs."

"Or zombies," added Buffy.

"Or drugs," said Shaun.

"Actually," said the senator, stepping into the room, "we're slightly disappointed by the lack of bombs, zombies, or drugs hidden in your gear. I thought you folks were supposed to be reporters, but there wasn't even any illicit booze."

"We're clear?" I asked, ceasing my pacing. Shaun and Buffy were already on their feet, nearly vibrating. I understood their anxiety; the senator's security crew had their hands on all our servers, which had Buffy unhappy, and on Shaun's zombie hunting and handling equipment, which usually makes him so restless that I wind up locking him in the bathroom just to get some peace and quiet. It's times like this that I'm truly glad of my role as the hard-nosed reporter in our little crew. Maybe Buffy and Shaun call me a Luddite, but when the government goons take away all our equipment for examination, they lose everything. I, on the other hand, retain my MP3 recorder, cellular phone, notebook computer, and stylus. They're all too basic to require much examination.

Of course, I can't keep my hands on the vehicles, which had me almost as restless as my companions. The van and my bike represent the most expensive articles we travel with, and most of our livelihood depends on their upkeep. At the same time, they're probably the easiest items to repair—a good mechanic can undo almost any damage, and my bike isn't that customized. As long as the feds didn't bust up the van, we'd be fine.

"You're clear," the senator said. He didn't bat an eye as Shaun and Buffy ran out of the room, despite the fact that neither of them said good-bye. I remained where I was, and after a moment, he turned toward me. "I must admit, we *were* impressed by the structural reinforcements on your van. Planning to last out a siege in that thing?"

"We've considered it. The security upgrades were our mother's design. We did the electrical work ourselves."

Senator Ryman nodded as if this explained everything. In a way, it did. Stacy Mason has been the first name in zombie-proof structural engineering for a long time. "I have to admit, I don't really understand most of your professional equipment, but the security systems... Your mother did a truly lovely job."

"I'll give her your compliments." I gestured toward the door. "I should join the feeding frenzy. Buffy's going to want to start assembling today's footage, and she always goes overboard without me standing over her."

"I see." The senator paused for a moment. His voice was uncharacteristically stiff as he continued, "I wondered if I might ask you a small favor, Miss Mason."

Ah, the first demand for censorship. I was going to owe Shaun ten bucks; I'd been betting that Senator Ryman could make it at least until we hit the actual campaign trail before he started trying to control the media. Keeping my voice level, I said, "And that would be, Senator?"

"Emily." He shook his head, a smile tugging at his lips. "I know you'll release whatever you want to, and I look forward to having the chance to read and watch it all. I don't figure we caught half the cameras and recorders you three had on you—some of the ones Miss Meissonier was carrying were barely in the range of our sensors, which leads me to believe that she had others we couldn't see at all, and if she ever wishes to pursue a career in espionage, I only pray she offers her services to us first—so you've doubtless got some great footage. And that's fabulous. But Emily, you see, well... she's not so comfortable with a lot of media attention."

I looked at him, thoughtfully. "So you want me to minimize the use of your wife?" That was odd. Emily Ryman was friendly, photogenic, and, except for the horses, just about the sanest politician's wife I'd ever met. I expected him to milk her as the asset she was. "She's going to have to feature in this campaign. And if you win—"

"She understands her role in things, and she doesn't mind being written about, but she'd rather her picture wasn't used excessively," he said. He was clearly uncomfortable with the request. That made me a lot more likely to grant it. "Please. If it's at all possible, I would see it as a great personal favor."

Lowering my sunglasses enough to let him see my eyes, I asked, "Why?"

"Because she raises horses. I know you don't approve of keeping mammals that meet the size for Kellis-Amberlee amplification, but you're polite about it. You write articles and you lobby for stricter controls, and that's fine, that's your right as an American citizen. Given your family connections, it's even unavoidable. Some people, however, get a little more... aggressive."

"You're talking about the bombing in San Diego, aren't you?" It was the darling of the news feeds for a while, because it was such a huge event: the world's largest remaining zoo and wild animal conservatory, bombed by activists who believed Mason's Law should be used to shut down every facility in the world that kept animals capable of undergoing viral amplification. The same fringe group, in other words, that supports lifting the bans on big-game hunting across the world, and wiping out North America's large indigenous mammals. They call themselves "pro-life," but what they really are is pro-genocide. Their proverbial panties get wet just thinking about the opportunity to go out and slaughter something under the illusion of following the law. Hundreds died in San Diego because of what they did, and I'm not just talking about the animals. We got a lot of firsts out of that stunt. "First confirmed Kellis-Amberlee transmission through giraffe bite" wasn't the weirdest.

Senator Ryman nodded, lips pressed into a thin line. "I have three daughters. All of them are at the ranch with their grandparents, waiting for their mother to rejoin them."

"Trying to avoid making them a target?"

"That's unavoidable, unfortunately. It's the nature of modern politics. But I can keep them out of the spotlight for as long as I can."

I kept my sunglasses pulled down, studying him. Unlike most people, he met my eyes without flinching. Having a wife with retinal KA probably helped with that. Finally, I slid my glasses back into place and nodded. "I'll see what I can do."

He offered a quick, boyish smile, his relief showing clearly. "Thank you, Miss Mason. Don't let me keep you any longer. I'm sure you're anxious to check the state of your vehicles."

"If your goons scratched my bike, I'll have to get bitchy," I cautioned, and left the room, following the path Shaun and Buffy had taken to the yard. Leaving Emily out of things would be relatively easy. The way the kitchen was lit meant we could limit footage of her without changing the overall tone of the afternoon, and without being too blatant—looking like you're hiding something is the fastest way to bring the vultures down. I'd have to leave it up to Buffy, of course. She's our graphics wiz.

The interesting part was that he was willing to ask for it at all. Senator Ryman knew he'd only get to ask us to leave things out so many times before we started resisting, and once that happened, he wasn't going to be a happy man. So why introduce us to Emily at all, if the introduction meant he'd have to use one of his limited "get out of jail free" cards to keep her out of a puff piece about meeting the candidate over some good old-fashioned fish tacos? It was possible he was just trying to play on our sympathies— "Golly, my wife doesn't like to be seen on camera, and it could endanger the kids, so you'll be good to us, right?"—but that didn't seem likely. It seemed a lot more realistic to me that she'd wanted the chance to meet us, and he was willing to go along with it, as long as it kept her happy with him. I've learned to trust my hunches, and they were telling me now that the senator and his wife were generally good folks, with the bad taste to choose politics and horse breeding as their respective careers.

Our vehicles were parked out front. The van had been scrubbed until it gleamed, and even the relay towers were clean. All the chrome on my bike had been buffed until it was almost too bright to contemplate, even through my sunglasses. "I don't think that thing's been this clean since before I bought it," I said, shoving my glasses back up my nose. The sunset was on the way, and as far as I was concerned, it was taking a little too much of its own sweet time about things.

Shaun stuck his head out of the van's rear door and waved, calling, "Hey, George! They got the fruit punch stain out of the upholstery!"

"Really?" I couldn't help being impressed. That stain had been in the van since three days after the parents gave it to us, and that was on our eighteenth adoption day. "Class A license means Class A equipment," Dad said, and that—well, that, and roughly three hundred hours of back-breaking work—was that.

"And they moved *all* Buffy's wires around," he said, with a certain degree of sadistic glee, before retreating back into the van.

I smothered a smile as I started toward the van, pausing to run one hand down the sleekly polished side of my bike. If the security crew had scratched the paint, they'd also buffed the scratch clean without leaving a trace. It was impressive work.

Things were less peaceful inside the van. Shaun was sprawled in a chair, cleaning his crossbow, while Buffy was flat on her back under one of the desks, heels drumming against the floor as she yanked wires out of their current, incorrect locations and jammed them into new holes. Every time she yanked a wire, one or more of the van's monitors would start to roll or be consumed by static, turning the scene into something abstract and surrealistic, like a bad B-grade horror movie. She was also swearing like a merchant marine, displaying a grasp of profanity that was more than a little bit impressive.

"Do you kiss your mother with that mouth?" I asked, stepping over the spools of discarded cabling and taking a seat on the counter.

"Look at this!" She shoved herself out from under the desk and into a kneeling position, brandishing a fistful of cables in my direction. I raised my eyebrows, waiting. "*All* of these were connected wrong! All of them!"

"Are they labeled?"

Buffy hesitated before admitting, "No."

"Do they follow any sort of normal, sane, or predictable system?" I knew the answer to that one. Shaun and I did most of the electrical work, but the actual wiring is all Buffy's, and she thought most people were too conservative with the way they managed their inputs. I've tried to understand her system a few times. I've always come away with a migraine and the firm conviction that, sometimes, ignorance really *is* bliss.

"They didn't have to unplug *everything*," Buffy muttered, and crawled back under the desk.

Shaun pulled back the string on his crossbow with one finger, checking the tension, and said, "You can't win. Logic has no power over her when her territory has been invaded by the heathens."

"Got it," I said. The monitor next to me rolled to static before it began displaying a video feed of the yard outside. "Buffy, how long before we're fully operational again?"

"Fifteen minutes. Maybe twenty. I haven't checked the wires on the backup consoles yet, so I don't know how big of a mess they made *there*." The irritation in her voice was unmasked. "No data loss so far, but none of the van's exterior cameras got anything but static for over an hour, thanks to their stupid monkeying."

"I'm sure we can live without an hour's recordings of the security team," I said. "Shaun, get the lights?"

"On it." He put his crossbow aside and rose, moving to drop the shade over the van's window and pull the rear door closed. Buffy made a small grunt of protest, and he flicked the switch to turn on the interior lights. The area was promptly bathed in a soft, specially formulated light designed to be gentle on sensitive eyes. The bulbs cost fifty bucks each, and they're worth it. They're even better than the black lights I use in my room at home. They don't just prevent headaches; sometimes, they *cure* them.

I removed my glasses with a sigh, massaging my right temple with my fingertips. "All right, folks, we have our first official, on-the-record encounter. Impressions?"

"Like the wife," said Shaun. "She's photogenic, and a definite asset. I still need a handle on the senator. He's either the biggest Boy Scout ever to make it past the local level, or he's playing us."

"The fish tacos were good," said Buffy. "I like Senator Ryman, actually. He's nice even when he doesn't have to be. This could be a pretty fun gig."

"Who cares about fun as long as it brings in the green?" asked Shaun, with a philosophical shrug. "We're made when this is over. Everything else is gravy."

"I agree with both of you, to a degree," I said, still massaging my temple. I could already tell I was going to need painkillers before we wrapped for the night. "Senator Ryman can't be as nice as he wants us to think he is, but he's also nicer than he has to be; it's not entirely a put-on. There's a degree of sincerity there that you can't fake. I'll do a pull-and-drop profile on him tonight, something like 'First Impressions of the Man Who Would Be President.' Puff piece, but still. Buff, how long is it going to take you to splice our footage?"

"Once everything is ready to run again, I'll need an hour—two, tops."

"Try for an hour. We want to hit the East Coast while they're still awake. Shaun, care to do a review of the security precautions? Hit up a few of the guards, find out what sort of ordnance they're carrying with them?"

His face split in a wide grin. "Already on it. You know the big blond guy? Built like a linebacker?"

"I did notice the presence of a giant on the security team, yes."

"His name's Steve. He carries a baseball bat." Shaun made an exaggerated swinging motion. "Can you imagine him hitting one out of the park?"

"Ah," I said, dryly. "The classics. Grab a few cameras, harass the locals until you get what you want. Which brings us to my last order of business—we have a request from the senator."

Buffy slid out from under the desk again, another bundle of wires in her hands, and gave me a curious look. Shaun scowled.

"Don't tell me we're being censored *already.*"

"Yes and no," I said. "He wants us to keep Emily out of things as much as we can for right now. Minimize her inclusion in the lunch footage, that sort of thing."

"Why?" asked Buffy.

"San Diego," I said, and waited.

I didn't have to wait long. Shaun doesn't feel as strongly as I do about the universal application of Mason's Law, but he still follows the debate. Expression changing from one of incomprehension to complete understanding, he said, "He's afraid somebody's going to target her at the ranch if we make too big a deal of things."

"Exactly." I switched my massaging to my other temple. "Their kids are out there with their grandparents, and he sort of wants the family alive. A little risk is unavoidable, but he'd like to keep them low-profile as long as he can."

"I can manage the footage edits," said Buffy.

"She wouldn't feature in my piece at all," said Shaun.

"And I'll sidebar her. So we're in agreement?"

"Guess so," said Shaun.

"Great. Buffy, let me know when we're back to live-feed capacity on all bands. I'm going to step outside for a few minutes." I slid my sunglasses back on and stood. "Just getting a little air."

"I'll get to work," said Shaun, and stood as I did, exiting the van a few steps ahead of me. He didn't stop or look back as I came out; he just kept going. Shaun knows me better than anyone else in the world. Sometimes I think he knows me better than I do. He knows I need a few minutes by myself before I can start working. Location doesn't matter. Just solitude.

The afternoon light had dimmed without dying, and my bike wasn't quite as painful to look at. I walked over and leaned against it, resting my heels on the driveway as I closed my eyes and tilted my face up into the dying light. Welcome to the world, kids. Things were moving now, and all we could do was make sure that the truth kept getting out, and getting where it needed to be.

When I was sixteen and told my father that I wanted to be a Newsie—it wasn't a surprise by that point, but it was the first time I had said it to his face—he pulled some strings and got me enrolled in a history of journalism course at the university. Edward R. Murrow, Walter Cronkite, Hunter S. Thompson, Cameron Crowe... I met the greats the way you should meet them, through their words and the things they did, when I was still young enough to fall in love without reservations or conditions. I never wanted to be Lois Lane, girl reporter, even though I dressed like her for Halloween one year. I wanted to be Edward R. Murrow, facing down corruption in the government. I wanted to be Hunter S. Thompson, ripping the skin off the world. I wanted the truth, and I wanted the news, and I'd be damned before I settled for anything less.

Shaun's the same, even if his priorities are different. He's willing to let a good story come before the facts, as long as the essential morals stay true. That's why he's so good at what he does, and why I double-check every report he writes before I release it.

One thing I did learn from those classes is that the world is not, in any way, what people expected thirty years ago. The zombies are here, and they're not going away, but they're not the *story*. They were, for one hot, horrible summer at the beginning of the century, but now they're just another piece of the way things work. They did their part: They changed everything. Absolutely everything.

The world cheered when Dr. Alexander Kellis announced his cure for the common cold. I've never had a cold, thanks to Dr. Kellis, but I understand they were pretty annoying; people didn't enjoy spending half their time sniffling, sneezing, and getting coughed on by total strangers. Dr. Kellis and his team rushed through testing at a pace that seems criminal in retrospect, but who am I to judge? I wasn't there.

What's really funny is that you can blame this whole thing on the news. One reporter heard a rumor that Dr. Kellis was intending to sell his cure to the highest bidder and would never allow it to be released to the man on the street. This was ridiculous if you understood that the cure was a modified rhinovirus, based on the exact virulence that enabled the common cold to spread so far and so fast. Once it got outside the lab, it was going to "infect" the world, and no amount of money would prevent that.

Those are the facts, but this guy didn't care about the facts. He cared about the scoop and being the first to report a great and imaginary injustice being perpetrated by the heartless medical community. If you ask me, the real injustice is that Dr. Alexander Kellis is viewed as responsible for the near-destruction of mankind and not Robert Stalnaker, investigative reporter for the *New York Times*. If you're going to lay blame for what happened, that's where it belongs. I've read his articles. They were pretty stirring stuff, condemning Dr. Kellis and the medical community for allowing this to happen. Mankind, he said, had a right to the cure.

Some people believed him a bit too much. They broke into the lab, stole the cure, and released it from a crop duster, if you can believe that. They flew that bastard as high as it would go, loaded balloons with samples of Dr. Kellis's work, and fired them into the atmosphere. It was a beautiful act of bioterrorism, conducted with all the best ideals at heart. They acted on a flawed assumption taken from an incomplete truth, and they screwed us all.

To be fair, they might not have screwed things up as badly as they did if it hadn't been for a team working out of Denver, Colorado, where they were running trials on a genetically engineered filovirus called "Marburg EX19," or, more commonly, "Marburg Amberlee." It was named for their first successful infection, Amanda Amberlee, age twelve and a half. She'd been dying of leukemia and considered unlikely to see her thirteenth birthday. The year Dr. Kellis discovered his cure, Amanda was eighteen, finishing her senior year of high school, and perfectly healthy. The folks in Denver took a killer, made a few changes to its instructions, and cured cancer.

Marburg Amberlee was a miracle, just like the Kellis cure, and together they were primed to change the course of the human race. Together, that's what they did. No one gets cancer or colds anymore. The only issue is the walking dead.

There were ninety-seven people in the world infected with Marburg Amberlee when the Kellis cure was released. The virus never left the system once it had been introduced; it would kill off cancerous cells and go dormant, waiting. All those people were quiet, noninfectious hot zones, living their lives without a clue of what was about to happen. Amanda Amberlee wasn't among them. She died two months earlier, in a car crash following her senior prom. She was the only one of the Marburg Amberlee test cases not to reanimate; she provided the first clue that it was the interaction of the viruses and not Marburg Amberlee itself that caused the apparently dead to rise.

The Kellis cure swept the globe in days. Those responsible for the release were hailed, if not as heroes, then at least as responsible citizens, cutting through red tape to better the lives of their fellow men. No one knows when the first Marburg Amberlee test subjects came into contact with the cure or how long it took from exposure to mutation. How long for the formerly peaceful filovirus to seize on the newly introduced rhinovirus and begin to change? Best estimates say that within a week of the introduction of the Kellis cure to Marburg Amberlee, the two had combined, creating the airborne filovirus we know as Kellis-Amberlee. It went on to infect the world, hopping from person to person on the back of the virulence coded into the original Kellis cure.

There is no index case for viral amplification. It happened in too many places at the same time. We can only pinpoint things to this degree because of what the movies got wrong: Infection wasn't initially universal. People who died before getting dosed with Kellis-Amberlee stayed dead. Those who died after infection didn't. Why it brings its hosts back to literal, biological life is anyone's guess. The best theories hold that it's an enhanced version of normal filovirus behavior, the urge to replicate taken to a new and unnatural level, one that taps into the nervous system of the host and keeps it moving until it falls apart. Zombies are just sacks of virus looking for something to infect, being "driven" by Kellis-Amberlee. Maybe it's true. Who knows? Whether it is or not, the zombies are here, and everything has changed.

That includes the shape of the political world, because a lot of the old issues shifted once the living dead were among us. The death penalty, animal cruelty, abortion—the list goes on. It's hard to be a politician in this world, especially given the xenophobia and paranoia running rampant through most of our more well-off communities. Senator Ryman was going to have a long, hard fight to the White House, assuming he could get there at all. And we'd be with him every step of the way.

I sat with my face toward the sun, ignoring the way my head was throbbing, and waited for Buffy to tell me that the time had come to begin.

BOOK II

Dancing with the Dead

You tell the truth as you see it, and you let the people decide whether to believe you. That's responsible reporting. That's playing fair. Didn't your parents teach you anything?

—Georgia Mason

Darwin was right. Death doesn't play fair.

—Stacy Mason

To explain my feelings for Senator Peter Ryman, I must first note that I am a naturally suspicious soul: that which seems too good to be true, in my experience, generally is. It is thus with the natural cynicism that is my hallmark that I make the following statement:

Peter Ryman, Wisconsin's political golden boy, is too good to be true.

As a lifelong member of the Republican party in an era when half the party has embraced the idea that the living dead are a punishment from God and we poor sinners must do "penance" before we can enter the Kingdom of Heaven, it would be easy for him to be a bitter man, and yet he shows no signs of it. He is friendly, cordial, intelligent, and sincere enough to convince this reporter, even at three in the morning when the convoy has broken down in the middle of Kentucky for the third time and the language has turned saltier than the Pacific tide. Rather than preaching damnation, he counsels tolerance. Rather than calling for a "war on the undead," he recommends improving our defenses and the quality of life in the still-inhabited zones.

He is, in short, a politician who understands that the dead are the dead, the living are the living, and we need to treat both with equal care.

Ladies and gentlemen, unless this man has some truly awe-inspiring skeletons in his closet, it is my present and considered belief that he would make an excellent President of the United States of America, and might actually begin to repair the social, economic, and political damage that has been done by the events of these past thirty years. Of course, that can only mean that he won't win.

But a girl can dream.

—**From *Images May Disturb You*,**
the blog of Georgia Mason, February 5, 2040

Seven

The civic center had been prepared for Senator Ryman's visit with row upon row of folding chairs and video screens angled to broadcast his image all the way to the rear of the cavernous room. Speakers were mounted every fifth row to make sure his words remained crystal clear as they fell upon the ears of the twenty or so brave souls who had actually dared to come hear him speak. The attendees were clustered in the front four rows, leaving the back of the room for the senator's entourage, security folks, and, of course, the three of us. Put together, we outnumbered the voting public almost two to one.

Not that this was a unique occurrence. We'd seen this scene play out in nearly two dozen states and more than three times as many locations in the six weeks since we had left California. People don't come out to "press the flesh" the way they used to, not even for the primaries that determine which candidates will be making it all the way to the presidential elections. They're too worried about contagion and too afraid that the weird guy who keeps muttering to himself isn't actually insane—there's always a chance that he's going through massive viral amplification and will take a chunk out of someone at any moment. The only safe people are the ones you know so well that they can't surprise you with the personality changes the virus causes during replication. Since few people have enough close personal friends to fill an auditorium, most folks don't come out.

That doesn't mean that things have been going unobserved. Judging by the ratings, page hits, and downloads, the campaign has been maintaining some of the highest viewer numbers since Cruise versus Gore in 2018. People want to know how it's going to turn out. There's a lot riding on this election. Including, incidentally, our careers.

Shaun's always said that I take things too seriously; since the start of the campaign, he'd started saying my sense of humor had been surgically removed to make room for more anal-retentiveness. Anyone else who said that would probably have gotten slapped, but from Shaun, I had to admit to an element of truth. Still, if I left things up to him, we'd be living with our parents and pretending we didn't mind the lack of privacy until we died. Someone has to watch the bottom line, and someone has pretty much always been me.

Glancing to Buffy, I stage-whispered, "How do our numbers look?"

She didn't look up from the text scrolling rapidly across her phone. The data feed was moving so fast I didn't have a prayer of following it, but it obviously meant something to Buffy because she nodded, with a small smile on her lips as she said, "We're looking at a sixty percent local audience on the video feed, and we just hit top six percent on the Web. The only candidate getting a higher feed ratio is Congresswoman Wagman, and she's lagging in the actual polls."

"And we know why *she's* getting the feeds, now, don't we children?" drawled Shaun, continuing to test the links in his favorite chain-mail shirt with a pair of lightweight pliers.

I snorted. Word on the blog circuit is that Kirsten "Knockers" Wagman had serious breast augmentation surgery before she went into politics, acting under the assumption that in today's largely Internet-based demographic, looking good is more important than sounding like you have two brain cells to knock together. That worked for a while—it got her a seat in Congress, partially because people enjoy looking at her—but it isn't going to get her very far in a presidential race. Especially not now that she's up against folks who understand the issues.

Senator Ryman didn't appear to have noticed the emptiness of the hall or the nervous expressions on his few actual, physical attendees. Most were probably local politicians coming out to show that they believed in the safety of their community, since several of them looked like they'd explode if you snuck up behind them and said "boo" in a commanding tone of voice. Most, not all. There was one little old lady, at least seventy years old, sitting dead center in the front row. She held her purse primly in her lap, lips set into a thin, hard line as she watched Senator Ryman go through his paces. She didn't look nervous at all. If any zombies tried to invade *this* political event, she'd probably wind up giving them what-for and driving them back outside to wait their turn.

The senator was winding down. You can only give your political platform in so many ways, no matter how much practice you have at saying the same thing from sixteen different angles. I adjusted my sunglasses, settling in my chair as I waited for the real fun to begin: the question-and-answer period. Most of the questions people come up with have something to do with the infected, as in, "What are you going to do about the zombies that the other guys haven't tried already?" The answers can get seriously entertaining, and honestly, so can the questions.

Most questions are e-mailed in by the home audiences and asked by the polite, slightly bland voice of the senator's digital personal assistant, which has been programmed to sound like a well-educated female of indeterminate age and race. Senator Ryman calls it "Beth" for no reason anyone has been able to get him to explain. I intend to keep trying. The *best* questions are the ones that come from the live audiences. Most of them are scared out of their minds after being out of the house for more than half an hour, and nothing loosens the tongue like fear. If I had my way, all questions would be asked by people who had just taken a trip through a really well-designed haunted house.

"—and now I'd like to take a few questions from our audience—both those watching this event through the electronic methods provided by my clever technicians," Senator Ryman chuckled, managing to telegraph his utter lack of understanding of such petty details as "how the video feeds work," "and the good people of Eakly, Oklahoma, who have been good enough to host us this evening."

"Come on, lady, don't let me down," I murmured. Sure enough, the lady in the front row had her hand in the air almost before the senator finished speaking, arm jutting upward at a fierce, near-military angle. I settled back in my chair, grinning. "Jackpot."

"Huh?" Buffy looked up from her watch.

"Live one," I said, indicating the lady.

"Oh." Suddenly interested in something other than the data feed, Buffy sat forward. She knows potential ratings when she sees them.

"Yes—the lady in the front row." Senator Ryman indicated the woman, whose tight-lipped face promptly filled half the monitors in the room. Buffy tapped two buttons on her phone, directing her cameras to zoom in. The senator's tech team is good, and even Buffy admits it; they understand camera angles, splicing footage, and when to go for a tight shot. Thanks to Chuck Wong, who does all their planning and design, they're probably near the top of their field. But Buffy is better.

The lady in question lowered her hand, fixing the senator with a stern gaze. "What is your stance on the Rapture?" Her voice was as clipped and thin as I'd expected. The sound system picked it up clear as a bell, reproducing every harsh edge and disapproving inflection flawlessly.

Senator Ryman blinked, looking nonplussed. It was the first time I'd seen a question take him completely by surprise. He recovered with admirable speed, though, saying, "I beg your pardon?"

"The Rapture. The event in which the faithful will be elevated to the Heavens, while the unfaithful, sinners, and infidels will be left to suffer Hell on Earth." Her eyes narrowed. "What is your stance on this holy, foreordained event?"

"Ah." Senator Ryman continued to look at her, thoughtfulness clearing away his confusion. I heard a faint clink and glanced to my left; Shaun had put down his chain mail and was watching the stage with open interest. Buffy was staring at her phone, furiously tapping buttons as she angled her cameras. You can't edit or pause a live feed, but you can set up the data to give you the best material to work from later. And this was the sort of material you just can't stage. Would he bow to the religious nuts who have been taking over more and more of the party in recent years? Or would he risk alienating the entire religious sector of the voting public? Only the senator knew. And in a moment, so would we.

Senator Ryman didn't break eye contact with the woman as he stepped out from behind his podium, walked to the edge of the stage, and sat, resting his elbows on his knees. He looked like a schoolboy approaching confession, not a man jockeying for the leadership of the most powerful country on the planet. It was a well-considered position, and I applauded it inwardly, even as I began to consider an article on the showmanship of modern politics. "What's your name, ma'am?"

"Suzanne Greeley," she said, pursing her lips. "You haven't answered my question, young man."

"Well, Ms. Greeley, that would be because I was thinking," he said, and looked out at the small gathering, a smile spreading across his face. "I was taught that it's rude to answer a lady's question without giving it proper thought. Sort of like putting your elbows on the table during dinner." A ripple of laughter passed through the crowd. Ms. Greeley didn't join in.

Turning back toward her, the senator continued: "You've asked me about my position on the Rapture, Ms. Greeley. Well, first, I think I should say that I don't really have 'positions' on religious events: God will do as He wills, and it isn't my place or my position to judge Him. If He chooses to lift the faithful into Heaven, He will, and I doubt all the politicians in the world saying, 'I don't believe you can do that' would stop him.

"At the same time, I doubt He's going to do anything like that, Ms. Greeley, because God—the God I believe in, anyway, and as a lifelong Methodist, I feel I know Him about as well as a man who doesn't devote his life to the Church can—doesn't throw good things away. God is the ulti-mate recycler. We have a good planet here. It has its troubles, yes. We have overpopulation, we have pollution, we have global warming, we have the Thursday night television lineup," more laughter, "and, of course, we have the infected. We have a lot of problems on Earth, and it might seem like a great idea to hold the Rapture now—why wait? Let's move on to Heaven, and leave the trials and tribulations of our earthly existence behind us. Let's get while the getting's good, and beat the rush.

"It might seem like a great idea, but I don't think it is, for the same rea-son I don't think it's a great idea for a first grader to stand up and say that he's learned enough, he's done with school, thanks a lot but he's got it from here. Compared to God, we're barely out of kindergarten, and like any good teacher, I don't believe He intends to let us out of class just because we're finding the lessons a little difficult. I don't know whether I believe in the Rapture or not. I believe that if God wants to do it, He will . . . but I don't believe that it's coming in our lifetime. We have too much work left to do right here."

Ms. Greeley looked at him for a long moment, lips still pressed into a thin line. Then, so slow that it was almost glacial, she nodded. "Thank you, young man," she said.

Those four words couldn't have been sweeter if they'd been backed by the hallelujah choir.

"Internet share just jumped to top three percent," Buffy reported, rais-ing her head. Her eyes were very wide. "Georgia, we're getting a *top-three feed.*"

"Ladies and gentlemen," I murmured, leaning back in my chair, "I do believe we've got ourselves a presidential candidate."

Top-three feed. The words were, if you'll pardon the cliché, music to my ears. The world of Internet percentages and readership shares is compli-cated. It all comes down to server traffic. There are thousands of machines dedicated to calculating the flow of data, then reporting back which sites are getting the most access requests from outside sources, and which sub-sidiaries are attracting the biggest number of hits. Those turn into our rat-ings, and those are what the advertisers and financial backers base their investments on. Top three was the top of the heap. Anything more would require adding click-through porn.

The rest of the question-and-answer period was pretty standard stuff, with a few hardballs thrown in just to keep things interesting. Where did the senator stand on the death penalty? Given that most corpses tended to get up and try to eat folks, he didn't see it as a productive pursuit. What was his opinion on public health care? Failure to keep people healthy enough to stay alive bordered on criminal negligence. Was he prepared to face the ongoing challenges of disaster preparedness? After the mass reanimations following the explosions in San Diego, he couldn't imagine any presidency surviving without improved disaster planning. Where did he stand on gay marriage, religious freedom, free speech? Well, folks, given that it was no longer possible to pretend that any part of the human race was going to politely lie down and disappear just because the majority happened to disagree with them, and given further the proof that life is a short and fragile thing, he didn't see the point of rendering anyone less free and equal than anybody else. When we got to the afterlife, God could sort us out into the sinner and the saved. Until we got there, it seemed to him that we were better off just being good neighbors and reserving our moral judgments for ourselves.

After an hour and a half of questions, more than half of which originated in the auditorium—a campaign first—the senator stood, wiping his forehead with the handkerchief he'd produced from a back pocket. "Well, folks, much as I'd like to stay and chat a while longer, it's getting on late, and my secretary has informed me that if I don't start cutting off these evening discussions, I'm going to seem a little dull to the folks I'm visiting in the morning." Laughter greeted this comment. Relaxed laughter; sometime in the previous hour, he'd managed to ease the audience out of their fear and into the sort of calm most people don't experience outside of their homes. "I want to thank you for having me, and for all your questions and viewpoints. I sincerely hope I'll have your vote when the time comes, but even if I don't, I have faith that it will be because you managed to find someone who was better for this great land."

"We're following *you*, Peter!" shouted someone from the back of the room. I twisted around in my seat and blinked, realizing that the shouter wasn't someone from the campaign; it was a woman I'd never seen before, holding up a hand-painted Senator Ryman for President sign.

"The campaign has groupies," observed Shaun.

"Always a good sign," said Buffy.

The senator laughed. "I certainly hope that you are," he said. "You'll have the chance to make me put my money where my mouth is soon enough. In the meantime, good night, and God bless you all." Waving to the audience, he turned and walked off the stage as "The Star-Spangled Banner" began to play from speakers around the room. The applause wasn't exactly thunderous—there wasn't enough audience for that—but it was enthusiastic. More so than it had been at the last engagement, and that one had been more enthusiastic than the one before it, and so on, and so on. Maybe you couldn't tell by looking at it, but the campaign was gathering steam.

I stayed where I was, observing the audience as they rose, and, surprisingly, began to talk among themselves rather than fleeing the hall for the safety of their cars. That was a new development, just like the applause. People were *talking*. Face-to-face, real-time *talking*, inspired by the senator and the things he had said.

More and more, I was beginning to feel like we were following a president.

"Georgia?" said Buffy.

"Go ahead and check the backstage feeds," I said, and nodded toward the knot of chattering attendees. "I'm going to go see what the buzz is."

"Make sure you're recording," she said, and started for the stage, gesturing for Shaun to follow. Grumbling good-naturedly, he snagged his chain mail and went.

I walked toward the group of attendees. A few of them glanced over at my approach, took note of my press pass, and went back to talking. The news is either invisible or something to be avoided, depending on what's going on and how many cameras the people around you can see. Since I didn't have any visible recording equipment, I was just part of the scenery.

The first cluster was discussing Senator Ryman's stance on the death penalty. That's one that's been going around since the dead first started getting up and walking. If you're killing someone for the crime of killing people, doesn't it sort of contradict the spirit of the thing if their corpse is going to get up and immediately start killing *more* people? Most death-row inmates stay there until they die of natural causes, at which point the government seizes their shambling corpses and adds them to the ongoing research on the cure. Everybody wins, except for the unlucky prisoners who get eaten by the newly deceased before they can be recovered.

The next group was talking about the potential candidates. Senator Ryman was definitely getting a favorable reception, since they were calling his closest competition respectively "a cheap show-biz whore"— that would be Congresswoman Wagman—and "an arrogant tool of the religious right"—that would be Governor Tate, originally of Texas, and currently the single loudest voice claiming the zombies would only stop eating good American men and women when the country got back to its moral and ethical roots. Whether this would stop the zombies from eating people of different national backgrounds never seemed to come up, which was a pity, since I liked the idea of zombies checking your passport before they decided whether or not they were allowed to bite down.

Satisfied that I wasn't likely to hear anything new in this crowd, I started casting around for a conversation worth joining. The one nearest the doors looked promising; there was a lot of scowling going on, and that's usually a sign that interest is warranted. I turned, walking close enough to hear what was going on.

"The real question is whether he can keep his promises," one man was saying. He looked to be in his late fifties, old enough to have been an adult during the Rising and part of the generation that embraced quarantine as the only true route to safety. "Can we trust *another* president who won't commit to an all-out purge of the zombie population of the national parks?"

"Be reasonable," said one of the women. "We can't simply wipe out endangered species because they might undergo amplification. That kind of rash action isn't going to do anything to make the average man safer."

"No, but it might keep another mother from burying her children after they get attacked by a zombie deer," countered the man.

"Actually, it was a moose, and the 'children' were a group of college students who crossed a proscribed stretch of the Canadian border looking for cheap weed," I interjected. All heads turned my way. I shrugged. "That's a Level 1 hazard zone. It's forbidden to almost everyone outside the armed forces and certain branches of the scientific community. Assuming you're talking about the incident last August and I didn't somehow miss an ungulate attack?" I knew I hadn't. I religiously follow animal attacks on humans, filing them under one of two categories: "We need stricter laws" and "Darwin was right." I don't think people should be allowed to keep animals large enough to undergo amplification, but I also don't believe wiping out the rest of the large mammals in the world is the answer. If you want to go foraging into the wilds of Canada without proper gear, you deserve what you get, even if that happens to include being attacked by an undead moose.

The man reddened. "I don't think I was talking to you, miss."

"Fair enough," I said. "Still, the facts of the event are pretty well documented. Again, assuming I didn't miss something."

Looking mildly amused, one of the other men said, "Well, come on, Carl, did the young lady miss an attack, or are you referring to the incident with the moose?"

He didn't need to answer; his glare was answer enough. Turning his back pointedly on the three of us, he moved to join a vigorous condemnation of the senator's stance on the death penalty that was going on just a few feet away.

"I don't think I've ever seen him deflated with facts before," said the woman, and offered her hand. "I'll have to remember that. Rachel Green. I'm with the local SPCA."

"Dennis Stahl, *Eakly Times*," said the remaining man, flashing his press pass in a brief show of solidarity.

Relieved that my sunglasses would cover the more subtle points of my expression, I took Ms. Green's hand, shook once, and said, "Georgia Mason. I'm one of the bloggers covering Senator Ryman's campaign."

"Mason," said Ms. Green. "As in...?"

I nodded.

She winced. "Oh, dear. Is this going to be unpleasant?"

"Not unless you're in the mood for a debate. I'm here to record reactions to the senator's agenda, not forward my own. Besides," I nodded to Carl's back, "I'm not as hard-line as some. I just have strong opinions about large animals being kept in urban areas, and I think we can agree to disagree on that point, don't you?"

"Fair enough," she said, looking relieved.

Mr. Stahl laughed. "Rachel gets a lot of flack from the local media for what she does," he said. "How's the campaign trail treating you?"

"Are you saying you haven't been reading our reports?" I asked the question lightly, but I wanted to hear the answer. Journalistic acceptance is one of the last things any blog gets. We may be accepted inside the community, but it's not until the traditional news media starts to take our reports seriously that a new feed can honestly be said to have established itself.

"I have," he said. "They're good. A little rough, but good. You care about what you're reporting, and it shows."

"Thanks," I replied, and glanced to Ms. Green. "Did you enjoy the presentation?"

"Is he as sincere as he seems?"

"I haven't seen any signs that he's not," I said, and shrugged. "Illusions of journalistic objectivity aside? He's a nice guy. He has good ideas, and he presents them well. Either he's the best liar I've ever met, or he's going to be our next president. Not that the two are mutually exclusive, but still."

"Mind if I quote you on that?" asked Mr. Stahl, with a sudden predatory intensity that I recognized quite well from my peers.

I smiled. "Go right ahead. Just make sure to give your readers a link to our site, if you would be so kind?"

"Of course."

The three of us chatted for a bit longer, eventually exchanging pleasantries and going our separate ways. I resumed moving from group to group, now mostly listening, and was amused to see that Carl—no last name given or requested—continually moved away from me, as if afraid that I'd taint his ranting with more of my unfortunate facts. I've encountered his type before, usually at political protests. They're the sort who would rather we paved the world and shot the sick, instead of risking life being unpredictable and potentially risky. In another time, they were anti-Semitic, antiblack, antiwomen's liberation, anti-gay, or all of the above. Now, they're antizombie in the most extreme ways possible, and they use their extremity to claim that the rest of us are somehow supporting the "undead agenda." I've met a lot of zombies. Not as many as Shaun and Mom have, but I'm not as suicidal as they are. In my experience, the only "undead agenda" involves eating you, not worming their way into public acceptance and support. There will always be people for whom hate is easier when it's not backed up by anything but fear. And I will always do my best to hoist them by their own petards.

The hallway lights dimmed once before returning to their original brightness, a sign that moving along was requested by the management. I glanced at my watch. It was a quarter to ten. Most zombie attacks occur between the hours of ten and two. Allowing people to gather during the "high risk" period can triple your insurance rate, especially if you live in an area with recently documented outbreaks. That includes much of the Midwest, where coyotes, feral dogs, and farm animals create a constant low-grade threat.

It doesn't take much to get most people moving after they realize they've managed to stay out past the unspoken world curfew. The conversational groups broke up as people grabbed their coats, bags, and traveling companions and turned to head for the doors. All of them had someone to walk with, even Carl. We are a nation equally afraid of gathering together and being alone. Is it any wonder that the average American is in therapy by the age of sixteen?

My ear cuff beeped, signaling a call. I reached up and tapped it on. "Georgia."

"You coming to join the party soon, or should I drink this beer by myself?" I could hear laughter in the background. The senator's entourage was celebrating another series of political minefields navigated with grace and charm. They were right to celebrate. If the numbers we'd been getting were anything to go by, Senator Ryman was a shoo-in for the Republican Party nomination once the convention rolled around.

"Just finishing out here, Shaun," I said. The hall lights began coming up from their ambient "event" setting, heading for the blazing fluorescents that would keep things lit for the cleaning crew. I squinted my eyes closed, turning to walk toward the stage exit. "Let folks know I'm coming through?"

"On it," he said. My ear cuff beeped again, signaling disconnection. I'm not much for jewelry, but disguised cellular phones are another matter. They're more convenient than walkie-talkies and have a longer battery life, with an average talk time of fifty hours before the battery gives out. Once the batteries go, it's cheaper to buy a new phone than it is to pay to have the case cracked and a new battery installed, but we all have to pay the price of progress. I have at least three phones on me at any given time, and only Shaun has all the numbers.

Two of the senator's security guards were waiting by the door, dressed in identical black suits, with sunglasses covering their eyes and blotting out most of their expressions. I nodded to them. They nodded back.

"Steve, Tyrone," I said.

"Georgia," said Tyrone. He produced a portable blood testing unit from his pocket. "If you would?"

I sighed. "You know they're just going to test me again before they let me into the convoy."

"Yes."

"And you know that a clean result now would be a clean result after the five-minute walk to the buses."

"Yes."

"But you're still going to make me prick my damn finger, aren't you?"

"Yes."

"I hate protocol." My ritual grumbling finished, I extended my hand, pressing my index finger against the contact pad. The lights on the top of the box flashed in the familiar red-green pattern, settling on a steady, uninfected green. "Happy?"

"Overjoyed," Tyrone replied, a faint smile on his lips as he withdrew a biohazard bag from his other pocket and dropped the test kit into it. "Right this way."

"How gracious," I said. Steve smothered a wider smile, and I smiled back, starting across the parking lot toward the distant lights of the convoy. The bodyguards fell into step beside me, flanking me as we walked. Being escorted through every open area we encountered had been a little annoying at first, but I was getting used to it.

The senator's crew—Shaun, Buffy, and I included—had been traveling in a convoy consisting of five luxury RVs, two buses, our van, and three converted military transport Jeeps, which were ostensibly for scouting runs before entering open territory but were mostly used for off-road rallies in whatever fields presented themselves. There were several smaller vehicles, ranging from my bike to the more substantially armored motorcycles favored by the bodyguards. With as much equipment as we need to carry to meet legal safety standards, it wouldn't make sense to break camp and check into hotels for anything less than a four-day stay, and so we often found ourselves spending a lot of nights "roughing it" in mobile homes that were better outfitted than my room back home.

Shaun, Buffy, and I had been assigned to share one of the RVs, although Buffy usually slept in the van with her equipment, claiming that the perpetual gloom of my special lights gave her, quote, "the heebie-jeebies." The senator's crew had been taking it as another sign that our resident techie is a little bit unhinged, and Shaun and I hadn't been making any efforts to discourage them, even though we knew that it was less of an obsessive-compulsive desire to protect the cameras and more of an ongoing quest for something resembling privacy. Unlike most of our generation, Buffy is an only child, and life in the convoy had been getting on nerves she may not have known she had.

Life in the convoy was also creating a new issue: her religion, and our lack thereof. Buffy prayed before she went to sleep. Buffy said grace before she ate. And Shaun and I...didn't. It was better to avoid the conflict by letting her have a little space. Besides, that gave Shaun and me the sort of privacy *we* were accustomed to—the kind that never actually leaves you alone, but doesn't put people in your personal space when you don't want them there, either.

Two more guards waited at the perimeter gates. Unlike Steve and Tyrone, who kept their pistols concealed beneath their jackets, these two openly held autofeed rifles I vaguely recognized from Mom's magazines. They could probably hold off the average zombie mob without outside assistance.

"Tracy, Carlos," I said, and extended my hand, palm down. "I'm tired, I'm filthy, and I'm ready to get drunk with the rest of the good boys and girls. Please confirm my uninfected status so that I can get on with it."

"Bring me a beer later, and it's a deal," Carlos replied, and shoved one of the tester units over my hand, while Tracy did the same for Steve. Tyrone stepped back, waiting his turn. These were midrange units, performing a more sensitive scan and taking a correspondingly longer time to return results. It would be possible for the finger-prick test to declare someone clean and for the full-hand unit to revoke that status less than five minutes later.

My results came back clean, as did Steve's. Tyrone stepped up to start his own tests and waved us off, toward the third RV in the chain. I could claim that my finely honed journalistic instincts told me which way to go, but they didn't have nearly as much to do with my choice of destinations as with the fact that it was the only RV with an open door, and was definitely the source of the pounding rock music that was assaulting our ears. The Dandy Warhols. The senator is a man who loves his classics.

Senator Ryman was standing on a coffee table inside the RV with his shirt half-unbuttoned and his tie draped over his left shoulder, saluting the room with a bottle of Pabst Blue Ribbon beer. People were cheering too loudly for me to tell what he was saying, but from the look of things, I'd just walked into the middle of a toast. I stopped by the door, stepping out of the way to let Steve get inside behind me, and took a wine cooler offered by one of the interns. I've given up trying to keep them straight; this was one of the brunette ones, which made her a Jenny, a Jamie, or a Jill. I swear, they should come with name tags.

Shaun pushed through the crowd, nodding to Steve before settling next to me. "Word?"

"Generally positive. People like our boy." I nodded to the senator, who had pulled a Jenny up onto the table with him. The audience cheered louder. "I think we might be able to ride this one all the way."

"Buffy said the same thing," Shaun agreed, taking a swig from his beer. "Ready to review tonight's footage?"

"What, and miss the bacchanal? Let me think...*yes.*" I shook my head. "Get me out of here."

The first postappearance party was fun. So was the third. And the fifteenth. By the twenty-third, I had come to recognize them as a clever method of controlling the locals: let the peons blow off some steam, reinforce the idea that you're just "one of the gang," and get down to the real business after most of the campaign had gone to bed. It was cunning, it was productive, and I salute Senator Ryman for thinking of it. All that being what it is, I saw no reason to spend any more time in an overly bright, overly crowded RV drinking crappy wine coolers than I absolutely had to.

Steve smiled wryly as we turned to push past him. "Leaving so soon?"

"I'll be back for the midnight football game," Shaun promised, and propelled me out the door with a solid push to the middle of my back. The dimness outside was like a benediction.

"Midnight football?" I asked, giving him a sidelong look as we moved away from the raucous RV, heading for our much quieter van. "Do you *sleep*?"

"Do you?" he countered.

"Touché."

Shaun spends his time moving, planning to move, and coming up with new ways to move, many of them involving heavy explosives or the undead. I spend my time writing, thinking about writing, and trying to come up with new things I can write about. Sleep has never been high on the priority list for either of us, which is probably a blessing in disguise. We kept each other amused as kids. If one of us had actually wanted to get some rest, we would have made each other crazy.

The van lights were on and the back door was unlocked. Buffy looked up as we entered, her expression remaining distracted even as she made note of our arrival. Once she was sure that we weren't being pursued by a rampaging horde of zombies, she turned back to her keyboard.

"Working on?" I asked, putting the wine cooler down next to my station.

"Splicing the footage from tonight and synchronizing the sound feeds. I'm thinking of doing a music video remix once it's all finished. Pick something retro and rock the house. Also, I'm chatting with Chuck. He's going to let me access his campaign footage to date and see if I can't put together a sort of retrospective."

I raised an eyebrow as I grabbed a Coke from the fridge. "Because you couldn't get at that footage without help?"

Buffy's cheeks reddened. "He's being helpful."

"Buffy has a crush," Shaun sing-songed.

"Play nice," I said, and sat, cracking my knuckles. "I need to hit the op-ed sites, see who's saying what, and start prepping the morning headlines. It's going to be a fun night, and I don't need you starting a fight and spoiling it."

Shaun rolled his eyes. "Riiiiight. You girls feel free to stay cooped up in here screwing around all night—"

"It's called 'making a living', dumb-ass," I said, flicking the screen on and entering my password.

"Like I said, screwing around all night. I'm going out with the boys. We're going to find some action, and I'm going to fuck with it, and tomorrow, we'll have a ratings bonanza like you've never seen." Shaun spread his hands, framing his illusionary triumph. "I can see it now: 'Flagging News Site Saved by Intrepid Irwin.'"

"Get glasses," said Buffy.

I snickered.

Shaun gave Buffy his best wounded look, opening his mouth to rebut.

Whatever he was going to say was drowned out by the gunshots from outside.

─────────────

You want to talk hypocrisy? Here's hypocrisy: the people who claim Kellis-Amberlee is God's punishment on humanity for daring to dabble where He never intended us to go. I might buy it if zombies had some sort of supernatural scientist-detecting powers and only went for the heretics, but when I look at the yearly lists of KA-related casualties—you can see the raw lists at the official CDC Web site, and a more detailed list is posted on the Wall every Rising Day—I don't see many scientists. What do I see?

I see children. I see Julie Wade, age seven, of Discovery Bay, California; I see Leroy Russell, age eleven, of Bar Harbor, Maine; I see a lot more than just them. Of the two thousand six hundred and fifty-three deaths directly attributed to Kellis-Amberlee within the United States over the past year, *sixty-three percent* were persons under the age of sixteen. Doesn't sound like a merciful God to me.

I see the elderly. I see Nicholas and Tina Postoloff, late of the Pleasant Valley Nursing Home in Warsaw, Indiana. Reports say Nicholas would have survived if he hadn't gone back for Tina, his wife of forty-seven years. They died and were reanimated by the virus before help could arrive. They were put down in the street like wild animals. Doesn't sound like divine judgment. Doesn't sound like divine *anything*.

I see men and women like you and me, people trying to live their lives without making any mistakes that will come back to haunt them later. I don't see sinners or people who have called down some sort of righteous plague. So stop. Stop trying to make people even more afraid than they already are by implying that, somehow, this is just a taste of the torments to come. I'm tired of it, and if there's a God, I bet He's tired of it, too.

**—From *Images May Disturb You*,
the blog of Georgia Mason, January 12, 2040**

Eight

Shaun didn't hesitate. Putting his beer on the nearest counter, he grabbed a crossbow off the wall and ran for the door. I was only a few feet behind him, Coke in one hand. Unlike my idiot brother, I have no intention of becoming a footnote on the Wall, but that doesn't mean I can't watch from a safe remove.

"Georgia!" There was enough anxiety in Buffy's voice to make me turn. She lobbed a handheld camera in my direction. I caught it, raising my eyebrows in question. "Better picture quality and sixty hours of battery life."

And audiences love a little hand-shot footage, as long as you cut to the smoother computer-operated stuff before they get motion sickness. "Got it," I said, and followed Shaun, opening my soda as I went.

The encampment was ablaze with activity. Guards swarmed everywhere I turned, weapons out and ready. I couldn't blame them for their excitement. Anyone who goes into private security in this day and age is likely to be a lot like Shaun, and he'd slowly been going nuts from the lack of dangerous things to pester.

More gunshots sounded from the south. I turned in that direction, flipping on the camera, and tapped my soda twice against the pressure pad on my belt. My ear cuff beeped. A moment later, Shaun's slightly breathless voice was in my ear: "Kinda busy, George. What gives?"

"Need a position if you want this on film." Distant moaning was audible as a whisper on the wind. Buffy's microphones are pretty sensitive. If she could get any sort of audio track, she'd be able to intensify it and play it back with the report, twice as loud and ten times as chilling.

"Location?"

"Just outside the van."

"Northwest. I'm at the fence."

That was directly away from the loudest signs of combat. "You sure about that?"

"Hurry and get over here!" he snapped, and clicked off. Shrugging, I turned toward the northern fence, breaking into a trot. I've learned not to argue with Shaun where zombies are concerned; he knows more about their behavior than I can imagine wanting to, and if he says "north," he's probably right. Gunshots continued to sound as the moaning, faint as it was, began getting louder.

The glare from the perimeter lights confused my night vision; I heard Shaun before I saw him. He was swearing merrily, using language that would make a longshoreman blush, as he taunted the infected closer to the fence. There were five of them, all fresh enough to look almost human, assuming you discounted the extreme dilation of their pupils and the slack, hungry way they stared at my brother as their fingers clawed against the fence. They'd died within the past few hours. I raised the camera, zooming in on their faces.

Shaun didn't even realize I was there until my soda hit the pavement. He stopped taunting the infected, stepping clear of the fence as he turned to stare at me. "George? What's wrong? You look like you've seen a ghost."

"I have." I indicated one of the zombies. Before amplification, she'd been a slender young woman, no heavier than Buffy. The wound that killed her the first time stood out livid and red against the still-pink flesh of her throat, and the fabric of her pale gray University of Oklahoma sweatshirt was stained bloody. "Recognize her?"

"Should I?" Shaun leaned closer to the fence. The zombie bared her teeth and hissed, increasing her attempts to break through. "She's definitely not one of my exes, George. I mean, she's cute, but way too dead for my tastes."

"Like you *have* any exes?" Shaun has dated as much as I have, which is to say "not at all." Buffy usually has five or six paramours at any given time, but Shaun and I haven't ever bothered. Other things keep getting in the way.

"Well, if I *did* have exes, they wouldn't look like her. Fill me in?"

"She was the cheering section at the senator's presentation." She'd looked a hell of a lot better when she was alive. I didn't remember seeing her after the Q&A broke up. If she left promptly and got caught on the street...given her body mass, she'd have had plenty of time to reach full amplification and rise again. It wasn't a difficult scenario to imagine. A young college student comes alone to a risky meeting in a public place and leaves the same way. No one would have been there to help her. A single bite is a death sentence, and not everyone has the guts to call the police and request a bullet to the brain before it gets too late to avoid rising.

Whoever she was, she died alone, and she died stupid. I couldn't help feeling bad for her.

"Oh, jeez, you're right." Shaun leaned closer still, moving well out of what most people would call the safe zone. All five zombies were clustering around the same stretch of fence now, hissing and snarling at him. "That was *fast*."

"This isn't the primary pack. They're too fresh." The most decayed of the zombies would still have been able to pass for human in a dark alley, assuming he could keep himself from trying to eat anyone in range. "Something had to bite them."

"Or one of 'em dropped dead of a heart attack," Shaun said. "You're right. The rest are south, harassing the guards." He gave the fence an assessing look. "I'd put this at what, twelve feet?"

"Shaun Phillip Mason, you are *not* thinking what I think you're thinking."

"Sure as hell am. Keep 'em distracted, okay?" He didn't wait for a reply before backing up, getting a running start, and launching himself at the fence. His fingers caught well above the reach of the tallest of the zombies. His toes didn't fare quite as well, but that didn't matter much—steel-toed combat boots are too tough for even the infected to gnaw their way through. Laughing at their moans, Shaun began pulling himself up toward the top of the fence.

"Next up, we have my brother, committing suicide," I muttered and focused the camera on him, tapping the pad at my belt again to dial Buffy. "Don't fall, asshole, or I'm telling Mom you did it for love of the dead girl."

"Bite me," Shaun called back. He swung his leading leg over the top of the fence and stood astride it, with one foot hooked into the chain on either side. Unhooking the crossbow from his belt, he loaded the first quarrel.

"Not while I'm breathing, oh brother mine."

"Buffy here," said Buffy's voice in my ear.

"Buffy, you getting the feeds on this? I want any positive IDs you can pull on our friends. You can cross-reference the one in the sweatshirt with footage from the—"

"I'm on it. Her name was Dayna Baldwin, age twenty-three, political science major at the University of Oklahoma. I'm running lookups on the other four. I have a few possible matches, but there's nothing confirmed."

Shaun pulled back the catch, taking careful, almost affectionate aim on the nearest of his admirers. I directed the handheld camera toward the mob as a crossbow bolt appeared in the center of their leader's forehead. He fell and two of the remaining four were suddenly distracted with cannibalizing his remains, leaving two to menace Shaun. The virus that drives the infected is only in it for the meat. Zombies generally choose the living over the dead, but something that won't put up a fight is always better than nothing at all.

"Keep looking," I said. Shaun reloaded his crossbow, moving with calm, unhurried precision. I have to give my brother this: He's damn good at what he does.

"Of course," said Buffy, sounding affronted. She hung up, presumably to focus on her cameras. We'd get a clearer picture of everything that had happened once Shaun finished having his fun and we could get back to the van. If there's a square inch of convoy that Buffy can't get on film, I'll eat my sunglasses.

Shaun was taking aim on the third zombie when I realized there was something wrong with the quality of the moans. They were getting louder and moving against the prevailing wind. I dropped the camera, hearing its case crack as it hit the ground, and turned to look behind me.

The leader of the zombies—another familiar face, opinionated Carl from the after-meeting—was ten feet away and closing fast, moving at that horrible, disconnected half-run that only the freshest zombies can sustain for long. He must have died even more recently than Dayna, because he'd been up and moving around less than an hour before. That implied multiple bites and a group attack, possibly by the pack that Shaun was in the process of dispatching.

Six more zombies followed the ill-fated Carl, moving at speeds ranging from a half-run to a shamble. Pulling the pistol from my belt, I shot Carl twice in the head, turning to aim at the zombie behind him. I didn't have enough bullets. Even if I were as good of a shot as Shaun, which I'm not, eight bullets and seven zombies didn't leave me in a position with much of a margin for error. I was already down below the one-for-one divide, and that made survival a lot less likely. I pulled the trigger and the second zombie fell.

The sound of gunshots attracted Shaun's attention. I heard his sharp intake of breath as he turned, surveying my attackers. "Holy—"

"We're past saying it and all the way to doing it," I snarled, and fired again. The shot went wild. Four bullets and only two zombies down; the odds were not in my favor. "*Buffy!*"

Buffy never sends out a camera without a two-way sound pickup. She says she doesn't trust us to manage our own levels, but really, I think she just likes being able to eavesdrop without leaving the van. Her voice emerged from the speaker a moment after I called her name, coming through crackly and distorted. "Sorry for the delay—distracted. We've had a perimeter breech on the south fence. One of the gates went down and they're reporting casualties. How're you two faring?"

"Let's just say that if you have a broadcast point near some unoccupied men with heavy weaponry, now would be a swell time to use it." I fired twice more. The second bullet hit its target. Six bullets and three zombies down, while the remaining four continued to approach. I fired at the new leader of the pack and missed. A crossbow bolt whizzed by my shoulder and the zombie toppled, the end of the bolt protruding from its forehead. Three zombies. "I didn't come out here expecting to actually *fight* anything—I'm only carrying a pistol, and I'm about to be out of bullets. Shaun?"

"Three bolts left," he called. "Think you can make it up this fence?"

"No." I'm a decent sprinter and I can gun a motorcycle from zero to suicidal in less than ten seconds, but I'm not a climber. I nearly washed out of the physical section of my licensing exams, twice, thanks to my lack of upper-body strength. If I was lucky, I'd be able to cling to the fence until the zombies grabbing my ankles hauled me down and ate me. If I wasn't, I'd just fall.

The speaker crackled. "There's a group of guards on the way," Buffy said. "They're having some problems, but they said they'd be there as fast as they could."

"Hope it's fast enough," I said. I started backing up toward Shaun and the fence. My father has always had just one piece of advice about zombies and ammunition, one he's drilled into my head enough times that it's managed to stick: When you have one bullet left and there's no visible way out of the shit you're standing in, save it for yourself. It's better than the alternative.

Two more crossbow bolts whizzed by, and two more zombies fell, leaving just one to shamble toward us, still moaning. There were no answering moans, either from the sides or from behind. Shaun's pack was down, and there didn't seem to be any further reinforcements coming.

"Fire any time now, Shaun," I said tightly.

"Not until I know that there aren't more coming," he said.

I kept backing up until I hit the fence and stopped, keeping my gun in front of me, muzzle aimed toward the shambler. Between the two of us, we had the ammo to take it down...as long as that was all there was. "It figures," I said.

"What figures?"

"We finally crack the global top five, so of course we're going to get eaten by zombies that same night."

Shaun's laughter managed to be bitter and amused at the same time. "Are you ever *not* a pessimist?"

"Sometimes. But then I wake up." The zombie was continuing to advance, moaning as it came. There were no answering moans. "I think it's alone."

"So shoot, genius, and we'll see."

"I may as well." I steadied my hands, lining up on the zombie's forehead. "If it eats me, I hope you're next."

"Always gotta go first, don't you?"

"You know it." I fired.

My shot whizzed past the zombie, punching a barely visible hole in the nearest RV. Still moaning, the zombie raised its arms in the classic "embracing" gesture of the undead, moving slightly faster now. No one's ever figured out how the zombies can tell when their victims are unarmed, but they manage somehow.

"Shaun…"

"We have time."

"Yeah, sure," I said. The zombie was still twelve feet away, well out of attack range, but it was closing on us. "I hate you."

"It's mutual," Shaun said. I risked a glance up at him, and saw that he was aiming for the zombie's forehead, waiting for the perfect shot. One bolt, one chance. Maybe that sounds like the odds he'd been playing before, but it wasn't. It's easier to get a bull's-eye when there's nothing actually at risk.

"Just so we're clear," I said, and closed my eyes.

The gunfire came from two directions at the same time. I opened my eyes to see the last zombie mowed down by a hail of chain-fed bullets being fired by no fewer than four of the guards, two closing on either side. Above me, Shaun gave a loud war whoop.

"The cavalry has *arrived*!"

"God bless the cavalry," I muttered.

Our tense stand-off was over in a matter of seconds. I ignored the fallen camera as I pushed away from the fence and strode toward the nearest pair of guards. The camera was a write-off. Buffy had the footage downloaded by now, and they were going to insist on destroying the damn thing anyway, since it had almost certainly been spattered with blood when the guards started firing. The electronics were too delicate to survive a full decontamination. That sort of thing is why we keep our insurance paid up.

Steve was there, scowling at the fallen infected like he was challenging them to get up and let him kill them again. Sorry, Steve, the virus only reanimates a host once. His partner was a few feet away, scanning the fence. It wasn't Tyrone. I paused, starting to get the vaguest idea of how the zombies had broken through the fence.

Ideas never drew ratings without confirmation. "What happened?"

"Not now, Georgia," said Steve, with a tight shake of his head. "Just... not now."

I considered pressing the matter. If this were a normal zombie attack, one of the hit-and-run outbreaks that can happen anywhere, I probably would have. It's always best to question the survivors before they can start deluding themselves about the reality of what they just went through. After the adrenaline fades, half the people who survive a zombie attack turn into heroes, having gunned down a thousand zombies with nothing but a .22 and a bucket of guts, while the other half deny that they were ever close enough to the undead to be in any actual danger. If you want the real story, you have to get it fast.

But Steve was a professional bodyguard, and that made him less likely than most men to lie to himself. Factor in the fact that unless he left the convoy after the paperwork was completed, I'd have to continue interacting with him on a regular basis, and getting the scoop wasn't worth alienating the large, potentially violent man who managed a lot of my blood tests. Shaking my head, I took a step back.

"Sure, Steve," I said. "Just let us know if there's anything we can do."

There was a clatter as Shaun jumped down from the fence. I didn't turn, and he trotted to a stop beside me, eyes narrowing as he took note of the attending guards. "Christ, Steve, where's Tyrone?" he said.

Shaun has done more to get close to the guards than I have. A little friendliness is unavoidable, but he'd actually gotten out there and made *friends*. Maybe that's why Steve answered his question with a quiet, "Conversion was confirmed at twenty-two hundred hours, twenty-seven minutes. Tracy put him down, but not before he was able to pass on the infection."

Shaun whistled, long and low. "How many down?"

"Four casualties from the convoy and an as-yet-undetermined number of locals. The senator and his aides are being moved to a secure location. If you'll gather your things and collect Miss Meissonier, we'll take the three of you to decontamination before relocating you as well."

"Are all the zombies down?" I asked.

Steve frowned at me. "Miss Mason?"

"The zombies. Shaun and I just eliminated the better part of two packs," ignoring the part where one of us nearly got eaten in the process, "and you seem to have handled the mess at the gates. Are all the zombies down?"

"Channels are showing a negative on infected activity within the area."

"Channels are not a one hundred percent guarantee," I said, keeping my tone reasonable. "You're down hands, and we've already been in primary contact, which means we'll need the same decon you will. Why not let Shaun and me stay and help? We're licensed, and if you have ammo, we're armed. Remove Buffy, but let us stay."

The guards exchanged uneasy glances before looking to Steve. Whatever he said would go. Steve frowned down at the bodies littering the tarmac, and finally said, "I hope you both understand that I won't hesitate to shoot either one of you."

"We wouldn't go out with you if we thought you'd hesitate," said Shaun. He held up his crossbow. "Anybody got bolts for this thing?"

Cleanup is the worst thing about a small-scale outbreak. For many people, this part of a rising is pretty much invisible. Anyone without a hazard license is confined outside the contaminated zones until the burials, burnings, and sterilizations are done. When the cordons come up, life goes back to normal, and this sort of thing is routine enough that, unless you know the signs, you could even fail to realize that there was an incident. We've had a lot of practice at cover-ups.

That changes if you have to be involved. Part of getting your hazard license is going along on a cleanup run, just to make sure you understand what you're getting into. George and I both threw up when we made our first cleanup run, and I almost passed out twice. It's horrible, messy work. Once a zombie's been shot through the head, it doesn't look like a zombie anymore. It just looks like somebody who was in the wrong place at the wrong time, and I hate the whole process.

Sterilization is horrific. You burn any vegetation the zombies came into contact with, and if they walked on any open ground, you drench it with a solution of chlorinated saline. If it's a rural or suburban area, you kill any animals you find. Squirrels, cats, whatever; if it's mammalian and can carry the virus in its live state, it dies, even if it's too small to undergo amplification. And when you're done, you shuffle back to the hazmat center that's been established for agent decon, and you go inside, and you spend two hours having your skin steamed off, which is a nice way to prepare for the two weeks of nightmares that you're going to have to live through.

If you ever start to feel like I have a glamorous job, that maybe it would be fun to go out and poke a zombie with a stick while one of your friends makes a home movie for your buddies, please do me a favor: Go out for your hazard license first. If you still want to do this crap after the first time you've burned the body of a six-year-old with blood on her lips and a Barbie in her hands, I'll welcome you with open arms.

But not before.

—From *Hail to the King*,
the blog of Shaun Mason, February 11, 2040

Nine

I collapsed onto our bed at the local four-star hotel a little after dawn, my aching eyes already squeezed shut. Shaun was a bit steadier on his feet and he stayed upright long enough to make sure the room's blackout curtains were drawn. I made a small noise of approval and felt him pulling my sunglasses off my face a moment later. I swatted ineffectually at the air.

"Stop that. Give those back."

"They're on the bedside table," he said. The bedsprings creaked as he sat down, taking the side of the bed that was closer to the window. Rustling followed as he removed his shoes and slumped sideways. I didn't have to open my eyes to know what he was doing. We shared the same room until puberty hit, and since then we've never been more than a closed door away from one another. "Christ, George. That was a clusterfuck."

"Mmm," I replied, and pulled the covers over my head. I was still wearing my shoes. The staff was paid to wash the sheets after every visit, and by the point we left the field, I'd dressed and undressed so many times in the course of decontamination that I never wanted to remove my clothes again. I'd just wear them until they dissolved, and then spend the rest of my life naked.

"How the hell did we get an outbreak that close to the convention hall? Primaries are coming up. We didn't need this, even if it's going to be great for ratings. Think Buffy has the initial edits up? I know you hate it when she releases footage without your say-so, but cleanup ran long. She probably won't wait. Waiting could mean we get scooped."

"Mmm."

"Bet this spikes us another half-point. More when I can get my POV stuff edited together. Think there were faults in the fencing? Maybe they broke through. Steve wasn't clear on where the attack started, and we lost both guards stationed on the gate."

"Mmm."

"Poor Tyrone. Jesus. Did you know he was putting his teenage son through college with this gig? Kid wants to be a molecular virologist—"

Somewhere in the middle of explaining the hopes, dreams, and character failings of the fallen guards, Shaun's voice trailed off, replaced by the soft, rhythmic sound of his breathing. I sighed, rolling over, and followed him into sleep.

The curtains were pulled away from the window some unknown length of time later, allowing sunlight to stream into the room and jerk me unceremoniously back into awareness. I swore, fumbling for the nightstand I vaguely remembered Shaun mentioning in conjunction with my sunglasses. My hand hit the side of the bed, and I squinted my eyes more tightly closed, trying to ward off the light.

Shaun was less restrained in his profanity. "Fuck a duck, Buffy, what are you trying to do, blind her?" My sunglasses were thrust into my hand. I unfolded them and slid them into place, opening my eyes to see Shaun, clad only in his boxer shorts, glaring at an unrepentant Buffy. "Knock next time!"

"I did knock, three times," she said. "And I tried the room phone, twice. See?" Both Shaun and I glanced toward the phone. The red message light was blinking. "When you kept not answering, I rerouted the locks to make them think your room was my room and let myself in."

"You didn't just shake us because?" I mumbled. A splitting headache was rushing in to fill the void left by my disrupted REM cycle.

"Are you kidding? You two sleep armed. I like having four limbs and a head." Seeming oblivious to the hostility in the room, Buffy activated the terminal on the wall, pulling down the foldable keyboard. "I'm guessing you guys haven't seen the daily returns, huh?"

"We haven't seen anything but the insides of our eyelids," Shaun said. He wasn't making any effort to hide his irritation, which was only increasing as Buffy ignored it. "What time is it?"

"Almost noon," Buffy said. The hotel start-up screen came up and she began typing, shunting the connection to one of our own server relays. The logo of After the End Times filled the screen, replaced a moment later by the black-and-white grid of our secure staff pages. "I let you guys sleep for, like, six hours."

I groaned and reached for the phone. "I am so calling room service for a gallon of Coke before she can do any more talking."

"Get some coffee, too," said Shaun. "A whole pot of coffee."

"Tea for me," said Buffy. The screen shifted again as she pulled up the numerical display that represents our feed from the Internet Ratings Board. It measures server traffic, unique hits, number of connected users, and a whole bunch of other numbers and factors, all of them combining to make one final, holy figure: our market share. It's color-coded, appearing in green if it's more than fifty, white for forty-nine to ten, yellow for nine to five, and red for four and above.

The number at the top of screen, gleaming a bright, triumphant red, was 2.3.

I dropped the phone.

Shaun recovered his composure first, maybe because he was more awake than I was. "Have we been hacked?"

"Nope." Buffy shook her head, grinning so broadly that it seemed like the top of her head might fall off. "What you're seeing is the honest to God, unaltered, uncensored Ratings Board designation for our site traffic over the past twelve hours. We're running top two, as long as you discount porn, music download, and movie tie-in sites."

Those three site types make up the majority of the traffic on the Internet—the rest of us are just sort of skimming off the top. Rising unsteadily, I crossed the room and touched the screen. The number didn't change.

"Shaun..."

"Yeah?"

"You owe me twenty bucks."

"Yeah."

Turning to Buffy, I asked, "How?"

"If I attribute it to the graphic design, do I get a raise?"

"No," said Shaun and I, in unison.

"Didn't think so, but a girl has to try." Buffy sat down on the edge of my bed, still beaming. "I got clean footage from half a dozen cameras all the way through both attacks. No voice reports, since someone went and volunteered to help with cleanup—"

"Not that going through decon without helping would have left me able to record," I said dryly, retreating back toward the phone. Incredible ratings or not, I needed to kill this headache before it got fully established, and that meant I needed something caffeinated to wash down the painkillers. "You know that wipes me out."

"Details," said Buffy. "I spliced together three basic narrative tracks—one following the outbreak at the gate as closely as possible, one following the perimeter, and one that followed the two of you."

I glanced in her direction as I waited for room service to pick up. "How much of our dialogue did you get?"

Buffy beamed. "All of it."

"That explains some of the jump," Shaun said dryly. "We always get a point spike when you say you hate me in a published report."

"Only because it's true," I said, quashing the urge to groan. It was my own fault for leaving Buffy alone with the unedited footage. She had to put *something* up. A news blackout doesn't heighten suspense; it just loses readers.

Shaun snorted. "Right. So you had three tracks, and...?"

"I tossed them up in their raw form, tapped some beta Newsies to throw down narrative tracks, got straight bio files on the confirmed casualties, and wrote a new poem about how fast everything can fall apart." Buffy cast an anxious glance my way, smile slipping. "Did I do it right?"

Room service confirmed that the assorted drinks were en route, along with an order of dry wheat toast. I hung up the phone. "Which betas?"

"Um, Mahir for the gate, Alaric for the perimeter, and Becks for the attack on the two of you."

"Ah." I adjusted my sunglasses. "I'm going to want to review their reports." It was a formality, and from the look on her face, Buffy knew it; she'd selected the same betas I would have chosen. Mahir is located in London, England, and he's great for dry, factual reporting that neither pretties things up nor dumbs them down. If I have a second in command, it's Mahir. Alaric can build suspense almost as well as an Irwin, fitting his narration and description into the natural blank spots in a recording. And Becks would have been a horror movie director if we weren't all practically living in a horror movie these days. Her sense of timing is impeccable, and her cut shots are even better. Of the betas we've acquired, I count my Newsies as the best of the bunch. They're good. They're hoping to ride our success to alpha positions of their own, and that makes them ambitious. Ambition is worth more than practically anything else in this business, even talent.

"Of course you will," Buffy said, clearly waiting for me to break down and say the words.

I smiled, faintly, and said them: "You did good."

Buffy punched the air. "She shoots, she scores!"

"Just don't get cocky," I said. There was a knock at the door. This hotel must have the fastest room service in the Midwest. "Remember, one successful set of executive decisions does *not* prepare you to take my—"

I opened the door to reveal Steve and Carlos. They were impeccably dressed, matching black suits so crisply pressed that you'd never have guessed they'd been in the field incinerating the bodies of their fallen comrades less than eight hours previous. I stood there in my slept-in clothes, with my uncombed hair sticking up in all directions, and stared at them.

"Miss Mason," said Steve. His tone was flat, even more formal than it was on our first encounter. Dipping a hand into his pocket, he produced the familiar shape of a handheld blood testing unit. "If you and your associates would care to come with us, a debriefing has been scheduled in the boardroom."

"Couldn't you have called first?" I asked.

He raised his eyebrows. "We did."

Shaun and I really had been sleeping like the unrisen dead. I pressed my lips into a thin line, and said, "My brother and I have only been awake for a few minutes. Can we have time to make ourselves presentable?"

Steve looked past me into the room, where Shaun—still clad only in his boxers—offered a sardonic wave. Steve looked back to me. I smiled. "Unless you'd prefer we came as we are?"

"You have ten minutes," Steve said, and shut the door.

"Good morning, Georgia," I muttered. "Right. Buffy, get out. We'll see you in the boardroom. Shaun, put clothes on." I raked a hand through my hair. "I'm going to wash up." One good thing about going to bed straight from a cleanup operation: Even after six hours of sleeping and sweating into my clothes, they were still cleaner than they'd been when I bought them. After you've been sterilized seven times for live virus particles, dirt doesn't stand much of a chance.

"Georgia—" Buffy began.

I pointed to the door. "Out." Not waiting to see whether she obeyed me—largely because I was pretty certain she wasn't going to—I grabbed my overnight bag off the floor by the foot of the bed and went into the bathroom, closing the door behind me.

There's only one way to prevent a migraine from the combination of too little sleep and too much light from fully establishing itself, and that's to wear my contacts. They come with their own little complications, like making my eyeballs itch all damn day, but they block a lot more light than my sunglasses. I pulled the case out of my bag, popped off the top, and withdrew the first of the lenses from the saline solution where they customarily floated.

Normal contact lenses are designed to correct problems with the wearer's eyesight. My eyesight is fine, except for my light issues, which the lenses can compensate for. Unfortunately, while normal contacts enhance peripheral vision, these ones kill the greater part of mine by covering the iris and most of the pupil with solid color films that essentially create artificial surfaces for my eyes. I'm not legally allowed to go into field situations while wearing contacts.

Tilting my head back, I slipped the first lens into place, blinking to settle it against my eye. I repeated the process with the other eye before lowering my head and looking at myself in the mirror. My reflection gazed impassively back at me, eyes perfectly normal and cornflower blue.

The blue was my choice. When I was a kid they got me brown lenses that matched the natural color of my eyes. I switched to blue as soon as I was old enough to have a say. They don't look as natural, but they also don't make me feel like I'm trying to lie about my medical condition. My eyes aren't normal. They never will be. If that makes some people uncomfortable, well, I've learned to use that to my own advantage.

I straightened my clothes, tucked my sunglasses into the breast pocket of my shirt, and ran a brush through my hair. There, that was as presentable as I was going to get. If the senator didn't like it, he could damn well refrain from allowing any more late-night attacks on the convoy.

Buffy was gone when I emerged from the bathroom. Shaun handed me a can of Coke and my MP3 recorder, wrinkling his nose. "You know your contacts creep me out, right?"

"That's the goal." The soda was cold enough to make my back teeth ache. I didn't stop gulping until the can was empty. Tossing it in the bathroom trash, I asked, "Ready?"

"For hours. You girls always take *forever* in the bathroom."

"Bite me."

"Not without a blood test."

I kicked his ankle, grabbed three more Cokes from the room service tray, and left the room. Steve was waiting in the hall, blood test unit still in his hand. I eyed it.

"Isn't this going a bit far? We went from cleanup to bed. I doubt there was a viral reservoir in the closet."

"Hand," Steve replied.

I sighed and switched my pilfered sodas to my left hand, allowing me to offer him the right. The process of testing me, and then Shaun, took less than a minute. Both of us came up unsurprisingly clean.

Steve dropped the used units into a plastic bag, sealed it, and turned to walk down the hall, obviously expecting us to follow. Shaun and I exchanged a glance, shrugged, and did exactly that.

The boardroom was three floors up, on a level you needed an executive keycard to access. The carpet was so thick that our feet made no sound as we followed Steve down the hall to the open boardroom door. Buffy was seated on a countertop inside, keying information into her handheld and trying to stay out of the way of the senator's advisors. They were moving back and forth, grabbing papers from one another, making notes on whiteboards, and generally creating the sort of hurricane of productive activity that signals absolutely nothing happening.

The senator was at the head of the table with his head in his hands, creating an island of stillness in the heart of the chaos. Carlos flanked him to the left, and as we crossed the threshold, Steve abandoned us to cut across the room and flank Senator Ryman to the right. Something must have alerted the senator to Steve's presence because he raised his head, looking first toward the bodyguard and then toward us. One by one, the bustling aides stopped what they were doing and followed the direction of the senator's gaze.

I raised a can of soda and popped the tab.

The sound seemed to snap the senator out of his fugue. He sat up, clearing his throat. "Shaun. Georgia. If the two of you wouldn't mind taking your seats, we can get things started."

"Thanks for holding the briefing until we got here," I said, moving toward one of the open chairs and setting my MP3 recorder on the table. "Sorry we took so long."

"Don't worry," he said, waving a hand. "I know how late you were out with the cleanup crews. A little sleep is hardly repayment for going above and beyond the call of duty like that."

"In that case, I'd like some groupies," said Shaun, settling in the chair next to mine. I kicked him in the shin. He yelped but grinned, unrepentant.

"I'll see what we can do." The senator rose, rapping his knuckles against the table. The last small eddies of conversation in the room died, all attention sliding back to him. Even Buffy stopped typing as the senator leaned forward, hands on the table, and said, "Now that we're all here...how the *hell* did that happen?" His voice never rose above a conversational level. "We lost four guards last night, three of them at our own front gate. What happened to the concept of security? Did I miss the meeting where we decided that zombies weren't something we needed to be concerned about anymore?"

One of the aides cleared his throat and said, "Well, sir, it looks like there was a power short on the anterior detection unit, which resulted in the doors failing to shut fast enough to prevent the incursion from—"

"Speak English at this table or I will fire you so fast you'll wind up standing at the airport wondering how the hell you got from here to there without any goddamn pants on," the senator snapped. The aide responded by paling and dropping the papers he'd been holding. "Can *anyone* here tell me what happened and how, in simple English words of two syllables or less?"

"Your screamer wasn't working," said Buffy. Every head in the room turned to her. She shrugged. "Every perimeter rig has a screamer built in. Yours didn't switch on."

"A screamer being...?" asked one of the aides.

"A heat-sensitive motion sensor," said Chuck Wong. He looked anxious—and with good reason. Most of his job involves the design and maintenance of the convoy's automated perimeter defenses. If there'd been a mechanical failure, it was technically his fault. "They scan moving objects for heat as well as motion. Anything below a certain range sets off an alert of possible zombies in the area."

"A really fresh one can fool a screamer, but the packs we saw last night were too mixed for that. They should have set off the alerts, and they didn't." Buffy shrugged again. "That means we had a screamer failure."

"Chuck? Care to tell us why that happened?"

"I can't. Not until we can arrange for a physical inspection of the equipment."

"It's arranged. Carlos, get three of your men and take Chuck for an inspection run. Report back as soon as you have anything." Carlos nodded, heading for the door. Three of the other bodyguards moved away from the walls and followed, not waiting to be asked.

"I'll need my equipment—" Chuck protested.

"Your equipment should be with the convoy, and since that's where you're going, I'm sure you'll have everything you need," the senator said. There was no arguing with his tone. Chuck obviously saw that. He stood, thin-boned hands twitching by his sides as he turned toward the door.

"Mind if I go along?" asked Buffy. The room looked at her again. She flashed her most winning smile. "I'm pretty good at seeing why field equipment decided to fry. Maybe I could be a second opinion."

And maybe she could get us some footage for a follow-up report. I nodded, and caught the senator watching the gesture before he, in turn, began to nod. "Thank you for volunteering, Miss Meissonier. I'm sure the group will be glad to have you along."

"I'll ring back," Buffy said, and hopped off the counter, trotting out the door after Chuck and the bodyguards.

"There she goes," Shaun muttered.

"Jealous?" I asked.

"Tech geeks trying to figure out why a screamer broke? Please. I'll be jealous if she comes back saying there were actual dead guys to play with."

"Right." He was jealous. I folded my arms, returning my attention to the senator.

He wasn't looking his best. He was leaning forward with his hands braced against the table, but it was clear even in that well-supported position that he hadn't had nearly as much sleep as Shaun and I. His hair was uncombed, his shirt was wrinkled, and his collar was open. He looked like a man who'd been faced with the unexpected, and now, after a little time to consider the situation, was getting ready to ride out and kick its ass.

"Folks, whatever the cause of last night's catastrophe, the facts are this: We lost four good men and three potential supporters right before the first round of primaries. This does *not* send a good message to the people. This sort of thing doesn't say 'Vote Ryman, he'll protect you.' If anything, it says 'Vote Ryman if you want to get eaten.' This isn't our message, and I refuse to let it become our message, even though that's the way my opponents are going to try to spin it. What's our game plan?" He glared around the room. "Well?"

"Sir, the bloggers—"

"Will be staying for this little chat. We try covering it up, they'll report it a lot less kindly when they manage to root it out. Now please, can we get down to business?"

That seemed to be the cue the room had been waiting for. The next forty minutes passed in a blaze of points and counterpoints, with the senator's advisors arguing the finer aspects of spin while his security heads protested any attempts to categorize their handling of the campaign to date as "lax" or "insufficient." Shaun and I sat and listened. We were there as observers, not participants, and after the argument had a little time to develop, it seemed as if most of the room forgot we were there at all. One camp held that they needed to minimize media coverage of the attack, make the requisite statements of increased vigilance, and move on. The other camp held that full openness was the only way to get through an incident of this magnitude without taking damage from other political quarters. Both camps had to admit that the reports released on our site the night before were impacting their opinions, although neither seemed aware of exactly how much traffic those reports had drawn. I opted not to inform them. Observing the political process without interfering with it is sometimes more entertaining than it sounds.

One of the senator's advisors was beginning a rant on the evils of the modern media when my ear cuff beeped. I rose, moving to the back of the room before I answered. "Georgia here."

"Georgia, it's Buffy. Can you patch me to the speakerphone?"

I paused. She sounded harried. More than that, she sounded openly nervous. Not frightened, which meant she probably wasn't being harassed by zombies or rival bloggers, but nervous. "Sure, Buff. Give me a second." I strode back to the table and leaned across two of the arguing aides to grab the speaker phone. They squawked protests, but I ignored them, yanking off my ear cuff and snapping it into the transmission jack at the base of the phone.

"Miss Mason?" inquired the senator, eyebrows rising.

"Sorry, this is important." I hit the Receive button.

"...testing, testing," said Buffy's voice, crackling slightly through the speaker. "Am I live?"

"We can hear you, Miss Meissonier," said the senator. "May I ask what was so important that it required breaking in on our conference?"

Chuck Wong spoke next; apparently, ours wasn't the only end on speakerphone. "We're at the perimeter fence, sir, and it seemed important that we call you as quickly as possible."

"What's going on out there, Chuck? No more zombies, I hope?"

"No, sir—not so far. It's the screamer."

"The one that failed?"

"Yes, sir. It didn't fail because of anything my team did." Chuck didn't keep the relief out of his tone, and I couldn't blame him. Carelessness can be a federal offense when it applies to antizombie devices. No one has managed to successfully charge a security technician with manslaughter—yet—but the cases come up almost every year. "The wires were cut."

The senator froze. "Cut?"

"The screamer shows detection of the zombies we saw last night, sir. The connection that should have set off the perimeter alarms wasn't made because those wires had been cut before the alarm was sounded."

"Whoever did it did a pretty good job," Buffy said. "All the damage is inside the boxes. Nothing visible until you crack the case, and even then you have to dig around before you find the breaks."

The senator sagged backward, paling. "Are you telling me this was sabotage?"

"Well, sir," said Chuck, "none of my men would have cut the wires on a screamer protecting the convoy that they were inside. There's just no reason for it."

"I see. Finish your sweep and report back, Chuck. Miss Meissonier, thank you for calling. Please, call again if you need anything further."

"Roger. Georgia, we're on server four."

"Noted. Signing off now." I leaned over and cut the connection before pulling my ear cuff out of the jack and sliding it back onto my ear. Only when this was done did I glance back up at Senator Ryman.

The senator looked like a man who'd been hit, hard and unexpectedly, from behind. He met my gaze, despite the alien appearance of my contacts, and gave a small, tightly controlled shake of his head. Please, that gesture said, not right now.

I nodded, taking Shaun's arm. "Senator, if you don't mind, my brother and I should be getting to work. We're a bit behind after last night."

Shaun blinked at me. "What?"

"Of course." The senator smiled, not bothering to conceal his relief. "Miss Mason, Mr. Mason, thank you for your time. I'll have someone notify you before we're ready to check out and move on."

"Thank you," I said, and left the room, hauling the still-bewildered Shaun along in my wake. The boardroom door swung closed behind us.

Shaun yanked his arm out of my hand, subjecting me to a sharp sidelong gaze. "Want to tell me what that was all about?"

"The man just found out his camp was sabotaged," I said. "They're not going to come up with anything useful until they finish panicking. That's going to take days. Meanwhile, we have reports to splice together and update, and Buffy's dumping her footage to server four. We should take a look."

Shaun nodded. "Got it."

"Come on."

Back in our hotel room, I turned the main terminal over to Shaun while I plugged my handheld into the wall jack and settled down to work. We couldn't both record voice feeds at the same time, but we could edit film clips for our individual sections of the site and we could write as much text as we needed. I skimmed the reports Buffy authorized while Shaun and I were on cleanup. All three of the betas had done excellent jobs. Mahir, especially, had done an amazing amount with his relatively straightforward video feed, and I saw from the server flags that both the footage and his voice tracking had already been optioned by three of the larger news sites. I tapped in a release, authorizing use of the footage under a standard payment contract that would give Mahir forty percent of the profits, with clear credit for the narrative. His first breakout report. He'd be so proud. After a pause, I added a note of congratulations, directed to his private mailbox. He and I have been friends outside of work for years, and it never hurts to encourage your friends to succeed.

"How're things in your department?" I asked, pulling up the raw footage of the attacks and setting it to run sequentially on my screen. I wasn't sure what I was looking for, but I had a hunch, and I've learned to follow my hunches. Buffy knows visual presentation, and Shaun knows shock value, but me? I know where to find the news. There had been sabotage. Why? When? And how had our saboteur been able to cut those wires without coming into the range of Buffy's cameras?

"I'm taking Becks away from you," he said. I glanced over. Shaun's screen was dominated by the footage of the two of us against the fence, holding off the last of the zombies. The audio was being fed directly to him via the earpiece plugged into his left ear. His expression was serious. "She wants to go Irwin. She's been begging for weeks. And this report—this isn't a Newsie report, George. You know that."

I scowled, but it wasn't like the request was a surprise. Good Irwins are hard to come by because the death rates during training are so damn high. You don't have time for a learning curve when you're playing with the infected. "What are her credentials?"

"You're stalling."

"Humor me." The footage on my screen was set to play in real-time, which meant some of the feeds would pause to let the others catch up again. The gate cameras had chunks missing from their narrative, while the attack at the fence was almost complete. I couldn't help wincing when I saw one of the women from the political rally come staggering up, clearly among the infected. I didn't need the dialogue tracks to tell me what Tyrone was saying: He was telling her to halt in her approach, back off, and present her credentials. But she just kept coming.

"Rebecca Atherton, age twenty-two, BA in film from New York University, Class A-20 blogging license, upgraded from a B-20 six months ago, when she passed her final marksmanship tests. She's testing for an A-18 next month."

An A-18 license would mean she was cleared to enter Level 4 hazard zones unaccompanied. "If you take her, my side of the site retains a six percent interest in her reports for the next year." The infected girl was sinking her teeth into Tyrone's left forearm. He screamed soundlessly and fired into the side of the zombie's head. Too late. The damage was done.

"Three percent," Shaun countered.

"Done," I said, not taking my eyes off the screen. "Draft an offer letter. If she agrees, she's yours." Tyrone was staggering in circles, clutching his arm against his body. I could see Tracy barking orders; Carlos turned and ran for the convoy, presumably to get reinforcements. That's why he survived—because he ran away. How must that kind of thing sit with a man like him? I can't imagine that it sits very well.

"George? What's up? I expected you to fight me more than that."

Instead of answering, I pulled the headphone jack out of my machine and let the sound start broadcasting to the room.

"Oh God Tracy oh God oh God," Tyrone was babbling. The moaning in the background was low and constant; the infected were coming, and the gate in the convoy fence was standing open.

"Shut up and help me close this thing," Tracy snarled, grabbing the gate with both hands. After a moment's hesitation, Tyrone ran over and joined her, placing his hands well away from hers. It was a good way of dealing with things. As long as she didn't encounter any of the live virus, she wouldn't begin amplification, and in someone Tyrone's size, full conversion would take longer than was needed to close a simple gate, even one that heavy. Once it was shut, she could wave him off to a safe distance and put a bullet through his brain. It wouldn't be pretty, but elimination of contagion rarely is.

The tape jumped. Tyrone was on the ground in a spreading pool of his own blood while Tracy screamed and struggled against the zombie gnawing at the side of her neck. The gate was closed, and yet there were six zombies on the screen, one chewing on Tracy, three closing, and the other two lurching onward, toward the convoy.

Shaun frowned. "Pause the feed."

I tapped my keyboard. The image froze.

"Rewind to the jump."

I tapped my keyboard again and the image ran backward to the blank spot. I left it there, frozen, and looked to Shaun for further instructions.

He wasn't looking at me at all. "Start it up again, half-speed."

"What are you—"

"Just start the feed, George."

I tapped my keyboard. The image began to move again, much more slowly now. Shaun scowled, and snapped, "Freeze!"

The frozen image showed Tracy screaming, the zombies shambling, and Tyrone dead on the ground. Shaun's finger stabbed out like an accusation, indicating the leg of Tracy's suit. "She didn't run because she *couldn't*," he said. "Someone shot out her kneecap."

"What?" I squinted at the screen. "I don't see it."

"Take out your damn contacts and try again."

I leaned back, blinking my right contact free and removing it with the tip of my index finger. After a moment to let my eye adjust, I closed my left eye and considered the screen again. With my low-light vision restored, it was much harder to miss the wetness of Tracy's leg, or the way the blood on the snow around her fanned out from her body, rather than falling straight down as I would have expected.

I sat up straight. "Someone shot her."

"During the missing footage," Shaun agreed, voice tight. I glanced to him, and he turned his face away, rubbing a hand across his eyes. "Christ, George. She was just doing this because it looked good on her résumé."

"I know, Shaun. I know." I put a hand on his shoulder, staring at my frozen video display, where Tracy battled for a life that was already lost. "We'll find out what's going on here.

"I promise."

> ...they come to us, these restless dead,
> Shrouds woven from the words of men,
> With trumpets sounding overhead
> (The walls of hope have grown so thin
> And all our vaunted innocence
> Has withered in this endless frost)
> That promise little recompense
> For all we risk, for all we've lost...

**—From *Eakly, Oklahoma*,
originally published in *By the Sounding Sea*,
the blog of Buffy Meissonier, February 11, 2040**

Ten

We were approaching the polls on Super Tuesday, and the mood in the senator's camp was grim. People should have been nervous, elated, and on edge; we were hours away from finding out whether the gravy train was about to take off like a rocket or come grinding to a halt. Instead, a funereal atmosphere ruled the camp. The guards continued to triple-check every protocol and step, and no one was willing to go out without an assigned partner. Even the interchangeable interns were beginning to get antsy, and they didn't notice much beyond their duties. It was bad.

The convoy was holding a position three blocks from the convention center, parked in what used to be a high school football field before the Rising rendered outdoor sports too dangerous. It was a good location for our purposes, providing power, running water, and sufficient clear ground for the perimeter fence to be established without anything—either physical or visual—obstructing the cameras. The number of people packed into Oklahoma City for the festivities necessitated running secure buses to the convention center every thirty minutes. Each of them was equipped with state-of-the-art testing units and armed guards.

We had received the final confirmation that Tracy McNally was shot through the right kneecap during the attack two days after Shaun and I first reviewed the tape and brought it to the attention of the senator's security team. This, on top of the cut wires in the perimeter screamers, had provided absolute confirmation that the attack had been a poorly managed assassination attempt. The convoy had been preparing to leave Eakly at the time, and it felt like we'd left the last of our high spirits behind.

It was Shaun who first identified the assassination attempt as poorly managed. When the senator asked him to defend his position, he shrugged and said, "You're alive, aren't you?" It wasn't a comforting point, but it was a good one. A few more zombies in the original wave or a few more guards taken out like Tracy and the convoy could have been overrun rather than suffering a few casualties. Either it hadn't been a full-fledged assassination attempt, or it was an incredibly badly planned one. The former seemed unlikely. They used infected humans.

The attraction of attempting to weaponize the infected has decreased exponentially since the Raskin-Watts trail of 2026, when it was officially declared that any individual who used live-state Kellis-Amberlee as a weapon would be tried as a terrorist. What's the point of using a sloppy, difficult-to-manage weapon if even failure means you're likely to be one of the few lucky souls to still qualify for the death penalty?

The screamers were the only piece of the convoy's equipment that seemed to have been sabotaged. Reviewing the cameras at the gate confirmed that the blank spots were caused by a localized EMP burst—something focused enough that it took out only the cameras within a certain range and didn't attract the attention of most of Buffy's sensors. You can get that sort of tech at RadioShack. It's portable, disposable, and entirely untraceable, unless you happen to have the make and model of the unit, which we don't. The senator's men had been going over every scrap of available evidence since the incident, and they were still no closer to finding answers. If anything, they were further away, because the trail had time to get cold.

Who would want to kill Senator Ryman? Try "practically everyone," and you'd be off to a good start. Senator Peter Ryman started out as a long shot, and somehow became a front-runner in the presidential race. Everything could change before the official party conventions, but there was no denying that he'd been doing well in the polls, that he'd been performing solidly across a wide spectrum of potential voters, and that his views on the issues tended to appeal to the majority. Being the first candidate to open his campaign to the blogging world certainly didn't hurt—he'd enjoyed a substantial boost in awareness among voters aged thirty-five and below. The other candidates took too long to realize that they might have missed a trick, and they'd all been scrambling to catch up. Two of our betas received invitations to follow competing politicians in the week immediately after Eakly. Both refused the offers, citing conflict of interest. When you've got a good thing going, you don't shoot it before you have to.

Beyond Senator Ryman's standing lead, he was photogenic, well-liked, and well-placed in the Republican Party, with no major scandals in his background. No one makes it that far in politics and stays completely clean, but he's about as close as they come. Literally, the biggest scandal

I've been able to find on the man is that his oldest daughter, Rebecca, was either three months premature or was conceived out of wedlock. That's it. He's like a big, friendly Boy Scout who just woke up one day and decided to become the President of the United States of America.

He doesn't even seem to belong to any of the major special-interest groups. Despite his wife's horse ranch, he supports the enforcement of Mason's Law, which means he's not in the pocket of the animal rights organizations, but he also opposes wide-scale hunting and deforestation, which means he doesn't belong to the militant antinature groups. He neither preaches damnation nor asserts that secular humanism was the only answer for a post-Rising world. I haven't even been able to find proof that his campaign received funding from the tobacco companies, and *everyone's* campaign receives funding from the tobacco companies. Once lung cancer stopped killing their customers, they rapidly became the number one contributors to most political campaigns. There's big money to be had in cigarettes that don't give anybody cancer.

A lot of people would benefit if Peter Ryman turned up dead. So maybe it's no surprise that things were fairly bleak around the convoy as the primaries approached. The playful atmosphere that had dominated the campaign for the first six weeks was gone, replaced by blank-faced, by-the-book bodyguards who sometimes seemed to think they should demand blood tests after you used a public toilet. Buffy was handling things pretty well, largely by spending her time either inside the van or with Chuck and his team over in the senator's equipment rig, but it was driving Shaun and me out of our minds.

We both have our own ways of dealing with crazy. That's why Super Tuesday found Shaun off with every other Irwin who'd shown up to cover the convention, looking for dead things to irritate, while I was packed onto a bus with six dozen other deeply uncomfortable-looking reporters, heading for the convention center. I didn't know why they looked so uneasy; I had to get my press pass scanned three times and my blood tested twice before they'd even let me board. The only way anyone was going into conversion before we hit the convention center was if they suffered from cardiac arrest from the strain of being surrounded by other human beings.

A tense-looking man whose shirt was deformed in a way that telegraphed "I am wearing poorly fitted Kevlar" got onto the bus, and the driver announced, "We are at capacity. This bus is now departing for the convention center." This garnered a smattering of applause from the riders, most of whom looked like they were rethinking their choice of careers. No one ever told them that being a reporter would mean *talking* to people!

If it seems as if I have little respect for the other members of my profession, that's because it's true: I frequently don't. For every Dennis Stahl who's willing to go out and chase down the story, you have three or four "reporters" who'd rather edit together remotely taped feeds, interview their subjects by phone, and never leave their homes. There's a fairly popular news site, Under the Lens, that makes that one of their selling points: They claim they must be truly objective, because none of their Newsies ever go into the field. None of them have Class A licenses, and they act like this is something to brag about, like being distanced from the news is a good thing. If the paparazzi clouds serve one purpose, it's keeping that attitude from spreading.

Fear makes people stupid, and Kellis-Amberlee has had people scared for the last twenty years. There comes a point when you need to get over the fear and get on with your life, and a lot of people don't seem to be capable of that anymore. From blood tests to gated communities, we have embraced the cult of fear, and now we don't seem to know how to put it back where it belongs.

The ride to the convention center was almost silent, punctuated only by the various beeps and whirrs of people's equipment recalibrating as we passed in and out of the various service zones and secure bands. Wireless tech has reached the point where you'd practically have to be in the middle of the rain forest or standing on an iceberg in uncharted waters to be truly "out of service," but privacy fields and encryption have progressed at roughly the same rate, which frequently results in service being present but unavailable unless you have the security keys.

No one's supposed to interfere with the standard phone service channels. This doesn't stop overenthusiastic security crews from occasionally blanking everything but the emergency bands. It was amusingly easy to spot the freelance journalists in the crowd: They were the ones hitting their PDAs against their palms, like this would somehow make the proper security keys for the convention center access points appear. Fortunately for the security techs of the world, this approach has yet to work for anyone, and the freelancers were still quietly abusing their equipment when we reached the convention center.

The bus stop was located in the underground parking garage, in a clear, well-lighted area equidistant from both the entrance and exit. The bus approached, the entry gate rose; the bus entered the garage, the gate descended. Assuming it was a standard security setup, there were circuit breakers in place to prevent the entry and exit gates from opening at the same time, and sounding the internal alarm would cause them both to descend and lock. In modern security design, "death trap" isn't always a bad phrase. The idea is minimizing casualties, not preventing them entirely.

Blank-faced security men approached the bus as the doors opened, each holding a blood testing kit. I bit back a groan as I exited and approached the first free guard, adjusting the strap of my shoulder bag before extending my hand toward him. He slipped the unit over my hand and clamped it down.

"Press pass," he said.

"Georgia Mason, After the End Times." I unclipped the pass from my shirt and offered it to him. "I'm with Senator Ryman's group."

He fed the pass into the scanner at his waist. It beeped and popped the pass out again. He handed it back and glanced at the testing unit, which was showing a flashing green light. He frowned. "Please remove the glasses, Ms. Mason."

Lovely. Some of the extremely sensitive units can get confused by the elevated levels of inactive virus particles caused by retinal KA. I didn't exactly want to expose my eyes to the harsh lights of the parking garage, but I didn't feel like getting shot as a security precaution either. I removed by sunglasses, fighting the urge to squint.

The guard leaned forward, studying my eyes. "Retinal Kellis-Amberlee," he said. "Do you carry a med card?"

"Yes." No one with naturally elevated virus levels goes out without a med card if they enjoy breathing. I withdrew my wallet and produced the card, handing it over. He slotted it into the back of the testing unit. The green light stopped flashing, turned yellow, and finally turned a solid green, apparently having satisfied itself that my virus levels were within normal parameters and nothing to be concerned with.

"Thank you for your cooperation." He returned my card. I replaced it in my wallet before sliding my glasses back on. "Will your associates be joining us?"

"Not today." The scan of my press pass would have told him everything there was to know about our organization: Our work history, what our ratings share was like, any citations we'd received for sloppy reporting or libel, and, of course, how many of us were traveling with the senator and his group. "Where can I find—"

"Information kiosks are inside, up the stairs, and to your left," he said, already turning toward the next of the waiting journalists.

Assembly-line hospitality. Maybe it's not that welcoming, but it gets the job done. I turned to head through the glass doors into the convention center proper, where I could hopefully locate a bathroom in short order.

The light had left dazzling spots dancing in front of my eyes, and the only way I was going to make them go away was by swallowing some painkillers before the migraine had time to finish developing. It was a small hope, but as I didn't exactly relish the idea of spending the day mingling with politicians and reporters while suffering from a headache, it was the best one I had.

The air conditioning inside was pumping full volume, ignoring the fact that it was February in Oklahoma. The reason for the arctic chill was evident: The place was packed. Despite the xenophobia that's gripped the world since the Rising, some things still have to happen face-to-face, and that includes political rallies. If anything, the rallies have gotten larger, growing as the smaller events dwindled. There's always the chance of an outbreak when you gather more than ten or twenty people in one place, but man is by his very nature a social animal, and once in a while, you just need an excuse.

Before the Rising, Super Tuesday was a big deal. These days, it's a three-ring circus. Beyond the expected political factions and special-interest groups, the convention center has exhibit halls and even a temporary mini-mall of service and sales kiosks. Place your vote for the next presidential candidate and buy a new pair of running shoes! You know everyone in here has been screened for signs of viral amplification, so have a ball!

The combination of sudden cold and the press of that many bodies was enough to make my impending headache throb. Hunching my shoulders, I began cutting my way diagonally across the crowd, aiming for the escalators. Presumably, the information kiosk would identify the locations of both the bathrooms and whatever was serving as a press staging area in this zoo.

Getting there was easier said than done, but after swimming my way upstream against the delegates, merchants, voters, and tourists who felt that the inconvenience of going through security was worth the chance to have a little fun, I managed to reach the escalator and stepped on, clinging to the rail for all that I was worth. I think the average American's tendency to hide inside while life goes whizzing by is an overreaction to a currently unavoidable situation, but I'm still a child of my generation; for me, a large crowd is fifteen people. The wistful looks older people sometimes get when they talk about gatherings of six and seven hundred are completely alien to me. That's not the way I grew up, and shoving this many bodies into one space, even a space as large as the Oklahoma City Convention Center, just feels *wrong*.

Judging from the makeup of the crowd, I wasn't alone in that attitude.

Except for the people dressed in the corporate colors of one exhibitor or another, I was the youngest person in sight. I'm better crowd-socialized than most people born after the Rising because I've forced myself to be; in addition to the paparazzi swarms, I've attended technology conventions and academic conferences, getting myself used to the idea that people gather in groups. If I hadn't spent the past several years working up to this, just stepping into the hall would have made me run screaming, probably causing security to decide there was an outbreak in progress and lock us all inside.

That's me. The eternal optimist.

I saw the information kiosk as soon as I stepped off the escalator: a brightly colored octagon surrounded by scantily clad young women handing out packs of cigarettes. I pushed past them, refusing three packs on the way, and squinted at the posted map of the convention center. "You are here," I muttered. "That's great. I already found me. The drinking fountain, on the other hand, would be exactly where?"

"Nonsmoker?" inquired a voice at my elbow. I turned to find myself facing Dennis Stahl of the *Eakly Times*. He was smiling and had a press pass clipped to the lapel of his slightly wrinkled jacket. "I thought you looked familiar."

"Mr. Stahl," I said, eyebrows rising. "I didn't expect to see you here."

"Because I'm a newspaperman?"

"No. Because this hall holds roughly the population of North America, and I wouldn't expect to see my brother without a tracking device."

Mr. Stahl laughed. "Fair enough." One of the scantily clad young women took advantage of his distraction and pushed a pack of cigarettes into his hand. He eyed it dubiously before holding it toward me. "Cigarette?"

"Sorry. Don't smoke."

He tilted his head to the side. "Why not? I'd expect a cigarette to be the perfect capper on your 'look at me, I'm hard as nails' air of journalistic integrity." I raised my eyebrows farther. He laughed. "Come on, Ms. Mason. You wear all black, carry an actual handheld MP3 recorder—I haven't seen anyone use one of those in years—and you never remove your sunglasses. You really think I don't know how to spot an image when I see one?"

"First off, I have retinal KA. The sunglasses are a medical necessity. Second…" I paused, smiling. "You got me. It's an image. But I still don't smoke. Do you know where the bathrooms are in this place? I need some water."

"I've been here three hours, and I haven't seen a bathroom yet," he said. "But there *is* a cunningly concealed Starbucks at the end of one of the exhibitors' rows, if you wouldn't mind my walking you?"

"If it gets me water, I'm all for it," I said, waving off another pack of cigarettes.

Mr. Stahl nodded, opening a path through the crowd with a sweep of his arm as he led me through. "Water, or a suitable substitute thereof," he agreed. "In exchange, I have a question for you...Why don't you smoke? Again, it seems like the perfect capper to your image. Personal reasons?"

"I like having sufficient lung capacity to run away from the living dead," I replied, deadpan. Mr. Stahl raised an eyebrow, and I shrugged. "I'm serious. Cigarettes won't give you cancer, but they still cause emphysema, and I have no desire to get eaten by a zombie just because I was trying to look cool. Besides, the smoke can interfere with some delicate electronics, and it's hard enough to keep most kits working in the field. I don't need to add a second level of pollution to the crap they're already trying to function through."

"Huh. And here I thought that once you took cancer out of the equation, we'd be back to a world where every hard-hitting journalist was up to eight packs a day."

The exhibitors' row was packed with people selling things of every shape and size, from freeze-dried food guaranteed to stay good for the duration of a siege to medieval weaponry with built-in splatter guards. If you were looking for fluffier entertainments, there were the usual assortment of new cars, hair-care accessories, and toys for the kids, although I had to admit a certain affection for the Mattel booth advertising Urban Survival Barbie, now with her own machete and blood testing unit.

"That assumes every 'hard-hitting journalist' comes equipped with parents who don't mind them living at home and stinking up the curtains," I said. "What about you? I don't see you lighting up."

"Asthma. I could smoke if I wanted to. I could also collapse in the middle of the sidewalk clutching my chest, and somehow, that makes it substantially less fun." He pointed to the end of the row. "There's the Starbucks. What brings you out this way?"

"The usual: following the Senator around like a kitten on a string. Yourself?"

"A little bit of the same, on a somewhat more general scale." There was no line at the Starbucks, just three bored-looking baristas leaning on the counter and trying to seem busy. Mr. Stahl stepped up to them and said, "Large black coffee, please, to go."

The baristas exchanged a glance, but they'd clearly had their fill of arguing with men wearing press passes. One of them moved to start filling his order.

Glancing to me, Dennis asked, "Want anything?"

"Just a bottled water, thanks."

"Got it." He collected his coffee and handed me my water, passing a debit card to the barista at the register.

I dug a hand into my pocket. "What do I owe you?"

"Forget it." He reclaimed his card and turned to head for an open table near the edge of the exhibit line. I followed, sitting down across from him. He smiled. "Consider it payback for the circulation figures I got off that little incident out at your encampment after the rally the other week. Remember?"

"How could I forget?" I pulled a bottle of prescription-strength pain-killers out of my shoulder bag, uncapping them with my thumb. "That 'little incident' has been defining my life for weeks."

"Got any juicy details for an old friend?"

It had been impossible to keep from releasing the fact that the scream-ers had been sabotaged. Even if we'd wanted to damage our ratings that way, the families of the victims could have sued us for interfering with a federal case if we'd attempted to suppress details. I shook my head. "Not that the press hasn't already released."

"The dangers of pumping industry sources," Mr. Stahl said, and sipped his coffee. "Seriously, though, how have things been around the camp? Everything going smoothly?"

"Relatively so," I said, shaking four pills into my palm and slamming them down with a long gulp of icy water. Once I finished swallowing, I added, "Tense, but smooth. There haven't been any real leads on who sabotaged our perimeter. Causes a bit of internal strife, if you understand what I'm saying."

"Unfortunately, I do." Mr. Stahl shook his head. "Whoever it was must have been careful to cover their tracks."

"With good reason. People died in that attack. That makes it murder and that means they could be tried under Raskin-Watts. Most folks don't commit acts of terrorism expecting to get caught." I took another slower sip of water, waiting for the painkillers to kick in.

Mr. Stahl nodded, lips pressed into a thin line. "I know. Carl Boucher was a blowhard and an opinionated bastard, but he didn't deserve to die like that. None of those folks did. Good or bad, people deserve better deaths than that." He pushed away from the table, taking his coffee with him. "Well, I need to go meet up with my camera crew. We're interviewing Wagman in half an hour, and she likes it when her news crews are prompt. You take care of yourself, Miss Mason, all right?"

"Do my best," I replied, with a nod. "You've got my e-mail address."

"I'll keep in touch," he assured me, and turned, striding off into the crowd. It swallowed him up, and he was gone.

I stayed where I was, sipping my water and considering the atmosphere of the room. In some ways, it was like a cross between a carnival and a frat party, with people of all ages, stripes, and creeds bent on having as much fun as they could before it was time to leave for less well-secured climes. Signs hanging from the ceiling directed voters of the various districts where they should go if they wanted to place their votes in the old, physical way, rather than doing them from home via real-time electronic ballot. From the way most folks were ignoring the signs, I guessed the majority had placed their votes online before hitting the convention center. The paper-voting booths are more of a curiosity than anything else, maintained because the law insists that anyone who wishes to do so be able to place their ballot via physical, nonelectronic means. What this really means is that we can't get exact results on any election until the paper ballots have been tabulated, even when ninety-five percent of the votes have been already placed electronically.

The tobacco companies weren't the only ones working the time-honored selling power of half-clothed female flesh to push their wares. Girls wearing little more than a bikini and a smile were weaving their way in and out of the crowd, offering buttons and banners with political slogans to the passersby. More than half the swag was finding its way into nearby trash cans or onto the floor. Most of the buttons that stayed on, I noted, were either promoting Senator Ryman or Governor Tate, who was definitely shaping up to be Ryman's closest in-party competitor. Congresswoman Wagman had been able to ride her one-trick pony pretty far, but the buzz was pretty uniform in agreeing that it wouldn't get her much further. You can take the "porn star" platform a long way, but it's never going to get you to the White House. Signs indicated it would either be Ryman or Tate for the Republican nomination.

The results of the day would probably solidify one of them in the lead and make the upcoming convention nothing but a formality. I'd been hoping for a third candidate to mix things up at least a little, but there hadn't been any real breakouts on the campaign trail. Among the Republican voters—and even some of the Democrats and Independents—it was either Ryman's brand of laid-back "we should all get along while we're here," or

Tate's hellfire and damnation that was attracting the attention, and hence the potential support, of just about everyone.

Tapping my watch to activate the memo function, I raised my wrist and murmured, "Note to self: See what you can do about getting an interview out of Tate's camp sometime after the primary closes, whatever the results." Technically, Shaun, Buffy, and I count as "rival journalists," given that we're mostly devoted to following Ryman's campaign. At the same time, we've all taken public oaths of journalistic integrity, and that means we can—at least supposedly—be trusted to provide a fair and unbiased report on any subject we address, unless it's in a clearly flagged editorial. Getting close enough to Tate to see how the man ticks might help with my growing objections to his political standpoints. Or it might not, and that could give me a renewed reason to rally for Ryman. Either way, it would make for good news.

My water was nearly gone, and I hadn't come to the convention center to people watch and cadge free beverages from the local newspapermen, no matter how much of an improvement that was over life at the convoy. I tapped my ear cuff. "Call Buffy."

There was a pause as the connection was made, and then Buffy's voice was in my ear, asking, "What glorious service may this unworthy one perform for her majesty on this hallowed afternoon?"

I smirked. "Interrupt your poker game?"

"Actually, we were watching a movie."

"You and Chuckles are getting a little cozy there, don't you think?"

Buffy's reply was a prim, "You don't ask about my business, and I won't ask about yours. Besides, I'm off-duty. There's nothing to edit, and all my material for the week has already been uploaded to the time-release server."

"Fine with me," I said. Contrary to my earlier fears, the painkillers were preventing the headache from becoming more than an annoying throb at the back of my temples. "Can you get me a current location on the senator? I'm over at the convention center, and the place is a madhouse. If I try to find him on my own, I may never be heard from again."

"I'd be able to track a government official because . . . ?"

"I know you have at least one transmitter planted on the man, and you never let a piece of equipment out of your sight without a tracking device."

Buffy paused. Then she asked, "Are you near a data port?"

I looked around. "There's a public jack about ten yards from me."

"Great. They don't have wireless maps of the convention center up for public access—something about 'preserving the security of the hall' or whatever. Go over and plug yourself in, and I can give you Senator Ryman's current location, assuming he's not standing within ten yards of a scrambler."

"Have I mentioned recently that I adore you?" I rose, chucked my bottle into a recycler, and walked toward the jack-in point. "So, Chuck, huh? I guess he's cute, if you like the weedy techie type. Personally, I'd go for something a little taller, but whatever floats your boat. Just make sure you know where he's been."

"Yes, mother," Buffy replied. "Are you there yet?"

"Plugging in now." Hooking my handheld to the wall unit was a matter of seconds. The standardization of data ports has been a true blessing to the technically inept computer users of the world. My system took a few seconds to negotiate a connection with the convention center servers, and most of that was verifying compatibility of antiviral and antispam software. It beeped, signaling its readiness to proceed. "I'm in."

"Great." Buffy quieted. I could hear typing in the background. "Got it. You're in the exhibition zone on the second level, right?"

"Right. Near the Starbucks."

"Drop the singular; there are eight Starbucks kiosks on that level alone. Bring me a sugar-free vanilla raspberry mocha when you come back. The senator is on the conference floor three levels down. I'm dropping you a map." My handheld beeped, acknowledging receipt. "That should have everything you need, assuming he doesn't move."

"Thanks, Buffy." I unplugged myself from the wall. "Have fun."

"Don't call back for at least an hour." The connection cut itself off.

Shaking my head, I focused on the map dominating my screen. It was fairly simplistic, representing the convention center in clear enough lines that my route was difficult to misinterpret. The senator's last known location was marked in red, and a thin yellow line connected him to the blinking white dot representing the data port where I'd downloaded the information. Nicely done. Pushing my sunglasses back up, I began making my way down the exhibition hall.

The crowd had grown thicker during my water break. That wasn't a problem: Buffy's mapping software was equipped with a full overview of the pedestrian routes through the convention center and had been programmed to come up with the fastest route between points, rather than the shortest. After estimating congestion levels, it displayed a route that made use of little-used hallways, half-hidden shortcuts, and a lot of stairwells. Since most people will use escalators whenever possible, taking the stairs is often the best way to avoid getting yourself lost in a crowd.

The human tropism toward illusionary time-saving devices has been the topic of a lot of studies since the Rising. There were an estimated six hundred casualties in one large Midwestern mall due entirely to people's unwillingness to take the stairs during a crisis. Escalators jam if you overload them. People got stuck on elevators or ambushed by zombies that had been able to worm their way into the crush of people trying to force their way up the frozen escalators, and that was all she wrote. You'd think that after something like that, folks would start getting better about expending a little extra effort, but you'd be wrong. Sometimes, the hardest habit to break is the habit of doing nothing beyond the necessary.

It took about fifteen minutes to descend three levels and make it past the cursory security checkpoint between the exhibition levels and the conference floor, which was closed to everyone save the candidates, members of their immediate family, official staff, and the press. The security check consisted of scanning my press pass to confirm that it wasn't a fake, patting me down for unlicensed weapons, and performing a basic blood check with a cheap handheld unit from a brand that I know for a fact returns false negatives three times out of ten. I guess once you're past the door in these places, they don't worry as much about your health.

The quiet of the conference floor was a welcome change from the hustle and bustle of the levels above. Down here, the business of waiting for results was exactly that: business. There are always a few hopefuls who stick it out even after the numbers indicate they don't have much of a shot at the big seat, but the fact of the matter is that the party nominations almost always go to the folks who take Super Tuesday, and without party backing, your odds of taking the presidency are slim to none. You're welcome to try, but you're probably not going to win. Nine out of ten of the folks who've been out pounding the pavement for the last few months will be heading home after the polls close. It'll be four more years before they have another shot at the big time, and for some of them, that's too long to wait; a lot of this year's candidates will never try for it again. Dreams are made and broken on days like this.

The senator and his team were in a plushly appointed boardroom about halfway down the hall. A placard on the wall identified the room's inhabitants as "Senator Ryman, Rep., WI," but I still knocked before trying the door, just in case something was going on that I wasn't meant to interfere with.

"Come in," called a brisk, irritated voice. I nodded, satisfied that I wasn't interrupting, and stepped inside.

When I first met Robert Channing, the senator's chief aide, my initial impression was of a fussy, egotistical man who resented anything that might get in his way. After a few months of acquaintanceship, I haven't been forced to revise that impression, although I've come to understand that he's very good at what he does. He doesn't travel with the convoy. He's usually at the senator's office in Wisconsin, arranging bookings, setting up the halls where Senator Ryman speaks, and coordinating outside news coverage, since "three amateur journalists with a vanity site doesn't exactly constitute wide-scale exposure." Oddly, much of my respect for him comes from the fact that he's willing to say things like that to my face. He's been very upfront about everything that affects the senator's chances at the White House from day one, and if that means stepping on a few toes, he's okay with that. Not a nice guy, but a good one to have on your side.

At the moment, he was looking at me with narrowed eyes, and it was clear that whoever's side he was currently on, it wasn't mine. His tie was askew, and his jacket had been tossed over a nearby chair. That, more than the senator's unbuttoned jacket and missing tie, told me they'd been having a rough day. Senator Ryman is quick to shed the trappings of propriety, but Channing only takes his jacket off when the stress is too much to tolerate in tweed.

"Thought I'd come see how things were going at the fort," I said, closing the door behind myself. "Maybe get some decent reaction quotes as the numbers come down."

"Miss Mason," acknowledged Channing stiffly. Several of the interchangeable interns were occupied at the back of the room, taking notation from the various monitors into their handhelds and PDAs. "Please try not to get underfoot."

"I'll do my best." I sat in the first unoccupied chair, folding my hands behind my head as I stared in his direction. Channing is one of those people who can't stand the fact that my sunglasses make it hard for him to tell whether I'm actually looking at him.

He met my stare with a disgruntled glower before grabbing his jacket and striding for the door. "I'm getting coffee," he said, and stepped out into the hallway, slamming the door as he went.

Senator Ryman didn't bother to conceal his amusement. Instead, he roared with it, as though my driving his chief aide out of the room was the funniest thing he'd seen in years. "Georgia, that wasn't nice," he said, finally, between gusts of laughter.

I shrugged. "All I did was sit down," I said.

"Wicked, wicked woman. I assume you're here to find out whether you still have a job?"

"I have a job whether you have a campaign or not, Senator, and I can monitor the public polls from the convoy just as well as I can monitor them from here. I wanted to get an idea of the mood around the camp." I looked around the room. Most of the people present had shed their jackets, and in some cases their shoes. Empty coffee cups and half-eaten sandwiches littered random surfaces, and the whiteboard was largely dedicated to a series of tic-tac-toe grids. "I'm going with 'guardedly optimistic.'"

"We're ahead by twenty-three percent of the vote," the senator said, with a short nod. "'Guardedly optimistic' is an accurate assessment."

"How are you feeling?"

He frowned at me. "How do you mean?"

"Well, sir, at some point in the next," I made a show of checking my watch, "six hours, you find out whether you have a shot at the party nomination, and hence the presidency, or whether you're looking at the second-banana consolation prize, or worse, nothing at all. Today begins the process of winning or losing the election. So, bearing all of that in mind, how are you feeling?"

"Terrified," the senator said. "This is a long way from turning to my wife and saying, 'Well, honey, I think this is the term when I make a run for the office.' This is the real deal. I'm a bit anticipatory, but not that much. Whatever the polls say, the people will have spoken, and I'll just have to abide with what they have to say."

"But you're expecting them to speak in your favor."

He fixed me with a stern eye. "Georgia, has this just turned into an interview?"

"Maybe."

"Thanks for the warning."

"Warnings aren't in my job description. Did you need me to repeat the question?"

"I hadn't realized it was a question," he said, tone suddenly wry. "Yes, I'm expecting them to speak in my favor, because you don't make it as far as I have without developing an ego, and I'm of the opinion that the average American is an intelligent person who knows what's best for this country. I wouldn't be running for office if I didn't think I was the best man for the job. Will I be disappointed if they don't pick me? A bit. It's natural to be disappointed when you don't get chosen for this sort of thing. But I'm willing to believe that if the American public is smart enough to choose their own president, then the American public is smart enough to know what they want, and if they don't choose me, I need to do some serious self-examination to see where I got it all wrong."

"Have you given any thought to your next steps, assuming you show strongly enough in today's polls to continue with the campaign?"

"We'll keep taking the message to the people. Keep getting out there and meeting people, letting them know that I won't be the sort of president who sits in a hermetically sealed room and ignores the problems plaguing this country." His dig at President Wertz was subtle but well-deserved. No one's seen our current president set foot outside a well-secured urban area since before he was elected, and most critiques of his administration have centered around the fact that he doesn't seem to realize not everyone can afford to have their air filtered before it gets to them. To listen to him talk, you'd think zombie attacks only happened to the careless and the stupid, rather than being something ninety percent of the people on the planet have to worry about on a daily basis.

"How does Mrs. Ryman feel about this?"

Senator Ryman's expression softened. "Emily is as pleased as can be that things are going so well. I'm on this campaign with the full support and understanding of my family, and without them, I'd never have been able to make it half as far as I have."

"Senator, in recent weeks, Governor Tate—who many view as your primary in-party opponent—has been speaking out for stricter screening protocols among children and the elderly, and increased funding for the private school system, on the basis that overcrowding in the public schools only increases the risk of wide-scale viral incubation and outbreak. How do you stand on this issue?"

"Well, Miss Mason, as you know, all three of my daughters have attended the excellent public schools in our home town. My eldest—"

"That would be Rebecca Ryman, age eighteen?"

"That's correct. My eldest will be graduating high school this June and expects to start at Brown University in the fall, where she'll be studying political science, like her old man. Supporting a free and equal public school system is one of the duties of the government. Which does mean increased blood screening for children under the age of fourteen, and additional funding for school security, but it seems to me that taking money from our public schools because they might be threatened at some point in the future is a bit of burning down the barn to keep the hay from going bad."

"How do you speak to the criticisms that your campaign depends too heavily on the secular issues facing our nation, while ignoring the spiritual?"

Senator Ryman's lips quirked in a smile. "I say when God comes down here and helps me clean my house, I'll be more than happy to help Him with cleaning His. Until then, I'll trouble myself with keeping people fed and breathing, and let Him tend the parts I can't do anything to help."

The door opened as Channing returned, balancing a tray of Starbucks cups on his outstretched arms. The interchangeable interns promptly mugged him. An open can of Coke was somehow deposited in front of me in the chaos that followed. I acknowledged it with a grateful nod, picked it up, and sipped before saying, "If the campaign ends today, Senator, if this is the culmination of your work to date...was it worth it?"

"No," he said. The room went quiet. I could almost hear heads turning toward him. "As your readers are no doubt aware, an act of sabotage committed at my headquarters earlier this month led to the deaths of four good men and women who were dedicated to supporting this campaign. They signed on to draw a paycheck and maybe, along the way, help an ideal find a place in this modern world. Instead, they passed on to whatever reward may be waiting for us—for heroes—in the *next* world. If those men and women had lived, then yes, I could have walked away from this a little sadder, a little wiser, but convinced that I'd done the right thing, I'd done my best, and next time, I'd be able to make that run all the way to the end of the road. At this point?

"Nothing I do is bringing them back, and if there *were* something I could do to change what happened in Eakly, I would have done it ten times over. From where I sit, there's only one thing left that I *can* do, and that's win. For the ideal they died supporting, and for the sake of their memories. So if I lose, if I have to go home empty-handed, if the next time I contact their families it's to say, 'Sorry, but I couldn't make it after all'...then no, it wasn't worth it. But it was the only thing I knew to do."

There was a long, stunned pause before the room erupted in applause. Most of it came from the interchangeable interns, but the technicians were applauding as well—and so, his hands devoid of coffee cups, was Channing. I noted this with thoughtful interest before turning back to the senator and nodding.

"Thank you for your time," I said, "and best of luck in today's primaries."

Senator Ryman flashed a practiced grin. "I don't need luck. I just need the waiting to be over."

"And I just need the use of one of your data ports, so that I can clean this up and transmit it over for upload," I said, pulling out my MP3 recorder and holding it up to the room. "It'll take me about fifteen minutes to do the surface edits."

"Will we be permitted to review your report before release?" asked Channing.

"Down, boy," said the senator. "I don't see where we need to. Georgia's been square with us so far, and I don't see where that's going to change. Georgia?"

"You can review it if you'd like, but all that's going to do is delay release," I said. "Leave me to work, and this hits my front page before the polls have closed."

"Go to it," said the senator, and indicated a free space on the wall. "You have all the data ports you need."

"Thanks," I said, and took my Coke, moving over to the wall to settle down and set to work.

Editing a report is both easier and harder for me than it is for Shaun or Buffy. My material rarely depends on graphics. I don't need to concern myself with camera angles, lighting, or whether the footage I use gets my point across. At the same time, they say a picture is worth a thousand words, and in today's era of instant gratification and high-speed answers, sometimes people aren't willing to deal with all those hard words when a few pictures supposedly do the job just as well. It's harder to sell people on a report that's just news without pictures or movies to soften the blow. I have to find the heart of every subject as fast as I can, pin it down on the page, and then cut it wide open for the audience to see.

"Super Tuesday: Index Case for a Presidency" wouldn't win me any awards, but once I cleaned up my impromptu interview with Senator Ryman and intercut the text with a few still shots of the man, I was reasonably sure that it *was* going to catch and hold an audience, and tell the truth as I understood it. Anything beyond that was more than I had a right to ask.

With my report uploaded and turned in, I settled to do what a lifetime of reporting the truth has equipped me for best of all: I settled to wait. I watched the interchangeable interns come and go, watched Channing pace, and watched the senator, aware that his fate was already determined, holding calm and implacable sway over them all. He just didn't know what that determination was.

The polls closed at midnight. Every screen in the room was turned to the major media outlets, a dozen talking heads conflicting with one another's words as they tried to string the suspense out and drive their ratings just a few degrees higher. I couldn't blame them for it, but that didn't mean that I had to be impressed with it.

My ear cuff beeped. I tapped it.

"Go."

"Georgia, it's Buffy."

"Results?"

"Senator Ryman took the primary with a seventy percent clean majority. His position jumped eleven points as soon as your report went live."

I closed my eyes and smiled. One of the talking heads had just revealed the same information, or something similar; whoops and cheers were filling the room. "Say the words, Buffy."

"We're going to the Republican National Convention."

Sometimes, the truth *can* set you free.

The importance of the Raskin-Watts trial and the failure of all subsequent attempts to overturn the ruling have been often overlooked in the wake of more recent, more sensational incidents. After all, what bearing can two long-dead religious nutcases from upstate Indiana have on the state of modern politics?

Quite a lot. For one thing, the current tendency to dismiss Geoff Raskin and Reed Watts as "religious nutcases" is an oversimplification so extreme as to border on the criminal. Geoff Raskin held a degree in psychology from UC Santa Cruz, with a specialization in crowd control. Reed Watts was an ordained priest who worked with troubled youth and was instrumental in bringing several communities "back to God." They were, in short, intelligent men who recognized the potential for turning the waves of social change engendered by the side effects of Kellis-Amberlee to their own benefit, and to the benefit of their faith.

Did Geoff Raskin and Reed Watts work for the common good? Read the reports on what they did to Warsaw, Indiana, and see if you think so. Seven hundred and ninety-three people died in the primary infection wave alone, and the cleanup from the secondary infections took six years to complete, during which time Raskin and Watts were held in maximum security, awaiting trial. According to their own testimony, they were intending to use the living dead as a threat to bring the people of Warsaw, and eventually of the United States, around to their point of view: that Kellis-Amberlee was the judgment of the Lord, and that all ungodly ways would soon be wiped from the Earth.

It was the finding of the courts that the use of weaponized live-state Kellis-Amberlee, as represented by the captive zombies, was considered an act of terrorism, and that all individuals responsible for such acts would be tried under the International Terrorism Acts of 2012. Geoff Raskin and Reed Watts were killed by lethal injection, and their bodies were remanded to the government to assist in the study of the virus they had helped to spread.

The moral of our story, beyond the obvious "don't play with dead things": Some lines were never meant to be crossed, however good your cause may seem.

—From *Images May Disturb You*,
the blog of Georgia Mason, March 11, 2040

Eleven

"Georgia! Shaun! It's so lovely to see you!" Emily Ryman was all smiles as she approached, arms spread wide in an invitation to an embrace. I glanced at Shaun and he stepped forward, letting her hug him while he blocked her from reaching me. I don't like physical contact from semi-strangers, and Shaun knows it.

If Emily noticed the deliberate way we positioned ourselves, she didn't comment. "I never quite believe you're alive after those reports you do, you foolish, foolish boy."

"It's good to see you, too, Emily," Shaun said, and hugged her back. He's much easier with that sort of thing than I am. I blame this on the fact that he's the kind of person who believes in shoving his hand into the dark, creepy hole, rather than sensibly avoiding it. "How have you been?"

"Busy, as usual. Foaling season kept us hopping, but that's mostly over, thank God. I lost two good mares this year, and neither managed to reanimate on the grounds, thanks to the help being on the ball." Emily detangled herself from Shaun, still smiling, and turned to offer her hand. Not a hug, just her hand. I gave her a nod of approval as I took it. Her smile widened. "Georgia. I can't thank you enough for your coverage of my husband's campaign."

"It hasn't just been me." I reclaimed my hand. "There are a lot of reporters keeping a close eye on the senator. Word on the street is he's receiving the party nomination tonight." The other political journalists were starting to smell "White House" in the water and were gathering like sharks, hoping for something worth seizing on. Buffy spent half her time disabling cameras and microphones set up by rival blog sites. She spent the other half writing steamy porn about the senator's aides and hanging out with Chuck Wong, who'd been spending a disconcerting amount of time in our van recently, but that was her business.

"Yes, but you're the only one I've met who's reporting on *him*, rather than the interesting things his campaign drives out from beneath the rocks, or the fictional affairs of his office aides," Emily said, wryly. "I know I can trust what you say. That's meant a lot to me and the girls while Peter was on the road, and it's going to mean a lot more from here on out."

"It's been an honor."

"What do you mean, 'it's going to mean a lot more'?" asked Shaun. "Hey, George, are you finally going to learn to write? Because that would be awesome. I can't carry you forever, you know."

"Sadly, Shaun, this doesn't have anything to do with how well your sister can write." Emily shook her head. "It's all about the campaign."

"I understand," I said. Glancing to Shaun, I continued, "Once he accepts the nomination—assuming he gets nominated—this gets real. Up until now, it's been a weird sort of summer vacation." After the nominations, it would be campaigning in earnest. It would be debates and deals and long nights, and she'd be lucky to see him before the inauguration. Assuming all that work didn't turn out to be for nothing; assuming he could win.

"Exactly," said Emily, expression going weary. "That man is lucky I love him."

"Statements like that make me wish that I didn't have quite so much journalistic integrity, Emily," I said. The statement was mild, but the warning wasn't. "You, expressing unhappiness with your husband? That's about to become sound-bite gold for both sides of the political fence."

She paused. "You're telling me to be careful."

"I'm telling you something you already know." I smiled, changing the subject to one that would hopefully make her look less uncomfortable. "Will the girls be joining you? I still need to meet them."

"Not for this silly convention," she said. "Rebecca is getting ready for college, and I didn't have the heart to drag Jeanne and Amber away from the foals to get their pictures taken by a thousand strangers. *I* wouldn't be here if it wasn't absolutely necessary."

"Understandable," I said. The job of a candidate's spouse at the party convention is simple: stand around looking elegant and attractive, and say something witty if you get a microphone shoved in your face. That doesn't leave much time for family togetherness, or for protecting kids from reporters itching to find something scandalous to start chewing on. Everything that happens at a party convention is on the record if the press finds out about it. Emily was doing the right thing. "Mind if I drop by later for an interview? I promise not to bring up the horses if you promise not to throw heavy objects at my head."

Emily's lips quirked up in a smile. "My. Peter wasn't kidding when he said that the convention had you feeling charitable."

"She's saving up her catty for her interview with Governor Tate," Shaun said.

"He's agreed to an interview?" asked Emily. "Peter said he'd been putting you off since the primaries."

"That would be why he's finally agreed to an interview," I replied, not bothering to keep the irritation from my voice. "Doing it before now was dismissible. I mean, what was I going to say about the man? 'Governor Tate is so busy trying to get elected that he doesn't have time to sit down with a woman who speaks publicly in support of his in-party opposition'? Not exactly a scathing indictment. Now we're at the convention and if he doesn't talk to me when he's talking to everyone else, it looks like censorship."

Emily considered me for a moment. Then, slowly, she smiled. "Why, Georgia Mason, I do believe you've entrapped this poor man."

"No, ma'am, I've merely engaged in standard journalistic practice," I said. "He entrapped himself."

An exclusive six weeks before the convention would have been something he could bury or buy off: No matter how good it was, unless I somehow got him to confess to a sex scandal or drug abuse, it wasn't going to be enough to taint the shining purity of his "champion of the religious and conservative right" reputation. Senator Ryman is moderate leaning toward liberal, despite his strong affiliation to and affection for the Republican Party. Governor Tate, on the other hand, is so far to the right that he's in danger of falling off the edge of the world. Few people are willing to stand for both the death penalty and an overturning of *Roe v. Wade* these days, but he does it, all while encouraging loosening the Mason's Law restrictions preventing family farms from operating within a hundred miles of major metro areas and encouraging tighter interpretation of Raskin-Watts. Under his proposed legislation, it wouldn't be a crime to own a cow in Albany, but it would be considered an act of terrorism to attempt to save the life of a heart attack victim before performing extensive blood tests. Did I want a little time alone with him, on the record, to see how much of a hole he could dig for himself when faced with the right questions?

Did I ever.

"When's your interview?"

"Three." I glanced at my watch. "Actually, if you don't mind Shaun escorting you from here, that would be a big help. I need to get moving if I don't want to make the governor wait."

"I thought you *did* want to make the governor wait," said Shaun.

"Yes, but it has to be on purpose." Making him wait intentionally was showing strategy. Making him wait because I didn't allow enough time to get to his office was sloppy. I have a reputation for being a lot of things—after the article where I called Wagman a "publicity-seeking prostitute who decided to pole-dance on the Constitution for spare change," "bitch" has been at the top of the list—but "sloppy" isn't among them.

"Of course," said Emily. "Thank you for coming out to meet me."

"It was my pleasure, Mrs. Ryman. Shaun, don't make the nice potential First Lady poke any dead things before you deliver her to security."

"You never let me have any fun," Shaun mock-grumbled, offering Emily his arm. "If you'd like to come with me, I believe I can promise an utterly dull, boring, and uneventful trip between points A and B."

"That sounds lovely, Shaun," said Emily. Her security detail—three large gentlemen who looked just like every other private security guard at the convention—fell in behind her as Shaun led her away down the hall.

When she'd e-mailed asking us to meet her, she said she'd be arriving at one of the delivery doors, rather than the VIP entrance. "I want to avoid the press" was her quixotic, but sadly understandable, justification. Despite the snide implications that have been made by some of my colleagues, my team and I aren't the lapdogs of what will hopefully become the Ryman administration. We're twice as critical as anyone else when the candidate screws up because, quite frankly, we expect better of him. He's *ours*. Win or lose, he belongs to *us*. And just like any proud parent or greedy share-holder, we want to see our investment make it to the finish line. If Peter screws the pooch, Shaun, Buffy, and I are right there in the thick of things, pointing to the wet spot and shouting for people to come quick and bring the cameras...but we're also the ones who won. We have no interest in embarrassing the senator by harassing his family or dragging them inap-propriately into the spotlight.

An example: Rebecca Ryman fell off her horse during a show-jumping event at the Wisconsin State Fair three years ago. She was fifteen. I don't understand the appeal of show-jumping—I don't care for large mammals under any circumstances, and I like them even less when you're stack-ing adolescents on their backs and teaching them to clear obstacles—so I can't say what happened, just that the horse stepped wrong somehow, and Rebecca fell. She was fine. The horse broke a leg and had to be put down.

The euthanasia was performed without a hitch; as is standard with large mammals, they used a captive bolt gun to the forehead, followed by a stiletto to the spinal column. Nothing was hurt except the horse, Rebecca's pride, and the reputation of the Wisconsin State Fair. The horse never had a prayer of reanimating. That hasn't prevented six of our rivals from airing the footage from that fair for weeks on end, as if the embarrassment of a teenage girl somehow cancels out the fact that they didn't make the cut. "Ha-ha, you got the candidate, but we can mock his teenage daughter for an honest mistake."

Sometimes I wonder if my crew is the only group of professional journalists who managed to avoid the asshole pills during training. Then I look at some of my editorials, especially the ones involving Wagman and her slow political suicide, and I realize that we took the pills. We just got a small portion of journalistic ethics to make them go down more easily. Emily knew she was safe with us because, unlike our peers, Shaun and I don't abuse innocent people for the sake of a few marketable quotes. We have politicians to abuse when we need that sort of thing.

I checked my watch as I strode down the hall toward the main entrance. A shortcut through the press pen would take me to the governor's offices, where his chief of staff would be happy to stall me for as long as possible. My interview wasn't for a guaranteed sixty minutes; I'd need a lot more pull if I wanted to achieve something like that. No, I just got whatever questions I could ask and have answered in the span of an hour, no matter what else came up during that time. I wanted to make him wait no more than ten minutes. That would make a point but still leave me the time to get the answers I both wanted and needed to have. His chief of staff would not only want to make *me* wait, he'd want to make me wait for at least half an hour, thus gutting the interview and proving once more exactly who was in control of the situation.

There are moments when I look at the world I'm living in, all the cutthroat politics and the incredibly petty, partisan deal mongering, and I wonder how anyone could be happy doing anything else. After this, local politics would seem like a bake sale. Which means I need to stay exactly where I am, and *that* means making sure everyone sees how good I am at my job.

People called greetings my way as I cut through the press pen. I waved distractedly, attention focused on the route ahead. I have a reputation for aloofness in certain parts of the press corps. I guess I deserve it.

"Georgia!" called a man I vaguely recognized from Wagman's press pool. He shouldered his way through the crowd, drawing up alongside me as I continued toward the door to Governor Tate's offices. "Got a second?"

"Not so much," I said, reaching for the doorknob.

He put a hand on my shoulder, ignoring the way I tensed, and said, "The congresswoman just dropped out of the race."

I froze, swinging my head around to face him before tugging my sunglasses down enough to allow me an unobstructed view of his face. The overhead lights burned my eyes. That didn't matter; I could see his expression well enough to know that he wasn't lying. "What do you want?" I asked, pushing my glasses back up.

He looked over his shoulder toward the rest of the gathered journalists. None of them seemed to have realized that there was blood in the water. Not yet, anyway. They'd catch on fast, and once they did, we were cornered.

"I bring you what I have—and there's footage, too, lots of stuff, all the votes, details on where she's throwing what's left of her weight—and you let me on the team."

"You want to follow Ryman?"

"I do."

I considered this, keeping my face impassive. Finally, incrementally, I nodded. "Be at our rooms in an hour, with copies of all your recent publications, and everything you've got on Wagman. We'll talk there."

"Great," he said, and stepped back, letting me continue on my way.

Governor Tate's security agents nodded as I stepped through the doorway into the governor's offices, holding up my press pass for their review. It passed muster; they didn't stop me.

Governor Tate's quarters looked just like Senator Ryman's, and were, I'm sure, close to identical to Wagman's. Since presidential hopefuls are packed into contiguous convention centers these days, the folks organizing the conventions go out of their way to prevent the appearance that they're "showing favor" to any particular candidate. One of our guys was going to come away the Crown prince of the party while the other went begging for scraps, but until the votes were counted, they'd be standing on equal footing.

The office was full of volunteers and staffers, and the walls were plastered with the requisite "Tate for President" posters, but the atmosphere still managed to be quiet and almost funereal. People didn't look frightened, just focused on what they were doing. I tapped the button on my lapel, triggering its internal camera to start taking still shots every fifteen seconds. There was enough memory to keep it doing that for two hours before I needed to dump the pictures to disk. Most of the shots would be crap, but there would probably be one or two that I could use.

I killed a few minutes pouring myself an unwanted cup of coffee and doctoring it to my supposed satisfaction before walking over to show my press pass to the guards waiting at the governor's office door.

"Georgia Mason, After the End Times, here to see Governor Tate."

One of them looked over his sunglasses at me. "You're late."

"Got held up," I replied, smiling. My own sunglasses were firmly in place, making it difficult, if not impossible, to tell whether the smile was reaching my eyes.

The guards exchanged a look. I've found that men in sunglasses really hate it when they can't see your eyes—it's like the air of mystique they're trying to create isn't meant to be shared with anyone else, especially not a silly little journalist who happens to suffer from an ocular medical condition. I held my ground and my smile.

Late or not, they didn't have a valid reason to keep me out. "Don't do it again," said the taller of the two, and opened the door to the governor's private office.

"Right," I said, and let my smile drop as I walked past them. They closed the door behind me with a sharp click. I didn't bother to turn. I'd only get one first look at the private office of the man who stood the best shot at putting me out of a job. I wanted to savor it.

Governor Tate's office was decorated austerely. He'd chosen to cover the room's two windows; shelves blocked them almost completely, and the ambient light was provided by soft overhead fluorescents. Two massive flags covered most of the rear wall, representing, respectively, the United States and Texas. There were no other personal touches in evidence. This office was a stopping place, not a destination.

The governor himself was behind his desk, carefully placed so he was framed by the flags. I could imagine his handlers spending hours arguing about how best to create the image that he was a man who would be strong, both for his country and for the world. They'd done it; he looked perfectly presidential. If Peter Ryman was all boyish good looks and all-American charm, Governor David Tate was the embodiment of the American military man, from his solemn demeanor down to his respectable gray crew cut. I didn't need to call up his service record; the fact that he had one while Senator Ryman didn't has been the source of a lot of ads paid for by "concerned citizens" since the campaign cycle began. Three-star general, saw combat in the Canadian Border Cleansing of '17, when we took back Niagara Falls from the infected, and then again in New Guinea in '19, when a terrorist action involving aerosolized live-state Kellis-Amberlee nearly cost us the country. He'd been wounded in battle, he'd fought for his nation and for the rights of the uninfected, and he understood the war we fight every day against the creatures that used to be our loved ones.

There are a lot of good reasons the man scares the crap out of me. Those are just the beginning.

"Miss Mason," he said, indicating the chair on the far side of his desk with a sweep of one hand as he rose. "I trust you didn't get lost? I was beginning to think you weren't intending to come."

"Governor," I replied. I walked over and sat down, pulling my MP3 recorder from my pocket and placing it on the table. The action triggered at least two video cameras concealed in my clothing. Those were the ones I knew about; I was sure Buffy had hidden half a dozen more in case someone got cute with an EMP pulse. "I was unavoidably detained."

"Ah, yes," he said, sitting back down. "Those security checks can be murder, can't they?"

"They certainly can." I leaned over to turn on the MP3 recorder with a theatrical flick of my index finger. Smoke and mirrors: If he thought that was my only recording device, he'd worry less about what was really going on the record. "I wanted to thank you for taking the time to sit down with me today and, of course, with our audience at After the End Times. Our readers have been following this campaign with a great deal of interest, and your platform is something that they're eager to understand in more depth."

"Clever folks, your readers," the governor drawled, settling back in his seat. I glanced up without moving my head; the ability to see your interviewees when they don't know you're looking is one of the great advantages to living your life behind tinted glass.

It was easier to look than it was to avoid flinching at what I saw. The governor was watching me with undisguised blankness, like a little boy watching a bug he intended to smash. I'm used to people disliking reporters, but that was a bit much. Sitting up again, I straightened my glasses and said, "They are among the most discriminating in the blogging community."

"Is that so? Well, I suppose that explains their unflagging interest in this year's race. Been glorious for your ratings, hasn't it?"

"Yes, Governor, it has. Now, your run for president was a bit of a surprise—political circles held that you wouldn't be reaching for the office for another cycle. What prompted this early entrance into the race?"

The governor smiled, erasing the blankness from his eyes. Too late; I'd already seen it. In a way, the sudden life in his expression was even more frightening. He was on script now. He thought he knew how to handle me.

"Well, Miss Mason, the long and the short of it is that I've been getting a mite worried watching the way things have been going around here. I looked out at the field and realized that, unless I was on it, there just wasn't anyone out there that I'd trust to watch after my wife and two boys when the dead decided it was time for another mass uprising. America needs a strong leader in this time of turmoil. Someone who knows what it means for a man to fight to hold what's his. No offense against my esteemed opponent, but the good senator hasn't ever fought for what he loves. He doesn't understand it the way he would if he'd ever bled to keep it." His tone was jovial and almost jocular, a father figure imparting wisdom on a privileged student.

I wasn't buying it. Keeping my expression professional, I said, "So you see this as a two-man race—between yourself and Senator Ryman."

"Let's be honest here: It *is* a two-man race. Kirsten Wagman is a good woman with strong Republican values and a firm grasp of the morals of this nation, but she's not going to be our next president. She isn't prepared to do what's needed for the people and the economy of this great land."

Resisting the urge to point out that Kirsten Wagman believed in using her breasts in place of an informed debate, I asked, "Governor, what do you feel is needed for the people of America?"

"This country was based on the three Fs, Miss Mason: Freedom, Faith, and Family." I could hear the capital letters in his voice; he said the words with that much force. "We've gone to great lengths to preserve the first of those things, but we've allowed the other two to slip by the wayside as we focused on the here and now. We're drifting away from God." The blankness was back in his eyes. "We're being judged; we're being tested. I'm afraid we're coming direly close to failing, and this isn't a test you get to take more than once."

"Can you give me an example of this 'failure'?"

"Why, the loss of Alaska, Miss Mason; a great American territory ceded to the dead because we didn't have the guts to stand up for what was rightly ours. Our boys weren't willing to put their faith in God and stand that line, and now a treasured part of our nation is lost, maybe forever. How long before that happens again, in Hawaii or Puerto Rico or, God forbid, even the American Heartland? We've gotten soft behind our walls. It's time to put our trust in God."

"Governor, you saw action in the Canadian Border Cleansing. I'd expect you to understand why Alaska had to be abandoned."

"And I'd expect you to understand why a true American never lets go of what's his. We should have fought. Under my leadership, we *will* fight, and we will by God win."

I suppressed the unprofessional urge to shudder. His voice held all the hallmarks of a fanatic. "You're requesting relaxation of Mason's Law, Governor. Is there a particular reason for that?"

"There's nothing in the Constitution that says a man can't feed his family however he sees fit, even if that way isn't exactly popular. Laws that limit our freedoms are needless as often as not. Why, look what happened when the Democrats stopped fighting for their unconstitutional gun control laws. Did gunshot deaths climb? No. They declined by forty percent the first year, and they've been dropping steadily ever since. It stands to reason that relaxation of other antifreedom legislation would—"

"How many of the infected are killed with guns every year?"

He paused, eyes narrowing. "I don't see what bearing that has on our discussion."

"According to the most recent CDC figures, ninety percent of the Kellis-Amberlee victims that are killed in clashes with the uninfected are killed by gunshot."

"Guns fired by licensed, law-abiding citizens."

"Yes, Governor. The CDC has *also* said that it's virtually impossible to tell a murder victim killed by a shot to the head or spinal column from an infected individual put down legally in the same fashion. What is your answer to critics of the relaxed gun control laws who hold that gun-related violence has actually *increased*, but has been masked by the postmortem amplification of the Kellis-Amberlee virus?"

"Well, Miss Mason, I suppose I'd have to ask them for proof." He leaned forward. "You carry a gun?"

"I'm a licensed journalist."

"Does that mean yes?"

"It means I'm required to by law."

"Would you feel safe entering a hazard zone without it? Letting your kids enter a hazard zone? This isn't the civilized world anymore, Miss Mason. The natives are always restless now. Soon as you get sick, you start to hate the folks who aren't. America needs a man who isn't afraid to say that your rights end where the grave begins. No mercy, no clemency, and no limits on what a man can do to protect what's his."

"Governor, there have been no indications that infected individuals are capable of emotions as complex as hate. Further, they're not dead. If rights end where the grave begins, shouldn't they be protected by law like any other citizen?"

"Miss, that's the sort of thinking you can afford when you're safe, protected by men who understand what it means to stand strong. When the dead—sorry, the 'infected'—are at your door, well, you'll be wishing for a man who speaks like me."

"Do you feel that Senator Ryman is soft on the infected?"

"I don't think he's ever been put into a position to find out."

Nicely said. Cast doubt on Senator Ryman's ability to fight the zombies *and* imply that he might be overly sympathetic to the idea of "live and let live"—a concept that gets floated now and then by the members of the far left wing. Usually for about fifteen minutes, until another lobbyist gets eaten. "Governor, you've spoken on wanting to do away with the so-called Good Samaritan laws that currently make it legal to extend assistance to citizens in trouble or distress. Can you explain your reasoning?"

"Simple as pie. Someone in distress likely got that way for a reason. Now, I'm not saying that I don't feel terrible for anyone who winds up in that sort of a position, but if you rush to my aid when I've been bit, and you violate a quarantine line to do it, well, odds are good that you're not saving me anyway, but you've also just thrown your own life aside." The governor smiled. It might have seemed warm if it had come close to reaching his eyes. "It's always the young and the idealistic who die that way. The ones America needs most of all. We have to protect our future."

"By sacrificing our present?"

"If that's what it takes, Miss Mason," he said, smile widening and turning beatific. "If that's what America requires."

──────────

Now that I've had my long-delayed meeting with the man, there's one question on everybody's mind: What did I think of Governor David "Dave" Tate of Texas, elected three times in a landslide of votes, each time from voters from both sides of the partisan fence, possessed of an incredible record for dispensing justice and settling disputes in a state famed for its belligerence, hostility, and political instability?

I think he's the scariest of the many frightening things I've encountered since this campaign began. And that includes the zombies.

Governor Tate is a man who cares so much about freedom that he's willing to give it to you at gunpoint. He's a man who cares so deeply about our schools that he supports shutting down public education in favor of vouchers distributed only to schools with government safety certifications. A man who cares so deeply about our farmers that he would reduce the scope of Mason's Law to allow not only large herding dogs but livestock up to a hundred and thirty pounds back into residential neighborhoods. Governor Tate wants us all to experience the glories of his carefree youth, including, it would seem, pursuit by infected collies and zombie goats.

To make matters worse, he has a good speaking manner, a parochial appearance that polls well in a large percentage of the country, and a decorated history of military service. In short, ladies and gentlemen, he is a legitimate contender to hold the highest office in our nation, as well as being the man who seems most likely to escalate the unending conflict between us and the infected into a state of all-out war.

I can't tell you to choose Senator Ryman as the Republican Party candidate just because I don't like Governor Tate. But I can tell you this: The governor's biases, like mine, are a matter of public record. Do your research. Do your homework. Learn what this man would do to our country in the name of preserving a brand of freedom that is as destructive as it is impossible to secure. Know your enemy.

That's what freedom really means.

—From *Images May Disturb You*,
the blog of Georgia Mason, March 14, 2040

Twelve

George?"

"Yeah?" I didn't look up. Editing Governor Tate's remarks into a coherent interview was easy, especially since I wasn't forcing myself to be evenhanded. The man didn't like me; there was no reason to pretend it wasn't mutual. Compiling everything into a readable format took less than fifteen minutes, and we were already getting a satisfactory number of hits. It was the follow-ups that were taking time. Not only did I have a lot of photographs and video footage to wade through, but the phenomenal amount of gossip and hearsay posted about the man bordered on appalling. The folks running the convention were about to start calling the votes— we'd have a formal party nominee inside the hour—and I wasn't anywhere near prepared to leave my computer.

"No, seriously, George?"

"*What?*"

"There's a man."

Now I did look up, squinting in the glare from the open office door before I reached for my sunglasses. The room faded into a comforting monochrome. Anyone who values colors has never had to deal with a KA-induced migraine. "You want to try that again? Because you almost told me something, and I'm thinking you might want to obfuscate your verbiage just a little more. Just for, y'know, giggles."

"He says you invited him here." Shaun leaned forward and smirked, his tone dripping with affected smarm. "Got a little election night itch you want scratched? I mean, he's not completely hideous, although I didn't think the corn-fed farm boys were your type—"

"Wait. Sandy brown hair, about your height, blue eyes, older than us, looks like butter wouldn't melt in his mouth?"

"Or anywhere else you wanted to shove it," Shaun confirmed, eyes narrowing. "You mean you really *did* tell him to come here?"

"He's a defector from Wagman's press corp. She's pulling out, and he's bringing everything he's got, providing it nets him a spot with us for the duration of Ryman's campaign."

Shaun's eyebrows rose. "Public domain materials?"

"Or he wouldn't be trying to bribe us with them. Buffy!" I hit Save and stood, looking toward the closet our resident Fictional had drafted as her private office. The door cracked open, and her head poked out. "Drop me all the personnel files you can pull on Wagman's press corps and get out here. We have an interview to conduct."

"Okay," she said, and withdrew back into the closet. My terminal beeped a moment later, signaling receipt of the files I'd requested. We're nothing if not efficient.

"Good." I looked to Shaun. "Let's find out whether the man's wasting our time. Go get him."

"Your wish, my command," Shaun said, and turned, closing the door behind him.

Buffy emerged from her closet, moving to take the seat next to me. She had her hair skimmed back in a loose ponytail and was wearing a blue button-up shirt I was reasonably sure belonged to Chuck. She looked about as professional as your average fifteen-year-old, which was close to perfect: If this guy couldn't handle us in our natural working environment, he didn't really want to work with us.

"You really thinking of hiring this guy?" she asked.

"Depends on what he's got and what his credentials say," I said.

She nodded. "Fair enough."

Further conversation was forestalled as the door swung open. Shaun stepped into the room, followed by the man from the press room. He was carrying a sealed folder under one arm, which he tossed to me as soon as he was clear of the door. I caught it and raised one eyebrow, waiting. Buffy sat up a little straighter, attention fixed on the newcomer.

"That's everything," he said. "Video, hardcopy, data files. Six months of following Wagman, plus the details on the deals she cut as she made for the door. Your boy's getting confirmed tonight, and it's going to be partially because of the amount of pull she tossed his way."

"I doubt she shifted the balance," I said. Handing the folder to Buffy, I said, "Run this. See if there's anything we can use."

"Got it." She stood and paused, tossing a studied, impish grin toward the newcomer. "Hey, Rick. You're looking all downtrodden and desperate."

The newcomer—Rick—returned the smile with one that looked substantially more sincere, and even, I thought, slightly relieved. "Ah, Buffy," he said. "You, meanwhile, look like you're wearing your boyfriend's clothes again. I hope this one is at least a Catholic?"

"That's between me and my prayers," she said, blowing him a kiss.

I turned to eye him, pulling my sunglasses far enough down my nose to make my expression plain. "I take it you two know each other?"

"No, I just call every strange blonde I see 'Buffy.' You'd be amazed how often I'm right." He offered his hand. Buffy snorted, amusement evident, and retreated to her closet.

I could pursue that line of questioning later. "Well, you've tagged our Fictional, and I know you know who I am. Care to even the odds?" I took his hand and shook it.

His grip was firm, but not overly so. "Richard Cousins—Rick to my friends. Newsie, currently unaffiliated, although I'm hoping we're about to change that; my biases are registered with Talking Points and Unvarnished Truth."

"Huh," I said, releasing his hand. Talking Points and Unvarnished Truth are two of the larger blogger databases; anyone can register a bias page with them and get it certified. Still, their signal-to-noise ratio is surprisingly good, largely because they self-police on a constant basis, looking for people who claim one set of biases while espousing another. "License level?"

"A-15. Wagman required it when she started aping your boy." He produced a data pad from inside his coat. "My credentials are there and ready for link, along with my most recent medical records and blood test results."

"Fabulous." I slid the data pad into the docking slot on my terminal. Files promptly filled my screen. I skimmed them as I unhooked the pad and passed it back to him. "No publications before two years ago, but you're already reporting at an A-15 level? I don't know whether that's impressive or suicidal."

"I vote 'blackmailed the license committee,'" contributed Shaun.

"Actually—" said Rick.

"Open the file on his print media pubs," said Buffy, emerging from the closet. "That'll explain everything. Won't it, Ricky?"

"Print media?" Shaun's eyebrows shot upward. "Like magazines?"

"Try newspapers," said Buffy, eyes on Rick. I had to give him this much: He was taking her poking with good grace, and he wasn't squirming. Yet. "That's why he's such a golden oldie."

"Newspapers," I repeated, disbelieving, and pulled up the next page in his file. The rest of his credentials filled the screen. I slid my glasses back up to cover my surprise. "Here we go—Buffy's right. Staff writer, *St. Paul Herald*, five years. Field reporter, the *Minnesota News*, three years. How old *are* you?"

"My recertification to virtual media was fully processed eighteen months ago. I got on Wagman's team fair and square," said Rick, before adding, "And I'm thirty-four."

"Fair and square means, what, you got on by waiting for her to realize Ryman had the right idea and then chasing her ambulance?" asked Buffy sweetly.

"All right, that's enough." Removing my glasses, I looked from Rick to Buffy and back. "What's the story, you two?"

"Richard 'Rick' Cousins, Newsie, stated biases are left-wing Dem without crossing any lines into actual psychosis, solid writer, good with deadlines, not too adept at use of imagery, and the bastard beat me in an essay contest six years ago," Buffy said.

"You can't hold that against me," Rick protested. "It wasn't a teen competition. You were sixteen."

"I can hold anything I *want* against you," said Buffy, glowering at him before her face split in a wide grin. "You didn't say you wanted the files on *Rick*, Georgia. Finally looking for a real story, you perverted ambulance chaser?"

"Don't flatter yourself, Buffy. Any story you've had your hands on can't possibly be real," Rick countered.

Shaun and I exchanged a look. "Think they know each other?" he asked.

"Getting the feeling. Buffy?"

She looked, briefly, like she didn't want to explain. Then she shrugged and said, "After Rick beat me, we started writing. He's a pretty cool guy, once you get past the part that he's older than the dawn of time."

"I choose to take that in the spirit in which it was offered," said Rick. "Especially since it comes from someone who thinks Edgar Allen Poe is socially relevant."

Buffy sniffed.

"Right, you know each other," I said. "How's his bribe? Do we hire him?"

"He's got good footage of Wagman from the last six months, a couple exclusive interviews, and a full recording of her chief of staff making the resignation calls," Buffy said.

I shot Rick a startled look.

He grinned. "He didn't say I had to stop taping."

"If I was interested in boys, I'd kiss you right now," said Shaun, deadpan. "George, in Newsie-speak, what does that mean for ratings?"

"Three percent increase for starters, more if he can write well enough to sustain an audience. Rick, we can take you as a beta, you get your own byline but you run everything through me or my second, Mahir Gowda, no direct access to the candidate; if Ryman doesn't get the nomination, you're on a six-month base contract. I can e-mail you the legalese."

"And if he does get the nomination?"

"What?"

"If he gets the nomination—which he will—what do I get?"

I smiled. "You get to stay with us until the bitter end, or until I fire your ass, whichever comes first."

"Acceptable." He held out his hand.

I shook it. "Welcome to After the End Times."

Shaun clapped him on the back before he had a chance to let go. "More testosterone on the field team! My man! What do you think about poking dead things with sticks?"

"It's a good way to get ratings and commit suicide at the same time," Rick said.

I snorted. "All right. You can stay."

There was a knock at the door. It opened before any of us had a chance to react, and Steve entered, sunglasses obscuring the majority of his expression. I stood.

"Is it time?" I asked.

Steve nodded. "Senator asked me to make sure you were ready."

"Right. Thanks, Steve." Grabbing my bag, I hooked a thumb toward our newest addition. "Rick, you're with me; we're on the floor. Buffy, I need you here, working the terminals. Hit my remotes and tell them we're streaming raw footage starting in ten minutes, and they should be ready to start doing the forum-facing clean and jerk."

"Editorial power?"

"Fact only, no opinions until I log on and start setting the baselines." I was checking equipment as I spoke, hands moving on autopilot. My recorder was charged, and the readout on my watch indicated that all cameras were operating at seventy percent or above. "See if you can rouse Mahir, and yes, I know what time it is in London, but I need *someone* sane stomping on the trolls. Shaun—"

"Outside the convention hall with my skateboard and my stick, watching to see if the protestors and picketers do anything worth reporting on," Shaun said, snapping an amiable salute. "I know my strengths."

"Play to them, and don't get dead," I said, turning to head for the door. Steve stepped out of the way, giving me a sidelong look as Rick followed in my wake. "It's okay, Steve. He's on the squad."

"They liked my backflip," Rick said, looking up at Steve. There was a lot of "up" to look at. "You're very tall."

"You *must* be a reporter," Steve said. He closed the door behind us, leaving Shaun and Buffy inside.

The convention center had seemed busy before. Compared to the madhouse that greeted us as we proceeded toward the main meeting hall, it was a mausoleum. People were everywhere. They ranged from staffers I recognized from the various campaigns to private security, members of politicians' families, and reporters who'd somehow managed to get out of the press pit and into the wild. Soon, they'd go feral and start inventing scandals for the sake of their ratings.

Rick greeted the scene with calm professionalism, sticking close as I followed in Steve's massive, crowd-clearing wake. Rick didn't seem to have any problems taking orders from a woman ten years his junior, either, which can be an issue with guys trying to jump from the traditional news media to the blogging world. They don't mean to bring their prejudices with them when they make the transition, but some things are harder to get rid of than an addiction to seeing your stories physically printed. If Rick continued to listen as well as he had been, things were going to be fine.

Steve steered a course through the back halls and into the screaming furor of the auditorium, where politicos and onlookers of every age, race, and creed were gathered for the solemn practice of screaming at the top of their lungs whenever they thought they caught a glimpse of one of the prospective candidates. A satisfying percentage of the crowd was sporting "Ryman for President" buttons. A group of clean-cut sorority girls in tight white T-shirts hung over one of the rails, shrieking with delight over the entire political process.

I elbowed Rick, indicating the girls. "See their shirts?"

He squinted. " 'Ryman's My Man'? Who comes up with this stuff?"

"Shaun, actually. He's got an amazing ear for doggerel." I tapped my ear cuff. "Buffy, we're in. How's my signal?"

"Loud and clear, O glorious recorder of really jumbled footage. Try to get yourself to a clean shot, I'm only getting fifty percent signal off the stationary cameras."

"You mean the stationary cameras that belong to the convention center and were installed for security purposes? The ones with the supposedly unbreakable signal feeds?"

"Those would be the ones. I won't be able to use them for anything but pan shots, and the networks have the wall-mount cameras under exclusive coding that I *can't* break through, so get something good!"

"Yes, ma'am," I said.

"Buffy out."

The connection clicked off, and I turned to Steve. "Where are we?"

"Mrs. Ryman has said you can sit backstage with her if you'd like, or you can stay out here and film the crowd," Steve said. "Either way, I need to head back there. We're hitting the wire."

"Got it." I looked to Rick, unclasping the recording array from my left wrist. "Take this. Three cameras, direct feed back to Buffy in the closet— just lift it up, the lenses are set to autofocus."

He took the wristband and snapped the Velcro around his own wrist. "You'll be backstage?"

"Got it. Meet back in the office when the crowd disperses, and we'll see where we're going from there." The footage I got backstage wouldn't be as sensational, but it would be more intimate, and that sort of thing has a staying power that crowd shots lack. We'd hook readers with the screaming and keep them with the silence. Plus, this was a good opportunity to test Rick's reactions in a field situation. The term "probationary period" doesn't mean much in the news. He'd work out or he wouldn't, starting tonight.

"Right." He turned toward the stage, raising his arm to give the cameras the best view. Satisfied that he wasn't going to screw around, I followed Steve along the edge of the hall toward the curtained-off area behind the stage.

You wouldn't think one little canvas curtain could make that much of a difference. Most little canvas curtains aren't equipped with enough private security to stop a full-scale invasion. The men at the entrance eyeballed our credentials but didn't bother to stop us or ask for blood tests—once we were this deep into the convention center, either we were clean or we were all dead already. So we just sailed on through, out of the chaos and into the calm harbor on the other side.

Once upon a time, in a political process far, far away, the candidate selection results were known before they were announced to the general public. With necessary enhancements in security and increases in the number of delegates who chose to vote remotely, this has changed over the last twenty years. These days, no one knows who's taking the nomination until the announcement is made. Call it part of a misguided effort to reinsert drama into a process that has become substantially more cut-and-dried as the years went by. Reality television on the grandest of scales.

Emily and Peter Ryman were sitting in a pair of folding chairs near the stage, his left hand clasped in both of hers as they watched the monitor that was scrolling current results. David Tate was pacing not far away; he shot me a poisonous look as I entered.

"Miss Mason," he said. "Looking for more muck to rake?"

"Actually, Governor, I was looking for more facts to pass along," I said, and continued for the Rymans. "Senator. Mrs. Ryman. I hope you're ready for the results?"

"Ask not for whom the bell tolls, Georgia," said the senator gravely. Then he laughed, releasing his wife's hand and standing to grasp and shake mine. "Whatever the numbers say, I want to thank you and your crew. You may not have changed the race, but you made it a hell of a lot more fun for everyone involved."

"Thank you, Senator," I said. "That's good to hear."

"After Peter's had a few weeks to rest, all three of you *must* come and visit the farm," Emily said. "I know the girls would love to meet you. Rebecca's very fond of your reports, especially. It would be a real treat for them."

I smiled. "We'd be honored. But let's not assume a break just yet."

"Far from it," said the senator, with a glance at Governor Tate. Governor Tate's return look wasn't a friendly one. "I think we're going to go all the way."

A bell rang as if to punctuate his words, and a hush fell over the convention. I stepped back, lifting my chin to bring the camera on my collar to a better angle.

"Let's see if you mean that," I said.

Over the loudspeaker, the voice of a third-rate celebrity who'd gone from bad sitcoms to convention announcements blared: "And now, the Republican Party's man of the hour, and the next President of these fabulous United States of America—Senator Peter Ryman of Wisconsin! Senator Ryman, come on out here and greet the people!"

The cheers were almost deafening. Emily gave a little squeal that was only half-surprise, and wrapped her arms around the senator's shoulders, kissing him on both cheeks as he lifted her off the ground in a hug. "Well, Em?" he said. "Let's go make the people happy." Beaming, she nodded her agreement, and he led her onto the stage. The cheers doubled in volume. Some of those people wouldn't be able to talk at all the next day. Right then, I doubted any of them particularly cared.

Tate stayed where he was, expression blank. Before I moved toward the stage exit, still filming, I paused long enough to get a reaction shot of a man whose dreams had just been dashed. "Go, Pete, go," I murmured, unable to keep from smiling. He had the nomination. That was our man out there on that stage, accepting the nomination.

We were going on the road.

My ear cuff beeped three times, signaling an emergency transmission. I tapped it, stepping away from the opening. "Shaun, what did you—"

Buffy's voice cut me off. It was all business, and so cold I almost didn't recognize it at first. "Georgia, there's an outbreak at the farm."

I froze. "What farm?"

"The Ryman farm. It's on all the feeds, it's *everywhere*. They think one of the horses went into spontaneous conversion. No one knows why, and they're still digging in the ashes and setting the perimeter. No one knows where the... where the—oh, God, Georgia, the girls were in there when the alarms went off, and no one knows—"

Slowly, as if in a dream, I turned back toward the opening. Buffy was talking, but her words didn't matter anymore. Senator Ryman had formally accepted the nomination and was standing there grinning, his beautiful wife holding his arm, waving to the crowd that chose him to bear their banner toward the highest office in the country. They looked like the happiest people in the world. People who had never known what a real tragedy was. God help them, they were about to learn.

"—you there? Mahir's trying to control the forums, but he needs help, and we need you to find the valid news feed into all this, we—"

"Tell Mahir to contact Casey at Media Breakdown and arrange a fact-only feed-through of the situation at the farm; tell him we'll trade an early release on my next candidate interview," I said, tonelessly. "Wake Alaric, get him backing Mahir until Rick finishes on the floor, then throw him in there, too. He wanted to join the party? Well, here's his invitation."

"What are you going to do?"

Emily Ryman was laughing, hands clasped together. She had no idea.

Grimly, I said, "I'm going to stay here and report the news."

BOOK III

Index Case Studies

The difference between the truth and a lie is that both of them can hurt, but only one will take the time to heal you afterward.

—GEORGIA MASON

We live in a world of our own creation. We've made our bed, ladies and gentlemen, whether we intended to or not. Now, we get the honor of lying down in it.

—MICHAEL MASON

I've done a lot of difficult things over the course of my journalistic career. Few, in the end, were pretty; most of the supposed "glamour" of reporting the news is reserved for the people who sit behind desks and look good while they tell you about the latest tragedy to rock the world. It's different in the field, and even after doing this for years, I don't think I grasped how different it was. Not until I looked into the faces of presidential candidate Peter Ryman and his wife and informed them that the body of their eldest daughter had just been cremated by federal troops outside their family ranch in Parrish, Wisconsin.

You've heard about Rebecca Ryman by now. Eighteen years old, scheduled to graduate high school in less than three months, ranked fifth in her class, and already accepted at Brown University, where she was planning to study law and follow in her father's footsteps. She'd been riding since she was old enough to walk; that's how she was able to bridle that postamplification horse and get her baby sisters off the grounds. She was a real American hero—at least, that's what all the papers and news sites say. Even mine.

If you'll allow a reporter her brief moment of sentiment, I'd like to tell you about the Rebecca that I met, if only for a moment, in the words and the faces of her parents.

Rebecca Ryman was a teenage girl. She was petulant. She was sulky. She hated being asked to sit for her sisters on a Friday night, especially when there was a new Byron Bloom movie opening. She liked to read trashy romances and eat ice cream straight from the container, and nothing made her happier than working with the horses. She stayed home from the Republican National Convention partially to get ready for college and partially to be with the horses. Because of that decision, she died, and her sisters lived. She couldn't save her grandparents or the men who worked the ranch, but she saved her sisters, and in the end, what more could anyone have asked of her?

I told her parents she was dead. That, if nothing else, qualifies me to say this:

Rebecca, you will be deeply missed.

—From *Images May Disturb You*,
the blog of Georgia Mason, March 17, 2040

Thirteen

The funeral services for Rebecca Ryman and her grandparents were held a week after the convention at the family ranch. The delay wasn't for mourning or to allow family members time to travel; that's how long it took for regional authorities to downgrade the ranch from a Level 2 hazard zone to a Level 5. It was still illegal to enter unarmed, but now at least nonmilitary personnel could enter unescorted. The area would return to its original Level 7 designation if it could go three years without signs of further contamination. Until then, even the kids would need to carry weapons at all times.

Most public opinion held that it wouldn't matter how long it took for the hazard rating to drop; no family would choose to stay in a home and a profession—viewed by many as a dangerous, glorified hobby—that claimed the life of one of their children. They said the ranch would be long deserted by the time that happened.

I wish I could say that attitude was confined to the conservative fringe, but it wasn't. Within six hours of Rebecca's death, half the children's safety advocacy groups were clamoring for tighter guidelines and attempting to organize legislation that would make the life led by the Rymans illegal. No more early riding classes or family farms; they wanted it shut down, shut down now, and shut down hard. It wasn't a surprise to anyone but the Rymans, I think: Peter and Emily never attempted to map out the scenarios leading to the martyrdom of their eldest daughter, and so they'd never considered what a boon her death would be to certain organizations. Americans for the Children was the worst. Its "Remember Rebecca" campaign was entirely legal and entirely sleazy, although its attempts to use pictures of Jeanne and Amber had been quashed by the Rymans' legal team. It didn't matter. The images of Rebecca with her horses—and of postamplification horses attempting to disembowel the federal authorities putting them down—had already done their damage.

In the chaos and noise surrounding the outbreak at the ranch, it wasn't really a surprise that Senator Ryman's selection of a running mate barely made anyone's radar, save for the hardcore politicos who couldn't care less that people were dead...and me. I wasn't surprised, although I must admit that I was more than slightly disappointed when it was announced that Governor Tate would accompany Senator Ryman on the ballot. It was a good, balanced ticket; it would carry most of the country, and it stood a good chance of putting Senator Ryman in the White House. The tragedy at the ranch had already put him twenty points up on his opponent in the early polls. The Democratic candidate, Governor Frances Blackburn, was a solid politician with an excellent record of service, but she couldn't compete with a teenage heroine who sacrificed herself to save her sisters. This early in the race, people weren't voting for the candidate. They were voting for his daughter. And she was winning.

My team and I offered to head back to California until after the services. While our contract with the senator said "constant access," there's a difference between honest reporting and playing the ghoul. Let the local news film the funeral. We'd do our laundry, give Buffy a chance to upgrade the equipment, and introduce Rick to the parents. Nothing says "crash course in working as a team" like starting with a major political convention, then moving on to meeting my mother on her home turf. Shaun can seem like a minor natural disaster sometimes, but Mom's *always* a seven point five on the Richter scale.

That plan was scotched on the drawing board by Senator Ryman, who took me aside the day after the convention and informed me that it would mean a great deal to everyone if we would attend—and cover—the funeral. Rebecca loved our coverage of the elections, and given his position as the Republican Party candidate, he knew there would be reporters trying to get in to report on the funeral. This way, he'd know the press was reputable.

What was I supposed to say? Buffy can order most of what she needs online, and they have Laundromats everywhere. The only thing that might have been a sticking point was Rick, since he was still moving his personal belongings out of the hotel that had been the base camp for the Wagman campaign, but I didn't anticipate it being much of a problem. He'd been forced to hit the ground running, and he'd done it without a murmur of complaint. His footage of Senator Ryman's acceptance speech was topnotch, especially after we had cut it with the video feed of the assault on the ranch. Our viewer numbers have jumped more than eighteen percent since the convention, and they're still climbing; I attribute it partially to adding Rick to the team. No one else got an exclusive on the Wagman pullout. Add that to the acceptance and the tragedy, and well...

Sometimes in the news, "luck" is just a matter of "capitalizing on someone else's pain."

March in Wisconsin is very different from March in California. The day of the funeral was gray and cold, with patches of snow dotting the struggling lawn of the O'Neil family cemetery. Emily's family had been in the area long enough to have their own graveyard. If the old zombie flicks had been right about the dead clawing their way out of the ground, the funeral would have been a blood bath.

Fortunately, that's one detail the movies got wrong. The earth was smooth beneath its uneven blanket of snow, save for the darker, recently dug patches in front of three headstones near the west wall. Folding chairs were set up on the central green and people sat close together, steadfastly not looking toward the displaced ground. A woman who bore a vague resemblance to Peter—enough that I was willing to tentatively place her as a cousin, if not a sister—murmured to her companion, "They're so *small*."

Of course. Cemeteries are an oddity in this modern world; since most bodies are cremated, there's no need for them unless you're fabulously wealthy, strongly religious, or clinging to tradition with both hands. When you do have an actual burial, you're not looking at the iconic rectangles of disturbed earth that you find in pre-Rising movies. Modern graves are little circles in the grass, big enough to hold a handful of ash.

The mingled Ryman and O'Neil clans were dressed in the mourning editions of their Sunday best: all blacks and charcoal grays, with the occasional hint of off-white or cream in someone's shirtfront or blouse. Even the little girls, Jeanne and Amber, were wearing black velvet. Shaun, Buffy, and I were the only attendees who weren't related to the family; the senator's security detail—a combination of the campaign agents and the new guys from the Secret Service—had stopped at the cemetery gates, guarding the perimeter without disturbing the ceremony. We were the privileged few, and everyone knew it. More than a few unpleasant looks had been tossed our way by the relatives as we moved into position.

Not that I cared. We were there for Peter, for Emily, and for the news. What the rest of the family thought didn't matter.

"...and so we have come together, in the sight of God, to commend the mortal remains of His beloved children into His keeping, to be held in trust, no longer subject to the dangers of the world, until the day we may be reunited in the Kingdom of Heaven," said the priest. "For His is the

Kingdom, the life and the glory, and through His grace may we be granted everlasting life. Let us pray." The family bowed their heads. So did Buffy, who was raised to a faith beyond "tell the truth, know the escape routes, and always carry extra ammunition."

Shaun and I didn't bow. Someone has to keep the lookout. After checking to make sure my shoulder cameras were still recording on an even keel, I turned my head, surveying the cemetery. It was completely indefensible; the low stone walls were more for delineation of boundaries than anything else and wouldn't have kept a determined horde of zombies out for more than a few minutes. The gates were spaced widely enough to make the whole place little more than a big corral for humans. I shuddered.

Shaun caught the gesture and put a hand at the small of my back, steadying me. I flashed him a smile. He knows I don't like being outside in poorly defended areas. He doesn't feel the same way; open spaces just make him think something worth poking is bound to come along sooner than later.

The service was winding down. I schooled my expression back to grim serenity and turned to face forward as the priest closed his Bible. The family rose, many of them in tears. Most turned to head for the gates, where cars were waiting to take them to the reception at the funeral home. Nothing says "deeply in mourning" like canapés and free beer. A few remained, still looking toward the graves as if shell-shocked.

"I just feel so bad," murmured Buffy. "How can things like this happen?"

"Luck of the draw?" Shaun shrugged. "Play with big animals, a little amplification is almost guaranteed. They're lucky it waited this long."

"Yeah," I said, frowning. "Lucky." Something wasn't right about this whole setup. The timing, the scope—you need safety precautions on a scale most millionaires wouldn't bother with to operate a horse ranch, even several miles from the nearest town, and you need to have them upgraded on a regular basis. If something went wrong, it would be contained in a matter of minutes. They might have to torch a barn, but they shouldn't have lost *anyone*. Certainly not three family members and half the working staff. "Shaun, get Buffy back to the van, okay? I'm going to give my regrets to the family."

"Shouldn't we come, too?" asked Buffy.

"No, you go back to the van. Call Rick, make sure nothing's caught fire while we were away from our screens."

"But—"

Shaun reached around me to take Buffy's arm. "C'mon, Buff. If she's sending us away, it's because she wants to poke something with a stick and see what happens."

"Something like that," I said. "I'll be there in a few minutes."

"Okay," said Buffy, letting Shaun guide her toward the cemetery gates. I turned to study the remaining members of the family. Peter and Emily were there, along with several other adults who looked enough like one another to be close relations. Emily had one arm around each of her two remaining daughters. She didn't look like she'd slept for a week, and both Jeanne and Amber looked like they were finding their mother's embrace more than a little smothering. Peter seemed older, somehow, his farm boy good looks strained by the speed and severity with which everything had gone wrong.

He caught the motion of my head as I looked toward them. He nodded slightly, indicating that it was safe for me to approach. I answered with a thin smile, beginning to pick my way across the slushy ground.

"Georgia," said Emily, as I reached them. Letting go of Jeanne and Amber, she put her arms around me in a too-tight hug. The girls moved to stand behind an elderly woman who looked like she might be their paternal grandmother, blocking their mother from grabbing them again once she was done with me. I couldn't blame them; Emily's grief had given her a measure of hysterical strength that seemed likely to crack one of my ribs. "We're so glad you came."

"I'm sorry for your loss," I said, patting her awkwardly on the back. "Buffy and Shaun send their regrets."

"Emily, let the nice girl go," said Peter, tugging his wife's arm until she released me. I stepped quickly backward, and both Jeanne and Amber cast understanding glances my way. They'd been their mother's targets since she ran out of the convention to get to them. "Georgia."

"Senator Ryman." He didn't try to hug me. I appreciated that. "It was a beautiful ceremony."

"It was, wasn't it?" He glanced toward the churned-up earth. "Becky hated these things. Said they were morbid and silly. She would've stayed home, if she weren't a required attendee." He laughed, bitterly. "She really wanted to meet you."

"I'm sorry she never got the chance," I said, pushing my sunglasses up to shield my eyes from the light glinting off the patchy snow. "Would you mind if I took you aside for a moment? It won't take long."

"No, of course not." He kissed Emily on the forehead, and said, "You just get back to the girls, all right, sweetheart? I'll only be a moment."

"All right," said Emily. She managed to force a wavering smile, and said, "We'll see you at the reception, won't we, Georgia?"

"Of course, Mrs. Ryman," I replied.

The senator and I walked until we were about eight feet from the group, far enough that they couldn't hear us, but close enough to maintain visual contact. "Now, Georgia," he said, without preamble. "What's this all about?"

I tilted my chin up until I was looking directly at him, and said, "Senator, if you don't mind, my team and I would like permission to go up to the ranch and take a look around." He was silent. I continued: "If we walk the grounds and post our footage..."

"You think it'll reduce trespassers looking for a little excitement?"

I nodded.

Senator Ryman looked at me for a long moment. Then, shoulders sagging, he nodded his acquiescence. "I hate this, Georgia," he said, in a voice that was a million miles away from the proud, self-confident man I'd followed most of the way across the country. "This is supposed to be the start of the most exciting fight in my career, and instead I'm standing here consigning my eldest unto God when I just want to shake the bastard until he gives her back to me. It's not fair."

"I know, Senator," I said. Glancing back to where Emily had managed to recapture her surviving children, I added, "But you're not the only one it isn't fair to."

"Are you telling me to mind my family, young lady?" he asked, with a mirthless chuckle.

"Sometimes family is all we have, sir."

"Very true, Georgia. Very true." He followed my gaze back to Emily and the girls. "I'll tell Em I've given you folks permission to go to the ranch. She'll understand. The guards, now..."

"We have the proper licenses."

"Good." Raking his hair back from his forehead with one hand, he sighed. "Ain't this just one hell of a mess?"

"Very much so," I agreed.

We made our good-byes without much conviction; he needed to get back to the business of mourning, and I needed to get back to my team before Shaun decided to go hiking or Buffy took the wireless network offline for upgrading. Rick hadn't been with us long enough for me to know what I didn't want him doing, but I was sure he'd come up with something. He was a journalist, after all, and we're all incurably insane.

I walked toward the cemetery gates, tapping my ear cuff. "Shaun, what's your twenty?"

"We're parked behind the security vans," Shaun said. Someone asked a question in the background, and he added, "Buffy wants to know if we need her or if she can go with Chuck. He's pretty torn up, and she wants to get in some 'couple time.'"

"Shaun Mason, you may be the only boy above the age of nine who still says 'couple time' like it was a dead rat." I nodded to the guards as I passed through the gates and scanned the parking lot for the security vans.

"I do not," said Shaun, sounding affronted. "I *like* dead rats."

"Sorry. My bad. Tell Buffy she's free to go, but I want her to have the field equipment ready, and she needs to be back for editing by nine."

"The field equipment...?"

"I have Senator Ryman's clearance. We're heading for the ranch." I grimaced at Shaun's whooping and tapped my ear cuff again, cutting off the connection. The van was in sight; I could let him yell in my ear once I was inside, rather than putting up with it remotely.

Buffy was seated on a counter doing something arcane to a shoulder-mount camera when I stepped through the rear door. She'd changed out of her funeral clothes into something more comfortable, if still subdued, and when she looked up, it was obvious that she'd redone her makeup to match. "Hey."

"Hey." I looked around, starting to unbutton my jacket. "Where's Shaun?"

"Up front checking his armor for holes." She peered into the camera, blew lightly on the exposed circuitry, and snapped the cover back into place. "Chuck's going to come pick me up, so you can leave me here when you head out. It'll only take a few more minutes to review the field equipment."

"Anybody call Rick?" I tossed my jacket onto a chair and started unbuttoning my dress shirt. I had a tank top under that; swap my skirt for jeans, add a Kevlar vest, my motorcycle jacket, and combat boots, and I'd be ready for a low-hazard field op. Most girls learn how to accessorize for dinner parties and dates. I learned to do it for hazard zones.

"He said he'd meet you at the ranch." Buffy offered me the camera. "Here. This whole generation is on its last legs. We're gonna need new ones sooner than later."

"I'll get it into the budget," I said. Peeling off my shirt, I dropped it to the floor and took the camera, eyeing Buffy over my glasses. "Something on your mind, Buff?"

"No. Yes. Maybe." She sat back on the counter, her gaze dropping to her hands. "You're going to the ranch."

"Yes."

"It's..."

"The area's been downgraded. We have the licenses to enter, as long as we're armed."

Buffy's head snapped up. "It's *disrespectful.*"

Ah. The crux of the problem. "Disrespectful to whom, Buffy? To the dead?" She gave a small, almost imperceptible nod. "Buffy, the dead aren't there. They've been buried." After they were cremated to prevent their corpses from coming back to life and doing disrespectful things to the living.

"They *died* there," she said, fiercely. "They died there, and now you're going to turn it into more *news.*"

"We aired the attack."

"That was different. That was something dangerous. This is just ghosts. Souls trying to sleep." Her expression turned pleading. "Can't we let them sleep? Please?"

"We're not going to disturb them. If anything, we're going so that they *can* sleep. The Rymans trust us to be respectful, and we will be, and by showing that there's nothing of any interest in those buildings, we'll keep *less* respectful journalists from breaking in looking for an 'exposé.'" I might be wrong—journalists seeking a scoop will break into almost anything— but I needed to get in there, and I needed Buffy to stay calm. Without her to enhance any footage we got, we might well come up with less than nothing.

She sniffled. "You swear you're not intending to upset their ghosts?"

"I'm not sure I believe in ghosts, but I swear we won't do anything to disturb any spirits that might be resting there." I put down the camera she'd handed me and shook my head as I opened the van closet and pulled out the rest of my field gear. I always keep a few pairs of thick denim jeans on hand, the kind with steel fibers woven into the fabric. "Be prepared" isn't just the Boy Scouts' marching song anymore. "Zombies are enough. I don't need to add poltergeists to the ranks of 'things that want to kill me.'"

She studied me for a moment before she nodded, offering a small smile. "All right. It just seems ghoulish to go there on the day of the funeral."

"I know, but time is sort of important right now," I said. A horn honked outside. I glanced over my shoulder toward the door. "Sounds like your ride's here."

"That didn't take long." Buffy slid off the counter. "Your kits are packed. I didn't review the auxiliary batteries, but you'd only need those if everything else failed. Technically, they're not even required."

"I know," I said. "Get out of here. Have a nice evening with Chuck, and I'll see you at the hotel at nine for editing and data consolidation."

"Work, work, work," she complained, but she was almost laughing as she stepped outside. I caught a glimpse of Chuck waving from his rental car before the van door banged shut, blocking them from view.

"Have a nice date, Buffy," I said to the closed door and pulled on my jacket before moving to assess the field kits.

Normally, Buffy would have done all the checks before she went anywhere. Normally, where she was going was "back to the van" or "home to her room," not out with her boyfriend. It's not like she's never dated; she's had at least six boyfriends since we met, and unlike a large percentage of our generation, they've all been face-to-facers, not virtuals. She doesn't date people she meets online unless they live locally and are willing to meet in the flesh, with all the security checks and blood tests that entails, and even then, she likes to keep her romantic relationships as offline as possible. Partly because she likes the interaction—it's a change from the amount of time she spends online—but I think it's partly been to keep them untraceable. She's never been comfortable with the fact that Shaun and I won't talk about why we don't date. She eventually gave up trying to hook us up with people she knew, but Chuck is still the first of her boyfriends who we've been allowed to spend any real time around, and I suspect it's only because they met on the campaign trail.

Everyone has their own little quirks. My brother and I avoid romantic entanglements, and Buffy runs hers like acts of international espionage.

Checking the field kits took about five minutes. Shaun emerged from the front of the van carrying a crossbow and moving with a slight stiffness that signaled how much body armor he was wearing. Straightening, I tossed him his pack.

"Light," he said, hefting it. "Did we decide to skip the cameras this time?"

"Actually, I decided to skip the weapons." Picking up the other two kits, I brushed past him on my way up front. "If we meet any zombies, we'll pacify them with Hostess snack cakes."

"Even the living dead love Hostess snack cakes."

"Precisely." I hooked open the door between the sections of the van with my foot and tossed Rick's field kit back to Shaun. "I'm driving."

"I'm not surprised," he said, with a mock annoyed look. Following me, he settled in the passenger seat and asked, "So what are we *really* doing?"

"Really doing? We're really visiting the scene of a tragic accident to determine whether it was caused by gross human negligence or a simple series of unavoidable events." I sat and pulled my seat belt across my lap. "Buckle up."

He did. "You aren't implying what I think you're implying."

"What am I not implying, Shaun?"

"They had to torch and burn the infection. Don't you think someone would have noticed if things weren't right?"

"Repeat the first part of your statement again."

"They had to torch and..." He stopped. "You're not serious."

"Shaun, the O'Neils have been raising horses for generations. They didn't even take a break after the Rising." I pulled out of the lot and started down the road. The countryside around us was wide, flat, and relatively unbroken by anything as plebian as signs of human habitation. Not the best hunting territory for the living dead. "They don't make mistakes on the level of allowing a massive outbreak that kills nearly half the hired help. It just doesn't happen. So either somebody screwed up big time—"

"—or someone cut the screamers," Shaun finished, hushed. "Why wouldn't anyone have found anything?"

"Was anyone going to *look*? Shaun, if I say, 'A big animal amplified and killed its owners,' do you think, 'Something is rotten in the state of Denmark,' or do you think, 'It was bound to happen sometime'?"

Shaun was quiet for several minutes as we drove toward the ranch. Finally, in a pensive tone, he said, "How big is this, George?"

I tightened my hands on the wheel. "Ask Rebecca Ryman."

"What are we going to do about it?"

"We're going to tell the truth." I glanced toward him. "Hopefully, that's going to be enough."

He nodded, and we drove on in silence.

———————

A lot of time was spent looking into the science and application of forensics before the Rising. How did this man die? What did he die for? Could he have been saved? It's been different since the Rising, as the possibility of infection makes it too dangerous for investigators to pry into any crime scene that hasn't been disinfected, while the strength of modern disinfectants means that once they've been used, there's nothing to find. DNA testing and miraculous deductions brought about by a few clinging fibers are things of the past. As soon as the dead started walking, they stopped sharing their secrets with the living.

For modern investigators, whether with the police or the media, this has meant a lot of "going back to our roots." An active mind is worth a thousand tests you can't run, and knowing where to look is worth even more. It's all a matter of learning how to think, learning how to eliminate the impossible, and admitting that sometimes what's left, however improbable, is going to be the truth.

The world is strange that way.

**—From *Images May Disturb You*,
the blog of Georgia Mason, March 24, 2040**

Fourteen

Rick was a good match for our team in more ways than one: He had his own transport, and he didn't leave home without it. I'd heard about the armor-plated VW Beetles—they're in a lot of Mom's antizombie ordnance reports, which she tends to leave lying all over the house—but I'd never actually seen one before Rick's. It looked like a weird cross between an armadillo and a pill bug.

An electric blue armadillo.

With headlights.

He was parked outside the ranch gates, leaning against the side of his car and typing something into his PDA's collapsible keyboard. He lifted his head as we drove up, folding the keyboard and stowing the entire unit in his pocket.

Shaun was out of the van before we'd stopped moving, pointing to Rick. "You do not lower your eyes in the field!" he snapped. "You do not split your attention, you do not focus on your equipment, and you *especially* do not do these things when you're alone at an off-grid rendezvous point!" Rick blinked, looking more confused than anything else.

I stopped the van, leaning over to close Shaun's door before opening my own. A lot of people don't think my brother has a temper. It's like they assume I somehow sucked up the entire quota of "cranky," and now Shaun's perpetually cheery and ready for a challenge while I glower at people from behind my sunglasses and plot the downfall of the Western world. They're wrong. Shaun has a bigger temper than I do. He just saves his fits of fury for the important things, like finding one of our team members acting like an idiot in the vicinity of a recent outbreak.

Rick was realizing he had a problem. Putting up his hands in a placating gesture, he said, "The area was cleared, and they did a full disinfect. I looked it all up before I came out here."

"Did they get a one hundred percent scratch-and-match between mammals meeting the KA amplification barrier, known victims, registered survivors, and potential vector points?" Shaun demanded. He knew they hadn't, because there's *never* been a one hundred percent return on the Nguyen-Morrison test array, not even under strict laboratory conditions. There's always the chance something capable of carrying the virus, either in its own bloodstream or by carrying tainted blood or tissue on its person, got away.

"No," Rick admitted.

"No, because it doesn't happen. Which means you? Have basically been standing naked in the middle of the road, waving your arms and shouting, 'Come get it, dead guys, I wanna be your next snack.'" He flung Rick's field kit at his chest. Rick caught it and stood there, blinking as Shaun spun on his heel and stalked off toward the gates. I let him go. Someone needed to start the process of presenting our credentials to the guards on duty, and it would calm him down. Bureaucracy generally did.

Rick stared after Shaun, still looking shell-shocked.

"He's right, you know," I said, squinting at him through my sunglasses. The glare outside the van was bad enough to make me wish it were safe to take painkillers in the field. It's not; nothing that dulls your awareness of your body and what it's doing is a good idea. "What made you get out of your car?"

"I thought it was safe," Rick stammered.

I shook my head. "It's never safe. Get your pack on, activate your cameras, and let's go." I started along Shaun's path to the ranch gates. Getting out of the car alone was a rookie mistake, but Rick's record wasn't heavy on field work. His reporting was good, and he knew enough to stick with the senior reporters in an area. He'd learn the rest if he lived long enough to get the chance.

If getting out of the car was a rookie mistake, going into the ranch on foot was blatant stupidity, but we didn't have any real choice. Not only would our vehicles have been impossible to fit into any of the standing structures, we wouldn't have been able to avoid getting hung up in potholes or in the ruts opened by the government cleaning equipment. Better on foot and paying attention than sucked into a false sense of security and taken out by hostile road conditions.

Shaun was outside the guard station, where two wary, clean-shaven men watched from behind thick sheets of safety glass. Both were wearing plain army jumpsuits. From the looks on their faces, this was their first outbreak, and we didn't fit their expectations of the sort of folks who would walk into a sealed-off hazard zone, even one that was due to be unsealed within the next seventy-two hours and had been the scene of a complete Nguyen-Morrison testing, including bleach bombs and aerosol decontamination. If it'd been the sort of ranch that grew crops instead of livestock, they'd have been forced to shut it down for at least five years while the chemicals worked their way out of the soil. As it was, they'd be importing feed and water for eighteen months, until the groundwater tested clear again.

The things we're willing to do to avoid the possibility of exposure to the live virus are sometimes awe inspiring. "Any trouble?" I asked, stopping next to Shaun and casting a tight-lipped smile toward the army boys. "My, don't they look happy to see us?"

"They were happier before I showed them we had Senator Ryman's permission to be here and the proper clearances to enter the property. Although I think they were kind of relieved when they realized our clearance levels mean they don't have to come in with us." Shaun grinned almost maliciously as he handed me and Rick the metal chits that served as our passes into the zone. Any hazard seals would react to the ID tags on the chits, opening to let us pass. "Somehow, I don't think the boys want to meet a real live infected person of their very own. It's amazing that they passed basic training."

"Don't tease the straights," I said, pressing the chit against the strap of my shoulder bag. It adhered to the fabric with a nearly unbreakable seal, turning on and beginning to flash a reassuring green. "How long's our clearance?"

"Standard twelve-hour passage. If we're inside the zone when the chits run out, we'll have to call for help and hope help answers." Shaun pressed his own chit to the collar of his chain-mail shirt. It flashed before dimming to standard metallic gray.

"Any recent signs of movement in or around the zone?" Rick asked. His chit was clinging to the earpiece of his wireless phone, where its green flashes contrasted with the blinking yellow LED.

"Not a one." Shaun jerked his up, indicating the guards. "Shall we move on before they book us for loitering outside a hazard zone?"

"Can they do that?" asked Rick.

"We're within a hundred yards of a recent outbreak," I said. "They can do just about whatever they want." I walked toward the gates. The chit on my bag flashed and they swung open, letting me enter the ranch grounds.

There were no blood tests on this side of the hazard zone. If I wanted to enter a known infection site when I was already infected, I'd just finish my transition behind a pre-established barrier. Not exactly what most people would consider a loss.

The gates shut behind me, only to open again as Shaun approached, and a third time for Rick. Only one person was allowed to pass at a time. If they'd followed standard procedure, the gates would also be electrified, with a current set to increase exponentially if anything grabbed hold. It wouldn't do much to stop a horde of zombies that really wanted to get through, but it was better than nothing.

"Dropping the first fixed-point camera, setting the feed to channel eight, and activating screamers," Shaun said, planting a small tripod. It extended an antenna, flashing yellow as it caught the local wireless. It would record everything it saw and feed it to the databases in the van. We wouldn't get anything useful unless there was an outbreak while we were on the grounds, but it never hurts to cover your bases. More important, it would sound the alarm if it detected any motion not connected to one of the team's identifying beacons. "George, we have a map?"

"We have a map," I confirmed, pulling out my PDA and unfolding the screen to its full extension. "Buffy pulled it down before she left." God bless Buffy. No team is complete without a good technician, and the word for an incomplete team is usually "fatality." "Cluster round, guys." They did.

The Ryman family ranch was laid out in the pre-Rising style, with a few adjustments to account for the increased security required by the senator's political career and the possibility of invasion by the rampaging undead. Most of the buildings were unconnected, with four separate horse barns—one for foaling, one for yearlings, one for older horses, and the last, constructed in isolation and using modern quarantine procedures, for the sick. The main house had more windows than any sane person would be comfortable with, but that had apparently suited the Rymans just fine.

Shaun studied the map before asking, "Do we have the outbreak grid?"

"We do." I started tapping. "Either of you boys care to place a bet as to where the outbreak started?"

"Isolation ward," Rick said.

"Foaling," said Shaun.

"Wrong." I hit enter. A grid appeared, crisscrossing the map with streaks of red. The largest red zone surrounded the yearling barn, covering the entire building and extending out in all directions. "The first outbreak was in the yearling barn. Where the strongest, healthiest, most resistant horses were housed."

Shaun frowned. "I don't know much about horses, but that seems a little funny to me. We have a full match-up on the index case?"

"Ninety-seven percent certainty on the Nguyen-Morrison," I said, pulling up a picture of a pale gold horse with a white streak down its nose. "Ryman's Gold Rush Weather. Yearling male, not gelded, clean vet reports every three months since birth, and a clean blood test registered every week for the same time period. No history of elevated virus levels. If you were looking for the cleanest horse on the planet, epidemiologically speaking, you'd have trouble going wrong with this one."

"And he's our index?" said Rick. "That's bizarre. Maybe something bit him?"

"They logged every movement these horses made, all day, every day." I closed the files, snapping the screen of my PDA into its collapsed formation before slipping it into my shoulder bag. "Goldie went out for a run the night before the outbreak, was rubbed down, and checked out clean, with no wounds or scratches. He didn't leave the barn again before things went south."

"None of the other horses top out in the Nguyen-Morrison?" Shaun reached into his own bag, pulling out a collapsible metal rod that he began uncollapsing as the three of us moved, by unspoken accord, toward the side of the ranch where the barns were clustered. If there was evidence to be found, it would be in the barns.

"The closest is the horse in the stall next to his, Ryman's Red Sky at Morning, which tested out at a ninety-one *and* had visible bite marks. Six percent pretty much says Goldie's our index."

"The only way that could happen is spontaneous amplification," Shaun said, with a deep frown. He snapped the last segment of the rod into place and hit a button on the handle, electrifying the metal. "No chance of heart attack or other natural death?"

"Not in a place like this," Rick said. We both looked toward him. Shaking his head, he said, "I did a piece on modern ranching a few years back. They have those animals so monitored that if they just up and die—a heart stops, or they suffocate on a piece of feed, or whatever—someone will know immediately."

"So you're saying the people on duty would have received some sort of notification that the horse had died, and they'd have been able to get there before he got up and started biting the other horses," I said, slowly. "Why didn't they?"

"Because when you convert instead of reanimating, there's no interruption in your vital signs," said Shaun. He was starting to sound almost excited. "One minute you're fine, the next minute, bang, you're a shambling mass of virus-spreading flesh. The monitors wouldn't catch a spontaneous conversion because a machine wouldn't be able to tell that anything was *wrong*."

"And people say modern technology doesn't do enough to protect us," I deadpanned. "All right, so if the horse checked out clean at a seven o'clock rubdown and went into spontaneous amplification in the night, the monitors wouldn't have caught it. That still doesn't tell us why it happened."

Spontaneous amplification is a reality. Sometimes, the virus sleeping inside a person decides it's time to wake up, and there's nothing anyone can do to stop it. Roughly two percent of the recorded outbreaks during the Rising were traced back to spontaneous amplifications. It usually hits only the very young or the very old, as the virus reacts to their rapidly changing body weight by making some rapid changes of its own. I'd never heard of spontaneous amplification occurring in livestock, but it's never been proven that it *couldn't* happen...and it seemed way too pat. The index case for equine spontaneous amplification happened to be in Senator Ryman's barn, on the day he was confirmed as the next Republican candidate for president? Coincidences like that don't exist outside of a Dickensian tragedy. They certainly don't wander around happening in the real world.

"I don't buy it," said Rick, voicing my thoughts. "It's too cut-and-dried. Here's a horse, the horse is healthy, now the horse is a zombie, lots of people die, isn't that tragic? It's what I would write if you asked me to pen a front-page human interest story that would never happen."

"So why isn't anyone digging deeper?" Shaun stopped in the courtyard between the four barns, looking first at Rick, then at me. "Not to be rude or anything, but Rick, you're new on this beat, and George, you're sort of professionally paranoid. Why isn't anyone else punching holes in this crap?"

"Because no one looks twice at an outbreak," I said. "Remember how pissed you got when we had to do all that reading about the Rising back in sixth grade? I thought you were going to get us both expelled. You said the only way things could've gotten as bad as they did was if people were willing to take the first easy answer they could find and cling to it, rather than doing anything as complicated as actually *thinking*."

"And you said that was human nature and I should be thankful we're smarter than they are," Shaun said. "And then you hit me."

"That's still your answer: human nature."

"Give people something they can believe, especially something like a personal tragedy and a teenage girl being heroic to save her family, and not only will everyone believe it, everyone will *want* to believe it." Rick shook his head. "It's good news. People like to believe good news."

"Sometimes it's great living in a world where 'good' and 'news' don't always combine to mean 'positive information.'" I looked to Shaun. "Where do we start?"

I'm in charge in the editing studio and the office. It's different in the field. Shaun calls the shots unless I'm demanding an immediate evac. Both of us are smart enough to know where our strengths lie. His involve poking dead things with sticks and living to blog about it.

"Everyone armed?" he asked—more for Rick's benefit than mine. He knows I'd stick my hand in a zombie's mouth for fun before I'd enter a field situation unarmed.

"Clear," I said, pulling out my .40.

"Yes," said Rick. His own gun was larger than mine, but he handled it easily enough for me to think it was a matter of preference, not machismo. He slid it back into the holster in his vest, adding, "I'd offer to take some marksmanship tests, but this doesn't seem like the place."

"Later," said Shaun. Rick looked amused. I smothered a snort of laughter. Poor guy probably thought my brother was kidding. "Right now, we're splitting up. George, you take the foaling barn. Rick, you hit the adult quarters. I'll take the hospital barn, and we'll meet up back here to go through the yearling barn together. Radio contact at all times. If you see anything, scream as loudly as you can."

"So we can all come together to help?" asked Rick.

"So the rest of us have time to get away," I said. "Cameras on, people, and look alive; this is not a drill. This is the *news*."

Splitting up made the most sense: All four barns were involved in the outbreak, but it started in a single place. We'd search the other areas individually, get some good atmospheric shots for background, and then get back together where we might actually find something. That didn't stop my heart from racing as I opened the door to the foaling barn feed room and stepped inside. The barn was dark. I removed my glasses and the burning in my eyes stopped almost immediately, pupils abandoning their futile efforts to contract and relaxing into full expansion as I walked into the main barn. This unvaried twilight was the sort of light they're best suited to. I saw in it the way the infected did, and like the infected, I saw everything.

The ranch was clearly a state-of-the-art establishment, on top of all the latest developments in animal husbandry. The stalls were spacious, designed to maximize the comfort of all parties involved. It was actually possible to ignore the federally mandated hazmat suits hanging from one wall and the yellow-and-red biohazard bins that marked the barn's four corners.

The smell of bleach was harder to ignore, and once I admitted it was there, the rest came clear. The stains on the walls that weren't paint or spilled feed. The way the straw in the stalls was matted down with the remains of some thick, tacky liquid. They hadn't finished the biohazard cleanup in here yet. That's standard operating procedure. First you remove all infected bodies and any...chunks...that were left behind. Then you seal the building as well as you can and fill the air with bleach. Finally, you set off the aerosol disinfectants and formalin bombs. Formalin is a formaldehyde-based compound that can kill almost anything, including the mobile infected, and standard decontamination procedures call for five waves of the stuff, releasing a new batch as the previous one is depleted by the organic materials around you. It's only after the area has been bleached so thoroughly that anything living is pretty much toast and has been allowed to sit long enough for all fluids to dry to a splatter-free state that it's considered safe to start removing and incinerating potentially infected materials, like the straw in the stalls.

My shoulder cam was already recording. I activated three more cameras, one attached to my bag, one at my hip, and one concealed in my barrette, and began to make my first slow turn, looking around the barn.

A pile of dead cats was under the hayloft, their multicolored bodies twisted from the brutal abdominal hemorrhaging that killed them. They'd survived the outbreak and the chaos that followed, but they couldn't outrun the formalin. I spent several seconds standing there, looking at them. They looked so small and harmless...and they were. Cats don't reach the Mason barrier. They weigh less than forty pounds. Kellis-Amberlee isn't interested in them, and they don't reanimate. For cats, dead is still dead.

I made it almost to the wall before I threw up.

It was easier once the initial wash of disgust was out of my system. My first pass brought up nothing. There were no signs that anything unusual had happened; it was just the site of an outbreak, tragic and horrible, but not *special*. Here was the place where one of the infected horses kicked its way inside, knocking the barn's sliding door off its rails. It would have hit the nursing mares in the first three stalls without slowing down, and the humans on duty were probably totally undefended. They had no idea anything was wrong until it was too late. If they were lucky, they died fast, either bleeding out or ripped to pieces before the virus had a chance to take hold and start rewriting them into another iteration of it. That was sadly unlikely. A fresh mob wants to infect, not devour.

It was easy to picture infected horses rampaging through the place, biting everything in sight and rushing on to bite still more. It was a nightmare image; it's how we almost lost the world at the beginning of the century, and it was probably accurate. We know how this sort of outbreak goes, even though we wish we didn't. The virus is dependable, not creative.

It took me twenty minutes to sweep the barn. By the time I was done, I was in such a hurry to get out of there that I forgot to put my sunglasses on before rushing out into the sunlight. The sudden glare was more than I could take. I staggered and caught myself against the barn door, eyes squinting shut.

"This is how we can tell she hasn't converted," Shaun commented to my left. "Real zombies don't get flash-blinded by sunlight when they forget their sunglasses."

"Fuck you, too," I muttered, as Shaun got his arm around me and hoisted me away from the barn.

"You kiss our mother with that mouth?"

"Our mother and you both, dickhead. Give me my sunglasses."

"Which are where?"

"Left-hand vest pocket."

"I've got it." That was Rick's voice, and it was Rick who pressed my glasses into my hand.

"Thanks." I snapped the glasses open, continuing to lean against Shaun as I pushed them on. Both their cameras were catching this. I really didn't care. "Either of you find anything?"

"Not me," said Shaun. For some reason, he sounded like he was... laughing? His barn couldn't have been any better than mine; if anything, it should have been worse, since more of the medical staff would have been on duty overnight. "Looks like Rick's the only one who got lucky."

"I've always had a way with the ladies," said Rick. Unlike Shaun and his evident amusement, Rick sounded almost embarrassed.

I clearly needed to see whatever was going on to understand it. Wary of the light, I opened first one eye, and then the other. There was Shaun, his arm still around me, holding me upright as best he could; my eyes are a lot of why I'm so leery to go into live field situations, and no one understands that better than him. And there was Rick, standing just a few feet away, his expression a mixture of anxiety and confusion.

Rick's shoulder bag was moving.

I jerked upright, demanding, "What is *that*?"

" 'That' would be Rick's new lady friend," Shaun said, snickering. "He's irresistible, George. You should've seen it. He came out of that barn and she was all *over* him. I've seen clingy girlfriends before, but this one doesn't just take the cake, she takes the entire *bakery*."

I eyed the junior member of my reporting staff warily. "Rick?"

"He's right. She latched on once she realized I was in the barn, not aiming a bleach gun at her face, and not planning to hurt her." Rick opened the flap of his shoulder bag. A narrow orange-and-white head poked out, yellow eyes regarding me warily. I blinked. The head withdrew.

"It's a cat."

"All the others were dead," Rick said, closing his bag. "She must have managed to burrow farther under the hay than they did. Or maybe she was outside when the cleaners came through and somehow got trapped inside when they left."

"A *cat*."

"She tests clean, George," Shaun said.

Mammals under forty pounds can't convert—they lack some crucial balance between body and brain mass—but they can sometimes carry the live virus, at least until it kills them. It's rare. Most of the time, they just shrug it off and carry on, uninfected. In the field, "rare" isn't something you can gamble on.

"How many blood tests?" I asked, looking toward Shaun.

"Four. One for each paw." He held up his arms, anticipating my next question. "No, I didn't get scratched, and yes, I'm sure the kitty's clean."

"And he already yelled at me for picking her up before I was certain," Rick said.

"Don't think that means I'm not planning to yell at you, too." I pushed away from Shaun. "I'll just do it when we're back inside. We have three clean barns and one live cat, gentlemen. Are we ready to proceed?"

"I've got nothing better planned for the afternoon," Shaun said, his tone still cheerful. This was Irwin territory. Very little makes him happier. "Cameras on?"

"Rolling." I glanced at my watch. "We have clean feeds and more than enough memory. You going to grandstand?"

"Do I ever not?" Shaun backed away until he was standing at the proper angle in front of the remaining barn, backlit by the afternoon sun. I had to admire his flare for the theatrics. We'd do two reports on the day's events—one for his side of the site, playing up the dangers of entering an area that had suffered such a recent outbreak, and one for my side, talking about the human aspects of the tragedy. My opening spiel could be recorded later, when I had a better idea of what happened. Irwins sell suspense. Newsies sell the news.

"What's he doing?" Rick asked, raising his eyebrows.

"You've seen those video clips of Irwins talking about fabulous dangers and horrible lurking monsters?"

"Yeah."

"That. On your count, Shaun!"

That was his cue. Suddenly grinning, suddenly relaxed, Shaun directed the smile that sold a thousand T-shirts toward the camera, flicked sweat-soaked hair out of his eyes with one gloved hand, and said, "Hey, audience. It's been pretty boring around here lately, what with all the politics and the sealed-room stuff that only the heavy-duty news geeks care about. But today? Today, we get a treat. Because today, we're the *only* news team being allowed into the Ryman ranch before decon is finished. You're gonna see blood, guys. You're gonna see stains. You're gonna do everything but taste the formalin in the air—" He was off and running.

I admit it: I tuned him out as he started getting into his spiel, preferring to watch rather than actively listening. Shaun has working his audience into a frenzy down to a science; by the time he's done with them, they get excited by the mysterious discovery of pocket lint. It's impressive, but I'd rather watch him move. There's something wonderful about the way he lets go, becoming all energy and excitement as he outlines what's coming next. Maybe it's geeky for a girl my age to admit she still loves her brother. I don't care. I love him, and one day I'll bury him, and until then, I'm going to be grateful that I'm allowed to watch him talk.

"—so come with me, and let's see what *really* happened here on that cold March afternoon." Shaun grinned again, winking at the camera, and turned to head for the barn doors. As he reached them, he called, "Cut segment!" and turned back, joviality gone. "We ready?"

"Ready," I said.

With all chances to gracefully decide, "You know what? This is a job for the authorities—the people we *pay* to risk their lives for information" behind us, Rick and I followed Shaun through the feed room and into the last of the Ryman's four barns.

The smell hit first. There's a stench to an outbreak site that you never find anywhere else. Scientists have been trying for years to determine why it is that we can smell the infection even when it's been declared safely dead, and they've been forced to conclude that it's the same viral sense that lets zombies recognize each other, just acting on a somewhat smaller scale. Zombies don't try to kill other zombies on sight unless they haven't had anything to eat in weeks; the living can tell where an outbreak started. It's probably another handy function of the virus slumbering in our own bodies—not that anyone can say for sure. No one has ever been able to put the smell into words. Not really. It smells like death. Everything in your body says "run." And, like idiots, we didn't.

Once the feed room door was shut, the barn was washed with the same dimness I experienced before. "George, Rick, lights," Shaun called. I had time to raise my arm to shield my eyes before the overhead lights clicked on. Rick made a faint gagging noise, and I heard him throwing up somewhere behind me. Not a real surprise. Everyone tosses their cookies at least once on this sort of trip—I had, after all.

When enough time had passed to let my eyes adjust to the limits of their capacity, I lowered my arm. What I saw was sheer chaos. The foaling barn seemed bad at first, but it was really nothing, just a few odd stains and some dead cats. The dead cats were here, too, strewn around the floor like discarded rags. As for the rest...

My first thought was that the entire barn had been drenched with blood. Not just sprayed; literally drenched, like someone took a bucket and started painting the walls. That impression passed as it became clear that the majority of the blood was in one of two locations—either smeared along the walls in a band roughly three feet off the floor, or soaking the floor itself, which had turned a dozen different shades of brown and black as the mixture of bleach, blood, and fecal matter dried into an uneven crust. I stared at it, unblinking, until I was over the urge to vomit. Once was fine. Twice was not, especially when round two happened in front of the others.

"These are labeled with the names of the horses," Shaun called. He was on the far side of the barn, studying one of the stalls. "This one was called 'Tuesday Blues.' What kind of name is that for a horse?"

"They liked weather names. Look for Gold Rush Weather and Red Sky at Morning. If anything odd happened here, we might find signs of it around their stalls."

"Under the six hundred gallons of gore," Rick muttered.

"Hope you brought a shovel!" Shaun called, sounding ungodly cheerful.

Rick stared at him. "Your brother is an alien."

"Yeah, but he's a cute one," I said. "Start checking stalls."

I was halfway down my own row of stalls—between "Dorothy's Gale" and "Hurricane Warning"—when Rick called, "Over here." Shaun and I looked toward him. He was indicating a corner stall. "I found Goldie."

"Great," Shaun said, and we started toward him. "Did you touch anything?"

"No," Rick replied. "I was waiting for you."

"Good."

The stall door hung askew. The hinges had been broken from the inside, and the wood was half-splintered in places, dented with the crescent shapes of a horse's hooves. Shaun whistled low. "Goldie wanted out pretty darn bad."

"Can't say that I blame him," I said, leaning forward to study the broken wood. "Shaun, you've got gloves on. Can you open that?"

"For you, the world. Or at least an open door on a really disgusting horse stall." Shaun swung the door open, latching it with a small hook to keep it that way. I bent forward, letting my camera record every inch, as Shaun stepped past us into the stall itself.

Something crunched under his feet.

Rick and I whipped around to face him. My shoulders were suddenly tight with tension. Crunching noises in the field are almost never good. At best, they mean a close call. At worst...

"Shaun? Report."

Face pale, Shaun lifted first one foot, and then the other. A piece of sharp-edged plastic was wedged in the sole of his left boot. "Just some junk," he said, expression broadcasting his relief. "No big deal." He reached down to pull it loose.

"Wait!"

Shaun froze. I turned to stare at Rick. "Explain."

"It's sharp." Rick looked between us, eyes wide. "It's sharp-edged, in a *horse stall*, on a breeding ranch. Do you see any broken windows around here? Any broken equipment? Neither do I. What is something *sharp* doing in the stall? Horses have hard hooves, but they're soft on the inside, and they get cut up really easily. Competent handlers don't allow anything with a sharp edge loose near the stalls."

Shaun lowered his foot, careful to keep his weight balanced on his toe, not pressing on the plastic. "Son of a—"

"Shaun, get out of there. Rick, find me a rake or something. We need to turn that straw."

"Got it." Rick turned and headed for the rear corner of the barn where, I supposed, he'd seen some cleaning equipment. Shaun was limping out of the stall, still pale-faced.

I hit him on the shoulder with the heel of my right hand as soon as he came into range. "Asshole," I accused.

"Probably," he agreed, calming. If I was calling him names, it couldn't be too bad. "You think we found something?"

"It seems likely, but it's not your concern right now. Get the pliers, get that goddamn thing out of your shoe, and get it bagged. If you touch it, I'll kill you."

"Gotcha."

Rick came trotting back, rake in hand. I took it from him and leaned over, starting to poke through the straw. "Rick, keep an eye on my stupid brother."

"Yes, ma'am."

Using the rake to turn over the straw where Shaun had stepped uncovered several more chunks of plastic, and a long, bent piece of snapped-off plastic in a familiar shape. Behind me, Shaun breathed in sharply. "George..."

"I see it." I continued stirring the straw.

"That's a needle."

"I know."

"If there's no reason for the plastic to be in there, why is there a *needle* in there?"

"For no good reason," said Rick. "Georgia, try a little bit to the right."

I glanced toward him. "Why?"

"Because that's where the hay is less crushed. If there's anything else to find, it's more likely to be intact if it's off to the right."

"Good call." I turned my attention to the right-hand side of the stall. The first three passes found nothing. I had already decided the fourth pass would be the last in that area when the tines pulled an intact syringe into view. Not just intact: loaded. The plunger hadn't been pushed all the way home, and a small amount of milky liquid was visible through the mud-smeared glass. The three of us stared at it.

Finally, Shaun spoke. "George?"

"Yeah?"

"I don't think you're a paranoid freak anymore."

"Good." I gingerly used the rake to pull the syringe closer. "Check the sharps bin and see if there are any isolation bags left. We need to vacuum seal this before we take it out of here, and I don't trust our biohazard baggies."

"Why?" Rick asked. "They did the Nguyen-Morrison."

"Because there's only one thing I can think of that someone would inject into a perfectly healthy animal that then turns around and becomes the index case for an outbreak," I said. Just looking at the syringe was making me feel nauseous. Shaun could have stepped on that. He could have put his foot down wrong and...

New thought, Georgia. New thought.

"Syringes are watertight," Shaun said, as he turned to head for the sharps bin. "Bleach wouldn't have been able to get inside."

"You mean—"

"Unless I'm wrong, we're looking at enough Kellis-Amberlee to convert the entire population of Wisconsin." I smiled without a trace of humor. "How's that for a front-page headline?

"Rebecca Ryman was murdered."

The Kellis-Amberlee virus can survive indefinitely inside a suitable host, which is to say "inside a warm-blooded, mammalian creature." No cure has been found, and while small units of blood can be purged of viral bodies, the virus cannot be removed from the body's soft tissues, bone marrow, spinal fluid, or brain. Thanks to the human ingenuity that created it, it is with us every day, from the moment of our conception until the day that we die.

We'll have multiple "infections" of the original Kellis strain during our lifetimes. It manifests to fight invading rhinoviruses seeking to attack the body and it acts to support the immune system. Some will also have minor flares of Marburg Amberlee, which wakes when there are cancerous growths to be destroyed. The synthesis of these wildly different viruses has not changed their original purposes, which is a good thing for us. If we're going to have to live with the fact that formerly dead people now rise up and attempt to devour the living, we may as well get a few perks out of the deal.

We only have problems when the conjoined form of these viruses enters its active state. Ten microns of live Kellis-Amberlee are enough to begin an unstoppable viral cascade that inevitably results in the effective death of the original host. Once the virus is awake, you cease to be "you" in any meaningful sense. Instead, you're a living viral reservoir, a means of spreading the virus, which is always hungry and always waiting. The zombie is a creature with two goals: to feed the virus in itself, and to spread that virus to others.

An elephant can be infected with the same amount of Kellis-Amberlee as a human. Ten microns. Speaking literally, you could pack more viral microns than that onto the period of this sentence. The horse that started the infection that killed Rebecca Ryman was injected with an estimated 900 *million* microns of live Kellis-Amberlee.

Now look me in the eye and tell me that wasn't terrorism.

—From *Images May Disturb You*,
the blog of Georgia Mason, March 25, 2040

Fifteen

It turns out that calling a United States senator from inside a quarantined biohazard zone to report that you've found a live cat and a syringe containing what you suspect to be a small but terrifying amount of live Kellis-Amberlee is a *great* way to get the full and immediate attention of both the army and the Secret Service. I've always known radio and cellular transmissions out of quarantine zones were monitored, but I'd never seen the fact so clearly illustrated. The words "intact syringe" were barely out of my mouth before we were surrounded by grim-faced men carrying large guns.

"Keep filming," I hissed to Rick and Shaun. They answered with small nods but were otherwise as frozen as I was, staring at the many, many guns around us.

"Put the syringe and any weapons you may be carrying on the ground and raise your hands above your heads," boomed a dispassionate voice, distorted by the crackle of a loudspeaker.

Shaun and I exchanged a look.

"Uh, we're journalists?" called Shaun. "On Class A-15 licenses with the concealed carry allowance? We've been following Senator Ryman's campaign? So we're carrying a lot of weapons, and we're sort of uncomfortable with this whole 'syringe' thing. Do you really want to wait while we take off *everything*?"

"God, I hope not," I muttered. "We'll be here all day."

The nearest of the armed men—one of the ones in army green rather than Secret Service black—tapped his right ear and said something under his breath. After a long pause, he nodded and called, in a much less intimidating voice than the one from the loudspeaker, "Just put down the syringe and any visible weapons, raise your hands, and don't make any threatening moves."

"Much easier, thanks," said Shaun, flashing a grin. At first, I couldn't figure out why he was wasting the energy to show off for the crowd, which was probably pretty high-strung and might be trigger-happy. Then I followed his line of sight and had to swallow a smile. Hello, fixed-point camera number four. Hello, ratings like you wouldn't believe, especially with Shaun doing his best to keep it interesting.

I stepped forward and placed the syringe on the ground. It was safe inside its reinforced plastic bubble, which was safe inside a second plastic bubble. A thin layer of bleach separated them. Anything that leaked out of that syringe would die before it hit the open air. Still moving with extreme care, I put my gun a few feet away, followed by my Taser, the pepper spray I keep clipped to my shoulder bag—there are dangerous things out there other than the infected, and most of them hate getting stinging mist in their eyes—and the collapsible baton Shaun gave me for my last birthday. Holding up my hands to show that I didn't have anything else, I began to step back into the line.

"The sunglasses too, ma'am," said the soldier.

"Oh, for crying—she's got retinal KA! You have our files from when we came in here, you should know that!" Shaun's earlier grandstanding was gone, replaced by genuine irritation.

"The sunglasses," repeated the soldier.

"It's all right, Shaun; he's just doing his job," I said, gritting my teeth and squeezing my eyes closed before tugging off my sunglasses and dropping them. Again, I moved to step back into the line.

"Please open your eyes, ma'am," said the soldier.

"Are you prepared to provide me with immediate medical attention?" I asked, not bothering to conceal my own anger. "My name is Georgia Carolyn Mason, license number alpha-foxtrot-bravo-one-seven-five-eight-nine-three, and like my brother said, you *have* my file. I have advanced retinal Kellis-Amberlee. If I open my eyes without protection, I risk permanent damage. Again, we're journalists, and I *will* sue."

There was another pause as the soldier conferred with whoever was giving him his orders. This one took longer; they were presumably calling up my file and confirming that no one was attempting to use a pair of sunglasses and some big words to conceal my impending conversion. "Return to your group," he said, finally. I stepped backward, letting Shaun's hand on my elbow guide me to a stop.

It took nearly ten minutes for Shaun and Rick to finish putting their weapons down and move back into place beside me, Shaun's hand going to my elbow in case we needed to move. I'm basically blind in daylight without my glasses. Maybe worse, since a real blind person doesn't have to worry about migraines or damaging their retinas just because there's no cloud cover.

"Under whose authority have you entered these premises?" asked the soldier.

"Senator Peter Ryman," said Rick, speaking with a calm that clearly said that he'd done more than his share of dealing with the authorities. "I believe it was Miss Mason's call to the senator that you intercepted?"

The soldier ignored his barb. "Senator Ryman is aware of your current location?"

"Senator Ryman gave full consent for this investigation," said Rick, stressing the word 'senator.' "I'm sure he'll be very interested in our findings."

There was another pause as the soldier conferred. This one was interrupted by a crackle of static, and Senator Ryman's voice came over the loudspeaker, saying, "Give me that thing. What are your people doing? That's my press corps, and you're acting like they're trespassers on *my* land—you don't see something wrong with that?" Another voice mumbled contrition outside the range of the speaker's microphone, and Senator Ryman boomed, "Damn right, you didn't think. You folks all right? Georgia, have you gone mental, girl? Get your glasses back on. You think a blind reporter's going to be much good at uncovering all my dirty little secrets?"

"These nice men told me to take them off, sir!" I called.

"These nice men with all the guns," Shaun added.

"Well, that was very neighborly of them, but now I'm asking you to put them back on. Georgia, you got a spare set?"

"I do, but they're in my back pocket—I'm afraid I'll drop them." Never go out without a spare pair of sunglasses. Preferably three. Of course, that anticipates contamination, not army-induced flash-blinding.

"Shaun, get your sister her glasses. She looks naked without them. It's creeping me out."

"Yes, sir!" Shaun let go of my elbow and reached into my pocket. A moment later, I felt him pressing a fresh pair of glasses into my palm. I let out a relieved sigh, snapped them open, and slid them on. The glare receded. I opened my eyes.

The scene hadn't changed much. Shaun and Rick were still flanking me, the armed men were still surrounding us, and fixed-point camera number four was still transmitting the whole thing back to the van on a band so low that it would look like white noise to most receivers. Buffy stays on top of what's happening in the field of wireless technology for just that reason; the more she knows, the harder it is to jam our signals. I didn't know whether our higher-band cameras were being blocked—probably, considering the army—but our low-band was going to be fine.

"Are your eyes all right, Georgia?" asked the senator. Shaun was giving me a look that asked the same question, in fewer words.

"Absolutely, sir," I called. That wasn't entirely true. My migraine was reaching epic proportions and would probably be with me for days. Still, it was close enough for government work. "We need to talk when these nice men are done, if you have time."

"Of course." There was a tension in the senator's voice that belied his earlier friendliness. "I want to know everything."

"So do we, sir," said Rick. "For one thing, we'd very much like to know what's in this syringe. Unfortunately, we lack the facilities to test its contents."

"The item in question is now in the custody of the United States Army," said the first voice, reclaiming the loudspeaker from Senator Ryman. "What it does or does not contain is no longer your concern."

I straightened. Shaun and Rick did the same.

"Excuse me," Rick said, "but are you saying that potential proof that live Kellis-Amberlee was used to cause an outbreak on American soil, on the property of a candidate for President of the United States of America, is *not* the concern of the people? Of, to be specific, three fully licensed and accredited representatives of the American media, who located that proof after being invited to perform an investigation that the armed forces had neglected to carry out?"

The soldiers surrounding us stiffened, and their guns were suddenly at angles that implied that accidents can happen, even on friendly soil. The Secret Service men frowned but remained more relaxed; after all, the original investigation hadn't been under their control.

"Son," said the original voice, "I don't believe you want to imply what you're implying."

"What, that you're saying we don't get to know what we found, even when we have a worldwide audience that really, *really* wants to know?" Shaun asked, folding his arms and sliding into a hip-shot pose that seemed casual, if you didn't know him well enough to see how pissed off he was. "That doesn't scream 'freedom of the press' to me."

"It won't say 'freedom of the press' to our readers, either," I said.

"Miss, there are things called 'nondisclosure forms,' and you'll find that I can have all three of you signing them before you take step one outside of this property."

"Well, *sir*, that might work if we hadn't been streaming our report live all along," I replied. "If you don't believe me, hit our Web site and see for yourself. We have a live feed, a transcript, the works." There was a pause before the sound of muffled swearing drifted through the loudspeaker. Somebody looked online. I allowed myself to smile. "If you wanted this kept secret, you shouldn't have left it for the journalists to find."

"And what I'd like to know," said Senator Ryman, in a voice that was suddenly colder than it had been before, "is what gives you the authority to seize materials found on my property without giving full disclosure to me, as the owner. *Especially* if said materials may have been involved in the death of my daughter and her grandparents."

"All sealed hazard zones—"

"Remain the property of the original owners, who must continue to pay taxes but will not benefit from any natural resources or profitable development of the land," said Rick. I gave him a sidelong look. Smiling serenely, he said, "*Secor v. the State of Massachusetts*, 2024."

"That aside, covering up evidence is rarely smiled upon in this country," Senator Ryman said. "Now, I believe what you intended to tell these nice folks was that they were free to leave the zone as soon as they've passed their mandatory blood tests, and that you'll be contacting me *and* them with an analysis of the contents of that syringe, given as how they found it and it was found on my property."

"Well—"

Senator Ryman cut him off. "I hope you understand that arguing with a senator—especially one who intends to be president, if only so he can make you realize what an imbecilic move this was—is not the best way to further your career."

There was a longer pause before the first voice spoke again, saying carefully, "Well, sir, I think perhaps you've gotten the wrong idea about this situation..."

"I hoped that was the case. I assume my people are free to go?"

Now falsely jovial, the first voice said, "Of course! My men are just there to escort them to their blood tests. Men? Get those citizens out of the field!"

"Sir, yes sir!" barked the soldiers. The Secret Service just looked faintly disgusted with the entire situation.

The soldier who asked me to remove my sunglasses consulted with the speaker on his shoulder before saying, reluctantly, "If the three of you would retrieve your weapons and follow me, I'll take you to the gate for testing and release. Please don't attempt to touch the article you removed from the outbreak site."

Rick looked like he was going to contest the phrase "the article" by bringing up the fact that we'd removed more than one thing from the outbreak site. Since I didn't think the cat would be happy to be dissected by army scientists, I kicked Rick in the ankle. He glared at me. I ignored him. He'd thank me later. Or the cat would.

Picking our weapons back up took longer than putting them down, since all the safeties had to be checked. The area was certified as clean as was reasonable under the Nguyen-Morrison—as clean as any area where you found a syringe full of potential live-state Kellis-Amberlee could be—but shooting yourself in the foot in the vicinity of a recent outbreak still strikes me as an all-around rotten plan. Our escort waited as we armed ourselves and then walked with us in lockstep to the gates, where, I was pleased to see, Steve and two other men from Senator Ryman's security detail were waiting with the blood test units.

I caught my breath as I saw the boxes. Leaning over slightly, I nudged Shaun with my elbow. He followed my gaze and whistled. "Pulling out the big guns, there, Steve-o?"

Steve cracked a thin smile. "The senator wants to be certain you're all right."

"My brother's never been all right, but Rick and I are clean," I said, holding out my right hand. "Rock me."

"My pleasure," he said, and slid the box over my hand.

Blood testing kits range from your basic field units, which can be wrong as often as thirty percent of the time, to the ultra-advanced models, which are so sensitive that they've been known to trigger false positives as they pick up the live Kellis infection harbored by nearly every human on Earth. The most advanced handheld kits are the Apple XH-237s. They cost more than I care to think about, and since they're field kits, they can only be used once without replacing the needle array, a process that costs more than most independent journalists make in a year. Once is more than enough. Needles so thin they can barely be felt, hitting at sites on all five fingers, the palm, and the wrist. Viral detection and comparison mechanisms so advanced that the Army supposedly bought the right to use several of Apple's patents after the XH-237 came out.

Shaun and I carry one—only one—in the van. We've had it for five years. We've never felt rich or desperate enough to use it. You only use the

XH-237 when you need to be sure, right here and now, with no margin for error. It's a kit for use after actual exposure. The army didn't wonder what was in that syringe. Somehow, they *knew*. The implications of that were more than a little disturbing.

Steve activated the kit. The lid locked down, flattening my palm until I felt the tendons stretch. There was a moment of pain. I tensed, but even waiting for it, I couldn't feel the needles as they began darting in and out of my hand and wrist. The lights atop the unit began to cycle, flashing red, then yellow, and finally settling, one by one, into a steady, unblinking green. The entire process took a matter of seconds.

Steve smiled as he dropped the unit into a biohazard bag. "Despite all natural justice, you're still clean."

"That's one more I owe to my guardian angel," I said. A glance to the side showed me that Shaun's unit was still cycling, while Rick's test was just getting started.

"Yeah, well, stop making that angel work so hard," said Steve, more quietly. I looked back to him, surprised. His expression was grave. "You can leave the zone now."

"Right," I said. I walked to the gate, where two blank-faced men in army green watched me press my forefinger against the much simpler testing pad. Another needle bit deeply, and the light switched from green to red to green again before the gate clicked open. Shaking my stinging hand, I stepped out.

Our van and Rick's car had been joined by a third vehicle: a large black van with mirrored windows that gleamed with the characteristic patina of armor plating. The top bristled with enough antennae and satellite dishes to make our own relatively modest assortment of transmitters look positively sparse. I stood, considering it, as Shaun and Rick made their own exits from the ranch and moved to stand beside me.

"That look like our friendly order-giver to you?" Shaun asked.

"Can't imagine who else it would be," I said.

"Well, then, let's go up, say hello, and thank them for the welcome. I mean, *I* was touched. A fruit basket might have been more fitting, but an armed ambush? Definitely a unique way to show that you care." Shaun went bounding for the van. Rick and I followed at a more sedate pace.

Shaun banged on the van door with the heel of his hand. When there was no reply, he balled his hand into a fist and resumed banging, louder. He was just starting to get a good rhythm going when the door was wrenched open by a red-faced general who glared at us with open malice.

"I don't think he's a music lover," I commented to Rick. He snorted.

"I don't know what you kids think you're doing—" began the general.

"Pretty sure they were looking for me," said Senator Ryman, stepping up behind him. The general cut off, shifting the force of his glare to the senator. Ignoring him, Senator Ryman moved around him and out of the van and clasped Shaun's hand. "Shaun, good to see you're all right. I was a bit concerned when I heard that transmission had been intercepted."

"We got lucky," Shaun said, with a grin. "Thanks for getting us through the red tape."

"My pleasure." Senator Ryman looked back at the glowering general. "General Bridges, thank you for your concern for the well-being of my press pool. I'll be speaking to your superiors about this operation, and I'll make sure they know your part in it."

The general paled. Still grinning, Shaun waggled his fingers at him.

"Nice to meet you, sir. Have a nice day." Turning back to Rick and me, he slung his arms around our shoulders. "So, my beloved partners in doing really stupid shit for the edification of the masses, would you say I bought us another three percent today? No, that's too conservative, for I am a God among men and a poker into unpokeable places. Make that five percent. Truly, you should all worship me in the brightness of my glory."

I turned my head enough to glance at the Senator. He was still forcing himself to smile, but the expression wasn't reflected in his eyes. That was the face of a man under considerable strain.

"Maybe later," I said. "Senator Ryman? Did you drive out here?"

"Steve was listening to your report," the senator said. "When he heard you'd found something, he called me, and we came out here immediately."

"Thank you for that, sir," said Rick. "If you hadn't, we might have had a few issues to contend with."

"Permanent blindness," said Shaun, looking at me.

"An all-expenses paid stay at a government biohazard holding facility," I countered. "Sir, did you want us to follow you back to the house and give you the details on what we found?"

"Actually, Georgia, thank you, but no. Right now, I'd like the three of you to return to your hotel and do whatever it is you need to do. Go do your jobs." There was something broken in his expression. I'd thought he looked old at the funeral, but I was wrong; he looked old *now*. "I'll call you in the morning, after I've had time to explain to my wife that our daughter's death wasn't an accident, and to get very, very drunk."

"I understand," I said. Looking to Rick, I said, "Meet us at the hotel." He nodded and turned to head for his car. I didn't want him to ride with us and leave it here. We'd just annoyed the army. A little accidental "vandalism" wasn't outside the realm of possibility. "You'll call if you need anything, sir?"

"You can count on it." The senator's voice was mirthless. So was his expression as he walked over to his government-issue SUV. Steve was already standing next to the passenger-side door, holding it open. I couldn't see any other security guards, but I knew they were there. They wouldn't be taking any chances with a presidential candidate this close to a recent hazard zone. Especially not after the things we'd just learned.

I watched the senator climb into the car. Steve shut the door behind him, nodded toward us, and got into the driver's side, pulling out. Rick's little armored VW followed a few minutes later, rumbling down the road toward civilization.

Shaun put his hand on my shoulder. "George? We okay to get going before the jerks in power come up with a reason to detain us? Other than the cat. Rick took the cat with him, so if there's going to be detention, it'll just be him. Beating erasers, getting electrodes strapped to sensitive parts of his body…"

"Huh?" I twisted around to look at him. "Right, leaving. Yeah, I'm ready to go."

"You feeling okay?" He peered at me. "You're pale."

"I was thinking about Rebecca. You drive? My head hurts too much for it to be safe."

Now Shaun was really starting to look concerned. I don't like to let him drive when I'm a passenger. His idea of traffic safety is going too fast for the cops to catch up. "You sure?"

I tossed him the keys. Usually, I don't like to be in the car when he's behind the wheel, but usually, I don't have a bunch of dead people, a distraught presidential candidate, and a splitting headache to contend with. "Drive."

Shaun gave me one last worried look and turned to head for the van. I followed and climbed into the passenger seat, closing my eyes. Showing rather uncharacteristic concern for my well-being, Shaun opted to drive like a sane human being, pulling out at a reasonably sedate fifty or so miles per hour, and actually acknowledging that the brakes could be used in situations other than "band of zombies blocking the road ahead." I settled deeper into my seat, keeping my eyes closed, and started to review.

When I said that the facts on the outbreak at the ranch didn't add up, I'd been half-expecting to find some sign of human neglect or possibly of an intruder who kicked off the whole mess and managed to get overlooked in the carnage, leaving it to be blamed on the horses. Some small thing that was nonetheless enough to trigger my sense of "something isn't right here." In short, a blip, a little bit of nothing that didn't change anything.

Rebecca Ryman was murdered.

This changed *everything*.

We'd known for weeks that Tracy's death—and thus probably the entire Eakly outbreak, although there wasn't anything conclusive that could be used to prove it—wasn't an accident, but we'd had no real proof that it was anything more than some lunatic taking advantage of an opportunity to cause a little chaos. Now…the chances of two random acts of malicious sabotage happening to the same group of people were small to nil. They just got smaller when you stopped to consider that the man who connected both incidents was one of the current front-runners for the office of President of the United States of America. This was big. This was very, very big.

And it was also very, very bad, because whoever was behind it thought nothing of violating Raskin-Watts, and that meant they'd already crossed a line most people don't even realize is there. Murder is one thing. This was terrorism.

"George? Georgia?" Shaun was shaking my shoulder. I opened my eyes, squinting automatically before I realized that I was facing blessed dimness. Cocking an eyebrow, I turned toward him. He smiled, looking relieved. "Hey. You fell asleep. We're here."

"I was thinking," I said primly, unbuckling my belt before admitting, "and maybe also dozing a little bit."

"It's no big. How's the head?"

"Better."

"Good. Rick's already here, and your crew is driving him up a wall—he's called three times to find out when we'd be on site."

"Any word from Buffy?" I grabbed my bag and opened the door, sliding out of the car. The parking garage was cool and fairly full. Not surprising; when the senator booked our rooms, he put us in the best hotel in town. Five-star security doesn't come cheap, but it comes with perks, like underground parking with motion sensors that keep constant track not only of who's where, but how long they've been there and what they're doing. Stay down here walking in circles for a while, and Shaun and I could get a whole new view of hotel security. That might have been appealing if we hadn't already been working a story that was almost too hot to handle. I was starting to miss the days when toying with rich people's security systems was enough to make our front page.

"She's still at Chuck's, but she says the servers are prepped to handle whatever load we ask them to and that the Fiction section won't have a response for a day or two anyway; we should go ahead and run without her." Shaun slammed his door, starting toward the elevators that would let us into the main hotel. "She seemed pretty shaken up. Said she'd probably sleep over there tonight."

"Right."

Like most of the senator's men, Chuck was staying at the Embassy Suites Business Resort, a fancy name for a series of pseudo-condos that offered less transitory lodgings than our own high-scale but strictly temporary accommodations. His place came with a kitchen, living room, and a bathtub a normal human being could actually take a bath in. Ours came with a substantial array of cable channels, two queen-sized beds that we'd shoved together on the far side of the room in order to make space for the computers, and a surprisingly robust electrical system. We'd only managed to trip the circuit breakers twice, and for us, that's practically a record.

The elevators were protected by a poor-man's air lock. The sliding glass doors opened at our approach, then slid closed, sealing us into a small antechamber. A second set of glass doors barred us from the elevator. Being a high-end hotel, they were configured to handle up to four entrances at a time, although most people wouldn't be foolish enough to take advantage of that illusionary convenience. If anyone failed to check out as clean, the doors would lock and security would be called. Going into an air lock with someone you weren't certain was uninfected was a form of Russian roulette that few cared to indulge in.

Shaun took my hand, squeezing before we split up. He took the leftmost station while I took the one on the right.

"Hello, honored guests," said the warm, mock-maternal voice of the hotel. It was clearly designed to conjure up reassuring thoughts of soft beds, chocolates on your pillow every morning, and no infections ever getting past the sealed glass doors. "May I have your room numbers and personal identifications?"

"Shaun Phillip Mason," said Shaun, grimacing. Our usual games worked on the security system at home, but with a setup this advanced, there was too much potential that the computer would mistake "messing around" for "confused about your own identity" and call security. "Room four-nineteen."

"Georgia Carolyn Mason," I said. "Room four-nineteen."

"Welcome, Mr. and Ms. Mason," said the hotel, after a fifteen-second pause to compare our voice prints to the ones on file. "Could I trouble you for a retinal scan?"

"Medical dispensation, federal guideline seven-fifteen-A," I said. "I have a registered case of nonactive retinal Kellis-Amberlee and would like to request a pattern recognition test, in accordance with the Americans with Disabilities Act."

"Hang on while I check your records," said the hotel. It fell silent. I rolled my eyes.

"Every time," I muttered.

"It's just trying to be thorough."

"*Every* time."

"It only takes the system a few seconds to find your file."

"How many times have we gone through this garage now?"

"Maybe they figure that if you were infected, you'd forget that stupid federal guideline."

"I'd like to forget your stupid—"

The speaker clicked back on. "Ms. Mason, thank you for alerting us to your medical condition. Please look at the screen in front of you. Mr. Mason, please proceed to the line marked on the floor, and look at the screen in front of you. Tests will commence simultaneously."

"Lucky disabled bitch," muttered Shaun, placing his toes on the indicated line and opening his eyes wide.

My screen flickered, resetting from scanning to text mode, and displayed a block of text. I cleared my throat and read, "Ah, distinctly I remember, it was in the bleak December, and each separate dying ember wrought its ghost upon the floor. Eagerly I wished the morrow, vainly I had sought to borrow from my books surcease of sorrow."

"Please hold," said the hotel. The black plastic doors on two of the test panels slid upward, revealing the metal testing panels. "Mr. and Ms. Mason, please place your hands on the diagnostic panels."

"Don't you love how it doesn't tell us whether we've passed or not?" said Shaun, putting his hand flat on the first panel. "They could be calling security right now and just stalling us until they get here."

"Gee, thanks, Mr. Optimism," I said. I pressed my hand to the second panel, feeling the brief sting of a needle against the base of my palm. "Got any other cheery thoughts?"

"Well, if Rick's frantic, Mahir may have experienced spontaneous human combustion by now."

"I hope somebody got it on film."

"Mr. and Ms. Mason, welcome to the Parrish Weston Suites. We hope you enjoy your stay; please let us know if there's anything we can do to make you more comfortable." The hotel finished delivering its sugar-soaked greeting as the doors between us and the elevator slid open, allowing us to proceed. They closed as soon as we were through, locking us out of the air lock. "Thank you for choosing the Weston family of hotels."

"Same to you," I said, and hit the Call button.

The science of moving people from point to point has improved over the past twenty years, since the infected have done a lot to discourage the once-natural human desire to linger alone in dark, poorly defended places. The Weston had nine elevators sharing a series of corridors and conduits. They were controlled by a central computer that spent the day dispatching them along the most efficient, collision-free routes. It took less than five seconds for the elevator doors to open. It promptly skidded sideways twenty yards once we were inside, beginning the rapid ascent to the elevator access closest to our hotel rooms.

"Priorities?" asked Shaun, as the elevator shot upward.

"Clear the message boards, perform a general status check-in, and debrief," I said. "I'll get my crew online if I have to haul them out of their beds. You get yours."

"What about the Fictionals?"

"Rick can handle them." If Buffy wanted to skip out on what might be the most important scoop the two more realistic sections of the site ever had, that was her prerogative, but she'd have to cope with us rousing her junior bloggers. Her department didn't get to hang up the blackout curtains just because she wanted to get laid.

Shaun grinned. "Can I tell him?"

The elevator slowed as it approached our floor, dumping inertia at such a rate that you'd never guess it had just been traveling in excess of twenty miles per hour. The doors slid open with a ding. "If it'll make you happy, by all means, tell him. Make sure he knows Magdalene is his to abuse. That should help things a bit." I approached our room, pressing my thumb against the access panel. It flashed green, acknowledging my right to enter. Shaun opened the door and shoved past me, leaving me standing in the hall. I sighed. "After you."

"Don't mind if I do!" he called back.

Rolling my eyes, I followed him.

When the senator booked our rooms, he gave us a pair of adjoining suites, assuming Buffy and I would take one room while Shaun and Rick took the other. It didn't work out that way. Buffy refuses to sleep without a nightlight, which I can't tolerate for obvious reasons; Shaun tends to respond violently to unexpected noises in the night. So Rick and Buffy wound up in one room, while Shaun and I were in the other with all the computers, turning it into our temporary headquarters.

Rick was at a terminal when we came in. The cat he'd saved was curled up in his lap, purring. I'd be purring, too, if I'd just eaten the better part of a tuna fish sandwich from room service.

"Lucky cat," I commented.

"Oh, thank God," said Rick, looking up. "Everyone wants to know what we're doing next. The raw footage has been downloaded so many times I thought we were going to blow up one of the servers, Mahir won't stop pinging me, and the message boards are—"

I interrupted him with a wave of my hand. "What are the numbers like, Rick?"

"Ah..." He recovered quickly, glancing to the top of his screen. "Up seven percent in all markets."

Shaun whistled. "Wow. We should uncover terrorist conspiracies more often."

"We haven't uncovered it yet; we've just found out that it existed," I said, and sat down at my own terminal. "Hit your boards and start pinging your people. We're doing the debrief in thirty, and then we start to edit and recap for the evening reports."

"On it." Shaun grabbed a chair and looked to Rick, adding carelessly, "You get to ping the Fictionals. Buffy isn't coming."

"Oh, great," said Rick, wrinkling his nose. He was already pulling up his IM lists as he asked, "Why do I get the honor?"

"Because you kept the cat," I said. "Kick Magdalene. She'll help you. Hush now. Mommy's working." He snorted but turned back to his computer. Shaun and I did the same.

It took thirty minutes to beat the message boards into something that looked less like a combination of a forest fire and a conspiracy theorist convention. No one had quite reached the point of linking the outbreak at the Ryman family ranch with the initial release of the Kellis cure and the death of JFK, but they'd have gotten there before much longer. As I'd expected, everyone in my department was already up, online, and doing their best to moderate the mess, and from the crossover threads, it looked like the same was mostly true for the Irwins and the Fictionals. Behold the power of the truth. When people see its shadow on the wall, they don't want to take the time to look away.

"My boards are clear," Shaun called. "Ready when you are."

"Same," Rick said. "The chat relay is humming nicely, and the volunteer mods have things under control."

"Excellent." Since the volunteers weren't technically employees of After the End Times, they didn't need to be included in the debriefing. I pulled up the employee chat and typed, *Log on now.* "Turn on your conference functions, boys. We're about to see the swarm."

"Logged on."

"Logged on."

"Logging on now. Room eleven, maximum security." Our conferencing system is half the standard Microsoft Windows VirtuParty setup—allowing people to share real-time socialization through webcams and a common server—and half Buffy's own homebrew. All eleven of our channels have varying degrees of security, from the base three, which clever readers can break into with relative ease, to eleven, which has never been successfully violated. Not even by the people we've paid to try.

Windows began spawning on my screen, each containing the small, pixelated face of one of our bloggers. Shaun, Rick, and I appeared first, followed almost immediately by Mahir, who looked like he hadn't slept in several days, Alaric, and Suzy, the girl I'd hired to replace Becks after she jumped ship to the Irwins. Becks herself appeared a moment later, along with a trio of Irwins I only vaguely recognized. Five more faces followed them as the Fictionals logged in; three of them were sharing one screen, proving that Magdalene was hosting another of her infamous grindhouse parties.

When all was said and done, we were only missing Dave—one of Shaun's Irwins, who was on a field trip in the wilds of Alaska and probably couldn't get to a conferencing setup—and Buffy. I looked from face to face, studying their expressions while the initial quiet still held. They looked worried, confused, curious, even excited, but none of them looked like they had anything to hide. This was our team. This was what we had to work with. And we had a conspiracy to break.

"All right, everyone," I said. "This afternoon, we led an expedition onto the Ryman family ranch. You've seen the footage by now. If you haven't, please log out, watch it, and come back. Here's the topic at hand: 'What happens next?'"

Following the campaign of Congresswoman Kirsten Wagman taught me one important fact about politics: Sometimes, style *can* matter more than substance. Let's face it: We're not talking about one of the great political minds of our age. We're talking about a former stripper who got her seat in Congress by promising her constituency that for every thousand votes she got, she'd wear something else inappropriate to the floor. Judging by the landslide of that first win, we'll be seeing congressional hearings graced by a lady in lingerie long after the end of her term in office.

But she didn't win. Despite the general malaise of the voting public and their willingness to put "interesting" above "good for them" in nine out of ten cases, Wagman's run for the presidential seat proved to be the tenth event. Why was this? I place the blame partially on Senator Peter Ryman, a man who proved that style and substance can be combined to the benefit of both, and, more important, that integrity is not actually dead.

I also blame After the End Times and Georgia Mason, for their willingness to get into the campaign in a way that has seldom been seen in this century. Their reporting hasn't been impartial or perfect, but it has something we see even more rarely than integrity.

It has heart.

It is with great joy that I report that the youth of America aren't actually riddled with ennui and apathy; that the truth hasn't been fully forsaken for the merely entertaining; that there's a place in this world for reporting the facts as accurately and concisely as possible and allowing people to draw their own conclusions.

I've never been more proud of finding a place where I can belong.

—From *Another Point of True*,
the blog of Richard Cousins, March 18, 2040

Sixteen

The discussion lasted late into the morning. People dropped off the conference one by one, until it was just Rick, Mahir, and me. Shaun had long since passed out at his terminal, leaning back in his chair and snoring. Rick's newly acquired cat was curled up on his chest with its tail tucked over its nose, occasionally opening an eye to glare at the room.

"I don't like this, Georgia," said Mahir, worry and exhaustion blurring his normally crisp English accent into something much softer. He ran his hand through his hair. He'd been doing that for hours, and it was sticking up in all directions. "The situation is starting to sound like it isn't exactly safe."

"You're on the other side of the planet, Mahir. I don't think you're going to get hurt."

"It's not my safety I'm concerned with here. Are you sure we want to continue to pursue the situation? I'd rather not be reporting your obituary." He sounded so anxious that I couldn't be angry with him. Mahir's a good guy. A little conservative, and generally inclined to avoid taking risks, but a good guy and a fabulous Newsie. If he couldn't understand why we were pursuing things, I just needed to make them clearer.

"Everyone who died at the ranch was murdered," I said. His image winced. "The people who died in Eakly were murdered, too, and that set of casualties nearly included me and Shaun. There's something connected to this candidate and this campaign that someone wants to see destroyed, and they're not above causing a little collateral damage. You want to know if we want to continue pursuing the situation. I want to know what makes you think we can afford not to."

Mahir smiled, reaching up to adjust his glasses. "I was assuming you'd say something along those lines, but I wanted to be certain of it. Rest assured that you have the full support of everyone here. If there's anything I can do, all you have to do is say so."

"You know, Mahir, your support is something I never worry about. I may have something for you very soon," I said. "Although if you play 'test the boss' again, I may kill you. For now, it's almost four in the morning, and the senator's going to want to talk before much longer. I hereby declare this discussion over. Rick, Mahir, thanks for sticking it out."

"Any time," said Rick, voice echoing as the relay raced to keep up with him. His window blinked out.

"Cheers," said Mahir, and logged off. I closed the conference, standing. I was so stiff that it felt like my spine had been replaced with carved teak, and my eyes were burning. I removed my sunglasses and rubbed my face, trying to relieve some of the tension. It wasn't working.

"Bed?" asked Rick.

I nodded. "Don't take this the wrong way, but—"

"Get out. I know. Wake me when it's time to go?"

"I will."

"Good night, Georgia. Sleep well." Rick opened the adjoining door with a faint creak. I opened my eyes, turning to wave as he slipped out.

"You too, Rick," I said. Then the door was closed, and I staggered to the bed, shedding clothes as I went. When I was down to T-shirt and panties, I abandoned the notion of looking for nightclothes and crawled under the covers, closing my eyes again as I sank into blessed darkness.

"Georgia."

The voice was vaguely familiar. I pondered its familiarity for a moment, and then rolled over, deciding I didn't need to give a damn.

"Georgia."

There was more anxiousness to the voice this time. Maybe I needed to pay attention to it. It wasn't the sort of anxiousness that said "Pay attention or something is going to eat your face." I made a faint grumbling noise and didn't open my eyes.

"George, if you don't wake up *right now*, I'm going to pour ice water over your head." The statement was made in an entirely matter-of-fact manner. It wasn't a threat, merely a comment. "You won't like that. I won't care."

I licked my lips to moisten them and croaked, "I hate you."

"Where's the love? *There's* the love. Now get out of bed. Senator Ryman called. You slept through me talking to him for, like, the whole time I was getting dressed. How late were you up last night?"

I opened my eyes and squinted at Shaun. He was wearing one of his bulkier shirts, the ones he puts on only when he needs to cover body armor. I pushed myself unsteadily into a sitting position, holding out my left hand. He dropped my sunglasses into it. "Sometime around four. What time is it?"

"Almost nine."

"Oh, my God, kill me now," I moaned, and rose, shuffling toward the bathroom. The hotel had been happy to switch our standard light bulbs for lower-wattage soft lights that wouldn't hurt my eyes, but management didn't have a way to swap out the built-in bathroom fluorescents. "What time will he be here? Or are we going to him?"

"You've got fifteen minutes. Steve's picking us up." There was a distinctly amused note in Shaun's voice as he relayed this piece of information. "Buffy's *pissed*. She and Chuck are already with the Rymans, and she didn't have spare clothes with her. I got the world's angriest text message while I was on the phone."

"She wants to have her night on the town, she can take the walk of shame the day after." The bathroom lights were searingly bright, even through my sunglasses. I looked in the mirror and groaned. "I look like death."

"Cute journalistic death?"

"Just plain death." I was washed-out and sallow, and it had been too long since I had my hair trimmed; it was getting long enough to tangle. My head wasn't throbbing, but it would be soon. The light seeping in around the edges of my glasses was telling me that. There was a way I could avoid that, if I was willing to deal with the inconvenience. Muttering under my breath, I grabbed my contact case off the sink and clicked the bathroom lights off. Even with as little as I voluntarily wear my contacts, the nature of my medical condition means I need to be able to put them in despite near or total darkness. Doing otherwise means risking retinal scarring, and I have things to do that require having eyes.

Shaun's feet shuffled on the carpet as he crossed to the bathroom door. "George? What are you doing in there in the dark?"

"Putting in my contacts." I blinked, and felt the first slide into place. "Find me clean clothes."

"What do I look like, your maid?"

"Nah, she's *way* better looking." I blinked my second lens into place before clicking the bathroom lights back on. Harsh white light flooded the room. I squinted slightly, studying my blue-eyed reflection before I turned to the important matter of brushing my hair and teeth. "Any time now, Shaun. I can't go see the senator in my undies."

"Hunter S. Thompson would go see a senator in his undies. Or your undies, for that matter."

"Hunter S. Thompson was too stoned to know what undies were." The bathroom door opened. I turned, catching the clothes Shaun pitched in my direction. "There, now, was that so hard? Go grab our gear. I'll be there in a second."

"Next time, I'll let you sleep in," he grumbled, backing up. "And those contacts make you look like an alien!"

"I know," I said, and shut the bathroom door.

Ten minutes later, Shaun and I were back in the elevator. I was running the final diagnostic checks on my equipment, and Shaun was doing the same, fingers tapping over the screen of his PDA in a series of increasingly complex patterns. This wasn't a field op, and odds were that Senator Ryman would request a privacy screen on anything we recorded, but that didn't matter. Leaving the hotel without our cameras and recorders set and primed to go would have been like leaving naked, and neither of us was up for that.

Some of my cameras were starting to show signs of misalignment, and the memory in my watch was almost full. Making a note to have Buffy take a look at things, I stepped out into the lobby with Shaun half a beat behind.

"Thank you for choosing the Parrish Weston Suites as your home away from home," the hotel chirped as we approached the air lock. "We know you have many choices, and we are grateful for your business. Please place your right hand—"

"That's enough," I said, slamming my palm down on the test panel as soon as it finished opening. Getting *out* of the hotel requires nothing but a clean blood test. They don't care if you want to go into massive viral amplification as long as you have the common courtesy to do it outside, preferably after you've paid your bills.

Shaun and I checked clean and the outer doors slid open, allowing us to exit while the automated voice of the hotel chirped pleasantries to an empty antechamber. It was cold and bright outside; a perfect Wisconsin day. There was only one car idling in the passenger pickup lane.

"Think that's us?" asked Shaun.

"That, or there's a pro-wrestling convention in town," I said. We started toward it.

When the senator sends a car, he doesn't screw around. Our intended transport was a solid-looking black SUV. The windows were tinted, and I would have placed bets on their being bulletproof. Possessing a personal fortune has its perks. Shaun nudged me and whistled, pointing to the inset gunner's windows on the back windshield.

"Even *Mom* doesn't have those," he murmured.

"I'm sure she'll be jealous," I said.

Steve was standing by the rear passenger door, holding it open for us—as much, I'm sure, as a reminder that we weren't allowed to ride up front as a gesture of civility. His eyebrows rose when he saw my contacts. To his credit, he didn't comment on them; he just held the door open a little wider. "Shaun. Georgia."

"I see you drew the short straw this morning," I said, hoisting myself into the SUV and scooting over to make room for Shaun. Rick was already inside. I offered him a small wave, which he dolefully returned.

"The senator prefers this meeting be conducted in a more secure location and thought you might appreciate the chance to take a break from driving." Steve glanced toward the parking garage and tapped his earpiece. I frowned. They thought our van had been bugged? It was possible—without Buffy running a full diagnostic on our systems, there was no way to tell—but it seemed a little paranoid.

I stopped that line of thought. Rebecca Ryman was murdered by someone who was willing to use live-state Kellis-Amberlee in an uncontrolled situation to achieve their goals, whatever they happened to be. There was no such thing as paranoia anymore.

"Looking good, Steve-o," said Shaun, slapping the security agent a high five as he slid into the car.

"One day you're going to call me that, and I'm going to punch your head clean off," said Steve, and slammed the door. Shaun laughed. The sound of Steve's footsteps moved around the car, where the driver's-side door opened and closed again. A sheet of one-way glass separated the front seat from the passenger compartment. He could see us, but we couldn't see him. How encouraging.

"He probably means that, you know," said Rick.

"As long as I get it on film, I'll be happy," said Shaun. Folding his hands behind his head, he stretched out on the seat and propped his feet in my lap. "This is awesome. We're being driven to a clandestine meeting with a man who wants to be president. Anybody else feel like James Bond right now?"

"Too female," I said.

"Too aware of the fact that I'm not immortal," said Rick.

"You realize you're both wimps, right?" scolded Shaun.

"Yes, but we're wimps with a life expectancy, and I have to respect that," I replied.

"I'll trade my life expectancy for a cup of coffee and a nice dark room," said Rick.

I craned my head to look at him. He was rubbing his eyes. He looked groggy, and I wasn't entirely sure he'd changed his shirt. "Didn't sleep well?"

"Cat kept me up all night," he said. Dropping his hands from his face, he did a classic double-take, eyes going wide. "Georgia? What's wrong with your eyes?"

"Contacts," I said. "They irritate the shit out of my eyes, but at least this way, I can't have some hopped-up asshole with a megaphone take my sunglasses away."

He tilted his head, studying me. "That really upset you, didn't it?"

"What, you mean the part where the nice guys with the big guns demonstrated over a live feed that I can be incapacitated by taking my glasses away? That didn't bother me a bit." I shoved Shaun's feet off my lap. "Sit up. This isn't a cruise."

"Behold the bitchiness of George when she hasn't had her beauty sleep," said Shaun, pushing himself upright. Twisting around to face Rick, he said, "So, Ricky-boy, you seen your ratings? Because I have some ideas to spice things up. Let's start with nudity—" And he was off and running, offering a plethora of insane suggestions as my overwhelmed fellow Newsie looked on in dismay.

Grateful for the save, I pulled out my PDA and started scrolling through the headlines. There'd been another outbreak in San Diego; that city hasn't had a break since the Rising, when bad timing and worse luck caused amplification to occur during the annual International Comic Convention, an event that drew over a hundred and twenty thousand attendees. The results were less than pleasant. In other news, Congresswoman Wagman had been asked to leave the floor for showing up in an outfit more suitable for a Vegas showgirl. Another nutcase in Hong Kong was claiming that Kellis-Amberlee had been engineered specifically to undermine those religions that depended on ancestor worship. In other words, a pretty quiet day…if you cut out the headlines that directly referenced or connected back to our expedition to the Ryman family ranch. At a rough glance, I estimated that sixty to seventy percent of the news sites were carrying us as their top story. *Us.*

I tapped my ear cuff. There was a pause as the connection was made; then Buffy was on the line, sounding irritated from her first curt "Go."

"Buffy, I need numbers. We're everywhere, and I have to know whether I'm hauling Mahir's ass out of bed to start manning the walls."

"Sec." We all have live feeds, but Buffy's are the most up-to-date. I need special equipment to get the data she pulls as a matter of course. That's why she's the techie, while I'm just in charge.

There was a long pause. Longer than I'm used to; Buffy can normally give me numbers in a matter of seconds. "Buffy?" Shaun stopped talking as both he and Rick turned toward me. I held up my hand, signaling for quiet. "Are you still there?"

"I'm here. I, uh…I think I'm here, anyway." She sounded a little bit scared. "Georgia? We're number *one*, Georgia. We have more current hits, references, link-backs, and quotations than any other news site on the planet."

My entire body seemed to go numb. I licked my lips. "Say that again."

"Number one, Georgia."

"You're sure?"

"I'm positive." There was a pause before she said, plaintively, "What do we do now?"

"What do we do now? What do we do *now*? Wake them up, Buffy! Call your people and wake them up!"

"Senator Ryman—"

"We're on our way! Ignore him! Get your people on the phone, and get them on the damn site!" I hit my ear cuff to kill the connection and twisted to face the others. "Shaun, start dialing. I want your entire team updating, ten minutes ago, and that means Dave, too. They have phones in Alaska. Rick, check your in-box, start clearing out any merchandise queries that got routed to you by mistake."

"George, what—"

"We have the ratings, Shaun. *We have the top slot.*" I nodded at his stunned expression. "Yeah. Now get them on the phone."

The rest of the ride was a blur of telephone calls, text messages, e-mails, and rousing person after person out of their well-earned rest in order to throw them back into the fray. Most of my crew was too disoriented by lack of sleep to argue when I ordered them out of bed and to their terminals, where the freshly updated site message that appeared as each of them logged in read "Number One News Site in the world" in flashing red letters. If that wasn't enough to jolt them into consciousness, they were probably already dead.

Mahir put it best: When I called him, he responded first with stunned silence, then by swearing a blue streak and hanging up on me so he could get to his computer. I love a man who keeps his priorities straight.

All three of us were so engrossed in work that we missed the rest of the drive to the senator's "secure location." I was in the process of giving Alaric and Suzy their marching orders when the car doors opened, filling the back seat with light and nearly spilling Shaun—whose feet were braced against the left-hand passenger window—into the parking lot.

"We're here," said Steve. The three of us continued frantically typing on our various handheld PDAs and output screens. Rick was managing to type on his Palm and his phone at the same time, using his thumbs for data entry. Steve frowned. "Uh, guys? We're here. The senator is waiting."

"Sec," I said, freeing one hand long enough to hold it up to him in the universal "stop" gesture. While he gaped at me, I finished tapping out the instructions Alaric and Suzy would need to keep their portions of the site functional until I could get back online. I wasn't confident they'd survive the day, but Mahir would back them up as much as he could, and he had most of the same administrative permissions as Shaun and I; it would have to do. I lowered my PDA. "All right. Where do we go?"

"You sure you don't need a few more minutes to check your e-mail or anything?"

I glanced to Shaun. "I think he's making fun of us."

"I think you're right," Shaun said, and slid out of the car, offering me his hands. "Ignore the philistine and get out here. We have government officials to annoy."

We were parked in a covered garage less than a quarter the size of the one at the hotel. The lights were bright enough that I hadn't even noticed the transition from real to artificial illumination. I used Shaun's hands for balance as I stepped out of the car, sliding my PDA into the carrier on my belt before turning to help Rick down. He glanced to me, and I nodded.

That was his cue. Rick goggled, sparing Shaun and me the trouble of playing hick, before asking, "Where *are* we?"

"The senator considers it wise to keep a second local residence for meetings of a sensitive nature," said Steve.

I gave him a sharp look. "Or meetings with people who didn't feel comfortable being around the horses?"

"I'm sure I wouldn't be qualified to speak to that, Miss Mason."

That meant yes. "Fine. Where do we go?"

"This way, please." He led us to a steel-reinforced door, where I was surprised to see a lack of the customary blood testing units. There also wasn't a doorknob. Shaun and I exchanged a glance as Steve tapped his earpiece, saying, "Base, we're at the west door. Release."

Something clicked, and a light above the door frame flashed green. The door slid open. There was a soft outrush of air as the hall on the other side was revealed; it was a positive-pressure zone, designed to force air out rather than allowing it to flow in and cause a contamination risk.

"No wonder they don't need blood tests." I followed Steve into the hall with Shaun and Rick close behind me. The hallway door slid shut behind us.

The lights in the hall were bright enough to hurt my eyes even through my contacts. I squinted, stepping closer to Shaun and letting the blurry motion of his silhouette guide me toward the door at the far end, where two more guards waited, each holding a large plastic tray.

"The senator would prefer this meeting not be broadcast or recorded," Steve said. "If you would please place all nonessential equipment here, it will be returned to you at the end of the meeting."

"You have *got* to be kidding," said Shaun.

"I don't think he is," I said, turning toward Steve. "You want us to walk in there naked?"

"We can put up an EMP privacy screen if you don't think we can trust you to leave your toys behind," said Steve. His tone was mild, but the tightness around his eyes said he knew exactly how much he was asking and he wasn't happy about it. "The choice is yours."

An EMP privacy screen sufficient to secure an area would fry half of our more sensitive recording devices and could do serious damage to the rest. Replacing that much gear would kill our operating budget for months, if not the rest of the year. Grumbling, all three of us began stripping off our equipment—and in my case, jewelry—and dumping it into the trays. The guards stood there impassively, waiting for us to finish.

Dropping my ear cuff into my hand, I looked to Steve. "So do we have to be totally radio silent, or are we allowed to keep our phones?"

"You can keep any private data recorders that will be used solely for the purposes of taking personal notes, and any telecommunications devices that can be deactivated for the duration of the meeting."

"Swell." I dropped my ear cuff into the tray and slipped my PDA back onto my belt. I felt strangely exposed without my small army of microphones, cameras, and data storage devices, as if the world held a lot more dangers than it had a few minutes before. "How's Buffy taking this?"

Steve smirked. "They said they wouldn't cut her off until we got here."

"So you're telling me your men are in there, right now, trying to take

Buffy's equipment away?" Shaun said, and looked toward the closed door with a sort of wary fascination. "Maybe we should stay out here. It's a *lot* safer."

"Unfortunately, Senator Ryman and Governor Tate are waiting for you." Steve nodded to the guards. The one on the left leaned over and took the tray from the one on the right, who opened the door. There was another inrush of air as the hallway's positive-pressure zone met the house beyond. "If you don't mind?"

"Tate's here?" My eyes narrowed. "What do you mean, Tate's here?"

Steve walked through the open door without answering me. Eyes still narrowed, I shook my head and followed, with Rick and Shaun close behind me. Once the last of us was through the door, the guards closed it, remaining outside in the garage.

"What," muttered Shaun, "no blood test?"

"Guess they figure there's no point," said Rick.

I kept my mouth shut, busying myself with studying the house. The décor was simple but refined, all clean, sleek lines and well-lit corners. Overhead lighting provided a steady level of illumination, with no visible dimmer switches or controls; it was either light or darkness, with nothing in between. It was less glaring than the hallway lights, but I still grimaced. The lights answered one question—this was nothing but a show home, intended for meetings and parties, but never for living in. Emily, with her retinal KA, couldn't possibly have lived here.

There were no windows.

We walked through the house to the dining room, where a brisk-looking security guard in a black suit was finishing the process of taking Buffy's equipment away. If looks could kill, the way she was glaring would have left us with an outbreak on our hands.

"We about done here, Paul?" asked Steve.

The guard—Paul—shot him a harried look and nodded. "Miss Meissonier has been quite cooperative."

"Liar," said Shaun, so close to my ear that I don't think anyone else heard him.

"Buffy," I said, swallowing my smile. "What's the sitrep?"

"Chuck's in there with the senator and Mrs. Ryman," Buffy said, as she continued glaring at Paul. "Governor Tate just got here. They didn't tell me he was coming, or I would've warned you."

"It's all right." I shook my head. "He's a part of this campaign now, like it or not." I looked to Steve. "We're ready when you are."

"This way, please." He opened a door on the far side of the room, holding it as the four of us filed through. When Rick stepped through the doorway, Steve closed the door behind him. The lock slid home with a final-sounding "click."

We were standing in a sitting room decorated in stark blacks and whites, with stylized white art deco couches flanked by glossy black end tables and carefully arranged spotlight lamps illuminating tiny pieces of art that probably cost more individually than our operating budget for the year. The only spots of color came from the faces of the senator and his wife, both red-cheeked from crying, and from Governor Tate, who was wearing a tailored dark blue suit that screamed "money" in a politely subdued way. All three turned toward us, and the senator rose, tugging his suit jacket down before offering his hand to Shaun. Shaun shook it. I looked past them to where Governor Tate was endeavoring to cover his own expression of disgust.

"Thank you for coming," said Senator Ryman, releasing Shaun's hand and reclaiming his seat. Emily's eyes were hidden behind mirrored sunglasses. She mustered a tiny smile as she folded her hands around her husband's. He tugged her closer, seemingly unaware of the gesture. He didn't have much strength to offer, but what he did have was hers without question. That's the kind of guy we need running this country.

"We had a choice?" asked Shaun, dropping onto one of the couches and sprawling with intentional untidiness. He'd clearly caught Tate's look, too; that, combined with the confiscation of our equipment, had him primed and ready to offend. Good. It's always easier to seem reasonable when my brother is providing a handy contrast.

"We were glad to come, Senator, but I'm afraid I don't understand why our equipment had to be confiscated. Some of those cameras are delicate, and I'm not comfortable leaving them with anyone who's not a member of our staff. If we'd been informed of the need for privacy before we left the hotel, we could have left them behind."

Tate snorted. "You mean you could have brought cameras that were easier to hide."

"Actually, Governor, I meant what I said." I turned to look him in the eyes, unblinking. One of the few handy side effects of retinal KA is the lack of a need for repeated ocular lubrication—or, in layman's terms, I don't blink much. Being stared at by someone with retinal KA can be very unnerving, at least according to Shaun. "I'm aware that you're a recent addition to this campaign, and may not be used to working with members of the reputable news media. We can make allowances for that. I would, however, appreciate it if you could also keep in mind that we've been working with Senator Ryman and his staff for some time now, and not once have we broadcast or distributed material we were asked to withhold. Now, I'll admit that part of that can be attributed to the fact that we've never been asked to withhold information without good reason. I still believe it establishes that we're capable of behaving ourselves with tact, propriety, and, above all, the patriotism inherent in the duty of serving as media corps of a major political campaign."

"Well, missy," said Tate, meeting my eyes without a flinch, "those are a lot of pretty words, but I hope you'll forgive me if I've been burned a few times by the media before landing here, and I prefer to proceed with caution."

"Well, *sir*," I replied, "you'll forgive *me* if I believe that our track record should count for something, given that we've never been anything other than appropriate in our dealings with sensitive information; further, if I might be so bold, there's a chance that the media has 'burned' you so many times because you persist in treating honest people like they're waiting for the opportunity to be criminals. For a man who says he's standing for American values, you're sure devoted to the suppression of media freedom."

The governor's eyes narrowed. "Now see here, young lady—"

"My name is neither 'young lady' nor 'missy,' and I think I see all too well." I turned to the others. "Shaun, get up. Rick, Buffy, come on."

"Where do you think you're going?" demanded Tate.

"Back to our hotel, where we'll cheerfully explain to our many readers that we have no news for them today because—after uncovering an act of criminal bioterrorism on United States soil—we were unable to attend a conference with our candidate since, oopsie, the new man on the ticket thinks the media can't be trusted." I smiled. "Won't that be fun?"

"Georgia, sit down," said Senator Ryman. He sounded exhausted. That was no surprise. "You, too, Shaun. Buffy, Rick, you can sit or not, as you prefer. And you, David, will please try to remember that these folks are the only ones who cared enough to really *look* at the ranch rather than writing it off as a simple outbreak. You'll be courteous, and we'll trust them to keep on being as they have been: perfectly reasonable and willing to work with us."

"There's still the matter of our recording devices, Senator," I said, staying still.

"That was a bad decision, and I'm sorry. That being said, I'm going to stand by it for now, and ask that you allow me to conduct this meeting."

I raised an eyebrow. "And what do we get?"

Governor Tate sputtered, growing red in the face. Senator Ryman waved him down, looking at me squarely, and said, "An exclusive interview with me, no editing, regarding what you found yesterday."

"No deal," said Shaun. The senator and I looked toward him, surprised. My brother was sitting up, suddenly alert. "No offense, sir, but you're not that impressive anymore. Our readers know you. They respect you, and if you keep on the way you have been, they'll elect you, but they won't be razzled and dazzled by the fact that we managed to *get* you."

The senator ran a hand through his hair, looking pained. "What do you want, Shaun?"

"Her." He nodded to Emily. "We want an interview with her."

"Absolutely n—"

"Yes," said Emily. Her voice was weary but clear. "I'm happy to. I only wanted to be left out of things for the sake of... for the sake of my family." Her voice broke. "That's not a concern anymore."

"You aren't worried about the safety of your younger daughters?" I asked.

"They aren't at the ranch. They have the best security in the world. They're safe. If I can prevent people from going out and killing other people's pets because of what happened to Rebecca and my parents, well." She managed to muster a smile. "It'll be worth the strain."

Senator Ryman reached for her arm. "Emily..."

"Accepted." I sat next to Shaun, ignoring the senator's stricken look. "We'll be setting up interview times with both of you later this afternoon. Now, I assume there's a reason we're all here?"

"The senator would like to discuss the tragic evidence of tampering that your crew discovered at his family ranch, Miss Mason," said Governor Tate smoothly, all traces of his earlier aggravation gone. The man was a natural politician; I had to give him that, even if I wasn't willing to let him have anything else if I could help it. "Now, I realize this may seem as if I'm questioning your journalistic integrity—"

"Hey, Rick, ever notice how dickheads only say that when they're about to question your journalistic integrity?" asked Shaun.

"Oddly, yes," Rick said. "It's like a nervous twitch."

The governor shot them a glare and continued. "Please understand that I don't ask this for personal reasons, but simply because we need to determine the truth of the situation."

I looked at him. "You're wondering if somehow, to drive up our ratings, we smuggled evidence of terrorist activity through the checkpoints and managed to plant it while our own cameras were broadcasting over a live feed to an audience that can be conservatively estimated, judging by yesterday's ratings, as being somewhere in the millions."

"I wasn't intending to put it in quite those—"

I held up my hand to cut him off, turning to face Senator Ryman. "Senator, you know I'll ask this again when I'm permitted to film the exchange, but in the interests of killing this line of questioning here and now, I'm going to sacrifice spontaneity in favor of clarity. Have the lab results come back on the syringe?"

"Yes, Georgia, they have," said the senator, jaw set in a hard line.

"Can you tell us what those results were?"

"I don't see how that's relevant to the original question," said Tate.

"Senator?" I said.

"The contents of the syringe were determined to be a suspension of ninety-five percent live-state virus, common designation 'Kellis-Amberlee' or 'KA', isolated in iodized saline solution," the senator said. "We're waiting on additional information."

"Like the viral substrain?" I asked. "Right. Governor Tate, my crew and I were several hundred miles from the ranch at the time of the outbreak at the Ryman family home, and security records will support this. Further, with the exception of Mr. Cousins, we were all traveling with the campaign for months prior to the outbreak. Mr. Cousins was traveling with the convoy of Congresswoman Wagman, who should be able to vouch for his whereabouts. I'm not a virologist, but I'm fairly sure it takes special equipment to isolate the live virus without risking infection, and that said special equipment would not only be delicate, but would require special training to operate and maintain. Do you see where I'm going with this, Governor Tate, or should we draw you a diagram?"

"She's right," said Emily. Governor Tate looked toward her, eyes narrowing. She met his gaze and said, "I took virology courses at college; they're required for an animal husbandry degree. What Peter is describing is lab quality. You'd need a clean room and excellent biohazard protections just to isolate it, much less load it into any sort of a...a weapon. They just didn't have the resources. You'd need something a lot more secure than a pressure cooker in a hotel room to do something like this."

"Furthermore," I said, cutting Tate off before he could speak again, "even assuming we could somehow come up with the resources to do something like this, *and* had some sort of 'silent partner' we could get out to the ranch while we were occupied at the convention, we'd have to be *idiots* to turn around and be the ones who found the proof that the outbreak was man-made. So now that you've insulted our patriotism, our sanity, and our intelligence, how about we move on?"

Governor Tate leaned back in his seat, eyes narrowed. I kept my own eyes wide, playing off just how disturbing the unbroken, too-too-blue of my contacts is to most humans. He looked away first.

Satisfied, I turned toward Senator Ryman. "So now that we've had that little throwdown, what else did you feel needed to be handled behind a firewall?"

To his credit, he looked embarrassed as he said, "We were wondering, given the circumstances, if, well…if it might not be the best idea for the four of you to go home."

I gaped at him. Rick did the same. Buffy, who had been uncharacteristically silent through the entire exchange with Tate, continued staring at her hands.

In the end, it was Shaun who spoke, slamming his feet flat against the floor as he stood up and demanded, "Are you people *fucking insane*?!"

"Shaun—" said Senator Ryman, raising both hands in a placating gesture. "If you'd just be reasonable here—"

"Pardon me, *sir*, but you gave up your right to ask me to do that when you suggested we run out on the story," Shaun snapped, voice tight. Out of everyone in the room, I was the only one who understood how much that degree of self-control was costing him. Shaun's temper doesn't show itself often, but when it does, "duck and cover" is the best approach. "Don't you think we owe it to our viewers to finish what we started? We signed up for the long haul! We don't get to cut our losses and run as soon as things start getting a little bit uncomfortable!"

"My daughter *died*, Shaun!" said the senator. He was suddenly on his feet, leaving Emily abandoned and looking lost on the couch. "Do you understand that this is more than a story to us? Rebecca is *dead*! Telling the truth isn't going to bring her back to life!"

"Neither is telling a lie," said Rick, his tone so calm that it seemed almost out of place among the heated exchanges. We all turned to look at him. His head was up, his expression clear as he looked from Senator Ryman to Governor Tate. "Senator, believe me when I say I understand your pain more than you can know. And I understand that concern is making you listen to bad advice," he glanced toward the governor, who had the grace to redden and scowl, "that says we're civilians, and you should get us out of harm's way. But, sir, it's too late for that. This is news. If you send us away, you're just going to get other reporters sniffing around, looking for a story. Reporters who, if you'll allow me to beg your pardon, you can't control. Now, we have a working relationship, and you know we'll listen to you. Can you honestly expect that from anyone else who might be attracted to this scoop?"

"I think we should go," said Buffy. I turned to her, eyes going wide. Still looking at her hands, she continued. "We didn't sign up for this. Maybe Rick's right, and maybe other people will come, but who cares?" She glanced up through the fringe of her hair and licked her lips. "If they want to come and die, that's their problem. But I'm scared, and he's right. We shouldn't be here anymore. If we were ever supposed to be here at all."

"Buffy," said Shaun, sounding stung. "What are you talking about?"

"This is just a *story*, Shaun, and everywhere we've gone, horrible things have happened." She raised her head, expression miserable. "Those poor people in Eakly. The thing at the ranch. Senator Ryman, I think you're a wonderful man, but this is just a story, and we shouldn't be in it. We're going to get hurt."

"That's exactly why we have to stay," I said. My disappointment didn't show in my voice; I found that astonishing. I wanted to slap Buffy. I wanted to shake her and demand to know how she could be so blind to the importance of telling the truth after everything we'd been through together. Instead, I faced the room, and my voice stayed calm as I said, "Everything is 'just a story.' Tragedy, comedy, end of the world, whatever, it's just a story. What matters is making sure it's *heard*."

"That attitude, young lady, is why it's time for you to go," said Governor Tate. "We can't trust you to keep your mouth shut when *you* decide it's time for the story to be told. Your judgment isn't the yardstick here. National security is. And I don't think you fully understand the dangers you could place us in."

"Now, David—" said the senator.

"Nice stand for freedom there, Governor," I snapped.

"Can you *believe* this bullshit?" demanded Shaun.

"On the plus side, 'Faithful Reporters Fired from Campaign as Veil of Censorship Descends' has a nice ring to it," said Rick. "I figure that's a rating spike, right there."

"Ratings! All you concern yourself with—"

"Be quiet," said Emily.

"—is your precious by God ratings!" Governor Tate was getting into it now, his face flushing with religious fire. He'd found his latest opponents, now that Senator Ryman was off the menu. Us. "A little girl dies, a family is shattered, a man's run to the presidency may not recover, and what do you care about? Your damn *ratings*! Well, you can take those ratings, and—"

We never found out what we could do with our ratings. The sound of Emily's palm striking Governor Tate's cheek rang through the room like a branch breaking; the only thing that could have been louder was the silence that came after it. Governor Tate raised his hand to his cheek, staring at her like he couldn't believe what he was seeing. I couldn't blame him. I couldn't believe what I was seeing either, and I wasn't the one who'd been slapped.

"Emily, what—" began Senator Ryman. She raised her hand for silence, and then slowly, deliberately, removed her sunglasses, eyes on Governor Tate the whole time. The unforgiving light flooding the room had caused her pupils to expand until her irises were entirely gone, drowning in blackness. I winced. I knew how much that had to be hurting her, but she didn't flinch. She kept staring at Tate.

"For the sake of my husband's political career, I will be pleasant to you; I will smile at you at public functions, and I will, whenever a camera or member of the undiscriminating press is present, endeavor to treat you as if you were a human being," she said, in a calm, almost reasonable tone. "But understand this: If you *ever* speak to these people in that sort of manner in my presence again? If you *ever* behave as if they have no judgment, no compassion, and no common sense? I'll make you wish you'd never joined this ticket. And if I come to believe that your attitude is in any way changing my husband—not damaging his oh-so-precious career, but changing who he is *as a man*—I will repudiate you, and I will *end* you. Do we have an understanding, Governor?"

"Yes, ma'am," said Governor Tate, sounding about as stunned as I felt. A glance to Shaun showed that he was probably feeling much the same. "I think you've made yourself clear."

"Good." Emily turned toward us. "Shaun, Georgia, Buffy, Rick, I hope you won't let this unpleasant little scene sour you against my husband's campaign. I speak for both of us when I say that I very much hope you'll continue doing exactly what you've been doing for us."

"We signed on for the good and the bad alike, Mrs. Ryman," said Rick. "I don't believe any of us are planning on going anywhere."

Looking at Buffy, I wasn't sure. "He's right, Emily," I said. "We're staying. Assuming, of course, the senator wants us to…?" I looked his way, and waited.

Senator Ryman looked uncertain. Then, slowly, he nodded and rose, moving to put his arm around his wife's shoulders. "David, I'm afraid I'm going to have to vote with Emily on this one. I very much want them all to stay."

"Well, Senator," I said, "I think our partnership is still good."

"Good," he replied. Reaching out, he took my hand and shook it.

————————

The trouble with the news is simple: People, especially ones on the ends of the power spectrum, like it when you're afraid. The people who have the power want you scared. They want you walking around paralyzed by the notion that you could die at any moment. There's always something to be afraid of. It used to be terrorists. Now it's zombies.

What does this have to do with the news? This: The truth isn't scary. Not when you understand it, not when you understand the repercussions of it, and not when you aren't worried that something's being kept from you. The truth is only scary when you think part of it might be missing. And those people? They like it when you're scared. So they do their best to sit on the truth, to sensationalize the truth, to filter the truth in ways that make it something you can be afraid of.

If we didn't have to fear the truths we didn't hear, we'd lose the need to fear the ones we did. People should consider that.

—From *Images May Disturb You*,
the blog of Georgia Mason, April 2, 2040

Seventeen

We spent three weeks in Parrish before it was time for the campaign to get back on the road. The voters would forgive the senator taking time to mourn for his daughter, but unless he got out there and made sure people remembered him as more than the victim of a senseless tragedy, he'd never make up the ground he was already losing. Voters are a fickle bunch, and Rebecca Ryman's heroic death was already yesterday's news. Instead, the news was buzzing with Governor Blackburn's exciting plans for heath-care reform, her suggestions for increasing school security, and her proposed alterations to the animal husbandry and care laws. In some ways, her campaign was using Rebecca as much as the senator's was, because when she said "tougher restrictions on keeping large animals," it was Rebecca's face people saw. The senator needed to get rolling or there wouldn't be anywhere for him to roll to.

Unfortunately, our swift departure from Oklahoma City left the convoy of RVs and equipment trucks we'd been depending on to get us across the country several states behind us. This became an issue as we were preparing to set out from Wisconsin, especially since our newly tightened schedule didn't leave time to go back and get them. How were we supposed to get ourselves, the senator, his staff, the security detail, and the equipment—some of which was new to the campaign, having joined us with Governor Tate—to our destination when we didn't have a means of protected travel?

The answer was simple: We weren't. Instead, the senator, his wife, the governor, their respective campaign managers, and the bulk of the staff flew ahead to our next stop in Houston, Texas, where they could meet up with the convoy and really get things started. The rest of us were left with the exciting task of getting ourselves and the equipment that *hadn't* been abandoned in Oklahoma to Texas via the overland express. There was no train from Parrish to Houston large enough to haul the additional equipment, but that worked out since Shaun and I were unwilling to abandon our vehicles. One way or another, we were driving it.

We initially planned to make the drive alone: just the After the End Times crew, reconnecting with one another through the time-honored ritual of the road trip. This plan got shouted down on all fronts, starting with Senator Ryman and moving down the chain to Steve. The argument that we'd travel faster without a bunch of extra bodies didn't hold water where they were concerned, but we managed to find a compromise after three days of shouting. We'd take a security team. We were exhausted enough after that fight to give in on the matter of Chuck, who needed to monitor the transportation of some of the more sensitive equipment. Besides, his presence might keep Buffy a little calmer, and we needed all the help we could get in that regard.

The tension between Buffy and the rest of us had been getting worse since our meeting with the Rymans and Governor Tate. None of us had expected her to endorse the idea that we should walk away. It was a betrayal of everything we worked for, and it came out of nowhere. Rick took it hardest. As far as I knew, he hadn't spoken to Buffy since we got back to the hotel. Buffy looked at him sorrowfully, like a dog that knew it had done something wrong, and went back to the task of getting our equipment ready for the road. By the time we were ready to roll, I think she'd rebuilt every piece of camera equipment we owned at least twice, in addition to upgrading our computers and replacing the memory chips in my PDA.

Shaun and I didn't have anything that practical to concern ourselves with. I managed to stay distracted by conducting remote interviews with every politician I could get my hands on, working with Mahir to update our merchandising, and cleaning up the message boards. Shaun lacked those outlets. The government had banned him from going back to the ranch during the investigation, and Parrish was otherwise short of things for him to poke at. He was restless, unhappy, and making me insane. Shaun doesn't handle idleness well. Make him sit still too long, and he winds up silent, sullen, and, above all, touchy as hell.

Shaun's crankiness, combined with everything else, was the reason for our caravan traveling arrangements. Rick was in his little blue armadillo with the barn cat, which he'd named "Lois" after it received a clean bill of health from the Ryman family veterinarian. Shaun was in our van, blasting heavy metal and brooding, while Buffy was riding with Chuck in the equipment truck at the rear of the convoy.

My own place in the driving order was a little less predictable since I was on my bike and unconstrained by the shape of the road. I kept my cameras running the whole time, privately hoping I'd find a shambler for Shaun to amuse himself with. That was all he'd need to bring his spirits up. We'd been driving for two days, with another two still ahead of us, and the silence was starting to wear on me.

My helmet speaker crackled. "On," I said to activate the connection, following it with, "Georgia here."

"It's Rick. What do you think about dinner?"

"The sun went down an hour ago, and dinner is traditionally the evening meal, so I think dinner is logically our next stop. What are we looking at?"

"GPS says there's a truck stop about two hours up the road that has a pretty decent diner."

"Any record on their screening protocols?" We'd run into multiple truck stops where the security agents wouldn't let us eat because their blood tests weren't good enough to guarantee we wouldn't have to worry about an outbreak between the coffee and the pie. I'd been driving all day. If we stopped, I wanted it to be for more than fifteen minutes and an argument.

"They're government certified. All their licenses up to date, all their inspection scores posted."

"Sounds good to me. I'll see if I can rouse Shaun and let him know what the plan is. You call Steve and the guys, give them the address, and tell them we'll meet there."

"Deal."

"Coffee's on me. Georgia out."

"Rick out."

"Great." I followed it with, "Disconnect and redial Shaun Mason." The speaker beeped acknowledgment, and began to ring as it signaled my brother.

He never picked up the call. He didn't have the time.

I didn't hear the gunshots until I went back to review the tapes and turned the low-level frequencies up enough to undo the work of the silencers. Eight shots were fired. The first two trucks, the ones containing the campaign guards and lower-level personnel, passed by unmolested. They were rolling ahead of the rest of the crew and passed out of the shallow valley without incident. The gun didn't start going off until Rick's car pulled into the ideal position, halfway between the valley's entrance and its exit.

Two shots were fired at Rick's little blue armadillo, two more were fired at the van, and the two after that were fired at my bike. The last two shots were fired at the equipment truck at the back of the caravan, the one Chuck was driving, with Buffy riding shotgun. The shots were very methodical, one following the other as fast as the skill of the shooter would allow. I'd have been impressed if they hadn't been aimed so effectively at me and mine.

The first shot fired at my bike punched a hole in my front tire, sending me weaving out of control. I screamed and swore, fighting with the handlebars as I tried to steady my trajectory enough to keep me from becoming a stain on the side of the road. Even with my body armor, falling wrong would kill me. I was focusing so hard on not toppling over that my driving became impossible to predict, and the second shot went wide. Maybe that's why I was able to believe I'd blown a tire as I let momentum carry me off the edge of the road, rolling onto the uneven ground beyond the shoulder.

I finished steadying myself, dumped speed, and wrenched the bike to a stop twenty yards after I left the road. Panting, I kicked the stand down and unsealed my helmet before turning to stare at the carnage that had overwhelmed the road.

Rick's car was still at the front of the pack, but now it was lying stranded on its back, wheels spinning in the air. The tires on the right-hand side were nothing but shredded rubber stretched over bent steel. The equipment truck was on its side fifty or so yards behind him, smoke oozing from its shattered cabin.

There was no sign of the van.

Suddenly frantic, I fumbled my ear cuff from my pocket and shoved it onto my ear with enough force to leave a bruise that I wouldn't feel until later. "Shaun? Shaun? Pick up your goddamn *phone*, Shaun!"

"Georgia?" The connection was poor enough that his voice crackled in and out, but the relief was unmistakable; it would have been unmistakable even if the connection had been worse. He never called me by my full name unless he was angry, scared, or both. "Georgia, are you okay? Where are you?"

"Twenty yards off the road on the left-hand side, near some big rocks. I'm between the car and the equipment truck. There's smoke, Shaun, has anyone else tried to—"

"Don't make any more calls. I don't know if they can trace them. You stay *right there*, Georgia. Don't you fucking *dare* move!" The connection cut with a sharp, final click. In the distance, I heard tires squealing against the road.

Shaun had sounded panicked. Rick and Buffy were out of communication, the truck was on fire, my bike was down, and Shaun was panicking. That could only mean one thing: It was time to take cover.

Slamming my helmet back over my head, I ducked behind my bike and started surveying the surrounding hills. Short of a rocket launcher, there wasn't much that stood a viable chance of killing me in my body armor. Hurting me, yes, but killing me, not really.

There was nothing. No lights, no signs of motion; nothing.

"—ia? Come in, Georgia?"

"Rick?" I nodded to the right, confirming the connection. "Rick, is that you? Are you okay? Are you hurt?"

"I'm fine. Air bag stopped me from hitting the roof." He coughed. "Chest's a little banged up, and Lois is pissed as hell, but otherwise, we're okay. You?"

"Didn't dump the bike. I'm fine. Any word from Buffy?"

There was a pause. Finally, he said, "No. I was hoping she'd called you."

"Did you try to call her?"

"No word."

"Damn. Rick, what *happened*?"

"You mean you don't *know*?" He sounded genuinely surprised. "Georgia, somebody shot out my damn tires."

"Shot? What do you *mean*, sh—" Shaun came blasting around the curve of the road and off the pavement, moving so fast that our hydraulically balanced and weighted van nearly rocked onto two tires. "Shaun's here. We'll be right there to get you. Georgia out."

"Clear." The connection clicked off.

I pulled my helmet back off and climbed to my feet, waving my hands in the air. Shaun spotted the motion and turned the van toward my location, screeching to a stop beside me. The doors unlocked, and Shaun was throwing himself out of the driver's-side door, his heels slipping on the gravel-covered ground as he ran over to throw his arms around me. I let him crush me against his chest, taking a deep breath.

"You okay?" he asked, not letting go.

"You didn't get a blood test before coming over here."

"Don't need one. If you were infected, I'd know," Shaun said, and let me go. "I repeat, you okay?"

"I'm okay." I climbed in the open van door, sliding over to settle in the passenger seat. Shaun got in behind me. "You okay?"

"Better now," Shaun said, turning the engine back on and slamming his foot down on the gas. The van leapt forward into a wide curve, rocketing toward Rick's car. "You hear the shots?"

"Bike was too loud. How many?"

"Eight. Two for each of us." He glanced at me. For a brief moment, I saw the raw worry in his eyes. "If they'd nailed both your tires..."

"I'd be dead." I leaned forward to open the glove compartment and pull out the .45 I keep there. Suddenly, being outside without a gun in my hand didn't seem like a good idea. "If whoever did this had done their damn homework, you'd be dead, too, so let's not dwell. Word from Buffy?"

"None."

"Great." I pulled back the slide, checking the chamber. Satisfied by my bullet count, I let the slide rack back into place. "So, is this enough excitement for you?"

"Maybe a bit much," he said. For once in his life, he sounded like he meant it.

It was true, though. If our attackers had done their homework, Shaun wouldn't have been driving; he'd have been dying. Normal tires blow when they take a bullet. Even armor plating won't prevent that. But some vehicles are too damn valuable to lose just because you lose a tire, and most vehicles in that class are the sort likely to draw heavy gunfire. So scientists developed a type of tire that doesn't give a damn about gunshots. They're called run flats: You put a bullet in them, and they keep on rolling. I might have skipped them—I did skip them on my bike, where they made the ride unbearably choppy—but Shaun insisted. He bought a new set every year.

For the first time since we got the van, it didn't seem like a waste of money.

Shaun focused on driving, and I focused on trying to page Buffy and Chuck, using every band and communications device we had. We knew communications weren't being jammed; at least some of my messages should have made it through. There were no replies on any channel. I'd been terrified. That's when I started to get numb.

Shaun pulled up next to Rick's car. "Think there's still a shooter out there?"

"Doubtful." I slid the gun into my pocket. "This was a targeted operation. They only took out *our* cars. If they'd been sticking around to make sure they killed us, you'd have kept taking bullets. And I made a damn good target when I first stopped my bike."

"Hope you're right," said Shaun, and opened his door.

Rick watched our approach through the car window, waving his arms to show that he was still alive. He was half-pinned by the air bag and blood was dripping into his hair from a small cut on his forehead, but other than that he looked fine. Lois and her carrier were strapped into the seat next to his. I didn't want to be the one to let that cat out of the box.

I knocked on the glass, calling, "Rick? Can you open the door?" Despite the urgency of the situation, I couldn't help but be impressed by the structural integrity of his little car. It had to have rolled at least once before coming to a stop on its roof, and yet it wasn't showing any dents: just scratches and a crack in the passenger-side window. The folks at VW really knew what they were doing.

"I think so!" he called back. "Can you get me out?"

Mirthlessly, I echoed, "I think so!"

"Not the most encouraging answer," he said, and twisted in the seat, movements constrained by seat belt and air bag, until he could kick the door. On his second kick, I grabbed the handle and pulled. I didn't have to pull that hard; despite the car's inverted position and the beating it had taken, the door swung open easily, leaving Rick's foot dangling in the air. He pulled it back into the car, saying, "Now what?"

"Now I get your belt, and you get ready to fall." I leaned into the car.

"Hurry up, George," said Shaun. "I don't like this."

"No one does," I said, and unsnapped Rick's belt. Gravity took over from there, sending Rick thumping against the roof of the car.

"Thanks," he said, reaching over to unhook Lois's carrier before climbing out. The cat hissed and snarled inside the box, expressing her displeasure. Straightening, Rick eyed his car. "How are we supposed to flip that back over?"

"Triple A is our friend," I said. "Get in the van. We need to check on Buffy."

Paling, Rick nodded and climbed in. Shaun and I were only a few feet behind him. I noted without surprise that Shaun had his own pistol— substantially larger than my emergencies-only .45—with specially modified ammo that did enough damage to human or posthuman tissue that it was illegal without a disturbing number of licenses, all of which Shaun obtained before he turned sixteen—out and at the ready. He wasn't buying my glib assurances of our safety. That was fine. Neither was I.

Shaun took my assumption of the driver's seat with just as little surprise and didn't bother fastening his belt as I slammed the gas pedal down, sending the van racing across the hard-packed ground between us and the still-smoking equipment truck. The truck wasn't likely to burst into flames; that only happens in the movies, which is almost a pity, given the number of zombies that arise from automotive accidents every year. Buffy and Chuck could die from smoke inhalation if we dawdled...assuming they weren't dead already.

Rick braced himself against the seat. "Has there been any word from Buffy?"

"Not since the truck went down," Shaun said.

"Why the hell didn't you go for her first?"

"Simple," I said, steering around a chunk of rubber torn from the truck's tires. "We knew you were alive, and we might need the backup."

Rick didn't say anything after that until we pulled up alongside the equipment truck. Shaun reached between the seats and pulled out a double-barreled shotgun which he passed to Rick. "What am I supposed to do with this?" Rick demanded.

"You see anything moving that isn't us, Chuck, or Buffy, you shoot," Shaun said. "Don't bother checking to see if it's dead. It'll be dead after you hit it."

"And if I hit emergency personnel?"

"We're stranded, and we've been the victims of a malicious attack in possible zombie territory," I said, stopping the engine and opening my door. "Cite *Johnston's*, and you'll get a medal instead of a manslaughter conviction." Manuel Johnston was a truck driver with several DUIs on his record, but when he gunned down a dozen zombies in highway patrolmen's uniforms outside Birmingham, Alabama, he became a national hero. Since Johnston, it's been legal to shoot people for no crime more defined than existing in rural hazard zones. We usually curse his name, since the precedent he set has gotten a lot of good journalists killed. Under the circumstances, he was a savior. "Shaun and I have the truck. You've got point."

"Got it," said Rick, grimly, and climbed out the van's side door as Shaun and I got out and moved toward the still-smoking truck.

It was obvious that the equipment truck had taken the worst of the beatings. Lacking the maneuverability of my bike, the armor of Rick's car, or the paranoia-fueled unstoppability of our van, it had taken two bullets to the front left tire and completely lost control. The cabin was half-smashed when the truck went over. The smoke had thinned without clearing, and that lowered visibility as we started toward the cab.

"Buffy?" I called. "Buffy, are you there?"

A piercing scream was the only answer, followed by a pause, a second scream, and silence. Zombies can scream. They just generally don't.

"Buffy? Answer me!" I ran the rest of the way to the truck and grabbed the handle of the nearer door, wrenching it as hard as I could. I barely noticed removing a layer of skin from my palms in the process. It didn't matter; the door was mashed in when the truck fell, and it wasn't budging. I tried again, yanking even harder, and felt it shudder on its hinges. "Shaun! Help me over here!"

"George, we have to make sure we're covering the area in case of—"

"Rick can do the goddamn covering! Help me while there's still a chance that she's alive!"

Shaun lowered his pistol, cramming it into the waistband of his pants and moving to put his hands over mine. Together, we counted, "One, two, *three*," and yanked. My shoulders strained until it felt like I would dislocate something. The door groaned and swung open, creaking along the groove of the broken frame. Buffy tumbled out onto the glass-sprinkled pavement, coughing hard.

That cough was reassuring. Zombies breathe, but they don't cough; the tissue of their throats is already so irritated by infection that they ignore little things like smoke inhalation and caustic chemical burns, right up until they render the body unable to function.

"Buffy!" I dropped to my knees next to her, feeling glass crunch through the reinforced denim of my jeans; I'd have to check for slivers before I put them on again. I put my hand against her back, trying to reassure her. "Honey, it's okay, you're okay. Just breathe, sweetheart, and we'll get you away from here. Come on, honey, breathe."

"Georgia..."

Shaun's voice was strained enough that he sounded almost sick. I looked up, my hand still flat against Buffy's back. "What—"

Shaun gestured for silence, attention fixed on the interior of the truck's cab. His right hand was moving with glacial slowness to the gun shoved into the belt of his jeans. Whatever he was looking at was outside my range of vision, and so I stood, leaving Buffy coughing on the ground as I reached up to remove my sunglasses. The smoke wouldn't irritate my eyes more than they already were, and I'd see better without them.

At first there seemed to be nothing but motion inside the cab of the truck. It was slow and irregular, like someone trying to swim through hardening cement. Then my pupils dilated that extra quarter-centimeter, my virus-enhanced vision compensating for the sudden change in light levels, and I realized what I was looking at.

"Oh," I said, softly. "Crap."

"Yeah," Shaun agreed. "Crap."

Buffy fell out of the cab when we opened the door; Buffy hadn't been wearing her seat belt. Buffy never wore her seat belt. She liked to ride cross-legged in her seat, and seat belts prevented that. Chuck, on the other hand, was a law-abiding citizen who obeyed traffic regulations. He fastened his seat belt every time he got into a moving vehicle. He'd fastened it before the convoy pulled out that morning. He was still wearing it now that he was too far gone to remember how to work the clasp, or even what a clasp was. His hands moved against the air in useless clawing motions as his mouth chomped mindlessly, stimulated by the presence of fresh meat.

There was blood around his mouth. Blood around his mouth, and blood on the seat belt, and blood on the seat where Buffy had been sitting.

"Cause of death?" I asked, as analytically as I could.

"Impact trauma," said Shaun. The creature that had been Chuck hissed at him, opening its mouth and beginning to moan. Unconcerned, Shaun raised his pistol and fired. The bullet hit the zombie square between the eyes, and it stopped trying to reach us, going limp as the message of its second, final death was transmitted throughout the body. Continuing as if he'd never paused, Shaun said, "It must have been instantaneous. Chuck was a small guy. Amplification would have been over in minutes."

"Source of the blood?"

Shaun looked toward me, and then back to Buffy, who was still down on her knees in the broken glass, hugging herself and coughing. "He didn't have time to bleed."

I stayed where I was for a seemingly endless moment, staring into the cab of the truck. Chuck remained slumped and unmoving. I wanted to find something, anything, I could use to explain the blood away. A scalp wound, maybe, or a nosebleed that started when he hit his head and didn't stop until he reanimated. There was nothing. Just one small, sad body, and bloodstains on the passenger seat that didn't match to any visible wounds.

I turned to Buffy, numbly unsurprised to see that Shaun had his pistol out. My feet crunched on the glass as I walked over to her. "Buffy? Can you hear me?"

"I'm dead, not deaf," she said, and lifted her head. Tears had left clean trails through the soot staining her cheeks. "I hear you just fine. Hi, Georgia. Is everyone all right? Is... is Chuck...?"

"Chuck's resting now," I said, crouching down. "Shaun, radio Rick. Tell him to come back here, and to bring a field kit."

"George—"

"*Do it.*" I kept my eyes on Buffy and felt, rather than saw, Shaun's angry stare. I was too close to her. Her body weight was too low, and I was too close; if she was undergoing amplification, I might not be able to move back fast enough. And I didn't care. "Buffy, are you hurt at all? There's some blood we can't identify. I need you to show me if you're hurt."

Buffy smiled. It was a small, utterly resigned expression, one that turned wry as she rolled up her right sleeve and turned her arm toward me, showing the place where a chunk had been bitten out of her forearm. Bone showed through the red. "You mean like this? I must've hit my head on the roof when the truck rolled, because I woke up when Chuck bit me."

The bleeding was already starting to slow. Rapid coagulation of blood; one of the first, classic signs of the Kellis-Amberlee virus going into amplification. I swallowed, saying in a soft, sickened tone, "That would probably account for it."

"I heard the gunshot, you know. If Chuck's 'resting,' it's the sort of rest you don't get better from." Buffy rolled her sleeve primly back down. "You should shoot me now. Take care of things while they can still be tidy."

"Rick's on his way with the field kit," said Shaun, stepping up next to me. He had his gun trained on Buffy the whole way. "She's right, you know."

"He'd just turned when he bit her. There's a chance his saliva hadn't gone live yet," I said, glancing at him over my shoulder. I was lying, to no one more than to myself, but he'd let me. Just for a few minutes, he'd let me. "We wait for the test."

"I was never any good at tests," said Buffy. She shifted on the ground, pulling her knees up against her chest in an unconsciously childlike gesture. "I always failed them in school. Hi, Shaun. Sorry about this."

"Not your fault," he said. His tone was gruff; anyone who didn't know him as well as I do might not have realized how upset he was. "You're taking this pretty well. Considering, y'know. The circumstances."

"Not much we can do about it now, is there?" Her tone was light, but her eyes were beginning to brim with tears. One escaped, running down the channel already cleaned by its peers. "I'm not happy about this. But I'm not going to take it out on you. I have faith that God will reward me for my forbearance."

"I hope you're right," I said, softly. The Catholic church declared all victims of zombie attack martyrs fifteen years ago, to deal with the messy little issue of last rites; it's hard to conduct them when death is fast, unexpected, and filled with teeth.

"I've got the kit!" shouted Rick, jogging up to the three of us. He had the shotgun tucked underneath his arm and a standard blood testing kit in his left hand. He came to a stop as he spotted Buffy, paling. "Please, please, tell me this isn't for you, Buffy."

"Sorry," she said and held up her hands. "Toss it here."

Eyes gone wide in his bloodless face, he tossed her the kit. She caught it with ease, sliding her right hand, the one nearest the bite, into the kit's opening. Then she closed her eyes, not watching the lights as they cycled green to red, green to red.

"You need to read my notes," she said, in a voice so tightly controlled as to be a model of reasonableness and calm. "They're stored on the server under my private directory. Log-in ID is the one I use for my poetry uploads, password is 'February dash four dash twenty-nine,' capital 'F' in 'February.' I don't have time to explain everything, so just read them."

February 4, 2029, was the day the United States government finally acknowledged that Alaska was too well-suited to the undead and would never be able to come below a Level 2 hazard zone. As that made it illegal for anyone without a very special and difficult to obtain license to even *enter* Alaska, much less live there, that was the day they began evacuating the last of the state's residents. Including Buffy's family. Like a lot of the displaced, they never got over losing Alaska.

"You're going to be fine," I said, watching the lights. They were still cycling, still measuring the viral payload of her blood, but the cycle was becoming irregular, hanging on red for six seconds before flashing back to green. The test results were being confirmed, and they were not in Buffy's favor.

"You're too attached to the truth, Georgia," she said. Her voice was serene, at peace with itself. "It makes you a crappy liar." The tears were falling faster now. "I swear I had no idea they were going to do those things. No idea at all. If I'd known, I would never have agreed to it. You have to believe me, I wouldn't have."

The lights had settled on a steady red, as damning as any doctor's report. The viral load Buffy picked up from Chuck's saliva might have been small, but it had been enough. That wasn't the only thing making me go cold. I stood, stepping back next to Shaun, and pulled the gun from my belt. "You wouldn't have agreed to what?"

"They said the country was drifting away from God. They said that we were losing sight of His desires for the nation, and that was why things are the way they are now. And I believed them."

"They who, Buffy?"

"They didn't give me a name. They just said they could make sure things went the way they needed to go. The way they *had* to go for this country to be great again. All I had to do was let them access our databases and follow the Ryman campaign."

Voice gone suddenly hard, Rick said, "When did you figure out what they were using that information to do, Buffy? Before or after Eakly?"

"After!" she said, opening her eyes and turning a plaintive look his way. "After, I *swear* it was after. It wasn't until the ranch that I realized...I realized..."

My hand shook, sending my aim wavering as I realized what she was saying and what it meant. "Oh, my God. With access to our databases, they'd known exactly where the senator was going to be, what sort of security he'd have, what times we had booked for any given location—"

"It gets worse," said Shaun. His own voice was flat. "She had our databases cued to the senator's databases. Didn't you, Buffy?"

"It seemed practical at the time, and Chuck said it wouldn't hurt anything as long as we stayed out of the more sensitive areas. It made things easier..."

"Lots of things," I said. "Like knowing when the ranch would be most vulnerable. You cut them off, didn't you? Told them you wouldn't be giving them anything else."

"How did you know?" She closed her eyes again, shuddering.

"Because they'd have no other reason to try to kill us all." I glanced toward Rick and Shaun. "We stopped being useful. So Buffy's 'friends' tried to take us out."

"My notes," said Buffy, with an air of desperation in her tone. Her tears were stopping. Another classic sign. The virus doesn't like to give moisture away. "You have to read my notes. They'll tell you everything I knew. I didn't know their names, but there are time stamps, there are IPs, you can try to...try to..."

"How could you do this, Buffy?" demanded Shaun. "How could you possibly have done this? To the senator? To *us*? People have *died*, for God's sake!"

"And I'm one of them. It's time to shoot me. Please."

"Buffy—"

"That's not my name," she said, and opened her eyes. Her pupils had dilated until they were as large as mine. She turned those unnaturally dark eyes toward me, shaking her head. "I don't remember my name. But that isn't it."

Shaun started to swing his pistol into place. I raised my hand, stopping him. "I hired her," I said, quietly. "It's my job to fire her."

I stepped forward, putting my left hand over my right to steady my grip on the gun. Buffy continued looking up at me, her expression calm. "I'm sorry," I said.

"It's not your fault," she replied.

"Your name is Georgette Marie Meissonier," I said, and pulled the trigger.

She fell without another sound. Shaun put his arms around my shoulders, and we stood there, frozen in the night.

Nothing would ever be the same.

BOOK IV

Postcards from the Wall

Alive or dead, the truth won't rest. My name is Georgia Mason, and I am begging you: Rise up while you can.

— GEORGIA MASON

If you asked me now "Was it worth it? Were the things you got, the things you wanted?" I'd tell you "no," because there isn't any other answer. So I guess it's a good thing that nobody's ever going to ask. They never ask the things that really matter.

— SHAUN MASON

It is the unfortunate duty of the management of After the End Times to announce that the maintainer of this blog, Georgette Marie "Buffy" Meissonier, passed away this past Saturday night, April 17, 2040, at approximately eight-fifteen P.M. Buffy was involved in an automotive accident that led, tragically, to her being bitten by her boyfriend, Charles Wong, who had died and reawakened only a few moments previously.

Please do not mistake the professional tone of this memo for a lack of compassion or mourning on the part of the staff here at After the End Times. Rather, take it for what it is, a sign of our respect and dismay over her sudden loss.

Buffy's family has been notified, and her entry has been transmitted to the Wall. Her blog and its archives will be maintained in her honor for the lifetime of this site.

Buffy, you will be missed.

—A message from Georgia Mason,
originally published in *By the Sounding Sea,*
the blog of Buffy Meissonier, April 18, 2040

Eighteen

My aim has never been as good as Shaun's, but it didn't matter at close range: Head shots get a lot easier when there's no real distance between you and your target. Even so, I kept my gun raised for several minutes, as much waiting to feel something as waiting for her to move. She was part of my team, part of our inner circle, and she was gone. Shouldn't I have felt *something*? But there was nothing beyond a vague sense of loss and a much stronger sense of onrushing dread.

The sound of Rick retching snapped me out of my fugue. I leaned back against Shaun's arm, sliding my sunglasses back on and feeling their familiar weight settle against my face before I lowered my gun and turned toward the other surviving member of our team. "Rick, what's your status?" He made more retching noises. I nodded. "About what I figured. Shaun, head for the van and get three more field kits."

"And you'll be doing what, exactly, as I leave you alone in the middle of nowhere with the dead things and Captain Vomit?"

I unzipped the pocket of my jacket and pulled out my PDA, holding it up. "I'll be standing here, keeping an eye on Captain Vomit and calling for help. We'll need to provide clean test results before they'll approach us with anything more useful than bullets. We're going to need a full biohazard squad out here; we have two corpses, we have a contaminated truck, we have Buffy's blood on the ground—"

Shaun froze, going white as he looked from the slivers of glass embedded in the knees of my jeans to my hands, which were red and raw from where the door handle had stripped the skin from my palms. "And we need clean test results," he said, in a voice that bordered on numb.

"Exactly," I said. He looked scared. I distantly wished I could find it in me to be scared, but I couldn't. It wasn't making it past that damned numbness. "Go."

"Going," he said, and wheeled, breaking into a run as he headed for the van.

Rick was still on his hands and knees making soft retching sounds, but the actual vomiting had stopped. I moved to stand beside him, attempting to comfort with my presence as I tapped in an emergency channel call on my PDA. Opening a broad emergency channel while standing near a state highway would broadcast my message to every police scanner, hospital hazmat department, and federal agency within the receiving range. If there was help to be had, we'd have it.

"This is Georgia Carolyn Mason, license number AFB dash one-seven-five-eight-nine-three, currently located between mile markers seventy-seven and seventy-eight on southbound Interstate 55 with a hazard zone upgrade for the vicinity and a priority-A distress call. Status is stable, awaiting test results on surviving party members. Request acknowledgment."

The reply was immediate. "This is the Memphis CDC. A biohazard team is being dispatched to your location. Please explain your presence in the hazard zone."

It isn't technically illegal to drive the federally maintained highways—people still have to get from place to place—but it's unusual unless you're a trucker, and even they have to file routes stating exactly where they expect to be at each step along the way. Caravans are held to many of the same restrictions. When the rulings first went into effect, some people complained that the government was limiting personal freedom, but they quieted when it was pointed out, rather harshly, that this wasn't as much a matter of tracking the movements of individuals as it was a matter of charting the mobility of potential outbreaks. Most people shut up as soon as "we just want to know where the zombies are going to be" came into the equation.

"Route registry forty-seven dash A, designation Ryman/Tate equipment caravan, registered drivers present at the scene are Georgia Carolyn Mason, Class M license; Shaun Phillip Mason, Class A license; Richard Cousins, Class C license; Charles Li Wong, Class A license. Registered passengers Georgette Marie Meissonier, Class C license. Purpose of trip registered as movement of heavy equipment from Parrish, Wisconsin, to Houston, Texas. Registered duration, four days, allowing for reasonable rest stops and sleeping periods for the available drivers. Two of our trucks are still on the road; I'm not sure of their status. If you give me your network key, I can transmit our precise route."

The man's tone was gentler when he spoke again; my information had been fed into his computer and was checking out clean. "That won't be necessary, Ms. Mason. Why are y'all calling for a hazard team?"

"Someone shot out the tires on three of our vehicles. We're down a car, with possible injuries to the driver. The rear equipment truck flipped. The driver, Charles Wong, was killed in the impact and reanimated before we were able to reach the vehicle. He infected his passenger, Georgette Meissonier. Her test results are recorded in a standard field test unit, manufacturer Sony, model number V dash fifteen dash eleven dash A, and were registered via wireless upload with the CDC mainframe at the time of confirmation. Due to the possibility of inaccurate positive with that model number, we did not take immediate action but maintained a safe distance until Ms. Meissonier began to experience pupil dilation and memory loss. Once her infection was confirmed, she was put down honorably." There was the grief and outrage, at last, beginning to chip away at the edges of my numbness. "We have hot blood in the cab of the truck and on the ground outside the truck, as well as two hot corpses in need of removal and disposal."

"The team will not approach until preliminary test results for the surviving members of your party have been uploaded, and they will not offer direct physical assistance until you've been tested again on the CDC field units they provide," the man cautioned, some of the warmth leeching from his tone. Two bodies and a lot of hot blood on the road outside Memphis could spell an outbreak much larger than our little team. We both knew it. Now we had to contain it.

"Understood." My PDA started beeping, signaling an incoming call. "Sir, may I ask, what is your name?"

"Joseph Wynne, Ms. Mason. Stand tight; our team will be there soon."

"Thank you, Joe," I said.

"God be with you," he said. The line clicked off.

Shifting my PDA to my other hand, I pressed the Receive button. "Georgia." Shaun was running toward me, the field kits clutched against his chest. I raised my free hand, and he lobbed one at me. It was more than a simple game of catch; there are a hundred small tests and checks for infection that don't depend on medical science. If he could throw, and I could catch, the odds were better that we were both clean. I saw him relax when I caught the kit, even though he didn't slow down.

Senator Ryman's voice came through the receiver, made sharp and tight by panic: "Georgia, what's this I'm getting on the scanner about an accident? Is everyone all right out there?"

"Senator." I nodded to Shaun. He put Rick's testing kit down next to him, and the two of us popped the lids off our respective kits in comforting unison. Routine is the most reassuring thing there is. "I'm afraid I have to answer in the negative, sir, but the CDC is dispatching a biohazard team to our location. Once we have an all-clear, we're going to need a fresh truck and a team to move the equipment." I hesitated before adding, "We're also going to need a new driver. Rick doesn't have his Class A license, and I don't want to leave my bike behind."

There was a long pause, during which I tucked my PDA between my shoulder and my ear, freeing my hand, and mouthed a silent "one, two" at Shaun. On two, we both rammed our forefingers down on the unit the other held. The prick of the needle puncturing my thumb made me wince, nearly dislodging the PDA.

Finally, while the lights were blinking red to green and back again, the senator said, "Georgia... is Chuck...?"

I closed my eyes, blocking those ever-hateful lights, and said, "I'm sorry, Senator."

He paused again. "Georgia..."

"Yes, Senator?"

"Buffy. Wasn't she..."

"I'm afraid that when the truck rolled, we were unable to save either of the occupants."

"Oh, Christ, Georgia, I'm sorry."

"So am I, sir; so am I. Can you arrange for another truck and driver to be sent to our location, and alert the rest of the convoy that we're being unavoidably delayed? We're just outside Memphis. You should be able to pull us up on the team GPS."

"I'll have someone on the way inside the next ten minutes." The third pause was longer than the other two, and when he spoke again, he sounded more exhausted than I'd ever heard him, even after we received the news of Rebecca's death. "Georgia, have the rest of you... have you..."

"The tests are running now. If anything changes, we'll call you."

"Thank you. I suppose I should let you get to it."

"That would be best."

"God save you, Georgia Mason," he said, and ended the call before I could say good-bye.

Lowering the PDA, I opened my eyes, looking to Shaun's face and avoiding the lights entirely. "He's sending help," I said.

"Good," he replied. "We're not infected."

I allowed myself to glance down to the field kits, whose lights had settled on a steady green. I took a single shallow breath, followed by another deeper one, and nodded. "Better." Turning, I looked at Rick. "Rick, we need a blood test."

"What?" He raised his head, eyes wide and blank.

"A blood test. The field kit is next to you. The biohazard team won't approach until we're either checked out clean or dead." I pulled my finger free, feeling the antiseptic tingle in the pinprick wound, and shook my hand briskly before depressing the signal button at the base of the kit. That would activate the built-in wireless transmitter, uploading the results into the CDC mainframe. A manual upload is only necessary in the event of a negative; the CDC doesn't care, under normal circumstances, about the fact that someone *isn't* about to turn into a zombie. Buffy's results uploaded themselves the second the lights settled on red. Once you've tested positive, the CDC knows. Disabling the upload functionality of a blood testing unit is a federal offense.

Shaun mirrored my actions. He held out his hand and I passed him his test kit, which he dropped into one of the plastic bags he pulled from his belt. My test kit went into a separate bag, which he handed to me. Again in semi-unison, we pressed down the pressure seals, leaving our respective thumbprints on the corners of our bags. If they were tampered with in any way, the seals would turn scarlet and the kits inside would become worse than useless; they would become suspect.

"I...I'm not sure I can," said Rick, swallowing. "Buffy..."

"Buffy's dead, and so is Chuck. We need to know if you're clean." I handed the bag back to Shaun and moved to crouch next to Rick, picking up his test unit and popping off the plastic cover to reveal the pressure pad and needle inside. "Come on. You know the drill. It's just a little pinprick."

"What if the lights go red?"

"Then we'll sit with you until the CDC gets here; they have better units than we do, and they're on their way," I said, keeping my voice as reasonable as I could. I felt like crying. I didn't dare. Rick looked like he was barely holding himself together; if I started to cry, his control might shatter. "Unless you actually start to convert, we'll take no actions."

"If the lights go red, you'll take action immediately," he said, and his voice was suddenly cold, devoid of hesitation. "I want that bullet in my brain before I know what's going on."

"Rick—"

He leaned forward, jamming his thumb down on the needle's point. "I'm not upset that you shot her, Georgia. I'm upset that she had to go that far before you could." He tilted his face upward, looking to Shaun, then to me. "My son converted before he died. Please do me the great kindness of letting me die while I remember his name."

"Of course," I said and straightened, stepping back to my customary place beside Shaun. He raised his right hand, placing it against the middle of my back, while his left hand moved to rest, ever so lightly, on the holster of his pistol. If we lost a second teammate today, the bullet wouldn't be mine. Sometimes you have to spread the guilt around.

"I didn't know you had a kid, Ricky-boy," said Shaun, his tone almost jovial. "What else haven't you been telling us?"

"I wear women's underwear," Rick said. Then, very slightly, he smiled. "I'll show you his picture sometime. He just…he's the reason I left print media. Too many people there remembered him, and too many of them had known his mother. Too many people looked at me differently after I lost them. I still loved the news. But I didn't want to *be* the news. So I found another way to get the story out there."

The lights were flashing, red to green to red. "What was your son's name, Rick?" I asked.

"Ethan," Rick said, his smile growing more sincere and coloring with sorrow. "Ethan Patrick Cousins, after my father and his mother's grandfather. Her name was Lisa. His mother, I mean. Lisa Cousins. She was beautiful." He closed his eyes. "He had her smile."

The lights stopped flashing.

"We'll remember their names for you, if it ever comes to that," I said, "but it won't be today. You're clean, Rick."

"Clean?" He opened his eyes, looking at the test kit like it was some alien thing he'd never seen before. Then, slowly, he removed his finger from the needle and pressed the transmission button. "Clean."

"Which is a damn good thing because there was no way I was taking care of your mangy cat," said Shaun.

"He's right," I said, moving to offer a hand to Rick, to help him off the ground. "Shaun would have tossed her out the window at the first truck stop we passed."

"Now, George, don't be silly," chided Shaun. "I would've waited for one that had a 'Beware of Dog' sign. It wouldn't do for Lois to not have any *friends*."

Rick and I exchanged a startled look before we burst out laughing. I started to cry at the same time, and pulled Rick to his feet before slinging my arms around his shoulders and using him to steady myself. Shaun walked over and put his arms around the both of us, joining our laughter and smashing his face into my hair to hide his own tears. I knew they were there; Rick didn't need to. Some secrets don't need to be shared.

We stayed that way until the sound of tires alerted us to the approach of the biohazard convoy. Hastily, we pulled apart, trying to get ourselves into something that approached composure; Rick wiped his face with one hand, while Shaun dried his cheeks and I raked my fingers through my hair before shoving my sunglasses up the bridge of my nose. Looking to Shaun, I nodded and started toward the sound of the approaching vehicles, carrying my bagged test in one hand, digging my license beacon out with the other.

The convoy stopped about twenty yards away from the forerunning vehicle; my poor, abandoned motorcycle. The Memphis CDC didn't play around. They'd sent a full unit: two troop carriers with their standard Jeep-style frames surrounded by steel-reinforced clear plastic armor, a white medical van nearly twice the size of ours, and, most ominously, two of the vast armored trucks media pundits call "fire trucks." They were huge, painted safety orange with red biohazard signs blazoned on all sides, and their hoses didn't squirt water; instead, they delivered a nasty high-octane variant on napalm mixed with a concentrated form of insecticide. Once a fire truck sprays something down, it's sterile. The soil would be dead for decades, and anything that happened to be in the radius and alive when the trucks came wouldn't be breathing afterward, but the area would be clean.

One of the men in the foremost troop carrier raised a microphone as we approached, and the loudspeaker at the front of the car blared, "Put down your testing units and step back. Clean units will be put in their place. Do not approach personnel. Failure to comply with instructions will result in termination."

The headlights of the convoy were almost blinding, even through my sunglasses. I raised the hand with my license to shield my eyes, and squinted at the troop carrier. "Joe? Is that you?"

"Got it in one, darlin'," the voice replied, less formally. "Just go ahead and set those units on down, if you'd be so kind?"

"I'm leaving my license beacon with the test," I called. "It includes important medical data." If these people made me take my glasses off, the glare from their headlights would probably blind me.

A new voice, female and substantially more clinical, came over the loudspeaker. "We know about your retinal condition, Ms. Mason. Please comply with instructions."

"We're complying, jeez!" shouted Shaun, dropping his bagged testing unit and putting his license beacon on top. I bent to put mine down, somewhat more gently, and Rick did the same. The three of us then started backing away.

We made it about twenty feet before Joe's voice came over the speaker again, saying, "That's far enough, darlin'. You three hold tight, now." The door of the medical van opened and three technicians in biohazard containment suits emerged. I could hear the chugging of their positive pressure unit as it cycled the air, keeping outside particles from entering their sterile zone.

Moving with the sort of grace that implied hundreds, if not thousands, of hours spent in the bulky suits, the technicians walked over to collect our test kits and beacons, putting three sealed kits in their place. With this accomplished, they retreated, and Joe's voice called, "Please approach, open the testing units, and stay where you are until you've checked out clean."

"It's like playing Simon Says," muttered Shaun as we started forward.

"Where I grew up, Simon didn't usually have a truck full of napalm pointed at you," said Rick.

"Pansy," said Shaun.

The testing units left by the CDC technicians were Apple XH-229s, only slightly less advanced than the top of the line. Shaun whistled low under his breath.

"Wow. We really are a threat."

"Something like that," I said. I picked up the first kit and broke the seals with my thumbnail before removing the plastic lid. It was designed to cover my whole hand, all the way to the base of my wrist. There were at least fifteen visible points of contact. Grimacing, I rolled my sleeve up and slid my hand inside.

The mist of antiseptic across my skinned palm was deceptively soothing, a feeling that lasted only a second before needles drove themselves into my already damaged flesh, starting to sift through my blood looking for active viral bodies. The lights began to cycle, moving from red to yellow to green as the more advanced medical processes kicked in.

I was so intent on the lights and what they could mean about my future that I didn't hear the footsteps behind me over the drone of the positive pressure units, or feel the hypo until it was pressed against my neck. A wash of cold flowed over me, and I fell.

The last thing I saw was a row of lights, settling on a steady green. Then my eyes closed, and I didn't see anything at all.

—————————————————

...the question I have been asked most frequently since my transition from the traditional news media to the online world is "Why?" Why would I want to give up an established career to strike out into a new field, one where my experience would not only be laughed at, but would actually work against me? Why would any sane man—and most people regard me as a sane man—want to do something like that?

For the most part, I've replied with the pretty, expected lies: I wanted a challenge, I wanted to test myself, and I believe in telling the truth and telling the news. Only that last part is true, because I *do* believe in telling the truth. And that's what I'm doing today.

I married young. Her name was Lisa. She was smart, she was beautiful, and, above all, she was as crazy in love with me as I was with her. We were still in college on our wedding day. I was going to be a journalist, and she was going to be a teacher—a career path that got put on hold when, three days after graduation, the pregnancy test came up positive. That was a test we passed, and gladly. It was the only test we passed.

Our son, Ethan Patrick Cousins, was born on April 5, 2028. He weighed eight pounds, six ounces. And routine testing of his bodily fluids and vital signs revealed a system crawling with the Kellis-Amberlee virus. His mother had condemned him without ever knowing it; further tests showed that the virus had set up camp in her ovaries, reproducing there without infecting her or changing her life in any way. Our son was not so lucky.

I was fortunate. I had nine good years with my son, despite the precautions and quarantines his condition entailed. He loved baseball. On his last Christmas, he wrote to Santa Claus and asked for a cure, so "Mommy and Daddy won't be sad anymore." He underwent spontaneous viral amplification two months and six days after his ninth birthday. Posthumous examination of his corpse displayed a final body weight of sixty-two pounds, six ounces. Lisa took her own life. And me? I found a new career.

One where I'm still allowed to tell the truth.

—**From *Another Point of True*,
the blog of Richard Cousins, April 21, 2040**

Nineteen

I woke in a white bed in a white room, wearing white cotton pajamas, with the cloying white smell of bleach in my nose. I sat up with a gasp, screwing my eyes shut in an automatic attempt to keep them from being burned by the overhead lights before I realized that I'd opened my eyes while I was lying on my back. I looked directly into the lights, and it hadn't hurt at all. A lack of sensitivity to pain is one of the many warning signs of early Kellis-Amberlee amplification. Was that why the CDC decided to attack us? Was I in some sort of fucked-up research facility? Rumors always abound, after all, and some of them just might be true.

Cautious now, I reached up to touch my face. My fingers found a thin band of plastic resting above my eyes, balanced to put next to no pressure on either the bridge of my nose or the sides of my head. I knew what it was when I felt it; they've been using polarized UV-blocker strips for hospital treatment of retinal KA for about fifteen years now. They're expensive as hell—just one can add five hundred dollars or more to your bill, even after insurance, and they're fragile, to boot—but they filter light better and less noticeably than any other treatment mechanism we've found so far. I relaxed. I wasn't amplifying. I was just a CDC kidnap victim.

It says something about the situation that I was able to find this reassuring.

I began studying the room. It was empty, except for me, the white bed with its white sheets and white duvet and white pillowcases, a white bedside table with foam-padded edges that rendered it effectively useless as a weapon, and a large tinted "mirror" that took up most of the wall next to the door. I squinted at the glass, looking into the sterile hallway beyond. There was no one watching my room. That spoke well for my continued nonzombie status. They'd have had guards out there if I was infected, assuming they had some reason not to have just shot me already.

If it hadn't been for my ocular condition, that "mirror" would have seemed like the real thing, allowing me the illusion of privacy while letting any attending physicians watch me from a distance. The days of beeping monitors and bulky machines are over; everything is streamlined now, all micromesh sensors and carefully concealed wireless monitors. It's as much for the protection of the doctors as it is for the comfort of the patients. After all, every reason to go into the room with someone who might go into viral amplification at any moment is another reason to stop practicing medicine and go into a safer profession. Like journalism.

Not that journalism seemed particularly safe at the moment. I closed my eyes. Buffy was right there waiting for me, looking up with virus-dark eyes as the infection took hold and the essential core of her dissolved. I got the feeling she always would be there. For the rest of my life, she'd be waiting.

Kellis-Amberlee is a fact of existence. You live, you die, and then you come back to life, get up, and shamble around trying to eat your former friends and loved ones. That's the way it is for everyone. Given what my parents do and what happened to their son, it might seem like it's had a huge impact on my family, but the fact is, all that happened before Shaun and I were old enough to understand. The virus is background noise to us. If it hadn't existed, Shaun and I would have found something else to do with our spare time, something that didn't involve poking zombies with sticks. Until Chuck and Buffy, it had never actually taken anyone away from me. It touched people I cared about. It killed acquaintances, like the security guards we lost in Oklahoma, or Rebecca Ryman, who I knew from pictures, if not from actual meetings. But it never touched *me*. Not until Memphis.

I opened my eyes. All the brooding in the world wasn't going to bring Buffy and Chuck back, and it didn't change the facts of the situation: The Memphis CDC had, for whatever reason, drugged us and transported us to a holding facility. I didn't have my clothes, my weapons, or any of my recording equipment. My ears were bare; they'd taken my short-range cellular devices along with everything else. Even my sunglasses were gone, replaced by a UV blocker that, while doubtless more effective, left me feeling naked.

My mother once told me that no woman is naked when she comes equipped with a bad mood and a steady glare. Fixing that fact at the forefront of my mind, I walked over to the room's single door and tried the knob.

It was unlocked.

That wasn't necessarily good.

The hallway was as sterile as the room where I woke up, all white walls, white floors, and stark white overhead lighting. More of those large faux-mirrors were spaced every ten feet, lining both sides of the corridor. I was in the isolation wing. That was even less reassuring than the unlocked door. Pushing the UV blocker up the bridge of my nose in a gesture that was deeply reassuring if not strictly functional, I started down the hall.

Rick was in the third room on the left, lying atop his bedcovers in white cotton pajamas identical to mine. The CDC isn't big on gender stereotyping. I knocked on the "window" to warn him that I was coming before opening the door and stepping inside.

"Do they actually have room service in this place? Because I'd just about die for a can of Coke right about now. Reanimation strictly optional."

"Georgia!" Rick sat up, relief and delight warring for control over his features. "Thank God! When I woke up in here alone, I was afraid—"

"What, that you were the last one left? Sorry, guy, but you don't get promoted that easily." I leaned against the door frame, assessing him. He wasn't visibly injured. That was good. If we needed to exit in a hurry, maybe he could keep up. "I am, in fact, immortal when annoyed."

"Wow."

"Wow?"

"You'll never die." He paused and raised his right hand, making vague gestures toward his eyes. "Georgia, you're not—"

"It's all right." I tapped the band. "UV-blocking plastic. The latest thing. Technically better than my sunglasses, even if everything is a little bright right now."

"Oh," he said. "Your eyes are brown."

"Well, yeah."

He shrugged. "I never knew."

"Life is an education." Keeping my tone as light as possible, I asked, "So were you just waiting for me? Have you seen Shaun?"

"No—like I said before, I woke up alone. I haven't seen anyone since the CDC Mickeyed us. Any idea what the hell is going on here?"

"I'm thinking it's more like they roofied us, and right now, I'm marginally more interested in finding my brother."

He gave me a speculative look. "You're more interested in your brother than in figuring out the truth?"

"Shaun's the *only* thing that concerns me more than the truth does."

"He's not here right now."

"Which is why we're going to find him." I stepped back into the hall. "Come on."

To his credit, Rick rose without argument. "They didn't lock the doors. That means they don't think we're infectious."

"That, or it means we're already in the middle of an outbreak, and they've sealed this whole wing."

"Aren't you just a little ray of happy sunshine?"

I slanted a tight smile in his direction. "I always have been."

"I understand your brother a little bit more with every day that passes."

"I'm choosing to ignore that remark." The hall was empty, stretching in both directions with no distinguishing features either way. I frowned. "Know anything about isolation ward layouts?"

"Yes."

His answer was surprisingly firm. I glanced toward him, eyebrows raised in silent question. He shrugged.

"Lisa and I spent a lot of time in places like this."

"Right," I said, after an uncomfortable pause. "Which way?"

"CDC iso wards all follow the same basic layout. We go left."

That made sense. Zombies don't learn, and if there's a chance your personnel are uninfected, you want them to know which way to run. It would also serve as a herding mechanism; those that had already amplified but were hoping for a way out would charge straight into the air lock, where a positive blood test would buy them a bullet to the brain.

Rick started walking. I hurried to keep up, and he glanced at me.

"I'm sure Shaun's fine."

"Mmm."

"If he'd amplified, we'd be seeing signs of the outbreak. Or at least smelling fresher disinfectant."

"Mmm."

"I'd like to take this opportunity to say, off the record, that your eyes are much more attractive when you don't hide them behind those freaky-ass contact lenses. Blue really doesn't suit you."

I gave him a sidelong look.

Rick smiled. "You didn't go 'mmm' at me that time."

"Sorry. I get a little anxious when I don't know where Shaun is."

"Georgia, if this is 'a little anxious,' I never want to see you when you're actually uptight."

I shot him another sidelong look. "You're awfully relaxed."

"No," he said, in a measured tone, "I'm in shock. See, the difference is that if I were relaxed, I wouldn't be walking along, waiting for the reality of Buffy being dead to hit me like a brick to the side of the head."

"Oh."

This time, his smile was small and tight and held not a trace of humor. "Ethan taught me about CDC isolation. Lisa taught me about shock."

I didn't know what to say to that. We walked through the white halls, our white-clad reflections flickering like ghosts in the tinted-glass "windows" until something new appeared up ahead: a steel-barred door with an intercom and a blood testing unit set into the wall next to it.

"Friendly," I said, as we approached.

"The intercom connects to the duty station, and the test unit has an automatic upload function," said Rick.

"Friendly *and* efficient," I amended. I stopped in front of the door and pressed the button for the intercom. "Hello?"

Shaun's voice answered immediately, full of the rampant cheer only I was likely to recognize as his way of masking grief and fear. "George! You decided to rejoin the world of the living!"

Something in the center of my chest unclenched and I could breathe again. "Good to see you haven't decided to leave it," I said. "Next time, leave me a damn note or something."

"Afraid that's my fault, Ms. Mason," said a deeper, Southern-accented voice. "We try not to leave anything that could serve for a weapon in the rooms. That includes paper. You understand the necessity."

I frowned. "Joe?"

"That's right, and I'm pretty properly glad to see you're both all right."

Both? Rick hadn't said a word since I activated the intercom. I turned and scanned the edge of the ceiling until I found a small discolored patch, off-cream against the white of the tile. Looking directly into it, finger still on the intercom button, I said, "You must have been real popular with the girls in high school. They love Peeping Toms."

"Hey, don't rag on the man, George. This way I get to see your adorable pajamas. You look like Frosty the Snowman. If he were on the rag, I mean."

"Frosty's going to be kicking your ass in a minute," I said. "Can someone tell me what the hell is going on here, before I get seriously pissed?"

"Door won't unlock without a blood test, George," said Shaun.

"Of course it won't." Turning, I slapped my hand down on the reader panel, barely even flinching as the needles bit into my skin. For every needle I felt, there were five more I didn't. The thicker needles on CDC kits are more for psychological reassurance than anything else—people don't believe they've been tested unless they feel the sting. Most of the information the CDC needs comes from hypos so small they're essentially acupuncture needles, sliding in and out without leaving marks.

A light over the door flashed on, going almost immediately from red to green, and the locks disengaged with a loud "click." I removed my hand from the panel.

"I assume alarms go off if Rick tries to follow right through?"

"Got it in one. Head into the air lock, let the door shut, and he can follow you."

"Right." I gave Rick a quick nod, which he returned, and opened the door and stepped through.

If the hallways seemed featureless, the air lock they fed into was antiseptic. The walls were so white that the stark light they reflected was enough to make my eyes ache, even through the UV-blocking strip. Half squinting, I shuffled to the middle of the room.

The intercom crackled, and Joe's voice said, "Stop there, Ms. Mason."

"Close eyes, hold breath?"

"Exactly," he said, with faint amusement in his tone. "It's always a pleasure to work with someone who knows the drill."

"I'm not really in a 'pleasure' place," I said. "Maybe after I have some pants on." Standing around and grousing wasn't going to get me to my clothes, or my brother, any faster. Closing my eyes, I removed the UV blocker, took a deep breath, and held it.

The smell of bleach and disinfecting agents filled the room as a cool mist drifted down from the vents in the ceiling, blanketing me. I forced myself to keep holding my breath, counting backward from twenty. I'd reached seventeen when the fans kicked on and the mist pulled away, sucked into drains in the floor. It would be pulled into channels of superheated air, baked until any traces of infection that had managed to survive the chemical bath were burned away, and then pumped into an incinerator, where it would be destroyed. The CDC does a lot of things, but it doesn't fuck around with sterilization.

"You can open your eyes now, Ms. Mason."

Sliding the UV blocker back into place, I opened my eyes and proceeded to the door on the air lock's far side. The light above it was green, and when I touched the handle, it swung open without resistance. I continued on.

The duty station was one of those hybrid beasts that have become so common in the medical profession over the past twenty years: half nurse's station and medical triage, half guard point, with alarm buttons posted at several spots around the walls and a large gun cabinet next to the water-cooler. A good medical duty station can provide an island of safety for the uninfected, even as an outbreak rages on all sides. If your air locks don't fail and you have enough ammo, you can hold out for days. One duty station in Atlanta did exactly that—four nurses, three doctors, and five security personnel kept themselves and eighteen patients alive for almost a week before the CDC was able to fight through the outbreak raging through the neighborhoods around the hospital and get them safely out. They made a movie about that incident.

Shaun, who had his own clothes on, the bastard, was sitting atop the counter with a cup of coffee in his hands. A man I didn't recognize was standing nearby, wearing a white doctor's coat over his clothes, and Senator Ryman was beside him, looking more anxious than the other two combined. Nurses and CDC techs moved past the station, talking among themselves like extras in a movie background—they completed the setting, but they weren't part of it, any more than the walls were.

The senator was the first to acknowledge my arrival. He straightened, relief radiating through his expression, and moved toward me, catching me in a tight hug before I had a chance to register what he was planning to do. I made a soft "*oof*" noise as the air was shoved out of my lungs, but he just squeezed tighter, seeming unfazed by the fact that my arms remained down by my sides. This was a hug for his comfort, not mine.

"Don't think she can breathe over there, chief," drawled Shaun. "Pretty sure she hasn't kicked the oxygen habit just yet."

The door opened and closed again behind me, and Rick said, sounding surprised, "Why is Senator Ryman trying to crush Georgia?"

"Post-traumatic shock," said Shaun. "He thinks he's a boa constrictor."

"You kids can laugh," said the senator, finally letting go. Relieved, I stepped back before he could decide to do it again. "You scared me to death."

"We scared ourselves pretty badly, too, Senator," I said, continuing my retreat until I was next to Shaun. He put his hand on my shoulder, squeez-ing. There was a world of relief in that simple gesture. I leaned into his hand, looking toward the stranger. "Joe, I presume?"

"Dr. Joseph Wynne, Memphis CDC," he said and walked over to extend his hand in my direction. I took it. His grip was solid without being crush-ing. "I can't begin to say how glad I am to speak with you face-to-face."

"Glad to still be in the shape to speak," I said. Pleasantries accom-plished, I frowned. "Now, can someone fill me in on why I was standing next to a highway, doing my civic duty, and suddenly woke up in a CDC iso ward? Also, if I could get hooked up with my clothes, that'd be awesome. I feel kind of naked here, and that's weird when there's a United States senator in the room."

"That's a funny story, actually," said Shaun.

Releasing Joe's hand, I craned my head around to eye my brother. "Define 'funny.'"

Shaun picked up a bundle from the counter on the other side of him and passed it to me. My clothes and a plastic bag containing my gun and all my jewelry. As I hugged the bundle to my chest, he said, with all apparent sincerity, "Someone called the CDC two minutes before you did and told them that we'd all been killed in the accident."

For a moment, all I could do was stare at him. Then, swiveling my head around to direct the stare to Joe and Senator Ryman, I demanded, "Is this true?"

Looking distinctly uncomfortable now, Joe said, "Well, darlin', we have to react to every call we get..."

"You had test results from us. You knew we weren't dead."

"Those types of test results can be falsified," Joe said. "We did the best we could."

I nodded grudgingly. Under the strict interpretation of the law, the CDC would have been within its rights to come into the valley, shoot us, sterilize the surrounding area, and deal with our remains. The fact that it took us alive for extensive testing was unusual, because it represented an unnecessary risk on its part—no one would have questioned it if the CDC had killed us.

"What made you take us alive?" I asked.

Joe smiled. "Ain't many people who can make a call that drastic to the CDC and sound that calm about it, Ms. Mason. I wanted to meet anyone who could do that."

"Our parents taught us well," I said. Raising the bundle of clothes and gear, I asked, "Is there a place where I could get dressed?"

"Kelly!" Turning, Joe flagged down a passing woman in a doctor's coat. She was fresh-faced and wide-eyed; she couldn't have been any older than Buffy, and her long blonde hair, clipped back with a barrette, created the illusion of resemblance. A knot formed in my throat.

Joe gestured from the woman to me. "Georgia Mason, Dr. Kelly Connolly. Dr. Connolly, if you could please show Ms. Mason to a changing room?"

Shaun slid off the counter. "C'mon, Rick. I'll show you the men's room."

"Much obliged," said Rick, snagging his own clothes from the counter.

"Certainly, Dr. Wynne," said Kelly. "Ms. Mason, if you'd come this way?"

"Sure," I said, and followed her.

We walked down a short hallway, this one painted a warm yellow, and Kelly opened a door leading into a small locker room. "The nurses change here," she said.

"Thanks," I said. Putting my hand on the knob, I glanced to her. "I can find my own way back."

"All right," she said. Hesitating, she looked at me. I looked back. Finally, she said, "I read your site. Every day. I used to follow you on Bridge Supporters, before you managed to schism off."

I raised an eyebrow. "Really? To what do I owe the honor?"

She reddened. "Your last name," she said, sounding abashed. "I did a report in medical school on human-to-animal transmission of the Kellis-Amberlee amplification trigger. I found you when I was looking for information on your . . . your brother. I stayed for the writing."

"Ah," I said. She seemed about to say something more. I waited, watching her.

Her blush deepened. "I just wanted to take this opportunity to say that I'm sorry."

I frowned. "About . . . ?"

"Buffy?"

It felt like all the blood in my veins had turned to ice. Careful to keep breathing, I asked, "How did you know about that?"

She blinked, surprise unconcealed as she said, "I saw the notice that she'd been added to the Wall."

"The Wall?" I said. "But how would they know to . . . oh, Jesus. The cameras."

"Ms. Mason? Georgia? Are you all right?"

"Huh?" At some point, I'd looked away from her. I looked back, shaking my head. "I just . . . I didn't realize she'd already be on the Wall. Thank you. Your condolences are appreciated." I turned and walked into the changing room without waiting for her to respond, closing the door behind me. Let her think I was rude. I'm a journalist. Journalists are supposed to be rude, right? It's part of the mystique.

Thoughts chased themselves through my head like leaves tumbling in the wind as I stripped off my CDC-issue pajamas and began getting my own clothes on. It took longer than normal because I had to pause every step along the way to get the appropriate recording devices, cameras, and wireless receivers into their assigned pockets. If I didn't, I wouldn't be able to find anything for weeks.

Buffy's death was on the Wall. I should have known it would be, since her family would have been notified, which meant there would have been an obituary, but somehow, knowing that simple fact—that she'd joined all the other victims of this endless plague on the Wall—made her death all the more impossible to deny. More, it reminded me of one crucial fact: We were connected to the rest of the world, even when we were isolated. The cameras were always rolling. And right now, that was what concerned me.

I slid my sunglasses into place, removing the UV blocker as I shoved them up the bridge of my nose. They made me feel less naked than anything else. Reaching up, I tapped my ear cuff. "Mahir," I said.

Several seconds later, Mahir's sleep-muddled voice came over the line, saying, "This had better be good."

"You realize your accent gets thicker when you're tired."

"Georgia?"

"Got it."

"Georgia!"

"Still got it."

"You're alive!"

"Barely, and we're in CDC custody, so I need to make this fast," I said. Mahir, being the good lieutenant that he is, shut up immediately. "I need you to download the footage from the external cameras on the van and my bike, check to make sure it's complete, and then wipe the originals."

"I'm doing this because...?"

"I'll explain later." When I wasn't making the call from inside a government installation, where all communications were likely to be monitored. "Can you do it?"

"Of course. Right away."

"Thanks, Mahir."

"Oh, and Georgia? I'm very grateful that you're still alive."

I smiled. "So am I, Mahir. Get the footage and get some sleep." I tapped my ear cuff, cutting off the call.

Adjusting the collar on my jacket, I schooled my face back toward neutrality and left the changing room, heading for the duty station. The cameras. How could I have forgotten about them, even for a few minutes?

We keep the external cameras recording constantly. Sometimes we've found things when we've gone back to do review, like the time Shaun was able to use some shots of a totally normal highway median to track a pack of zombies hunting near the Colma border. Depending on the angle the shooter was working from, we might be able to use the latest footage to find a murderer. Assuming, of course, that whoever it was hadn't already been able to get to our hard drives, and that Buffy hadn't told any of her "friends" about our filming habits.

I was starting to feel like a conspiracy theorist. But that was all right because this was starting to feel very much like a conspiracy.

Rick had less equipment than I did; he and Shaun were back at the duty station when I arrived, and Rick had acquired a mug of coffee from somewhere. I started to give it a longing look, and stopped as Shaun handed me a can of Coke, still cold enough to have condensation beading on the sides.

"Truly, you are a God among men," I said.

"Now I'm a God, but tomorrow, when you have to stop me from playing with dead things again, you'll be right back to calling me an idiot, won't you?" Shaun said.

"Yup." I lifted the can, cracked the tab, and took a long drink before exhaling. "CDC has decent taste in soda."

"We try," said Joe.

That was the opening I needed. Lowering the can, I turned toward him, secure behind my sunglasses. "You received a call reporting us dead?"

"Time stamp puts it at two minutes before your call came in. The report flashed my screen while I was talking to you."

That explained his request for detailed credentials. "Did you get a name? Or better, a number?"

"Afraid not, on either," Joe said.

Shaun broke in: "It was an anonymous tip made from a disposable mobile phone."

"So the number's in their records—"

"But it doesn't mean anything."

"Cute." I continued watching Joe. "Dr. Wynne—"

"Joe, please. A girl comes back from the other side of 'legally dead,' she gets to call me by my Christian name." My surprise must have shown because he chuckled without amusement, saying, "The CDC gets a call that says you're virus-positive, you're dead until we confirm it's a hoax. It's a standard legal and safety precaution."

I stared at him. "Because it's not like anyone would hoax the CDC."

"No one should be, and believe me, Ms. Mason, when we find the people responsible, they'll be learning that lesson right well." Joe's smile drew down into a scowl. An understandable one: Most of the people who go to work for the CDC do it out of a genuine desire to better the human condition. If anyone's going to find a cure for Kellis-Amberlee, it's almost certainly going to be the Centers for Disease Control, with its near-global approval ratings and even more extensive pocketbooks. Young idealists fight tooth and nail over CDC postings, and only the best ever get them. That means the CDC employs a lot of very proud people, ones who don't take things that besmirch the honor of the institution sitting down.

"I'd be willing to bet that whoever made that call was also responsible for shooting out our tires," I said.

"Well, Ms. Mason—"

"Georgia, please."

"Well, Georgia, it seems like a bit of a sucker bet, and I don't customarily take those. It isn't often someone tries to pull a fast one on the CDC, and a fast one that happens to center on a convoy that's been attacked by snipers, well…"

"Do we have any ballistics on the gun the shooter used?"

Joe's expression turned remote. "I'm afraid that's classified."

I glanced at the senator. His own expression was equally distant, his eyes fixed on some point beyond our heads.

"Senator?"

"I'm sorry, Georgia. Doctor Wynne is right; information relating directly to the police investigation of this matter is classified."

I looked at him, grateful for the way my sunglasses concealed the bulk of my expression. Only Shaun was likely to realize how upset I was. "You mean it's classified from the media."

"Now, Georgia—"

"Are you seriously telling me that if I were some random Joe Public, you'd answer my questions, but because I work for a news site, you won't?" His silence was all the answer I needed. "God*dammit*, Peter. We are *dying* for you, and you won't tell us what kind of bullets they're using for the job? Why, because being reporters means we automatically have no sense of discretion? Is that it? We're going to run right out and cause a public panic, because, gee, no one's going to suspect a cover-up when one of our own gets dead and we don't say anything but 'Death sucks'!" I started stepping toward him and stopped as Rick and Shaun each grabbed me by an arm. "Screw you," I spat, not bothering to fight their hold. "I thought you were better than this."

Senator Ryman looked at me, shaking his head in open bewilderment. "She's dead, Georgia. Buffy's dead. Chuck's dead. You *should* be dead, all of you, dead and sanitized, not here and alive, shouting at me for not wanting you to rush right back out and keep getting yourselves killed! Georgia, I'm not keeping this from you because you're a reporter. I'm keeping it from you because I'd rather you didn't die."

"With all due respect, Senator, I think that's a decision you have to let us make for ourselves." I shook my arm free of Shaun's grasp. As soon as Shaun released me, Rick did the same. We looked at Senator Ryman together, waiting for his answer.

The senator glanced away. "I don't want your deaths on my conscience, Georgia. Or on my campaign."

"Well, then, Senator, I guess we'll just have to do our best not to die," I said.

He turned back to us. His expression was bleak. It was the face of a man who'd spent his life chasing a dream and was only now beginning to realize how much it might cost to get it.

"I'll have the reports sent to you," he said. "Our plane leaves in an hour. If you'll excuse me." It wasn't a question, and he didn't wait for an answer. He just turned and walked away.

...first time I met Buffy. Man, I didn't even know I was meeting her, y'know? It was one of those types of things. Me and George, we knew we needed a Fictional if we wanted to get hired at one of the *good* sites because you can't just log in and be like "Yo, we're two-thirds of a triple threat, give us our virtual desks." We needed a wedge, something to make us complete. And that was Buffy. We just didn't know it yet.

They do these online job fair things in the blogging community, like Craigslist gone even more super-specialized. Georgia and I flagged our need for a Fictional at the next fair, opened a virtual booth, and waited. We were about to give up when we got a chat request from somebody who IDed herself as "B.Meissonier" and said she didn't have any field experience but she was willing to learn. We talked for thirteen hours straight. We hired her that night.

Buffy Meissonier was the funniest woman I knew. She loved computers, poetry, and being the kind of geek who fixes your PDA before you know it's broken. She liked old TV and new movies, and she listened to all kinds of music, even the stuff that sounds like static and church bells. She played guitar really badly, but she meant every note.

There are people who are going to say she was a traitor. I'll probably be one of them. That doesn't change the fact that she was my friend. For a long time, before she did anything wrong, she was my friend, and I was with her when she died, and I'm going to miss her. That's what matters. She was my friend.

Buffy, I hope they have computers and cheesy television and music and people laughing where you are now. I hope you're happy, on the other side of the Wall.

We miss you.

—From *Hail to the King*,
the blog of Shaun Mason, April 21, 2040

Twenty

The senator and his security team came from Houston to Memphis via the Houston CDC's private plane. Every CDC installation has one fueled and ready at all times. Not because there could be an evacuation—any outbreak large enough to require evacuating an entire CDC installation would leave a distinct lack of uninfected people to actually *evacuate*—but for the transfer of specialists, patients, and, yes, politicians and other such notables from one location to another in a quick, efficient, and, above all, discreet manner. It wouldn't do to set off a public panic because someone had seen, say, the world's leading specialist in Kellis-Amberlee-related reservoir conditions being flown into a populated area. The nation is constantly poised on the edge of a riot, and the CDC is very aware of how easy it would be to be the match that starts the fire.

The last time I was on a CDC plane and conscious of the experience, I was nine and on my way to visit Dr. William Crowell. Dr. Crowell was that "world's leading specialist" I mentioned before, and he thought he might've found a cure for retinal KA. My parents, ever eager to do stupid shit in the name of a good story, flew me to Atlanta to let him test his treatment on me. His cure proved as artificial as his toupee and his "light therapy" left me seeing spots for a month, but I got to ride in an airplane and have an adventure without Shaun. For my nine-year-old self, that was almost enough.

They give you more snacks when you're nine. Also, airplane captains may be willing to let cute little girls in dark glasses hang out in the cabin, but they're not as understanding of adult journalists who just want to get away from their traveling companions. When you added the fact that the senator wouldn't look me in the eye, while Shaun spent the entire flight trying to take his seat apart with a screwdriver swiped from one of the guards, it's no surprise that I was happy as hell to touch down at our destination, even though landing came barely an hour after taking off.

My relief was partially fueled by the fact that CDC regulations forbade the use of wireless devices while in flight, and I hadn't heard from Mahir before we left Memphis. I was switching things on before they even opened the cabin doors. Mail alerts began sounding immediately. I had more than five hundred pending mail messages, and none were the message I wanted.

Six more guards were waiting on the runway, including Steve, who held a wicker cat carrier in one hand. Rick let out a wordless exclamation and pushed past Shaun to snatch the carrier, starting to make cooing noises at the wide-eyed, brush-tailed Lois.

"Cat didn't die," I said, adjusting my sunglasses.

Shaun shook his head. "Man needs a girlfriend."

"Hush. This is a touching reunion."

"I stand by my statement." Shaun tilted his head back, looking up at Steve. "You brought the man his cat."

Looking amused, the enormous security nodded. "I did."

"So where's *my* present?"

"Will the location of your van do?"

"I think so." Shaun glanced to me. "George?"

"I was planning on holding out for a million dollars, but as long as my bike's included in the deal, I guess I can let you off easy. This time." I flashed a thin smile. "Hey, Steve."

"Good to see you breathing, Georgia."

"It's good to be breathing, Steve."

Robert Channing—who got elevated from "chief aide" to "Chief of Staff" as soon as it became apparent that the campaign might have a genuine shot at the White House—pushed past the substantially larger guards, arrowing in on Senator Ryman like a hunting dog going for the kill. "Senator! We have twenty minutes to get halfway across the city, and you *can't* be late or Tate's going to take the stage alone." His tone implied that this would be a horror beyond all reckoning.

"And we can't have that, now, can we?" Senator Ryman grimaced, shooting an apologetic glance our way. "I'm sorry, but…"

"The job comes first," I said. "Rick, give me the cat."

Looking alarmed, Rick hugged the carrier to his chest. Lois yowled. "Why?"

"Because despite recent events and rampant stupidity, we're still reporters, assuming we're still allowed to be." I slanted a sidelong glance at the senator. He met my eyes and nodded. Turning back to Rick, I said, "You're

going with the senator to cover whatever sort of appearance this is supposed to be—"

"Speaking to the Daughters of the American Revolution," said Robert.

"Right, whatever," I said, waving a hand to indicate my lack of interest
in the specifics. "Rick, you're going to attend whatever sort of appearance
this is supposed to be, and you're going to find something interesting to
say about it. We're going to go check the equipment and see what sort of
dive we're supposed to be camping out at."

Rick nodded with obvious regret, holding the carrier out to me. I
almost felt bad taking it from him. Only almost. I needed to talk to my
brother, and loath as I was to admit it, I needed to do that talking alone.
Rick and Buffy had a past; Buffy betrayed us; Rick was still in the equation.
If we were going to keep working with the illustrious Mr. Cousins, we had
to decide to do it together, and without Rick participating in the discussion. And if we weren't, we needed to have all our ducks in a row before we
invited him to seek employment elsewhere.

Sounding affronted, Robert said, "You're staying at the Plaza with the
rest of us. It's five stars, all the latest in amenities, and fully licensed security. Senator, I'm sorry, but there isn't any more time to stand around and
chat. Come on, please." Not pausing to allow any further discussion, he
grabbed the senator by the arm and began steering him toward the waiting
car. Rick followed, along with all but two of the security guards.

Steve was one of the guards remaining behind. The other was a Hispanic man I didn't recognize but whose sunglasses were dark enough to
either be prescription strength or render him effectively blind. He would
have seemed tall next to anyone else; next to Steve, he looked like a normal
human.

Shifting Lois's carrier to my left hand, I looked toward Steve.
"Babysitters?"

"Bodyguards," Steve replied, without levity. "You folks came close to
dying out there on the road. We'd like to see to it that you don't do it
again."

"So we don't do any long-distance driving."

"Not good enough."

Shaun stepped up beside me. "Are you planning to stop us from doing
our jobs?"

"No. Just to keep an eye on you while you do them."

I could feel Shaun starting to bristle. Being an Irwin means frequently
taking stupid chances for the amusement of the cameras. A good Irwin
can make going to the corner store for a candy bar and a Coke look death

defying and suicidal. The idea of trying to post reports with a security guard looking over his shoulder was probably about as appealing to Shaun as the idea of censorship was to me. I put a hand on his arm.

"So you're saying our jobs have become *so* dangerous that we need to be protected not from the hazards of the living dead, but from the hazards presented by our fellow man?" I asked.

"Not exactly how I would've put it, but you're in the neighborhood," said Steve.

Shaun relaxed grudgingly. "I guess it'll sound good in the headlines," he said, his tone implying that it wouldn't do anything of the kind.

At least he was mollified. Leaving my hand on Shaun's arm, I swung my head around until I was facing the second agent, not depending on my questionable peripheral vision. "I'm Georgia Mason; this is my brother, Shaun Mason. You would be...?"

"Andres Rodriguez, ma'am," he replied. His tone was level. "Do I pass muster?"

"That's a question for the grand jury. You can, however, take us to our hotel now." Lois yowled. I amended: "*Right* now. I think someone's getting cranky."

"The cat isn't the only one," Shaun said.

"Behave," I said. Keeping the hand that wasn't holding the carrier on his arm, we turned and followed the agents to the car.

Steve and Andres took the front, leaving us with the back seat. A sheet of soundproof safety glass cut us off from our bodyguards, turning them into vaguely imposing silhouettes that might as well have been in another car. It was a small blessing, even if I couldn't quite bring myself to relax. I didn't trust it. I didn't feel like I really trusted anything anymore.

Shaun opened his mouth when the engine started, but I shook my head, gesturing toward the overhead light. He quieted. Without Buffy and her tiny armada of clever devices, we had no way of knowing whether the car was bugged. It turned out that even with Buffy we'd had no real way of knowing whether the car was bugged, since she'd sold us out, but at least we'd *believed* we could protect our privacy.

Brow furrowed, Shaun mouthed "Hotel?" I nodded. Once we were in our own space with our own things, we could sweep for bugs and set up an EMP field. After that, we could talk in something resembling security—and we needed to talk. We needed to talk about a lot of things.

The drive from the CDC airstrip to the hotel took approximately twenty minutes. It would have taken longer, but Steve took advantage of the priority override available to government officials and law enforcement, turning on the car's beacon and sliding us straight into the fast side of the carpool lane. The tollbooths flashed green as soon as we came into receiving range. Electronic pay passes have led to a general speed-up, but nothing moves your average driver as fast as knowing that someone else is picking up the ticket for his commute. We must have provided a free pass for dozens of commuters. That almost made up for the fact that we were cutting ahead of them during the beginning rush hour, when five minutes can make the difference between "home at a reasonable hour" and "late for dinner."

Lois yowled the whole way, while Shaun made a vague, disinterested show of trying to pick the lock on his side of the car. My brother's good with locks; the car's security was better. He'd made no progress by the time we pulled off the freeway and turned toward the hotel, and he put away his lock picks with a silent expression of disgust.

The Downtown Houston Plaza was one of those huge, intentionally imposing buildings built just after the Rising, when they still hadn't figured out how to walk the fine architectural line between "elegance" and "security." It looked like a prison coated in pink stucco and gingerbread icing. Palm trees were planted around the exterior, where they utterly failed to blunt the building's harsh angles. There were no windows at ground level, and the windows higher up the building were the dull matte of steel-reinforced security glass. The infected could batter on them for years without breaking through. Assuming they somehow made the intellectual leap necessary to figure out how to use a ladder.

Shaun eyed the building as we circled. It wasn't until the car pulled off at the parking garage entrance that he offered his professional opinion: "Death trap."

"Many of the early 'zombie-proof' buildings were." I adjusted my sunglasses. The garage doors creaked open as Steve waved a white plastic fob in front of the sensors, and we drove on into relative darkness. "What makes this one so deadly?"

"All that froufrou crap on the front of the building—"

"You mean the trim?"

"Right, the trim. It's supposed to be ornamental, right? Doesn't matter. I bet it would bear my weight. So if I get infected but I haven't converted, I can use the trim to climb the building looking for shelter. There are plenty of handholds. So I can get to the roof. And if this place followed the standard floor plan for the time period, there's a helicopter pad up there, and multiple doors connecting it to the interior, so any survivors could use it to evacuate during an outbreak." Shaun shook his head. "Run for the roof, it's covered in the people who ran there before you. And they're not looking for a rescue. They're looking for a snack."

"Charming," I said. The car pulled into a parking space and the engine cut off. "I guess we're here."

The front driver's-side door opened. Steve emerged, heading across the garage floor to the air lock. I tried my own door, but it was still locked; the safety latches hadn't disengaged.

"The hell—? Shaun, try your door."

He did, and scowled. "It's locked."

The car intercom clicked on. Andres's voice, distorted by the speakers, said, "Ms. Mason, Mr. Mason, if you could be patient for a moment. My colleague is going to pass through the air lock and will wait for you on the other side. The lock on the right will be disengaged as soon as he's tested clean, and Ms. Mason will be permitted to proceed. Once Ms. Mason has passed through the air lock, Mr. Mason will be permitted to go."

Shaun groaned. "Oh, you have *got* to be kidding me."

The intercom clicked again. "Standard safety precautions."

"You can take those safety precautions and shove 'em sideways up your—" Shaun began, pleasantly. I put a hand on his arm. He stopped.

"Mr. Rodriguez, it looks like Steve's made it through," I said, keeping my voice level. "If you'd unlock my door now, please?"

"Very well." My door unlocked. "Mr. Mason, please remain seated. Ms. Mason, please proceed toward the—hey! What are you doing? You can't do that!"

Ignoring the shouts from the intercom, Shaun finished sliding out of the car, blowing a kiss back toward the agitated shape of Andres before slamming the door and following me to the air lock. True to expectations, Andres remained seated, mouth moving as he swore at us through the glass.

"Nobody who cares that much about security is going to come out into the open with a possible infection," I said, taking Shaun's hand in my left, swinging Lois's carrier in my right. She yowled, punctuating the statement. "We're dangerous."

"Man thought he could make us do this separately," said Shaun. Taking the still-yowling Lois from me, he slid the carrier into the luggage hatch. The sensors would record the fact that the box contained a living thing, but they would also record its weight. Lois was too small for amplification and would slide straight through. "Man's an idiot."

"No, he's an amateur," I said, moving into position in front of the blood testing panel. I raised my right hand. Shaun stepped into position next to me and raised his left. "One..."

"Two."

We pressed our palms flat.

Steve was waiting on the other side of the air lock, shaking his head. "You probably just scared Agent Rodriguez out of a year of his life," he scolded, without conviction.

"Given that Agent Rodriguez just annoyed me out of a year of *my* life, I'd say we're even," I said, retrieving Lois from the luggage bin. "Do we need to wait on him, or can you show us to our rooms?"

"And our van," Shaun said. "You promised me our van."

"Your van is in the parking garage, along with Georgia's bike," Steve said. Fishing two small plastic rectangles out of his jacket pocket, he passed them to us. "Shaun, you're in room two-fourteen. Georgia, you're in room two-seventeen."

We exchanged a look. "Those don't sound adjoining," I said.

"Originally, you were going to be sharing a room with Ms. Meissonier, Georgia, while Shaun and Mr. Cousins shared a room down the hall," Steve said. "It seemed best to let you keep your privacy, given recent... events."

"Right." Shaun handed his key back to Steve. "I'll just stalk along with George until you can get me my own key. Rick and Lois can have some valuable alone time to re-bond after their separation." As if on cue, Lois yowled.

Steve's eyebrows arched upward. "You two would rather share a room?"

His expression was a familiar one. We've been seeing it from teachers, friends, colleagues, and hotel concierges since we hit puberty. It's the "you'd rather share a room with your opposite-gender sibling than sleep alone?" face, and it never fails to irritate me. Social norms can bite me. If I need to have someone guarding my back when the living dead show up to make my life more interesting than I want it to be, I want that someone to be Shaun. He's a light sleeper, and I know he can aim.

"Yes," I said, firmly. "We two would rather share a room."

For a moment, Steve looked like he might argue. Then he shrugged, dismissing it as none of his business, and said, "I'll have them send up a second key and get your luggage moved. Georgia, all your things and the equipment that you had marked as vital are already in your room."

That meant they'd been searched—standard security—but I didn't particularly care. I make it a rule never to keep sensitive data unencrypted where other people might get at it. If Senator Ryman's security detail wanted to waste their time looking for answers in my underpants, they could be my guests. "Excellent. We'll just head for our room, then, if you don't mind? Assuming you don't feel the need to accompany us."

"I'm going to trust the two of you not to get yourselves killed between here and the elevator," said Steve.

"Thanks for the vote of confidence," I said. Shaun snapped a salute and we walked away, Lois still yowling, to follow the wall-mounted signs leading us to the elevators in the lobby.

The hotel was old enough that the elevators still ran up and down in fixed shafts. It would have been an interesting novelty if I hadn't been so wired and exhausted. As it was, I stared at the mirrors on the walls, trying to ignore my growing headache and the increasingly fevered pitch of Lois's complaints. She wanted out of the box, and she wanted out *now*. I understood the sentiment.

Our hotel room was as old as the elevator, with hideous wallpaper striped in yellow, green, and brown, and a steel-reinforced window looking out over the central courtyard. Sunlight reflecting off the pool three floors down turned the water into a giant flare of light, shining directly through our window. I whimpered involuntarily, whipping my face around and squeezing my eyes shut. Shaun shoved past me to close the blackout curtains, and I stumbled blind into the room, letting the door swing closed.

The lights were off, and when Shaun got the curtains fastened the room was plunged into blessed darkness. He walked back across the room, putting a hand on my elbow. "It's safe now," he said. "The beds are this way."

"That was a rotten trick," I complained, and let him guide me.

"But funny."

"Not funny."

"I'm laughing."

"I know where you're planning to sleep tonight."

"And yet somehow, still funny." He stopped walking, pushing down on my shoulder as he took the cat carrier out of my hands. "Sit. I'll get things set up."

"Don't forget the EMP screen," I said, settling on the bed and flopping backward. The mattress was younger than the décor. I bounced. "And get the servers up."

"I *have* done this before," said Shaun. The amusement was evident in his tone, but it wasn't enough to conceal the concern. "You look like hell."

"You can tell that with the lights off?"

"You looked like hell before the evil day star punched you in the face. Now you look like hell in a darkened room. Easier on the eyes, no less hellish."

"Why didn't you say anything before?"

"We were surrounded by people, and you were getting your bitchy-and-thwarted on. It didn't seem appropriate." Rattling noises marked his passage across the room, followed by a thump and the sound of a lightbulb being unscrewed. "I'm swapping the bulbs in the bedside lights."

"Thanks."

"No worries. You're more pleasant when you haven't got a migraine."

"In that case, toss me my big painkillers when you're done with that?"

There was a pause. "You actually want them?"

"I'm going to need them after we talk." I take a lot of generic drugs for the headaches my eyes give me. That's not the same thing as my "big painkillers," a nasty narcotic mix of ergot alkaloid, codeine, caffeine, and a few less-pronounceable chemical agents. They kill the pain. They also kill all higher brain functions for at least six hours after I've taken them. I avoid drugging myself whenever possible, because I don't usually have the time to waste, but I was getting the feeling this might be the last "free" time we were going to have for a while. If spending it drugged out of my mind meant I had the stamina to handle the rest, well, I've done worse in my pursuit of the truth.

"Georgia—"

"Don't argue."

"I was just going to say that there's time for a nap before we talk, if you want it, and painkillers after that. The Daughters of the American Revolution always talk for hours."

"No, there isn't. We ran out of time when someone decided we'd out-lived our usefulness. Time is now officially something we don't have. Hit the lights as soon as you're ready."

"Right," said Shaun. There was a click. The room brightened before I heard him move away again. "Servers need to initialize, and I'll turn on the screens. Your computer's on the desk if you want to get it hooked up."

"Got it." My headache screamed when I opened my eyes. I ignored it. The lower-wattage bulbs Shaun put in were bearable, if not exactly pleasant; I could deal. Sitting up, I bent forward to open the cat carrier, which was still sitting on the floor near the base of the bed. Lois was out in a flash, vanishing into the bathroom.

I rose and walked over to take a seat at my desk, where I started connecting cables. I was moving gingerly, to upset my head as little as possible, and that slowed me down; I was only halfway done when Shaun called, "Clear." I put down the plug I'd been holding, and the air filled with an electrical buzz that made all the hair on my arms stand on end.

"You'd better have that set low enough not to fry anything," I said, going back to work.

"What do you take me for, an amateur?" Shaun was trying to sound affronted. I wasn't buying it. It's easy to slip when you're setting up a privacy screen—that's part of why I'm not fond of using them. They also make my teeth itch. "It'll short out anything around the perimeter, but as long as you don't get any closer to the walls, you'll be fine."

"If you're wrong, you owe me dinner."

"If I'm right, you owe me dessert."

"Deal." I swiveled in my chair. Shaun was sitting on the bed, leaning back on his hands in a pose of such sheer relaxation that it had to be forced. Skipping the preamble, I said, "Buffy sold us out, and someone tried to kill us."

"I got that."

"Did you get the part where, legally, we were dead as soon as the CDC got the call saying we were infected?"

"I did." Shaun frowned. "I'm surprised they didn't come in shooting."

"Call that the last of our luck," I said. "The way I see it, they weren't just gunning for Buffy. If they were, they wouldn't have bothered calling the CDC after they saw her truck go down. Horrible accident, very tragic, but there's no need to do that sort of mopping up."

"Makes sense," Shaun said and flopped over backward. "So what do we do? Pack our things and go running home?"

"That might not work, since presumably we already know something that's worth killing us for."

"Or Buffy knew something worth killing us for."

"Whoever's behind this has already proven that it's the same thing. I can't imagine we've got two conspiracies running in parallel. That means whoever had our tires shot out was also responsible for the ranch."

"And for Eakly," said Shaun. "Don't you dare forget Eakly."

"I wouldn't," I said. "I can't."

"I dream about Eakly." The statement was almost offhanded, but there was a depth of hurt to it that surprised even me, and I usually know what Shaun's thinking. "They never saw it coming. They never had a chance."

"So leaving isn't an option."

"Leaving never was."

"What are we going to do about Rick?"

"Keep him on, of course."

Raising my eyebrows, I leaned forward to rest my elbows on my knees. "There was no hesitation there. Why not?"

"Don't be an idiot." Shaun sat up, falling into a posture that was the natural mirror image of my own. "Buffy got bit, right?"

"Right."

"Buffy was dying—that's not right. Buffy was *dead*, and she knew it. She told us what she'd done and how to find out more about it, right? Rick was there, and she didn't finger him for a snitch. She was sorry for what she'd done, George. She didn't mean for anyone to die. So why would she've gone and left us with a cuckoo in our birdhouse?"

"What if she didn't know?"

"What if?" Shaun shook his head. "They tried to kill Rick, too. If his car was a little less reinforced, or if he'd hit at a slightly different angle, he'd have been a goner. There's no way to stage that. And the call to the CDC said we were all toast, not just the two of us. So what if Buffy didn't know? Rick's not a moron. He'd have said something by now."

"So you say he stays."

"I say we can't afford to lose anyone else. And I also say that with Buffy gone, I'm an equal partner in this enterprise, so get up."

I blinked. "What?"

"Get up." Shaun stood and pointed to the bed. "You're going to take a nap, and you're going to do it right now."

"I can't nap. I'm waiting for Mahir to call me back."

"He can talk to your voice mail."

"No. He can't."

"Georgia—"

"Just wait."

"No." Shaun's voice was firm. "I'll get the rest of the equipment set up, I'll get the servers running, and I'll check your caller ID every time your phone rings. If Mahir calls, I'll wake you, without consideration for the fact that you're going to work yourself to death. I'm agreeing to that, but I'm also making an executive decision, and my decision is that you, Georgia Carolyn Mason, are going to bed. If you do not like this decision, you may appeal to the court of me hitting you in the back of the head as soon as you turn around."

"Can I have my painkillers?"

"You can have two pills and a pillow," Shaun said. "When you wake up, the world will be a magical wonderland of candy canes, unicorns, and fully assembled servers. And Rick stays. Deal?"

"Deal." I stood, stepping out of my shoes before sitting back down on the bed. "Bastard."

"Close your eyes." I did. Shaun removed my sunglasses, pressing two small round objects into my hand. "Swallow those and you can have these back when you wake up."

"That's dirty pool," I complained, popping the pills into my mouth. They dissolved almost instantly, leaving the bitter taste of codeine behind. I wobbled and let myself fall sideways, eyes still closed. "Dirty pool player."

"That's me." Shaun kissed my forehead. "Rest, George. It'll be better when you wake up."

"No, it won't," I said, resigning myself to the inevitable. "It'll just be later. Later isn't better. Later is just when we have less time."

"Sleep," said Shaun.

So I did.

This is the truth: We are a nation accustomed to being afraid. If I'm being honest, not just with you but with myself, it's not just the nation, and it's not just something we've grown used to. It's the world, and it's an addiction. People crave fear. Fear justifies everything. Fear makes it okay to have surrendered freedom after freedom, until our every move is tracked and recorded in a dozen databases the average man will never have access to. Fear creates, defines, and shapes our world, and without it, most of us would have no idea what to do with ourselves.

Our ancestors dreamed of a world without boundaries, while we dream new boundaries to put around our homes, our children, and ourselves. We limit our potential day after day in the name of a safety that we refuse to ever achieve. We took a world that was huge with possibility, and we made it as small as we could.

Feeling safe yet?

—From *Images May Disturb You*,
the blog of Georgia Mason, April 6, 2040

Twenty-one

Iawoke to the sound of Rick and Shaun arguing quietly, undercut by the comforting static buzz of servers and computers; true to his word, Shaun had managed to get the network up and running while I slept. I stretched experimentally and was pleased to discover that my head neither hurt nor felt like it was stuffed with medicated cotton wool. I'd live. I'd pay for it later—my headaches come from minor damage to the optical nerves, and the more I use artificial stimulants to ignore it, the more likely it becomes that the damage will be permanent—but I'd live.

"—telling you, we're letting her sleep until she wakes up. Work on your report."

"It's the Daughters of the American Revolution. They haven't said anything new *since* the American Revolution."

"So it should be an easy report."

"Asshole."

"Hey, man, I just want you to do your job and let my sister get some sleep. Is that so wrong?"

"Right now? Yes."

"Pet your cat and finish your report." Shaun sounded exhausted. I wondered how long I'd been asleep, lost in my dreamless, drug-induced wonderland while he wrangled the servers and waited for Mahir to call.

I must have sighed because I heard footsteps. The mattress bowed as Shaun leaned against the edge, asking, anxiously, "George? Did you want something?"

Another eight hours of sleep, replacement eyes, and Buffy back from the dead. Since I wasn't likely to get any of the things I really wanted, I sighed and answered, "My sunglasses?" My voice was dry and scratchy.

I turned my face toward Shaun, my eyes still closed and eyebrows raised in silent punctuation to the question.

He touched my hand with the tips of his fingers before he pressed my sunglasses against my palm, saying, "You've been out for about ten hours. I've tried Mahir three times, but there's been no response. Becks says she spoke to him after we did, when she had to request a delete and re-upload of some of her journal files, but that's the last time stamp anybody has."

Becks…? Oh, Rebecca Atherton, the Newsie he stole from me after things went wrong in Eakly. I slipped my sunglasses on and opened my eyes, taking a moment to orient myself before sitting up. Getting my eyes to focus took a little longer. Shaun put a hand on my knee, steadying me, and I covered it with my own, turning my still blurry eyes toward the distant glow of the computers against the far wall. There was a patch of blobby darkness there that looked out of place against the green, and I nodded to it, saying, "Hey, Rick."

"Hey, Georgia," the blob replied. "Feeling any better?"

"I'm half-blind, and it feels like a flock of seagulls crapped inside my head, but it doesn't hurt, so I guess I'll live." I squeezed Shaun's hand. "How was the DAR meeting?"

"Boring."

"Good. At least something in this world can be counted on to stay dull." My eyes were starting to work. The blob had a head now. "You planning on sticking around, or do we need to post your job opening, too?"

Rick paused. "Shaun said you'd already discussed it."

"The two of us, yes. The three of us? Not so much." I shrugged. "I figured you should get a say. You plan to stick around? We're not doing so well on the survival figures, I'm afraid. One out of four sort of sucks."

"I'd rather take my chances with you than anyplace else I can think of, if it's all the same."

I raised my eyebrows high enough that they crested above the tops of my sunglasses. "Oh? What's the logic behind that?"

"I know I haven't known you or your brother for long, and you don't have much reason to trust me; what I'm about to say probably won't help with that. But Buffy was a friend of mine for years. She was a good person, and she never meant to hurt anyone, but if I don't stay with this team long enough to make sure you remember that, one day the news is going to get out, and she's going to be remembered not as a great writer and a good friend, but as the cause of the Eakly Massacre and the cat's paw behind the death of Rebecca Ryman. The best she'll be able to hope for is 'traitor.'

And I won't have that." I could hear the frown in his voice. "I'm staying because I have to. You can try to make me leave if you want to, but it's not going to be fun for any of us."

"I wouldn't dream of it." Giving Shaun's hand a final squeeze, I stood and walked over to sit down at my computer. This close up, my screen was a little fuzzy, but it was nothing I couldn't handle. "If you feel that strongly about staying, you stay. We're glad to have you." My screen blinked at me, prompting for a password. I entered it. Shaun could get me online, but that didn't mean he could access my files. Starting to type, I asked, "What's our general status?"

"Buffy's death hit the newswires five minutes after it happened," said Shaun, moving back to his own machine. "But that's not the fun part." He paused, portentously, until I glared at him. He's good at detecting glares, even through dark glasses. "You want the fun part?"

"Yes, Shaun," I said. "I've been asleep for ten hours, and I want the fun part."

"Fine. Here's the fun part: Our deaths hit the wires at the same time."

My eyes widened. *"What?"*

"We were all reported dead," Shaun said. "Half the news sites had the story before anyone could contradict it, and half of them are still listing you as deceased."

I looked to Rick, who nodded.

"Whoever called the CDC made sure the call was 'accidentally' made on a channel that several local news sites monitor for gossip," he said. "We all got listed as dead before we even made it to Memphis. They printed a retraction about Shaun when he posted to complain about the CDC coffee, and about half the sites did the same for me when I threw up the DAR blurb." He quirked a smile. "I'm not interesting enough to spread as quickly as a *Mason*."

"And me?" I asked, too annoyed not to.

"Still dead," said Rick. "They've got some great conspiracy theories going, too, about Shaun and me concealing your death until we can prove you weren't doing something forbidden by your licensing."

"Thus invalidating my life insurance," I said, putting a hand over my face. "Is there any more good news?"

"Only Buffy made it to the Wall," Shaun said. "She's the only one whose death has actually appeared in the public CDC database."

I bit back a groan. "How many people think we faked our own deaths to up ratings?"

"A lot," Shaun said, voice going grim. "On the plus side, if we'd really been doing that, it would've worked. We gained another three points of market share while people waited for the grisly details to pop up."

"And have they?"

"On us? No. On Buffy? Yeah. It's all over the place. Somebody broke into our main camera upload and—"

"I get the picture. I'll get our official report up tonight so we can put these damn hoax rumors to rest and let people know I'm still breathing. Buffy deserves better than to have her death tarred with some publicity stunt we didn't pull."

"How official is this official report going to be?" asked Rick.

"You mean, 'am I going to include the call the CDC got?'" I asked. He nodded. So did I. "Yes, I am."

"Is that—"

"Wise? Safe? A good idea? No, on all three counts, but I'm going to do it anyway." I pulled up my e-mail and started scanning the list of senders, looking for Mahir's name. "Somebody who's depending on secrecy wants us out of the way. So screw 'em. We're taking that secrecy away."

"And when they start shooting?"

"Who says they've stopped?" Even with Buffy's astonishingly well-constructed filters, the amount of spam that had managed to get through was daunting. I began deleting. "That reminds me. We need to hire a new head for the Fictionals."

Rick shot me a sharp look. "Doesn't that seem a little abrupt? Buffy just died."

"Buffy's death was abrupt; this is necessary. The Fictionals aren't like the Newsies or the Irwins. They won't keep working just because they don't know how to hold still. They need management, or it turns into a million works in progress and nothing that actually *progresses*. Unless we want to start getting angry letters from people wanting to know where the next installment of some fifty-part serial romance is, we need a new division head."

Shaun blinked. "Buffy didn't name anyone?"

"Buffy thought she was immortal. Talk to Magdalene; even if she won't do it, she can probably suggest somebody who will." Suddenly tired again, I set my spam purge to run on auto and minimized the window, pulling up the staff LW&T directory. That archive contained a current copy of the last will and testament of every employee currently on the After the End Times payroll, including details on the dispensation of their intellectual property. Properly filed and witnessed wills are legally required for all businesses whose normal routine brings them into contact with federally established hazard zones, the infected, or members of the working press. Journalists: as dangerous as zombies under modern American law. According to the directory time stamps, Buffy's file hadn't been updated since we left California.

I entered my password to open the file. Both Shaun and I possess the legal authority to access all files stored on our servers, just in case of situations like this. The document flashed open. It was a read-only copy of the actual document, which was being held, according to the header information, by the Meissonier family lawyer back in Berkeley. For our purposes, it was more than sufficient.

Shaun slid out of his chair and stepped up behind me, resting a hand on my shoulder. Buffy left the bulk of her personal possessions to her family, her written works and literary estate to the site as a whole, and her nonfiction—which is to say, her personal files—to Shaun and me. We had the right to use her data however we saw fit. There was no mention of a successor, but that didn't matter because that last rider told me everything we needed to know.

"Son of a bitch," I muttered. "She knew she was going to die over this. And she knew she was doing the wrong thing, even if she didn't want to admit it to herself. She *knew*."

"How can you say that?" asked Rick.

Shaun answered for me, saying, "She left us her personal files. Why would she do that if she didn't know we'd need something that's in them? Maybe she felt like she had to do this, but that doesn't mean she managed to convince herself that it was right. George…"

"Rick, I need you to find a new head for the Fictionals." I hit Print and closed the file. "That's your assignment for right now. Well, that and the DAR report. Shaun, I'm going to need to do a news report on what happened, but—"

"But the bulk of it's an Irwin thing. Got it." Shaun squeezed my shoulder before returning to his own machine. "What about Buffy's files? The server she told us to access?"

"I'd really like that camera footage Mahir has; I was hoping to get that out of the way first. But yeah, the files. I'll head over there now."

"George—"

"Just be quiet while I deal with this," I said, almost more curtly than I'd meant to, and began to type.

After the End Times maintains two file servers for employee use. One, the so-called "public" server, is open to uploads and downloads by every blogger we employ, as well as every blogger even remotely affiliated with the site. If you do any work for us at all, we open an account for you on the public server, and those accounts are rarely revoked unless there's active abuse. There's just no point, especially since we have a tendency to reuse freelancers. Why burn goodwill on a server purge? More important, why waste time by forcing your IT person to set up the same accounts more than once? When we're a little bigger—if we live that long—we'll need to reconsider that policy, but it's served us well so far.

The private server is a lot more locked down. There are presently seven people whose accounts include access to that server, and one of them is dead. Me, Mahir, and Rick from the Newsies; Buffy and Magdalene from the Fictionals; Shaun and Becks from the Irwins. That's where we keep the important things, from private financial records to stories about the campaign that still need to have their facts verified. That server is as hack-proof as it can be because one unverified story leaked under my byline would be enough to seriously cripple, if not kill, the news section of our site.

The news is serious business. If you're not willing to treat it that way, you shouldn't be anywhere near it.

I opened an FTP window and fed in the address for our secure server. When it prompted me for a user name and password, I typed in *sounding-sea*, followed by the password *February-4-29*. Shaun and Rick abandoned their workstations and moved to stand behind me, watching as the screen flickered once, twice, and then rolled as a video player seized control of my machine. Tapping the Escape key did nothing to stop the program from opening, and so I settled back in my seat, comforted by the presence of my team. We weren't much, and we were dwindling by the day, but the three of us were all that we had left.

The screen stopped rolling as the much-beloved face of Buffy Meissonier became clear. She was seated cross-legged on the counter of our van, wearing her patchwork vest and a tattered broomstick skirt. I recognized that outfit; she'd been wearing it the day we left Oklahoma City, when we'd barely been speaking to one another. She'd wanted us to give it up. Hindsight is twenty-twenty, they say. Well, it was a little late now, but at least I understood why she'd wanted so badly to make us all head home. She'd been trying, in her misguided way, to save our lives.

Looking into the camera, Buffy smiled. "Hey," she said. Her voice and expression combined to paint the picture of a woman tired beyond all reckoning, so worn through that she was no longer sure she could be patched back together again. "I guess you guys are watching this. Schrödinger's video recording—if you can see it, it's too late for you to tell me what the picture quality is like. Isn't that always the way? It's my masterpiece, and I'll never see the reactions. I guess that means I won't have to live with the reviews, either. I should get down to business, though, because if you're watching this, you probably don't have much time left to waste.

"My name is Georgette Marie Meissonier, license number delta-bravo-echo-eight-four-one-two-zero-seven. I am of sound mind and body, and I am making this recording to testify that I have willingly and knowingly participated in a campaign to defraud the American public, beginning with my business partners, Shaun Phillip Mason and Georgia Carolyn Mason. As a part of this campaign, I have fed news reports and private feeds to third parties, with the understanding that they would use this information to undercut the presidential campaign of Senator Peter Ryman, and planted recording devices in private spaces, with the understanding that the material thus collected would be used to further undermine the campaign."

On the screen, Buffy paused to take a deep breath, looking suddenly very young behind her exhaustion. "I didn't know. I knew that what I was doing was wrong, and that I'd never work in the news again, but I didn't know anyone was going to get hurt. I didn't know until the ranch, and by then, I was in too deep to find a way out again. I'm sorry. That doesn't bring back the dead, but it's the truth, because I didn't want anyone to get hurt. I thought I was doing the right thing. I thought that when this was over, we'd be a stronger nation because of what I'd done." A tear escaped her left eye, running down her cheek. It would have seemed overly theatrical if I hadn't known Buffy as well as I did—knowing her, it wasn't theatrical *enough*. She was really crying. "I see them when I dream. I close my eyes, and they're all there. Everyone who died in Eakly. Everyone who died at the ranch. It was my fault, and I'm so afraid we got this job because someone who could manipulate the numbers knew I was for sale, if you offered the right price. I'm so sorry. I didn't mean it. I didn't mean any of it.

"If I knew who I'd been sold to, I'd tell you, but I don't. I went out of my way to never know, because if I'd known...I think, if I'd known, I would have realized it was wrong." Buffy looked away from the camera, wiping her eyes. "I got in too deep. I couldn't get back out. And you won't let us go home. Georgia, why can't we go home?" She turned back toward the lens, both eyes brimming with tears. "I don't want to die. I don't want you to see this. Please. Can't we just go *home*?"

"God, Buffy, I'm sorry," I whispered. My words dropped into the silence that followed her plea like rocks into a wishing well, with as little effect.

On the screen, Buffy took a deep breath and held it before letting it slowly out. "You're going to see this," she said, lips tugging up into a small and bitter smile. "You have to see it. Or you'll never know the truth. By triggering this file, you've mailed a video to my parents telling them how sorry I am, and how much I loved what I did. When it closes, you'll have access to my private directory, including a file named 'Confession.' It's locked and time stamped. If you don't open it, it'll be admissible in court. I didn't trust everything to the servers. I think I know better than anyone else right now just how dangerous it is to trust people. You have something of mine that no one else has. Look there. You'll find everything I've got, including the access codes for all those listening devices. Good luck. Avenge me if you can. And I'm sorry."

Buffy paused, smiling for real this time, and added, "This—being here, with you, following this campaign—really was what I wanted. Not all of it, maybe, but I'm glad I came. So thank you. And good luck." The picture winked out.

The three of us stayed frozen in our silent tableau for several minutes. A sniffle from behind my left shoulder told me Rick was crying. Not for the first time, I damned Kellis-Amberlee for taking that simple human comfort away from me.

"What did she mean, something we have that no one else does?" Shaun asked, putting his hand on my right shoulder. "All her luggage was in the truck."

"But we have her laptop," I said. Pushing my chair back from the desk, I rose, turning to face them. "Get me a tool kit and her computer."

Never steal another reporter's story; never take the last of another reporter's ammo; never mess with another reporter's computer. Those are the rules, unless you work for a tabloid, where they replace "never" with "always"...but once you're dead, you're meat, and all bets are off. I had to keep telling myself that as I used a screwdriver to work the bottom panel off Buffy's laptop. Shaun and Rick stood nearby, watching. We'd already scanned the machine itself and found nothing—literally nothing. She wiped the drives at some point, probably before we left on the drive that killed her. When it came to paranoia, Buffy was world class. She'd had good reason to be, after Eakly.

It was somehow anticlimactic when the laptop's bottom panel came free, tearing the tape stretched between it and the battery case and dropping a data stick into my hand. I held it up, showing it to the two of them. "The plot thickens," I said. "Shaun, Becks used to be a Newsie. How's she with computers?"

"Not as good as Buffy—"

"No one's as good as Buffy."

"But she's good."

"Good enough?"

"Only one way to find out." He held out his hand. I gave him the data stick without a moment's hesitation. The day I couldn't trust Shaun, it was over. Simple as that.

"Get her online and get her going through these files. Buffy said there were time stamps and IPs. We need to see what they can give us." I stood. "Rick, get back on that report."

"What are you going to do?"

"Rouse Mahir," I said, moving back to my machine. The chair was still warm; things were moving faster than they seemed. "I don't care what it takes. We need to get a copy of whatever's on that disk stored off-site, and I think 'London' qualifies."

"Georgia?" Rick's tone was soft. I glanced toward him. He hadn't moved back to his own machine; he was just standing there, looking at me.

"What?"

"Are we going to survive this?"

"Probably not. You want out?"

"No." He shook his head. "I just wanted to know whether you realized that."

"I do," I said. "Now get to work."

Both nodding, Rick and Shaun did exactly that.

For all that Mahir seemed to be out, or asleep—or, God forbid, if this was somehow even bigger than it looked, already dead—his machine address still registered on the network. I tapped it in along with my priority code, activating a personalized screamer. If he did *anything* online he'd start getting loud, intrusive pings demanding that he contact me immediately. Screamers are generally viewed as extremely poor form outside of emergencies. As far as I was concerned, this qualified as an emergency.

Satisfied that I'd done everything I could be reasonably expected to do in order to find my second, I bowed my head, set my fingers to the keys, and went to work.

There's something deeply reassuring about doing a factual report. You have every bit of information you need at your fingertips waiting to be smoothed out and turned into something that makes sense. Take the facts, take the faces, take the facets of the truth, polish them until they gleam, and put them on paper—or, in my case, put them in pixels—as an exercise for the reader. I set my feed for a live page-by-page, with a license confirmation on the upload. Anyone who really thought this was some sort of cover-up for my death could report the site to the licensing committee for abuse of my number, and that would cancel the rumors faster than anything else I could do. It'd make good news, too.

The e-mail started coming in as soon as my first page was uploaded. Most of it was positive, congratulating me on my survival and assuring me that my readers had known all along that I'd get out alive. A few letters were less friendly, including one I tagged for upload with the op-ed piece I was planning to write; it said Shaun and I deserved to die at the hands of the living dead, since sinners like us were about as ethically advanced. It would fit perfectly with the reality of how Buffy had been bought.

Page six had just gone up when Shaun called, "Becks says she's cross-checking the IPs now. Most of them look to be scrambled."

"Meaning?"

"Meaning she can't follow them."

Damn. "How about the time stamps?"

"They prove it wasn't any of us, or the senator, but not too much other than that. Just going by the times, it could even be Mrs. Ryman."

Double damn. "Got any good news for me?"

Shaun looked up from his screen, grinning. "How does access codes on all Buffy's bugs sound?"

"Like good news," I said. I would have said more, but my computer beeped, flashing an urgent message light at the bottom of the screen. I double-clicked the prompt.

Mahir's face appeared in a video window, his hair unkempt and his eyes wild as he demanded, "What's going on? What's wrong?"

"You weren't answering your phone!" I said, embarrassed even as the words left my mouth. He was on the other side of the world; there was no way this situation could hold the same urgency for him.

"The local Fictionals were holding a wake and poetry reading in Buffy's honor." He brushed his hair out of his face. "I attended to report on it, and I'm afraid I had a bit too much to drink." Now he sounded sheepish. "I fell asleep as soon as I got home."

"That explains how you slept through the screamer," I said. Twisting in my seat, I asked, "Shaun, we have a local copy of those files?"

"In the local group directory," he confirmed.

"Good." I turned back to my computer. "Mahir, I'm going to upload some files to your directory. I want you to save them locally. Make at least two physical copies. I recommend storing one of them off-site."

"Should I delete them from the server once I've finished reading?"

His tone was light, attempting to joke with me. Mine wasn't light at all.

"Yes. That would be a good idea. If you can pull the rest of your files long enough to reformat your sector, that wouldn't be a bad idea, either."

"Georgia..." He hesitated. "Is there something I should be aware of?"

I bit back the urge to start laughing. Buffy was dead; we'd been reported dead to the CDC; someone had tried to use us to undermine the United States government. There was a *lot* going on that he needed to be aware of. "Please," I said, "download the files, read them, and give me your honest opinion."

"You want my *honest* opinion?" His expression was filled with naked concern. "Get out of that country, Georgia. Come here before something happens that you can't bounce back from."

"England wouldn't want me."

"We'd find a way."

"Entertaining as political exile might be, Shaun would go crazy if I forced him to move, and I wouldn't go without him." Impulsively, I removed my sunglasses and offered Mahir's image a smile. "I'm sorry I may never get to meet you."

Mahir looked alarmed. "Don't talk that way."

"Just read the files. Tell me how to talk after you do that."

"All right," he said. "Be safe."

"I'll try." I tapped the keys to start the upload and his image winked out, replaced by a status bar.

"Georgia?"

Shaun's voice; the wrong name. I turned toward him, a cold spot forming in my stomach as I registered the fact that he hadn't called me "George." "What?"

"Becks has one of the bugs online."

"And?"

"And I think you ought to hear this." Reaching over, he pulled his headset jack out of the speakers. The crackle and hiss of a live transmission promptly blared into the room, seeming all the louder in the sudden silence. Even Lois, crouched next to Rick's monitor, was silent and still, her ears slicked back and her eyes stretched wide.

"—hear me?" Tate's voice was almost impossibly loud, amplified by the bug's internal pickups and Shaun's speakers. "We are going to solve this problem, and we're going to solve it now, before things get any worse."

Another voice, this one indistinguishable. Shaun caught my eye and nodded. He'd have Becks running it through a filter as soon as we finished listening, trying to clean it up enough to determine the speaker. That was all we could really do.

"And I'm telling you, they're getting too close. With the Meissonier girl gone, we can't steer them anymore. There's no telling how many of those damn bugs she planted around the offices. I told you we couldn't trust a spook."

I caught my breath as Rick started swearing under his. Only Shaun was completely silent, his lips pressed into a tight line. Unaware that he was being listened to, Tate continued: "I'm in her little boyfriend's portable office. If there was any spot she wouldn't bug, it'd be the one where she was doing her own share of the sinning."

"He really didn't know her very well," Rick said, in a bitter, distant tone.

"Neither did we," Shaun replied.

"I don't care how you take the rest of them out," Tate barked. "Just do it. If the CDC couldn't finish them off, we'll find another way. Understand me? Do it!" There was a slam, as if a receiver was being thrust rudely into its cradle, followed by the sound of footsteps. The hiss continued for a few more seconds, then cut off as suddenly as it had started.

"They only cut and save when there's sound being received," said Shaun needlessly. We all knew how Buffy's saver bugs worked. Plant them and they'd press anything they heard to file, going dormant to save their batteries when the space around them was silent. She must not have been listening to her files. Just saving and transmitting them, serene in her own certainty that her side was the right one.

"Tate," snarled Rick. "That *fuck*."

"Tate," I said. My eyes were burning. Finally sliding my sunglasses back into place, I looked from one to the other. "We have to see the senator."

"Can we trust him not to be a part of this?" Shaun asked.

I hesitated. "How good is Becks?"

"Not that good."

"Fine." I swiveled back to my screen. "Screamers on everyone. Get the whole team online. I don't care *where* they are, I want them here."

"Georgia . . . ?" said Rick, uncertainly.

I shook my head, already beginning to type. "Shut up, sit down, and get started. We have work to do."

⸻

Every life has a watershed moment, an instant when you realize you're about to make a choice that will define everything else you ever do, and that if you choose wrong, there may not be that many things left to choose. Sometimes the wrong choice is the only one that lets you face the end with dignity, grace, and the awareness that you're doing the right thing.

I'm not sure we can recognize those moments until they've passed us. Was mine the day I decided to become a reporter? The day my brother and I logged onto a job fair and met a girl who called herself "Buffy"? The day we decided to try for the "plum assignment" of staff bloggers to the Ryman campaign?

Or was it the day we realized this might be the last thing we ever did...and decided not to care?

My name is Georgia Mason. My brother calls me George.

Welcome to my watershed.

—From *Images May Disturb You*,
the blog of Georgia Mason, April 8, 2040

Twenty-two

It took two hours and seventeen minutes to gather every blogger, associate blogger, administrative employee, system administrator, and facilities coordinator employed by After the End Times together in one hastily opened virtual conference room. Our conferencing system has eleven rooms, and the eleventh had never been successfully hacked, but Buffy "built" them all. The code was hers, and I didn't feel like we could trust it anymore. We would have invited the volunteer moderators—leaving them out didn't seem right—but we didn't have a way of contacting them without using unsecured channels. And that was the last thing I was willing to do just now.

With Becks, Alaric, and Dave—who was finally back from Alaska, having acquired several hundred hours of footage, and a minor case of frostbite—working in tandem, we almost had a functional replacement for Buffy. Alaric and Dave did most of the heavy lifting of setting up the room, freeing Becks to keep trying to sift through Buffy's data. There was a lot to sort through.

The atmosphere started out jovial, if tinged with unavoidable melancholy. Buffy was dead; we weren't, and every person who logged on seemed to feel the need to comment on both facts, congratulating us on our survival even as they mourned for her. The Fictionals were taking it the hardest. No surprise there, although I was pleased to see Magdalene stepping up to comfort the ones who seemed the most distraught. No fewer than four of the network connections we were getting off the Fictionals were coming from her house—Fictionals tend to be the most social and the most paranoid of the bloggers you're likely to encounter, but Maggie, with her sprawling old farmhouse with the military-grade security system, has a talent for getting them to set the second aside in favor of the first. She could've been an alpha at her own site, if she'd wanted it, but what she'd wanted was to work with Buffy. That wasn't an option anymore. I tapped an IM to Rick, reminding him to ask her about taking the department; if she was handling the mourning period this well, she'd definitely be an asset.

The grumbling started about an hour in, when the congratulatory celebration of our survival died down and it became apparent both that there were people online but working on some sort of secret project, and that we weren't planning to tell *anyone* what was going on until *everyone* arrived. No exceptions, no allowances. Not this time.

The last person to log on was a Canadian Fictional named Andrea, mumbling something about hockey games and cold-weather romances as her connection finished rolling and her picture stabilized. I wasn't really paying attention by that point. That wasn't why we were here.

"Is everyone's connection stable and secure?" I asked. Tapping out a predetermined sequence of characters on my keyboard caused the borders of the dozens of tiny video windows to flash yellow. "If the answer is yes, please input the security code now appearing at the bottom of your screen. If the answer is no, hit Enter. We will be terminating this conference immediately if we can't confirm security."

The grumbling slowed. People had been relieved to see us when we first called them, confused as I refused to let them off the line, and finally annoyed by our group refusal to tell them what was going on. Add draconian security measures and it became clear that something was up. One by one, the borders of the video windows representing our staff flashed white and then green as their security status was confirmed. Shaun's window was the last to change states; we'd agreed on that beforehand. He would close the loop.

"Excellent." I picked up my PDA, which had been cued to my e-mail client since the conference began, and tapped Send. "Please check your e-mail. You'll find your termination notice, along with a receipt confirming that your final paycheck has been deposited to your bank account. Due to California's at-will status and the fact that you're all employed under hazard restrictions, I'm afraid we're not required to give you any notice. Sorry about that."

The conference exploded as everyone started talking at once, voices overlapping into a senseless barrage of sound. Almost everyone. Mahir, Becks, Alaric, and Dave stayed silent, all of them having ascertained from the process of getting the conference online that something huge was going on.

Shaun, Rick, and I sat quietly, waiting for the furor to die down. It took a while. The Irwins shouted the loudest, while the Newsies shouted the least; they knew me well enough to know that if I was supporting a grand gesture—and this *was* a grand gesture—there had to be a reason. They trusted me enough to wait and see what it was. Good team. I hired well.

I set my PDA aside when the shouting began to quiet, saying, "None of you work for us. None of you have any legal ties to keep you here. If you choose to log off at any point during the next five minutes, I'll see to it that you have a letter of recommendation stating that your value as a journalist is entirely beyond measure. You'll never have this easy a time finding another job in your life because I'll pull strings to get you hired, I'll make sure you're settled, and then I'll write you off. This is the all-or-nothing moment, folks: Walk away now if you want to walk, but if you do, you're walking for keeps."

There was a long silence, broken when Andrea asked, "Can you tell us why you're doing this?"

"Buffy's dead, and now we're fired," interjected Alaric. "You don't think these things might be connected?"

"I just—"

"Not very well, you didn't."

"Do me a favor, dears, and shut up so our former boss can speak?" Magdalene sighed. "You're giving me a headache."

"Thank you, Maggie." I looked around my screen, studying each video window in turn. "Andrea, the answer to why we're doing this is a simple one: We don't want any of you to feel obligated to stay with this site any longer than you already have. I'm sure you've all heard about the call the CDC received, reporting our deaths?" Murmurs of agreement. "It was received before we placed the call to tell *them* we were still alive. Someone shot out our tires, there was no one else on the road, and yet somebody told the CDC that we'd been killed."

"Do you have time stamps on that?" asked Alaric, suddenly alert.

"We do," I confirmed, nodding to Shaun, who began to type. Alaric glanced away from his video transmitter, signaling the arrival of the appropriate files, and quieted. "Buffy didn't die in an accident; Buffy was murdered, and her killers thought they'd killed us too. There's a lot more going on, but that's the important part right now: Buffy was *murdered*. Her *murderers* would have been happy to do the same to the three of us, and that means I can't put it past them to do the same to any of you. This is your chance to make a graceful exit before I tell you why they want us all dead." I tapped my PDA again. "If you check your e-mail, you'll see an offer of new employment—everyone but you, Magdalene, and you, Mahir. We need to talk to you off-line." From Magdalene's nod, it was apparent that she'd been expecting that request, or something similar. Mahir just looked floored. I'd been anticipating both responses. "Again, if you want to refuse, that's fine. You will have five minutes to make your decision. If you haven't decided within that time, I'll disconnect you from this conference. Should you choose to leave this organization, you will have twelve hours to remove your personal files from our servers. At the end of that time, your access will be revoked and you'll need to contact a member of the senior staff to obtain anything you haven't downloaded."

I paused, giving the others a chance to speak. No one said a word. "All right. Please review your contracts. If you accept, enter the security code listed under the space for your license number. If you do not accept, it's been a pleasure working with you. I wish you all the best in your future endeavors."

More silence followed this announcement as people opened and read their new employment agreements. Nothing had really changed from their original contracts; they got the same number of shares and the same percentages of the various merchandising lines, and they were expected to hold to the same deadlines and levels of journalistic conduct. In another way, everything had changed from their original contracts because when those contracts were signed, nobody was trying to kill us. We weren't offering hazard pay or guaranteed ratings. We were just offering a lot of danger, and the only real reward was the chance to be a part of telling a truth that was bigger than any of us on our own.

Andrea was again the first to speak, saying, "I...I'm sorry, Georgia. Shaun. I just...I was here because Buffy asked me to come. I never wanted to deal with this sort of thing. I can't."

"It's all right, Ace," said Shaun, soothingly. He's always been good with this sort of thing. That makes one of us. "Thank you for all your hard work."

"I'm sorry I couldn't stay longer," said Andrea. "I...good luck, all of you." Wiping her cheeks with the back of her hand, she looked away from her webcam just before the picture blinked off, leaving a black rectangle on the corner of my screen.

That was the pebble that kicked off the avalanche. Screen borders started blinking white as people agreed to their new contracts; video windows started blacking as people mumbled their apologies and logged off. Some of the answers we got weren't a surprise. I knew Alaric and Becks would stay. Shaun had given me the same reassurance about Dave. With

Buffy gone, there was no one to vouch for the Fictionals, but it seemed likely that we'd lose at least half of them. What I wasn't expecting was how many of my Newsies would be making their apologies along with them.

Luis put it best. "It's not that I don't think you're doing the right thing. I know you. You're doing the only thing you *can*. But people are going to get hurt, and I can't afford to be one of them. I have a family. I'm sorry." And then he was gone, disconnected like half the Fictionals and most of the administrative staff.

We were left with less than half of our original connections when the disconnections stopped, and the only windows not outlined in white were those belonging to Magdalene and Mahir. I looked to the window that held my anxious, former second-in-command and said, "I'll call you when this is over," before tapping out the code to close the connection. "Magdalene, you can stay, if you understand that you're not currently employed by this site."

"I'm assuming you're about to go over the current risk situation, and that you're not hiring me right away because my contract needs review, since you want me to do Buffy's job," said Magdalene, matter-of-factly. "Sound right?"

"Sounds exactly right," said Rick.

"I'll stay. It's my problem as much as it is yours, and my department's going to need me to know what's going on."

"Thank you," I said. I meant it. She'd never really replace Buffy, but her response told me that she was willing to try. "Rick, transmit the files."

"Done."

"Everyone, please check your mail. You'll find an attachment detailing what we currently know, including that whoever ordered Buffy's death was highly placed in the current government. Tate is involved. This information isn't just sensitive; it's potentially enough to get any one of us killed. Read it, transfer it to off-line storage, and wipe your mail. Whether you're involved with our ongoing efforts to find out what's going on is going to be up to you, but if we're convicted of, say, treason against the United States government, all of you have just placed your asses on the line. Welcome to our party." I stood. "Shaun and Rick will be remaining to answer any questions you may have; Shaun speaks for the Irwins, and Rick, as my new second, will be speaking for the Newsies. Thank you for coming. Now, if you'll excuse me, I need to make a phone call." Ignoring their protests, I walked into the bathroom, turning off the interior lights before closing the door behind me.

While Dave and Alaric were cobbling together a new conference room,

Shaun and I had been isolating the bathroom in its own frequency screen, creating an envelope that could only be broken by transmissions made on a very specific set of bandwidths. Most of my equipment was as good as dead on the other side of that door, which was exactly how I wanted it to be. If I had that much trouble dialing out, the rest of the world was going to have one hell of a time dialing in.

Even with the screen's keys coded into my PDA, it took almost five minutes to establish a connection with Mahir's phone. His first words were delivered in a sharp, wounded tone: "What the hell was that about? Have I given you some reason to doubt my dedication to this site? Have I ever done anything other than precisely what you asked of me? Because I'm not feeling terribly valued at the moment, *Miss* Mason."

"Hello to you, too, Mahir," I said, leaning against the bathroom sink and removing my sunglasses. The glow from my PDA was enough for me to see by. It wasn't enough to relieve my headache, but it was a start. "You *are* terribly valued. That's why I fired you."

There was a long pause as he tried to sort through that sentence. Finally, he admitted, "I'm afraid I'm not following you."

"Look. There's every chance in the world that things are going to go wrong." I wished that I was lying to him. I've never wanted to be a liar so badly in my life. "We're playing in an arena we're not equipped for, and there's nobody we can call who has the tools we need to *get* equipped for it. We're either going to find what we're looking for, or we're going to go down in flames."

"What does that have to do with firing me? You seem happy to take everyone else down with you. What robs me of my right to a seat on the *Titanic*?"

"The fact that I need you to be receiving the signals in the Coast Guard tower."

There was a pause. Then: "I'm listening."

"If this goes as badly as it has the potential to go—if it goes *all the way* wrong—we could wind up dead, and everyone who works for the site could wind up charged with treason against the United States government. If whoever's behind all this can somehow turn it from *their* plot into *our* plot, that means every employee of After the End Times is in a position to be charged with terrorist involvement in the use of live-state Kellis-Amberlee to bring about human viral amplification."

"...oh, my God," said Mahir, sounding horrified. "I hadn't considered that."

"I didn't think you had," I said, grimly.

The Raskin-Watts ruling of 2026 didn't impact just America. How could any country, however opposed to the United States government it might be, afford to look like it was soft on the matter of the infected? It couldn't. Every industrialized nation in the world with an extradition treaty had stepped forward by the end of 2027 to state that any individual found guilty of using or conspiring to use Kellis-Amberlee as a weapon would be turned over to the government of the affected nation or nations in order to stand trial. Being outside the boundaries of a country no longer protected you from that country's laws, if you were foolish enough to cross the one line everyone had agreed to draw in the sand.

The United States doesn't apply the death penalty to many crimes these days. Terrorism remains an exception to this particular rule. Use Kellis-Amberlee as a weapon and die. That plain. That simple. That universal.

"Georgia, I appreciate the thought, I truly do, but I don't think sparing me is going to save the rest of you."

"It's not intended to," I said.

"Well, then, what *is* it intended to do?"

"It's intended to give you time to download everything off the server, burn it to disk, and run for Ireland," I said. Ireland has never had an extradition treaty with the United States. It still doesn't. "If you can get across the border, you can probably lie low for years."

"And do what? Hope they forget that I'm an international terrorist?"

"Make sure the world finds out the truth."

The pause this time was even longer. When Mahir spoke again, his voice was quiet and very distant. "I'm not sure whether I should be flattered that you trust me this much, or disturbed that you've just informed me that my life is your contingency plan."

"Does that mean you won't do it?"

"Are you mad? Of course I'll do it. I'd have done it if you'd asked me upfront, and if you'd asked me in a month. It's the only way." He hesitated before adding, wistfully, "I just wish I were better with the notion of you doing this unsupported. Rick's a good fellow, but I've not worked with him long enough to feel like I'm leaving you in competent hands."

"What he can't manage, Shaun will," I said. "I'm going to cut off your official server access at midnight. I'll be mirroring all our findings on the old server address. You remember the old server?" The "old server" was a box we rented from Talking Points when we were all part of Bridge Supporters. We'd used it to back up our files when we were on the road, since Bridge Supporters wouldn't post anything that hadn't been through full validation and didn't store anything uploaded by a beta blogger for more than twenty-four hours. We hadn't used it since well before the campaign trail began, and almost no one outside the clerical staff at Talking Points knew I still had the lease. It wasn't entirely secure, but it wasn't ours, either. Mahir could access it without leaving a trail that would prove he was still a part of our group.

"I do," he said. "I suppose I shouldn't call you after this."

"Not a good idea. I'll contact you when I can."

"Right." He chuckled. "Cloak and dagger, that's us."

"Welcome to journalism."

"Indeed. I do wish I'd met you in the flesh, Georgia Mason. I truly do. It's been an honor and a privilege working with you."

"You may still get the chance, Mahir; I'm not ready to count us out yet." I slid my sunglasses back on. "Be good, be careful, and be alert. Your name is still connected to After the End Times. I can't change that."

"I wouldn't want you to. You do the same, won't you?"

"I'll try. Good night, Mahir."

"Good night, Georgia...and good luck."

The click of the call disconnecting sounded more final than it had any right to. Snapping my phone closed, I straightened, sighed, and reached for the door. It was time to get back to my team.

We had an awful lot of work to do.

It is with regret but without shame that I must announce my resignation from this site. We part, not over differences of politics or religion, but merely over a desire to explore different things. I wish the Masons the best in their future projects, and I look forward to seeing what they will accomplish.

I am sure it will be something spectacular.

—From *Fish and Clips*,
the blog of Mahir Gowda, April 9, 2040

Twenty-three

Six weeks is a long time in the news, even when you're not working on a big project. Following a political campaign is a big project, one that's capable of taking up the resources of an entire team of dedicated bloggers. Training a new division head is also a big project. The Fictionals tend to require the least amount of hand-holding, being largely content to sit around, tell each other stories, and look surprised when other people want to read them, but the person in charge of keeping them on-task needs to be more focused than the rest of the breed. There were contracts to sign and review, permissions to change, files to transfer, and a thousand little administrative things to handle that none of us wanted to deal with. Not with Buffy's blood still fresh in our minds.

Buffy caused her share of problems during those six weeks. Maybe she was gone, but she was still very much a part of the team—and not a productive one. Becks spent the bulk of her time hunting through our code and communications feeds looking for bugs and back doors. I'd clearly never realized how paranoid Buffy really was, because the number of confirmed recording devices hidden *internally* was over three digits, and Becks was still finding feeds for wireless listening devices hidden in just about every office, public gathering place, and conference center we'd been to since this whole thing started. "If she'd wanted to go CIA, she could have owned the place," Shaun muttered on the day Becks confirmed that there were still bugs running in Eakly.

"But would they have put up with her fixation on sappy purple poetry?"

"Guess not."

Alaric and Dave followed Becks through our systems, rebuilding the mess she made as she rooted out Buffy's worms. Together they were almost up to the task of remaking the things Buffy had built alone, although it was starting to wear on them; they'd signed on as journalists, not computer technicians. "Hire new field systems maintainer" was near the top of my to-do list, right under "uncover massive political conspiracy," "avenge Buffy's death," and "don't die."

And even with all of this going on, we still had a job to do. Multiple jobs, really. Not only did we need to keep following the Ryman-Tate Campaign—which continued to gather steam, now buoyed by not one, not two, but *three* major tragedies, earning us a lot of extra news cycles in the traditional media outlets, as well as online—we needed to keep our beta bloggers on-task and updating the rest of the site. The news marches on, whether you're walking wounded or not. That's one of the beautiful things about the news. It's also one of the most frustrating.

Two weeks in Houston. Two weeks of sending Rick on every assignment we could get away with sending him on, while Shaun and I locked ourselves in our hotel room and planned for a war we'd never signed up for, against an adversary we'd never volunteered to fight. Whose side was Ryman on? I was guessing he wasn't a part of Tate's plan; no sane man would sacrifice his daughter like that. Then again, Shaun and I were adopted to satisfy the Masons' desire to prove the zombie war had been won by the living, and they've never stopped us from walking into the jaws of death—if anything, they've encouraged it, living for the ratings, because when they lost Phil, the ratings were all they had. So who are we to judge the sanity of parents? We sat up until almost dawn every night, working through the darkness, making plans, making contingencies for those plans, looking for a way out of a maze we didn't see before we were already lost inside it.

Shaun pretended he didn't know I wasn't sleeping, and I pretended not to hear him punching the bathroom walls. Caffeine pills and surgical tape; that's what I'll always think of when I think of Houston. Caffeine pills and surgical tape.

I tried to talk to Ryman twice; he tried to talk to me three times. None of our attempts synchronized. I couldn't trust him when I didn't know whether or not he was working with Tate; he couldn't understand why we'd pulled away, or why we were overworked and snarly with exhaustion. Even Shaun was visibly withdrawn. He'd stopped going out in the field with Steve and the boys when he didn't need to file reports, and while he was still meeting his contracted duties, he wasn't doing it with anything like the flair and enthusiasm Ryman had come to expect from him. From all of us. There wasn't anything we could do about it. Until we knew if we could trust him, we couldn't tell him what was going on—what we suspected, what we knew, anything. And until we told him what was going on, we couldn't be sure we could trust him. It was a Möbius strip of a problem, endlessly twisting back on itself, and I couldn't see a way out of it. So we pushed him away and hoped he'd understand the reasons when things were over.

After Houston, it was time to get back on the road, rolling across the country like nothing had ever gone wrong. Not nothing; Chuck was gone, replaced by a pale-faced drone who scuttled around doing his job and avoiding anything that resembled socialization. Our security detail tripled while we were moving, and Shaun was no longer allowed to ride out unescorted. He took an almost malicious glee in forcing his babysitters to follow him into the nastiest, most dangerous terrain he could find, and some of the footage he got out of it has frankly been amazing. The Irwin community has been buzzing about putting him up for a Golden Steve-o award this year, and I'll be surprised if he doesn't win.

We spent a month glad-handing our way across the western half of the country while the other candidates stayed in the air and the major cities, assuming major metro areas would have better anti-infection measures. Tell that to San Diego. The devil-may-care approach was winning Ryman big percentage points, enough to keep him in the news even as the media flurry kicked up by this latest tragedy died down. "Man of the People Keeps the World Grounded"—human interest gold. A few outlets made the requisite noises about how Ryman's insistence on an old-fashioned campaign had dogged him with tragedy from the beginning, but the facts of Rebecca and Buffy's deaths were enough to pretty much silence them. Maybe you could blame the senator for Eakly if you reached, but you couldn't blame him for terrorist action or assassination attempts. America is the land of the free and the home of the paranoid, and yet, blessedly, we haven't fallen that far. Yet.

Six weeks after Memphis, we were overworked, overtired, and about to hit the crowds in one of the country's toughest, most essential markets: Sacramento, California.

You'd think Shaun and I would be excited about a stop in our state's capital, being California kids bred and raised. You'd be wrong. California is essentially a bunch of smaller states held together by political connections, water rights, and the stubborn refusal of any segment to cede the cash-cow name "California" to any of the others. The California secessionist movement has been around since before the Rising—not the state quitting the country, but the various parts of the state quitting each other. Sacramento has no love for the Bay Area. We get the good weather, the good press, and the big tourism dollars, and they? They get the state government and a lot of hard to defend farmland. To say that there's a little resentment there is to understate the case just a little. Whatever fellow-feeling Sacramento had for the rest of the state died when it stopped hosting the annual state fair and started hosting the annual "everybody hide in their houses and pray they don't die"-a-thon in its place.

The air was hot and so dry it seemed to suck the moisture out of my throat as we stepped out of the Sacramento Airport and onto the partitioned-off loading zone where we'd be meeting the senator's convoy. It was late afternoon, and the sun was bright enough to stab at my eyes through the lenses of my sunglasses. I staggered, catching myself on Rick's shoulder. He shot me a questioning glance. Silent, I shook my head. We were all feeling the strain, Shaun as much as any of us, and if Rick said anything, Shaun would spend the rest of the afternoon fussing over me. There was too much to do for me to let him do that.

Senator Ryman had flown in the day before, along with Governor Tate and most of the senior staff. We were supposed to be right behind them, flying commercial air rather than via private jet; unfortunately, a medical emergency grounded our plane in Denver, forcing us to wait on the tarmac with a hundred terrified passengers to see whether our aircraft was about to be declared a closed quarantine zone. I'll admit, for a few guilty moments, I was almost hoping it would be. At least then we'd be able to get some sleep before heading back to our home state. I was really starting to worry about Shaun. It had gotten to where he only went to bed when I *put* him there.

A familiar black car pulled up to the curb, and the door opened to reveal Steve, implacable and hulking as ever. "Miss Mason," he said, with a nod in my direction.

One corner of my mouth curled upward. "Nice to see you, too, Steve. What's our plan for the afternoon?"

"I'm your escort to the Assembly Center. The convoy leaves for the hall in ninety minutes."

"That doesn't leave much time." I grimaced, grabbing a suitcase in each hand as Steve got out of the car and moved to start hoisting our equipment. Senator Ryman was giving a keynote speech to the California Republicans, and it promised to be the sort of evening that resulted in lots of sound bites, accidental quotes, and competitive reporting. We all needed to be on our game. I'd been hoping to manage it with more rest and less caffeine, but you can't always get what you want. "Thanks for coming to meet us."

"Of course." A second car pulled up behind the first, Carlos getting out and joining in the collection of luggage. Our keepers—the unfortunate

Andres and a blank-faced woman named Heidi, who I suspected had only been assigned to accompany us because my eyes meant I would have to go for a private security screening, and they didn't want "private" to mean "away from our guards"—joined him, first in moving the luggage, then in his car. I suppose a night at the airport with the three of us had rather soured them on our company.

"Ready?" asked Steve.

"Ready," Shaun confirmed, and we piled into the car, where blessed air conditioning washed over us. Steve glanced in the rearview mirror to be sure we were wearing our seat belts before turning on the flashers and pulling away from the curb.

I raised an eyebrow, and Shaun, taking his cue like a pro, asked, "We expecting trouble, sport?"

"There are a great many politicians in town," Steve said.

I knew what that meant: It meant Senator Ryman was concerned that whoever had been responsible for the attacks on his campaign was here in the city and would try to take care of unfinished business. They only got Buffy on their first try, after all. I forced the jet of fury rising in my chest down, refusing to let myself get riled. He didn't know the snake was in his camp; he didn't know it was Tate he needed to be watching out for. So why the *fuck* did he let us fly commercial?

Shaun put his hand on my arm, seeing my sudden tension. "Easy," he murmured.

"Hard," I said, and subsided.

In the carrier Rick was clutching, Lois yowled. I knew exactly how she felt.

Our diminutive convoy cut through the airport traffic in a bubble of open space created by the flashers, heading for the outskirts of town. Once, Sacramento was known for hosting the state fair, along with various rodeos, horse shows, and other large outdoor gatherings. After the Rising made those impractical, the city found itself missing a lot of vital revenue and it started looking for another way to make money. Several local taxes, a few private donations, and several major security contracts later, the fairgrounds reopened, given new life as the Sacramento Secure Assembly Center. Open-air, with standing structures and mobile home hookups for traveling convoys, a four-star hotel, a conference center...and the country's largest outdoor space certified as safe for public assembly. If you wanted to see a candidate speak outside, looking heroic and all-American against a blue summer sky, you did it in Sacramento. Presidencies were *made* there; no matter what your politics were or how clean a campaign you ran, it all came down to how the people reacted when they saw your silhouette against that sky.

According to the itinerary, Senator Ryman and Governor Tate were going to be spending the next seven days in Sacramento, giving speeches, meeting the press, and getting endorsements from California's political leaders. Not just the Republicans. My notes indicated that several prominent Democrats and Independents would be coming to have their pictures taken with the man many were beginning to suspect would be our next president. Assuming the scandal when we outed Tate didn't kill his career, of course.

"Jesus," said Rick, whistling as the fence around the Center came into view. "You people don't do anything small, do you?"

"Welcome to California," I said, rolling up my sleeves. Shaun was doing the same. Rick glanced at us, wincing, and I smiled. "Don't worry. They'll leave you a little bit."

After four blood tests and a call to the CDC databases to confirm that my retinal KA was legitimately registered and not a recent affliction, we were permitted to move into the Center. From here, blood tests would be required if we wished to enter a standing structure or leave the grounds; we'd also be subject to random testing by the Center's staff, which could happen as often as twice an hour or as rarely as once a week. Shaun made a game of pointing out the security cameras and motion detectors as we drove toward the spot assigned to the convoy.

"Start moving like a dead thing and they'll be on you in less than a minute," he said, with some satisfaction.

"Please tell me you're not speaking from experience," Rick said.

"I'm smarter than that." Shaun tried to sound affronted. He failed.

"Someone else got there first," I said. "How long did he get in state prison?"

"Two years, but it was for science," said Shaun.

"Uh-huh," I said. I might have gone on, but the car was turning, pulling down a narrow drive whose signpost identified it as "Convoy Parking #11." I sat up straighter, resetting my sunglasses. "We're here."

"Thank God," said Rick.

The Sacramento sun hadn't gotten any cooler during our drive. I shed my jacket and grabbed my laptop bag, scanning the assembled vehicles and trailers until I spotted my objective. A slow smile spread across my face.

"Van sweet van," murmured Shaun.

"Exactly." I started walking, trusting the security detail to bring the rest of our things. Our vehicles and the majority of our equipment were already in place.

"In a hurry?" Rick asked, trotting to catch up with me. Shaun gave him a look. He ignored it.

"I want to see if the boys have made any progress," I said, pressing my palm against the pressure pad on the van door. Needles bit into my hand. The door unloaded a few seconds later. Looking back over my shoulder, I asked, "Steve, which trailer are we?"

"The one on the far left with your name over the door. Mr. Cousins is in the trailer next to it," Steve said. "I assume you're anxious to get to work?"

"Yes, actually—crap." I paused, dismayed. "The keynote speech."

"I've got it," said Shaun. I must have looked stunned, because he shrugged. "I can wear a monkey suit and take notes like a Newsie. They'll never know the difference, and I bet the invite just says 'Mason.' Steve?"

"Yes..." said Steve, looking perplexed.

"It's settled. C'mon, Rick. Let's let George get some work done." My brother grabbed the startled Newsie by the arm and hauled him away. Steve smirked and followed, leaving me standing at the entrance to the van, wondering what had just happened. Then, not being one to look a bit of gift productivity in the mouth, I stepped inside.

We removed a few vital system components before letting them ship the van, like the backup drives, our files, and—most important—the data sticks that would unlock the servers. I made my way around the interior, taking my time as I brought each system up and online, ending with the perimeter cameras. There was a certain feeling of homecoming as the screens Buffy had worked so long to get installed began flickering on, showing rotating camera views of the outside. Nothing was happening. That's the way I like it. Once everything was stable, I flipped on the security systems. They would generate enough static to block any outside surveillance less sophisticated than the CIA's, and if we were being monitored by the CIA, we'd have been dead already. Sitting down at my console, I opened a chat window.

Most online networking is done via message boards—totally text, not quite real-time—or streaming video these days. Very few people remember the old chat relays that used to dominate the Internet. That's good. That means that if both sides of the chat are on servers you control, you can fly so far under the radar that you're essentially invisible.

Luck was with me. Dave was waiting when I connected.

What's the story? I typed. My words appeared white against the black command window.

Georgia? Confirm.

Password is 'tintinnabulation.'

Confirmed. Have you checked your e-mail?

Not yet. We just got in.

Log off. Go read. I don't want to waste your time with a reframe.

I paused, staring at those stark white words for a long moment before I typed, *How bad?*

Bad enough. Go.

I went.

Reading the files Dave and Alaric provided took the better part of an hour. Getting myself to stop hyperventilating took another twenty minutes. When my lungs stopped burning and I was sure I could control myself, I shut down my laptop, returned it to its case, and rose. I needed to get myself dressed; it was time to crash a party.

I always knew I wanted to be a journalist. When I was a kid, I thought they were the next best thing to superheroes. They told the truth. They helped people. I wouldn't find out about the other things journalists did—the lies and espionage and back-stabbing and bribes—for years, and by that point, it was too late. The news was in my blood. Like every junkie in the world, I needed my next hit too badly to give it up.

I've wanted nothing but the news and the truth and to make the world a better place since I was a little girl, and I never regretted it for a minute. Not until now. Because this is bigger than me, and it's bigger than Shaun, and God, I'm scared. And I'm still a junkie. I still can't walk away.

—From *Postcards from the Wall*,
the unpublished files of Georgia Mason, June 19, 2040

Twenty-four

Unfortunately for my need to hurry, the instructions regarding the senator's keynote speech and the dinner party to follow were clear: Formal attire was required for all attendees, even media representatives. Maybe especially media representatives—after all, everyone *else* paid fifteen hundred dollars for the privilege of eating rubber chicken and rubbing elbows with Senator Ryman, while we were getting in on that damned "freedom of the press" loophole. If they shut us out, we'd be free to start playing dirty. If they let us in, cosseted us, petted us, and put us in our places, they could maintain the semblance of control. Maybe it's never stopped a real scandal from growing legs, but it's done a lot to keep the little ones under the table where they belong.

The campaign staff had been careful with our luggage, placing mine and Shaun's on our respective sides of the trailer we'd be living in for the duration of the Sacramento stop. That was, sadly, before Shaun tore through like a hurricane, looking for his own formalwear. My suitcases were buried beneath a thick layer of Shaun's clothing, weaponry, paperwork, and other general debris. Locating them took the better part of ten minutes, and determining which case contained my own formalwear took another five. I cursed Shaun the whole time. It kept me distracted.

Men's formal attire is sensible: pants, suit coats, cummerbunds. Even ties can be useful, since they work as makeshift tourniquets or garrotes. Women's formal attire, on the other hand, hasn't changed since the Rising; it still seems designed to get the people wearing it killed at the first possible opportunity. Screw that. My dress was custom-made. The skirt is breakaway, the bodice is fitted to allow me to carry a recorder and a gun, and there's a pocket concealed at the waist for extra ammo. Even with all those alterations, it's the most confining garment I own, and the situations that call for me to wear it almost invariably require hose and heels. At least modern pantyhose are made with a polymer weave that's virtually puncture proof.

I'd wear the heels. I'd wear the hose. I'd even wear a layer of tinted lip gloss, since that would make it look like I'd applied makeup for the occasion. There was no way I was going to put my contacts in for what was, essentially, a snatch-and-grab to get me to the senator and my team, convince them I had news, and get them back to the compound. Still swearing, I yanked the shawl that went with the dress out of the side pocket of my garment bag, clipped my ID badge to the right side of my chest, and went storming back out of the trailer, heading for the motor pool.

Steve was on duty, standing at a relaxed sort of attention as he monitored the radio channels for security or vehicular needs. He straightened when he saw me coming, chin bobbing downward as he took in the way that I was dressed. It was impossible to see his eyes behind his sunglasses, but he took no pains to disguise the motion of his head, which rose again as he studied the tailoring of my dress, the shawl around my shoulders, and finally, with a quirk of one eyebrow, my sunglasses.

"Going somewhere?" he asked.

"I was planning on doing a little gate-crashing," I said. "Give a girl a ride?"

"Didn't you send your brother in your place?"

"Something came up. It's important that I get over there."

Steve studied me for a moment, his expression implacable. I looked back at him, keeping my own expression just as composed. We both had a lot of practice, but I was the one who had more to lose if I slipped up. It was Steve who gave in, nodding marginally before he said, "This got something to do with Eakly, Georgia?"

His partner died there. We knew there was a conspiracy. How likely was it that we'd still be alive if our security detail was a part of it? There might be listening devices. There was nothing I could do about that, and we were in the end game. It was time to go all-in. "This has everything to do with Eakly, and with the ranch, and with why Chuck and Buffy died. Please. I need you to get me to that dinner."

Steve remained still for a moment more, mulling over what I'd said. He was a big man, and people often assume big men must be slow. I never assumed that about Steve, and I didn't assume it now. He was getting his first real look at a situation my team and I had been living with for months, and it took some getting used to. When he did start to move, he moved quickly and with no hesitation. "Mike, Heidi, you cover this gate. Anybody radios for me, you say I'm in the can and I'll radio back when I'm done. Tell them I had franks and beans for dinner, if you think it'll keep them from asking more."

Heidi tittered, a high, nervous sound entirely out of keeping with her professional exterior. Mike frowned, expression betraying a slow confusion. "Yeah, we can do that," he said. "But why...?"

"We hired you after the ranch, so I'm not going to smack you for asking that question. There's reasons." Steve glanced at me. "I'm guessing that if it was safe to give those reasons in a place as open as this one, they'd have already been given."

I nodded. I wouldn't have said as much as I had if he hadn't invoked the specter of Eakly first, but I wasn't going to lie to the man when I was asking for his help. Even if I thought I could pull it off, which I didn't, it would have been wrong.

"Just do it, Mike," said Heidi, aiming an elbow at the unfortunate Mike's side. He bore the blow stoically, only allowing a slight grunt to escape. Heidi withdrew her elbow. "We got it, Steve. Watch the gate, monitor the radio, don't tell anybody you're gone."

"Good. Miss Mason? This way." Steve turned, his legs eating ground with frightening efficiency as he led me to one of the motor pool's smaller vehicles. It was a modified Jeep with a hard black exterior that made it look like nothing so much as a strange new type of beetle. He produced the keys from one pocket and hit a button; the doors unlocked with a beep. "You'll forgive me if I don't open the door for you."

"Of course," I said. In a two-person vehicle this new, there would be blood test units built into the door handles to prevent some unfortunate driver from ending up sealed in an enclosed space with one of the infected. Chivalry wasn't dead. Chivalry just wanted to be certain I wasn't a zombie before I got into the car.

Even when concerned enough to abandon his post—and that's what he was doing, given that he hadn't radioed our whereabouts to base—Steve remained a careful, cautious driver. He sped down the roads back toward town at precisely the speed limit, without turning the flashers on. They would have attracted too much attention, especially from any members of our own camp who might start to wonder what he was doing out there. Our departure from the compound had been recorded, but those records were legally secured, save in the instance of an outbreak causing privacy laws to be suspended.

The hall where Senator Ryman's keynote speech and the associated dinner party were being hosted was downtown, in one of the areas that was rebuilt after the Rising. Shaun and I did a series of articles on the "bad" parts of Sacramento a few years ago, taking cameras past the cordons and into the areas that were never reapproved for human habitation. Burnt-out husks of buildings stare out on cracking asphalt, the biohazard tape still gleaming across their doors and windows. In the white marble and clean chrome paradise of the government assembly hall, you'd never know that side of Sacramento existed. Not unless you'd been there.

It took three blood tests to reach the foyer. The first was at the entrance to the underground parking garage, where valets in plastic gloves brought the test panels, clearly expecting us to allow the polite fiction that there weren't guards with automatic weapons flanking the booth. Those men stood there like statues, sending goose bumps marching across my arms. It wasn't the security; it was how blatantly it was displayed. No one would argue if they gunned us down. I had my recorders running, but without a security schematic, I couldn't afford to transmit across what might be compromised airspace, and without Buffy, I didn't have a security schematic I could trust. We needed her so badly. We always had.

Steve stayed behind in the garage, standing silent guard over the car; without my press pass and invitation, he'd never make it into the party without making a scene, and we didn't want to do that. Not yet. I was pretty sure there were a lot of scenes in my future. Assuming the senator listened long enough that we could keep on *having* a future.

It took a second blood test to get out of the garage and into the elevator. The third blood test came as a bit of a surprise; it was required to get *out* of the elevator. How they expected me to have been exposed to the virus during the ten seconds I'd spent between floors was a mystery to me, but they wouldn't have spent the money on a testing unit if it hadn't happened at least once. The elevator doors didn't open until the light over the door went green, and I spared a moment to wonder what happened when more than one person took the elevator at a time. Then I stepped out into the foyer and into a world that had never known the Rising.

The mystery of the extensive security was solved in an instant, because this huge, lavishly appointed room looked like it was lifted straight from the pre-infection world. No one carried visible weapons or wore protective gear. A few folks had the clear plastic strips over their eyes that signaled the presence of retinal Kellis-Amberlee, but that was it. The place even had picture windows, for God's sake. It took careful scrutiny to see that they were holograms, looking out over an image of a city too perfect to be real.

Maybe that's how it was once, but I doubt it; corruption's been with us a lot longer than the living dead.

Even without visible weapons, there was security. A man with a portable bar-code scanner in one hand stopped me not two steps out of the elevator. "Name?"

"Georgia Mason, After the End Times. I'm with the Ryman campaign." I unclipped my badge, handing it over. He swiped it through his scanner and passed it back, frowning at the display. "You should have me on your list."

"According to this, Shaun Mason has already checked in with those credentials."

"If you'll check your list of associated journalists, you'll see that we're *both* registered as being attached to the Ryman campaign." I didn't bother trying to win him over with my scintillating wit. He had the look of a natural bureaucrat, and that sort of person almost never yields from the stated outline of their job.

"Please wait while I access the list." He made a seemingly careless gesture with one hand. Only seemingly careless; I could see four people in the crowd who were now looking in our direction, and none of them was holding a drink or laughing. If four of the guards on duty were being that blatant, the math of professional security meant there were four more who weren't.

The scanning unit beeped as it connected to the wireless network and queried the files available on the press corps cleared for entrance. Eventually, it stopped beeping, and the officious little man's frown deepened.

"Your credentials are in order," he said, sounding as if the very fact that I hadn't lied was inconveniencing him. "You may proceed."

"Thank you." The watchers had melted into the crowd now that they were sure I wasn't gate-crashing. I clipped the badge back to my chest, putting several feet between myself and the man with the scanner before reaching up to tap my ear cuff. "Shaun," I muttered, quietly.

There was a pause, the transmitter beeping to signal that it was making a connection. Then Shaun's voice, close by and startled: "Hey, George. I figured you'd be neck-deep in site reviews by now. What gives?"

"Remember the punch line I forgot yesterday?" I asked, scanning the crowd as I moved toward what I presumed was the entrance to the main dining hall. "The *really* funny one?"

Shaun's surprise faded, replaced by wariness. "Yeah, I remember that one. Did you figure out the rest of the joke?"

"Uh-huh, I did. Some friends of mine found it online. Where are you?"

"We're at the podium. Senator Ryman's shaking hands. What's the punch line?"

"It'll be funnier if I tell you in person. How do I get to the podium?"

"Straight through the big doors and head for the back of the hall."

"Got it. Georgia out." I tapped the ear cuff, killing the connection, and walked on.

Shaun and Rick were a few feet to the left of the crowd of people the senator was glad-handing his way through. They'd paid for the privilege of meeting the man being predicted as our next president, and they were by God going to meet him, even if it was only for the few seconds it took to shake a hand and share a smile. On those few seconds are presidencies made. Here, behind the believable "safety" of a double-checked guest list and that guest list's triple-checked infection status, old-school politicians felt free to revert to their old habits, pressing the flesh like it had never gone out of style. You could tell the ones who were genuinely young from the ones who'd had all the plastic surgery and regenerative treatments money could buy, because the young ones were the ones looking nauseated by all the human contact around them. They hadn't grown up in this political culture. They just had to live with it until they became the old men at the top of the hill.

The senator didn't look uncomfortable at all. The man was in his element, all toothy smiles and bits of practical wisdom sliced down to sound-bite size in case one of the nearby reporters was broadcasting on an open band. He'd known to do that sort of thing long before we joined his campaign, but having a constant press entourage had forced him to master the art. He was good. Given enough time, he'd be great.

Shaun was watching for my arrival, his shoulders set at the angle that meant he was tenser than hell and trying to hide it. They relaxed slightly as he saw me cutting through the crowd, and he nodded for me to approach. I shook my head, mouthing 'Where's Tate?'

Holding up a finger to signal me to quiet, Shaun pulled out his PDA and scrawled a message with the attached stylus. My watch beeped a second later, the message *other side o/room w/investors what's going on?????* scrolling across the screen. The message *I need to talk to Sen. Ryman w/o Tate hearing* would have taken too long to type on the tiny foldout keypad. I deleted the message and kept walking.

"Georgia," Rick greeted as I drew close. He was holding a flute of what appeared to be champagne, if you didn't pay too much attention to the bubbles. Sparkling cider: another trick of working the crowd. If people think you're getting as drunk as they are, they forget to be careful around you.

"Rick," I said, with a nod. Shaun was shooting me a concerned look, and failing in his efforts to hide it. I put a hand on his arm. "Nice tux."

"They call me Bond," he said, gravely.

"Figured they might." I looked toward the senator. "Gonna need to wade in there. I wish I had a cattle prod."

"Are we going to find out what the situation is any time soon, or are we supposed to follow you blindly?" asked Shaun. "I ask because it determines whether I'm hitting you in the head sometime in the next eight seconds. Very vital information."

"It's a little hard to explain here," I said. "Unless you know who's broadcasting locally?"

Shaun groaned, attracting startled glances from several bystanders. A plastic smile snapping instantly into place, he said, "Jeez, George, that was a *terrible* joke."

"I didn't say it was a *good* punch line, just that I'd remembered it," I said, stepping a little closer. Pitching my voice so low it verged on inaudible, I said, "Dave and Alaric had their big breakthrough. They followed the money."

"Where'd it go?" Shaun was even better at this than I was. His lips didn't even seem to move.

"'Where'd it *come* from?' would be a better question. It *went* to Tate. It *came* from the tobacco companies, and from some people they haven't traced yet."

"We knew it was Tate."

"The IPs they're pulling are from D.C. . . . and Atlanta."

There's only one organization in Atlanta important enough to bring me running the way I had, especially when we'd already known at least a part of the conspiracy. Shaun's eyes widened, need for secrecy eclipsed by sudden shock. If the CDC had been infiltrated . . .

"They don't know for sure?"

"They're trying, but the security is good, and they've nearly been caught twice."

Shaun sighed. That *was* audible, and I elbowed him in the side for it. He shook his head. "Sorry. I just wish Buffy were here."

"So do I." Palming a data stick, I slipped it into his pocket. To an observer, it would have looked like I was going for his wallet. Let them call security. It's not like there'd be anything for them to find. "That's a copy of everything. There are six more. Steve doesn't know he has one."

"Got it," said Shaun. Always back up your data, and scatter it as far as you can. I can't count the number of journalists who have forgotten that basic rule, and some have never recovered from the stories they lost. If we lost this one, getting discredited was going to be the least of our worries. "Off-site?"

"Multiple places. I don't know them all; the guys did their own backups."

"Good."

Rick had been observing our semi-audible conversation without comment. He raised his eyebrows as it stopped, and I shook my head. He took the refusal with good grace, sipping from his glass of "champagne" and continuing to scan the crowd. There were a few people who seemed to be holding the bulk of his interest. Some were politicians, while others were people I recognized from the campaign. I glanced to Rick, who nodded toward Tate. Got it. These were people whose loyalties he thought he knew, and thought belonged to our resident governor. Who just happened to be the man most likely to have caused the deaths of an awful lot of innocent people, as well as being responsible for the corruption and death of one of our own.

None of those people was standing close enough to hear our conversation unless one of them had listening devices planted on or around the senator. If I was going to risk anything, I needed to do it now. "I'm going in," I murmured to Shaun, and began working my way through the crowd surrounding Senator Ryman.

I'll give the flesh-pressers this: They didn't give ground easy, not even as I was none too gently elbowing my way into their midst. A lady old enough to have been my grandmother drove the heel of her left shoe down on the top of my foot with a degree of force that would have been impressive in a younger woman. Fortunately, even my dress shoes are made of reinforced polymer. Even so, I bit my tongue to keep myself from swearing out loud. Casual assault might be A-okay with security, but I was reasonably sure shouting "cock-sucking bitch" wouldn't be.

After a lot of shoving and several painful kicks to my shins and ankles, I found myself to the right of the senator, who was busy having his hand pumped up and down by a barrel-chested octogenarian whose eyes burned with the revolutionary fervor one only ever seems to see in those who discovered either religion or politics at a very young age. Neither man seemed to have registered the fact that I was there. I was neither the assaulting nor the assaulted, which left me on the outside of their present closed equation.

The handshaker showed no signs of stopping. If anything, his pumps were increasing in vigor as he started hitting his stride. I weighed the potential danger of octogenarian assault against waiting for him to tire, and settled on action as the better part of valor. Smoothly as I could, I moved to place my hand on Senator Ryman's free arm and said, in a sugar-sweetened tone, "Senator, if I could have a moment of your time, I'd be most appreciative."

The senator jumped. His assailant looked daggers at me, which moved up the scale to full-sized swords as the senator turned and flashed his best magazine-cover smile my way. "Of course, Miss Mason," he said. He deftly twitched his fingers free of the handshaker, saying, "If you wouldn't mind excusing me, Councilman Plant, I need to confer with a member of my press pool. Everyone, I'll be right back with you."

Fighting into the throng had taken almost five minutes. Getting out of it required nothing but the senator's hand at the small of my back, propelling me along as we made our way to the clear space to the left of the dais. "Not that I mind the save, Georgia, since I was starting to worry about the structural integrity of my wrist, but what are you doing here?" asked Senator Ryman, his voice pitched low. "Last I checked, you'd stayed at the Center, which is why your brother's been here annoying the staff and eating all the shrimp canapés all evening."

"I *did* stay at the Center," I said. "Senator, I don't know if you're aware of this, but—" Someone shouted congratulations to the senator, who answered it with a grin and a broad thumbs-up. It was a perfect photo-op moment, and I snapped the shot with my watch's built-in camera before I even thought about what I was doing. Instincts. Clearing my throat, I tried again. "Buffy was working for someone who wanted to keep tabs on your campaign."

"You've told me this before," he said, more briskly. I recognized the impatience in his eyes from dozens of media briefings. "It's all some big shadow conspiracy looking to bring me down. What I don't understand is why this is suddenly so pressing that you need to rush over here and risk making a scene on what might be one of the most important political evenings of my life. There are a great many movers and shakers here tonight, Georgia—a *great* many. These are the men who could hand me California, as you'd know, if you'd bothered to read the briefing papers and attend my speech." *If you'd bothered to do your job,* said his subtext, so clearly that it might as well have been spoken aloud. I'd let him down. My reporting, which he'd come to depend on as one of the tools of his campaign—the objective reporter, won over by his politics and his rhetoric—was supposed to have been there, and it wasn't.

The senator had heard my excuses with increasing frequency in the time since Buffy's death, and it was clear that he was getting tired of them.

More than tired; he was getting frustrated with them, and by extension, with me.

Talking faster now, in an effort to keep him from shutting me out before I could finish, I said, "Senator, I've had two of my people running traces for weeks now on every bit of data we could find. They've been following the money. That's what it always comes back to—the money. And they've managed to find—"

"We'll talk about this later, Georgia."

"But Senator Ryman, we—"

"I *said* we'd talk about this later." He was frowning now, his stiff, political smile, the one he used during debates, or when chastising recalcitrant interns. "This is neither the time nor the place for this discussion."

"Senator, we have proof Tate was involved in what happened to Buffy." The senator froze. Finally sensing that he might listen, I pressed my case. "We've had audio for a while, but my team found the payments. We found the contacts. Buffy wasn't the start. Eakly was the start. Eakly and the ranch—"

"No."

The word was soft but implacable. I stopped dead, run up against the side of that refusal like I'd just slammed into a wall. After a frozen moment, I tried again, saying, "Senator Ryman, please, if you'd just—"

"Georgia, this is not the time, and it's not the place, especially if those are the accusations you've come here to make." His face was cold. I'd never seen him look that cold toward anyone who wasn't a political rival. "David Tate and I may not have always seen eye to eye on this campaign trail, and God knows, I've always known there was no love lost between the two of you, but I'm not going to stand here and listen to you say these things about a man who spoke at my daughter's funeral. I can't have that."

"Senator, that man was just as responsible for your daughter's death as if he'd infected her himself."

Senator Ryman's shoulders tensed, and his hand actually rose several inches before he forced it down. He wanted to hit me; that truth was written so clear across his face that even Shaun could have seen it. He wanted to, but he wouldn't. Not here, not in front of all these witnesses.

"It's time for you to go, Georgia."

"Senator—"

"If the three of you aren't off the premises in the next fifteen minutes, you'll be spending tonight in the Sacramento County jailhouse, as I'll have had your press clearance pulled." His tone was calm, even reasonable, but there was no kindness in it, and kindness was the thing I was most accustomed to hearing from him. "When I get back to the Center, I'll come by your trailer, and you'll show me every scrap of proof you think you have."

"And then?" I asked, despite my own better judgment. I needed to know how seriously he was willing to take this.

"And then, if I believe you, I'll back you up when we call for the federal authorities, because what you're saying, Georgia, what you're *accusing* is terrorism, and if that accusation gets made without absolute proof behind it, well, there's more than one man's career it could destroy."

He was right. If it got out that the Ryman campaign had been harboring a man who'd use Kellis-Amberlee as a weapon—hell, that a man who'd use Kellis-Amberlee as a weapon was actually *on the ticket*—it would ruin him. His political enemies would never let the scandal die. Some of them would probably say he'd supported Tate's actions, even to the point of killing Rebecca, for the votes it bought him.

"If you don't believe me?" I asked, shaping the words with lips that had gone numb.

"If I don't believe you, you're all on the next bus to Berkeley, and we're parting ways before the sun comes up," the senator said and turned his back on me, all smiles as he shifted his attention to the crowd. "Congresswoman!" he said, joviality coming back into his voice as if he'd flipped a switch. "You're looking lovely tonight—is that your wife? Well, Mrs. Lancer, it surely is a pleasure to finally have the opportunity to meet you in the flesh, after seeing you in so many of those Christmas card photos—"

And then he was moving away, leaving me standing alone in the middle of the crowd, the important people of this little modern Babylon pressing all around me as they struggled for a moment of his attention, my colleagues standing not ten feet away, waiting to hear what I'd accomplished.

The truth had never felt like it was further away, or harder to make sense of. And I had never in my life felt like I was more lost, or more alone.

We were eleven when I first understood that we weren't immortal. I always knew the Masons had a biological son named Phillip. Our folks didn't talk about him much, but he came up every time someone mentioned Mason's Law. It's funny, but I sort of hero-worshipped him when

I was a kid, because people remembered him. I never really considered the fact that they remembered him for dying.

George and I were hunting for our Christmas presents when she found the box. It was in the closet in Mom's office, and we'd probably overlooked it a thousand times before, but it caught George's eye that day for some reason, and she hauled it out, and we looked inside. That was the day I met my brother.

The box was full of photographs we'd never seen, pictures of a laughing little boy in a world where he'd never been forced to worry about the things we lived with every day. Phillip riding a pony at the state fair. Phillip playing in the sand on a beach with no fences in sight. Phillip with his long-haired, short-sleeved, laughing mother, who didn't look anything like our mother, who wore her hair short and her sleeves long enough to hide the body armor, whose holster dug into my side when she kissed me good night. He had a smile that said he'd never been afraid of anything, and I hated him a little, because his parents were so much happier than mine.

We never talked about that day. We put the pictures back in the closet, and we never found our Christmas presents, either. But that was the day I realized...if Phillip, this happy, innocent kid, could die, so could we. Someday, we'd be cardboard boxes at the back of some-body's closet, and there wasn't a thing we could do about it. George knew it, too; maybe she even knew it before I did. We were all we had, and we could die. It's hard to live knowing something like that. We've done the best we could.

No one gets to ask us for anything more. Not now, not ever. When history looks our way—stupid, blind history, that judges everything and never gives a shit what we paid to get it—it better remember that no one had a right to ask us for this. No one.

**—From *Hail to the King*,
the blog of Shaun Mason, June 19, 2040**

Twenty-five

G eorgia, what just happened?"

"George? You okay?"

Both of them sounded so concerned it left me wanting to scream. I settled for grabbing a flute of champagne from a passing server, draining it in one convulsive gulp, and snapping, "We have to go. Now."

That just redoubled their concern. Rick's eyes went wide, while Shaun's narrowed, accompanied by a sudden frown. "How pissed is he?" he asked.

"He's pulling our press passes in fifteen minutes."

Shaun whistled. "Nice. Even for you, that's impressive. What'd you do, suggest that his wife was having an affair with the librarian?"

"It was the tutor, that was the Mayor of Oakland's wife, and I was right," I said, starting to stalk for the exit. True to form, they followed. "I didn't say anything about Emily."

"Excuse me, but does one of you mind telling me what's going on?" interjected Rick, putting on a burst of speed to get in front of me. "Georgia just got us kicked out of a major political event, Senator Ryman's clearly pissed, and Tate's glaring. I'm missing something. I don't like that."

I went cold. "Tate's glaring at us?"

"If looks could kill—"

"We'd be joining Rebecca Ryman. I'll fill you in once we're in the car."

Rick hesitated, licking his lower lip as he registered the anxiety in my tone. "Georgia?"

"I'm serious," I said, and sped up, going as fast as I could manage without starting to a run. Shaun took the cue from me, linking one arm through mine and using his longer legs to give me a little extra speed. Rick hurried along behind us, holding his questions until we got outside. Bless him for that much, anyway.

It took only one blood test to get back to the car. Since everyone on the banquet level was assumed clean after the checks they'd endured to get there, the elevator came at the press of a button, no needles involved until we wanted to exit. Like a roach motel—the infected could check in, but they couldn't check out. My earlier curiosity about what would happen if more than one person took the elevator at the same time was answered as the interior sensors refused to let the doors open until the system detected three different, noninfected blood samples. Someone who unwittingly boarded the elevator with a person undergoing viral amplification would just die in there. Nice.

Steve was still next to the car, arms folded across his chest. He straightened when he saw the three of us come marching out of the elevator but he restrained his curiosity better than Rick had, waiting until we were reaching for the doors before he asked, "Well?"

"Threatened to yank our press passes," I said.

"Nice," said Steve, raising his eyebrows. "He pressing charges?"

"No, that'll probably come after tonight's episode of 'meet the press.'" I climbed into the back seat.

Shaun did the same on the opposite side of the car, commenting, "She means 'beat the press,' don'cha, George?"

"Possibly," I said.

"*Now* will you tell me what's going on?" asked Rick, getting into the front passenger seat and twisting around to face us.

"It's simple, really," I said, sagging into the seat. Shaun already had his arm in place to support me, offering as much comfort as he could. "Dave and Alaric followed the money and proved that Governor Tate was behind the attacks on Eakly and the ranch. Also, PS, the CDC is potentially involved, which isn't going to make me sleep any easier tonight, thanks. The senator wasn't thrilled with the idea that his running mate might be the goddamn devil, so he's asked us to go back to the Center to prepare our notes while he decides whether or not to fire our asses."

There was a long silence as the other three people in the car attempted to absorb what I'd just said. Surprisingly, it was Steve who spoke first, in a low rumble closer to a growl than a normal conversational tone. "Are you *sure*?" he asked.

"We have proof," I said, closing my eyes and leaning into Shaun's arm. "People have been funneling him money, and he's been funneling it on to the sort of folks who think weaponizing Kellis-Amberlee is a good thing. Some of that money's been coming from Atlanta. Some of it's been coming from the big tobacco companies. And a lot of people have died, presumably so that nice ol' Governor Tate can be Vice President of the United States of America. At least, until the president-elect has some sort of tragic accident and he has to step into the position."

"Georgia..." Rick sounded almost awed, overwhelmed with the possibilities. "If we know this for sure—Georgia, this is a really big deal. This is...Are we allowed to know this and not just report it to the FBI, or the CDC, or *somebody*? This is *terrorism*."

"I don't know, Rick; you're the one who worked in print media. Why don't you try telling me for a change?"

"Even in cases of suspected terrorism, a journalist can protect his or her sources as long as they aren't actually sheltering the suspect." Rick hesitated. "We're not, are we? Sheltering him?"

"Pardon me for breaking in, Mr. Cousins, but if Miss Mason's proof is as good as she seems to think, it doesn't matter whether she plans on sheltering him or not. My partner died in Eakly." Steve's tone was normal now, almost casual. Somehow that was even more disturbing. "Tyrone was a good man. He deserved better. Man who started that outbreak, well. That man *doesn't* deserve better."

"Don't worry about it," I said. "I have no intention of sheltering him. I'll talk it over with the senator, and if he wants to throw us off the campaign, he's welcome to. I'll mail our files to every open-source blog, newspaper, and politician in the country while we're on the road for home."

"This is crap," Shaun said, withdrawing his arm.

"Right," I agreed.

"Absolute fucking crap."

"No argument."

"I want to punch somebody right about now."

"Not it," Rick said.

"I punch back," Steve said. A note of amusement crept into his voice, making him sound a little less likely to explode. That was good. Not that I'd object to seeing Tate get the crap kicked out of him—I just didn't want to see Steve go to federal prison over it when the FBI would be just as happy to do the honors. Hell, after they had Tate in custody, and considering what had happened in Eakly, they might be willing to let Steve have his licks. Just as long as they got theirs first.

"Just have patience; this is all going to be over soon," I said. "One way or another, I guess we're finishing things tonight."

"Let's pick one way, okay?" said Shaun. "I don't like another."

"That's okay," I said. "Neither do I."

We finished the drive in silence, pulling through the Center gates and enduring the barrage of blood tests that followed with as much grace as we could muster. Three of us were exhausted, scared, and angry; Steve was just angry, and I almost envied him. Anger's easier to run on than exhaustion. It doesn't strip your gears as badly. Less than two hours after convincing him to abandon his post for my fool's errand, Steve drove back into the motor pool, his car heavier by two journalists and a whole lot of free-floating worry.

"Don't say anything, please," I said, as we climbed out of the car. "I'm meeting with the senator tonight, when he gets back from his dinner. After that—"

"After that, I guess what needs doing is going to be clear one way or the other," said Steve. "Don't worry. I wouldn't have gone into security if I didn't know how to keep my mouth shut."

"Thanks."

"Don't mention it." Steve smiled, briefly. I smiled back.

"George, c'mon!" Shaun called, already a good four or five yards from the car. "I want to get out of this damn monkey suit!"

"Coming!" I shouted, muttering, "Jesus," before I turned to follow him back to the trailers.

Rick walked with us as far as the van; then he turned left, toward his trailer, while we turned right, toward ours. "He's a good guy," said Shaun, pressing his thumb against the lock on the trailer door. It clicked open, confirming Shaun's right to enter. "A little old-fashioned, but still a good guy. I'm glad we got the chance to work with him."

"You think he'll stay on after we all get home?" I started rummaging through the mass of clothing on the beds and floor, looking for the cotton shirt and jeans I'd been wearing earlier.

"He can write his own ticket after this campaign, but yeah, I think he may stick around." Shaun was already halfway out of his formal wear, shedding it with the ease of long practice. "He knows he can work with us."

"Good."

I was doing up the last of the buttons on my shirt when I heard the shouting. Shaun and I exchanged a wide-eyed, shocked look before we both went running for the trailer door. I made it out half a beat ahead of him, just in time to see a shell-shocked-looking Rick come staggering up the path with Lois cradled against his chest. I didn't have to be a veterinarian to know that something was horribly wrong with his cat. No living animal has a neck that bends that way or hangs that limply in its owner's arms.

"Rick...?"

He stopped in his tracks, staring at me, the body of his cat still clutched against his chest. I ran the last fifteen feet between us, and Shaun ran close behind me. That was probably the part they didn't figure on: those fifteen feet.

Those fifteen stupid little feet saved our lives.

"What happened?" I asked, putting out a hand, as if there were a damn thing I could do. Seen this close, it was even more obvious that the cat had been dead for a while. Her eyes were open and glazed, staring blankly off at nothing.

"She was just... I got back to the trailer and I almost tripped on her." For the first time, I realized Rick was still wearing his formal clothes. He hadn't even had time to change. "She was just inside the doorway. I think... even after they hurt her, I think she tried to get away." Tears running down his cheeks. I'm not sure he was even aware of them. "I think she was trying to come and find me. She was just a *little* cat, Georgia. Why would anyone do this to such a *little* cat?"

Shaun stiffened. "She was inside? Are you *sure* this wasn't natural causes?"

"Since when do natural causes break your neck?" asked Rick, in a tone that would have been reasonable if he hadn't been crying so hard.

"We should go to the van."

I frowned. "Shaun—?"

"I'm serious. We can talk about this in the van, but we should go there. Right now."

"Just let me get my gun," I said, and started to turn toward the trailer. Shaun grabbed my elbow, yanking me back. I stumbled.

The trailer exploded with a concussive bang, like an engine misfiring.

The first bang was followed by a second and larger bang, echoed in the distance as another trailer—probably Rick's—went up in a ball of blue-and-orange flame. Not that there was much time to make estimates about where the blast was coming from. Shaun still had my arm and he was running, dragging me in his wake as he rushed toward the van. Rick ran after us, clutching Lois's body to his chest, all of us bathed in the angry orange glare of the blast. Someone was trying to kill us. At this point, I didn't even have to wonder who. Tate knew we knew. There was no reason for him to play nice anymore.

Once he was sure I'd keep running, Shaun let go of me, dropping back as he tried to cover our retreat toward the van. I quashed the urge to worry about him, keeping my focus on the running. Shaun could take care of himself. I had to believe that or I'd never be able to believe anything else. Rick was running like a man in a dream, Lois bouncing limply in his arms with every step. And I just ran.

Something pricked my left biceps when we were about halfway to the van. I ignored it and kept going, more focused on getting to cover than on swatting at some mosquito with shit for timing. No one's ever been able to tell the insects of the world that they shouldn't interrupt the big dramatic moments, and so they keep on doing it. That's probably a good thing. If drama kept the bugs away, most people would never emotionally mature past the age of seventeen.

"Rick, get the doors!" shouted Shaun. He was hanging about five yards back, still moving fast. He had his .45 drawn, covering the area as we retreated. The sight of him was enough to make my heart beat faster and my throat get tight. I knew he was wearing Kevlar under his clothes, but Kevlar wouldn't save him from a headshot. Whoever blew up the trailers might be out there watching, and once they saw us scattering into the open, there was every chance they'd decide to finish what they'd started. And none of that mattered, because someone had to watch the rear, and someone had to open the van, and if we clustered together to make me feel better, neither of those things would happen, and we'd *all* die.

Knowing the realities of the situation didn't do a damn thing to make me feel better about leaving Shaun to twist in the wind. It just meant I understood that we didn't have a choice.

Rick put on a burst of speed, reaching the van a good twenty feet ahead of me. He finally seemed to realize he was carrying Lois because he dropped her body, reaching out to grab the handles of the rear doors and press his forefingers against the reader pads. There was a click as the onboard testing system ran his blood and prints, confirming he was both uninfected and an authorized driver before the locks released.

"Got it!" he yelled, and wrenched the doors open, motioning for us to get inside.

He didn't need to tell me twice. I sped up, breath aching in my chest as I raced to get out of the open. Shaun continued moving at the same pace, swinging his gun unhurriedly from side to side as he covered our retreat.

"Shaun, you idiot!" I yelled. "Get your ass in here! There's no one out there to save!"

He glanced over his shoulder, eyebrows rising in apparent surprise. Something in my expression must have told him that it wasn't worth arguing because he nodded and turned to run the rest of the way.

I didn't start really breathing again until he and Rick were both inside with the doors closed behind them. Shaun flipped the dead bolts on the rear doors, while Rick moved to do the same on the movable wall that shut the driver's cabin off from the rest of the vehicle. With those latches thrown, we were effectively cut off from the rest of the world. Nothing could get in, and unless we opened the locks, nothing could get out. Barring heavy explosives, we were as safe as it was possible to be.

I took a seat at the main console and brought up the security recordings for the last day. The scanner came up clean, showing no attempted break-ins or unauthorized contact with the van's exterior during that time. "Shaun, when was the last security sweep?"

"I ran one remotely while I was waiting for the senator's speech to finish."

"Good. That means we're clean." I leaned over to turn on the exterior cameras—without them, we were flying blind and would have no way of knowing when help arrived—and froze.

"George?"

It was Shaun's voice, sounding distant and surprised. He'd seen me reach for the switches, and seen me stop; he just hadn't seen why. I didn't answer him. I was too busy staring.

"George, what's wrong?"

"I..." I began, and stopped, swallowing in an effort to clear the sudden dryness from my mouth. Forcing myself to start again, I said, "I think we may have a problem." Raising my right hand, I wrapped numb fingers around the hollow plastic dart projecting from my left biceps and pulled it free, turning to face the other two. Rick paled, seeing the red stain spreading through the fabric of my shirt. Shaun just stared at the dart, looking like he was seeing the end of the world.

In a very real and concrete way, there was an excellent chance that he was.

If you want an easy job—if you want the sort of job where you never have to bury somebody who you care about—I recommend you pursue a career in whatever strikes your fancy...just so long as it isn't the news.

**—From *Another Point of True*,
the blog of Richard Cousins, June 20, 2040**

Twenty-six

Shaun broke the silence. "Please tell me that didn't break the skin," he said, almost pleading. "The blood came from something else, right George? Right?"

"We're going to need a biohazard bag." There was no fear in my voice. Really, there was nothing there at all. I sounded...empty, disconnected from everything around me. It was like my body and my voice existed in different universes, tethered by only the thinnest of threads. "Get one from the medical kit, put it on the counter, and step away. I don't want either of you touching this." Or me. I didn't want them touching *me* when there was a risk that I could infect them. I just couldn't say that. If I tried, I'd break down, and any chance of containing this would go right out the window.

"George—"

"We need a testing kit."

Rick's voice was surprisingly strong, considering the circumstances. Shaun and I turned to face him. He was white-faced and shaking, but his voice was firm. "Shaun, I know you don't want to hear this, and if you want to hit me later, that's fine, but right now, we need a testing kit."

Storm clouds were gathering in Shaun's expression. He knew Rick was right; I could see it in his eyes and in the way he wasn't quite willing to look at me. If he hadn't known, he wouldn't have cared that Rick was calling for a blood test. But because he did, it was the last thing in the world he wanted. Well. Maybe not the *last* thing. Then again, it was starting to look like the last thing had already happened.

"He's right, Shaun." I placed the dart on the counter next to my keyboard. It was so small. How could something so small be the end of the world? I barely noticed when it hit me. I never thought it was possible to overlook your own death, but apparently it is. "Don't just grab a field box.

Get the real kit. If we're going to do this, we're going to do it right." The XH-237 has never had a false result; it's one hundred percent accurate, as far as anyone can tell.

Shaun would never believe anything else. He was staring at me in open disbelief. He was denying this as hard as he could. So why wasn't I? "Georgia..." he began.

"If I'm overreacting, I'll buy a new one with my birthday money," I said, sagging backward in my chair. "Rick?"

"I'll get it, Georgia," he said, starting for the medical supplies.

I closed my eyes. "I'm not overreacting."

Almost too quiet for me to hear, Shaun whispered, "I know."

"I brought the bag," said Rick. I opened my eyes, turning toward his voice. He held up a Kevlar-reinforced biohazard bag. I nodded and he put the bag on the counter, before stepping away. We knew proper protocols. They'd been drilled into us for our entire lives. Until we knew I was clean, no one touched me...and I knew I wasn't clean.

Moving with exaggerated care, so both Shaun and Rick could see me every inch along the way, I reached for the bag and thumbed it open before picking up the dart. Dropping it into the bag, I activated the seal. It was a matter for the CDC now. Its people would break the seal after it was turned over to them, and what happened after that wasn't my concern. I wouldn't be around to see it.

I looked up once the bag was sealed and set aside. "Where's the test kit?" It felt like the muscles in my eyes were relaxing. It could be psychosomatic, but I didn't think so. The viral bodies responsible for the perpetual dilation of my pupils were moving on to greener pastures. Like the rest of my body.

"Here," said Shaun, holding it up. He stepped closer and knelt in front of me. He was only inches outside the federally defined "danger zone" for dealing with someone who might be amplifying. I shot him a sharp look, and he shook his head. "Don't start."

"I won't." I extended my left hand. If he wanted to administer the test himself, he had the right. Maybe it would make him believe the results.

"You could be wrong. You've been wrong before," Shaun said, sliding the testing kit over my hand. I flattened my palm until I felt the tendons stretch, and gave him the nod to clamp down the lid. He did, pinning my fingers in their wide, starfished position.

"I'm not wrong," I said. Dull pain lanced my hand as the needles—one for each finger, and five more set in a circle at the center of the palm—darted out, taking blood samples. The lights on the top of the unit began to flash, cycling from green to yellow, where they remained, blinking on and off, until one by one, they started settling into their final color.

Red. Every one of them. Red.

Tears prickled against my eyelids. It took me a moment to realize what they were, and then I had to resist the urge to blink them back. Kellis-Amberlee never let me cry before. It was damn well going to let me cry now. "Told you I was right," I said, trying to sound lighthearted. All I managed to sound was lost.

"Bet you're sorry," Shaun replied. I raised my head and met his shocked, staring eyes with my own.

We sat that way for several moments, looking at each other, waiting for an answer that wasn't going to come. It was Rick who spoke, voicing the one question we all wanted to ask and that none of us was quite prepared to answer.

"What do we do now?"

"Do?" Shaun frowned at him, looking utterly and honestly perplexed. That expression was enough to terrify me, because he looked like someone who didn't understand the idea that before too much longer, I was going to be making a concerted effort to eat him alive. "What do you mean, 'What do we do?'"

"I mean exactly what I said," Rick said. He shook his head, gesturing to me. "We can't just leave her like this. We have to—"

"No!"

The vehemence of Shaun's reply startled me. I turned toward him. "No?" I repeated. "Shaun, what the hell do you mean, 'no'? There isn't room for 'no.' 'No' is over."

"You don't know what you're saying."

"I know exactly what I'm saying." Rick was pale and shaking, beads of sweat standing out on his forehead. Poor guy. He didn't sign up for political assassinations when he decided to join the so-called "winning team." Despite that, he met my eyes without flinching and didn't try to avoid looking at me. He'd seen the virus before. It held no surprises for him. "You're the closest thing we've got to a virologist, Rick. How long do I have?"

"How much do you weigh?"

"One thirty-five, tops."

"I'd say forty-five minutes, under normal circumstances," he said, after a moment's consideration. "But these aren't normal circumstances."

"The run," I said.

He nodded. "The run."

Viral amplification depends on a lot of factors. Age, physical condition, body weight—how fast your blood is moving when you come into contact with the live virus. If someone gets bitten in their sleep without waking up, they may take the rest of the night to fully amplify, because they'll be calm enough that their body won't be helping the infection along. I, on the other hand, got hit with a viral payload a lot bigger than you'd find in a bite, and it happened while I was running for my life, heart pounding, adrenaline pushing my blood pressure through the roof. I'd cut my time in half. Maybe worse.

It was already getting harder to think; harder to focus; harder to *breathe*. I knew, intellectually, that my lungs weren't shutting down. It was just the virus enclosing the soft tissues of my brain and starting to disrupt normal neurological functions, making normally autonomic actions start intruding on the conscious mind. I've read the papers and the clinical studies. I knew what to expect. First comes the lack of focus, the lack of interest, the lack of capability to draw unrelated conclusions. Then comes hyperactivity as the circulatory system is pushed to overdrive. Then, when the virus reaches full saturation, the coup de grace: the death of the conscious mind. My body would continue to walk around, driven by raw instinct and the desires of the virus, but Georgia Carolyn Mason would be gone. Forever.

I was dead before the lights flashed red. I was dead the second the hypodermic hit my arm, and there was nothing anyone could do about it. But there was something I could do before I went.

Turning to Shaun, I nodded. There was a long pause—almost too long—before his expression calmed and he returned the gesture, looking more sure of himself, more *like* himself, despite the tears running down his cheeks.

"Rick?" he said.

Rick turned to him, shaking his head. "You can't beat this. There's no beating this. She's gone. You need to realize that. She's gone, and I'm sorry, but we have to—"

"Get me the medical kit from under the server rack," Shaun said. I had to envy him the calmness in his voice. I couldn't have stayed that calm if he were the one undergoing explosive viral amplification. "The red one."

"What do you—"

"*Do it!*"

The words were barely out of his mouth before Rick was rushing to the front of the van, digging under the seat for the med kit. Mom packed it for us a million years ago, for use in absolute emergency. When she put it in my hands, she said she prayed we'd never have to use it. Sorry, Mom. Guess we let you down good this time. But hey, at least the ratings will be high.

I let out a long, shuddering sigh that somehow transformed into hysterical giggling. I bit my tongue before the giggles could turn to sobs. There wasn't time for that. There wasn't time for anything except the red box, and the things it held, and maybe—maybe, if I was lucky—one last article.

Rick came back to Shaun's side, holding the box at arm's length. His expression was cold. He didn't think Shaun would be able to do it. He didn't know him as well as he thought he did. I closed my eyes and leaned my head against the seat, suddenly tired.

"You can go now, Rick," I said. "Take my bike and the gray backup drive. Get as far away as you can, then hit a data station and upload everything to the site. Free space. No subscription required. Creative Commons licensing."

"What is it?" he asked, curiosity briefly overriding his determination to see me dead. Bless you, Rick. A journalist after my own heart, right up to the end.

"Everything I died for," I said. My eyes were starting to itch. I took my sunglasses off and threw them aside as I rubbed my eyes. "Files, bank records, everything. It's just everything. Now get out of here. You've done everything you can."

"Are you—"

"We're sure," said Shaun. I heard the box pop open and the distinctive snap of polyvinyl-Teflon gloves. They're nearly impossible to tear and so expensive that even the military only uses them under special circumstances. Shaun always insisted we carry a pair. Just one. Just in case. "Take my extra body armor. There's always a chance they're still shooting out there."

"Do you think they are?"

"Does it matter?"

"No. I guess it doesn't."

I listened as Rick moved around the van. He pulled Shaun's body armor out of the closet where it was stored and yanked it on over his clothes, snaps and zippers fastening with their quiet, distinctive sounds. It kept me distracted from the sounds that were coming from Shaun's direction, the sloshing, snapping sounds as he got the injector cartridges ready.

"Thanks, Rick," I said. "It's been one hell of a ride."

"I... right." I heard Rick's footsteps approach; the scrape of metal as he lifted the drive from beside my computer; then his retreat, until the door creaked open and he stopped, hesitating. "I... Georgia?"

"Yes, Rick?"

"I'm sorry."

I cracked my eyes open, allowing him a small, mirthless smile. For the first time that I could remember, the light didn't hurt. I was going into conversion. My body was losing the capacity to understand pain. "That's all right. So am I."

For a moment, he looked like he might say something else. Then his lips tightened and he nodded, before undoing the latches on the door. That was the last exit: When the van was locked again, it would detect infection and refuse to open for anyone inside.

"Shaun? Train's leaving," I said, quietly. "You want to jab and go?"

"And let you finish this without me?" He shook his head. "No way. Rick, you be careful out there."

Rick's shoulders tightened and he was gone, stepping out into the evening air. The door banged shut behind him.

Shaun sat down on the floor in front of me, the injector in his hands. It was a two-barrel array, ready to deliver a mixed payload of sedatives and my own hyper-activated white blood cells. Together, the mixture could slow conversion...for a while. Not for long, but if we were lucky, for long enough. Expression staying neutral, he said, "Give me your right arm."

I held it out.

Shaun pressed the twin needles to the thin skin at the bend of my elbow and a wash of coolness flowed into me as he pressed the plunger home.

"Thanks," I said, shivering.

"That's all we've got." He opened a biohazard bag and dropped the used injector into it before sealing the top. "You've got half an hour, tops. After that—"

"There's no guarantee I'll be lucid. I know." He rose, walking stiff-legged across to the biohazard bin and dropped the bag inside. I wanted to run after him, wrap my arms around him, and cry until there weren't any tears left in me, but I couldn't. I didn't dare. Even my tears would be infectious, and the sedatives he'd shot into my arm weren't going to work any miracles. Time was short.

I still had work to do.

I swung back to my monitor, trying to swallow away the dryness as I heard Shaun moving behind me, taking one of the spare revolvers out of the locker by the door and loading it, one careful cartridge at a time. What was it the reports said? The dryness of the mouth was one of the early signs of viral amplification, resulting from the crystal blocks of virus drawing away moisture and bringing on that lovely desiccated state that all the living dead seem to share? That seemed about right. It was getting harder to think about that sort of thing. Suddenly, it was all just a little too immediate.

My hands were still hovering above the keyboard while my mind struggled to find a beginning when I felt the barrel of the gun press against the base of my skull, cold and somehow soothing. Shaun wouldn't let me hurt anyone else. No matter what happened, he wouldn't let me hurt anyone else. Not even him. Not more than I already had.

"Shaun..."

"I'm here."

"I love you."

"I know, George. I love you, too. You and me. Always."

"I'm scared."

His lips brushed the top of my head as he bent forward and pressed them to my hair. I wanted to yell at him to get away from me, but I didn't. The barrel of the gun remained a cool, constant pressure on the back of my neck. When I turned, when I stopped being me, he would end it. He loved me enough to end it. Has any girl ever been luckier than I am?

"Shaun..."

"Shhh, Georgia," he said. "It's okay. Just write." And so I began. One last chance to roll the dice, tell the truth, and shame the devil. One last chance to make it all clear. What we fought for. What we died for. What we felt we had to do.

I never asked to be a hero. No one ever gave me the option to say I didn't want to, that I was sorry, but that they had the wrong girl. All I wanted to do was tell the truth and let people draw their own conclusions from there. I wanted people to think, and to know, and to understand. I just wanted to tell the truth. In the van that had carried us across a country, and through the last months of my life, with my brother standing ready to pull the trigger, my hands came down, and I wrote.

Was it worth it?

God, I hope so.

RED FLAG DISTRIBUTION RED FLAG
DISTRIBUTION RED FLAG DISTRIBUTION

CREATIVE COMMONS LICENCE ALERT
LEVEL ALPHA SPREAD TO ALL NEWS SITES IMMEDIATELY

REPOST FREELY REPOST FREELY REPOST FREELY
FEED IS LIVE

My name is Georgia Mason. For the past several years, I've been provid-ing one of the world's many windows into the news, chronicling current events and attempting, in my own small way, to offer context and per-spective. I have always pursued the truth above all other things, even when the truth came at the cost of my own comfort and well-being. It seems, now, that I pursued the truth even when it would mean my life, although I was unaware of it at the time.

My name is Georgia Mason. According to the time stamp on the field test unit (model XH-237, known for reliability and, God help me, accuracy), I legally died eleven minutes ago. But for now, at this moment, my name is still Georgia Mason, and this is... I guess you can call this my last postcard from the Wall. There are some things you need to know, and we don't have much time.

As I write this, my brother is standing behind me with the barrel of a gun pressed against the back of my neck, where a blast will sever the spinal cord with the smallest possible spray radius. In my bloodstream, a large dose of sedatives mixed with a serum based on my own immune system is running a race against the virus that is in the process of tak-ing over my cells. My nose isn't clogged and I can swallow, but I feel lethargic, and it's hard to breathe. I tell you this so you'll understand that this isn't a hoax, this isn't some sophomoric attempt to increase ratings or site traffic. This is real. Everything I am about to tell you is the truth. Believe me, understand, and act, before it is too late.

If you're viewing this from the main page of After the End Times, you'll see a download link labeled "Campaign_Notes.zip" on the left-hand side of your screen. Possession of the documents behind that link may be considered treason by the government of the United States of America. Please. Click. Download. Read. Repost to any forum you can, any message board or photo-sharing site or blog that you can reach. The data contained in those files is as essential to our freedom and survival as the report of Dr. Matras proved to be during the Rising. I am not overstating the data's importance. There isn't enough time for that.

Neither is there enough time for me to repeat the facts that are already codified and ready for you to download. Let this suffice for all the things I cannot say, do not have the time to say, will never say, and wish I could: They are lying to us. They are willfully channeling research away from the pursuit of a cure for this disease, and they are doing it under the auspices of our own government. I don't know who "they" are. I didn't live long enough to find out. Governor Tate served their interests. So, I regret to say, did Georgette Meissonier, previously a part of this reporting site.

They want us to stay afraid.

They want us to stay controlled.

They want us to stay sick.

Please, don't let them do this to our world. I am begging you from the Wall, because it's all that's left for me to do. It's all I *can* do. Don't let them keep us frightened and hiding in our homes. Let us be what we were intended to be: human and free and able to make our own choices. Read what I have written, understand what they intend for us, for all of us, and decide to live.

They made a mistake in killing me because, alive or dead, the truth won't rest. My name is Georgia Mason, and I am begging you. Rise up while you can.

Mahir I'm so sorry.

Buffy I'm so sorry.

Rick I'm so sorry.

Shaun I'm sorry I'm sorry I'm sorry I didn't mean it I would take it all back if I could but I can't I cant I I I I I I I I all fading words going cant do this cant Shaun please Shaun please I love you I love you I always you know I Shaun please cant hold on everything jfdh cant do this jhjnfbnnnn mmm have to my name my name is Shaun I love you Shaun please gngn please SHOOT ME SHAUN SHOOT ME N—

TERMINATE LIVE FEED
RED FLAG DISTRIBUTION RED FLAG
DISTRIBUTION RED FLAG DISTRIBUTION

REPOST FREELY

BOOK V

Burial Writes

I've spent my whole life imagining worlds other than the one that I was born in. Everybody does. The one world I never imagined was a world without a Georgia. So how come that's the world I have to live with?

— SHAUN MASON

I'm sorry.

— GEORGIA MASON

It is the sad duty of the management of After the End Times to announce the death of Georgia Carolyn Mason, the head of our Factual News Division, most commonly called "the Newsies," and one of the original founders of this site.

I've been trying to find the words for this announcement since I was asked to make it, some three hours ago. The request came with a promotion to which I never aspired, and a position made bitter by the knowledge of what it cost. I would sooner have my friend than all the promotions in the world. But that option is not open to me, or to any of those who will mourn for her.

Georgia Mason was my friend, and I will always regret that we never met in the flesh. She once told me she lived each day hoping and praying she would find the truth; that she was able to keep going through all life's petty disappointments because she knew that someday, the truth would set her free.

Good-bye, Georgia. May the truth be enough to bring you peace.

—From *Fish and Clips*,
the blog of Mahir Gowda, June 20, 2040

Twenty-seven

George's blood didn't all dry at the same rate.

Some of the smaller streaks dried almost immediately, staining the wall behind her ruined monitor. The gunshot collapsed the screen inward, safety-tempered glass holding its form as well as it could, even when the plastic casing shattered. It was like looking at some modern artist's reinterpretation of an old-school disco ball. "The party's in here, and we're just getting started." As long as you didn't mind the blood on the glass, that was. *I* minded the blood on the glass. I minded the blood on the glass a lot. I just didn't see a way to put it back where it belonged.

The bigger splashes were drying slow and sticky, the color maturing from bright red to a sober burgundy, where they seemed content to stay. That bothered me. I wanted the blood to dry, wanted it to settle in funeral colors and stop taunting me. I'm a good shot. I've been on firing ranges since I was seven years old, in the field—legally—since I was sixteen. Even if the virus still allowed her to feel pain, George didn't have *time* for pain. It was just the roar of the gun, and then she was slumping forward, face-first on her keyboard. That was the only real mercy. She landed face-first, so I didn't have to see what I'd... so I didn't have to see. She didn't have time to suffer. I just have to keep telling myself that, now, and tomorrow, and the next day, for as long as I can stay alive.

The sound of the gun fired inside the van would've been the loudest thing I'd ever heard if it hadn't been followed by the sound of George falling. That's the loudest thing I've ever heard. That's *always* going to be the loudest thing, no matter what else I hear. The sound of George, falling.

But I'm a good shot, and there was no shrapnel unless you wanted to count the aerosolized blood released when the bullet hit my... when I shot... not unless you counted the blood. I had to count the blood because it was enough to turn the entire damn van into a hot zone. If I was infected, I was infected—too late to worry about that kind of shit now—but that didn't mean I needed to make my chances worse. I moved as far away as I could and sat down with my back against the wall, the gun dangling loose against my left knee, to watch the blood dry, and to wait.

George turned the security cameras on before things got too...before it was too late to worry about that sort of stuff. I watched the Center's security forces rush around with the senator's men and some dudes I didn't recognize. Ryman wasn't the only candidate working Sacramento. There was no sign of Rick. Either he got dead or he got out of the quarantine zone before things went to hell. And things *had* gone to hell. I could spot at least three of the infected on every monitor, about half of them being gunned down by frantic guards who'd never dealt with a for-real-and-true zombie before. They were shooting stupid. They would have *known* they were shooting stupid if they'd paused to think for five seconds. You're not a sharpshooter, you don't go for the head, you go for the knees; a zombie that's been hobbled can't come at you as fast, and that leaves more time to aim. You're out of ammo, you leave the field. You don't reload where you stand unless there isn't any choice. When you're fighting a disease, you have to fight smarter than it does, or you may as well put down your weapons and surrender. Sometimes they just bite enough to infect if you don't put up a fight and if the pack's too small. You can avoid being eaten if you're willing to defect to the enemy's side.

Part of me wanted to get out there and help them, because it was clear they were pretty fucked without some sort of backup. Most of me wanted to stay where I was, watching the blood dry, watching the last signs of George slipping away forever.

My pocket buzzed. I slapped at it like it was a fly, fumbling out my phone and clicking it on. "Shaun."

"Shaun, it's Rick. Are you okay?"

It took me a moment to recognize the high, wavering sound in the van as my own distorted laughter. I clamped it down, clearing my throat before I said, "I don't think that word applies at this point. I'm alive, for now. If you're asking whether I'm infected, I don't know. I'm waiting until someone shows up to get me before I run a blood test. Seems a little pointless before that. Did you get out before the quarantine came down?"

"Barely. They were still reacting to the explosions when I got to Georgia's bike; they hadn't had time to do anything. I think they closed the gates right behind me. I—"

"Do me a favor. Don't tell me where you are." I let my head tilt back to touch the van's wall and discovered more blood I'd need to keep an eye on. This was on the ceiling. "I have no idea how tapped our phones are or who might be listening. I'm still in the van. Doors are probably locked anyway, since we confirmed an infection in here." The van's security system wasn't going to trust any attempt to open it from the inside, even if I registered uninfected. It would need an outside agent to free me. That or a rocket launcher, and even I don't pack *that* heavy for a little political rally.

Rick's reply was subdued. "I won't. I...I'm sorry, Shaun."

"Aren't we all?" I laughed again. This time the high, strangled sound seemed almost natural. "Tell me her last transmission got out. Tell me it's circulating now."

"That's why I called. Shaun, this is—it's insane. We're getting so many hits that it's swamped two of the servers. *Everyone* is downloading this; *everyone* is propagating it. Some folks started the usual 'it's a hoax' rumors, and Shaun, the *CDC* put out a press statement. *The CDC.*" He sounded awed. He damn well should. The CDC *never* puts out a statement with less than a week to prepare it. "They confirmed receipt of her test results with a time stamp and everything. This story doesn't just have legs—it has *wings*, and it's flying around the world."

"The name on the press release. It wasn't Wynne, was it?"

"Dr. Joseph Wynne."

"Guess our trip to Memphis did some good after all." The blood on the ceiling was more satisfying than the blood on the walls. It was thinner up there. It was drying so much faster.

"She didn't die for nothing. Her story—*our* story—it got out."

Suddenly, I was tired. So goddamn tired. "Sorry, Rick, but no. She died for nothing. No one should have died for this. You get away from here. Far as you can. Dump your phones, dump your transmitters, dump anything that could be used to bounce a signal, stick Georgia's bike in a garage, and don't call again until this is over."

"Shaun..."

"Don't argue." A bitter smile touched my lips. "I'm your boss now."

"Try not to die."

"I'll think about it."

I hung up and chucked my phone across the van, where it shattered against the wall with a satisfying crunch. Rick was out of the quarantine, and he was still running. Good. He was wrong—George damn well died for nothing—but he was also right. *She* would have thought this justified things. *She* would have said this was enough to pay for my being forced to put a bullet through her spine. Because she put the truth ahead of absolutely everything we ever had, and this had been the biggest truth of all.

"Happy now, George?" I asked the air.

The silence supplied her answer: *Ecstatic.*

The sound of beeping intruded on my contemplation of the bloody ceiling some ten minutes later. The fight outside was winding down. Bemused, I looked toward my shattered phone. Still broken. There were countless things in the van that could be beeping like that, about half of them on George's side. Hoping whatever it was happened to be voice activated, I said, "Answer."

One of the wall-mounted monitors rolled, the body of a dead security guard and the two infected feasting on his torso being replaced by the worried face of Mahir, my sister's longtime second and our secret weapon against government shut-down. Guess that cat didn't need to stay in the bag any longer. His eyes were wide and terrified, the whites showing all the way around, and his hair was disheveled, like he'd just gotten out of bed.

"Huh," I said, distantly pleased. "Guess it was voice activated after all. Hey, Mahir."

His focus shifted down, settling on where I sat against the wall. It wasn't possible for his eyes to get any wider, but they tried when he saw the gun in my hand. Still, his voice struggled to stay level as he said, with great and anxious seriousness, "Tell me this is a joke, Shaun. Please, tell me this is the most tasteless joke in a long history of tasteless jokes, and I will forgive you, happily, for having pulled it on me."

"Sorry, no can do," I said, closing my eyes rather than continuing to look at his worry-stricken face. Was this how it felt to be George? To have people looking at you, expecting you to have the answers about things that didn't involve shooting the thing that was about to chew your face off? Jesus, no wonder she was tired all the time. "The exact time and cause of death for Georgia Carolyn Mason has been registered with the Centers for Disease Control. You can access it in the public database. I understand there's been a statement confirming it. I'm gonna have to get that framed."

"Oh, dear God—"

"Pretty sure God's not here just now. Leave a message. Maybe He'll get back to you." It was nice, looking at the inside of my eyelids. Dark. Comfortable. Like all those hotel rooms I fixed up for her, because her eyes got hurt so easy...

"Shaun, where *are* you?" Horror was overwhelming the anxiety in his tone. He'd seen the van wall. He'd seen the gun. Mahir wasn't an idiot—he could never have worked for George if he'd been stupid—and he knew what my surroundings meant.

"I'm in the van." I nodded, still letting myself take comfort in the dark. I couldn't see his face. I couldn't see the blood drying on the walls. The dark was my *friend*. "George is here, too, but you can't really say hi just now. She's indisposed. Also, I blew her brains out all over the wall." The giggle escaped before I could bite it back, high and shrill in the confined air.

"Oh, my God." Now there was nothing *but* horror in his tone, wiping everything else away. "Have you activated your emergency beacon? Have you tested yourself? Shaun—"

"Not yet." I found myself beginning to get interested against my better judgment. "Do you think I should?"

"Don't you want to *live*, man?!"

"That's an interesting question." I opened my eyes and stood, testing my legs and finding them good. There was a moment of dizziness, but it passed. Mahir was watching me from the screen, his dark complexion gone pale with panic. "Do you think I should? I wasn't supposed to. George was supposed to. There's been a clerical error."

"Turn on your beacon, Shaun." His voice was firm now. "She wouldn't want it this way."

"Pretty sure she wouldn't want *any* of this. Especially not the part where she's dead. That would be the part she liked the least." My head was starting to clear as the shock faded, replaced by something cleaner and a lot more familiar: anger. I was furiously angry because it wasn't supposed to be this way; it was *never* supposed to be this way. Georgia would attend my funeral, give my eulogy, and I would never live in a world she wasn't a part of. We agreed on that when we were kids, and this...this was just plain wrong.

"Regardless, now that she's gone and you're not? She'd want you to make at least a small effort to stay that way."

"You Newsies. Always bringing the facts into things." I crossed the van, keeping my eyes away from the mess at my sister's terminal and the surrounding walls. The beacon—a button that would trigger a broadcast loop to let any local CDC or law enforcement agents know that someone in the van had been infected, and that someone else was alive—was a switch on the wall next to what had been Buffy's primary terminal, before she went and died on us.

First Buffy, now George. Two down, one to go, and the more I forced myself out of the comfort of my shock, the more I realized that the story wasn't over. It didn't have an ending. George would have *hated* that.

"It is, as you might say, our job," Mahir said.

"Yeah, about that." I flipped the switch. A distant, steady beeping began, the beacon's signal being picked up and relayed by the illegal police scanner in the sealed-off front seat. "Who are you working for right now?"

"Ah...no one. I suppose I'm a free agent."

"Good, 'cause I want to hire you."

Mahir's surprise was entirely unfeigned as he demanded, *"What?"*

"This day can't be good for your blood pressure," I said, crossing to the weapons locker. The revolver wasn't going to cut it. For one thing, it was probably contaminated, and they'd take it away when they let me out of the van. For another, it lacked class. You can't go hunting United States governors with a generic revolver. It simply isn't done. "After the End Times has found itself with a sudden opening for a new Head of our Factual Reporting Department. I mean, I could hire Rick, but I don't think he's gonna have the guts for the job. He's one of nature's seconds. Besides, Georgia would've wanted me to give it to you." We'd never discussed it— the topic of her dying was so ludicrous that it never came up—but I was sure of what I was saying. She would've hired him if she had any say in the matter. She would've hired him, and she would've trusted him to take over the site if my death followed hers. So that was all right.

"I...I'm not sure what you..."

"Just say yes, Mahir. We have so many recorders running right now that you know a verbal contract will stand up in court, as long as I don't test positive when they come to let me out of here."

Mahir sighed, the sound seemingly summoned up from the very core of him. I glanced up from the process of loading bullets into Georgia's favorite .40, and saw him nod. "All right, Shaun. I accept."

"Good. Welcome back onboard." I've done my own hiring and firing from the start and I know what it takes to activate a new account or reactivate an old one. Leaning over the nearest blood-free keyboard, I called up an administrative panel and tapped in his user ID, followed by my own, my password, and my administrative override. "It'll take about ten minutes for your log-in to turn all the way back live." Just about as long as it had taken Georgia's typing to degrade. "Once you can get in, *get in*. I want you monitoring every inch of the site. Draft any-damn-body you can get your hands on—I don't care *what* department they belong to, you get them working the forums, watching the feeds, and making the goddamn news *go*. You need to hire people, you hire people. Until I come back, you're in charge. Your word is law."

"What's the goal here, Shaun?"

I looked toward the screen, teeth bared in a grin, and he recoiled. "We're not letting them kill my sister's story the way they killed her. She gets buried. It doesn't."

For a moment, it looked as if he might protest, but only for a moment. It passed as quickly as it had come, and he nodded. "I'll get on that. Are you about to do something foolish?"

"You could say that," I agreed. "Good night, Mahir."

"Good luck," he said, and the screen went black.

I had just finished loading Georgia's gun when the intercom buzzed. "Answer," I said, pulling down my Kevlar vest and slamming the weapons locker shut before starting to fasten the buckles around my chest.

"—there? I repeat: Shaun, are you in there?"

"Steve, my man!" I didn't have to feign my delight at the sound of his voice. "Dude, you're like a *cat*! How many lives you got, anyway?"

"Not as many as you," Steve replied, the rumble of his voice not quite hiding his concern. "Georgia in there with you, Shaun?"

"She is," I said, sliding a Taser into my pocket. It wouldn't stop someone who'd amplified all the way, but it would slow them down. The virus doesn't like to have the electrical current of its host messed with. "She's not really interested in talking, though, Steve-o, on account of the bullets I put through her spinal column. If you're not infected, and you'd be good enough to open the doors, I'd be greatly obliged."

"Did she bite, scratch, or come into contact with you in any way after exposure?"

They were routine questions. They'd never made me so angry in my life. "No, Steve, I'm afraid she didn't. No bites, no scratches, no hugs, not even a kiss good night before that Bible-thumping bastard's assassins sent my sister off to the great newsroom in the sky. If you've got a blood test unit and you'll open the doors, I'll prove it."

"You armed, Shaun?"

"You gonna leave me in here if I say yes? 'Cause I can lie."

The pause that followed was almost enough to make me think Steve had decided safe was better than sorry and was leaving me in the van to rot. That was a goal, sure, but not yet. The story wasn't done until the last of the loose ends were tied off, and one of those loose ends was slated to be George's honor guard. Finally, voice low, Steve said, "I haven't read her last entry all the way. I read enough. Stand back from the door and keep your hands where I can see them until you've tested out clean."

"Yes, sir," I said, and stepped backward.

The air that rushed in when the door opened was so fresh it almost hurt my lungs. The scents of blood and gunpowder were heavy, but not as heavy as they'd been inside the van. I took an involuntary step forward, toward the light, and stopped as a large dark blur raised what I could only assume was an arm and said, "Don't come any closer until I've moved away."

"You got it, Steve-o," I said. "You guys dealt with the little outbreak you had going out here? Sorry I didn't come to join your party. I was preoccupied."

"It's been contained, if not resolved, and I understand," said Steve, coming into focus as my eyes adjusted. He knelt, placed something on the ground, and retreated, allowing me to approach the object. As expected, it was a blood testing unit. Not the top of the line, but not the bottom, either; solidly middle of the road, enough to confirm or deny infection within an acceptable margin of error. "Acceptable." That's always seemed like such a funny word to use when you're talking about whether somebody lives or dies.

It weighed less than a pound. I broke the seal with my thumb, looking toward Steve as I did. "He doesn't walk away from this," I said.

"I promise," Steve replied.

Good enough for me. "Count of three," I said. "One…"

Inside my head, Georgia said, *Two…*

I slid my hand into the unit and pressed the relays down, watching as the lights started cycling through the available colors. Red-yellow-green, yellow-red-green. Every damn one of those lights danced between red and gold for a few seconds, long enough to make me sweat, before settling on a calm and steady green. You're fine, son; just fine. Now go and be merry.

"Merry" wasn't exactly in my plans. I held up the testing unit, letting Steve get a good long look. "This good enough?"

"It is," he said, and tossed me a biohazard bag. "What the hell happened, Shaun?"

"Just what George said. Some sick fucker killed Rick's cat and rigged our trailers to blow. When the blast didn't kill us, they hit George with one of those hypodermic darts like the one that triggered the outbreak at the Ryman place. Shit, I wish we'd been looking for the things back at Eakly. I bet we would've found one."

"I bet we would have, too," said Steve, watching as I dropped the testing unit into a biohazard bag. He was holding his sunglasses loosely in one hand, and his eyes were the eyes of a man who's looked into hell and found he couldn't cope with what he was seeing. I wouldn't have been willing to bet that my eyes were any better. "You got a plan from here?"

"Oh, the usual. Get a vehicle, head for whatever site they have the candidates under lockdown at—"

"Right where you left them," Steve interjected.

"Well, that's convenient. I know the security layout there. Anyway, head back to the candidates and have a chat with Governor Tate." I shrugged. "Maybe blow his brains out. I don't know. The plan is still in the formative stage."

"Need a ride?"

I grinned, the expression feeling foreign on my face. "I'd love one."

"Good. Because my boys and I—what's left of my boys—wouldn't like to see you get hurt just because you felt like being stupid and going it alone."

The ludicrousness of it all was enough to make me laugh. "Wait, you mean this was all I had to do to get myself a bigger security detail?"

"Guess so."

"Get your boys." The laughter faded as I looked at him. "It's time we got on the road."

━━━━━━━━━

Sometimes we leave the connecting door between our rooms open all night. We'd still share a room if they'd let us, turn the other room into an office and have done with it. Because both of us hate to be alone, and both of us hate to have other people—people outside the country we've made together—around when we're defenseless. We're always defenseless when we're asleep.

We leave the connecting door open, and I wake up in the night to the sound of him snoring, and I wonder how the hell I'm going to stay alive after he finally slips up. He'll die first, we both know it, but I don't know... I really don't know how long I'll stay alive without him. That's the part Shaun doesn't know. I don't intend to be an only child for long.

—From *Postcards from the Wall*,
the unpublished files of Georgia Mason, June 19, 2040

Twenty-eight

The outbreak was still going strong. The infected weren't actually everywhere; it just seemed that way, as they lurched and ran out of the shadows, following whatever weird radar signals the virus uses to tell the active hosts from the ones where the potential for infection is still just that, potential, sleeping and waiting for a wake-up. The scientists have been trying to figure out *that* little trick for twenty years, and as far as I know, they're no closer than they were the day Romero movies stopped being trashy horror and started being guides to staying alive. I should have been thrilled—it's not every day I get to walk through the center of an actual outbreak—but I was too busy being angry to really give a damn. Zombies didn't kill George. People did. Living, breathing, uninfected people.

I recognized a lot of faces among the infected. Interns from the campaign; a few security staffers, one long-faced man with thinning red hair who'd been traveling with us for about six weeks writing speeches for the senator. *No more speeches for you, buddy*, I thought, and put a bullet through the center of his forehead. He fell soundlessly, robbed of menace, and I turned away, nauseated.

"If I get out of this alive, I may need to look for another line of work."

"What's that?" asked Steve, between breathless radio calls to his surviving men. He was pulling them back to the motor pool. Several were moving slowly due to the need to herd less-well-armed survivors, going against the recommended survival strategies for an outbreak as they responded like human beings. You want to stay alive in a zombie swarm? You go alone or in a small group where everyone is of similar physical condition and weapons training. You never stop, you never hesitate, and you never show any mercy for the people that would slow you down. That's what the military says we should do, and if I ever meet anybody who listens to that particular set of commands, I may shoot them myself just to improve the gene pool. When you can help people stay alive, you help them. We're all we've got.

"Nothing," I said, with a shake of my head. "How're we looking for support?"

His mouth drew down in something between a wince and a scowl before he said, "Our last call from Andres came while I was on my way to get you. He was backed against a wall with half a dozen of the aides. I don't think we'll be seeing him again. Carlos and Heidi are at the motor pool; that zone's relatively clear. Mike...I haven't heard from Mike. Not Susan or Paolo, either. Everyone else is either on the way to meet with us or holding fast in a safe zone."

"Andres—crap, man, I'm sorry."

Steve shook his head. "I never was very good at partners." He turned and fired into the shadows at the side of a portable office. Something gurgled and fell. I gave him a sidelong look, and he actually smiled. "You thought we wore these sunglasses for our health?"

"I have *got* to get a pair of those."

We kept walking. What started as a pleasant, well-configured camp for visiting politicians had become a killing ground, full of cul-de-sacs and blind alleys that could hold almost anything. Complacency had long since destroyed the functionality of the layout. I couldn't blame them—there hadn't been an outbreak in Sacramento in years—but I didn't appreciate it, either. Luck was on our side: With the senator and most of his senior staff off the grounds for the keynote speech, we had fewer bodies to deal with than we might have otherwise. Our chances of survival had gotten better with every person who left the compound. "Just wish we hadn't come back," I muttered.

"What's that?" asked Steve.

I started to answer but was cut off as something hit me from behind, the momentum forcing me to the ground as hands clawed at my shoulders. Steve shouted. I was too occupied with trying to shake the zombie off to understand what he was saying. It was tearing at my back, trying to bite through the Kevlar. It would move up before too much longer, and my scalp was unprotected. The idea of having my brain literally eaten was really failing to appeal.

"*Shaun!*"

"Busy now!" I rolled to the left, ignoring the growls behind me as I struggled to get the Taser out of my belt. "Can you shoot it?"

"It's too close!"

"So get it off me before it figures out where to bite!" The Taser came free, almost falling into my hand. I twisted my arm as far behind me as I could, praying the thing wouldn't catch the unprotected flesh of my lower arm before the electricity could do its job. "Dammit, Steve, grab the fucking thing!"

Electricity spat and arced as the Taser made contact with the zombie's side. Luckily for me, it had been an intern, not a security guard; it wasn't wearing protective clothing. The thing screamed, sounding almost human as the viral bodies powering its actions became disoriented in the face of an electric current greater than their own. I hit it again, and Steve finally moved, grabbing the zombie and yanking it off. I rolled onto my back, reaching for Georgia's .40, and starting to fire almost as soon as I had it drawn. My first shot hit the zombie high in the shoulder, rocking it back. The second hit it in the forehead, and it went down.

My heart was pounding hard enough to echo in my ears, but my legs were steady as I scrambled back to my feet. Steve looked a lot more shaken. Sweat stood out on his forehead, and his complexion was several shades paler than it had been before I fell. I glanced around. Seeing that nothing else was about to rush me, I bent, picked up the Taser, and replaced both it and the gun in my belt. "You okay over there, Steve-o?"

"Did you get bit?" he demanded.

There was a predictable response. "Nope," I said, raising my hands to show the unbroken skin. "You can test me again when we hit the motor pool, okay? Right now, I think we should stop being out here, like, as soon as possible. That wasn't my favorite thing ever." I paused, and added, almost guiltily, "Besides, I didn't have a camera running." George would've kicked my ass for that, after she finished kicking my ass for getting that close to a live infection.

"You don't need the ratings," said Steve, and grabbed my arm, hauling me after him as he resumed moving, double-speed, toward the motor pool.

Maybe it was because Carlos and Heidi had access to an entire ammo shed, and maybe it was because the motor pool wasn't a popular hangout for the living, but the infected tapered off as we moved toward it, and we crossed the last ten feet to the fence without incident. Good thing; I was almost out of bullets, and I didn't feel like trusting myself to the Taser. The gate in the fence was closed, the electric locks engaged. Steve released my arm, reaching for the keypad, and a shot rang out over our heads, clearly aimed to warn, not wound. Small favors.

"Stop where you are!" shouted Carlos. I looked toward his voice and watched as he and Heidi stepped out from behind the shed, both bristling with weapons. I clucked my tongue disapprovingly. Sure, it *looked* good, but you can't intimidate a zombie, and they had so many things piled overlapping that they'd have trouble drawing much of anything when their primary guns ran out of bullets.

"Overkill," I muttered. "Amateurs."

"Stand down," barked Steve. "It's me and the Mason kid. He tested clean when I picked him up."

"Beg your pardon, sir, but how do we know you test clean *now*?" Heidi asked.

Smart girl. Maybe she could live. "You don't," I said, "but if you let us through the fence and keep us backed against it while you run blood tests, you'll have the opportunity to shoot before either of us can reach you."

She and Carlos exchanged a look. Carlos nodded. "All right," he said. "Step back from the gate."

We did as we were told, Steve giving me a thoughtful look as the gate slid open. "You're good at this."

"Top of my field," I said, and followed him into the motor pool.

Carlos chucked us blood testing units while Heidi reported on the status of the other units, still remaining at a safe distance. Susan was confirmed as infected; she'd been tagged by a political analyst as she was helping Mike evacuate a group of survivors to a rooftop. She stayed on the ground after she was bitten, shooting everything in sight before taking out the ladder and shooting herself. About the best ending you could hope for if you got infected in a combat zone. Mike was fine. So, surprisingly, was Paolo. There was still no word from Andres, and three more groups of security agents and survivors were expected to reach the motor pool at any time. Steve absorbed the news without changing his expression; he didn't even flinch when the needles on his testing unit bit into his hand. I flinched. After the number of blood tests I'd had recently, I was getting seriously tired of being punctured.

Heidi and Carlos relaxed when our tests flashed clean. "Sorry, sir," said Carlos, walking over with the biohazard bags. "We needed to be sure."

"Standard outbreak protocol," Steve said, dismissing the apology with a wave of his hand. "Keep holding this ground—"

"—while we break quarantine," I said, almost cheerfully. George snorted amusement in the back of my head. All for you, George. All for you. "Steve-o and I need to take a little trip. Loan us a car, give us some ammo, and open the gates?"

"Sir?" Heidi sounded uncertain; the idea of leaving a quarantine zone without military or CDC clearance is pretty much anathema to most people. It's just not done, ever. "What is he talking about?"

"One of the armored SUVs should do," said Steve. "Find the fastest one that's still on the grounds." Carlos and Heidi stared at him like he'd just gone into spontaneous amplification. "Move!" he barked, and they moved, scattering for the guard station where the keys to the parked vehicles were stored. Steve ignored their burst of activity, leading me to the weapons locker and keying open the lock. "Candy store is open."

"So all you have to do to break quarantine is shout 'move'?" I asked, beginning to load my pockets with ammunition. I considered grabbing a new gun, but dismissed the idea. Nothing but George's .40 was going to feel right in my hand. "Wow. Normally, I need a pair of wire cutters and some night-vision goggles."

"Gonna pretend you never said that."

"Probably for the best."

Carlos emerged from the guard station and tossed a set of keys to Steve, who caught them in an easy underhand. "We can unlock the rear gate, but once the central computer realizes the seal's been broken—"

"How long can we have?"

"Thirty seconds."

"That's long enough. You two hold your ground. Keep anyone who makes it here safe. Mason, you're with me."

"Yes *sir*!" I said, with a mocking salute. Steve shook his head and pressed the signal button on the key fob. One of the SUVs turned its lights on. Showtime.

Once we were inside, belts fastened and weapons secured, Steve started the engine and drove us to the gate. Carlos was already waiting, ready to hit the manual override. The manual exits exist in case of accidental or ineffective lockdown, to give the uninfected a chance to escape. They require a blood test and a retinal scan, and breaking quarantine without a damn good reason is a quick way to get yourself sent to prison for a long time. Carlos was risking a lot on Steve's order.

"That's what I call a chain of command," I said to myself, as the gate slid open.

"What's that?" asked Steve.

"Nothing. Just go."

We went.

The roads outside the Center were clear. That's standard for the time immediately following a confirmed outbreak in a noncongested area. The people inside the quarantine zone will survive or not without interference; it's all up to them the minute the fences come down. So the big health orgs and military intervention teams wait until the worst of it's had time to burn itself out before they head in. Let the infection peak. Ironically, that makes it *safer*, because it's trying to save the survivors that gets people killed. Once you know everyone around you is already dead, it gets easier to shoot without asking questions.

"How long since the quarantine went down?" I asked.

"Thirty-seven minutes."

Standard CDC response time says you leave a quarantine to cook for forty-five minutes before you go in. Given our proximity to the city, they wouldn't just be responding by air; they'd be sending in ground support to make sure nobody broke quarantine before they declared it safe. "Shit." With eight minutes between us and the end of the cooking time, we needed to get out of sight. "How good's the balance on this thing?"

"Pretty good. Why?"

"Quarantine. It's going to be forty-five minutes since the bell real soon here, and that means we're gonna have company. Now, I've got a way out, but only if you trust me. If you don't, we're probably gonna get the chance to tell some nice men why we're out here. Assuming they don't just shoot first."

"Kid, I'm already committed. Just tell me where to go."

"Take the next left turn."

Being a good Irwin is partially dependant on knowing as many ways to access an area as possible. That includes the location of handy things like, say, railroad trestle bridges across the American River. See, they used to run trains through Sacramento, back when people traveled that way. The system's abandoned now, except for the automated cargo trains, but they run on a fixed schedule. I've had it memorized for years.

Steve started swearing once he realized where we were going, and he kept swearing as he pulled the SUV onto the tracks and floored the gas, trusting momentum and the structure of the trestle to keep us from plunging into the river. I grabbed the oh-shit handle with one hand and whooped, bracing the other hand on the dashboard. I couldn't help myself. Everything was going to hell, George was dead, and I was on my way to commit either treason or suicide, but who the hell cared? I was off-roading across a river in a government SUV. Sometimes, you just gotta kick back and enjoy what's going on around you.

We were halfway across the river when the first CDC copters passed overhead, zooming toward the Center. Three more followed close behind, in closed arrow formation. Fascinated, I leaned over and clicked on the radio, tuning it to the emergency band. "—repeat, this is not a drill. Remain in your homes. If you are on the road, remain in your vehicle until you have reached a safe location. If you have seen or had direct contact with infected individuals, contact local authorities immediately. Repeat, this is not a drill. Remain in—"

Steve turned the radio off. "Breaking quarantine is a federal offense, isn't it?"

"Only if they catch us." I settled back in my seat. "Doesn't bother me much, and they're not looking down."

"All right, then." He hit the gas again. The SUV rolled faster, hitting the end of the trestle and blazing onward toward the city. He glanced at me as we drove, saying, "I'm sorry about your sister. She was a good woman. She'll be missed."

"That's appreciated, Steve." The idea of looking at his face—it would be so earnest, if his words were anything to judge by, so anxious for understanding—made me tired all over again. There was nothing I could do now, nothing I could do until we got to the hall and to the man who had killed my sister. So I looked at my hands as I cleaned and reloaded Georgia's gun, and I was silent, and we drove on.

—————

   ...but they were us, our children, our selves,
These shades who walk the cloistered dark,
With empty eyes and clasping hands,
And wander, isolate, alone, the space between
Forgiveness and the penitent's grave.

—From *Eakly, Oklahoma*,
originally published in *By the Sounding Sea*,
the blog of Buffy Meissonier, February 11, 2040

Twenty-nine

Quarantine procedures hit different social and economic classes in different ways, just like outbreaks. When Kellis-Amberlee breaks out in an urban area, it hits the inner cities and the business districts the hardest. That's where you have the largest number of people coming and going, experiencing the closest thing we have these days to casual contact. Interestingly, you tend to have more fatalities in the business districts. The slums may not have the same security features and weaponry, but they're mostly self-policing and fewer people try to conceal injuries when they know amplification isn't just going to cost them their coworkers; it's going to cost them their families. Inner cities and business districts turn into ghost towns when the quarantines come down. If you pass through while they're under quarantine, you can feel the inhabitants watching you, waiting for you to make a move.

Middle-class zones also tend to seal themselves off, but they're less blatantly aggressive about it; windows too small or too high for a person to get in through can be left open, and not every glass door has a steel shield in front of it. You can enter those areas and still believe people live in them, even if those folks aren't exactly setting out the welcome mats. They'll kill you as quickly as anyone else will if you try to approach them. If you don't, they won't interfere.

The hall where they held the keynote speech was far enough from the Center that it wasn't technically in the quarantine zone. Street traffic was down to practically zero, but there were no retractable bars over the windows and no steel plating over the doors. Local businesses were open, even if there weren't any customers. I looked around as Steve pulled up to the first checkpoint, and I hated these people for being able to ignore what was

going on outside their city. George was dead. Rick and Mahir said the whole
world was mourning with me, but that didn't matter, because the man who
did it—the man I intended to blame—wasn't even inconvenienced.

If the guard thought there was something odd about us arriving in a
dusty, dented SUV over an hour after the Center went into lockdown, he
didn't say anything. Our blood tests came back clean; that was what his
job required him to give a damn about, and so he just waved us inside. I
clenched my jaw so hard I almost tasted blood.

Calm down, counseled George. *It's not his fault. He didn't write the news.*

"Go for the writers," I muttered.

Steve shot me a look. "What's that?"

"Nothing."

We parked next to a press bus that had doubtless been loaded with
reporters who were now thanking God for their timing, since being on
assignment with a bunch of political bigwigs meant they weren't available
to be sent out to report on the quarantine. Local Irwins would be flock-
ing to the perimeter, getting footage of the CDC men as they locked and
secured the site. I would've been with them not that long ago, and been
happy about it. Now . . . I'd be just as happy if I never saw another outbreak.
Somewhere between Eakly and George, I lost the heart for it.

Steve and I got into the elevator together. I glanced at him as he keyed
in our floor, saying, "You don't have a press pass."

"Don't need one," he said. "The Center's under quarantine. By contract, I'm actually obligated to circumnavigate any security barricade
between myself and the senator."

"Sneaky," I said, approvingly.

"Precisely."

The elevator opened on a sickeningly normal-looking party. Servers
in starched uniforms circulated with trays of drinks and canapés. Politicians, their spouses, reporters, and members of the California elite milled
around, chattering about shit that didn't mean a goddamn thing compared
to George's blood drying on the wall. The only real difference was in their
eyes. They knew about the quarantine—half of these people were staying
at the Center, or worked there, or had a stake in its continued success—
and they were terrified. But appearances have to be maintained, especially
when you're looking at millions of dollars in lost city revenue because of an
outbreak. So the party continued.

"Poe was right," I muttered. The man with the blood tests was waiting
for us to check in. I slid my increasingly sore hand into the unit he held,

watching lights run their cycle from red to yellow and finally to green. I wasn't infected. If being shut in a van with George's body didn't get me, nothing was going to. Infection would have been too easy a way out.

I yanked my hand free as soon as the lights went green, held up my press pass, and ducked into the crowd. Steve was right behind me. I dodged staff and guests, arrowing toward the room where I had last seen Senator Ryman. They wouldn't allow him to leave after the Center went into lockdown, and if he couldn't leave, he wouldn't have left the room where he had his surviving staff and supporters gathered. It just made sense.

People recoiled as I passed them, eyes going wide and suppressed fear surging to the front of their expressions. I paused, looking down at myself. Mud, powder burns, visible weapons—everything but blood. Somehow, I'd managed to avoid getting George's blood on me. That was a good thing, since she'd died infected and her blood would have made me a traveling hot zone, but still, it was almost a pity. At least then she would have seen the story find an ending.

"Shaun?"

Senator Ryman sounded astonished. I turned toward his voice and found him half standing. Emily was beside him, eyes wide, hands clapped over her mouth. Tate was on his other side. Unlike the Rymans, the governor looked anything but relieved to see me. I could read the hatred in his eyes.

"Senator Ryman," I said, and finished my turn, walking to the table that looked like it held all the survivors of the Ryman campaign. Less than a dozen of us had been at this stupid speech; less than a dozen, from a caravan that had swelled to include more than sixty people. What kind of survival rate were we looking at? Fifty percent? Less? Almost certainly less. That's the nature of an outbreak, to kill what it doesn't conquer. "Mrs. Ryman." I smiled narrowly, the sort of expression that's always been more Georgia's purview than my own. "Governor."

"Oh, God, Shaun." Emily Ryman stood so fast she sent her chair toppling over as she threw her arms around me. "We heard the news. I'm so *sorry*."

"I shot her," I said conversationally, looking over Emily's shoulder to Senator Ryman and Governor Tate. "Pulled the trigger after she started to amplify. She was lucid until then. You can increase the duration of post-infection lucidity with sedatives and white blood cell boosters, and first-aid classes teach you to do that in the field. So you can get any messages they may have for their family or other loved ones."

"Shaun?" Emily pulled away, looking uncertain. She glanced over her shoulder at Governor Tate before looking back to me. "What's going on here?"

"How did you get out of the quarantine zone?" asked Tate. His voice was flat, verging on emotionless. He knew the score. He'd known it since I walked through the door. The bastard.

"A little luck, a little skill, a little applied journalism." Emily Ryman let me go entirely, taking a step backward, toward her husband. I kept my eyes on Tate. "Turns out most of the security staff liked my sister more than they ever liked you. Probably because George tried to *help* them, instead of using them to further her political ambitions. Once they knew what happened, they were happy to help."

"Shaun, what are you talking about?"

The confusion in Senator Ryman's voice was enough to distract me from Tate. I turned to blink at the man responsible for us being here in the first place, asking, "Haven't you seen Georgia's last report?"

"No, son, I haven't." His expression was drawn tight with concern. "Things have been a bit hectic. I haven't had a site feed since the outbreak bell rang."

"Then how did you—"

"The CDC puts out a statement, that tends to go around in a hurry." Senator Ryman closed his eyes, looking pained. "She was so damn *young.*"

"Georgia was assassinated, Senator. Plastic dart full of live-state Kellis-Amberlee, shot straight into her arm. She never had a prayer. All because we figured out what was really going on." I swung my attention back to Tate and asked, more quietly, "Why Eakly, Governor? Why the ranch? And why, you fucker, why *Buffy?* I can actually understand trying to kill me and my sister, after everything else, but *why?*"

"Dave?" said Senator Ryman.

"This country needed someone to take real action for a change. Someone who was willing to do what needed to be done. Not just another politician preaching changes and keeping up the status quo." Tate met my eyes without flinching, looking almost calm. "We took some good steps toward God and safety after the Rising, but they've slowed in recent years. People are afraid to do the right thing. That's the key. Real fear's what motivates them to get past the fears that aren't important enough to matter. They needed to be reminded. They needed to remember what America stands for."

"Not sure I'd call terrorist use of Kellis-Amberlee a 'reminder.' Personally, I'd call it, y'know. Terrorism. Maybe a crime against humanity. Possibly both. I guess that's for the courts to decide." I drew Georgia's .40, and aimed it at Tate. The crowd went still, honed political instincts reacting to what had to look like an assassination attempt in the making. "Secure-channel voice activation, Shaun Phillip Mason, ABF-17894, password 'crikey.' Mahir, you there?"

My ear cuff beeped once. "Here, Shaun," said Mahir's voice, distorted by the encryption algorithms protecting the transmission. Secure channels are only good once, but, oh, how good they are. "What's the situation?"

"On Tate now. Start uploading everything you receive and down-load Georgia's last report directly to Senator Ryman. He needs to give it a glance." Governor Tate was glaring. I flashed him a smile. "I've been recording this whole time. But you knew that, didn't you? Smart guy like you. Smart enough to get around our security. To get around our *friends*."

"Miss Meissonier was a realist and a patriot who understood the tri-als facing this country," said Tate, tone as stiff as his shoulders. "She was proud to have the opportunity to serve."

"Miss Meissonier was a twenty-four-year-old journalist who wrote poetry for a living," I snapped. "Miss Meissonier was our partner, and you had her killed because she wasn't useful anymore."

"David, is this true?" asked Emily, horror leeching the inflection from her voice. Senator Ryman had taken out his PDA and seemed to be grow-ing older by the second as he stared at its screen. "Did you . . . Eakly? The ranch?" Fury twisted her features, and before either I or her husband could react, she was out of her chair, launching herself at Governor Tate. *"My daughter! That was my daughter, you bastard! Those were my parents! Burn in hell, you—"*

Tate grabbed her wrists, twisting her to the side and locking his arm around her neck. His left hand, which had been under the table since I arrived, came into view, holding another of those plastic syringes. Unaware, Emily Ryman continued to struggle.

The senator went pale. "Now, David, let's not do anything rash here—"

"I tried to send them home, Peter," said Tate. "I tried to get them off the campaign, out of harm's way, out of *my* way. Now look where they've brought us. Me, holding your pretty little wife, with just one outbreak left between us and a happy ending. I would have given you the election. I would have made you the greatest American president of the past hundred years, because together, we would have remade this nation."

"No election is worth this," Ryman said. "Emily, be still now, baby." Looking confused and betrayed, Emily stopped struggling. Ryman lifted his hands into view, palms upward. "What'll it take for you to release her? My wife's not a part of this."

"I'm afraid you're all a part of this now," Tate said, with a small shake of his head. "No one's walking away. It's gone too far for that. Maybe if you'd disposed of the *journalists*," the word was almost spat, "it could have gone differently. But there's no use crying over spilled milk, now, is there?"

"Put down the syringe, Governor," I said, keeping the gun level. "Let her go."

"Shaun, the CDC is piggybacking our feed," said Mahir. "They're not stopping the transmission, but they're definitely listening in. Dave and Alaric are maintaining the integrity, but I don't know that we can stop it if they want to cut us off."

"Oh, they won't cut us off, will you, Dr. Wynne?" I asked. I was starting to feel a little light-headed. This was all moving so damn fast.

Keep it together, dummy, hissed George. *You think I want to be an only child?*

"I've got it, George," I muttered.

"What's that?" asked Mahir.

"Nothing. Dr. Wynne? You there?" If it was him, the CDC was with us. If it was anybody else...

There was a crackle as the CDC broke into our channel. "Here, Shaun," said the familiar southern drawn of Dr. Joseph Wynne. Mahir was swearing in the background. "Are you in any danger?"

"Well, Governor Tate's holding a syringe on Senator Ryman's wife, and since the last two syringes we've seen have been full of Kellis-Amberlee, I'm not betting this one's any different," I said. "I've got a gun on him, but I don't think I can shoot before he sticks her."

"We're on our way. Can you stall him?"

"Doing my best." I forced my attention back to Governor Tate, who was watching me impassively. "Come on, Governor. You know this is over. Why not put that thing down and go out like a man instead of like a murderer? More of one than you already are, I mean."

"Not exactly diplomatic, there, Shaun," said Dr. Wynne in my ear.

"Doing the best I can," I said.

"Shaun, who are you talking to?" asked Senator Ryman. He looked edgy. Having a crazy dude holding a syringe of live virus on his wife probably had something to do with that.

"Dr. Joseph Wynne from the CDC," I said. "They're on the way."

"Thank God," breathed the senator.

"Want to put it down now, Governor?" I asked. "You know this is over."

Governor Tate hesitated, looking from me to the senator and finally to the horrified, receding crowd. Suddenly weary, he shook his head, and said, "You're fools, all of you. You could have saved this country. You could have brought moral fiber back to America." His grip on Emily slackened. She pulled herself free, diving into her husband's embrace. Senator Ryman closed his arms around her and rose, backing away. Governor Tate ignored them. "Your sister was a hack and a whore who would have fucked Kellis himself if she thought it would get her a story. She'll be forgotten in a week, when your fickle little audience of bottom-feeders moves on to something more recent. But they're going to remember me, Mason. They always remember the martyrs."

"We'll see," I said.

"No," he said. "We won't." In one fluid motion, he drove the syringe into his thigh and pressed the plunger home.

Emily Ryman screamed. Senator Ryman was shouting at the top of his lungs, ordering people to get back, to get to the elevators, behind secure doors, anything that would get them away from the man who'd just turned himself into a living outbreak. Still looking at me, Governor Tate started to laugh.

"Hey, George," I said, taking a few seconds to adjust my aim. There was no wind inside; that was a nice change. Less to compensate for. "Check this out."

The sound of her .40 going off was almost drowned out by the screams of the crowd. Governor Tate stopped laughing and looked, for an instant, almost comically surprised before he slumped onto the table, revealing the ruined mess that had replaced the back of his head. I kept the gun trained on him, waiting for signs of further movement. After several moments had passed without any, I shot him three more times anyway, just to be sure. It never hurts to be sure.

People were still screaming, pushing past each other as they rushed for the doors. Mahir and Dr. Wynne were trying to shout over each other on our open channel, both demanding status reports, demanding to know whether I was all right, whether the outbreak had been contained. They were giving me a headache. I reached up and removed my ear cuff, putting it on the table. Let them shout. I was done listening. I didn't need to listen anymore.

"See, George?" I whispered. When did I start crying? It didn't matter. Tate's blood looked just like George's. It was red and bright now, but it would start to dry soon, turning brown, turning old, turning into something the world could just forget. "I got him. I got him for you."

Good, she said.

Senator Ryman was shouting my name, but he was too far away to matter. Steve and Emily would never let him this close to a hot corpse. Until the CDC showed up, I could be alone. I liked that idea. Alone.

Taking two steps backward, I pulled out a chair and sat down at a table that would let me keep an eye on Tate. Just in case. There was a basket of breadsticks at the center, abandoned by fickle diners when the trouble started. I picked one up with my free hand and munched idly as I kept George's gun trained on Tate. He didn't move. Neither did I. When the CDC arrived to take command of the site fifteen minutes later, we were still waiting, Tate with his pool of slowly drying blood, me with my basket of breadsticks. They seized the site, sealed it, and ushered us all away to quarantine and testing. I kept my eye on him as long as I could, watching for some sign that it wasn't over, that the story wasn't done. He never moved, and George didn't say a word, leaving me alone in the echoing darkness of my mind.

Was it worth it, George? Well, was it? Tell me, if you can, because I swear to God, I just don't know.

I don't know anything anymore.

CODA:

Dying For You

The next person who says "I'm sorry" is going to get punched in the nose. Because "I'm sorry" doesn't do a damn thing except remind me that this can't be fixed. This is my world now. And I don't want it.

—Shaun Mason

I love my brother. I love my job. I love the truth. So here's hoping no one ever makes me choose between them.

—Georgia Mason

Somebody once asked me if I believed in God. It was probably the windup to some major proselytizing, but it's a good question. Do I believe in God? That somebody made all this happen for a reason, that there's something waiting for us after we die? That there's a purpose to all this crap? I don't know. I'd like to be able to say "Yes, of course" almost as much as I'd like to be able to say "Absolutely not," but there's evidence on both sides of the fence. Good people die for nothing, little kids go hungry, corrupt men hold positions of power, and horrible diseases go uncured. And I got Shaun, maybe the only person who could make it seem worthwhile to me. I got Shaun.

So, is there a God? Sorry to dodge the question, but I just don't know.

—From *Postcards from the Wall*,
the unpublished files of Georgia Mason, April 17, 2040

Thirty

It took three months for the CDC to release Georgia's ashes. It would normally have taken longer, given the way she died. Lucky me, my sister died an international celebrity. That sort of thing gets you friends in high places. Even inside the CDC itself, which has been preoccupied with internal reviews as it tries to find the source of Tate's anonymous "donors." When Dr. Wynne went to his superiors and petitioned them for the right to let us have Georgia's ashes, they listened. Guess they didn't want to risk being our story of the week. No one does, these days. That'll fade with time—Mahir says we're losing percentages daily, as people move on to newer things—but we're always going to have a certain cachet after everything that went down. "After the End Times: So dedicated to telling you what you need to hear that they'll die to do it." I'd probably be a lot more disgusted by the whole thing if it weren't for the part where it let us bring George home.

Dr. Wynne brought the box containing her ashes to me himself, accompanied by a fresh-faced, yellow-haired doctor I remembered from Memphis. Kelly Connolly. She's the one who gave me the pile of cards, handwritten by CDC employees from all over the country, and said they had three more as large from the WHO and USAMRIID. Her eyes were red, like she'd been crying. Buffy died, and we got accused of trying to hoax the world. George died, and that same world mourned with me. Maybe that should have been a comfort, but it wasn't. I didn't want the world to mourn. I just wanted George to come home.

She would have needed a forwarding address to find me. I came back from the campaign trail battered, exhausted, and ready to collapse, and discovered that home wasn't home anymore. My room was connected to George's room, and George wasn't there. I kept finding myself standing in her room, not sure how I got there, waiting for her to start yelling at me and tell me to knock first. She never did, and so I started packing my things. I wanted to get away from the ghosts. And I wanted to get away from the Masons.

George died, and the world mourned with me, sure. All the world but them. Oh, they did the right things in public, said the right things, made the right gestures. Dad did a series of articles on personal versus public responsibility and kept invoking the "heroic sacrifice" of his beloved adopted daughter, like that somehow made his platitudes more relevant. Guess it did, because it got him the highest ratings he'd had in years. George died a celebrity. Can't blame a man for capitalizing on that. Except for the part where I can. Oh, believe me, I can.

George and I've had our last wills and testaments filed since before we were required to, and even though we both always assumed I'd go first, we both still filed with predeceasement clauses. If I went first, she got everything I had, including intellectual property, published and unpublished. If she went first, I got the same. We both had to die before anyone else had a shot at our estates, and even then, we didn't leave them to the Masons. We left them to Buffy, and, in the event that she hadn't survived whatever event managed to kill us both—since we always figured the only way we'd die together was something like the van breaking down in the middle of an outbreak—it all rolled to Mahir. Keep the site going. Keep the news in the right hands. The Masons haven't been in the chain of inheritance since we were sixteen. Only they didn't seem to have realized that because I hadn't been home for three days before they started harassing me to sign over George's unpublished files to them.

"It's what she would have wanted," Dad said, doing his best to look solemn and wise. "We can take care of things and leave you free to build a career of your own. She wouldn't have wanted you to put your life on hold to take care of what she left behind."

"You're one of the top Irwins in the world right now," Mom added. "You can write your own ticket. Whatever you want to do, you can do it. I bet you could even get a pass to visit Yosemite—"

"I know what she wanted," I said, and I left them sitting there at the kitchen table, not quite certain how they'd failed. I moved out the next morning. Two weeks couch-surfing with local bloggers who knew the score, and then I was in my own apartment. One bedroom, security controls so far out of date that the place would have been condemned if it hadn't been in such a well-certified hazard zone, and no ghosts or opportunistic parents waiting to ambush me in the halls. George followed me, of course, in the form of all her things, tucked into neat cardboard boxes by the movers that I'd hired...but she'd never been there while she was alive, and so sometimes, I was able to forget she wasn't there anymore. For minutes at a time, even, it seemed like the world was the way it was supposed to be.

Doctors Wynne and Connolly cut the delivery of George's ashes pretty close; they didn't bring them until the day before the funeral. I wouldn't have scheduled it at all, not until I had her back in hand and maybe had a little time to come to terms with things again, but circumstances didn't leave me much of a choice. It was the only day Senator Ryman could make it, and he'd asked that we hold the service when he could attend. I might still have put it off, except for the part where our team couldn't come out of the field if the senator—who was fighting, and apparently winning, an increasingly vicious battle for his political position—was still out there. Magdalene, Becks, and Alaric deserved their chance to say good-bye to George, too. Especially since they'd taken over where she and I, and Buffy, had to leave off.

Becks runs the Irwins now; I meant it when I said I didn't have the stomach for it anymore. Site administration is enough excitement for me, at least for right now. Mahir and Magdalene are doing fine with their departments. Ratings have actually gone up for the Fictionals. Magdalene is better at staying focused than Buffy ever was, even if she doesn't have a flair for technical things or espionage. And maybe that's good, too. We've been down that road before.

Mahir's flight from London landed at eleven the day of the funeral. I drove to the passenger collection zone at the edge of the airport's quarantine border, hoping I'd be able to pick him out of the crowd. I didn't really need to worry. His plane had been almost empty, and I would've known him anywhere, even if I hadn't been seeing him on video screens for years. He had the same empty confusion in his eyes that I saw in my mirror every morning, that odd sort of denial that only seems to come when the world decides to jump the rails without warning you first.

"Shaun," he said, and took my hand. "I'm so glad to finally meet you. I just wish it could have been under better circumstances."

"This is from George," I said, and pulled him into a hug. He didn't hesitate. He just hugged me back, and we stood there, crying on each other's shoulders, until airport security told us to clear out or be held in contempt of quarantine regulations. We left.

"What news?" Mahir asked, as we pulled onto the freeway. "I've been incommunicado for hours. Blasted flight."

"Mail from Rick—Senator Ryman's plane touched down about the same time yours did. They'll be meeting us at the funeral home. Emily couldn't make it, sends her regrets." I shook my head. "She sent a pie last week. An actual pie. That woman is so weird."

"How's Rick handling the transition?"

"He's taking it pretty well. I mean, he quit when the senator asked him to be the new VP candidate, and it doesn't seem to be driving him crazy. Who knows? Maybe they'll win. They're definitely bread and circuses enough for the general populace."

"American politics." Mahir shook his head. "Bloody bizarre."

"We work with what we've got."

"I suppose that's the way of the world." He hesitated, looking at me as I turned off the freeway and onto the surface streets. "I'm so sorry, Shaun. I just...There's nothing I can say that says how sorry I am. You know that, don't you?"

"I know you cared about her a lot," I said, shrugging. "She was your friend. You were hers. One of the best ones she ever had."

"She said that?" he asked, wonderingly.

"Actually, yeah. All the time."

Mahir wiped the back of his hand across his eyes. "I never even got to meet her, Shaun. It's just...it's so damned unfair."

"I know." I didn't bother wiping my own tears away. I stopped bothering weeks ago. Maybe if I let them fall they'd get around to stopping on their own. "It is what it is. Isn't that how these things always go? They are what they are. We just get to cope."

"I suppose that's true."

"At least she got her story." The parking lot of the funeral home was choked with cars. Packing the staff of multiple blog sites and a presidential campaign, as well as friends and family, into a single building will do that sort of thing. Their security must have been freaking out. The thought was enough to bring the ghost of a smile to my face, and the ghost of a chuckle from George in the back of my head.

Mahir glanced at me as I pulled into the last parking slot reserved in the "family" section of the lot. "I'm sorry, did I miss something? You're smiling."

"No," I said, unlocking the door. There'd be men with blood tests at the funeral home doors, and mourners waiting to tell me how sorry they were, to share their tears like I could understand them when I could barely understand my own. "You didn't miss anything at all, I guess. You got as much as I did." I climbed out of the car, Mahir still looking at me strangely.

And then I stood there, waiting, until he followed me. "Come on. There's a whole bunch of people waiting for us."

"Shaun?"

"Yeah?"

"Was it worth it?"

No, whispered George, and, "No," I said. "But then again, when you get to the end, what really is?"

She told the truth as she saw it, and she died for it. I came along for the ride, and I lived. It wasn't worth it. But it was the truth, and it was what had to happen. I tried to hold onto that as we walked into the funeral home to say as many of our good-byes as we could. It wouldn't be all of them. It never could be. But it was going to have to be enough, for me, and for George, and for everyone. Because there wasn't going to be anything more.

"Hey, George," I whispered.

What?

"Check this out."

We stepped inside.

Acknowledgments

This is a book that truly could not have been written without the help of a dedicated and industrious team of editors, continuity checkers, and subject matter experts. From doctors and epidemiologists to people willing to attempt riding luggage carts over railroad trestles for the sake of research, there was as much field work as sit-down study. It was a group effort in many ways, and I owe an enormous debt of gratitude to all the people, named and unnamed, who helped me bring the world of *Feed* to life.

Rae Hanson and Sunil Patel were two of the first to join the proofing pool, providing valuable advice about technology, politics, the media, and the way the entertainment world would change after the zombies rose. (Rae also carved a jack-o-lantern with Shaun and Georgia riding the bike over a crowd of zombies. I have excellent friends.) Amanda and Steve Perry were my point people for everything having to do with wireless and cellular technology, and taught me a great deal about the miniaturization going on in the real world. Between them and Mike Whitaker, who did the majority of the technical design on Shaun and Georgia's van, I have much more accurate tech than I have any right to.

Matt Branstad was responsible for verifying the accuracy of my firearms design, and was invaluable when it came to finding new, exciting ways to kill zombies. Michelle and David McNeill-Coronado provided regional details on Sacramento (David actually suggested the railroad trestle), as well as providing active, engaging sounding boards for the political climate of the book.

Medical assistance was provided by Brooke Lunderville and Melissa Glasser, who rebuilt my medical technology from the ground up several times, while Debbie J. Gates helped out with the animal action. Alison Riley-Duncan, Rebecca Newman, Allison Hewett, Janet Maughan,

Penelope Skrzynski, Phil Ames, Amanda Sanders, and Martha Hage were on tap for general proofreading and plot consultation; I couldn't have done this without them.

Finally, acknowledgment for forbearance must go to Kate Secor and Michelle Dockrey, who received the bulk of my "talking it out" during the writing process; to my agent, Diana Fox, who is never anything short of heroic; to my editor, DongWon Song, who understood the story from the first; and to Tara O'Shea and Chris Mangum, the incredible technical team behind www.MiraGrant.com. This book might have been written without them. It would not have been the same.

Rise up while you can.

DEADLINE

I am honored to dedicate this book to
Brooke Amber Lunderville
and
Rae Hanson.

The Rising would have been very different without them.

BOOK I

Point of Infection

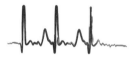

Sometimes you need lies to stay alive.

—SHAUN MASON

The only thing we have in this world that is utterly and intrinsically ours is our integrity. If we give that away, we may as well stop fighting, because losing that battle is what loses the war. There's nothing worth that.

—GEORGIA MASON

I got another interview request yesterday from some brand-new baby blogger who's looking for a scoop and wants to know how I'm "coping." That's apparently the only thing anyone thinks I'm doing these days. I'm "coping." There are days when I feel like I'm never going to be allowed to do anything else. I'm going to walk through my life being Shaun Mason, the Dude Who Copes. Copes with a world filled with stupid people. Copes with a life that doesn't include the one person who ever really mattered. Copes with everyone asking him whether he's "coping," when the answer should be totally obvious to anyone with a brain.

How am I coping? I miss George, and the goddamn world is still full of zombies, that's how. Everything else...

Everything else is just details. And those don't really matter to me anymore.

**—From *Adaptive Immunities*, the blog of Shaun Mason,
February 17, 2041**

One

Our story opens where countless stories have ended in the last twenty-seven years: with an idiot—in this case, Rebecca Atherton, head of the After the End Times Irwins, winner of the Golden Steve-o Award for valor in the face of the undead—deciding it would be a good idea to go out and poke a zombie with a stick to see what happens. Because, hey, there's always the chance that this time, maybe things will go differently. I know I always thought it would be different for me, back when I was the one doing the poking. George always told me I was an idiot, but I had faith.

Too bad George was right.

At least Becks was being smart about her stupidity and was using a crowbar to poke the zombie, which greatly improved her chances of survival. She'd managed to sink the clawed end under the zombie's collarbone, which was really a pretty effective defensive measure. The zombie would eventually realize that it couldn't move forward. When that happened, it would pull away, either yanking the crowbar out of her hands or dislocating its own collarbone, and then it would try coming at her from another angle. Given the intelligence of your average zombie, I figured she had about an hour before she really needed to be concerned. Plenty of time. It was a thrilling scene. Woman versus zombie, locked in a visceral conflict that's basically ground into our cultural DNA by this point. And I didn't give a damn.

The guy next to her looked a whole lot less sanguine about the situation, maybe because he'd never been that close to a zombie before. The latest literature says we're supposed to call them "post-Kellis-Amberlee amplification manifestation syndrome humans," but fuck that. If they really wanted some fancy new term for "zombie" to catch on, they should have made it easy to shout at the top of your lungs, or at least made sure it formed a catchy acronym. They're zombies. They're brainless meat puppets controlled by a virus and driven by the endless need to spread their infection. All the fancy names in the world won't change that.

Anyway, Alaric Kwong—the dude trying not to toss his cookies all over Becks's dead friend—had never been a field-situation kind of a guy. He was a natural Newsie, one of those people who are most comfortable when they're sitting somewhere far away from the action, talking about cause and motivation. Unfortunately for him, he'd finally decided that he wanted to go after some bigger stories, and that meant he needed to test for his Class A journalism license. To get your Class A, you have to prove you can handle life in the field. Becks had been trying to help him for almost a week, and I was rapidly coming to think that it was hopeless. He was destined for a life of sitting around the office compiling reports from people who had the balls to pass their exams.

You're being hard on him, Georgia chided.

"I'm being realistic," I muttered.

"Shaun?" Dave looked up from his screen, squinting as he turned in my direction. "Did you say something?"

"Not a thing." I shook my head, reaching for my half-empty Coke. "Five gets you ten he fails his practicals again."

"No bet," said Dave. "He's gonna pass this time."

I raised an eyebrow. "Why are you so sure?"

"Becks is out there with him. He wants to impress her."

"Does he now?" I returned my attention to the screen, more interested now. "Think she likes him back? It'd explain why she keeps wearing skirts to the office..."

"Maybe," said Dave, judiciously.

On the screen, Becks was trying to get Alaric to take the crowbar and have his own shot at holding off the zombie. No big deal, especially for someone as seasoned as Becks. At least, it wouldn't have been a big deal if there hadn't been six more infected lurching into view on the left-hand monitor. I flipped a switch to turn on the sound. Not a thing. They weren't moaning.

"...the fuck?" I murmured. Flipping another switch to turn on the two-way intercom, I said, "Becks, check your perimeter."

"What are you talking about?" She turned to scan her surroundings, raising one hand to shield her eyes. "Our perimeter is—" Catching sight of the infected lurching closer by the second, she froze, eyes going wide. "Oh, *fuck* me."

"Maybe later," I said, standing. "Keep Alaric alive. I'm heading out to assist with evac."

"Empty promises," she muttered, barely audible. "Alaric! Behind me, *now!*"

I heard him swearing in surprise. The sharp report of Becks shooting their captive zombie followed immediately after. The more zombies you have in an area, the more intelligent they seem to get. If Becks and Alaric wanted to get out of there alive, they needed to reduce the number of infected as much as possible. I didn't see her make the shot; I was already heading for the door, grabbing my rifle from the rack as I passed it.

Dave half-stood, asking, "Should I...?"

"Negative. Stay here, get the equipment secured, and get ready to drive like hell."

"Check," he said, scrambling from his seat toward the front of the van. I didn't really pay attention to that, either; I was busy kicking open the doors and stepping out into the blazing light of the afternoon.

When you're going to play with dead things, do it during the daylight. They don't see as well in bright light as humans do, and they don't hide as well when they don't have the shadows helping them. More important, the footage will be better. If you're gonna die, make sure you do it on camera.

The GPS tracker in my watch showed Becks and Alaric remaining in a stationary position roughly two miles away. Two miles is the federally mandated minimum distance between an intentional zombie encounter and a licensed traveling safe zone, such as our van. Not that the infected would avoid coming within two miles out of some sort of respect for the law; we just aren't allowed to lure them any closer than that. I did some quick mental math. If they'd already attracted a group of six, and the infected weren't moaning yet, that implied that we had enough zombies in the immediate vicinity to form a thinking mob. Not good.

"Right," I said, and swung myself into the driver's seat of Dave's Jeep. The keys were already in the ignition.

Unlike most field vehicles, Dave's Jeep has no armor to speak of, unless you count the run-flat tires and the titanium-reinforced frame. What it has is speed—and lots of it. The thing has been stripped down to the bare minimum, rebuilt, and stripped down again so many times that I don't think there's a single piece left that conforms to factory standards. It offers about as much protection during an attack of the infected as a wet paper bag. A very fast wet paper bag. It's evac only in hostile territory, and we haven't lost a man yet while we were using it.

I braced my rifle between the seats and hit the gas.

Large swaths of California were effectively abandoned after the Rising, for one reason or another. "Difficult to secure" was one; "hostile terrain giving the advantage to the enemy" was another. My personal favorite applied to the small, unincorporated community of Birds Landing, in Solano County: "Nobody cared enough to bother." They had a population of less than two hundred pre-Rising, and there were no survivors. When the federal government needed to appoint funds for cleanup and security, there was nobody to argue in favor of cleaning the place out. They still get the standard patrols, just because letting the zombies mob is in nobody's best interests, but for the most part, Birds Landing has been left to the dead.

It should have been the perfect place to run Alaric's last field trial drill. Abandoned, isolated, close enough to Fairfield to allow for pretty easy evac if the need arose, but far enough away that we could still get some pretty decent footage. Not as dangerous as Santa Cruz, not as candy-ass as Bodega Bay. The ideal infected fishing hole. Only it looked like the zombies thought so, too.

The roads were crap. Swearing softly but steadily to myself, I pressed the gas farther down, getting the Jeep up to the highest speed I was confident I could handle. The frame was shaking and jerking like it might fly apart at any second, and, almost unwillingly, I started to grin. I pushed the speed up a little farther. The shaking increased, and my grin widened.

Careful, cautioned George. *I don't want to be an only child.*

My grin died. "I already am," I said, and floored it.

My dead sister that only I can hear—and yes, I know I'm nuts, thanks for pointing out the obvious—isn't the only one who's been worried about my displaying suicidal tendencies since she passed away. "Passed away" is a polite, bloodless way of saying "was murdered," but it's better than trying to explain the situation every time she comes up in conversation. Yeah, I had a sister, and yeah, she died. Also yeah, I talk to her all the damn time, because as long as I'm only that crazy, I'll stay sane enough to function.

I stopped talking to her for almost a week once, on the advice of a crappy psychologist who said he could "help." By the fifth day, I wanted to eat a bullet for breakfast. That's one experiment that won't be repeated.

I gave up the bulk of my active fieldwork when George died. I figured that might calm people down, but all it did was get them more worked up. I was Shaun Mason, Irwin to the president! I wasn't supposed to say "Fuck this noise" and take over my sister's desk job! Only that's exactly what I did. Something about shooting my own sister in the spine left me with a bad taste in my mouth when it comes to getting my hands dirty.

That didn't change the fact that I was licensed for support maneuvers. As long as I kept taking the yearly exams and passing my marksmanship tests, I could legally go out into the field any time I damn well wanted, and I didn't even need to worry about getting decent footage anymore. I was getting close enough to Becks and Alaric's position that I could hear gunshots up ahead, accompanied by the sound of the zombies finally beginning to moan. The Jeep was already rattling so hard that I probably shouldn't try to make it go any faster.

I slammed my foot down as hard as I could.

The Jeep went faster.

I came screeching around the final bend in the road to find Becks and Alaric standing on top of someone's old abandoned toolshed, the two of them back to back at the center of the roof like the little figures on top of a wedding cake. Only the figures on wedding cakes aren't usually armed, and even when they are—it's amazing what you can order from a specialty bakery these days—they don't actually shoot. They also aren't customarily surrounded by a sea of zombies. The six I'd seen on the monitors were quiet because they didn't need to call for reinforcements; the reinforcements were already there. A good thirty infected bodies stood between my people and the Jeep, and even more were shoving their way forward, into the fray.

Becks had a pistol in either hand, making her look like an illustration from some fucked-up pre-Rising horror/Western. *Showdown at the Decay Corral* or something. Her expression was one of intense and unflagging concentration, and every time she fired, a zombie went down. Automatically, I glanced at the dashboard, where the wireless tracker confirmed that all her cameras were still transmitting. Then I swore at myself, looking back toward the action.

George and I grew up with adoptive parents who wanted ratings more than they wanted children. We were a coping mechanism for them, a way of dealing with grief; their biological son died, and so they stopped giving a damn about people. Lose people, they're gone forever. Lose your slot on the top ten and you could win it back. Numbers were safer. We were a means to an end.

I was starting to understand why they had made that decision. Because I woke up every day in a world that didn't have George in it anymore, and I looked in my mirror expecting to see Mom's eyes looking back at me.

That won't happen, you idiot, because I won't let it, said George. *Now get them out of there.*

"On it," I muttered, and reached for the rifle.

Alaric was a lot less calm about his situation than Becks was. He had his rifle out and was taking shots at the teeming mass around them, but he wasn't having anything like her luck: He was firing three or four times just to take down a single zombie, and I saw a couple of his targets stagger back to their feet after he'd hit them. He wasn't taking the time to aim for the head, and I had no idea how much ammo he was carrying. Judging by the size of the mob around them, it was nowhere near enough.

Neither of them was wearing a face shield. That put grenades out until I could get them to move out of the blast radius, since aerosolized zombie will kill you just as sure as the clawing, biting kind. The Jeep wasn't equipped with any real defensive weapons of its own; they would have weighed it down. That left me with the rifle, George's favorite .40, and the latest useful addition to my zombie-hunting arsenal, the extendable shock baton. The virus that controls their bodies doesn't appreciate electrical shocks. It won't kill a zombie, but it'll disorient the shit out of it, and sometimes that's enough.

The mob still hadn't noticed my arrival, being somewhat distracted by the presence of already-targeted meat. Attempting to lure them off wouldn't have done any good. Zombies aren't like sharks; they won't follow in a group. Maybe a few would have followed me, but there was no way to guarantee I'd be able to handle them, and Becks and Alaric would still have been stranded. Recipe for disaster.

Not that what I was about to do was likely to be any better, in the long run. Moving to a position about ten feet behind the mob, I pulled George's gun from its holster and fired until the magazine was exhausted, barely pausing between shots. My aim might still be good enough for the exams, but it was getting rusty in field situations; seventeen bullets, and only twelve zombies went down. Becks and Alaric looked up at the sound of gunshots, Alaric's eyes widening before he started to do a fascinating variant on the victory shuffle.

Becks was more subdued in her delight over my brainless cavalry charge. She just looked relieved.

There was no time to pay attention to my team members. My shots had alerted the zombies to the presence of fresh, less-elevated meat. Several outlying members of the mob were turning in my direction, starting to lurch, shuffle, or run toward me, depending on how long they'd been in the grips of full infection. After snapping another magazine into George's pistol, I holstered it and raised the rifle, aiming for the point of greatest density.

Fact about zombies that everyone knows: You have to aim for the head, since the virus that drives their bodies can repair or route around almost every other form of damage. This is very true.

Fact about zombies that almost no one knows, because you'd have to be a damn fool to take advantage of it: An injured zombie *does* slow down, since you've just forced the relatively single-minded virus controlling the body to try its hand at double-tasking. What's more, the *right* kind of injury can make the difference between having time to reload and getting mowed down.

Bracing the rifle against my shoulder, I fired wildly into the throng. I was starting to get their attention; heads turned toward me, and the moaning changed timbre. I fired the last three shots in fast succession. Too fast to be productive, but fast enough to signal Becks. She hit the roof of the shed, dragging Alaric down with her. I dropped the rifle onto the seat and opened the glove compartment.

Using live grenades when you have people on the ground is antisocial at best and grounds for a murder charge at worst. Still, if you get the right kind—the ones that are calibrated to be explosive without being *too* explosive, since you want to minimize your aerosolized zombie bits—they can be damn handy. The wind still has to be with you, but as long as your people are more than eight feet up, you should be fine. I grabbed all four of the available grenades, pulling their pins one at a time as I sent them sailing into the thick of the zombie mob.

There were several loud, wet bangs as the projectiles found their targets, fragmented into multiple slammer pieces, and exploded. The zombies that caught shrapnel in the head or spinal column went down. Others fell as their legs were blown out from under them. Those last didn't stay down; they started dragging themselves forward, the entire mob now moaning in earnest.

Say something witty now, moron, prompted George.

I reddened. I never used to need coaching from my sister on what it took to do my job. I hit the general channel key on my watch, asking, "You guys mind if I join your party?"

Becks responded immediately, relief more evident in her voice than it had been in her face. Maybe she just wasn't as good at hiding it there. "What took you so long?"

"Oh, traffic. You know how it goes." The entire mob was moving toward me now, apparently deciding that meat on the hoof was more interesting than meat that wouldn't come out of its tree. I snapped the electric baton into its extended position, redrawing George's .40, and offered the oncoming infected a merry smile. "Hi. You want to party?"

Shaun . . . said George.

"Yeah, yeah, I know," I muttered, adding, louder, "You guys get down from there and try to circle to the Jeep. Hit the horn once you're in. There's more ammo under the passenger seat."

"And you're going to do what, exactly?" asked Becks. She sounded sensibly wary. At least one of us was being sensible for a change.

"I'm going to earn my ratings," I said. Then the zombies were on top of me, and there was no more time for discussion. Quietly, I was glad.

There's an art to fighting the infected. It was almost a good thing that this mob had started off so large; we were cutting down the numbers rapidly, since we had the ability to think tactically, but the survivors were still behaving like members of a pack. They wanted to eat, not infect. "They wanted to kill me" may not sound like much of an advantage, but trust me on this one. A zombie that's out to infect will try to smear you with fluids. That gives it a lot more weapons, since they can bleed and spit—even puke, if they've eaten recently enough. A zombie that wants to eat you is just going to come at you with its mouth, and that means it has only one viable avenue of attack. That evens the odds, just a little.

Just a little can be more than enough.

I used my baton to sweep a constant perimeter around myself, shocking any zombie that came into range and trusting the Kevlar in my jacket to keep my arm from getting tagged before I could pull it back. The electricity slowed them down enough for me to keep firing. More important, it kept them from getting positions established behind me. I could track Becks and Alaric by the sound of gunshots, which came almost as regularly as my own. I was taking out two zombies for every three shots. Not the best odds in the world. Not the worst odds, either.

The zombies pressed forward. I backed toward the Jeep, letting them think they were herding me while I kept thinning out their ranks. I realized I was grinning. I couldn't help it. Maybe facing possible death isn't supposed to make me happy, but years of training can't be shrugged off overnight, and I was an Irwin for a long time before I retired.

Aim, fire. Swing, zap. Aim, fire. It was almost like dancing, a series of soothing, predictable movements. When George's gun ran out of ammunition, I switched to my own backup pistol, the motion as smooth and easy as it could possibly have been. I couldn't hear gunshots anymore, so either Becks and Alaric had made the Jeep or my brain had started filtering out the sounds of their combat as inconsequential. I had my own zombies to play with. They could deal with theirs. Even George had fallen quiet, leaving me to move in a small bubble of almost perfect contentment. It didn't matter that my sister was dead, or that the assholes who'd ordered her killed were still out there somewhere, doing God knows what to God-knows-who. I had zombies. I had bullets. Everything else was just details, and like I keep saying, I don't care about the details.

"Shaun!"

The shout came from behind me, rather than over the intercom or from the inside of my head. I barely squashed the urge to turn toward it, a motion that could be fatal in the field. I put two bullets into the zombie that was lunging at me, and shouted back, "What?"

"We've made the Jeep! Can you retreat?"

Could I retreat? "Well, that's an interesting question, Becks!" I shouted. Aim, fire. Aim again. "Is there anything behind me? And what the fuck happened to honking?"

"Don't move!"

"I can do that!" I fired again. Another zombie went down. And hell opened up behind me. Not literally, but the sound of an assault rifle can be similar. Becks, it seemed, had found more than just ammo under the seat. Dave and I were going to have a long talk about making sure I knew what my assets were before we let me head into the field.

"Clear!"

"Great!" My throat was starting to ache from all the shouting. I surveyed the zombies remaining in front of me. None of them looked fresh enough to put up a real chase, and so I did exactly what you're not supposed to do in a field situation if you have any choice in the matter:

I took a chance.

I turned my back on the mob and ran for the Jeep, whacking anything that looked likely to move with my electric baton. Becks was in the back, covering the area, while Alaric sat in the passenger seat, looking shell-shocked.

Nothing grabbed me, and in just a few seconds, I was using the stripped-down frame to swing myself into the driver's seat. I didn't bother with the seat belt as I hit the gas, and we went roaring out of there, leaving the moaning remains of the Birds Landing zombie mob behind.

California is a fascinating place to live. Thanks to the weird geography and the microclimate zones, we have everything from mountain tundra to verdant forest, and that means we can be used as a case study for zombie preservation in almost any climate you can think of. We have some of the largest metro zones, and they're close to some of the first counties to be declared legally abandoned. It's like the whole state has multiple personality disorder.

Sometimes I think about moving someplace like New York or Washington, D.C., where the news is valued, but there aren't as many actual outbreaks to worry about. Only Shaun would be totally miserable if I did that, because he'd follow me. He'll always follow me, just like I'll always follow him. That's what being together means, right?

Neither of us ever has to be alone.

—From *Postcards from the Wall*,
the unpublished files of Georgia Mason,
originally posted January 9, 2041

So Becks and Alaric got themselves into a sticky spot today—for the moment-by-moment, uncensored report, check Alaric's status feed, but be prepared for lots of adult language. Did you know he knew some of those words? I did not know he knew some of those words! Our little boy is growing up.

But Becks and Alaric getting into trouble is practically old news around here, right? So what makes this such a big deal? Only the fact that our Lord and Master Shaun "The Boss" Mason made his triumphant return to the field to pull their asses out of the fire. And I have to say, seeing him out there...

It was good in a way I don't think I can put into words, and I do this for a living. Maybe we're going to recover from what happened last year after all. Maybe we can move on.

Maybe we're going to be okay.

—From *The Antibody Electric*,
the blog of Dave Novakowski, April 12, 2041

Two

I stopped the Jeep in front of the van before turning to really look at Becks and Alaric, scanning them for signs of visible injury or blood. Their clothing was filthy, but I didn't see any gore on either of them. "Either of you bit?"

"No," said Becks.

Alaric just shook his head. Poor guy still looked like he was going to puke.

"Scratched?" I hate this part. Before she died, George always took care of the postfield briefing and blood tests. I didn't want to deal with them, and she didn't make me. These days, I'm the boss, and that makes it my problem.

"Negative."

"No."

"Good." I leaned across Alaric to open the glove compartment, pulling out three blood tests. "You know what happens now."

"Oh, great," Alaric said, with a grimace. "Bloodshed. Because I haven't had nearly enough of that so far today."

"Stop your whining and poke your finger," I commanded, passing out the small plastic boxes.

Moaning and grumbling about needle pricks aside, I have to give the blood test units this: They're awesome pieces of technology, and they get better every year. The basic units I was handing out were ten times more sensitive than the units George and I were using in the field before we signed up to follow then-Senator Ryman's presidential campaign, where we'd had access to much better equipment. All we had to do was prick our fingers, and the sensors inside the disposable little boxes would go to work, filtering through our blood, looking for the active viral bodies that would signal an unstoppable cascade ending in amplification and zombification.

Blood tests are a part of daily life, especially if you're going out into the field. Most people don't consider them a big deal anymore, which is fascinating to me. This is a test where failure means death—no negotiation, no makeup exams. You'd expect there to be a lot more anxiety. I guess people just put the possible consequences out of their heads. Maybe it helps them sleep at night.

It sure as hell doesn't help me.

I popped the lid off my own test, saying, "One..."

Two, said George, half a second out of synch with Alaric.

I rammed my finger down on the test pad, closing my eyes.

"Three," said Becks.

I don't watch the lights on test units when I can help it. They flash between red and green while your blood is being examined to prove that either result is possible. It's partially a psychological device and partially to protect the makers of the test units from lawsuits. "I shot my wife, officer, but the green light on her unit didn't work." The man who could muster that defense would get a healthy settlement and possibly a movie deal. No one likes to get sued, and so any unit that finds a malfunction in either light will automatically reset itself, requiring you to try again. So the flashing makes sense, but I don't really give a shit. I've seen that light go red for real too many times. There are things that just hurt too much to be worth watching.

"Clean," said Alaric, relief naked in his voice.

"Me, too," said Becks.

"Good." I opened my eyes and looked at my own test. The light was shining green. No surprise there. Kellis-Amberlee won't ever kill me. That would be too merciful.

"Get back in the van before your new friends catch up with us," I said. "Dave's ready to get us the hell out of here. Aren't you, Dave?"

Dave had been eavesdropping, as I knew he would be. His response over the group channel was an immediate "Foot's on the gas, boss."

"You heard the man." I grabbed a reinforced plastic bag from the glove compartment, passing it around to collect the test units. "Becks, get these into the biohazard container. Both of you, start your footage cleanup while you're on the road, and we'll regroup at the office after cleanup and downtime."

"And what are you going to do?" asked Becks, somewhat warily.

"I'm getting the Jeep home. Now get out."

She looked like she wanted to argue with me. Luckily for my blood pressure, she didn't do it. "Come on, Alaric," she said, taking the shaken Newsie by the elbow and tugging him out of the Jeep as she climbed out of the backseat. "Let's get some walls between us and the idiots."

She didn't have to tell him twice. I'd never seen him move that fast. Becks and I exchanged a semi-surprised look as the van door slammed shut behind Alaric's retreat, and I actually laughed before waving her to follow him.

"Go on," I said. "I'll be fine."

"Sure thing, boss," she said, and turned to go.

I waited until she closed the door and I heard the van's engine turn over before starting the Jeep again. We were cutting it pretty close; I could hear the approaching moan of the hunting mob before the rumble from our vehicles drowned it out.

Good for ratings, George offered.

"Like that means anything?"

She didn't have an answer to that. Dave pulled the van back onto the road, such as it was, and I followed.

It was after midnight in London according to the clock on the dashboard. Bad, but not too bad, especially not when you're talking about professional blogging hours. "Time delay broadcast for editing," I said. My headpiece beeped to signal that my personal cameras were now being fed into a buffer, rather than recording live. Not as good for ratings as a live feed, but the only way to get even the pretense of privacy. I could delete anything I didn't want hitting the Internet. "Phone, dial Mahir."

"Local time in London is approximately twelve thirty-seven A.M.," said the automated operator, with mechanized politeness. "Ms. Gowda has requested that calls be held until eight A.M. local time."

"Ms. Gowda doesn't have the authority to block my calls, as I am, in fact, her husband's boss," I said amiably. "Please dial Mahir."

"Acknowledged," said the operator, and went quiet, replaced by the faint beeping of an international connection in process. I hummed under my breath, watching the abandoned California countryside rolling out on either side of me. It would have been pretty if not for, y'know, all the dead stuff.

"Shaun?" Mahir's normally smooth voice was blurry with exhaustion, making his British accent stand out more than usual.

"Mahir, my main man! You sound a little harried. Did I wake you?"

"No, but I really do wish you'd stop calling so late at night. You know Nandini gets upset when you do."

"There you go again, assuming that I'm not actually trying to piss off your wife. I'm really a much nicer person inside your head, aren't I? Do I give money to charity and help old-lady zombies across streets so that they can bite babies?"

Mahir sighed. "My, you *are* in a mood today, aren't you?"

"Been monitoring the boards?"

"You know that I have been. Or was, until I went to sleep." I also knew he'd called up the numbers the second I got him out of bed, because that was how Mahir's mind worked. Some men check their wallets; he checked our ratings.

"Then you know why I'm not in the mood for sunshine and puppies." I paused. "That expression makes no sense. Why the hell would I *ever* be in the mood for puppies?"

"Shaun—"

"I could go with sunshine, though. Sunshine is useful. It should really be 'sunshine and shotguns.' Something you'd actually be happy about."

"Shaun—"

"How'd the footage go over?"

There was a pause as Mahir adjusted to the fact that I'd suddenly decided to start making sense. Then, clearing his throat, he said, "We're getting some of our highest click-through rates and download shares in the last six months. There have been eleven outside interview requests, and I think you'll find as many, if not more, when you check your in-box. Six of the more junior Irwins have already been caught on the staff chats trying to figure out whether this means you'd be willing to do a joint excursion." A pause. "None were hired during your tenure as department head."

That meant they knew me, but had never worked with me in the field. I sighed. "Okay, so I won't shoot them. What's the worst headline?"

"Are you quite sure you want to do this while you're driving?"

"How did you—"

"You've gone to time delay, but there are still quite a few people watching you through the van's rearview window camera, hoping to see you get attacked again."

Of course there were. "There are days when I really think I should go be an accountant or something."

"You'd go mad."

"But no one would be staring at me. What's the worst headline, Mahir?"

He sighed, heavily. "You're sure?"

"I'm sure."

"All right, then. 'Shaun of the Dead, Part Two.'" He stopped. I said nothing. He must have taken that as a cue because he continued: "'Shaun Phillip Mason, the world's most well-known and well-regarded action blogger (known as an 'Irwin' to the informed, named in honor of a pre-Rising naturalist with a fondness for handling dangerous creatures), returned to the field today after almost a year of full-time desk duty. Does this mark the end of his much-debated 'retirement,' a career choice made during the emotionally charged weeks following the death of his adoptive sister, Georgia Mason, a factual news blogger? Or does it—'"

"That's enough, Mahir," I said quietly.

He stopped immediately. "I'm sorry."

"Don't be. I wouldn't have called if I hadn't expected them to be bad. At least this tells me what I'll be dealing with when I get back to the office." George was as pissed off by the world's refusal to leave me the fuck alone as I was, and she was swearing steadily in the back of my head. It was more reassuring than distracting. The things that get under my skin don't always get under hers, and I feel the closest to crazy when I'm disagreeing with the voice in my head.

"Are you all right?"

I paused before answering, trying to find the best words. If George had a best friend—a best friend who wasn't me, anyway—it was Mahir. He was her second-in-command before she died and gave him a promotion that he'd never wanted. Sometimes, I thought he was the only person who fully understood how close we'd been, or how much her death had broken me. He was the only one who never questioned the fact that she still talked to me.

Frankly, I think he was jealous that she never spoke to *him.*

"Ignoring the part where you know the answer to that is 'fuck, no,' I'm fine, Mahir. Tired. I shouldn't have gone out there."

"If you hadn't—"

"Becks had it under control. It's her department now. I shouldn't have interfered."

"You know that isn't true."

"Do I?"

Mahir paused before saying, "I was actually pleased to see you out there. If you don't mind my saying so, Shaun, you looked more like yourself than you have in quite some time. You might want to consider making this the beginning of a true... well, revival, if the word isn't in poor taste. You could do with something beyond spending all your time in an office."

"I'll take that under consideration."

No, you won't.

"No, you won't," said Mahir, in eerie imitation of George.

"Now you're ganging up on me," I muttered.

"What?"

Sometimes Mahir was a little too sharp for my own good. "Nothing," I said, more loudly. "I'm signing off now, Mahir. I need to concentrate on the drive."

"Shaun, I really think you should—"

"Tell the management I won't call back until it's a decent hour in your part of the world. Say, five minutes before the alarm clock?"

"Shaun, really—"

"Later." I hit the manual switch on the dashboard, cutting Mahir off midsentence. The silence that followed was almost reassuring enough to distract me from the fact that I was still apparently being filmed. I raised a hand and amiably flipped off the van.

Not nice, chided Georgia.

"George, please."

She fell sullenly quiet. For a change, I didn't mind. A sulking sister is better than a scolding sister, especially when I'm trying to wrap my head around the fact that the world wants me back in the field on a regular basis. One dead Mason just isn't enough for some people.

To distract myself, I hit the gas, sped up, and passed the van. It was a deviation from our standing driving formation, but not enough of one that it was likely to cause any real distress with the occupants of the van. With our viewing audience, maybe—especially the percentage that was hoping to see me fight off a horde of the infected through the rearview cam—but the staff would understand.

Hitting the gas harder, I sped off toward Alameda County, and home.

Prior to George's death, the two of us lived with our adoptive parents in the genteel Berkeley house where we were raised, a former faculty residence sold by the university after the Rising. I went back there initially, and quickly found that I couldn't take it. I could handle having George's ghost in my head, but I couldn't deal with the years of memory in those halls. More important, I couldn't handle watching the Masons hover around looking for ways to capitalize on the death of their adopted daughter. We always knew what they were to us and what we were to them, but it took George dying to really make me realize how unhealthy it was. I moved out as soon as I could manage it, renting a crappy little apartment in downtown El Cerrito. I moved again six months later, after the site really started pulling in the bucks. Oakland this time, and one of the four apartments in the same building that we'd rented under the name of After the End

Times. One apartment for the office; one apartment shared by Alaric and Dave, who spent half their time as best buddies and half their time as mortal enemies; one apartment open for visiting staffers who needed a place to crash.

One apartment for me and George, who didn't take up any physical space but was so much a part of every room that sometimes I could fool myself into thinking she had just stepped out for some fresh air. That she'd be right back, if I were just willing to wait. If I were still seeing a psychiatrist, I'm sure I'd be getting lectured on how unhealthy my attitude is. Good thing I fired my shrink, huh?

Oakland's a pretty awesome place to hang your hat, whether or not you've got a dead sister to deal with. Twenty-five years ago—roughly, I'm not big on math—Oakland was an urban battlefield. They had a gang problem in the early nineteen-eighties, but that cleared up, and they were fighting a different war by the time the Rising rolled around. Oakland had become the site of an ongoing conflict between the natives who'd lived there for generations and the forces of gentrification that really wanted a Starbucks on every corner and an iPod in every pocket. Then the zombies showed up, and gentrification lost.

More things we learned from the Rising: It's hard to gentrify a city that's on fire.

The new folks turned tail and ran for the hills—the ones who lived long enough, anyway. But the people who'd grown up in Oakland knew the lay of the land, and they knew what it meant to fight for what's yours. Maybe they didn't have the advantages some of the richer cities started out with, but they had a lot of places they could hole up, and they had a lot of guns. Maybe most important of all, thanks to that gang violence I mentioned earlier, they had a lot of people who actually knew how to *use* the guns.

Oakland's inner city fared better than almost any other heavily populated spot on the West Coast. When the dust of the Rising settled, the city was battered, bruised, and still standing—no small accomplishment for a city that most of the emergency services had already written off as impossible to save. It's still a proud, heavily armed community today.

It's about fifty miles from Birds Landing to Oakland, and the safest route is even longer. Thankfully, having a journalist's license means never having to explain why you didn't want to take the safe way. I hit the first of the checkpoint entrances to I-80 after about twenty miles on the rocky, poorly maintained California back roads. According to pre-Rising records, the checkpoints used to be called toll booths, and they actually accepted currency, rather than automatically deducting usage fees from your bank account. Also, they didn't have armed guards or require a clean blood test for passage. Road trips must have been pretty boring before the zombies came.

Despite the ongoing decrease in personal travel—the number of miles logged by the average American goes down every year, with many people telecommuting and ordering their groceries delivered so that they'll never even need to leave their homes—we still need freeways for things like truckers and journalists. I-80 is actually fairly well-maintained, assuming you like your roads with concrete walls and fences all around them. Most accidents are fatal, not because of the other cars but because spinning out and hitting one of those walls doesn't leave much of a margin for recovery. It also doesn't leave much of a margin for reanimation. That's probably the point.

My GPS said that I was seventeen miles ahead of the van when I hit the freeway. I sped up, accelerating to the posted speed limit of eighty-five miles per hour. The van wouldn't be able to go that fast—not unless they wanted to risk flipping over. I could reach the apartment, get through decontamination, and hole up somewhere before they had a chance to grab me and ask me to do a postrun interview. The last thing I wanted to deal with was some idiot asking me how I was *feeling*, even if it was an idiot who worked for me.

Cameras mounted atop the I-80 gun turrets swiveled to follow me as I blazed down the road. Just one more government service, keeping the world safe from infection, the living dead, and the terrifying risk of privacy. For my generation, the concept of personal privacy was one more casualty of the Rising—and not one that many people take the time to mourn.

The Rising: casual parlance for the mass amplification and outbreak following the initial appearance of the mutated Kellis-Amberlee viral strain. It started three years before my sister and I were born, during the hot, brutal summer of 2014. More people died during that summer than have ever been properly accounted for, and they kept dying for five years.

Before the Rising, zombies were the stuff of fiction and crappy horror movies, not things that you could encounter on the street. The Rising changed that. It changed the world forever.

Oh, the world didn't change in the big, apocalyptic "tiny enclaves of people fighting to survive against a world gone mad" way most of the movies suggested it would, but it still changed. George used to say we'd embraced the culture of fear, willingly letting ourselves be duped into going scared from the cradle to the grave. George used to say a lot of things I didn't really understand. I understood this much, anyway: Most people are scared of more than just the zombies, and there are other people who like them that way.

I rode I-80 to another checkpoint and another blood test, even though it would almost take a miracle to amplify on a closed freeway system. Only almost: It's happened a few times. Spontaneous amplification is rare but possible, and that, combined with the culture of fear, keeps the checkpoints in operation. As I'd expected, my infection status hadn't changed during my solitary, zombie-free drive; also as I'd expected, the guards eyed my stripped-down Jeep like it was some sort of rolling death trap and waved me through just as fast as federal regulations would allow. I offered them a brilliant smile, making their nearly identical looks of discomfort deepen, and drove off the freeway to the surface streets.

My crew's apartment building is less than half a mile from the freeway, a quirk of location that makes it perfect for our needs and less desirable to the rest of the population, keeping the rent lower than it might otherwise be. We don't even have our own parking garage. Instead, we share a secure "community structure" with half the other buildings on our block. Every local resident and business pays into a neighborhood fund that goes to pay for security upgrades and salaries for the guards. It's definitely money well-spent. After the End Times regularly contributes extra cash, just to make sure things stay as close to top-of-the-line as possible.

I arrived to find James on duty at the guard station, his feet propped on the desk next to the monitor and the latest issue of *Playboy* open on his knees. He was studying the centerfold without shame, although he was paying enough attention to raise his head when I pulled up to the gate. Smiling, he hit the button for the intercom.

"Afternoon, Mr. Mason. Have a good day out there?"

"The best, Jimmy," I said, returning his smile. "You want to buzz me through?"

"Well, that depends, Mr. Mason. How do you feel about passing me your residency card and sticking your hand in my little box?"

"Pretty damn lousy, Jimmy," I said. Digging out my wallet, I produced my residency card and dropped it into the guard station's miniature air lock. It would be disinfected before James ever touched it, and he'd still wear Teflon-coated gloves when he picked it up to run it through his scanner. Protocol. Gotta love it, because anything else would lead to madness.

While James ran my card through his system and checked it for signs of tampering, I stuck my hand into the guard station's built-in blood test unit, gritting my teeth as the needles unerringly managed to hit right on top of my freshest puncture wounds. The worst thing about going into the field isn't the zombies or the driving. It's all the damn blood tests.

"Well, Mr. Mason, everything looks to be in order," James said, still cheerfully. He dropped my card back into the lockbox. "Welcome home."

"Thanks, Jimmy," I said, withdrawing my hand. His welcome was the only confirmation that I'd actually passed my blood test. Unlike the private units, which have to show you your results, business units often display only to the people who need to know—that is, the ones whose job it is to kill you if you fail.

Offering him a wave, which he amiably returned, I retrieved my card and drove on, leaving him to his comfortable Plexiglas box and his pornography.

Building underground in California isn't strictly safe, but neither is walking on the streets. That's the brilliant logic that led to the construction of underground tunnels connecting the community structures to their associated buildings. Our building's tunnel is about the length of a football field. As I walked along it, I amused myself by pondering just how many zombies would be able to pack themselves inside if there were ever a lapse in security. I had just reached the conclusion that the tunnel could hold somewhere around two hundred infected bodies, assuming they were all of average size, when I reached the door, swiped my residency card through the scanner, and was home.

The building consists of three floors and ten apartments: two on the first floor, four each on the second and third. My staff has three of the four third-floor apartments, and the fourth belongs to old Mrs. Hagar, who's so deaf that she probably wouldn't notice if we started holding weekly raves on the roof. Becks calls her "an old dear" and brings her cookies. In exchange, Mrs. Hagar no longer threatens to lob grenades at us every time we run into each other in the downstairs lobby. A few chocolate chips are a small price to pay to avoid getting vaporized while you're picking up the mail.

The manager has one of the first-floor apartments. He's almost never there, and we're all pretty sure he has another residence somewhere outside of the city. Someplace safer. A lot of people think they're safer in the country because there aren't as many bodies capable of amplification. Not as many bodies means not as many guns, as George used to say. I'll take my chances with the cities.

The other first-floor apartment is mine. It's not much distance from the staff apartments, but it's enough to let me feel like I have a little privacy. A little privacy can make all the difference in the world. I pressed my palm to the test pad for yet another blood test, unlocked the front door, and stepped inside, alone at last.

Alone? asked George, sounding dryly amused.

"My apologies." Closing my eyes, I let my head tilt backward until it hit the door. "Apartment, give me lights in the living room, news scroll on mute on the main monitor, and prep the shower for a decontamination."

"Acknowledged," said the polite voice of the apartment's computer system, following the word with a series of muted beeps as it activated the various requested utilities. I stayed where I was for a few more seconds, stretching out the moment. I could be anywhere in that moment. I could be in my apartment. Or I could be back in my bedroom in my parents' house, the room that was connected to Georgia's room, waiting for my turn at the shower. I could be anywhere.

I opened my eyes.

My apartment is never going to win any beautiful-home competitions. It consists of a living room full of boxes, computer equipment, and racks of weaponry; a bedroom full of boxes, computer equipment, and racks of weaponry; an office full of boxes, computer equipment, and racks of weaponry; and a bathroom where the floor space is almost completely consumed by a top-of-the-line shower and decontamination unit. No weaponry in there, at least—just ammunition. Bullets are waterproof enough these days that I could probably take them in the shower with me, if I were feeling particularly weird that day.

The air in the apartment always smells like stale pizza, gun oil, and bleach. Several people have said it doesn't feel like anybody lives there, and what they don't seem to understand is that I like it that way. As long as I'm not really living there, I never have to think about the fact that I'm living there alone.

It took me fifteen minutes to complete standard decontamination procedures and get myself into some clean clothes, leaving the old ones in a biohazard-secure bin for later sterilization. I checked the GPS readout on my watch. According to the van's tracking coordinates, the rest of the team was just now reaching the guard station and getting their chance to check out Jimmy's substandard taste in porn. Good. That meant I still had time to square myself away. Grabbing a clean jacket off a stack of survivalist magazines, I started for the door, swerving almost as an afterthought to pass through the kitchen and snag a Coke from the fridge.

Thanks, said George, as I stepped out into the hall.

"No problem," I murmured, cracking open her soda and taking a long drink before heading toward the door to the roof-access stairs. In most buildings, tromping around on the roof is likely to get you shot. Just another advantage of living where I do: Mrs. Hagar can't even hear us up there unless we're setting off land mines, and we've done that only once, for quality control purposes.

There used to be a padlock on the door leading to the roof-access stairs. As if the infected were going to be mounting a top-down attack? That stopped happening when the mass outbreaks stopped driving the wounded to the rooftops to wait for rescue that never came. The manager periodically realizes that the lock is missing and replaces it, and someone on my staff comes along and cuts it off the next day. That's the circle of life around here. Nothing stays locked away forever.

You're depressing today.

"It's a depressing sort of day," I said. George quieted, and I climbed the stairs in something that was chillingly close to solitude.

I don't deal well with being alone. Maybe that's why I decided to go crazy instead.

My crew's been working on converting the roof to suit our needs since we took over the third floor. It's one of those projects that's never going to be finished; there's something new every time I go up there. Dave has what he calls his "outdoor theater," a little grouping of folding chairs and a collapsible movie screen under a pavilion he bought at the Wal-Mart in Martinez. He brings out a projector on warm nights and shows pre-Rising horror movies. I think he's trying to lure Maggie out of her house and into the city by competing with her grindhouse parties, and if he keeps it up, he just may succeed.

Becks has a small firing range with targets designed for everything from basic handguns to her personal favorite weapon, the wrist-mounted crossbow. That girl reads too many comic books. Still, I have to say, the sight of a zombie's head catching fire after it gets hit with one of her trick arrows isn't something I'm going to forget anytime soon. Neither are our viewers.

And me? I have a corner of the roof where no one does anything else, where I can go and sit and drink a Coke and watch the clouds chase themselves across the sky, and where I don't have to be the boss for a little while. I can just be me. When I go up there, my staff'll move heaven and earth to keep anyone from following me, because they know I need the escape. They've mostly gotten over treating me like I'm made of eggshells, but there are exceptions.

A pigeon was sitting on the edge of the roof when I walked up, cooing contentedly to itself. It looked at me suspiciously, but waited to see what

I would do before going to the trouble of flying away. When I just sat, it resumed its cocky back-and-forth strut without a second thought.

"Must be nice to be a pigeon," I said, taking another swig of Coke and making a face. "You sure I can't sell you on the idea of coffee? Nice, bitter, hot coffee that doesn't taste like going down on a hooker from Candyland?"

You never objected to me drinking Coke before, George replied.

"Yeah, George, but you didn't live inside my head before. You can use this stuff to clean car batteries. *Car batteries*, George. You think that's doing anything good to my internal organs? Because I'd bet good money that it's not."

Shaun, said George, in that all-too-familiar, all-too-exasperated tone, *I don't* live *anywhere. I'm not alive. Remember?*

"Yeah, George," I said, taking one last drink from the can of Coke before tossing it, still half full, off the edge of the roof. It sprayed soda in an impressively large arc as it fell. I leaned backward against the building's air-ventilation shaft and closed my eyes. "I remember."

As I've mentioned several times, I have a sister. An adopted sister, to be precise, fished out of the state system by Michael and Stacy Mason after the Rising left us both without our biological parents. That was George. She's the reason I got into blogging, and the reason we wound up running a site of our own. She was never meant to be one of nature's followers. And technically, I guess the tense is wrong there, because it ought to be "I *had* a sister." The death of Georgia Carolyn Mason was registered with the Centers for Disease Control on June 20, 2032. Her official cause of death is recorded as "complications from massive amplification of the Kellis-Amberlee virus," which means, in layman's terms, "she died because she turned into a zombie."

It would be a lot more accurate to say that she died because I shot her in the spine, spraying blood all over the interior of the van that we were locked in at the time. It might be even more accurate to say that she died because some bastard shot a needle full of the live Kellis-Amberlee virus into her arm. But the CDC says she died of Kellis-Amberlee, and hey, we don't argue with the CDC, right?

If I ever find out who fired that needle, their official cause of death is going to be Shaun Mason. That's the thought that keeps me going. I sleepwalk through my job, I pretend I'm administrating our site while Mahir does all the work, I delete calls from my crazy parents, I hold conversations with my dead sister, and I look for the people who had her killed. I'll find them someday. All I have to do is wait.

See, when the zombies came, it was an accident. Researchers in two totally unconnected facilities were working on two totally unrelated projects that involved genetically engineering "helper viruses"—new diseases that were supposed to make life better for the whole damn world. One of them was based on a really fucking nasty hemorrhagic fever called Marburg, and was designed to cure cancer. The other was based on a strain of the common cold, and was supposed to get rid of colds forever. Enter Marburg Amberlee and the Kellis Flu, two beautiful pieces of viral engineering that did exactly what they were supposed to do. No more cancer, no more colds, just happy people all over the world celebrating the dawn of a new age. Only it turns out the viruses were just like the people who made them in at least one sense, because when they met, through the natural chain of transmission and infection, it was basically love at first sight. First comes love, then comes marriage, then comes the hybrid viral strain known as "Kellis-Amberlee." It swept the planet before anyone knew what was happening.

And then people started dying and getting back up to munch on their relatives, and we figured out what was happening damn fast. People fought back, because people always fight back, and we had one advantage the characters in zombie movies never seem to have: See, we'd *seen* all the zombie movies, and we knew what was likely to be a bad idea. George always said the first summer of the Rising was possibly the best example of human nobility that history had to offer, because for just a few months, before the accusations started flying and the fingers started pointing, we really were one people, united against one enemy. And we fought. We fought for the right to live, and in the end, we won.

Sort of, anyway. Look at the movies from before the Rising and you'll see a whole different world from the one that we live in; a world where people go outside just because they think that, hey, going outside might be fun. They don't file paperwork or put on body armor. They just *go*. A world where people travel on a whim, where they swim with dolphins and own dogs and do a hundred thousand things that are basically unthinkable today. It seems like paradise from where I'm sitting, a generation and a couple of decades away. If you ask me, that world was the single biggest casualty of the Rising.

The Rising didn't just showcase the nobler side of human nature; it was a war, and as long as there have been wars, there have been war profiteers. There's always somebody willing and waiting to make a buck off somebody else's pain. I'm not sure most of them meant to do what they did— I'm sure most of them really meant to do the right thing—but somehow, an entire world full of people who had managed to take arms against an enemy that was straight out of a Romero flick was convinced that what they really wanted was fear. They put down their guns, they locked their doors, they went inside, and they were grateful for all the things that they were scared of.

I used to think the Irwins were great warriors in the ongoing fight to live a normal life in our post-Rising world. Now I'm starting to suspect that we're just tools of some greater plan. After all, why leave your house when you can live vicariously through a dumb kid willing to risk his life for your amusement? Bread and circuses. That's all we are.

You're getting bitter, George observed.

"I got reason," I said.

Bread and circuses is what got George killed. We—her, me, and our friend Georgette "Buffy" Meissonier—were the original After the End Times news team, and we got hired by President Ryman to follow his campaign. He was Senator Ryman then, and I was a dumb, optimistic Irwin who believed...well, a lot of things, but mostly, that I'd die before George did. I was never going to be the one who buried her, and I was sorry that she was going to bury me, but we'd both made our peace with that years before. We were chasing the news, and we were chasing the truth, and we were on the adventure of our lives. Literally, for George and Buffy, because neither one of them walked away from it. Turns out there were people who didn't want Ryman to make it to the White House. Oh, they were happy to have him elected. They just didn't want him to be president. They were backing their own candidate.

Governor David Tate. Or, as I prefer to think of him, "the fucking asshole pig that I shot in the head for being part of the conspiracy that killed my sister." He admitted it before he died. Well, before he injected himself with a huge quantity of live Kellis-Amberlee and forced me to shoot him. During the after-investigation, I got asked why I thought he'd decided to pull the classic super-villain rant before he killed himself. I got asked a lot of other questions, too, but that was the one I had an answer for.

"Easy," I said. "He was a smug fucker who wanted us to know how awesome the world would have been if we'd let him take it over, and he was stalling for time, because he knew that if he managed to inject himself, we'd never find out whom he was working with. He wanted us to think he was the mastermind. It was all him. But it wasn't. It never could have been."

They asked me why not.

"Because that asshole was never smart enough to kill my sister."

They didn't have any questions after that. What could they have asked? George was dead, Tate was dead, and I'd put the bullets in both of them. Before the Rising, a statement like that would have been an invitation to a murder charge. These days, I'm lucky no one tried to give me a medal. I think Rick probably convinced then-Senator Ryman that even the suggestion would result in me assaulting a federal official, and nobody wanted to deal with that. Although I might have welcomed the distraction.

Speaking of distractions, there was something poking me in the knee. I cracked one eye open and found the pigeon was now industriously pecking at my jeans. "Dude, I'm not a breadcrumb vending machine." It kept pecking. "Has Becks been putting steroids in your birdseed or something? Because don't think I don't know she's been feeding you. I found the receipt from the last time she hit the pet store."

"Since I haven't made any attempts to hide it from you, it would be a little bit upsetting if you didn't know," said Becks, from about three feet behind me. "As it is, you noticed the receipt and not the twenty-pound bags of birdseed in the office coat closet. That doesn't say much about your powers of observation."

"But it says a lot about my attention to detail." I twisted around to face her, sending the pigeon fluttering off to find a safer place to perch. "Is there a reason the sanctity of the roof has been violated?"

Becks crossed her arms across her chest in a gesture that was only semi-defensive. I don't know why she looks at me that way. I've never hit her. Dave a few times, and I broke Alaric's nose once, but never her. "Dave says you've been up here for three hours."

I blinked. "I have?"

I thought you needed the sleep, George said.

"Gee, thanks," I muttered. You'd think having my dead sister living inside my head might have some helpful side effects, like, say, insomnia, but no such luck. I get all the negatives of being insane, with none of the bonuses.

"You have," said Becks, with a small nod. "We've been going over the footage. We got some great shots, especially from the sequence where Alaric was holding the crowbar. Before everything got bad, I mean."

"You checked your license allowances before you let him do that, right?" I asked, levering myself to my feet. My back was stiff enough to confirm that whole "three hours" thing; I'd been sitting in one position for way too long.

"Of course," she said, sounding affronted. "As long as I stayed within five feet and he was in no immediate nonconsensual danger, I was totally within my legal rights as a journalism teacher. What do you think I am, some sort of field newbie?" She sounded even more offended than the question would justify, because there was another question underneath it: *When did you stop being any fun?* Becks hired on as a Newsie under George and switched to my department almost before the ink on her contract was dry. She's one of nature's born Irwins, and she and I worked together really well. That's why I gave her my department when I stepped down. And that's probably also why she seems to really believe, deep down, that all she needs to do is find me a stick and a hole to poke it into and I'll be fine.

It's really a pity that I don't think it's ever going to work that way for me. Because damn, it would be nice.

"I don't think you're a field newbie, Becks, I just think there are some people who'd love to have an excuse to slap us with more violation charges. I mean, how much did we pay to get those 'standing too close to a goat' charges off Mahir's record? And he's in England. They still *like* goats over there."

"All right, fair enough," she admitted. "But still, Alaric did really well out there today. I think he's almost ready for his exams."

"Well, good."

"He just needs a senior Irwin to sign off on him."

"So sign."

"Shaun—"

"Was that the only reason you came up here to poke at me? Because it doesn't seem like enough."

You're trying to distract her.

I gritted my teeth and didn't answer. No one heard George but me; everyone heard me when I talked to her. Not exactly the fairest deal I've ever been a part of, but, hey, I'm the one who gets to keep breathing, so I probably shouldn't complain all that much. George wouldn't complain if our positions were reversed. She'd just glare at people, drink a lot of Coke, and write scathing articles about how our judgmental society called her crazy for choosing to maintain a healthy relationship with a dead person.

Becks gave me a sidelong look. "Are you all right?"

"I'm fine," I said, teeth still gritted as I willed George to shut up until I'd managed to get Becks to go away. "Just stiff. And that didn't answer my question. What else made you come up here?"

"Ah, that. You have company." Becks unfolded her arms, shoving her hands into the pockets of her jeans. She'd changed her clothes, which only made sense; the clothing she'd worn in the field needed to be thoroughly sterilized before it was safe to wear again. The logical need to change didn't explain why she'd put on new jeans and a flowery shirt that wouldn't offer any protection in an outbreak, but girls have never made much sense to me. I never needed them to. George was always there, ready and willing to play translator.

I raised an eyebrow. "Company? Define 'company.' Is this the kind of company that wants an interview? Or the kind of company I have a restraining order against?" Most people don't think I'm handling Georgia's death very well, what with the whole "hearing her inside my head even though she's not here anymore" aspect of things. Well, if I'm not handling it well, the Masons aren't handling it at all, since they've spent the last year alternately pleading with me to see reason and threatening to sue me for ownership of her intellectual property. I always knew they were vultures, but it took someone actually dying for me to understand just how appropriate that comparison really was. They'd started hovering around before the man who paid her killer was even cold, looking for a way to make a profit off the situation.

I mean that literally. I checked the time stamps on the first e-mails they sent me. I don't think they even took the time to pretend to grieve before they started trying to make sure they'd get their piece of the action. So yeah, I took out a restraining order against them. They've taken it surprisingly well thus far. Maybe because it's done wonderful things for their ratings.

"Neither," said Becks. "She says she knows you from the CDC, and that she's been trying to get hold of you for weeks—something about needing to talk to you about a research program that Georgia was involved with back when you were—Shaun? Where are you going?"

I was halfway across the roof the moment the words "research program" left her lips, and by the time she asked where I was going, it was too late; I was already gone, hand on the doorknob, barreling back down the stairs toward the hallway.

My line of work, combined with George's virological martyrdom and my ongoing, if somewhat amateur, attempts to locate the people behind the conspiracy that killed her, has brought me into contact with a lot of people from the CDC. But there's only one "she" who has my contact information and would even dare to bring up George around me.

Dave was waiting outside the office apartment door, looking agitated. I stopped long enough to grab his shoulders, shake briskly, and demand, "*Why* haven't I been seeing her e-mail?"

"The new spam filters must have been stopping her," he said, looking a little green around the edges. It appeared that I was scaring him. I was having trouble getting worked up about that when I was already so worked up about more important matters. "If she was using the wrong keywords—"

"Fix them!" I shoved him backward, hard enough that he smacked his shoulders against the wall. Turning, I opened the apartment door.

Alaric was in the process of handing my "company" a cup of coffee, making polite apologies about my absence. He stopped when I entered, turning to face me, and she half rose, a small, almost timid smile on her face.

"Hi, Shaun," said Kelly. "I hope this isn't a bad time."

There were many would-be saviors during the Rising, but some stand above the rest. One such is Dr. William Matras, a virologist working out of the Centers for Disease Control's Atlanta office. With a governmental decree forbidding any discussion of what they called "the Walking Plague," the CDC was unable to warn the populace of the coming crisis. Dr. Matras co-opted the one channel of communication he knew to be unmonitored: the blog of his daughter, Wendy. He posted everything he knew about the epidemiology of the Walking Plague, and he armed a world against the disease.

Dr. Matras was tried for treason, acquitted on all counts, and given a posthumous commendation for valorous service. His son, Ian Matras, is the current director of the WHO. His eldest daughter, Marianne Matras-Connolly, is an instructor at Georgetown University. Of his five grandchildren, three are in the family business, with the youngest, Kelly Connolly, currently studying under Dr. J. Wynne of the Memphis CDC.

We owe this family a great debt for everything that they have done. Without men like Dr. Matras, the future of the human race would be much bleaker.

**—From *Epidemiology of the Wall*,
authored by Mahir Gowda, January 11, 2041**

Three

The last time I saw Kelly Connolly, she was delivering George's ashes for the funeral. The time before that, she was at the Memphis CDC installation where George, Rick, and I were taken into quarantine after an anonymous call claimed we'd gone into amplification. Not exactly the sort of encounters that lend themselves to easy companionship. I'm never really sure how to deal with people who aren't a part of my team and aren't trying to either kill or interview me. My usual tactics—gunshots and punches to the face—just don't seem to apply.

Kelly was looking at me expectantly, the cup of coffee she'd taken from Alaric still held in front of her. I almost wished she'd throw it at me, just so I'd have some idea of what I was supposed to *do*.

Say hello, George prompted.

"Why—" I began, and caught myself, snapping my jaws closed on my tongue so hard I tasted blood. Talking to George in front of my friends and coworkers was one thing: It weirded them out a little, but they were essentially used to it. Talking to her in front of someone who was still practically a stranger was something else entirely. I didn't have the time or the patience to deal with the questions it would inevitably raise.

Kelly was still looking at me with the same expectant air, now becoming slowly tinged with concern. I know that look. I get that look a lot. If I didn't say something soon, she was going to start asking whether I was all right, and then I was going to need to decide whether or not I was going to deck her.

Punching visitors from the CDC would be a new low for me. It wasn't one I was particularly eager to reach. I swallowed away the taste of blood and forced myself to smile as I stepped forward, offering my hand. "Dr. Connolly. It's nice to see you again."

Kelly took my hand, the edge of concern not leaving her face. Her handshake was surprisingly firm. I looked closer and realized that the concern was masking an even more pronounced expression of fear. Fear? She was with the CDC. Short of Kellis-Amberlee deciding to jump species and start infecting birds, what did she have to worry about?

"You don't need to be so formal, Shaun." Her smile tightened for a moment before she dropped it. She let go of my hand at the same time. I kept studying her face, taking note of the dark circles under her eyes. The good doctor hadn't been sleeping much recently...if she'd been sleeping at all. "I won't call you Mr. Mason if you won't call me Dr. Connolly."

"Deal." I stepped back, tucking my hands into my pockets. "Welcome to the madhouse, Doc. Have you had a chance to meet the rest of the team?"

"Well, I met Alaric here when he buzzed me into the building," she said, smiling brightly at him. He ducked his head, blushing and slanting a glance toward Becks at the same time, like he was checking her reaction. He shouldn't have bothered. Becks was staring straight ahead, giving Kelly her best "I am an ice-cold action bitch and you'd better not forget it" look.

Dave had managed to slink back into the room while I was gaping at Kelly. He hunched his shoulders as he sat down next to the bank of monitors, trying to make himself look small. If we hadn't had company, I would have rushed over to tell him I was sorry and promise—again—that this was the last time I'd ever lay a hand on him. I'd mean it, too, even if we'd both know I'd never be able to keep my word. Dave would say it was okay, that I hadn't actually hurt him, and we'd both feel better...at least until the next time I lost my temper.

That's how things worked around the office without George. We were used to it; comfortable, even. Having Kelly Connolly standing there, clearly waiting for an introduction to the rest of the team, was just screwing everything up.

"Uh," I said. "Well, that cool cat over on the news desk is one of our Irwins, Dave Novakowski." Dave raised a hand and waved. "Alaric here is Mahir's second-in-command. Mahir is...uh...Mahir Gowda runs the Newsie division remotely from London." I still couldn't bring myself to call him George's replacement. The word was just too bitter to say.

Kelly nodded, offering a quick smile in Dave's direction. Dave answered with a distracted nod, hands beginning to move rapidly across his keyboard. "Mr. Gowda interviewed me earlier this year," Kelly said, looking back to me. "He was a very nice gentleman."

"He did?" I asked blankly.

Alaric was staring. A note of excitement crept into his voice as he asked, "Wait—are you *the* Kelly Connolly?"

Becks and I exchanged a blank look, Becks mouthing "What the fuck?" I shrugged.

Kelly, meanwhile, was smiling half-smugly, with that look on her face that famous people always seem to get when they're pretending not to be pleased about being recognized. Mom used to walk around with that expression permanently locked in place. "I am."

"Oh, wow," said Alaric, eyes going even wider. "It's an honor to meet you, ma'am. I mean a real, genuine honor."

"Uh, excuse me for asking, but does someone want to explain to the nice Irwins," I caught the hopeful look in Becks's eyes, and hastened to clarify, "nice Irwins and *former* Irwins exactly what '*the* Kelly Connolly' is supposed to mean? Because I have to say, I'm clueless."

"Truer words were never spoken," Becks muttered, almost under her breath.

"Dr. Matras was her grandfather," said Alaric, like that explained everything.

I paused, filtering through my recollections of college history seminars. Finally, I ventured, "You mean the CDC treason guy?"

They dropped the charges, George chided.

"Sorry," I said, automatically.

Kelly must have assumed the apology was directed at her, because she shook her head and said, "It's okay; that's how most people outside of epidemiological circles remember him. His trial was a pretty big deal. They made us watch the tapes when I was in medical school."

"Right," I said. I was starting to remember more, probably because George was practically yelling in my inner ear. "He's the guy who hijacked his kid's blog so he could get the word out." I could vaguely recall seeing Kelly in CDC press releases and interviews, always in the background, but pretty steadily there all the same. I always figured it was because she was photogenic. Turns out it was because she was an asset.

"His eleven-year-old kid's blog," said Becks, eyeing Kelly suspiciously. "You're at least twenty-one. How did you manage that?"

"My Aunt Wendy was the youngest of six," Kelly replied, with the ease of someone fielding an all-too-familiar question. "She was actually the flower girl at my mother's wedding. My mother is Deborah Connolly, born Deborah Matras, age twenty-five at the time of the Rising."

Becks nodded, her former Newsie's instincts mollified. "So what brings you to our neck of the woods?"

"Uh, guys?"

"Dave, I told you, we'll edit that report together in a minute," Becks said impatiently.

My phone beeped. Holding up a hand to excuse myself, I took a step backward and pulled the phone out of my pocket, clicking it open. "Shaun here."

"Why aren't you online?"

"Hello to you, too, Mahir. Why are you still awake? Shouldn't the Bride of Bollywood be threatening to withhold sex for a month if you don't put down your keyboard and crawl back to the nuptial bed?"

"She's asleep," he said, flatly. "No thanks to you. Why aren't you online?"

"There are a great many answers to that philosophical question, but for right now, I'm going to settle for 'because we have company, and my mama taught me it was rude to use your computer in front of company unless you've got enough for everybody.'"

"You're a bloody bad liar, Shaun Mason. Your mother didn't teach you anything of the sort."

"Maybe not, but she should have. Why do you need me online?"

"Guys?" Dave again, a little more insistent this time.

"Turn on the news and see for yourself. I'm blocking the live feeds out of the office and claiming site issues. You can thank me for it later."

Mahir hung up.

Mahir *never* hung up on me like that.

Frowning, I lowered the phone. "Dave? What are you trying to tell us?"

"I was looking for CDC-related reports from the last few days, to see if I could figure out why we have company, and there's a report from this morning of a break-in at the Memphis CDC."

"So?"

"So they're saying one of the doctors died."

I didn't need to ask which one. The answer was in Kelly's sudden pallor, and the way her eyes darted from side to side, like she was looking for an escape route from the apartment. There wasn't one. With the entire resident staff inside, the door had automatically sealed itself, and it wasn't going to open for anyone who didn't have a key.

Or couldn't pass a blood test.

I wasn't the only person who'd put two and two together. Alaric took two quick steps backward, nearly tripping over a beanbag chair someone had abandoned in the middle of the floor. Becks stayed where she was, tucking her hands behind herself. She always kept a firearm of some sort in a holster at the small of her back, where it wouldn't necessarily be spotted. I knew from field trials that she could have it out and aimed in under a second.

Take charge of this situation, or it's going to get messy. George sounded worried. That worried me, in a "less important than the possibly infected CDC doctor in our apartment" sort of a way. If my inner George was becoming more nuanced, did that mean I was getting more crazy? And if I was, did I mind?

"What do you want me to do here?" I asked, forgetting the whole "don't talk to George in front of strangers" rule in the face of a bigger problem.

You trained Becks and Dave. That means they'll shoot first and ask questions later. Alaric might have been helpful if this had happened yesterday, but he's too wound up from the field to think clearly right now. You need to settle them down.

Great. It wasn't enough that my sister was dead and living inside my head; now she was giving me orders. "It never stops," I muttered, and looked back toward Kelly. "If you died, want to tell us how it is you're standing here and not trying to eat us?" I paused, then added, "That wasn't actually a request."

"If you listen to the report, it doesn't say I died. It just says they found my body," she said, in a careful tone that I recognized from way too many press conferences. It was the voice people use when they aren't saying something.

The silence in the room for the next few seconds was almost palpable, as all four of us struggled with that statement. Dave spoke first, asking, "So you're listed as dead because you've started amplification?"

"No," Kelly said emphatically. "I'm not infected. I'm willing to submit to as many blood tests as you need in order to prove that."

She was technically lying: We're all infected. Anyone born after the Rising was infected in the womb, since Kellis-Amberlee is totally untroubled by the placental barrier. It's just that in most of us, the virus is sleeping peacefully, rather than taking over our bodies and turning us into something from a horror show. That's what the blood tests look for. Not infection; amplification. Which raised another question: amplification takes minutes, not hours. If Kelly was exposed to the live virus in Memphis, how could she possibly have traveled all the way to Oakland without fully amplifying?

"So why do they think you're dead?" Becks sounded pissed, like she was considering drawing on Kelly just to make the confusing situation stop. I shot her a warning look. She glared back.

George was right. I needed to take control of things before they got bad.

"Becks—" I said, cautioning.

"It's all right, Shaun. I knew I'd have to answer some questions." Kelly looked toward Becks, saying calmly, "They think I'm dead because the body they found was mine."

Pandemonium. I doubt there was anything else she could have said that would cause that much chaos, that quickly, amidst my staff. Even "Look, a zombie" would probably have inspired only general interest and a search for things to poke it with. It's only because we were viewing her as friend, not foe, that she didn't get a bullet in the forehead as soon as she finished speaking. As it was, the sentence was barely out of her mouth before Dave was on his feet, guns drawn and aimed in her direction. Becks provided a mirror image on the other side of the room. Meanwhile, Alaric was showing a rare degree of common sense for a Newsie and had resumed his retreat, taking cover behind the couch.

All three of them were shouting. Dave and Becks were coordinating their actions; Alaric was just yelling. And through it all, Kelly stood perfectly still, keeping her hands clearly in view. She was trembling, and the whites showed all the way around her eyes, but she didn't move. I had to admire that. It was the smartest thing she could possibly have done.

"Guys!" I clapped my hands. I didn't need to draw, since Dave and Becks were already holding guns on her. I could actually be the one playing Good Cop in the potentially life-threatening situation for a change. "She had to pass a blood test to get inside, remember? Chill the fuck out. I'm sure she has a good explanation." I glanced toward Kelly. "Just a friendly hint, Doc: This would be a really, really good time to say something that makes enough sense that it can keep my people from shooting you. Because around here, dead things are for target practice."

Kelly turned toward me, making the motion as economical as possible. Even so, Dave's hands twitched, putting the slightest degree of extra pressure on the triggers. Catching his eye, I shook my head. He eased off. Not enough. If Kelly didn't have a truly excellent explanation, we were going to need a new carpet.

"Cloning," she said.

That qualified as a truly excellent explanation.

"What?" I demanded, almost in unison with Becks's "You can't be serious!" and Dave's "No fucking way." Alaric stuck his head up from behind the couch, expression disbelieving.

"We've been using cloning technology in hospitals for fifteen years," said Kelly, a certain bitter amusement in her voice. "What makes you think this is so unreasonable?"

"Full-body cloning is illegal, immoral, and impossible," said Becks, slowly. "Try again, princess."

"If we can clone a kidney, why can't we clone a Kelly?" asked Kelly.

Becks didn't seem to have an answer for that.

"Actually…" Alaric stood up, eyes still fixed on Kelly. He wasn't coming back to the center of the room, but he was abandoning at least a small measure of cover. That was a good sign. "Full-body cloning isn't *impossible*. It's just illegal for anyone outside the three major medical research entities. They use clones to study the progression of Kellis-Amberlee. The World Heath Organization, USAMRIID—"

"—and the CDC," I finished. Everyone turned to look at me, Dave and Alaric included. I shrugged. "I can count. So we can clone people?"

"Yes," said Alaric.

"And the CDC gets cloning privileges?"

"Yes," said Kelly.

"And they decided to clone you because…?"

"I think at this point, it's going to be easier for me to explain if I can do it without people holding guns on me." Kelly glanced at Becks, licking her lips in agitation. "I'm not used to it."

"You're going to need to get used to it if you're planning to hang out around here." I crossed to the rack of medical supplies next to the weapons locker. Grabbing a high-end testing unit—not the best the market has to offer, but good enough that we could have faith in the results—I tossed it overhand at Kelly. She fumbled the catch, nearly dropping the unit before she got a good grip.

"Loss of manual dexterity is an early sign of amplification," said Becks.

"Loss of manual dexterity is also a sign of a lab rat surrounded by people who seem likely to shoot her in the face," I said. "You'd better go ahead and get some results for us, Doc, before one of my people decides they're done being civilized."

"You sure do know how to treat a guest," said Kelly. She popped the test open, shoving her hand inside.

"We try," I said.

Becks was right about the loss of manual dexterity: It's related to the virus basically hip-checking the brain out of the way and taking over. Once Kellis-Amberlee amplification begins, victims lose motor control at a fairly impressive pace. Viruses—even genetically engineered viruses designed to better the human condition—aren't all that smart, and they don't have to pass driver's ed before they get a shot at driving *us*. So zombies don't know how to use their fingers very well, and most of them are a little clumsy even when we're talking about things like "walking" and "not getting shot in the head."

About the only thing a zombie can do with any reliable accuracy is bite, spit, and scratch. The easiest routes to infection.

The lights on Kelly's test unit were just beginning to flash when my phone beeped again. I clicked it on, not bothering to check the caller ID. "Hey, Mahir."

"Is she still there?"

"Yeah, she's still here." I watched the lights flash between red and green, resisting the urge to look away.

"Is the situation contained?"

Red, green, pause. Red, green, pause. "I'm not sure. Dave and Becks have guns trained on her head right now."

"What, only the pair?"

"Alaric's busy hiding behind the couch—"

"Hey!"

"—and I figured I'd try being the reasonable one for a change."

"Really? How's that going, then?"

Not well, muttered George.

"Not bad," I said, wishing I had a way to glare at the inside of my own head. The lights were slowing down, lingering on green for longer and longer periods of time. "We're just about done with the blood tests over here. Do you want to video conference in or something? Because it's time to play twenty questions with Doc, and you might have some good ones."

"I can't." There was genuine regret in his tone. This was news, happening right in our company headquarters, and as the head of the Newsies, Mahir had a serious jones for information. That was part of what made him so good at his job. "This is a secure connection, but if I go for a video link, it'll attract attention, and I'll have to answer questions."

"I take it from your tone that this would be a bad idea right about now?"

The lights on Kelly's unit settled on a firm, unblinking green. She held it up, smiling a little, like she'd known the answer all along. Dave lowered his guns, sliding them back into their holsters. Becks lowered one of hers, hesitated, and lowered the other. I gave her an approving nod. The Masons may not have taught me much about how to treat a guest, but they taught me not to shoot at them unless it was absolutely necessary.

Mahir sighed. "Yes. A very bad idea."

"I told you not to marry her, Mahir."

"I'm not having this conversation again."

"Just saying, you didn't have to worry about this shit when you lived the happy bachelor life. Look, I need to go—the Doc's just checked out clean, so it's probably time to find out what she's doing here."

"Call me when you know what's going on."

"Got it," I said, and clicked off.

Kelly lowered her test unit, apparently satisfied that everyone had seen it, and said, "I'm clean. Do you have a biohazard receptacle I can dispose of this in?"

"It's next to the medical supplies." I walked toward the kitchen. "I need a Coke. Anybody else need anything before story time commences?"

No one did.

The kitchen gave me just enough privacy to feel comfortable saying quietly, "Can we try to keep the interjections down for a little bit? I don't want Kelly thinking I'm crazy." I paused. "Not yet, anyway."

You have a plan? asked George.

"More making it up as I go along," I replied, and grabbed my soda before turning to walk back into the living room.

When I got there, Kelly was on the couch, Alaric was sitting on the beanbag he'd tripped over before, and Dave was back at his terminal, watching the scrolling data feed with one eye while remaining half-turned toward the room. Only Becks was still standing, eyeing Kelly like she expected the other woman to spontaneously amplify at any second.

"Aren't we a cheery bunch?" I grabbed a folding chair from against the wall and set it up in front of the entrance hall. Nobody was getting in or out without going through me, and that wasn't exactly an easy proposition. Potentially entertaining; not easy.

"I'm cheerier when there isn't a corpse sitting on the couch," said Becks, before moving to her computer chair and slowly sitting down.

"Most people are." I turned to Kelly. "That brings us back to story time. Well, Doc? What's going on?"

Kelly sighed. It was a soft, exhausted sound, conveying a vast amount of information in a very small amount of time. This was a woman who'd been run to the limits of her endurance before being forced to find reserves she didn't think she had. Now even those reserves looked about to run out. Maybe the word "corpse" was more accurate than it sounded. I tensed, waiting for the other shoe to drop.

"Dr. Wynne sends his regards."

There it was: the other shoe.

Dr. Joseph Wynne was Kelly's supervisor at the Memphis CDC. He was also the man who answered when George called the CDC for help on the night Buffy died. We knew we'd been set up—it was hard to miss that part, what with people shooting at our tires and everything—but we didn't realize how thoroughly screwed we were until we talked to the CDC. Somebody else called them before George did. That first caller reported that we'd all gone into amplification, not just Buffy. Since we were outside in a confirmed outbreak by that point, Dr. Wynne would have been legally justified in ordering our immediate executions. He didn't do it. That meant, in a strange sort of sidelong way, that I owed him.

"Does he?" I asked, as neutrally as I could.

"He sent a data card for you to review." She picked up her briefcase from the floor next to the couch and popped it open, rummaging for a second before producing a plain white plastic rectangle. I raised an eyebrow. A smile ghosted across Kelly's face as she offered the card to me. "What, did you think I managed to grow a full-body clone and stage my own death without *help*?"

"Guess not," I said. "Alaric, run the card." He jumped to his feet, snatching the card from her hand and running for his terminal so fast that I almost expected him to leave skid marks on the floor. I snorted with amusement before turning back to Kelly. "Now it's *really* story time, Doc."

"Yes, it is," she agreed. She took a stack of manila envelopes from the briefcase and stood, walking a loose circuit around the room. Each of us got an envelope before she returned to the couch and sat, looking almost serene. I know that look. That's the look I get from people who've done their civic duty by reporting the zombie outbreak to the local news media and are now planning to sit down and let it be our problem instead of theirs. It's the expression of someone who knows, deep down inside, that the buck is about to be passed.

Buck-passing rarely comes with handouts. I peered into the envelope, natural paranoia demanding that I confirm it wasn't filled with mousetraps or funny white powder before I removed the contents. Paper. Some paper-clipped reports, a few loose memos, and a few sheets of statistical data. I didn't understand most of what I saw, which really wasn't surprising. I never was much of one for the numbers.

I looked up. Kelly was watching me intently. Everyone else was flipping through the contents of their respective envelopes. It looked like it was up to me to keep her talking. I waved a sheet of statistics and asked, "What's all this?"

"It's the story." She sagged back in the couch, closing her eyes. The "passing the buck" expression faded, replaced by one of deep and abiding weariness.

She kept her eyes closed as she began to talk. It may have been because she was concentrating on getting her facts straight, but I don't think so.

I think she just didn't want to risk seeing the look on my face.

"The first cases of confirmed Kellis-Amberlee occurred in 2014. That's when the viruses were introduced to the biosphere, met, and managed to successfully combine. The viral substrains are either descendants of different initial cases of Marburg Amberlee or the result of very minor natural mutation, occurring within isolated geographic areas. Everywhere in the world, Kellis flu met Marburg Amberlee, and Kellis-Amberlee was the result. It's not natural virus behavior. Neither of the pathogens involved was a natural virus. Kellis-Amberlee has been stable, and effectively identical, since it was 'born.'"

Becks looked perplexed. "Did we sign up for a seminar or something?" I held up a hand for quiet. She snorted, and subsided.

Kelly continued: "The first cases of confirmed Kellis-Amberlee infection going 'live' in isolated parts of the body—the reservoir conditions—were identified in 2018. They may have been cropping up before then, but we didn't have the capacity to track them. The infrastructure was still too broken down for that to be an option."

"Makes sense," I agreed. The Rising left the medical community in tatters. Frontline doctors and nurses were among the first to be infected, leaving the hospitals of the world severely understaffed even after the initial battles of the Rising had been fought and technically won. I say "technically" because it's hard to call a conflict with that kind of casualty rate a victory. There are still hospitals and people who can use them, so I guess we'll have to count that as a win, for now.

A smile tugged at the edges of Kelly's lips. "I could start listing the index cases for the known reservoir conditions, but I doubt you really care, and they aren't that applicable in this situation. They showed up one by one, they didn't follow any perceptible pattern, and they were as incurable as the parent virus. That's what matters to the story: Once you have a reservoir condition, you have it for the rest of your life."

She's got that right, said George bitterly. She developed retinal Kellis-Amberlee while we were little, and she had it until the day she died. Kids in our high school used to tease her about it and threaten to steal her sunglasses. They never did, though. There was always too much of a chance that her "cooties" might be contagious.

That's bullshit, by the way. You can't catch the live form of Kellis-Amberlee unless you come into contact with it, and George didn't sweat the live virus. It just lived inside her eyes, all the time. Waiting for the day when it would get loose to play with the rest of her body.

Which it eventually did.

I had to force myself to start talking again, before I could really start dwelling on what had happened to George. This wasn't the time. "So what's the moral of our story?" I asked, relieved when my voice sounded halfway natural. "Reservoir conditions suck?"

"Reservoir conditions represent a viral behavior with no known purpose or explanation," contributed Dave. Everyone but Kelly turned to look at him. He shrugged. "I took a couple of virology courses before I went to Alaska. It seemed like it might help with that whole 'not dying' thing."

"Ah." Dave was in Alaska last year when half the staff died. He was probably safer on the frozen, zombie-infested tundra than we were in Sacramento. There was something ironic about that. I paused. "Wait, are you saying no one knows what the reservoir conditions *do*?"

"There are theories." Kelly sounded suddenly evasive. I eyed her. Her expression was practically a mask; with her eyes closed, she could have been thinking anything at all.

She should get some sunglasses if she wants to pull that trick, said George.

I didn't say anything. I just waited.

Kelly gave a small shake of her head and continued: "I've spent the last year studying reservoir conditions. The CDC tracks anyone with a KA-related medical condition, but nothing's ever really been done with the data. So I thought I'd start."

"Hey, that's not true," I protested. "George was in all kinds of studies. There was always some new specialist asshole wanting to poke her in the eyes and see what happened."

"There have been studies of the individual *kinds* of reservoir conditions, but nobody's really looked into the syndrome as a whole." Kelly sank, if anything, farther back into the couch. "Why does it happen? Why does it happen in specific parts of the body? How is it that the virus is contained? Everything we know says that anyone with a reservoir condition should amplify immediately, but they don't. They just keep going until they die. It doesn't make sense."

"And that's what you were studying?"

A marginal nod. "Uh-huh. That's when I found it."

"Found what?" asked Alaric.

"Look at the statistics." Kelly sighed, tilting her face up toward the ceiling. "The first column is population. The second column is percent of population with a known reservoir condition—type is irrelevant in this instance."

I squinted at the numbers. I'd seen the number on the third column somewhere before. I hazarded a guess: "Column three is KA-related deaths in the last year?"

"Yeah."

"So what's the fourth column?"

Becks spoke, voice heavy with dawning horror. She'd managed to figure things out just a little faster than the rest of us, and she didn't sound happy about her epiphany. "Oh, my God. It's—that's the number of people with reservoir conditions who died, isn't it?"

Kelly nodded.

I squinted at the numbers. They didn't seem to mean anything. I was about to open my mouth when George said, very quietly, *Look at column two again, Shaun.*

I looked. And I understood.

"This can't be right," I said, suddenly cold. Reservoir conditions don't increase the odds of viral amplification; they actually tend to reduce them, since most people who suffer from a latent form of KA wind up even more paranoid about infection than the rest of the population. People like George, who went out into the field, or Emily Ryman, who kept raising horses even after she developed retinal KA, were the exception rather than the rule.

Kelly sighed, opening her eyes for the first time since her lecture had begun. "That's what I thought," she said, looking right at me. "I ran the numbers over and over. I had an intern pull the census data six times. It's all accurate."

"But—"

"Less than eleven percent of the population suffers from reservoir conditions. Last year, they accounted for thirty-eight percent of the KA-related deaths." Kelly's tone was grim. Suddenly, her exhaustion was starting to make a lot of sense. "Statistically speaking, this can't be happening."

"Maybe it was a glitch," suggested Dave. "Statistical anomalies happen, right?"

Becks snorted. "Yeah, and respected CDC doctors totally help their employees fake death by clone over statistical anomalies. It happens all the time."

"The data goes back ten years, and it's consistent all the way through. Every year, more people with reservoir conditions die than can be supported by reasonable projections—not from spontaneous amplification, not because they were stupid, not for any reason that I can find. And no one's ever said, 'Hey, maybe something's wrong here.'" She paused, shaking her head a little. "That's not right. There have been project proposals that would have addressed these numbers, and somehow they always get shut down. There's always something more important, more pressing, more impressive. Politics get involved, and the reservoir conditions get pushed to the back burner. Again, and again, and again."

"So what, you think it's intentional suppression?" asked Alaric.

"Last year, there was a six-billion-dollar study on a new strain of MRSA that's cropped up in two hospitals in North Carolina. We could have done it on a third of the budget and half the manpower. It was busywork. There's so damn much busywork." She rubbed her temple with the heel of one hand, frustration evident. "The CDC is supported by the government. We're supposed to be an independent organization, but that isn't how the funding works out."

"Was Tate involved?"

The question was soft, reasonable; it took me a moment to realize that I'd asked it.

"Not with that study," said Kelly. Hope flared and died immediately as she continued: "He was one of the supporters of continuing cancer research. You know, since cancer will become a threat again once Kellis-Amberlee has been cured. So more and more of our budget goes to things like that, and reservoir conditions just get ignored."

"How big a chunk of the CDC budget are we talking about?" asked Alaric.

"Eleven billion dollars."

Dave whistled, long and low. "That's not chump change."

"No, it's not. I'd say maybe twenty percent of our research budget is actually being spent on research into Kellis-Amberlee-related conditions. The rest of it keeps getting siphoned off into studies that look good, but don't *do* anything." Her frustration was evident. "It's like we're being stopped from finding out what this virus really does."

Probably because you are, said George.

"I didn't know that was possible," I said. "You're the CDC."

"And somebody has to pay the bills."

"Right." I stood abruptly, stalking back into the kitchen with my mostly full Coke in one hand and the stack of papers in the other. Behind me, Kelly started to ask where I was going, and was quickly hushed by Becks. Becks understood. Becks always understands.

The kitchen was cool and dark and, most important, empty. I put my things down on the counter, turned to face the wall, and began, methodically, punching it as hard as I could. The sound echoed through the room, gunshot-loud and soothing. My knuckles split on the fourth blow. I started feeling a lot better after that. I generally do. Pain clears the fog in my head, enough that I can *think* again. Besides, as long as I'm punching walls, I'm not punching people.

Someone was using the CDC's budget to control their research. Someone was funneling research *away* from Kellis-Amberlee, into diseases that weren't an issue anymore and problems that shouldn't even have been on the CDC's radar. And Governor Tate had been involved. The man who killed my sister. The man who changed everything. If Tate had his bloody little fingers in the pie...

If Tate was involved, so was whoever he worked for, said George, as calmly as I couldn't. *We have to help her. We have to find out what's going on. This could be our chance, Shaun. This could lead us straight to the ringleaders.*

"Yeah." I stopped punching the wall, taking a shaky breath as I studied the new dent I'd created next to the half a dozen that were already there. We lost our security deposit a long time ago. "I know."

Good.

If we helped Kelly, we could find out who was manipulating the CDC. We could find the people who ordered Tate to kill George. After that...

Maybe after that we'd both be able to rest.

I rinsed my hand in the sink, applying gauze and antibiotic cream before returning to the living room. There was no point in freaking Kelly out any more than the pounding noises doubtless already had. "Sorry about that," I said. "I just needed to work through a few things."

"It's okay, boss," said Dave. Alaric and Becks nodded their agreement.

Kelly bit her lip. "Is...is everything okay?"

"Not really, but we can pretend." I walked back to my seat, belatedly realizing that my things were still in the kitchen. Oh, well. "So no one ever tried to figure out why so many people with reservoir conditions were dying?"

"Um." Kelly blinked, apparently thrown by my return to the earlier topic. Then she nodded. "We got a new crop of interns recently. Very enthusiastic, very eager to prove themselves. One of them noticed the statistical anomaly while he was doing some filing, and he brought it to Dr. Wynne. What he said just didn't sound right. I asked if I could look into it. Dr. Wynne was as surprised as I was, and he agreed."

"That's how you got started on this?" asked Alaric.

"I thought it was bad data. I thought I was chasing down a reporting error. Instead...this was huge. I put together a team of people I trusted once I realized what I was really looking at. Someone's killing people with reservoir conditions in truly terrifying numbers." She took a shaky breath. "And when my team started digging, they started killing us, too."

"What?" Becks demanded.

Oh, shit, said George. I privately echoed the sentiment.

"There were eight people on my team when I started this study. Now I'm the only one left." Kelly sniffled. I realized without any real surprise that she was on the verge of tears. "I need help. I didn't know where else to go."

Becks and I exchanged a look. Dave and Alaric did the same. Then everyone turned toward me, like they expected me to make the call. Oh, wait. With George gone, they did.

Crap.

⸻

It seems like everyone I work with has some great story about how their family shows support of their career in the news. Alaric's father paid for his college education, no strings attached—scholarship by Daddy. Dave comes from this huge Russian family, and they're all so proud of him they could explode. Maggie's parents buy her everything her little Fictional heart desires, and Mahir's parents are so happy with what he does that they send care packages to the office. Care packages from *England*, sent to an office where he doesn't even work. That's how cool with things they are.

Shaun may hate the Masons, but at least they supported what he chose to do with his life. No cotillions, no coming-out parties, no "Oh, honey, this is just a phase" or "Please, darling, it's just one night." Just one night, just one dance, just one silk dress, and the next thing I knew, I'd be just one more product of the Westchester Trophy Wife Factory, proudly producing quality goods since the days of the Mayflower. I am a card-carrying Daughter of the American Revolution. I can foxtrot, quickstep, waltz, and tango. I know how to plan a cocktail party, make small talk, and overlook a man's personality, manners, and hygiene in favor of what matters: his bloodline and his bank account.

These are the things my parents taught me. They raised me to be just like my sisters—sweet, pliant, pretty, and available to the highest bidder. It's too bad I had other ideas. I am the shame of my family, the bad seed whose name will be quietly erased from the family tree the day after my picture gets posted on the Wall. I am the one who couldn't be content playing nicely with the other children, and who had to go out and get her hands all dirty.

It's days like this when I miss Georgia most of all. I may have abandoned the Newsies to go Irwin the second the opportunity presented itself, but she understood what I meant when I talked about my family, about not being sorry that I let them down. The things that made her a pretty lousy friend made her an excellent boss, and I think this would all be a hell of a lot easier if she were here.

Mom, Dad? The next horrible thing I do in public is for you. I hope you choke on it.

—From *Charming Not Sincere*,
the blog of Rebecca Atherton, March 8, 2041

Hello, darlings! I hope you're ready for some sizzling romance, swashbuckling adventure, tragic love, and mysterious happenings, because all those and more are on the schedule for this week. I'll be on the live chat every night from seven to ten Pacific time, and I'm always happy to talk about anything your little hearts desire. I'm your private Scheherazade, and I'm here to tell you stories all night long. Welcome to Maggie's House of Horrors—I hope you're planning to stay for a while.

After all, you know I always miss you when you're gone.

—From *Dandelion Mine*,
the blog of Magdalene Grace Garcia, April 11, 2041

Four

W hat are we going to do?"

Becks asked the question, but all three of my staffers were look-ing at me with near-identical expressions of impatient expectation on their faces. It was all I could do to not turn and flee the room. They were expect-ing me to give them a direction; they were expecting me to make the call; they were expecting me to be George.

"What are we going to do?" I echoed, hoping they'd take the question as rhetorical.

The person it was aimed at didn't. There are small mercies. *We're going to find out what's going on, and we're going to scream it from the mountaintops,* said George. I repeated each word a half-beat behind her, creating a weird delay that no one outside my head could hear. *We're going to do our jobs. We're going to go out there, and we're going to get the news.*

All four of the people in the room were staring at me by the time I— we—finished our little speech. Alaric was the first to look away, ducking his head slightly as he turned back to his computer screen. Dude always wanted me to be my sister when it came time to make a decision, but he was never okay with it when I actually did.

"That's great and everything, but there are a few things to work out," said Dave. He held up a finger. "What do we do with Doc here?" A second finger. "If we don't know whether it's safe to talk to the CDC, where the hell are we supposed to start?" A third finger. "What are we going to say to the rest of the site? This isn't you and a little team and a van anymore. This is a business. We can't go chasing a story we can't talk about, maybe even disappear on everybody, and expect them to be cool with it."

"Call Rick, see what he says," said Becks.

"I'm pretty sure we can't call the vice president of the United States with 'Hey, we have a dead CDC researcher who says somebody's trying to suppress her research,'" I replied. "We're going to call Rick, but we need more than we have before we do it."

Becks looked mollified. Rick Cousins used to be one of our staff Newsies. Now he's helping run the country. That gave us a certain degree of access to the president, but if we were going to announce that the sky was falling, we needed to have some proof.

"And the rest?" asked Dave.

"Starting with your third question, we're going to tell Mahir, because he already knows, and we're going to tell Maggie," I said. "We can figure out the rest as we go."

Dave frowned. "Why are we getting Maggie involved?"

"Because she's in charge of the Fictionals. If there's any chance this is going to end up getting big enough that we have to bring the whole site in on it, I want her to have had time to figure out how she's planning to tell her people," I said.

Plus, it's the right thing to do, added George.

"Well, yeah," I muttered. "I knew that."

My team had learned not to comment on my conversations with George. Kelly hadn't. Frowning, she asked, "Are you wearing an earpiece?"

"What?" Shit. "Uh...no, not exactly."

"Then who are you talking to?"

There was no way out but straight ahead. Shrugging, I said, "Georgia."

Kelly hesitated, emotions chasing themselves across her face like a gang of zombies chasing a government hunting party. Finally, she settled for the easiest possible answer: "I see."

The urge to get up in her face and try to start something was almost too strong to suppress. That's how I usually dealt with people who gave me the look that she was wearing now, that horrible mix of surprise and shock and pity. Six months ago, I probably wouldn't have been able to stop myself. Six months ago, I was thinking a lot less clearly. Maybe I'm crazy. But I'm going to be the kind of crazy that's careful until it blows everything in its path to kingdom come.

"We all cope in our own ways," I said briskly. "Dave, is Maggie online? We can conference her in right now."

"Negative," he said, without a moment's hesitation. I gave him a curious look. He shrugged. "She had a movie party last night. She won't be up for another few hours."

"Is she actually nocturnal or just trying to train herself to act that way?"

asked Becks. Glancing to me, she added, "I'm not sure I'm comfortable with this."

"What, with telling Maggie?"

"With not telling everyone else."

"How many people work for this site?"

Becks paused. "Uh…I'm not sure."

"That's why we have to do things this way, because right off the top of my head, *neither am I*." I gestured at the server bank. "Like Dave says, this isn't just me and a team that fits in a van anymore; this is a *business*. You know why corporate espionage keeps happening, no matter how bad they make the penalties for getting caught?"

"Greed?" ventured Alaric.

"Poor judgment brought on by possession of insufficient data?" said Kelly.

"People stop caring," said Dave.

I pointed at him. "Give that man a prize. People stop caring. Once you reach the point where you're working with more people than can comfortably go for drinks together, folks stop giving as much of a shit. Politics creep in. Do I trust everyone who works for us with the day-to-day? Yeah. I'd trust every Irwin we have at my back in a firefight, and every Newsie we've got to tell the truth according to their registered biases. But we go dangling a giant cherry of a story like 'The CDC has illegal clones, and their dead researcher isn't really dead, oh, and maybe there's a conspiracy blocking certain research paths,' somebody's going to leak it. They'll do it for profit, they'll do it because it gives them the leverage to get a better job with another site, or they'll do it because it's just too damn good not to share. Every person we bring in on this is another chance that this gets out before we're ready, and we're all fucked."

"Some of us more than others," muttered Kelly, sotto voce.

"You trusted us with Tate," said Becks.

"We didn't have a choice with Tate, and we didn't understand the stakes the way we do now," I said. "We tell Mahir, we tell Maggie, and we stop there until we know what's going on. Anyone really feel like arguing?"

No one did.

"Good," I said, after taking another look around the room. "Doc? From what you're saying, the CDC's out of the picture. I'm assuming that means WHO is also compromised."

She nodded marginally. "WHO and USAMRIID. There's no way we can go to them without the CDC finding out what we're doing. But…" She hesitated.

"But what?" asked Becks. "I'm sorry, Doc, you can't just show up here with your corpses and your conspiracy and your craziness and not give us at least a place to *start*."

Kelly wiped her eyes, managing to do it without smearing her mascara, and said, "I mentioned that the funding wasn't really there for researching the reservoir conditions. My team had the director's blessing, and we were still working on a shoestring budget. Our interns kept getting reassigned, our lab spaces...anyway. That doesn't matter. What matters is that almost all the specialists have gone into the private sector to pursue their own research. I have a list."

"Thank you, God," said Dave, rolling his eyes theatrically toward the ceiling.

"Dave, cut it out." I focused on Kelly. She was holding it together better than I would have expected. Pure researchers don't usually do well when suddenly hurled out of their labs and into the real world. "Is that everything, Doc?"

Kelly took a deep breath, and said, "No one outside the CDC knew what my team was researching."

Dead silence engulfed the room as Dave and Alaric stopped typing and Becks and I just stared. There was a moment where I wasn't sure I'd be able to control my temper—a moment where her statement was one thing too many in the "Why didn't you say that first?" column. Was it her fault? No. But it was suddenly our problem.

Calm down, cautioned George. *We need to keep her talking.*

"Says you," I snapped. Kelly blinked, looking to Becks, who shook her head. My team's had time to learn the difference between me talking to them and me talking to George. Thankfully.

It's not her fault.

"I know." I whirled around and punched the wall. Kelly jumped, making a small squeaking noise. That was satisfying, even as it made me feel worse about the whole situation. Like she wasn't scared enough already? "Sorry, Doc. I'm just...I'm sorry. I was a little surprised, is all."

"It's okay," she said. It wasn't—not according to the look in her eyes—but it was going to have to do.

I shook my hand to ease the ache as I counted to ten, considering the implications of Kelly's words. We'd always known somebody inside the CDC was involved with Governor Tate's doomed attempt to claim the presidency through the use of weaponized Kellis-Amberlee; Kelly's information just confirmed it. What we'd never had was the proof necessary to make a concerted inquiry into one of the most powerful organizations in the world.

"Get me facts and I'll convince the president," that's what Rick had said. But the facts had been awfully slow in coming.

As for me...I'd been ready to take the CDC on single-handedly, if that was what it took. Mahir and Alaric talked some sense into me. Getting myself killed wouldn't bring George back. If we wanted the people responsible for her death punished, we needed to be slow, we needed to be careful, and we needed to nail them to the wall. Kelly's information didn't change any of that, and at the same time, it changed everything, because it meant the conspiracy was still alive and well. If someone inside the CDC decided that the study needed to stop, then someone inside the CDC was involved in whatever was raising the death rates among individuals with reservoir conditions.

Somebody *knew*. Somebody knew George was in danger—before the campaign, her condition pre-existed the campaign by years—and they didn't do a thing. Somebody *knew*—

Shaun!

Her tone was sharper this time, cutting cleanly through my anger. I took another deep breath, counting to ten before I straightened, tucking my bruised hand behind my back. "Doc, give Dave the list." I paused. "Please."

"Sure." Kelly produced a flash drive from her briefcase and leaned over the back of the couch to pass it to Dave. He took it without a murmur of thanks, slamming it straight into a USB port and beginning to type.

"Thanks. Now take off all your clothes."

"*What?*" demanded Kelly, eyes going wide. "Shaun, are you feeling all right?"

"I'm fine. I just need you to strip."

"I'm not going to take off my clothes!"

"Actually, princess, you are," said Becks, standing and moving to stand beside me. "We need to check you for bugs. Don't worry. You don't have anything we haven't seen before."

Being asked by another woman seemed to do the trick, even if it was overly generous to call what Becks was doing "asking." Kelly sighed deeply and began removing her clothing, holding each piece up to show us before dropping it to the floor. Finally, when she was standing stark naked in the middle of the living room, she spread her arms and asked, "Happy?"

"Ecstatic." I glanced to Becks. "Take her clothes with you." Becks nodded, and grabbed a laundry bag before beginning to gather Kelly's things.

"Wait, what?" Kelly dropped her arms. "Where is she taking my clothes?"

"Don't worry, you're going with them. Becks, get the countersurveillance kit from the closet and take her to the bedroom. I want everything she has swept for trackers, bugs, anything that might transmit. Don't bring her back until you're sure she's clean." I gave Kelly a reassuring look. "It's not personal, Doc. We just need to know."

Kelly surprised me: She didn't argue. She just sighed, looking resigned, and said, "I understand decontamination procedures," before picking up her briefcase and turning to Becks. "Where do we go?"

"This way." Becks slung the laundry sack over her shoulder and led Kelly from the room. The door closed behind them with a snap as Becks engaged the interior locks. They'd be a while.

Alaric and Dave were watching me warily when I turned to face them. I smiled faintly. "It's a fun day, isn't it? Alaric, turn on the wireless speaker. I want the two of you to hear this."

"Hear what?" he asked, beginning to type again.

"I'm going to play the concerned citizen and call the Memphis CDC. I want to extend my heartfelt condolences to my good friend Joseph Wynne," I said blandly, pulling out my phone. "Dave, start the server recording."

"It's on," he said.

"Good." With all the necessary steps taken, I flipped my phone open. Most guys my age have girlfriends and drinking buddies on their speed dial. Me, I have the Memphis CDC. Sometimes I really think I never had a chance in hell of having a normal life.

"Dr. Joseph Wynne's office, how may I direct your call?" The receptionist's voice was bright, perky, and generic. I might have spoken to him before; I might not have. Office staff at the CDC seemed trained to behave as interchangeably as possible.

"Is Dr. Wynne available?"

"Dr. Wynne has asked not to be disturbed today."

"And why is that?"

"There has been a recent personnel change, and he is attempting to redistribute tasks in his department," said the receptionist pertly.

That was the coldest way I'd ever heard to describe somebody's death. Rolling my eyes, I said, "Tell him it's Shaun Mason calling with condolences for his recent loss."

"One moment please." There was a click and the speaker was suddenly playing the elevator music version of some bloodless pre-Rising pop hit. Removing the lyrics and most of the subliminal bass actually improved the song.

Dave and Alaric got up and came to stand beside me, as much for the psychological benefit as to hear what was going on; the speaker was broadcasting every tortured, tuneless note to the entire room, and it kept broadcasting as the music clicked off, replaced by the tired, Southern-accented voice of Dr. Joseph Wynne: "Shaun. I wondered when you'd be calling."

"I just finished processing the news, sir. How are you holding up?"

"Oh, as well as can be expected, I suppose," he said. Someone who thought Kelly was dead might have taken the strain in his voice for grief. Since Kelly was in the next apartment showing Becks parts of her anatomy that only her gynecologist would normally see, I recognized his hesitance for what it was: fear.

I was talking to a man who was scared out of his mind.

"What happened?" I asked.

"We don't rightly know yet, although I wish we did. There's a group of folks here from the Atlanta office going over our security tapes and checking all the facilities. There's no way anyone should have been able to get this far into the building, but they managed it somehow."

"I'm so sorry, sir," I said, exchanging a nod with Dave. It was good tactical thinking. Set up a convoluted enough break-in and distract the security teams with picking it apart, rather than looking too closely at "Kelly" while she was still in the morgue. The body would be cremated almost immediately—hell, it might have been cremated already, depending on her family's wishes—and any chance of them identifying it as a clone would be lost. Sure, Dr. Wynne would be fucked beyond belief if the break-in was revealed as a fake, but Kelly would be in the clear.

"I'm still a bit in shock," he said. "I'm sorry to say it, Shaun, because I know the wounds are still raw for you, but it's like Georgia all over again."

Shit, hissed George.

"George?" I said, automatically.

Luckily for me, Dr. Wynne was one of the few people I knew who hadn't received the "Shaun has lost his marbles" memo. Him and my parents. "The way we lost her was just so damn sudden," he said, continuing our conversation without missing a beat.

He's saying it was an emergency evacuation, you idiot, said George. *She may not know it, but he got her out to save her life. God, I wish there was a way you could ask if he was sure she wasn't bugged.*

"Uh, yeah," I said. "It really was. Was there any way anyone could have predicted this was coming?"

"I don't think so," said Dr. Wynne, quickly. Not quickly enough. I could hear the hesitation in his voice, that split second of uncertainty that told me everything I'd been hoping I didn't really need to know. Did he think he'd managed to get Kelly out clean? Yeah, because if he didn't, he wouldn't have risked sending her to us. But was he absolutely one hundred percent sure that he'd succeeded?

No, he wasn't.

"Let us know if there's anything we can do over here, but you may have to wait a little while for a response," I said. "The team and I are going on location for a little while. I'm not sure when we'll be back."

"Really?" There was deep reluctance in his voice as he asked the natural next question: "Where are y'all heading?"

The reluctance was the last piece of evidence I needed to support the idea that Kelly might not have gotten out as cleanly as she thought she had. Dr. Wynne didn't want to ask in case I was serious about the trip; he didn't want me to tell him the truth about where we were going. "Santa Cruz," I lied. "Alaric's testing for his field license soon, and we want to get some footage of him on his provisional to build into a supporting report. We're trying to up his merchandise sales among the female demographic, and our focus groups agree that the best way to do that involves getting him shirtless in a pastoral setting. Danger is just a bonus." Alaric shot me a confused look. I waved him down.

"You kids," said Dr. Wynne, with a forced chuckle. "Y'all be careful out there, all right?"

"As careful as you can be when you're looking for the living dead," I said. "Take care of yourself, Dr. Wynne."

"You, too, Shaun," he said, and disconnected the call.

I took a second to just stand there with my phone in my hand, closing my eyes and listening to George swearing in the back of my head. "Here we go again," I said, voice barely above a whisper.

"What?" asked Dave.

"Nothing." I opened my eyes, slamming the phone into my pocket before stalking back into the kitchen for a fresh Coke. I popped the tab and downed half the can in one large, carbonated gulp. The frozen sweetness made my molars ache and snapped the world back into a semblance of focus. "I need you to tear down your workstations, and then get started on everybody else's," I said, returning to the living room. "Dave, where are you with that list?"

"It's encoded. I need—"

"Forget what you need. Upload it to the main server and the mirrors; pack the physical drive."

"Boss?" asked Alaric, uncertainly.

"Gear up like you're never going to see this place again. Alaric, as soon as Becks confirms that there's nothing standard on the Doc, I need you to take over. Do a second scan of everything she brought with her. You find anything that looks like it might be related to something that might be a bug, kill it." I raised a hand before he could protest. "Don't study it, don't dissect it, don't try to subvert it, *kill* it. We don't have time to risk the sort of heat that might be coming after her."

"But—"

I turned away from him to open the closet door. The shelf on the right was crammed with ammo boxes. I started grabbing them three at a time. "He said it was like George, Alaric. Not like Buffy, who was actually unexpected; not like Rebecca Ryman, or any of the other people he and I wound up having in common."

"So what?"

Go easy on him, said George. *He wasn't there. He doesn't really understand.*

"I know," I muttered darkly. More loudly, I said, "So there were people at the CDC who were involved with what happened to her, and we never caught them. George had a reservoir condition. I thought you were the Newsie here. Do I have to draw you a picture?"

My favorite hunting rifle was leaning against the closet wall. I grabbed it, relaxing slightly as its satisfying weight fell into my hand. Letting it rest against my shoulder, I went back to grabbing ammo.

"Fuck," muttered Dave.

"My thoughts exactly," I said. "Go tell Becks she needs to hurry it up; we're getting out of here. Any bugs she can't find without a subdermal sweeper, she's not going to find with an extra ten minutes."

"On it," said Dave, and trotted out of the room.

We got to work, Alaric dismantling the equipment that wasn't needed for final uploads, while I emptied and packed down the contents of the closet. Dave came back and started helping Alaric break things down. I was filling a backpack with protein bars and spare laptop batteries when the bedroom door opened and Becks emerged, followed by a rumpled-looking Kelly.

"She's clean," Becks announced, tossing Kelly's briefcase to Alaric. He caught it and turned back to what remained of his workstation, reaching for a scanner.

"Good. We roll in twenty. Grab whatever you think you're going to need, and pack like we're not coming back."

"Where are we going?" asked Becks.

"Maggie's," I replied. She nodded, looking relieved. Even Dave and

Alaric relaxed a little. If we were heading for Maggie's, they knew that we were at least going to wind up someplace safe.

Maggie lives in the middle of nowhere and has the best security money can buy. Literally. Some of the systems on her house are military grade or better, and her parents make sure she gets the latest upgrades. Hell, sometimes I think the latest upgrades are designed specifically for her and then just shared with everybody else. She started out as one of Buffy's friends—and Buffy had interesting friends.

The apartment buzzed with renewed activity as Dave and Alaric redoubled their work. Becks started picking up stray ammo boxes. Only Kelly stayed where she was, looking utterly confused. "I don't understand," she said.

"We're leaving," I informed her. "Which sort of brings up the next question on the table: Do you have a cover story that lets us take you with us, or are we going to be smuggling you out and then shipping you off to one of the Amish compounds to live a camera-free existence?"

"They always need trained medical personnel who don't have a major addiction to electricity and running water," said Becks sunnily. Kelly shot her an alarmed look before turning to me. She seemed to view me as the stable one in the room. I might have found that comic under better circumstances.

"I have a cover story," she said. "A whole ID, even. Dr. Wynne paid to have it built for me. The files are on that card I gave you."

"Who did he pay?" asked Dave, sounding suddenly wary. Alaric didn't say anything; he just stiffened as both of them turned toward Kelly. They looked like they were waiting for something to explode.

Their reaction wasn't surprising or as over the top as it might look. Dave and Alaric wound up taking over the bulk of the computer maintenance after Buffy died, at least until we could hire some permanent IT staff. They never approached Buffy's level of competence—she was some kind of crazy computer virtuoso, and those don't come around very often—but they'd learned a lot, and they hadn't exactly started out as idiots. If anyone knew how easy it was to crack a cheap cover story, it was them.

"I don't know who did the programming," said Kelly, with increasing annoyance. "Dr. Wynne mentioned 'the Brainpan' once, but that was all. Everything was done through electronic transfer and encrypted messages. I never saw a face."

Dave and Alaric exchanged glances, saying, almost in unison, "The Monkey."

"It's creepy when you two do that, so stop." I raised a hand. "Somebody want to share the reason this makes us not panic?"

"The Monkey is possibly the single best identity counterfeiter in the country." Dave shook his head. "If you want an ID that can stand up to anything, you find a guy who knows a guy who might be able to put you in touch with one of the Monkey's girlfriends, provided you're willing to pay a deposit on faith."

"How much 'anything' are we talking here?" I asked.

"Scuttlebutt says one of the news anchors at NBC has three felony convictions and an ID by the Monkey," said Alaric.

"First, never say 'scuttlebutt' again," I said. "Second, good to know. All right, Kelly, you've got an ID. So who, exactly, are you supposed to be?"

"Mary Preston," she promptly replied. "Dr. Wynne's niece."

"Right. Alaric, can you—"

"Already on it," said Alaric, turning to one of the computer terminals that had yet to be torn down.

"Good. So 'Mary,' does this mean you have a paper trail?" I turned back to Kelly, who was starting to nod. "How much of a paper trail?"

"Mary's a real person, and she's really Dr. Wynne's niece," said Kelly. "Born in Oregon, joined Greenpeace straight out of high school, and got her conservationist's pass to move across the Canadian border five years ago. Last Dr. Wynne heard, she was working on one of the dog preservation farms and had no intention of ever coming back to the States."

"So she's disreputable enough to get along with journalists, and unlikely to come demanding her identity back when you're still using it." I looked over at Alaric. "Well?"

"Damn. I mean, just…damn." He was staring at his screen in open admiration. The rest of us took that as an invitation and put down whatever we were holding as we clustered around to peer over his shoulders, leaving Kelly by herself. Alaric shook his head. "I've never had a confirmed piece of the Monkey's work to look at. This is…it's not just amazing; it's *elegant*."

I frowned. "What are we looking at?"

The entire screen was filled with pictures of Kelly. Kelly in elementary school. Kelly at what looked like her senior prom. Kelly holding up one end of a banner that read STOP SHARK FISHING in big yellow hand-painted letters. Pretty standard snapshots, the kind you'd find on anybody's personal site or bias page.

Look again, prompted George, sounding exasperated.

I looked again, and actually saw what I was looking at. "Holy...are all those pictures fakes?"

"Yes and no," Alaric said, pulling up another set of pictures, including what looked like a still frame from an ATM's security camera and a shot where she was clearly drunk and flipping off the camera. "They're not really pictures of the Doc," he nodded toward Kelly, "but they're real pictures. The Monkey must've taken every picture of Mary on the entire Internet and somehow forced Kelly's physical isometrics over them. Seamless transition. Add the paperwork I'm finding, and—"

"No one ever knows the difference," Becks finished. "Slick."

"I'm glad you all understand what the fuck that means, because I don't," I said sharply.

"Magic computer pictures make old Mary go bye-bye, put pretty new Mary instead. Now pretty new Mary not get shot by CDC for failure to be her own dead clone," said Dave, in the lilting voice of a children's teaching-blog host.

"Great. So you've got an ID that's unbreakable as long as some chick in Canada doesn't get homesick, a bunch of numbers I don't understand, and a bunch of dead researchers. Oh, and folks like George are dying way too fast for anything short of a massive conspiracy. Okay, people, can anyone come up with a way to make this day any worse?"

That's when everything started to happen at once.

The building's siren began blaring almost at the instant that my phone started screaming with Mahir's emergency ringtone. I smacked it without taking it out of my pocket, triggering my headset to pick it up. "We're having a situation here, Mahir," I snapped. I could see Dave and Alaric out of the corner of my eye, rushing through the effort of tearing down our gear. "Sirens just started going off. We don't know why yet."

"Yes, well, I bloody well do!" he shouted. "Your building's surrounded, you've got no evac routes, and the civic authorities are declaring a state of general emergency through the surrounding cities! I don't know how you're supposed to do it, but you need to get the hell out of there, and you need to do it *now*!"

"Wait—Mahir, what the fuck are you talking about?" Becks started to say something. I held up a hand for quiet. It was already hard enough to hear Mahir over the siren.

"Good God, man, you mean you didn't know?" Mahir managed to sound horrified and unsurprised at the same time. It was a nifty trick, but I didn't have long to appreciate it; his next words took all the appreciation out of the world:

"There's an outbreak in Oakland, Shaun. And you're right in the fucking middle of it."

<hr>

The formation of the modern health-care system was an organic process, guided almost entirely by the stresses imposed by the Rising and by the panic of the general populace. Given the death rates at hospitals during the worst of the outbreak, it wasn't a surprise that people would be afraid of them. Given the risk of amplification, it wasn't a surprise that people would need medical attention more than ever. The answer was complex, involving the restoration of house calls and private care, increased access to home medical technology . . . and the sudden semi-autonomy of the CDC and the World Health Organization. If they couldn't do what needed to be done, when it was needed, there was the risk that none of us would live long enough to make a better choice about how things should be handled.

The CDC enjoys relative freedom from all ethical medical laws and local restrictions. The WHO enjoys absolute freedom in almost every nation in the world. Maybe it's time we stopped and thought about that a little more.

**—From *The Kwong Way of Things*,
the blog of Alaric Kwong, April 15, 2041**

Five

I dropped my phone and lunged for the window, swearing. The sirens were making it difficult to focus on anything but the noise. Outbreak alarms are supposed to get your attention and make you focus on the problem at hand. They work well for the first, and not so much for the second. Behind me, Alaric and Becks were shouting at Dave to shut the damn thing off already, while he shouted at them to be quiet, he was trying, and they were making it harder for him to concentrate.

Only Kelly seemed to realize that my reaction meant something was seriously wrong. She clenched her hands together, stress-whitened knuckles resting against the underside of her jaw, and watched me with eyes that seemed suddenly too large for the rest of her face.

I jerked the window as far open as it would go before leaning out over the fire escape and looking down at the street. The siren in the apartment stopped shrieking as Dave finally managed to crack the case and yank out the wires, but with the window open, the neighborhood sirens were right there to take its place—and so was the screaming.

At least the sirens took the edge off the screams. At least the sound of gunfire meant that someone was still standing.

At least.

Oh, fuck me, said George.

"My thoughts exactly," I muttered. "Guys?"

"What?" asked Alaric.

"I think it's time for an evacuation. Nice, easy, and oh, say, yesterday." I pushed away from the window. "I hate to say it, but this is not a drill."

There was a moment of relative silence as everyone stared at me, trying to rationalize what I'd just said. Then they exploded into motion, Becks and Alaric lunging for the weapons cache in the closet, Dave lunging for his keyboard. Only Kelly stayed where she was, hands still clenched beneath her chin.

Shaun—

"I'm on it," I said, and started for the server rack.

It had been almost fifteen years since the last major outbreak in Oakland. You want the recipe for a relatively zombie-free existence? It's easy. Take an armed population, give them an ingrained bunker mentality, and tell them they can't depend on anyone outside the community. They'll police their borders so well that you'll probably never need to worry about them again. Trouble is, that sort of border patrol can wind up hurting as much as it helps. Sure, Oakland had all the security features you'd expect to find in a major urban center, but most people didn't know exactly how they worked or how to take full advantage of them. They could handle their home defense systems. The public defenses were a little more difficult.

At least half the storefronts I'd seen during my brief survey of the street had been standing open, with their emergency gates fully retracted. Some of the blast shutters had managed to descend, but not nearly enough of them to make a difference, especially when the doors weren't locked. Sealed blast shutters on a building whose doors were standing open wouldn't save anyone. They'd just make sure no one could get out once the infected got in.

About half the unsealed windows had been broken—shatterproof glass is a much more academic concept when the infected are involved. They don't have any functioning pain receptors to slow them down, and they'll keep beating themselves against the glass until something gives way. When you're talking about civic-use storefronts in a relatively low-income neighborhood, it's going to be the glass that gives. There had been blood splashed all around the sidewalk, and there wasn't much screaming coming from our immediate vicinity. For most of the locals, it was long past too late.

I stepped up to the server rack and started to disconnect drives and flip the switches to transfer as much of our data as possible to secured off-site backups. There are some files we try never to keep live on an out-facing network, including most of the research we've done into the conspiracy that killed my sister. Even that data gets backed up daily, both to the drives I was shoving into my pockets and to other, off-site drives, stored in safety deposit boxes, hidden caches, and stranger places all over the Bay Area. I feel I've earned my paranoia.

I could hear the reassuring sound of Becks loading her rifle behind me, underscored by the equally reassuring sound of Alaric emptying the contents of the primary weapons locker onto the apartment floor. He might not be a field man, but he's one of the most well-informed weapons geeks I've ever met. That's not a contradiction in terms. Being comfortable on the firing range doesn't mean you'll have a damn clue what to do when a zombie comes at you. The belief that the two skill sets translate directly gets a lot of people killed.

You're getting distracted, chided George. She sounded anxious. I couldn't blame her. *Focus, asshole. This would be a stupid way to die.*

"I know, I know." I shoved the last of the drives into my pocket. Time to start moving.

The sound of my voice snapped Kelly out of her fugue. "What do we do?" she asked, in a low, tightly controlled voice. Her gaze darted around the apartment like she expected zombies to come bursting through the walls. She'd probably never been in an actual outbreak before. Talk about your trial by fire: from illegal cloning and faking your own death to trying to survive your personal slice of the zombie apocalypse in just one afternoon.

I'm man enough to admit that under most circumstances, I might have enjoyed watching the biological error messages flash across Kelly's face. Maybe it's cruel, but I don't care. There's nothing funnier than seeing somebody who thinks of the infected as somebody else's problem realize that they, too, could join the mindless zombie hordes. Most medical personnel fall into that category; by the time they have hard proof that they're not somehow above all harm, they're usually either dead or infected. Either way, they're not exactly making reports after that.

There's a time and a place for laughing at the suffering of others. This wasn't either. "We get the hell out of here," I said, striding toward Dave. "What's the situation at the parking garage? Do we have vehicle access, or are we just fucked?"

"They managed to take out the human security, but the autolockdown kept them from getting inside," Dave reported, his eyes never leaving the screen. His fingers flew across his keyboard and the ones to either side of it like a concert pianist in the middle of a symphony, never missing a beat. The screens connected to the secondary keyboards flickered windows and blocks of code so fast that they were almost strobing. None of it seemed to bother Dave. This was his element, and he was damn well in control of it. "The tunnel's clear—for the moment. The building's automated defense systems include bleach and acid sprayers. I've managed to suppress the acid. I can't stop the bleach."

"That's what gas masks and goggles are for. You sure there's nothing in the parking garage?"

"It should be clear all the way to the van." His hands didn't slow down once. "Outer perimeter hasn't been breached yet. I give it fifteen minutes if they keep slamming on the doors the way they are. Ten minutes if anybody gets bitten, panics, and drives their car into one of the fuse boxes on the street."

"How likely is that?"

"Move fast."

"Got it." I turned. "Alaric, Becks, status?"

"Almost ready." Becks tossed me a grenade. I clipped it to my belt. "We could blast our way out of anything, but..."

"But we need to assume the entire population of Oakland now wants to eat us. I know the drill. Alaric, how are we for gas masks?"

"Good." He looked up, face flushed. "Kelly, what's your weapons rating?"

She blanched. "I—it wasn't a priority for lab work, and so I didn't—"

All activity stopped as people turned to stare at her. Even Dave's fingers ceased their tapping. The screams and sirens from outside seemed louder without our preparations to blur them.

"Please tell me you didn't let it expire," I said, quietly.

"It wasn't necessary for lab work," she said, her voice practically a whisper.

I didn't need to swear. George was doing it for me, loudly and with great enthusiasm. The fact that no one else in the room could hear her was purely academic; it was making *me* feel better, and at the moment, that was all I gave a shit about. "That changes things," I said. "Alaric, you're on Kelly. Where she goes, you go, at all times. And Kelly, before you make the privacy protest, there are no potty breaks during a zombie outbreak."

Becks raised her eyebrows, looking at me.

"You've got another job to take care of." Dave's typing resumed as I spoke. The sound took the edge off the screaming from outside. Gesturing toward the pile of weaponry, I said, "Suit up, take what you need, and hit the garage. I want that tunnel absolutely secured, and I want a thorough sweep of the vehicles before we get out of here. You're going to be taking the van."

Her eyes widened as she realized what I wasn't saying. "Oh, no."

"Oh, yes."

"Shaun, you're not driving a motorcycle out through an active outbreak. That's not just stupid; that's suicidal."

"You've all been saying I was suicidal for months now, so I guess it's time I proved you right." I shook my head. "This isn't open for negotiation. Get ready, and get moving. Alaric, after you're done dealing with the ammo, go up and check the roof, see if any of our neighbors are up there, and check for helicopter evacuations on the nearby buildings. Once you've got an idea of the situation, regroup downstairs next to the door to the parking garage."

"Got it," he said, nodding once. He didn't argue with my orders or try to negotiate for leaving Kelly behind; he just stood and headed for the door. George trained her people well, and Alaric started out as one of hers.

Kelly hesitated on the cusp of following him into the hall, clutching the police baton Becks had shoved into her hands against her chest like a child would clutch a teddy bear. "Where are you going?"

"My apartment." I grabbed the rifle I'd taken from the closet, resting it against my shoulder. "I need to get something."

Dave glanced away from his keyboard. "Shaun—"

"Don't. Stay here, keep the network traffic moving, keep shifting the files we're going to need later, and just don't." Kelly stepped out into the hall, following Alaric. I looked from Dave to Becks, shaking my head. "I'll be right back."

I don't believe you just said that.

"I've been saying it all my life," I muttered, and left the apartment.

The emergency lights were on all the way along the hall, bathing it in bloody red light that was supposed to "convey a feeling of urgency" while "reducing the mental trauma of possible biological contamination." Government doublespeak for "red freaks people out so they move faster" and "it's harder to see what you're stepping in that way." To make matters worse, the emergency shutters on our building had activated, at least in the public areas where we hadn't bothered to install any overrides. The shutters blocked out the screaming. They also blocked out the daylight.

Leave it, Shaun. It's not that important.

"Pretty sure me being the one with the body means I get to decide what's important." The stairs were clear. I took them two at a time, ready to start shooting if anything moved in a way I didn't like. Nothing did.

Shaun—

"Shut up, George," I said, and opened my apartment door.

Every blogger keeps a black box in case something goes wrong. No, that's not right. Every *good* blogger keeps a black box in case something goes wrong. Every *sane* blogger keeps a black box in case something goes wrong. Every blogger you should be willing to work with keeps a black box, because every blogger you should be willing to work with understands that "things going wrong" isn't an *if*. It's a *when*.

Black boxes take a lot of forms. They're named after the boxes the FAA puts on airplanes to record information in the event of a crash. The idea behind a blogger's black box is basically the same: That's where we record the information that we need to survive when nothing else does. George's black box was built to withstand every known decontamination protocol, and a few that were still just theoretical. It was the first thing I got back from our van after she died. Becks and the others might think it wasn't worth going out into the open for, but they'd be wrong. It was the only thing worth going out into the open for.

George and I basically grew up online. What with the Masons cheerfully exploiting our childhoods for ratings and our own eventual entry into the world of journalism, we never had many secrets. Everything we ever did wound up in somebody's in-box. Almost everything, anyway. There were always the things we didn't want to share, or didn't know how to. That's why we kept paper journals. It was the only way to steal ourselves a little privacy. That "we" is intentional, by the way; George was always the thinker, while I was always the doer, but we kept one diary between us for almost twenty years. We still do. I write my pages, and then I close my eyes and let her take care of hers.

I don't read them anymore. It's better if I just imagine that they're real.

The black box contained our paper journals. Her medical records, her extra sunglasses, her first handheld MP3 recorder, and data files from the start of the campaign up until the point where she stopped recording. Her bottles of expired pain medication. All together, it was the most physical part of my sister that I had left, and there was no way I was going to run off and leave it behind.

Getting my shit together took less than five minutes. I crammed the black box into a duffel bag, along with all the weapons I could grab, and crammed extra ammo into the space remaining. There was a picture of us on my bedside table. I grabbed it and slipped it into the pocket of my jacket. Whenever you have to evacuate, there's always the chance that you won't be able to come back. Take whatever you're not willing to live without.

I paused at the door, glancing back at the boxes and the barren walls. Everything I cared about could fit in one bag, the pockets of my coat, and my head. There was something tragic about that. Or there would be, if I let myself think about it.

Don't, whispered George in the back of my head, almost too softly for me to hear.

It's scary when she fades out like that. It reminds me that, technically, her presence makes me crazy, and sometimes, crazy people get sane again. "I won't," I said brusquely, and pulled the door shut as I hurried toward the stairs.

My headset connector started beeping angrily when I was only halfway there. I unsnapped it from my collar and jammed it into my ear, demanding, "What?"

"We've got a problem." Dave sounded so calm that he might as well have been telling me to update the shopping list. "Alaric just got back from the roof."

"That was fast." I kept walking, stretching my legs until I was taking the stairs three at a time. It still didn't feel fast enough. It was the best I could do.

"Well, it turns out that he's had enough field training to know that when you open the roof door on a mass of the infected, you should stop and turn around."

My toe caught on the lip of the stair I was stepping over, sending me tumbling forward. I grabbed the railing, banging my elbow in the process. *"What?!"* I barked, in almost perfect unison with George.

"There's a mob up there. Kelly says twenty, Alaric says eleven, I'd say the real number is somewhere in the middle." Dave paused. "He got a positive ID on Mrs. Hagar before he slammed and barred the door. The rest didn't come from this building."

"Meaning what?" I asked, picking myself up and resuming the trek toward the third floor.

Meaning this "outbreak" is somebody's idea of cleaning house.

"Somebody had to put them there," said Dave, unknowingly supporting George's statement. "There's no way our building is generating spontaneous zombies."

Swearing steadily now, I took the last of the steps in four long strides, kicking open the door to the apartment. Kelly jumped, staggering back against Alaric. She was as white as a sheet. Alaric's complexion was too dark to let him pull the same trick; he was settling for turning a jaundiced yellow-tan. Dave didn't even turn around. He just kept typing, hands moving across his conjoined keyboards like he was conducting the world's biggest orchestra.

"Prep for evac," I snapped. "We're out of here as soon as Becks gets back."

"Why don't we go meet her?" demanded Kelly, a thin edge of hysteria slicing through her voice. "Why do we have to wait up here? There's a *live outbreak* on the roof! Those people, they're *infected*!" The hysterical undertones were getting louder, like she wasn't sure we understood that this was supposed to be a big deal.

Deep breaths, counseled George. *Count to ten if you have to.*

I actually had to count to thirteen before I felt calm enough to speak without shouting. "We're aware of outbreak protocol, Dr. Connolly," I said. My tone was cold enough to make Dave glance away from his screen and shake his head before going back to work. "Rebecca is currently confirming whether it's safe for us to proceed, or whether we need to find an alternate route. The rooftop door is locked, and the front of the building is sealed. We're safer sitting here than we would be rushing blindly toward what we think might be an exit."

"The building design makes that tunnel a perfect kill-chute," added Dave. "If there's anything down there, Becks is probably clearing it out before she reports back. If not, she's confirming that we can get out of the garage without dying."

"Actually, she's right behind you."

We all turned toward the sound of Becks's voice. She was standing in the doorway, smelling of gunpowder, with a grim set to her expression. I raised my eyebrows in silent question. Becks held up a bagged blood testing kit, lights flashing green, and tossed it to the floor next to the biohazard bin. That was an answer in and of itself: She wouldn't have ignored proper biological waste disposal protocols if she thought there was any chance we'd be staying.

"Three guards and two civilians who had no good reason to be there, all infected. None of them made it within ten feet of me. The rest of the garage is clear, and our transport's prepped and ready."

"Excellent." I glanced around the apartment one last time, looking for things we might have missed. Our outbreak kits have always been well-maintained and ready for something to go wrong. That doesn't stop the feeling that something major has been forgotten. "Everyone, grab your masks and goggles. We're out of here."

Suiting up for a run through a tunnel that might or might not fill with bleach while we were inside it took only a few minutes—God bless panic, the best motivator mankind has ever discovered. Kelly looked oddly calmer once she had her goggles on and a gas mask bumping against her collarbone, waiting to be secured over her nose and mouth. Maybe it reminded her of being back at the CDC, where all the "outbreaks" were carefully staged and even more carefully controlled. She'd need to get over that eventually. Now wasn't the time. If pretending this was all a drill would keep her calm, I was all for it.

We left the apartment in a tight diamond formation. I was on point and Becks was at the rear, with Dave and Alaric flanking Kelly in the center. If there were any other people in the building, they didn't show themselves as we descended. That's the right thing to do when you're caught in an outbreak and don't have an evacuation route: stay put, stay quiet, and wait for the nice men with guns to come and save you. Sometimes they'll even show up in time.

We were halfway down the last flight of stairs when the sirens changed, going from a continuous shriek to a rising series of piercing air-horn blasts, like a car alarm with rabies. Alaric stumbled, knocking Kelly into Becks and nearly sending all three of them sprawling. I took two more steps down to get out of the way, and then turned, looking back toward the others.

That's not a good sound.

"I know," I muttered, before saying, more loudly, "Dave? What's going on?"

Dave might as well have been a statue. He was standing frozen, eyes gone wide in a suddenly pale face. My question startled him back into the moment. He blinked at me twice, shook his head, and whipped his PDA out of his pocket, fingers shaking as he tapped the screen.

"We should be moving," said Becks.

"We should be waiting," I replied.

"We should be praying," said Dave, glancing up. "This block has been declared a loss."

Alaric closed his eyes. Becks started swearing steadily in a mixture of English, French, and what sounded like German. Even George got into the action, uttering some choice oaths at the back of my head. Only Kelly didn't seem to share the group's sudden distress. Sweet ignorance.

"Meaning what?" she asked. "Why are we stopping?"

"Meaning they salt the ashes," said Becks, before starting to swear again.

Dave swallowed, squaring his shoulders as he looked at me. "Boss..."

"No."

"Yes."

"There's got to be another option."

There isn't, said George, quietly. *You know that. You have to let him.*

"I can delay the lockdown. Not forever, but long enough."

I shook my head. "No. There's got to be—"

"There's not," said Alaric. I turned toward him, not quite fast enough to miss the mixture of terror and relief washing over Dave's face. Alaric had pulled off his goggles, presumably so we could see his eyes. He was looking at me with something close to pity in his expression. "The computers in the apartment are wired into the building's security systems. They can't be controlled remotely, but they work just fine if you're tapped directly into the cable. He can do it. But only if he does it from up there."

"Do you know what you're asking me to do?" I demanded. "You're asking me to let him kill himself."

"I'm asking you to let me do my job." Dave's voice was quiet, almost serene. "I didn't become an Irwin because I wanted to live a long and happy life, boss. I sure as shit didn't stay with this site because I thought it was going to be a cushy job. The math's pretty simple. It's me or it's everybody. Pick one."

"Can't someone else—"

"Unless you're planning to bring Buffy back from the dead, no."

My hand clenched into a fist. I forced myself to lower it, gritting my teeth all the way. "You're trying to piss me off," I accused.

"Yeah, I am," Dave agreed. The air-horn blasts were getting louder and closer together, breaking up our conversation like gunshots. "Keep fighting me, and we all die here." And then, the killing blow: "You'll never find out who killed your sister."

I stiffened. There was a moment where it could have gone either way; a moment where I could have grabbed him and dragged him along with us, where we would have been caught in the government lockdown when it hit our building.

Please, George whispered.

The moment passed.

"Who has the ID Dr. Wynne made for Kelly?" I demanded. Kelly blinked as she produced the card from her pocket. I snatched it from her hand and passed it to Dave. She started to protest. I cut her off, saying, "You're not carrying any trackers, and your equipment checks clean. This is the *only* thing with circuitry we can't decode, and somebody traced you here. Understand?"

Mutely, she nodded, face gone white with increasing terror. I'm not sure she'd realized before that moment that she could still be followed.

Dave shot me a pained look, saying, "Shaun—"

"Just don't. You fucker, you better make this count." I turned my back on him and continued down the stairs, snapping, "Move out!" to the others. I heard steps going up as he started back toward the apartment. Then the others were moving with me, Alaric and Becks hustling Kelly along.

We were halfway down the tunnel when the bleach jets came on, but that was all; no acid, no nerve toxins designed to target the infected and the healthy alike. We just got decontaminated, and then we were out, moving through the empty garage to our vehicles. Becks got Alaric and Kelly into the van while I donned my helmet and straddled George's bike, shoving the key into the ignition.

Cameras ringed the parking garage; cameras with feeds that plugged into the building's security system. I turned to the nearest of them, blinking back the tears that were suddenly threatening to blur my vision, and saluted.

"Move it or lose it, boss," said Dave, voice cracked and distorted by the speakers in my helmet. "You've got ten minutes at most before the fire rains down."

"Don't you dare move into my head after you die, you fucker," I said. "It's crowded enough in here."

"Boss?"

I closed my eyes. "Open the doors."

Whatever whack-ass computer voodoo he'd worked on the security system was good; the doors slid open as soon as I gave the command. Only a few of the infected were visible on the street outside, but they'd start to mob soon enough. I gunned my engine, waving for Becks to follow, and roared out into the light. She followed about fifteen yards behind, both of us cutting a path toward the closest major street—Martin Luther King Boulevard—and our hopeful survival.

Dave was wrong about one thing. We didn't have ten minutes. The building went up in a pillar of flame six minutes later, along with every other structure in its immediate vicinity. Slag and ash rained down on the entire neighborhood. Collateral damage for a major urban outbreak; the only way to be sure the infection wouldn't spread.

We were outside the quarantine by that point, outside the kill zone, but the light from the explosion was still enough to hurt my eyes. I pulled off to the side of the road and kept watching it all the same. When the glare got to be too much, I put on the extra pair of sunglasses George always kept in a case clipped to her handlebars, and I kept watching.

I kept watching while Oakland burned, and a good man burned with it. A lot of good men, I'm sure, but only one who'd answered to me. The first man lost on my watch, instead of on my sister's.

"All right, George," I said. "Now what?"

For once, she didn't have an answer.

BOOK II

Vectors and Victims

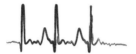

Life's more fun when you take the chance that it might end. I have no regrets.

—Dave Novakowski

A martyr's just a casualty with really good PR. I'd rather be a living coward any day.

—Georgia Mason

—transmitting? You fucking useless piece of crap, don't you cut out on me n—

—fixed it. I hope that means I fixed it. If this is getting out, this is Dave Novakowski reporting live from the headquarters of the After the End Times. Well. This *was* Dave Novakowski reporting live. By the time this report finishes bouncing to our servers, and Mahir sees it and clears it by the boss, I'm going to be long d—

—shit, the sirens just stopped. That means they're not letting evacuees out anymore. Too late, ha-ha, joke's on me, couldn't get out if I wanted to. I take my hands off the controls, the building goes into lockdown. I stay here, I can let people out—or I could, if there were any people left—but I can't escape. Irony in action, ladies an—

—dalene? Even if this entry stays in-house, I know you'll see it, somehow. God, Maggie, I'm sorry we screwed around so much. We should've just gone for it. That's what people ought to do. They should just go for it. I loved you a lot. I loved my job a lot. I guess that makes me one of the lucky ones. I guess—

—can hear the bombs now; I can hear them coming, I can he—

—From *The Antibody Electric*,
the blog of Dave Novakowski, April 12, 2041. Unpublished.

Six

Maggie's place is located six miles outside a town called, I swear to God, Weed. Weed, California, one of the smallest urban areas intentionally reclaimed after the Rising. What made them so special? Choice of location: Weed offers convenient access to three of California's major rivers, and with red meat permanently off the menu, the fishing industry is one of the hottest things going. If you want river-fished trout to be one of your menu options, you need to reclaim your fishing towns. Weed was rescued from the oblivion that claimed most of the towns and cities built too close to the wild, and it was rescued *because* it was so close to the wild. Sometimes, logic just doesn't work.

Driving from Oakland to Weed takes about four and a half hours if there aren't any quarantine barriers on I-5. According to the GPS, we were looking at clear sailing the whole way. I signaled for Becks to follow and pulled back onto the road, turning north. It was time for us to get the hell out of Dodge.

Shaun?

"I'm not in the mood right now, George." The roar of the wind ripped my words away as soon as they were spoken, but that really didn't matter; she'd hear me. She always heard me, even when I didn't say a word.

I lost him, too.

"He died on my watch, George. *My* watch. That's not supposed to happen."

Bitter amusement tinged her tone as she replied, *So, what, they're only supposed to die on mine?*

I didn't have an answer for that, and so I didn't answer her at all. She took the hint, falling silent as the bike chewed away at the miles between us and our eventual destination. The van stayed visible in my mirrors, following at a close but careful distance. There were no other cars to be seen anywhere along the highway in either direction. A reflective yellow sign caught the light and threw it back at me as we went roaring past: CAUTION—DEER HABITAT.

Deer can grow to more than forty pounds and meet the standards necessary for Kellis-Amberlee amplification. We can't wipe them out wholesale—ecological concerns aside, they're herbivores, which means their food supply hasn't been compromised, and they breed like the world's biggest rabbits. Periodically, somebody introduces legislation to firebomb the forests and take care of the deer problem once and for all, and promptly gets shouted down by everyone from the naturalists to the lumber industry. I don't have an opinion one way or the other. I just find it interesting that kids apparently used to cry when Bambi's mother died. George and I both held our breaths, and then cheered when she didn't reanimate and try to eat her son.

A small orange light started blinking at the top right-hand corner of my visor, signaling that the van was trying to open a connection. Did I want to talk to any of the people who were in the van? No. No, I did not. Did that mean I could get away with ignoring the call?

Unfortunately, no, it didn't. Smothering the urge to hit the gas and drive away from the trappings of responsibility as fast as I could, I said, "Answer call."

Becks spoke in my ear a moment later, voice rendered irregular and crackly by the sound of the wind whipping by outside my helmet. "Shaun, you there?"

"No, it's the Easter Bunny," I said. "Who do you expect is going to be answering my intercom? What do you want, Becks? We're a long way from Maggie's."

"That's actually what I wanted. We didn't have time to prep the vehicles for another road trip before we left the—" She stopped, choking off the sentence with a small hiccup. Her voice was softer when she spoke again, making it even harder to hear above the roaring of the wind. "I mean, we're not all that good for gas over here. I don't know what your status is, but we've got about another fifty miles, tops, before we're going to have an emergency."

Fuck. "What does the GPS say?"

"There's a truck stop about twenty miles up the road that takes journalist credentials and has a good safety rating. Clean, reliable blood tests, no outbreaks in the past nine years."

With our luck, we'll fix that for them.

"Probably," I said, my shoulders sagging with relief. George had been quiet since I told her I wasn't in the mood, and I'd been irrationally afraid that somehow, the trauma of losing someone else who mattered to me had combined with my anger and managed to repair my brain, making me fit the normal standards for "sane." Screw sane. I don't want anything that makes her stop talking to me. That would drive me crazy for real.

"Shaun? What was that?"

"Nothing, Becks. The truck stop sounds fine. Why don't you call ahead and let them know we're coming?" If the truck stop was ready for our arrival, they'd have someone waiting at the gate to run the blood tests and let us inside. Much faster and more convenient than calling from the driveway and chilling our heels while some underpaid attendant tried to pull himself away from his coffee.

I was about to hang up when a thought struck me, making my stomach drop all the way to my toes. "Fuck—what about the Doc? She's legally dead, and her only clean ID just went up with Oakland."

She's died twice in under a week, commented George. *Even I never managed that.*

"Hush," I muttered.

Becks ignored my interjection as she replied, "We're way ahead of you. Alaric dug out one of Buffy's old clubbing IDs for her. It won't hold up to major scrutiny, but it'll do until we get to Maggie's and he can find something more stable."

"Awesome. Get a hat or something on her—we don't want anybody getting a good look at her face. And she stays in the van; somebody else can buy her drinks."

"Got it," said Becks. "Terminate call." There was a click, and I was alone with the sound of the wind once more.

The wind and the voice that lurked inside my head. "George?"

Yeah?

"Is it always like this? Losing somebody that counted on you?"

You say that like it happened all the time.

"You did it first."

Yeah. A long pause, and the faintest sensation of a sigh at the back of my mind. *But what else is new?*

George always did everything first. She talked before I did, read before I did...about the only thing I ever did first was figure out the game the Masons were playing with us, and that was as much luck as anything else. She was the one who decided to become a professional journalist, hauling me along in her excitement. I went along with it in the beginning to make her happy, and later because it turned out I was actually pretty good at poking things with sticks for the amusement of others. It was the first thing I'd ever found that I was really good at, that I really enjoyed doing, and I never would have found it if it weren't for her. She was the one who suggested we follow Senator Ryman's presidential campaign. She was the first one to recognize what it had the potential to do for our careers.

She was the first one to die.

I drove quietly, giving her time to collect herself. Finally, slowly, she said, *It's different every time. Losing Buffy was… It was basically the end of the world, but I held it together. I had to hold it together.*

"Why?"

Because, she said, like it was the most obvious thing in the world, *you needed me to.*

There was nothing I could say to that. I put my head down, gunned the throttle, and drove straight down the highway until the neon sign of a truck stop beckoned, promising food, fuel, and lots of burly rednecks with guns who were just aching for the chance to put down an outbreak. Everyone's got the places where they feel safe. My top three would probably be the middle of an Irwin meet-up, inside a CDC lockdown facility, and any truck stop in North America. You want to talk scary survivalist mentality, go find yourself a trucker, and then get back to me.

Three guards in oil-stained denim met us at the gates with handheld blood testing units. One guard for me, two guards for the van. My attendant was an unsmiling, pimple-faced teenager whose nametag identified him, probably inaccurately, as "Matt." I didn't bother trying to engage him in conversation. I just pulled off my glove and held out my hand to let him do his job. He grunted appreciatively at the professionalism, jamming the test unit over my hand without pausing to make sure my fingers were straightened properly. It wouldn't change the test results; all one of those boxes cares about is blood. I winced as he bent my pinkie, but didn't say a word. Better to let him take care of things before I made him think of me as a person.

The lights on the top of the unit cycled from red to green, stabilizing. A grin split his cratered face, transforming it into something that was almost endearing. "Looks like you're clean and clear, Mr. Mason," he said, further confirming that Becks had radioed ahead with our credentials. "Love your site. Those reports you sent out of Sacramento last year? They were amazing." He paused before adding shyly, "I was really sorry to hear about your sister."

I plastered my best "Gosh, no, it doesn't hurt at all when you bring up George randomly in conversation. Thanks so much for checking with me first" smile across my face, glad that the helmet's visor mostly obscured my eyes, and said, "Thanks. It's been an interesting time."

"Well, welcome to Rudy's. I hope we've got everything you need."

"Thanks," I repeated, and tugged my glove back on before starting the bike and rolling past the gates, into the truck stop proper. The other two guards were still busy testing the occupants of the van; maybe even double-checking Kelly's credentials. I felt better knowing that she was using something Buffy built. The Monkey might be the best in the business, but Buffy was the one whose work I knew and trusted.

I set my bike to auto-fuel while I ducked into the truck stop's generously designed convenience store, wandering past racks of real artificial cheese nachos and withered all-soy hot dogs to find the sodas. I paused in the act of opening the Coke cooler, looking longingly at the pot of coffee simmering next to the hot dogs. That stuff was probably ancient, tarlike, created through the slow compression of the bones of prehistoric creatures until their fossilized blood was pumped up from the very center of the planet to fortify long-distance truckers.

Go ahead.

"Huh?" I stopped where I was, blinking like an idiot. Not exactly a safe thing to do, since disorientation and jerkiness are early signs of Kellis-Amberlee amplification. My team may be used to my conversations with my dead sister, but the rest of the world isn't quite so understanding.

You want coffee. Get some coffee.

"But—"

I already made you drink a hooker from Candyland once today. I can show a little mercy. There was amusement tinged with sadness in her tone. It took me a while to learn to read how she was feeling—I wasn't used to watching for cues in a disembodied voice—but now that I knew, I couldn't un-know. *Besides, you've earned it.*

"Blow up one employee for one cup of coffee, huh?" I murmured, stepping away from the coolers and heading for the steaming prehistoric coffee. George always hated the taste of the stuff. I just don't understand why anyone would want to get their caffeine in a less-efficient form.

Alaric must have lost the "who has to leave the car" coin toss; he was coming into the convenience store as I was coming out, the biggest cup of coffee they were willing to sell me clenched firmly in my hands. Alaric glanced at the steaming cup and blinked, raising his eyebrows. The question was clear in his expression. Lucky for me, I've had a lot of time to practice being the oblivious one.

"I'm going to go double-check the bike and make sure all the windows on the van are clean while you take care of things in here." I sipped my coffee, reveling in the feeling of it searing its way down my throat. It was as thick and bitter as I'd hoped. "Make sure you remember to get something for Becks and the Doc to snack on. It's a long way to Weed, and Maggie may not have dinner on the table when we get there."

Alaric frowned. "Boss—"

"Go ahead and use the company card. When I get the bill, I'll tell me that I authorized it, and I'm sure I'll be willing to let the charge stand." I offered him a bright, disingenuous smile and brushed quickly past as I left the convenience store, heading for the fueling stations.

The sun was dipping lower in the sky; we'd be making most of the drive to Weed in full darkness. Even in today's safety-oriented society, there aren't lights on most of I-5; just around the exits to inhabited areas. Those are also the places where the guard stations are actually staffed, and where nice men with guns will be happy to "help" if you go and get yourself infected. Good Samaritans, every single one of them. Thanks to the laws regarding infection, they don't even have to be certain before they shoot; anything that can stand up as reasonable doubt in a court of law is enough to excuse them putting a bullet through your skull. The farther into the wild you go, the less reasonable that doubt has to be.

"Night-riding," I said, sipping my coffee again. "Gosh. That's just what I was hoping I'd be doing tonight. Driving down a deserted highway in the dark is always superfun."

I'd do it for you if I could.

"I know," I said. Alaric was coming out of the convenience store, practically staggering under his load of junk food and bottled sodas. I tossed my half-full coffee cup into the nearest trash can and pulled my helmet over my head, offering him a quick salute as I kicked one leg over my bike. The faster I made for the gate, the less time we'd have to talk about what happened. There'd be time for talking when we got to Maggie's place. We wouldn't be able to help it. For now, all I wanted to do was drive, and I didn't even particularly feel like doing that.

I had my bike pulled out from the pump and idling by the time Alaric reached the van. He dumped the supplies into the passenger seat and waved to me, a questioning expression on his face. I've learned to recognize the "Do you want to talk about it?" look—God knows I got it enough after George died. I shook my head, jerking a thumb toward the gate.

My team knows my signals as well as I know theirs. Alaric nodded, getting into the van. A moment later, Becks flashed me the thumbs-up signal out the driver's-side window and started the engine. The van pulled away from the pump and stopped behind me, waiting for my sign.

"Amateurs," I muttered, and gunned the engine.

The rest of the drive to Weed was the sort of uneventful that leaves every nerve on full alert, ready to freak out at the slightest provocation. Pre-Rising horror movies used to build suspense before a big scare by making the audience wait. They'd do something horrible, maybe kill off a few protagonists, and then make people sit around waiting for the next terrible thing to come along. They called it "setting up a jump scare." Well, the drive to Weed felt exactly like that. We blasted down the abandoned length of I-5, and with every mile that passed without something going wrong, the paranoia grew.

It was almost eleven when we pulled off the freeway and onto the surface streets of Maggie's hometown. Floodlights lit a billboard located near the city center, large block letters proclaiming CONGRATULATIONS JAMES! WEED'S CITIZEN OF THE MONTH!

There's something in the mentality of small towns that I'll never understand. Shaking my head, I signaled for the others to follow as I turned onto the frontage road leading to Maggie's.

Houses took on a distinctly utilitarian feel after the Rising, as people suddenly figured out that maybe being able to withstand the zombie apocalypse was more important than having a showy picture window. I've always had a soft spot for pre-Rising buildings. Sure, they're basically death traps and most of them should be torn down before something goes horribly wrong, but they're death traps with *style*. Pre-Rising houses are the Irwins of the architectural world. Maggie's place, well…it could easily win a Golden Steve-o just for existing.

We turned off the lackadaisically maintained frontage road and onto the smooth pavement of Maggie's two-mile driveway, which wound like a ribbon through the trees to make an almost perfect circle around the house. Less impractical than you might think: Every segment of the driveway was surrounded by automatic sensors and motion trackers, right up until you hit the wall, which looked like stone but was actually specially treated polymer over a steel core. The gates were set to slam shut in less than half a second, and they were guaranteed to shear straight through anything short of a tank. The twisting driveway sliced the surrounding woods into sectors, and each sector contained a series of trip wires and cameras that would make sure nothing ever snuck up on Maggie or her guests.

I stopped the bike just shy of the first gate, shifting to neutral and activating my helmet's intercom. "Uh, Becks? Did anybody call Maggie to tell her we were coming?"

A long pause greeted my question before Becks said, "No. I thought you did."

"Slipped my mind." I sighed, starting forward. "Let's see if her security system kills us, shall we?"

The first two gates were set to open for anyone with After the End Times credentials. The third required a blood test—you could get into the kill chute after you were infected, but you'd be stopping there in a hurry. The fourth performed a mandatory ocular scan. George never had the occasion to visit, which was a pity. It would have been fun to watch the hard-coded security system try to deal with her retinal KA. Maggie might have needed to actually call some of the live guards out of the woods where they usually lurked unseen.

We could see the house after we passed the third curve in the drive. Every window was lit, and the yard was illuminated by floodlights concealed in the carefully manicured garden. It was practically bright enough to be daylight. The light led us the rest of the way up the hill. I started to relax after we'd passed the fourth gate without anything coming out of the trees to kill us all. The fifth gate—the final gate—was standing open. I drove through to the yard, parking to the side in order to leave the van with plenty of space to pull in past the gate.

The front door opened while I was taking off my helmet and Becks was parking the van. A small flood of furry bodies poured out into the yard, Maggie walking at the center of the rollicking, barking pack. I had to smile. I couldn't help it.

The barrier weight for Kellis-Amberlee amplification—that is, how heavy something has to be before it won't just die, but will also come back from the dead and have a go at eating Grandma—is forty pounds. That seems to be a reasonably hard cut-off point; some things may not reanimate under fifty pounds, but nothing reanimates under forty. Logically, you'd think this would mean the dog fanciers of the world would go, "Gosh, aren't teacup poodles nice?" Logic has never been the human race's strong suit. Breeding programs sprang up the minute the risk of apocalypse was past, with people all over the world trying to miniaturize their favorite canine companions.

George used to say it was disgusting, and that people should get over themselves. Me, I've always found Maggie's miniature bulldogs endearing, in a fucked-up, epileptic sort of a way. The miniature bulldog's tendency to develop epilepsy is actually the reason rescues like Maggie's exist, since a surprising number of families wanted a dog "just like Grandpa's," but didn't read the new breed specs.

"Hey, Maggie," I said, shifting my attention from the sea of bulldogs to their owner. "Are we too late for dinner?"

"Not if you like emu meatloaf," she said, with a forced attempt at a smile. Her eyes were red and slightly swollen, like they'd been wiped too many times in the past few hours. "I assume you guys are planning to stay for a while?"

"If that's all right with you." She looked miserable, standing there in the midst of her little swarm of rescue dogs and trying to seem like nothing was wrong. I wanted to comfort her. Only I didn't have any idea how.

I was better with that sort of shit when George was alive, because I had something to protect. She didn't like touching people, so I touched them for her. She didn't like emotional displays, so I took up the slack. Only without her around to give me an excuse, it was like I didn't even know where I was supposed to start.

We always figured she was the one whose emotional growth got stunted by the way we were raised. It was sort of weird to realize that the damage extended to cover both of us.

Alaric saved me from needing to figure out what I was supposed to do. He was out of the van almost before Becks had the engine off, running toward Maggie with total disregard for the dogs surrounding her. Luckily, miniature bulldogs are smart enough to get out of the way when they're about to be stepped on, and he made it to her without incident. Putting his arms around her shoulders, he pressed his face into her shoulder. She did the same to him, and they simply held each other. That was all. That seemed to be enough.

Breathe, George said.

"I'm trying," I murmured. Watching Maggie and Alaric embrace felt weirdly like spying. I turned away.

"Hey," said Becks, stepping up beside me. Kelly was close behind her, clutching one of the spare blankets we kept in the back of the van around herself for warmth. They both looked exhausted, but of the pair, it was Becks who looked like she was going to be okay. The circles under Kelly's eyes were deep enough to be alarming, and her face was pale.

"Hey," I replied. Nodding toward Kelly, I asked, "Doc get through the drive okay?"

"I slept some," said Kelly, in a distant tone.

"No," said Becks, half a second later.

"Didn't think so." I glanced over to where Alaric and Magdalene were still clinging to each other, and said, "Maggie made emu meatloaf. It's inside. Maybe we should join it."

"That sounds like an excellent idea to me," Becks said. "I'll get my bag."

Now Kelly began to look alarmed. "Wait—this is where we're *staying*? Here?"

"Yup," I answered, turning to unhook the bike's saddlebags and sling them over my shoulder. "Welcome to Maggie's Home for Wayward Reporters and Legally Dead CDC Employees."

"But this isn't—it's not—" She waved her hands, encompassing the wide green lawn, the patches of tangled, seemingly untended greenery, and the trees outside the wall. "This isn't safe!"

Becks and I exchanged a look. Then, almost in unison, we started to laugh. It had the ragged, almost hysterical edge that always seems to come with laughter that's halfway born from exhaustion, but still, it felt damn good to laugh about *something*. Just about anything would have been okay by that point.

Kelly looked between us, eyes widening with alarm that turned quickly into irritation. "What?" she demanded. "What are you laughing at?" That made us laugh harder, until I was bent almost double, and Becks was covering her face with her hands. Even George was laughing, an eerie, asynchronous echo inside my head. Alaric and Magdalene ignored us, lost in the private world of their grief.

Becks was the first to get control of herself. Wiping her eyes, she said, "Oh, Shaun, I don't think anybody ever bothered to tell the Doc here exactly where it was that we were going."

"Apparently not," I said, rolling my shoulders back and forcing my expression to sober as I turned to Kelly and said, "Doc, we are fortunate enough to enjoy the hospitality of Miss Magdalene Grace Garcia."

"Please don't steal the silver," added Becks.

Kelly's mouth dropped open.

If Kelly's family was responsible for many of the medical advancements of the past twenty-five years, it was Maggie's family who made sure they had the equipment they needed to keep moving forward. Her parents were heavily into software before the Rising; their company had already made millions when the dead began to walk. They were savvy people, and they saw the writing on the wall: Either everybody was about to die, in which case money had just become an outdated concept, or we were going to beat back the infected, and folks were going to get real concerned about their health. They managed to shift most of their financial capital into medical technology before the markets froze. They didn't make millions. They made *billions*, and that was after taxes.

They weren't only heavily into software: They were also heavily into philanthropy, and their contributions were a large part of what made saving Weed possible. Of course, that left them owning a controlling share in two of the town's four major fisheries, as well as most of the hospital. We're talking about the kind of people for whom a thousand dollars is a perfectly reasonable price for a bottle of wine. When Maggie turned twenty-one, they asked her what she wanted, said that the sky was the limit, nothing was too good for their precious little girl.

She asked for the farmhouse that belonged to her grandparents, a military-grade security system, a private T1 line, and permanent access to the interest generated by her trust fund. Nothing else. And her folks, being the sort of people who try to keep their word, agreed. We might have been safer in an underground CDC bunker. Maybe. If it was protected by ninjas or something.

"But..." Kelly said finally. "Shouldn't she be doing something, I don't know, important with herself?"

"She is," I said, and smiled. "She hosts grindhouse film festivals and writes for me. Come on. Last one to the table has to do the dishes." I started for the door, skirting a wide circle around Alaric and Maggie. Kelly followed me, still looking confused, and Becks came after her. She left the front door standing open. The privileges of security are many, and not always visible.

None of the other Fictionals were evident in the large, bookshelf-lined living room, which was cluttered with boxes of dusty papers, dog beds, and comfortable-looking couches. That was unusual; Maggie was almost never home alone, having opened her house on a semipermanent basis to all the Fictionals working for the site, as well as a few of the Irwins and Newsies. She liked company, Maggie did. She grew up in a level of society where it was still possible to be a party girl, and even though she walked away from her roots in a lot of ways, she couldn't walk away from everything she'd learned. Normal people like being alone. Being alone means being safe. Maggie got lonely.

Kelly stuck close behind me, drinking in her surroundings with a coolly assessing expression that I recognized from watching Irwins sizing up hazard zones. Most homes are decorated for utility these days, resulting in a lot of sleek lines, brightly lit corners, and modernistic furniture that looks like it came from a pre-Rising horror movie, all of it designed to be easy to disinfect. Maggie decorated in antiques and homemade furniture, with clutter covering every surface, and dust covering all the clutter.

I've always assumed that Maggie lives the way she does partially out of sheer contrariness. If everyone expects her to run around partying with the kids she grew up with, moving in a virtual bubble of overpaid security guards and the sort of safety that only money can buy, fine; she'll live in the middle of nowhere with a pack of epileptic dogs instead of a purse poodle and a posse. If people expect her to have three brain cells to knock together, she'll become a professional author and manage a crew of twenty more. The list goes on. She's a fun girl, our Maggie, even if the way she lives implies that her sanity is somewhat dubious.

The thought barely had time to form before George interrupted it, saying, *You're one to talk.*

I didn't mind. At least she was talking to me. And she sounded amused, which is always nice. It's good to know that I can still make my sister smile. "Hush, you," I said.

Kelly gave me a startled look. "I didn't say anything," she protested.

"It was George," I said, with a quick shake of my head.

"You know," said Kelly carefully, "if it's anxiety that leads you to continue conversing with her, there are medications that will—"

"New topic time," I said pleasantly. "Continuing this topic is going to lead to somebody getting punched in the face. It could be you."

"Shaun has no compunctions about hitting girls," said Becks.

"You try growing up with George, see how many compunctions about hitting girls you come out with." I led our motley little parade into Maggie's kitchen. It was decorated like the rest of the house, in middle-class pre-Rising shabby. Maggie hadn't been kidding about the meatloaf. It was sitting on the kitchen table, alongside a platter of sliced vegetables, a big bowl of mashed potatoes, and half a sponge cake.

"I'll get the plates," said Becks.

When Maggie and Alaric finally came in fifteen minutes later, they found the three of us seated around the kitchen table, stuffing our faces. Becks and I were stuffing our faces, anyway. Kelly was watching us with a sort of horrified bemusement, like she couldn't believe her life had gone so terribly wrong in just one day. She'd catch on. If she lived long enough.

Maggie and Alaric had clearly both been crying, although it showed more on her than it did on him; her eyes were puffy and her cheeks were even redder, whereas Alaric looked about as normal as he ever did. He tried to explain his consistently camera-ready appearance to me once, but I didn't listen. Largely because I didn't care.

"Alaric tells me you're the dead girl from the CDC," said Maggie, arrowing in on Kelly with the laser-point accuracy that has made her editing skills feared throughout the Fictional world. "Nice trick. Explain it."

"Hello to you, too, Maggie," I said brightly, reaching for the mashed potatoes. "Do you need an introduction to our guest, or do you prefer the tornado approach? Just so it's said, she's had a pretty shitty week, and I wouldn't blame her if she freaked out on you. I mean, it's been a shitty day for all of us, so I'd really appreciate it if you could take it easy on the Doc."

Maggie stiffened. I looked at her calmly, waiting to see which way the dam was going to break: raging flood or anguished trickle.

Finally, her shoulders dropped, and she said, "Mahir kept Dave's last post from going live, but he sent me a copy and said he thought you might be coming here. That's why I sent everybody home."

"That was a good idea," I said, neutrally.

"I didn't get to say good-bye, Shaun." Maggie shook her head. "I should've been able to say good-bye. I should've been able to tell him…I should've been there."

That was the sort of grief I can handle. Sadly enough, it's the kind I've been on the inside of, because even saying good-bye isn't enough. There's always one more thing you should have had the time to say, or do, or ask. There's always going to be that one missing piece.

I put my fork down and stood, shifting dogs out of the way with the side of my foot as I walked over to Maggie. She looked at me. I nodded, once, and put my arms around her, feeling the tension in her shoulders. "I won't tell you it's going to be all right, because it's not going to be all right," I said. "I won't tell you I understand what you're going through, because nobody who isn't inside your head can understand, and I won't say that we're here to help. We're not. We're here to save our asses, and we're here to find out what the fuck is going on. But I'll say this: Dave made his decision, and they're going to put him up on the Wall with all the other heroes. He's going to be there forever because of what he decided was the right thing to do. I guess I can't be too angry at him for that. George wouldn't have hired him if she didn't think he knew how to make the hard calls, and I wouldn't have kept him if she wasn't right."

"I think I loved him," said Maggie, her voice soft and almost muffled by her face pushing up against the side of my shirt.

I sighed deeply, looking over her head toward the others. Becks and Alaric had barely had time to get over being the walking wounded after losing Buffy and George. I'd barely had time to learn how to look like I was coping. And now it was all starting up again. The conspiracy theories, the confusing evidence, the deaths, the whole fucking mess.

The worst part was that deep down in my heart, in the part of me that no one got to see but George, I was glad. Because if all the old shit was starting up again, that meant that we were moving again. Moving toward an answer to the question that kept me from sleeping at night, and probably kept me from killing myself:

Who really killed my sister?

Kelly met my eyes and looked away, expression guilt-stricken. I'd have to talk to her about that. This wasn't her fault, any more than it was mine, or Alaric's, or Maggie's. She was a victim, just like the rest of us. None of us did anything wrong. But that could be dealt with tomorrow, when we'd had time to sleep, reassure Mahir that we were still alive, and really look at Kelly's data.

"I think we all loved him at least a little," I said, with complete honesty, and I stood in that homey-smelling kitchen surrounded by the remains of my team, and I held her while she cried.

Screw you, David Novakowski. Screw you for being noble and good and earnest and staying in that damn building, and screw you for that last transmission, and screw you twice for taking so fucking long to say anything. You idiot. You stupid, stupid idiot.

I loved you, too, you idiot.

I can't post this. I want to post this. I can't post this. But writing it down helps, a little, because writing it down is what we *do.* They're on their way here—they have to be, because if they're not...I won't think about it. The house feels so empty. God.

—From *Dandelion Mine*,
the blog of Magdalene Grace Garcia, April 12, 2041. Unpublished.

I'm sorry, my darlings, but I won't be able to make tonight's chat. I know, I promised, and I'm sorry, but Auntie Maggie has a headache right now and needs to have a nap. Normal transmissions will resume tomorrow. Be good. Be kind to each other. And if there's somebody you love, tell them. The world always needs more love.

—From *Dandelion Mine*,
the blog of Magdalene Grace Garcia, April 12, 2041

Seven

S haun?"
  I raised a hand to rub my temple as I raised my head, trying to ward off the headache I could feel brewing there. I'd turned off most of the lights when the rest of the house went to bed, but I hadn't stopped reading. Maybe that wasn't such a good idea. "In here, Maggie." I was sitting on the living room floor, back against the couch. I'd been sitting long enough that I wasn't sure I could still stand.

Maggie made her way down the darkened hall to the doorway without tripping over anything. I had to admire how well she knew where everything was. I couldn't have navigated that hall without causing my shins some serious damage. "How's Mahir?"

"Relieved that we're not dead. Broadcasting some old camping footage George and I took the last time we went to Santa Cruz. As long as he strips the dates, he should be able to make it look like we were all off having a grand time with the infected when they firebombed our building."

Maggie swallowed. "And Dave?"

"Stayed behind to take care of the servers. We figure the cleanup on Oakland should be done by morning. They'll contact his family, and we'll announce it after they contact us." It was heartless. It was unforgivable. It was the only choice we had. "I figure we can fake being out in the field for three or four days before we need to find somewhere else to be."

"Don't be an idiot." The edge on her voice was surprising. I blinked. Drawing her tattered terrycloth bathrobe around her shoulders like it was a form of armor, Maggie scowled at me. "You'll stay right here. My security systems can bounce your signal anywhere we want it to be."

"Maggie—"

"Don't you dare tell me it isn't safe, Shaun Mason. Don't you *dare*." She stalked to the nearest overstuffed armchair and sat, curling her legs under herself and eyeing me like an aggravated cat. "I've never been safe in my life. I'm not planning to start now."

"You can't tell me that," I protested. "I've seen your security system."

Maggie's laugh was rich, bright, and surprising. "I'm going to inherit enough money to buy a small country someday. My parents don't have anyone else to leave it to. There's a reason I live in the middle of nowhere and surround myself with reporters. Do you have any idea how good the security on this place *really* is? If I scream, someone comes. They can't fake an outbreak on us here that won't be immediately obvious as a setup. So unless the dead decide to rise en masse again—"

"Which is thankfully not very likely."

"Exactly. You won't be safe when you leave here."

I looked at her measuringly. "Nice cage you've got here."

"Thanks." She smiled thinly. "The food's pretty good, but, man, does the company suck."

"We do our best." I sighed. "I'm really sorry about all this."

"Don't be. Just get some sleep." Maggie pulled her almost waist-length braid over one shoulder, picking aimlessly at the trailing end. "You've had a long day."

"Yeah, well. Objects in the rearview mirror don't get smaller just because they're getting farther away." I held up one of the folders from Kelly's briefcase. "I'm trying to make sense out of all this crap while nothing's catching on fire. I figure that won't last for long."

"It never does," Maggie agreed. "How bad is it?"

"On a scale of one to oh fuck, we're all gonna die?" I flipped the folder open and read, "'Considering the risk of mutation, the concept of the reservoir conditions as the next stage in Kellis-Amberlee's evolution cannot be ignored. We would be severely remiss to ignore the opportunities, and dangers, that such an evolution may present.'" I closed the folder, but didn't look up. "What the fuck does it even mean? Somebody's killing the folks with reservoir conditions. The numbers aren't lying, even if everybody else is. But what does it *mean*?"

"It means we have a job to do, I guess."

"Yes." I glanced toward the hall. "Everybody else asleep?"

"Yes, they are. I think a few of them may have helped themselves get that way with chemical aid, but whatever works."

"Good."

Maggie had prepared the guest rooms while we were still on the road, swallowing her grief long enough to break out fresh bedding and clean towels. I'm pretty sure the process was a sort of good luck charm for her; if she got the rooms ready, we'd show up alive. As it was, when bedtime came, she apologized for having only three guest rooms, since the other two spare rooms had been converted, respectively, into a home theater and a study. Like there's anything "only" about a house with six bedrooms. George and I grew up in a house with three, and ours were connected enough to practically count as a single room. Three guest rooms meant one each for Alaric, Becks, and the Doc. I've slept on couches before. It doesn't bother me.

Besides, I wanted to stare at those numbers until they started making sense. After almost two hours, I wasn't getting any closer. I sighed. "I'm missing something. I know I'm missing something."

Don't be so hard on yourself, said George. *You're tired.*

"That's easy for you to say," I snapped, before I could stop myself. Then I froze, casting a careful glance toward Maggie. I was expecting…I don't know what I was expecting. I get a lot of reactions to the fact that I still talk to my sister. Most of them aren't good ones.

Maggie's fell somewhere in the middle of the spectrum. She was looking at me thoughtfully, head tilted slightly to one side. "She really talks to you, doesn't she?" she asked. "It's not just you talking to her. She talks *back*."

"Hell, half the time she starts it," I said, half-defensively. "I know it's weird."

"Well, yes, it's weird. Technically, I think it's insane. But who am I to judge?" Maggie shrugged. "I live in a house most people view as the setting of a horror movie waiting to happen, with an army of security ninjas and a couple dozen epileptic dogs for company. I don't think I'm qualified to pass judgment on 'weird.'"

That's a new one, said George, bemused.

"Tell me about it," I muttered, adding, louder, "That's, uh, different."

"At least you know that you're crazy. That means you have the potential to recover."

I hesitated. There are a lot of people who'd say that my steadfast refusal to give up on George means I'll never get over my grief. I sort of hope they're right. I don't want to get over it. "Well, um, thanks," I said. The words sounded even lamer outside my head than they did inside.

Maggie didn't seem to notice. She was gazing off into one of the darkened corners of the room, expression gone even more wistful. "I knew Dave loved me, you know," she said, with a studied casualness to her tone. Whatever she was going to say, she was going to say it whether she got the right conversational prompts from me or not. I was an audience, not a participant. "But I was still getting over losing Buffy, and Dave and I, we were doing this…this weird circling thing, like we needed to figure out every single line of the script before we could even start the movie. I knew, and he knew, and we didn't do a damn thing about it." She sniffled. A very small sound that seemed loud in the sudden silence of the room. "It's like we thought everything had to be perfect, or it wouldn't work. Like it was a story."

I wanted to say something, but there was nothing to say. I sat frozen, my fingers twitching slightly on the folder I still held. I wanted to reach for her. I wanted to take her hand. Only I knew it wasn't her hand I wanted—the hand I wanted had been reduced to ash and chips of bone before being scattered down the length of California Highway 1—and so I didn't move.

"Have you ever been in love?" Maggie looked back toward me, the faint light glittering off the tears running down her cheeks.

There's never been a good answer to that question. I didn't even try. I just shrugged.

"Love sucks," said Maggie, and stood. "Everyone I fall in love with dies. Try to get some sleep tonight, okay, Shaun? And…thanks for listening. I can't post that." She chuckled, the sound barely managing to escape turning into a sob. "You know, it seems like every time I wind up with a real tragic love story to tell, I can't post it. It wouldn't have been fair to Buffy, and now it wouldn't be fair to Dave. It's…there's so little that's personal anymore."

"Yeah," I said, swallowing past the dryness in my throat. "I'm pretty sure he knew you loved him, too. He had this theater thing set up on the roof—"

"I know." Her smile was brief, but it was real. "Get some sleep. Tomorrow's not going to be any better."

Can't be any worse, muttered George.

I swallowed the urge to answer George, and said, instead, "I'll try."

"Good enough for me," said Maggie, and turned to go, leaving me alone with my pile of folders, my tiny pool of light, and the voice of my sister echoing inside my head.

You used to make me sleep, said George.

"Yeah, well, you had a body then." I looked at the folder in my hands, willing it to open of its own accord. That way I wouldn't actually have to decide whether or not I was going to stop. Once it was open, I could just read.

Shaun—

"Leave it."

She sighed. I knew that sigh. I knew all her sighs. This was the "Shaun, stop being stupid" sigh, usually reserved for when I needed to be pushed into doing something she considered sensible. *I won't let you dream.*

I froze.

George didn't say anything after that. I could feel her waiting at the edges of my mind, eternally patient, at least where my well-being was concerned. I swallowed again before I leaned back in the chair, closing my eyes. "You can still surprise me," I said.

Good. Now get up, and get on the couch.

"Yes, ma'am."

Maggie's couch proved to be surprisingly comfortable once I'd cleared everything off it and piled it all on the floor. I turned off the light before taking off my shirt and shoes, leaving my jeans on, just in case we needed to make an early-morning getaway. I was asleep almost before my head hit the pillow.

George was true to her word. If I dreamed that night, I don't remember it.

I woke to the sound of voices in the next room, pitched at that harsh semi-stage-whisper level that everyone seems to think is unobtrusive, despite being impossible to ignore. Something about the sound of people whispering touches off a primordial red alert in the back of the brain. I probably wouldn't have noticed if they'd just spoken quietly in normal voices. At least no one was screaming; that meant we'd all probably managed to live through the night. Survival is always a nice thing to wake up to.

Sitting up was hard. My back was stiff from spending several hours on the bike, followed by several more hours sitting on the floor and trying to study. I may not spend as much time in the field as I used to, but that hasn't made me a bookworm or anything. Who knew being a geek would *hurt*? Groaning, I braced my elbows on my knees and dropped my head into my hands. The voices from the kitchen stopped. Zombies don't groan, they moan, but the two can sound almost identical to the untrained ear. Of the four people in the house with me, only Becks had the field experience necessary to know that whatever had made that sound was alive. Just cranky.

Becks and Alaric both had enough general experience working with me to know better than to come poking before I was at least standing under my own power. The voices from the kitchen resumed, a little louder now that they knew they didn't have to worry about waking me anymore. Leaving my head cradled in my hands, I considered my options. Going back to sleep was at the top of the list and had the extra added bonus of not requiring me to think about anything. Unfortunately, whoever was killing the people with reservoir conditions wasn't going to wait around for me to get my shit together, and if anyone realized Kelly was still alive, we probably didn't have all that much time.

There was always the possibility that time had already run out. If Kelly's original fake ID was compromised, they might have tracked her across the country with it. That didn't explain why they waited for her to reach us before going on the offensive, but maybe she just hadn't held still long enough before that. They wouldn't be tracking her that way again. Her fake ID was so much slag in the remains of Oakland, and nobody outside the team knew she was alive.

Now we just had to keep it that way.

The outbreak could have been triggered in response to my call to Dr. Wynne, but that didn't seem likely. The timelines didn't synch. That level of outbreak would take time to set up. Even if it had started the second my call was connected to the CDC, there wasn't time for all those people to amplify and get into position. Whoever targeted us—assuming it was a "who," which had to be my operating assumption, at least until something came along to make a strong case for coincidence—had more time than my phone call gave them.

I lifted my head, groaning again, and stood. One of the bulldogs had turned my discarded shirt into a makeshift doggy bed, probably as revenge for my taking up the entire couch. It opened one eye to watch me as I approached, and made a small "*buff*" noise that might have been intimidating, if it hadn't been roughly the size of an overweight housecat. "Whatever, dude," I said, putting up my hands. "I wasn't that cold anyway."

Alaric, Becks, and Kelly were gathered around the kitchen table when I came shuffling in, making a half-hearted attempt to push my spiked-up hair back into a semblance of order. All three looked over at my entrance. Becks raised her eyebrows.

"You're looking bright and shirtless this morning," she said, dryly. "Did you decide that clothes were for sissies?"

"Dog took my shirt," I replied. "Where's Maggie? Is there coffee? If Maggie's hiding because she drank all the coffee, it's not going to be pretty."

"Ms. Garcia is, um, out back, in the garden," said Kelly. She gestured toward the back door as she spoke, looking distinctly uncomfortable. Understandable. She'd probably never been in a private residence open to the scary, scary outside world before. Sometimes I think George was right when she said that people want to be afraid.

"Coffee's on the stove," said Alaric, before adding quickly, "Do we have a plan, or are we just going to sit around here drinking coffee and waiting to see what happens next?"

"That depends on the Doc." I walked over to the stove. A half-full pot of coffee was on the central heating plate. "We know what happened yesterday wasn't just bad timing. So I guess the question is, Doc, were they after us, or were they after you?"

Silence fell behind me. I took a mug from the rack and poured myself a cup of coffee, taking a slow, patient sip as I waited for someone to say something. The liquid was almost hot enough to be scalding, and it tasted like it had been brewed just this side of Heaven. I'll drink Coke for George all day if I have to, but there's nothing like that first cup of coffee to get the morning started.

Finally, in a small voice, Kelly said, "Dr. Wynne thought we were managing to get me out before our plan could be compromised. With most of my team dead, it's not like there were that many people who knew about the clone, or what we were going to do with it. It should have been a clean escape. He did say... When I left, he said you were probably in danger anyway, because of..." She stopped. A lot of people have trouble talking about what happened to George when I'm in the room. I can't decide whether it's because they don't want to remind me that I was the one to pull the trigger, or if it's because they can't deal with the fact that she's still with me. Maybe they just don't feel like getting punched in the face.

The *why* doesn't matter much to me. The end result is the same: George stays dead, and no one talks about it.

"You knew we were in danger before you reached us?" I recognized the warning in the tone Becks was using. She started as a Newsie, and she processes facts a little faster than most Irwins. That gives her the ability to sound very reasonable, and the more reasonable she sounds, the more danger you're in. "And you didn't say anything?"

"There will be no killing the Doc," I said, walking over to the settle at the table. "She's just as screwed as we are, so play nicely, okay? This isn't her fault."

Kelly nodded firmly, looking more frustrated than anything else. "I *tried* to say something. I was e-mailing you for three weeks before we hit the point where I couldn't hang around in Memphis anymore."

The spam filters, said George quietly.

I winced.

"A secure phone line would have been noticed in a facility as locked down as the CDC," Kelly continued. "When Dr. Wynne evacuated me, I wound up drugged and stuffed into the back of a truck that was hauling dry goods to California. I barely had a pulse for a few thousand miles. I definitely wasn't in any condition to make phone calls."

"You could still have opened the conversation with the fact that we might want to evacuate," said Becks.

"Would you have listened?" asked Kelly.

Becks looked away.

Kelly sighed. "I thought not. Look: I had no way of knowing things would get that bad, that fast. The world doesn't work like that in the lab. Things go slower there." She took a shaky breath, calming herself. "Our research team was down to three when we realized none of us were safe. We had to get someone out alive if we wanted to preserve our results. Dr. O'Shea wasn't willing to take the risk, and Dr. Li had a family. It had to be me. So I went to Dr. Wynne."

"And he had you cloned," I deadpanned. "Naturally. Why didn't I think of that?"

"I had to seem to die—it was the only way that I'd have a chance at getting away with our results. Dr. O'Shea was working on a nerve study that required full-body subjects. She set up the clone. It was supposed to be her DNA."

"Swap-off happened at the techie level?" asked Alaric, suddenly paying attention. He always paid attention when something started smelling like a story.

"Yes," said Kelly. "One intern handed the sample to another intern, who handed it to a lab tech when Dr. Wynne asked him to run an errand instead, and by that point, it was easy enough to get the sample from the incubator and swap in one of my own samples instead."

Ask her why the source DNA matters, prompted George.

"Right," I muttered, before saying, in a more conversational tone, "Why does the source DNA matter? I thought the CDC was exempt from the prohibition against cloning."

"Clones are illegal for moral reasons. The CDC's dispensation allows researchers to do full-body cloning for research purposes, and the moral questions are skirted by permitting only self-cloning," said Kelly. "That way the question of the clone having a soul can be politely ignored, and the religious community doesn't feel the need to shut us down."

"Because presumably there's just one soul per genetic pattern, and the original donor holds the copyright?" I asked. Kelly nodded. I snorted. "That's a fun piece of bureaucratic jump rope if I've ever seen one. So fine, they think they cloned this other lady, and they actually cloned you. What's going to keep somebody from doing the math when they crack the factory seal on her and there's nothing there?"

"Dr. O'Shea died two weeks ago. There was an error in her car's electrical system and she lost control on the freeway." Kelly looked at me, lips drawing back in a smile that looked more like a rictus. "It was very sad. Our superiors were quick to offer their regrets and let us know that if we wanted to shut down the program, they'd support our moving on to other research projects. An immediate destruction notice was issued on her clone, since the original was deceased. It was officially destroyed four days before my 'death.'" She hesitated before adding, much more softly, "Dr. Li was killed in a lab accident the day after that."

"How come no one noticed they were short a clone?" asked Becks.

Kelly shrugged, shaking off her brief malaise. "Clones are considered lab waste. Anyone can dispose of them."

"So you disposed of the clone that didn't exist."

"Exactly."

"What did I miss?" asked Maggie, coming in with a basket full of tomatoes over one arm. "Hey, Shaun, you're up. Can I get you anything? Toast? Omelet?"

"An omelet would be great, and you got here just in time to hear the Doc explain how they broke her clone out of storage and slaughtered it like a chicken so she'd be free to come and make herself our problem." I took another drink of coffee and stopped, grimacing. "Also, you got any Coke?"

Alaric and Becks exchanged a look. Maggie simply nodded, saying, "I'll get you one in a minute," as she continued across the kitchen to begin fussing with her harvest. "Keep talking, everybody. I'm sure I'll catch right up."

"Great." I looked back to Kelly. "Carry on, Doc. We're burning daylight here, and you've just made that a rare commodity around these parts."

"My clone wasn't slaughtered like a chicken," she protested. "Dr. Wynne knows some people. Professional people. He hired them to break in and shoot the clone after we'd decanted it. They guaranteed a kill on the first shot. It didn't have time to suffer."

"And then you ran for us."

"And then I ran for you." Kelly glanced away. Her gaze fell on the open door and she grimaced, looking down at her lap instead. "Your... There were a lot of records detailing the progression of Georgia Mason's retinal Kellis-Amberlee. The particular nature of your mutual upbringing provided an invaluable source of data."

"Meaning what, exactly?" asked Maggie, putting a skillet on the stove.

"She means there were cameras on us all the time when we were kids, and we got a lot of med tests so we could follow the 'rents into proscribed areas." I watched Kelly. Kelly kept watching her lap. "It made George a great case study, without any of those pesky release forms getting in the way."

"Mm-hmm," said Kelly, looking up. "That also makes you a great case study."

"Me?"

You, confirmed George, quietly. *Prolonged exposure to someone with a reservoir condition is odd enough, but for you to be my—*

"—makes your immunological reactions uniquely fascinating," said Kelly, her words overlaying Georgia's until she drowned out the voice in my head. I managed not to jump. My hand still shook hard enough to slosh the remainder of my coffee dangerously close to the edge. I put the cup down on the table. Kelly didn't seem to notice. "We would have been asking you to come in for some tests later this year if our study had been allowed to develop normally. Just to see if there were any deep abnormalities that might explain why she developed retinal Kellis-Amberlee and you didn't. Of course, with Georgia dead, there's always the possibility whoever's killing the people with reservoir conditions could come after you, instead. We don't know what the motive is there."

"So combine Shaun's possibly fucked-up immune system with all the footage we've got, and our known connections to the research team, and we're a target, is that it?" asked Becks. "Note for the future? This is the sort of shit you should maybe lead off with. 'Hi, nice to see you, just faked my own death, and PS, the people who want me dead are probably after you, too.'"

"Yes," said Maggie pleasantly, as she started cracking eggs into the pan. "It might've saved Dave's life."

"That's not fair," interjected Kelly.

Maggie ignored her. "Two eggs or three, Shaun?"

"Three, please. I doubt we're going to be stopping for a big lunch."

"Good. Will you need to bury her body in the forest behind my house tonight, or will you be keeping her around a little longer for informational purposes?" This question was asked just as pleasantly as the last. Maggie's tone didn't hold anything to indicate that killing Kelly was of any more or less importance than my omelet.

Maggie can be like that sometimes. She's grown beyond her upbringing, for the most part, but sometimes she's still a spoiled little rich girl whose response to things she doesn't like begins and ends with getting rid of them.

It's better not to argue with her when she gets that way. "Informational purposes, but I promise to let you know when that changes," I said. Kelly paled. I decided that the polite thing would be to ignore it. "Any news out of Oakland?"

"The announcement of Dave's death went up about an hour ago," said Alaric, quietly.

"Okay." I looked at my coffee, and sighed. "What do our site stats look like?"

"Up five percent globally, Dave's reports are up thirty-five percent, and we have three syndication requests for his Alaska material from last year." Alaric sounded a lot more confident in this answer. That wasn't surprising. Next to Mahir, there's nobody who tracks our standings as carefully as Alaric does.

"Did Maggie fill you in on the cover story?" Everyone nodded. "Good. Has anyone posted?" Everyone shook their heads. "Not so good. I need you all online. We were camping in Santa Cruz, our apartment got blown up, we're shaken, we're going to stay in the field for a few days while we recover. Maggie, I want you to make it clear that you're here alone. Tack on a poem I don't understand, with lots of creepy-ass death imagery— the usual—and then if you can double security, that would probably be a bonus. Nobody say anything about the Doc. She's not here."

"I'll get right on that," Maggie said, walking over and slapping a can of Coke into my hand before putting the plate with my omelet next to my discarded coffee cup.

"Good. Becks—"

"Come up with some believable outdoor footage." She stood, picking up her plate. "I'll set up out in the van."

"Good. Alaric—"

"Ground-level analysis of the Oakland tragedy, short memorial piece on Dave." He rose as he spoke, expression already far away. "I should be able to cobble something together fast enough to let me hit the forums and do some damage control after."

"That's excellent. Now what are we going to do about the Doc?"

"I thought you'd ask that," said Alaric, looking briefly smug. He likes being efficient. "I checked Buffy's stock of precoded IDs. Kelly looks enough like Buffy did that she can use most of them."

"Any of them come with medical credentials?"

"No strict medical, but three scientific. I have an ichthyologist—a fish scientist," Alaric added, seeing my look of blank incomprehension. "Also a theoretical physicist and a psychologist."

"I minored in psychology," said Kelly, sounding relieved to have something to contribute to the discussion. "I've never practiced, but I can fake it if I have to."

"Great. Alaric, get the ID up and running, make sure it passes any surface checks people are likely to run, and go from there. You're still a doc, Doc. We're going to hire you to replace Dave as soon as we come back to civilization." Kelly looked faintly alarmed. I grinned. "Don't worry. Mahir will ghostwrite your articles, and we'll just publish them under—what byline are we publishing these under, Alaric?"

"Barbara Tinney."

"Great. We'll publish them under the Barbara Tinney byline. It reinforces the impression that you're legit—and we can just call you 'Doc' in public."

"You're crazy," pronounced Becks.

"And you're carrying eight guns," I replied. "Now that we've covered what everybody knows, can we move on? When I post, I'll say a few words about Dave and how honored we all are to have worked with him, bullshit, bullshit, blah, blah, blah." I waved my free hand vaguely before cracking open the Coke and taking a deep drink. The acidic sweetness hit the back of my throat like a slap. I choked a little, getting my breath back, and finished: "I'll hit the staff boards. Give everybody the edited version of the situation. Be done with your reports and ready to roll by ten."

"Where are we going?" asked Kelly, looking like she couldn't tell whether she should be relieved to be getting away from Maggie or worried about what was coming next.

"And why are we going *now*?" asked Alaric.

I couldn't blame him for the question. He wasn't there when we lost Buffy, or when we lost George. I took a deep breath, held it long enough to be sure I'd stay calm while I answered him, and said, "If we sit here until we feel ready to move, we're never going to move again. We're going to get comfortable, and we're going to stay here until we die. We don't want to run off half-cocked, either, but there's a line between the two, and if we don't find it, we're fucked. As for where we're going..." I turned a predatory smile on Kelly. "That's what the Doc here is going to tell me."

"Me?" she asked, sounding surprised.

"You. Come on. We're using the living room terminal, and you're going to explain what I'm not getting out of all those lovely notes you brought for us." Picking up my omelet, I added, "You have your assignments, everybody. Two hours. Be ready."

Kelly followed me to the living room and sat next to me at the desk.

"Perk up. It's not like you went out of the frying pan and into the fire. It's more like out of the frying pan and into the industrial-strength toaster."

"I don't understand." She shook her head, looking perplexed. "This is our chance to go to ground. Why aren't we doing it?"

"And where would we go? Canada? We're not going to get any answers there. I trust Maggie's system to keep us off the grid, and whoever arranged to have Oakland deleted is going to have trouble sweeping it under the rug if they pull it a second time. I know my job, okay?" I tapped the side of my head, smile fading. "I've got a few brain cells still working up here."

"I didn't mean—"

"Don't start. My mood stays better if you don't start." I turned to the keyboard. The terminal turned itself on as soon as its sensors "saw" me looking at it, and I typed my password to unlock the home network.

"Noted," she said. She didn't sound like she approved, but at the moment, that was at the bottom of my priority list.

"Good." All Maggie's computer equipment was top of the line. Having parents with money and Buffy Meissonier as your original technical consultant will do that. "I spent a few hours after the rest of you went to bed going through those files you brought us last night. Didn't understand half of what I was reading, but George managed to explain some of it for me."

Kelly's expression went very still, like she was fighting an inner battle to keep herself from pointing out that George couldn't explain anything, because, guess what, George was dead. I've seen that look a lot since the funeral. As long as she could keep herself from saying anything, I could keep myself from getting angry that she'd want to.

"Really," she said finally, in a neutral tone that could have meant just about anything.

Good enough for me. "Really," I confirmed. "What I'm curious about is the list of labs. How many of those are going to be safe for us to visit? Where can we go to get the fieldwork side of the equation?" Kelly's files gave us numbers, but they didn't give us the rest of the picture. If we were going to understand, we needed to talk to someone who could confirm or contest the data—and if the CDC had been steered away from researching the reservoir conditions for as long as Kelly said, the labs on our list might have pieces of the puzzle we didn't even know existed yet.

"All the labs on list A are ones with head researchers a member of the team worked with directly at some point, either before or after they went into the private sector," she said, sounding much more relaxed now that she was dealing with verified facts instead of crazy reporters. "List B contains the labs where someone had personal experience with the supporting researchers, but not the head of the lab, and list C is made up of the labs where we had only secondhand information on the people working there. Reputations, credentials, whether or not they bothered to check their sources..."

"What about list D?" My hands were moving as we spoke, spewing out line after line of borderline coherent claptrap. It was the day after a death. We'd be expected to update—nothing was going to get us out of that, not even actually dying; George's blog may have changed names when she died, but her backlog of files meant she missed less than a week. That didn't mean we were expected to be profound.

"Ah." Kelly's tone was disapproving enough that I actually glanced toward her. Her lips were pursed into a tight moue of distaste. "That would be the labs where the researchers have been confirmed as following less than ethical paths in their research."

"What, vivisection? Human test subjects?" I pressed Post on my first entry of the day, switched from my own feed to the administrative, and started typing again as I asked, "Full-body cloning?"

"It's different when the CDC does it," she said sharply. "We have a dispensation."

"So?" I shrugged, continuing to type. "That doesn't make it right. How many of the labs on list D would have been on list A if you weren't being judgmental?"

Kelly sighed. "Two, at most."

"Okay. Either of them anywhere near here?"

There was a horrified pause as she realized what I was asking. "Shaun, you don't understand! These people were blacklisted from reputable scientific circles for a lot of reasons, and not all of them were as petty as you seem to think! These are not the secret heroes of some underground resistance against the evil CDC—they're bioterrorists and crazy people, and they're *dangerous*. We could get seriously hurt if we go to them. We could get *killed*."

"And we could get killed if we stay here. I'm not seeing a difference in results." I picked up George's Coke and took another swig. "Your objections are noted. Can any of these people be trusted? At all? Or do I just pick one at random and hope they aren't on the Frankenstein end of the 'mad doctor' scale?"

Kelly swallowed, throat working as she struggled against some clear inner impulse not to answer. Finally she said, "Dr. Abbey. I read some of the work she did on reservoir conditions before she went off the grid. I think she'd be able to help us."

"Fine. Where is she?"

She sighed. "Portland, Oregon."

"That's a five- or six-hour drive if we take the direct route," I said, sipping again from the can. "Annoying, but manageable. What was the big crime that got them blacklisted?"

"Unethical experiments involving the manipulation of the viral structure of Kellis-Amberlee. None involving human subjects, thank God, or she and her staff would be in federal prison for the rest of their lives."

"I'm surprised they aren't in federal prison anyway. How much blackmail material did she have?"

"Enough." Kelly shook her head. "I don't know much—it was all before my time—but she worked for Health Canada. Joint research team, theirs and ours. Some bad things happened, and she quit. Ever since then, she's been pretty careful about who she lets get anywhere near her or her research."

"Better watch out, Doc. That sounded almost like respect."

"I like people who are serious about their work." She shrugged. "Dr. Abbey was devoted to figuring out Kellis-Amberlee."

"Somebody has to be." I swung back around to the keyboard. "Better go see if Maggie's got something you can wear, Doc. We're going on another road trip."

———

We made it out of Oakland alive. I'm still not sure how we did it, except that my team is made up of some of the best people I've ever known, and I don't deserve them. I keep making it out of places alive. I think the universe is fucking with me.

I did something during the evacuation that you shouldn't ever do. I went back for George's black box. I'd do it again, too. Because there's already not enough of her left in this world, and I'm running out of things to hold onto.

Fuck, I miss her.

**—From *Adaptive Immunities*,
the blog of Shaun Mason, April 12, 2041. Unpublished.**

Santa Cruz is gorgeous this time of year. I realize it's a zombie-infested wasteland, but hell, at least the rents are good, right? Besides, there's a reason this used to be one of the state's most popular vacation destinations, and I doubt it had very much to do with their boardwalk, no matter what the old tourism brochures try to tell you.

We're still working on getting Alaric ready for his field trials. Next up, Becks is going to take him down to the beach and see if they can find a zombie seal to poke at. Never a dull moment around here. Oh, well. It's better than a desk job.

—From *Adaptive Immunities*,
the blog of Shaun Mason, April 12, 2041

Eight

Maggie didn't look *happy* about being sent off to outfit the Doc, but she did it; that was really all I could ask of her. I stayed in the living room, getting a few posts up on the site and making it clear that we'd been nowhere near Oakland when the bombs came down. While I was at it, I surfed over to the medical blogs to see what they had to say about the "death" of Dr. Kelly Connolly. With the way they were going on about her—lost scion of one of the CDC's proudest heritage families, rising young star of the virology world—you'd think she'd been on the verge of curing Kellis-Amberlee, not just slaving in the CDC salt mines with the rest of the peons.

That's the power of good press, said George dryly.

I chuckled, and got back to work.

Alaric came into the room with a half-eaten piece of toast in one hand as I was firing off an e-mail to authorize the continuing sale of Dave's merchandise line. "Did you see the crime scene photos on the gossip sites?" he asked. I nodded. He continued: "This is, like, *Invasion of the Body Snatchers* levels of scary. I always knew cloning technology was better than we saw here on the fringes, but the CDC employs the best doctors in the world, and even they couldn't tell it was a clone."

"Could be worse."

"How?"

"I have no idea. But it can always be worse." I glanced toward the kitchen door. "Where's Becks?"

"She's helping Maggie with Dr. Connolly." He took a bite of toast, sitting down at the monitor next to mine. "I don't think she wanted to leave them alone together."

"I always knew she was smart."

Alaric grunted as he logged on and started working the message boards. I leaned over to "supervise," which really meant "look over his shoulder, drinking a Coke and pretending to pay attention." He ignored me. I took his tendency to shut me out while he worked personally at first, until George assured me that he'd always done the same thing to her. He was just one of those people who really liked to focus on his work.

I love how you ignore the inherent impossibility of me telling you something you didn't already know, George said.

"Don't start with me," I said, and took another drink of Coke. That's normally enough to shut her up for a little while. When that doesn't work, I zone out in front of the news feeds. Comforting for her, educational for me. Everybody wins.

It's true.

"It's a shitty thing to say and you know it."

Alaric ignored my conversation with the air. He learned the hard way that sometimes it was best to turn a blind eye. During our first few months in the office, he asked who I was talking to every time I forgot and answered George aloud, and he pointed out that she was dead more than once. He stopped after I finally lost my temper and introduced my fist to his face, resulting in skinned knuckles on my part and a broken nose on his. He still flinches if I move too fast. Guess I can't blame him. If my boss were a potentially crazy man with a mean right hook, I'd probably be a little jumpy, too.

The title of one of the threads caught my eye. I leaned forward, tapping Alaric's screen. "There. Can you expand that thread?"

"Sure." He clicked the header line: *CDC Safety Precautions Insufficient?* "I don't see what it has to do with—"

"Just scroll."

"Right," he said, and started scrolling.

The thread started as a discussion of the break-in at the Memphis CDC and devolved into a discussion of CDC security precautions over the course of half a dozen posts. As I'd hoped, the posters quickly started naming names, citing every CDC doctor, intern, affiliate, and publicity person to have died during the last eighteen months. "Alaric, can you grab the names of the deceased and start calling up obituaries and circumstance-of-death reports? If anyone looks at you funny, you can say you're basing a report off this thread."

"Sure," he said, warming to the idea as he saw where I was going with it. "I can do you one better. I still have a few of Buffy's old worms live and functional. I'll set one of them digging for connections between the deceased employees, Kelly Connolly, Joseph Wynne, and any other unusual or unexplained deaths in their circle of friends."

"Just don't get caught or traced and you can do whatever you want."

"Awesome." Alaric bent forward, starting to type. He had the same focus I've seen from George, Rick, and every other Newsie I've ever met. I could probably have danced naked on his desk without getting him to do more than grunt and shove me out of the way of his screen. Content that I'd done something useful, I got up and walked to the kitchen. A fresh Coke would keep me from thinking too hard about the tools he was using to do the job.

There are people who say that Kellis-Amberlee and its undead side effects are going to bring about the end of the human race. I tend to disagree with this perspective. I'm pretty sure that if the zombies were going to destroy humanity, they would've done it back in 2014, when they first showed up. I think that if anything destroys the human race at this point, it's going to be the human race itself.

With my posts done, Alaric working, and Becks and Maggie sequestered with Kelly, I didn't know what to do with myself. I settled for sitting at the kitchen table with my fresh can of Coke, waiting for something to happen. My patience was rewarded about fifteen minutes later, when something happened.

Footsteps descended the stairs and Becks appeared in the kitchen doorway, hands raised in a warding gesture. Not the best sign. "Okay, Shaun, before you freak out, this was the best way to do it."

I raised an eyebrow. "That's a really shitty elevator pitch, and I would never buy your project based on that. Just so you know."

"I'm just saying, don't freak out." She finished stepping into the kitchen, looking back over her shoulder. "Come on, Kelly."

"I feel like an idiot," said Kelly. She moved into view, Maggie half a step behind her.

I stared.

Buffy left a lot of her shit to me and George when she died. Her parents gave us even more. We were her best friends, and they couldn't think of anything else to do with her collection of gaudy jewelry and hippie skirts. The fact that I'm not a cross-dresser and George wouldn't have been caught dead in that sort of thing didn't matter: They were grieving parents, we were Buffy's friends, and we got it all. Only we didn't have much room in the apartment, and the idea of getting rid of her things left me feeling sick. So we stored them at Maggie's.

Becks was looking at me with rare anxiety, clearly waiting for me to say something. I swallowed the lump that was blocking my throat and said the first thing that came to mind:

"Wow. That's...different."

Kelly was wearing a multicolored broomstick skirt, a white peasant blouse, and a patchwork vest with little mirrors sewn all over it. They twinkled when she moved, not quite as gaudily as the dozen or so bangle bracelets crusted with LED "jewels." There were matching "jewels" on the straps of her sandals, which looked entirely impractical. I knew better. Buffy was an idealist and sort of an idiot, but she knew the importance of being prepared, and she didn't own a single pair of shoes she couldn't run in.

God, I miss her, said George, almost too quietly for me to hear.

"Me too," I murmured, just as softly.

Georgette "Buffy" Meissonier was the original head of the Fictional News Division. She designed almost all of the After the End Times network and computer systems. She was one of the only people I ever met who could make George smile on a reliable basis. She was sweet, and she was funny, and she was smart as hell, and she was an enormous geek, and every time her name comes up, I have to remind myself that she didn't do any of the things she did on purpose. Sure, she let Tate's men into our system, and sure, a lot of people got killed because of that, but she had the best intentions.

Buffy died because of what she did. On the days when I'm really getting my crazy on, that seems like sufficient payment. Of course, those are the days when I can convince myself that George isn't dead, just, I don't know, mysteriously intangible and pissed off about it. Most of the time, well...

I'm just a little bit bitter.

Either Maggie or Becks—I was betting on Maggie—had hacked off most of Kelly's hair, leaving her with a spiky mess that stuck up in all directions. I'd never been so glad a woman was blonde in my life, because that was exactly the way George always wore her hair—too short for the zombies to grab, long enough to be controllable with a minimum of effort—and if Kelly had been a brunette, I think I would have screamed.

"Well?" asked Maggie.

"Right." I swallowed several more possible responses, starting with "dead friend's clothes, dead sister's haircut, good job" and going downhill from there. "She definitely looks, uh, really different." That seemed insufficient, so I added, "Good job."

Becks grinned, looking unaccountably pleased.

Kelly, meanwhile, reached up to touch her hair with one hand, saying, "I haven't kept my hair this short since I was a little kid. I don't even know what to do with it."

"Better cropped than arrested for hoaxing the CDC, Doc," I said.

Kelly sighed. "I wish I could argue with that."

"I wish a lot of things," I said, and stood. "Come on, gang. Let's get moving."

Herding everyone out of the house was more difficult than it should have been, since Kelly was exhausted and wanted to stay behind, leading to loud protests on Maggie's part. She said she didn't trust people alone with her dogs. What Kelly was supposed to do to a pack of epileptic bulldogs wasn't entirely clear to me, but Maggie was firm: No one was staying home unsupervised—and, apparently, the enormous army of security ninjas lurking in the bushes didn't count as supervision. To complicate matters further, Maggie refused to stay behind.

"I just lost Dave," she said. "I'm not letting you drive off and leave me here. If I'm going to lose everyone, I'm going to go with you."

I couldn't really bring myself to argue with that.

After a lot of shouting, some plea bargaining, and an outright threat to leave Alaric sitting by the side of the road, we wound up with Becks driving the van, Alaric manning the forums from the passenger seat, and Kelly riding in the back. I drove the bike, Maggie riding pillion. She insisted, probably because she didn't trust herself in an enclosed space with Kelly. Dave's death wasn't the Doc's fault. Maggie would realize that eventually. I hoped.

I'd never driven any real distance with a passenger—not unless you counted George, who didn't actually change the way the bike was balanced, or make it necessary for me to compensate for additional weight. Oh, I'd *been* a passenger on the bike often enough, back when George was doing the driving, but it wasn't the same thing by a long shot. It didn't help that Maggie wasn't used to riding a motorcycle and didn't know to shift her weight to help me keep us balanced. If we'd encountered any real problems, we would have been screwed.

There aren't many real problems along I-5. The combination of tight security, large stretches with little to no human habitation, and most motorists being unwilling to drive more than a few miles has done a lot to make distance travel safer for those of us crazy enough to attempt it.

Buffy died during a long-distance road trip, when a sniper shot out the wheels of the truck she was riding in. But beyond little things like that, it's perfectly safe.

Safe. Now there's a laugh.

Nearly six hours and fifteen security checkpoints later, we were approaching Eugene. I-5 is the fastest route to damn near any major city on the West Coast, but it has its downsides, like the constant barricades.

We had to stop every time we drove into or out of a city, or even too close to one, by whatever the local definition of "too close" happened to be. It was always the same song and dance: Where are you going? Why? Can we see your licenses? Can we see your credentials? Would you like to submit to a retinal scan? Do you really think you have a choice?

The CDC had no reason to be tracking our movement—not yet, anyway. Our papers were in order, and every checkpoint wound up waving us through, but the stops still made me nervous. I was being paranoid. After the past twenty-four hours, I figured it was justified.

The orange light in the corner of my visor started blinking, signaling an incoming call. "Answer," I said.

"Hey, boss." There was a note of tension underscoring Alaric's normally laid-back tone. "We're an hour and a half out of Portland, according to the GPS. You going to give us the actual address soon, or are we going to play guessing games with the surface streets?"

"We're not going to Portland," I said. Becks started swearing in the background. I almost laughed. "Tell Becks to keep her panties on. We're going to a town *near* Portland. It's called Forest Grove. We're heading for an old business park that got shut down during the Rising and never officially reopened. The address is in the GPS. I uploaded it under the header 'Shaun's secret porn store.'"

Charming, commented George.

"Ew," said Alaric. "Okay, accessing coordinates now. Is there anything else we need to know?"

"You know what I do, and you can pump the Doc for information if you need to." I swerved to avoid a pothole, feeling Maggie's arms tighten around my waist. She was staying amazingly calm for a woman who almost never left her house. I was starting to wonder exactly what was in that "herbal tea" she drank right before we left. "We're heading for an illegal biotech lab to talk to somebody the CDC is too afraid of to fuck with. What could possibly go wrong?"

There was a long silence before Alaric said, "I'm hanging up on you now."

"That's probably for the best."

"You're fucked in the head."

"That's probably true. See you in Forest Grove." The amber light flicked off. I allowed myself a grim chuckle and hit the gas. Our little road trip of the damned was well under way.

Do you have a plan? asked George.

"You know better," I replied. I wasn't worried about Maggie hearing me talk to myself; the roar of the wind would keep my voice from reaching her. Weird as it might seem, George and I actually had a measure of privacy, despite having another human being with her arms wrapped around my waist. If Maggie had been driving, I might have actually been able to fool myself into thinking everything was the way it was supposed to be, even if the illusion would only last until the bike stopped.

George laughed. I smiled, relaxing, and kept on driving. Next stop: Forest Grove.

The Caspell Business Park was located at the edge of town, in what was probably considered an area ripe for expansion before the dead decided to get up and walk around. It was built on a model popular before the Rising, all open spaces and broad pathways between the buildings. I'd be willing to bet that more than half those buildings had automatic doors at one point, totally unsecured against the shambling infected. It was no wonder the local authorities hadn't bothered trying to reclaim the place; if there was anything remarkable about it, it was that it hadn't been burned to the ground.

According to the Doc's instructions, the place we were looking for was in the old IT complex, where the buildings had been constructed according to much more sensible schematics: airtight, watertight, no windows, no real danger of contamination if you remembered to lock the damn doors. Georgia and I went to preschool in a pre-Rising IT complex, and we were just as secure as we could possibly be. Locating the lab in that sort of structure made a lot of sense, especially with the rest of the business park providing excellent, if hazardous, cover. Not even the bravest Irwin was going to stumble on the place by mistake, and the ones who were dumb enough to think it was a good idea would all be eaten before they arrived.

The parking garage had developed a worrying leftward tilt. I eyed it, shook my head, and kept driving. The last thing we needed was to get a parking garage dropped on our heads, or worse, dropped on our vehicles while we were inside the building. On the other hand, we'd be dead if the garage fell on us, and we wouldn't have to worry about this shit anymore.

You're in a fabulous state of mind today, said George.

"Enjoy it while it lasts," I said, and continued to blaze a trail through the deserted business park. Maggie clung a little tighter every time we hit a bump, but she didn't jerk around enough to make me lose my balance. That was a good thing. The broken pavement was littered with rusted metal, broken glass, and other debris; if we went sprawling, we'd be lucky to get away with just a tetanus shot.

The loading dock behind the IT complex was clear and showed signs of semirecent upkeep. That was promising. I pulled up and killed the engine, waiting for Maggie to dismount before deploying the kickstand and sliding to the relatively unbroken pavement. My thighs ached from too many hours on the road, but my head was clearer than it had been in weeks. Knowing that I'm actually *doing* something has that effect on me.

The van pulled up a few yards away. The side door was open before the wheels had fully stopped turning, and Alaric jumped down, fumbling his field pack on as he trotted toward us. I pulled off my helmet and smirked at him. "Did you have a nice drive?"

"I hate you," he said flatly.

"That's nice," said Maggie. Alaric shot her a look, and she smiled, removing her helmet. Her pupils were slightly enlarged—not in the exaggerated manner that would indicate a live infection, but in a softer, more relaxed manner that I recognized from dealing with high-strung reporters at press conferences. Her herbal tea definitely contained a few extra ingredients.

I considered pulling her aside for a talk about taking psychoactive substances before going into the field and decided to let it pass. It wasn't like she was a combatant. She and Kelly were so much dead weight if we got attacked. She might as well be pre-anesthetized dead weight, in case things went poorly. As it was, she was only legal to be with us because the town zoning regulations made this place technically safe. Very technically.

Becks was the next out of the van, her own field pack already in place. Her scowl looked like it had been permanently affixed to her face. "You owe me," she said, coming to a stop next to Alaric.

"Me or Maggie?"

"*Yes*. No. I don't know. The only way to keep her quiet was to keep the radio turned to the medical news channel. If I'd been forced to spend another minute listening to the exciting new developments in the world of pharmaceuticals, I would have taken her head and—"

Kelly's hesitant emergence saved us from the details of what Becks would have done to her. She gave the parking lot a horrified look before hurrying toward us, demanding, "What are we doing *here*?"

"This is the address your file said we should be at, Doc."

"There must be some mistake."

"Nope. Underground lab, underground facilities." I tucked my helmet under my arm, looking at the low-slung buildings spread out around us. "Can anybody see the numbers on these things? We're looking for eleven."

"You can't mean we're actually going to go *inside*," said Kelly.

"No, Doc, we just drove a couple hundred miles to pose on the sidewalk." Becks shook her head before turning to stalk off toward the buildings, scanning for more signs of habitation.

Kelly sighed. "This day just gets better and better."

"Don't worry. I'm sure that soon, we'll be looking back on this moment as one of the good times." I followed Maggie, Alaric close behind me. Kelly stayed where she was for a few moments, staring after us. I could see her out of the corner of my eye. It was all I could do to not start laughing—which would have been entirely inappropriate, true, but it would have felt so damn good.

Be careful, George cautioned. *Push her too far and she'll freak out. We need her to stay calm, stay cooperative, and keep talking.*

"I thought she'd already told us everything," I muttered, as Kelly started running to catch up. Alaric cast a glance in my direction, but didn't say anything.

You're not that dumb.

There was nothing I could say to that. I kept walking, assessing the buildings surrounding us as I moved. I wasn't exactly expecting a big sign that said ILLEGAL VIROLOGY LAB HERE, but it would have been nice. The buildings in the IT complex seemed to be essentially identical, all square, boxy, and in reasonably good repair, as long as you weren't judging by the paint jobs. The building closest to us even had its original set of cell tower repeaters bolted to the roof, their narrow antennae making a familiar lightning-jag outline against the afternoon sky.

I stopped in my tracks. Looking bemused, Alaric did the same. "What year did we go to block-by-block private cell towers? Anybody know?"

"Uh...two thousand twenty," said Alaric, after a long pause to do the math inside his head. "I remember when they put ours in."

"Uh-huh. This is a pre-Rising complex. So who installed that?" I jerked a thumb toward the antennae.

Alaric's eyes went wide. "Oh."

"Yeah, oh. Over here, guys." I waved for the others to join us and started up the cracked pathway leading to the building door. Locked. No real surprise, that; if I were running an illegal biotech lab, I wouldn't exactly want scavengers or thrill-seekers dropping in on me unannounced. I rapped my knuckles against the metal of the door itself, hearing the echoes they sent ringing dully into the space beyond.

No one answered. That really wasn't a surprise, either. "Maybe we should shoot the lock out," suggested Becks.

I gave her a dubious look. "Did you just suggest discharging a firearm into a door that may be attached to a lab? Like, 'explosive chemicals and weird machinery and God knows what else' lab?"

Becks shrugged. "At least we'd be doing something."

"We *are* doing something. We're getting inside." I knocked again. After a several-second pause, I cleared my throat, and shouted, "This is Shaun Mason, from After the End Times. We're here to speak to Dr. Abbey. Is she available? It's about the reservoir conditions."

The echoes of my knock were still ringing when the door swung open, revealing a short, cheerfully curvy woman with spiky brown hair streaked with bleach-white lines that looked more accidental than anything else. She was wearing an electric orange T-shirt that read DO NOT TAUNT THE OCTOPUS, jeans, and a lab coat, and was pointing a hunting rifle at the middle of my chest.

"Got any ID?" she asked. Her voice was light, even charming, with an accent I couldn't quite identify. She followed the question with a pleasant smile that didn't warm her eyes. This was a woman who wouldn't hesitate to pull the trigger if she thought we were giving her reason.

Not the friendliest greeting ever, and yet, not the least friendly, either, said George. Kelly gasped, either in shock or indignation. I wasn't sure which, and I really didn't care; it gave me something to respond to that wouldn't convince the woman with the large gun that I was insane right off the bat. That could come later, when she no longer had a weapon aimed at us.

"Hush," I said, making sure to slant my eyes toward Kelly, to at least give the impression that I was talking to her. Looking back to the woman in the doorway, I asked, "May I reach into my jacket for my press pass? I promise to do it slowly."

"Fine by me," she said, still smiling. "Joe! Come over here, boy." The largest dog I'd ever seen came ambling up behind her, its flapping jowls oozing strings of gooey white saliva. Its head looked like it was bigger than my chest. That may have been shock speaking, but there was no way I was going to volunteer to do the measurements. It didn't help that the damn thing was solid charcoal black, making it look unnervingly like the classic hellhound.

Kelly drew her breath in again. This time, I didn't blame her. Even Becks gasped, and I heard Maggie mutter something that sounded suspiciously like "Holy shit."

"Joe, guard," said the woman with the rifle. The massive canine obediently padded out onto the walkway, standing between her and the rest of us. It wasn't growling, glaring, or doing anything else actively hostile; it was simply standing there, being enormous. That was more than enough.

Reaching slowly into my jacket, I asked the most sensible question I could come up with under the circumstances: "Lady, what the *fuck* is that?"

That's right. Antagonize the woman who accessorizes with Cujo. I was tired of being the only dead one in this relationship.

I ignored her, choosing instead to focus on the woman who had the capacity to kill me. Call me single-minded. I tend to pay more attention to the immediate threats to life and limb, and leave the sarcastic dead people for later.

"That's Joe," said the woman, keeping the rifle aimed solidly at my chest. "He's shown me his ID. He's in no danger of getting himself shot."

"He's an English Mastiff," breathed Maggie, almost reverently. She started to step forward, one hand outstretched in a gesture I'd seen her use on her video blog whenever she was adding a new rescue to her miniature pack. She froze midgesture, eyes darting toward the woman with the rifle. "Is he friendly?"

"He will be, once I've seen your ID." Still, shotgun lady's smile took on a slightly more honest edge. "Joe's a good boy. He only eats the people I tell him to eat."

"How encouraging," I muttered, and held out my journalist's license. "Here. All my credentials are on file. Just run the code."

"And your people?" She jerked her chin toward the others, not bothering to take the license from my hand.

"Rebecca Atherton, head of the Irwins. Magdalene Garcia, head of the Fictionals. Alaric Kwong, he's with the Newsie division; the actual division head lives in London and isn't with us today. And this is—" For a sickening moment, I couldn't remember Kelly's alias.

Barbara Tinney, prompted Georgia.

"—Barbara Tinney," I echoed. "She's a social scientist on loan to the site for a few months. Getting some field experience."

From the look on the woman's face, she wasn't buying it. "Uh-huh. What are you folks doing here? Take a wrong turn on the way to a real story?"

I had two choices. I could try to come up with a plausible lie or I could tell her the truth. Once, I would have gone straight for the lie, the more interesting the better. I'm not really comfortable with that sort of thing anymore. "We came to see Dr. Abbey," I said, still holding out my license. "I have some files from the CDC that I need to have explained to me, and I thought she might be the person who could do it." Her brows lifted slightly; she was interested. I decided to press my luck. "I don't know if you follow the news, but my sister, Georgia Mason—"

"Retinal Kellis-Amberlee, wasn't it? I remember her. That was a real tragedy. I was very sorry to hear about it." The rifle wavered slightly. "I need a better reason for you to be here, and not at a 'real lab' somewhere."

Tell her. George's mental voice held a venom I rarely heard from her, even when she was alive. Then again, I couldn't blame her. The CDC's secret keeping might be the reason she was just a voice in my head.

In for a penny, in for a pound. "Barbara Tinney is a cover ID for Dr. Kelly Connolly of the CDC. The researcher who was killed in a break-in recently—that was a full-body clone. The real Dr. Connolly wasn't killed, and this is her." This time, Kelly's horrified expression was more than a bit betrayed. I did my best to ignore it. "She's how we got the files, and those same files identified this lab as being disreputable enough that no one would suspect we'd go to you, while still having staff who know how to find their asses with both hands. It didn't mention the giant dog, or we might have gone somewhere else. Now, are you Dr. Abbey, or can you tell us where to find her? I'm getting a little uncomfortable standing out here in the middle of nowhere."

"Well, why didn't you just say so?" The spiky-haired woman lowered her gun, suddenly smiling with genuine sincerity. "I'm Dr. Abbey—you can call me Shannon—and it's a pleasure to have guests. Especially guests with such interesting connections." Her smile dimmed as her gaze fell on Kelly, who was too busy staring at me to notice. "How about you all come inside, and we'll sort this out."

Alaric managed to find his voice, swallowing hard before he asked, "Will—will the dog be coming?"

"Of course he will. Joe's my lab manager, aren't you, Joe?" The enormous canine responded with a bark loud enough to make my ears hurt, tail beating against the ground. Maggie looked like she was physically restraining herself from running over and throwing her arms around his neck. Catching the look, Dr. Abbey laughed. "He doesn't bite. Joe, guest passes for all these folks. Got it?" The dog stood, tail still wagging.

"Does that mean I can pet him?" asked Maggie eagerly.

"Can you pet the moving legal violation after we get inside?" I asked.

"Come on." Dr. Abbey stepped aside, waving a hand at the open door. "Ladies first."

"That means us, princess." Becks looped her arm through Kelly's, tugging the reluctant doctor along with her as she went striding through the door to the lab. Maggie followed, still casting longing looks at the dog. Alaric gave me an uneasy glance and went after her, presumably unwilling to leave her alone in the company of a bona fide mad scientist.

Dr. Abbey crooked an eyebrow, studying me. "Will you be joining us?"

"Yeah. Thanks." I did my best to swagger as I walked toward the door, even going so far as to give her enormous pet a pat on the head as I passed him. "Good doggie."

Joe made a deep buffing sound in the back of his throat. I hoped that meant he was happy, rather than planning to bite my hand off at the shoulder. The law forbidding urban ownership of any domestic animal large enough to undergo Kellis-Amberlee amplification was named after my family. That means I never got much experience with dogs beyond Maggie's epileptic teacup bulldogs.

Dr. Abbey snorted with amusement and followed me inside. Joe padded after her, killing any lingering hope that I might have had about the big dog staying outside to, I don't know, guard the sidewalk or something.

I was so busy watching what the dog did that I walked right into Becks, bumping her forward a half step. "Hey, watch it," I began.

Shaun, hissed Georgia. *Look*.

I looked. And promptly understood why the rest of the team was standing frozen in their tracks at the end of the short entrance hall, staring into the gutted warehouselike depths of the former IT building. I'd been expecting a dingy little basement operation, something barely more technically advanced than a bunch of kids running their own pirate news site out of their parents' house. This was a functional lab, operating totally outside all sane safety precautions, but still equipped way beyond anything I might have anticipated.

All the interior walls not essential for structural support had been knocked out at some point, replaced with a maze of cubicles, portable isolation tents, and live animal cages. Racked computer servers stood side-by-side with rabbit hutches. Hydroponic beds studded the floor, growing healthy-looking crops of things I vaguely recognized from Maggie's garden. The light was an even, brilliant white, and about half the people I could see moving around the computers were wearing either sunglasses or the clear plastic bands hospitals sometimes used to protect the eyes of individuals with reservoir conditions.

Kelly was staring at the scene with her lip curled upward, looking utterly disgusted. "This is...horrific," she breathed, turning toward me. "We have to get out of here. This is an abomination. It's a violation of so many medical and ethical regulations that I can't even start to count them, and—"

"And it's not under CDC control, which means it's not okay to break the rules, is that it?" asked Maggie. Her tone was icy.

Kelly stopped midtirade, taking a shaky breath. "You don't understand," she said, slowly. "This is…the things they could do here, with this sort of equipment, are practically unthinkable. That's a genetic sequencer." She indicated a machine I didn't recognize. "They could build a whole new version of the virus, if they wanted to."

"Let's not antagonize the nice people, okay?" I asked. "You can be offended by their ethics later. When we aren't outnumbered." A lab this size would make body disposal distressingly easy. The last thing I wanted to do was give Dr. Abbey a reason.

The massive dog—Joe—ambled up and stopped beside me, panting amiably. Maggie promptly knelt down and offered her hand, knuckles first, like she was trying to attract the attention of one of her own, much less scary-looking, canines. Joe deigned to sniff it. A moment later, he was slobbering all over her palm, tail wagging with delight as she used her other hand to start scratching behind his ears.

"Most people are a lot less relaxed about Joe," said Dr. Abbey, rejoining the rest of us. She'd shed her rifle somewhere between the door and the lab floor, but she was still wearing the lab coat. At least some of the overhead lights must have been using George's beloved blacklight frequencies, because the fabric fluoresced slightly in the glare.

"Most people don't like risking infection when they don't have to," said Kelly.

"Well, those people have sticks shoved half a mile up their asses," said Dr. Abbey. "Besides, Joe's no threat. He's immune, aren't you, sweetheart?" The mastiff looked around at the sound of his name, tail still wagging frantically back and forth.

The rest of us, with the exception of Maggie—who was still deeply involved in her dog-worshipping duties—turned to stare at her. Surprisingly, it was Alaric who found his voice first, asking, "Are you serious? Immune? But he's got to weigh more than sixty pounds. How can he possibly be immune?"

Dr. Abbey shrugged. "He's got the canine forms of five reservoir conditions, and the initial signs of developing a sixth. He's never going to be a daddy, since the fourth one he developed was testicular Kellis-Amberlee—I had to have him neutered after that, poor guy—but he's never going to amplify fully, either. He's immune."

My thoughts raced as I tried to absorb her words. It didn't help that George was shouting in my head, demanding answers and denying the possible truth of Dr. Abbey's claims at the same time. Kelly turned to look at Dr. Abbey, her mouth moving silently as she tried to form a protest that wasn't willing to come out. Even Becks was just staring, looking as surprised as I'd ever seen her. That was saying something, because Becks doesn't *do* surprised. No one who's done field time as both a Newsie and an Irwin goes around being easy to knock off balance.

Maggie looked up from her enthusiastic worship of Joe, a narrow line forming between her eyebrows as she considered Dr. Abbey. "Five reservoir conditions in one dog?" Dr. Abbey nodded. "But how? I've never heard of anything, canine or human, developing more than one."

"Oh, that part was simple," said Dr. Abbey, and beamed. This smile was pure professional pride. "I induced them."

All of us fell silent at that, even George. Maggie's hands stilled, dropping away from the dog. The distant beeping of the computers, the occasional squeal or bark from a lab animal, and the footsteps of the other technicians provided a strange sort of background music. Joe looked between the humans and let out a resonant, echoing bark.

Dr. Abbey reached down to pat him on the head. "Well, since we've obviously got a lot to talk about, why don't you come to my office? There's cookies and tea, and I can tell you all about how I've managed to pervert the laws of nature. Come on, Joe." Waving for the rest of us to follow, she walked forward, into the bustling lab.

"Are we going with her?" asked Alaric.

"Got a better idea?"

"Nope," he said, glumly.

"All right, then. Following the crazy lady to our deaths it is." I shrugged and walked after her, trying to look nonchalant. The day was getting more interesting by the minute. I just had to hope it was the sort of interesting we'd live to talk about later.

The nature of the so-called reservoir conditions has never been fully explained, although a great many theories have been proposed, some reasonable, some not. Why does the KA virus manifest its live state in certain parts of the body? Why does that live virus then fail to spread the infection according to the laws that govern all of its other manifestations? Why is retinal KA most common in females, while cerebrospinal is most common in males? Nobody really seems to have a clue.

We do know that reservoir conditions are becoming more common, with reported cases of retinal, cerebro-spinal, ovarian, testicular, and pituitary KA in both human and animal hosts up by more than eighteen percent over the last eleven years. There are rumors of new reservoir conditions manifesting themselves, conditions with scary names like "cardiac" and "pulmonary." Yet still, no one knows why.

Taken all together, it's enough to make one question whether we truly dodged the end of the human race...or merely delayed it by a decade or two.

—From *Epidemiology of the Wall*,
authored by Mahir Gowda, January 11, 2041

Nine

D r. Abbey's "office" was a euphemistically named cubicle only slightly larger than the ones around it. It didn't help that it was jammed with file boxes, outmoded computer equipment, and—best of all—clear plastic tanks full of assorted insects and arachnids. I don't have a problem with spiders. Spiders can't carry Kellis-Amberlee. Ditto giant hissing cockroaches and squiggly things with way too many legs. Becks didn't share my disregard. Every time the squiggly thing moved, she sank farther back into her chair.

It's called a millipede, said George.

"It's called comedy," I muttered, and turned my attention back to Dr. Abbey.

She had shrugged out of her lab coat before pulling a bag of Oreos out of a filing cabinet and dumping them onto a paper plate. Now she was rummaging through the minifridge shoved under her desk, crouching in a way that I recognized as designed to put a minimum of stress on her knees. Joe the Mastiff was stretched out between her and us, enormous head resting between his forelegs. His pose was relaxed, but his eyes were alert, focusing on whoever had moved most recently. That meant his focus was mostly on Becks, who couldn't stop flinching.

"So there's apple juice, water, beer, and something unlabeled that's either a protein shake or algae." Dr. Abbey looked up. "Who wants what?"

"I want to know how you managed to induce a reservoir condition," volunteered Kelly, the need for knowledge apparently overwhelming her reluctance to work with unsanctioned researchers.

Dr. Abbey fixed her with a flat stare. "That's not a beverage. *I* want to know how you managed to justify violating a couple dozen international laws when you used a clone for personal benefit. Don't they train you out of that at the CDC? I thought that was their job. That, and restricting research to party-line channels while people were dying."

"I'll take an apple juice," I said.

"Nothing for me, thanks," said Alaric. He was looking at Dr. Abbey with the same sort of intent focus that Joe was turning on the rest of us, eyes slightly narrowed.

"Uh, water," said Maggie.

Becks said nothing. She was too busy watching the millipede.

"Got it." Dr. Abbey straightened, passing a bottle of water to Maggie and a bottle of apple juice to me before sitting in the chair next to her dog. "So you're finally here about the reservoir conditions. Damn. I've had a bet going with Dr. Shoji in Oahu for years now. He's been swearing you'd come someday. I thought you'd just keep treading water until we were all completely fucked."

"Shoji?" asked Alaric, eyes narrowing further. "Would that refer to Joseph Shoji, the director of the Kauai Institute of Virology?"

"Why are you asking me questions you know the answers to already? Nobody here needs the exposition." Dr. Abbey picked up her own drink, sipping calmly before she said, "If you think you can sell me to your government, think again. They already know who I'm in contact with, how often, how we communicate, basically everything but how often I change my underwear. If they wanted to take me, they'd take me. They just don't want to risk it."

"Actually, I sort of need the exposition, since I have no clue what you people are talking about," I said. "Why doesn't the government want to risk it? I mean, no offense, but it's not like you're sitting on a nuke here or anything."

"Oh, but I am." Dr. Abbey's gaze went to Kelly, and stayed there, guileless and steady as she continued: "See, the CDC knows damn well and good that something's wrong. I don't know how many of the people working there know what it is, but you can't have half a brain, work in the medical field, and not realize that something's not right."

"That's not fair," protested Kelly. "The research—"

Dr. Abbey cut her off: "That's an excuse."

"You're talking about the reservoir conditions," said Becks. It was a relief to have her join the conversation. Her training was a lot more analytical than mine. I didn't know what questions to ask. She and Alaric did, and that could save our asses.

"Exactly." Dr. Abbey kept looking at Kelly. "What do you know?"

"I don't know who Dr. Shoji is," I volunteered. "But I know that people with reservoir conditions are dying faster than they should be, and I know that my sister was one of those statistics, so we're here because we need you to tell us what the CDC doesn't want to say."

Kelly shot me a look. "Control of sensitive information is a key duty of all government organizations," she said. "Given your own need for information security, I would have thought—"

"Drop the party line, Doc," I said pleasantly. "I still don't have a problem with hitting girls."

Her mouth snapped shut with an audible click.

Dr. Abbey studied me for a moment before looking toward Alaric, nodding in my direction, and asking, "Is he for real?"

"He's for real," said Alaric. "Infuriating, impossible, and probably insane, but for real."

"Huh." Dr. Abbey took another sip of her drink. "Joe has five fully developed reservoir conditions. Retinal, cerebro-spinal, cardiac, testicular, and my personal favorite, thyroid. He's the first documented case of a canine thyroid reservoir condition, aren't you, Joe?" Joe turned his massive head toward her, tongue lolling as he drooled agreement with her words.

"You said you induced them?" said Becks.

"That's impossible," said Kelly. "The virus doesn't behave that way."

"It's not impossible. It's just hard," said Dr. Abbey. "I started injecting him with the live-state virus when he was six weeks old. That gave his body time to learn to deal with it before he got big enough to amplify. The first two conditions developed on their own, as a consequence of the inoculations. The others took more doing, since they had to be induced after adulthood."

"I just don't understand," said Kelly. "I mean, the risk of amplification alone—"

"Who says he didn't amplify?"

We all turned toward Maggie—I'd almost forgotten she was there, I was so busy trying to understand what the hell was going on—who was looking at Dr. Abbey with wide, solemn eyes.

"What?" asked Kelly.

"Who says he didn't amplify?" repeated Maggie. She picked up her water, took a thoughtful drink, and continued: "I mean, if you can induce reservoir conditions...You said he'd never amplify *fully*. It seems like there's only one way you could know, and that's by testing it. I'm not sure how you'd do it; it's not like I'm a doctor, but it seems...possible."

"Doesn't it?" asked Dr. Abbey. "Gold star for you."

A slow, horrifying picture was beginning to come together in my head, a picture that I didn't want to see. George was silent, making it even harder to ignore the conclusions my mind was drawing. Whatever those conclusions were, she was drawing them, too, and she didn't like them any more than I did. My mouth was suddenly desert-dry, as parched as the ground outside of Memphis, where snipers opened fire on our convoy, where Buffy died...where the CDC took us in for the very first time.

"Dr. Abbey?" I asked. She looked toward me, expression that of a teacher who wanted to encourage a favorite student to come up with the right answer before the final bell. "What do the reservoir conditions really do? Do you know?"

"Of course I do." She smiled, setting her drink aside as she stood. "Come on. I think it's time I took you for a tour of the lab. You need to understand what we're doing here."

"I've always liked a good perversion of science," said Becks. At least one of us was remembering to keep things light. "Let's take the tour."

Yes, said George, sounding oddly subdued. *Let's.*

Kelly didn't say anything. Maybe that was for the best.

We left our drinks behind and followed Dr. Abbey from her cramped cubicle to the main floor of the lab. Joe padded along at the rear of the group, claws making an unnerving clacking sound against the bare linoleum. It was impossible to forget that he was there, or that he was—all protests aside—more than large enough to undergo full amplification. He could kill us all before anyone had a chance to reach for a weapon.

But he won't, said George, picking up on the thought. *I don't think Dr. Abbey's quite that crazy.*

"Says the one with the least to lose," I muttered.

Dr. Abbey looked back at me, brows raised. "What was that?"

I offered her a sunny smile. "Just talking to my dead sister. She lives inside my head now. She says you're not crazy enough to let your dog go zombie and eat us all."

"She's right," Dr. Abbey agreed, seemingly unperturbed by the fact that I was talking about carrying on conversations with a dead person. It was weirdly jarring. "Even if Joe *could* amplify—which he can't, after all the work we've done—I wouldn't let him do it outside a sealed room. There's too much here that he could damage."

"Like these?" Alaric stopped, frowning at a tank that contained about a dozen things that looked like guinea pigs with too many legs. Becks followed his gaze and let out a shriek, jumping backward.

"Goliath tarantulas," said Dr. Abbey. "Average weight of the specimens in that tank is between four and six ounces. It's taken generations to breed them up that large."

"Why would you *want* to?" demanded Becks. "They're horrible."

"They're infected," said Dr. Abbey. We all turned to stare at her. She continued blithely, "The biggest female has amplified twice so far. Once she got sick enough that she started displaying stalking behavior and infected three other spiders before she could be contained. One of them didn't recover. A pity. He was from a very encouraging line. Come on, there's a lot to see." She resumed walking, obviously trusting us to follow her.

"Spiders can't amplify," said Kelly, sounding uncertain.

"Keep telling yourself that," said Dr. Abbey, and kept walking.

The rest of us hurried to catch up, with Joe once again lingering long enough to bring up the rear. I found myself wondering what would happen if one of us tried to split the party, the way they always seemed to do in the horror movies Maggie and Dave liked so much. Given the size of Joe's head, and the number of teeth it contained, I wasn't in any real hurry to find out. Let Becks take the suicidal risks. She was the group's remaining Irwin, after all.

Dr. Abbey waited for us at the head of a narrow alley that smelled of salt water and damp. "I was starting to think I needed to send search parties," she said, and ducked between the racked-up tanks, starting into the darkness.

"I don't like this," said Alaric.

"Too late now," I replied, and followed her.

The source of the smell quickly became apparent: The tanks making up the sides of the alley were filled with salt water and contained a variety of brightly colored corals and plastic structures. I paused to peer closer and recoiled as a thick, fleshy tentacle slapped the glass from the inside. Dr. Abbey snickered.

"Careful," she said. "They get bored sometimes. They like to mess around with people's heads when they're bored."

"They who?" I asked, pressing a hand against my chest as I waited for my heart to stop thudding quite so hard against my ribs. There was a distinct heaviness in my bladder, telling me that I needed to find a bathroom before I lined myself up for too many more exciting surprises. "What the fuck is that thing?"

"Pacific octopus." Dr. Abbey tapped the offending tank. The tentacle responded by slapping the glass again, before it was joined by two more near-identical appendages, and a large octopus slithered out from a crack between two pieces of coral. "We do a lot of work with cephalopods. They're good subjects, as long as you can keep them from getting bored enough to slither out of their tanks and go around wreaking havoc."

I glanced to Becks. "Isn't this the part where you should run screaming?"

"Nah," she said. "I've got no problem with octopuses. It's bugs and spiders that I don't like. Octopuses are cute, in their own 'nature did a lot of drugs' sort of way."

"Girls are fucking weird," I said.

You should know, George replied.

I smirked and leaned in for a closer look at the octopus. It settled against the glass, watching us with its round, alien eyes. "That is a freaky-looking thing," I said. "What's it for?"

"Barney here is for testing some of the new KA strains we've been developing," said Dr. Abbey, removing the cover from the tank. The octopus promptly switched its focus to the surface of the water. She stuck in a hand, and it reached up with two tentacles, twining them firmly around her wrist. "We haven't been able to infect him yet, although he's shown some fascinating antibody responses. If we can just figure out what's blocking infection in the cephalopod family, we'll be able to learn a lot more about the structure of the virus."

"Wait, you mean you're actually *trying* to develop new strains of the virus?" Kelly looked at her with wide, baffled eyes, like this was the last thing she could imagine anyone wanting to do.

Dr. Abbey took her attention away from the octopus—which was now trying to pull her arm all the way into the tank—as she frowned at Kelly. "What did you think we were doing here? Growing hydroponic tomatoes and talking about how nice it'll be when the CDC finally decides to get around to saving us all?" She began untangling her hand from the octopus's grasp, not appearing to take her attention off Kelly. "Please. Are you really going to stand there questioning my medical ethics while you tell me you people haven't been working with the structure of the virus at all?"

Kelly bit her lip and looked away.

"Thought not." Dr. Abbey pulled her hand out of the tank and replaced the lid. The octopus settled back at the bottom in a swirl of overlapping arms, appearing to sulk. "If you'll all walk this way, I think we're about ready to conclude our little tour. You should have all the information you need by this point." She turned and strode down the alley, shoulders stiff.

"Think we should follow?" asked Alaric, sotto voce.

"I'm not sure Joe here is going to give us a choice." I glanced at the mastiff. He was sitting calmly behind our little group, blocking the only other exit from the narrow row between the tunnels. "Besides, we've come this far. Don't you want to find out what the big secret the Wizard has to share with us is?"

"Maybe she's planning to give you a brain," deadpanned Becks.

"If she does, I hope that means you're getting a heart," I replied, and started walking.

Behind me, Alaric said, almost mournfully, "I just want to go home."

Kelly and Maggie didn't say anything at all. But they followed, and that was more than I had any right to ask of them.

Dr. Abbey was waiting on the other side of the alley, in front of a wide safety-glass window that looked in on what was obviously a Level 4 clean room. The people inside were wearing hazmat suits, connected to the walls by thick oxygen tubes, and their faces were obscured by the heavy space-helmet-style headgear that's been the standard in all high-security virological facilities since long before the Rising. Dr. Abbey was looking through the glass, hands tucked into the pockets of her lab coat. She didn't turn as we approached. Joe trotted up, and she pulled one hand free, placing it atop his head.

"I started this lab six and a half years ago," she said. "I've been waiting for you—or someone like you—ever since. What took you so long? Why didn't you show up years ago?"

"I didn't even know you were here," I said. "I still don't really understand."

Yes, you do, said George. Her voice was small, subdued, and almost frightened.

"George?" I asked. My own voice sounded almost exactly like hers had.

"We should go," said Kelly, sounding suddenly alarmed. She took my elbow. I looked down at her hands, but she didn't let go. "Or we should ask her about the research. You know, what we came to ask about."

"Dr. Abbey?" asked Alaric. "What's going on? What are you doing here? Why did you give your dog reservoir conditions, and what do you mean when you say he can't amplify? And what does it have to do with the deaths of the people with the natural reservoir conditions?"

"The Kellis-Amberlee virus was an accident," said Dr. Abbey, still looking at the pane of safety glass. Her hand moved slowly over her dog's head, stroking his ears. "It was never supposed to happen. The Kellis flu and Marburg Amberlee were both good ideas. They just didn't get the laboratory testing they needed. If there'd been more time to understand them before they got out, before they combined the way that they did...but there wasn't time, and the genie got out of the bottle before most people even realized the bottle was there. It could have been worse. That's what nobody wants to admit. So the dead get up and walk around—so what? We don't get sick like our ancestors did. We don't die of cancer, even though we keep pumping pollutants into the atmosphere as fast as we can come up with them. We live charmed lives, except for the damn zombies, and even those don't have to be the kind of problem that we make them out to be. They could just be an inconvenience. Instead, we let them define everything."

"They're zombies," said Becks. "It's sort of hard to ignore them."

"Is it really?" Dr. Abbey's hand continued caressing Joe's ears. "There's always been something nasty waiting around the corner to kill us, but it wasn't until the Rising that we let ourselves start living in this constant state of fear. This constant 'stay inside and let yourself be protected' mentality has gotten more people killed than all the accidental exposures in the world. It's like we're all addicted to being afraid."

Ask her about the reservoir conditions, prompted George.

"George—I mean, *I* want to know, what do the reservoir conditions have to do with any of this?" My voice sounded unfamiliar to my own ears, like someone else was asking the question.

"The immune system can learn to deal with almost anything, given sufficient time and exposure. How else could we have stayed alive for this long?" Dr. Abbey turned to look at me, eyes dark and very tired beneath the erratically bleached fringe of her hair. "The reservoir conditions are our bodies figuring out how to process the virus. How to work around it. They're our immune responses writ large and inconvenient, like the autoimmune diseases people used to suffer from before the Rising."

Just about everyone with an autoimmune syndrome either died during the Rising or found their suffering greatly alleviated as the body's immune responses got something much better to waste their time on than attacking their own cells: the sudden burgeoning Kellis-Amberlee infection doing its best to wipe out everything in its path. Autoimmune disorders still crop up, but they're nothing compared to their numbers before the Rising turned the medical world on its ear.

The facts flashed across my mind like puzzle pieces falling inexorably into place, each of them notching smoothly into place with the ones around it. The things Kelly was surprised by. The illegally massive dog with the induced reservoir conditions, and the casual way Dr. Abbey said he wouldn't amplify, like she knew, absolutely, what she was talking about. The spiders, the bugs, and the octopuses with their grasping limbs and their staring, alien eyes. All of it made sense, if I just stopped trying to force it.

I turned toward Kelly before I realized that I was intending to move. Her eyes widened, and she took a step back, almost pressing herself against Maggie. Maggie gave her a puzzled look as she stepped out of the way.

"I don't know what he's so pissed about, but I'm not going to get in his way," she said, in a tone that bordered on the sympathetic. "Better you than me."

Alaric and Becks were watching me with confusion. Dr. Abbey turned to watch me advancing on Kelly, and there was no confusion in her expression, just calm satisfaction, the teacher's face once more watching her student finally understand the lesson.

"The reservoir conditions are an immune response," I said. It wasn't a question; it didn't need to be. I could see the confirmation in Kelly's widening eyes. "They're the way the body copes with the Kellis-Amberlee infection, aren't they?" She didn't answer me. *"Aren't they?!"* I shouted, and slammed my hand into the safety glass.

Maggie and Alaric jumped. Becks stepped up beside me. And Kelly flinched.

"Yes," she said. "They are. They just...they just happen. We think it has something to do with exposure in infancy, but the research has never been...it's never..."

All my sympathy for her was gone, like it had never existed at all. I wasn't seeing a person anymore. I was seeing the CDC, and the virus that took George away. "I'm going to ask you one question, Doc, and I want you to think really hard about your answer, because you're legally dead, and if we want to hand you to this nice lady," I gestured toward Dr. Abbey, "for her experiments, well, there's really not much you can do about it. Don't lie to me. Understand?"

Kelly nodded mutely.

"Good. I'm glad to see that we have an agreement. Now, tell me: The reservoir conditions. What do they do? What do they *really* do?"

"They teach the immune system how to handle an ongoing live Kellis-Amberlee infection," said Kelly, meeting my eyes at last. She sounded oddly relieved, like she'd known we were going to wind up here and just hadn't known how to force the issue on her own. "They teach the body what to do about it."

"Meaning what?"

Alaric spoke abruptly, his own voice glacially cold: "That's the wrong question, Shaun."

"All right, you're the Newsie. What's the right question? What should I be asking her?"

"Ask her what would have happened if you hadn't pulled the trigger." Alaric looked at Kelly for a long moment, and then looked away, like he couldn't bear the sight of her. "Ask her what would have happened to Georgia if you'd just left her alone in the van and hadn't pulled the trigger."

Kelly's answer was a hushed whisper, so soft that, for a moment, I couldn't believe what I was hearing. The words seemed to get louder and louder as they echoed inside my head, repeating over and over again until I couldn't bear the sound of them. I slammed my fist into the safety glass as hard as I could, so hard I could feel my knuckles threaten to give way. Then I turned on my heel and stalked away, back down the dank-smelling alley where the octopuses watched with their alien eyes, back past the tanks of massive spiders, past the working lab technicians, who barely even looked up as I passed them. I was running by that point, running as I tried to outpace the words still echoing in my ears—those horrible, condemning, world-destroying words. It didn't do any good. No matter how fast I ran, no matter how hard I hit the world, nothing could take those words back again.

Those five small, simple words that changed everything:

"She would have gotten better."

Shaun and I had one of those awkward talks today—the ones that hurt the most because they're the ones you don't want to have, ever, but *have* to have eventually. This one was about our birth parents. Who they were, why they gave us up, whether they survived the Rising, all those things they say adopted kids are supposed to ask. Whether they wanted us. That's a big one for Shaun. He's always been more forgiving of the Masons than I am, but for some reason, it's really important to him that we were wanted before we wound up here.

I know what triggered it. I got the same e-mail he did, from a service promising to "reunite the orphans of the Rising with their families." According to the e-mail, these people would—for a modest fee, of course—run blood and tissue samples through every public and military database in the country, looking for a genetic match. Satisfaction guaranteed; they were clear on that point. We Find Your Family, Or Your Money Back.

That sort of scam fascinates me, but I don't want the answers that they're offering. I've had my genes tested for every nasty recessive and surprise health hazard we can test for, and that's most of them—anything they don't have a chromosome type for is so damn rare that at least it would be interesting to write about as it killed me. I have no pressing need to find the family that created me. The one thing I have in this world, the one thing I'm not willing to risk losing, is Shaun. And if I went out and found another family, I'd run the risk of losing him.

Whether the Masons rescued us from certain death—like the press releases say—or stole us, or hell, bought us on the black market, I don't *care*. The girl I would've been if I'd grown up with a mother with my nose and a father with my funny-looking toes never got the opportunity to exist. *I* did. *I* was the one who got to grow up, and I grew up with Shaun, and that's all I give a damn about. We got lucky. If he doesn't see it, well... I guess there's no way to make him.

But I still know.

—From *Postcards from the Wall*,
the unpublished files of Georgia Mason,
originally posted May 13, 2034

The good thing about Kellis-Amberlee, as a virus, is that it only goes after mammals. I mean, think about it. Can you imagine an infected giant squid? It would be like the Sea World Incident of 2015 all over again, only this time with bonus tentacles. Not my idea of a good scene. If that doesn't disturb you, consider this: The average crocodile is well over the amplification threshold.

Yeah. That was my thought, too.

The bad thing about Kellis-Amberlee, as a virus, is that it goes after *all* mammals. From the smallest field mouse to the largest blue whale (assuming there are any blue whales left down there), if it's a mammal, it's a carrier. That means that any cure we devise will also have to work for all mammals, because otherwise there's always the chance that Kellis-Amberlee can mutate and come back for another try. Viruses are tricky that way. At least we're used to dealing with this form of the disease. I'm not sure how quickly we'd adjust if it somehow changed the rules.

—From *The Kwong Way of Things*,
the blog of Alaric Kwong, April 12, 2041

Ten

The outside air slapped me hard across the face as the door to Dr. Abbey's lab clanged shut behind me. I stumbled to a stop, realizing two things at the same time—first, that I was alone in the middle of a mostly abandoned industrial park, and second, that while I had my standard field arms, I wasn't wearing any armor beyond my basic motorcycle gear. It was like a recipe for suicide, and while it might have been acceptable when I was too out of it to realize what I was doing, that moment had passed. I let my gaze flick wildly around my surroundings, looking for signs of movement. I didn't find any. What I did find was the van, sitting like an island of serenity among the ruins.

I took another step forward, barely aware that I was going to do it until it was already done. The van. That's where I was going when I ran away. To the van, where George and I saved each other's lives a thousand times... where I pulled the trigger and killed the woman who was my sister, my best friend, and my only real family, all with a single bullet.

She would have gotten better, whispered Kelly's voice, in the black space behind my eyes where only George was supposed to speak. The world blanked out again.

The sound of the van door slamming forced me back into my surroundings for the second time. My index finger was slightly numb, with the deep, subcutaneous ache that meant I'd taken—and passed—a blood test to open the doors. No amplification for me. Not yet, anyway. I looked dully around the van's interior, eyes flicking toward the ceiling in an automatic check for the Rorschach test that was formed by George's blood immediately after I pulled the trigger. For a moment, I could see it, streaks of red trending into a dozen shades of brown as it dried. Then I blinked, and the blood was gone, replaced by pristine white paneling.

"Breathe, Shaun," said George. Her voice came from behind me, rather than from inside my head. It was calm, soothing, even slightly amused; she was just talking me down from a panic attack. Nothing important, all part of a day's work. I've never been terribly prone to that kind of episode, but when you spend your days playing with dead things, one or two flip-outs are bound to come with the territory. "You're going to give yourself an aneurysm."

"Didn't you hear her?" I demanded, clenching my hands into fists. The urge to look toward the sound of her voice was nigh irresistible. I kept looking at the ceiling instead, waiting for the blood to repeat its flickering appearance. "You would have gotten better."

"Says her," George said. The amusement vanished, replaced by the barely chained irritation that was practically her trademark. "The test results were locked in—the CDC knew I was dead. If you'd walked away, something would have happened, and you know it. Worst-case scenario, you would have been treated to the delightful sight of men in hazmat suits dragging me into the open while I screamed for them to take another test. My last post might not have gone out. The *truth* might not have gone out." She paused before delivering what I was sure was meant to be the killing blow: "Tate might have walked away clean."

"You don't know," I said. "We could have claimed there was something wrong with the test. It's happened before."

"How often?"

I didn't answer her.

George sighed. "Three times, Shaun. With a top-of-the-line test, three times. In all three cases, there was proof of mechanical failure—and in two of the cases, the people were killed anyway. Their families won their suits on the basis of secondary testing units. We both know what a secondary test would have shown in my case. There's no point in pretending that we don't."

That was too much. The blood flickered back into visibility a second before I spun around, feeling my fingernails cutting into my palms as I shouted, "For fuck's sake, Georgia, there was a *chance*!" The empty chair would fix it. I'd see the empty chair, and she'd go back to being a voice in my head, just a voice in my head, because she was dead, I killed her. I just had to see the empty chair.

Instead, I saw George.

She was sitting in her customary place at the counter, her chair turned to face me. The computer monitor behind her framed her head like a technological halo, and the position, the lighting, all of it was so familiar that I didn't know whether I wanted to laugh, scream, or thank God that I'd finally gone all the way insane. She was wearing her usual fashion-impaired ensemble: black jacket, white dress shirt, black slacks. Only her face was wrong—no, not even her entire face; just her eyes. Her sunglasses were missing, and her eyes were the clear, undistorted coppery-brown that I remembered from the years before the progression of her retinal Kellis-Amberlee turned her irises into outlines.

I stared at her. She ignored it, the way she always did when she wasn't willing to wait for me to catch up. "Was," George agreed. "Not *is*. There *was* a chance. But we're past that now, aren't we? We're way, way past that."

My mouth went dry, and the room, already unsteady, started to spin. "George…?"

"Glad to see you haven't suffered any major head injuries lately," she said, wistfully, and smiled.

I kept staring until she sighed and said, "It's not like we have all day, you know. They're going to come looking for you sooner or later—probably sooner—and you really don't want them to find you like this."

"They're used to me talking to myself," I said quietly.

"To yourself, yes; to me, no." George shook her head. "Don't get me wrong, we both know that I'm not really here. There's no such thing as ghosts. But if you're actually *looking* at me, they're going to have a harder time taking you seriously, and you have a lot of work to do. *We* have a lot of work to do."

I decided against asking how "we" could do anything, if we both knew that she wasn't really here. If I did that, she might decide to stop talking to me altogether, and then I really would go crazy. The kind of crazy that puts you in a rubber room, rather than chasing conspiracies and running a news site. I forced a smile of my own, wondering how believable it would be, and said, "It's good to see you."

"I'd say it's good to be seen, but it's not," said George, looking at me steadily. "Just how crazy are you?"

"On a scale of one to ten?" I bit back a laugh. "Crazy enough that we're having this conversation. How's that for a starter?"

"Can you function?" She leaned forward, bracing her elbows against her knees. It was such a familiar gesture that my chest tightened, making it hard to breathe. "The way I see it, this is either where you man up and stop letting yourself freak out, or where you admit that you're too cracked to do the job and hand things over to somebody else. It's your call. You're the one who isn't actually dead."

I winced a little at the word "dead." "Can you not—?"

"Can I not what? Call myself dead? It's true, you dumb-ass. You're talking to me because I represent the part of you that still has a fucking clue how bad things are going to get. You've been fucking around since Tate decided to play martyr, and I'm tired of it. The team needs you. *I* need you. You can either step up, or you can step down, but you can't keep treading water like this."

She would have gotten better, whispered Kelly.

"Be quiet," I muttered.

"You're only saying that because you know I'm right," said George implacably. Apparently, the voices in my head couldn't hear each other. That was just another slice of crazy pie. "God, you never could take an honest critique. You would never have made it as a Newsie."

"Then it's a good thing I never tried to." My knees were shaking. I sagged back against the counter on my side of the van, resting my weight on my hands. It was as much to keep myself from trying to grab hold of my hallucination as it was to keep from falling over. "How do you expect me to step up for something like this? This wasn't the plan."

"No, the plan was to make me do it." She looked at me solemnly, alien eyes wide and grave in that familiar face. "We always knew one of us was going to be finishing things alone. Maybe we didn't know why, exactly, but we always knew this would happen somehow." Her solemnity broke, replaced by the half smile that meant she didn't want to be as amused as she was. "I have to admit, even when I was being self-important, I never thought they'd put 'assassinated to conceal a massive political conspiracy' on my Wall entry. I always figured it'd be something less...I don't know. Something less your department."

"Yeah, well." It was hard to swallow past the lump in my throat. It was the damn smile that did it. I knew she was a hallucination. I just didn't *care.* "You zigged when you should've zagged."

"What's done is done. So are you up for this?"

I didn't say anything.

More sharply: "Shaun? Are you even listening to me?"

"I miss you so much." I looked down at my feet. I couldn't keep looking at her, not if I wanted to hold on to what little was left of my sanity. "I mean, you know that, and I know I've been talking to you this whole time, but I also know it's because I'm really not all here without you, so I'm talking to myself in order to pretend I can ever be all the way here again, and this isn't even really a sentence anymore, so I'm going to stop now, but God, George, I miss you so much." I stopped, and hesitated before adding, very softly, "I don't think I know how to do this without you."

"You have to." I heard her stand, heard her footsteps as she crossed the van to stop in front of me. Her knees were on a level with my field of vision. If there's a rating system for quality of hallucination, I can say I was definitely scoring pretty high; I could see the wrinkles in her slacks where they fell over her knees, and a bit of carpet lint sticking to the sole of one sensible shoe. "Shaun, look at me."

I raised my head. This close, her eyes were even more alien...but they were still her eyes. It was still her behind them.

"Step up or step down," she said, very quietly. "Those are the choices."

I swallowed. "Do I get anything more than that? Step up or step down?"

"This isn't a news story, Shaun. The only reward you get for making it to the end is making it to the end—you get to know the truth, and that's it. I don't come back. The last year doesn't unhappen. Life doesn't go back to the way that it was; life never goes back to the way it was, no matter how hard we try to make it. But you'll know. You'll have the truth. You'll have the pieces that we're still missing." She smiled again, despite the tears welling up in her eyes. I'd never seen her cry, even when we were kids. The retinal KA atrophied her tear ducts years before her eyes actually changed in a visible way. But she was crying now. "The only happy ending we can have is the ending where you take the bastards down and make them pay for what they did to us. Can you do it? Because if you can't, I need you to call Mahir and tell him that he's in charge now. Someone has to find the truth. *Please*."

"I can do it," I said. My voice was unsteady, but it was there, and that was really all that I could ask. "For you, I can do it."

"Thank you." She leaned forward. My breath caught as she pressed a kiss against my forehead and stepped away again, leaving me with a clear path to the exit. "I miss you, too."

I stood, glancing up as I did. The blood on the ceiling was gone. When I looked down again, so was George. I wiped my cheeks with the palm of my hand until it came away dry, still looking at the spot where George had been. She didn't reappear. That was probably a good sign. "Love you, George," I whispered.

She would have gotten better, hissed Kelly's voice, but its power was gone. Oh, I was still going to have to deal with the reality of it, but I'm good at dealing with stupid shit. If the CDC wanted to play hardball, we'd play hardball. And we'd win.

I was unsurprised to find Becks standing outside the van with her pistol resting against her knee, lazily sipping from a bottle of water. She straightened when I stepped out onto the blacktop, asking. "Everything okay?"

"I think I just had a minor psychotic episode or maybe a breakdown or something, but it's cool; I'm feeling basically okay now," I replied, closing the van doors. "You?"

Becks blinked at me, momentarily thrown by the flippancy of my reply. Even after working with me for as long as she has, she hasn't learned to take statements like "minor psychotic episode" in stride. I'll give her this: She recovered fast, saying, "Well, I just watched my boss have a minor psychotic episode, and I thought I'd come out and make sure he didn't get his damn fool ass eaten by a zombie before he settled down." She hesitated, then added, "I didn't shoot her. After you ran out of the room? I didn't shoot her."

I wasn't sure whether she was looking for praise or expecting me to condemn her for showing mercy. I elected for the praise. "Good call," I said, nodding. "We're going to need that pretty little head of hers intact if we're going to crack it open, pry out all its secrets, and use them to bring down the CDC."

"Right," said Becks, slowly. "Were you on the line to Mahir just now? Because I thought I heard voices in there."

"Psychotic break, remember?" I shrugged. "Look, Becks—Rebecca—you know what you're getting out of this team. We're damaged goods, some more than others. I'm so damaged I'm practically remaindered. If you can cope with that, I can promise you the ride of your life. If you can't, I have the feeling that when we go back in there," I hooked a finger toward the door to Dr. Abbey's lab, "you lose the last chance to cash in your ticket on the crazy train."

"I like trains," said Becks. Her expression sobered before she added, "And I loved your sister. She was the first person who gave me a chance to prove myself in the field. She was a damn good reporter. So if you're a little nuts, so what? I think it's pretty obvious that we're all mad here."

"Great," I said. We were the only things that moved as we walked toward the door. "She didn't want to let you go. I had to haggle like a bastard to get you away from the Newsies."

"She recognized talent when she saw it," said Becks, with a small smile.

"Yes, she did," I replied, with utter seriousness. Becks blinked, smile fading as she saw the look on my face. "So did I. I'm about to ask all of you to go all-in—put up or shut up, because we're done treading water." I was echoing some of what George had said to me, but that was okay. She was a figment of my insanity, and she probably wouldn't sue me for plagiarism. "Not all of us are going to walk away from this one alive."

"You're kidding, right?" Becks actually laughed out loud, the sound echoing through the empty structures around us. "If there's one thing I've learned since I started working with you people, it's that no one gets out alive." She leaned over, kissing me lightly on the cheek and then speed-walking the rest of the way to the door. "No one," she repeated, and was gone.

I stopped, touching my cheek and staring after her in bewilderment. "What the fuck was that?"

A complication, said George. She sounded amused. *Also, a girl thing.*

"Right." I dropped my hand. "Glad to see you're back where you belong."

I'm right here. Until the end.

"Great." I started forward again. "Come on, George. Check this out."

BOOK III

The Mourning Edition

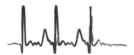

All I wanted was a little excitement in my life. Was that such a horrible thing to ask?

— Rebecca "Becks" Atherton

I guess in the end, it doesn't matter what we wanted. What matters is what we chose to do with the things we had.

— Georgia Mason

Here's how it used to work: George told you the unvarnished facts, no matter how nasty they were or how lousy they made you feel, and then I came in to dance like a monkey and make you feel better about this shitty world we're living in. I was the carrot, and she was the stick. Well, guess what, folks? The stick got broken, and that's not how things are going to work anymore. Those days are behind us.

This is the new deal: I'm going to tell you the unvarnished facts, no matter how nasty they are or how lousy they make you feel...and that's it. If you want news that makes you feel good, go somewhere else. If you want wacky adventures, laughter, and an escape from your miserable life, go somewhere else.

If you want the truth, stay here. Because from here on out, that's all I'm going to give you. No more carrot-and-stick. No more dancing monkeys. Just the truth. And if it kills us, well, at least this way we died for something. It's better than the alternatives.

—From *Adaptive Immunities*, the blog of Shaun Mason,
April 15, 2041

Eleven

Becks was half a step behind me as I stopped at the end of Octopus Alley to take in the scene. Kelly was sitting in a folding chair with her hands clasped white-knuckle tight and resting on her knees. Alaric sat across from her, watching her like he thought she'd start making sense to him if he waited long enough. Best of luck with that, buddy. Maggie and Dr. Abbey leaned against the safety-glass window, watching this little tableau. Only Joe didn't seem to be disturbed by the current mood in the room. He was sprawled at Dr. Abbey's feet, gnawing on a massive length of animal bone.

Dr. Abbey offered me a nod. "Welcome back. Feeling better?"

"No, but I think I'll live. That's more than some people can say." Kelly shot me a look. I ignored her. "Dr. Abbey, how secure is your network? If we made a call, could it be traced?"

"A call to, say, the CDC?" She straightened. "I have a few burn phones I've been saving for just such an occasion. Wait here." Dr. Abbey made a complicated gesture toward Joe, who was in the process of standing, presumably so he could follow her. The dog subsided, staying where he was as she turned and strode out of the room.

Kelly looked at me with open alarm. "Shaun? What are you going to do?"

"Break your fucking jaw if you don't shut up, right now," I said, pleasantly enough. "I'm not ready for you to talk to me yet."

"That means it's time for you to be quiet," said Maggie.

There was a time when I would have told her not to taunt the Doc. That time was over and done with. "Becks, why don't you make sure the Doc stays quiet while I take care of things. I wouldn't want her to get any funny ideas about saying hi."

"My pleasure." Becks drew her pistol and moved to stand behind Kelly, adopting an easy, comfortable-looking stance. She could stand that way all day if she needed to. I'd seen her do it in field recordings.

Kelly stared straight ahead, unflinching. If I hadn't been so mad at her, I might have been impressed. As it was, I couldn't really look at her without wanting to punch her face in.

Dr. Abbey walked briskly back down the hall and slapped a phone into my hand. "This is voice activated and will stay untraceable for about five minutes. Give it the number you want and tell it to dial. You might also tell it to set itself to speaker, since I'd like to know what my resources are being used to do."

"Happily," I said. I pulled my normal phone from my pocket and brought up Dr. Wynne in my address book, reading off the numbers in a slow, clear voice before saying, "Dial and set to speaker."

The phone beeped. Three rings later, a CDC receptionist came on the line, perky as always as he said, "Dr. Joseph Wynne's office, how may I direct your call?"

"This is Shaun Mason. Please connect me to Dr. Wynne."

"May I ask the nature of your call?"

"No, you may not. Now connect me to Dr. Wynne."

"Sir, I'm afraid I—"

"*Now!*"

Something in my tone must have made it clear that I wasn't fucking around. The receptionist stammered an apology before the line gave a click, replacing his carefully cultivated blandness with the hum of hold music. That lasted only a few seconds. There was another click, and Dr. Wynne said, "Shaun, thank God. Now what the blazes is going on? You nearly gave poor Kevin an attack."

"I'll be sure to send a nice card and some flowers." The acid in my voice surprised even me. I thought I was better trained than that. "I left several people in Oakland before the outbreak, so you'll forgive me if I'm not on my best behavior."

There was a pause as Dr. Wynne took in what I was saying: that Dave hadn't been the only casualty of Oakland. It was a lie, sure, but it was one he had no reason not to believe. "Oh," he said finally, voice gone soft. "I see. I'm so sorry to hear that."

"It is what it is. Look, I've been doing some research, Dr. Wynne, and I wanted to confirm the results I'm getting. Got a second to answer a few questions for me?"

"I'm always happy to answer questions for you."

"Maybe not this time." I glared at Kelly as I spoke. Tears were start-ing to roll down her cheeks as she stared at the wall, expression otherwise remaining impassive. I didn't care. Bitch deserved to cry. "Dr. Wynne, are reservoir conditions an immune response?"

He hesitated. When he spoke again, his tone was slower, more careful, and more heavily accented. "Well, I suppose it depends on who you ask. Some people think they might be."

"What do *you* think?"

"I'm not sure that's relevant."

"I think it is. So what do you think? Are reservoir conditions an immune response or not?"

"Shaun..." He sighed heavily. "Yes. I think they are."

"So if Dave had managed to scan and e-mail me some documents before Oakland went kerplooey, and if the people I'd gone to with them said that George would have recovered if I hadn't decided to go ahead and shoot her, would they be fucking with me? Or was that little slice of good news somehow omitted from my handbook?"

He was silent.

"Fine. Whatever." Making my voice light was almost impossible, but I did it. Somehow. "I guess I'll just publish everything I've got here, let people with a more scientific background than mine sort it out. Right?"

"Shaun..." He sighed again. "Yes. Yes, she might have recovered. *Might.* The tests we ran on her blood were inconclusive."

My vision flashed red. The CDC had George's blood for weeks after her death. Logically, I knew they'd been using that time for tests, as well as decontamination, but I'd never really allowed myself to think about it. The idea of them doing God knows what to her had never been a pleasant one, and the more I knew, the less pleasant it became. "You're an asshole," I said, conversationally. "We trusted you."

"Shaun—"

"Fuck off." I hung up and tossed the burn phone back to Dr. Abbey. "Thanks."

"You're welcome." She tucked the phone into the pocket of her lab coat. "Satisfied now?"

"No. But it's a start." I turned to Kelly. "It's your turn to talk, Doc. Make it count."

"I..."

I glared at her. "*Talk.*"

She talked.

She kept her eyes on the floor the whole time, her voice tight and bordering on monotone. It was like she was trying to convince herself that she was giving a lecture, rather than being interrogated at gunpoint. The few times she did glance up, her eyes were filled with guilt, darting between us almost too rapidly to be followed. Then she'd look down again, her monotonous monologue never stopping. The expression on Dr. Abbey's face—calculating and predatory—probably didn't help. Then again, the fact that Becks was holding a gun pointed at the Doc's head probably helped even less.

"The first reservoir conditions were identified in 2018. Four years isn't long in human terms, but it's centuries in virus generations. The Kellis-Amberlee virus had been replicating the whole time. Spreading. Changing. I mean, the first infected didn't demonstrate mob behavior, but they started by the early twenties. That wasn't an adaptation on the part of the infected. It was an adaptation in the behavior of the viral substrains driving them. Six of the fifteen strains we had identified by that point would cause the pack behavior. Nine wouldn't. Ten years later, we could find only two strains that didn't come with that instinct to infect before eating. Outside the ones we had stored in our freezers, that is." She hesitated, shoulders tightening for an instant. Then, like some impossibly difficult decision had been made, she continued: "We tried cross-infection. Well. When I say 'we,' I mean scientists working at the CDC and USAMRIID. I wasn't working with...I wasn't a part of that project." Kelly glanced up again, eyes searching desperately for a sympathetic face. "I wasn't involved."

"That's when Dr. Shoji went off the reservation—he stuck it out as long as he could, but those cross-infection tests were the last straw," said Dr. Abbey, in a casual, matter-of-fact tone. "You want to talk about the cross-infection tests? What those entailed, precisely? I'm sure these nice people would really love the gory details."

Kelly took a deep breath as she looked back down. "They took... volunteers..."

"Prisoners," said Dr. Abbey.

"They volunteered," said Kelly, a stubborn note in her voice. "Yes, they were prisoners. They had no chance of parole, no chance of ever being released back into the public, and use of human test subjects has a...it has a long and time-honored place in medical science. Sometimes it's the only thing you *can* do. That's how they discovered that yellow fever was spread by mosquitoes, you know. How...how they proved that smallpox inoculation worked. A lot of people's lives were saved by human testing. When there wasn't any other choice. When there wasn't any other way."

"How many lives did this save?" asked Dr. Abbey.

"What did you *do?*" asked Alaric.

His was the question Kelly chose to answer. Darting a glance toward him, she said, "The choice was offered to certain inmates whose viral profile matched the criteria. Let us inject them with a potential vaccine and, if they recovered, we'd enter them in the witness-protection program. Whole new identities. Whole new lives. They could start over."

"If they lived," said Alaric, softly.

Kelly winced.

"Come on, princess," said Becks. "Story hour isn't over yet. I want to know what happens next."

"The volunteers were injected with a serum containing deactivated viral particles from the opposing strain. The theory was that maybe one strain would destroy the other. Best-case scenario, they'd *both* destroy the other, and we'd finally have a treatment. Worst-case scenario…" Her voice tapered off.

Dr. Abbey took up the thread when it became clear that Kelly wasn't going to, saying, "Worst-case scenario is what they got. Not only did every single one of their 'volunteers' go into spontaneous amplification when the two strains met, but they bred a new strain—one that increased mob behavior in exposed infected. They fucked up gloriously. And then they swept it all under the rug, with the rest of their failures."

"What did you want us to do?" Kelly's head snapped up, eyes narrowing as she glared at Dr. Abbey. "Did you want us to just sit back and watch the virus do its thing, not even *try* to find the answer? Yes, people died. Yes, mistakes were made, and mistakes will *be* made, and someday, maybe, because of those mistakes, we'll have a cure. Wouldn't you like that? A cure? An end to all the fear? Because that seems like a really good thing to me, and if I have to work with the CDC to make it happen, that's what I'm going to do."

"I'd love that idea, if I thought it was anything but a pipe dream." We all turned toward Maggie. She'd moved to sit on the floor next to Joe, one arm slung lazily across the dog's back. She looked completely at peace, despite the fact that she was leaning against an animal that could take off her face with a single bite. "People laugh at me because I watch a lot of horror movies, but horror movies are educational, if you know how to pay attention to them. They tell you about societal trends—about the things that people are afraid of. In the ones before the Rising, they were afraid of actual *things*. The new ones…they're just afraid of not being afraid."

Kelly snorted. "No one makes horror movies anymore."

"Yes, they do," said Maggie. "These days, everything's a horror movie."

"To get back to the original point, before we went on this fascinating and informative tangent, you said the virus was adapting," said Alaric. He leaned forward, eyes fixed on Kelly. The Newsie in him sensed blood in the water. I could see it in his face. "No mob behavior, then, mob behavior. What are the reservoir conditions supposed to *do*?"

"No one really knows." Kelly stole a glance in my direction, testing my reaction, before focusing on Alaric. She sounded less like she was lecturing and more like she was trying to make herself understood, like it suddenly *mattered* that we understand. "We think they stem from exposure to the live virus that somehow fails to cause full amplification. You see it mostly in people who risked exposure when they were under the threshold weight, although there have been exceptions. We're still trying to figure out what causes the exceptions. Why it happens in some adults, and not in others. We don't really know yet, and it's not the sort of thing you can easily test."

"So wait," said Becks. "Are you saying that people who got exposed when they were really little, they get reservoir conditions instead of getting the whole zombie combo pack?"

Kelly nodded. "Exactly."

My eyes were normal until I was almost at the amplification threshold, said George thoughtfully. *The retinal distortion didn't kick in until then.*

"I know," I mumbled, keeping my voice low, so as to hopefully avoid reminding my team that I was crazy. Louder, I asked, "What does that mean, exactly?"

"It means their bodies were exposed to live Kellis-Amberlee when they were still incapable of suffering the full effects of the virus," said Dr. Abbey. There was a lunatic good cheer in her voice, like being allowed to make that statement was a great and glorious gift. "Ever hear of chickenpox?"

"Well, yeah," said Becks. "It's part of the standard set of field vaccines."

"For a long time, they didn't have a vaccine for chickenpox—it was a childhood disease, and almost everybody caught it. Only that was a good thing back then, because most kids get over the chickenpox pretty easy. They itch for a week and then they're fine. Better than fine. Having the virus once makes them resistant to catching it again, and for adults, chickenpox is no laughing matter. It can cause permanent nerve damage, severe scarring, all sorts of nasty side effects." Dr. Abbey looked placidly at Kelly. "People used to have chickenpox parties, where they'd deliberately expose their young children to somebody who was already sick."

"That's disgusting," said Becks.

"Now that we have a vaccine, sure. Back then, it was a way to save your children from suffering a lot more. It wasn't safe—kids died of chickenpox—but it was a damn sight better than the alternative."

"I don't understand," I said.

I do, said George, very quietly.

"I do," echoed Alaric. I turned to look at him, and he said, "When infants are exposed to live Kellis-Amberlee, they can't amplify, but they still get sick. Only they can get better, can't they? They can actually recover from the virus."

"Bingo." Dr. Abbey, touching her nose with her left index finger while she pointed at Alaric with her right. "Princess CDC, tell the nice man what he's won!"

Kelly was silent.

I swallowed away the dryness in my throat, and said, quietly, "Please."

My voice seemed very loud in the enclosed space of the lab. Kelly turned to face me and said, "Yes, sometimes early exposure can lead to individuals successfully fighting off a live Kellis-Amberlee infection. It's impossible to run a standard blood test on an infant, because they can't amplify, so we can't find the usual amplification markers. But they'll get sick. It's been seen. And then, after a little while, they aren't sick anymore." Kelly stopped, choosing her next words with care: "Most of the individuals who undergo a potential infectious episode as infants develop one of the reservoir conditions when they get older, because their immune systems are preconditioned to respond."

"Their bodies remember that the virus is bad, and they set up their own little kennels, filled with their own little packs of domesticated viral bodies," clarified Dr. Abbey, leaning down to thump Joe on the side. He looked up at her adoringly, tongue lolling. "That's what humanity does when faced with wolves. We take them in, tame them, and teach them how to keep us safe."

"Yes," agreed Kelly. "The reservoir conditions are a marker that the immune system has learned it needs to fight back when Kellis-Amberlee starts taking over."

"That's why you said she would've gotten better, isn't it?" Kelly didn't answer. I slammed my fist into the safety-glass window, hard enough to make everyone jump—everyone but Dr. Abbey, who looked like she'd plugged herself into some inner reservoir of contentment. "Answer the damn question, Doc."

"Yes." Kelly looked up at me, expression drawn. "Dr. Wynne and I reviewed her test results. Her immune system was already starting to respond to the new infection when the test was taken. The chances that she would have been able to fight off the infection were very good. Better than eighty percent."

"Spontaneous remission," said Alaric, sounding awed.

I didn't take my eyes off Kelly as I said, "Explain."

"It's supposed to be an urban legend. Supposedly, there are people who've been infected—like, full-on ready-to-eat-the-neighbors infected—but they miraculously recovered before they could be put down. Nobody ever seems to know anyone who's had a spontaneous remission. It's always a guy who knows a guy who used to know a guy. But the stories keep cropping up, and then the CDC reminds everyone that there's no cure and they get written off again."

"Guess it's not that much of a legend, huh, Doc?" I glanced toward Dr. Abbey. "Is that what we're talking about here? This remission thing?"

"The CDC is telling the truth about one thing: There's no cure for Kellis-Amberlee, and if someone offered me one, I wouldn't take it, for a lot of reasons. They're also lying, because if you can live with the virus from the time you're born, why the hell should it be able to wake up but not able to go back to sleep?" Dr. Abbey smiled encouragingly. "Isn't story hour fun?"

"Like a heart attack," I said.

"Two in ten thousand," said Kelly sharply.

"What?" I asked.

"Two in ten thousand." She stood, ignoring the gun Becks had trained on her. "That's how many people *with* existing reservoir conditions are likely to recover from a live infection. Two in ten thousand. No one who didn't have a reservoir condition has ever recovered. The rate of recovery seems to be tied to the density of the viral particles in the individual reservoir, but we don't have any hard-and-fast proof of that. It's not like we've had much opportunity for study, since you can't exactly get volunteers for that sort of thing."

"Not even from the prison system," deadpanned Maggie.

Kelly winced again. I didn't really give a fuck. If she wanted to feel guilty, she'd damn well earned her guilt. "It's not like that," she said.

"Bullshit," said Dr. Abbey. "There are plenty of ways to test that sort of thing. Take Joe. I exposed him as a puppy: He got sick, he got better, he developed his first reservoir condition. I exposed him again when he hit amplification weight: He got sick, he got better, he developed his second reservoir condition. At this point, I could bathe him in the damn virus and he wouldn't amplify. He might get a little dehydrated and have some chest pains, but they'd pass quickly. Test passed."

"How many puppies did you start with?" countered Kelly.

Dr. Abbey looked uncomfortable for the first time. "Joe wasn't the first subject, true. But he's been the most successful."

"So wait a second," said Becks. "Are you people saying what I think you're saying?"

"That depends. Rebecca, do you think they're saying that a person with a pronounced enough reservoir condition can come back from zombie-dom, and that we could intentionally give babies reservoir conditions by exposing them before they're big enough to go zombie? Because that's what *I* think they're saying. But I'm the big, dumb Irwin, remember?" I punched the window again. "George was the smart one. Too bad she's the one who died."

"Two in ten thousand," repeated Kelly, like it was some sort of magic charm. "Could you have pulled the trigger if you had that figure? Could you have put the gun to her head and let her go to keep anybody else from getting hurt if you knew there was a chance—even a tiny, tiny little chance—that she'd get better?"

No, said George.

"Yes," I said, but there was no strength behind the word. I think everyone knew that I was lying. I don't think any of them had the right to blame me.

Kelly shook her head. "Society would collapse. Everyone would start to think *they* were special, *they* would be the ones whose mothers or fathers or children would get better. They'd start hesitating before they fired."

"Shoot first, ask questions later," said Becks, very quietly. "I hate to say this, Shaun, but she's right. If people stopped shooting, it'd be a bloodbath. Nobody would be willing to risk killing somebody who might recover."

"And while they're sick, they're really sick. The virus isn't any kinder to their bodies than it would be to yours, or to mine," said Kelly. "They can hurt people, and they can infect people, before their fevers start to go down. Can you imagine? Getting bit, and then coming out of it and learning that you'd killed and eaten your entire family? And what happens if your family isn't actually dead, just sick? As soon as you stop registering as part of the mob, they'll rip you apart. We won during the Rising because we learned that once someone gets bitten, you shoot. Take that away, and we're all going to die."

"Nice speech, but there's something you forgot, Doc," I said, as mildly as I could.

"What's that?"

"She," I hooked a thumb toward Dr. Abbey, "managed to give a dog a reservoir condition. So why the fuck aren't we starting a program to do that for people? Why are we just sitting back and...and not trying to change things?"

"Ask her how many of the puppies didn't have to get bitten before they amplified," Kelly countered.

"Aw, hell," said Alaric. "Rick's kid."

"What?" asked Becks.

"He had a son. He also had a wife with ovarian KA. He did a piece for the site about it, before he went off to become vice president. Their son amplified as soon as he hit the threshold weight. He was born with the live virus in his blood, and he never managed to fight it off." Alaric looked to Kelly. "That's what you're talking about, right?"

"It is." She lifted her chin a little, trying to look confident. She was only succeeding in looking scared. "We can't start a vaccination program unless you want to start turning every baby into a little time bomb. Maybe they'll fight it off and just have messed-up eyesight or weird headaches. Or maybe they'll stay sick, and then one day, they'll turn around and try to rip your throat out. We don't have enough control over the virus to do it. And we can't tell people because it changes things too much." She shot a pleading look in my direction. "Your sister was passionate about the truth, Shaun, but there are truths the world isn't ready to hear. There are truths that are just too big."

"Who made you the judge of that?" I asked quietly.

"Nobody." She shook her head. "There was nobody we could ask."

"Boo-hoo," said Dr. Abbey. "Let me know when you people want to grow a pair and join the scientific community. We're looking for answers. We'd love access to your lab equipment."

"You mean join the mad scientists," spat Kelly, guilt turning into anger in an instant.

"You say potato, I say pass the jumper cables," said Dr. Abbey.

Alaric looked at her thoughtfully. "You said Dr. Shoji left the mainstream medical community after the cross-infection trials. What made you do it? Why aren't you working with the CDC, trying to take them over from the inside out?"

"Simon Fraser University," said Dr. Abbey.

Kelly stiffened before sinking back into her seat and covering her face with her hands. Alaric's reaction was nowhere near as dramatic. His eyes widened slightly, and then he nodded, sympathetic comprehension filling his expression. "Who did you lose?"

Dr. Abbey looked down at Joe the mastiff. Maggie was stroking his ears, and he looked utterly blissful. "My husband," she said calmly. "Joseph Abbey. He was a software engineer. I was still working for the provincial CDC back then, looking for solutions through 'safe' channels. I followed protocol, I maintained my lab at their professional standards, and I was stupid enough to think that meant something."

The name of the school was familiar, but it wasn't connecting to anything, and for once, George wasn't helping. "Somebody fill me in," I said.

"Joe used to give lectures to software engineering classes. They said it was good for the students to deal with someone who had 'real-world experience.' I always thought it was partially to remind them that there was a world off campus." Dr. Abbey glanced my way. "Simon Fraser was a closed school. No student or faculty in and out during the semester. You came in clean, you stayed clean, you left clean. Pretty much the only risk of infection came from the outside speakers and the maintenance staff, and they were tested in every way possible. Joe used to say he couldn't sit down for a week after he did one of his lectures." She fell abruptly silent.

"There was an outbreak," said Alaric, taking up the thread where Dr. Abbey left off. "The security footage was mostly destroyed, but what we have indicates that it must have started in the gym. Maybe someone pushed themselves a little bit too far and had a coronary. We'll never know."

"Oh, fuck," I said.

"My thoughts exactly," said Dr. Abbey.

An outbreak is never good, but an outbreak on a sealed campus is close to a worst-case scenario. The healthy would be locked in with the infected until someone could come and let them out, and the mop-up would probably take weeks, if not months, after which the school would almost certainly be decommissioned for several years while they waited for the hazard level to go down again. "What was the student body size?"

"About eleven thousand," said Dr. Abbey. "It was a larger school before they closed it to nonresident students. Add another three hundred or so for the faculty and staff."

"How many got out?" asked Maggie.

"None," whispered Kelly.

"None," echoed Dr. Abbey. "See, the outbreak started near the school walls, and they were located on a hill that made it difficult to get to the campus any way but via the main road. Whoever was in charge that day—whatever genius was at the switch—decided that it was too dangerous to try for an evacuation. That the infection was already too close to breaking out. So they called down the wrath of fucking God on that little school."

"I remember that," said Becks, sounding faintly awed. "We studied it when I was in training. Almost all the security footage went missing, even the stuff that should have been beamed straight into the Health Canada and CDC databases. It was just gone."

"Except for the pieces that somehow ended up on private servers," said Alaric. "I've seen some of the footage. It's clearly an outbreak, but it doesn't look…"

"It doesn't look that bad," said Dr. Abbey. She seemed to have regained a bit of her composure. She looked challengingly around at our little group before she continued: "It looks like the sort of thing you handle with an insertion team and a general quarantine. Not by ordering a firebombing on Canadian soil. My *husband* was in that school. He called me fifteen minutes before they hit the news, and he was *laughing*. He said there was 'a little ruckus' near the track, and that he'd be home in time for dinner. Told me to get an ice pack ready for the bruises left by all those blood tests they insisted on running. Everything was fine, and that was *after* the outbreak started. But they treated it like the end of the goddamn world."

"So you went rogue?" I asked.

"Is that what they're calling it these days?" Dr. Abbey shook her head. "I tendered my resignation immediately. They refused it. Three times. Said that I was a 'valuable researcher,' and that they'd be happy to give me the time I needed to get my affairs in order before I returned to work. So I got my affairs in order. I packed my things, I emptied out my lab, and I left while they were still congratulating themselves on being so understanding in my time of need."

"You quit," said Kelly.

"You never started," countered Dr. Abbey. "Don't you look at me like that, you little Barbie girl with your big moral ideals that go out the window as soon as you think you know best. My husband died because a bomb was cheaper than a cleanup squad. That's the simple truth of things. Joe died because somebody didn't want to pay the bill. His sister," she jabbed her finger at me, "died because you people won't do the research into the reservoir conditions that needs to happen if we're going to survive this damn virus. As a species, and as a society. You may think you're doing the right thing, and hell, you may even be right, but when you don't let anyone watch over your shoulder, how the fuck are the rest of us supposed to know?"

Kelly took a slow breath, visibly calming herself before she said, "I wouldn't be here if I was still willing to play by their rules."

"And again bullshit." Dr. Abbey slid off the desk, taking a quick step forward. "You don't make them, but you're sure as shit defending them, and it's time to stop. Because if you're far enough off the reservation to be sitting here, they're not going to let you come back. It's cheaper to drop the bomb than it is to offer medical assistance, remember?" She leaned in until her face was almost up against Kelly's, and said, voice suddenly soft, "I was you, once upon a time. Remember that. I was *you*, and the organization you still believe in made me who I am now. They'll do the same to you, if you don't get smart in a hurry."

Kelly gaped at her. Before any of us could formulate a response, Dr. Abbey was turning and striding off down the hall. Joe lumbered to his feet and went trotting after her, nearly knocking Maggie over in the process. The rest of us joined Kelly in gaping.

We were still staring when she shouted back, not turning, "I want you people out of my lab in ten minutes!" Then she was gone.

I glanced at Alaric. "I think I like her."

I think I do, too, said George.

Becks eyed the rest of us with poorly restrained impatience. "Well?" she asked. "Now what the fuck are we supposed to do?"

"That part's easy." I smiled, slowly. "We have a conspiracy. Let's go bust this fucker open and see what comes tumbling out."

But when the springtime turns to dust
(A thousand shades of blood and rust)
And everything is ash and stone
(Contagion writ in blood and bone)
Then what exists to have or hold?
(What story, then, has not been told?)
Let this be my sacred vow
(Oh Mother Mary, hear me now):
I will not fail, I will not fall
(Though Heaven, Hell, and Chaos call).
We are the children of the Risen.
This world our home, this prayer our prison.

—From *Dandelion Mine*,
the blog of Magdalene Grace Garcia, April 16, 2041

I am officially tired of camping. I am tired of eating fish. I am tired of watching the boys wander around scratching themselves and pretending that we're "roughing it" while living out of a van that's better appointed than many mobile homes. I am tired of shooting zombie deer that wander past our safety zone. Well, okay. I'm not really tired of that part. That part is pretty cool. Suck it, Bambi.

So I'm going to do something else today. No, I'm not going to tell you what; you're going to have to tune in and find out for yourself. But I promise you, you're going to have a *blast*.

—From *Charming Not Sincere*, the blog of Rebecca Atherton,
April 16, 2041

Twelve

Most major cities have their own CDC offices, although three out of four are just satellites, built mostly to keep people calm. The big offices are rarer, and they're the ones with the real resources—they're the ones where things get *done*. The nearest big office was smack in the middle of Portland, which conveniently put it less than an hour's drive from Dr. Abbey's lab.

Less conveniently, we couldn't exactly pull up stakes and go running straight to the CDC to start shaking them down for answers. "They're a government agency," said Becks. "It's their *job* to make things confusing."

"Besides, if we just go charging in there, we're all going to die," added Alaric.

"I hate trying to argue with you when you use logic on me," I said. The sun had dipped substantially lower in the sky while we were getting our Virology 101 from Dr. Abbey, and the shadows were long enough to have become menacing. Sunsets were considered beautiful before the Rising. Now they just mean night is coming, and staying out after dark is a good way to get yourself killed. "We need to get in there. We need to plant some bugs and see if we can knock the CDC off balance enough to tell us anything."

"This isn't a good idea," said Kelly. There was no room for disagreement in her tone. "The CDC has the right to shoot first and ask questions later. All they need to do is formulate a reasonable case for you having been a threat."

"Then I guess we'd better not be threats, huh?" I looked at her and shook my head. "We're going in there, Doc. We need to."

Seeing that Kelly still wasn't following me, Alaric said, "It's like putting together an academic defense. Sometimes you need to look for negative results, as well as positive ones. If we don't learn anything from the CDC, we get footage of them outright denying what everybody will eventually know is true. If we do learn something, we've made progress."

"And I need to know how much of the CDC is involved."

Kelly looked between us, frowning slightly. "You're all insane," she said.

"Yeah." I unlocked the van doors. "But look at it this way: At least you don't have to come."

Kelly snorted and got in.

Sadly, I meant what I said. No matter how pissed I was at Kelly, she was the one who spoke their language, and having her with us would have made things infinitely easier. But with Dr. Wynne assuming she'd died in Oakland, and everyone else believing she'd died in Memphis, we couldn't exactly march her into the office and expect to get actual answers. Shot at, yes, but answers, no.

Alaric was the one to come up with the obvious solution: "It's too late for us to do anything serious tonight. Why don't we get a couple of hotel rooms, and then you can leave me and Maggie to babysit Dr. Connolly while you and Becks go off to wreak havoc."

"I'm not normally in favor of splitting the party, but I have to say that Alaric's plan is a good one. It also keeps those of us—namely, me—who don't have much field experience from standing in the line of fire," added Maggie. "I'd rather not have the CDC call my parents to report that I've come storming their castle."

I nodded. "All right. Let's get out of here. Of course, if there's anyone who'd like to skip their all-expenses-paid ticket on the crazy train, you're welcome to stay here. At that point, your options are going back to the lab and trusting Dr. Abbey not to turn you into her private Frankenstein, or staying out here and praying that whatever comes to find you is in a killing mood, rather than an infecting one."

"Actually, Frankenstein was the doctor, not the monster," said Maggie. "Common misconception."

"Way to ruin the moment, Maggie." I walked over to the bike, picking up my helmet. "Everyone cool?"

"I still say this is a very poorly conceived idea," said Kelly. "I mean, maybe you'll get lucky. Maybe the CDC will let you walk out alive. But I wouldn't place bets on it."

"Maybe *you'll* get lucky and they'll let us leave," I corrected, gently. "Becks here may be the one voted most likely to point a gun at somebody's head just for kicks, but Maggie…"

"They'll never find the body," said Maggie. Her tone was blithely chipper, like she was talking about the latest fund-raiser for the Bulldog Rescue Association. That made it worse. "Not that anyone's going to be looking, since you're legally dead, but even if they looked for you, they'd never come close. All I'd need to do is call my father and tell him I finally had a problem he could fix. You could be the best Father's Day present I've ever given him. He's *so* hard to shop for."

Kelly's eyes widened, fear flickering in their depths. "Is she serious?"

"Almost certainly, but I wouldn't worry about it just yet," I said. "Come on, crew. Let's find us a hotel."

In the end, we wound up checking into the first hotel we found in downtown Portland, a nondescript little Holiday Inn whose front door boasted about their recent security upgrades. I was barely picking up any wireless frequencies, which meant "recent" was probably more like ten years ago, but that didn't matter. Their clearances were up-to-date, and the local review sites said that the rooms were generally clean. We didn't need five-star accommodations. We just needed a place to stash our semi-hostage and regroup without being attacked by zombies.

We got two rooms, one for the boys, one for the girls. If Alaric was uncomfortable about rooming with me—and hence with George—he didn't say anything about it. He just started hooking up his equipment and plugging things in to recharge, while Becks marched Maggie and Kelly into the room across the hall with all the tenderness of a drill sergeant. Maggie took the barked orders gracefully, while Kelly just looked unsettled. I found myself feeling sorry for her, even after everything. After all, I liked her before she told me what the reservoir conditions really meant. It wasn't like she designed the disease.

She's out of her element, said George.

"We all are," I muttered. Alaric glanced my way but didn't say anything. He just kept connecting cables, getting the mobile office of After the End Times up and online.

The message boards had been busy while we were off gallivanting around the Pacific Northwest, harassing mad scientists, and uncovering corruption in the CDC. I skimmed the comment feeds as I waited for my mail to finish downloading. The usual cadre of trolls, assholes, and conspiracy nuts were out in force, almost drowning out the more reserved forum participants. Mahir and the rest of the Newsies had them essentially under control. Technically I'm in charge of the site, but it can be easy to lose track of how big we really are these days. It used to be me, George, and Buffy. Now it's dozens of people, half of whom I've never met and probably never will. Thank God for Mahir. Without him, we'd fall apart, becoming another fringe site clinging to the edges of extinction. He manages the marketing and merchandising that George used to handle, and somehow all the bills get paid. Even the ones relating to ammo supplies for the Irwins, which I know from experience can get pretty damn expensive.

"Anything on fire?" asked Alaric.

"Not as such, but that's okay. I'm sure tomorrow's field trip will supply us with plenty of matches." I put my laptop on the bedside table, stretching until I felt my shoulders pop. "For right now, I'm going to see about catching a little sleep before I go back to professionally risking my life. You have things under control on your end?"

"Yeah. I'm going to write up a few articles on medical ethics and the lack of high-level oversight; I figure Mahir should be up by the time I finish, and I want to check in with him before I crash." As the head of the Newsie division, Mahir was Alaric's direct superior and the one who actually approved his articles. They worked together well, which was a relief. I don't know how I would have dealt if they'd hated each other. Probably by punching the walls until the two of them settled down and said they'd play nicely.

You never did have any people skills, said George, tone managing to be dry and fond at the same time.

"You're one to talk," I mumbled, and closed my eyes, sinking into the too-soft hotel mattress. The sound of Alaric typing away was soothing, helping me relax even further. George and I shared a lot of rooms exactly like this one, one of us dozing while the other kept working, the staccato click of keys providing the white noise that meant it was safe to sleep.

Hush, chided George. *You need to get some rest. You're running yourself too hard.*

"I learned from the best." I sighed, letting out my breath in a deep, slow exhalation. Somewhere in the middle of breathing out, the world slipped away, and I slipped into sleep.

In my dreams that night, George had coppery eyes that she didn't need to hide behind her sunglasses, and we walked in the sunlight, and we didn't have to be afraid. Everything was perfect. Those are the worst dreams of all, because in the end, I can't stay asleep forever.

I woke to the sharp, sweetly metallic tang of gun oil. It had managed to perfume the entire room, overwhelming the less-intrusive smells of toast and greasy hotel turkey bacon. I scrubbed my eyes with the back of a hand, clearing the gunk away before sitting up and squinting at the figure perching on the end of the bed.

"I was starting to think you'd sleep until we got attacked again," commented a female voice. For a single, heart-stopping moment, it sounded like George—but the moment passed. Becks raised her eyebrows at my expression, asking, "You see something green, Mason? Or are you just pissed that I messed up your beauty sleep?"

"Some of us don't *need* beauty sleep, Atherton," I shot back, pushing myself into a sitting position and reaching for the room-service tray someone had kindly placed on the bedside table next to my laptop. "What's the status?"

"Alaric's in the other room keeping an eye on the princess while Maggie makes a grocery run and checks in with the staff at her house. She's worried they'll forget to feed the dogs if she doesn't remind them." Becks continued wiping a silicon cloth along her gunstock, removing the marks her fingers left behind. Her entire kit was open in front of her, explaining the scent of gun oil in the air.

"And the princess herself?" I started making a sandwich from fake bacon and dry toast. It didn't look all that appetizing, but I was hungry enough not to give a damn.

"Awake, anxious, the usual." Becks started packing up her kit. "She's a good kid, but she's also a liability. We should find a safe house and turn her into someone else's problem."

"She's a useful liability—and what do you mean 'kid'? She's the same age you are. We need her, at least for now."

"I wish I were as sure about that as you are."

"I thought you were the one who started out as a Newsie." I took a bite of my sandwich, swallowing before saying, "She knows things we don't know—and if worst comes to absolute worst, I bet she knows the layout of the Memphis CDC pretty darn well. Whoever tracked her to Oakland may not have thought to rekey the biometric sensors to take her retinal scans and fingerprints off the security locks yet. Everyone thinks she's dead, right? So why waste the money to do a rekey when they don't have to?"

Becks blinked before admitting, "I hadn't thought of that one."

"That's why I'm in charge." A drop of hot grease hit me below the collarbone. I hissed and wiped it away, realizing as I did that I'd managed to remove my shirt sometime during the night. This led to the unpleasant but suddenly important question of whether or not I was wearing pants. "Kelly has more to tell us, and she's *going* to tell us. We just have to give her time to realize that she doesn't have a choice."

"I don't like it."

"Never asked you to. Look, I'm pretty sure I don't trust Dr. Wynne, but I still have to admit that he's a damn good doctor, and she worked with him. Maybe she's not the most efficient data-delivery mechanism ever. She still risked a lot to come here and help us out. She's a dead woman walking. She's got nothing left to lose. That makes her a damn good ally."

"It also makes her a damn big suicide risk." Becks stood, taking her gun kit with her. "How long before you're ready to roll?"

"Give me twenty minutes to shower and clean up. We want the CDC to let us in, don't we?" I gave her my best camera-ready smile. Becks rolled her eyes, looking unimpressed, and stomped out of the room.

The door slammed behind her. I yanked the sheets off, relieved to see that I'd managed to keep my jeans on through the night. Accidentally flashing my female colleagues has never been one of my secret aspirations.

The hotel might be shabby, but it was good enough to have a full decontamination shower, with an attached clothing sterilization unit for people who didn't have sufficient gear for fieldwork. It was a nice touch that probably didn't get used too often. I stripped down and shoved my clothes into the sterilizer, hopping into the shower and triggering the bleach nozzle. The water came on at the same time, spraying me down with a heated combination of sterilizing chemicals, bleach-based antiseptics, and something that smelled like cheap lemon disinfectant. I squeezed my eyes tightly shut and started scrubbing.

The amount of bleach in the average shower is why blonde highlights have become so common. They're almost a badge of safety for some people—"See, I've been decontaminated so many times that my hair has lost all natural color." George always hated that. She re-dyed her hair at least twice a month, keeping it dark brown and snarling at anyone who said she was being girly. I always liked the way her hair dye smelled, caustic and sweet at the same time. A lot like George.

The shower finished running the decontamination cycle a few seconds after the clothing sterilizer beeped to signal that my clothes were once more safe to wear around other humans. I dried off, dressed, and stepped back out into the main room to find Alaric waiting for me in an eerie, unintentional imitation of Becks.

"Ready to go?" he asked.

"Ready to stay?" I countered.

To my surprise, he shook his head, and said, "No. Maggie and I were talking, and we want to take the van—and the Doc—back to the house while you're at the CDC."

"Why?" I asked, as I moved to shut down my laptop and start packing it to go.

"Maggie's starting to get twitchy about being away from home this long, and I'd rather not be in the city when you make your trip." Alaric shrugged. "Maybe I'm being paranoid, but if things go wrong, I don't want Dr. Connolly this close to a CDC installation."

"Afraid she'll run for cover? Pretty sure that ship has sailed."

"Afraid they'll come and take her away from us."

I froze in the act of zipping my laptop case. "Fuck. I didn't even think of that. You really think it's a risk, even after we torched her first ID?"

"It depends on whether she's here to play decoy and herd us into danger, or whether she really was sent because they're afraid someone's killing CDC researchers." Alaric shrugged. "Any institution large enough to have different departments is going to have infighting. I don't think she's here to stab us in the back, and that means she's in danger as long as she's in Portland—and we're in danger as long as we're here with her."

"Damn." I chuckled, shaking my head as I shoved the laptop case into my bag. "I bow before your logic. Yeah, take Maggie and the Doc and head for Maggie's place. Becks and I will meet you there after we finish up at the CDC, assuming they don't shoot us on sight. If we haven't checked in by five o'clock this afternoon..." I paused before finishing. "Run. Got it?"

"Got it." Alaric stood, picking up his own laptop as he did. "Kinda like old times, huh, boss?"

"What, walking into certain danger with eyes open, one hand on the recorder, and one hand on the gun?" I flashed him a quick smile. "Exactly like old times."

"I wish—" He faltered before finishing lamely, "Anyway, you and Becks be careful out there today, okay?"

I nodded. "Do my best. Drive safe."

"Will do."

Maggie, Becks, and Kelly were waiting in the hall. Becks cast a thin smile my way. "So you're good with the plan?"

"You guys don't have to conspire against me, you know," I said, shaking my head. "It's a good plan; I am good with the good plan. Maggie, I want you messaging Mahir every twenty miles until you get home, you hear me?"

"No problem," she said. Taking Kelly by the elbow, she said, "Come on. Let's get out of here before somebody gets hurt."

"Where's the fun in that?" asked Becks, and turned to lead the way down the hall and out of the hotel.

Watching the van drive off with Alaric at the wheel left me strangely numb, like somehow their departure meant I would never see them again, like this was some sort of an ending, rather than another step along the road to learning why George really died. I stood frozen in the parking lot, staring after them, a hard lump blocking my throat when I tried to swallow.

"Hey." Becks touched my elbow. I turned to face her. She raised her eyebrows. "Are you okay?"

I managed a small smile. "I'm always okay. You ready to go and piss off the CDC?"

"Why, Shaun," she said, flirting her eyelashes coquettishly, "I thought you'd never ask." She turned to head for the bike. After a moment's pause, I followed her.

The Portland CDC was located in its own facility, a large, meticulously clean collection of low, white-painted buildings that could easily have been repurposed as a hospital or maybe a medical college. From a distance, it looked friendly and inviting, the sort of place that would make a routine checkup almost enjoyable. That first impression didn't survive getting close enough to see barbed wire topping the fence that circled the entire installation, or the small yellow-and-black signs indicating that the fence itself was electrified. Pre-Rising, they would have used a low wattage and backed it up with guard dogs.

Post-Rising, well, let's just say they probably cranked things up to lethal levels at the slightest excuse.

Becks kept her arms looped around my waist as I pulled the bike up to the guard station. It was a small, featureless gunmetal booth that gave no indication whether it was occupied or automated. I held up our IDs, careful to keep both of my hands visible, and said, "Shaun Mason, After the End Times, and Rebecca Atherton, same."

"Please place your identification in the slot," said a mechanized voice. A slot hissed open in the side of the guard station, right next to the speaker. I dropped our ID cards into the slot, which hissed shut. "Please wait."

"Because I was totally planning to zoom off and leave you with our IDs," I muttered.

Shaun, said George warningly. Becks pinched me on the back of the neck.

"Your identification has been confirmed," announced the guard station. The slot opened again, allowing me to reclaim our cards as the first gate began sliding open. "Please proceed onward for blood testing and examination."

"How I love the CDC," I said, passing Becks her ID card and hitting the gas.

The procedure from there was exactly as the guard station threatened—sorry, "indicated." We reached a second gate about ten yards onto the campus, this one accompanied by men wearing Kevlar vests and clutching assault rifles. There were also blood testing units waiting there, one for each of us. We both passed our blood tests, robbing the sentries of the chance to use the weapons they clutched so carefully, and drove on to the third station, where the retinal scanners were waiting.

"I'd think this was excessive if I hadn't just been to Maggie's place," I muttered to Becks, who snorted with quiet laughter. I wasn't kidding, either; I wouldn't be surprised to learn that Maggie and the CDC get their security designs through the same firm. God knows her family has the money, and they've never been shy about spending a few extra bucks for the sake of a little bit more safety.

Finally, after running the security gamut, we were allowed to enter the CDC parking lot, where I parked in a space marked VISITOR in large yellow letters. Becks slid off, removing her helmet and producing a hairbrush from her pack while I was still getting the kickstand positioned. She began briskly brushing out her hair, making adjustments in accordance with some secret set of female rules that even George had never been willing to share with me.

"You look fine, especially for this sort of visit," I said, securing my own helmet to the handlebars. "Nobody's going to be looking at your hair."

Becks gave me a frosty look. "So says you," she said stiffly. "I've found that good hair can open many doors for the female investigative reporter. It certainly doesn't hurt my ratings when I take steps to avoid looking like I just rolled out of bed."

I had to admit she had a point: Becks paid more attention to her appearance than any other Irwin I knew, male or female, and her merchandise sales were even higher than mine. She wore her hair longer than was strictly safe for fieldwork, with blonde highlights and dark brown lowlights that made her otherwise medium-brown hair seem somehow exotic, especially in the sort of light conditions she was usually filming under. Combined with naturally green eyes and a fondness for wearing tight white tank tops, well, it wasn't a mystery why eighty percent of her viewers were male. It was more of a mystery that she seemed to want me to approve of it. I was never going to get that one.

Let her brush her hair so we can get moving, said George.

"Fine," I said, digging my equipment out of the bike's saddlebag more briskly than was strictly necessary.

"What?" asked Becks.

"Nothing."

"Right." She shoved the brush back into her bag. "There, all done."

"Really?" I lifted my eyebrows, giving her an appraising look. "You sure you don't need to touch up your makeup or something before we can go in?"

Becks flashed me a sunny smile that didn't come close to masking the sarcastic lilt in her voice as she said, "Nope. My mascara's designed to stay on for twenty-four hours in a heavy rainstorm under combat conditions. My eye shadow practically has to be removed with an acid wash, and this lipstick is so long-lasting that I haven't seen the natural color of my lips since I was fifteen. I'm totally ready."

"I'm sure the CDC will be thrilled to know that you made such an effort on its behalf," I said, and started down the path that was labeled ENTRANCE in more large yellow letters. At least these ones were on a sign, not painted onto the pavement. Becks made an entirely unladylike snorting noise, and followed me.

After all the security checks required to get to the parking lot, walking up to the front doors of the Portland CDC was almost anticlimactic. They were clear glass, making a point with their total lack of reinforcement— this was the CDC. If the infected made it this far in, the city was already lost, so why bother wasting money that could be put to better use else- where? These were *scientists*. They didn't feel the need to squander public funds on fripperies.

Those fripperies included furniture for their front lobby. A wave of comfortably chilly climate-controlled air hit us as we walked into the build- ing, so devoid of character that it might as well have been an unused movie set. The floor was black marble, and the walls were white, except for the large steel sign proclaiming this to be the Portland office of the Centers for Disease Control. "Got that part, thanks," I muttered, arrowing toward the one piece of furniture in the room: the sleekly futuristic reception desk.

The receptionist herself was also sleekly futuristic, possibly because she felt the need to live up to her workstation. Her hair was pulled into a bun so severe it looked almost molded, her jacket was impeccably cut, and the eyes behind her black-framed glasses were cold. "Names and business?" she asked as we approached. Her fingers never stopped darting across her keyboard, even as she glanced in our direction, looked us up and down, and dismissed us as unimportant.

"We're with the After the End Times news site, and we'd like to speak to the director of this installation," I said mildly, leaning against the edge of her desk as I flashed her my ID. Becks did the same, unsmiling. "Don't worry, we can wait if we have to."

The receptionist gave us another of those quick, cold, up-and-down glances before asking, "The nature of your business, sir?" The "sir" was grudging, purely a formality to check off some internal list marked "proper procedure."

"That's for us to discuss with the director," said Becks.

"I see." The receptionist sniffed. "If you'd like to make an appointment, I'm sure we can fit you in sometime this week. In the meanwhile—"

"Sometime this week? Really? That's *awesome*." I smacked the edge of the desk for emphasis as I straightened, and was only a little gratified to see the receptionist jump. "Okay, Becks, you start setting up the cameras, and I'm going to analyze the light levels in here, see where it's best for us to start shooting."

"Excuse me?" The receptionist half rose from her seat, revealing a pencil skirt as precisely tailored as the jacket. I found myself wondering if she starched her underpants to keep them from ruining her mood through excessive softness. "What are you doing?"

"Well, this is a government building, right?" I asked, guilelessly. "Which means that we, as citizens, are totally entitled to be here whenever and whyever we want, as long as we're not actively disrupting normal business or committing acts of vandalism? No appointments required unless there's an active state of emergency?"

"Yes, but—"

"So we're going to be streaming live from the lobby here until we get in to see your director. Let the good citizens of Portland—and the world, did I mention we're a top-rated global news site? Right, I may have left that little tidbit off when we were making introductions—see what an awesome job the CDC does responding to visitors."

"I think we can set the cameras up right over there," said Becks, stabbing a finger at a random patch along the wall.

"You can't do that!" said the receptionist. She sounded agitated. Poor thing. She'd probably sprain herself if she tried for any real facial expressions with her hair pulled back that tightly. "I'm sorry, there was a little—this is all a misunderstanding, give me a moment and I'll get Director Swenson for you."

"Thanks," I said, flashing a wide grin in her direction. "It's cool, Becks, you can hold off on setting things up."

"Check," said Becks. She re-shouldered her pack. We watched as the increasingly anxious-looking receptionist picked up her phone, muttering into it with her palm cupped around the receiver, like that would magically keep us from hearing what she was saying. It worked, a little; most of her side of the conversation was too garbled to understand, although I was pretty sure I caught the words "crazy," "reporters," and "threatening to." As press went, it wasn't bad, and might actually give the director an idea of what he was about to be dealing with.

Nothing could ever prepare him for you, said George.

"Flatterer," I murmured. The receptionist shot me a wary look, hand still cupped around the receiver. I smiled at her. Brightly. She looked away again.

"Yes, sir; of course, sir," she said, and set the receiver back into its cradle, not looking in our direction as she said, "Director Swenson is on his way down and apologizes for any inconvenience that you may have experienced in being forced to wait so long."

"It's cool," I said.

The receptionist didn't say anything. She leaned slightly forward, shoulders hunched as she focused her attention on her computer. It was obvious that she couldn't entirely dismiss our presence as a bad dream—we were a little too solid for that—and it was equally obvious that she was giving it the old college try. I rocked back on my heels, content to let her ignore us. There's pushing the envelope of polite behavior to get what you want, and then there's just plain being mean. I try not to cross the line when it can be avoided.

We'd been waiting less than five minutes when the sound of crisp footsteps echoed through the lobby and an immaculately groomed man in a white lab coat stepped around a corner and into view. He was dressed like a generic midlevel bureaucrat at any corporation in the country, assuming you could overlook the lab coat: gray slacks that were probably some sort of insanely expensive natural fiber, white button-up shirt, sedate blue-and-green tie, and immaculately polished black shoes. Even his lab coat looked like it was tailored for him, rather than being the standard off-the-rack lab wear. If the CDC was running in the red this season, his wardrobe definitely wasn't feeling the pinch.

Neither was his plastic surgeon. His hair was thick and well-styled, but still uniformly silver, and his unwrinkled skin had the characteristic tightness of a man in his late fifties paying through the nose to maintain the illusion that he was a well-preserved thirty-seven or so. He walked to the receptionist's desk with the calm assurance of a man who knows himself to be in absolute control of his environment, extending a hand in my direction. "Shaun Mason, I presume?"

"The same." I took his hand and shook it. Even with all the training I've had to desensitize me to the necessity of occasional contact with strangers, the gesture felt *wrong*. You aren't supposed to touch people you don't know.

Not unless they've just demonstrated their infection status with a successful blood test, and maybe not even then. "This is my colleague, Rebecca Atherton. She works with our action news division."

"Ah, an Irwin," said the man, reclaiming his hand and turning to study Rebecca. His gaze started at her face, swept down her body, and returned to her face again, all without a trace of hesitation or shame. "You know, I've always liked that term. Irwin, for the late, great Steve Irwin. He died in the field, you know. Just the way he would have wanted to go."

"No shit, asshole," muttered Becks.

"Actually, sir, I'm pretty sure the way he would have wanted to go was in his sleep, sometime in his late nineties, but that's beside the point." Something about him was putting my hackles up. Maybe it was the way he looked at Becks. Maybe it was his tone, which was slick enough to grease a rusty chainsaw. "I'm guessing you're Director Swenson."

"Precisely so. I apologize for making you wait. Next time, please be sure to call ahead. That will allow us to avoid these little delays."

Yeah, because we'll never get past security again.

I forced my expression to remain composed as I said, "I'll keep that in mind. If you don't mind, though, my colleague and I were in the area and had some questions we wanted to ask you—in person, hence the dropping by. Is there a place where we could talk?"

A flash of discomfort crossed his face, there and gone before I could blink. "Of course," he said, smoothly. "If you'd both come with me, I believe one of the conference rooms is available. Miss Lassen, as you were."

The receptionist—Miss Lassen—nodded, looking deeply relieved as Director Swenson turned and began retracing his steps, leaving the front lobby behind. She might not have been able to keep us out, but at least we weren't going to be her problem anymore. Becks and I exchanged a look, shrugged, and followed the director to the back of the lobby, around a corner, and into a nondescript hall that seemed to stretch on for the better part of a mile.

Director Swenson walked past three identical doors before stopping at a fourth and pressing his thumb against a small sensor pad. The light above the door changed from red to green, and the door swung open. "Past this point, you'll need blood tests as well as someone with the proper clearances to open any doors, including the restrooms," he said, sounding self-indulgently amused. "I recommend not wandering off unescorted."

"I'll keep that in mind if I need to pee," muttered Becks. I gave her a speculative look, which she met with a glare.

Funny, normally you're the one pissing off the natives, said George.

I bit my lip to keep myself from answering as we followed Director Swenson through the door and into one of the long, featureless white hallways characteristic of CDC installations everywhere. It's like they're afraid to spend money on interior decorating when there's such a good chance of the place needing to be hosed down with bleach at any moment. We didn't pass any doctors, although we did walk past several large glass "windows" looking in on empty patient rooms. White walls, white beds, white floors—white everything. I woke up in one of those rooms once, after the CDC team picked us up outside of Memphis. I thought I'd died and gone to the sterilized afterlife.

Director Swenson stopped in front of a door that looked exactly like every other door in the place, except for the larger, more elaborate-looking testing unit built into the wall next to it. "The cycle takes approximately fifteen seconds," he said, pressing his palm flat against the test pad. "Once I go through, the door will close and the unit will reset. Please don't try to follow without a clean test. I'd really rather not send the entire facility into lockdown today."

"It's cool," I said. "We know how to do our jobs."

The light over the door turned green and the door swung open with a hydraulic hiss, saving Director Swenson the trouble of answering me. Instead, he raised an eyebrow and stepped through the doorway before the door swung closed again.

"Scale of one to ten, how stupid is this?" asked Becks, pressing her own palm against the testing panel.

Ten, said George.

"Oh, five, tops," I said, and smiled brightly. "Don't worry about it. We're just here to ask the scientists some questions about science. Scientists like that sort of shit."

"Right," said Becks dubiously as the light turned green and the door hissed open again. She stepped through.

"Hey, George," I muttered, flattening my hand against the testing panel. "Check this out."

When does telling the truth become an act of terrorism? At what point does a lie become an act of mercy? Is it cruel to tell a parent their child will die, even if it's true? Is it kind to tell an accident victim they're going to recover, even though all evidence says they won't? Where's the line dividing honesty from harm, deceit from decency, and misinformation from malice? I don't know. All the clever wordplay in the world won't somehow grant me that knowledge. I'm sorry. I wish it would.

This is what I do know: A lie, however well-intended, can't prepare you for reality or change the world. The accident victim will die whether they're promised recovery or not, but the parent told that their child is dying may have time to prepare, and may be able to treasure those final days together even more. To tell the truth is to provide armament against a world too full of cruelties to be defeated with simple falsehoods. If these truths mean the world is less comforting than it might have been, it seems like a pretty small price to pay.

It seems to me we owe the world—more, we owe ourselves—the exchange of comfort for the chance that maybe the truth can do what people always say it can. The truth may, given the opportunity, set us free.

**—From *The Kwong Way of Things*,
the blog of Alaric Kwong, April 16, 2041**

We had another meeting with the senator today. We're about to head out, and he wants to be sure that we all understand our roles in the campaign. I don't think he trusts us to have our heads in the game right now, and frankly, neither do I. Shaun is barely talking to anyone, including me, and Buffy simply isn't talking. I keep running the footage of the attacks so far over and over again, looking for something that we might have missed, looking for some clue to who is responsible for all of this.

When I sent in the application for this position, I thought I was doing us a favor. I thought I was giving us the opportunity to make a name for ourselves, and that we could change the world by telling the truth. I thought I was doing the right thing. But now I watch Shaun punching the walls, and I wake up as tired as I was when I went to bed, and I just wish that I could take it back. I wish I could take it all back. I'm tired, and I want to go home.

But oh, God, I'm so afraid that we're not all going to make it home alive.

**—From *Postcards from the Wall*,
the unpublished files of Georgia Mason,
originally posted April 18, 2041**

Thirteen

The CDC conference room lived up to the design aesthetic I was coming to expect from them: white on white on white. It was like they'd looked at the uniforms American nurses wore during World War II and said "Yeah, that's what we're talking about." Maybe they bleached the place on such a regular basis that they didn't want to deal with paying to have all the furnishings re-dyed. Whatever the motivation, the combination of white walls and white carpet with a glass-topped conference table and white faux-leather chairs was enough to make me feel grubby and unwashed. CDC employees probably took a lot of showers, just to keep themselves from feeling like they were too dirty to be allowed to touch the furniture.

Director Swenson walked the full length of the conference table to sit at the head. Alpha male posturing if I'd ever seen it. The gesture was designed to say "This is mine and I am in charge here"—I was sort of surprised he didn't lift his leg and piss on something. Urine's a natural bleaching agent, right? It would explain how they kept everything so damn white.

Becks and I trailed along behind him like good little peons, finally sitting down next to each other on the left-hand side of the table. Becks took the seat closer to the director. Sure, I was technically in charge of our little fact-finding expedition, but of the two of us, I was the one more likely to launch myself for his throat, and we wanted to avoid that if at all possible. Attacking high-ranking CDC officials isn't really the best way to get what you want.

"Now, then," said the director, gracing us with a fatherly smile as warm as it was artificial. "What can I do for the two of you? I'll admit, I was a bit surprised that you didn't phone ahead. That's standard for most representatives of the media."

"Yeah, we're really sorry about that," I said, not bothering to inject the slightest note of apology into my tone. "See, we'd usually call ahead, only I managed to leave my address book—where did I leave that again, Becks?"

"In your office," said Becks promptly. She knows her cues. With as long as we've been working together, she'd better.

"Right, in my office." I bared my teeth at Director Swenson in an approximation of his smile. The corners of his mouth twitched downward, confusion flickering in his eyes. That was good. I wanted him off balance. "That's sort of the problem, since my office is—my office *was*, I guess—in Oakland, basically right at the center of the zone that got firebombed. We were out camping when the quarantine came down, but not all my people made it out."

"I see." Director Swenson leaned back in his chair, expression smoothing into careful neutrality. The confusion in his eyes faded, replaced by wariness. "You're very fortunate. That outbreak was particularly bad."

"Yeah, how *did* that happen as fast as it did? Isn't the CDC supposed to prevent things like that?" asked Becks. I shot her a sharp look. She ignored me, attention focused on Director Swenson like a sniper focuses on a target.

She had friends inside the blast zone, said George. *Not just Dave. Civilian friends.*

It was all I could do not to wince. I'd been withdrawn since George died, which meant I never really bothered getting to know the neighbors in our bucolic little part of Oakland. Becks was a hell of a lot more gregarious. She probably knew everyone on our block, not just in our building, and could recite the names of the deceased without cross-referencing the Wall. And now we knew, beyond a shadow of a doubt, that the CDC was involved in something nasty. Put it all together, and I'd basically primed her to go off. The question was whether being stuck in the blast radius was going to be a good thing or a bad thing.

"It appears that someone in the area had been illegally breeding American pit bull terriers for use in dogfights," said Director Swenson, smoothly as you please. "From what we've been able to reconstruct, one of the dogs became infected and attacked the others. The pack attacked their handler when he came to see what all the noise was about. The dogs were able to escape, and those large enough to amplify went on to infect individuals all around the area. It became too large to contain shortly after."

It was a textbook example of a no-win infection scenario. That was the problem. Textbook examples almost never happen in the real world. I saw Becks opening her mouth, probably to say just that. I clamped my hand down on her thigh under the table, squeezing hard. The pressure was enough to cut her off. She shot me a confused look. I tried to look like I was ignoring her, and cleared my throat.

"Would've still been nice if you'd sent, I don't know, a rescue helicopter or something for folks inside the blast radius, but that's beside the point," I said smoothly, keeping my hand clamped on Becks's thigh. "Anyway, I'm sure you understand why we couldn't call ahead, having lost your number in the explosion and all."

The explosion didn't wipe the CDC's phone number off the Internet, but that didn't really matter; my excuse was plausible enough that Director Swenson couldn't get away with calling me a liar, and artificial enough that we both knew I was lying. His nostrils flared slightly from the strain of keeping his expression neutral. I smiled.

"Yes, absolutely," said Director Swenson. "Now, to what do we owe the honor of this visit?"

"To get a little background, make sure we're on the same page and everything, you remember my sister, Georgia Carolyn Mason?" Becks winced at the sound of George's name, probably thinking of my recent tendency to fly off the handle whenever George came up in conversation. In the back of my head, George snorted with brief amusement but didn't say anything. This was my party. She was going to let me be the one to send out the invitations.

Director Swenson nodded. "I've seen her file. Her death was—any death is tragic, but what she accomplished, even after the point of initial amplification, was—it was amazing. You must be very proud."

"She died in the field," I said, as flatly as I could. "Just the way she would have wanted to go."

"I'm sure that must be a great comfort to you." He sounded like he meant it, too. My hand clenched tighter on Becks's thigh. It took every inch of self-control I had to peel my fingers away. She didn't make a sound, even though the way I was squeezing must have hurt.

"To be honest, I'd rather have her alive and pissed off than dead and happy," I said, putting my hands flat on the table before I could grab hold of Becks again. "If you've seen her file, you must know she suffered from retinal Kellis-Amberlee."

"Yes, I saw that. It's amazing that she accomplished so much, given her disability."

I somehow managed to smile at him. I may never know how I did that. "She did a lot with her life, it's true. Now I've got to soldier on and take care of the things she wasn't able to finish."

"Oh?" Director Swenson gave me an attentive look. "What was she working on?"

"Reservoir conditions. See, she knew a lot of people through her support groups and mailing lists—"

Support groups? asked George, sounding horrified. *I never joined a support group in my life.*

I ignored her. "—and she started noticing this crazy pattern." Was it my imagination, or was Director Swenson going still? "It was like her friends died faster than anybody else's. I mean, even faster than *my* friends, and most of my friends are Irwins, which is sort of like waving a big red flag in the face of Darwinism. So she started to dig."

"Funny, I don't remember seeing any received queries in her file," said Director Swenson. His voice had gone completely blank, neither excited nor cold. The voice of a man in the process of disconnecting.

"She didn't query the CDC," said Becks, before I could open my mouth. I decided to let her take the conversation and run. Her training was better for this bluff than mine was. "She figured that if there wasn't a pattern, she didn't want to bother you, and if there was..." She let the sentence trail off before lifting her shoulders in a "What are you going to do?" shrug, and said, "It was a pretty big scoop. If the reservoir conditions were that dangerous, and somebody was going to break the story, why couldn't it be her?"

"I suppose her notes were lost along with your address book," said Director Swenson, looking at me.

"Oh, no, not at all," I replied. "I've been studying them, actually. I mean, they're a little outside my reading level, but hey, what's life without learning? She's right, too. The death rate is, like, crazy. Some of these people, statistically, should have lived to see their great-grandkids. Which means either the overall mortality rates for the country need to be recalculated, because we're calibrating something really, really wrong, or folks with reservoir conditions are dying at a *really* accelerated rate." I gave him my best big-dumb-Irwin face, and asked, "Which do you think it is?"

"Well, now that you bring it up, there is some documentation to support your sister's conclusions. I only wish she'd brought them to us before she died. It would have been a real pleasure working with her." Director Swenson stood, motioning for Becks and me to stay where we were. "If you two will excuse me for just a moment, I'll go and get the files that relate to this particular issue. I think you'll find them very enlightening."

"We'll chill here," I said, offering him a half-salute. Director Swenson mustered a wan smile and turned, walking quickly out of the conference room. He shut the door as he exited. Probably another of those crazy CDC security precautions...or he wanted us to think so, anyway.

Relaxing in my chair, I pulled out my phone and fiddled with it, saying carelessly, "It's cool that he's going to share his research, huh?" as I texted Becks with *He's up to something. Watch yourself.*

Becks didn't look even slightly surprised when her phone started buzzing. Unclipping it from her belt, she read the screen and started to key in a reply as she said, "I told you the CDC was the place to go with this. They're going to have files on anything and everything she could have found on her own, if she just hadn't been so damn stubborn." *You think? That man couldn't have rushed out of here faster if you'd been spurring him on with an electric prod. He's not happy that we're here, and he's really not happy about this line of discussion.*

"You know George. Stubborn to the end." *At least this confirms that it's more than just Memphis. Did you keep track of escape routes on the way in?*

"It was her best quality." *There really aren't any, other than the way we came. These buildings are designed as giant kill chutes. If there's an outbreak, staff is supposed to hole up and stay where they are until help shows up.*

"You can say that again." *Isn't that fucking awesome.* While Becks keyed in her response, I dipped a hand into my pocket and withdrew one of our increasingly limited supply of Buffy-built bugs. You can buy listening devices from sources both legal and extralegal all over the world, and mail order makes it possible to make those purchases essentially untraceable. None of them hold a candle to Buffy's work.

Hey, you're the one who thought coming here was a good idea. I was following your lead. Do we want to scout while we wait for him to come back and get us?

I can't imagine it would be a worse idea than coming here in the first place. I snapped the bug onto the bottom of the table, flattening its edges until they were flush to the frame. The CDC would need to be looking real hard to stand even a chance of finding it.

Got it. Becks glanced up from her phone, asking, "You think Director Swenson is going to be back soon? I need to tinkle, and he didn't show us where the bathrooms were."

I bit my lip to keep from laughing out loud. Everything gets funnier when you're waiting to find out whether you're in mortal danger, and Becks saying "tinkle" would have been hysterical under the best of conditions. This was, after all, a woman who once pissed off the side of a moving RV while fleeing from a mob of hungry zombies. On camera, no less. We got a lot of down-loads that day, even with the modesty filters in place. "Well, last time we went to a CDC office, they were—hell with it, he won't mind if I show you, and it'll be faster this way." I stood, sliding my phone back into my pocket.

"Thanks, Shaun." Becks followed me. She was doing her best to look embarrassed, and she was doing a decent job. I would have believed it if I'd been watching the scene through a security feed, and if I hadn't known her so well. "It'll only take me a minute."

"It's cool. Keeps me from getting twitchy while we wait." I hesitated, looking at the door. Something about it was wrong in a way that was so weird that I couldn't figure out what it was. It was like waking up one morning to find that my hair had changed color—impossible, and hence invisible, at least for a little while.

Look at the light, advised George.

The light above the door—the light that should have been green, signaling that the standard security features were active, and that the door would open after a successful blood test had been run—was glowing a strong and steady yellow. I nodded toward it, watching as Becks followed the direction of the gesture. She went pale. A green light means everything is good, all systems go. A red light means a lockdown: Either there's live viral material in the room with you or there's live viral material right *outside* the room, where you don't want to go. Either way, if you sit tight, the problem will resolve itself. A yellow light...I wasn't sure what a yellow light could possibly mean, beyond the chilling "this door has not been properly locked."

Ignoring the testing panel waiting for my palm, I reached out and gently grasped the doorknob. Nothing shocked or stung me. The light didn't change. I gave a gentle tug. The door swung just as gently inward. There was no hydraulic hiss; the hydraulics were not engaged.

"I don't think there's a place anywhere on this planet where that's a good thing," said Becks, reaching under her jacket to rest her hand against the grip of her pistol. "Suggestions?"

"I suggest we go and find Director Swenson, let him know that he's having some kind of security problem—and I don't mean two reporters loose in his building. You're going to have to wait for that tinkle."

"I can hold it," said Becks gravely.

"Good."

We left the white-on-white confines of the conference room for the white-on-white of the hall we'd come in through. There was no one in sight in either direction, making it seem like we might be the last two people on Earth.

Something isn't right here, said George.

"Got that right," I muttered, drawing my own pistol and releasing the safety. Becks was looking at me intently, waiting for me to clarify whether I was talking to George or to her. I gestured down the hall in the direction we'd come from. "I think I can get us out if we go this way. But I'll bet you a dollar our good director went the other way."

"Then that's the way we're going," said Becks, turning to scan the hall ahead of us. "Looks clear from here."

"I think that's the problem." I started walking, keeping my pistol at a low, defensive angle. Technically, it's legal for me to be armed anywhere I want to be, since I've passed my tests and I keep my licenses up-to-date at all times. Less technically, I'm not sure it's a good idea for anyone, be he blogger, God, or the president of the United States, to go around waving a gun in a government building. It tends to give them the crazy idea that you might shoot, and things tend to get real unpleasant real fast after that happens.

The not-rightness of the situation became more and more apparent as we walked. We passed labs, break rooms, and more of the one-way windows into rooms intended for patient care. We passed bulletin boards, signs, and even the bathrooms. What we *didn't* pass was anyone who demanded to see our IDs and asked what we were doing wandering around the building unescorted. Near as I could tell, the Portland CDC had been quietly and effectively deserted. All we needed was a creepy minor-key soundtrack to reinforce the idea that this was a bad situation. George waited silently inside my head, not making any comments that might distract me. That was good. I was already jumpy enough.

"We should be catching up to the director soon, assuming he hasn't taken a turn we missed," I said. "If he has, we better hope there's an emergency exit somewhere in this place."

"Pessimism doesn't become you."

"But I'm so *good* at it." We kept walking, Becks trailing about three feet behind me and turning every few steps to sweep the corridor. If anything came lunging after us, she'd have time to gun it down before it caught up. "Hey, did you ever see those fucked-up first-person shooter games that were so big before the Rising? The ones with the zombies chasing you through government buildings and creepy old houses and shit?"

"Shut up, Shaun."

"That's what this feels like. One big maze, and we're the rats unlucky enough to be in it." A reassuring exit sign marked one of the doors ahead, and the light above it was a steady, reassuring green. I started to think that maybe there was an innocent explanation for all this, like a broken circuit somewhere that had required a quick, quiet evacuation of the unsecured areas. The director might have been intending to come back for us.

Yeah, and pigs might fly. I slapped my hand down on the test panel as soon as it came into reach. The metal was cool and nonresponsive. No needles appeared to sample my blood, no anesthetics sprayed to numb the nonexistent sting. The light over the door stayed green. "Fuck."

"What?" Becks stepped closer, still scanning the halls around us for signs of movement. "What's it doing?"

"Nothing." I took my hand off the panel. The light over the door went out. A moment later, so did the lights in the hall, plunging us into total darkness.

Fuck, said George.

"Yeah, tell me about it," I muttered, trying the door handle. It was unsurprisingly locked. It didn't deliver an electric shock or shoot a sedative needle into my palm—both standard defensive measures for a sealed door in a government compound—but that was all I could say in the positive. I pulled my hand away and started rummaging through my pockets for a flashlight. "We could really use your eyes about now. Done being dead yet?"

Sorry, no.

"Shaun?" An amber light clicked on to my left as Becks produced the field light from her backpack and held it up between us. She still had her pistol in her other hand. That was probably a good idea. "I hate to interrupt, but can you maybe focus on the living for a little bit? I'd like to keep breathing long enough to get mad at you for this shitty idea."

"You went along with it." My fingertips grazed the hard metal base of my portable flashlight. I pulled it out and clicked it on, aiming it for the floor. The amber field light was night-vision friendly, but we'd need the extra illumination at floor level if we didn't want to risk tripping over something in the dark.

"I never said I was the smart one. Thoughts?"

"These places are designed as kill chutes—they're supposed to herd you deeper, so the infected can be picked off easily and the uninfected will stand a chance in hell at getting themselves to safety." I gestured back toward the conference room with my pistol, keeping my flashlight pointed down. "We walk this way and hope we trip over a maintenance guy."

"And if we don't?"

"Then we hope we trip over an exit."

"This plan sucks."

"I know."

We started back down the hall, me leading, Becks so close behind that her shoulders brushed mine every time she turned to do another sweep behind us. George had gone silent again. That was good; that let me narrow my focus until there was nothing that mattered but the sound of our slow progress. Field training involves learning how to step lightly and breathe slowly, so as to reduce your auditory impact on the environment. Viral amplification doesn't give zombies superpowers, but it makes them really focused. Consequentially, they're occasionally capable of feats of tracking that seem to border on the unnatural. They're not. They're just incredibly good at homing in on the little things. The little things are what get people killed.

We hit the first corner. I spun around it, raising my flashlight to light up the entire hallway ahead. What it cost us in night vision was more than balanced by its effectiveness as a defensive weapon: The retinal condition that kept George behind prescription sunglasses for most of her life is universal among the infected. They can adjust to going out during the day, but they always prefer to stay in the dark when possible, and having a flashlight shine directly into their eyes is never fun.

An empty hall greeted my sweep. I lowered the flashlight. "Clear," I said, and we walked on, following the gently herding design of the CDC building. We were walking into a kill chute. Sadly, it was the smartest thing we could do. Going the other way would just take us farther from any help that might be waiting for us—assuming there was any help to be had.

We repeated the same procedure at the next three corners we reached. Each time, I spun around to blind any lurking infected with my flashlight, while Becks watched my back and got ready to start shooting. Each time, the light revealed nothing but featureless, utterly empty hallway. The white walls glimmered like ghosts through the dimness as we walked. My skin crawled, claustrophobia and paranoia beginning to speed my heart rate. Not enough to put me in danger of panic, but enough that I could feel it rising. From the way Becks's breath was starting to hitch—just a little, every third inhale—she was in a similar state. It's not the action that kills you. It's the *waiting*.

At the very next corner, the waiting ended.

It started out like the turns before it: Becks braced to shoot, while I stepped around the corner and swept my flashlight over the hall. Only this time, the hall in front of us extended for only about five feet before splitting into a T-junction...and this time, something up ahead and to the left responded to the light with a moan. It was still out of sight around the turn, but that didn't matter; once you've heard the moaning of the infected, you never forget it. It's the sort of sound that hardwires itself into your primitive monkey brain, and the message it sends is simple: run.

I took a hasty step backward, keeping my flashlight pointed in the direction of the moan. It wouldn't ward off the infected—nothing stops a hungry zombie once it has an idea of where a free lunch can be found—but the pain would slow them down. "Becks?"

"Yeah?"

"Is the other direction clear?"

"I think so."

"Good. Becks?"

"Yeah?"

"Run."

There was no grace or artistry in our flight. Becks was running almost before the word was out of my mouth, waiting only for the confirmation that I didn't have a better idea, and I was only half a heartbeat behind. We ran as fast as we could, our footfalls echoing off the walls around us and making it impossible to tell whether we were running for safety or into the arms of another mob. The moaning started behind us, distant at first, but growing louder with bone-chilling speed. That's one thing the old movies got wrong. Real zombies—especially the freshly infected kind—can *run*.

Call for help!

"What?" I gasped, still running. Becks shot me a look. I shook my head, and she returned her attention to the serious business of running for her goddamn life.

You have a phone! Think, *Shaun!*

It was hard to focus on running and think about what George was trying to tell me at the same time. She was always the smart one, and that's held true even now that she's nothing but a ghost in my machine. I struggled to make sense of her words, and nearly stumbled as it hit me.

"Oh, mother*fuck*," I said, causing Becks to shoot me another sharp look. "Becks, I need you to buy us some time. Don't worry about the interest rates."

"Got it," she said, obedience winning out over confusion. She turned to face the direction of the moaning, still pacing me down the hall. If she tripped, it was all over, but that didn't seem to bother her. Her hands were steady as she pulled a ball-shaped object from her belt. The motion was followed by the distinctive sound of a pin being pulled, and then she flung the grenade in the direction of the moaning. She whipped around as soon as she let go, grabbing me by the arm. It was her turn to haul me down the hall, and she did it with admirable force. "*Run!*"

I ran.

The grenade Becks had thrown exploded about six seconds later. It wasn't a big enough boom to come with a back draft but it was big enough to fill the hall briefly with light. I risked a glance back over my shoulder. The walls were burning. That should be enough to slow the infected for at least a little while. "Cover me," I said.

Becks nodded, slowing enough to let me pull a few feet in front of her before speeding up again, holding a position about a foot and a half behind me. I felt like a total shit putting her between me and the danger we knew, but I needed the breathing space. It might be the one thing that could save us.

Fumbling an ear cuff from my jacket pocket without dropping my flashlight wasn't easy, especially not at a dead run. Somehow, I managed. I slammed the ear cuff into place, pressing the Call button as I snapped, "Secure connection, command line 'Hi, honey, I'm home,' open channel to Alaric Kwong."

The ear cuff beeped. For a long, undying moment, the only sounds were footsteps, harsh, exhausted breathing, the distant moans of the infected, and the overstrained beating of my heart. We couldn't run forever. Eventually, the kill chute was going to close, and if we were in the wrong place when that happened...

The ear cuff beeped again as Alaric came on the line: "Secure connection confirmed, please verify your identity before I hang up on you."

"Fuck you, Alaric, I don't have the *time* to remember some stupid code word." That was a lie: "some stupid code word" was the current call sign. If the CDC was recording, which they probably were, this might make them think our security wasn't as good as it really was. I could hope, anyway. "We're in a little bit of trouble here. Is the Doc there?"

"Shaun? Why are you breathing like that? What's—"

"I need you to put the Doc on the line *right fucking now*, Alaric, or you're getting a goddamn field promotion! Am I making myself clear, here, or do I need to get footage of the zombies trying to eat our asses?"

"I'll get her," said Alaric. The line beeped again, going silent.

Becks pulled up almost even with me. Sweat was adding that new-penny shine to her cheeks. "What are you *doing*?"

"CDC installs are all built on the same basic floor plan, right?" Another T-junction came into view ahead of us, my flashlight barely illuminating it enough to give us warning before we hit the wall.

"Right, but—"

"Doc gets us out or we're dead, Becks." The moaning from behind us was still getting louder, and that wall was getting closer. "Keep running!"

The ear cuff beeped, and Kelly's hesitant voice took the place of the silence, asking, "Shaun? Is that really you?"

"In a pickle, Doc! Zombies are chasing us through the Portland CDC, and we need out before we're on the menu! There's a T ahead of us—which way do we go?"

I had to give Kelly this: She recovered damn fast to what must have seemed like a totally random question. "Have you already passed a T-junction?"

"Yes! We went right!"

"You went—damn. Okay. At the T ahead, take the left, and try the third door you pass. Is the place in lockdown yet?"

"Do you mean 'Are the lights all fucking out, and did half the doors go amber before the power failed'? Because then yeah, we're in lockdown!" I grabbed Becks by the wrist, hauling her along as I veered left. "What kind of door?"

"Same size as the rest, but it should open when you push it."

One door flashed by on our right, followed about six feet later by a second door, this one on the left. I slowed to keep from overshooting the third door and grabbed for the knob, all too aware of the advantage I was throwing to our opponents if Kelly was wrong. The zombies weren't going to slow down just to keep the playing field even.

The knob turned without any resistance and the door swung inward, nearly spilling me—and by extension, Becks—into a pantry-sized room with glowing amber tubes running all along the edges of the ceiling, like supersized versions of the portable field light. I recovered my balance and stumbled fully into the room, thrusting Becks behind me before slamming the door shut. There were three old-fashioned deadbolts on the inside, the kind of things that can never go down, not even in a power failure. I slid all three of them into the closed and locked position before I'd even finished processing the impulse to do it.

"Shaun?" Kelly's voice was strident enough to make me wince. "Where are you? Are you okay?"

"We're in some sort of weird closet." I backed away from the door, keeping my pistol trained just above the knob. If the infected started trying to batter their way inside, I'd make them pay for every inch they gained.

"Are the lights red, yellow, or green?"

"Yellow." It was close enough to the truth, and closer than either of the other options.

Kelly sighed in obvious relief. "That means the security system is engaged, but you're not in one of the sections already locked down. The door is soundproof, scent-proof, and splatter-proof, so as long as everyone inside is clean, you should be okay."

"As long as we don't mind dying like rats in a cage, you mean. How do we get *out* of here, Doc?"

"There should be a door directly opposite the one you came in through."

The wall was blank and featureless. "No door."

"Touch the wall."

"What?"

"Just do it."

If Kelly was trying to kill us, she wouldn't have given us a bolt hole. I nodded toward the far wall, saying, "Doc wants us to touch it."

"Touch it?"

"Yeah."

"Anything's better than going back out there." On this philosophical note, Becks slapped her left palm flat against the wall—which immediately wavered and turned translucent, revealing a second wall behind it. There was a door at the center, twin to the one we'd entered through.

Becks yanked her hand away, swearing loudly. In my ear, Kelly said, "I hear shouting. Do you see the real wall now?"

"You could've warned us!" The newly revealed wall included three testing panels, all with reassuringly green lights shining next to them.

"I wasn't sure it would be there," said Kelly. Her tone was sincere; either she really meant it, or she was a much better actress than she'd been letting on. "Put your hands against the test panels. You're going to need to check out as clean if you want the glass to lift. If you're not…"

If we weren't, we'd never get out of this room. "Are you sure the tests will work?"

"It's a secondary system. It doesn't run off the main grid. If the screen was still in place and the interior lights are on, it should work."

"I'm trusting you on this one, Doc. Don't fuck us." I holstered my pistol and walked over to join Becks at the wall, slapping my hand against one of the testing units. She lifted her eyebrows. I nodded to her, and she mimicked the motion. From her grimace, the needles bit into both of us at the same time. These tests were built for crude effectiveness, not reassurance. They didn't waste time with any of the niceties like stinging foam or pre-test hand sterilizer—or full-sized needles. The feeling of the test engaging was like brushing my palm across the surface of a cactus, all tiny pinprick stings that didn't hurt because they didn't last long enough to totally register. They just itched like a sonofabitch.

"Step away from the testing center," intoned a pleasant female voice.

Becks and I exchanged a look as we took a long step backward. "Doc, the room's talking," I reported.

"That's normal," she said. Somehow I didn't find that particularly reassuring.

The lights next to the two units we'd used began to flash through the familiar red-green pattern as the units themselves filtered our blood looking for live viral bodies. There was still no sound from the hall outside, which wasn't helping. Sure, we knew that we weren't going to be eaten in the next thirty seconds, but the entire infected staff of the Portland CDC could be out there, and we'd have no idea. Not the sort of thing I really wanted to be thinking about.

Breathe, said George.

I took a deep breath as the lights next to the testing units turned a uniform, steady shade of green. "Thank you," said the female voice. "You may proceed." The glass slid to one side, vanishing into a groove in the far wall.

"This is your fucking fault, Mason," growled Becks, starting for the now-accessible door.

"How are you coming to that conclusion?"

"You're the one who said this was like a pre-Rising video game."

I had to bite my lip to keep from laughing. I didn't really want to give Kelly any reason to doubt our infection status—not when I still needed her to guide us to safety. "Okay, Doc, the clear wall's open now. There's a door. What do you want us to do?"

"Listen closely: You're in one of the secondary escape corridors. They're designed to get essential staff out if at all possible, even during an outbreak. They aren't public, and they're never used for the transport of biological materials, just evacuations. Do you understand what I'm trying to say?"

My skin crawled. "They're set to autosterilize if there's any sign of contamination, aren't they?"

"Yes, they are. My suggestion?" Kelly paused before finishing, grimly, "Go as fast as you possibly can. Follow the yellow lights. They'll lead you to an exit. As long as your infection status hasn't changed, it'll let you out."

"And if it has?"

"If anyone in the escape corridor goes into conversion, the autosterilize initiates."

"Fuckin' swell. Okay. Tell Alaric I'll call back if we're not dead." I cut the connection over her protests, yanking the ear cuff off and shoving it into my pocket as I turned to Becks. "We're pulling a last run. Once this door is open, you haul ass, and if the lava comes down while we're inside, it was nice knowing you."

"Got it," said Becks, with a small, tight nod. It wouldn't actually be lava. It would be a highly acidic chemical bath, followed by flash irradiation, followed by another chemical bath, until everything organic in the corridor had been reduced to so much inert slime. That sort of thing can't really happen in places where humans are expected to be on a regular basis, since it tends to render the environment permanently toxic, but for a rarely used, last-ditch exit, it made perfect, if horrible, sense.

I hesitated, and then offered her my hand. "It was nice knowing you, Rebecca," I said.

"The same, Shaun. Believe me, the same." She laced her fingers into mine and smiled wistfully. "Maybe when we get out of this alive, you and me can go for coffee or something."

"Sure," I said. She didn't let go of my hand, and I didn't pull away. Leaving our fingers tangled together like computer cables, I reached for the second door and pulled it open. An amber light clicked on across from us. Becks and I exchanged one final look before stepping through the doorway, into the relative darkness on the other side.

The door swung shut as soon as we were through, hydraulics engaging with a loud hiss that was almost reassuring. It meant all systems were go; even if those systems got us dissolved, they'd be doing so while fully operational. Another amber light clicked on to the left of the first one, and another, and another, until a line of tiny glittering beacons led the way deeper into the dark.

There was no other way to go, and Kelly's instructions said to follow the light. We'd trusted her this far. The worst that trusting her the rest of the way could get us was dead. "Come on," I said. We started in the direction indicated by the lights, moving as fast as we dared.

Distances always seem longer in the dark. The greater the darkness, the longer the distance. The amber lights were meant to guide us, not show us where we were going, and even my flashlight wasn't enough to beat back the shadows. We probably traveled no more than a few hundred yards, but it felt like ten or twelve times that. Our breath was impossibly loud in the confines of the tunnel, and my toes kept catching on the floor, which wasn't completely level. After the third time I almost tripped, I realized we were running across the floor of an enormous shower, complete with drains every ten feet. They'd be essential if the CDC ever needed to sluice the place down—say, after melting a few unwanted guests. I sped up, pulling Becks along with me. She didn't argue. She was smart enough to want out of there as badly as I did.

The amber lights winked out about thirty seconds after we passed them, winking on ahead of us at the same rate. After the second time I looked back into the encroaching darkness, I forced myself to stop looking. It wasn't doing a damn bit of good, and it was doing damage to my nerves that I really couldn't afford.

I'm here, said George.

I squeezed Becks's hand and kept going.

The amber lights led us around a corner and into a narrower hallway with lights lining the walls on either side. They were still small, but they were plentiful enough to show the outline of Becks's face and shoulders. Being able to see her walking beside me lowered my stress levels like nothing else. I saw her head turn toward me, and I felt her fingers relax around mine as the same wave of relaxation washed over her. Maybe it was going to be okay.

The lights continued lighting up in front of us, finally circling a door frame directly ahead. Becks and I broke into a sprint at the same time, heading for the exit at full speed. I got there half a step before she did, purely by virtue of having longer legs, and I grabbed the door handle with my free hand. Needles stung my palm, biting deep and then—unlike every other blood test I'd ever taken—staying where they were as the light above the door flashed between red and green. The light stopped on green, and then went out, replaced by a single green bulb off to the left. The needles withdrew. The door didn't open.

"Oh, those slick bastards," I muttered, pulling my hand away. "Your turn, Becks. They're not going to let us out of here until we're both clean."

"Yippee," she deadpanned, and stepped up to take my place. The lights repeated their flickering dance, and a second green bulb came on next to the first. The latch released and the door swung inward, knocking us both back a step. Cool air rushed into the hallway like a benediction. I took a deep breath, glorying in the taste of clean air, and let Becks pull me for a change, hauling me into the light.

Kelly's emergency exit let out on the edge of the employee parking lot. About a dozen people were already there, most wearing lab coats...and there, off to one side, was Director Swenson. He was standing in a small cluster with two of the people in lab coats and Miss Lassen, the receptionist. She was the first to see us. Her shoulders went stiff as she straightened, whispering something urgently to the director. He turned his head in our direction, and his eyes widened before he could compose himself.

Becks squeezed my hand. I hadn't even realized she was still holding it. "Don't," she whispered. "We have what we need. The recorders were running the whole time. This story will end him. We have everything we need."

I nodded curtly as I pulled my hand away. Then I smiled. "Director Swenson!" I called, raising my arms and waving them overhead like I was signaling a plane to land. "Good to see you made it out! What happened, dude?"

"Mr. Mason—Ms. Atherton," said the director. He'd managed to compose his face, but there was still a quaver in his voice. The bastard really didn't think we'd make it out. "I'm so glad to see you both. I was so afraid you wouldn't realize what had happened in time to make it to an exit." His eyes flickered toward the door that we'd emerged through. "I had no idea that you knew about the evacuation tunnels."

Which explains why he didn't have them purged while you were still inside, said George. She sounded furious. No one threatened me and got away with it.

"We've done our homework." I kept smiling. It was that or punch him in the face, and that seemed a hell of a lot less productive, if a hell of a lot more fun. "So seriously, dude, what happened? Was it pit bulls again? Another illegal breeding program like the one in Oakland?"

"I—we're not quite sure yet." Director Swenson's eyes darted toward the door again. He clearly hadn't prepared a cover story. Why should he have bothered? We weren't intended to survive. "There will be a press release as soon as we have a better idea of what went wrong."

"Cool. Make sure we get a copy. Oh, and also, that documentation you said you had, the stuff that related to Georgia's research? I'll expect copies, since we couldn't, y'know, go over it together. I guess if I don't get it, I'm going to have to assume you've got something to hide." I turned, still smiling, and started for the visitor parking area.

"Wait—where are you going?"

I turned back to Director Swenson long enough to flash him the biggest shit-eating grin I could muster. It felt more like I was baring my teeth. Maybe it looked that way, too; he took an involuntary step backward, eyes going wide. "We're going to do what we're paid to do," I said. "We're going to go and tell everybody the news." I waved to the rest of the survivors of the Portland CDC and kept on walking, with Becks following close behind me. Neither one of us looked back as we got to the bike, stowed our gear, put on our helmets, and drove away.

Fuck you all. If that's the way you want to play things... If that's the way you want things to go... Then fuck you all. You have no idea what you're dealing with. You have no idea what I'm capable of. And you have no idea how little I have left to lose.

You're about to be sorrier than you could possibly believe, and I am going to laugh while I'm pissing on your grave.

—From *Adaptive Immunities*,
the blog of Shaun Mason, April 18, 2041. Unpublished.

Fourteen

According to the bike's GPS, the drive from the Portland CDC to Maggie's place should have taken a little over five hours on the main highway. It actually took us closer to eight. Since the chances that we were being tracked by the CDC had just gone way, way up, we stuck to the back roads, keeping our cameras off and avoiding checkpoints whenever we could. I won't say we drove through the ass-end of nowhere, exactly, but we had to stop twice to gun down the zombie deer trying to chew their way through the fence between the road and the undeveloped land around us.

"I wish to God I could post this," bemoaned Becks, shooting another infected herbivore squarely between the antlers.

"Yeah, well, I wish to God I had a cup of coffee," I replied, and gunned the bike's engine. "Come on."

There was a time when I thought George was paranoid for asking Buffy to build a jammer into her bike's tracking system. I'm over it, especially since that jammer allowed us to duck back onto the highway three times for fuel and twice more for caffeine. Becks kept scanning through the newsfeeds as I drove, listening for reports of the outbreak in Portland. "We can't be too careful," she said when we stopped for drinks and enough greasy snack food to get us to Maggie's without crashing. I agreed with her. We'd come too far to die because we weren't paying attention to the news.

None of the initial reports mentioned our presence. They were all bland, tragic, and carefully sanitized. We'd been on the road for about two hours when the "official record" began admitting that perhaps some journalists had been present for the outbreak, but they didn't identify us by name and they didn't try to pin things on us. That was good. That meant it would be a little longer before we needed to kill them all.

George stayed uncharacteristically quiet during the drive. She wasn't gone—that would've left me too shaken to control the bike, especially after everything that had happened since Kelly's arrival—but she wasn't talking, either. She was just quiet, sitting at the back of my head and brooding over God knows what. I figured she'd tell me when she was through working it out for herself. Maybe it says something about my mental health that I didn't find the idea even a little strange. We were too far away from normal for strange to have any meaning anymore.

The sun was hanging low in a mango-colored sky when I turned onto Maggie's driveway. I had to keep one foot on the ground to keep the bike upright while we navigated the various security gates, until my clutch hand was cramping and I started to feel like we would have made better time if we'd ditched the bike on the street and made the rest of the trip to the house on foot. Becks clearly shared my frustration. By the time we cleared the ocular scanner, she was all but twitching with the anxious need to be back in the safety of friendly walls.

The fifth gate was standing open, just like it was when we first arrived as refugees from the ashes of Oakland. A casual observer might have thought Maggie never closed the damn thing. They would have been proven wrong almost immediately, because as soon as I coasted to a stop, the gate slid slickly shut. The sound of the locks engaging was the sweetest thing I'd ever heard.

Becks barely waited for the bike to stop before she dismounted; my foot was still on the kickstand when she hopped off. She stayed where she was for a few brief seconds, jittering in place as she worked the feeling back into her legs. Then she grabbed her bag off the side of the bike, announced, "I'm going to go take a shower," and took off for the kitchen door. I watched her go without commenting. She didn't want to give the live breakdown on what happened at the CDC, and, since I was the boss, she was leaving that little luxury for me.

"She's such a sweetheart," I said dryly.

Be careful. George sounded concerned. I jumped. It wasn't just the worry in her tone: She'd been quiet for so long that I'd almost forgotten she was there, like sitting in a room with someone who hasn't spoken in hours, until they finally get up to leave. *I don't think you really understand what's going on with her.*

"What, are you saying she might be working with the CDC? I don't think so. I'm usually better at reading people than that."

Shaun... I could almost see the exasperated shake of George's head, the way she'd be glowering at me behind her sunglasses. *I don't think Becks is a traitor, but you need to be careful with her. Okay? Can you do that for me?*

"Sure, George." I slid off the bike, stretching. The muscles in my calves and thighs protested the movement but were overruled by my ass, which was so sore from the drive that I doubted I'd ever sit down again. "Whatever you say."

One nice thing about working with people who know how crazy I am: Maggie, Alaric, and Kelly were in the kitchen when I stepped inside, all three of them in easy view of the window, and not one of them commented on the fact that I'd stopped to talk to myself before following Becks into the house. It's a lot easier to deal with people who are already used to me.

"Becks tore through on the way to the shower," said Maggie. She was next to the sink, drying the last of the dinner dishes. The kitchen smelled of savory pastry and fresh-cooked chicken. My stomach rumbled, reminding me that all I'd eaten since leaving Portland was some soy jerky, half a bag of potato chips, and a candy bar. The corner of Maggie's mouth turned up in a smile. "There's a potpie for each of you in the oven. We left them there so they'd stay warm."

"Awesome. Thanks." George was hovering at the back of my mind, casting a veil of anxiety over everything. I walked to the fridge and opened it. Someone had gone to the store while Becks and I were out; there was a twelve-pack of Coke on the bottom shelf, and what looked like sufficient fresh provisions for us to survive a siege, so long as no one cut the power.

I grabbed a can of Coke and swung the door shut, turning toward the table as I popped the tab. "Hey, guys," I said, as amiably as I could manage. "So how were things while Becks and I were on location?"

"Mahir announced the hiring of 'Barbara Tinney' and helped Kelly get her first post up while I monitored the footage you were beaming out of the CDC," said Alaric.

"Really? Cool. What was it about?"

"The psychological impact of isolationism on the development of human relationships," said Kelly. I looked at her blankly. She amended: "Cabin fever makes people shitty roommates."

"I'm sure it's a real ratings grabber," I said, after a suitable pause. "Alaric?"

He took the cue with grace, saying, "I was able to get about a dozen reports cobbled together after things went south, and we had them online before anyone else picked up on the outbreak. Mahir has every on-duty Newsie and about half the Irwins running follow-ups now. The CDC's only comment so far called it 'an avoidable tragedy,' and said they were looking into possible failure of the airlock seals that are supposed to separate the treatment areas from the employee locker room."

"Which is bullshit," said Kelly. "Those air locks were designed to withstand a nuclear war. There's no way they could just *fail*."

"Good to know," I said, sipping my Coke.

Ask whether any of the reports include the conference room, said George, with a sudden, strange urgency in her tone.

"Okay," I muttered. More loudly, I asked, "Uh, hey, Alaric? Did any of the reports Mahir put together include footage of me and Becks sitting in the conference room waiting for the director to come back?"

Alaric blinked and nodded. "How did you know? That was the second one he put up. He said the time stamp was important to get out there in the public record."

George started to explain. I cut her off, saying, "The time stamp on the conference room footage means they can't try to pin the outbreak on us. There's no way for us to have spent that much time sitting together, waiting, *and* be the ones who damaged the air lock seal."

You're learning, said George, approvingly.

"Time stamps can be forged," said Maggie. Alaric, Kelly, and I all turned to look at her. She shrugged. "You just shouldn't put too much faith in the time stamp. It's not going to save you by itself. That's what my family has lawyers for."

"Thanks for that little ray of sunshine, Maggie." I turned to Kelly. "So, Doc, was there any way to know that we were walking into a deathtrap? I mean, at this point, I trust the CDC about as far as George can throw you, but it still seems a little extreme, burning a whole installation to take out two reporters."

Kelly frowned. "But Georgia is—oh." She stopped midprotest, comprehension flooding her expression. "No. I didn't. I'm starting to realize that my...my former employers"—she spat out the word "former" like it tasted bad—"may be capable of some pretty horrible things, but I never suspected they'd do anything like that. I wouldn't have let you go if I knew."

"The sad part here is that I bet they have more nasty surprises for us. Just wait." I sipped my Coke, studying Kelly's face for signs that she was fraying. The Doc was holding up better than I expected; all I saw in her eyes was exhaustion, both physical and mental. The rest of us were tired, but we were also trained for this sort of shit—or as trained as you *can* be for something that's never supposed to happen. "Well, we got out alive. That's something. Alaric, how's our market share?"

"Up four points last time I checked, with the expected uptick in our closest competitors," said Alaric, not missing a beat. "Three of them are crying hoax and two more are claiming that we're endangering our licenses by behaving recklessly in hopes of increasing our ratings."

I snorted. "Because 'behaving recklessly' is suddenly not in the job description? Amateurs. Let 'em find their own potentially fatal government conspiracies."

"Can we not?" Maggie picked up a stack of plates and began putting them away in the cupboard. "I think one is more than enough at any given time, and since they have a tendency to spread, I'm not sure a second one wouldn't wind up getting all over us, too."

"Fair enough." I tossed my empty can into the recycling bin. "You said there was a potpie?"

"Yes, and you said you'd tell us what happened." Maggie put away the last of the plates before taking down the oven mitts and opening the oven, producing a covered ceramic dish that smelled like it was less than half a mile shy of Heaven. She set it down on one of the open spaces at the table.

"Caffeine, then food, then exposition." I grabbed a fork from the dish drainer before moving to sit down. The potpie smelled even better up close. The bulldogs agreed: two promptly appeared from the next room, sitting by my feet in perfect, implacable begging positions. "Remind me again why we didn't all move in with you years ago?"

"Because I live in the middle of nowhere, and that isn't actually an asset for anyone who isn't a pure Fictional." Maggie went back to putting dishes away. "Now talk, or I'm going to take back your dinner."

"Anything but that." I stabbed my fork into the piecrust. "How much of the footage have you guys watched?"

"Enough," said Alaric grimly.

I nodded. "Okay, then." I took a bite of potpie, swallowed, and began talking, starting with the point where Becks and I drove away from the motel. Most of our time at the CDC had been fairly well-documented by the cameras we carried, but they'd been simple recorders, not full-on field deployments. There were things they missed, like most of Director Swenson's reactions, and everything in the emergency tunnels.

"Your recording feeds cut off as soon as you went through that second door," said Alaric. "They picked up again once you were outside."

"Really?" I glanced to Kelly. "Did you know that was going to happen?"

"No, but it makes sense. Those tunnels are heavily shielded, to prevent contamination if there's ever need for an actual flush. We're not even supposed to stay in them during drills, if we can help it."

"Radiation?" asked Alaric.

Kelly shrugged. "I really don't know. I'm sorry."

I took advantage of their brief side-conversation to shovel another few bites of potpie into my mouth, barely chewing. Finally, I said, "Okay, so you didn't get any of that footage. It wasn't bright enough in there to get much worthwhile, but unless their shielding fried our electronics—" I glanced at Kelly. She shook her head, indicating that it shouldn't have done anything of the sort. That made sense, since the CDC probably had recording devices of their own in the tunnels. They'd need to know what went wrong if there was ever an emergency purge. "You should be able to extract the audio track."

"Don't forget the pretty amber lights. Those are probably worth a screenshot or two." We all turned toward the sound of Becks's voice. She was wearing one of Maggie's bathrobes, knotted loosely around her waist, and her hair was still half-wet, tousled from the postshower drying. "Is there another potpie, Maggie? I'm hungry enough to eat a dog."

"Please don't," said Maggie. "It's hard enough to socialize them without making them think that people will decide to randomly eat them. Your potpie is in the oven."

"You're an angel." Becks arrowed for the oven, dismissing the rest of us in favor of food.

I stabbed my fork into my own potpie, spearing a chunk of chicken as I focused my attention back on Kelly. "So, Doc, that was a good job you did, getting us to the tunnels. Pretty quick thinking, too."

"We do evacuation drills and infection simulations every month in order to minimize the loss of life in case of an outbreak," said Kelly. "There are differences between offices, but they're reasonably minor, and the central floor plan doesn't change. Plus, they shuttle us to different offices once a year to run evacuation trials there, to make sure we don't get too hung up on familiar landmarks."

"What, like the white door, the white door, or, that old favorite, the white door?"

Kelly cracked a slight, brief-lived smile. "Something like that. It's amazing how much two identical halls can differ when you work in them every day for a year or more. We have to learn to strip them down to nothing but the architecture."

"Does that mean you have entire installations memorized?" asked Alaric, suddenly interested. Kelly nodded. "Could you draw a map if I gave you some basic drafting software?"

"I think so. Why?"

"Because that may not be our last trip into the CDC, and I'd rather we didn't need to count on an open phone line to get us out next time," I said. Kelly's attention switched back to me. "Alaric, get her that drafting software and see if you can find some public databases to check her work against."

"The public databases won't have the emergency access tunnels," said Kelly.

"It's still never a bad idea to have a backup plan." I flashed her a toothy smile. "Besides, the public databases will have full blueprints of the general-access areas, and that should be enough to jog your memory. It's not that I don't trust you to tell us the truth as you see it, Doc. It's just that after what we learned from Dr. Abbey, I don't trust you not to leave things out if you think they're too sensitive for us."

Her expression hardened. For a moment, I thought she was going to challenge my authority. The others saw it, too: Alaric pushed his chair back from the table by a few inches, while Maggie and Becks both stopped moving around the kitchen, their attention going solely to Kelly. The house seemed to hold its breath. Finally, grudgingly, Kelly shook her head.

"Fair enough. We're in this together, whether we like it or not. I guess we're all going to need to learn how to trust each other."

"There's the spirit," I said.

"I just have one question," said Alaric. "How do we know the CDC isn't going to run an audio comparison on your call and figure out that Kelly's still alive? The last thing we need is another major raid."

"No, the *last* thing we need is them figuring out where we are. Them figuring out that the Doc's still breathing is second to last, at best." I pushed my half-eaten potpie away and stood. "I guess we'll need to keep an eye on the news feeds, see whether anything comes through accusing us of identity theft."

"Can you steal your own identity?" asked Kelly.

"Guess we'll find out." Becks moved to take my seat as I stepped away. "Becks, you need to update as soon as you finish eating. I'm going to go and get the untransmitted footage loaded to the server. Alaric, I want you cleaning and screenshotting inside the hour."

"Got it," said Alaric.

"I've got a few poems and a bunch of garden pictures to put up," said Maggie. "I'm officially still in mourning for Dave, which is why I'm all alone here in my big, spooky old house."

"Good," I said. "Doc, work with Mahir and get started on another post about whatever the hell psychology crap you're writing about. See if you can come up with a plausible excuse for why we don't have a picture of you. I don't want anyone getting overzealous and looking for you in the public broadcast footage."

"All right."

I grabbed another Coke from the fridge and went back to the living room, where the computer wouldn't argue with me, ask me questions, or do anything but help me clear my head. George was still quiet, her normally constant presence numbed to a dull ache at the back of my skull. It didn't hurt, precisely. It just felt weird as hell.

The computer woke at the touch of a finger. I navigated the company log-in menus to reach my mailbox, which was comfortingly over-full of spam, date offers, naked pictures, suggestions of things that would make good articles, and the seemingly obligatory elevator pitches on places I should go and dead things I should bother. Sometimes it seems like the entire world is out to get me back into the field. What they don't understand—and I can't tell them—is that I've lost one of the integral traits of a good Irwin: I'm not having any fun. When I wind up in the field, it's a chore to be survived, not an adventure to be relished. Without that little spark of gosh-golly-wow to drive me on, I'm essentially a dead man walking. Don't think I don't see the irony. George is the one who stopped breathing, but I'm the one who gave up on living.

The forums were as big a mess as I'd expected from Alaric's report. The moderators were trying to be six places at once, and failing pretty spectacularly. I sat back for a few minutes sipping my Coke and watching the message notifications as they popped up next to thread after thread. The team currently on duty were all beta bloggers, trying to prove their credentials by doing the sort of shit job that George and I used to do back when we were still bylines on the Bridge Supporters site. In those days, we couldn't think of anything we wanted more than to be out on our own, telling the stories we wanted to tell, not answering to anybody but ourselves.

"Look at where *that* got us," I muttered, leaning forward in the chair and reaching for the mouse. "Stay where you are, guys. You'll be a hell of a lot happier in the long run."

George didn't say anything, and kept not saying anything as I went back to my in-box and started skimming, looking for messages that actually needed my attention. I needed to start editing footage. I needed to post and let people know that I was still alive, but most of all, and first of all, I needed to calm down a little bit. My heartbeat was starting to speed up as my body realized that the running away was over—we'd reached our destination, and now it was finally safe for me to freak out.

My hand was shaking. I sat perfectly still, waiting for the tremors to pass. I didn't have time for another breakdown. One a month is about my limit, and since this one was unlikely to come with the extra-bonus "full visual hallucinations of your dead sister," I didn't see the point of doing it again. Eventually, the shaking stopped, and I started again.

I hit Important when I was halfway down my in-box. It was buried in thread updates, private messages from the moderators, and random posts from my mailing lists, and I almost didn't click because I didn't recognize the sender's e-mail address. "Who the fuck uses 'TauntedOctopus' for a handle, anyway?" I asked myself. It wasn't entirely a rhetorical question. I was hoping the sheer stupidity of it would be enough to make George speak up.

Instead, it was enough to make me stop, swear, and open the message. Who uses "TauntedOctopus" as a handle? Probably a woman who wears T-shirts telling you not to do it. Dr. Abbey.

From: TauntedOctopus@redacted.cn.com
To: Shaun.Mason@aftertheendtimes.com
Subject: Aren't you a busy boy?

I admit I was surprised when I heard that the Portland CDC had been overrun by the infected less than twenty-four hours after you left me. You don't waste time, and I respect that. Then again, it's not like you have much time to waste. You're not the only one who knows how to operate a camera, and I bet you dollars to donuts that somebody got footage of you and your little band of Merry Men on the trek out here. It's just a matter of time before somebody figures out we were in contact, and then the shit you're in will be so deep that it'll make your current shit look like chocolate pudding. Don't come back. We started tearing down the lab as soon as you left, and by the time you get this message (assuming you live long enough to get this message, which is by no means guaranteed), we'll be on our way to a new location. The little "arrangement" I have with the CDC depends on a certain status quo, and you're playing in dangerous enough waters that I can't count on it right now. So hurry up and get your answers or get yourselves killed, will you?

The attachments on this message contain everything I've done to date involving mapping the structure of Kellis-Amberlee against the autoimmune oddities that cause the formation of stable reservoir conditions. I don't have a mechanism for reversing them, or a reliable way to induce them in adult subjects, but there's more than enough to prove that reservoir conditions are the result of the immune system beginning to learn to cope under supposedly impossible conditions. Most of the research won't make any sense to you, but it'll make perfect sense to the little CDC flunky who introduced us. Make sure she sees it. Tell her it all goes public if you think she's holding out on you. See what she has to say after that.

You're a brave idiot, Shaun Mason, and I'm sorry I never got to meet your sister. Almost as sorry as I am that you never got to meet my husband. Give my regards to the Merry Men, and tell them to sleep with one eye open, because you're well on the way to pissing off some pretty damn important people. Good for you. Keep doing what you're doing. Somebody has to.

Best wishes, and stay the fuck away from me,
Dr. Shannon L. Abbey

A flare of guilt rose, washed over me, and died as I contemplated the fact that talking to us cost Dr. Abbey her lab. She knew what she was doing when she let us through her door. Maybe she didn't invite us to come for a visit, but once we were there, she was perfectly happy to tell us what she knew. If she wasn't going to blame us for showing up, I wasn't going to feel bad for doing it.

The attachments on her message downloaded clean, and they opened to reveal huge, detailed medical charts and graphs that made about as much sense as abstract art. I recognized some of the labels, but that was about it. That was okay because Dr. Abbey was right: It didn't matter if her research made sense to me. What mattered was that her research would make sense to *Kelly*, and once she'd seen it, maybe she'd know where we needed to look next. Given the situation we were in, every little bit was about to start counting, big time.

I forwarded Dr. Abbey's message to Alaric and Mahir with a priority flag, printed copies of the attachments, and returned to cleaning out my in-box. Nothing else was nearly as interesting as that message, which wasn't much of a surprise. "Here's my Kellis-Amberlee research, enjoy" was a pretty hard act to follow.

According to the site log, Mahir was logged in, which meant that either he was awake or I had reasonable cause to think he might be. That was good enough for me. Leaning back in my chair, I dug my phone out of my pocket and snapped it open.

Luck was with me: Mahir, not his wife, answered the phone. "Shaun. Thank God."

"Hey, Mahir. There a reason you always feel the need to invoke the divine when I call you? Is that just how they're saying hello in London these days?"

"It's four o'clock in the bloody morning, Shaun, and I'm awake to take your call. That might tell you a little something about how worried I've been." A door closed in the background, and the sound of distant traffic filtered through the phone. "Try remembering that I'm eight hours off your time zone and give me the all-clear a little sooner next time, won't you?"

"Hey, sorry, dude. I figured Alaric would keep you posted." One of the London magazines did a profile on Mahir after the Ryman election—he was a local boy involved in a huge American political scandal, which was sort of a big deal. The picture they ran with the article was of him standing on the wide balcony outside his apartment, looking out over the Thames River with the sort of serious "I am an intellectual artist" expression that George and I always used to make fun of. That was the scene I pictured now, listening to the traffic rushing past behind him: Mahir on the balcony, surrounded by the weight of the London night, while cars packed with paranoid commuters went whizzing past below.

"He did. So did Magdalene. But at the end of the day, Shaun, the only person I trust to tell me your condition is you."

"I'd feel flattered if I didn't know that you expected me to die."

"Isn't that your intention?"

I stopped for a moment, suddenly and sharply aware of George's silent presence at the back of my head. Lying to Mahir would border on impossible, even if George was willing to let me, and in the end, I didn't bother trying. "Eventually, yeah. But not until after we've found the people who killed George. Did you get those files I sent you?"

"I did," Mahir admitted. "How much of them did you understand?"

"Not enough. I'm guessing you understood a little bit more."

"Enough to make me think I'll never sleep again."

"That's good—means the files are what Dr. Abbey said they were. I need you to do something for me."

"What's that?"

"Find a virologist with nothing left to lose and get them to check her work."

Now it was Mahir's turn to fall briefly silent. Finally, tone wary, he asked, "Do you understand what you're asking me to do?"

"Yeah, I do. I feel like a total ass for doing it, but I do."

Mahir went silent again. Honestly, I couldn't blame him.

North America lost a lot during the Rising. Big chunks of Canada and the lower parts of Mexico have never been reclaimed from the infected. We held the line in Alaska as long as we could, but in the end, the infection was too strong and we had to let the entire state go. Almost every part of the United States has its little dead zones, places that are too damn dangerous to take back. None of that can hold a candle to what India lost. Because what India lost... was India.

The conditions in pre-Rising India formed a perfect model for pandemic spread of Kellis-Amberlee. We studied it in school as part of the standard epidemiology curriculum: Combine highly concentrated populations with large stretches of rural farmland, a polluted water supply, and large, unconfined animals, and you were basically setting up the ideal conditions for losing everything. According to the reports—the ones that made it out of India, anyway; there aren't many—the virus first started showing up in Mumbai, where it went from zero to chaos in the streets in less than thirty-six hours. While India was throwing all its resources at trying to save the city, the infection was taking hold in the country, claiming villages and small towns so quickly that no one had time to sound the alarm. By the time anyone realized that the quarantine couldn't possibly have held, it was way too fucking late to do anything but evacuate.

The first handheld blood testing unit was invented by an Indian scientist named Kiran Patel. Dr. Patel had isolated his family when the first signs of trouble started to show; thanks to his quick thinking and willingness to use lethal force against the infected, he managed to keep his entire apartment building clean of the live virus during a six-day siege that should have left them all casualties. When he wasn't standing watch, Dr. Patel was modifying his own diabetes kits to look for something a little more crucial than blood sugar. By the time the UN soldiers fought their way into that sector of Mumbai, he had a crude but reliable way of proving someone's infection status in minutes. The whole building checked out. Two of the troops who'd come to their rescue didn't. Acceptable losses for a piece of technology that no one else had even taken the time to think about, much less put together.

Dr. Patel went into a diabetic coma on the helicopter that airlifted him and his family out of the city. He never made it out of India. His widow went to the UN and demanded refuge for the survivors of her country in exchange for her husband's notes. She got everything she asked for. The people who made it out of India were allowed to settle anywhere they wanted, bypassing all the normal citizenship requirements. The Indian consulates stayed open and issued passports to the children of the survivors; as far as I know, they still do. When the disease is defeated, they say, they'll be ready to go home.

Whether that's true or not, London has one of the largest Indian communities on the planet, second only to Silicon Valley—although Toronto is a pretty close third. Mahir was born in London. He's never been to India, and as far as I know, he's never wanted to go. That's not true for everyone. A lot of people want to reclaim their heritage. They may like living where they are, but they want it to be a choice, not an exile. There are doctors and scientists in the Indian community who answer only to the government of a nation that currently doesn't exist, pursuing research whose only motive is "get us home." But racism doesn't die just because the dead start walking, and there are some folks who watch the displaced communities carefully for signs that they might be "turning against us." If Mahir did what I was asking him to do—if he went to one of the virologists who was working out of his home, rather than out of a government lab, and asked him to explain Dr. Abbey's work—he was putting them both at risk of a terrorism charge.

Finally, Mahir said, "I'm going to ask a question that sounds insane, Shaun, and you're going to answer. Refuse, and I hang up, and we both pretend this conversation never happened."

That sort of thing never works. Once you're past the age of five, you can't make something unhappen just by refusing to think about it. "Sure," I said. "Whatever you say."

"All right." He laughed, a little unsteadily, and asked, "What does Georgia have to say about this plan?"

Mahir had never questioned the fact that George still talks to me, but he'd never gone out of his way to address her, either. Maybe my crazy was starting to rub off on the people around me. Is crazy contagious? "Hang on. I'll ask her." *George,* I thought, *if you're just being quiet because you're pissed or something, I could really use your help right about now . . .*

Sorry. I was thinking. Tell him . . . She hesitated. *Tell him that if this research means what I think it means, the world has a right to know, and without his help, we might not be able to tell them. This is for everybody.*

"...okay." I cleared my throat. "She says that if this research means what she thinks it means, the world has a right to know, and that if you're not willing to help, we might not be able to figure out enough to know what to tell them. She says this is for everybody." I paused before adding, "And I say it looks like they were willing to blow up Oakland and infect an entire CDC facility to keep the news from getting out without it looking like they were trying to hide something. I want to get at least part of the work off this continent, so somebody can keep on going after they drop the bomb on Maggie's place."

"I swear, I'm going to move to San Francisco just to make you people stop using me as your off-site backup." Mahir sighed deeply. "Fine."

"Fine? You mean you'll do it?"

"I'm clearly out of my mind, and I'm going to regret this for the rest of my life, and my wife is probably going to leave me, but yes, I'll do it. Someone has to. I'm going to have to involve my local beta bloggers. This is a rather large project."

"Whatever you need, but keep it limited to people you know and can trust, okay? We can't risk this getting out early."

"Silence is expensive."

"That's not a problem. I'm sure if we shake the merchandising hard enough, the money will fall out." If nothing else, I had a standing offer to print a book of George's posts from the campaign trail. I'd been refusing—somehow that felt more like making money off her corpse than continuing to run her blog did—but it would be a good way to make some reasonably quick cash. And then there was Maggie's trust fund. Normally, I wouldn't think of going there. These were some pretty special circumstances.

"Oh, believe me, I wasn't intending to worry about the budget, and if I'm still married when this is over, you're financing the second honeymoon it's going to take for me to stay that way."

"Totally fair. Thank you. Really, thank you. You're a good guy."

"Your sister had excellent taste in men. Now update your damn blog, Shaun. Half the readership thinks you're dead, and I'm entirely out of the passion it takes to refute conspiracy theories." The sounds of distant traffic cut off as Mahir killed the connection, leaving me listening to nothing but the sound of my own breath. I clicked the phone shut and slid it back into my pocket, staring thoughtfully at the computer screen. Dr. Abbey's research looked back at me like the world's deadliest abstract art. The lines of it were strangely soothing when I looked at them long enough. They reminded me of the faint traceries of iris surrounding George's pupils, little lines of brown that no one got to see unless they got close enough to look past her glasses.

Lifting my hands, I tugged the keyboard toward me and begin to write.

—————————

I like to think of myself as a reasonable man. I suppose that's true of everyone. Even the people we'd paint as the villains of the piece, given leave, doubtless consider themselves reasonable. It's a part of the human psyche. Still. My needs are simple. I have my flat, which is paid for. I have my work, which I enjoy and do reasonably well. I have a beautiful wife who tolerates the strange hours and stranger company I keep. I love the city I live in, its sights and sounds and brilliant culture, which has managed to not only recover but to thrive under adversity. London is the only place I have ever truly wished to be, and I am privileged beyond all measure to call it home.

I like to think of myself as a reasonable man. But I have buried too many friends in the too-recent past, and I have seen too many lies go unquestioned, and too many questions go unasked. There is a time when even reasonable men must begin to take unreasonable actions. To do anything else is to be less than human. And to those who would choose the safety of inaction over the danger of taking a stand, I have this to say:

You bloody cowards. May you have the world that you deserve.

**—From *Fish and Clips*, the blog of Mahir Gowda,
April 20, 2041**

Fifteen

Writing up the events of the day was enough to leave me utterly exhausted. I just wanted to go upstairs, shower, go through a proper decontamination cycle, and crash for six to eight hours before something else demanded my attention. If I did that, though, my post would go up in plain text and I'd have eager beta bloggers flooding my in-box with offers to "help." Their "help" would probably end in tears—theirs, after I dismissed them from the site for pissing me off beyond all hope of recovery. It was easier to force myself to stay where I was and go combing through the footage of the day, looking for suitable clips and screenshots.

There are times when I miss Buffy. I mean, I always miss her—she was one of my best friends, right up until she sold us out—but there are times when I *really* miss her. I could have handed her my report and told her to make it pretty, and she would have had a multimedia extravaganza ready to go almost before I could finish making the request. She was the best at what she did. Everything she did, which was sort of the problem, since in the end, what she did included betraying us and getting a lot of people killed. She said she was sorry when she came clean. I believed her then, and I believe her now. Sometimes people make mistakes, and sometimes those mistakes are the sort that don't allow for second chances.

Doesn't make her any less dead, or make me miss her any less.

In the end, I chose three short film clips and ten stills and called it a day, slapping them into my article in the places where they'd have the most impact, or at least look like they were there for a reason. I dropped a note in the mod forum to let folks know I'd be going off-line for a few hours and that I was only to be disturbed if the world was ending. Even then, they were supposed to get clearance from Mahir before they called me. That wouldn't guarantee I'd be left alone, but it would slow people down. Sort of like setting a snooze button on reality.

It wasn't until I stood that I realized how sore I was. I stretched until something in my shoulders popped. That was the cue for half the muscles in my body to start complaining, while the other half seemed to turn to jelly. "Fuck. I'm not getting any younger," I said, and walked toward the kitchen.

Alaric was gone, probably off doing his time on the message boards. I'd say better him than me, but I've done that gig more times than I can count, and it's not something I'd wish on anybody. Becks and Maggie were still sitting at the table, watching the uncomfortable-looking Kelly the way cats watch mice. She turned toward me when I entered the kitchen, expression going pathetically relieved. If I was her idea of salvation, things must have been really nasty while I was in the other room.

"Hey," I said. "I'm going to go upstairs and get a shower."

Kelly's look of relief died. "Don't you want to finish your potpie?"

"No, I'm good. Maggie, can you take care of any comments I get for the next few hours? I need to catch some sleep or I'm going to be useless tomorrow."

"Absolutely." Maggie smiled. "Now go. You're running yourself too hard."

"You're probably right." I paused, a thought hitting me. "Maggie, tell Alaric to check on the bug we planted in the conference room. It should be showing up on the live index now, and I want to know the second it picks anything up."

"Decontamination will take a few days," said Kelly. If she had opinions about the legality of bugging CDC installations, she was keeping them to herself. "You won't be getting anything until that's done."

"Well, then, I guess I'll have plenty of time to catch up on my beauty sleep. All of you, good night, and try to get some rest."

"I will," said Becks, giving me a thoughtful look as I turned to go.

Making it up the stairs took more effort than it should have. I was so damn tired. It seemed like too much trouble when I could sit down and sleep perfectly well on the steps. I knew I needed to shower. Strict field protocols said I should have showered the second I got to the house, like Becks did. It can really screw up your insurance if you don't go through proper decontamination after every logged trip into the field, but there are loopholes to the law, if you know how to use them. We didn't log the trip to Dr. Abbey's lab, and CDC offices are counted as some of the few public places *not* considered hazard zones. My failure to scrub up like a good little boy was strictly legal, and I was aware enough of my exposure risks to know that I hadn't been dangerously close to anything infectious. I just didn't want to go to bed feeling like I'd never be clean again.

The showers in Maggie's house are another amazing example of what you can achieve if you have enough money and don't care how much of it you spend. The showers in the Oakland apartments were bare-bones, consisting of air locks, computer-controlled water sprays, and simple blood test panels. Using them was like getting scrubbed down by industrial robots that didn't give a damn whether you were comfortable with the process. They didn't quite perform involuntary enemas, but God, they came close. Maggie's place, on the other hand...When her parents set her up with a place of her own, they took "spare no expense" seriously. Some of the bells and whistles she had were things I'd seen only in magazines and in articles about people with more money than sense.

The entire bathroom was decorated in pre-Rising tile, with genuine porcelain fixtures, the kind that can get broken or splinter, thus becoming infection risks and requiring full replacement. It was easy to miss at first glance that the room was divided into two sections, since the main section contained the toilet, a full-sized sink, and an antique claw-footed bathtub. All you had to do to get inside was open the door—no blood tests required. If you were the sort of person who could ignore the heavy curtain covering one wall, you could pretend that it really *was* a pre-Rising bathroom, and that all that zombie nonsense had never actually happened.

I closed the bathroom door and crossed to the sink, where I emptied my pockets into one of the mesh baskets Maggie keeps for exactly that purpose. Once I was sure I wouldn't accidentally sanitize my press pass or something, I stripped, tossing my clothes—shoes and all—into the bathroom hamper. As soon as I activated the shower, a chute in the bottom of the hamper would open and send my clothes for automatic sterilization. No human hands would touch them until they were certified infection-free. I glanced at my reflection and scowled. I looked exhausted, and I was starting to develop bags under my eyes. Good thing I wasn't doing the Irwin circuit anymore. An Irwin who looks tired is an Irwin who's losing merchandising points with every frame of footage he posts.

Pulling back the curtain revealed the hermetically sealed air lock door separating the shower from the rest of the bathroom. There was a testing panel to one side. I pressed my hand against it, feeling the needles bite into the base of my palm. The light over the shower began flashing between red and green. I cleared my throat, and said, "Shaun Mason, guest, requesting standard decontamination protocols."

There was a pause as the shower's computer ran my blood sample and checked my voice print against the house logs. The light stopped flashing, settling on a steady green. A chime rang, and a pleasant voice that sounded suspiciously like Maggie said, "Welcome, Shaun. Please enter." The air lock hissed as the seal released and the door swung slowly open. I shuddered as I stepped through. The sound of hydraulics wasn't going to sit easily with me for a while—not until something else horrible happened to make me forget about the events of the Portland CDC.

The door swung closed behind me, locking with a second, louder hiss. Once the decontamination cycle started, there was no way to cut it short.

"What sort of shower would you prefer?" The voice of the shower came from a speaker set high in the rear wall. Everything but the air lock door was tiled, the floor and ceiling in white, and the walls in a soothing shade of blue. There were four showerheads, set at levels ranging from shoulder height to almost ceiling level. A recessed nook in the left-hand wall held shampoo, conditioner, and a variety of shower gels.

"Hot, short, thorough," I said. I hesitated before adding, "Please." It never pays to insult computers that are smart enough to form sentences. Not when they're in control of the locks, and especially not when they have the capacity to boil you in bleach.

"Absolutely," said the shower. "Please close your eyes." That was all the warning I got before the water turned on, cascading with a vengeance from all four showerheads. I closed my eyes half a second too late and sputtered as I tried to wipe them dry. At least this shower started with water. Some of them just go straight to bleach.

The initial blast of water lasted for thirty seconds, letting me get warmed up before the shower announced, still politely, "I will be commencing sterilization on the count of three. Please prepare yourself."

"Got it," I said, and screwed my eyes more tightly shut. The liquid raining over me cooled, taking on the sharp smell of industrial-strength bleach. I did my best not to breathe too much as I scrubbed myself down, working the bleach into my skin. It stung like a bitch, just like it always does, but it was a good sting; it was the sting of getting all the way clean and staying alive for another day.

The bleaching stuck to the absolute legal minimum, lasting only a few seconds longer than the water. Finally, the shower said, "Normal bathing cycle is beginning. You have four minutes. Please speak if you want to extend this time."

The bleach stopped immediately, replaced by rapidly warming water. I rinsed my face clean before saying, "Four minutes is fine, thanks."

"You're welcome, Shaun," said the shower.

Creepy. I hate it when machines get chatty with me. I wiped my eyes before opening them and reaching for the shampoo. George and I used to have shower races. Who could get in and clean and out again in the shortest amount of time. All the guys we went to school with insisted that their girlfriends and sisters took forever in the bathroom, but George always beat me. She could scrub down in under three minutes if she was in a hurry and hadn't been out in the field—bleaching added time to both our totals, so we started subtracting it when we compared times. It was the only way to keep the contest fair. Of course, once a month or so, she'd take over the bathroom for an afternoon to dye her hair back to its original color, which inevitably resulted in her shouting for me to come in and help her dye her roots. The sink on our old bathroom was stained a permanent shade of brown by the time we were sixteen, and we ruined so many towels—

The water cut off, leaving me with soap behind one ear and a goony expression on my face. I hadn't realized four minutes could go so quickly. "Thank you for showering with me today, Shaun," said the shower, as the air lock door unsealed and hissed open. "It's been a pleasure serving you."

"Uh, thanks," I said, stepping out. "Same here."

I grabbed two towels from the pile by the sink. I wrapped one around my waist and used the other to dry my hair, rubbing briskly all the way around my head before slinging the towel around my shoulders. I needed to sleep. The basket full of my crap would be safe on the counter for the night, and it was long past time for me to get to bed.

I started for the door, and stopped in the process of reaching for the doorknob. "Oh, crap." When we arrived, Maggie apologized for having only three guest rooms—one each for Alaric, Becks, and Kelly. That left me sleeping on the front room couch, which was fine, when I had, y'know, clothes. Nudity was definitely going to be an issue if I was intending to sleep there again, and since I hadn't exactly taken time to pack when the building was exploding, I didn't have spare jeans.

I was too damn tired to make a decision. I was still standing there, trying to figure out what to do, when somebody knocked on the bathroom door. I let out a relieved sigh; saved. Clearly, Maggie had realized I was going to have a problem and was bringing me a bathrobe, if not actual pants left behind by one of her Fictional houseguests. "You have no idea how glad I am that you're here," I said, opening the bathroom door.

Becks was on the other side. She looked at me with wide, solemn eyes, and said, "I hoped you would be." Then, before I had a chance to react or say anything, she stepped into the bathroom and closed the door behind herself.

She stayed there for a moment, one hand behind her back and clutching the doorknob, the other hand resting against her upper thigh. It was somewhere between a pose and a pause, and I had no idea what it meant.

"Uh." I took a step backward, making room for her to do, well, whatever it was she was getting ready to do. "Hey, Becks, are you okay? I was just about to clear out, so if you need the bathroom—"

"Shut up, Shaun." She let go of the doorknob and walked toward me. Once she reached me, she took the towel from my shoulders and tossed it carelessly to one side. "For once in your life, just *once*, why don't you. Just. Shut. Up." She stepped a little closer, leaning up onto her toes, and kissed me.

I wasn't expecting the kiss. I didn't have a chance to step aside or deflect it. So, no, I couldn't have prevented it from starting...but I could have pulled away from her. I could have stopped it right there.

Instead, I kissed her back.

Becks pressed herself hard against me as soon as I started to respond to her kiss, arms tightening around my shoulders and holding me where I was. I wrapped my arms around her waist, as much to have a place to put them as anything else, and almost involuntarily pulled her closer. The heat coming off her skin felt like it would steam the remaining dampness from the shower right off me. Through it all, she kept on kissing me, the urgency in her movement growing with every second. Suddenly exquisitely aware of how close to naked I was, I raised my hands and took hold of her forearms, pushing her gently away. She fought to maintain the kiss for another few seconds before the distance between us made it impossible.

Her eyes were bright and her cheeks were flushed. She was still wearing the bathrobe she'd borrowed from Maggie, and the belt was half-untied, letting the top gape open enough to give me a really good view of her cleavage. I swallowed. Hard. Tired or not, I was still male, and it had been a long damn time since I'd had a look at that particular vista. Parts of my anatomy that I'd been willing to write off completely were waking up and announcing their interest in the situation. Loudly.

"Becks, I don't know if—"

"Do you want me to stop?" She twisted out of my grasp, moving with a simple grace that made my breath catch in my throat. Then she reached up to take my hands, sliding her fingers into mine. "I'll be totally honest. I don't want to stop. But I will, if that's what you want."

"I...I don't know, I just..." I looked at our joined hands, studying the short, practical shape of her nails. She had the nails of an Irwin. That made me feel better, oddly enough. I was just another hazard zone for her to explore. "I don't know if this is such a good idea."

"Hey. Look at me." I raised my head. Becks met my eyes and said, "I'm not going to ask you for a commitment. I don't want to go steady. You're my boss, and you're my colleague, and I respect that. But we almost died today, and I'd like to remind myself that we didn't." She stepped back, still holding my hands. "I'm lonely. Don't you ever get lonely?"

It was suddenly hard to breathe. "Every damn night," I said, and closed the distance between us with a step, yanking my hands free before wrapping my arms around her waist again. This time, I was the one initiating the kiss; this time, I was the one pressing with increasing urgency as she kissed me back, bringing one hand up so she could curl her fingers through my hair and pull my head a little farther down. We kissed until my lips felt bruised and my chest hurt with the effort of continuing to breathe.

Becks pulled back, fingers still knotted in my hair. "Does that mean you don't want me to stop?"

"Don't stop," I managed, and kissed her again.

Somehow we made it out of the bathroom and down the hall to the guest room where she'd been sleeping. I managed to keep the towel on until the door was closed behind us, when Becks resolved the question of what I was supposed to do with it by removing it from my waist and throwing it to one side. She untied her bathrobe and pressed herself hard against me before resuming her frantic kisses. The feeling of her skin touching mine was almost more than I could handle. I groaned. She moaned appreciatively, the sound of a living woman desiring and being desired, rather than the sound of the dead. God, I needed to hear that. I didn't spend nearly enough time among the living.

The ringing silence in my head was forgotten, drowned out by the sounds our bodies made—skin sliding against skin, fingers rustling through hair, lips meeting and parting and meeting again. Becks kept moving steadily backward, forcing me to follow if I wanted to keep kissing her. I wanted to keep kissing her, and so I kept going until she pulled me onto the bed and slung one leg over mine, keeping me there. I didn't resist. I didn't want to. For the first time since George died, I really didn't give a shit about anything but the present. It was a nice feeling. I'd missed it.

"Shaun."

I started kissing her neck, tasting the slightly salty flavor of her skin. I'd missed that, too. The taste of a woman's neck, the way it moved when she breathed—

"*Shaun.*"

It took a moment for the fact that Becks was talking to me to sink all the way into my brain. I stopped kissing her in order to push myself back and look at her face. Her hair was rumpled, making her look like she'd just finished running a marathon after holding off an entire horde of zombies with nothing but a shotgun. I was starting to understand why she kept it long. It might be impractical as hell, but it made views like this one possible, and that was worth a little inconvenience. "What? Did I do something wrong?"

"No." She smiled, a little wryly. "I just wanted to let you know that I have condoms."

I hadn't even thought that far ahead. I blinked for a moment, and then nodded. "Cool, because if I have any, they're downstairs." Actually, I wasn't sure whether I had condoms in my pack or not. I hadn't needed that sort of thing in so long that I'd stopped thinking about it, since thinking about it didn't do me a damn bit of good. Sex wasn't a factor in this post-George world. There just wasn't time.

Becks smiled a little more, looking surprisingly shy, considering that we were buck-ass naked and twisted around each other. "Will you let me up?" she asked.

"Um, right." It took some effort to untangle our limbs. She stood, stretching to give me the best possible view of her body—and I had to admit, the girl was stacked—before crossing to her pack and bending to rummage through one of the inside pockets. I stayed on the bed, feeling suddenly awkward and not exactly sure where I was supposed to put my hands. That was another thing I never had to worry about before. I wasn't even sure I was supposed to be looking at her when she wasn't in the bed. I settled for sitting up with my hands resting loosely between my thighs, looking in her direction, but trying to keep myself from really *looking*. She might get upset if I looked away. She might decide I didn't like the way she looked or something.

Jesus. When did life get so damn complicated?

"Here we go." Becks turned, a foil-wrapped condom held between her thumb and forefinger, and walked back toward the bed. "I've got a birth control implant, but you can't be too careful, right?"

"Right," I echoed, faintly. The pause had given me time to think, which wasn't such a good thing. My body was still voting in favor of going through with things, but now my brain was trying to weigh in on the topic, and it wasn't convinced that this was a good idea. It was reasonably sure that this was a really *bad* idea, and if there was any time to stop, this was it.

Becks tore the foil.

My brain found itself outvoted in a sudden upset sponsored by the body and supported by every hormone I had. I was reaching for her, and she was reaching for me, and then her fingers were unrolling the condom along the length of my cock, and then coherent thought took a backseat for a while. Its services were no longer required, or really wanted. Everything that mattered was in the bed, and none of it took the slightest bit of thinking. All I had to do was act. So I closed my eyes, cupped my hands against the side of her waist, and let the moment do the driving.

I don't know how long the moment lasted. Long enough that when it ended, I was even more exhausted. It was a better exhaustion, it was just...all-consuming, the kind of tired that it's almost impossible to fight. I helped clean up the mess with my eyes half-closed, fumbling as we got the damp sheets and the used condom into the appropriate hampers and waste baskets. Then I sagged back into the mattress, relaxing utterly as my head hit the pillow. It felt like all the tension was finally running out of me, leaving me floating in that wonderful horizon between half-asleep and all the way gone.

Fingers trailed down the length of my chest, coming to rest just above my navel. "Good night, Shaun," whispered a voice, inches from my ear.

God. For the first time in longer than I could remember, the world felt like it was actually back the way that it was supposed to be. I brought up a hand to brush my knuckles against her cheek, smelling the sweet-salt-sex smell of her, and smiled.

"Good night, George," I said, and slipped away into sleep.

Mankind's history is littered with singularities—big moments that changed everything, even if nobody knew they were coming. The discovery of antibiotic medicine was a singularity. Before that, it was normal for women to die of "childbed fever," a simple staph infection making them die slowly and in great agony. Cavities killed. Antibiotics changed all that, and less than fifty years later, the thought of living the way people lived before antibiotics was alien to almost everyone.

The industrial revolution was a singularity. As you sit reading this, consider that, once, electric lighting was considered a luxury, and some people weren't even sure it would catch on. The idea that someday the entire world would be run by machines was crazy, preposterous science fiction...but it happened.

The Rising was a singularity. The way we live today isn't just a little different. It's alien. Our paradigm has shifted, and it can't be shifted back. That's why so many of the old rules of psychology don't apply anymore. Once the dead are walking, crazy's what you make it.

—From *Cabin Fever Dream*,
guest blog of Barbara Tinney, April 20, 2041

———

Tonight's watch-along film is that classic of the genre, *The Evil Dead*, wherein a truly spicy young Bruce Campbell—yum—is menaced by demons, evil trees, and his own hand. I'll be opening the chat room at eight Pacific, and live blogging the whole movie for those of you whose attention spans won't tolerate anything longer than a few hundred characters.

I hope to see you all online, and remember, last person to log on owes me a drink.

—From *Dandelion Mine*,
the blog of Magdalene Grace Garcia, April 20, 2041

Sixteen

I woke sprawled buck-ass naked on the guest room bed, surrounded by the furry mounds of sleeping bulldogs. Groaning, I pushed myself up onto my elbows. The door was open about a foot—just enough to explain my unwanted guests. I scrubbed at my face with one hand, trying to wake up enough to start worrying about my clothes. "Guess it's time to deal with another fucking morning, huh, George?"

Ringing silence answered me. I pulled my hand away from my face and sat all the way up. "George?" Still no answer. "You're starting to freak me out here, George. What did I do to earn the silent treatment? I'm doing what you asked me to do. I'm actually stepping up to the plate. So could you stop fucking around?"

She didn't stop fucking around. She was still there—I remember what sane felt like, and this wasn't it; sane didn't come with the constant low-grade awareness of George sitting at the back of my head—she just wasn't talking. I scowled.

"Fine. If you want to play silent treatment, we'll play silent treatment. See how *you* like it." I scooched my butt along the mattress, eventually getting to the point where my feet hit the floor. Every muscle in my legs ached. I could already tell I was going to be applying Icy-Hot and gulping aspirin like M&Ms all day. I guess that's what you get when you go and outrun an outbreak.

"And yet somehow better than the alternative," I muttered.

The mystery of how the door got open was answered by the stack of clothing and crap on the bookshelf just inside. I sent a silent thanks to Maggie's in-house laundry service—silent because with her computer systems, I was vaguely afraid the program in charge of the laundry service might respond if I thanked it out loud—and began getting dressed. Even the things I'd left in the bathroom were clean, down to the rust on my ancient Swiss army knife. I shook my head. Sometimes it's possible to be a little *too* efficient. It was unnerving to think of the house sending out tiny cleaning devices and using them to polish my thumb drive and pocket change to a mirror sheen.

At least nothing was missing. I shoved things into their respective pockets, fastened my belt, and sat down on the bed to put my boots on. That's when the reality of my position finally filtered through my sleep-addled, George-less brain:

I was the only person in the room. Where the hell was Becks? I looked back at the bed, which didn't offer any answers. From the way I'd been sprawled when I woke up, there was nothing to prove that anyone else had been in the bed to begin with. That was a little worrisome. If I'd gone even further over the edge and started hallucinating being seduced by random members of staff, the time remaining before I went totally insane was probably pretty low.

With that cheerful thought at the front of my mind, I started trying to get my boots on. The process was complicated by the dogs, who thought attacking the laces was a fantastic game. The main difference between dogs that size and cats seems to be that cats, while crazy, are at least *meant* to be little, whereas the process of shrinking dogs seems to drive them insane. "At least we have that much in common," I muttered, and stood, stretching for a final time before walking out of the room. I left the guest room door open. No point in depriving the bulldogs of a nice warm bed.

Alaric was sitting at the kitchen table with his laptop, tapping industriously away. A half a pot of coffee sat in front of him, wafting the delicious smell of hot caffeine toward me as I entered. I stopped to sniff appreciatively. The sound got his attention; he looked up, nodded briefly, and looked back down again. "Hey."

"Hey," I said. I grabbed a mug from the counter and poured myself a cup of hot black coffee. Morning is the only time I normally get coffee without complaining from my inner peanut gallery. If George wanted to sulk, maybe I could get a second cup in before going back to Coke.

A pang of guilt followed on the heels of the thought, although it wasn't enough to stop me from taking a mouthful of throat-searing liquid. I'd rather have George than all the coffee in the world. Still, if focusing on self-caffeination distracted me from the question of her silence, it was worthwhile. Alaric kept typing as I sat down across from him, seeming to ignore me completely. I sipped my coffee. He typed. George didn't say anything.

This went on for a few minutes before I cleared my throat and asked, "So what have I missed? Other than the sunrise and, apparently, breakfast?"

Alaric raised his head. "Maggie took Becks and the Doc into town to go grocery shopping. Something about us eating her out of house and home."

The image of that particular trio tackling the Weed supermarket was fascinating. I paused for a moment to ponder it. I've seen pictures of pre-Rising grocery stores. They were weird, cramped things, with narrow aisles filled with milling consumers—and of course, when the zombies came, they turned into effective little death traps, full of places for the infected to hide. Even the sprinkler systems they used to run over the vegetables worked to spread the outbreak, since all it took was a few drops of blood getting into the water system and, bam, you were literally misting live infection throughout the produce aisle. It didn't help that people kept freaking out and running for places where they could try to hole up until it was all over—like the nearest warehouse megastore. The body counts at Costco and Wal-Mart were nothing short of stratospheric.

For a few years post-Rising, everyone bought their groceries online. Some people still do that, preferring a small delivery charge to the inherent risks of going out among the rest of the population. Unfortunately for them, not everything lends itself to the online model. Fresh fruit and vegetables, meat—fish and poultry, anyway, those being the meats still sold for eating—and anything with the word "bulk" attached to it are much better bought in person. The rise of the modern grocery store has been a reflection of people's twin needs to eat and not get eaten. The layout is closer to the old megastores than anything else, but only a certain number of people are allowed in each department at any one time. Groups cycle through according to the store's floor plan, with air locks and blood testing units between each distinct part of the store. The process takes hours. Grocery shopping is not an activity for the faint of heart.

I paused. "Isn't Maggie afraid they'll be spotted?"

"I'm pretty sure her parents own the store."

"Oh, that'd do it. Has the Doc ever actually *been* in a grocery store?" I asked. My coffee was starting to cool down. I took a longer swallow, letting comforting bitterness cover the back of my throat. It was weird, drinking coffee without apologizing to George or asking permission before doing it. I took another drink, almost daring her to comment.

She didn't.

"I don't think so," said Alaric. "She turned sort of white when Maggie told her where they were going."

"God, I hope somebody's got a camera running." Or four, or five, or maybe an even dozen. We couldn't use the footage for anything, but seeing Kelly confronted with an actual fish counter would be comedy gold.

"I'm sure they do," said Alaric. "They know their jobs."

"True." I refilled my mug. "Anything else going on?"

"Not really."

"Huh. Okay. How are the overnights?"

"Good."

"Not great?"

"Really good." Alaric seemed to realize I wasn't going anywhere. He pushed his laptop to one side and reached for his own mug. "Your report got a ridiculous number of downloads. I mean, really ridiculous. Every time you go anywhere near the field, we see a ratings spike of insane proportions."

"Yeah, well, every time I go anywhere near the field, I wind up not sleeping for a month, so I guess it evens out in the end. Has the CDC said anything about what happened in Portland?"

"There's no official statement yet, but Talking Points managed to get an interview with Director Swenson—"

I snorted. Talking Points is a lousy site, and they have a reputation for editing reports to match the requests of the highest bidder. Giving them an exclusive was sort of like buying a commercial slot during prime time: a great use of your money, but a terrible abuse of the truth.

Alaric narrowed his eyes. "Mind if I continue?"

"Sorry." I waved my mug in his direction. "I'm all ears. No more interruptions, I promise."

"I'll believe that when I see it," Alaric muttered, before continuing: "He repeated the lab accident story and added a cute little 'maybe if they hadn't somehow wandered into a secure area, they wouldn't have been forced to use the emergency access tunnels' rider, trying to make it look like you and Becks had been negligent, or worse, trespassing."

"How did we answer that?"

"Mahir uploaded your footage, sans dialogue, of everything from the director leaving you in the conference room to the lights going out. Time stamps visible for the entire thing. If you were someplace you weren't supposed to be, it was because the director left you there."

"Remind me to give that man a raise."

"How about you get the rest of us out of the line of fire, first?" Alaric's tone was harsh, verging on nasty. I'd never heard him talk to anyone like that before. Not even after the time I broke his nose for suggesting that my ongoing need to talk to George was a sign of mental illness. I know it's a sign of mental illness; I knew it then, too. I just think the alternative to going crazy is even worse.

I put my mug down, frowning as I studied Alaric. He looked tired, but that wasn't really a surprise. We *all* looked tired, and with good reason. "Dude, what's going on? Did somebody decide to piss in your cereal or something?"

"I'm just not sure you have your priorities straight anymore. That's all." Alaric looked at me steadily, lips firming into a thin line. "It's not like any of us can quit at this point, is it? Not when they're blowing up buildings to make us stop poking at things."

"What, and you think that's my fault?" I waved an arm toward the front door. "I didn't ask the Doc to show up, and they started shooting at us as soon as they had a bead on where she was, remember? You can*not* pin that one on me, Alaric. You want to be pissed off at somebody, I recommend her."

"*She* brought us a hook into the greatest conspiracy of our generation! *You* just want it to be about revenge! It's not all about you, Shaun. It's *never* been all about you. You're not the only one being lied to, and you're not the only one who's lost people. I guess I'm just getting tired of you acting that way."

I blinked. "I...what?"

"You heard me."

"I never said this wasn't everybody's fight."

"Could've fooled me."

I slammed my hand down on the table hard enough to make the coffee slosh over the lip of my mug. Alaric jumped. "Dammit, Alaric, this is *not* the time to play pissy bitches. What the fuck is bothering you? Did you get trolled on the message boards? Is your revenue share down? Do you not like the guest room you're in? What?"

"Was there a particular reason Rebecca came down the stairs this morning looking like she hadn't slept, and ran out of here the second she was given the opportunity to do so?" You could have used the edge on his voice to cut steel. Closing his laptop with one hand, Alaric continued: "You were asleep at the time. That may be why she left so quickly. Avoiding an unpleasant encounter."

"Oh, crap." Any relief I might have felt at hearing that I wasn't going crazier—Becks and I really did have sex—was destroyed by the realization that I'd hurt her in the process. I put a hand over my face, resting my elbow on the table. "Oh, fuck."

"That was what I assumed you'd been doing."

"Alaric, man—" I raised my head, looking at him. He was still glaring at me. That was fine. I felt like glaring at myself. "How upset was she?"

"I'm not sure, really. She wasn't exactly in the mood for handing out details."

That was one I owed her. Two, if you counted the monumental apology I was going to be making as soon as she got back. "I guess not. Look, Alaric, I never meant for any of that to happen, I swear. I wasn't trying to get her into bed, and I sure as hell wasn't trying to hurt her once she was there."

"I know." He sighed, deflating somehow as he looked down at the table. "I know she likes you. I've known for ages. I just kept hoping she'd see that you weren't interested. That she had better options available. But it was like she couldn't see anything but the fact that you were playing hard to get."

"I wasn't playing," I said softly. This sort of thing was easier to handle when George was around. She was always the one who noticed when girls started crushing on me, and she made them go away. One way or another. I'd never tried to deal with this sort of situation on my own before. "I really wasn't."

Alaric laughed. It was a short, dry sound, utterly devoid of humor. "The tragedy of all this is that I know. If you'd been playing, she might have gotten over you faster."

"I'll apologize."

"You'd better." He stood, taking his laptop with him. "We can't afford to be at each other's throats right now."

"No, we can't," I said bleakly, and watched as he turned and walked out of the room. Once he was gone I let my head fall to the table, forehead knocking gently against the wood. "Fuck, George. How do I get myself into this shit?"

Leaping before you look, mostly. It's always been your biggest weakness. Her laugh was superficially similar to Alaric's, all sharp, hard edges, but there was amusement there, too. The sort of amusement that comes right before the execution. *That, and me, anyway.*

"Oh, thank God." I sat up and sagged backward in the chair, closing my eyes. "You scared the crap out of me."

You needed some time to think.

"Yeah, and look how much good that did me. Now Becks is pissed, which means Maggie's going to be pissed, too, and Alaric thinks I'm an asshole."

Well, you sort of are. I told you to be careful with her.

"How was I supposed to know she was going to jump me in the bathroom?"

I love you, but there are times when I really don't understand the way your brain works. She's been getting ready to jump you for a while now. All the signs were there.

"Why would I know what the signs *were*, George? I never had to read them before."

She sighed. *True enough. You shouldn't have called her by my name, Shaun. This is going to complicate everything.*

"I know. Now what am I supposed to do about it?"

She didn't have an answer for that one.

Maggie's van pulled up half an hour later. I heard doors slamming in the driveway, and then, like magic, the kitchen was full of women with arms full of groceries, covering every flat surface with brown paper sacks. I was still at the kitchen table, although I'd exchanged my coffee for a can of Coke. The acidic sweetness of it was actually pleasant for once; the fact that I was drinking it meant that George was speaking to me again. That was worth doing a little damage to my tooth enamel.

Becks cast a wounded look in my direction as she dropped her armload of grocery bags onto the stove. Then she fled out the back door, vanishing in the direction of the van. I winced and stood. "Aw, hey, Becks, hang on a second—"

"Freeze," said Maggie, in an amiable tone.

I froze.

"Kelly, why don't you go and get Alaric. Tell him we need help unloading the van." Maggie's voice stayed pleasant, but there was an edge to it that made arguing with her seem like a seriously bad idea. Kelly nodded and left the room even faster than Becks had. She didn't even bother putting down her last bag of groceries.

I stayed where I was, watching Maggie cautiously. She put down the bag she was holding and walked over to me, stopping a few feet away as she studied my face. Finally, shaking her head, she sighed.

"How crazy *are* you, Shaun?"

It was an echo of the question George asked me in the van, after Kelly dropped her little bombshell about the reservoir conditions. There was no possible way for Maggie to have heard Georgia's side of the conversation, even if she'd been listening in. I flinched all the same, answering without thinking about it: "Pretty damn crazy." I winced. "Okay, that was maybe not the best answer. Can I try again?"

"It was an honest answer, which is what I needed." Maggie looked me slowly up and down. "Did you know what you were going to do to Rebecca when you let her take you to bed?"

"God, no. Maggie, I didn't even know she was...y'know, *interested* in me. That way."

"I thought that might be the case." Maggie sighed. "Have you ever had a girlfriend?"

That was another question without a good answer. I settled for being as honest as I could. "Not as such, no."

Again that slow look up and down before Maggie said, "I thought that might be the case, too. Will you let me give you some advice?"

"At this point?" I barked a short, bitter laugh. "I'd take advice from the bulldogs if I thought it would help. I didn't mean to fuck things up with Becks. I mean..." It was my fault because she'd been there, and she'd been willing, and she'd been offering me something I thought I wanted. She came with full disclosure, all her baggage right there on the table. Me, I'd been hiding how far gone I was for so long that I...didn't. She had no idea what she was getting into. I knew that. And I should have known better.

"Are you blaming her?"

"I'm blaming myself."

"Good." Maggie nodded, looking satisfied. "You're both adults, and it's none of my business what you do, as long as nobody's getting hurt. Becks got hurt. Maybe she should have been more careful about weighing the risks, but that doesn't matter right now. You need to apologize to her. You need to make this right, because if you wait for her to get better on her own, I don't think you're going to be able to work together anymore."

"Yeah, I can do that." I would even mean it. Becks deserved a hell of a lot better than the way I'd treated her, whether I meant to treat her badly or not.

She deserved a hell of a lot better than me.

"I'm glad." Maggie stepped forward and hugged me. Her hair smelled like vanilla and strawberries. She held on just long enough that I was starting to get uncomfortable before letting go and turning to start taking groceries out of bags, leaving me blinking dumbly after her. Catching my look, she arched her eyebrows, and said, "Well? What are you waiting for? Get out there and talk to her. *Go.*"

I went.

The grass was damp, probably from some overnight rainfall, and my boots were wet by the time I'd crossed it to Maggie's van, which sat in the driveway with doors open and groceries on the front seat. There was nobody there. I turned to look around, unsurprised to see footprints in the wet grass leading away, toward Maggie's vegetable garden.

I followed the trail all the way around the house and to the edge of the carefully tilled plot of ground that Maggie used for growing vegetables and fresh herbs. A few pre-Rising park benches had been set up inside the garden border, providing a decorative touch of retro chic to the place. Becks was sitting on the bench farthest from where I stood, her back to me. I wasn't quiet as I approached her, and she didn't move. I guess she'd been expecting me.

"Hey," I said, when I was close enough. "You mind if I sit down?"

"Yes, I do mind." She turned in my direction, tilting her chin up as she looked at me. Her eyes were only a little bloodshot. She'd clearly mastered the Irwin art of crying without making yourself look bad for the cameras. That just made me feel worse. "But I guess we have to do this, so you might as well." She scooted to the side, waving a hand in invitation.

"Thanks." I sat, letting my hands rest on my knees. Silence fell between us. She was waiting for me to start, and I had no clue how.

Say you're sorry, prompted George.

She'd never led me wrong before. "I'm sorry, Becks. I mean, Jesus, I'm so fucking sorry, I don't think I can even say it. I was stupid, and I was selfish, and I'm sorry."

Becks took a shaky breath. There was an edge of laughter to her voice when she spoke, like she couldn't quite believe that we were doing this. "So that's it? You're sorry? I knew you had issues, Shaun, and I'm a big girl—I thought I could handle them. I guess I was wrong. I shouldn't blame you for that." *But I do.* The subtext in her words was impossible to miss, even for me.

"Maybe you shouldn't blame me, but I should still have been smart enough to tell you that it wasn't a good idea for us to be...intimate like that."

"You mean we shouldn't have fucked like bunnies?"

I coughed, partly from surprise, partly to cover the phantom sound of George's laughter. "Uh, that, too. I just...I guess I wasn't expecting it and does that sound unbelievably lame, or is it just me?"

Becks frowned, slowly. "You really mean that, don't you? You really had no idea."

"No idea of what?"

She stared for a moment before letting her chin drop and saying, "Oh, my God. You *really* had no idea."

I was starting to get concerned. Apologizing for something I knew I'd done was one thing—I may not have much experience with girls, but I'm smart enough to know that calling them by somebody else's name is *never* a good thing, especially when that somebody else is dead and also technically my sister. Apologizing for something I didn't know I'd done was a bit more of a problem, if only because I couldn't be sure I was doing it right. "Uh, Becks, I'm sorry, but you're kinda losing me here. I'm happy to keep apologizing, but I do need to know what I'm apologizing *for*."

This time her laughter was bright and brittle, like broken glass glinting in the sunlight. "I've been throwing myself at you for *months*, Shaun. The flirting, the frilly tops, the requests for hands-on review of my reports—I mean, what the hell did you think I was doing?"

"I don't know," I replied honestly. "I figured you just wanted to make sure your facts were solid before you posted, and all that frilly stuff looked like a girl thing. Sort of like the way you wear your hair."

"I wasn't getting any ratings based on what I wore to work," she said.

I shrugged.

Becks sighed. "Fine. So you wrote all that off. What about the flirting? Did you write that off as 'a girl thing,' too?"

If I was telling the truth, I might as well go for the whole truth. I was pretty sure it couldn't get me into any more trouble than I was already in. "Until you showed up and took my towel away, I really didn't notice."

"If Dave weren't dead, I'd owe him ten bucks." Becks looked away from me, staring out at the forest past the fence. It looked completely untamed; Maggie's security precautions were very well concealed. "He said you didn't get it. I thought you were playing hard to get."

"That's what Alaric said, too. I'm really sorry. I never did the whole flirting thing."

"No, I guess you didn't, did you?" She slanted a sidelong glance my way, considering me. "You didn't need to."

I thought about lying to her. After everything else, there didn't seem to be any point. "No, I guess I didn't."

She nodded, once, mouth twisting in that too-damn-familiar way before she went back to looking at the forest. I hated that look. I'd hated it on every face that I'd ever seen wearing it. The one that said, clearly, "But she's your *sister*," and ignored the part where she was also the only person who'd ever really given a damn what I thought. About anything.

Finally, in a soft, almost contemplative tone, Becks said, "I guess I sort of knew, deep down. Maybe that's why you were so safe to chase. I didn't think I'd ever have a chance to catch you."

I wasn't sure what to say to that. I settled for what seemed like the safest of my available options. "I'm sorry."

"I am, too, Shaun. Believe me, I am too. I...I know we can't exactly go back to the way things were. That's my fault as much as it is yours, I guess. I just don't know..."

"How we're supposed to go on from here?" I ventured. She nodded. I bit back the urge to laugh, mostly because I wasn't sure I'd be able to stop again. "Dude, Becks, I've been asking myself that question pretty much every day since George died."

"Have you figured out the answer yet?"

"There isn't one." I slumped against the back of the bench, tilting my head back until I couldn't see anything but sky, going on for what might as well have been forever. "I figure I'll just keep on going the way I am until something starts making sense."

"What if nothing ever does?"

"I guess if that happens, I'll start hoping all the God freaks are right, and there's some superior intelligence up there treating us all like laboratory rats."

Fabric rustled against wood as Becks turned to peer at me. I couldn't see her, but I knew her well enough to know exactly what her expression looked like: confusion mixed with wary suspicion that whatever I said next was going to be so completely off the wall that she couldn't stand to hear it. Finally, she said, "Why are you going to start looking for God?"

"I didn't say I was going to start looking. If there's a God, there are plenty of people who know where he is." I shrugged, still watching the sky. It was easier than watching Becks. "I just want to know that he's there, so that I can die knowing there's going to be someone I can punch in the mouth on the other end."

Becks laughed. Some of the tension in my shoulders slipped away. I'd done a terrible thing to her, but I didn't mean to, and the tone of her laughter told me that maybe—despite everything—we could manage to be okay again. She was right; we'd never be exactly the same kind of okay that we were before. But we'd be more okay, and that was better than nothing.

Violence isn't the only solution, George said. She sounded as relieved as I felt.

"Sometimes it's the most fun one," I answered, without thinking about it. Becks stopped laughing. I tensed, looking away from the sky and back to her as I waited for us to start arguing again.

Instead, she just looked at me. Her eyes were hazel. I'd never noticed that before—not really. That made me feel even worse about what we'd done. I should never have slept with her if I couldn't even remember the color of her eyes. "You're pretty lucky, you know," she said.

I blinked at her. "What?"

"Most people, we lose the people that we love, and they're just *gone*. We don't get to have them anymore. But you..." She raised a hand, brushing her fingertips across my forehead. Her skin was cool. "She's always going to be there for you, isn't she? As long as you live."

"I don't know how to live in a world that doesn't have her in it," I said. My voice came out raw with a longing that surprised me. I never start thinking I'm getting over losing her. It still startles me sometimes, when I realize just how damn much I miss her.

"Here's hoping you never have to." Becks stood. "We're okay, Shaun. Or at least, I'm okay, and I'd like you to be okay with me."

I nodded. "I'd like that."

"Good. I'll go tell Maggie that we talked things through." She hesitated, and then added, "Keep the guest room. I'll sleep on the couch tonight." She shoved her hands into her pockets and walked away before I could say anything, footsteps plodding heavily on the damp garden earth. I watched her go, and then sagged back into the bench, closing my eyes.

"When do things get to be simple again, George?" I whispered. "Ever?"

They weren't simple to begin with, she said.

I didn't have a comeback for that, and so I just sat in the sunlight in the garden and breathed in the smell of rain-soaked grass, waiting for the world to slow down. Just a little bit. Just long enough to let us rest before the next storm came crashing through. Was that really so much to ask? I just wanted to rest.

Just for a little while.

Things it is not polite to discuss at the dinner table: politics, religion, and the walking dead.

Things we wind up discussing at the dinner table every single night: politics, religion, and the walking dead. Along with small-caliber versus large-caliber weapons for field use, personal security gear, Maggie's garden, our ratings, and vehicle maintenance. It's very claustrophobic and intense, with everyone on top of everybody else pretty much all the time. There's no real privacy, and there's so much security on the house that getting out is almost as big a production as getting *in*. It's like a fucked-up combination of prison and summer camp.

Is it weird that this is what I always dreamed the news would be like? Because, God, maybe I'm fucked in the head or something, but this is the most fun I've ever had. I want someone to remind me I said that when it all turns around and bites us in the ass.

—From *Charming Not Sincere*,
the blog of Rebecca Atherton, May 9, 2041. Unpublished.

Check it out, folks! I can add "survived an unplanned zombie encounter while visiting the CDC to discuss the outbreak in Oakland" to my résumé! Not to brag or anything, but why don't you all download my reports, and then go fill out your Golden Steve-o nominations for the year? I'll be your best friend...

—From *Charming Not Sincere*,
the blog of Rebecca Atherton, May 9, 2041

Seventeen

Five days ticked by with little fanfare. Becks and I went shooting in the woods outside of town, clearing out a mixed mob of zombie humans and cows. Once the disease takes over, species isn't an issue anymore. Maggie spent a lot of time writing poetry, weeding her garden, and avoiding Kelly, who took over the dining room table with Dr. Abbey's research and kept muttering things none of the rest of us could understand. Alaric hung out with her, listening, taking notes, and nodding a lot. It was almost unnerving, in a geeky sort of way.

Those five days may have been the last good time for us. Maybe the universe had been listening when I made my wish out in the garden; I don't know. I just know that I asked for time to rest, and somehow, miraculously, I actually got it. Nothing exploded. There were no outbreaks and no emergencies, nothing to pull us away from the difficult task of turning ourselves back into a team. The hours turned into days, and the days blended together, distinguished from each other only by the activity in the forums and the reports we were posting.

Kelly continued her series of guest articles under the Barbara Tinney byline. It wasn't exactly a runaway hit, but it was popular—surprisingly so. I always forget how much people like getting excuses for their crazy. The profits Kelly's column brought in went directly to Maggie, where they could help pay for our room and board. She snorted and waved it off like it was no big thing. She also took the money. It made me feel a little bit less guilty about the way we were intruding.

Becks moved into the study, saying that the air mattress was better for her back than the couch was for mine. That meant I could move to the guest room, which was a relief, since I wasn't really sleeping in the living room. And I needed my sleep. I went to bed every night with my head stuffed full of science, and woke up every morning ready to cram in some more. I needed to understand the research Dr. Abbey had given us. More important, I needed to understand the research Mahir was hopefully sweet-talking some British professor into doing. If I was going to march everyone off to get themselves killed on my behalf, I was by God going to be certain I knew what they were dying for. It was the only promise I could make that I felt reasonably sure of being able to keep.

When I wasn't studying, I was making calls. My little team of reporters might not have much in the way of manpower, but we had connections, and it was time to exploit them. Rick's ascent from Newsie to vice president of the United States isn't a normal career path for either a journalist or a politician, but hey, it's worked out pretty well for him. I started calling his office, once a day at first, then twice a day, until it became clear that he wasn't going to call me back. That wasn't like him. Not even a little bit. And that worried me.

The days rolled on. Alaric started a series on the rise of digital profiling and its applications in the medical field. Becks took a trip up into Washington, looking for zombies she could harass on camera; she came back with powder burns, bruises, and twice as many articles about her adventures. Reading the first one made my throat get tight with half a dozen emotions it was hard to put into words. That used to be me running into the woods to play tag with zombie deer and gathering "no shit, there I was" stories from truckers who remembered the roads during the Rising. That used to be all I wanted in the world. Everything changed when George died. Sometimes I read the articles that Becks posts and I wonder whether the man I used to be would even recognize the one I'm becoming. I don't think he'd like the new me very much.

I know I don't.

I told Mahir and Maggie about the silence from Rick's office, and they agreed that it was best if we kept it between us, at least for now. Everyone was freaked out enough without adding that little wrinkle to the mix. Maggie's Fictionals didn't help; at some point, she'd given at least half of them the all-clear. They went back to dropping in without warning, appearing on the doorstep and in the kitchen like they'd been there all along. Most of them brought pizza, or cookies, or samosas. I'd never met two-thirds of them before, even though they were all technically part of the site staff. They walked on eggshells around everyone but Maggie, and we started using their visits as excuses for equipment repair and trips into Weed for more groceries. Once their grindhouse parties got started, they could go for hours, watching crappy pre-Rising horror movies and eating gallons of popcorn. I didn't realize how antisocial I was becoming until the Fictionals started to descend, and all I could think of was how quickly I could get away.

The bug at the Portland CDC yielded nothing useful; either they'd managed to find and destroy it, or it hadn't survived the decontamination process. One more possible information source down the drain. The worms Alaric activated back in Oakland were doing a little bit better. They kept finding old research papers and short-lived projects buried in the bowels of one server or another. We added them to the data we already had, and kept on working.

Mahir had a few local scientists who were willing to at least discuss the situation with him; he didn't tell us their names, and I didn't press. There were some things I was better off not knowing until I had to. It seemed to be going well, at least in the beginning, but after the second day, he stopped calling or e-mailing. His reports still went up on time, and he still did his time on the forums—from the outside, everything looked fine—but he wasn't keeping up normal contact.

Don't push him, said George. I listened, more out of habit than because I agreed with her. She was usually right about when I needed to wait and when it was okay to barrel on ahead. I just wasn't sure how much longer my patience could last.

The waiting ended a little over two weeks after the destruction of Oakland and our arrival at Maggie's. The house phone rang, ignored by the humans currently present—myself, Maggie, and the Doc, who was struggling to write an article about the pros and cons of exposing children to the outside world. She was having a lot more trouble meeting her deadlines now that she didn't have Mahir to help.

The answering machine picked up after the second ring. There were a few minutes of silence, followed by the voice of the house computer saying politely, "Excuse me, Shaun. Do you have a moment?"

I hate machines that sound like people.

"Hush," I muttered. The house computer had learned not to pay attention when I spoke that quietly—I guess even machines have a learning curve for crazy—and continued to wait for my reply until I said, "Yeah, sure. What's up?"

"There is a call for you."

"I guessed that part. Who is it?"

"The caller has declined to identify himself. By his accent, there is an eighty-seven percent chance that he is of British nationality, although I am unable to determine his region of origin with any accuracy. The call has been placed from a local number. The exact number is blocked. Would you like me to request additional information?"

I stood so fast that I knocked my Coke over. Soda cascaded across the table and onto the carpet. I ignored it, lunging for the phone next to the kitchen door. Maggie was right behind me, demanding, "House, is the line secure?"

"This end of the line is secured according to protocol four, which should be sufficient to block anything but a physical wiretap. I am unable to determine the security standards of the other end of the line. Do you wish to proceed?" The voice of the house was infinitely patient, mechanical calm unbroken by the fact that Maggie and I looked like we were on the verge of hysterics.

"Yes, dammit," I said, and grabbed the receiver from the wall. Dead air greeted me. I gave the phone a panicked look. "Where is he?"

"House, *connect*," ordered Maggie.

The phone clicked, and suddenly, wonderfully, Mahir's voice was in my ear, muffled slightly, like he had his hand over the receiver. "—Promise you, sir, I'm phoning my ride now. I apologize for loitering within your isolation zone, but as my original flight was delayed, it was unfortunately unavoidable." His tone was clipped, carefully polite, and shaded with a bone-deep weariness that made me tired just listening to it.

"Mahir!" I said, loudly enough that he would be able to hear me through his hand.

There was a scraping sound before he said, "About bloody time, Mason. Come get me."

"Uh, sorry if I'm a little bit behind the program here, but come get you *where*?"

The house said the call was coming from a local number, said George sharply. *He's* here. *Mahir is in this area code.*

"I'm at the Weed Airport."

I froze, staring stupidly at the wall. Maggie nudged me with her elbow, and I said the first thing that popped into my head: "Weed has an airport?"

Maggie dropped her forehead theatrically into her hand. "The man's been here for weeks and he hasn't even checked the phone book..." she moaned.

"It had best, or I'm in the wrong place entirely." Mahir sounded like he was too tired to be amused. "I'm inside twenty minutes of being toted off for loitering, which would be a bit of a problem for me, so will you *please* come pick me up?"

"I—" I shot a glance at Maggie, who was still covering her face with her hand. "We'll be right there. Just stay where you are."

"That's not going to be a problem," Mahir said.

There was a click, and the calm, pleasant voice of the house said, "The other party has disconnected the call. Would you like me to attempt to restore the connection?"

"No, he hung up," I said, and did the same. My fingertips were numb, probably from the shock. "Maggie, you know how to find the airport?"

"I can get us there."

"Good. Doc! Get your shoes on. We're taking a road trip."

Kelly emerged from the dining room, hugging a notepad against her chest. "We are?" she asked, sounding bemused. "Where are we going?" After a pause, she added, "Why am *I* going?"

"We're going to the airport to pick up a friend, and you're coming because Maggie has to tell me how to get there." By group consensus, Kelly was never left alone in the house for any reason, not even for a few minutes. The closest we'd come was leaving her in the custody of a few of Maggie's Fictionals, and even then, it was never for more than an hour. We weren't afraid she was going to run—not anymore—but there was always the chance the CDC would finally track her down when we weren't there to protect her.

To her credit, Kelly had stopped arguing about our refusal to leave her by herself after the first week, and she wasn't arguing now. She nodded, saying, "I'll go get my coat," before disappearing back into the dining room.

Maggie and I exchanged a glance. "I didn't think he'd come *here*," she said. "I've only met him the once, at... the last time he came to California."

The event she wasn't naming was Georgia's funeral. I nodded, both in acknowledgment and as silent thanks for her not saying the word "funeral" out loud. "He's a good guy. If he's here, he must have found something pretty big."

"Or he's running from something pretty big."

"That's also possible." Mahir hadn't said anything about his wife being with him, and somehow I couldn't imagine that she'd approved this little jaunt without a good reason. "Let's go find out, shall we?"

"I'm pretty sure we don't have a choice," Maggie said, and patted my arm lightly before heading for the door.

I paused long enough to grab my gun belt and laptop, and followed. "I guess this means the break is over," I muttered.

I think you're right.

Maggie and Kelly were waiting next to Maggie's van when I made it outside, miniature bulldogs frolicking around their feet. Maggie smiled wryly. "They can't imagine any reason for us to be outside that doesn't involve playing with them."

"I'll throw tennis balls for an hour once we finish the debriefing," I said, holding up my hand. "Keys?"

"You're driving?" asked Maggie, as she lobbed them to me underhand.

"At least that way we'll get there alive."

Maggie's laughter was echoed by George, the two of them setting up a weird reverb that no one but me could hear. George always *hated* letting me drive, said I was trying to send the both of us to an early grave every time I swung around a corner without slowing down. I do the driving for both of us these days, by necessity, and she mostly doesn't give me shit about it, but still, the irony wasn't escaping either one of us.

Even when she was alive, George would have admitted that I was a better driver than Maggie. I've never let the car spin out just to see what would happen, for example, and I don't view rainy days as an excuse to hydroplane. I may be crazy, but I think there's a pretty good chance that Maggie's suicidal.

Kelly crawled into the backseat. Maggie and I took the front, Maggie programming an address into the GPS as I started the van. I drove slowly down the length of the driveway, pausing only for the exit checkpoint—a small, almost cursory confirmation that we were aware of the dangers inherent in choosing to leave the property—before turning onto one of the winding two-lane roads that pass as major streets in a town the size of Weed. There weren't many potholes. That was about as far as the civic planners went in terms of preparing the citizenry for an outbreak. In places like Oakland and Portland, there are standing defenses, blood test checkpoints, and lots of fences. In places like Weed, there are doors with locks, safety-glass windows, and room to breathe. I'd never spent much time in a stable rural area before; I always thought the people who chose to live that way were sort of insane. It was sort of surprising to realize that I liked it.

When all this is over, I'll make sure you can retire on a farm with lots of room to run around and play with the other puppies, said George dryly.

I managed to turn my laughter into a shallow cough, ducking my head to the side before Maggie and the Doc could see me smile. With as good as things had been going, I was trying not to shove reminders of my relationship with George in their faces. Knowing the boss is crazy is one thing. Dealing with it is something else.

"How far is the airport?" asked Kelly, leaning between the seats so she could see the road. Her hair was starting to grow out, and it tangled in front of her eyes in a tawny fringe. It made her look more like herself, and that made it easier for me to deal with her, especially since she was still wearing Buffy's clothes everywhere. One ghost was more than enough for me.

"About ten miles," said Maggie. She picked up the radio remote, beginning to flick through the frequencies. Our van has a sophisticated antenna array capable of picking up police and even some military bands, thanks to Buffy's tinkering and George's endless willingness to throw money into improving our access to information. Maggie's van, on the other hand, has six hundred channels of satellite radio. Prior to riding with her, I didn't know there was enough, say, Celtic teenybopper surf rock to fill a podcast, much less an entire radio station. Live and learn.

Maggie settled on a station blaring pre-Rising grunge pop, cranking the volume a few notches before she put the remote down and reclined in her seat. "That's better."

"Better than what?" asked Kelly.

"Not having the music on." Maggie twisted to face me, delivering a firm jab of her forefinger to my ribs at almost exactly the same time. "Now spill. Did you have any idea he was coming?"

"I really had no idea, Maggie, I swear." I slowed at a stop sign—not quite coming to a full stop—before gunning the engine again and going barreling down a narrow, tree-lined street at a speed that only bordered on unsafe. As long as I didn't cross that line and kill us all, I figured I was doing pretty well. "He was doing some research for me, but I honestly never expected that particular phone call."

Neither did I, and that worries me, said George.

"Who are we talking about?" asked Kelly. She sounded worried. "I'm already a little uncomfortable with the number of people who've been in the house lately. Is this guy going to be staying?"

"For a while, yeah," I said. "We're on our way to pick up Mahir Gowda. You met him at the funeral." Not that they'd had very much time to talk, or reason to; Kelly was only in attendance because the FBI had seized George's body as evidence in the case against Governor Tate, and the CDC doesn't allow human remains to be shipped without an escort. Thanks to that little rule, I wound up with two extra guests at a party I never intended

to hold: Kelly and her boss, Dr. Wynne. I left George in the van and went
to confront the man who really killed her—I shot her, but Tate ordered her
infection, and I held Tate responsible for what happened—and I didn't see
her again until she was nothing but a heap of sterile ash—

Steady, said George, breaking my black mood before it could fully form.

"Right, sorry," I muttered. Mahir's unexpected visit had me on the edge
of panic, and every little thing—like the reminder of how Kelly and Mahir
had first met—was enough to send me over the edge into seriously brooding. That wasn't something I could afford just now.

Maggie gave me a sidelong look that was thoughtful and, oddly,
relieved. "He was the one in the really unfortunate brown pants," she said,
directing her words toward Kelly.

"He flew in from London, didn't he?" Kelly paused, eyes widening.
"Wait, did he just fly in from London *again*?"

"That's what it I looks like," I said. We were approaching a large green
sign that read WEED AIRPORT (MUNICIPAL FIELD 046) AHEAD. I slowed to
match the posted speed limit, turning into the lane that would take us to
the quarantine zone.

Air travel changed a lot after the Rising. According to the history books,
it used to be a pretty simple process. Older movies show airports packed
with people coming and going as they pleased, and the real old ones show
really crazy shit, like guys who aren't even passengers pursuing their runaway girlfriends through security and people buying tickets from flight
attendants, in cash. Every flight attendant I've ever seen has been carrying
more ordnance than your average Irwin, and if somebody ran onto a flight
without the proper medical clearances and a green light from the check-in
desk, they'd be dead long before they hit the floor. Working for the airlines
teaches a person to shoot first and ask questions later, if ever.

People who can't hack it as Irwins because they're too violent go into
the air travel industry. There's a thought to make a person want to stay at
home.

Travel between the major airports requires a clean bill of health from
an accredited doctor, followed by inspection by airport medical personnel
before even moving into the ticketing concourse. Nonpassengers aren't
allowed past the first air lock. Once you're inside, you're herded from
blood test to blood test, usually supervised by people with lots and lots
of guns. That's another thing that seems unbelievable about pre-Rising
air travel: Nobody in those old movies is ever carrying a weapon unless
they work for the police or the air marshals. Something about the fear of
hijacking. Well, these days, the fear of zombies ensures that even people

who have no business carrying a gun will have one when they want to get on a plane. You get on, you sit down, and you stay sitting unless one of the flight attendants is escorting you to the restroom—after a blood test, of course. It takes their clearance to even unbuckle your seat belt once the plane is in motion. So yeah, air travel? Not simple, not fun, and definitely not something people undertake lightly.

Weed's airport was tiny, three buildings and a runway, with only the minimum in federally mandated air lock and quarantine space between the airport and the curb. Several airport security cars were parked nearby. Overkill most of the time, especially for an airport this small, but I was willing to bet they wouldn't be nearly enough if a plane actually flew in with an unexpected cargo of live infected. That's the trouble with being scared all the time. Eventually, people just go numb.

I stopped the car in the space marked for passenger pick-up and drop-off, hitting the horn twice. Kelly winced, but didn't question the action. Only an idiot gets out of their car unprompted at even the smallest of airports.

We didn't have to wait long. The echoes from the horn barely had time to die out when the air lock door opened and Mahir came walking briskly toward us, dragging a single battered carry-on bag behind him. The formerly black nylon was scuffed and torn and patched with strips of duct tape in several places. At least that probably made it easy to recognize when it came along the conveyor belt at baggage claim—not that Weed's airport was large enough to *have* a conveyor belt. I was pretty sure Mahir hadn't arrived on any commercial flight.

He pulled open the van's rear passenger-side door without saying anything, putting his carry-on bag on the seat before he climbed in and pulled the door shut again. Even then, he didn't say anything, just fastened his seat belt and met my eyes in the rearview mirror, clearly waiting.

I started the engine.

Mahir held his silence until we were half a mile from the airport, and the rest of us stayed silent just as long, waiting for him to say something. Finally, closing his eyes, he pinched the bridge of his nose and said, "Magdalene, how far is it from here to your home?"

"About ten miles," she said, twisting in her seat to look at him with wide and worried eyes. "Honey, are you okay?"

"No. No, I am not okay. I am several thousand miles from okay. I am quite probably involved in divorce proceedings even now, I am present in this country under only the most tenuous of legal umbrellas, I am entirely unsure as to what time zone I am in, and I want nothing more than to rewind my life to the point at which I permitted myself to first be hired by one Miss Georgia Mason." Mahir dropped his hand away from his face, eyes remaining closed as he sagged backward. "I believe that if I were any more exhausted, I would actually be dead, and I might regard that as a blessing. Hello, Shaun. Hello, Dr. Connolly. I would say it is a pleasure to see you again, but under the circumstances, that would be disingenuous at best."

"Hello, Mr. Gowda," said Kelly. I didn't say anything. I kept driving, listening to George swearing loudly in the space between my ears. If there had been any question about what Mahir had found—whether it was good, bad, or just weird—his demeanor answered it. There was no way he'd look that beat down over anything but the end of the world, and somehow, I was starting to suspect that the end of the world was exactly what he represented.

Maggie looked around the car, a crease forming between her brows as she considered the expressions around her. Then she reached for the remote and turned the volume on the radio up. Somehow, that seemed like exactly the right thing to do, and we drove the rest of the way home without saying a word, blasting the happily nihilistic pop music of a dead generation behind us as we went.

Mahir opened his eyes when we reached Maggie's driveway, watching with interest as we passed the first and second gates. As we approached the third gate, he asked, "Does it know how many people are in the vehicle?" I hit the switch to roll down the van windows as I glanced to Maggie for her answer. Metal posts telescoped up from the bushes around the driveway, unfolding to reveal small blood test units with reflective metal panels fastened to their sides. The tiny apertures where the needles would emerge glittered in the sunlight.

"The security grid runs on biometric heat-detection, equipped with low-grade sonar," Maggie said, with the sort of rote precision that implied she knew because she'd read the manual, not because she really understood what the security system was doing. At least she read the manual. Some people trust their safety to machines without even doing that much. "It always knows how many people need to be tested. We ran a bus up here once, when we did the group trip to Disneyland, and the gate wouldn't open until all thirty-eight of us had tested clean."

"It made you run all thirty-eight?" I asked, punctuating the question with a low whistle. "That's impressive." Also terrifying, since I was willing to bet the designers hadn't considered all the possible loopholes in that model. Maggie's security system made us each lean out the window long enough for a blood test, but it didn't actually make us get out of the car and walk through an air lock while everyone else was tested. It would be entirely possible for someone to test clean and then go into amplification while the rest of the group was still being checked out. The ocular scan at the next gate would catch them—probably—but it would increase the number of potential infected from one to everyone in the group.

Maggie smiled blithely, missing the subtext of my comment. That was probably for the best. "It's the best on the private market." She stuck her hand out the window as she spoke, pressing it down against the passenger-side testing panel.

"It's not *on* the private market," said Kelly. I twisted to look at her as I slapped my hand down on my own testing panel. She shrugged, sticking her hand out the window, and said, "This technology isn't supposed to be available outside of government agencies for another two years."

"Oopsie," said Maggie. She flashed a smile at Kelly and pulled her hand back into the van as the green light next to the testing unit flashed on. "I guess Daddy must have pulled some strings."

Again, added George dryly. I swallowed a chuckle.

"He did an excellent job," said Mahir. The light next to his testing panel flashed green. Withdrawing his hand, he slumped in his seat and closed his eyes again. "Good lord, this nation is enormous. Wake me when there's coffee."

"You'll need to open your eyes for the ocular scan in a minute," said Maggie.

Mahir groaned.

I glanced at him in the rearview mirror, taking in the fine stress lines etched around his eyes. Those weren't there a year ago. George's death was almost as hard on him as it was on me—something I wouldn't have believed possible for almost anybody else. Mahir had been her beta blogger, her colleague, and her best friend, and sometimes I got the feeling he would have tried to be more if they hadn't lived on different continents. At least I had the constant reassurance of going crazy. He just had the silence, and now, thanks to me, the strain of whatever it was he'd learned that was bad enough to drive him out of England.

"Hope this was worth it," I muttered, and started the engine again.

The ocular scanners were calibrated to test only two people at a time; it took us nearly five minutes to clear the fourth gate. Mahir and I went first—me because safety protocols say to clear the driver as fast as possible, him because I was afraid he'd actually fall asleep if we made him wait too long. His exhaustion was becoming more obvious by the moment. I wasn't going to insist he stay awake long enough to tell us everything he knew, but I wanted to know if we were looking at another Oakland. Last time we let an unexpected visitor have time to calm down before telling us everything, our apartment building got blown up, Dave died, and we wound up running for our lives. I'd like to avoid having that happen again if I get any say in the matter.

Maggie's bulldogs were waiting on the front lawn, and they mobbed our feet as soon as we got out of the van. Mahir backpedaled frantically, winding up sitting on the armrest of the passenger seat with his feet drawn up, out of reach of inquisitive noses. This didn't stop them from jumping at his shoes, yapping in their oddly sonorous small-dog voices. "Good lord, don't you keep these things leashed?"

"Not when they're at home," Maggie replied. "Bruiser, Butch, Kitty, down." The three dogs that had seemed the most intent on getting to Mahir dropped to all fours and trotted over to Maggie, tongues lolling.

"They grow on you," I said, leaning past Mahir to grab his bag. It was deceptively heavy. I'd been expecting it to weigh maybe twenty pounds, but it was heavy enough to throw me off balance for a moment. "Jeez, dude, what's in this thing, bricks?"

"Computer equipment, mostly. I hope you have a few shirts I can borrow. It seemed like a poor idea to travel with more than I could fit in a single bag." Mahir watched the dogs warily as he slipped out of the van and edged toward the house. The dogs, for their part, stayed clustered around Maggie, looking up at her with adoring eyes.

"You can borrow my shirts, my man, but you're going commando before you're borrowing my boxers." I slung my arm around his shoulders and started walking toward the kitchen door. "Coffee awaits, unless you'd rather have tea. You look like shit, by the way."

"Yes, I've gathered," said Mahir wearily. "Tea sounds fantastic."

He kept trudging onward as I glanced back at Maggie. Kelly had emerged from the van and was standing next to her, frowning thoughtfully. Maggie nodded, signaling her understanding. I answered her nod with a brief, relieved smile. I needed a few minutes alone with Mahir before he fell into an eight-hour coma, and Maggie was telling me she'd keep Kelly out of the way until I was ready for her.

The kitchen was empty. Alaric and Becks were still off-site, and all the bulldogs were outside, probably harassing Maggie into playing catch with them. I guided Mahir to a seat at the table. "You have a tea-based preference? Maggie has something like five hundred kinds. I think they all taste like licking the lawnmower, so I really can't make recommendations."

"Anything that isn't herbal will be fine." Mahir collapsed into the chair, his chin dipping until it almost grazed his chest. "Soy milk, no sugar, please."

"You got it." I kept one eye on him as I filled the electric kettle and got down a mug.

He's worn out.

"I got that," I muttered. Mahir raised his head enough to blink at me. I offered an insincere smile. "Sorry. I was just—"

"I know what you were doing. Hello, Georgia. I hope your ongoing haunting hasn't driven your brother too far past the edge of reason to justify this visit."

There's no such thing as ghosts, said George, sounding peevish.

The idea of getting into that particular argument was too ludicrous to consider, especially given my position. I got the soy milk from the fridge instead, answering, "George says hey. Your tea will be ready in just a minute. Want to tell me why you decided to be a surprise? We could've at least made up the couch for you, if we'd known that you were coming."

"I didn't want to broadcast it anywhere," Mahir said, with a calm that was actually chilling. This wasn't a spur-of-the-moment decision. I hadn't really expected it would be, but still, the tone of his voice, combined with the exhaustion in his face, made me want to put away the tea and break out the booze. "I purchased a flight from Heathrow to New York via an actual travel agency, rather than online, and flew from there to Seattle, where I switched from my own passport to my father's and caught a flight to Portland. From there, I took a private flight to Weed. The gentleman who owns the plane took payment in cash, and his manifest will show that I was a young woman of Canadian nationality visiting the state for a flower show."

"How much did that cost?"

"Enough that you should be deeply grateful I'm paid in percentage of overall site income, rather than drawing a salary, or you'd owe me quite a bit of money." Mahir removed his glasses in order to scrub at his eyes with the heel of his hand. "I'm not going to be useful much longer, I'm afraid. I've been awake damned near a day and a half as it is."

"I sort of figured." The kettle began to whistle. I turned it off, dropping a teabag from Maggie's disturbingly large collection into a mug and covering it with water before walking the mug and soy milk over to Mahir. "Give me the short form. How bad is it?"

"How bad is it?" Mahir took a moment to doctor his tea, not speaking again until he was settled with both hands wrapped firmly around the mug. Looking at me steadily, he said, "I took the data you gave me to three doctors I was reasonably sure were reputable. One laughed me out of his office. Said if anything of the sort were going on, he'd have heard about it, since the trending evidence would be virtually impossible to overlook. Further said that if anything of the sort were going on, the national census would reflect it. I challenged him to prove that it didn't."

"And?"

"He stopped taking my calls three days later. I'd wager because the national census reflected exactly what he said it wouldn't." Mahir sipped his tea, grimaced, and continued: "When I went to confront him about this in person, he was gone—and he didn't leave a forwarding address."

Well, shit, said George.

"I had more luck with the second doctor I approached—largely, I think, because he was Australian and didn't really give two tosses what the local government thought of his work. He said the research was sound, if a bit overly dramatic, and that he'd rather like a chance to test its applications in a live population."

"It had applications?" I asked, mystified.

"In the sense that… Well, look, it's sort of like the research they were doing on parasites at the turn of the century. They found quite a few immune disorders that could be controlled by the introduction of special-ized parasites, because the parasites provided a sufficient distraction for the immune system as a whole. They kept the body from attacking itself. Part of what makes Kellis-Amberlee so effective is that it acts like a part of the body—it's with us all the time, so our immune systems don't attack it. There'd be no point; they'd rip us apart trying to kill it. The trouble is that when the virus changes states, the body still doesn't think of it as an enemy. It still regards it as a friendly component."

I frowned. "You lost me."

"If the body regards the sleeping virus as a part of itself, it isn't prepared to fight the virus when it wakes. But people who somehow survive a bout with the activated virus—those who get exposed when they're too small to amplify, for example, or those with a natural resistance—can 'store' a cer-tain measure of the live virus in themselves, like a parasite. Something that teaches the body what it's meant to be fighting off."

"So this dude wanted to, what, go expose a bunch of kangaroos and watch to see what happened as they got bigger?"

"Essentially, yes."

"What happened with him?"

"He got deported on charges of tax evasion and improper work permits."

Silence stretched between us as I considered what he was saying—and what he wasn't. Even George was quiet, letting me think. Finally, I asked, "What about the third guy?"

"His files are in my bag." Mahir looked at me levelly as he sipped his tea. "He read the files. Three times. And then he called me, told me his conclusions and where he'd sent his data, hung up the phone, and shot himself. Really, I'm not certain he had the wrong idea."

"What...what did he say?"

"He said that were we braver and less willing to bow to the easy path, we might have had India back a decade ago." Mahir put his cup down and stood. "I'm tired, Shaun. Please show me where I can sleep. You can read what I've brought you, and we'll discuss it later."

"Come on." I stood and started for the hallway. "You can use my room. It's not huge, but it's quiet, and the door latches, so you shouldn't wake up with any surprise roommates."

"That's a relief," he said, following me up the stairs. His presence, strange as it was, felt exactly right, like this was exactly what had to happen before we could finish whatever it was we'd started.

We were all refugees now. None of us would stop running until all of us did.

BOOK IV

Immunological Memory

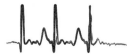

It's better to go out with a bang and a press release than with a whimper and a secret.

— GEORGIA MASON

Fuck this. Let's just blow some shit up.

— SHAUN MASON

George and I never technically knew our birthdays. The doctors could estimate how old we were and make some educated guesses about our biological parents, but it really didn't matter. We knew we were born sometime in 2017, toward the end of the Rising, when most of North America had been taken back from the infected, because the doctors said so. We knew she was older by about six weeks. Everything else was details, and details weren't important. Not to me. What was important was that I had her, and she had me, and we had each other, and that meant we could face anything the world threw at us. Sometimes I was even arrogant enough to think the Rising happened so we could be together.

It's as good an explanation as any.

As of today, no matter when my birthday really is, I've had a birthday without George. As of today, I've spent a year going to sleep and waking up in a world she isn't in, a world that seems meaningless because she's never going to make it mean anything ever again. I was always sort of afraid she'd turn suicidal when I died. I asked her once if she ever worried about me like that.

"You're already suicidal, you asshole," she said, and laughed. Only it turns out she was wrong, because losing her made me more careful about almost everything. I miss her every day. I miss her every *minute*. But if anything happens to me, she may never get the ending she deserves, and I refuse to be selfish enough to die before I'm finished taking care of the things she left behind.

Happy birthday, George. You made me better than I could ever have been without you, and you hurt me worse than I could ever have been hurt by anybody else. I love you. I miss you. And I'm starting to get the feeling that I'll see you pretty soon, because I'm starting to feel like, maybe, things are coming to an end.

God, I miss you.

**—From *Adaptive Immunities*,
the blog of Shaun Mason, June 20, 2041**

Anybody who messes with Shaun is messing with me. And of the two of us, I swear, I am the one you do *not* want to mess with. He'll kill you. But I will make you sorry, and I will make you pay.

Trust me. I'm a journalist.

—From *Postcards from the Wall*,
the unpublished files of Georgia Mason,
originally posted June 20, 2041

Eighteen

Alaric, what's your twenty?" Silence answered me. I bit back a snarl and tried again: "Alaric, where are you?" Getting mad at him for not knowing the weird mix of military and ham radio pidgin used by the Irwin community was pointless. That didn't stop me from doing it.

This time he answered, his voice coming clear and easy through the phone: "I'm finishing up my edits while Becks does some final recon for her report."

"Not an answer." I raked a hand through my hair, watching Maggie try to guide Kelly through the steps required to mix pancake batter. Either Kelly was the worst cook in the world or Maggie was really shitty at giving instructions. It could have gone either way. "Where are you, exactly?"

"Down near Mount Shasta." My silence must have told Alaric he needed to give me more information, because he added, "About an hour out. Why? Do you need us to stop at the store or something on our way back in?"

Back when Buffy was alive, we could trust our network against anyone on the planet, including the CIA. Our security isn't that stellar anymore, but thanks to upgrades cobbled from Maggie's house system, Becks's jury-rigging skills, and Alaric's computer know-how, we're pretty stable. Stable enough for what I was about to say, anyway: "Mahir's here."

It was Alaric's turn to go briefly silent. Finally, he said, "Mahir sent in a report?"

"No, dumb-ass, Mahir's *here*. Mahir is asleep upstairs in the guest room I've been using. He showed up with pretty much the clothes on his back and a suitcase full of research, and he looks like hammered shit."

Maggie looked over. "Is that Alaric? Tell him to stop by the House of Curries on his way home. I'm going to send in an order."

"Got it. Alaric, Maggie says—"

"I heard her," he said, managing to sound annoyed and astonished at the same time. "You're serious, aren't you? Mahir is actually *here*."

"Yeah, that's what I've been saying." Alaric began swearing. I listened, impressed. I hadn't realized he knew that much Cantonese. I let him go for a few minutes, then interjected, "You kiss your mother with that mouth?"

Play nice with my Newsies, or I swear I'm going to make you sorry, said George flatly.

"I am being nice."

Luckily, Alaric was still swearing, finishing off an elaborate phrase that started in Cantonese and switched to English as he said, almost wonderingly, "—son of a chicken-fucking soy farmer and a diseased convention-center security guard. How did he *get* here? Is he all right? Are we going to need to move again?"

"I'd rather wait and explain everything to you and Becks at the same time. Right now, he's exhausted but I'm pretty sure nobody's been shooting at him—yet, anyway—and that's something else I'd like us all to talk about at once. So when can you be here?"

There was a clattering sound as Alaric shoved his keyboard away, knocking something to the van floor in the process. "Give me ten minutes to get Becks back here, and I'll break a couple of dozen speed limits getting over to you."

"Don't forget to pick up dinner," called Maggie.

"Maggie says—"

"I heard her. Do you need anything else?"

"Just drive safely, don't get pulled over, and don't crash into anything. If we're going to die horribly, we're all going to do it together."

"Great pep talk, boss. Very touching. I'll always remember the day when you told me not to drive into a tree on the way home." Alaric said something caustic sounding in Cantonese—what little I remembered from my course on field communications made me think he'd just called me a goat fucker—and hung up.

Smirking, I pulled off my ear cuff and dropped it into my shirt pocket, twisting to face Maggie and Kelly. "They're on their way, and yes, Maggie, Alaric's going to pick up dinner. He said they'd be about an hour. Why are we ordering dinner if you're making pancakes?"

"It gives me something to do with my hands, and Mahir's got to be hungry after becoming an international fugitive from justice." Maggie handed Kelly another egg. "I'll tell the house to transmit our normal order, plus three."

"Fair enough." I got up and crossed to the fridge, pulling out a can of Coke. "Make me a couple of pancakes, will you?"

"Already planning to." Maggie took the bowl from Kelly. She looked inside, sighed, and started picking bits of eggshell out of the batter. "I'm assuming things are pretty bad for him to have come to us this way."

"I don't know that they're any worse than they were yesterday, but I think they're about to get pretty bad, yeah." I couldn't stop thinking about Mahir's casual mention of divorce papers. I'd given his wife shit since the day they got married, but that didn't mean I wanted her to leave him. He was risking everything to be here with us. Hell, he'd been risking everything since the day he agreed to come back to the team. I just hoped we could live up to the degree of faith that he was putting in us, because I really wasn't sure anymore.

Just keep breathing, advised George. *It's too late for any of us to turn back now.*

"Got that right," I muttered, and cracked open the Coke, taking a drink before asking, "Doc, what do you know about viral parasitism?"

Kelly stared at me. "What?"

"It was something Mahir said before he went upstairs to crash—the virus acts like a parasite in people with reservoir conditions, and that teaches their bodies how to cope with it better. I'm not quite sure what he meant, but I figure you'll be able to translate for us when we sit down for the big meeting."

"I..." Kelly frowned thoughtfully. "It's not a *common* theory, but I've heard it before. It basically says that the virus can change its behavior, go from being a strict predator to a sort of symbiotic parasite."

"Isn't that what both source viruses were originally supposed to do?" asked Maggie, turning on the stove. She began pouring dollops of batter onto the griddle, filling the room with the hot, sweet scent of cooking pancakes. "We were supposed to catch them and then keep them forever, like...I don't know, weird immortal hamsters that cured cancer."

"Only these hamsters developed rabies." I sipped my Coke. "If it's something people already know about, is there any reason for someone to get deported for studying it? Viral parasitism, I mean. Not hamsters."

"No," Kelly said, firmly. "There's no good reason for someone to be deported for studying viral parasitism."

"That's what I thought." I leaned back in my seat, sipping my Coke, and watched Maggie make pancakes. Kelly went quiet, a speculative expression on her face. I could almost see the wheels turning as she got herself a glass of water and sat down across from me, both of us waiting for the pancakes to be ready.

Mahir's arrival changed everything. We'd been treading water, writing our reports, studying the material we got from Dr. Abbey, and waiting for something to happen, because something always happened when we got too comfortable. We'd long since passed the point where we could back out safely—maybe we passed that point the day George and I decided it would be a good idea to go out for the Ryman campaign. I don't know—but that didn't mean we'd exactly been hurrying toward the end game. We'd been waiting to see what would happen next. Now that Mahir was with us, it was time for things to start moving again.

I wasn't ready. I don't think any of us were, or really could be. I just knew that it was too damn late to back out. It had been too late since George died.

Maybe it was too late before that, and we couldn't see it. I don't know.

Mahir hadn't come downstairs by the time Alaric and Becks showed up. The security system announced their approach long before the familiar growl of the van's engine became audible. Maggie had plenty of time to clear away the mess from the pancakes and set out dishes for dinner. "Shaun, go wake our guest," she said, starting to rummage for forks. I blinked at her, and she grinned. "I figure he's likely to hit someone if he's startled, and he'd probably feel bad if he hit a girl."

I couldn't argue with that—it was too true—and so I grunted my assent, finished off the last of my Coke, and went trudging up the stairs to the room that had been mine until just a few hours before. The door was shut, and there were no signs of motion from the other side. I raised my hand, hesitating before I actually brought it down in a knock.

"He looked exhausted," I said.

We're all exhausted, George replied. *He needs to explain things sooner or later.*

As soon as he explained all the way, any chance we had of postponing the future would be gone. It would end when he opened his bag and pulled out the files he hadn't shown me yet, and there would be no taking it back, because there never is when the truth gets involved. "Can't it be later?" The plea in my voice surprised us both, I think, me more than her; George has always known me better than I know myself. I used to do the same favor for her.

It already is, she said, quietly.

She was right, and because she was right, I brought my hand down and knocked on the guest room door. "Yo, Mahir. Alaric and Becks are here with dinner."

There was no response.

I knocked again, harder this time. "Mahir! We can sleep when we're dead, my man!" Part of me couldn't help remembering how bleak he'd looked, how deep the circles under his eyes had been. *If we can sleep when we're dead*...

Stop it. You're just freaking yourself out, and that's not going to do anyone any good. Knock again.

I didn't knock: I hammered. *"Mahir!"*

The door opened. Mahir was still dressed, his clothes no more wrinkled than they'd been before—they'd long since passed the point where a little thing like a nap was going to do anything to hurt them—and his hair was sticking up in uneven spikes, making him look like some sort of apocalyptic prophet. "Is it morning already?" he asked. Exhaustion thickened his accent, making it border on unintelligible. "I'd murder for a cuppa."

"Not sure what that is, but there's coffee and tea downstairs. Also dinner. Maggie had Becks and Alaric swing by the House of Curries on their way back from whatever the fuck it is they were doing out there." I probably should have cared more about what my team was up to when they weren't working directly on the whole "possible globe-spanning conspiracy" thing, but to be honest, I didn't have the time or the energy. I trusted them not to get themselves killed while I wasn't looking. That was all I had left to give them, and it needed to be enough.

"Right." Mahir rubbed a hand through his hair, doing nothing to improve its spiky disarray. "Is there someplace I can wash my face and slap on a couple of stimulant patches before I have to come down and face humans?"

"Bathroom's across the hall."

"Brilliant." He offered me a wan, distracted smile and stepped into the hall, heading for the bathroom. I put a hand on his elbow. He stopped, blinking at me. "Yes?"

"I'm glad you're here, even if it does mean the shit's finally hitting the fan," I said, and hugged him.

George and I weren't raised to be physically demonstrative. Having parents who treat you as a ratings stunt will do that. Mahir knew that. There was a pause no longer than the time it took for him to catch his breath, and then he was hugging me back, shoulders sagging slightly as he let go of some weight I wasn't quite aware of yet, but doubtless would be soon.

"Thank you," he said. His smile as he let me go was a little stronger. I turned to head downstairs as he walked into the bathroom, shutting the door behind himself.

The air downstairs smelled like hot curry, garlic naan, and the sweet, pasty nothingness of white rice. Maggie was unpacking bulging paper sacks from the House of Curries onto the counter while Alaric, Becks, and Kelly sat at the table, trying to stay out of her way. The bulldogs were gone, and the connecting door to the front room was closed, indicating the location of their banishment.

Hail, hail, the gang's all here, said George, quietly.

"Yeah," I muttered, pausing in the doorway and watching them. Becks was hiding a laugh behind her hand, probably in response to something Alaric had said. Maggie kept rocking onto her toes, like she was dancing to a private beat. Even Kelly was relaxed, sitting in her chair and watching the others with a faint, puzzled smile on her face. This was my team. Maybe it wasn't the one I would have put together on my own—out of all of them, Becks was the only one I really trusted in the field, and she was also still the one I had the most trouble talking to. Alaric was never actually field certified, since the shit hit the fan while he was still prepping for his tests, and Maggie had never needed to be, being a Fictional and all.

Footsteps behind me signaled Mahir's approach. I turned to face him, asking, "Hey, you're cleared for fieldwork, right?"

Mahir frowned at me. He'd slicked back his hair and done something to wipe away most of the more visible signs of exhaustion. He hadn't been kidding about the stimulant patches. He'd pay for that later. Then again, we were going to be paying for a lot of things later, assuming we lived that long.

"In the United Kingdom and European Union, yes, in the United States, no, although I can travel on my U.K. license for up to ninety days as a visiting journalist. Why?"

"Just wondering." I stepped to the side, sweeping one arm grandly toward the kitchen. "Ladies and gentlemen, Mahir Gowda!"

"Boss!" said Alaric, sounding delighted. As a Newsie, he answered directly to Mahir, and counted on Mahir to make me understand when I was being unreasonable. Having us both in the same house probably seemed like an excellent way to cut out the middleman. I couldn't honestly say that he was wrong.

Becks didn't do anything as gauche as shouting. Standing, she walked over to Mahir and threw her arms around his shoulders, hugging him tightly. He hugged her back, just as tightly. "I'm so glad you're here," she said.

I looked away, feeling uncomfortably like a voyeur, and found myself looking at Kelly instead. She was watching the scene in front of her with an almost wistful expression on her face, like a kid who wasn't invited to the party.

She gave up her whole life to come here and tell us what she knew, and she can never go back. The people in this room, we're all she has. And she's never going to be part of things the way Mahir is.

"Right," I muttered. Louder, pitched for an audience of people who actually existed *outside* my head, I said, "Something smells great, Maggie. Please tell me it's dinner, and not a sadistic new kind of air freshener." I brushed past Mahir and Becks, still embracing, and moved toward the counter.

Maggie flashed a smile my way. "Oh, it's dinner. All the containers are labeled, and I made sure to get extra Aloo Gobi this time, so you won't be able to eat it all."

"You're seriously underestimating my capacity for devouring curried cauliflower." I reached for a plate.

That was the signal for everyone to start grabbing plates, utensils, and whatever combination of things they were planning to eat for dinner. Mahir ate like he was starving, and the rest of us weren't much better. I wasn't the only one who understood what Mahir's arrival meant. This might be the last peaceful meal we had for a while, and none of us wanted to be the one to disrupt it.

Cramming six people around Maggie's table was surprisingly easy. I've never known anyone who entertained as much as she does, or was as willing to adjust for strangers on a moment's notice. Being in her kitchen was almost like being in one of those old pre-Rising TV shows, the ones where everyone seemed to wind up sitting around eating from the same bowl of mashed potatoes and talking about their day. We didn't have mashed potatoes, and I wasn't interested in sharing the Aloo Gobi, but we did have rice and samosas and other things to pass around. Mahir turned out to be surprisingly good at talking to Kelly, who got a little more relaxed with every minute that passed.

The best intentions weren't enough to stop the clock. All too soon, we were putting down our forks, finishing our drinks, and falling into an expectant silence. Maggie stood, starting to clear the table; Alaric and I moved to help her. She waved me back to my seat. "Stay where you are," she said. "You're going to need to ride herd on this madhouse, and that works better when you don't have something to distract yourself." She didn't wave Alaric back down. I guess she figured he could do his part from the sink if he had to.

Mahir cleared his throat. "I'll just go get a few things, shall I?"

"I think it's about that time," I agreed. "Get ready to explain some crazy science, Doc."

Kelly smiled a little. "It'll be my pleasure."

Maggie returned to the table, handing me a Coke as she sat down to my left. Alaric sat next to Becks, leaving a space between us for Mahir. The air in the kitchen seemed to be getting heavy, pressing down on us like a lead weight.

It was almost a relief when Mahir returned with an armload of manila file folders, their contents bristling with multicolored tab dividers. At least this meant that we weren't going to be waiting anymore. "I have virtual copies of everything here," he said, dropping the files onto the table without any preamble. "I didn't want to e-mail things, since there was a chance I was being watched after what happened with Dr. Christopher."

"The Australian?" I asked.

Mahir nodded. "Precisely. I might not have been under surveillance before that, but the odds increased rather substantially after I got someone deported. That's when I realized it might be best for everyone if I came here."

"Makes sense." I glanced toward Alaric and Becks, saying, "One of the scientists Mahir went to talk to about Dr. Abbey's research got kicked out of the country."

Alaric whistled, long and low. "That's not fooling around."

"No, it's not," said Mahir, with dry gravity. "What we have here is a combination of the material that was originally sent to me, the material provided by Doctors Tiwari and Christopher, some supplemental research I was able to request from Dr. Shoji of the Kauai Institute of Virology before I felt it was unsafe to make any further out-of-country contacts, and finally, the files I was able to retrieve from Professor Brannon's mail drop before it was shut down. I don't have copies for everyone, but there's enough here to keep us all predicting the end of the world until well past dawn."

"Who's Professor Brannon?" asked Becks. "Because I'm feeling a bit like I missed a memo somewhere."

"Professor Brannon..." Alaric frowned. "He was a world-renowned expert in the behavior of Kellis-Amberlee. He spent his entire professional career identifying and studying viral substrains. He..." Alaric's eyes went wide. "He shot himself last week. It was a devastating blow to the epidemiological community. No one saw it coming."

"I'm afraid that was my fault." Mahir handed him one of the file folders. "He'd been studying the virus in lab conditions. He'd never had the time to devote to studying it in the wild. I suppose we all require some measure of specialization in order to keep our heads above water."

Alaric started flipping through the folder in his hand, eyes narrowing in a focused "the rest of the world might as well not be here" way. I used to see that look on George's face a lot.

Kelly, meanwhile, looked horrified. "Professor Brannon is *dead*?" she asked. She sounded genuinely stunned. "But…but…Professor Brannon *can't* be dead. He *can't* be."

"You knew him?" I asked, reaching for a folder.

"I attended one of his lectures while I was in medical school. It was about the ways that Kellis-Amberlee inherently differs from a naturally occurring virus—" She glanced around at the rest of us, taking in our expressions, and cleared her throat before saying, "Naturally occurring viruses have a primary host, something where they, um, retreat when there isn't an outbreak going on. Like malaria, which is bacterial, but still sort of applies. Even when there isn't a malaria outbreak going on, the mosquitoes are still infected. That's how it can keep coming back, no matter how many times we think we've cured it in a human population."

"What does that have to do with Kellis-Amberlee?" asked Maggie.

"Nothing. That's sort of the point." Kelly shrugged. "Kellis-Amberlee doesn't have a natural reservoir. It's infectious across all mammalian species. Even things too small to amplify can sustain the virus—mice, squirrels, everything. It's completely endemic. Curing the human race wouldn't do any good unless we could cure the rest of the planet at the same time."

"Huh. Okay." I looked to Mahir. "So he was a lab guy, you showed him Dr. Abbey's work, and then he shot himself. Why?"

"There are several potential reasons, but I think this is the main one." Mahir began laying out a series of graphs. They didn't make much sense to me, at least on the surface; each showed two jagged lines, one red, one blue, one going up as the other went down. The red line would occasionally fight against its descent, managing a brief upward spike, but it would inevitably get quashed by the blue line as it arced unstoppably toward the top of the paper.

All of us squinted at the pages. Kelly paled, clapping a hand over her mouth. She looked like she was going to throw up. Alaric shook his head.

"This can't be right." He tapped one of the pages, next to the start of the blue line. "This strain occurred in Buenos Aires only six years after the Rising. It was one of the first signs we had that Kellis-Amberlee was mutating outside a lab setting."

Those are strain designations, said George. Her voice was very small.

Those are the strain designations for some of the most widespread varieties of Kellis-Amberlee.

Everyone has Kellis-Amberlee, but most of us have only one strain at a time. Some are more aggressive than others and will basically wipe out an existing infection in order to take over a body. The original Kellis-Amberlee strain developed when lab-clean Kellis flu met lab-clean Marburg Amberlee. That was the first infection anybody had to deal with, the one that swept the world during the Rising. It took years of study and analysis of the structure of the virus before anyone realized that it was doing what viruses have done since the beginning of time: It was mutating, changing to suit its environment. For a while, people hoped it was becoming less virulent and that it would eventually turn into something that didn't do quite as much damage. Honestly, I think we'd have been happy if the virus just started killing people, rather than doing what it does now. At least then the dead would stay dead and the world could start moving on. Instead, Kellis-Amberlee has continued doing what it does best: making zombies and unleashing them on the world whenever it gets the opportunity.

I guess it's consistent. That's something, anyway.

"It's correct," said Mahir. His voice was dark, and there was something dangerous in his tone, something I'd never heard there before. He adjusted his glasses and continued: "There was a spike in deaths in Buenos Aires right before the substrain was isolated and identified for the first time. Eighty percent of the dead were confirmed as suffering from an early form of reservoir condition. It was five years before that substrain was identified in connection with a live reservoir condition."

Kelly paled further.

"As part of his research into the behavior of the various substrains, Professor Brannon had access to census and death records from multiple parts of the world," said Mahir. "Much of this data hadn't previously been incorporated into the model—Dr. Abbey is unable to acquire information through many normal channels, due to her lab's lack of accreditation, Dr. Christopher's focus is on treatment, not the structure of the virus itself, and Dr. Tiwari doesn't do statistics."

"I'm not following you," I said.

"I am," said Kelly. She directed her words at the wall, looking faintly stunned. "He's saying that once they were able to feed the substrain analysis and the census data into the same model, they started getting some results they didn't want to get. The kind of results a man who spent his life working to save lives would commit suicide over."

Maggie frowned. "I thought results were sort of the goal."

"They are, in the general sense, but there are negative and positive results from any analysis. Look at this." Mahir tapped the paper, shoving it toward Maggie. "Every time a new viral substrain is identified—*every* time—it comes immediately after a spike in the local death rate. Buenos Aires. San Diego. Manchester. It isn't a coincidence, and it isn't confined to any specific country or part of the world. It's everywhere, and it's every time."

Becks shook her head. "What does that prove? Maybe the new strains are more virulent when they're first getting started, and they're killing all these people."

"Unlikely." He produced another sheet of paper, this one with a brightly colored pie chart on it.

"Eye-catching," I said, tugging it closer to my side of the table.

"That was the intent." Mahir pulled another copy of the chart from his file and handed it to Alaric. "This shows the aggregate causes of death among the people with reservoir conditions killed immediately prior to the identification of a new substrain."

"These wedges are too small to read," said Alaric.

"My point exactly. There is no dominant cause of death among the victims in these regions. They just...die. They get hit by cars, they fall from ladders, they take their own lives, they die. As if it were any other day, as if theirs were any other deaths. The pattern is in the absolute lack of a pattern, and it's *everywhere*, and a month later, there's a new strain of Kellis-Amberlee running about, more virulent than the one that was in that region prior to the deaths. Three to five years after that, the first reservoir conditions linked to the new strain start showing up, and then it's another two years before the cycle starts over again." Mahir removed his wire-rimmed glasses, wiping them on his shirt. "Dr. Connolly, would you care to tell me what conclusions you draw from this data?"

"I can't make any firm determinations without studying the material more thoroughly, but..." Kelly wiped her eyes with the back of her hand, voice hitching a little as she continued: "I would say there are no naturally occurring viral substrains of the viral chimera generally referred to as Kellis-Amberlee."

"What are you talking about?" I demanded. "He just *said* there were new strains appearing all the damn time. This dead professor dude made his career studying them. They have to exist."

She didn't say they don't exist, Shaun. She said they don't occur naturally.

Georgia sounded subdued, even resigned, like this was the answer she'd been expecting all along, like the part of me that kept her with me understood perfectly and was just waiting for the rest of me to catch up. I went very still, the skin tightening into goose bumps along my arms as I looked, helplessly, at Mahir. He looked back, waiting. They were all waiting, and they all knew I'd get there if they just gave me a minute. They knew George had the answers, and I...well, I had her.

"They exist, but they aren't natural," I said.

"Exactly." Mahir picked up another folder and started passing its contents around the table. "These are CDC analyses of the structure of Kellis-Amberlee. They were acquired legally; they've all been published for public use. People have been trying for years to figure out how something this intricate and stable has been able to mutate without once creating a strain that behaved in a manner different from its parents. The answer is simple: It can't, and it hasn't. Every strain after the original has been created in a laboratory and has been released following what can only be an intentional culling of the individuals afflicted with reservoir conditions. It's a bloody global study, and we've all been invited to participate."

Silence fell hard. None of us knew enough to say that he was wrong, except for maybe Kelly, and she wasn't saying anything; she was just sitting there, tears running slowly down her cheeks as she looked at the papers covering the table. That, maybe more than anything, told me that Mahir's conclusions were correct. After all the years she had spent living the CDC party line, if Kelly could have argued, she would have.

Becks was the one to eventually break the silence, asking, "So what do we do now?"

"Now?" I stood, slapping my palms down on the table. "We get packing. We're hitting the road in the morning. All reports will be made while mobile—I don't want us to be sitting ducks when the shit comes down."

"Where are we going?" asked Alaric.

"The only place I think we might have half a chance of breaking into that's going to have the resources to tell us where we're supposed to go next." I looked challengingly at Kelly. She didn't look away. Instead, she nodded, acceptance blossoming in her expression.

"We're going to Memphis," she said.

I wanted to be a sport reporter. I wanted to report on sport. Sounds good, doesn't it? Rhymes a little. "Mahir Gowda, Sport Reporter." I'd watch the cricket matches and the obstacle courses and the stockcar races, and I'd write pithy little articles about them and make buckets of money, buy a huge house somewhere on the outskirts of London, and raise a family big enough to field a cricket team of my own.

Enter Georgia Carolyn Mason. She knew I'd never be happy reporting on sporting events and the lives of professional athletes. "The news is in your blood": That's what she said to me, and she hounded me until I agreed to give it a shot. A year later, when she struck out on her own, she hired me. She was right too much of the time. She was right about me, and about what I was meant to do.

I have to say as I rather wish that she'd been wrong.

—From *Fish and Clips*,
the blog of Mahir Gowda, June 21, 2041

Nineteen

It's a little over two thousand miles from Weed, California, to Memphis, Tennessee. That would have been about a two and a half days of solid driving pre-Rising, complete with miserable traffic jams and lots of rest stops. Distance is less of a barrier these days, since the average highway speed is between eighty and ninety miles per hour, and the average traffic jam involves having three cars on the same three-mile stretch.

Our problem was simpler: getting there without getting ourselves killed. Travel that crosses more than one state line needs to be registered with the Highway Commission, so that your movement can be monitored. Your updated location gets added to your file every time you stop for gas or check into a motel. It's a nifty system. George did an article on it once, and I didn't think it was completely boring. That's saying something. The trouble was that if we couldn't trust the CDC to be secure, we sure as hell couldn't trust the Highway Commission, an organization whose databases have been hacked so many times that they might as well put out a welcome mat and stop pretending they're secure.

I was the subject of a highway ambush once before—an ambush that landed me, my sister, and our friend Rick in the Memphis CDC, ironically enough. The three of us got out alive. The other two members of our group, Georgette Meissonier and Charles Wong, didn't. If we assumed the people responsible for the destruction of Oakland were waiting for another opportunity to take a shot at us, the last thing we wanted to do was put ourselves on the open road, where accidents could—and doubtless would—happen.

Trouble was, we didn't have a choice. We couldn't take the train; the few passenger lines still in existence are luxury-oriented and would take a week to get there. Flying with Mahir and Kelly wouldn't work, since one of them was legally dead and the other was in the country under the sketchiest of legal pretenses. What's sad is that I didn't know which was the bigger concern.

Maggie's bedrock streak of practicality came to the rescue around the time Mahir and I were starting to brainstorm about stealing a crop duster and somehow riding it across the country to Tennessee. "Why don't you idiots take my van and get it over with?" she demanded, flinging her keys down on the table. "The VIN's registered to Daddy so I don't get stopped when I have to cross the border to Canada, and nobody's going to risk nuking it if they think there's even half a chance that I'm inside. Kill the heir to the Garcia pharmaceutical fortune while my parents are still alive to destroy them? No government conspiracy is *that* stupid."

Privately, I thought she was being a little complacent—anyone who was willing to nuke a *city* wouldn't hesitate before killing a pharmaceutical heir and would have the resources to make it look like an accident—but I didn't say so. I just scooped the keys into my pocket. "You really have no qualms about abuse of power, do you? Thanks, Maggie. You're badass."

"Not a single one," she said amiably. "Believe me, I know how badass I am. You'll have to leave the bike behind, you know."

I'd been trying to avoid thinking about that. The idea of leaving George's bike when I didn't know if we'd ever make it back was almost physically painful. "I know."

"Good, just so long as it isn't going to be a fight. Now you'd better get moving. I want my guest rooms back in time for this weekend's film festival."

"What are you watching?" asked Mahir.

"All thirteen *Nightmare on Elm Street* movies, back to back," Maggie replied. "We're starting with the original and going from there."

I shuddered. "I'll take my chances with the CDC."

"I thought you might," said Maggie, and smiled.

After a day of arguing about what to pack and how many bullets we'd need, Maggie's van was loaded and ready to go. She didn't normally drive on run-flats—something about the way they changed the steering made them too much trouble for her to deal with—but one of the faceless security men we normally never saw walked up the driveway with a brand-new set and installed them before I could even ask if it was an option.

She's been expecting this for a while, said George.

I said nothing.

Kelly and Mahir were coming along, naturally; they'd both come too far and been through too much to do anything else. Becks was coming, too, despite our mutual misgivings about spending that much time crammed into a van together. We'd need another Irwin on hand if things turned bloody, and after what had happened to Dave, this was almost as personal for her as it was for me. Alaric and Maggie were staying behind.

"I'm no good in the field. I don't even have my licenses yet," said Alaric, not meeting my eyes. I think he was afraid I'd start yelling—or worse, that I'd somehow talk him into coming with us. "You'll be better off if I stay here."

"You're right."

That wasn't the answer he'd been expecting. He glanced to me, eyes gone wide.

I shrugged. "We can't pretend we're here if we're posting reports from the road, and we can't all go silent at once, either. Like that's not going to look suspicious? So we'll bounce them to you, and you can post everything from here. Same IP address. Business as usual."

"Right." Alaric smiled, either not bothering or not managing to hide his relief. "I can do that."

"While you're at it, keep digging, okay? I don't think we're at the bottom of this yet."

"On it," he said.

There was nothing to do after that but leave.

Maggie packed us a cardboard box of sandwiches and potato chips on the morning we finally started for Tennessee, along with a cooler full of sodas. She loaded everything into the backseat with Kelly before turning around and handing me two things: a large envelope packed with cash, and a debit card. "Don't use the card unless the money runs out. It draws on the company account. Seeing charges from it that match the van's movements shouldn't set off any red flags, and my parents won't care unless you buy a submarine or something."

"And here I always wanted a submarine," I said.

"Where would you put it?" asked Mahir.

"I'd have to buy a lake."

"Well, that's reasonable, I suppose."

Maggie laughed—a short, sharp sound that had a lot in common with the confused yipping of the teacup bulldogs milling at her feet—and threw her arms around my shoulders, hugging me close before I had a chance to step back. "Come *back*," she whispered, voice small and tight and right next to my ear, so only I could hear it.

We'll try, said George.

"Don't worry about us," I said. I hugged her back, feeling awkward until she let go and stepped away, turning her face to the side to hide the tears that were glinting in her eyes. I sighed. "Maggie—"

"Go," she said.

I swallowed the things I still wanted to say and turned to walk toward the van. Behind me, I could hear Maggie and Mahir exchanging their last good-byes, too softly for me to make out the words. The words didn't matter, really, because we all knew that we might not be coming back.

Becks was in the passenger seat with a laptop propped open on her knees when I slipped behind the wheel. "File transfer and backup is almost complete; when it finishes, we'll have files stored in twenty different places, ten outside the United States." Becks kept her eyes on the screen, fingers tapping out rapid patterns across the keyboard.

I fastened my seat belt. "How solid is the encryption?"

"Solid enough that I wouldn't want to be the one who was trying to break it. Not unless I had a week to waste."

"I hope that's good enough." I slid the key into the ignition before letting my hands rest on the wheel, trying to feel the shape of it the way I felt the shape of my own van, the one George and I rebuilt almost on our own. It wasn't going to happen, but I could at least force myself to be comfortable with the idea that I was about to drive across the country in someone else's car. "Alaric's going to drop the security keys to Dr. Abbey's last known e-mail address in an hour and a half. If there's no response within half an hour, he's sending a coded message to Dr. Shoji to let him know that we need to reach her."

"Do you think it's going to work?"

"Jesus, Rebecca, I don't know. This cloak-and-dagger shit was never my first choice for a career. I think it stands a chance, anyway, and if there's any way we can get this to Dr. Abbey, we should. She'll know what to do with it."

"If we don't come back from Memphis?" Becks kept her eyes on her laptop, but I could hear the tension in the question.

"Pretty much," I said.

She didn't say anything. She just sighed, shoulders straightening a little, and got back to work. In the backseat, Kelly pulled out one of Mahir's research files and started reading. She'd been over it all a thousand times, but that didn't stop her from trying to find something the rest of us might have missed. I stayed where I was, hands resting on the steering wheel, and waited.

It can't have been more than ten minutes before Mahir pulled open the van's side door and climbed inside. It felt more like ten years. Becks kept typing the whole time, fingers dancing across her keyboard without missing a single stroke. She was brilliant, beautiful, and brave as hell. If anything proved how fucked-up I was, it was my inability to tell her any of those things. All I could do was hurt her, and having already done it once, I wasn't exactly racing to do it again.

"Right," said Mahir, settling next to Kelly as the door shut and locked behind him. "Unless we've got any more messy good-byes to make, I suppose we'd best be on our way."

I nodded and started the engine.

Maggie stayed on the lawn as we drove away, waving at first, and then just standing there, a small figure surrounded by a teeming sea of tiny dogs. Her image dwindled in the rearview mirror, disappearing and reappearing as we went around the curves in the driveway, until finally she was out of sight for good. Sanctuary was behind us, and we were well and truly on our way.

The plan called for us to drive down the length of California before cutting across through Arizona, New Mexico—the desert states. It wasn't the most efficient route, but it took good advantage of one of the bigger weaknesses of the infected: the heat. We had to cede Alaska because frostbite doesn't do much but slow a zombie down until it becomes fatal. The deserts, on the other hand, were one of the first things we managed to take back completely. The human host of the active virus still needs water, still needs shade, still collapses with heatstroke and sunstroke, still putrefies, and maybe even dies from the bite of a rattlesnake or the sting of a scorpion. There are no resident zombie mobs in the deserts of America, and while even the driest desert can sustain life, very little of that life is big enough to cross the Kellis-Amberlee amplification barrier. If we encountered any real threats, they'd be fresh ones, and that limited their potential numbers.

The relative safety of the desert made our route less suspicious, even as it meant that we'd need to stop regularly for water and watch the van to be sure it didn't overheat. It was a small price to pay for potentially making it to Memphis alive. Most of the checkpoints just waved us through, the guards too anxious to stay cool to do more than the most cursory of tests. That suited our needs perfectly.

Becks and I did the driving in shifts, six hours on, six hours off. After the first two shifts, the one who'd just finished a shift would move to the backseat to sleep, while one of the passengers would move up front to keep the driver from passing out. Mahir didn't have a license to drive in the USA, and while Kelly could drive, she didn't have her field license, and was too jumpy to drive safely. So it was just the two of us, and that meant taking turns.

Mahir and I worked on our strategy—such as it was—when Becks slept, using Kelly as a sort of a sanity check. "It's not that I'm not willing to die for this story," Mahir said, reasonably. "It's just that I'd rather not be martyred and leave the tale half-told if there's any other option." Even George had to admit that this was a sound approach, and so the four of us put our three heads together and tried to come up with something that wouldn't get us all killed for good. It was harder than it sounded, which was impressive, since it sounded pretty damn difficult. Finally, we decided to go with what we had: surprise, and the threat of going public without letting the CDC tell their side of the story.

The farther we got from Maggie's house, the dumber our makeshift plan looked...and the more obvious it became that there *wasn't* another way. When the corruption seems to go all the way to the end of the world, the only good approach is through the front door with a gun in each hand. No one was going to help us take on the CDC, not with our resources and reputation, and not with the radio silence coming out of the White House. That meant we needed to play to our strengths, and our strengths came from lifelong training in shoving microphones at danger and demanding that it explain itself. It wasn't much. It was going to have to be enough.

We stopped at a seedy motel in Little Rock, Arkansas, the night before we got to Memphis. They took cash and didn't look too hard at our IDs. No matter how high-tech the world gets, there will always be places designed for people who are looking to slip between the cracks. This was one of them. The man behind the desk didn't know who we were, and better, he didn't want to know. Becks and I checked in together, letting Mahir and Kelly wait in the van until the necessary transactions had been completed. The man was disinterested. He was also a modern American, which meant he might have seen Kelly's face on the news, and might well wonder what a dead woman was doing wandering around Arkansas with a couple of disreputable-looking types like me and Becks.

After the better part of two days spent driving down empty highways and eating out of truck-stop diners, all four of us smelled like road trip— that funky mix of stale corn chips, sweat, dirty hair, and ass that seems to show up any time you drive more than a couple hundred miles in one stretch. We had two rooms, which meant two of us could shower at once, after all four of us had cleared the blood test required to get inside.

Somehow, even though one room was supposed to be for the men and one for the women, Becks and Kelly managed to snag the first showers. It was like a magic trick. I asked "Does anybody want a shower?" and they were *gone*, disappearance punctuated only by the steady hiss of the water.

Mahir and I settled in the room where Kelly was taking her shower, again, just in case. We were too close to her home ground for us to want her left alone. The motel security could be worked around, and I didn't trust her to shoot her way out of a paper bag if something happened while she was unguarded.

I sat on the edge of one of the two queen-sized beds, rubbing my face with one hand like I could wipe the exhaustion away. It never worked. "So the Doc says most folks get to work around nine. The janitorial staff arrives at seven. That gives us two hours to evade one of the best security systems in the world, get inside without taking any blood tests that would announce our presence, and make our way to Dr. Wynne's lab."

"Correct," said Mahir. Paradoxically, he looked *less* tired than he did when he first arrived in Weed. The bastard. I hadn't been able to get any real sleep in the van—too many years of training telling me never to let my guard down in the field—but he'd been out like a light every time he didn't need to be working on something. The rest had been good for him. He was going to need it.

"Is it just me, or is this essentially fucking impossible?"

"If they haven't changed the timing of the security sweeps since Dr. Connolly's death, it's going to be bloody difficult, but no, I wouldn't call it 'fucking impossible.' Fucking impossible requires rather more in the way of, I don't know, ninjas." Mahir smiled. It was a small thing, half-buried in stubble and his own natural restraint, but it was there. "I'm not sure where one goes about ordering ninjas."

"Same place you get the submarines." I looked toward the bathroom door, listening to the sound of running water for a moment before I asked, "Does this shit *ever* end, Mahir? I mean, really, is there a point where we get to say 'enough' and let things go back to normal?"

"No."

I blinked at him.

He shrugged, smile fading. "Your sister trained me, and she never stood for liars. No, Shaun, I don't think this ever ends, not for us, not until we're dead. Maybe not even then. You're a haunted house pretending to be a man these days, and Georgia may be dead, but she's still not out of the game, is she?"

Bet your ass I'm not, said George. Her tone was grimmer than I'd ever heard it.

Mahir looked at my face and nodded. "I thought not. You get distant when you're listening to her. Either you're truly haunted, or you're the most reasonable madman I've ever known, and it doesn't much matter either way: The end result's the same, and she's not going to be resting in peace anytime soon."

"What if we all die here?"

"What makes you think we won't find people of our own to haunt?" Mahir dug into his pocket, producing a slim nylon wallet. He flipped it open and passed it to me. "My wife, Nandini. Nan. You never once asked to see a picture of her. You realize that? You called at all hours of the night, you drove her mad with your nonsense, and you never asked me a damn thing about her."

I took the wallet, too abashed to know what else to do. It was open to a picture of a slim, sharp-eyed woman with dark hair that she must have dyed regularly, to keep the bleach from showing. She was wearing a cowl-necked sweater the color of cherry cola, and frowning at the camera.

The resemblance wasn't perfect. Her skin was too dark and her clothing was too impractical and her nose was a little bit too long. But something in the way she held herself, something about the expression in her eyes . . .

"She looks like George."

"Yes." Mahir leaned over and plucked the wallet from my hand. I didn't fight him. "It was an arranged marriage, but she wasn't the first bride they offered me, or even the fifteenth. She was just the first one I fancied enough to have a go with. Traditional enough to suit my family, but fierce enough to be worth fighting with. I'm not sure whose parents were more relieved, hers or mine." He gave the picture a fond look, snapped the wallet shut, and slid it back into his pocket. "I told her to divorce me when I bought my tickets out of London. She's not much for listening—still, I've no doubt she listened this time, for spite if nothing else."

"I didn't mean to . . . I mean, I didn't know . . ."

"What, that I loved your sister? Of course you didn't, just like you had no idea Rebecca fancied you. You never had to go searching like the rest of us. She was haunting you a long time before she died, and if you'd been the one to go, you'd be haunting her the same way." Mahir stood as the water turned off. "We're all hauntings waiting to happen, Shaun. The sooner you realize that, the sooner you'll get past wondering when our normal lives will be starting up again."

He didn't look back as he walked out of the motel room, letting the door swing gently shut behind him. I stayed where I was, listening to the silence inside my head and the soft sounds of Kelly drying herself off behind the bathroom door. We were all hauntings waiting to happen? Really?

"I guess I can live with that," I said, to the silence.

"Live with what?"

I turned to see Kelly standing in the bathroom door, wearing an outfit I hadn't seen before. She must have bought it on one of her innumerable shopping trips with Maggie. Tan slacks, a white button-down blouse, and a pair of low, black heels. A starched white lab coat completed the illusion that she'd left the CDC only yesterday, not months before. I blinked and said the first thing that popped into my head: "What the hell happened to your hair?"

Kelly reached up to self-consciously touch her long blond ponytail. It was the hairstyle she'd been wearing when she first arrived in Oakland, if maybe a shade or two lighter. "Maggie found it for me at a beauty supply shop. Don't you like it?"

"Shit, Doc, anyone who sees you is going to think they're seeing a ghost."

Very funny, said George.

"That's the idea," said Kelly, and smiled. There was a bitterness in that expression I don't think she would have been capable of before she came to us. Even if she survived, the things she knew now had broken her, maybe forever. "Wiping my biometric information from the scanners would be expensive and time-consuming, and these people are arrogant bastards—I know, because I'm one of them. My profile will still be there. We won't have any issues with the automatic doors. The night guards don't really know any of the junior staff by name—we're just faces to them, and with all the traveling we do, it's not unusual for us to disappear for weeks at a time. As long as we don't wander into a spot check, we'll be fine."

"What about the part where we've been hiding you all the way across the country, on account of that whole 'faking your own death' thing? This seems risky as hell."

"It would be, if we were planning to deal with anyone but security, the janitorial staff, and Dr. Wynne. Security won't stop anyone the scanner says is allowed to be there, and janitorial doesn't care. We'll get past them."

"That leaves us with only the automatic systems to navigate." We'd gone over all of this before. I was so thrown by her appearance that my mouth was running on autopilot.

"So we'd better hope the servers haven't been updated." Was that doubt in her voice? It could have been. It didn't really matter either way. We were miles past the point of no return, and she was as committed as the rest of us.

"Good." I stood. "Let's get you across the hall to Becks. If we're going to invade the Centers for Disease Control, I want to do it while I'm at least remotely clean."

Kelly nodded and ducked back into the bathroom to grab her street clothes before following me to the room across the hall. It was the mirror image of the room we'd just left, with the exception of Becks. She was sitting cross-legged in the middle of one of the room's two beds, field-stripping a sniper rifle I hadn't even been aware she had. I raised an eyebrow.

Becks looked up, hands continuing their work as she glanced at Kelly and gave an encouraging nod. "That's good. You look like a CDC flunky."

"Thank you?" said Kelly, raising an eyebrow.

"That's good," I assured her. "A sniper rifle, Becks? Really?"

"Better overprepared than totally screwed."

"Fair enough." I took a step backward. "You're on Doc duty until Mahir gets out of the shower. As soon as I'm done, we can regroup and get some grub."

"Good," said Becks, and smiled. "I'm starving."

"Yeah," I said, a little dumbly. Looking at her smile, I felt a small pang of regret. We could never have really been lovers, no matter how much she wanted it or how much I tried; that just wasn't what I was wired for. But sometimes, when she smiled at me like that, I wished things could have been different.

I realized I was staring. "Later, Doc," I said, and left.

My shower was an exercise in minimalism. I spent no more time than was legally necessary under the spray of bleach and the steaming water that followed. If anyone checked the hotel's records, they'd see that the rooms had been let to four occupants, and that all four had gone through proper decontamination procedures before leaving the grounds for any reason. That's the sort of detail people don't always think about, and that makes it the sort of detail you shouldn't forget for any reason. Follow the rules whenever possible. That makes it a lot more surprising when you break them.

The bleach was cheap as hell. It stung my eyes, and even after I rubbed myself down in citrus-based lotion—designed for swimmers pre-Rising, back when they were the only people bleaching themselves on a regular basis—my skin kept itching. "Isn't this going to be an absolutely *awesome* night?" I muttered, yanking on a clean pair of khakis.

Better than tomorrow, said George.

"Yeah, I guess that's true." I hesitated. This seemed to be my night for heart-to-heart talks, maybe because I wasn't entirely sure I'd still be alive in twenty-four hours. "George—"

Yes?

I swallowed. "How long is it going to be like this? I mean, how long am I going to be your haunted house, or are you going to be my imaginary friend, or whatever the fuck the cool kids are calling it these days? Is this forever?"

George's answer, when it came, was thoughtful and slow. *Are you asking because you're scared of losing me, or because you're hoping I'm going to go away one day?*

"Yes. No. I mean…I mean I don't know, George, and I sure as shit need you right now, but I have to wonder sometimes if this is my life. If this is the rest of my life."

I think I'm here as long as you keep me here, Shaun. I think one day you're going to look at a mountain and say "I should climb that," or hell, look at a pretty girl and say the same thing. I think when that happens, I'll go. She laughed a little, and added, *But what do I know? I'm just the dead girl in your head.*

"You know everything, George. You always did." I put my hand flat against the steamed-up mirror. If I squinted a little, and didn't let myself really look, I could pretend it was her looking back at me and not my own blurred reflection. "I miss you."

I know. But that won't keep me here forever.

The others were waiting for me in the girls' room. Mahir was in the process of towel drying his hair, and Kelly was back in street clothes. The CDC costume was for tomorrow, when we'd storm the gates or die trying. The hair extensions were gone, and she had a baseball cap pulled low over her eyes to hide her features from any bored bloggers taking pictures for background color. Becks had put her rifle away. She was leaning against the wall next to the door, expression one of bland detachment.

"Hey," I said, stepping inside. "Who feels up for pizza?"

"What took you so long?" asked Becks.

I shrugged, smiling a little. "I had to talk something out with myself before I could come over here. That's all."

"Well, I'm starving," said Mahir, dropping the towel and grabbing his jacket off the bed. Kelly and Becks followed. I brought up the rear, pausing to close and lock the motel room door.

George didn't say anything as we walked toward the van...but in the back of my head, I was pretty sure I could feel her smiling.

It has been a pleasure and a privilege blogging for you over these past few weeks. Thank you for your insightful questions and for your commentary in the forums, where I have learned a great deal about what does—and doesn't!—work in this form of reporting. I promise to take these lessons, and this experience, with me in my future endeavors.

Also, while I'm being sappy...thank you, all of you, for continuing to care as much as you do about the world. This is the only one we're going to get, and I think it's important that we continue to give a damn about every single part of it, even the ones that aren't currently a part of our lives. You are the reason that someday, when this disease has been defeated, the amusement parks will become family fun lands once again, and people will laugh and live and love just the way they always have. Thank you for sharing yourselves with me.

Thank you.

**—From *Cabin Fever Dream*,
guest blog of Barbara Tinney, June 23, 2041**

Twenty

I'm not sure any of us slept that night. We were on an Internet blackout while stationary: no uploads, no message forums, nothing that could be traced to prove we were ever here. That also meant no phone calls, since turning on our phones could activate their GPS chips. We'd been scrupulously careful since leaving Weed. We just had to hope we'd been careful enough.

It was the blood tests that worried me. You can't survive in America without at least one blood test a day, and possibly—probably—more than that. We'd been taking blood tests at toll booths and convenience stores all the way across the country, and if the CDC was somehow tracking clean results, we were screwed.

Oh, the CDC swears they don't track clean results, only the ones that come back positive for a live infection, but no one knows for sure. Legally, they're not *allowed* to track clean results. It's considered an invasion of privacy. If there's nothing to indicate that a person is at risk of amplification, you can't use their tests for anything. Not tracking, and not medical profiling—which is why we have that handy little ruling to depend on. See, the insurance companies would love an excuse to analyze the blood of every person in the country, looking for pre-existing conditions. Ironically, the insurance companies may have the sort of big pockets that can normally shove something like blood test tracking through, but the pharmaceutical companies make them look like paupers, and the pharmaceutical companies didn't want to lose their customer base because people couldn't afford coverage anymore. That's one more thing we can thank Garcia Pharmaceuticals for.

We left the motel at four-thirty in the morning. The sky was still pitch-black, and the streets were deserted. We planned to arrive at the CDC about fifteen minutes before the janitorial staff, stash the van in the maintenance parking lot, and enter through a side door while the grounds were still mostly deserted. It was a risky approach, but it was no worse than any of the other ideas we'd come up with, and it was way better than some of them. Maggie's van was generic enough to be ignored, without crossing into the overly generic "plain white van with blacked-out window." That sort of thing attracts attention by virtue of being designed to be ignored.

Kelly and I were the only ones awake in the van for the first hour of the drive. She sat next to me in the passenger seat—another risky approach, since her death was big news for weeks in the Memphis area. "Local hero doctor dies in the saddle" is the sort of headline that has legs. Newsies like stories like that; they can go back to that well again and again when things get slow, milking them until they go dry. At the same time, Kelly was the one who could steer me down the frontage roads and through the shortcuts only a local would know. The thing that made her a possible danger also made her a major asset.

Then again, hadn't that been the case all along?

The sun was starting to burn a smoky line along the horizon when we hit the outskirts of Memphis. I clicked the radio on, cranking the volume as the scrambler grabbed the nearest station and blasted Old Republic through the van. "Classic rock!" I shouted to Kelly. I had to shout or she wouldn't have been able to hear me. "That's awesome! I hate this shit!"

Judging by the loud swearing now coming from behind me, Becks and Mahir hated it even more. "Turn that crap off!" shouted Becks, smacking me hard on the back of the head.

I grinned as I turned the volume down. "Good morning, sunshine." Kelly was hiding a smile behind her hand. That was good. The more relaxed we all were going into this, the better our chances of getting out alive. "Sleep well?"

"I should shoot you in the bloody head, dump you on the side of the road, and go back to the motel for another six hours of not being in this van," said Mahir.

"That's a yes. Water's in the cooler. Who needs caffeine pills?"

Everyone needed caffeine pills. Kelly handed them out, three to a person. We all gulped ours, me with Coke, Mahir and Kelly with water, and Becks dry. I didn't say anything. Some people blast pre-Rising rock music, some people put on lab coats, and some people try to prove they're the biggest badass around. If it made her feel better, I didn't have a problem with it.

The maintenance lot was just as easy to access as Kelly said it would be.

Only one blood test was required to pass the gate, and it was conducted by an unmanned booth. "Can't say I think much of their security," I said. "Portland was a lot harder to get into."

"Portland was also open when you went there," Kelly said. "Trust me. It only gets worse from here."

Somehow, I didn't want to argue with her about that.

I parked as close to the building as I dared, maneuvering the van into a space tucked mostly behind a large steel generator cage. Becks was out before I'd even turned off the engine. She turned in a slow circle, pistol out and held low in front of her, where she wouldn't be slowed by the process of trying to draw. Mahir followed her out, looking less immediately aggressive as he took up his position next to the van. I glanced to Kelly.

"You ready for this?"

"No," she said, and got out of the van.

I sighed. "Am *I* ready for this?"

No, said George. *But it's too late to turn back now.*

"I guess that's fair." I opened the ashtray and dropped the keys inside. If I didn't make it out of the building, the others wouldn't need to worry about trying to hotwire the van before they could escape. "Check this out."

I opened the door and got out.

We must have made an odd sight as we made our way across the parking lot. Kelly took the lead for once, her white lab coat glowing like a banner in the dimness of the early-morning light. Becks walked close behind, covering her. She was wearing camouflage-print cargo pants, running shoes, and an olive-drab jacket with Kevlar panels sewn into the lining. She actually had her hair up, pulled back in a tight bun that would look lousy on camera but was less likely to get in her eyes than her usual waves. Mahir walked almost alongside Becks, his white running shoes the only thing keeping him from looking like a visiting professor from Oxford, and I brought up the rear in my usual steel-reinforced jeans, cotton shirt, and tweed jacket. Not exactly the sort of group that normally goes parading into the Memphis CDC before the sun is all the way up.

The first door was locked with an actual, manual lock, the sort that requires a key to open. "No blood test to get in?" asked Becks, incredulous.

"Not at this stage," said Kelly, digging in her purse. "If you're going to amplify on the property, we'd much rather you did it in the clear zone between the parking lot and the labs. That way we can catch or kill you at our leisure, and you don't eat the staff." She produced a key.

"Practical," said Mahir.

Kelly unlocked the door and we entered the CDC, Becks now taking point while I stayed at the rear. Our effective noncombatants would walk between the two of us for as much of the trip as possible. Our little formation wouldn't stop a sniper, but it might give us a chance to react before they both went down.

Taking civilians into a fire zone, said George. *What* would *your mother say?*

"That I should keep the cameras rolling," I muttered, and kept following Kelly.

That first door led to a narrow hallway, which opened after about ten feet into a wide concrete corridor that looked like it had been sliced from a pre-Rising bomb shelter. Turbines hummed in the distance. There were no windows and no natural light; instead, huge fluorescents glowed steadily overhead, protected by grids of steel mesh. Kelly kept walking, forcing the rest of us, even Becks, to hurry if we wanted to keep up.

"What is this?" asked Mahir, looking warily around.

"Isolation zone. If we lock down, this area goes airtight, and the negative-pressure venting system kicks in. It can be flooded with formalin from the central control center, or manually from any of the booths along the walls. In case of an outbreak, the doors to the main building open and the security system starts trying to herd the infected here, where they can be kept until we decide what to do with them."

"Ever hear of just shooting the damn things?" asked Becks.

"We have to get our test subjects somewhere." The statement was matter-of-fact; this was, for Kelly, another part of what it meant to work for the CDC. "We all sign body release waivers when we accept our employment offers. As soon as you amplify, you become company property."

"Because that's not creepy." I scanned the walls. "I don't see any cameras." What I did see was a series of sniper slits in the walls, probably leading to a second airtight corridor where the gunmen could be locked until their job was done and their blood tests were clean. This was a storage room. It was also a kill chute, and we needed to remember that. "Is there one of those nifty escape tunnels here, too?"

"Underground. It lets out on the other side of the property." Kelly stopped at a door with a keypad and retinal scanner next to it. She started hitting buttons, narrating her actions, probably to keep one of us from getting trigger-happy and putting a bullet through her head. "I'm giving the system the visiting technician security code, along with the security code for Dr. Wynne's lab, and telling it I have three guests with me. This level of security doesn't distinguish between entry points. It's a known hole, but we keep it open in case we need to bring people in the back way."

"To avoid the media?" asked Mahir mildly.

Kelly reddened but kept tapping for several more seconds before she pulled her hand away. A panel opened in the wall, exposing four blood test units. "We all need to test clean before we can proceed." She slapped her hand down on the first panel, starting her retinal scan at the same time. It was a good maneuver: It cut off any further questioning, and we had *plenty* of questions. Starting, at least for me, with "How the fuck are we planning on getting out of here?"

"Too late to back out now," muttered Becks, and initiated her own blood test. Mahir and I shrugged and did the same. Becks was right; too late now.

The tests came back clean—no surprise, given that we'd only just arrived—and the door swung open, revealing a long white corridor that looked a lot more like what I expected from the CDC. Only about half the lights were on, filling the corners with shadows. A sign on the nearest door read CAUTION—BIOHAZARD.

"All the comforts of home," I said, following Mahir into the hall. I was the last one through; the door closed behind me, locks engaging with a hydraulic hiss that reminded me chillingly of Portland. The hairs along my arms and the back of my neck stood on end as I realized that we were well and truly locked in now.

"The lab is this way," said Kelly, turning to the left and starting to walk with a confidence I'd never seen from her before. We were on her home ground. Only the best and brightest actually go from medical school into careers with the CDC; she must have worked for years for the right to call these hallways hers.

This has to be killing her, said George quietly.

I nodded, not wanting to say anything out loud. George and I grew up not trusting anything anyone said to us. We always knew there were things people didn't say when the cameras were running. For Kelly, the CDC's betrayal had to feel like the end of the world. I was incredibly sorry for her…and at the same time, I was privately glad to know that she had to be hurting like hell. The CDC was her life, and the CDC was part of the reason my sister died. I could feel bad for Kelly. I couldn't forgive her for being naive enough to believe the things she'd been willing to believe for the sake of her career.

At least she'd judged the janitorial schedules correctly. We walked the length of one hall and then another before we reached Dr. Wynne's lab, and we didn't see a single soul. I didn't see any cameras, either, and I was watching for them. Their security was incredibly well-concealed. That was a little worrisome. They'd been nowhere near this good in Portland, and in my experience, when the security cameras go invisible, that means they have something they really need to hide.

"Here," whispered Kelly, stopping at an unlabeled door with a blood test panel next to it. She started to raise her hand, and then hesitated, expression turning unsure. "We're going to have to go through one at a time," she said, slowly.

I winced. Becks scowled. Going one at a time meant that either one of us walked in ahead of Kelly—which would mean walking blind into unfamiliar territory—or we sent her through alone, which could split the party permanently. I didn't want us on opposite sides of a door when the CDC shock troops swept in and gunned us all down.

And I didn't have a choice. We'd followed Kelly's research across the world, and we'd followed her directions into the guts of the Memphis CDC. If we called it off now, a lot of people had died for nothing. "Go ahead, Doc," I said. She shot me a surprised look. "We'll be right behind you. Don't worry. We're not going anywhere."

Kelly nodded and slapped her hand down on the panel. A moment later, the light over the door flashed green and she stepped through, vanishing.

"I hope you know what you're doing," said Becks, stepping up to start her own test.

"I never have before," I said. "I figure, why start now? I wouldn't want to ruin a good thing."

The light went green before she could say anything. That was probably for the best. She still glared as she stepped through the door, and flipped me off as it slid shut again behind her.

Mahir sighed as he pressed his hand against the panel. "I do wish you wouldn't taunt her while we're in the field."

"She wouldn't know what to do with me if I didn't."

"I suppose not," said Mahir, and stepped through the newly open door, leaving me alone in the hall.

Not entirely alone. *Your turn*, said George.

"Yours, too," I said, and pressed my hand down.

The lab on the other side of the door was standard-issue CDC: equipment I didn't understand, refrigerator full of things I didn't want to know about, desk heaped with paperwork that was probably several weeks overdue. A dry-erase board, covered in what looked like meaningless gibberish, took up most of one wall. Kelly was staring at it, transfixed.

"He's figured out the settlement problem," she said, as much to herself as to the rest of herself. "I don't know how, but he's figured out the settlement problem in the immune response. This whole thing, it's so *simple*, it's so..."

"It's elegant," said Mahir.

Kelly smiled. "Yes, it is."

"Good for it," I said, stepping up behind her. "Want to explain it to the rest of us?"

"Oh! Well, this here—" She waved a hand at a segment of the board and began to talk, medical jargon flowing from her lips too fast for me to follow. That didn't matter. I didn't need to follow it live; I never go anywhere without half a dozen active cameras running, and I could review the recording at my leisure. Assuming we all got out of here in one piece. Since we couldn't transmit, I couldn't make backups. If we died inside the CDC, it was all for nothing.

I pushed that grim thought aside. Kelly was still talking, and at least Mahir seemed to understand whatever the hell she was saying. He interjected periodically, asking questions and restating things that had been particularly confusing when she said them.

"I love having a smart guy around," I said to Becks, sotto voce.

"Me, too," she said, and grinned, all that familiar field excitement filling her face. Irwins are never more alive than when they're five minutes away from getting slaughtered.

Kelly finished her explanation fifteen seconds before we heard the door unseal itself. It was barely louder than a whisper, but we were all so on edge that it felt like we could have heard a pin drop a mile away. I signaled to Becks, who nodded, and the two of us moved smoothly into position, flanking the doors while Mahir pulled Kelly back, out of immediate view. The door slid open and a tall man in a white lab coat stepped through, attention fixed on the clipboard he was carrying.

The door slid closed again, and Becks and I moved to stand shoulder to shoulder, pistols raised until their muzzles barely pressed against the back of the man in the lab coat. He froze. Smart guy.

"Hello, Dr. Wynne," I said amiably. "We figured you might like to know how things have been going, so we swung by to say hello."

"*Shaun?*"

"Last time I checked." I took a half step forward, digging the muzzle of my gun in a little harder. "How about you? How's it been going for you?"

"I—ah. I wasn't expecting to see you here."

"We didn't think you would be," said Mahir, stepping into Dr. Wynne's line of sight. Kelly hung back, face still hidden in the shadows. "I saw you at the funeral, but I don't believe we've been properly introduced."

"Mahir Gowda, replacement head of the Factual News Division at the After the End Times," said Dr. Wynne, not missing a beat. "I've been keeping up with the site. I must admit, I didn't expect to see you, either. Ever."

"We're full of surprises tonight," said Becks, and nudged him forward with her gun. "Move away from the door. Center of the room, hands at your sides. Please don't make any sudden moves. I'd really hate to have to shoot you."

"It's true, she would," I said. "We told her she'd have to mop up any messes she made while we were here, and Becks *hates* cleaning."

Dr. Wynne shook his head as he followed her instructions, walking to the middle of the floor before turning to face me. "Shaun, what are you doing here? You shouldn't have come."

"There was too much that didn't add up. We needed you to check our math."

Ask him about the strains.

"I'm getting to that," I muttered.

"What?" asked Dr. Wynne.

"Nothing." I flashed him a glossy photo-op smile. "Doc? You want to say hello?"

"Happily." Kelly stepped out of the shadows, heels clicking against the floor. Dr. Wynne went white. "Hello, sir. How have you been?"

"I...you..." He stopped for a moment, composing himself, and said, "Shaun told me you died in Oakland."

"The dead have a tendency to come back these days, remember?" She looked at the whiteboard. "You solved the immune response issue. I recognize some of these figures. Every time I posited them, you said I was off base. But it looks like it worked."

"Kelly, how did you—"

She turned back to us, giving me a small nod.

That was my cue. I offered Dr. Wynne another smile, and said, "We've been doing some digging, and we didn't have a way of reaching you that wouldn't send up too many red flags, especially since the Doc wanted to be involved. We figured you'd want to know what we'd managed to find."

"And the guns were what? Just a precaution?"

"Pretty much." I lowered my gun. "You can't be too careful these days."

"You let me think Dr. Connolly was dead."

"That's true," I said agreeably. "Mahir?"

"On it." Mahir produced a handheld reader from inside his coat and walked around to offer it to Dr. Wynne. "The information you'll want to see is presently up on the screen. Read carefully. The implications can be rather unpleasant."

"When I sent Dr. Connolly to you, I expected you to disappear immediately," said Dr. Wynne, running one big hand through his thinning hair as he looked at the screen. "It would have been the smart thing to do. If you'd dropped off the grid as soon as she got there, you could have been safe."

"You know we've never worked that way," I said, surprised by the apologetic note creeping into my tone. I really *was* sorry. If we were wrong, and he only wanted to protect us—

Shaun, said George. *Shaun, stop a second. You need to stop.*

Dr. Wynne nodded as he scrolled through the material we'd collected. "This is some very good work. How difficult was this to find?"

"Not terribly," said Mahir, before I could speak. He looked at Dr. Wynne neutrally, and added, "It's amazing how much of this was out there, floating around, and simply needed to be put together in the correct order."

Shaun—

"Wait a second, George," I said softly, watching Dr. Wynne's expression. He was frowning with concentration, studying the data. "I want to hear what he has to say."

"Was any of it commissioned?" Dr. Wynne glanced up. "Is there anything here that you needed a lab or special access to find?"

All Dr. Abbey's research was conducted in a lab, and I didn't know how much of it was available to the general public. We'd released some of it in the process of getting the rest of the data, but not everything, and not in a collected format. I opened my mouth to tell him that... and stopped, frowning.

George spoke into the silence: *He lost track of Kelly as soon as the building blew and destroyed her ID—the ID he gave her. He never questioned her death. He must have known. Shaun—*

"I know," I whispered. And I did know, suddenly, and without room for argument: Dr. Wynne ordered the destruction of Oakland. Dr. Wynne killed Dave.

"Know what, son?" he asked.

"Nothing." I swallowed my revulsion, forcing my face to stay neutral. "Is Kelly the last living member of her research team?"

Dr. Wynne hesitated before nodding. "Yes. That's why I knew I needed to get her out of here. I was worried that something might happen to her if she stayed."

"So you sent her to us?" He would have known her arrival would bring us all in from the field; he couldn't send her out with false data—she'd know; she'd been on the research team too long for him to slip that by her—and the real stuff was more than enough to keep us stationary for hours. We were all home when Kelly got there. Even if we hadn't been, I would have called anyone who was out on assignment and demanded they come in. Let her get there. Wait a few hours. And then unleash the hounds, knowing we'd all be in one place.

"I knew I could trust you."

"Huh. Okay." I raised my gun again, aiming it at him. Mahir and Kelly blinked at me, looking startled. "See, I would have sent her to Canada. Or maybe to one of the unsanctioned labs, the ones where they'd know what to do with the stuff she had. We were grateful for the story we couldn't break and all, but it wasn't the best use of your illegal resources."

"I don't see what you're getting at, Shaun," said Dr. Wynne, looking up. His eyes widened when he saw the gun. "What's that for? We're all friends here."

"I'm starting to not be so sure about that." Becks stepped up next to me, raising her own gun into firing position. "Why did you send her to us? What the hell made us so special?"

"You were dangerous," said Kelly, and gave the dry-erase board another glance before looking toward Dr. Wynne. "That was it, wasn't it? You sent me to them because they were dangerous."

Dr. Wynne said nothing.

I gave Kelly an amiable nod. "I think that means yes. So what screwed you up, Dr. Wynne? Did somebody read the time wrong?"

Dr. Wynne frowned. "I don't understand what you mean."

"We checked the Doc real carefully for trackers, but there weren't any after we trashed the ID you gave her," I said. "If there had been, I don't think we'd have made it out. Somebody cared enough about killing us that they were willing to blow up half of downtown Oakland—"

"I think you're exaggerating a bit there, son," said Dr. Wynne.

"—but they lost track of us after that, didn't they?" I kept my gun trained on Dr. Wynne, watching his face as I spoke. "Why do you care where we got our research, Dr. Wynne? Shouldn't it be enough that we got it? If we can do it, anybody can."

"No, Shaun, not anybody." Dr. Wynne shook his head, smiling a little as Mahir snatched the reader away from him. "You'd need some pretty specialized resources. People with inside data." Kelly paled. "People who aren't bound by American law."

Mahir's eyes narrowed, expression going suddenly dangerous. "Are you saying, sir, that we were a perfect testing ground for the spread of information?"

"I'm saying I expected you to run," said Dr. Wynne. His tone was reasonable enough, still the warm, Southern-accented voice of the man who'd been there to welcome me and George back from the dead when the CDC took us off the highway. He ran a hand through his thinning hair, looking at me steadily. "I never gave you much credit for brains, Shaun—that was your sister's department, God rest her soul, and if she made any errors in judgment, it was in trusting you to watch her back—but I still thought you were smarter than this."

My throat felt dust dry, making it impossible to swallow. "You take that back," I whispered.

Don't listen to him, said George. *All he's doing is messing with you. He knows damn well that we would never have run. He didn't expect us to.*

"That's easy for you to say, George," I muttered. "You're the dead one."

Dr. Wynne's eyebrows rose. "You really do talk to her. That's...fascinating. I'd heard that, but I thought it was an exaggeration. Does she answer?"

I glared at him.

He raised his hands. "Now, son, I'm not trying to be insulting. I'm just interested. It seems a bit, well, crazy, if you don't mind my saying it."

"Oh, don't worry. I've heard it all before," I said flatly.

"We've said it," added Becks. "Frequently."

"Dr. Wynne?" Kelly sounded...lost. For the first time since she'd shown up in Oakland, she sounded utterly and completely lost. She'd been scared, she'd been confused, and she'd been angry, but she'd never sounded like that. "Is he right? Is what Shaun's saying...Is he right?"

He half turned toward Kelly, lowering his hands. "It was never personal, darling. You have to believe that."

She shook her head, eyes narrowing. "I don't know what to believe... but I do believe you sent me out there to die. The facts aren't on your side."

"I suppose I should have considered this as a risk. They've managed to get to you, haven't they? These silly people with their silly crusade against the status quo. Well, that's why you went in blind, isn't it?" He took a step toward her. "You know I never wanted to hurt you. You were one of my favorites."

Her lip trembled as she looked at him. The urge to believe was naked in her eyes. "I just don't understand."

"Don't worry. You don't have to." He smiled a little. "Just know that you helped me a great deal with my research, and someday—when the world is ready—your work will help a lot of people. Isn't that enough?" He took another step forward.

"Stop right there," I said, sharply.

And he lunged.

I never would have guessed that a man that size could move that fast. In the time it took to shift my aim, he grabbed hold of Kelly, swinging her against his chest, and produced a gun from his lab coat pocket, pressing it against her temple. She squeaked once, sounding terrified.

"Drop it!" barked Becks.

"I don't think so," said Dr. Wynne mildly. "But thank you for asking." He took a step backward, dragging Kelly with him. "You know, Shaun, I would never have tried this if we'd hit our original target. I wouldn't have needed to. Georgia would have gotten the point when Tate made his grand, villainous exit. She would have left well enough alone."

"Don't you talk about her!" I snarled.

I didn't realize I'd stepped forward until Dr. Wynne tapped the gun against Kelly's temple again, making a "*tsk*" sound. "Now, you wouldn't want me to slip and shoot this little peach, would you? She's such an earnest girl. Never could believe the worst of anyone. That's why this was inevitable. She could be useful only so long."

Mahir, meanwhile, was gaping. "You mean... I always thought he was a bit overblown at the end, a bit too much of a movie-reel villain. That was *intentional?*"

"No need to look for shades of gray when an absolute black-and-white is in front of you," said Dr. Wynne, reasonably. "We offered you a perfect bad guy, with no motives to question and no thought required. You were just too damn dumb to take it."

"Dr. Wynne?" whispered Kelly.

"Hush now, darling, you be still." He took another step backward. "You like stories, don't you? Here's a story for you. Once upon a time, there was a young doctor who wanted to save the world. But worlds don't save easy, and this one needed to be damned a little longer before it would properly appreciate salvation. Salvation came with... complications. So he agreed to help some men who knew better than the rest of the world. Men who would be angels. And he learned that a man who controls enough can become an angel, too, in his own time."

"Okay, you win," I said. "You get to be the crazy one. I give you the crown."

Dr. Wynne shook his head. "Here's another story for you—one that's going to be the truth very soon. I was stunned when the security cameras reported a break-in. It's fortunate I came to work on time or there's no telling what sort of damage you might have done before I could stop you. Of course, we suspected you might have had some involvement with the outbreak in Portland, but it wasn't until you tried to repeat the event here that we understood just how far astray you'd gone. Without your sister to shore you up, and without a conspiracy to chase, you simply couldn't face reality. You started making monsters out of thin air."

"Why is it you assholes always feel the need to tell the media your evil plans before you kill us?" asked Becks. She sounded totally calm. I have never been more proud of her. "Is it a union requirement or something?"

"I thought you might like the truth before you died. You people are always so fixated on the truth. Like it's more righteous than a lie, even when the lie protects what the truth would destroy." His lips quirked in a regretful smile, making him look like the sympathetic figure who once greeted me with the news that I was going to live. I hated him even more for that. "I'm not afraid of being recorded. You can't transmit from here, and it's not like you'll be leaving."

I forced myself to lower my gun, saying, "How about this. We all put down our guns, you give Kelly back, and we go. Okay? Nobody needs to die. It's not like we can prove anything's actually happening here."

"Oh, but you did prove it, you did—and you exposed some holes we hadn't even considered patching. You did the work for us, and you've brought me everything we'll need to repair the situation. Half a dozen researchers, a few dozen assistants, and all this goes away for another decade. That should be more than long enough for us to make some real progress on the problem, without sending the world into a panic." He chuckled. At least he wasn't backing up anymore; his back was to the counter, Kelly locked against his chest. "You get so hung up on your precious truth that you can't see the big picture. If this information got out…"

"What? People would know something?" Becks glared. "Your evil plan sucks."

"Why tailor new strains of the virus?" asked Mahir. "What does it serve?"

"We'll find one that doesn't trigger reservoir behavior," said Dr. Wynne. "Once that's done, we'll be in the position to pick the virus apart at our leisure. No more pesky moral issues with shooting the infected. No more unexpected behavior. Once it's been normalized, once it *conforms*, we can finally get to work on a virus that does what *we* want it to do, that follows *our* orders, not anyone else's. We'll save the world the way we want to, in our own time, and we'll get the proper credit. The reservoir conditions complicate things, and we can't have that. Still, I'm sorry the strike on Oakland was called in early, Shaun. I really did like you. I'd hoped to spare you this very situation."

"What makes you think the information won't get out *anyway*?" I asked, mildly. "I didn't bring my whole team here. If we don't check in, it all goes public."

"Ah, but by the time it goes public, we'll have tied you to the outbreak in Portland, and possibly to the attacks on President Ryman's campaign. You may even be the reason your sister died. You won't be a hero, Shaun. You won't even be a martyr. You'll be the man who killed his sister for ratings, and the world will hate you." Dr. Wynne smiled beatifically as he let go of Kelly and reached for the counter behind them. She didn't move. Something about the gun pressed to her temple seemed to be dissuading her. "Nothing that comes out of your little tabloid press will be believed. It'll just be the final thrashings of a madman."

You bastard, whispered George.

For once, I was calmer than she was. "You're an asshole," I said.

"Yes, but I'm an asshole who's going to walk away from here alive, which is more than I can say for you," he replied. He locked his arm around Kelly again, pulling her toward the door. "Security is on the way. There's nothing you can do."

When he moved his hand, I saw what he'd picked up from the counter: two plain ballpoint pens. "What are you going to do when security gets here?" I asked. "Scribble us to death?"

Kelly's eyes widened. She didn't look lost anymore. Now she looked terrified. Even having a gun against her head hadn't elicited that response. "What?" she whispered.

"In a manner of speaking, yes," said Dr. Wynne.

"It's a *pen*," I said.

Appearances can be deceiving, said George.

Kelly looked at me, eyes still wide, and mouthed, "I'm sorry." Then she reached behind herself, fumbling a scalpel from the tray of surgical instruments before driving it into the back of Dr. Wynne's neck. He bellowed like a wounded bull, gun falling as he clapped his hand over the side of his neck. The hand that held the pens snapped upward, some sort of trigger releasing in one of them. A thin dart whistled through the air past my ear, embedding itself in the wall. Becks fired twice, one shot catching Dr. Wynne in the arm, the other going wild. I brought my own arm back into firing position and shot him squarely in the chest, right in the spot where he'd been aiming the pen at me.

The impact whipped him hard to the side, and Kelly lost her grip on the scalpel, falling back. She slammed into Mahir. Dr. Wynne, still bellowing, raised the pens again, aiming at them. Kelly screamed and shoved Mahir to the side, sending him sprawling as Dr. Wynne's knees buckled.

Dr. Wynne fell hard to the floor, and Becks immediately shot him twice in the head. That was one body that wouldn't be getting back up.

Mahir staggered to his feet, careful to avoid touching Dr. Wynne's blood. "Oh my God—"

"Mahir, are you clean?" I demanded.

He looked down at himself, scanning his clothing. "I—I think so. Nothing seems to have gotten on me."

"Great. Well, avoid fluid transfer until we can get you to a test unit. A *non*-CDC unit. Suddenly, I don't trust anything in this damn building." I lowered my gun, but didn't put it away. "Come on, Doc. We need to get the fuck out of here."

"I don't think so," she said, sounding dazed.

My head snapped up.

There was a clear plastic needle embedded in her chest, glittering with a faint, oily sheen. "He shot me," she said, staring at it. "Dr. Wynne shot me before he fell down. With the pen. Only it's not a pen—it's a defense mechanism. You can load them with knock-out darts, or lethal injections, or...all sorts of things." She swallowed. "All sorts of things."

"That doesn't mean anything," said Becks.

"Right. Because he obviously shot me with a sedative or something." Kelly shook her head, looking actively annoyed. "Don't be stupid. We don't have time for this."

"Fuck, Doc, just come on."

"No." She turned and yanked open a drawer, pulling out a test unit. She slammed it down on the counter, popped off the lid, and shoved her hand inside. "I'm so sorry. I swear, I didn't know. Maybe I should have known, maybe I was being a naive little idiot—I was so busy trying to do what I was supposed to do, and save the world, that I didn't open my eyes—but I didn't know."

"I believe you," Becks said, softly.

The lights along the top of Kelly's test unit were turning red, one after the other.

She pulled her hand out when the last light stabilized on red, shooting a challenging glare in our direction. "*Now* do you believe me? Dr. Wynne shot me, and I've gone into amplification. I'm done. It's over. And I really think it's time for you to leave."

I winced. "Fuck. Doc, I'm sorry." Becks raised her arm, gun up, and pointed at Kelly's head. From this distance, there was no chance she'd miss.

"So am I." Kelly pulled the needle free. She held it up for a moment, long enough for the rest of us to see it clearly, and then she dropped it to the floor. It made a faint clinking noise when it hit the tile, before rolling to a stop in a puddle of Dr. Wynne's blood. "Leave the door open when you go. I'll stay here and distract security."

I reached to the side and pushed Becks's arm slowly down, shaking my head in negation. "Doc, are you sure? Amplification's not something to fuck around with."

"I think I know that better than you do." A thin smile tilted her lips up. That, combined with the ponytail, made her look briefly, heartbreakingly like Buffy. I'd seen the resemblance when Kelly first showed up in Oakland, and now here it was again, at the worst possible time.

I guess they have more in common than we thought, said George.

Kelly shrugged out of her lab coat, letting it fall. The blood on the floor began to soak through the cotton almost instantly, but she didn't seem to notice. She just kept talking as she bent to pick up Dr. Wynne's gun. "At my body weight, you have approximately eleven minutes before I become a danger. That's long enough for you to get out of here, and that gives me long enough to make sure the security team has a really, really bad morning. Exit, take a left, and head for the end of the hall. Security will be coming from the other direction. Turn left again when you reach the T-junction, and open the fourth door you see. That should put you—"

"Same place as before?" I asked.

She nodded. Her smile faded slowly, and her lower lip quavered for a moment before she said, "The security systems in the evacuation tunnels are independent of the rest of the building, in case of malfunction or . . . or something like this. As long as you can test clean, you can get out, no matter what else is happening in here."

"I remember." I took a step back, away from her. "Becks, Mahir, come on."

"Yeah." Becks hesitated before asking, "You got enough bullets?"

Kelly smiled again, this time directing it at Becks. It was a small thing, and it hurt to see, because it might be the last smile she'd ever wear. At least this one didn't make her look like Buffy. "I do. Thank you."

"If you decide you can't do this—if you want to die remembering who you are—just make sure you save one for yourself."

"I will." Kelly sighed, looking at the gun in her hands. "Under the circumstances, I think my grandfather would want me to do this. He thought the truth was important...and so do I. I really didn't know Dr. Wynne was sending me to hurt you. And I'm sorry. I didn't want any of this."

"I know," said Becks.

I took a breath, letting it out slowly before I tried to speak. "Thanks, Doc." A whisper at the back of my mind brought a sad smile to my lips. "George says thanks, too. She's sorry she didn't trust you."

"You're welcome—and tell her it doesn't matter."

Kelly's smile faded. She stepped back, bracing herself against the cabinet before sinking to the floor. That was my last image of her, just sitting there with her knees drawn up to her chest, staring at Dr. Wynne's unmoving body like she expected it to tell her some sort of a secret—to say something that would magically make everything she'd been through start making sense.

The three of us who were still standing left the office at a walk that turned rapidly into a run and left us with no time for dwelling on what had just happened. We were too busy racing for the exit, looking for an escape from what I was raised to believe was the safest place on the planet.

We were halfway to the end of the first hall when the alarm started to blare, flashing amber lights snapping on at the top of every wall. Mahir sped up, passing us both to take the left. Becks reached back to grab my elbow, hauling me around the corner and out of sight just before the sound of running footsteps filled the hall, coming hard and fast enough to be audible under the alarm. Security was finally on the way.

"You need to keep up," she hissed. I could barely hear her; it was mostly the shape of her lips that told me what she'd actually said.

"Yeah, I know." Becks started to let go of my arm. I grabbed her hand. "Come on, you two. Let's get the fuck out of here."

Neither of them argued. We started moving again, traveling at a pace that was just short of a run as we followed a dead woman's instructions to freedom. Kelly was true to her word; she kept security busy in Dr. Wynne's lab. The sound of gunfire started as we were making our way into the evacuation grid, only to be cut off when the hidden door swung shut behind us. The secure tunnels were silent and dark, just like before.

We didn't see a soul during our escape. I still barely breathed until the outside door swung open to let us out on the far edge of the parking lot, half-hidden from the building by a short fence made of steel strips. It took me a moment to realize what it was for: If the facility had been taken by the infected, the metal would hide us from view and might give us the time to either run like hell or go back underground to wait for rescue. It was a nifty idea. Too bad "escape" didn't mean anything but getting the hell off the grounds before we were spotted.

I waited for gunshots as we ran to Maggie's van, crouched to minimize our visible profiles, with guns in our hands and ready to fire. They never came. Security was still inside, searching for Kelly's phantom guests. No one had checked the logs showing the evacuation tunnels, possibly because they hadn't compared notes with Portland, possibly because they didn't think we'd get that far. My heart hammered against my ribs, George making soothing, incoherent noises at the back of my head to try and keep me calm. It did, barely. I didn't really start breathing until we were safe inside the van with the doors closed against the outside. Then I was slamming the key into the ignition, and we were racing away into the brittle golden light of morning, leaving the CDC—and Kelly Connolly, who was naive, but never bad—behind.

We've left too many people behind. And somehow, the running never seems to end.

The sweetest summer gift of all
Is knowing spring gives way to fall
And when the winds of winter call,
We'll answer as we must.
Persephone chose to descend
Into the night that has no end,
In Hades' hands she goes to spend
Her nights amidst the dust.
For Hades holds his loved ones dear,
Away from life, away from fear,
And so when death is drawing near,
In Hades' hands we trust.

—From *Dandelion Mine*,
the blog of Magdalene Grace Garcia, June 23, 2041

Twenty-one

I kept my foot slammed down on the gas as we blazed along a frontage road, taking one of the more obscure ways out of town. Mahir rode in the passenger seat with a smartphone in his hand, entering alterations to our route every few minutes as he received updates from the GPS satellites. Every change had to be registered with the Highway Commission, but our credentials were in order, and unless there was a stop order out on our vehicle, registering our route was less dangerous than dealing with the smackdown if we got caught crossing state lines without the proper paperwork in place.

Our weird little hopscotch of twists and turns wasn't the fastest way to get where we were going, even if I don't think we ever dropped under eighty miles per hour, but it was definitely the most confusing. I wouldn't have been able to track us—not without an actual tracking device planted somewhere on the van, and if the CDC was that deep into our shit, we were already dead. Hacking the highway registry wouldn't give them any of the vehicles known to be registered to our site or its employees, and I seriously doubted they had a full catalog of vehicles registered to Garcia Pharmaceuticals.

Becks rode in the rear with a rifle clutched in her hands, waiting for the moment when an unmarked car would come roaring up behind us and she'd have to start shooting. Maybe we were being paranoid, but I seriously doubted it. The CDC has had a lot of power for a long damn time now. Our deaths wouldn't register on anybody's radar, except for maybe Maggie's, and there wouldn't be too much even she could do about it. Her parents had money, political pull, and a lot of patience. That didn't mean she'd be able to convince them to take on the CDC, even if she could convince them that the research we'd collected was the real deal.

I allowed the shuddering van to drop back to a more reasonable sixty miles per hour after we passed the halfway point between Memphis and Little Rock. There was still no visible pursuit. "Becks? How's the road looking?"

"Clear." I could see her in the rearview mirror. All her attention was focused on the road, shoulders tense as she waited for the moment when the ambush would be sprung. "Not a soul since we passed that tour bus."

"With your driving, the poor bastards probably thought we were running from an outbreak," said Mahir. There was a smothered chuckle in his tone. I knew that edge of hysteria better than I wanted to, although I hadn't heard it that clearly in a long time. It went away after you'd spent enough time in the field. Hysteria takes too much energy to be maintained forever. "They likely turned around as soon as they found a wide enough spot in the road."

"As long as their turn didn't take them in our direction, I don't care where they went." Becks managed to sound like she was muttering even while pitching her voice to be heard at the front of the van. It's a trick from the basic Irwin handbook: The lower and more urgent your tone, the more exciting and dangerous the situation will seem to the people at home. It's just a matter of learning to whisper as loudly as some people shout, to make sure the cameras can pick you up. I knew exactly what she was doing. I was still impressed. She was damn good at it.

"We have enough gas to get us past Little Rock—after that, I want to get freaky," I said. "Mahir, get us a route that doesn't involve the roads we used to reach Tennessee. Try to get a whole new set of states if you can."

"Why are you asking *me*?" Mahir asked peevishly. He started tapping a staccato pattern on the screen of his phone, calling up a more sophisticated GPS mapping program. "I'm the only one in this car not native to this damn continent."

"Great. That means you won't have any stupid preconceptions about what to avoid."

"What, bad neighborhoods?"

"I was thinking more like Colorado, but sure, whatever." I made a sharp turn onto yet another frontage road, causing Becks to whack her shoulder against the window. She swore, but didn't yell at me. Our escape was too important to interrupt for silly things like fighting amongst ourselves. "Becks, we still clear?"

"Unless the CDC has invisible cars, yes," she snarled.

"Good enough for me." I pulled a disposable ear cuff out of my pocket and snapped it on, tapping the side to trigger the connection. "This is

Shaun Mason activating security protocol Campbell. The bridge is out, the trees are coming, and I'm pretty sure my hand is evil. Now gimme some sugar, baby."

Mahir stared at me with undisguised confusion. "What the fuck was all that about?"

"Single-use phone. I wanted to make sure I wouldn't activate it by mistake." The ear cuff beeped as the connections were made, routed through half a dozen dummy servers and half a dozen more firewalls.

Fire-and-forget phones are about as secure as it gets, providing you don't mind spending a few hundred bucks to make one call. That call can't last for more than six minutes, and it has to end with the total destruction of the phone you used to make it. But yeah, it's secure.

"Well, that's definitely one thing no one's going to say on bloody accident!"

"Exactly. Now get back to finding us a rabbit hole to dive down."

The beeping stopped, and Alaric's voice came down the line, asking, "Shaun? Is that you? Where *are* you?"

"That's a good question, and no matter how secure I think this line is, it's one I'm not going to answer. We have a maximum of six minutes talk time before we become traceable, so I want you to get Maggie and set your phone to speaker. Got me?"

"She's right here," said Alaric. There was a clicking sound. When he spoke again, his voice was tinny and a little distant, like it was coming down a tube. "Go."

"Right. Wynne sold us out. I don't know if he was always dirty or if they got to him after the election, but I'm not sure it matters. He's dead. So's Kelly." I winced as I realized that there was one more unexpected tragedy to her death. "Shit. We can't even put her on the Wall. She officially died months ago, and it wasn't because of the infected."

"Damn," whispered Alaric. The seconds were ticking away from us, but we still fell silent for a moment, considering the magnitude of the tragedy in front of us. The Wall is a virtual monument to the people who've died because of Kellis-Amberlee. It started during the Rising with bloggers and doctors, college students, and soccer moms—anyone and everyone who came out on the losing end of the zombie apocalypse. We've kept it up since then. The blog community views it as a public service and a vital reminder that none of us is safe; that it never really ended. Maybe the infected don't roam the streets the way they did once, but they're still here. They're never going away. And names keep going up on the Wall.

George's name is up there. So is Buffy's, and Dave's, since he died during an outbreak. Hell, even Tate's name is on the Wall. He killed my sister, but the Wall doesn't judge. George used to call it the ultimate monument to truth, a universally accepted model of the world as it is, not as we want it to be. There was no way we could pretend Kelly died because of any reason other than Kellis-Amberlee...and because of that goddamn clone, she was never going to go up on the Wall.

I guess there's nothing in the world that can't lie to us, said George, sounding subdued. *I think I'm glad I died before I found that out.*

There was nothing I could say to that. I cleared my throat, shattering the silence. "We're on our way home. I can't tell you how we're going to be coming—it's not safe, and I'm not sure—but I want you to stay inside, lock yourselves down, and don't go out for *anything*. I mean *anything*."

"The dogs—" started Maggie.

"That's what you have security for! Call them out of the woods and make *them* take the little crap factories out for walkies. Dammit, Maggie, I don't think you understand how deep the shit is right now. Alaric, start backing up our databases everywhere you possibly can. Send encrypted copies to everyone in the employee database, everyone who's ever *been* in the employee database, your ex-girlfriend, your ex-girlfriend's new boyfriend, *everyone*."

"Everyone?" asked Alaric.

I hesitated.

Do it, said George.

"Yeah—everyone," I said. "Make the flat-drop. Encrypt the files first, to slow things down, but make it. We'll deal with it later, assuming there *is* a later. Both of you, make sure your wills are up-to-date. Maggie, tell your Fictionals to stay the fuck home until further notice. I don't want anyone coming within a hundred miles of Weed if they have a choice in the matter."

"All right, boss," said Alaric, quietly.

"Turn left at the next intersection," said Mahir.

"Got it." I slowed slightly as I took the turn. There were still no other cars in sight. "I'm dead serious here, guys. We're on lockdown until further notice. Treat every door and window as a sealed air lock, and open them only if your lives depend on it. Your lives probably *do* depend on keeping them closed, since these assholes have clearly demonstrated that they wouldn't know a scruple if it bit them on the ass. Mahir, how's our network security?"

"I have no fucking idea, Shaun. If you've got a way of bringing Buffy back from the dead, maybe *she* could tell you. The only thing *I* can tell you is that you've got a right turn coming up in a block and a half."

"Right. Well, the dead are walking, boys and girls, but they're not doing it in our favor, so for right now, we're on our own. I don't have a safe way of transmitting our files to you."

Maggie broke in. "I'll tell my Fictionals I've had another problem with the plumbing, and keep anything more detailed to the secure servers. Will you be able to call in again at all?"

"Maybe," I hedged. "I'm not going to promise anything, but I'll try. For the moment, assume you won't be hearing from us until we arrive, and that we won't be staying long before it's everybody out. We wouldn't be coming back at all if there was anywhere safer to go." The CDC would figure out that we'd been staying at Maggie's place, eventually. I was just praying that their fear of her parents would keep them from doing anything drastic before we had time to grab our shit and hit the road. "Pack a bag and be ready to move."

"On it."

"Good. This shouldn't be more than a three-day drive, and that's assuming we actually stop to sleep. If we're not there inside of the week—"

"If you're not here in a week, don't bother coming," she said. "We won't be here when you arrive."

"That's the right answer." I glanced over at Mahir. His attention was still focused on the phone in his hand. "Mahir? You want to send a message for your wife?"

"No." He looked up, offering me a strained smile. "She knew where I was going. She knew I might not come back. It's best if we don't complicate that further, don't you think?"

I didn't really know what to say to that. I shook my head and checked the rearview mirror. Becks was still in watch position, expression grim as she scanned the windows. "Becks? Any messages you wanted to send?"

"Fuck that shit." Her narrowed eyes met mine in the rearview mirror, almost daring me to argue. "We're going to make it home, and then we're going to take them all down."

"Sounds like a plan to me. Alaric? Maggie? You've got your marching orders. Now march. We'll check in if we can, and if we can't, just keep the porch light burning until our time runs out."

"It's been good working with you, boss," said Alaric.

"Same here, buddy, but it's not over yet."

"Your lips to God's ears," said Maggie. "All of you, stay safe, and don't pull any stupid heroics. I don't want to flee to the Bahamas with nobody but Alaric for company."

"Truly a fate worse than death," deadpanned Mahir.

"We'll do our best," I said. "Stay safe."

There was nowhere good that the call could go from there, and we were almost at the limit of what the phone's security would allow. I killed the connection before pulling off the ear cuff and dropping it into the coin tray between the van's front seats. "We'll stop and torch that as soon as we can," I said.

"Better make it sooner rather than later," said Becks.

"On it. Mahir?"

"Take the right."

I took the right.

Our original route took us to Tennessee by way of the American Southwest, hour upon hour of desert unspooling outside the van's windows. Mahir's adjusted route followed roughly the same roads, at least until we got to Little Rock. Then things got weird. Instead of heading down to avoid the mountains and the hazard-marked farmland, we turned *up*, heading out of Arkansas and into Missouri. We stopped for gas in Fayetteville.

Mahir stayed in the van while I filled the tank and Becks visited the station's obligatory convenience store. She'd done a remarkable job of changing her appearance while standing guard against possible CDC pursuit. Her hair was down and she'd somehow managed to trade her jacket and cargo pants for a halter top and a pair of hot-pink running shorts that might as well have been painted on and left absolutely nothing to the imagination.

I didn't need to imagine what she'd looked like without them, and it was still hard to keep from staring at her ass as she sauntered toward the convenience store doors. The only aspect she hadn't been able to change were her shoes, still clunky, solid, and more "fight club" than "fashion show," but in that outfit, I doubted anyone was going to be looking at her feet.

Sometimes you're such a guy, said George.

"Yeah, well, I'm the one who isn't dead yet, remember?"

I was stating a fact, not making a complaint.

I snorted and hit the button to start fueling up. If the CDC clued to the fact that we were using a Garcia Pharmaceuticals company ID to pay our bills, we were fucked, but our cash ran out in Little Rock and it wasn't like we had another choice. The truth may set you free. It won't fill your fuel tank.

Mahir's proposed route was a good one, cutting through the corner of Missouri and into Kansas. From there, we'd travel through Colorado, Wyoming, and Utah before hitting the home stretch across Nevada. Of the six states we'd be crossing before we got to California, only two had laws forbidding self-service fueling stations, and those were the two we'd be spending the least overall time in: Colorado and Utah. If we paced ourselves right, we'd be able to avoid stopping in either state for anything longer than a bathroom break. That was good. The more we could stay away from people, the better.

While the tank filled, I washed the windshield, checked the tires, and did my best not to think about the fact that we were running from an organization that had the power to declare martial law without any justification more sophisticated than a sneeze. I couldn't believe the CDC was doing this alone, or that the entire CDC was involved—Kelly clearly hadn't been, and I was willing to bet that all the other team members who'd died hadn't been either. Still, a properly seated cabal of people willing to do anything to get their way is more than enough to be a major problem, especially when they have essentially infinite resources to throw around. At the same time, they were obviously trying to stay at least somewhat under the radar, or they wouldn't be bothering with artificial outbreaks and assassinations made to look like natural deaths. All that spy shit is necessary only when you're trying to pretend you don't exist.

Becks came sauntering out of the convenience store with a paper sack in each arm and a smug, cat-that-ate-the-canary smile curling her lips. It faded as soon as she was close enough to be out of the cashier's sight, and she yanked the van's rear door open without so much as a hello as she scrambled to get herself and our supplies inside. I unhooked the fuel pump and opened the driver's-side door, sliding myself behind the wheel.

"Any problems?" I asked, twisting to watch Becks unpack bottles of water, sodas, and snack food all over the backseat. We'd told her to buy as much as she could without attracting suspicion. Apparently, this meant focusing on things that made it look like she was heading for a bachelorette party, including a bottle of cheap Everclear knockoff and seventeen bags of M&Ms.

"Next time *you're* wearing the 'look at my titties' shirt, and *I'm* filling the tank." She chucked a bag of M&Ms at my head. I caught it and passed it to Mahir. "No, no problems. If they're running our pictures on the news, the dickhead working the counter didn't know anything about it. There's been a minor outbreak alert in Memphis, and the area around the CDC there is on lockdown, but it wasn't a big enough deal to peel Dicky's eyes off my ass."

"See, I wouldn't get the same results with that shirt. I just don't have the figure for it. Mahir might do a little better. We can try it next time we stop." I leaned into the back to grab a bottle of Coke before she could chuck that at my head, too. "We're good to go, then?"

"Should be." Becks pulled her jacket back on before opening one of the bags of M&Ms. "Mahir, make sure you're running weather projections on our route. They had a storm advisory up while I was checking out."

"Right," he said, and grabbed a drink before he started pecking away at his phone.

I slid my soda into the van's drink holder and started the engine. We'd been holding still long enough, and we had a long damn way to go before we'd be anything resembling safe.

We crossed into Kansas an hour later, and I risked pulling off the road, into the parking lot of an abandoned pre-Rising rest stop. The gate across the entrance wasn't even chained. If we wanted to go in there and get eaten, that was our problem, not the local government's. "We should report them for negligence," muttered Becks, as we pushed the gate out of our way.

"That's good," I said agreeably. "How are we going to explain what we're doing out here? Are we on a sightseeing tour of the haunted corn-fields of North America or something?"

She glared at me. I shrugged and got back into the van, pulling forward until we were completely hidden from the road by the overgrown trees surrounding what must have once been a pretty nice picnic area. People used to bring kids and their dogs to places like this, letting them run wild on the grass to burn off a little energy before they got back into the car and continued their drive toward the American dream. These days, that kind of thing will get you thrown in jail for child abuse. Not even the Masons were that crazy, and they did a lot of dangerous things with me and George while we were growing up. Running around in the grass near an unsecured structure and a bunch of trees is a good way of taking yourself out of the gene pool.

Becks stood guard with her rifle while I took the fire-and-forget phone over to the remains of a barbecue pit. Mahir followed me, observing without comment as I beat the phone with a large rock, tossed it into the hole, and set it on fire. A few squirts of lighter fluid from the travel kit made sure that it kept burning, delicate circuitry and memory chips melting into slag under the onslaught of the flames.

"Hey, check it out, Mahir—the green wires burn purple. What's up with that?" No answer. I looked up. "Mahir?"

He was staring toward the low brick building that contained the rest-rooms and water fountains like a man transfixed. "Why haven't they torn this thing down?" he asked. "It's like a bloody crypt, right in the middle of what ought to be civilization."

"I don't know. Maybe they don't have the money. Maybe they think it's better to give the infected someplace they can hide, so they'll know where to go when they start getting outbreak reports." I squirted more lighter fluid onto my makeshift pyre. "Maybe the people who live around here would feel like it was too much like giving up. Leave the walls standing so we can build a new roof when the crisis is over. Don't tear down something you're going to want to use later."

"Do you really think people are going to want to go to places like this ever again? Even if we kill all the damn zombies, we'll remember where the dangers were."

"Will we?" I stuck the lighter fluid back into my pocket. My hands were smudgy with old ash from the barbecue pit, and I wiped them carelessly clean against the seat of my jeans. "People have pretty short memories when they want to. It'll take a few generations, but give them time, and things like this will be all the rage again. Just watch."

"Assuming we ever get to that point."

"Well, yeah. Which is going to take people not trying to kill us for a little while." The bottle of knockoff Everclear Becks picked up at the convenience store turned out to make an excellent accelerant. I dumped it out over the fire. The flames leapt up and then died back down, burning off the additional fuel in seconds.

Mahir snorted. "That would be a rather impressive change."

"Wouldn't it?" I kicked some dirt onto the remaining flames. "If we burn this place down, you think we'll get in trouble for arson?"

"I think we'll get medals from the bloody civic planning commission."

"Cool." I kicked more dirt onto the fire. That would have to be good enough; we didn't have time to dawdle. "Come on. Let's get out of here before Darwin decides we need a spanking."

Becks looked over as we approached, nodding her chin curtly toward the smoke still wafting up from the barbecue pit. "We done here?" she asked.

"Unless you want to stick around and make s'mores, yeah, we are."

She snorted. "I suppose we'd roast our marshmallows on sticks and tell each other ghost stories after the sun went down?"

"Something like that." I reached for the van door and paused, looking at Mahir, who was staring up at the sky. "What now?"

"Look at those clouds." He sounded faintly awed. Becks and I exchanged a glance, tilted our heads back, and looked.

Growing up in California meant George and I never really experienced that much in the way of what most people would consider "weather." We got more in the way of "climate." Still, even California gets rained on, and I know what a cloud looks like when it's getting ready to storm in earnest. The clouds forming overhead were blacker than any that I'd ever seen, hanging low in the sky and visibly heavy with rain. They were coming together at a disturbing rate. The sky wasn't exactly clear when we pulled off, but it hadn't been anything like this.

Becks whistled low. "That is *some* storm," she said.

"Yeah, and we get to drive in it." I opened the van door. "As long as we don't get washed away, this could actually work in our favor. If that sucker comes down as hard as it looks like it's going to, we're gonna be a bitch to track."

"Saved by the storm," said Mahir. "I suppose it's true that stranger things have happened."

Becks rolled her eyes. "I hate to be the one to get all negative on you two, but we're in Kansas, and we're planning to *be* in Kansas for hours. Isn't this where Dorothy was when that whole 'twister ride to Oz' thing happened? Does either of you know how to recognize a tornado? Because I don't. It might be a good idea for us to find a motel and hole up until this blows over."

I shook my head. "That might be the smart thing to do, but it's not an option. If the CDC is following us, they're going to expect us to wait out the storm. This could be the best shot we have at getting clear." Becks still looked unconvinced. I didn't blame her; I wasn't entirely convinced myself. "Look, we'll keep the weather advisory running on Mahir's phone. It's a nonspecific enough program that no one should be able to use it to track us, and if it starts flashing 'Get off the road, assholes,' we'll pull off until the storm passes. Okay?"

"Okay," she said, slowly. "But if we get blown to Oz, I'm going to drop a house on your ass."

"See, that's the sort of compromise I can live with." I got into the van. Becks and Mahir did the same.

You really sure this is the right plan? asked George.

"Absolutely not," I muttered, and started the engine.

We backed out of the rest area a little at a time. Once we were on the road, Mahir got out to close the gate, Becks covering him with her rifle the whole time. The highway was clear in all directions. What travelers we might have had to deal with were clearly all smarter than we were and had chosen to get out of the path of the oncoming storm. The van shuddered as the wheels left the cracked pavement of the rest area entrance for the smooth, well-maintained asphalt of U.S. 400, running west, toward California.

The light faded out a little bit at a time, until I was driving with the lights on in what should have been the middle of the day. The wind picked up as the light slipped away, and the flatness of Kansas offered no real shelter. The van rattled and fought against me until I was forced to slow to forty miles an hour, Mahir still tapping away in the front passenger seat. Becks stayed crouched in the back with her rifle in one hand and a chocolate bar in the other, munching as she watched out the window. As long as it kept her awake, I really didn't care what she wanted to do. I was going to need her to take over driving duties before too much longer, at least if we wanted to get out of this storm without smashing the van by the side of the road.

Kansas stretched out in front of us like a bleak alien landscape, the shadows cast by the clouds turning everything strange. I turned the radio on just to break the silence, pushed down the gas a little more, and drove onward, into the dark.

We didn't know. There was nothing we could have done, and we didn't know. You can't shoot the wind. You can't argue with the clouds. There was nothing, *nothing* we could have done to stop the storm, and even if there had been, we didn't know. There was no fucking way for us to know. Nothing like that had ever happened before, and we didn't know.

It wasn't our fault. And if I say that enough times, maybe I'll start believing it. Oh, fuck.

It wasn't our fault. We didn't know.

Oh, God, we didn't know.

—From *Adaptive Immunities*,
the blog of Shaun Mason, June 24, 2041. Unpublished.

Twenty-two

We crossed Kansas on the leading edge of the storm, chasing the light until the sun went down and we were driving in darkness so absolute that it was oppressive. The clouds covered the sky until they blocked out all traces of the stars, and when the rain started—about half an hour after the sun went down—visibility dropped to almost zero, even with the high beams on.

Becks took over driving after the rain started, while I moved to the back and the increasingly futile task of watching for pursuit. We hadn't spotted anybody yet, but that didn't mean no one was coming; it just meant they'd been careful enough to stay out of sight. There was a chance the rain would make them careless, driving them closer as they tried to keep from losing us. Of course, there was also a chance I'd wind up shooting myself in the leg if I tried to fire under these conditions. Sadly, that was a risk we had to take.

There was one good thing about the way the wind was howling; with Becks and Mahir in the front seat and me at the rear, they wouldn't be able to hear me over the storm. "Christ, George, will you listen to that?" I whispered. "It's like it wants to blow us all the way back to California."

I don't like it, she said, tone clipped and razor-sharp with tension. It felt almost like I'd see her if I turned my head just a little to the side, watching the other side of the van with her favorite .40 in her hands as she scanned the road for trouble. I didn't turn. She added, *There's something not right about all this. Why aren't they coming after us yet?*

"Maybe they're not sure it was us." The excuse sounded stupid almost before it was out of my mouth. The people Dr. Wynne was working with had to know he'd sent Kelly to infiltrate us—he couldn't have triggered the outbreak in Oakland remotely, and he certainly couldn't have called in an air strike without somebody to approve it. Finding Kelly dead in his lab might confuse the legit members of the CDC, but the corrupt ones would know exactly who must have brought her back to Memphis, and they'd be watching the roads. So where were they?

This is too easy.

"I know." I took a breath, scanning what little of the road was still visible through the darkness and the pounding rain. I almost wished there was someone else out there. At least a second pair of headlights would have broken up the black a little bit. "I think we fucked up, George. I think we fucked up big."

We should have come up with a better plan. There has to have been another way. Her voice turned bitter. *If anyone should have known better, it was me.*

I didn't argue with her. George was stubborn even when she was alive. Dead, she was basically impossible to convince of anything she didn't agree with. "So now we head home, we regroup, and we head someplace where we can be invisible. We can't stay with Maggie anymore. It's not safe."

We can't leave her there alone, either. I could almost see the resignation on her face as she added, in an intentional echo, *It's not safe.*

"Fuck," I whispered, and settled against the seat, eyes still on the road.

Maggie never needed to be a blogger. She never needed to be anything. She had her parents' money and could have spent her entire life doing nothing as ostentatiously as possible. I've never been sure how she and Buffy met. It never really mattered. They were friends when Maggie joined the site, and they stayed friends right up until the day that Buffy died. She was our only real choice to take over the Fictionals, and she'd done an amazing job from day one...and she never needed to. Most people come to the news because there's something driving them, something that they need to find a way to cope with. Maggie was just looking for something to do with her time. She did it well, she did it professionally, and now she was in just as much danger as the rest of us.

She knew the job was dangerous when she took it, George said. She was trying to be reassuring. She was failing.

"Really?" I asked. "Because Buffy didn't."

Not even George had an answer to that one.

"Shaun?" Mahir pitched his voice just short of a shout to be heard above the roaring wind. "The wireless has gone out. We've no more GPS connection from here, so we're going to need to pray for clarity of road signs."

"That's awesome," I called back, as deadpan as I could manage. "What's our last known position?"

"We crossed into Colorado about twenty minutes ago," shouted Becks.

"I'm going to go around Denver—cut through Centennial and skip Wyoming entirely. You can have the wheel when we hit Nevada."

"Deal." I crawled over the back of the seat, turning to face the front of the van. "But I have to get some sleep before I drive again. Mahir, can you watch the back? Just scream if anything looks funny."

"I think I can manage that," said Mahir, unbuckling his belt.

I stretched out on the middle seat as he worked his way past me. A bag of cheap potato chips from the first convenience store made a decent, if funky-smelling, pillow, and my jacket was a better blanket than I've had in some motels. I closed my eyes, listening to the howling wind and the sound of modern country drifting from the radio. George's phantom fingers stroked my forehead, soothing some of the tension away, and the world faded out as I slipped into a shallow doze.

I woke up several hundred miles and five and a half hours later. Mahir was asleep in the rear seat of the van, and the radio was blasting—not that you could really tell. The cloud cover seemed lighter here, allowing a few traces of what might have been sunlight to cut through. The wind was still committed to playing storm, screaming even louder than it had been when I went to sleep. I sat up groggily, rubbing the grit from my eyes, and swallowed twice to clear my throat before I rasped, "Where are we?"

"About thirty miles into Nevada," said Becks. She sounded exhausted. I was going to ask how she was still awake when I noticed the drift of Red Bull cans covering the floor. Those hadn't been there when I went to sleep.

I rubbed my eyes again. "Another supply run?" I guessed.

"Sort of." Becks met my eyes in the rearview mirror, and I realized with a start that she was on the verge of panic. "The wireless is still out. I can't get a decent radio signal. I stopped for gas about twenty minutes ago, and the place was deserted. *Open*, but there was no one there. I grabbed what I could, filled the tank, and ran."

"Did you grab anything but Red Bull?"

"Generic donuts, enough Coke to get you through Nevada, and some salmon jerky." She returned her attention to the road. "I don't think we should stop again if we don't have to. Something's really wrong out there."

"How do you mean?" I dug around between the seats until I found the bag with the Cokes. I grabbed one of those and a box of donuts, the kind so cheap that they may as well have been dipped in faintly chocolate-flavored plastic. Then I half stood and made my way to the front passenger seat, dropping down next to her.

"I haven't seen another person since Burlington," Becks said. Her hands were clenched on the wheel hard enough to turn her knuckles white. "The streets were pretty normal there, people trying to get home before the storm really hit, people trying to stock up on the things they didn't keep in the house—about what you'd expect. We rolled through Centennial so late that it wasn't weird that the streets were empty, but the sun's been up for an hour now. There should be cars. There should be *commuters*, even all the way out here. So where the fuck is everybody?"

"Maybe it's a holiday?"

"Or maybe something's really, really wrong." Becks pressed the radio scan button, scowling as it skipped through a dozen channels of static before settling back on the canned modern country station she'd been listening to the night before. "All my live news is off the air. There's nothing running but the preprogrammed music channels. I'd kill for an Internet connection right now, I swear to God. Something's really wrong."

"Have you tried to call anyone?" Making a call on an unsecured phone line could potentially blow our position. It was a last resort. With what Becks was saying, I wouldn't have questioned the choice.

She exhaled slowly, and nodded. "I did."

"And?"

"And I couldn't get a connection." Her hands clenched even tighter on the wheel. "The circuits were all full. I couldn't even get through to nine-one-one. Nobody's home, Shaun. Nobody's home anywhere in the country."

"Hey." I put a hand on her shoulder. "Take a deep breath, okay? I'm sure there's a totally reasonable explanation for all this. There usually is."

"Really?" asked Becks.

Really? asked George.

"No," I said. "But we've got a long way to go before we get back to Maggie's, so let's try to stay calm until we get there. I'd like to avoid having a fatal accident, if that's cool with you." I glanced back at Mahir, who was still flopped in the rear seat with his eyes closed. He was using one of Kelly's sweaters as a blanket. I guess there was no reason for him not to. It's not like she was going to be wearing it again.

Becks sighed. "I guess you're right."

"You know I'm right. It's the most annoying thing about me."

She actually smiled a little at that one. "True."

"When did Mahir go down?"

"Half an hour or so outside of Centennial. I figured there wasn't any harm in it. The only thing that's going to kill us on a road this empty is an air strike, and it's not like he could watch for that. Besides, he was falling asleep anyway. I just gave him permission to stop pretending he wasn't."

"Poor guy. He's really not used to field conditions."

"Shaun, *no one* is used to this kind of field condition. Zombie mobs, abandoned malls, skateboarding through ghost towns, sure, we're trained for that. Going up against the Centers for Disease Control in order to figure out who's behind a global conspiracy? Not so much. That's not why I became an Irwin."

"So why did you?"

She blinked at me, surprised. "What?"

"Why *did* you become an Irwin?" I waved a hand at the windshield, indicating the storm. "Worrying about what may or may not be going on out there isn't going to get us to Weed any faster. Now tell me why you became an Irwin while I try to get enough caffeine into my system to be safe behind the wheel."

"Right. I—right." Becks took a deep breath, drumming her fingers against the wheel. "How come you never asked me this before?"

"We were already busy when you hired on with the site, and then the Ryman campaign kicked into overdrive and there wasn't time. After that... I don't know. After that, I guess I was too busy being an asshole to realize it was something I needed to ask about. I'm sorry. I'm asking now."

"Okay." Becks shook her head a little. "Okay. You know I'm from the East Coast, right?"

"Yeah. Westminster, like the X-Men."

"No, Westchester, in New York. No mutants. Lots of money. *Old* money." She glanced my way. "My parents aren't in the same weight class as the Garcias, but they're well-off enough that my sisters and I had what must have looked like a fairy-tale childhood. Dance lessons at three, riding lessons at five—yes, on actual horses. That may have been the only dangerous thing my parents ever approved of. I was supposed to go off to school, get a degree in something sensible, and come home to marry a man as well-bred and well-mannered as I was."

"So what happened?"

"I went to Vassar. My concentration was in English, with a minor in American history. Wound up getting interested in the way the nation has changed, and realized that what I really wanted was to go into the news." Becks slowed as she swerved to avoid a fallen tree branch that spanned half the road. "So I told my parents I wanted to study politics at New York University, transferred, and went for a degree in film, with a journalism minor. My parents disowned me when they found out what I was really doing, naturally."

"Naturally," I echoed, disbelieving.

Becks continued like I hadn't spoken. Maybe that was for the best. "I'd been freelancing for about eight months when I saw the job posting for the Factual News Division at your site. I was doing Action News, I was doing Factual News...I was doing everything but supporting myself. I was living in a walk-up in Jersey City, eating soy noodles for every meal. I applied almost as a Hail Mary. And I got the job."

"George was really excited about your application," I said.

"Thanks." Becks smiled a little. "I knew the Newsies weren't for me after my second press conference. I kept wanting to slap people until they got off their asses and *did* something. So I started trying to transfer. I just wanted...I don't know. I guess I wanted to do something fun for a change. I wanted to have a life before I died."

"Cool." I finished my Coke in one long swallow before wiping my mouth with the back of my hand and tossing the bottle into the back. "Thanks for telling me. I'm ready to drive, if you want to pull over."

"Yeah, well, I figure we're past the point of keeping secrets, right?" Becks began to slow. "Which reminds me. What's the flat-drop you told Alaric to do?"

I grimaced.

She shot a sharp look in my direction as she pulled the van to a stop on the shoulder of the road. "Hey, I answered yours."

"I know, I know. It's not that I don't want to answer. It's just that it's complicated." I unfastened my belt as I spoke and moved to slide between the seats, creating the space for Becks to move to the passenger side. "So. You know the situation with the Masons, right? The whole thing where they adopted George and me after their biological son died in the Rising?"

"I've read Georgia's essays on the adoption process," said Becks carefully, as she moved to take the seat I had so recently vacated.

"Yeah, well, after she died, they tried to take her files away. We even went to court over her estate. They lost. George had a really solid will. But they weren't happy about it."

"So the flat-drop—"

"Was to the Masons." I fastened my seat belt and resettled the seat, adjusting it to my height before taking the wheel. "Once those ratings-hounds get involved, there's no way this story is getting buried again. Hell, maybe we'll get lucky, and if anybody else needs to die, it'll be them."

"That's a pretty horrible thing to say about your parents."

"If they were my parents, I might feel bad about it." I looked over at Becks. "Get some sleep. I'll get us home from here."

She nodded, an expression I couldn't identify on her face. It might have been understanding. Worse, it might have been pity. "Okay."

I didn't look at her again as I pulled away from the shoulder and back onto the highway. The rain made the asphalt slick and a little hazardous, but it had been raining long enough that most of the oil had washed away, and the very structure of the highway was working in our favor. Roadwork got a lot more dangerous after the Rising, and the American highway system wound up getting some adjustments that hadn't been necessary before zombies became an everyday occurrence. In areas where flooding was a risk, the roads were slightly raised, and the drainage was improved over pre-Rising standards. It would take a flood of Biblical proportions to knock out any of the major roads, and that included the one that we were on. Let it pour. We'd still make it home.

Becks was right about one thing: The roads were deserted. I didn't see anyone else as we roared across Nevada. Even the usual police patrols were missing, which struck me as more disturbing than anything else, and every checkpoint had been set to run its blood tests on unmanned automatic. I expected the cars to come back when the rain tapered off, but they didn't. Driving along an empty, sunlit road was even more disturbing than driving alone through the darkness. At least when the storm was hanging overhead, I could blame it for the sudden desertion of America.

The radio remained mostly static, with a few stations playing preprogrammed playlists, and I couldn't restart the wireless when I was the only one awake. I kept trying the phone, but the lines were all tied up. It didn't change when we crossed the border into California, although Mahir woke up around that time, moving up to the middle seat before he asked, blearily, "Where are we?"

"California, and we're about to need to stop for gas. Becks got donuts. They're crap, but they're edible. In the bag behind me."

"Cheers." Mahir fished out a box of donuts covered in something that claimed to be powdered sugar. I didn't want to take any bets on what the covering really was. I also didn't want to put it in my mouth. Mahir didn't have any such qualms. A few minutes passed in relative silence before he asked, through a mouthful of donut, "'ow much 'ther?"

"Don't talk with your mouth full, dude. That's disgusting. We've got about another five hours to go. There's a truck stop ahead. I'll fill up while you get the wireless working, cool?"

He swallowed, and nodded. "Absolutely."

"Good."

I didn't want to admit it, but I'd been afraid to stop the van with both the others asleep. Something about the world outside the van was just too eerie, and somehow, deep down, I knew that if I stepped into that emptiness alone, I'd never come back.

The truck stop didn't help with that impression. The diner was closed, metal shutters drawn over the windows and locked into place. There were no vehicles in sight. I kept one hand on my gun during the fueling process, and I didn't mess around with wiping down the windows or checking the grill. Something about this whole thing was making my nerves scream, and you can't be a working Irwin for more than a few months without learning to trust the little voice in the back of your head that tells you to get the fuck out of a bad situation.

This is not good, said George.

"You got that right," I muttered, and got back into the van. "Mahir, what's the story with the wireless?"

"No luck. All the local networks are either locked down tight or offline. I think we're running blind until we get home."

"Because we really needed this day to get worse." I jammed the key into the ignition. The van started easily—thank God, car troubles were the one thing we hadn't been forced to deal with—and we got back out on the road.

We reached the base of Maggie's driveway an hour before sunset. Becks was driving, and I was in the passenger seat, while Mahir sat in the back with his laptop plugged into the car charger, tapping relentlessly away. He'd been writing for about four hours, recording everything we'd seen or heard in true Newsie fashion. It was a comforting sound. George used to do the same thing, back when she still had fingers.

The first two gates opened like they were supposed to, recognizing our credentials and letting us drive on through. "Looks like we're home free," said Becks. "Just a little farther and—holy shit!" She hit the brakes, hard. I slammed forward, my seat belt keeping me from hitting myself on the dashboard. There was a crash from the back as Mahir—who wasn't wearing a seat belt—went sprawling.

"Jesus, Becks, what the fuck?" I demanded.

She didn't answer me. She just raised one trembling finger and pointed to the driveway ahead of us. I turned to look where she was pointing, and stared.

Normally, the third gate on Maggie's driveway is the first one that requires authorized visitors to interact with the security system. The normal system wasn't in operation today. Instead, the gate stood open, and three men in full outbreak gear stood to block the road, assault rifles at the ready. Their faces were concealed by the biohazard masks they wore, filtering their air and blocking them from all fluid or particle attacks. That, more than anything else, told me this wasn't a drill. Those masks are hell to wear. Nobody would do that without good reason.

One of the men beckoned for us to come closer. Becks crept forward until the same man waved for us to stop. He walked over to the van and tapped the muzzle of his rifle against the glass of my window. "Please lower the window, sir," he said, in case his message hadn't been clear enough.

Swallowing hard, I did as I was told. "Uh, hey," I said. "You're one of Maggie's security ninjas, aren't you? I was starting to think you were a myth."

"Credentials."

"Right." I dug out my wallet and handed him my license card.

"All three of you."

"Got it. Becks? Mahir? A little help here?"

"Here," said Becks, shoving her card into my hand. Mahir followed suit.

I passed both cards to the security ninja. "So does this have anything to do with the total disappearance of the population of the American Midwest? Because we're a little creeped out right now, and I'd really like to get to the bathroom." I was babbling to cover my sudden conviction that something, somehow, had happened to Maggie and Alaric. We were driving into a murder investigation. We had to be. It was the only thing that made sense.

The security ninja didn't answer me. He fed our cards into a handheld reader, one at a time, before handing them back to me and waving one of the other men forward. This man carried a stack of top-of-the-line blood testing units—the same model we used to confirm that George had been infected.

"Please distribute these to the rest of your party," said the first man, as the second man carefully passed the test units through the window to me. He avoided touching my fingers, like I might be carrying a contagion that could somehow travel through his triple-lined Kevlar gloves and burrow into his skin. Not even Kellis-Amberlee can do that. The live virus has only ever traveled through direct fluid contact, thank God, or we'd all have been shambling our way around the world a long damn time ago.

I handed a test unit to Becks and held another out behind me, waiting until I felt Mahir take it out of my hand. I didn't take my eyes off the man in the outbreak gear. This wasn't outbreak *protocol*. They shouldn't have been outside at all, and if they were, they should have started firing as soon as we came into range. "What's going on?"

"Please open your test unit."

There were three security ninjas I could see, which meant there were probably half a dozen more that I couldn't. If they were all armed as heavily as the ones guarding the road, making trouble would be a good way to get dead without actually accomplishing anything. I frowned and popped the lid of the testing unit up, sliding my entire hand inside. The lid clamped down, holding my hand in position with the fingers spread for optimal sampling. Small snaps from beside and behind me told me that Becks and Mahir were doing the same. I kept watching the security ninja, trying to figure out what was going on.

The security ninja's mask wasn't directed toward my face anymore. It was directed at the lights on my testing unit. I realized with a start that his companions had moved to flank the van, putting them into position to shoot any one of us the second a test came back positive. That would fill the interior of the van with blood, turning it into a mobile hot zone, filling the enclosed space with the sharp tang of gunpowder—

Blood drying on the walls in half a dozen different shades, reds and browns and oh, God, George, I don't think that I can do this without you. I don't think I'm allowed to do this without you. So take it back, okay? Take back the blood, open your eyes, and if you've ever loved me, come back, take the blood away and come back—

George's voice cut through the sudden jangle in my head with clear, soothing calm: *That was a long time ago; that was a different van. Your test is clean.*

"What?" I said, before I could remember that talking to myself in front of strangers isn't a good idea.

The security ninja either didn't notice or had been briefed on my little idiosyncrasies. "I appreciate your cooperation, Mr. Mason," he said. A fourth man had appeared from somewhere—I wasn't sure I wanted to know exactly where, or how many friends he had lurking out there. He was carrying a large biohazard bag. "If you would collect the units and return them, we'll be glad to allow you to continue on your way."

"Uh, yeah." I took the bag with my free hand, dropping my green-lit testing unit inside before passing the bag to Becks. "Now do you want to tell us what's going on? Because seriously, we have no idea, and you're freaking me out more than a little."

"Me, too," contributed Becks.

"Myself as well," said Mahir. He leaned forward to drop his testing unit into the bag in Becks's hands. "I think we can safely declare this the worst vacation I have ever taken."

"Mr. Mason, Ms. Atherton, Mr. Gowda." The security ninja held out his hand. After a pause, Becks handed the bag back to me, and I handed it to him. He pulled it out of the van, handing it to the fourth man, who promptly vanished back into the brush surrounding the road. "If you would please continue on to the house, Ms. Garcia is anxiously awaiting your arrival."

And had probably been notified by the security system as soon as we passed the first gate. "You're not going to tell us what's going on, are you?"

"Please continue on to the house." The security ninja paused. When he spoke again, he sounded a lot more human, and a lot more frightened. "It isn't safe for you to be out here. It isn't safe for anyone to be out here. Now roll up those windows, and *go*."

"Got it. Thanks." I rolled up my window and turned to Becks, who looked like she couldn't decide between being terrified and being furious. "You heard the man. Let's get the hell out of here before they decide to shoot us just to be sure."

"Oh, right." Becks slammed her foot down on the gas, and we roared onward, up the circling driveway.

The other gates were standing open, each one flanked by a pair of men in outbreak gear. Whatever was happening, it was bad enough to mobilize the private security force that Maggie's parents maintained for her. That was terrifying, in and of itself.

Maggie's door was closed, and all the shades were drawn. They didn't twitch as we pulled to a stop in front of the house. Becks turned off the engine and simply sat there, staring through the windshield.

"Now what?" she asked.

"Now we grab whatever we absolutely can't live without and run for the house," I replied, picking up the bag with my laptop and guns in it. "Whatever the fuck is going on, it's bad enough to have men in outbreak suits on Maggie's driveway. Assume that once we're inside, we're not coming out again for anything short of the apocalypse."

"Funny, that," said Mahir. "I'm rather concerned that's what we're going in to hide from."

On the count of three, said George.

"Okay. One, two—" and I was out of the van, slinging my bag over my shoulder as I ran for the house. Doors slammed behind me as Becks and Mahir followed, the one only slightly faster than the other.

There was no blood test required to get inside the house. Once you were past the security on the driveway, you were clean—or that had always been the assumption before, anyway. I swung open the front door to find myself staring at an emergency air lock, the kind that can be slotted into place to block any standard hallway or door frame. This one was set far enough into the front hall that it left room for the three of us, and not much more than that.

There was no doggy door in the air lock. Whatever was going on, the bulldogs weren't being allowed out either.

Mahir and Becks piled in behind me while I was still staring at the air lock in dismay. As soon as Mahir was past the door frame, the door slammed itself shut. He twisted to try the knob, eyes widening. "The bloody thing's gone and locked on us," he said.

"Somehow, not surprised."

"Greetings," said the air lock.

We all jumped.

It was Becks who collected herself first, clearing her throat before she said, "Hello, house. What do you need us to do?"

"Please remove all exterior layers of clothing and place them in the chute for sterilization." A panel slid open at the base of the air lock, displaying a metal box.

"You want us to *strip*?" The words burst out before I could stop them.

"Please remove all exterior layers of clothing," repeated the house, with the infinite patience of the mechanical. "Once all potentially contaminated materials have been placed in the chute for sterilization, blood testing can begin."

Mahir cleared his throat. "Excuse me, but—"

"Failure to comply will result in sterilization."

Okay, maybe not *infinite* patience. "What about our equipment?" I asked. "Our laptops can't survive a full sterilization."

A second panel slid open next to the first. "Please place your equipment inside," said the house. "Anything that is not contaminated will be returned to you. All fabrics will be isolated and sterilized. Any materials that test positive for contamination will be destroyed. You have five minutes remaining in which to comply."

"Let's stop arguing with the creepy house and just do what it says, okay?" I slung my bag into the equipment chute before hauling my shirt off over my head and stuffing it into the clothing chute. "I don't really feel like getting sterilized today."

"The things I do for journalism," muttered Mahir, and took off his shirt.

In under a minute, the three of us were standing there barefoot in our underwear, trying to look at anything but each other. Since we were crammed in like sardines, that wasn't easy. The panel in the air lock door didn't close until the last of our clothing had been shoved through. "Please place your hands on the test panels," said the house, voice still mechanically calm. "Your testing will commence as soon as everyone is in compliance."

"I fucking hate talking machines," I muttered, and slapped my palm down on the nearest panel.

Getting Mahir and Becks access to their respective panels practically required us to play a game of standing Twister in the hall. I'd never noticed how narrow the damn thing was until I was penned in it. Finally, all three of us were in skin contact with the house security system. Three sets of lights clicked on, beginning to cycle rapidly between red and green.

"We haven't encountered any contagions between here and the gate," said Mahir. He sounded uncertain. I didn't blame him. I wasn't feeling all that certain myself.

"What if that's the problem?" asked Becks, giving voice to the one thought I was trying desperately not to have. "Maybe that's why there was no one on the roads—why those men were all wearing masks. Maybe the virus has finally gone airborne."

"It's already airborne," I said. That was true—Kellis-Amberlee is an airborne virus with a droplet-based transmission vector—but it wasn't the point. Becks wasn't talking about the passive, cooperative version of Kellis-Amberlee, the one that protects us all from colds and cancer. She was talking about the live version, the one that turns us into shambling zombies who'd eat our own families in order to fuel the virus powering our bodies.

"I suppose we'll know in a moment, won't we?" said Mahir. As if on cue, the lights started settling on green. Becks was the first, followed by Mahir's. Mine kept flashing for a few seconds more, just long enough to start making my chest get tight. Then the light settled on green, and the air lock hissed as it unsealed.

"Thank you for your compliance," said the house.

I directed my middle fingers at the ceiling.

Mahir and Becks pushed past me while I was distracted by telling the house to go fuck itself, stepping out of the air lock and into the living room where Maggie and Alaric were waiting. Becks ran to hug Alaric, while Mahir stepped off to one side, crossing his arms over his chest and looking self-conscious. I stepped out of the air lock, looking cautiously around.

Inside the house, it was obvious that the shades weren't just drawn; they were locked down, reinforced with sheets of clear plastic. The floor was practically covered with diminutive bulldogs, the entire pack forced inside by whatever emergency was at hand.

Maggie walked calmly over to me, slapped me hard across one cheek, and then, while I was still staring at her in confusion, throwing her arms around my shoulders. "We thought you were dead," she hissed, through gritted teeth. "You didn't call, and you didn't call, and we thought you were *dead*. You *asshole*. Next time, find a way to send a fucking message."

"How about there's not a next time? Can we do that, instead?" Maggie was clothed. I essentially wasn't, which was making this hug even more awkward than it would normally have been. I extricated myself from her embrace, looking around the room again. "I know we said to close the windows, but I didn't mean you had to go quite this far."

"Wait—what?" Alaric pulled away from Becks, looking utterly bemused. "What do you mean? After you told us to close the windows—don't you know what's going on out there?"

Maggie studied my face for a moment, horror dawning in her expression. "Oh, my God," she whispered. "You really don't know. You have no idea, do you?"

"No idea about what?" I shook my head. "We haven't seen anyone since Kansas, but we thought it was just the storm keeping people inside—"

"It's not just the storm." Alaric walked across the room with sharp, jerky motions and grabbed the television remote, turning the TV on. He hit another button and the infomercial that had been playing disappeared, replaced by CNN.

The picture showed a flooded street, helpfully labeled "Miami—Live Footage." A newscaster was speaking in a low, anxious tone, saying something about death tolls and tracking survivors. I didn't really hear him. I was transfixed by the picture, my brain refusing to accept what my eyes were telling me.

As always, it was George who grasped the reality of the situation first, and her understanding allowed me to understand. *Oh, my God . . .* she said, horrified.

I couldn't argue.

The street was choked with debris and abandoned cars, brown-and-white water swirling everywhere as it tried to force itself down clogged sewer drains. They should have been cleared before the flooding could get this bad, and the city had tried to clear them; that much was obvious from the number of people in fluorescent orange shirts who were shambling down the street, moving jerkily along with the rest of the mob. I had never seen that many infected in one place. I counted fifty before my brain shut down, refusing to process any more.

"—we repeat, the federal government has declared the state of Florida a hazard zone. Uninfected citizens are urged to stay in your homes and await assistance. Anyone found on the street may be shot without warning. Anyone leaving their home will be assumed infected and treated with the appropriate protocols. Please stay in your homes and await assistance. Please..." The newscaster faltered, losing the rhythm of his carefully prepared statement. The footage of the flood was silent. Even recorded moaning can bring zombies to your position.

Recovering himself, the newscaster said, "Reports of similar outbreaks are coming in from Huntsville, New Orleans, Baton Rouge, and Houston. We don't have numbers yet, but the death tolls are estimated to be in the thousands, and are climbing steadily." He paused again, longer this time, before saying, "Some sources are referring to the event as the second Rising. God forgive me, but I'm not so sure they're wrong. God forgive us all."

There was a rattling noise, like someone putting a microphone down, and then the sound of footsteps. The silent footage of the flood, and the infected, continued to play.

"That's what's going on," Alaric said. His voice was toneless, and I remembered with a start that his family lived mostly in Florida. "The second Rising. You drove right through the middle of it, and you didn't notice."

"Oh, my God," I whispered, echoing George's earlier statement. The picture on the TV jumped, the label at the bottom changing to "Huntsville." The newscaster didn't return. "Is this for real?"

"It's real," said Maggie.

It's the end of the world, said George, and I silently agreed.

Maggie was crying without any sign of shame, tears running down her cheeks. Her nose was chapped; she'd been crying off and on for a while. She reached for my hand, and I didn't pull away, letting her lace her fingers through mine. Becks moved to stand next to Alaric, and he took her in his arms again, holding her against his chest. All five of us stood transfixed, staring at the television.

Staring at the end of the world.

BOOK V

The Rising

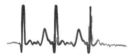

The one thing I have absolute faith in is mankind's capacity to make things worse. No matter how bad it gets, we're all happy to screw each other over. It's enough to make me wonder if we should have let the zombies win.

—Shaun Mason

I believe in the truth. I believe in the news. And I believe in Shaun. Everything else is extra.

—Georgia Mason

Shaun had a close call today.

He won't tell me exactly what happened; I wouldn't even know anything *had* happened if it weren't for the glitches in his video feed, the places where the picture cut out and picked back up again a few hundred seconds later. The footage he posts from the field is usually seamless, smooth and easy and effortless looking. Not this. This is amateur-hour stuff, and that tells me more clearly than anything else possibly could that whatever happened out there, it was bad.

He came home stinking like bleach and rank terror-sweat, the kind that comes after the adrenaline fades, and he didn't stop hugging me for almost ten minutes. I stopped laughing and trying to get away when I felt his shoulders shaking. My own shoulders started shaking when I realized what that sort of fear from Shaun—Shaun! Who once called a zombie in our backyard the best present I'd ever given him—actually meant.

Maybe life was always fragile and easy to lose, and maybe all those people who talk about how good things were before the Rising are full of crap, but we don't live in that world; we live in this one. And in this world, it takes only one slip, one unguarded moment, to lose every-thing. I don't know how close I came to losing him today. He won't tell me, and maybe this makes me a coward, but I'm not going to ask. This is one truth I have no interest in knowing. There are some truths we're better off without.

I don't know what I'd do without him. I really don't. I'd never tell him to stay out of the field—I know how much it means to him—but one day, the close call is going to cross the line into "too close," and after that...I don't know.

I just don't know.

**—From *Postcards from the Wall*,
the unpublished files of Georgia Mason,
originally posted June 24, 2041**

My parents, Yu and Jun Kwong, are dead.

My brother, Dorian Kwong, is dead.

My colleague, Dr. Barbara Tinney, is dead.

While reports are currently sketchy, it is entirely possible that the state of Florida, and much of the surrounding region, is dead.

Welcome to the end of the world.

—From *The Kwong Way of Things*,
the blog of Alaric Kwong, June 24, 2041

Twenty-three

Yes, I'll hold," snarled Mahir, and continued pacing. I barely noticed. I couldn't take my eyes away from the television, where CNN continued to faithfully record the worst disaster to strike the human race since the summer of 2014, when the dead first decided to get up and nosh on the living.

Maggie sat next to me on the couch, even more fixated on the news than I was. Her interest in the situation was a little more proprietary than mine; Garcia Pharmaceuticals owned three factories and a research center in the affected area, and with the fatality reports updating every few seconds, a moment's inattention could mean missing the deaths of people she'd known her entire life.

Alaric and Becks had retired to the kitchen after the first hour. Alaric was trying to get the wireless up and running, while Becks was cleaning her guns and checking the catches on the windows—just in case. It was a sentiment I could appreciate, even if I couldn't find it in myself to move.

That's enough, said George abruptly. The television was showing a school bus packed with refugees being besieged by the living dead. The people inside were screaming; I could see their faces through the windows. As long as they were screaming, they were still essentially human. They were past saving. I hoped that infection took them quickly, or that someone had enough bullets to—

Shaun! George's shout was enough to shock me out of my stupor. It's amazing how loud something like that can seem when it's coming from inside your head.

I turned to glare at the air to my left. Maggie, sunk deep in her own fugue state, didn't appear to notice. "What?" I demanded.

George folded her arms and glared back. "You're not doing anyone any good sitting there like a media consumer, you know. You need to be finding out what the hell is going on."

"And how do you suggest I do that, huh?" I spread my arms, indicating the television and Mahir—still pacing and snarling into his phone—with the same gesture. "Things are sort of shitty right now, George, in case you failed to notice."

"Oh, trust me, I noticed, I just don't see where I need to *care*." George grabbed my arm and hauled me to my feet. "Come on. You've got work to do." Giving me a slow look, she added, "And some clothes to put on. God, Shaun, are you really sitting around watching television in your boxers? That's just sad."

"If there's all this work, why don't you do it?"

"Because I'm dead, remember?" She kept hold of my wrist as she spoke, pulling me toward the kitchen. "You need to ask Alaric whether Maggie moved our van into the garage before things locked down." Catching my blank expression, she sighed. "Come on, Shaun, try to keep up for, like, thirty seconds while you're losing your mind, okay? If we can get to the van without going outside, we can get to our emergency wireless booster."

My eyes widened. "Crap, you're right. We still have that thing, don't we?"

"Unless you threw it away in a moment of unrepeated sanity and then didn't tell me about it, yeah, we do."

Being on a news team with Buffy Meissonier meant dealing with a girl who was occasionally twenty pounds of crazy crammed into a ten-pound sack, and who eventually sold us out to the government conspiracy that got George killed. It also meant working with the best espionage technician I've ever encountered, either in the private sector or working for the government. She could make computers do things I'm not sure even science fiction considers possible, and she did it all while wearing holo-foil butterflies in her hair and T-shirts claiming that some dude named Joss was her master now. People say Buffy was good. They're wrong. Buffy was *great*.

Mahir was still shouting at the phone when George pulled me past him. He gave me a harried glance and nodded, eyes skipping straight past George. That made sense, I guess, since it's not like she was really there.

"I'm pretty sure this represents a whole new level of fucked-up crazy," I muttered, as George yanked me into the kitchen.

"I'm not the cause of your psychotic break; I'm just a symptom," she replied waspishly, and shoved me toward Becks and Alaric.

Becks, like Mahir, had managed to dress while I was staring at the television and was wearing combat boots, a black tank top, and camouflage pants—the Irwin equivalent of a uniform. She and Alaric were sitting at the table, him with his laptop pulled as close to his body as it would go, leaving the rest of the space for her. She had what looked like a small armory spread out in front of her, and was in the process of reassembling a semiautomatic handgun that had yet to be legally cleared for private ownership. They looked up when they heard my footsteps.

"What's the update?" asked Becks. She snapped the magazine into place with a *click* that echoed through the kitchen, eliciting a startled yip from one of the bulldogs sprawled next to the sealed-off door.

"Nothing that's good," I replied. George had released my wrist when she got me where she wanted me, and I realized without surprise that she was gone again. That was okay by me. Her appearing and physically hauling me around the house represented a whole new level of crazy, and I wanted to avoid thinking about it for as long as possible. "Forever" seemed like an excellent place to start. "They've declared martial law in the areas that haven't been officially marked as hazard zones, and it's starting to look like they're going to mark the entire damn Gulf Coast as a Level 1 hazard."

Alaric paled. "They can't do that."

"Yes, they can." Becks put down the gun she'd been working on. "In case of an outbreak confirmed to impact more than sixty percent of the population in a given area, USAMRIID and the CDC will both recommend that a Level 1 designation be applied for the protection of the surrounding area. The government reserves the right to take their recommendation." A smile that looked more like a grimace twisted her lips upward. "Our parents voted that little jewel into law, and we never repealed it, because why should we? Outbreaks are tiny things. Bad things. It's better if we can let fifteen people die and save five thousand, right?"

"Only this time, we're going to let fifteen million die," I said. "That sounds a little different, don't you think? Alaric."

He turned to me and blinked. He was pale and stunned looking, like he still couldn't believe what was happening. That was understandable. I couldn't believe it either. "What?"

"Where's the van?" His expression didn't change. I took a careful breath, and amended, "Where's *our* van? Did Maggie have you move it to the garage after we left, or is it still parked out back?"

If the van was parked outside, there was no way I'd be able to get at it. Maybe one of Maggie's security ninjas—but that would mean trying to talk them through finding the wireless booster, and I wasn't sure my memory was good enough for that.

"I..." Alaric stopped, frowning. "It's in the garage. It was out back until you called—Maggie wanted to keep the garage open for her Fictionals when they came through—but she got spooked when you told us to hole up, and she had me move it inside, where it wouldn't be visible to satellite surveillance."

"God bless justified paranoia," I said fervently, and started toward the garage door. The bulldogs lifted their heads and whined, watching me.

"Where are you going?" asked Becks, half-rising.

"The van." I looked between them, noting their matching blank looks, and explained, "I'm pretty sure Buffy's old wireless booster is still out there. If I can get it running—"

"—we can get back online," said Alaric, his eyes widening in comprehension. "I forgot all about that thing!"

"We haven't exactly needed to use it in the last year." I started walking again. "I'll be right back. If I'm not right back, well…fuck, I don't know. If I'm not right back, throw some gas grenades into the garage and call for the security dudes to come and shoot me until I stop bleeding."

"We'll shoot you ourselves," said Becks, causing Alaric to shoot her a distressed look. She ignored it. You learn to shrug that sort of thing off after you've been in the field for a while. That, or you stop trying to talk to people who aren't Irwins.

"Thanks." I opened the garage door, shoving a bulldog aside with my foot before it could sneak by me, and slipped through.

The garage lights were motion-activated white fluorescents. They clicked on as soon as the door to the kitchen swung shut, filling the enclosed space with an even, sterile glow. I scanned the area, automatically assessing the load-bearing capacity of the shelves lining the walls and the security of the pipes connecting to the water heater and emergency backup generator. Maggie used the garage primarily for storage, cramming most of the shelves with boxes and using the ones nearest the door as an extension of the pantry. One entire floor-to-ceiling shelving unit was dedicated to bags of dried dog food. At least the bulldogs wouldn't be going crazy with hunger anytime soon.

Our van was sitting at the center of the room. It had been washed before it was put away, and its paint almost gleamed in the antiseptic light. I took a step toward it.

"Hello, Mr. Mason," said the voice of the house. It managed to sound chiding, which was a nice trick, since it didn't have normal human intonations. I stopped where I was, looking vainly for the speaker. "I am afraid the house is presently in a sealed state. You will be unable to exit, and should return to the interior."

"That's cool. I'm not trying to get out." I forced myself to relax, one inch at a time. "I just need to get something from the van."

"Attempts to break the isolation seals will be met with necessary force."

"Necessary force" was a polite way of saying that the house security system would shoot me where I stood if I looked like I was trying to get the doors open. "Noted," I said. "I'm not trying to get out, I swear. The van is right there, and I won't even be turning on the engine. Promise."

"Your compliance is appreciated," said the house, and went silent. I waited a few seconds to see if it was going to try to evict me from the garage. Nothing happened. I started for the van, moving faster this time—if the house decided I was dawdling, it might decide I was planning to escape, and then things could get really messy, really fast. Use of lethal force by private security systems has been authorized since some jackass in Arizona loaded his house guns with dummy bullets and got himself ripped apart by a pack of starving infected. His estate tried to sue the security firm that managed his defenses, and the security firm turned right around and sued the state, saying they hadn't been allowed to do the things they had to do if they wanted to keep their client alive.

"*Mangum v. Pierce Security v. the State of Arizona*," supplied George. She reached the van a few steps ahead of me, folding her arms as she leaned against the door. "Do you remember where Buffy kept the booster?"

"Hi, George. Nice to see you." I pressed my thumb against the scanner, letting the van identify me as an authorized driver. The locks clicked open. "So does this mean I'm finally going *really* crazy?"

She shrugged. Her face still looked wrong without her sunglasses, alien and familiar at the same time. "I think it means you already have a way of coping with things that are too big for you to handle. So Maggie goes into vapor lock, and Mahir shouts at the embassy trying to get a call through to his wife, and you…"

"I see dead people walking around and giving me orders. Great." I offered her a pained smile as I pulled the van door open. "At least I like having you here. This would get old damn fast if you were Mom."

George grimaced exaggeratedly. "There's a bright side to everything."

"Really? What's the bright side for Florida? Because I'm really not seeing one." Our field equipment was piled haphazardly around the van's interior, stacked on counters and taking up most of the floor space. It would take an hour, maybe more, to get the thing ready for an excursion. I couldn't blame Maggie and Alaric for putting it away in this condition—they weren't expecting to leave the house without a lot of notice, and they weren't field operatives—but I still had to grit my teeth when I saw that the weapon racks hadn't been properly secured. If we had to run for any reason, we'd all wind up getting killed by our own carelessness.

"If you're not seeing one, I can't see it either. You know that."

I bit back the urge to swear at her. Fighting with George used to be one of my best ways of blowing off steam. I've mostly tried to avoid it since she's been gone; it doesn't seem fair to start something when neither of us can really leave the room. Besides, in my saner days, I was always afraid I'd say something unforgivable and she'd leave me alone with the dark behind my eyes, and no more George, ever. I wasn't so much afraid of that anymore. We just didn't have *time* to fight.

"Hey, George, do me a favor, will you? Either go away, or stop pointing out how you're just a figment of my imagination and help me find the damn booster. I can't handle having you hanging around calling me crazy. I get enough of that from everybody else."

"Your wish is my command," she deadpanned, before climbing up to join me in the van. She couldn't touch anything, naturally, but her feet still made soft echoing sounds when they hit the floorboards, and her shadow on the walls moved just the way that it was supposed to. I had to admire the realism of my hallucinations, even though I knew that probably wasn't what most people would consider to be a good sign.

"Really? 'Cause right now, what I'm wishing for is a tank." I paused. "Maybe two tanks. Becks will probably want one, too, and I don't want to be greedy."

"Always thinking of others, that's you." Her fingers brushed the back of my neck as she moved past me. I shivered. "The last time I saw the booster, Buffy was stowing it back here, with the rest of the backup network hardware."

"We moved that around Valentine's Day, when Becks did her 'romantic places to take an Irwin' article series." I snapped my fingers. "The lockboxes!"

George leaned against the counter to watch as I dropped to my knees, rolled back the industrial rug covering the van floor, and pried up the trapdoor it had been concealing. We don't have a complete second floor in the van—the weight would have been prohibitive, not to mention the structural instability it would have introduced—but we had a few extra storage compartments built in for a rainy day during the first major retrofit. They made good hiding spots for contraband when we were doing certain types of articles, and the rest of the time, they were a convenient place to hide snack foods...or excess hardware.

The first compartment held nothing but weird-looking cartoon porn and Russian girlie magazines. I smiled despite myself. "Damn, Dave. You had smarts and you had guts, but what you did *not* have was taste."

"He was pretty much in love with Magdalene," said George.

I amended: "Most of the time, what you didn't have was taste. Sometimes, you were spot on." I pried open the second compartment. A metal box with half a dozen antennae welded to the sides was nestled in the bottom, padded by wads of duct tape. I reached down to wriggle it loose, lifting it carefully out of its cradle. "There we go."

"Remember, there's supposed to be a detached battery pack that goes with it."

"Right." I stuck my hand into the welter of duct tape, rummaging for a moment before pulling up a small metal square with a power adapter at one end and a USB port at the other. "Got it!" I held it up, turning to show her.

George was gone. Again.

I stopped for a second, looking at the space where she'd been—hadn't been—had appeared to be—only a moment before. Then I sighed, lowering the battery pack as I picked the wireless booster back up and pushed myself to my feet. "This stage of the crazy is going to get real old, real fast, you know."

Sorry. But you're still too sane to sustain that sort of breakdown for very long.

"Guess this means that whole 'not forever' thing we talked about before is sort of moot, huh?" My hands moved automatically as I spoke, pulling a bag from under the counter and sliding the wireless booster inside.

I think that depends on you, said George apologetically. *I'm not the one who needs to move on. I'm the one who's here because you still need me.*

"Yeah, well, right now? Right now, I think being crazy may be the only thing that's keeping mc sane. Come on."

I closed the van door and made my way back across the garage. The house security system didn't say anything. I guess it was smart enough to recognize that I hadn't gone near any of the exits. That, or it just wasn't in the mood to argue with me. I didn't care either way.

Alaric and Becks were still at the kitchen table, in the exact positions they were in when I went into the garage. There was one difference: Half of Becks's guns were gone, making room for me to put down the bag. "Alaric, you got an extension cord?"

"In my laptop bag," he said. As he bent to retrieve it, he asked, "Did you find the wireless booster?"

"I did. Got any idea how it works?"

"Not really."

"That explains why we stopped using it. I guess we're going to have to hope that my classic 'smack it until it works' approach can save the day." I sat, unpacking the wireless booster and connecting it to the battery pack. Alaric passed me an extension cord. I hooked it to the battery, and Becks took thc other end, plugging it into the wall.

Try not to break anything you can't fix.

"Hush, you," I said vaguely. "Working now."

Becks and Alaric exchanged a glance, but didn't say anything. That was probably the best thing they could have done.

Buffy built all her own equipment. That would have been fine—a lot of people build their own equipment—if it weren't for the fact that her idea of what equipment should look like was almost completely defined by pre-Rising television. She could put more wires, switches, and buttons on a single remote than anybody else I've ever met, and each one had a specific purpose. She also understood that by her standards, she worked with a bunch of ham-handed techno-illiterates. After the fifth time George tried to reboot a server by putting her foot through it, Buffy started putting idiot buttons on everything. They wouldn't provide access to the more complicated functions, but they'd get things going.

"Red," I mumbled. "Red, red, red…" Red buttons used to be common. They were visible, hard to miss, and universally understood as important. After the Rising, red took on another meaning: It became the color of infection, the color of danger…the color of death. Red buttons were installed on things that needed the capacity to self-destruct, and they represented the things that you should never, under any circumstances, touch. So of course Buffy, with her perverse sense of humor and pre-Rising aesthetic, made all the really good stuff red.

The center button on the booster's control panel was a glossy shade of strawberry red. Becks and Alaric knew Buffy by reputation and through staff meetings, but she was dead before they joined the standing office team. They never learned some of her little quirks. So it wasn't really surprising to see Alaric come halfway to his feet when I hit the button. Becks managed not to stand. She did have to stop herself before she grabbed my arm, but hey, at least she stopped herself.

I took my finger off the button. The wireless booster made a cheerful beeping sound as it started scanning the local network, looking for exploitable cracks in the security. I looked from Becks to Alaric, smiled, and stood.

"Give it five minutes," I said. "I'm going to get myself a Coke. Either of you want anything?"

Neither of them did.

The wireless booster clicked to itself, occasionally beeping as it verified some part of the network structure to its own satisfaction. It had been running for three of the five minutes I'd requested when Mahir came into the kitchen, rubbing his face with one hand. His glasses were propped up on his forehead, and he looked exhausted. Seeing the beeping, blinking box on the kitchen table, he slid his glasses back down and frowned. "What in bloody hell is that thing supposed to be, and what is it doing?" he asked.

"Hey, Mahir." I took a swig of Coke before saluting him with the can. "The embassy get you a connection?"

"No." He scowled. "All international lines are locked down until the cause of this incident can be determined. The damned government's thinking terrorist action, naturally. I've just had an offer of extraction back to Britain. As if the United States could hold an Indian citizen against his will."

"If this is declared an act of terrorism, I think they can," said Alaric.

Mahir paused. "You may be right," he said finally. "I'll try to avoid thinking about that for the moment. Now, does someone want to tell me what that thing is supposed to be?"

The wireless booster beeped, louder this time, and the lights along the top turned a bright sunshine yellow. I pushed away from the counter. "Hey, Alaric, check your connection."

"On it, boss." He tapped his keyboard. Then he punched the air, thrusting his arms up in a victory salute. "We have Internet!"

"Girl was a genuine genius." I finished my Coke and tossed the empty can into the sink. "That 'thing' is the original Georgette Meissonier wireless Internet booster and satellite access device. I have no clue how it works. I don't *care* how it works. All I know is that you have no signal, you plug it in, you get it to turn on, and then it finds you a signal. It—"

None of them were listening to me anymore. Alaric was typing furiously, while Becks and Mahir were in the process of hauling out their own laptops and setting to work. I looked around and shook my head.

"Thank you, Shaun. We really appreciate your getting us back into contact with the rest of the world, Shaun. You're awesome, Shaun," I said dryly.

Becks flipped me off.

"You're welcome," I said, and walked out of the kitchen.

My laptop bag was on the couch next to Maggie, who was still staring, transfixed, at the television. Her lap was full of bulldogs. I hadn't noticed that before. I touched her shoulder. She didn't react. "Hey. Maggie?" Still no response. "Maggie, hey, come on. You need to stop looking at that now. It's not doing you any good, and I think it's probably doing you a lot of bad." She still didn't react. "George…"

Just do it.

"Gotcha." The remote was on the arm of the couch. I picked it up and switched off the television before stuffing the remote into my pocket, where no one would be able to get it without my knowledge.

Maggie's protest was immediate. "Hey!" she exclaimed, looking blindly around for the missing remote control. "I was watching that!"

"And now you're not," I replied. "We have Internet again."

"We do?" Brief hope suffused her face. "Are things...did we...?"

"I dug Buffy's semilegal wireless booster out of storage. We're probably tapped into a Department of Defense satellite or something, but I think there's a good chance your parents own the satellite, so I don't give a shit. If they get pissed, you can bat your eyelashes at them and say we're sorry. Alaric's already online, Becks and Mahir are in a footrace to join him, and I figured you might want to log in and check your Fictionals. Make sure they're okay." Or as close as anyone was likely to be, under the circumstances.

Maggie isn't the sort of person who falls apart often, or for long. Her eyes cleared when I mentioned her Fictionals, and she nodded. "I'm not sure how many of them will have connectivity, but the ones who do will be worried sick." She lifted the bulldogs from her lap and set them on the couch. Two jumped down to the floor and went trotting off on unknowable bulldog errands. The third one made a fussy grunting noise, curled up, and went back to sleep.

I've never envied a dog before.

"The cities must still be online," I said. "If they knocked San Francisco off the network, they'd have riots to go with their zombies. I figure we lost connection because we're too far out in the boonies for anyone to give a shit about what happens to us."

These cold equations, said George, with a sigh.

"Exactly," I said.

Maggie pretended not to notice as she stood, brushed the dog hair from her legs, and said, "If we have Internet, we have VOIP again," she said. "I'm going to go call my parents."

I blinked. Maggie was generally happy to spend her family's money, but I'd never heard her say she was going to contact them. That was a part of her life that the rest of us really weren't invited into. "Really?"

"Really." She gave me a wry look. "Unless you want a private army descending to extract me."

"Go call your parents."

Half the dogs followed Maggie out of the living room, leaving the other half sprawled around in various stages of repose. I sat down on the couch, bracing my elbows on my knees and dropping my head into my hands as I tried to figure out our next move. No pressure or anything. It was just the end of the world.

I went through a science fiction phase when I was in my teens, around the time George was having her American history and angry beat poetry phase. We always shared the best stuff, so she learned a lot about ray guns, and I learned a lot about revolutions. There was this one story—I don't remember who the author was—about a dude who was flying a bunch of vaccine to a sick planet. The fuel was really precisely calculated, because fuel was expensive and the ship was pretty small. And this teenage girl who didn't understand stowed away on his ship. She wanted to get to her brother. Only there wasn't enough fuel to get them both to the sick planet, and she didn't know how to land the ship or deliver the vaccine. If she lived, everybody died. That was the cold equation. How many lives is one person, even a totally innocent person, going to be worth? We used to argue about that, more for fun than anything else, but we never managed to get that equation to equal anything but death.

If the outbreak was bad enough, they'd start diverting all but the most essential services to the big cities. Cold equations again: An outbreak in Weed would have a limited amount of fuel to feed it, and be geographically isolated enough to mop up without too much secondary loss of life. An outbreak in Seattle or San Francisco would kill millions, and then spill out of the city to kill millions more. We were the stowaways on this ship, and there was only enough fuel to get one person safely to the other side.

"You should call a staff meeting," said George, sitting down next to me and resting her head against my shoulder. She was affectionate like that only when we were alone, even when we were kids. She never wanted the Masons to see.

"I know." I left my head in my hands. "Maggie's crew won't be the only worried ones."

"Did we have anyone in Florida?"

"Not Florida, but we had a Newsie in Tennessee, and I think a couple of Irwins in Louisiana. They were doing the bayous." Their faces flashed behind my eyes, still photos that would have looked totally natural up on the Wall. I was grimly afraid they'd be going up there soon. Alana Cortez, who loved reptiles and had been bitten by more venomous snakes than any person has a right to survive encountering, and Reggie Alexander, a walking mountain of a man whose biggest claim to fame was the time that he punched a zombie and survived to brag about it. They were both solid, well-trained, and on the way to having lucrative careers in the news. But they'd been in Louisiana. And Louisiana wasn't there anymore.

"That makes calling a meeting even more important. If we've lost anyone, people are going to be convincing themselves that we've lost everyone."

I sighed. "Yeah, I know."

George put a hand on the back of my neck. Maybe I should have been disturbed by the fact that I could feel it, but I just couldn't work up the energy. I was too busy being grateful that she was there at all.

"Hey, George?"

"What?"

"That stuff I said before...before." Before Kelly died, before Dr. Wynne turned on us, before we fled the CDC hours ahead of a disaster of Biblical proportions—before everything. Before the world changed.

"Yeah?"

"I didn't mean it. I really, really didn't mean it." I lifted my head and she was there, looking at me with open anxiety, alien eyes grave. "Don't leave me. Please don't leave me. I can't do this without you, and if you try to make me, I don't think I'm going to be okay."

"Don't worry about that." Her smile was sad, and her hand continued to rest against the back of my neck, feeling solid and warm and alive. If this was crazy, God, I wasn't sure I was capable of wanting anything else. "I'm not going anywhere."

"Good," I whispered. I sat on the couch with my dead sister, listening to the voices from the kitchen, and wondered just how the fuck I was going to get us through this one in one piece.

...fuck it. I don't have the energy to be profound right now. Turn off your goddamn computer and go spend some time with your family before the world decides to finish ending. That's about the only profound thing that I have left.

We ran out of time, and we didn't even know that it was being metered.

—From *Adaptive Immunities*,
the blog of Shaun Mason, June 24, 2041

What he said.

—From *Charming Not Sincere*,
the blog of Rebecca Atherton, June 24, 2041

Twenty-four

The feeling of George's hand against the back of my neck eventually faded. I looked up to find myself alone. Even the usual soft sense of her at the back of my mind was gone. That didn't worry me the way it would have, once; I'd had plenty of time to adjust to the idea that her presence came and went depending on how stressed I was, how much pressure I was under, and I guess how sane I was feeling at any given moment. If she wasn't there, that must mean I was feeling better.

In the kitchen, Mahir and Alaric were typing furiously, while Becks was finishing the reassembly of what looked like her last gun for the day. Maggie was wearing a wireless headset and sitting in front of her laptop, chattering in a rapid mixture of English and Spanish. She sounded calmer. That was good, since the speed of her responses implied that whomever she was talking to wasn't calm in the least.

I hooked my thumb in her direction as I walked toward the coffee machine. George being out of the picture for the moment meant I could down a cup of real caffeine before I had to go back to caffeinated sugar water. "Who's on the line?"

"Her folks," said Becks, glancing up. "They've been talking for half an hour." The subtext—that I'd been sitting by myself in the living room for half an hour—wasn't subtle. Somehow, I didn't really care.

"Good job with the wireless booster." Mahir kept typing as he spoke, his head bowed in what could have been either concentration or prayer. "I believe Mr. Garcia was on the edge of commanding an armed extraction when she was finally able to get through and notify them as to her continuing safety."

"I could do with a little armed extraction." I took a large gulp of coffee, letting it sear the back of my throat before adding, "As long as they were willing to stay and be our private army. You think they'd stay and be a private army?"

"No," said Alaric tonelessly.

Mahir did look up at that, shooting a worried glance toward Alaric before turning to me and saying, "Internet journalists have been largely expelled from the impacted areas, and those attempting to take pictures or live blog from inside have been cited with practicing journalism without a license."

"What?" I straightened. "That's not legal."

"Becoming a blogger requires only that one establish a blog, and not necessarily even that, if one is willing to exist solely through commentary on the blogs of others. Becoming a journalist requires that one take the licensing exams, take the marksmanship exams, pass accreditation, and possess a license sufficient to allow entry to any given hazard zone, lest fines and possible charges be applied."

"Well, yeah, Mahir. Everybody knows that. What does that have to do with—"

"The individuals involved were in established hazard zones, taking actions of the sort that journalists must be properly licensed to perform." Mahir shook his head, light glinting off his glasses. "They're being held while charges are brought against them."

I gaped at him. "Wait—so—what, they're saying that when you combine 'has a blog' with 'is inside a hazard zone,' you automatically become a journalist?"

"Poof," muttered Becks.

"That's insane!"

"Insane, and very, very clever, as it's going quite a long way toward reducing the number of unapproved reports making it out of the impacted areas." Mahir's gaze skittered toward Alaric. Just for a moment, but long enough for me to see where he was looking. "Reduction doesn't mean elimination, thankfully. Some things are still getting out."

"Some things always do," I said, putting my mug down. I wasn't thirsty anymore. "Alaric? You okay, buddy?"

"The updates to the Wall started this morning," he said. Tears ran down his cheeks as he turned to look at me. He didn't bother wiping them away. Maybe he knew that drying his face wouldn't be enough to make the crying stop. "My little sister posted for our parents and our brother. Dorian shot our parents, and Alisa shot Dorian, after he'd started to turn. I always knew getting her shooting lessons for her birthday was a good idea, even if Mother wanted her to take dance classes."

I winced. "Fuck, Alaric, I'm—"

"Did it help you when I said I was sorry George died?"

Everyone said they were sorry when George died, even the Masons. And not a single apology had made a damn bit of difference. "No. It didn't help."

"Then don't say it." He looked back to his computer. "The forums are exploding. We're one of the only major sites that has people actually responding to queries."

"That's because we don't know anything."

"That's not entirely true," said Mahir. "We know the outbreak started when Tropical Storm Fiona made landfall—and that it spread with the storm. *Only* with the storm."

"Wait, what?"

"All the index cases have matched up with the initial footprint of the storm."

I stared at him. What he was saying didn't make sense. An outbreak starting when a major storm hit was reasonable, if horrifying. Storms cause devastation, they cause injuries, and they can cause a hell of a lot of cross-contamination. There have been documented cases of someone being injured in a major storm, only to have the wind carry their infected blood onto a bystander before anyone knew what was happening. But that outbreak would be geographically contained, and even though it would be horrible, it wouldn't be anything unique enough to cause the sort of devastation they were showing on the news.

If the live state of the virus had gone airborne, it would be reasonable to assume that it would spread with the storm. It would also spread *without* the storm, and while its initial footprint might have been defined by Fiona, it wouldn't stay that way. If this was a purely airborne outbreak, it should have been breaking out of any containment not defined through a complete absence of uninfected bodies.

"Wait…" I said again, slow dread worming its way into my stomach. I hadn't realized I still had the capacity to be frightened. Somehow, it wasn't a welcome discovery. "Alaric, your sister. You said she posted to the Wall. Is she all right?"

"She's scared out of her mind, and she's alone in the attic of the family condo, but she's physically fine." Alaric looked up, expression challenging me to say something as he added, "She's using the company server to chat with me."

"Good. Make sure she has a log-in of her own. If she wants to coauthor reports with you on what's going on out there, use your own discretion, but I say let her. It may take her mind off things until she's evacuated. Can you ask her a question for me?"

Alaric eyed me suspiciously. "What do you want me to ask?"

"Ask whether any of them had been outside since the start of the storm." The idea that was unfolding in the back of my head wasn't a pleasant one. It also wasn't one that I could categorically ignore.

Alaric frowned. "I don't think—"

"Please."

He hesitated, then turned back to his computer and began to type. Mahir and Becks looked up from their respective tasks, watching him. Maggie continued to chatter in the background for a few minutes more before saying her good-byes and walking over to stand beside me. "What's going on?"

I gestured toward the still-typing Alaric. "Alaric's asking his sister a question for me."

"The one in Florida?" She gave me a sidelong look. "That seems a little..."

"I know how it seems. But it's important."

"All right," said Alaric. "Alisa says Dad was the first to...he was the first to get sick, and he went outside just after the storm started, to bring in the recycling bins before they could blow away."

"Did she say whether anyone else went outside before they got sick?"

"No. I mean, no, no one else went outside. Mother was trying to make Dad feel better—no one really understood what was happening; Kellis-Amberlee doesn't *transmit* like that—when he bit her. Dorian tried to separate them, and Dad bit him, too."

"So only your father went outside, and only your father got sick without a recognizable vector?"

Alaric was starting to scowl. "*Yes.* I just told you that."

Becks and Mahir kept looking at me blankly. It was Maggie—daughter of pharmaceutical magnates, fan of bad horror movies, the girl who'd grown up steeped in the medical community—whose eyes widened with a shocked horror that perfectly mirrored my own. "You can't be serious."

"I wish I weren't." I could feel George at the back of my head again, watching the proceedings. I moved to grab a Coke out of the fridge as I said, "Alaric, tell your sister to close all the windows she can get to, and not to open the door for *anyone*. How long is it to sunrise there? Another five hours or so?"

He nodded mutely.

"Okay. If I'm right—and let's all hope I'm not—it should get a little safer after the sun comes up." I started for the door back to the living room.

"Hey!" Becks half rose. "Where are you going?"

Maggie didn't look at her. She just kept watching me, suddenly paler than I'd ever seen her. "He's going to go send an e-mail, aren't you, Shaun?"

"Yeah." I nodded. "I am. Mahir, hold the fort, keep everybody working—and if anybody sounds off from the hazard zones, tell them to stay inside and close the windows. I'll be back in a few minutes."

No one else spoke up as I left the kitchen; no one but George. *How sure are you?* she asked, voice tight.

"Sure enough to know that I'd give just about anything to be wrong." I stepped over piles of bulldogs on my way to the house terminal, where I sat and tapped the keyboard to wake the computer from its slumber. "But I don't think I am wrong. That's the problem. I really don't think I am."

I'm sorry.

I laughed, a little wildly. "Times like this, I really wish you weren't dead, you know. When you were alive, I could count on you to think of these things first. Then I got to sit back looking shocked, and let you do all the doom-saying."

Sorry my deadness is inconveniencing you.

"Don't worry about it. It was probably my turn to do the shit jobs." I logged in and called up my e-mail client, ignoring the multiple messages flashing *Urgent* as I scanned for a single sender. She wasn't there.

"Damn," I sighed, and opened a new message window. I paused long enough to be sure that I wanted to do this and, when no other ideas presented themselves, began to type.

From: Shaun.Mason@aftertheendtimes.com
To: TauntedOctopus@redacted.cn.com
Subject: The current outbreak.

Hey, Dr. Abbey. I know you said we needed to stay away from you and all, but we have sort of a problem, and I was hoping you were the person who could tell me what's up with it.

I'm pretty sure you've heard about the outbreak on the Gulf Coast. It's been eating all the news cycles for at least a day, and maybe longer. I can't say for sure, since we spent the first chunk of it on the road running away from the CDC—oh, right, remember what happened in Portland? Well, it sort of happened again, in Memphis this time. The doctor who sent Kelly to us turned out to be on the side of the bad guys. Kelly died. The rest of us (Mahir, Becks, me) got away. I sort of wonder whether that would have been possible if the storm hadn't hit; if maybe the storm is what distracted them from following us. But whatever. You can't base a report on maybe. That's what George always says, and I need to get some facts.

Alaric's family was in Florida when Tropical Storm Fiona hit. His father went outside after the storm made landfall, and he got sick. Two more members of Alaric's family got sick after he bit them, but the only one to actually amplify without a confirmed vector was the father.

The outbreak is spreading with the footprint of the storm—with the *wind*. It's moving with the wind, and not against it, and not away from it, even though the survivors are doing their best to get away. I've been trying to think of every disease vector I've ever encountered, and I'm coming up with only one that works for this. You're the one who understands the structure of this virus. You're the one who can infect anything. So I'm asking you, and I think the whole world may depend on your answer:

Dr. Abbey, is it possible for Kellis-Amberlee to be spread via an insect vector?

Please reply. I need to know.

Shaun Mason

I clicked Send and sat back in my chair, leaving my hands resting limp against the keyboard. More mail was pouring into my client. The view refreshed every few seconds as things passed the filters and landed in my in-box, their subject lines screaming for attention. For the most part, I ignored them. I was waiting for an answer, not another death notice or demand for information.

You really think it's insects?

"I don't think anything else has this kind of distribution pattern." One of the few saving graces of Kellis-Amberlee has always been the fact that it's a very hands-on virus. Unless you're in the unfortunate two percent of the population at risk for spontaneous amplification, you have to either die or get bitten by someone who's been infected before you have a problem. Giving it any sort of a distance-based vector changed the entire game… but it was still a speed killer, taking over bodies and rewriting instincts in a matter of hours. With modern quarantine procedures and our constant, comfortable societal paranoia, even an airborne strain could be controlled.

But an insect vector changed everything. Just ask the people living in parts of the world where malaria is still a problem. Ten-dollar mosquito nets can save entire families from a slow, agonizing death—assuming they don't get torn. Or stolen. Or left ever so slightly ajar one night, allowing one tiny bug to slip unnoticed through the mesh and deliver a stinging bite filled with microscopic death. But malaria's a parasitic infection. That's part of why it does so well with the whole mosquito gig. It's little and it's quick and it's very well-suited to the life cycle it's evolved for. Kellis-Amberlee is a huge, unwieldy virus, microscopically speaking, and it doesn't have the flexibility of malaria. Marburg Amberlee provided most of the structure when it combined with the Kellis flu strain, and it was a filovirus. They're *big*. So I had to be wrong. I had to be totally off-base, taking swipes at shadows. I just needed Dr. Abbey to tell me that, so we could move on to looking for answers in someplace a little bit more realistic.

Shaun? George sounded almost timid for a change. She didn't like this theory any more than I did. *Check your mail.*

I allowed my eyes to focus on the screen. The top item in my in-box was from an e-mail address I recognized all too well, and it was flagged *Urgent*. The little status marker was blinking bright red, which meant every possible "read this immediately" switch had been flipped, some of them maybe more than once. I took a breath, sent a silent prayer to anyone who might be listening, and opened the message.

For a long moment, everything was silent.

Oh, said George, finally. *I guess that answers that.*

"Yeah," I said. "I guess it does."

From: TauntedOctopus@redacted.cn.com
To: Shaun.Mason@aftertheendtimes.com
Subject: Re: The current outbreak.

Ten points, kid: You got it faster than I expected you to. The yellow fever epidemic of 1858 happened after a tropical storm blew infected *Aedes aegypti* mosquitoes over from Cuba. The city of Memphis was nearly wiped out. Hundreds of thousands died.

Tropical Storm Fiona originated in Cuba.

This time is going to be much, much worse, because the mosquitoes may have been blown in by the storm, but they're not tethered to it—some of them are probably already breaking away and infecting random people in the countryside. It's just not enough to cause the mass horror we're seeing in the storm zones. People and their shotguns can keep up with it, and as long as Fiona keeps going, the majority of the bugs will stay with the winds. That means they're concentrated, creating a steady critical mass of new infected to share the joy and make it a real community barbecue.

My lab has moved. If you need to evacuate your current location, download the attached file and upload it to a GPS unit you don't mind destroying. The directions will last for approximately five hours before the virus included with the file burns out your CPU. Attempts to extract the directions without uploading them will result in the file self-destructing and possibly giving you a nice little surprise as an added "you shouldn't have fucked around with me when I'm in this kind of a mood" bonus.

If you must go outside while the sun is down, wear long sleeves and bug spray. I recommend Avon Skin-So-Soft. It's a bath product. It smells like someone fed a Disney Princess through a juicer, but it works better than anything else on the market. Really, I recommend DDT and prayer. Sadly, those aren't available for sale.

You have twenty-four hours before I move again. I will not transmit directions a second time.

Good luck. You assholes are going to need it.

Dr. Shannon L. Abbey

I read the e-mail twice, making sure I understood exactly what it said. Finally, I sent two copies to the house printer and leaned back in my chair, bellowing, "*Mahir!*" A minute passed with no reply. I tried again: "*Mahir!*"

"What in the bloody blue blazes are you shouting about *now*?" he demanded, shoving open the kitchen door and storming toward me. The bulldogs scrambled out of his way, demonstrating more in the way of self-preservation than I would have credited them with. One small brindle even mustered the courage to bark at Mahir's ankles. I felt an unexpected pang. We were going to have to evacuate. If not immediately, then soon. The CDC knew where we were, and in the chaos of the second Rising, not even Maggie's parents would have the reach to keep us all safe.

Between the van and George's bike, we could easily take the five surviving members of the team. But there was no way we'd be able to take the dogs.

"I need a thumb drive," I said.

Mahir stared at me. "Do you mean to tell me," he said, in a measured tone, "that you just yelled like there was some sort of emergency on—when there *is* an actual emergency on, no less, which means we're all a trifle jumpy—because you needed a *thumb drive*?"

"Sort of, yeah." I held out my hand. "Got one?"

"I always thought the stories my staff told about you being impossible to work with were exaggerated, you know." Mahir dug a hand into his pocket and pulled out a thumb drive, which he slapped down on my palm. "This isn't the time to be acting the bastard, Shaun."

"I know." I plucked a sheet of paper from the printer and held it out to him. "Here's the latest from the lab of Dr. Abbey, crazy-ass scientist who knows more about the structure of Kellis-Amberlee than anybody else I've ever met. Just in case you needed a few more things to keep you awake at night."

Mahir took the paper wordlessly and started to read. I took advantage of the lull and uncapped the thumb drive, plugging it into an open USB port. It checked out clean, so I started downloading Dr. Abbey's embedded file for transfer. We'd need a way to get the information to the GPS when the time came.

That takes care of one GPS, said George. *Are you leaving the bike?*

"I'll follow the van," I replied, disengaging the thumb drive. It was another cold equation, and one that I liked just as little as I'd liked the first one. The more times we copied the information, the higher the odds were that someone could get hold of it. The van would be better armed and better-equipped to get away if something went wrong. The only person on the bike would be me, and I...

I wasn't quite at the end of my usefulness, but with the way I'd been slipping, I wasn't sure how much longer that was going to be true. If only one vehicle could reach Dr. Abbey's safely, it wasn't going to be mine. I was oddly okay with that.

That made one of us. *Shaun, you'd better not be thinking what I think you're thinking.*

"Or what? You'll haunt me?" I chuckled. "You're gonna have to do better than that."

George's rebuttal was cut short as Mahir raised his head and stared at me. The circles under his eyes were standing out like bruises against his suddenly pale skin. I'd thought he looked tired when he first came off the plane, but compared to this, he'd been in top fighting condition. We'd been running for too long. I wasn't the only one running out of go.

"Good lord, Shaun," he said. His voice was shaking. Not for the first time, I wished that I'd died and George had lived—at least she could have given him a hug and told him things might not be all right but they'd take a few of the bastards out with them. I didn't even know where to start. "Is this woman serious?"

"I don't think she's ever not serious. I also don't think she's ever wrong where Kellis-Amberlee is concerned. She's the one who collected most of the data I gave you. She's crazy. She's dangerous. But I think she's right."

"But I…" He stopped, licking his lips nervously before he said, "If she's right, we can't stay here."

"That's true."

"So what are we going to do?"

"Well, we can't stay here, and we can't go home." I stood, slipping the thumb drive into my pocket. "I suggest it's time we head off to see the Wizard. The wonderful Wizard of Jesus We Are All So Fucked."

I don't think you can make that scan, said George.

"I don't think so either," I replied. Mahir gave me an odd look. I ignored it. We were past the point of me feeling self-conscious about talking to someone nobody else could hear. "Dr. Abbey's right about the Avon Skin-So-Soft—it's sold as a cosmetic, but it's the best bug repellent on the domestic market. I have a couple of bottles in my kit. So should Becks."

Mahir blinked. "Kellis-Amberlee has never *had* an insect vector. I'm not sure I'm willing to believe that it has one now. Why are you already carrying this stuff?"

I smiled thinly. "Because it's the best bug repellent known to man. When you're an Irwin, poking into places men were not meant to poke, being chased by the living dead, the last thing you want to do is stop to deal with mosquito bites all over your ass."

"I suppose that makes sense."

"I'm going to go get the others up to speed. We need to start packing, and we need to give Maggie time to tell the house security systems to stand down." If I doused myself in bug repellent and wore my full-field armor, I'd be able to take the bike. Any mosquito that could bite through Kevlar deserved to get a piece of me. "We're taking the work van. If it doesn't fit in there, it isn't coming."

"What are you talking about? We need to wait—"

"The sun rises in five hours. The instructions will wipe themselves in five hours. If we want to get to Dr. Abbey alive, we need to leave now."

Mahir hesitated, eyes searching my face. Finally, carefully, he said, "Shaun, are you sure? I mean, are you really sure we should be going to this woman, rather than staying here, where it's safe?"

"*Is* it safe here? Maggie's folks know where we are. The security staff knows. It's only a matter of time before one of us slips and our readership knows. We're on the verge of full-blown martial law, which means that eventually some asshole at the CDC is going to put two and two together and realize that we're sitting ducks. It's going to be Oakland all over again. They just have to make sure their fall guy knows enough to be believable as the one who pressed the button and blew the only heir to Garcia

Pharmaceuticals to hell. If we want to stay alive through this, we need to get the fuck out of here."

"I…" Mahir stopped. Squaring his shoulders, he looked me in the eye, and asked, "What is it you need me to do?"

"Check with your Newsies. See who's posting what and how much they have ready to go up. Also see who can play phone-tree. We're going to want to hold a short staff meeting before we get out of here—and by 'we,' I mean you, me, and Maggie." Becks and Alaric weren't department heads. They could be packing the van and gathering any essential supplies from the house while we made the requisite reassuring noises and made it seem like we'd be staying where we were for the foreseeable future. I hated the idea of lying to my crew, I *hated* it, but I didn't see any alternative. Not if we wanted to stay alive. I didn't think any of them were secretly working for the enemy—Buffy was a special case—and I was pretty sure they were all willing to do whatever it took to help us spread the truth. George had a gift for hiring good people, and the best thing about hiring good people is that they'll recommend other good people when it comes time to expand.

I would trust our staff with my life, and had, on several occasions. But we couldn't take them all with us, and that meant they couldn't know where we were going. More cold equations. If someone came looking, it was important there be no one who could give our location away.

Mahir was clearly doing the same math I was because he looked stricken before he nodded. "I'll get them to report in, and I'll pass the word about the staff meeting. How long do you think we need?"

"Tell 'em to be online in fifteen minutes. Anyone who isn't there when we get started can join late and try to catch up as best they can." I paused. "Also…tell them I'm not my sister. I'm not going to pull a grand gesture like she did. But if they want to quit without consequences, now would be the time to do it."

George called a staff meeting when we first started to realize the size of the conspiracy we were facing. She made sure everyone was connected—and fired them all. Anybody who wanted to stay on could stay, but they had to sign another contract first. They had to *understand* what they were getting into. It was a big deal. It was incredibly important. And there just wasn't time for that kind of theater. They'd stay or they wouldn't. Anyone who'd signed on during the meeting with George knew the score, and so did anyone who'd signed on since.

"All right," said Mahir. He was already moving toward the house terminal, my printout clutched in one hand.

I leaned over and plucked it from his grasp, offering a wan smile in his direction before I turned and started for the kitchen. It was time to get everybody on the same page, get Maggie to start packing, and get ready to go on the run.

Bet you wish we'd never signed up for the Ryman campaign, huh?

"The thought has crossed my mind," I admitted. "When you said, 'Hey, Shaun, let's be journalists,' I'm pretty sure this part wasn't in the brochure."

Would it have made any difference?

I paused with my hand raised to push the kitchen door open. Mahir and Buffy, Maggie, Alaric, and Becks, we knew them all because of what we'd chosen to do with our lives. More important, they were *our* lives, not mine. If I'd said no, that I wanted to be something else when I grew up, George would still have become a blogger, and I would have lost her long before I actually did.

"Not a bit," I said, and stepped into the kitchen.

I am a poet, and I am a storyteller, and it is with these two callings in mind that I make the following statement, which comes from my heart, my soul, and my middle fingers:

Fuck you people and the horses you rode in on. You better watch yourselves, because we are done screwing around, and we are going to take your bitch asses down.

This is for Dave.

**—From *Dandelion Mine*,
the blog of Magdalene Garcia, June 24, 2041**

The world has gone insane, and you can't get a decent pint of lager anywhere in this bloody country. I think I can safely say that my schoolmates were correct when they predicted my eventual destination, and I am now in hell.

**—From *Fish and Clips*,
the blog of Mahir Gowda, June 24, 2041**

Twenty-five

The staff meeting went better than I was afraid it would. That's about the only good thing that I can say about it. Everyone was scared, and everyone was expressing that fear in a different way. The Irwins were restless and pissed off about being forbidden to go into the field. The Newsies were split into two distinct camps—the ones who wanted to grab an Irwin, get outside, and find out what the hell was going on out there, and the ones who were happy to stay as far away from the disaster zone as possible but wanted information to flow freely while they stayed indoors. That's the kind of Newsie attitude that's always pissed me off, since it seems to come with a blanket assumption that the Irwins are overjoyed to be risking their lives for the benefit of the Newsies' careers.

The Fictionals, on the other hand, were uniformly glad to be staying inside, but were all scared out of their minds and spent half the call going off on tangents that required all business to come grinding to a halt while Maggie calmed them down. She was good at her job, maybe better than I ever realized, and not even she could keep them on track for more than a few minutes at a time. After twenty minutes, I was ready to kill someone—and I wasn't all that picky about who.

Mahir saved everyone's asses. He took over the call and led it with calm and grace, pausing when Maggie needed to play kindergarten teacher, and otherwise keeping us moving forward. He fielded every question that was tossed his way, somehow prompting the rest of us to speak up just often enough that no one forgot we were there. If he'd wanted to go into event planning instead of journalism, he probably could have made a fortune.

The whole time the call was going, Alaric and Becks were packing up supplies and moving them to the back of the kitchen, just outside the closed garage door. Maggie and Alaric had done a lot of packing before the rest of us got there, but neither of them was an Irwin, and Becks felt the need—probably rightly—to go through everything and make sure that we had enough supplies to reach our destination in one piece.

"All right, folks," I said, breaking into the fifth near-identical argument over who was getting more screwed by the current embargos, the Newsies or the Irwins. "I'm glad we're all on the same page now, but the wireless booster is about to shut down from lack of juice, so I figure we should wrap this up. I don't know how long it'll be before they get our little slice of the Internet back online. In the meantime, everybody has their assignments, and we have our temporary department heads. Are there any questions?"

There were no questions. That was practically a goddamn miracle. Our three temporary department heads—Katie in Connecticut, for the Fictionals; Luis in Ohio, for the Newsies; and Dmitry in Michigan, for the Irwins—were nervous enough that their tiny digital pictures looked faintly ill. Still. We wouldn't have asked them to do the jobs if we didn't think they were ready. Not that anyone could really be considered ready to take over one-third of a major news site during a disaster this large, but they were about as prepared as the rest of us, and no one was shooting at them yet. That had to count for something.

"Okay, then, I'm going to shut this baby down before something manages to actually catch fire and we have to kill it with sticks." I looked at my screen. The faces of After the End Times looked back at me, all filled with the same anxiety. The world might actually be ending. That was a bit more than we were used to dealing with on a normal workday.

Say something inspirational, prompted George. *They need to hear it from you. You're the leader.*

That was a job I never applied for. I managed to bite back the words "Like what?" before they could quite escape, and cleared my throat instead, trying to think of a single damn thing to say. My mind was a blank. This was a threat way too big to prod with a stick.

You can do it, said George, quietly.

I cleared my throat again. "Guys…" Everyone looked at me expectantly. I faltered, losing my place for a second before I tried again: "This has been one hell of a year. For those of you who hired on with us after the campaign, I'm sorry. You've never seen me at my best. Hell, if it weren't for the fact that we have the best damn administrative staff in the known universe, you would never have seen me at all, because we would have gone under a long time ago."

"He's quite right about that," said Mahir.

Ignoring him seemed like the best idea, so I did. "And for those of you who've been with us since the beginning, I know this isn't what you signed on for. Hell, it's not what *I* signed on for, and you'd think I might have some say in what we do, right? But the thing is, regardless of when you came on with us, whether it was day one or yesterday, you have all done an amazing, amazing job. If I were asked to put together a team to record the end of the world, there's not one of you who I wouldn't want to have on board—and yeah, I don't know all of you that well, but I know the people who recommended you, and since I would trust them with my life, I figure you're worth taking the gamble on."

Laughter followed this statement, some nervous, most not. A few people were nodding. That was sort of unnerving.

"I don't know how much worse things are going to get before they get better. We're in the same place now that we were in twenty years ago—the dead are rising, the situation looks grim as hell, and no one really knows what's going on. I won't lie to you. If the first Rising is anything to go by, we're not all going to live to see the end of this. Some of us will be going up on the Wall before this is over." I paused, the litany of the dead running in the back of my mind. Buffy, Georgia, Dave, Kelly. The convoy guards in Eakly, Oklahoma. All our neighbors back in Oakland. Alaric's family. Too damn many people. "Some of us already have. But see, the thing is, that isn't what matters. What matters is that we're going to keep doing what we do. We're going to keep getting the news out. We're going to keep telling the truth. And if we go up on the Wall, we're by God going to know that we did the best we could—and that we've left behind as much information as we can for the ones who'll tell the truth after us."

There was a long pause. *Well said*, said George.

And then someone—one of the Irwins, I think, since we're the ones trained to start making noise whenever we get the excuse—cheered. Several more people joined in, and the ones who didn't clapped their hands, or just grinned. I stared at them, dumbfounded.

They like you.

I kept staring.

Mahir saved me by leaning forward and saying, "That's the end of our motivational speaking for the day, and the end of our power supply, I'm afraid. Ladies and gents, it's been fabulous chatting with you all, and we'll do our best to keep updating you as things progress here, but for now, assume that we're off-line for the foreseeable future. Ask your interim department heads if you have any questions or troubles, and stay safe." He moved his mouse cursor to the button for Terminate Conference, and clicked.

The screen went black, all those little windows blinking out in an instant. It felt weirdly final, like I'd never speak to any of these people again. In some cases, I probably wouldn't. I coughed into my hand to clear the tightness in my throat, and straightened.

"Okay," I said. "Let's go."

Packing the rest of the equipment took less than ten minutes. Maggie spent the time in the living room, feeding treats to the bulldogs and telling them how good they were. They were happy to receive the attention, if a little confused by all the fuss that she was making; people came and went all the time, after all, and she didn't normally make such a big deal out of it. To their canine minds, this excursion didn't look any different from the hundreds of others she'd taken. Maybe it was better that way.

While she was dealing with the dogs, I went upstairs to the guest room and changed into my body armor. I slathered Avon Skin-So-Soft over every inch of skin I had, even the skin that would be covered by three layers of Kevlar and leather. I was going to be as soft as a baby's ass, and more important, I wasn't going to get infected if I had any choice in the matter.

I paused in the doorway before heading back down to join the others, looking at the guest room. The bed was made, the nightstand was empty, and there was nothing to indicate that I'd ever been there at all.

"Will we ever stop just passing through?" I asked aloud.

George didn't answer, and so I went back downstairs.

Maggie had joined the others in the kitchen while I was getting changed. She offered me a nod, wiping her eyes with the back of one hand before turning to walk up to the back door. "House," she said, clearly, "please contact Officer Weinstein. Tell him it's time for the matter we discussed earlier."

"All right, Magdalene," said the house. Its tone was blandly pleasant as always.

"Thank you, house." Maggie looked over her shoulder to me. "I warned Alex we might need to go, and that we'd need it to be as quiet as possible. He's been waiting for my word."

"And the house will let us out?" asked Becks.

"If the security crew outside says that we're opening the isolation lock, even for a few minutes, the house won't have a choice. My security logs are only uploaded if there's an unapproved breach, so unless the infected take the house, no one will know for sure that we're gone." Maggie wiped her eyes again. "I hate this."

"I know," I said, quietly.

The house speaker crackled as someone switched to manual, and a man's voice came through, asking, "Ms. Garcia? Are you sure this is what you want to do?"

Maggie smiled unsteadily at a point just above the door—probably the location of a hidden security camera. "No. But I'm sure it's what I have to do. Please let us out, Alex."

"Your father—"

"Signs your checks, but you work for me, remember? That was always the deal. Now please, just give us ten minutes to get out of here, and you can lock the place down again."

He sighed heavily. "If anything happens to you, your father will have all our asses. You understand that, right?"

"I do."

"Just checking. You have ten minutes. Now please, try not to make me regret this."

The speaker crackled again as he hung up his end, and the house said, sounding almost perplexed, "The isolation order has been rescinded. Thank you for your patience. You are now free to leave the premises if you so choose."

"Grab your gear, folks," I said, picking up a duffel bag with one hand and my helmet with the other. "We need to get rolling."

"On it," said Alaric, grabbing the wireless booster.

Becks didn't say anything. She just picked up a box filled with dry cereal and cans of soda and kicked the garage door open.

The van was inside, which was good. The bike was outside, which was not good. Working in tight tandem, the five of us were able to load the van in just under five minutes, cramming boxes and bags into every inch of available space. I didn't question the amount of stuff that we were bringing. Since the odds of us coming back were pretty damn slim, we needed to take everything that was even potentially useful and assume that it was easier to throw shit away than it would be to find it once we were on the road.

We were halfway through the packing process when Alaric realized there wasn't going to be room for everyone. "Wait," he said. "We need to leave some of this. We're filling the backseat."

"It's all good." I raised my helmet. "I'm taking the bike."

"But—"

"We need someone riding point. And besides," I said and grinned, "you know I'm going to get the *best* footage."

He gave me an uncertain look. "You're going to be exposed."

"We've all basically bathed in insect repellent—if they bite me,

I probably deserve it. Now come on, finish packing the van. We have a pretty narrow time frame here, and we need to get out before it closes."

Becks lobbed a duffel bag at him. He caught it with an *oof*, and gave me a wounded look before turning to resume packing the van. I didn't really care if he thought I was being an idiot. Maybe I was. I was also being a realist.

When the last box was wedged into place and the last bag was stowed, the four of them got into the van, rolling the windows all the way up. I put on my helmet, sealing it tightly before nodding to activate the intercom. "How's our connection?" I asked.

"Loud and clear," Mahir replied.

"Great. Now let's roll."

The garage door rolled smoothly upward in answer to some unseen signal from Maggie, and the night air came flooding in, chilling me even through my leathers. It wasn't the temperature so much as the uncertainty that the air represented: the risk of a kind of infection we'd never been afraid of before. Kellis-Amberlee was a known quantity; it was, for lack of a better phrase, a safe virus, something that could kill you, but which we understood. The thought of a new vector made it all terrifying again.

Becks started up the van engine and turned on the headlights. I didn't need them to see where I was going, since the exterior house lights were turned up so far that it practically looked like noon out in the yard. I walked over to the bike and swung my leg over it, balancing myself. "Go," I said, into the microphone in my helmet. "I'll be right behind you."

The van pulled out of the garage. I let them get to the first gate before I started the ignition and followed.

The trip down the driveway was harrowing. We moved slowly enough that I had to walk the bike about two-thirds of the time. When that wasn't possible, I had to coast, trying to keep from either overbalancing or stalling out. Neither would be good. And I'd be dealing with it alone either way, since there was no way I was letting the others stop the van to help me. That wasn't part of the plan.

All the gates stood open, allowing us to keep moving through as we wound our way toward the street below. Maggie's security guards flanked the open gates, their guns held at the ready. I'm not sure they really believed that we were going until we'd passed the third gate. That was when they started locking things down behind us, each gate sliding shut and sealing itself with a clang that was audible even through my helmet. The guards moved forward as the gates closed, reforming their ranks around each new opening.

They stayed behind as we passed the last gate. One of them—Officer Weinstein, most likely—raised his assault rifle in salute. Then Becks hit the gas, speeding off down the road in answer to the instructions in the van's GPS, and I had to gun the throttle in order to catch up. It took only a few seconds for the house to recede entirely out of sight. The view of the hill that it was on lasted for a little longer, slipping in and out of sight as we followed the curve of the road.

The lights from the house stayed visible even after the house itself was out of sight. They blazed up into the night, painting the clouds with tiered bands of light and shadow. I was relieved when they finally faded. They reminded me too much of everything that we were leaving behind.

The speaker in my helmet beeped to signal an incoming call. I nodded to activate it. "Go."

"We're heading for I-5 toward Portland," said Becks, right in my ear. "We're going to have to take the main highway for about forty miles, just to get past the worst of the forest."

"Got it." Under most circumstances, taking the highway would have been the safest thing to do. It was well-guarded, was well-maintained, and had access to multiple emergency services, including bolt holes we could flee to if things took a turn for the worse. It was also the single route most likely to be monitored by anyone who was watching to see if we were on the move and, because of the nature of modern highway design, would be relatively easy to isolate from the rest of the grid. It was possible that some innocent bystanders might be caught up in an attack designed to target the five of us...and after everything we'd been through, I no longer had any illusions that the people we were running from would care.

"Watch yourself out there," said Becks. Then the connection was cut and the van sped up, racing away from the lights of Weed, racing into the darkness up ahead.

The only thing I could do was follow her.

I-5 was eerily deserted. Even the guard stations were dark, proving once again that, when faced with a true national emergency, no amount of "duty" is going to be sufficient to get people to leave their homes. Half the men who should have been guarding the road were likely to be charged with treason if they were caught, and right now, they had absolutely no reason to care. Treason wasn't as bad as infection and death. At least treason was something you stood a chance of surviving. We took the automated blood tests and rolled on.

Every time the occupants of the van had to roll down a window, I stopped breathing, waiting for the screams to start. They never did. We were far enough outside the footprint of the storm that we were probably safe...but "probably" isn't something I believe in banking on. Thank God for bug repellent.

With the road empty and both of us driving as fast as we dared, we cleared forty miles of highway driving in just under thirty minutes. From there, Becks led us onto a frontage road that paralleled I-5 but was mostly concealed by the concrete retaining wall meant to protect passing motorists. I guess if you were one of the people who lived in the tiny houses and aging trailer parks we passed, you were shit out of luck. That's something almost everyone does their best to forget: The world may have changed, but some people still can't afford to come in out of the cold. The poor didn't have advanced security systems or hermetically sealed windows, and now that Kellis-Amberlee had found itself a new vector...

It didn't really bear thinking about.

We were passing Ashland, Oregon, when my helmet beeped again. "Go," I said.

"Shaun?" Becks sounded uncertain. "The GPS just gave me our final destination."

"And?"

"And it's Shady Cove."

I managed to keep control of the bike, but only because I had George to take care of the vital business of swearing like a madwoman at the back of my head while I focused on the road. "Are you *sure*?"

"I'm sure." There was a long pause before she asked, "What are the odds that she's driving us into a trap?"

"I don't know. What are the odds that we have anywhere else to go?" She didn't answer me. "I figured as much. We're going to Shady Cove, Becks. Tell everybody to take off the safeties and keep their eyes on the mirrors."

"I hope to God you know what you're doing, Mason," said Becks, and cut the connection.

"So do I," I muttered. "So do I."

A lot of small towns were declared uninhabitable after the Rising. They're little dead zones scattered around the map of the world, places where no one goes anymore—no one but well-prepared, heavily armed Irwins looking for a story, and even then, we never go in at night. Going into a dead zone at night is like signing your own death warrant. Santa Cruz, California, is a dead zone. So is most of India. And so is Shady Cove, Oregon. It used to be a small but comfortable town of about two thousand people, surrounded by woodlands, comfortably close to the popular tourist attraction of several state and county parks. They did okay.

Until the zombies came, and the very things that made it such a nice place to live turned Shady Cove into a deathtrap. The same thing could have happened to Weed, if not for the fisheries, and Shady Cove didn't have anything that vital to the local economy. It just had people. We lost a lot of people in the Rising. A town that size was barely even a blip in the statistics.

This is bad, said George. *We need to turn back.*

"This makes perfect sense. If Dr. Abbey is trying to go off the grid, a dead zone is the best place to do it, and Shady Cove was never burned." I forced a smile. "Besides, you only know the place exists because of the number of times I begged you to let me go there."

There's a reason I always said no.

"I know. But it's not like we've been left with a whole lot of options."

George didn't have an answer to that one.

The frontage roads gave way to smaller frontage roads, which gave way in turn to roads that were barely even paved. The lights of the freeway guard walls stayed in view the whole time, almost taunting me with the idea of smooth surfaces and well-marked exit signs. We were still within Dr. Abbey's time frame, and the GPS was clearly still feeding Becks directions, because she kept driving and didn't stop to yell at me for getting us into this mess.

When I drove past a sign reading SHADY COVE—5 MILES, I actually started to believe that we might reach our destination alive.

Then the first zombie came racing out of the woods on my left.

It was moving with the horrible, disjointed speed that only the freshly infected can manage. A normal human will always be faster in a short sprint, but the freshly infected win every time in a long race. They don't care about pain, and they don't really notice when their lungs stop pulling in enough air. The uninfected will eventually stop chasing you. A zombie will run until it collapses from exhaustion, and there's a good chance that even that won't keep it down for long.

The van swerved to avoid the zombie. I did the same. I was so busy trying to keep the bike upright that I didn't see the other three infected lunging out of the shelter of the trees until one of them was scrabbling at the handlebars of my bike, with absolutely no awareness of the sheer stupidity of attacking a man on a moving motorcycle. "Holy—"

I slammed on the brakes, sending the zombie tumbling away from me. The van was back on track, moving away at top speed. I twisted the throttle, starting after them, only to come up short as an arm was hooked around my neck and I was jerked off the bike.

The Kevlar jacket I was wearing absorbed most of the impact with the road, but it couldn't save me from the hands that were pulling me down, uncoordinated fingers trying to find an opening in my body armor. I smacked them away, flailing to get free. If I could get to my guns, either of them, I would stand a chance of getting away from this. Not a good chance, but a chance.

My questing fingers found the grip of a pistol. I yanked it from the holster hard enough to break one of the snaps and fired it into the face of the first zombie without pausing to aim. The report was loud enough to make my ears ring, even through the still-sealed helmet. The zombie fell back, leaving me with just enough leverage to push myself into a sitting position and shoot the zombie to my right. That left—crap. That left at least three, by a quick count, and all of them focused entirely on me. The bike was on its side up ahead. There was no way I'd be able to get it righted and running again unless I took all the zombies out, and the numbers were *not* on my side.

Don't be an idiot. You've survived worse.

"Says you," I muttered, and took another shot.

I was so focused on the zombies I could see that I forgot one of the first rules of dealing with any zombie mob larger than three: Remember that they're smarter than you think they are. Surprisingly strong hands grabbed me from behind, jerking me back.

Maybe it was the fall I'd taken earlier, and maybe it was just a natural flaw in the construction of my body armor, but when the zombie pulled, I heard something tear. I whipped my head around, looking for a shot, and saw to my horror that the entire left sleeve of my jacket was ripped along the main seam, leaving my arm—protected only by a flannel shirt— exposed.

The infected who was holding me hissed, showing me his shattered, blackened teeth, and brought his head down as I brought my gun up. The bullet caught him in the crown of the head, blowing a jet of brain matter out onto the pavement. The zombie's hands went limp, and he fell, a look of comic bewilderment on the remains of his face. More infected were coming out of the woods. For the moment, however, I wasn't sure how much concern I could spare for them.

Most of my concern was for the new hole in my flannel shirt, and the blood welling up through the fabric. The pain hit half a second later, but the pain wasn't really that important. The blood had already told me everything I needed to know about the situation.

I grabbed the sleeve and yanked it back into place before running toward the bike, shooting as I went. The speaker in my helmet was beeping insistently. I didn't know how long that had been going on. The encounter felt like it had started years ago, even if I was reasonably sure it had been only a few seconds. I nodded sharply.

"—there? Shaun, please, are you *there*?"

"I'm here, Mahir." I shot another zombie as it ran for me, and snickered. "Hey, did you know that rhymes? Where are you guys?"

"We're coming back for you. Can you hold your position?"

"I can, but I gotta tell you, buddy, that's not the best idea you've ever had."

He took a sharp breath. "Shaun, please don't tell me..."

"No test results yet, but I'm definitely bleeding." The lights of the van blazed back into sight ahead of me. I groaned. "I told you not to come back!"

"Not in so many words, you didn't, and if you think we're leaving you without a test, you're an arsehole. Now down!"

Mahir's command was sharp enough that I obeyed without thinking, hitting the road on my hands and knees a second before bullets sprayed through the air where I'd been standing. The rest of the undead fell in twitching heaps. The gunfire stopped, leaving the night silent.

"Get on the bike and go," said a voice in my ear. For a dazed second, I couldn't tell whether it was George or Mahir. Then it continued: "We want the turnoff for Old Ferry Road."

"Mahir, I really don't think—"

"If you amplify before we get there, you'll lose control of the bike. If you don't, I'm sure Dr. Abbey will appreciate the chance to check your blood for signs that this is a new strain." Mahir's voice gentled. "Please, Shaun. Don't make us leave you out here."

"This is idiotic," I said.

"Yes."

"Just wanted to be sure you were aware." I nodded again to cut the connection and took a moment to pull my sleeve closed as best as I could before righting the bike and getting back on. It started easily. There went that excuse for staying behind. I could want to protect them, but I couldn't lie to them.

"Well?" asked George, next to my ear. "Are you going to follow them, or what?"

"I'll follow," I said.

The van turned laboriously around on the narrow road, taillights gleaming red through the darkness as Becks hit the gas and started forward once again. I squeezed the throttle, whispered a prayer for swift amplification, and followed them.

We took a tour of the government zombie holding facility on Alcatraz today.

A lot of people don't like having it there, even though it's been scientifically proven that Romero was wrong about at least one thing: Zombies can't survive without oxygen. Since they're too uncoordinated to swim, and they don't know how to operate boats, if there were ever an outbreak, it would be naturally confined. That doesn't matter. "Not in my backyard" comes out loud and clear where the dead are concerned.

I looked through the safety glass into the pens, into the dozens of eyes that looked just like mine, and I searched them as hard as I could for a sign of something, anything that would tell me they were still human. There was nothing there. Only darkness.

If I pray for anything tonight, it will be that when Shaun eventually does something insane and gets himself bitten, I'll be there to shoot him. Because I couldn't live with myself knowing I'd allowed him to amplify. No one deserves to end up like that. No one.

—From *Postcards from the Wall*,
the unpublished files of Georgia Mason,
originally posted June 24, 2034

Twenty-six

The building housing Dr. Abbey's new lab must have started life as the local forestry center. The front looked like pure glass until you got close enough to see that it was backed with sheet metal. Better yet, the trees had been cut back on all sides, making room for a massive parking lot that provided clear sightlines for anyone trying to guard the building from the infected... or, as we pulled up to park near what looked like the front entrance, from us. There was even a structure on the roof that might have started out as an observatory but would make a damn good shooter's nest, if necessity demanded.

Becks was the first out of the van, and she had a gun pointed at my head before I could get my helmet off. I could have kissed her for that, if it weren't for the history between us and the fact that I was probably contagious. Field protocol said I was to be kept under constant guard until I could be confirmed as uninfected, and somehow that didn't seem likely to me.

I pulled off my helmet. The night air was cool, and even cold where it hit the sweat on the back of my neck. "Hey," I said, wearily. My throat was a little dry, but that was all; I wasn't experiencing any of the other symptoms I knew would signal the start of amplification. Just my luck. I would have to go and develop a sturdy immune system.

"Hey," Becks agreed, with a small tilt of her head. "How are you feeling?"

"Like I want to go redline a test and get this over with." Mahir, Alaric, and Maggie got out of the van, all three looking shaken and nauseated. I offered them a nod. "Hey, guys, you know how to set up a guard formation?"

"Yes," said Alaric.

"No," said Maggie.

"I have absolutely no idea," said Mahir.

"That's fine. Becks, Alaric, you guard me. Mahir, you guard Maggie." I stepped away from the bike, leaving the helmet on the seat, and linked my hands behind my head. "Let's go tell Dr. Abbey she has guests, shall we?"

I felt almost like we were parodying our approach to the CDC as we walked toward the building. Mahir and Maggie went first, followed by Becks, who walked backward so as to keep her gun trained on me. Alaric brought up the rear, his own gun out and, I knew, pointed at my head. If I showed any signs of turning, they'd take me down before I could do any serious damage. It was reassuring.

At least they're well-trained, said George.

"There's that," I muttered. Them being well-trained might actually keep them alive for a little bit longer, now that they weren't going to be my responsibility anymore.

We were still about ten yards away when the door opened. Dr. Abbey stepped into view with a shotgun braced against her shoulder and Joe the Mastiff standing next to her, looking more massive than ever. Maybe she'd been feeding him trespassers.

"So you came after all," she said, eyes flicking over the group before settling on me. Her eyebrows rose. "And you're under armed guard because...?"

"I was bitten about five miles back," I replied. "There was a pack of infected in the woods. I'm pretty sure we killed them all, but you may want to send a cleanup crew, just to be certain."

"We didn't run a blood test because we didn't want the results uploaded to the CDC database," said Mahir. "Given the circumstances, it seemed somewhat...less than wise."

My stomach sank. I hadn't even considered that. "Shit," I whispered.

Nobody expects you to be doing any heavy thinking right after a zombie tried to take your arm off.

"Says you."

"So you brought him here?" Dr. Abbey shrugged, lowering her gun. "I would have settled for a bottle of wine, but I guess a new test subject and the location of some fresh corpses will do. Come on, all of you. Shaun, don't try to touch anyone, or my lab techs will have to blow your head off."

"That's fair," I agreed.

"Good boy." Dr. Abbey smiled and stepped back, letting Becks lead the rest of us inside.

The new lab wasn't as established as the old one, which meant it was more cluttered, with boxes everywhere, and didn't yet have that ground-in "science" smell—strange chemicals, bleach, sterile air, and plastic gloves. This lab smelled rather pleasantly of cedar wood. That would change as things got up to speed. Maybe they could hang some of those little air fresheners, try to bring it back.

Of course, that assumed they were going to have *time*. Most of the shelving units had a distinctly temporary look to them, like this was just a stop on the way to some more distant destination. The mad science equivalent of pitching camp for the night.

Lab-coated assistants scurried here and there, unpacking boxes, carrying trays of samples from one place to another. The assault rifles they all had strapped around their waists were new, making it clear just how seriously they were taking their situation. That was a bit of a relief. I wouldn't be leaving my team with no one to defend them.

"Molena, Alan," said Dr. Abbey, flagging down two of the nearest techs. "Take this group to the cafeteria. Get them coffee and blood tests, and see if you can't scrape together something resembling food. *Not* that god-awful lasagna we had for dinner. That's not even suitable for feeding to the pigs."

"Yes, Dr. Abbey," said the taller of the lab techs. He turned to the group. "If you'll come with me?"

"Of course," said Mahir. "Shaun—"

"Don't." I gave him a pleading look. "All of you, please, don't. We've said everything that needs to be said. So don't, okay?"

"All right," he said, and turned to follow the lab tech. Maggie cast an uncertain glance back in my direction and did the same.

Alaric lingered for a moment, shifting his weight from foot to foot. Finally, he said, "Say hello to Georgia for me," and fled, leaving only me, Becks, and Dr. Abbey behind. And Joe, of course. He sat next to Dr. Abbey, tongue lolling and tail wagging. He was the only one of us not equipped to understand the gravity of the situation, and I sort of envied him that.

Dr. Abbey looked at Becks. "Not hungry?"

"I'm not leaving until I know what you're going to do with him." She kept her gun trained on me as she spoke, professional to the last. Her hand was shaking only slightly. I didn't do as well when I was in her position.

"Fair enough. Come on, Shaun." Dr. Abbey waved for me to follow her as she turned and started down the nearest hall. She didn't call for anyone else to keep an eye on me. I guess she figured Becks would be enough.

We walked maybe twenty yards deeper into the building, moving around towers of cardboard boxes and past hastily constructed metal racks. Lab techs moved past us constantly, grabbing this and that and vanishing down hallways or through doors. I guess moving an entire virology lab isn't a simple task.

Dr. Abbey grabbed a blood testing unit from one of the shelving units and kept walking, offering nods and quiet greetings to some of the lab techs we passed. She stopped only when we reached a door labeled ISOLATION III. "In here," she said, and opened it. I didn't move. "What are you waiting for, an invitation? Get in."

"I thought—"

"We're not going in there with you. Don't be an idiot." She held the unit out toward me. "Go inside, sit down, and start your test. You won't be able to get out. You can't hurt anyone."

Relief washed over me, strong enough to make my shoulders unlock. "Thank you," I said. I flashed Becks one last smile, aware that it was strained, and not really that concerned about it. I wasn't going to hurt anyone. That was all I needed to know.

Becks smiled back. She was crying. I was sorry about that, but there was nothing I could do about it. So I stepped forward to take the testing unit from Dr. Abbey's hand and walked past her into the darkened isolation room.

The door swung shut behind me, the locks sealing with a hydraulic hiss that went on long enough to make it clear that this wasn't casual security. This was the real thing. The hissing stopped and the overhead lights clicked on, illuminating a room about the size of my bedroom back when George and I still lived with the Masons. The walls were painted a shiny, neutral beige, and there were three pieces of furniture: a narrow cot against one wall, a metal table bolted to the floor, and a folding chair. There was a blanket and a small pillow on the cot. Make the condemned as comfortable as possible, I guess.

I wasn't interested in comfort. I walked to the chair and sat down, placing the testing unit on the table in front of me. It seemed to stare back accusingly, like it didn't understand why I wasn't getting on with it already.

"It's not like this is important or anything," I said sourly, and unfastened my gloves, dropping them on the table. Blood had run down my left arm and onto the hand, crusting under my nails. I looked at it and shuddered, wishing there were some way to wash it off. After I amplified, I probably wouldn't care, but until then, I'd know it was there. I flexed my fingers, checking my joints for stiffness, and turned my attention to the testing unit.

It wasn't a model I'd seen before—if anything, it looked like the pictures of Dr. Patel's original design, the one that just measured your viral levels but didn't give you real-time results, and definitely didn't upload anything. I picked it up, checking it for lights, and didn't find any. Apparently, once I was in the isolation room, I didn't need to know whether I was infected or not. I scowled. "Isn't this just dandy?"

"Get it over with," said George, beside me.

I jerked my head up, looking for her. She was nowhere to be seen. I scowled more. "I don't exactly feel like rushing right now."

"The results won't change if you wait." Her voice came from the other side this time. I somehow managed not to look. I just sighed.

"Can you just appear already?"

"No. I'm sorry, but that's your choice, not mine."

"Okay. Right. Well...if you won't appear, will you at least stay?"

I felt the ghost of her hand brush the back of my neck, there and gone in an instant. "Until the end. I promise."

"Okay," I said, and popped open the lid on the unit. "One..."

"Two..."

I slammed my hand flat on the metal pressure pad, triggering the needles to start their business. They bit deep, and I hissed, biting my tongue against the pain. I thought amplification was supposed to make this sort of thing easier. I didn't feel any difference at all. Blood tests always hurt, but this one was worse than most, maybe because the unit was so primitive.

When the last of the needles disengaged, I pulled my hand away. The test unit beeped once and was silent. No lights, no alarms, nothing to indicate whether I'd passed or failed. Not that I really needed the confirmation that I was infected—"Get a bite, say good-night," as they said when I was in training—but it still would have been nice. You were supposed to see your results. That was how the testing worked.

"Hey." George put her hand on my shoulder. "Why don't you go lie down? You're exhausted."

I shrugged her hand off. "No, I don't want to sleep through this. If this is the end of me being me, I don't want to miss it." A thought struck me, and I chuckled bitterly. "I can't be too far gone if I'm still hallucinating you, can I? You're a pretty complicated delusion. Zombies probably can't manage this quality of crazy."

"Thanks a lot."

"You're welcome."

She fell silent, and so did I. I was too tense to carry on a conversation, even with a dead person who lived only in my head. I'd just keep trying to pick a fight, and she'd keep trying to stop me, until we wound up screaming at each other and I spent the last minutes of my conscious life arguing with the one person I least wanted to argue with. I just wanted to know that she was there, and that I wasn't going through this alone.

So I stared at the test unit instead of talking to her, willing it to develop lights and tell me what I needed to know. All I needed was for it to confirm that my life was over. Nothing difficult. Nothing any fucking toaster couldn't manage these days.

I don't know how long I sat there staring at the test unit, feeling my throat getting dryer and waiting for the other symptoms to set in. The difficulty breathing, the sensitivity to light, the murkiness of thought—all the little dividing lines that separated human from zombie. Dryness of the throat was only the beginning, and my training was extensive enough to tell me exactly what the progression would be. Every little step along the way.

The door opened.

My head snapped up, tensing as I waited for the gunmen to enter. I wondered whether they'd send Becks to shoot me; I wondered whether she'd insist. We'd been colleagues for a long time, and Irwins tend to view shooting infected comrades as part of the job. It's a sign of respect.

Dr. Abbey stepped into the room.

I stopped breathing for a second, eyes going wide. They went even wider as Joe pushed past her, his tail wagging wildly from side to side. "You're going to let him be in here while you put me down?" I asked. "That's cold. I mean, not that I'm one to judge, but that's *cold*."

Dr. Abbey smiled. "Hello, Shaun." She shut the door behind herself, waiting until the locks finished hissing before she walked over to the other side of the table. She was carrying a folding chair, which she set up and sank into, watching me the whole time. "How are you feeling?"

"You shouldn't be in here," I said. Joe walked around the table and shoved his enormous head into my crotch in canine greeting. I barely remembered the blood on my hand in time to stop myself from pushing him away. "This isn't safe."

"Oh, right. You're contagious." She reached into the pocket of her lab coat, pulling out a can of Coke and putting it down on the table between us. "You must be thirsty. You've been sitting in here for a while." I stared at her. "No, really, open the can. I want to see how good your manual dexterity is."

Still staring, I reached out and picked up the can. Its cold heaviness was soothing, even before I popped the tab, closed my eyes, and took a long, freezing drink. It was the best thing I'd ever tasted, sugary syrupy sweetness and all.

Dr. Abbey was watching me intently when I opened my eyes. "How's the throat feeling, Shaun?" she asked.

"A little dry. I don't understand what you're doing—" I stopped. The dryness in my throat was gone, replaced by the residual carbonated tingle that always came after I drank one of George's Candyland hookers. "—here," I finished, more slowly. "Dr. Abbey?"

"I'm here because I wanted to talk to you about your test results, Shaun." She reached into her pocket again, this time producing a standard, run-of-the-mill field testing unit. Catching my surprise, she said, "Don't worry. It's been modified so it won't upload—it'll think it has, but it won't. This won't give our position away to the CDC, or to anybody else."

"I don't understand. Did something go wrong with my first test?"

"No, nothing went wrong with your first test. Now please." She gestured toward the unit. "Humor the woman who's willing to risk her life by offering sanctuary to your team, and take the goddamn test."

"Right." At least this one had lights. I popped off the lid, whispering, "One," and waiting for George's answering *Two*, before pressing my hand against the pressure pad. The needles bit in, quick and painful as always, and the lights began to flash through their complex analytic series of reds and greens. They flashed fast to begin with, then slowed as they settled on their final determination. It only took about thirty seconds for the last light to stop flashing.

All five of them settled on green.

I frowned, looking up at Dr. Abbey. Joe shoved his nose into my hand. I ignored him, focusing on her instead. "Is this a side effect of blocking the transmission? You change something internally so it registers negatives as positives?"

"No, Shaun. I didn't." Dr. Abbey calmly picked up the lid to the testing unit, snapping it back into place. She watched my face the entire time, moving with slow, methodical gestures, so that I wouldn't be surprised. She didn't really need to worry. I was somewhere past surprise by that point. "None of the adjustments we've made to our equipment would do something as suicidal or idiotic as showing a positive result as a negative one. We'd just disable the readouts, like we did with your first test. Those results came to my computer, and no one else's. I was able to study your entire viral profile."

"What are you trying to say?"

"I'm not *trying* to say anything. What I *am* saying is that your test results—both times, the ones you didn't see and the ones you just witnessed—came back clean." Dr. Abbey looked at me gravely, a wild excitement barely contained in her expression. "You're not sick, Shaun. You're not going to amplify.

"I don't know what your body did, but it encountered the live virus… and it fought it off. You're going to live."

I didn't know what to say. So I just stared at her, the green lights on the testing unit glowing steadily, like an accusation of a crime I had never plotted to commit. I'd been right all along; amplification would have been too easy an exit, and when given the chance, my body somehow refused to do it. I was going to live.

So now what?

CODA:

Living for You

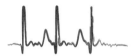

I have no idea what's going on anymore. When did the world stop making sense?

— SHAUN MASON

What the fuck is going on here?

— GEORGIA MASON

One of the Fictionals asked me this morning, if I could have one wish—any wish in the world, no matter how big or how small—what would I wish for? This would be a universe-changing wish. I could wish away Kellis-Amberlee. Hell, I could wish away the Rising if I wanted to, restore us to a universe where the zombies never came and we never wound up hiding in our houses, scared of everything we couldn't sterilize. And I stared at him until he realized what a stupid question that was and went running off, probably figuring that I was going to start hitting next.

He wasn't wrong.

If I could have any wish, no matter how big, no matter how small, I'd wish to have George back. Without that, nothing else I could wish for would be worth a fucking thing. And if you don't like that, you can shove it up your ass, because I don't care.

—From *Adaptive Immunities*,
the blog of Shaun Mason, January 5, 2041

Twenty-seven

I woke up in a white bed in a white room, with the cloying white smell of bleach in my nose and the tangled white cobwebs of my dreams still gnawing, ratlike, at the inside of my brain. I sat up with a gasp, realizing as I did that I was wearing white cotton pajamas and covered by a white comforter with no buttons or snaps. I took a breath, then another, trying to force my heart rate down as I looked around the room, seeking some clue as to where I was.

The only furnishings were the bed I was in and a single bedside table with rounded edges. I reached out and gave it an experimental shake. It was bolted to the floor. The bed probably was, too. Nothing in the room could be used as a weapon, unless I wanted to try strangling myself with the sheets. Even hanging was out of the question, since there was nothing for me to hang myself from.

A huge, inset mirror that almost certainly doubled as an observation window took up one entire wall. That sort of fixture in this sort of room can mean only one thing: medical holding facility, probably owned by the CDC. That fit with the dreams I'd been having, horrible, tangled things about some sort of major outbreak. No, not a major outbreak—there weren't that many people involved, at least not when we closed the doors. And we had to close the doors. We had to close the doors, because—

"I see you're awake."

The voice came from a speaker in the wall above the mirror and caught me entirely by surprise. I screamed a little, clutching the blanket against my chest before I realized I was being an idiot. Whoever had me in here could do a lot worse than talk to me, if they decided that was what they wanted. I eyed the speaker suspiciously, letting go of the blanket.

"I'm awake," I confirmed.

"Good, good. Now, you may be a little shaky at first. I don't recommend trying to walk before you've had a little time to get adjusted."

I was out of the bed before the voice was finished with its warning, stalking across the floor toward the mirror. Then I stopped again, stunned by the sight of my own reflection in what should have been—for me—a completely transparent surface. My eyes make one-way glass a pretty fiction.

Or they're supposed to, anyway. Only for some reason, things weren't working that way this time, and instead of looking at the hallway beyond the glass, I was looking at myself.

The pajamas I was wearing were at least two sizes too big, or maybe it was just that I'd lost weight: I looked like I was recovering from a long illness, all pale skin and bird-boned limbs. The lines of my collarbone stood out like knives, making me seem downright frail. My hair was too long, falling to hit my shoulders in those annoying thick curls that always seemed to form when I let it grow out, and my eyes ... There was something wrong with my eyes. Something very, very wrong.

I was still staring at my reflection when the speaker crackled on again. The voice from before came smoothly into the room, saying, "We're very glad to see you up and about. Some disorientation is normal at first, and you shouldn't let it bother you. Now, the speakers in your room are voice-activated; you don't need to look for a button or anything like that. Just speak loudly and clearly, and we'll understand you. Can you please tell us your name, and the last thing that you remember?"

I took a deep breath, holding it for a moment before letting it slowly out. Looking directly into my reflection—and hence, directly at anyone who happened to be standing in the hallway outside the one-way mirror, watching their little test subject, I answered.

"My name is Georgia Mason," I said. "What the *fuck* is going on here?"

Acknowledgments

Writing a follow-up volume to *Feed* was both elating and terrifying, and it wouldn't have been possible without the assistance of a wonderful group of people. I can't thank them enough. They ranged from medical professionals who worked with both humans and animals to gun experts and epidemiologists. *Deadline* is the work of many hands, and I am grateful to each and every one of them, because they were the ones who made this all possible.

Michelle Dockrey is a longtime editor of mine who chose to sit out *Feed* because it included zombies. Upon reading it, she promptly demanded the manuscript for *Deadline*, and just as quickly used her red pen and insightful eye for blocking to improve the book beyond all measure. (Also, I no longer need to worry about her trying to "sit this one out." I win at proofreader.) Brooke Lunderville stepped up to become primary medical consultant on this volume, and her keen sense of what you should and shouldn't do with a syringe can be seen on every page.

Alan Beatts joined the proofing pool as my new weapons expert, and his patient efforts to make me understand why a shotgun isn't the ideal zombie-fighting weapon did a lot to improve my combat scenes. I am incredibly grateful, especially given that it was really, really late in the process when I decided to say, "Hey, do you think you could..." Thanks also to Torrey Stenmark, Dave Tinney, and Debbie J. Gates for their well-timed, well-considered technical suggestions.

The Machete Squad must also, and always, be thanked. Amanda Perry, Rae Hanson, Sunil Patel, Alison Riley-Duncan, Rebecca Newman, Allison Hewett, Janet Maughan, Penelope Skrzynski, Phil Ames, and Amanda Sanders were all on tap for general proofreading and plot consultation. Through their efforts is this book made incalculably better. Meanwhile, at Orbit, DongWon Song was applying a keen editorial eye to the text, Lauren Panepinto was rocking the cover design, and Alex Lencicki was just plain rocking. Thanks so much, guys. I couldn't have done this without you.

Finally, acknowledgment for forbearance must go to Kate Secor, Shaun Connolly, and Cat Valente, who put up with an amazing amount of "talking it out" as I tried to make the book make sense; to my agent, Diana Fox, who remains my favorite superhero; to Betsy Tinney, for everything; and to Tara O'Shea and Chris Mangum, the incredible technical team behind www.MiraGrant.com. This book might have been written without them. It would not have been the same.

If you're curious about the American yellow fever epidemic and mosquito-based vectors, check out *The American Plague: The Untold Story of Yellow Fever*, by Molly Crosby.

Rise up while you can.

BLACKOUT

This book is dedicated to
Kathleen Secor,
Diana Fox,
and
Sunil Patel.

Without their efforts, I would never have made it this far.

BOOK I

From the Dead

People say things like "it wasn't supposed to go this way" and "this isn't what I wanted." They're just making noise. There's no such thing as "supposed to," and what you want doesn't matter. All that matters is what happened.

—Georgia Mason

I honestly have no idea what's going on anymore. I just need to find something I can hit.

—Shaun Mason

My name is Georgia Carolyn Mason. I am one of the Orphans of the Rising, the class of people who were under two years of age when the dead first started to walk. My biological family is presumably listed somewhere on The Wall, an anonymous footnote of a dead world. Their world died in the Rising. They didn't live to see the new one.

My adoptive parents have raised me to ask questions, understand the realities of my situation, and, in times of necessity, to shoot first. They have equipped me with the tools I need to survive, and I am grateful. Through this blog, I will do my best to share my experiences and opinions as openly and honestly as I can. It is the best way to honor the family that raised me; it is the only way I have to honor the family that lost me.

I'm going to tell you the truth as I understand it. You can take it from there.

—From *Images May Disturb You*,
the blog of Georgia Mason, June 20, 2035.

So George says I have to write a "mission statement," because our contract with Bridge Supporters says I will. I am personally opposed to mission statements, since they're basically one more way of sucking the fun out of everything. I tried telling George this. She told me that it's her job to suck the fun out of everything. She then threatened physical violence of a type I will not describe in detail, as it might unsettle and upset my theoretical readership. Suffice to say that I am writing a mission statement. Here it is:

I, Shaun Phillip Mason, being of sound mind and body, do hereby swear to poke dead things with sticks, do stupid shit for your amusement, and put it all on the Internet where you can watch it over and over again. Because that's what you want, right?

Glad to oblige.

—From *Hail to the King*,
the blog of Shaun Mason, June 20, 2035.

One

My story ended where so many stories have ended since the Rising: with a man—in this case, my adoptive brother and best friend, Shaun—holding a gun to the base of my skull as the virus in my blood betrayed me, transforming me from a thinking human being into something better suited to a horror movie.

My story ended, but I remember everything. I remember the cold dread as I watched the lights on the blood test unit turn red, one by one, until my infection was confirmed. I remember the look on Shaun's face when he realized this was it—it was really happening, and there wasn't going to be any clever third act solution that got me out of the van alive.

I remember the barrel of the gun against my skin. It was cool, and it was soothing, because it meant Shaun would do what he had to do. No one else would get hurt because of me.

No one but Shaun.

This was something we'd never planned for. I always knew that one day he'd push his luck too far, and I'd lose him. We never dreamed that he would be the one losing me. I wanted to tell him it would be okay. I wanted to lie to him. I remember that: I wanted to lie to him. And I couldn't. There wasn't time, and even then, I didn't have it in me.

I remember starting to write. I remember thinking this was it; this was my last chance to say anything I wanted to say to the world. This was the thing I was going to be judged on, now and forever. I remember feeling my mind start to go. I remember the fear.

I remember the sound of Shaun pulling the trigger.

I shouldn't remember anything after that. That's where my story ended. Curtain down, save file, that's a wrap. Once the bullet hits your spinal cord, you're done; you don't have to worry about this shit anymore.

You definitely shouldn't wake up in a windowless, practically barren room that looks suspiciously like a CDC holding facility, with no one to talk to but some unidentified voice on the other side of a one-way mirror.

The bed where I'd woken up was bolted to the floor, and so was the matching bedside table. It wouldn't do to have the mysteriously resurrected dead journalist throwing things at the mirror that took up most of one wall. Naturally, the wall with the mirror was the only wall with a door—a door that refused to open. I'd tried waving my hands in front of every place that might hold a motion sensor, and then I'd searched for a test panel in the vain hope that checking out clean would make the locks let go and release me.

There were no test panels, or screens, or ocular scanners. There wasn't anything inside that seemed designed to let me out. That was chilling all by itself. I grew up in a post-Rising world, one where blood tests and the threat of infection are a part of daily life. I'm sure I'd been in sealed rooms without testing units before. I just couldn't remember any.

The room lacked something else: clocks. There was nothing to let me know how much time had passed since I woke up, much less how much time had passed *before* I woke up. There'd been a voice from the speaker above the mirror, an unfamiliar voice asking my name and what the last thing I remembered was. I'd answered him—"My name is Georgia Mason. What the *fuck* is going on here?"—and he'd gone away without answering my question. That might have been ten minutes ago. It might have been ten hours ago. The lights overhead glared steady and white, not so much as flickering as the seconds went slipping past.

That was another thing. The overhead lights were industrial fluorescents, the sort that have been popular in medical facilities since long before the Rising. They should have been burning my eyes like acid…and they weren't.

I was diagnosed with retinal Kellis-Amberlee when I was a kid, meaning that the same disease that causes the dead to rise had taken up permanent residence in my eyeballs. It didn't turn me into a zombie—retinal KA is a reservoir condition, one where the live virus is somehow contained inside the body. Retinal KA gave me extreme light sensitivity, excellent night vision, and a tendency to get sickening migraines if I did anything without my sunglasses on.

Well, I wasn't wearing sunglasses, and it wasn't like I could dim the lights, but my eyes still didn't hurt. All I felt was thirst, and a vague, gnawing hunger in the pit of my stomach, like lunch might be a good idea sometime soon. There was no headache. I honestly couldn't decide whether or not that was a good sign.

Anxiety was making my palms sweat. I scrubbed them against the legs of my unfamiliar white cotton pajamas. *Everything* in the room was unfamiliar...even me. I've never been heavy—a life spent running after stories and away from zombies doesn't encourage putting on weight—but the girl in the one-way mirror was thin to the point of being scrawny. She looked like she'd be easy to break. Her hair was as dark as mine. It was also too long, falling past her shoulders. I've never allowed my hair to get that long. Hair like that is a passive form of suicide when you do what I do for a living. And her eyes...

Her eyes were brown. That, more than anything else, made it impossible to think of her face as my own. I don't *have* visible irises. I have pupils that fill all the space not occupied by sclera, giving me a black, almost emotionless stare. Those weren't my eyes. But my eyes didn't hurt. Which meant either those *were* my eyes, and my retinal KA had somehow been cured, or Buffy was right when she said the afterlife existed, and this was hell.

I shuddered, looking away from my reflection, and resumed what was currently my main activity: pacing back and forth and trying to think. Until I knew whether I was being watched, I had to think quietly, and that made it a hell of a lot harder. I've always thought better when I do it out loud, and this was the first time in my adult life that I'd been anywhere without at least one recorder running. I'm an accredited journalist. When I talk to myself, it's not a sign of insanity; it's just my way of making sure I don't lose important material before I can write it down.

None of this was right. Even if there was some sort of experimental treatment to reverse amplification, someone would have been there to explain things to me. *Shaun* would have been there. And there it was, the reason I couldn't believe any of this was right: I remembered him pulling the trigger. Even assuming it was a false memory, even assuming it never happened, *why wasn't he here?* Shaun would move Heaven and Earth to reach me.

I briefly entertained the idea that he was somewhere in the building, forcing the voice from the intercom to tell him where I was. Regretfully, I dismissed it. Something would have exploded by now if that were true.

"Goddammit." I scowled at the wall, turned, and started in the other direction. The hunger was getting worse, and it was accompanied by a new, more frustrating sensation. I needed to pee. If someone didn't let

me out soon, I was going to have a whole new set of problems to contend
with.

"Run the timeline, George," I said, taking some comfort in the sound
of my voice. Everything else might have changed, but not that. "You were
in Sacramento with Rick and Shaun, running for the van. Something hit
you in the arm. One of those syringes like they used at the Ryman farm.
The test came back positive. Rick left. And then...then..." I faltered, having trouble finding the words, even if there was no one else to hear them.

Everyone who grew up after the Rising knows what happens when you
come into contact with the live form of Kellis-Amberlee. You become a
zombie, one of the infected, and you do what every zombie exists to do.
You bite. You infect. You kill. You feed. You don't wake up in a white room,
wearing white pajamas and wondering how your brother was able to shoot
you in the neck without even leaving a scar.

Scars. I wheeled and stalked back to the mirror, pulling the lid on my
right eye open wide. I learned how to look at my own eyes when I was
eleven. That's when I got my first pair of protective contacts. That's also
when I got my first visible retinal scarring, little patches of tissue scorched
beyond recovery by the sun. We caught it in time to prevent major vision
loss, and I got a lot more careful. The scarring created small blind spots
at the center of my vision. Nothing major. Nothing that interfered with
fieldwork. Just little spots.

My pupil contracted to almost nothing as the light hit it. The spots
weren't there. I could see clearly, without any gaps.

"Oh." I lowered my hand. "I guess that makes sense."

I paused, feeling suddenly stupid as that realization led to another.
When I first woke up, the voice from the intercom told me all I had to
do was speak, and someone would hear me. I looked up at the speaker. "A
little help here?" I said. "I need to pee really bad."

There was no response.

"Hello?"

There was still no response. I showed my middle finger to the mirror
before turning and walking back to the bed. Once there, I sat and settled
into a cross-legged position, closing my eyes. And then I started waiting.
If anyone was watching me—and someone *had* to be watching me—this
might be a big enough change in my behavior to get their attention. I
wanted their attention. I wanted their attention really, really badly. Almost
as badly as I wanted a personal recorder, an Internet connection, and a
bathroom.

The need for a bathroom crept slowly higher on the list, accompanied by the need for a drink of water. I was beginning to consider the possibility that I might need to use a corner of the room as a lavatory when the intercom clicked on. A moment later, a new voice, male, like the first one, spoke: "Miss Mason? Are you awake?"

"Yes." I opened my eyes. "Do I get a name to call you by?"

He ignored my question like it didn't matter. Maybe it didn't, to him. "I apologize for the silence. We'd expected a longer period of disorientation, and I had to be recalled from elsewhere in the building."

"Sorry to disappoint you."

"Oh, we weren't disappointed," said the voice. He had the faintest trace of a Midwestern accent. I couldn't place the state. "I promise, we're thrilled to see you up and coherent so quickly. It's a wonderful indicator for your recovery."

"A glass of water and a trip to the ladies' room would do more to help my recovery than apologies and evasions."

Now the voice sounded faintly abashed. "I'm sorry, Miss Mason. We didn't think...just a moment." The intercom clicked off, leaving me in silence once again. I stayed where I was, and kept waiting.

The sound of a hydraulic lock unsealing broke the quiet. I turned to see a small panel slide open above the door, revealing a red light. It turned green and the door slid smoothly open, revealing a skinny, nervous-looking man in a white lab coat, eyes wide behind his glasses. He was clutching his clipboard to his chest like he thought it afforded him some sort of protection.

"Miss Mason? If you'd like to come with me, I'd be happy to escort you to the restroom."

"Thank you." I unfolded my legs, ignoring pins and needles in my calves, and walked toward the doorway. The man didn't quite cringe as I approached, but he definitely shied back, looking more uneasy with every step I took. Interesting.

"We apologize for making you wait," he said. His words had the distinct cadence of something recited by rote, like telephone tech support asking for your ID and computer serial number. "There were a few things that had to be taken care of before we could proceed."

"Let's worry about that *after* I get to the bathroom, okay?" I sidestepped around him, out into the hall, and found myself looking at three hospital orderlies in blue scrubs, each of them pointing a pistol in my direction. I stopped where I was. "Okay, I can wait for my escort."

"That's for the best, Miss Mason," said the nervous man, whose voice I now recognized from the intercom. It just took a moment without the filtering speakers between us. "Just a necessary precaution. I'm sure you understand."

"Yeah. Sure." I fell into step behind him. The orderlies followed us, their aim never wavering. I did my best not to make any sudden moves. Having just returned to the land of the living, I was in no mood to exit it again. "Am I ever going to get something I can call you?"

"Ah..." His mouth worked soundlessly for a moment before he said, "I'm Dr. Thomas. I've been one of your personal physicians since you arrived at this facility. I'm not surprised you don't remember me. You've been sleeping for some time."

"Is that what the kids are calling it these days?" The hall was built on the model I've come to expect from CDC facilities, with nothing breaking the sterile white walls but the occasional door and the associated one-way mirrors looking into patient holding rooms. All the rooms were empty.

"You're walking well."

"It's a skill."

"How's your head? Any disorientation, blurred vision, confusion?"

"Yes." He tensed. I ignored it, continuing. "I'm confused about what I'm doing here. I don't know about you, but I get twitchy when I wake up in strange places with no idea how I got there. Will I be getting some answers soon?"

"Soon enough, Miss Mason." He stopped in front of a door with no mirror next to it. That implied that it wasn't a patient room. Better yet, there was a blood test unit to one side. I never thought I'd be so happy for the chance to be jabbed with a needle. "We'll give you a few minutes. If you need anything—"

"Using the bathroom, also a skill." I slapped my palm down on the test panel. Needles promptly bit into the heel of my hand and the tips of my fingers. The light over the door flashed between red and green before settling on the latter. Uninfected. The door swung open. I stepped through, only to stop and scowl at the one-way mirror taking up most of the opposite wall. The door swung shut behind me.

"Cute," I muttered. The need to pee was getting bad enough that I didn't protest the situation. I glared at the mirror the entire time I was using the facilities, all but daring someone to watch me. See? I can pee whether you're spying on me or not, you sick bastards.

Other than the mirror—or maybe because of the mirror—the bathroom was as standard-issue CDC as the hallway outside, with white walls, a white tile floor, and white porcelain fixtures. Everything was automatic, including the soap dispenser, and there were no towels; instead, I dried my hands by sticking them into a jet of hot air. It was one big exercise in minimizing contact with any surface. When I turned back to the door, the only things I'd touched were the toilet seat and the floor, and I was willing to bet that they were in the process of self-sterilization by the time I started washing my hands.

The blood test required to exit the bathroom was set into the door itself, just above the knob. It didn't unlock until I checked out clean.

The three orderlies were waiting in the hall, with an unhappy Dr. Thomas between them and me. If I did anything bad enough to make them pull those triggers, the odds were good that he'd be treated as collateral damage.

"Wow," I said. "Who did you piss off to get this gig?"

He flinched, looking at me guiltily. "I'm sure I don't know what you mean."

"Of course not. Thank you for bringing me to the bathroom. Now, could I get that water?" Better yet, a can of Coke. The thought of its acid sweetness was enough to make my mouth water. It's good to know that some things never change.

"If you'd come this way?"

I gave the orderlies a pointed look. "I don't think I have much of a choice, do you?"

"No, I suppose you don't," he said. "As I said, a precaution. You understand."

"Not really, no. I'm unarmed. I've just passed two blood tests. I *don't* understand why I need three men with guns covering my every move." The CDC has been paranoid for years, but this was taking it to a new extreme.

Dr. Thomas's reply didn't help: "Security."

"Why do people always say that when they don't feel like giving a straight answer?" I shook my head. "I'm not going to make trouble. Please, just take me to the water."

"Right this way," he said, and started back the way we'd come.

There was a tray waiting for us on the bolted-down table in the room where I'd woken up. It held a plate with two pieces of buttered toast, a tumbler full of water, and wonder of wonders, miracle of miracles, a can of Coke with condensation beading on the sides. I made for the tray without pausing to consider how the orderlies might react to my moving faster than a stroll. None of them shot me in the back. That was something.

The first bite of toast was the best thing I'd ever tasted, at least until I took the second bite, and then the third. Finally, I crammed most of the slice into my mouth, barely chewing. I managed to resist the siren song of the Coke long enough to drink half the water. It tasted as good as the toast. I put down the glass, popped the tab on the can of soda, and took my first post-death sip of Coke. I was smart enough not to gulp it; even that tiny amount was enough to make my knees weak. That, and the caffeine rush that followed, provided the last missing piece.

Slowly, I turned to face Dr. Thomas. He was standing in the doorway, making notes on his clipboard. There were probably a few dozen video and audio recorders running, catching every move I made, but any good reporter will tell you that there's nothing like real field experience. I guess the same thing applies to scientists. He lowered his pen when he saw me looking.

"How do you feel?" he asked. "Dizzy? Are you full? Did you want something besides toast? It's a bit early for anything complicated, but I might be able to arrange for some soup, if you'd prefer that…"

"Mostly, what'd I'd prefer is having some questions answered." I shifted the Coke from one hand to the other. If I couldn't have my sunglasses, I guess a can of soda would have to do. "I think I've been pretty cooperative up to now. I also think that could change."

Dr. Thomas looked uncomfortable. "Well, I suppose that will depend on what sort of questions you want to ask."

"This one should be pretty easy. I mean, it's definitely within your skill set."

"All right. I can't promise to know the answer, but I'm happy to try. We want you to be comfortable."

"Good." I looked at him levelly, missing my black-eyed gaze. It always made people so uncomfortable. I got more honest answers out of those eyes… "You said you were my personal physician."

"That's correct."

"So tell me: How long have I been a clone?"

Dr. Thomas dropped his pen.

Still watching him, I raised my Coke, took a sip, and waited for his reply.

Subject 139b was bitten on the evening of June 24, 2041. The exact time of the bite was not recorded, but a period of no less than twenty minutes elapsed between exposure and initial testing. The infected individual responsible for delivering the bite was retrieved from the road. Posthumous analysis confirmed that the individual was heavily contagious, and had been so for at least six days, as the virus had amplified through all parts of the body.

Blood samples were taken from the outside of Subject 139b's hand and sequenced to prove that they belonged to the subject. Analysis of these samples confirmed the infection. (For proof of live viral bodies in Subject 139b's blood, see the attached file.) Amplification appears to have begun normally, and followed the established progression toward full loss of cognitive functionality. Samples taken from Subject 139b's clothing confirm this diagnosis.

Subject 139b was given a blood test shortly after arriving at this facility, and tested clean of all live viral particles. Subject 139b was given a second test, using a more sensitive unit, and once again tested clean. After forty-eight hours of isolation, following standard Kellis-Amberlee quarantine procedures, it is my professional opinion that the subject is not now infected, and does not represent a danger to himself or others.

With God as my witness, Joey, I swear to you that Shaun Mason is *not* infected with the live state of Kellis-Amberlee. He should be. He's not. He started to amplify, and he somehow fought the infection off. This could change everything...if we had the slightest fucking clue how he did it.

—Taken from an e-mail sent by Dr. Shannon Abbey to Dr. Joseph Shoji at the Kauai Institute of Virology, June 27, 2041.

Times like this make me think my mother was right when she told me I should aspire to be a trophy wife. At least that would have reduced the odds of my winding up hiding in a renegade virology lab, hunting zombies for a certifiable mad scientist.

Then again, maybe not.

—From *Charming Not Sincere*, the blog of Rebecca Atherton, July 16, 2041. Unpublished.

Two

"Shaun! Look out!"

Alaric's shout came through my headset half a second before a hand grabbed my elbow, bearing down with that weird mixture of strength and clumsiness characteristic of the fully amplified. I yanked free, whirling to smack my assailant upside the head with my high-powered cattle prod.

A look of almost comic surprise crossed the zombie's face as the electrified end of the cattle prod hit its temple. Then it fell. I kicked the body. It didn't move. I hit it in the solar plexus with my cattle prod, just to be sure. Electricity has always been useful against zombies, since it confuses the virus that motivates them, but it turns out that when you amp the juice enough you can actually shut them down for short periods of time.

"Thanks for the heads-up," I said, trusting the headset to pick me up. "I've got another dead boy down. Send the retrieval team to my coordinates." I was already starting to scan the trees, looking for signs of movement—looking for something else that I could hit.

"Shaun…" There was a wary note in Alaric's voice. I could practically see him sitting at his console, knotting his hands in his hair and trying not to let his irritation come through the microphone. I *was* his boss, after all, which meant he had to at least pretend to be respectful. Once in a while. "That's your fourth catch of the night. I think that's enough, don't you?"

"I'm going for the record."

There was a click as Becks plugged her own channel into the connection and snapped peevishly, "You've already *got* the record. Four catches in a night is twice what anyone else has managed, ever. Now please, *please*, come back to the lab."

"What will you do if I don't?" I asked. Nothing seemed to be moving, except for my infected friend, who twitched. I zapped him with the cattle prod again. The movement stopped.

"Two words, Shaun: tranquilizer darts. Now come back to the lab."

I whistled. "That's not playing fair. How about you promise to bake me chocolate chip cookies if I come back? That seems like a much better incentive."

"How about you stop screwing around before you make me angry? Immune doesn't mean immortal, you know. Now please." The peevishness faded, replaced by pleading. "Just come home."

She's right, said George—or the ghost of George, anyway, the little voice at the back of my head that's all I have left of my adopted sister. Some people say I have issues. I say those people need to expand their horizons, because I don't have issues, I have the Library of Congress. *You need to go back. This isn't doing anybody any good.*

"I don't know," I said. I used to be circumspect about talking to George. That was before I decided to go all the way insane. Madness is surprisingly freeing. "I mean, *I'm* having fun. Aren't you the one who used to nag me to get my butt back into the field? Is this field enough for you?"

Shaun. Please.

My smile faded. "Fine. Whatever. If you want me to go back to the stupid lab, I'll go back to the stupid lab. Happy now?"

No, said George. *But it's going to have to do.*

I poked my latest catch one last time with the cattle prod. It didn't react. I turned to stalk back through the trees to the ripped-up side road where the bike was parked. Gunshots sounded from the forest to my left. I paused. Silence followed them, rather than screaming. I nodded and started walking again. Maybe that seems callous, but I wasn't the only one collecting virtual corpses for Dr. Abbey, the crazy renegade virologist who'd been sheltering us since we were forced off the grid. Most of her lab technicians were either ex-military or trained marksmen. They could take care of themselves, at least in the "killing stuff" department. I was less sure about bringing the zombies home alive. Fortunately for me, that was their problem, not mine.

Alaric's sigh of relief made me jump. I'd almost forgotten that he and Becks were listening in from their cozy spot in the main lab. "Thank you for seeing sense."

"Don't thank me," I said. "Thank George."

Neither of them had anything to say to that. I hadn't expected them to. I tapped the button on the side of my headset, killing the connection, and kept walking.

It had been just under a month since the world turned upside down. Some days, I was almost grateful to be waking up in an underground virology lab. Sure, most of the things it contained could kill me—including the head virologist, who I suspected of having fantasies about dissecting me so she could analyze my organs—but at least we knew what was going on. We had a place, if not a fully functional plan. That put us way ahead of the surviving denizens of North America's Gulf Coast, who were still contending with something we'd never anticipated: an insect vector for Kellis-Amberlee.

A tropical storm had blown some brand-new strain of mosquito over from Cuba, one with a big enough bite to transmit the live virus to humans. No one had heard of an insect vector for Kellis-Amberlee before that day. The entire world had heard of it on the day after, as every place Tropical Storm Fiona touched discovered the true meaning of "storm damage." The virus spread initially with the storm, and then started spreading on its own as the winds died down and the mosquitoes went looking for something to munch on. It was a genuine apocalypse scenario, the sort of thing that makes trained medical personnel shit their pants and call for their mommies. And it was really happening, and there wasn't a damn thing we could do about it.

The worst part? Even if no one wanted to say it out loud, when you looked at the timing of everything going wrong—the way it all happened just as we started really prodding at the CDC's sore spots—I thought there was a pretty good chance it wasn't an accident. And that would mean it was our fault.

There was no one standing watch over the vehicles. That was sloppy; even if we cleared out the human infected, there was always the chance a zombie raccoon or something could take refuge under one of the collection vans and go for somebody's ankles when they came back with the evening's haul. I made a mental note to talk to Dr. Abbey about her tactical setup as I swung a leg over the bike. Then I put on my helmet—Becks was right, immune doesn't mean immortal—and took off down the road.

See, here's the thing. My name is Shaun Mason; I'm a journalist, I guess, even though right now all my posts are staying unpublished for security's sake. I'm not technically wanted for anything. It's just that places where I show up have a nasty tendency to get wiped off the map shortly after I get there, and that makes me a little gun-shy when it comes to telling people where I am. I think that's understandable. Then again, I also think my dead sister talks to me, so what do I know?

About a year and a half ago—which feels like yesterday and an eternity at the same time—George and I applied to blog for Senator Peter Ryman's presidential campaign, along with our friend Georgette "Buffy" Meissonier. Before that, I was your average gentleman Irwin, wanting nothing beyond a few dead things to poke with sticks and the opportunity to write up my adventures for an adoring populace. Pretty simple, right? The three of us had everything we needed to be happy. Only we didn't know that, so when the chance to grab for glory came, we took it. We wanted to make history.

We made it, all right. We made it, Buffy and George *became* it, and I wound up as the last man standing, the one who has to avenge the glorious dead. All I know is that part wasn't in the brochure.

The road smoothed as I got closer to our current home-sweet-home. Shady Cove, Oregon, has been deserted since the Rising, when the infected left the tiny community officially uninhabitable. We had to be careful about how visible we were, but Dr. Abbey had been sending her interns—interning for what, I didn't know, since most universities don't offer a degree in mad science—out at night to patch the worst of the potholes with a homebrewed asphalt substitute that looked just like the real thing.

Fixing the road was a mixed blessing. It could give away our location if someone came looking. In the meantime, it made it easier for supply runs to get through, even if no one seemed to know how we were getting those supplies, and it would make it easier for us to evacuate the lab when the time came. Dr. Abbey didn't care how many of us died, as long as her equipment made it out. I had to admire that sort of single-minded approach. It reminded me of George.

Everything reminds you of me, George said.

I snorted but didn't answer. The roar of the wind in my ears was too loud for me to hear my own voice, and I like to pretend that we're having real conversations. It helps. With what, I can't quite say, but... it helps.

Barely visible sensors in the underbrush tracked my approach as I came around the final curve and entered the parking lot of the Shady Cove Forestry Center. The building was dark, its vast pre-Rising windows like blind eyes staring into the trees. It looked empty. It wasn't. I drove around to the back, where the old employee parking garage had been restored and strengthened to provide cover for our vehicles.

Since it was a pre-Rising design, I didn't need to pass a blood test to get inside, and was able to just drive straight to my assigned slot, shutting off the bike. I removed my helmet and slung it over the handlebars, leaving it there in case I needed to leave in a hurry. I approach everything as a potential evacuation these days. I've got good reason.

Cameras tracked my progress toward the door. "Hello, Shaun," said the lab computer. It was pleasant and female, with a Canadian accent. Maybe it reminded Dr. Abbey of home. I didn't know.

What I *did* know was that I don't like computers pretending to be human. It creeps me out. "Can I come in?" I asked.

"Please place your palm on the testing panel." An amber light came on above the test unit, helpfully indicating where I needed to put my hand. Like any kid who lives long enough to go to kindergarten doesn't know how to operate a basic blood testing panel? You learn, or you die.

"I don't see the point of this." I slapped my hand down on the metal. Cooling foam sprayed my skin a bare second before needles started biting into my flesh. I hate blood tests. "You know I'm not infected. I *can't* be infected. So why don't you stop fucking around and let me inside?"

"All personnel must be tested when returning from the field, Shaun. There are no exceptions." The amber light blinked off, replaced by two more lights, one red, one green. They began flashing.

"I liked this place a lot better before Dr. Abbey got you online," I said.

"Thank you for your cooperation," replied the computer blithely. The red light winked off as the green one stabilized, confirming my uninfected status. Again. "Welcome home."

The door into the main lab unlocked, sliding open. I flipped off the nearest camera and walked inside.

Dr. Abbey's people have had lots of practice converting formerly abandoned buildings into functional scientific research centers. The Shady Cove Forestry Center was practically tailor-made for them, being large, constructed to withstand the elements, and best of all, in the middle of fucking nowhere. Entering from the parking garage put me in the main room—originally the Visitor's Welcome Lobby, according to the brass sign by the door. That explained the brightly colored mural of cheerful woodland creatures on the wall. People used to romanticize the natural world, before the Rising. These days, we mostly just run away from it.

Interns and technicians were everywhere, all rushing around on weird science errands. I don't understand most of what Dr. Abbey's people do, and that's probably a good thing. Mahir understands a lot more than I do, and he says it makes it hard for him to sleep at night.

Speaking of Mahir, the man himself was storming across the room, a look of profound irritation on his face. "Are you *trying* to get yourself killed?" he demanded.

"That's an interesting philosophical question, and one that would be better discussed over a can of Coke," I replied amiably. "It's good to see you, too."

"I have half a mind to punch your face in, you bloody idiot," Mahir said, still scowling.

Mahir used to be George's second in command. Since she can't run a third of the staff as a voice in my head, Mahir took over the Newsies when she died. I sometimes think he's angry with me for not being angrier with him over taking her place. What he never seems to quite understand is that he's one of the only people in this world who loved George the way I did, and having him on my side makes me feel a little better.

Besides, it's funny as hell when he gets pissed. "But you won't," I said. "What's our status?"

Mahir's glare faded, replaced by weariness. "Alaric is still attempting to find out what keeps happening to our mirror sites. We've put up six new reports from the junior bloggers in the past hour, none of which touch on the Gulf Coast tragedy, and three of them have vanished into thin air. I think he's going to start pulling his hair out before much longer."

"This is what happens when you piss off a government conspiracy." I started walking toward the kitchen. "How's Becks doing on the extraction plan?"

Mahir answered with a small shake of his head.

"Aw, damn." Alaric's little sister, Alisa, was in Florida when Tropical Storm Fiona made landfall. She managed to survive the first wave of infections, through a combination of quick thinking and dumb luck. After that...Alaric was unable to step forward to claim her, since Dr. Abbey said that if one of us left, all of us left. We thought Alisa might wind up placed with a foster family, but things in Florida were too bad for that. She wound up in a government-sponsored refugee camp. She was sending regular updates and had managed to stay mostly out of trouble. Still, it was clear that if we didn't find a way to get her out of there soon, Alaric was going to do something stupid. I understood his motivation. Family's the most important thing there is.

"Yes, well. It is what it is." Mahir paced me easily. He wasn't always a field man, but he'd been working out since we arrived at Dr. Abbey's—something about not wanting to die the next time we wound up running for our lives. "Dr. Abbey requests the pleasure of your company once you've had the opportunity to clean yourself up."

I groaned. I couldn't help it. "More blood tests?"

"More blood tests," he confirmed.

"Motherfucker." I scowled at nothing in particular. "Immunity is more trouble than it's worth."

"Yes, absolutely, being mysteriously immune to the zombie plague which has devastated the world is a terrible cross to bear," said Mahir, deadpan.

"Hey, you try giving blood on a daily basis and see how you feel about it."

"No, thank you."

I sighed. "Is this another of those 'no caffeine before donating' days? Did she say?"

"I believe it's not."

"Thank God for that." Don't get me wrong. No one knows why I seem to be immune to Kellis-Amberlee amplification—something the CDC has been telling us is impossible since the Rising, by the way. You get bitten, you amplify, simple as that. Only it turns out that with me, it actually goes "you get bitten; you get annoyed; you have to take a lot of antibiotics, because human mouths are incredibly dirty and dying of a bacterial infection would suck; you get better." I understood why Dr. Abbey needed blood almost every day. It was just a *lot* of needles.

Becks was in the kitchen when we arrived. She was sitting on the counter, holding a can of Coke. "Looking for this?" she asked.

"My savior." I walked toward her, making grabbing motions. "Gimme. Gimme sweet, sweet caffeine."

"The word is 'please,' Mason. Look it up." She tossed me the can, a gentle underhand lob that wouldn't shake the contents up too much. The team does that a lot these days—throws me things to double-check my manual dexterity. My recovery after being bitten was too miraculous to believe. We're all waiting for it to wear off and for me to go rampaging through the lab.

I made the catch and cracked the tab, taking a long, cold drink before putting the can down on the nearest table and asking, "Have any of the new guys made it in yet?"

"The first batch is in processing now," Becks replied. "We managed to net twenty-four infected tonight, including your four."

"Cool." Our lovely hostess needed a constant supply of fresh subjects, since her experiments required a couple dozen at any given time, and her lab protocols didn't leave many of them alive past the three-day mark. Snatch-and-grab patrols were going out twice a week, minimum, and at the rate they were working, Shady Cove was going to be free of the infected in under three months.

"I guess." Becks slid off the counter, giving me a calculating look. "What were you doing out there tonight, Mason? You could have been killed."

"That wasn't my first solo in these woods."

"It was your first one at night." She shook her head. "You're starting to scare me."

"And me," said Mahir.

And me, said George.

"You don't get a say in this," I muttered. Mahir didn't look offended. He knew I wasn't talking to him. In a more normal tone, I asked, "So what do you want me to do, Becks? I don't speak science. I barely speak research. Things are a mess out there, and we're stuck in here, spinning our wheels."

"So maybe it's time you stopped spinning." The three of us turned toward Dr. Abbey's voice. Like the lab computer, it was pleasant and Canadian-accented. Unlike the lab computer, it was coming from a short, curvy scientist with bleached streaks in her shaggy brown hair. Her lab coat was open, exposing a bright orange CEPHALOPODS UNION #462 T-shirt.

I raised an eyebrow. "Okay, I'm listening. What have you got in mind?"

Dr. Abbey held up a thumb drive. "Get your team and meet me in the screening room. It's time we had a little talk about what's going on in Florida." She quirked a small smile. "You can bring popcorn."

"Science and snacks, the perfect combination," I said. "We'll be there."

"Good," said Dr. Abbey, and left.

Mahir stepped up next to me. "Do you have any idea what that's all about?"

"Nope." I shrugged, picking up my Coke again. The second drink was just as good as the first had been. "But hey. We may as well get started. What's the worst that can happen?"

Managing things without Georgia has never been what I would term "easy," but it's never been harder than in the past few months. The devastation wreaked by Tropical Storm Fiona would have been terrible even without the additional horror of a newly discovered insect vector for Kellis-Amberlee infection. The loss of life would have been appalling even if so many of the lost had not gone on to attack and infect their fellow men. I find myself watching the news feeds and wishing, more than ever before, that Georgia Mason were with us today.

Georgia had a gift for reporting the news without letting sentiment color her impressions: She saw the world in black and white, no shades of gray allowed. It could have been a crippling disability in any other profession, but she made it her greatest strength. If she were here, she would be the one reducing bodies to statistics, rendering disasters into history. But she's not here. She, too, has been reduced to a statistic, has been rendered into history. All of which means that I, unprepared as I am, have been forced to do her job.

May posterity show mercy when it looks back upon the work we do today. We did what we could with what we had.

—From *Fish and Clips*,
the blog of Mahir Gowda, July 16, 2041.

Subject 7c is awake, responsive, and self-aware. Subject has asked several conditionally relevant questions, and does not appear to suffer any visual or cognitive disorders. Subject self-identifies as "Georgia Mason," and is able to recount events up to the point of physical death (see GEORGIA C. MASON, AUTOPSY FILE for details of injury).

We are prepared to continue with this subject for the time being. Full medical files are being transmitted under a secure encryption key.

—Taken from an e-mail sent by Dr. Matthew Thomas,
July 16, 2041.

GEORGIA MASON LIVES.

—Graffiti from inside the Florida disaster zone,
picture published under Creative Commons license.

Three

I have to give Dr. Thomas this: He recovered quickly from the question I obviously wasn't supposed to be asking yet. "I don't think you understand what you're saying." He retrieved his pen from the floor. "Maybe you need to sit down."

"My eyes are wrong. I could possibly be convinced to believe in a regenerative treatment that erased my scars. I could even accept that it was a deep enough dermal renewal to remove my licensing tattoo." I raised my wrist, showing him the spot where my personal information should have been permanently scribed. "But there's nothing that could have repaired my eyes. So I ask again: How long have I been a clone?"

Dr. Thomas narrowed his eyes. I stood up a little straighter, trying to look imposing. It wasn't easy to do in a pair of CDC-issue pajamas.

"This is highly irregular..." Dr. Thomas began.

"So is cloning reporters." I took a final sip of Coke before forcing myself to put it down. The caffeine was already starting to make me jittery. The last thing I wanted to do was finish the can and have my hands start shaking. "Come on. Who am I going to tell? I'm assuming you're not planning on giving me a connection to the outside world anytime soon."

Dr. Thomas gave me a calculating look. I looked back, wishing I had the slightest idea of how to look earnest and well meaning with my strange new eyes. Living life behind a pair of sunglasses was so much easier.

Finally, he nodded, a familiar expression flickering across his face. I'd seen it worn by a hundred interview subjects, all of whom thought they were about to pull one over on me. None of them ever seemed to realize that maybe my degree in journalism included one or two classes in human psychology. I may not be good at lying, but oh, I know a lie when I hear one.

"As I said before, this is highly irregular," he said in a lower, warmer tone of voice.

Trying to win my trust through confession. Pretty standard stuff, even if the situation was anything but standard. "I know, but please. I just want to know what's going on." I've never done "vulnerable" well. It wasn't on the final exam.

Maybe the fact that I was actually feeling vulnerable behind my facade of journalistic calm was showing through, because Dr. Thomas said, "I understand. You must be very confused."

"Also frightened, disoriented, and a little bit trying to convince myself this isn't a dream," I replied. I picked up my Coke again, not to drink, but to feel it in my hand. It was a poor substitute for the things I really wanted—my sunglasses, a gun, Shaun—but it would have to do.

"You have to understand that this is an experimental procedure. There was no way we could predict success, or even be sure that you would be yourself when you woke up." Dr. Thomas watched me as he spoke. He was telling the truth, or at least the truth as he understood it. "To be honest with you, we're still not sure how stable you are."

"I guess that explains the men with the guns, huh?" I took a sip of Coke without thinking about it, and decided against putting the can back down. I deserved a little comfort. Resurrection turns out to be really hard on a person. "So you're waiting for me to flip out and...what, exactly?"

"Cloning is a complicated process," said Dr. Thomas. "Modern generations are infected with the Kellis-Amberlee virus while in the womb. Their bodies grow up handling the infection, coming to...an agreement with it, if you will. Adult infections have been rare since the Rising."

"But cloned tissue is grown under clean-room conditions," I said. "How did you introduce the infection?"

"Aerosol exposure when the..." He stuttered to a stop, obviously unsure how to proceed. Their reports probably referred to me as "the subject" or "the body" at that stage of the process. Using a proper pronoun would involve giving too much identity to something he'd been treating as a lab experiment.

The temptation to point that out was there. I let it pass. I needed an ally, even one who thought he was getting me to cooperate, more than I needed to score a few points just to make myself feel better. "How far along in the growth cycle was the tissue?" I asked.

"Halfway," he said, visibly relieved. "We used techniques developed for organ cloning to accelerate the growth of the entire body. The immune and nervous systems were fully mature. We even used a blood sample on file at the Memphis installation, to be sure the exposure involved the strain of Kellis-Amberlee with which you were originally infected. It seemed the most likely to be compatible with your system. For all that we work with this virus every day, things like this, well, they aren't precisely an exact science…"

Things like this absolutely *are* an exact science. They're exactly what the Fictionals tell us to expect once mad science gets involved. I decided that was something else that didn't need to be pointed out. Instead, I seized on the thing he was doing his best to avoid saying. "The men with guns are here because there's a chance I'm going to spontaneously amplify, aren't they?"

"Yes," said Dr. Thomas. He looked genuinely sorry as he continued. "It will take a few days to be sure your system has properly adjusted to the infection. Until then, I'm afraid your movements will be carefully monitored. You can use the intercom to request food or drinks, and there will always be an escort ready if you need to visit the sanitary facilities. Showers will be available to you on a regular basis."

"Can I ask for an Internet connection?" I asked.

He looked away as he answered. "That isn't a good idea yet. We're still running tests, and we don't want to stress you more than is absolutely necessary. Hard copy reading material can be provided, if there are specific subjects you're interested in."

"Carefully censored, so as not to 'stress' me?" He had the good grace to look embarrassed. That didn't make me feel any better. "If you're trying to avoid stress, you should know that isolation stresses me."

"That may be, but you're going to have to live with it for a little while longer. I'm sorry. It's necessary for your health."

Something about the way he said that made my throat close up. A dozen nightmare scenarios flashed through my mind, all of them beginning in the dangerous seconds following the gunshot that killed me. I took a long drink of Coke to steady myself, and asked, "Is Shaun okay? Did he make it out of Sacramento? Please. Just tell me if he made it out of Sacramento."

"It's July of 2041. It's taken us a little over eight months to get you to the point of being both awake and aware of your surroundings," said Dr. Thomas. He delivered this apparent non sequitur in a hurried almost-monotone, like he wanted to get what he was about to say out of the way as quickly as possible. "A great deal has changed during that time."

"You didn't answer my question."

"I know."

"Why aren't you answering me? What are you trying to—"

"Miss Mason, I can't give you the answers you're asking me for. But I am truly and sincerely sorry for your loss."

I gaped at him, openmouthed. I was still gaping when he stepped out of the room, the door closing behind him. I didn't move. Not until my Coke hit the floor with a metallic *clink*, so much like the sound of a bullet casing being dropped. My knees went weak, and I sank into a kneeling position, my eyes fixed on the blank white door.

My cheeks were wet. I reached up with one hand, touching my right cheek. My fingertips came away damp. "I'm crying?" I said numbly. Retinal Kellis-Amberlee robs its victims of the ability to cry. Somehow, the idea that I could cry now was even more unbelievable than the idea that I was a CDC science project.

I staggered to my feet and stumbled over to the bed, where I collapsed atop the covers and curled into a ball, hugging my knees to my chest. The tears came hard after that, leaving me shaking and barely able to breathe. Somewhere in the middle of all that, I fell asleep.

I dreamed of funerals. Sometimes they were mine, and Shaun was standing in front of a room full of people, awkwardly trying to pretend he knew what he was doing. Those were the good dreams. Those were the dreams that reflected life as I knew it. Other times—most of the times—it was his face on the picture in front of the funeral urn, and either I was delivering a eulogy in a robotic monotone, or Alaric was standing there, explaining how it was only a matter of time. Once I was gone, no one really expected anything else.

The room was dark when I opened my eyes. They ached in a totally unfamiliar way. I shifted enough to free a hand to rub them, and discovered that my eyelids were puffy and slightly tender. I considered getting upset about it, but dismissed the idea. Either this was a normal side effect of crying, or Dr. Thomas had been right to be concerned, and I was starting to amplify. If it was the first, I needed to learn to live with it. If it was the second, well. It might be somebody's problem. It wasn't going to be mine.

I sat up on the bed, squinting to make out shapes in the darkened room. Even with the retinal Kellis-Amberlee, I probably couldn't have seen in a room this dark. Still, dwelling on it gave me something to do for a few seconds, while I waited for my eyes to stop aching and let my thoughts settle down into something resembling normal. I wasn't usually this scattered. Then again, I hadn't usually just come back from the dead. Maybe I needed to cut myself a little slack.

Minutes slipped by me almost unnoticed. It wasn't until my butt started going numb that I realized how long I'd been sitting there, paralyzed by the simple reality of the dark. "Fuck that," I muttered, and slid off the bed, only stumbling a little as my feet hit the floor. There. Step one had been successfully taken: I was standing up. Everything else could come from there.

If I remembered correctly, the wall with the door would be about six feet in front of me. I started forward, holding my hands out in a vain effort to keep myself from walking face-first into anything solid. I felt a little better with every step. I was *up*. I was *doing something*. Sure, what I was doing was basically creeping my way across a dark room like a heroine from one of Maggie's pre-Rising horror movies, but it was *something*, and that was a big improvement over what I'd been doing before.

It's amazing how effective simple disorientation is as a mechanism for controlling people. Reporters use it whenever we think we can get away with it. We try to be the ones in control of the environment, using everything from props and street noise to temperature to keep people either completely relaxed or totally on edge, depending on the needs of the piece. Well, the CDC was trying to disorient me, and I'd been playing right into their hands. Who cared if I was a clone of myself, being kept under lock and key in a secret facility somewhere? I was still Georgia Mason—call it "identity until proven otherwise." And if I was going to be Georgia Mason, I couldn't sit around feeling sorry for myself. I needed to do something.

My hands hit the one-way mirror. I stopped, leaning forward until my forehead grazed the surface of the glass. If I squinted, I could make out the hallway on the other side. It was like trying to look through a thick layer of fog; if the lights in the hall hadn't been on, I wouldn't have been able to see anything at all. As it was, I was only getting outlines. The walls. The equally deceptive "windows" looking in on those other, empty rooms. Were they waiting for their own secretly cloned residents? Was I the first, the last, or somewhere in the middle?

"Stop it," I muttered, wrenching my way out of that line of thought. It was something I needed to think about—probably at great length, and potentially as part of an exposé on illegal human cloning being conducted by the CDC—but this wasn't the time. Here and now, it didn't matter if they had a damn *army* of clones. I was the only clone I cared about.

I was the only...

I stepped away from the mirror, staring into the darkness in front of me. If the CDC was monitoring me on a hidden video feed—and I had absolute faith that the CDC was monitoring me on a hidden video feed, that's what hidden video feeds are *for*—they'd probably think I was having a seizure. Let them think what they wanted. My frozen stare was as close as I could allow myself to come to cheering and punching the air in raw triumph.

They'd almost managed to catch me in their little logic puzzle, I had to give them that, but I've spent my entire life pursuing the truth ahead of all other things, and I know a lie when I don't hear one. Dr. Thomas tried so very hard not to give me any firm answers...and that was the problem. He said he was sorry for my loss. He wouldn't let me have an Internet connection, not even one that wasn't capable of transmitting, only receiving. And he never, not once, went so far as to say that Shaun was dead. Why wouldn't he tell me Shaun was dead?

Because he didn't have any proof. The old Internet rallying cry: pics or it didn't happen. There was no way he could invent a believable story that I wouldn't be able to poke holes in, and if he'd been telling the truth, he would have been happy to prove it.

Shaun was alive.

I could be a clone, up could be down, and black could be white, but Shaun had to be alive. If I were in their shoes, the only thing that would have convinced me to clone a potentially recalcitrant reporter—and let's face it, I was renowned for my stubbornness, especially when people were trying to tell me what to do—was the need to have that *specific* reporter on my side. The CDC wouldn't have brought me back unless they needed me to do something for them. And there was only one thing I could do that no one else could.

I could make Shaun stop.

Shaun was alive, and he was doing something they didn't approve of. Shaun was doing something they wanted stopped. But this was the CDC—they were the good guys. Whatever he was doing had to be something I would support stopping, right? Shaun was always good at making trouble, and I was usually the one in charge of stopping him. Take me out of the picture, and well...

For a moment, I lost myself in the pleasant fantasy of the CDC telling me that they were done processing me, everything was fine, and I could go. They'd hand me a pair of sunglasses and show me the door, sending me out into the world to find Shaun and give him a brisk smack upside the head. I was the only one he'd listen to, after all.

Regretfully, I set that pretty daydream aside. If they just wanted to make Shaun settle down, they'd hit him with a tranquilizer dart or something. Cloning a single sterile organ for a transplant patient cost millions of dollars. My shiny new factory-issue body probably came with a price tag somewhere in the billions. Shaun could cause a lot of trouble if he wanted to, but he wasn't capable of *that* much trouble—certainly not enough to justify the cost of resurrecting me.

So what had he done that justified it? What did they want from me that they couldn't get from him? My fingertips brushed the edge of the door. I stopped, turned, and paced in the opposite direction, letting the fingers of my other hand whisk along the wall. Fine; so they hadn't brought me back from the dead for purely altruistic reasons. I knew that when I woke up. I represented too much money and too much time to be a purely scientific exercise. If this had happened before the Rising, human cloning might have been seen as a way to enhance and extend life. Worn out your body? Get a new one! Every cosmetic procedure imaginable in one easy step. Well, assuming you considered having your brain—whatever it was they did to my brain—having your brain somehow extracted and inserted into a whole new body "easy."

That was before the Rising. Our modern zombie-phobic society would never embrace something that brought people back from the dead, even if they came back without all those antisocial cannibalistic urges. When I got out of here—if I got out of here—I was going to have a lot of extremely fast explaining to do, unless I wanted to find myself getting shot dead for the second time in my life.

There was something wrong with that phrase. I reached the wall, turned, and continued pacing.

Shaun was alive, Shaun was causing trouble, and they weren't willing to risk getting caught in a lie if they told me he was dead. That might mean they were planning to use me against him somehow, convince me to spill private information about where we hid our network keys and offsite backup drives. That idea felt thin, like there was something I was missing, but it was a start. Every article begins with a line that can be twisted, somehow, into a hook.

Fine: The CDC brought me back so they could use me as a weapon against the only person in the world I loved more than I loved the truth. How they were planning to do that, I had no idea. Shaun knew I was dead. If anyone in the world knew, without question, that I was dead, it was Shaun; he's the one who pulled the trigger. Seeing a woman who looked like me might make him pause for a second, but it wouldn't be enough to bring him running.

Would it?

The door opened abruptly, sending light flooding into my absolute darkness. I recoiled, more from the expectation of pain than anything else, stumbling to a stop and catching myself against the wall.

The light didn't hurt my eyes the way it would have before my resurrection, but it still made them sting, blinding me for a few disorienting seconds. I raised a hand to shield them, squinting through the brightness at the man standing in the doorway. He wasn't moving, and hadn't moved, as far as I could tell, since he opened the door.

I dropped my hand. "Hello?" I hated the uncertainty in my voice. I was still unsteady, and the CDC was controlling too damn much of my environment. I hate being controlled.

Having two things to hate actually helped. I stood up straighter, frowning at the man silhouetted in the doorway. Being in pajamas should probably have made me feel vulnerable. Instead, it just made me angrier, like it was one element of control too many. Let them take away my connection to the outside world, my autonomy, and hell, even my body, but they weren't allowed to *dress* me.

"I said hello," I said, more sharply. I took a step forward. "Who are you? What are you doing in here?" Belatedly, it occurred to me that maybe walking toward a man I couldn't really see was a bad idea. Human cloning was illegal, after all, and it was entirely possible that there might be people at the CDC who didn't want me up and walking around.

"I saw you on the monitors," said the man. He had a low, pleasant voice, with just a hint of a Midwestern accent. He stepped out of the doorway, moving back into the hall, and giving me my first real look at his face. His skin was a medium brown with reddish undertones, a few shades lighter than Mahir, a few shades darker than Alaric, with a bone structure I thought might be Native American. He had straight, dark hair, worn loose and almost as long as mine. It grazed his shoulders, tucked behind his ears to keep it from getting in his face. I'd have to remember that trick, at least until I could get my hands on a pair of scissors. He was smiling cautiously in my direction, like a man facing a snake that could decide to bite at any second.

I'd never seen him before in my life. But he was wearing hospital scrubs, with a CDC nametag pinned to his chest. That made him, if not an ally, at least a vaguely known quantity.

"Who are you?" I asked, taking another step forward. "Did Dr. Thomas send you to check up on me?"

"No," he said, with careful patience. "Like I said before, I saw you on the monitors. You looked unsettled. I thought I'd come down and see if you needed anything. A glass of water, another blanket..."

"What if I wanted to go to the bathroom?"

He didn't miss a beat. "I'd call for guards to escort us there, so I didn't get fired. But I'd be happy to get you some water and an extra blanket first." He took the clipboard from under his arm, flipping back the top sheet. "Are you having trouble sleeping? This says you had some caffeine earlier. I know that when I have too much coffee, I can't sleep for love or money."

"I was sleeping just fine," I said. "Then I woke up. My internal clock is all messed up. It might help if I knew what time zone we were in."

"Yeah, it probably would," he agreed. "I'm Gregory, by the way, Miss Mason. It's a pleasure to see you up and about." He turned his clipboard as he spoke, holding it against his chest with the paper facing me. "You had everyone concerned for a while there."

I've had a lifetime of experience in the fine art of not reacting to things. Still, I froze as my eyes found the block letters on the top sheet of Gregory's clipboard, clearly intended for me to see.

YOU ARE NOT SAFE HERE.

Gregory's expression begged me not to react, like he knew he was taking a risk, but had gauged it a worthwhile one. I managed to school my face into something close to neutrality, tilting my chin slightly upward to hide the unavoidable wideness of my eyes. I would have killed for my sunglasses in that moment, if someone had offered me the opportunity.

"I'm not sure you can blame me for that. I was technically dead at the time."

Relief flooded Gregory's expression. He nodded, turning his clipboard around like he was reading from it, and said, "That's true. You weren't legally alive until you started breathing independently."

"That's interesting. Who got to make that fun call?"

"It's part of the international agreement concerning the use of human cloning technology for medical research," Gregory said, flipping over another page. "As long as the clone never breathes independently of the life-support machines, it's not a living entity. It's just meat."

"So you're allowed to call me a clone?"

"Dr. Thomas said you'd reached that conclusion on your own, and that we were allowed to reinforce it, if it came up. Said it would make you more confident in your own identity." Gregory glanced up from his clipboard and smiled. "I don't think anyone expected you to figure it out so soon."

"That's me, refusing to meet expectations," I said, struggling to keep my tone neutral. This man said I wasn't safe. Did I trust him? *Could* I trust him?

Did I have a choice?

"All we expect from you now is that you keep getting better," said

Gregory, with the sort of firm, bland sternness I'd been getting from medical authority figures since I was seven years old. He turned his clipboard around again, showing me the second sheet of paper.

I AM WITH THE EIS. WE ARE GOING TO GET YOU OUT OF HERE. GO ALONG WITH EVERYTHING THEY ASK YOU TO DO. DO NOT ATTRACT ATTENTION.

I nodded. "I'll do my best," I said, replying to both what he'd said aloud, and to what he'd written down for me to see. "Thanks for stopping by."

"Well, you'll be seeing a lot of me. I'm one of your night attendants. Now, are you sure I can't get you anything?"

"Not just yet," I said, and paused, suddenly alarmed by the idea of being left alone, again, in the dark. "Actually...I don't know if this is something you can do, but can you turn the lights back on? Please? It's so dark in here with the door shut that I'm not sure I'll be able to get back to sleep."

"I can turn the lights back on," Gregory assured me. "I can even turn them up halfway, if you'd like, so that you're not trying to sleep with things lit too bright."

"That would be great," I said. Tomorrow, I'd have to start trying to talk Dr. Thomas into giving me a lamp.

"I'll do it as soon as I get back to the monitoring station," said Gregory, putting a subtle stress on the word "soon." "If you decide you need anything else, all you need to do is say the word. The monitors will alert me immediately."

"Got it," I said, suddenly glad I didn't talk in my sleep. "It was nice meeting you."

"Likewise, Miss Mason," said Gregory. He turned his clipboard around one final time, hiding the message written there, and took another step back. The door slid shut almost instantly—too fast for me to have rushed out of the room after him, even if I'd been inclined to try—and I was plunged back into darkness.

I stayed where I was, counting silently. The lights came on as I reached a hundred and forty-five. The monitoring station, wherever it was, was approximately two and a half minutes away for a man walking at normal speed. That was good to know. That meant it would take at least thirty seconds for someone to run from there to here. There's a lot you can do in thirty seconds, if you're really committed.

I walked back over to the bed and climbed under the covers, stretching out with my hands tucked under my head as I stared up at the ceiling. So the EIS was getting involved...and they weren't on the side of the CDC. That was interesting. Interesting, and potentially bad.

The EIS—the Epidemic Intelligence Service—was founded in 1951 to answer concerns about biological warfare in the wake of World War II. EIS agents were responsible for a lot of the earliest efforts against infectious pandemics. Without them, smallpox, wild polio, and malaria would never have been eliminated…and if they'd been aware of the Marburg Amberlee and Kellis flu trials, the accidents that led to the creation of Kellis-Amberlee might never have occurred. They've always had a reputation for ruthlessness, focus, and getting the job done. It's too bad the Rising put an end to most of what they did. In a world where there's only one disease making headlines, what are a bunch of disease detectives good for?

But the branch held on. No matter how much the CDC restructured, no matter how the funding shifted, the EIS endured. Every time there was a whisper of corruption from inside the CDC, the EIS was there, dispelling the rumors, cleaning up the mess. Most people wrote them off as a bunch of spooks who refused to admit they weren't necessary anymore. I'd always been one of those people.

Maybe it was time for me to reevaluate my position.

Gregory came from the EIS; the EIS was part of the CDC; the CDC brought me back to life. Gregory said I wasn't safe here; Gregory spoke to me on his own, without barriers or guards. Dr. Thomas wouldn't come near me without an armed guard. Dr. Thomas was willing to let me believe Shaun was dead. I probably couldn't actually afford to trust either one of them. But given a choice between the two…

If the EIS was willing to get me out of here, I was willing to bank on my ability to escape from the EIS. I let my eyes drift closed, rolling onto my side. It was time to start playing along and find out what was going on, because when Gregory and his friends broke me out I was going to break the whole thing open.

I didn't dream of funerals this time. Instead, I dreamed of me and Shaun, walking hand in hand through the empty hall where the Republican National Convention was held, and nothing was trying to kill us. Nothing was trying to kill us at all.

The difficulty with knowing what something is and how it operates is that you're likely to be wrong, and just as likely to be incapable of admitting it. We form preconceptions about the world, and we cling to them, unwilling to be challenged, unwilling to change. That's why so many pre-Rising structures remain standing. Our generation may be willing to identify them as useless, archaic, and potentially deadly. The generations that came before us regard them as normal parts of life rendered temporarily unavailable, like toys put on a high shelf. They think someday we'll have those things again. I think they know they're wrong. They just can't admit it, and so they wait to die and leave the world to us, the ones who will tear all those death traps down.

Sometimes the hardest thing about the truth is putting down the misassumptions, falsehoods, and half-truths that stand between it and you. Sometimes that's the last thing that anybody wants to do. And sometimes, it's the only thing we *can* do.

—From *Postcards from the Wall*,
the unpublished files of Georgia Mason,
originally posted on July 16, 2041.

I keep writing letters to my parents. Letters that explain what happened, where I went, why I ran. Letters that tell them how much I love them, and how sorry I am that I may never see them again. Letters about how much I miss my house, and my dogs, and my bad-movie parties, and my freedom. I sometimes think this must be what it was like for everyone in the months right after the Rising, only the threat of the infected was never personal. They didn't kill all those people because they wanted to, or because their victims knew some inconvenient truth. They did it because they were hungry and because the people were there. So maybe this isn't like the Rising at all. With us, it's personal. We asked the wrong questions, opened the wrong doors, and Alaric will try to say that it was never *my* fault, it was never *my* idea, but he's wrong.

I always knew there was an element of danger in what we did, and I went along with it willingly because these people are my heart's family, and this is what I wanted. So I keep writing letters to my parents, saying I'm sorry, and I miss them, and I may not make it home.

So far, I haven't sent any of my letters. I don't know if I ever will.

—From *Dandelion Mine*,
the blog of Magdalene Grace Garcia, July 16, 2041. Unpublished.

Four

Dr. Abbey's screening room was originally the Shady Cove Forestry Center's private movie theater, intended for teaching bored tourists and wide-eyed school groups about safely interacting with the woods. I've watched a few old DVDs that Alaric dug out of the room's back closet. Most of them said "safely interacting with the woods" meant being respectful of the wildlife, and backing away slowly if you saw a bear. Personally, I think "safely interacting with the woods" means carrying a crossbow and a sniper rifle whenever you have to go out alone. I'll never understand the pre-Rising generation...but sometimes I wish I could. It must have been nice to live in a world that didn't constantly try to kill you.

The screening room was in disarray when we started crashing with Dr. Abbey. Now, barely a month later, it was as close to state-of-the-art as could be achieved with secondhand parts and cobbled-together wiring. That was Alaric's doing. I'm sure Dr. Abbey's people could have handled everything eventually—this wasn't the first time she'd uprooted her entire lab with little warning—but Maggie got uncomfortable when she didn't have access to a big-ass screen. So she batted her eyes at our last surviving tech genius, and Alaric, who was probably glad to have something to distract him from his sister's situation, started flipping switches. The result was something even Buffy might have been proud of, if she hadn't been, you know, dead.

The room was set up theater style, with gently curved rows of chairs descending toward the hardwood floor. Dr. Abbey was standing in front of the screen with her arms crossed, leaning against the built-in podium.

"Sorry we took so long." I held up my bowl of popcorn as I descended the steps, shaking it so she could hear the kernels rattle. "You said we could stop for snacks."

"That's true; I did. One day you'll figure out how to tell when I'm serious." There was no actual rancor in Dr. Abbey's tone. I stopped being able to really piss her off the day she learned that I couldn't amplify. I guess there are some advantages to being a human pincushion.

"Did you bring me any?" Maggie was sitting in the middle of the front row. She turned to look over the back of her seat. Her curly brown-and-blonde hair—brown from nature, blonde from decontamination and bleaching—half hid her face. She was one of the only women I knew who managed to make that combination look natural, largely on account of having a Hispanic father, a Caucasian mother, and really good skin.

"Sure." I started down the steps. Becks and Alaric followed me.

"Hey, Dr. Abbey," said Becks.

"Hello, Rebecca," said Dr. Abbey.

"Gimme popcorn," said Maggie. I leaned over to hand her the bowl. She beamed, blew me a kiss, and started munching.

Out of all of us, Maggie was the one who didn't have to be here. Alaric, Becks, and I were the ones who broke into the CDC facility in Memphis. While we were there, a man we thought was our ally showed his true colors, and the newest member of our team was killed. Her name was Kelly Connolly. She worked for the CDC, and she wanted to do the right thing more than almost anyone else I knew. The fact that her name will never go up on The Wall is a crime and a sin, and there's nothing I can do about it. There's nothing anyone can do about it.

Maggie wasn't there for any of that. Maggie could have said, "It's been fun; see you later," and left the rest of us to carry on without her. I wouldn't have blamed her. She had a life, one that didn't involve becoming a fugitive, or sleeping on an army cot in an abandoned park building. When her house was rendered unsafe, she could have just asked her parents to buy her a new one. She was the heir to the Garcia family fortune, possibly the richest blogger in the world, and she had absolutely no reason to be standing by us. But she *was* standing by us, and that meant she could have all the popcorn she wanted.

Dr. Abbey straightened, taking the remote control from the podium. "If you're all settled, I've got a few things to show you."

"We're good," I said, dropping into a seat.

Behave, said George. *You could learn something.*

"You mean *you* could learn something, and explain it to me later," I said, making only a cursory effort to keep my voice down. The others ignored me. After everything we've had to deal with, I guess knowing the boss is crazy isn't such a big deal anymore. That's fine by me. I have no particular interest in ever being sane again.

Becks and Alaric took the seats to either side of me. Maggie got up and moved to sit next to Alaric, bringing the popcorn with her. Becks smiled at them a little wistfully. I tried not to let my discomfort show. Becks and I slept together once—just once—before she realized exactly how crazy I really was. I hurt her pretty badly over that. I didn't mean to, but that doesn't excuse it, as both she and George were happy to point out. Sometimes I regret the fact that I'm probably never going to have a normal adult relationship with a woman who has a pulse of her own. And then I remember how deep the shit we're in already is, and I'm just glad I don't have anyone left for them to take away from me.

"Finally," said Dr. Abbey, and pointed her remote at the back of the room. The projector came on, filling the screen with an outline of the Florida coast. "Florida," said Dr. Abbey needlessly. She pressed a button. The image pulled back to show the entire Gulf Coast. A red splash was overlaid across the characteristic shape of Florida itself, covering almost two-thirds of the landmass.

Alaric winced, fingers tightening around a handful of popcorn with an audible crunch. That was the only sound in the screening room. That, and the sound of George swearing in the back of my head, inaudible to anyone but me.

Dr. Abbey gave us a moment to study the image before she said, "This is the most recent map showing the airborne infection following Tropical Storm Fiona. I know of six labs that are currently trying to sequence the genetic structure of the mosquitoes involved."

"Why?" asked Becks. "What does that matter?"

"This isn't a new strain of virus, which means it has to be a new strain of mosquito. If we know what species they were derived from, we'll know what temperature range they can tolerate."

A voice spoke from the back of the theater: "Derived from?"

"Mr. Gowda. Glad you could join us. And yes, derived from. Surely you don't think this happened naturally?" Dr. Abbey shook her head. "Mosquitoes can't spread Kellis-Amberlee because the virus is too large. You can't make it smaller; it would become unstable. That means you need a larger mosquito if you want an insect vector."

"Yeah, because who wouldn't want *that*," muttered Becks.

"Who made it?" asked Mahir. I turned in my seat to see him descending the stairs. He was frowning deeply. That was nothing new. I honestly couldn't remember the last time I'd seen him smile.

"Good question," said Dr. Abbey. "Now, as I was saying, if we know what species the mosquitoes are derived from, we'll know what temperature range they can tolerate. If we're looking at *Aedes aegypti*—the mosquito responsible for the American yellow fever outbreaks—then we're dealing with a mosquito confined to warm climates. Like so." She pressed another button. The image progressed, printing an orange zone on top of the red. "That's the maximum projected range for *Aedes aegypti*. They won't be able to get a foothold on the colder parts of the country, although it's doubtful we'll be cleaning them out of the Gulf Coast anytime soon."

"What are our other options?" asked Mahir.

"We have about a dozen possible candidates, although some are more likely than others. If you want to see the doomsday option, look no farther than *Aedes albopictus*, the Asian tiger mosquito. It's been nominated for the title of 'most invasive species in the world,' in part because the damn thing can survive anywhere. It sets up housekeeping, and that's the end of that. Reach for your bug spray and kiss your ass good-bye." Dr. Abbey clicked her remote again. The image pulled back, showing the entire continental United States. A third band of color appeared around the first two. This one was yellow, and extended almost all the way to the Canadian border. "Good night, North America. Thank you for playing."

"Isn't there anything we can do?" asked Maggie.

Becks leaned forward in her seat. "I have a better question. Why are you telling us this? We already knew things were bad. You could have just given us a written report."

"Because I wanted you to understand exactly *how* bad things are out there." Dr. Abbey pressed a different button. The map was replaced by a slideshow of pictures out of the flooded streets of Florida—still flooded, for the most part, even this long after the storm, because no one had been able to get past the ranks of the infected long enough to clear out the drains.

Mobs of blank-eyed, bloody-lipped zombies waded through the dirty water, their arms raised in instinctive fury as they closed ranks on the rare remaining uninfected humans. Their numbers were great enough that they clearly weren't trying to infect anymore; they had the critical mass the virus always seemed to be striving for. There was nothing left of the people they'd been before the storm touched down. All that remained was a single, undeniable command: feed.

Maggie gasped as a still picture of a young boy with his abdomen ripped completely open flashed across the screen. She twisted and buried her face against Alaric's shoulder. He raised one hand to stroke her hair, his own eyes never leaving the screen.

This is horrific, said George.

"Yeah," I whispered. "It is."

We knew how bad things were—there was no way we could avoid knowing—but the government had been doing a surprisingly good job of suppressing images from the infection zones. Something about the way journalists who tried to sneak into the cordoned areas kept winding up infected, shot, or both was doing a lot to discourage the curious. Most of the pictures that made it out were fuzzy things, shot from a distance or using cameras attached to remote-controlled drones. These pictures weren't fuzzy. These pictures were crystal clear, and the story they told was brutal.

"Where did you get these?" asked Mahir. He seemed to remember that he should be descending the stairs. He trotted quickly down the last few tiers, settling at the end of our row.

"I have my sources," said Dr. Abbey. "Most of these were taken in the last week. Since then, the body count has continued rising. We're looking at a death toll in the millions."

"I heard a rumor that the government is going to declare Florida officially lost," said Becks.

"It's not a rumor. They're making the announcement next week." Dr. Abbey pressed another button. The still pictures were replaced with a video, clearly shot by someone with a back-mounted camera as they were running for their life. A mob of infected pursued the unseen filmmaker down the flooded, debris-choked street, and they were gaining. Maggie glanced up, hearing the change in the room. As soon as she saw the screen, she moaned again, and pressed her face back into Alaric's shoulder.

"They can't do that," said Becks.

Yes, they can, said George.

"Yes, they can," I said. The others looked at me, even Maggie, who raised her head and stared at me with wounded, shell-shocked eyes. "Alaska. Remember? As long as they can prove they've made every effort to preserve the greater civilian population, the government is not only allowed to lock down a hazard zone, they're *required*." Shutting down a state would mean proving they'd done it to save the nation. Somehow, I didn't think that would be all that hard of a sell. Things were too bad, and people were too frightened.

"We have to go to Florida," said Alaric abruptly. "We need to get Alisa." He sat up in his seat, almost dislodging Maggie. "The refugee camp is inside the state borders. When they closed Alaska, they didn't evacuate all the camps."

Becks, Maggie, and Alaric started talking at once, all of them raising their voices to be heard. Even George got in on the action, although I wasn't relaying her comments to the others—yet. If they didn't settle down quickly, I'd probably start.

Mahir beat me to it. "*Quiet!*" he roared, standing. He walked over to the rest of us, focusing his attention on Alaric. "I'm sorry, Alaric, but there's no way. Going into Florida would be suicide."

"I don't care." Alaric stood, stepping forward so that he and Mahir were almost nose to nose. Mahir was easily four inches taller. At the moment, that didn't seem to matter. "Alisa is the last family I have left. I'm not letting them abandon her in a hazard zone."

"And as your immediate superior, I'm not letting you throw your life away running *into* a hazard zone."

"Does he really think that's going to work?" asked Becks.

"Would you have done it for *his* sister?" Alaric thrust out his arm, pointing at me. "If it were George in that hazard zone, would you have stopped *him*? Or would you have been putting on your protective gear and saying it was an honor to die trying to save her?"

"Hey, guys, let's settle down, okay?" Maggie cast a nervous look in my direction as she stood and tried to push her way between them. "Inciting Shaun to kill us all isn't anybody's idea of a good time."

"I don't know," said Dr. Abbey. "It might take care of a few problems. It would definitely cut down on the grocery bills."

She's really not fond of helping, is she? asked George.

"No, she's not," I replied, and stood. Becks, who was now the only one still sitting, gave me a worried look, like she wasn't sure whether I was about to try defusing the situation or start punching people. I couldn't blame her. Before Memphis, I wouldn't have been sure either, and it wasn't like I'd been exactly stable since then.

But the one thing I learned in Memphis—the one thing I was sure of now, even if I hadn't been sure of it before—was that my team was the only thing I had, and if I didn't want to lose them, I needed to take care of them. Somehow.

"Okay, everybody," I said. "Settle down."

"Shaun—" Alaric began.

"You're part of everybody. So shut up. Mahir? We're not abandoning Alaric's sister. We wouldn't abandon yours, we're not abandoning his."

"I don't have a sister," said Mahir.

"Yeah, well, join the club. Alaric?" I took a step toward him, letting my anger show in my eyes for a fraction of a second. Alaric paled. I might not be willing to lose my team, but that didn't mean I was willing to let certain things go. "Calm down. We'll figure this out. And don't you ever, *ever* use George against any of us, ever again. Do I make myself clear?"

Alaric nodded, pushing his glasses back up the bridge of his nose. "Extremely."

"Good. Thanks for trying to calm things down, Maggie."

She didn't say anything. But she smiled wanly, and I knew the comment was appreciated.

Good job, said George.

"Thanks," I replied. I looked to Dr. Abbey and asked, "Why are you telling us this? It's like Becks said—you would have just left a note on the refrigerator, if all you wanted to do was make us aware that things are shitty. Everyone knows things are shitty. This isn't news."

"Not that it's stopping 'everything in Florida is shitty' from dominating the news cycles right now," said Becks. "What impresses me is the way it's dominating them without most people actually knowing anything."

"Welcome to the modern media world," said Alaric.

Dr. Abbey had been waiting while we got the last of the nervous chatter out of the way. Not saying a word—not yet—she pressed a button on her remote. The video froze and vanished, replaced by an atlas-style road map. It could have been anywhere in the world, if not for the label identifying the thickest line as the border between Florida and Alabama. A small red star popped up on the Florida side of the line.

"The Ferry Pass Refugee Center," said Dr. Abbey serenely. She'd been setting us up for this moment. I would have been impressed, if I hadn't wanted to punch her. "The middle school has been turned into a holding area for people who were evacuated from the primary outbreak zones before evacuations ceased."

"You know where Alisa is?" Alaric's voice was suddenly small. We'd been getting updates from his sister since she was transferred to the camp, but she'd never been able to tell us where that camp was located. Alaric thought it was because things were too hectic, and the rest of us were willing to let him keep thinking that until we had something better to tell him. Because in my experience, when people are kept isolated "for their own safety" and not told where they are, those people are probably never going to be seen or heard from again.

"Camps were established in Florida, Georgia, and Alabama after Tropical Storm Fiona hit. People were assigned to them supposedly at random, although the Florida camps received a higher than average percentage of the poor, children without surviving parents, and journalists who'd been arrested inside the quarantine zone. The Georgia camps were evacuated last week. They're evacuating the Alabama camps tomorrow."

"And the Florida camps?" asked Mahir.

"Are considered a lower priority, due to the chance that they've already been contaminated. Luck of the draw, I suppose." Her tone was blackly amused, like it was that or start breaking things. "One more tragedy for a summer already packed chock-full of tragedies."

"They can't do this," said Becks.

"It's already done. The only question is whether they're going to get caught, and so far, the answer's been 'no.' Things are chaotic. No one knows exactly what's going on, and the people carrying out the orders aren't the ones giving them. As long as no one ever gives the order that says 'let those people die, they don't matter,' nothing illegal is being done." A small, bitter smile twisted the edges of Dr. Abbey's lips. "Trust me. I'm a scientist. We know all about the art of skirting ethics."

"We have to go to Florida," said Alaric. He grabbed my sleeve, eyes wild. "We have to! They're going to let her die! Shaun, you have to help me; you can't let my sister die!"

He's right; you can't, said George. *You can't go to Florida, either. So what are you going to do?*

The answer was obvious, at least to me. I gave Alaric's hand a reassuring pat before removing it from my sleeve, folding my arms, and focusing on Dr. Abbey. "What do you want us to do?"

She lifted her eyebrows. "What do you mean?"

"You made a big production out of telling us things suck in Florida. We knew things sucked. You just wanted us to really *believe* it. So you've got us. We believe." I let my smile mirror hers. "It's classic media manipulation. Present the facts in the scariest way possible, and wait for your audience to sell their souls for whatever you think they need."

"And what could I possibly have that you would need?"

"Beyond the whole 'shelter and hiding us' thing, which we already have, you know where Alaric's sister is. That means you know someone who's involved with the camps in Florida. Can you get her out?"

Alaric's eyes widened, and he focused on Dr. Abbey with new hope. "Is that why you told us all this? Can you get Alisa out of Florida?"

"It's possible," said Dr. Abbey, putting her remote back on the podium. "I could pull a few strings."

"Thought so." I looked at her appraisingly. "Now I know you don't want to cut me open, because I'm a better test subject alive than I'd be dead. And I know you don't want to kick us out for basically the same reason. So what do you want?"

"I do want you to leave, actually. I just don't want you to stay gone." Dr. Abbey shook her head. "Remember what I said about the mosquitoes?"

"Which part?" asked Maggie. "The scary part, the really scary part, the legitimately terrifying part, or the part that makes suicide sound like an awesome way to spend an evening?"

"That last one, probably. As I said before, there *are* labs working to sequence the genetic code of the mosquitoes. But they're working with inherently damaged data, because they're working with dead specimens."

Becks stared at her. "You want us to go out and catch mosquitoes for you?"

"Not all of you. Just him." Dr. Abbey pointed at me. "If you can get into one of the infection zones and catch some live specimens, we may be able to determine their base species—or at least make a better, more educated guess—without needing to wait for the gene sequencers to finish running. Plus, we can study their behavioral patterns, maybe come up with ways to avoid being bitten."

"This is all assuming I survive the bug hunt," I said dryly.

"You've survived everything else you've run up against, even when there's no way you should have. I'm willing to take the chance." Dr. Abbey sighed, raking her brown and bleach-yellow curls back with one hand. "Look. I realize this isn't exactly the nicest thing I've ever done to you people."

"You're a mad scientist," said Maggie, in what may well have been intended as a reassuring tone. "We don't expect you to be nice. We just go to bed every night hoping you won't mutate us before we wake up."

Dr. Abbey blinked at her. "That's…almost sweet. In a disturbing sort of a way."

"Maggie's good at sweet-but-disturbing," said Mahir. "Are you genuinely telling us you have the capacity to extract Alaric's sister from danger, and will not do so unless we agree to your request?"

"I'm telling you I have the capacity to *try*." Dr. Abbey shook her head. "Please don't misunderstand what I'm offering here. I can't guarantee anything. The mosquitoes haven't reached Ferry Pass, but that doesn't mean they won't. It also doesn't mean there won't be another form of outbreak before we can get there. All I'm offering is a chance, and yes, sometimes, chances have to be paid for."

Alaric gave me a pleading look. The others followed suit, even Dr.

Abbey, all looking at me with varying degrees of hope, or reluctance, or resignation. In that instant, I knew that what came next was entirely my decision. Maybe I was the crazy one, maybe I was the one who felt like he had nothing left to lose, but I was also their leader, and the only one my team had left. They needed someone to tell them what to do. Even Mahir, for all that half the time it seemed like *he* was the one who was actually in charge, needed me to be the one to pull the trigger.

"I didn't sign up for this shit," I muttered, as quietly as I could.

Good thing you're such a natural, then, isn't it?

I managed to bite back my laughter before it could escape. The team might be used to me talking to myself, but that didn't mean they'd forgive me for laughing at a time like this. I turned my laugh into a smile, calling up all the old tricks I'd been forced to learn back when I was a working Irwin and needed to smile despite pain, or terror, or just plain not wanting to be the dancing monkey for a little while.

"You know we can't all go, right, Doc?" I asked.

Dr. Abbey nodded. "I know."

"Alisa's going to need ID, papers, everything. There's no way she can use her real name. It wouldn't hurt for the rest of us to have a fallback plan, either. I want to send Mahir and Maggie up the coast. There's an ID fixer there who comes pretty highly recommended."

"The Monkey," said Alaric.

"I've heard of him. He's supposedly the best, and things *are* going to get worse before they get better," said Dr. Abbey, apparently unperturbed by my desire to split the team. "I'm even willing to supply an unmarked car, to help them get there."

"And someone's staying with you, to coordinate."

"I wouldn't have it any other way."

"I'm going with you," Becks said, stepping up next to me before Alaric could speak. She raised a warning finger in his direction. "*Don't* argue. You aren't good at fieldwork, you don't like being away from your computer, and if Dr. Abbey can get Alisa out of Florida, your sister will want to know that you're safe. We won't be."

Alaric deflated slightly, looking ashamed. I couldn't blame him. He was clearly relieved not to be the one going, and just as clearly felt like he should have insisted on it.

"Hey," I said. He didn't look at me. "*Hey.*"

This time Alaric's attention swung my way. "What?"

"Becks is right. Alisa needs you more than we do. Stay with Dr. Abbey.

Keep the crazy science lady happy, or at least non-homicidal. We'll be back as soon as we can. Okay?"

For a moment, I didn't think Alaric was going to give in. Finally, he nodded. "Okay," he said. "If that's the best way."

"It is." I looked to Dr. Abbey. "Well? What are we waiting for? Let's get this show on the road."

She smiled. "I thought you'd never ask."

But I'm scared a lot, too. There are ten girls sleeping in the classroom with me, and also our chaperone, Ms. Hyland. I don't think anyone here realizes my e-diary can also transmit. They're not supposed to be able to do that. That's why the people let me keep it. I don't know what I'd do if they took it away from me. Thank you, thank you, thank you for giving me this for last Christmas. I think it's saving my life.

They're starting to say scary things when they think none of us are listening—or maybe they don't care anymore whether we're listening or not, and that's scary, too. Please come get me. Please find a way to come and get me. I don't know what's going to happen next, but I'm really scared, and I need my brother.

Please come.

—Taken from an e-mail sent by Alisa Kwong to Alaric Kwong, July 19, 2041.

This morning I woke up, and for almost ten minutes, I forgot that George was dead. I could hear her in the bathroom, getting her clothes on and waiting for her painkillers to kick in. I could even see the indent her head left in the pillow. And then I turned to get something from my bag, and when I looked back, the indent was gone. No one was in the bathroom. I was alone, and George was dead again.

It's been happening more and more often. Just those little moments where something slips, and it becomes possible, for one beautiful, horrible moment, to lie to myself about the world. I won't pretend that I mind them, or that I'm not sorry when they end. I also won't pretend that I'm not afraid.

The last big break with reality is coming. I can practically hear it knocking at the door. And I'm terrified I won't have time to finish everything I need to do before it gets here.

I'm sorry, George. But I'm afraid I might want you back so much that I'm willing to let myself let you down.

—From *Adaptive Immunities*,
the blog of Shaun Mason, July 17, 2041. Unpublished.

Five

I barely glanced up from my book when the door slid open. It was an outdated sociology text written when people still lived in the middle of Canada, but it was a *book*, and in the absence of access to the Internet, I was so starved for data that I'd take what I could get. They still wouldn't let me have anything but hard copy, for fear that I'd somehow figure out a way to hopscotch off the local wireless network. As if. Techie tricks were Buffy's forte, and Buffy had left the building.

The door slid closed. I kept reading. Dr. Thomas cleared his throat. The sound was a dead giveaway. After a week with nothing to distract me, I'd learned to recognize my regular visitors by the things they couldn't help, like the way they breathed—or, in Dr. Thomas's case, the annoying way he cleared his throat. I turned a page. Dr. Thomas cleared his throat again.

"I can keep this up all day," I said pleasantly, even though the fact that I was the first one to speak proved I couldn't actually stand spending any more time sitting silently and pretending I wasn't bothered by Dr. Thomas standing there, watching me. "You know what you need to do."

"I think you're being unreasonable."

"I think that I legally became a human being as soon as you detached me from your crazy mad science clone incubator, which means I'm entitled to basic human courtesy." I turned another page. "It's up to you." Gregory wanted me to play along. Well, I was playing, but that also included a certain amount of understandable resistance. A totally complacent Georgia Mason would never have been believable, to anyone.

Dr. Thomas sighed. Finally, he said, "Hello, Georgia. May I come in?"

"Why, hello, Dr. Thomas." I looked up, dog-earing the top of the page to keep my place. "Would it make any difference if I said you couldn't?"

"No," he said curtly. I was starting to learn the limits of his patience. It was difficult, more so than learning to tell his footsteps from the footsteps of the guards who usually accompanied him. If I pushed him too far, they'd gas the room, and I'd wake up to find that whatever tests I'd been balking at had been run while I was unconscious.

When I finished with my exposé of this place, the CDC was going to wish they'd been willing to leave me dead. I kept that thought firmly in mind as I plastered a smile across my face and said, "Well, then, come on in. What can I do for you?" I paused, something else about the situation registering. I'd only heard one set of footsteps. "Where are your guards?"

"That's part of why I'm visiting. We've been reviewing your test results, and we've decided I don't need them in your quarters." Dr. Thomas's smile looked as real as mine. Whoever made the decision to send him into my room without protection had done it without asking how he felt about it. And clearly, how he felt wasn't good.

"Does that mean they've also decided I'm not a danger to society?"

"Don't be too hasty, Georgia. It simply means they've decided that spontaneous amplification is not an immediate danger. We still have a lot to do before we can be confident your body is prepared to function outside a laboratory setting." Dr. Thomas adjusted his glasses with one hand, something I'd learned to read as a nervous tic. "You may not feel particularly protected, but I assure you, this is the cleanest, most secure environment you have ever been in."

"It's definitely the most boring," I agreed, twisting around to face him. I'd been sitting cross-legged on my bed for long enough that my thighs ached when I moved. That was good. It looked like I wasn't doing anything. I was actually tensing and relaxing the muscles of my core, strengthening them as best I could without a better means of using them. I'd asked a few times about getting access to an exercise room, or at least a treadmill. So far, I'd had no luck. That meant I was getting my exercise where I could, and through whatever means available.

I never thought I'd be so grateful to Buffy for making me and Shaun sign up for that stupid virtual Pilates class.

The thought of Shaun, even that briefly, was painful. I pushed it away. I was still holding tightly to the belief that he was alive, but it was hard, and getting harder as Dr. Thomas continued not giving me anything to work with. I had to believe Shaun was alive. If I didn't, I was going to go insane.

Assuming the CDC didn't drive me crazy first.

"I thought you'd been provided with reading material?" Dr. Thomas gave my book a meaningful look. "That was what you requested, wasn't it?"

" 'Something to read' was on the list, yes, but I provided authors and titles, and nothing I've been given has been remotely like the things I asked for." I blew a wayward strand of hair out of my face. "I've been asking for a haircut, too. Any idea when I might be able to get one? If it's too hard to find someone on your staff who's cut hair before, you can give me a pair of scissors and I can do it myself."

"No, I'm afraid I *can't* give you a pair of scissors, Georgia, and I'll thank you not to make a suggestion like that again, unless you'd like to have your silverware privileges revoked." Dr. Thomas frowned in what I'm sure was intended to be a paternal manner. He'd been trying that a lot recently, acting like he had a fatherly interest in my welfare. Maybe if my own father had ever shown that sort of interest, I would have believed it. As it was, all he'd managed to do was get on my nerves. "Asking for potential weapons is not a sign of mental stability."

"Pardon me for arguing, Dr. Thomas, but I'm a clone living in a post-zombie America. I'm pretty sure *not* asking for potential weapons would be a much worse sign. Besides, I'm not asking for weapons, I'm asking for a haircut, and giving options if there's no way to get me someone willing to do it." I kept smiling. It was better than screaming.

Dr. Thomas sighed. "I'll see what I can do. In the meanwhile, you're going to need to do something for me."

I stiffened. "What kind of something?" I asked carefully.

"We need to run some special tests tomorrow, in addition to the ones on your usual schedule. There's some concern about your internal organs. These tests won't be quite the noninvasive sort that you've become accustomed to, I'm afraid. They'll be rather painful, and unfortunately, the nature of the needed data requires you to be awake during the process."

"And they're dealing with my internal organs?" I raised my eyebrows. It was a sign of how numb I was becoming to their endless tests that I couldn't even work up a mild level of concern over the idea of my kidneys shutting down. "Are my internal organs doing something they're not supposed to be doing?"

"No, no, not at all. We just want to be sure they're not going to *start* doing something they're not supposed to be doing. They're much younger than you look, after all, and there's always a chance for biological error."

"I don't really have a choice about this, do I?"

"Not really," said Dr. Thomas. "I hoped you'd be accommodating, since we're only concerned about your health."

"If I don't fight you on this, can I get some of the books from my list?"

"I'll see what I can do."

"How about that haircut?"

Dr. Thomas shook his head. "All things in good time, Georgia. For now, don't push it. I'm going to need you to go on an all-liquid diet for the next twelve hours, and then we'll be taking some fluid and tissue samples in the morning."

That was one of the first indicators I'd had of the actual time. I perked up a little. "If the tests are being run in the morning, that makes it, what, four in the afternoon? Five?"

"Don't push it," Dr. Thomas repeated, and withdrew a pair of clear plastic handcuffs from his pocket. "It's time for today's tests."

"This is really unnecessary," I said, and presented my wrists.

"Hopefully, we won't have to go through this for much longer." Dr. Thomas snapped the cuffs into place, careful not to touch my skin. He never touched me when he could help it. The few times that I'd "tripped" and touched him with my bare hands, he'd practically injured himself lunging away from me. It was a funny response, but it wasn't useful, especially not when I was trying to convince him that I was harmless.

"That would be nice," I said, and stood, pausing a moment as my rubber-soled socks found traction on the hard tile floor. I would have preferred shoes—even slippers—but the orderlies responsible for my clothing wouldn't let me have anything but socks. At least the rubber treads made it easier for me to walk with my hands restrained.

The cuffs didn't come out until the third time they took me out of my room. They'd been a constant reality since then. If I left the room to go anywhere but the bathroom, I left it in handcuffs. Presumably, whoever was actually in charge of my care—and it wasn't Dr. Thomas; if he'd been in charge of me, he would never have come near me—wanted to be sure I wasn't going to make some sort of daring escape. I was never sure whether I should be flattered by their apparent faith in my ingenuity or insulted by the fact that they thought handcuffs would stop me. That was the sort of thing I had a lot of time to think about these days. Solitary confinement punctuated only by intrusive medical testing will do that for a person.

The guards were waiting in the hallway. I recognized both. Not surprising, but reassuring in its own way. If I was starting to know the guards on sight, that meant they didn't have an infinite number of them. Eventually, they'd start thinking of me as a person, rather than as a test subject, and that would make them easier to get around when the day finally came for me to escape. Assuming I didn't spontaneously amplify or suffer acute organ failure before then. Also assuming Gregory didn't find a way to smuggle me out with the laundry, or do something else out of a bad pre-Rising heist movie.

Also, if the guards had never been repeated, I would have started to worry that they were being taken out back and shot after their shifts were finished. Call me sentimental, but I'd really rather not be the human equivalent of a death sentence.

One of the guards led us down the empty hall, while the other walked behind us. In the time since I woke up, I hadn't seen anyone aside from Dr. Thomas, Gregory, the constantly shifting crew of guards, and the lab technicians who were waiting at the end of this little journey. If there were any other patients in the building, my handlers were doing an excellent job of keeping me away from them. Whether that was for my protection or for theirs, I couldn't say.

We reached the end of the hall. The first guard pressed his hand against a blood test panel, waiting for the light over the door to go from red to green. The door opened, and the guard stepped through. Dr. Thomas repeated the process. The second guard gestured for me to do the same, not saying a word. None of the guards liked to talk to me. I'm pretty sure I made them nervous.

Dr. Thomas and the first guard were waiting on the other side. Dr. Thomas motioned for me to start walking, not waiting for the second guard. "Come along. The faster we get this done, the faster we can get you back to your room."

"Yes, empty rooms without Internet are absolutely the sort of place I yearn to get back to." This hall was colder. I shivered. This was a negative-pressure zone, and whoever was responsible for the environmental controls kept them turned lower than was strictly necessary.

"It's for your own good," said Dr. Thomas. There was no conviction in his words. He was parroting the argument we'd been having almost constantly since we met, and somehow, the thought of having it one more time was enough to make me tired.

"Right," I said, and kept plodding steadily along.

Dr. Thomas stopped at a door that looked like every other door in the vicinity. "Here we are. I don't have to remind you again how important it is that you cooperate with the technicians, do I?"

"No, Dr. Thomas, you do not," I replied blandly. "I'm going to be a good girl today. I'd like you to make note of that in my file, since maybe it can help me get Internet privileges faster. How would that be?"

Dr. Thomas smiled, the expression not quite managing to mask the fact that he was grinding his teeth. "We'll see," he said, and opened the door.

I was becoming quite the expert in CDC labs, at least as they were configured locally; like the guards, they seemed to rotate, with every battery of tests conducted in a different place. Even when I saw the same rooms, they'd been rearranged, equipment swapped around until my head spun. I couldn't tell whether they were intentionally trying to disorient me or just doing a really good job by mistake. Either way, I'd started making note of the things they couldn't rearrange—or wouldn't, anyway, unless those things were pointed out to them. I glanced up as I entered the room, making note of the pattern of holes on the ceiling. This was the one I called lab three, then. The last time I'd been in lab three, my afternoon test array included a bone marrow sample.

"Won't this be fun," I muttered.

Lab three was about the size of every other lab I'd been in at the CDC: twice the size of my current bedroom, and roughly the size of a large living room. It just seemed small because it was so packed. My stomach sank as I realized I didn't know what half of the machines were for. Technicians in lab coats bustled around the room, making tweaks and adjusting settings.

I used to try guessing which technicians would be running my tests. That was before I realized the person in charge was never one of the people operating the machines. Operating machines was beneath anyone chosen to supervise testing on a real live clone of a dead journalist. This session was no different. As soon as the door closed behind us, another door opened on the opposite side of the lab, revealing a small office. A tall, Nordic-looking woman with ice-blonde hair scraped into a tight bun stepped out, offering a chilly smile in our direction.

She was beautiful, in a "touch me and get frostbite" sort of way. Her lab coat was the normal white, but she had accessorized it with an indecently red silk shirt the color of the lights on a testing unit. Her shoes matched her blouse. I found myself envying them, despite their three-inch heels. I hate high heels. Having actual shoes would have been enough to make up for my dislike. Besides, in a pinch, high-heeled shoes can make good improvised weapons. Sure, that gets you right back to barefoot, but at least then you're armed.

"Ah, Dr. Thomas," she said, directing her words at my escort, even as her gaze settled firmly on me. "You're just in time. Thank you for bringing the subject to see me."

"It was no trouble, really, Dr. Shaw. If there's anything I can do to assist—"

"There's nothing you can help me with," she said, still not looking in his direction. She was studying my face avidly, like she expected it to provide the answer to some question she hadn't told me anything about. "I'll have you contacted when it's time to return her to her holding cell. Thank you."

"Dr. Shaw, I'm not sure—"

Annoyance flashed across her features as she looked away from me for the first time. "I have tests to perform, Dr. Thomas, and as you have made so abundantly clear, we are on a schedule, one that required me to jump through a ludicrous number of hoops in order to get even this much access. I refuse to waste any of my allotted time in shepherding you around my equipment. You may go, and take your trained monkeys with you. I will send one of my assistants to collect you when I'm prepared to remand the subject to your care."

Dr. Thomas hesitated, looking like he was going to argue. Dr. Shaw narrowed her eyes very slightly, and took a single half step forward. The heel of her shoe hit the floor with a loud snapping sound, like a pencil being broken in half.

That seemed to decide the matter. "Georgia, Dr. Shaw is in charge until I return," he said. "Cooperate with whatever she requests." He turned and stepped quickly out of the room, gesturing for the guards to follow him. Looking uncertain about the whole situation, they did.

Dr. Shaw waited for the door to shut before returning her attention to me. Something about her expression made me want to squirm, which just annoyed me even more. I stood up a little straighter, narrowing my eyes, and met her stare for stare.

Finally, surprisingly, she laughed. "Oh, *very* good! They really did bring you back, didn't they? Or good as, one supposes. If you would be so kind as to step behind the screen there and remove your clothing, we can begin."

"Sorry. Can't." I held up my hands, showing her the cuffs. "I'm too much of a threat to run around without restraints."

"I see." Dr. Shaw reached into her pocket, producing a key. She smiled at my startled expression. "They're standard CDC issue, for control of troublesome subjects. It wouldn't do to have someone require the services of a locksmith simply because their primary physician was unavailable when their cuffs needed to be removed."

I kept still as she unlocked me, waiting until the cuffs had vanished into her pocket before I asked, "Does the CDC make a practice of handcuffing patients?"

"Only the potentially dangerous ones." Her amusement vanished as quickly as it had come. "Now please. Behind the screen, and remove your clothing. Kathleen will supply a robe once you're done."

"Why is it that you people always try to get me naked first thing? It's not like I have any weapons to hide in my pajama pants." I rubbed my wrists as I walked to the indicated screen and stepped behind it. Then I stopped, my heart jumping up into my throat as I saw what the screen had been concealing from the rest of the room.

"Go ahead, Georgia," said Dr. Shaw's voice from the main room. "We really must get started as quickly as possible."

I stepped slowly forward, barely breathing as I picked up the tiny pistol that was sitting on the stool, almost like it was waiting for me. I revised that thought to remove the "almost" as I felt the way the gun fit into my palm, vanishing behind my fingers. Firearms this small were usually mass-manufactured, but this was a custom job. There was no other way to explain the rightness of it sliding into my hand. It felt like it was made for me because it *was* made for me.

It was made of hardened ceramic and heat-resistant plastic polymer. All the metal detectors in the world wouldn't be able to catch the fact that I was carrying it, and the guards' reluctance to touch me when they didn't have to meant I was pretty much safe from a pat down. It was mine. They wouldn't take it away from me, because they wouldn't know I had it. Not until I needed them to.

The gun had been holding down a piece of folded paper. I picked it up with my free hand, unfolding it, and read.

Georgia—

This is all the protection we can give you right now. We're still working on an exit plan. Trust Dr. Shaw. She's been working with me for a long time. Keep cooperating. They can't know you're planning to escape. You have to keep trusting me.

The gun was enough to buy a *lot* of trust. I kept reading, and stopped breathing for the second time in as many minutes as I saw the second part of his message:

I have received confirmation from my West Coast contact: Shaun Phillip Mason is alive. I repeat: Shaun is alive. He's been off the grid for a little while, for reasons I hope to have the opportunity to explain soon, but he *is* alive, and he *will* be waiting when we get you out of here. Whatever they say, whatever lies they try to make you believe,

believe *me*: Shaun is alive. All we have to do now is keep you that way long enough to get you back to him.

Yours—G.

I sank onto the stool, staring at the letter. My fingers were creasing the paper, rendering some of the words almost illegible, but that didn't matter. I knew what they said. They were burning behind my eyes, lighting up a darkness that I hadn't even realized was there.

Shaun was alive. I wasn't making educated guesses. I wasn't just telling myself something I wanted to believe: Shaun was actually and genuinely alive. That, or the CDC had planted Gregory to earn my trust... But the gun nixed that line of thinking. I paused, turning my attention from the paper to the pistol just long enough to eject the clip and check that it was loaded. It was. Those tiny bullets made all the difference, because no matter how hard the CDC was trying to make me believe them, they weren't going to give me a gun.

"There you are." Dr. Shaw stepped around the screen, moving with a silence that made it plain how much she'd been exaggerating the sound of her footsteps before. She plucked the paper from my hand, not seeming to mind when she ripped it in the process. "Thank you for cleaning up the lab, Georgia. I'll just go feed this through the shredder while you finish undressing. You can leave your clothing here. No one will disturb it."

My eyes widened as I glanced from her to the gun and back again. Dr. Shaw followed my gaze and nodded understandingly.

"I appreciate that you have little privacy in your current circumstances, but I assure you, no one will touch your things while you're here. I take privacy concerns *very* seriously." Her smile was thin and cold, briefly recalling the way she'd first presented herself. "You have my word."

Gregory said I could trust her, and she wasn't sounding the alarm over my possession of a weapon. I swallowed to clear my throat, and nodded. "I'll get ready."

"Thank you. Call for Kathleen when you want the robe." She paused, as if one more thing had just occurred to her, and added, "You may keep your underwear."

"I appreciate that."

"I thought you might." Dr. Shaw walked away, her heels clacking on the floor, as if to illustrate that outside this small, screened-in space, we were playing by the CDC's rules.

I may not enjoy playing by other people's rules, but I've had enough experience to be good at it. I slid off the stool, putting the pistol back where I originally found it, and disrobed, piling my white pajamas over the gun. If any of Dr. Shaw's technicians weren't in on things—and I had no real reason to believe that *any* of them were in on things—they'd need to actively look before they found anything awry.

While I stripped, I heard the oddly reassuring sound of a shredder coming from the main room. Dr. Shaw had been telling the truth about disposing of Gregory's message. I just hoped she'd have the sense to take the trash with her when she left.

Kathleen was waiting when I stuck my head around the screen. She held a plain white robe out to me, smiling pleasantly. "Dr. Shaw is ready for you now."

"Tell Dr. Shaw I'm almost ready for her," I said, and ducked back behind the screen to shrug into the robe. With one last, regretful glance toward the pile of clothing concealing my new gun, I turned to head out into the room.

Kathleen was still waiting. Her smile brightened as she saw that I was dressed. "This way," she said, beckoning. "We're going to begin by measuring your basic neurological responses."

"Meaning what?" I asked, following her.

"Meaning we'll be applying electrodes to your scalp, asking you neutral questions and watching to see how your brain waves change as you respond. Dr. Shaw has been petitioning for permission to do a sleep study, but so far, they've refused." Kathleen frowned, like the refusal was somehow a personal insult. She led me toward a complicated-looking machine where Dr. Shaw and two of the technicians were waiting. "I'm sure she'll be granted permission sooner or later. For the moment, conscious brain wave studies will have to do."

"For *today*," said Dr. Shaw, snapping a connector into place. "Georgia. So glad you could join us. If you would be so kind as to take a seat, we can begin getting you ready. Please remove the robe."

I froze. "Please *what*?"

"Remove the robe."

"Why did you give it to me if—?"

"Modesty and science are not always compatible," said Dr. Shaw. "Kathleen?"

"Yes, Dr. Shaw," said Kathleen, and took hold of my robe's collar, tugging just hard enough to make sure I knew she was there. "If you would be so kind?"

I bit back a sigh. I've never been the most modest person in the world, and my time as the CDC's favorite new lab rat was rapidly eroding what little modesty I possessed. I undid the belt, letting Kathleen peel the robe away, and took a seat in the indicated chair. It was covered in clear plastic that made little crunching noises as I slid myself into position. Worse, it was cold.

So was the greenish gel that Dr. Shaw's technicians began applying to my throat, shoulders, and stomach. I frowned. "I thought this was going to be a brain wave test?"

"Yes, but since we have limited time, and you're going to be immobilized anyway, I'm taking this opportunity to get a clear picture of your vital signs." Dr. Shaw smiled. "I'm very fond of efficiency."

"I'm beginning to see that." The technicians, including Kathleen, were taping sensor pads to my front.

"There's just one more thing that you might object to. I apologize, but I assure you, it's necessary to ensure the accuracy of my tests."

I gritted my teeth, steeling myself for something I wasn't going to enjoy. "What's that?" I asked. "You need me to sing Christmas carols while you measure my brain activity?"

"That could be entertaining, and you should feel free if it helps you relax, but no." Dr. Shaw produced a pair of scissors from her pocket, holding them up for me to see. "Your hair will interfere with the placement of the sensors on your scalp. I'm afraid I'm going to have to cut most of it off if we're going to get a clear result."

For a moment, I simply stared at her. Then I started to laugh. I was still laughing when she began cutting my hair, and barely got myself under control in time for the testing to begin. The real test—the test of whether or not I could survive the CDC—was still ongoing. But I was starting to feel like I might actually stand a chance.

———

Subject 7c continues to respond to stimulus, and has begun questioning the conditions of her containment. She—and it truly is impossible to avoid assigning a gender, and even an identity, to a subject that has been awake and interactive for this length of time—continues to adhere closely to the registered template. Her responses are well within the allowable parameters. Perhaps too well within the allowable parameters; early concerns about cooperation and biddability were not unfounded.

It may be necessary to begin preparing the 8 line for release. I will continue to observe and study 7c, but do not believe that 7d would offer any substantial improvement in the problem areas.

**—Taken from an e-mail sent by Dr. Matthew Thomas,
July 23, 2041.**

Preparations to separate the members of our group are nearly complete. Maggie keeps saying we shouldn't split the party. Privately, I agree with her. This is madness. We will separate, and we will each of us die alone. And yet...

Something must be done. If Shaun's paranoid ravings are correct, and the mosquitoes were engineered for release when a news cycle truly needed to be buried—one such as the cycle we were prepared to unleash when we left Memphis—then it is our responsibility to find a way to save the world from them. How arrogant that looks! "Save the world." I'm not in the world saving business. I'm a journalist.

But it seems the world has other ideas. Maggie and I leave for Seattle tomorrow. I'm terrified that I will never see London, or my wife, again. And a small, traitorous part of me is elated. I thought we no longer lived in an age of heroes.

I was wrong.

**—From *Fish and Clips*,
the blog of Mahir Gowda, July 23, 2041. Unpublished.**

Six

Deciding to hit the road took only a few seconds—the amount of time necessary for a thought to travel from my brain to my big mouth. Actually leaving took longer. Dr. Abbey wasn't sending us out to die; if anything, she was sending us out *not* to die, something she took great pains to make sure I understood.

"This isn't just about the mosquitoes, Shaun," she'd said, while running yet another blood test and getting yet another negative result. "I wasn't exaggerating when I showed you those distribution maps, or when I talked about the number of lives you could save by bringing me some live specimens. But it was never just about the mosquitoes."

George had sighed in the back of my head then, sounding so tired it made my chest ache. She was dead. She shouldn't have been tired anymore. But she was, and it was my fault, for refusing to let her go. *She wants you to get exposed again.*

"Are you fucking kidding?" I'd asked, too startled to remember to keep my voice down.

And Dr. Abbey had smiled, that bitter half twist of her lips that I normally saw only when she thought no one was looking, or when she murmured endearments to her huge black dog, the one with her dead husband's name.

"Someday you're going to have to explain how it is you've managed to create a subconscious echo that's smarter than you are." Still smiling, Dr. Abbey had looked me squarely in the eye and said, "I need to know if you can shrug off the infection a second time, outside lab conditions. If you can, that changes everything."

Swell.

The next four days rushed past in a blur, with all of us preparing to do the one thing I'd sworn I'd die to prevent: We were getting ready to go our separate ways. After everything I'd done to keep us together, to keep us alive, I was going to scatter us to the winds, and pray everyone came home again. We started as a news site. Somewhere along the line, we became a family. Me, and George, and After the End Times. That was all I needed. I'd already lost George. Did I have to lose everyone else, too?

Alaric would be staying with Dr. Abbey; that hadn't changed. He was our best technician. If it became necessary for the lab to move while we were still on the road, he'd be too useful for Dr. Abbey to just ditch, and he'd be able to keep the rest of us aware of its location. Besides, I didn't trust him in the field when his sister's safety was on the line. He was likely to do something impulsive and get himself hurt, and I wasn't sure I'd be able to force myself to stay on the road instead of running straight back to Dr. Abbey and her advanced medical facilities. Especially since by "advanced," I meant "better than a first aid kit." We were still off the grid. If one of us got messed up, the hospital wasn't going to be an option.

Maggie and Mahir, meanwhile, were going to head farther up the coast, leaving the wilds of Oregon for the dubious safety of Seattle. Maggie's plan was to go back *on* the grid as soon as possible, reclaiming her position as heir to the Garcia family fortune, and presenting Mahir as her latest boy toy. "People like their circuses when the news gets bad," she'd said, a perverse twinkle in her eyes. "I'm a Fictional, remember? I'm going to tell them a story so flashy they won't even think to ask where I've been." Alaric wasn't thrilled about the "boy toy" part, but it was solid. They would use her celebrity as a cover while they made contact with the Seattle underground, and located the man everyone called "the Monkey." He could cook new IDs for my whole team, IDs that were good enough to let us disappear forever, if things came to that.

Most of us, anyway. Maggie came to see me on the fifth day after we began planning our departure. I was clearing my things out of the van. I'd been sleeping there most nights, preferring the illusory privacy of its familiar walls to the dubious comforts of the dormlike sleeping arrangements inside the Forestry Center. The garage wasn't secure, but the van was, once the doors were locked.

She knocked once on the open rear door, and then just stood there, waiting.

I looked up. "Yeah?"

"You know we're not getting me an ID from the Monkey, don't you?" Her expression was a mixture of resignation and resolve. She looked like a heroine from one of the horror movies she loved so much, and in that moment, I really understood what Dave—one of the many teammates I'd buried since this whole thing started—and Alaric saw in her. She was beautiful.

And she was right. "Yeah, I do." I put down the toolbox I was holding, moving to take a seat on the bumper. "You can't disappear."

"If it weren't for the fact that my bio-tracker is still registering with my parents, I wouldn't even be able to stay underground for this long." Maggie touched the skin above her collarbone. Her parents had implanted a subdermal bio-tracker beneath the bone when she was still in diapers. It didn't come with a "trace" function—Maggie's misguided teenage years before she discovered journalism were proof that they'd been telling her the truth about that—but it enabled them to sleep soundly at night, serene in the knowledge that their only child was still alive.

"We could have it removed."

"If *anything* would switch this thing from transmitting my vitals to actively giving them a location, that would do it." Maggie sat down next to me. "It's too risky."

I looked at her levelly. "It's too risky, and you don't really want to disappear, do you?"

"It's not that! It's just...it's..." She took a breath, stopping herself before she could go any further. Finally, reluctantly, she nodded. "You're right. I don't want to disappear. I don't want to do that to my parents, and I miss my house. I miss my dogs. I miss my Fictionals. They have to be so worried. I've never done this to them before, not once. Alaric and I talked about this. He's not happy, but...it's what has to happen."

Tell her you understand, said George.

"I understand," I said, and even if I had to be prompted into the words, I meant them. Maggie had already given up a lot to stay with us this long, more than any of my team members except for maybe Mahir. Alaric's family would have been in Florida no matter where he worked. Becks hadn't spoken to her family in years. She was a lot like Georgia that way; both of them found the news and ran for it with open arms, not caring what got left behind in the process. But Maggie wasn't like that. Maggie was different.

Maggie was looking at me hopefully, like she could barely bring herself to believe I was really saying the words she was hearing. "I know I'm letting you down."

"You're not." I'm not a huggy person. I used to be more physically affectionate—not excessively so, but enough that I didn't seem standoffish. That was George's job. I took the hugs that were aimed at her. I haven't felt like hugging people very often since she died. I still leaned over and put my arm around Maggie's shoulders, giving her a brief squeeze. The situation seemed to call for it.

"Really?" she whispered.

"Really. Your parents would tear down the world trying to find you if you stayed gone too long. That's cool. That's sort of awesome, if you think about it. Becks's family hates her. Alaric's family is dead. Mahir's family is in England, and they probably think he's insane. And the Masons…" I stopped, the sentence coming to a halt.

"It's not your fault," said Maggie, filling the space with the words she assumed I needed to hear. "They were broken a long time before you came to live with them. It's not your fault you couldn't fix them."

"The flat-drop."

"What?"

"The flat-drop!" I turned to face her, grabbing her shoulders in my excitement. "We sent them a copy of our files when we were on the run from Memphis. I mean, we were going to die, so *someone* needed to have the data, right? Only I told Alaric he could encrypt the fuck out of them if he wanted to, and since the Masons haven't suddenly started 'discovering' lots of corruption inside the CDC, I guess he must have used a pretty damn good encryption."

"You're not making any sense," said Maggie, eyes wide.

"No, see, this is *perfect*! I was worried about how Becks and I were going to get into the hazard zone without getting caught, but the Masons practically invented breaking into hazard zones! They're pioneers in the field!" I laughed, mainly from relief. "All we have to do is show up on their doorstep and offer to crack those files in exchange for a low-risk route into Florida, and they'll jump at it. They'll have to."

"What if they don't?"

"Then I'll shoot their kneecaps out." I didn't realize I meant it until the words were said. The Masons raised me. The Masons gave me the greatest gift anyone has ever given me: George. But they were never really my parents, because they never wanted to be, and if they were what stood between me and what I needed to do, then they needed to be moved.

"Um," said Maggie. She pulled away from me and stood. "Well, okay, if that's what works. Really, though. Thank you for understanding."

"Thank you for being willing to go to Seattle with Mahir," I replied. "You heading back inside?"

"Yeah. Will you be out here long?"

"Not too long."

"If you're not inside by dinner, I'll send someone to get you." She walked away, her long brown braid swaying with every step. It was hard to believe that she was planning to use "bored heiress" as her cover during the trip up the coast. It was harder to believe that the news media would probably buy it.

"You need to be careful what you say around people, asshole," said George. I hadn't felt the van settle when she sat down, because she wasn't really there. I couldn't keep myself from feeling vaguely disappointed all the same. "Look at me when I'm talking to you."

"Sorry." I turned to face my dead sister, offering her a small smile. "Hi, George. How're you tonight?"

"Worried," she said. "You need to be careful. Everyone's already on edge without you going around talking about shooting people."

"I haven't hit anyone since we got here."

"That doesn't mean they're not waiting for you to start." Her expression dared me to argue. I couldn't, and so I just looked at her instead.

Maybe the fact that George sometimes appears to me is a symptom of the fact that I'm sliding farther and farther down the funhouse chute into insanity, but at moments like these, I can't force myself to care. When she died—when I shot her—I thought that was it; I would never see her again, except in pictures, and in my dreams. Only it turns out that's not true, thanks to my slipping grasp on reality. See? There are upsides to going crazy.

She still looked almost exactly like she did on that last day in Sacramento, pale-skinned from her near-pathological avoidance of sunlight, with dark brown hair cut in a short, efficient style she sometimes maintained with a pair of craft scissors. She was frowning. Since that was the expression she wore most often when she was alive, that was right, too. Really, if it hadn't been for the clear brown of her irises, she would have been indistinguishable from herself. If I could just convince my hallucination to put on a pair of sunglasses, the illusion would be perfect.

George frowned. "Shaun. Are you listening to me?"

"I am. I swear, I am." I reached one hand toward her face, stopping just short of the point where my fingertips would have failed to brush her skin. "I always listen to you."

"You just ignore what I have to say about half the time, is that it?" George sighed. I let my hand drop. As long as I didn't try to touch her, I didn't have to think of her as what she was. Dead. "Shaun—"

"It's good to see you."

"It's *bad* that you can see me. You need to talk to Dr. Abbey. Maybe she can put you on antipsychotics or something until this is all over."

"I'll go psychotic if I go on antipsychotics, which sort of defeats the purpose, don't you think?" I was trying to make it sound like a joke. We both knew I wasn't kidding. The one time I'd tried to block her out, I'd nearly committed suicide. "I can't take the silence, George. You know that."

"You asked once if I was going to haunt you forever, remember?"

"That was before Florida." I held up my left hand, showing her the faint scarring on my biceps. "That was before we found out that I'm immune to Kellis-Amberlee. That was before a lot of things."

"You know you're immune because we—"

"I know." I sighed, letting my hand drop. "Things are all fucked up. I was supposed to be the one who died. I'm not equipped to deal with this shit."

"You're wrong." Her voice was firm enough to surprise me. She met my eyes without flinching, and repeated, "You're *wrong*. Dr. Wynne wasn't kidding when he said that whoever's behind this would have been able to get away with everything if you'd been the one who died. You know that, right? I would have believed Tate when he started ranting about how he was behind everything, just him, from the start. I would have been so eager for a black and white solution, for a villain I didn't have to feel any conflict about...I would have believed him."

"I believed him," I whispered.

"Not all the way. If you'd believed him all the way—if you'd believed him the way I would have believed him—you would have done what we both know I would have done. You would have written your reports, held my funeral, gone home, and killed yourself." She smiled faintly. "Probably by overdosing on everything in our field kit before blowing the top of your head off. You never were one for leaving things to chance."

"What would you have done?"

"Slit my wrists in the bathtub," she said matter-of-factly. "Even if I amplified before I bled out, the bathroom security sensors would never have let me out into the house. I would have been bleached to death. The Masons would have had to pay if they wanted to clear the outbreak off their home owner's insurance, and you and I could have sat in the afterlife and laughed at them until we both cried."

Now it was my turn to smile. "That sounds like something you'd do," I agreed.

"But I didn't get the chance." She leaned over. This time, she was the one to reach for me, and when her fingertips grazed my skin, I felt it. Tactile hallucinations aren't a good sign of mental health, but sometimes I feel like they're the only things letting me keep body and soul together. "You got it. And you were stronger than I would have been. You're stronger than you think you are. All you've ever needed to do was let yourself see it."

"I don't know how much longer I can keep this up."

"Not too much longer, I'd wager," said Mahir, from behind me. His normally crisp accent was blurred around the edges, like he was too tired to worry about being understood by the Americans. "How's it coming?"

"About as well as can be expected," I said, stealing one last look at Georgia before I turned, casting an easy smile in his direction. I didn't need to look back to know that George was gone. She generally disappeared as soon as I took my eyes off her. I was seeing her more often with every day that passed, and that was wonderful, because I missed her so much, and it was terrible, because it meant I was running out of time.

We can cure cancer. We can cure the common cold. But no one, anywhere, ever, has found a reliable cure for crazy.

"Maggie spoke with you?"

I nodded. "She wanted to make sure I knew she wouldn't be coming back from Seattle."

"And you were all right with that?" Mahir walked toward me, stopping when he was still a few feet clear of the van. Maggie was a much more touchy-feely kind of person than he was. I appreciated that. One hug per day was pretty much my limit.

"No," I admitted. "I don't want her to go. The rest of us... You're going to be able to put your own name back on when you get home, but the rest of us, we're done. We'll be lucky if we don't wind up hiding in Canada being chased by zombie moose for the rest of our lives."

"There's always the chance we'll successfully manage to bring down the United States government somehow, and that will negate the need to flee to Canada," said Mahir helpfully.

I gave him a startled look. He smirked, fighting unsuccessfully to keep himself from smiling. Somehow, that was even funnier than what he'd said. I started laughing. So did he. We were both still laughing five minutes later, when Becks came out to the garage with a can of soda in one hand and a perplexed look on her face.

"Did I miss something?" she asked.

"We're going to topple the US government!" I informed her.

Becks appeared to think about that for a moment. Then she shrugged, cracking the tab on her soda at the same time, and replied, "Okay. Works for me."

Mahir and I burst out laughing again. Becks waited patiently for us to stop, taking occasional sips from her soda. Finally, I wiped my eyes with the heel of my hand, and said, still snickering, "Okay. Okay, I think we're done now. Did you see Maggie?"

"I did. She said something about you and me heading to Berkeley to kill your parents?"

"That's not quite what I said, but I guess it's close enough. We're going to Berkeley to ask the Masons if they'll tell us how to find a clear route into the Florida hazard zone."

"And what will you be giving them in return?" asked Mahir.

I sighed. "You know, I really kind of miss the days when I could just e-mail a memo to the team, and everybody would know what was going on, and I wouldn't have to repeat things seventeen times."

Not that you ever remembered to send the memos, said George.

"Because you did that *so* often," said Becks, saving me from the need to respond to someone no one else could hear. Again.

"I *could* have done it, if I'd wanted to," I countered. "That made the endless repetition a choice, and hence way less irritating. I'm going to tell them how to unlock the flat-drop of all our files. The one I had Alaric send while we were running from Memphis."

"And when they post our research far and wide? What happens then?" Mahir didn't sound annoyed, just curious. Even so, I was relieved when Becks crunched her empty soda can in her fist and chucked it into the trash can against the wall, where it landed with a rattling clunk.

"If the Masons post the things we've been withholding, they'll be the target of the firestorm that follows," she said. She sounded utterly calm. Her calm continued as she added, "Which means we can't let them do it."

"Hey!" I frowned at her. "I thought you were supposed to be on my side here."

"I'm on the side that doesn't get us slaughtered, Mason. Think about this for thirty seconds, why don't you? We give them the key to the files. They unlock them, and go all kid in a candy store over the contents, since hey, their stupid son just gave them the scoop of the century. They toss it all online. And people everywhere stop shooting zombies because they think their loved ones might get 'better.'"

I grimaced. "Not good."

"Not good at all. And then the government will lean on the Masons to tell them where to find us, so we can be used to 'prove' that it was all a hoax."

"Lovely," said Mahir.

Becks shrugged. "If you're going to think like a paranoid, you need to really *commit* to thinking like a paranoid."

Mahir looked at her quizzically. "What makes you so good at it?"

"I'm from Connecticut," said Becks. "It's not a *bad* idea—going to the Masons may be the fastest way to get ourselves access to a reasonably safe way through some pretty bad territory, and since I'm not leaving the van without dipping myself in DDT, I'd like it if we could make the trip in reasonable safety. But you're going to need another carrot to dangle in front of your freaky parents. Telling them how to get at our data isn't the way."

Yes, actually, said George, very quietly. *It's exactly the way.*

"What are you—" I began, and froze. "Oh, no. No, you can't be serious."

You know I'm serious. It's the best shot you've got.

"I won't."

You will.

Mahir and Becks had gotten good at knowing when I wasn't actually talking to them. They watched me with varying degrees of impatience, waiting until I stopped protesting before Mahir broke in, asking, "What does Georgia say we should do?"

"You know, addressing my crazy by name doesn't exactly help me stay sane," I said.

"Nothing can help you stay sane at this point, Mason," said Becks. "That ship has sailed. Now what does she say?"

I took a deep breath. "She wants me to sign her unpublished files over to the Masons. The stuff they were willing to take me to court over." I stopped, waiting for them to protest. Neither of them said a word. I scowled. "Well?"

"It's not a bad idea," said Mahir slowly. "I mean, it's true that her unpublished op-ed pieces were reasonably lucrative when we were able to publish regularly, but her news articles have been timing out at a fairly high rate. We've had our exclusive. If what's left can be used to benefit us—"

"You're fucking with me, right?" I stood, glaring at them, barely aware that my hands were balled into fists. I could hear George at the back of my head, telling me sternly to calm down, but I didn't pay any attention. That was nice, in its way. I so rarely felt like I could ignore her anymore. "Those files are her *private thoughts*. They're the last privacy she has left in this world. And you want me to just sign it over to those...those...those *people*?"

"Yes," said Mahir, sounding utterly calm. "That's exactly what we want. And I'd wager it's what Georgia wants as well, or you'd not be so angry about it. You'd be laughing it off."

"We've been using her private thoughts for our gain since she died," said Becks. "I've been okay with that, because you're okay with it. But, Shaun, you're the one who *really* knows what she would have wanted. You're the one who really knows *her*. If she were alive, would she be saying no, no way, not going to happen? Or would she be suggesting we stop fucking around and get our asses to Berkeley with the transfer papers already?"

George didn't say anything. George didn't need to say anything. I forced my fingers to unclench, waiting until I could feel my palms again before I looked away from Becks and Mahir, and said, "I'll get the transfer papers drawn up before we leave. That way, all we have to do is hand them over and get the hell out of town."

Thank you, murmured George. I felt the shadow of a hand brush my cheek, and shivered. I don't believe in ghosts. Never have, never will. George is a figment of my overactive imagination, nothing more, and nothing less. But moments like that, when she touches me with other people in the room...

At moments like that, I genuinely believe that I'm haunted.

"You're doing the right thing," said Mahir. I glanced up, meeting his eyes without meaning to. He smiled. Just a little. Enough for me to see that he meant it. "You're a crazy bastard, Shaun Mason, and I think sometimes you're not going to be happy until you've managed to get every last one of us killed, but you're a good man, all the same."

"Remind me to have that inscribed on my urn," I said, and Becks laughed, and things felt like they might be okay again. We had a direction. I didn't like it; I didn't have to. All I had to do was follow it, and let it lead me to whatever the next step on this increasingly insane journey would prove to be.

"Can I help you finish getting the van ready?" asked Becks. "Since we're going to be sleeping in the thing for God only knows how long, I want to be absolutely sure that there are no old tuna sandwiches moldering under the seats."

"Be my guest," I said, waving toward the open van doors. "Mahir, tell Alaric and Maggie we're rolling out in the morning. Team meeting at five."

Mahir grimaced. "A.M.?"

"Naturally."

"I take back what I said about you being a good man."

"Too late. There are no take-backs in real life."

Becks chuckled darkly. "Ain't that just the truth?"

"Sadly?" I asked. "Yes. It is. Now let's get back to work. We have a lot to get done, and not much time to do it in."

Mahir was opening his mouth to answer when a scream rang out from the other side of the garage door, followed by the sound of gunfire. In the brief pause between the first volley of shots and the second, we could all hear the moaning coming from inside.

"Never a dull moment, is there?" I asked. Grabbing my pistol, I ran for the door. Becks was there just ahead of me. She pushed it open, and we ran together into chaos.

Dr. Abbey gave me a dressing-down this morning for yelling at her staff. "They didn't sign up for this." That's what she said. Like it made all the difference in the world, somehow. "They didn't sign up for this. Don't treat them like they did."

You know what, lady? None of us signed up for this. Not me, not Mahir, not George, not anyone. And I definitely didn't sign up for keeping my mouth shut while a bunch of amateurs treat zombies like lab rats.

Zombies are dangerous. Science doesn't protect you from that reality. If anything, science makes it worse.

I didn't sign up for that, either.

**—From *Adaptive Immunities*,
the blog of Shaun Mason, July 23, 2041. Unpublished.**

Yes. You were right.
We will proceed.

**—Taken from a message sent by Dr. Danika Kimberley,
July 23, 2041. Recipient unknown.**

Seven

Dr. Shaw's tests were actually soothing, despite the partial nudity and the being touched by strangers. She was calm and professional, leading her team with an unwavering precision that gave them a degree of serenity I hadn't previously encountered at the CDC. Everyone else I'd dealt with had been uneasy when forced to come into direct contact with my skin, like being a clone was somehow catching. Dr. Shaw's assistants showed no such discomfort. They affixed their sensors without hesitation, even peeling them loose and sticking them back down in new configurations. It was so matter-of-fact and impersonal that it was almost wonderful.

I didn't realize I was starting to drift off until Dr. Shaw cleared her throat and said, "It would help us measure your waking brain wave patterns if you would do us the favor of remaining awake while they're being recorded."

"Oh." I opened my eyes, offering her a sheepish smile. "I'm sorry."

"It's understandable. You've been through a great deal. Still, the cause of science must take precedence over comfort." She leaned forward to affix a sensor to my forehead. Her lips almost brushed my ear as she murmured, barely audible even at that range, "The locks will be reset tonight at midnight. You can answer many of your questions then, if you're quick about it."

Pulling back before I could react, she pressed the edges of the sensor down and said, "Begin the next phase, James, if you would be so kind." One of her assistants nodded. Dr. Shaw turned away, attention seemingly fixed on the machine in front of her.

Right. Information exchange time was over, at least for the moment. Her words had definitely had one effect, at least—there was no way I was going to start nodding off again.

All the tests I'd been through since I'd woken up had been different. That was unusual, all by itself. Blood tests, muscle memory response tests, even psychological exams performed by people who didn't seem to understand the questions, much less the answers I was giving. The medical teams changed constantly, and each was directed by a different administrator. So what did that mean, exactly? What were they looking for that didn't require a single supervising doctor to find?

Dr. Shaw was the first to outright admit to measuring my brain waves. I was reasonably sure she wasn't the first one to do it. The chance to study a cloned brain that was actually functional and responsive had to be irresistible to them—and despite my fervent wish to believe otherwise, I knew my brain was as cloned as the rest of me. Nothing else made *sense*. When the virus went live in my original bloodstream, it attacked the brain with a ferocity unequaled by any naturally occurring pathogen. I'd been able to *feel* my memories eroding as I typed up the final entry on my blog. If they'd placed my infected old brain in my clean new clone body, I would have gone straight into amplification, and all their hard work would have been for nothing.

I watched the colored lines representing my brain's activity spike and tangle on the monitor across from me. None of them made a damn bit of sense. I never studied medicine, beyond the first aid required for field certification. Mahir might have been able to decode the peaks and valleys, turning them into comprehensible data. Mahir wasn't with me.

One of Dr. Shaw's assistants was trying to peel the sensor from my left biceps. I lifted my arm, tightening the muscle to give him more traction. He shot me a relieved look. "Thanks," he said. "This bio-adhesive can be tricky."

"What is it?" I asked, half from sincere curiosity, and half to keep him talking to me. It's easier to get information from people who think you're interested in the same things they are.

"Slime mold," said the assistant. He sounded happy about it, too.

"Oh," I said, unable to quite mask my dismay. Then again, I *was* the one who had living goo smeared on something like fifteen percent of her skin. I think I was allowed a little dismay. "That's . . . special. What happens to it when you're done with me?"

"We'll dust it with a powder that makes it go dormant, and then just roll it off your skin," he said. "Can you relax your arm for me?"

"Sure." I let my arm drop back to its original position. He attached the sensor to the inside of my elbow. "I guess that makes sense. No residue, no medical waste . . ."

"It's self-cleaning, so even if it gets bloody, it's safe to use again after eight hours. It also reacts to the presence of live virus."

"Really?" I asked, blinking. "How?"

"It tries to ooze away."

This time, I couldn't suppress my shudder. Several alarms went off on the machines connected to the various sensors, earning me dirty looks from a few of the assistants. "Sorry!" I said.

"George, please refrain from making the subject wiggle," said Dr. Shaw, not looking away from the monitor she was studying.

The assistant—George—reddened. "Sorry, Dr. Shaw."

I waited for him to get the sensor on my elbow firmly seated, then asked, "So you're another George, huh? The original form?"

"George R. Stewart," he replied. "And yes, the 'R' stands for 'Romero.' My parents were grateful, not creative."

"Georgia, here," I said. "One of my best friends was a Georgette."

"Georgette Meissonier, right?" George caught my startled expression and reddened again. "I, um. I'm a big fan of your work. Your last post was...it was amazing. I've never read anything like it."

I wasn't sure whether I should feel flattered or embarrassed. I wound up mixing both reactions as I said awkwardly, "Oh. So you know the part where I'm dead."

"The dead have been walking for a quarter century." He moved to my other side, adjusting another sensor. Dr. Shaw's other assistants all seemed to have machines to tend, leaving George with the dubious honor of working with the living equipment. Me, and the slime mold. "I'm glad you're back. If anyone deserves to be back..."

"Let's hope the rest of the world feels the same way when I start doing the celebrity blog circuit," I said, putting a lilt in my tone to show that I was joking. I wasn't joking.

"They're waiting for you," he said, cheeks getting redder still. He stopped talking after that, focusing all the more intently on the sensors he was shifting. I blinked a little, watching him. I'd expected a lot of reactions. That wasn't one of them. My last post...it made me another name on The Wall, but that was all, wasn't it?

Wasn't it?

The idea that I'd become some sort of symbol worried me. I'm a realist. I've been a realist since the day I looked at the Masons—who'd been Mommy and Daddy until that moment—and realized that Shaun was right, and they didn't love us.

I'd already known the CDC was never going to let me go. Whatever they brought me back for—blackmail or science project or just because I was the most convenient corpse when they decided to prove they could do it for real—it wasn't going to include opening the doors and telling me to go on my merry way. I was a prisoner. I was a test subject. I was, in a very real way, as much a piece of lab equipment as the machines that I was connected to. The only difference was that the machines couldn't resent the fact that they had no choice in their own existence.

And if I was a symbol, I was also a weapon, whether I wanted to be one or not.

"Are any of them pinching you?" asked George.

"No," I said, resisting the urge to shake my head. I didn't want to trigger any more alarms if I didn't have to. "I think we're good to continue."

"We're almost done," he said, and offered one more awkward, almost worshipful smile before moving away.

The remainder of the tests passed without incident. More living slime was applied to my limbs and torso, sometimes by George, sometimes by one of the other assistants; more sensors were attached or moved, allowing Dr. Shaw's equipment to record a detailed image of everything going on inside me. I resisted the urge to spend the whole time staring at the monitors. I didn't understand them. All I could do was upset myself more by watching them.

I'd almost managed to drift off again when the assistants began pulling the sensor pads off, letting George sprinkle what looked—and smelled—like baby powder on the sticky green residue the sensors left behind. True to his word, the green stuff rolled into tight little balls, which he scraped off me with the edge of his hand, gathering it all into one gooey-looking mass.

"Please don't forget to feed the slime mold," said Dr. Shaw, moving to disconnect the sensors at my temples. "I have no desire to listen to a week of complaints because we have to culture ourselves a new colony."

"Yes, Dr. Shaw," said George, and hurried off with his handful of inert green goop. Most of the other assistants followed him, leaving me alone with Dr. Shaw and Kathleen, the assistant who had initially brought me my currently discarded robe. She was holding it again, face a mask of patience as she waited for Dr. Shaw to finish freeing me from their equipment.

"Kathleen, what is our time situation?" asked Dr. Shaw, working a thumbnail under one of the sensors on my forehead. Either these had been pressed down harder, or they'd used a particularly robust batch of slime mold to glue them to my head and neck; it felt like she was trying to chip her way through concrete.

"We have fifteen minutes remaining in your original research appointment," said Kathleen serenely. "We have ninety-three seconds of previously untransmitted sensor data, which James is now feeding through the main uplink. It will remain unquestioned for approximately fifty-four more seconds."

I was still blinking at her in confusion when Dr. Shaw nodded, said, "Good," and ripped the recalcitrant sensor from my forehead. I yelped, clapping a hand over the stinging patch it left behind. Dr. Shaw watched me, calm appraisal in her eyes. "Are you paying attention?"

"Yes!" I gasped, half glaring at her. "I was paying attention *before* you tried to scalp me!"

"There will be an accident with the building's EMP shield tonight, at six minutes past midnight. The shift change will have occurred an hour previous, and you will have a thirty-minute window before anyone realizes they've lost the visual feed to your quarters." The certainty in her voice told me this wasn't the first time she'd had to give this little spiel. "Your contact will come to collect you. There's something we feel you need to see."

"Eleven seconds," said Kathleen.

"Do you understand?" asked Dr. Shaw.

I understood that they'd obviously timed this little window of stolen security so as to leave me no room for asking questions. "Yes," I said. "I understand."

"Good."

"Four seconds."

Dr. Shaw bent to remove the last sensor from the underside of my jaw. This time, her fingers were gentle, and the slime mold let go without resistance. The professional chill was back in her eyes as she stepped back, saying, "You may get dressed now. We appreciate your cooperation."

"Yeah, well, you're welcome," I said, standing. My legs were surprisingly shaky; I'd either been sitting still for longer than I thought, or there was some form of muscle relaxant engineered into their adhesive slime. Possibly both. Kathleen passed me the robe, and I leaned against the side of the chair to shrug it back on. Being clothed didn't make me feel any better. As the tests Dr. Shaw and her team had been running proved, I was always naked here. What difference did fabric make when these people could look inside my body, and understand it in ways that I didn't?

Kathleen and Dr. Shaw waited as I got my balance back. "Better?" asked Dr. Shaw.

"I think so."

"Good. Make yourself decent; I'll go unseal the door before Dr. Thomas decides to knock it down." She almost smiled as she turned and walked away from us, her heels clacking against the floor.

"This way," said Kathleen, motioning for me to follow her—in case, I supposed, I had somehow managed to forget where I left the screen that was protecting my flimsy CDC-issue pajamas... and the gun Gregory had somehow managed to smuggle to me. That was the last thing I was going to forget.

Becoming a licensed journalist requires passing basic gun safety and marksmanship exams; even if you're planning to do nothing but sit at home typing to an anonymous audience, having the phrase "accredited journalist" after your name means having a carry permit. Becoming a licensed field journalist, like I am—like I *was*—means taking a lot more exams, and learning how to handle a lot more varieties of weapon. I never shared Shaun's interest in the more esoteric firearms. The basics suited me just fine, and I'd been carrying at least one gun at pretty much all times since I got my first permit. I was twelve that summer. Knowing that I had a gun again, that I had a means of protecting myself if I needed it... that made a lot of difference. The robe didn't make me feel any less naked. The gun would.

Kathleen waited outside the screen while I went behind it and put my pajamas back on. The small plastic gun tucked easily into the top of my right sock, not even creating a noticeable bulge once my pants were on. As long as I could act natural, Dr. Thomas would never know that it was there. That was probably what Gregory was counting on.

Gregory, and the EIS. There was no way Dr. Shaw wasn't working for them, and if she was one of theirs, her assistants probably were, too. Definitely Kathleen; no one who was loyal to the CDC would have stood there calmly counting down our privacy window. Not unless she was a double agent hidden in the EIS, and that idea was too James Bond for me to worry about, since there was nothing I could do if it was true. The CDC had been infiltrated. The EIS might not be the good guys by any objective measure, but given the choices I had in front of me, I was going to go with the team that gave me firearms and told me Shaun wasn't dead.

Dr. Thomas and the guards were standing just inside the lab when I emerged. His eyes widened at the sight of me, and then narrowed. "What have you done to her hair?" he demanded, attention swinging back toward Dr. Shaw.

She watched him with cool, if evident, amusement and said, "It was interfering with the placement of my sensors. As none of the tests scheduled for the remainder of the month required uncut hair, I thought it best to eliminate the issue in the most efficient manner possible. Is there a problem?"

"No, but…" Dr. Thomas stopped, obviously torn as to how to complete that sentence. Finally, looking almost sullen, he said, "You should have consulted with me before cutting her hair. Sudden changes to her environment can be stressful at this stage in her recovery."

Dr. Shaw's laugh was surprisingly light and delicate, like it belonged to someone much younger and less put together. "Oh, come now, Matthew. You can't really expect me to believe that you consider a *haircut* a sudden change in her environment. I understand the necessity of controlling all variable factors while she gets her strength back, but no sensible young woman would take something this simple and medically necessary as a new source of stress."

"I like it," I contributed, before Dr. Thomas could say anything else. He turned to frown at me as I made my way across the lab to where he was waiting for me. "It's going to be a lot easier to brush. I've never tried to deal with long hair before."

"I suppose the convenience will make up for the aesthetic failings," he said stiffly.

I frowned. I couldn't stop myself, and quite frankly, I didn't want to. "This is the length I prefer my hair to be," I said. "The only 'aesthetic failing' is that I keep taking bleach showers without access to hair dye. I'm going to wind up blonde if this keeps up much longer, and that's not a good look for me."

"We all have our trials in this life," said Dr. Shaw. "Georgia, thank you for your cooperation today. You were very easy for us to work with, and I appreciate it."

"No problem, Dr. Shaw," I said. "It was my pleasure."

"It's time for us to go, Georgia," said Dr. Thomas. There was an edge to his voice that I normally heard only when I was pushing for privileges he didn't want to give. My curious look just seemed to fluster him. He scowled, cheeks reddening. "It's time to *go*," he repeated.

"Okay," I said, trying to look unconcerned as I followed him out the door. He hadn't put the handcuffs back on me, and with every step, it became a little harder not to panic. I'd been so sure I could get the gun back to my room without getting caught, but now…now…

I made it to the hall without either of the guards so much as batting an eye. I'd done it. Maybe not forever—maybe not even until the next day— but I'd done it. I had a weapon, and I was loose in the halls of the CDC.

For one brief, drunken moment, I fantasized about opening fire and running like hell, heading for the nearest exit and never looking back. It would never have worked. It would have been a poor way to repay Dr. Shaw and Gregory for arming me. But God, I wanted to do it.

The only thing that stopped me was knowing that Shaun really was alive, somewhere. If I ran, they'd shoot me. I was smart enough to know that. And then Shaun would be alone again, in a world where people would do this sort of thing to a girl who'd been innocently going about the business of being dead. He needed to be warned. I needed to survive long enough to be the one who warned him. They could make another Georgia Mason if I didn't survive...but I wanted it to be me. Not some other girl who shared my memories. *Me.*

Dr. Thomas scowled all the way back to my room. He didn't say a word, and neither did the guards. Once we were there, he slapped his palm against the exterior sensor to open my door, and spoke his first words since we left the lab: "Do you need to use the lavatory?"

"Not right now," I said. "I am hungry, though."

"Your diet is still restricted, but I'll see about having some soup sent." His eyes flicked to my hair, expression hardening. "You may have to wait. I recognize that you have little experience with waiting."

"I didn't ask her to cut my hair," I said, too annoyed by the way he was looking at me to watch what I was saying. "She did it so she could get the sensors to stay on. Sensors she glued down with *slime mold*, mind you. I think I've paid for this haircut."

"I'm sure you didn't argue with her either, Georgia. If you don't need to use the facilities, you can enter your room now."

"Thank you," I said sourly, and kept my head up as I walked inside. The door slid shut behind me, leaving me with the appearance of solitude. It was a lie—it was always a lie. I was being watched, possibly even by Dr. Thomas, who could be standing on the other side of that stupid mirror for all that I knew. I never thought I'd miss my fucked-up eyes. Then I died, and I learned that there are things a lot worse than needing to wear sunglasses all the time. Things like being spied on, knowing you're being spied on, and not being able to do a damn thing about it.

Lacking anything else to do to distract myself, I climbed into bed. Eventually, the lights were dimmed. I closed my eyes, feigning sleep, and waited.

False sleep turned into the real thing at some point. I awoke to the sound of the door sliding open. Sitting bolt upright, I squinted into the glare from the hall, trying to make out the figure standing there. Even shading my eyes with my hand couldn't turn him into anything more than an outline.

"It's all right, Georgia," said a familiar voice—Gregory. He motioned for me to get up, the gesture clear even without fine details. "Come on. If you want to understand what's really going on here, you need to come with me."

"I'm coming," I said. Taking a breath to steady my nerves, I slid out of the bed and walked to the door, where the chance to get my answers was waiting.

BOOK II

Lost Souls

Fuck survivor's guilt. I'm not supposed to be the guilty one here. The people who made me the last man standing . . . they're the guilty ones. And they're the ones who should be afraid.

—SHAUN MASON

There are three things in this world that I truly believe in. That the truth will set us free; that lies are the prisons we build for ourselves; and that Shaun loves me. Everything else is just details.

—GEORGIA MASON

Tomorrow morning, my boss and Becks will be heading to Berkeley to deal with his crazy parents. Why? So they can get a map to lead them past the government barricades between here and Florida. Maybe. If my boss's crazy parents don't sell them out for the ratings boost. And once they get there, they'll have to deal with government patrols, rampaging zombies, killer mosquitoes, and God knows what else, all of which are going to try to kill them. Why are they doing all this?

To get my sister safely back to me. I don't know whether to be grateful to them for going, or ashamed of the fact that I'm genuinely glad it's not going to be me out there. I'm even glad I'm not going to Seattle with Maggie, and I think I'm about halfway in love with her.

I guess I'm a coward after all.

**—From *The Kwong Way of Things*,
the blog of Alaric Kwong, July 23, 2041. Unpublished.**

Let us, who are the lost ones, go and kneel before the dead;
Let us beg them for their mercy over all we left unsaid,
And as the sun sinks slowly, the horizon bleeding red,
Perhaps they'll show us kindness,
Grant forgiveness for our blindness,
Perhaps they'll show us how to find the roads we need to tread.

Let us, who are the lost ones, ask the fallen where to turn,
When it seems that all the world is lost, and we can only burn,
For in dying they have learned the things that we have yet to learn.
Perhaps they'll see our yearning,

And may help us in returning
To the lands where we were innocent, that we have yet to earn...

—From *The Lost Ones*,
originally posted in *Dandelion Mine*,
the blog of Magdalene Grace Garcia, July 23, 2041. Unpublished.

Eight

Becks slammed her back against the open door, keeping it pinned against the wall. That gave her a good vantage position on the rest of the room, while defending her against rear attacks. She held her pistol in front of her in a classic shooting stance that would have sold a thousand promotional posters for her blog if she'd been wearing something other than jeans and a bleach-spotted gray tank top.

I couldn't admire the precision of her pose; I had issues of my own to worry about, like the screaming lab technicians running for the doors. Half a dozen of our previously captured zombies were shambling after the fleeing technicians. Three former technicians were shambling with them, only their increased speed and bloody lab coats distinguishing them from the rest of the mob. All the zombies were moaning in a pitch that made my bones itch. No one knows why zombies moan. They just do, and it's enough to drive you crazy if you listen to it too long.

Mahir stopped behind me, managing only a startled "Oh dear Lord…" before I whirled and shoved him back.

"Get in the van," I snapped. "Lock the doors, engage the security. If we don't come back for you, drive. Drive until you get back to England, if you have to."

"Shaun—"

"You're not made for fieldwork! Now get back in there!"

"Don't argue, Mahir," said Becks. Her tone was calm, like she was asking us not to raise our voices during a business meeting. "I need his gun, and you're not equipped for this."

Mahir's mouth set in a thin line, and for a moment, he looked like he was seriously pissed. Someone else screamed in the main room, the sound cutting off with a gurgle that told me the infected had stopped trying to spread the virus, and started trying to feed.

"Get the others on the com," I said, more gently. "Make sure they're safe, and that they've managed to get themselves under cover. I don't want to lose anyone today."

The line of Mahir's mouth softened slightly as he nodded. "Be careful," he said, and turned to walk toward the van. I watched him just long enough to be sure he was actually going to get inside.

"Any time now, Mason," said Becks. The moaning was getting louder. So were the screams. The fact that we hadn't been attacked yet was nothing short of a miracle—one we could probably attribute to the fact that we were standing relatively still in a room full of much more active targets. Faced with a choice between someone who isn't moving and someone who is, a zombie almost always goes for the runner. It's something in their psychology, or in what passes for psychology inside the virus-riddled sack of goo that used to be a human brain.

"On it," I said, and turned to face the main room, bracing myself in the doorway. As long as we held our positions, we knew we had a clear line of retreat.

"About fucking time," said Becks, tracking the progress of one of the infected with her gun. As soon as one of us fired a shot, they'd stop looking at us like furniture and start looking at us as potential meals. That would be bad. Even if I was immune, Becks wasn't, and immunity wouldn't stop them from tearing me apart. "Got any bright ideas?"

"Prayer would be good, if either of us believed in a higher power."

Becks's eyes widened, disrupting her carefully schooled expression. "I don't say this often, but you're a genius."

"Because I don't believe in God?" I trained my gun on another of the infected, one that was drawing a bit too close to our position for me to be comfortable. The screams seemed to be getting quieter. I had to hope that was because most of the technicians were out of danger, and not because most of them were dead.

"No. Because there *is* a higher power at work here." Becks removed one hand from her gun long enough to tap her ear cuff, saying in a calm, clear voice, "Open general connection, main lab." There was a single loud beep.

Too loud. The nearest of the infected looked up from her meal—the torso of a technician whose name had either been Jimmy or Johnny; I wasn't sure, and it didn't matter now. Her eyes searched the area, looking for new prey, and settled on Becks. With a low moan, she stood.

"Becks, whatever you're doing, do it fast," I muttered, adjusting my stance so that I was aiming directly at the standing infected. "Once the shooting starts, this is going to turn into one hell of a duck hunt."

"I can handle myself," she said. More of the infected were turning to face us, their attention attracted by the strange silence of the one nearest our position.

Steady, cautioned George. I thought I felt her fingers ghost across the back of my neck, and that was more frightening than anything else about our situation. If I started hallucinating during combat, there was no telling who I'd shoot, or what I'd let get past me.

"Not now," I whispered. "Please, not now."

Becks's ear cuff beeped again, and Dr. Abbey's voice said loudly, "A little busy right now, children! Maybe you could do something to help with that?" Joe—her English mastiff—was barking in the background, almost drowning out the sound of moaning.

"Working on it," said Becks. She must have realized there was no way we could fade back out of sight. The sound of Joe barking would have guaranteed that, even if nothing else could. "Mahir's secure, but the lab's in chaos. What's your twenty?"

Dr. Abbey's answer was drowned out by the local infected, all of whom started moaning at the top of their lungs as they lunged, shambled, and even ran toward us. "Less talky more shooty!" I snapped, and started firing.

"We'll be there," said Becks. She tilted her head, studying our onrushing attackers, and chose her first two shots with an almost languid care. Two of the infected went down, each with a hole in the middle of its forehead.

"Show-off," I muttered, and kept firing, trying to assess the tactical options presented by the room. I counted eight active infected in closing range; five of those were old, probably from the most recent batch of catches, while the other three wore lab coats and scrubs that identified them as former members of Dr. Abbey's staff. I recognized one of them as the tech I'd yelled at the day before for being careless around the infected.

Guess he'd learned his lesson, even if it hadn't done him any good. Anyway, those three would be the fastest movers, and the slowest to react. The virus that drove their bodies was still adjusting to being in control. Even the smartest zombie is pretty damn stupid, but new zombies are the dumbest, nastiest of them all.

I don't think they've got the density to start reasoning, said George.

I nodded, acknowledging her words, and stepped forward as I kept firing. "Becks! Fall in, and tell me where we're going!"

"On it, Boss!" She moved to flank me, our shoulders almost touching as we began to make our way forward. The door, freed from her weight, swung shut, slamming with an ominous bang. "Dr. Abbey's in her office on the second floor! They're holding the line, but they can't do it forever!"

"Got it!" I took aim and fired again, silently counting my bullets. There were two of us; that was good. That meant we might have time to reload, assuming we didn't both run out at the same time. I had a second pistol on my belt, for emergencies—and this qualified—but I didn't have my cattle prod, or anything as convenient as, say, a brace of grenades. That would teach me not to stay fully armed at all times.

"Look at it this way." Becks shot a former technician in the throat, sending the man backward. We continued to advance, moving in smooth, long-practiced tandem. "If we run out of bullets, we can just let them chew on you for a little while."

"I feel much better." I fired again. One of the older infected went down. "Any idea how many of these things we're dealing with?"

"Not a fucking clue!"

"My favorite kind of duck hunt." My breathing was starting to settle, the adrenaline in my bloodstream slipping away. The endorphins that replaced it were soothing, my old, familiar drug of choice. This was the feeling that used to drive me into the field with a baseball bat and a cocky grin, this floating, flying, nothing-can-hurt-me feeling. Georgia's death clipped my wings. In moments like this, I could almost forget that. There were no voices in my head that shouldn't be there, but they were replaced by contentment, and not the yawning void that usually opened when George stopped talking. This used to be what I lived for. I couldn't live for it anymore. But oh, God, I missed it.

Fire. Step forward. Fire. Becks ducked behind me, letting me cover her while she reloaded her gun. I pulled my second pistol, buying us a few more steps before she needed to repeat the favor.

"This is not cool," I muttered. "Becks? You got another reload on you?"

"No," she said grimly.

"Didn't think so. On my signal, we're going to run."

I didn't need to see her face to know what her expression looked like. "That's a *terrible* idea."

"So is staying here! Either Dr. Abbey's been doing independent collections, or the locals called for friends. Either way," I aimed, fired, and took down another zombie, "we're going to run out of bullets before we run out of walking corpses. We run or we die. Got a preference?"

"I like running."

"Good. One..." I took another shot. This one went wild, barely grazing the zombie I was aiming for.

"Two…"

"Three!" I shoved Becks in the direction of the stairs, firing rapidly to cover her. She'd been right about one thing; if one of us was going to get chewed on, it needed to be me. One bite and it was game over for her. I'd consider a few more scars to be a fair trade for getting Becks out of this alive.

They can still kill you, hissed George.

"Maybe I deserve it," I replied, and ran after Becks.

One nice thing about stairs: Zombies can navigate them, but they can't do it fast. There's a certain comedy to watching them try, as long as you're not in a position to get knocked over by an infected body tumbling back down to the ground floor after it manages to misjudge the positioning of its feet. A few zombies had already fallen by the time we reached the bottom step.

Becks shot the first of them and ran on, leaving me to take out the other two. Both of them were wearing lab coats. They moaned, reaching for me. I grimaced as I jumped over them, and paused long enough to turn back and shoot them in the head. It took a few seconds to be absolutely sure they were dead, not just incapacitated. I spent the time. I knew these people. I might not know their names, but I knew them, and this was at least partially my fault. I could have forced Dr. Abbey to up her security. I could have helped more. I could have stopped this from happening.

You need to stop taking responsibility for things that aren't your fault, said George, sounding cranky enough that I could almost see her frown.

"You need to stop telling me that things aren't my fault," I countered, turning to shoot a zombie that had been lurching up behind me. It went down hard. I kept my gun raised and began backing up the stairs, scanning the lab below me. The occasional gunshot from above told me that Becks was doing her part to clear the landing.

My ear cuff beeped. I jerked my chin upward, answering the call. "Kinda busy, so this better be good."

"Maggie's upstairs, locked in one of the cold storage rooms. She's not injured, but she's bloody pissed at whoever it was that shoved her in there," said Mahir. "Dr. Abbey says she made contact with Becks?"

"We're en route now." I took another shot. That left three. Four if I decided to use all my bullets, rather than going with the traditional approach to zombie-killing, and saving the last one for myself. The thought made me crack a smile. Saving bullets for myself was something I didn't have to worry about anymore.

You are so fucking morbid, muttered George.

"Learned from the best," I replied. There were only two visible zombies left on the floor, and both of them had been infected for long enough that they were moving slowly, in that classic Romero shuffle. Better yet, killing so many of their pack mates meant the viral intelligence driving them all had been reduced from mob level smarts back to individual stupidity.

No one knows why zombies get smarter when you have a bunch of them in one place, but they do, and it's a problem. Tactics that work against one or two lone undead will get you killed when you go up against a mob. I've seen them demonstrate complicated hunting techniques, like actual ambush preparation, and it's scary as hell. If nothing else, it forces you to remember that the things inside those rotting shells used to be human, and on some level, still might be. They just got sick. It could happen to anybody.

Anybody but me.

"Shaun? Shaun, are you there? Shaun?" Mahir's voice in my ear dragged me out of my thoughts and back into the situation.

"Sorry, just assessing." I turned, running up the stairs. Becks was waiting on the landing. She had her gun up, and was braced against the banister; two infected were shambling toward her, neither moving fast enough to be a major threat at their current distance. She was letting them set up the shot. It's a classic field tactic, and a good way to save your ammunition. There was just one problem with it.

If there were only two zombies out here, where was all that moaning coming from?

"What's your assessment?" asked Becks.

"We're fucked. Where's Alaric? I'm pissed off, I'm almost out of bullets, and I'm not having any *fun*." And that, right there, was the reason I stopped doing active fieldwork, even before we stopped really being a news site. You can't be a professional Irwin when you can't at least pretend to enjoy what you're doing. It doesn't work. The center does not hold.

"He's with Dr. Abbey."

"Good."

Becks took the first of her shots as I reached her. The zombie went down. She didn't even glance in my direction. "We clear below, Mason?"

"Two zombies, both too uncoordinated to handle the stairs. I made an executive decision. We need to conserve bullets more than we need to perfectly secure the area."

"Well, just don't forget that they're down there and sound the all-clear without going back to mop up your mess." She squeezed off her second shot. This wasn't a clean hit; her bullet took the infected in the throat, reducing it to a mass of torn flesh and visible bone. It kept shuffling forward.

"Uh, Becks—"

"One," she said. "Two. Three..."

The zombie went down, the virally enhanced clotting factors in its blood finally giving up the task of repairing the arteries shredded by her bullet.

"Three," she said, and flashed me a self-satisfied smile. "Just like getting to the center of a Tootsie Pop."

"Did you know they made that commercial in the 1970s?" I asked. There were no more infected in sight. The moaning in the distance continued. "How are you for bullets?"

"I did know that, yes. Three bullets left. You?"

"Four."

"Great. Let's hope this party isn't strictly BYOB." She turned and ran in the direction of the dead.

"We're on our way, Mahir," I said, and ran after her.

"Do they train you people to say stupid things when in mortal danger? I'm just curious, you understand, I'm not judging you."

"Yes, you are."

"Yes, I am."

"There are classes." I followed Becks around a corner, skidding to a halt. "Uh, Mahir? I'm going to need to call you back."

"What are you—"

I reached up to tap my ear cuff, breaking the connection. Becks raised her hand, signaling for silence. I nodded understanding. And then we both just stood there, staring at the five-deep wall of zombies that was trying to claw its way through the door into Dr. Abbey's office. They weren't paying any attention to us yet. That was the good part. The bad part was that they would inevitably either break down that door or lose interest in what was behind, and either way, we'd eventually wind up on the menu.

"Here," I mouthed, pressing my gun into Becks's hand. I shook my head at her questioning expression, nodding back the way we'd come. Slow understanding bloomed in her face, and she nodded, pressing herself against the wall as I turned and crept quietly away. Once I was back in the main hall, out of sight of the infected, I broke into a run.

This floor's armory was located at the far end of the building, in what used to be a bathroom. Dr. Abbey's technicians couldn't get the water working in the corroded old second-story pipes, and so the room had been converted to hold all the weapons of mass destruction that a bunch of geeks who insisted on playing with dead things could possibly need. I don't know what science geeks were like before the Rising, but these days?

After seeing the kind of armaments they pack, you couldn't pay me to get on their bad side.

It was just too bad they hadn't been carrying more of those armaments while they were "at home" in the lab. Maybe I wouldn't have needed to shoot so many of them.

I passed the bodies of three dead technicians as I ran. Really dead—they'd been torn apart, practically shredded by the hungry infected. Their screams probably saved the lives of everyone who was now huddling behind a locked door. The people who ran toward the trouble—or toward the armory, wanting to get ready to face the trouble head-on—had been the second wave of victims. That was how it almost always went in an outbreak. The first wave dies. The second wave rises.

The last of the bodies was right in front of the armory door, fallen like he had almost reached it when they finally managed to run him down. I grimaced as I stepped over him, leaning into the armory to turn on the light.

The zombie that had been lurking there lunged, the moan escaping from its lipless mouth bare seconds before the startled shout of "Whoa!" escaped from mine. I managed to jerk my arm back before it could get its teeth into me, and they clacked shut on empty air. The zombie lunged again.

"Back off, ugly!" I grabbed it by the hair, using its own momentum as I shoved it past me, into the hallway. If Dr. Abbey was wrong about my being immune, I was going to regret that in a minute. I would have regretted it a hell of a lot more if the thing had managed to get its teeth into me.

The zombie stumbled as I released it, taking several steps forward before it could get its balance back and remember how to turn itself around. I took advantage of those precious seconds, darting into the armory and looking frantically around me. I didn't use this room very often. We had our own equipment, and while Dr. Abbey was perfectly willing to be generous with the ammo, she usually didn't want us fetching it ourselves. The grenades were—were—

"Over here, Shaun," said George. I turned. She was standing in the far corner of the room, next to a stack of beautifully familiar olive-green boxes. "This what you were looking for?"

"Yeah. Thanks, George."

"Not a problem. Now kill your friend." She was abruptly gone, blinking out like she had never been there at all. That was reasonable. She *hadn't* been there.

I grabbed the nearest pistol that looked like it might be loaded—bad gun safety, good zombie safety, it balances—and whirled, taking aim right at the place I estimated my dead friend's head would be. "Bang, ugly," I said, and pulled the trigger.

Thank God for paranoia and overpreparedness. The gun barked and a large chunk of the zombie's skull vanished, transformed into red mist and a hail of bone fragments. I shoved the pistol into my belt and tapped my ear cuff, heading for the back of the room.

"Shaun?"

"Mahir, listen. If you can get a connection to Becks, tell her she needs to back up. I'm coming in with grenades." I grabbed guns as I walked, dropping anything too light to be loaded and cramming the rest into my belt. If I was making a last stand, I was doing it so ridiculously overprepared that I'd rattle when I walked.

Mahir sighed deeply. "Of course you are. Couldn't you try something a little less, I don't know, insanely idiotic?"

"I could, but they don't have a flamethrower here. Now let her know."

"I'm on it." The connection died.

Grabbing the top box of grenades, I paused only long enough to check that its contents were both intact and well secured. Then I ran.

Becks met me halfway down the hall, somehow managing to run silently in her combat boots. There was one more skill I'd never mastered. "What are you *doing*?" she demanded, tone barely above a whisper. "Mahir called me! He said you told him to do it! I could've been killed! Are you really planning to use *grenades*?"

"You got a better idea?"

"No, but the risk of structural damage—"

"Is minimal. Are the zombies where you left them?"

"What? Yes."

"Then you *would* have been killed if you'd still been in that hallway." I kept moving, holding the box up just enough for her to see the shape of it. "I'm going to aerosolize me some dead guys."

"You're insane."

"Yeah, probably." I pulled the first pistol I'd snagged out of my waistband, passing it to her. "Stay out here and guard my back. Oh, and if you could call Dr. Abbey and tell her to turn off the lab ventilation system until the spray settles, that would probably be good. I don't want to zombie-out the whole room trying to save them."

"You're *dangerously* insane," Becks amended—but she took the pistol, and added a quick, "Good luck," before retreating farther down the hall.

I felt better knowing she was out there. One close call per day is pretty much my limit. I walked until I reached the end of the short hall leading to Dr. Abbey's lab. The zombies were still trying to claw their way inside, their moaning echoing through the confined space until it seemed loud enough to drive a man insane. They were still focused on the prey in front of them, and not on things moving around behind them. That was good. I'd be changing that in a moment, but for now, distracted zombies were in my best interests.

Putting the box of concussion grenades on the floor, I opened the lid and pulled out the top two. They were designed for use in situations like this one, and would do maximal damage to soft tissue—such as zombies— while doing minimal structural damage to the building surrounding the zombies. They were usually used for large government extermination runs. A series of helpful cartoon thumbnails on the inside lid of the box used stick figures and the universal sign for NO to remind me that I shouldn't use concussion grenades without putting on a gas mask first, since aerosolized zombie isn't good for anybody.

"Too bad I have no respect for safety precautions," I muttered, and pulled the pin on the first grenade.

I might be willing to stand in the open air while I created a fine red mist of viral particulates, but that didn't make me stupid. I chucked the first grenade into the middle of the mob, causing about half of them to turn in my direction. I threw the second grenade about three feet in front of the mob. Then I ran, pausing only to grab two more grenades out of the top of the box. I pulled the pins and threw them behind me, into the path of the onrushing mob.

One, said George. *Two, three...*

"Four, five," I added, and kept running.

The first grenade went off with a low crumping sound, muffled enough to tell me that it had been buried by a substantial number of bodies when it exploded. The other three went off in rapid succession, each of them a little louder and less cushioned by the weight of the bodies on top of it. I kept running. When Becks came into sight ahead of me, I stepped to the side, giving her a clear line of fire, and pulled two of the guns from my waistband.

"God, I wish we had cameras on this," I said...and then the infected who'd managed to survive my little party tricks came shambling and running down the hall, and I forgot about cameras in favor of keeping us both alive.

They were a sorry-looking bunch, even for zombies. It's true that you can kill a zombie with trauma to the body; once they lose enough blood, or a sufficient number of major internal organs, they'll die like everybody else. The trouble is that they don't feel pain like uninfected humans do, and they can keep going long after their injuries would have incapacitated a normal person. Some of the zombies making their way down the hall were missing arms, hands, even feet—those stomped along on the shattered remains of their ankles, shins, or knees, giving them a drunken gait that was somehow more horrifying than the normal zombie shuffle. One had a piece of grenade shrapnel stuck all the way through his cheek, wedged at an angle that would make it impossible for him to bite even if he managed to grab us. That wasn't going to stop him from trying.

"Becks? You clear?"

"Clear!" came the shout from behind me.

"Great," I said, and opened fire.

The bad thing about setting up a kill chute like the one we were in is that it can just as easily turn into a "die" chute. The good thing about setting up a kill chute—the reason that people keep using them, and have been using them since the Rising—is that as long as your ammo holds out and you don't lose your head, you can do a hell of a lot of damage without letting the dead get within more than about ten feet of you.

The injuries to our mob were extensive enough that most of them weren't moving very quickly, and the ones who'd been shielded from the worst of the blast by the bodies of their companions were hampered in their efforts to move forward by those same bodies. The fast zombies got mired in the slow zombies, and their efforts to break free of the mob just slowed everything down a little more. Becks and I didn't bother aiming for the fast ones. We just went for the head and throat shots, and kept on knocking them down.

"Shaun!" called Becks. "Dr. Abbey just called! They're opening the lab door!"

"Awesome!" I shouted back, barely a second before gunfire started from the direction of the lab. I fell back several yards, pulling another gun from my waistband and holding it out behind me. "Reload?"

"Thanks." Becks snatched the pistol from my hand, taking aim on another of the infected. "So this is fun. This is a fun time."

"Sure." I fired twice, taking down two more zombies. I was about to shoot a third one when Joe came bounding into my line of fire. He grabbed a zombie by the leg, shaking so hard that the entire leg came off. The gunfire continued behind him, but for Joe, the party was all out here in the hall.

It probably says something about Dr. Abbey that she named her massive black English mastiff after her dead husband and used him for illegal medical experiments. I'm not sure *what* it says, exactly. I just know that Joe is now functionally immune to Kellis-Amberlee—he can get sick, but he can't go into conversion—and that meant that the enormous, angry carnivore now spreading zombie guts around the hall was on our side. Thank God for that.

"That's disgusting," said Becks, and shot a zombie who was continuing to advance on our position, ignoring the chaos behind him. "Oh, jeez. Is that a spleen?"

"I think that's a spleen, yes." I fired one more time, taking down a zombie that had gotten a little too close for comfort. Joe looked toward the sound of the shot, ears perked up questioningly, and barked once. "It's cool, Joe. We're not hurt."

"How cute. The giant dog is concerned."

"Someone's got to be." I leaned against the rail, watching Joe work. The gunshots from behind him were starting to taper off. Only three zombies that I could see were still making any real progress, and all of them were badly wounded. Becks raised her gun to fire. I pushed her arm gently down again. "Let him have his fun. He's had a long day, and he deserves the chance to kill some things."

"If you say so." Becks looked at me, seeming to tune out the sounds of slaughter coming from the hall in front of us. She frowned. "You have blood in your hair. And on your face."

"Great. I've been exposed. Dr. Abbey will be thrilled."

The gunshots from the hall had stopped. Becks and I exchanged a look, nodded, and waited where we were for a few more minutes before starting to make our way in that direction. Joe barked again as we approached him, the sound only slightly garbled by the fact that he had most of a human throat in his mouth.

"Don't talk with your mouth full," I told him. He dropped the throat, chuffing happily, and fell into step beside us. I patted his blood-tacky head with one hand. "Good dog." There was no possible way of minimizing my exposure at this point. I might as well just go with it.

Dr. Abbey, Alaric, and four of her technicians were in the hall, their faces covered by ventilator masks and eye protectors. "You made it," she said, sounding unsurprised. "Are we secure?"

"Not quite. There are at least three shamblers on the ground floor, Mahir's in the van, and Maggie's locked in a storage room," I replied. "Alaric? You okay, buddy?"

"Shaken, but intact," he said.

"Good." I looked to Dr. Abbey. "I've been exposed."

"There's a shocker." She shook her head, shoulders slumping. She looked tired. That wasn't normal. Not for Dr. Abbey. "Help with the cleanup, and I'll get blood test kits for both of you. Shaun—"

"I know, I know," I said. "I'll be donating a few more vials to the cause of science."

"We're still leaving in the morning," said Becks. I turned to blink at her. She shrugged. "There's always something, isn't there? We have to go. It's never going to stop long enough for there to be a good time."

"She's right," said Alaric. "Alisa can't wait."

"Well, then, I guess we're leaving in the morning," I said. "Let's get this place cleaned up, and figure out what happened with the security. Oh, and can someone go let Maggie out before she kills us all?" I looked at the mess surrounding us, and sighed inwardly.

It was going to be a long night.

We lost over a dozen techs, Joey—people who've been working with me for years, people who trusted me to keep them safe. And for what? So I could learn some more things we already knew? This was my fault. Half the people who were bitten knew better than to engage the infected the way they did, but they believed the treatment I've been working on could protect them, and they weren't careful enough. Looking into Laurie's post-conversion eyes . . . it was enough to break my heart. Shaun Mason may hold the answer to this pandemic, but if he does, I haven't found it yet.

I know you don't think I should send them to Florida. I have to. We need to know what they used when they built those mosquitoes—and I need to know who built them. If I can pick apart their genetic structure, we may stand a chance in hell.

—Taken from an e-mail sent by Dr. Shannon Abbey to Dr. Joseph Shoji at the Kauai Institute of Virology, July 24, 2041.

I don't know how much longer I can do this. I don't know how much longer I can keep convincing my team that I can do this. I don't know how much longer I can trust myself to keep them alive.

And I don't know if I could live with myself if I didn't keep trying.

We've been frozen here, just like we were frozen in Weed, back when the world seemed a lot less fucked up. It's time to start moving again, and I'm terrified, and I'm so damn relieved. I don't think I'll be coming out of this alive. I'm going to go out there, find out what really happened to George, make sure the whole damn world knows what she died for, and then I'm going to come home, and I'm going to go to where she is. I don't know how much longer I can do this, but that's okay, because I'm not going to be doing it for much longer.

—From *Adaptive Immunities*,
the blog of Shaun Mason, July 24, 2041. Unpublished.

Nine

Gregory motioned for silence as we left my room. I nodded, for once grateful for my lack of shoes. My socks didn't squeak against the tile. Somehow, he managed to walk so that his shoes didn't make any noise, and we passed through the darkened CDC building like ghosts.

The door at the end of the hall was open, the light above it glowing a steady amber. Alarm lanced through me. Green lights mean there's no danger; red lights mean the danger is near. Amber lights mean something has gone wrong.

Gregory's hand landed on my shoulder, stopping me before I could do more than stiffen. "It's part of our window," he said, keeping his voice low. "Come on. We're almost there."

"Where are we going?" I asked, taking his words as license to break my own silence. He led me through the door and into another hall, one I'd seen only in passing, when they were taking me from one lab to another.

"Someplace they'd rather you didn't see," he said. He didn't need to tell me who "they" were. "They" were the people who'd brought me back from the dead, and who gave Dr. Thomas his marching orders. "They" were the people behind all of this.

"So it's something that's going to cause me some of that stress they're so interested in minimizing," I guessed, more for the comfort of speaking than out of any serious desire to have my thoughts validated.

"You could say that," Gregory said. We reached a corner. He raised a hand, signaling me to stop, and stepped around it alone. "We're clear. Come on."

I came.

We walked to another door with an amber light above it. This one led to a hall I hadn't seen before. It was less pristine than the others. There were whiteboards on the walls, scribbled with notes about cafeteria menus and security sweeps. There were even a few flyers taped up, advertising cars for sale or asking if anyone knew a good tutoring service for high school biochemistry. It looked so much more real than the place I'd been since I woke up, so much more *human*, that it almost made my chest hurt. The world still existed. I'd died and come back, and the whole time I was gone, the world continued.

Gregory started walking faster, saying, "We're almost there. We allowed six minutes transit each way, which gives us fifteen minutes at our destination. I'm going to need you calm at the end of that time. I can't drag you down these halls if you're not working with me."

"Meaning what?" I asked, trying to sound like my stomach wasn't balling itself into a small, hard knot of fear.

"Meaning that if you lose it, I'll leave you." The words were kindly spoken—he wasn't trying to be cruel, just stating a fact. If I couldn't control myself, he'd leave me. The other half of that statement didn't need to be spoken: The EIS couldn't afford to have his cover blown because I couldn't keep myself calm. If he left me, he probably wouldn't be leaving me alive.

"I understand."

"Good," he said. He stopped at a door marked AUTHORIZED PERSONNEL ONLY, producing a thumb drive from his pocket. He plugged it into the side of the blood testing unit. The unit beeped twice, and the light above the door went out. Gregory put his hand on the doorknob, but didn't turn it. Instead, he looked at me gravely and asked, "Are you ready?"

"No," I said. "I'm pretty sure I've never been ready for anything that had to be prefaced with that question. Now open the door."

A small smile crossed his lips. "That's the answer I wanted to hear," he said, and opened the door, revealing a darkened lab. A dim blue glow filled the back third of the room. I looked back at Gregory, raising my eyebrows. "It's okay," he said. "Go on."

"There's an invitation to die for," I said, and stepped across the threshold. The overhead lights clicked on immediately, starting low and climbing to a normal level of illumination. I appreciated that small courtesy. I may not be as photosensitive as I used to be, but that doesn't mean I enjoy being blinded.

Gregory stepped in behind me, closing the door. "Here we are," he said.

"Where is 'here,' exactly?" I asked, squinting as I looked around the room. It looked like it had been cast on the same mold as all the other CDC labs I'd visited, with undecorated walls, stain-proof linoleum floors, and lots of equipment I didn't recognize. My heart leapt a little at the one thing I *did* recognize: a computer terminal.

Gregory followed my gaze and grimaced, looking genuinely sorry as he said, "I can't let you get on the Internet from here, Georgia. It's not safe."

"But—"

"That's not why we're here." He nodded toward the back of the room. The blue glow was less evident now that the lights were on, but it was still there.

"Right," I muttered, and turned to look in that direction. From where I was, it looked like a fish tank filled with luminescent blue liquid. I frowned and started toward it, trying to figure out what it was, and why it was important enough for Gregory to risk both our lives by bringing me here.

I think, on some level, that I knew what it was even before I saw it; I just had to put off understanding for as long as possible if I wanted to be able to handle what I was about to see. But maybe that's hindsight, me trying to justify things to myself. I don't really know. What I do know is this:

The blue liquid wasn't fully opaque; it just looked that way from a distance. It cleared as I approached, and by the time I reached the tank, I could see the outline of a human figure through the blue. I squinted, but couldn't make out any real details beyond the fact that it was female, and surrounded by a forest of tangled cords.

Gregory stepped up behind me and leaned to my left, pressing a button at the top of a control panel I hadn't noticed until then. The glow brightened, and the liquid began turning transparent, small lines of bubbles marking the spots where filters were cleansing some element out of the mix. In only a few seconds, I could see the figure floating in the tank.

She was naked, in her mid-twenties, and curled in a loose fetal position, like she had never needed to support her own limbs or head. Her hair was dark brown and badly needed to be cut. It was long enough that the movement of the liquid around her made it eddy slowly, wrapping around her neck and arms. Sensors were connected to her arms and legs, running up to join with the main cable. Her mouth and nose were exposed—she was breathing the liquid; I could see her chest rise and fall—and a thicker tube was connected at her belly button, presumably providing her with oxygen and nutrients. I stared at her, watching the way her fingers twitched and her eyes moved behind the thin shields of her eyelids.

Gregory waited, watching me watch her. The room seemed to be holding its breath, both of us waiting to see what I would do, whether I would be able to look at what was in front of me without snapping. For a moment, I didn't know the answer.

The moment passed. I took a shaky breath, followed it with another, and asked, "How many of us are there?"

"At the moment, three." Gregory turned his attention to the tank where another Georgia Mason floated. Her hair had never been bleached, and was still the dark brown that mine was supposed to be. I felt a brief flare of jealousy. She looked more like me than I did. "This is subject number 8c. It's the last member of the subject group following yours."

"Wait—subject group?" I turned my back on the tank, unsure of my ability to keep my cool while I watched my own silent doppelganger floating in the blue. "What does *that* mean?"

"Your designation is 'subject 7c.' Subject 7a didn't mature properly; 7b went into spontaneous amplification during the revivification process." He gestured at the tank. "Subject 8a was shut down due to issues with spinal maturation at about this stage."

"And 8b?" He wasn't using names for any of the other subjects, I noticed—he wasn't even giving them genders. They were just things to him, at least until the moment they woke up and turned into people. That was actually reassuring, because he treated *me* like a person. I wasn't the same as them.

I wasn't.

"Subject 8b is part of why we're here. Subject 8c is just the backup, in case something goes wrong." Gregory looked at me carefully. "Are you ready to proceed?"

"You mean, do I want to scream and throw things and maybe vomit, but can I keep myself together a little longer? Yes, and yes." I shook my head, taking comfort in the fact that I could feel the air against my ears. I might have started out like that girl in the tank, but I wasn't her anymore. I was awake, and alive, and my hair had been cut. We have to take our comforts where we can find them.

"All right," said Gregory. "Follow me."

He led me to a large metal rectangle on the far wall. He tapped a button on a control panel next to it, and stepped back as a whirring sound began to emanate from the wall itself. The metal rectangle slid slowly upward, revealing the room on the other side of the thick, industrial-grade glass. He tapped the control panel again, and the lights came on.

The walls of the room were featureless and white. The only thing that even resembled furniture was a narrow hospital bed with white sheets, surrounded by IV drips and beeping monitors. Thick black straps secured the room's single occupant to her bed, holding her in place. Unlike the girl in the tank—unlike me, when I first woke up—her hair was cut short, in a precise replica of the haircut I'd worn since I was twelve. I touched the close-shorn hair at the back of my neck without realizing I was going to do it, feeling how uneven the strands were. Dr. Shaw had done her best, but she was no hairdresser.

"This is 8b?" I asked. My voice was weaker than I wanted it to be. I swallowed hard, trying to clear away the dryness that was growing there. "What are they doing with her?"

"They're stabilizing her." Gregory touched another button. A video projection appeared on one side of the window, obscuring that half of the room. It showed subject 8b being removed from her tank and shifted onto a gurney. Her hair was long in the recording, and it stuck to her face and shoulders like seaweed. "This was taken a week ago."

"A week—but that was after they knew that I wasn't going to amplify. They knew I was viable." Panic tried to rise inside me like a small, biting animal. I forced it down again as hard as I could, breathing in and out through my nose several times before I asked, "Why are they stabilizing her? What are they planning to *do* with her?"

Gregory touched another button. The recording skipped, the image of the extraction being replaced by an image of the clone, now clean, clothed, and dry, with her head held up by a wedge-shaped foam pillow. Voices were speaking softly, just offscreen. I almost jumped when Dr. Thomas said, in a loud, clear tone, "Georgia, open your eyes."

And the recording of subject 8b opened her eyes.

A squeaky moaning sound escaped my lips before I could hold it in. Gregory put a hand on my shoulder, but he didn't say anything. There was nothing for him to say.

Her eyes were black, her pupils so enlarged that there was no band of color between them and the surrounding sclera. Shark's eyes, zombie eyes...or the eyes of a person with retinal Kellis-Amberlee, the reservoir condition I'd lived with for most of my life. With those eyes, she looked more like me than I ever could. Someone who was shown a picture of me would probably allow that I looked a lot like a reporter who died during the Ryman campaign. Someone who was shown a picture of *her*...

"How?" I managed to rasp.

"Surgical alteration," said Gregory. He took his hand off my shoulder. "They couldn't induce a specific reservoir condition—when they tried, it either caused immediate amplification, or it triggered a reservoir condition in a different part of the body. Getting one with stable retinal Kellis-Amberlee in both eyes could have taken years."

I didn't say anything.

"They've had to do more procedures than originally planned. It turns out we don't really understand the changes retinal Kellis-Amberlee makes to the structure of the eye as well as we thought we did. As soon as they removed the irises, the retinas began to detach. They've been replaced with artificial lenses, and the eyes have been stabilized."

And since I was known to have retinal Kellis-Amberlee, no one would raise any red flags over anomalies in her retinal scans, and the surgical tampering would never be caught. "Slick," I said. My voice sounded flat, like all the emotion had been somehow pressed out of it. That was a reasonably accurate assessment of how I was feeling. I swallowed again, and asked, "How much time do I have?"

Gregory shot me a sharp look. "What do you mean?"

"They didn't fix my eyes. They wouldn't have fixed…her…eyes if they didn't expect people to see her. Logically, that means they didn't expect people to see *me*. If I was the finished product, they would have stopped once I was stable." My voice was starting to rise at the end of my sentences. I forced it back down, and repeated, "How much time do I have?"

"We think it'll take about two weeks for them to finish all the tests they have scheduled, and for them to get subject 8b all the way functional. Again, they expected everything to be ready sooner, but they don't want any lingering pain from the operations to distract from the recovery process."

I wouldn't have paid any special attention to my eyes hurting when I woke up. I'd been too busy freaking out over not being dead. I decided to let that go for the moment. "After that?"

"Another two weeks, to be sure the subject won't spontaneously amplify or suffer organ failure."

So that had been a genuine risk, not just another way to scare me. Funny thing; even knowing that, I was still scared plenty. "What's going to happen to me?"

"They're going to keep you as long as you stay useful, and then…" Gregory's voice trailed off. "I'm sorry."

I sighed. "Right. That was a bad question. Why are they doing this? Why waste all this time with me if they're just going to bring her out of her chemical coma and drop me down the incinerator chute? What are they *gaining* from keeping me around?"

"You're the display model. Why do you think Dr. Thomas was so upset when you went and got your hair cut? They want you to be as pretty as possible, to show the investors that this process is safe and painless and yields the best possible results." Gregory touched the control panel. The image of subject 8b's eyes vanished, replaced by a four-way split-screen of me being…me. Me, sitting on the bed, one leg tucked under my body, the other rhythmically kicking the mattress. Me, pacing around the edges of the room, my fingers snarled in the short hair above my ears. Me, eating. Me, walking down the hall. The views flickered from perspective to perspective, making it clear both that I had been recorded from multiple angles, and that someone had taken the time to edit it all together into a single continuous feed.

"What?" I asked, staring at the screen. My face stared back at me from a dozen different angles, and every angle showed the eyes that didn't look as much like my own as the eyes on the clone intended to replace me.

"Everyone knows who Georgia Mason is. The girl who broadcast her own death and turned the tide of a political election. The one who told us to rise. You were the perfect candidate to prove that a person—a real, recognizable person—can return from the grave as *themselves*, rather than as a pretty, mindless toy." Gregory glanced at me as he spoke. "They made you as accurate as possible, so that you could be the showroom model. You didn't think the CDC bankrolled you on their own, did you?"

"I didn't really think about it," I said. "So what's…the other one…supposed to be?"

"The street model. They spent a lot of money getting you right, and while you have a certain 'unwitting celebrity spokesperson' cachet, there's no reason to waste good research. Building an accurate Georgia Mason taught them how to make an inaccurate one."

For a moment, I just froze. It was like everything in me shut down, my brain refusing to cope with the enormity of what it was being asked to process. Then, slowly, I took a breath, nodded, and said, "How inaccurate are we talking? If I'm Georgia Mason, who's she?"

"Not quite Georgia Mason." He tapped the control panel again. There was a single muted beep before the servos engaged, followed by the deeply comforting whir of the metal shutter descending. I wouldn't have to look at her anymore. Thank God.

"But I'm not quite Georgia Mason either, am I?" I looked up at him. "I *can't* be. I'm willing to believe that the CDC can clone people. Hell, I've known for years that the CDC could clone people. But there was no convenient backup of my—of her—memories. So who am I?"

"You're Georgia Mason." Gregory stepped away from the wall, moving back into my field of view. "The point of all this was proving that the CDC *can* conquer death. I don't understand all the science. My field is virology and corporate espionage, not human cloning and memory transfer. But

I've seen your charts, and while you're not a perfect replica of yourself, you have a ninety-seven percent accuracy rating. You're as close as science can get to bringing a person back from the dead."

"But *how?*"

"Neural snapshotting."

I had to allow that it made sense, as much as I understood it, which wasn't all that well. Thought, memory, everything that makes a person who they are, it's all electricity, little sparks and flashes encoded in the gray matter of our minds. The Kellis-Amberlee virus takes us over, but it also preserves the brain long after the point of what should be death. It turns those electrical impulses back on, over and over again. If the CDC had a way of taking a picture of those electrical patterns, and then somehow imprinting them on a blank mind...it could work.

I shook my head, frowning at Gregory. "How can you be so calm?"

"How can you?" he shot back. "You're not the first Georgia I've brought here, although you're the most accurate. The highest transfer score before yours was seventy-five. She started screaming as soon as she saw the clone, and she didn't stop. You're the only one who hasn't cried."

"I'll cry later, I promise," I said, and I meant it. This was the sort of thing that needed to be processed before I could really let myself get upset. "How close is she? If I'm the ninety-seven percent girl, what's she?"

"Subject 8b has been prepared through a modified conditioning process, which should, if fully successful, result in a forty-four percent accuracy rating when compared to the original, but with some behavioral adjustments," said Gregory. "She'll look like you. She'll act like you..."

"She won't *be* me," I finished. "So what's she for?"

For the first time since we'd arrived in the lab, Gregory looked at me like I'd said something wrong. "You mean you don't know?" he asked.

"No. How would I—" I stopped mid-sentence, a sudden horrible certainty flooding over me. "They wouldn't."

"Wouldn't what?"

Somehow, the one word I needed to say was harder to force out than all the others had been. "Shaun?"

Gregory nodded. "That's the plan. You'll stay here as long as you're useful, and she'll be put where he can find her. Mr. Mason is not particularly stable these days, and they're reasonably sure he'll believe whatever he's told if he thinks it's going to get you back. He's not going to ask questions. He's not going to look for double-crosses. He's just going to open the doors and let her in."

My lips thinned into a hard line. Maybe I wasn't really who I thought I was. Maybe I wasn't really anyone at all—if I wasn't Georgia Mason, but I shared her DNA and ninety-seven percent of her personality profile, who else could I be? The one thing I was absolutely sure of was that none of that mattered, because these bastards were *not* going to use my genetic code to honey-trap the only human being in this world that I had ever been willing to die for.

"Then that's just not going to happen," I said. "What do we need to do?"

Gregory glanced at his watch. "Right now, we need to get you back to your room before our window closes. I should be able to get another message to you tomorrow night. You need to keep your eyes open. Keep behaving normally. They're not going to take you off display unless you do something that makes it look like you're beginning to destabilize."

"By 'take me off display,' you mean kill me, right?"

He nodded.

"Got it," I said. "And after that?"

"After that?" said Gregory. He smiled a little, clearly trying to look encouraging. I didn't have the heart to tell him that all he was really managing to do was look scared. "I think it's about time that we got you out of here, don't you?"

"My thoughts exactly," I said. "Let's go."

I don't know why I bother writing these entries. It feels less like a blog and more like a diary every day, like I should be drawing hearts in the margins and writing stupid shit like "OMG I wonder if he'll ever get over his stupid dead sister and love me" or "wish I could go shopping, I've had to burn half my favorite shirts due to contamination." But it's routine, and it's a form of saying "fuck you" to the people who've driven us to this. Fuck you, government conspiracy. Fuck you, CDC. We'll keep writing, and someday, we'll be able to post again, and when that happens, you'd better pray we have something better to talk about than you.

But I don't think we will.

Shaun is starting to crack. He's covering it well, but I can see the fractures. During the outbreak yesterday, there were points where he just *froze*. It was like he wasn't even a part of the situation anymore. I don't know if he knows he's doing it, and I'm scared. I'm scared he's going to get one of us killed, and he's never going to forgive himself. I'm scared he's going to get even worse, and we're going to let him, because we love him, and because we loved Georgia.

And I'm still going to follow him to Florida. God. My mother was right. I really am an idiot.

—From *Charming Not Sincere*,
the blog of Rebecca Atherton, July 25, 2041. Unpublished.

She remained calm and reasonable throughout the encounter. She was able to ask coherent questions and give coherent answers. She remained controlled during the walk back to her room, and was able to return to her bed and feign normal sleep successfully enough to convince the orderly who came to relieve me. Stress fractures are still possible, but I believe we should continue as planned. I think this one is stable.

—Taken from a message sent by Dr. Gregory Lake,
July 25, 2041. Recipient unknown.

Ten

The morning dawned bright and clean, with a clear blue sky that afforded absolutely no cloud cover. Any spy satellites that happened to pick up on our anomalous route—not many people take the back roads anymore, and fewer still do it in a way that allows them to skip all security checkpoints—would have a perfect line of sight.

"If we get picked up by the DEA on suspicion of being Canadian marijuana smugglers, I'm going to be pissed," I muttered.

Becks looked up from her tablet, fingers still tracing an intricate dance across the screen. It was sort of unnerving that she could do that by nothing but the memory of where her apps were installed. *I need a keyboard, or I lose my place in seconds.* "What's that?"

"Nothing." I kept my eyes on the road.

Liar.

I didn't answer. We'd get into a fight if I did, and then Becks would have to pretend she didn't mind sitting there listening while I argued with myself. Back at the lab, she'd been able to leave the room when that started. Now that we were on the road again, she had nowhere to run. And neither did I.

The reality of what we were doing was starting to sink in. Dr. Abbey had insisted we get some sleep after the lab cleanup was finished—although not before she'd drawn enough blood from me to keep her surviving lab monkeys busy for a couple of weeks. "Some of us have to work while you take your little road trip," she'd said, like this was some sort of exciting pleasure cruise. Just me and Becks and the ghost of George, sailing gaily down the highway to meet our certain doom.

Not that we were actually *on* the highway unless we absolutely had to be. Dr. Abbey had installed a new module on our GPS, one programmed with all the underground and questionably secure stops between Shady Cove and Berkeley. Once that was done, Alaric and Mahir worked together to reprogram our mapping software, convincing it the roads we should take were the ones the system flagged as "least desirable." So we left Shady Cove not via the convenient and well-maintained Highway 62, but on a narrow pre-Rising street called Rogue River Drive.

We'd been on the road for almost four hours, playing chicken with major highways the entire time. Alaric and Mahir's mapping software sent us down a motley collection of frontage roads, residential streets, and half-forgotten rural back roads, all of them combining to trace roughly the same directional footprints as first Highway 62, and then Highway 5, the big backbone of the West Coast. As long as we stuck to the directions and didn't get cocky, we'd be able to stay mostly off the radar. As for the rest of the time...

"We're going to need to stop for gas in fifty miles or so," said Becks, attention focusing on her tablet. She tapped the screen twice; out of the corner of my eye, I saw the graphics flash and divide, changing to some new configuration. "Do we have any viable gas stations?"

"Let me check the map." I took one hand off the wheel and pushed a button at the front of our clip-on GPS device, saying, "Secure gas."

"Recalculating route," replied the GPS. The module had the same pleasant Canadian voice as Dr. Abbey's main computer. "Please state security requirements."

"Uh, we'd like to not die, if that's okay with you," I said.

"Recalculating route."

"Notice how she says that no matter what we ask for?" I slanted a glance at Becks. "Half the time she doesn't even change her mind about where we're going."

"Maybe she's just fucking with you."

"The thought had crossed my mind."

"The nearest secure gas station is approximately twenty-seven miles from your current location," announced the GPS. "Do you wish to continue?"

Becks looked up. "Define 'secure.'"

"The station is located in a designated hazard zone, and has been officially abandoned for the past eighteen years. Security systems are running at acceptable levels. The last known transmission was received three days ago, and indicated the availability of fuel, food, and ammunition."

"Works for me," I said. "Let's go."

"Recalculating route," said the GPS, and went silent, a new set of street names flashing on the tiny screen.

"I so wish we could do an exposé on all of this," said Becks wistfully. "I mean, the actual smuggler's railroad? Think about the *ratings*!"

"Too bad we're not purely in the ratings business these days, isn't it?"

"Yeah. But still..."

"Think about it this way, Becks. If these people had been exposed a year ago, they wouldn't be here to help us now. Everything's a tradeoff." I turned off the frontage road we'd been traveling down, onto a smaller, even less well-maintained frontage road.

Becks sighed. "I guess that's true."

I grew up in California, and if you'd asked me two years ago whether it was possible to drive from Oregon to my hometown without taking I-5, I would have said no. The longer I drove the route assembled by our modified GPS, the more I realized how wrong I'd been—and how much of the country we actually lost during the Rising. Most of the roads we were following didn't appear in normal mapping software anymore, because they'd been abandoned to the dead, or were located in places that were considered impossible to secure. Deer and coyotes peeked out of the woods at us as we drove past, showing absolutely no fear. I couldn't tell whether that was because they'd been infected, or because they had forgotten what humans were. As long as we stayed in the van, it didn't really matter.

"There used to be bears out here, you know," I said.

"Really?" Becks glanced up, frowning suspiciously in my direction. "Is there a reason you're telling me this? Should I be going for the biggest gun I can get my hands on?"

"No. I'm just wondering if there might not be bears out here again. I mean, California used to have a grizzly bear on the state flag, even."

Becks shuddered. "I do *not* understand how anyone ever thought that was appropriate. I like the current flag a lot better."

"You don't think it's a little, well...sanitized?" The old bear flag might not have been politically correct in a post-Rising world, but it felt like there was passion behind it, like once upon a time, someone really *cared* about that symbol and the things it represented. Its replacement—a crossed redwood branch and California poppy—always struck me as something cooked up by a frantic marketing department for a governor who just needed something to hang over the state capitol.

"There's a reason the word 'sanitized' contains the word 'sanity.' Using a giant carnivore as your state symbol is insane, zombies or no zombies."

"What's the Connecticut state flag?"

"A shield with three grapevines on it."

What? George sounded confused.

"My sentiments exactly," I muttered. Louder, I asked, "What's that supposed to mean? 'Welcome to Connecticut; we'll get you nice and drunk before the dead start walking'?"

"I have no idea what it means. It's just the stupid flag. What did the bear mean? 'Come to California; you won't have to wait for the zombies if you're looking to get eaten'?" Becks shot me a glare, expression challenging.

I couldn't help it. I started to laugh.

"What? What's so funny?"

"We're on the run from the Centers for Disease Control, heading for a gas station that caters to drug-runners and mad scientists, and we're fighting about the meaning of state flags."

Becks blinked at me. Then she put her tablet down on her knees, bent forward to rest her forehead on the dashboard, and began to laugh. Grinning, I hit the gas a little harder. If we were laughing, we weren't thinking too hard about what was waiting for us down the road.

Years before I was born, President Richard Nixon declared a "war on drugs," like drugs might somehow realize they were under siege and decide they'd be better off going somewhere else. That war went on for decades even before the Kellis-Amberlee virus gave us something more concrete to fight against. A sane person might think the dead rising would be a good reason to stop stressing out over a few recreational pharmaceuticals. It turns out the lobbyists and corporations who stood to benefit from keeping those nasty drugs illegal didn't agree, and the war on drugs continued, even up to the present day.

Smuggling is a time-honored human tradition. Make something illegal, create scarcity, and people will find a way to get it. Better, they'll find a way to make it turn a profit. In some ways, the Rising was the best thing that could have happened to the world's drug smugglers, because suddenly, there were all these roads and highways and even entire towns with no population, no police force, and best of all, no one to ask what those funny smells coming out of your basement windows were. They had to be constantly vigilant, both against the threat of the infected and the threat of the DEA, but they had more space than they'd ever had before.

The question remained: How were they supposed to move their product into more civilized areas? If drugs had been the only things in need of smuggling, maybe the answer would have involved tanks, or strapping backpacks to zombies before releasing them back into the wild. But drugs weren't the only things people needed to move. Weapons. Ammunition. Livestock—the illegal breeding farms on the other side of the Canadian Hazard Line were constantly looking for fresh genetic lines, and would go to incredible lengths to get them. George and I once followed a woman all the way to the California state border as she tried to get her Great Dane to safety without being stopped by the authorities.

I don't know whether she made it or not. We lost track of her shortly after she crossed into Oregon. But Buffy convinced George to let her scrub the identifying marks from our reports. These days, after spending some time on the wrong side of the rules, I sort of hope that woman and her dog made it over the border, into a place where they could live together the way she wanted them to.

That's because you're a sentimental idiot, said George.

"Probably," I said, getting my laughter under control. "But isn't that why you love me?"

Becks lifted her head from the dashboard, still chuckling, and went back to tapping on her tablet. "How much farther?"

"About ten miles," I said. "Get the trade goods."

"On it."

The smuggler's supply stations were largely maintained by people in the business of stealing the most forbidden commodity of all: freedom. They were the ones who chose to live in the places we'd abandoned, not because they were breeding large dogs or making meth, but because they wanted to live the way they always had. They wanted to open their doors on green trees and blue skies, not fences and security guards. I couldn't blame them. Oh, I was pretty sure they were insane, but I couldn't blame them.

Living off the grid came with its own set of problems, including limited access to medical care. So while the people we were on our way to buy gas from *might* take cash, they were likely to be a lot more interested in fresh blood test units, antibiotics, and birth control. More than half the "trade goods" we'd received from Dr. Abbey were contraceptives of one type or another.

"They choose their lives, and they love their lives, but bringing children into that environment isn't something you want to do by mistake," was her comment, as she showed Becks how to load the contraceptive implant gun. "This stuff is worth more than anything else you could possibly carry, and it'll keep them from trying to barter for your ammunition. Just make sure they see that you're armed, or you're likely to find yourselves at the center of a good old-fashioned robbery."

Becks unbuckled her seat belt and climbed over her seat into the rear of the van. I could hear her banging around back there as she got our kits ready. Glancing into the rearview mirror, I could see the back of her head. Her medium-brown hair was pulled into a no-nonsense braid, the streaks of white-blond from Dr. Abbey's chemical showers striping it like a barber pole.

"We need gas, and maybe some munchies," I called. "I think we can make it another eight or nine hours before we need to stop for the night."

"Got it," she called back. "Should I pack any of the antibiotics?"

"No, but grab the poison oak cream. That probably has some local demand." I turned my attention back to the road. The counter on the GPS indicated that our turn was somewhere just up ahead. "How we wound up here is a mystery to me," I said, almost under my breath.

The part where we're about to bribe criminals for gas, or the whole situation? asked George.

"A little bit of both."

"I wish I'd known about this while I was alive." It wasn't that surprising when I heard her voice coming from the seat Becks had vacated. I glanced over to see George with her feet braced on the dashboard and her knees tucked up almost against her chest. "I mean, Becks is right. This would have made a fantastic exposé."

"And destroyed these peoples' way of life. They've never done anything to earn that."

"How many of the people we exposed did? I mean, we were never tabloid journalists—"

"And thank God for that," I muttered.

"—but we weren't saints, either. If a story caught our eye, we chased it down, and sometimes people got hurt. Like that woman with the dog that you were just thinking about."

"Can you not remind me that you can read my mind? That's where I keep all my private thoughts."

"Please. Like there's anything in your head that could shock *me*?" George leaned forward, resting her cheek on her knee as she smiled at me. "The woman with the dog, Shaun. Even if she got out, how many of the routes we documented her taking were closed by Homeland Security immediately afterward? How many people like her tried to run when they saw our report, and got driven straight into a trap we'd created?"

"That's not our fault."

"Was it Dr. Kellis's fault when Robert Stalnaker decided to write a sensationalistic article about his cure for the common cold, and kicked off the whole stupid Rising? We're supposed to be responsible journalists. How do we cope when the stories we report get people hurt?" She sighed. "Do you honestly think Buffy and I were the first casualties?"

"Right now, I just think I'm lucky Buffy isn't haunting me, too," I said sourly.

"Shaun?"

I twisted in my seat to see Becks standing behind me. She looked concerned. I couldn't blame her. I'd have looked concerned, too, if I were the one in her place.

"Hey, Becks," I said, glancing to the empty passenger seat as I turned my eyes back to the road. George was gone. She'd be back. "Everything okay back there?"

"Yeah, everything's fine—is everything okay up front?"

"Just arguing with myself again. Nothing new."

"Please turn left," said the GPS, cutting off any reply from Becks. That was probably for the best. Ignoring my crazy might seem okay when we were in a nice, relatively safe lab environment, but that didn't mean her tolerance was going to extend to the field. I really didn't feel like arguing about whether or not I could decide to be sane again.

The road the GPS directed us down was barely more than a dirt path winding into the trees. Tires had worn deep ruts into the earth, and the van shuddered and jumped as we jounced along. Becks dropped into her seat, grabbing hold of the oh-shit handle with one hand and bracing the other against the dashboard.

"Are you sure this is the right way?" she demanded.

"Destination in one hundred yards," said the GPS.

"According to the creepy computer lady, yeah, it's the right way." I eased off on the gas. No sense in killing our shocks over a road that didn't even come with any zombies.

"I hate this road."

"It clearly hates us, too."

"Destination in twenty yards," said the GPS.

I frowned. All I could see ahead of us was more dirt road...at least until a pair of men stepped out of the trees, each holding a shotgun large and impractical enough to be essentially useless. Sure, you could shoot a zombie with one of those things, and sure, it would go down, but the kick from a shotgun that size would probably knock you down at the same time. Not

to mention the weight of the ammunition. If you wanted to carry something like that *and* have the option to run for your life when the need inevitably arose, you'd be carrying less than two dozen rounds.

"Shaun…"

"It's cool, Becks," I said, turning off the engine. The men with the shotguns trained them on our windshield. I responded by blowing them a kiss
and waving cheerfully. "They're not planning to shoot us. Those guns
wouldn't make sense if they were planning to shoot us."

"So what *are* they planning to do? Please, enlighten me." Becks scowled.

I undid my seat belt. "They're trying to scare us," I said, and opened the
van door. I kept my hands in view as I slid out of the driver's seat. The men
with the guns shifted to train them squarely on me. I smiled ingratiatingly
at them, stepping far enough from the van that they could see for themselves that I wasn't hiding anything. "We come in peace," I called. More
quietly, I added, for Becks's benefit, "I have *always* wanted to say that."

Sometimes you are an enormous dork, said George.

"True," I agreed. The men were still pointing their guns in my direction.
I sighed and raised my voice, trying another approach: "Dr. Abbey sent us.
We just need gas, and then we'll be on our way."

The man to my left lowered his gun. The one to my right did not. Eyes
narrowed with suspicion, he asked, "How do we know you're telling the
truth?"

"You don't, although I suppose you could make us stand out here while
you try to find someone who has the current number for Dr. Abbey's lab
and get her to give us her okay. But I really am telling the truth. I'm Shaun
Mason. The lady in the car is Rebecca Atherton. We're from After the End
Times, we're hiding from the CDC, and Dr. Abbey sent us."

Most of that would qualify as "too much information" if I were talking
to anyone else. But these were men who had chosen, for whatever reason,
to remove themselves from the grid of modern existence—no small task,
with government surveillance and public health tracking becoming more
invasive with every year that passed. Telling them we were hiding wouldn't
give them a lever to use against us; it would give *us* a point of commonality
with *them*. We were all hiding from the world together.

The second man lowered his gun. "How's that damn dog of hers
doing?" he asked. I could barely see his mouth through the bushy red
thicket of his beard. He was wearing denim overalls and a plaid lumberjack
shirt with the cuffs pegged up around his elbows. It was like being questioned by Paul Bunyan's much, much shorter brother.

"Still the size of a small tank," I said.

"She tell you we don't take plastic?" asked the first man, apparently unwilling to let his companion do all the talking. If the second man was Paul Bunyan's midget cousin, the first man would have made a decent stand-in for Ichabod Crane, even down to the prominent Adam's apple and impressively oversized nose.

I wish we were filming this, said George.

I swallowed my automatic "Me, too," focusing instead on looking as harmless and sincere as possible. It wasn't easy. Most of my training had focused on looking daring and oblivious, which probably wasn't going to fly here. "She told us our money wouldn't be any good," I said, still smiling. "She also said you might be willing to consider blood test units that wouldn't give you tetanus as a fair trade for some gas and a couple of sandwiches."

Paul Bunyan frowned for a moment—long enough that I was starting to wonder whether Becks would be able to move into the driver's seat and hit the gas before we *both* got shot. Then he grinned, showing the gaps where his front teeth had presumably been, once upon a time. "Well, hell, boy, why didn't you open with that?"

"We're still new at this," I replied. "Does that mean we can come in?"

"Sure does," said Ichabod. He and Paul started toward the van, leaning their guns against their shoulders in an almost synchronized motion. "Hope you're not averse to giving us a lift."

This had all the hallmarks of a test. "Sure," I said, motioning for them to follow me as I moved to climb back into the van. As expected, Becks had her pistol out, and was holding it just out of view behind the dashboard. I gestured for her to put it away before one of our new "friends" saw it.

"Are you *sure* this is a good idea?" she hissed, voice barely above a whisper.

"Nope," I said. I would have said more, but Paul and Ichabod had reached the van. "It's open!" I called.

"Much obliged," said Ichabod. He opened the van's rear door and climbed inside, with Paul close behind him. "I'm Nathan. This is Paul."

"Nice to meet you folks," said Paul.

"Charmed," said Becks, with a professional smile. Anyone who didn't know her would have trouble telling it from an expression of actual pleasure. Anyone who did know her would recognize it as a cue to grab a weapon and run.

"You look like a Paul," I said, ignoring the danger inherent in Becks's expression. She might not be happy about having strangers in our van, but she could cope. In the back of my head, Georgia laughed. "Go ahead and close the door. I assume you know where we're going?"

Paul slammed the van door and replied, "Just keep heading up the road. You'll see the turnoff in about another twenty yards."

"Awesome." I started the van's engine and began driving slowly down the uneven dirt road. Much to my surprise, the surface leveled out dramatically before we'd gone very much farther. The van stopped jarring and jouncing, settling into a more normal, smooth ride. The look on my face must have been good, because Nathan and Paul both burst out laughing.

"Oh, man, that gets you newbies every time!" said Paul, slapping his knee with one meaty lumberjack hand. "We maintain the road once you get far enough off the surface streets. Never know when you're going to need to burn rubber without blowing an axle."

"Yeah, that was high comedy," I said, barely managing to keep the annoyance out of my voice. I couldn't *afford* to get annoyed. Becks was already halfway there, and one of us needed to be the reasonable one.

I could do it, offered George.

One of us who actually had a *body* needed to be the reasonable one, I inwardly amended. "Where to next?" I asked.

"Keep going," said Nathan. "You'll know the turnoff when you see it."

"Sure," I said, and hit the gas a little harder, accelerating from two miles an hour to a more respectable five. The turnoff came into view a few seconds later, leading to a broad gravel road. Trees shaded it almost completely; I could tell just by looking at the branches that it would grant almost total protection from aerial surveillance.

Even Becks abandoned her suspicious observation of our passengers as she leaned forward to study the road, and pronounced her verdict: "Cool."

"Very cool," I agreed, and made the turn.

The trees that sheltered the road also cut off most visibility as we drove. That, too, was almost certainly intentional. We had been following the gravel road for about five minutes when it curved gently to the side, a last veil of foliage fell away, and we found ourselves facing a pre-Rising building that looked almost unchanged from those careless, bygone days. Unchanged except for the electrified fence with the barbed wire around the top, that is. The fence didn't fit with any of the pictures I'd seen of pre-Rising architecture. The rest of the structure, however, was almost certainly older than I was, built when this area was a thriving tourist corridor, and not the blasted back end of nowhere. Two men were pulling the gate open.

A row of fuel pumps sat off to one side, inside the fence but distanced from the main building, as if they had been an afterthought. There was also a row of portable toilets, and what looked like a portable decontamination shower. These people had thought of everything, and then they'd jury-rigged it all with plastic sheets and duct tape.

"Welcome to Denny's," said Nathan.

I glanced over my shoulder at him as I pulled the van through the open gate and steered to a stop just outside a second, shorter fence. This one only encircled the main building. "I thought that was a diner chain."

"It was. So was this." He grinned. "We're handy out here."

"Really?" I turned back to the building, blinking. "I've never seen one with the windows intact."

"We got lucky out here," said Paul. "The Denny's was already closed down when the Rising hit. They said it was an 'economic downturn,' and then the zombies came before anybody had to admit that we were having a depression. Good timing for everybody."

"Except the people who got eaten," said Becks.

"Well, true; probably not for them," allowed Paul. He opened the van door, sliding out. His boots crunched when they hit the gravel. "Come on. Let's see what we can work out in terms of trade."

Nathan followed him out of the van. The two of them seemed to be perfectly at ease as they ambled toward the refitted diner. I stayed where I was for a moment, squinting at the trees.

Becks paused in the process of unbuckling her seat belt. "What?"

"We're in the woods. Even if there aren't any bears out here, there should be deer. So why are our friends so calm?" A glint of light high in a tree—in a spot where light had no business glinting—caught my eye. I jabbed a finger toward it, not caring if anyone saw me. "There. They have cameras in the trees. Possibly snipers, too. They were stalling us on the road while their people got into position."

"Did anyone ever tell you that you really know how to make a girl feel all warm and fuzzy inside, Mason?"

"It's one of my best qualities," I said. I climbed out of my seat to exit through the van's rear door, grabbing the first of the boxes of trading supplies as I passed it. Becks followed me, muttering something under her breath. Not for the first time, I was glad that George was the only woman who had a direct line to the inside of my head.

You'd go crazy if there was more than one of us in here, said George.

I smothered a snort of laughter and didn't say anything at all.

Nathan and Paul were waiting by the second fence when Becks and I came walking up to them. This gate was standing open, with no blood test in evidence. Nathan must have seen the surprise in our faces. He shrugged, scarecrow shoulders jerking up and down in a sharp, birdlike motion as he said, "We can't afford the kind of paranoia you get out there in civilization. Unless we've got reason to think you've been exposed, we handle our outbreaks the old-fashioned way."

"With bullets," added Paul, just in case we were too dumb to get the point.

"Yeah, thanks for that," I said. Hoisting my box of trade goods, I asked, "Is this where we get down to business, or can we go inside first?"

"Sure thing," said Nathan. "Indy's got coffee on." He beckoned for us to follow as he stepped into the circle of ground protected by the fence. Paul stayed where he was. They weren't going to let us get behind them both once we were past the gate. Smart. I like people who can manage to be paranoid and smart at the same time. They're usually the ones who make it out of any given situation still breathing.

"Any chance I could get a Coke?" I asked. Becks glared at me as we followed him past the fence. Unsurprisingly, Paul swung the gate shut behind us, leaving himself on the other side.

"I'm not comfortable leaving the van unattended," said Becks.

"If you're worried we'll loot it, don't be," said Nathan. "If you pass the last checkpoint, we'll give you gas and supplies and whatever else you need, and no one will touch anything you don't trade freely. We're civilized here. That's probably why the Doc told you to come see us."

I winced a little. One of our former team members, Kelly Connolly, went by "Doc" most of the time. My choice, not hers. She's dead now, like so many others. "And if we fail the last checkpoint?" I asked.

"It's not looting to take from the dead," said Nathan implacably. He opened the diner door and stepped inside.

"And on that cheery note..." muttered Becks.

Durno v. Wisconsin was the case that decided the dead had no rights regarding property on or around their immediate persons at the time of death, making it perfectly legal to take a zombie's car and claim it as your own. It's been abused a few times over the years. It's still seen, and rightly, as one of the best legal decisions to come out of the Rising. I mean, who has the time to transfer a pink slip in the middle of a zombie uprising?

"At least there's coffee." I caught the diner door as it was in the process of swinging closed, indicating the doorway with a grandiose sweep of my free arm. "Ladies first."

"What, assholes second?" asked Becks—but she smiled as she stepped inside, and that was what I'd been shooting for. I followed her into the surprisingly bright interior. The windows must have been tinted to make it harder to tell that people still used the place. That made a lot of sense. The infected don't seem to recognize light as a sign of possible human habitation. The police do.

The last Denny's in California closed years ago, when the new food service and hygiene laws were still shaking out. I was pretty sure this one had been heavily modified from the original floor plan, since I can't imagine many "family diners" would have ammo racks or hospital beds in the middle of their dining areas. A few booths were intact, cherry-red vinyl upholstery patched with strips of duct tape. Most had been ripped out, replaced with wire convenience store shelving. About half the shelves were empty. The rest were filled with packaged snack foods, first aid supplies, and the necessities of life: toilet paper, tampons, and cheap alcohol.

The diner's original counter was also intact. Standing behind it was a tall African-American woman with strips of bright purple fabric wound around her dreadlocks and a suspicious expression on her face. She had a pistol in either hand. I was relieved to see that they were pointing downward, rather than aimed at us. Somehow, I didn't think she'd hesitate for a second before shooting us both.

"Indy, these are the folks that our cameras caught coming down the old post road," said Nathan. "They say the Doc sent 'em. They need to gas up."

"Hi," I said. "Nice place you've got here."

"Hello," said Becks.

Indy frowned, eyes narrowing. "What's the password?" she asked.

Becks blinked. "There isn't one." Then she froze, tensing. I did the same. If these people had been looking for an excuse to shoot us, our not knowing the password would probably count.

Hold on, cautioned George. *Look at her face.*

Indy was smiling. She looked a lot less menacing that way. "See, if you hadn't been from the Doc, you would have tried to make something up. Welcome to Shantytown."

"Is that the name of this place?" asked Becks.

"Hell, no. They're all Shantytown. That way, no one can ever really give away a location. Nathan says you've come looking for fuel?"

"Snacks would be good, but gas is the primary objective," I said. Holding up my box again, I said, "We brought contraceptives."

"And poison oak ointment."

Indy laughed. "Those are two things that go together more often than not out here. Come on over, kids. Let's look at your toys, and see if we can't come to some sort of an agreement about what they'll buy you."

Becks and I exchanged a relieved glance as we walked over to the counter. Indy held out her hands for the box. I briefly considered refusing to hand it over, since that would reduce our bargaining power. Stupid idea. Bargaining power wouldn't do us any good if we didn't get out alive. I gave her the box.

"Where you kids heading?" Indy asked, as she put the box down and began picking through its contents.

"Berkeley," said Becks.

"Florida," I said at the same time.

Indy glanced up, a glint of amusement in her eyes. "Long-term and short-term goals, I see. The Doc put you up to this?"

"She wants mosquitoes," I said with a shrug. "There are some people in Berkeley who may be able to help us get to Florida and back out again without getting arrested for suspected bioterrorism. I'm pretty sure the people maintaining the blockades out there won't like the idea of us just popping in."

"The Masons can probably help you," agreed Indy, pulling three packs of contraceptive implants out of the box and setting them on the counter. "Don't look so surprised. I looked you up as soon as you told my boys who you were."

"We know what the Internet is," contributed Nathan.

"Not all the old networks have been shut down," said Indy, and straightened, pushing the box toward me. "The implants—we have our own injection gun—two boxes of condoms, four test kits, and some antibiotics. We'll give you a full tank of gas, feed you lunch, and let you leave here alive. We'll even throw in a shower, if you want one."

"I'll pass on the shower for now, but the rest works," I said.

"It's amazing that you can live out here like this," said Becks.

"Well, honey, if you grew up before the whole world was behind walls, this can seem like the only way to live." Indy smiled a little wistfully. Then she caught herself. Wiping her hands briskly against her jeans, she straightened. "Come on. Let's get you fueled up."

Paul was still standing at the gate when we emerged. He and Indy exchanged a nod, and he watched silently as I got back into the van and pulled it up to the fuel pumps. Becks went back inside while I pumped the gas, emerging a few minutes later with a brown paper sack of something that smelled spicy and delicious.

Indy followed her, watching with folded arms as I finished pumping. "You want some free advice?" she asked. "It's worth what you'll pay for it."

"I'm listening," I said, hanging the fuel pump back on its hook.

"Trust the Doc as long as you're not between her and whatever crazy-ass thing she's working on right now. Trust the Masons as far as you can throw them."

"I learned that second part a long time ago," I said, with what I hoped was a wry smile. "Thanks for your hospitality." I wanted to ask what she knew about the Masons. I didn't think it would be a good idea, and so I kept my mouth shut.

"Any time." Indy turned to smile at Becks, who was staring at her like she'd just seen a ghost. "Drive safely, kids." She walked back inside before either of us could answer.

Becks followed me back to the van in stunned silence, climbing into the passenger seat without saying a word. I waved to Paul and Nathan as I started the engine, and navigated the van carefully around the closing gate, back onto the gravel road.

It wasn't until we reached the end of the gravel and started down the uneven dirt road that she spoke. "That was Indigo Blue," she said.

"What?" I asked, only half listening as I fought to keep from losing control of the van. "I hate this road."

"I said, that was Indigo Blue. The Newsie? The one who disappeared after she collaborated with your father?"

"Adoptive father," I said automatically. Then I blinked. "Wait, really? Are you sure?"

"We covered her in my History of Journalism class. I didn't recognize her immediately, but yes, I'm sure."

"Huh. I wonder what she's doing out here?"

"I wonder why she isn't *dead*! Everyone thought she was."

"Want to go back and ask her?"

"No!" Becks's answer was fast enough to make me take my eyes off the road and frown at her. She sighed. "If she's out here, she's got a reason. I want to know what it is, but I'll respect it. We're not here for that."

"I guess not." I turned my eyes back to the road. "I wonder if Dr. Abbey knew."

"I wonder if Dr. Abbey cared."

"There's always that. I—" My sentence went unfinished as I hit the brakes, causing my seat belt to cut painfully into my shoulder. Becks yelped as she was flung forward.

"Shaun! What the *fuck*?"

I didn't answer her aloud. I just raised my hand, pointing at the shaggy hulk that was standing at the end of the dirt road. Becks turned to follow my finger, her eyes going wide.

"Shaun. Is that...is that a bear?"

"Yeah," I said, not quite managing to keep the glee out of my voice. "You ever killed a zombie bear before?"

"Can't say as I have."

"Maybe we'll be going back to use their showers after all." I unbuckled my seat belt, moving slowly. "First one to get the headshot gets first shower."

"Deal," said Becks, and grabbed her gun.

Please make it back alive. Please make it back alive. Please make it back alive. Please make it back alive. Please make it back...

—From *Dandelion Mine*,
the blog of Magdalene Grace Garcia,
July 26, 2041. Unpublished.

My dearest Nandini;

You will only see this letter if I die during the fool's errand I am about to undertake—one more foolish quest in a life that has been defined by them. Do you ever regret that you chose a husband who would forever be leaving you to chase some elusive platonic ideal of the truth? I wouldn't blame you if you did. Please, consider this letter my blessing, and remarry when you're ready. Find an accountant or a computer programmer—a nice, stable profession that won't lend itself to this breed of madness.

Oh, but I loved you. Maybe not at first, when our parents brought us together and said we should marry, but it didn't take me as long as some thought it would. I am truly sorry I have not been the husband you deserved. You were always more wife than I was worthy of. I love you, my Nan. Believe me, even if you believe nothing else I have ever said. I love you, and I am blessed beyond all words that you were willing to take a risk, and marry me.

—Taken from an e-mail composed by Mahir Gowda,
July 26, 2041. Unsent.

Eleven

Dr. Thomas smiled indulgently across the table separating us. "Now, Georgia, I know things have been very stressful for you these past few weeks—"

"Boredom and stress aren't the same thing," I said. "You can check the dictionary if you want. I'll wait."

He made a note on his tablet. "Inappropriate humor is a defense mechanism, isn't it?"

"No, Shaun was a defense mechanism. Since he's not here, I have to fill in." I took a breath, trying to look miserable. It wasn't easy. I've never had to worry about what my eyes were doing. People say the eyes are windows to the soul, and I was accustomed to having blackout curtains over mine. Without my retinal KA, they might be giving me away without my even knowing it. "Are you ever going to tell me what happened?"

"When your system is ready to stand the stress," said Dr. Thomas, making another note on his tablet. "Dr. Shaw says you were very cooperative with her tests, and confirms your story about the haircut. I'm sorry to have doubted you."

"Yeah, well." I shrugged, trying to look frustrated and innocent at the same time. The frustration was easy. The innocence wasn't. "I've never been much of a liar."

That little dig hit home; Dr. Thomas winced. I made my reputation as a Newsie based on my refusal to lie—a refusal that got me fined several times early in my career, when I was found in places I wasn't supposed to be and couldn't come up with an even half-decent excuse for what I was doing there. I never got better at making excuses. I just got better at refusing to let Shaun talk me into climbing over fences marked No Trespassing.

My memories of those early escapades were fuzzy, like I'd reviewed them so many times that the edges had begun to blur. A lot of my earlier memories were like that, and had been since I'd woken up. I'd been trying to figure out what that meant. Given what Gregory had shown me the night before, I was pretty sure I finally knew.

The memories weren't fuzzy because the things I remembered happened a long time ago, or because there was a glitch in the process that transferred my consciousness into a freshly cloned body. The memories were fuzzy because the things I remembered never happened at all—not to me, anyway. I was "remembering" an implanted incident extracted from the mind of a dead woman. A certain loss of fidelity was only to be expected.

Somehow, knowing that I wasn't *really* who I thought I was—knowing that Georgia Mason was dead and gone and never coming back—made dealing with Dr. Thomas easier. I don't like lying. I've never liked lying. And when I was myself, I wasn't any good at it. Now that I was someone else who just thought she was me, it seemed like a skill worth developing. I wasn't compromising my values. I was creating my values, and compromising the values of a dead woman.

And maybe if I told myself that enough times, I'd convince myself to believe it.

Finally, Dr. Thomas cleared his throat, and said, "Your test results have been good so far. I believe you may be stabilizing."

"Bully for me."

"The people who have been monitoring your case remotely are very encouraged. You're getting high marks."

After Gregory's revelation that I was being used as a display model, that announcement made me want to start smashing things. I forced the urge back down, asking coldly, "Will any of these people be coming to see me in person?"

Dr. Thomas smiled, chuckling in practiced amusement. It was so at odds with his generally nervous demeanor that it made me want to slap him and send him to acting classes at the same time. "Vice President Cousins is too busy to come to the CDC for social calls, even when he's calling on an old friend."

I sat up a little straighter, old journalistic instincts locking my shoulders tight as his words sunk in. "*Vice President*? Rick? *My* Rick? From After the End Times?"

"Ah…" Dr. Thomas looked suddenly uncomfortable, realizing he'd said more than he should have. "Yes. Governor Tate was another unfortunate casualty of the incident which claimed your…I mean to say, the incident that resulted in your untimely..." He stopped, looking even more uncomfortable.

"Death?" I suggested. "Murder? Martyrdom? I always wanted to be a martyr." That was my second lie for the day. I *never* wanted to be a martyr. I wanted to live long enough to bury Shaun, however long that happened to be, and I wanted to die in my time, and on my own terms.

"Yes." Dr. Thomas nodded, looking relieved. "After the governor's death, President Ryman selected your colleague to stand with him. He said it was the least he could do to honor your memory, and to show the blogging community that it would still have a voice."

My shoulders tightened. He said "blogging community" the way most people would say "dead rat." Choosing my words carefully, I asked, "So Ryman won the election?"

"By a good margin. The events in Sacramento, unfortunate as they were, only provided his campaign with additional exposure."

"Yeah, I'm sure they did." What happened in Sacramento would have given Ryman's campaign virtual domination over the news cycles, regardless of what his opposition did to try to force themselves back into the picture. As long as Ryman himself made it out alive, he'd been all but guaranteed the White House. "Can you let Rick know I'd like to see him?"

"I'll pass the word, but the vice president is a very busy man."

I'm sure you will, I thought. Aloud, I said, "Thank you. It would be nice to have someone to talk to. I'm going a little stir-crazy in here."

"I understand, but, Georgia, things have changed since your death. Your face is very well known in the outside world, and even some of our personnel are...uncomfortable...about the implications of your presence. I'm sure you can see where it would be bad for everyone if someone assumed you had amplified because they were aware of your current legal status."

"Right." I forced a smile. From the look on Dr. Thomas's face, I could tell that it didn't look any more genuine than it felt. Given the circumstances, that was probably okay. There was no way the comment about "current legal status" was intended as anything but a warning: He was telling me I was still listed as deceased in all the government databases that mattered, and that if someone shot me, they wouldn't be guilty of murder. They'd be acting within the law.

Life was easier when I was dead.

Dr. Thomas stood. "Now, if you'd come with me, we've prepared a little treat for you."

"A treat?" The gun in my sock pressed reassuringly against my calf as I stood, reminding me that whatever else I might be, I was no longer defenseless. Sure, I'd be lucky if I could take out more than one of them before they were on top of me, and that assumed that my memory of knowing how to fire a gun could overcome the fact that my new body had no muscle memory, but there was a *chance*. That was more than I'd had before. I was going to hang on to it with everything I had.

"Come with me." Dr. Thomas turned and walked toward the door, confident that it would open at his approach. It did, of course, sliding smoothly aside to reveal the hallway. Envy burned my throat as I walked after him. The doors wouldn't respond to me. I walked toward them and they stayed stubbornly closed, like I was infected.

Like I was still dead.

The ever-present guards were waiting outside the lab. They fell into position ahead and behind us. We walked the length of the familiar hall, passing the doors I was accustomed to stepping through. I was starting to get worried—maybe this whole thing had been a test; maybe Gregory was working for the CDC after all, and I'd failed by going along with his grand conspiracy theory—when Dr. Thomas finally stopped. The lead guard did the same.

"Here we are," said Dr. Thomas. He touched the apparently featureless wall. A piece of paneling slid aside to reveal a blood test unit. "Georgia. You understand that this is a privilege, and that any inappropriate behavior on your part will result in your being sternly reprimanded."

I didn't want to think about what a reprimand might constitute, given that I already lived in a small, isolated box with no privacy. "I understand," I said.

"Good. I told them we could trust you to be cooperative." Dr. Thomas slapped his hand down on the blood testing unit. The light above the door clicked on, going from red to green, and the door swung open. Swung—not slid.

Light lanced into the hall, so bright it seemed almost like a physical attack. I automatically moved to shield my eyes, the part of my brain that handled reflexes kicking in before my conscious mind realized my retinas weren't burning. I slowly forced my arm down, raising my head and squinting into the brightness.

Sunlight. It was sunlight. I could smell green things, the sharp bitterness of tomato plants, the sweet bland scent of grass. I started hesitantly forward, my feet carrying me almost without consulting the rest of my body. The guards followed me, but at a distance, giving me a few meters of space as I moved out of the antiseptic CDC hall, and into the green.

I've never been an outdoorsy person. Shaun used to say the only reason I ever left my room was to yell at him for doing dangerous shit. He wasn't entirely right, but he wasn't entirely wrong, either. And stepping through that door was still just shy of stepping into Heaven.

It wasn't the actual outdoors; a quick glance upward was enough to confirm that I was actually in a moderately sized biodome, with a ceiling of steel and clear, bulletproof glass protecting me from any chance of feeling an actual breeze. I was standing in a lie. A big green lie, filled with flower beds and vegetable gardens and an expanse of grass even bigger than our yard in Berkeley. I didn't care. In that moment, the lie was as good as the truth would have been, because I was standing in the green, and there were butterflies—butterflies—fluttering past like it was no big deal. Like there were green things and butterflies everywhere in the world.

"What is this?" I asked, turning back to Dr. Thomas. My eyes were burning; that weird tingling burn that I was learning to recognize as a sign of tears. I fought the urge to swipe my hand across them. I'd been capable of crying for a little under a month, and I already hated it.

"Those of us involved with your care thought you might benefit from a little fresh air." Dr. Thomas was smiling that paternal smile again. I stopped fighting the urge to wipe my eyes, and started fighting the urge to punch him in the nose. "Welcome to Biodome six-eighteen."

Something croaked in one of the apple trees to my left. I glanced over just in time to catch a flash of black wings as what could only have been a crow took off, presumably to find a tree that wasn't next to unwanted humans. The distraction gave me the time I needed to get my breathing—and threatened tears—under control. My expression was one of wide-eyed amazement as I turned back to Dr. Thomas.

"You mean this has been here all along?" I asked.

His smile widened. Asshole. "This is one of the larger CDC establishments. This habitat allows us to grow some of our own food, and studies have shown that access to outdoor environments can assist in psychological recovery."

"Wow. I had no idea." I might have been laying it on a little thick with that last one, but I was too distracted to care. I was busy reviewing everything my damaged memory contained about the North American CDC facilities.

"I thought it would make a nice treat for you."

Nice how he was willing to take credit for it, now that I'd stepped "outside" without losing my shit. "It's amazing," I said, trying to infuse my words with an air of wonder.

It must have worked, because Dr. Thomas didn't say anything. He just kept smiling, watching as I apparently soaked in the wonders the CDC had prepared to impress me. I was impressed, all right; impressed by how much of Mahir's series on the various CDC installations had managed to survive the transfer of my memories. He'd broken them down by region, listing their major features, like helipads, private airstrips...and biodomes.

There were eight CDC facilities equipped with biodome simulators. Only four used them for agricultural purposes. Assuming this was one of the facilities that had existed when Mahir wrote his report, I was in one of those four.

None of the staff I'd spoken to had Southern accents. Dr. Thomas sounded like he was from the Midwest, but his accent was blurry, like he hadn't been home in a long time. Dr. Shaw sounded sort of like Becks, which meant she was probably from somewhere in New England. Everyone else had the Hollywood non-accent that meant West Coast, and I doubted the CDC was bussing in guards and orderlies just to confuse my sense of place.

So we weren't in the South—that took Huntsville off the list—and while we might be in the St. Paul facility, I didn't think so. The accents were wrong. That left either Seattle or Phoenix.

My smile was genuine as I turned back to Dr. Thomas. "Thank you so much for letting me see this," I said. "I think you're right. I feel better just being here."

Being in either of those two cities meant we were near a dozen bloggers who knew me. More importantly, we were near a dozen bloggers whose hunger to be the first at the scene would mean they listened first and shot second if I managed to show up on their doorsteps. All I had to do was find a way out of the building, and while I wouldn't be exactly in the clear, I would be in a much better situation than I could have been. I would have a chance.

"Well, as long as your recovery continues without any setbacks, and as long as you continue to cooperate, I believe I can see clear to letting you out for a constitutional every other day. How does that sound?"

My smile froze again. *It sounds like you think I'm some sort of house pet, you patronizing bastard*, I thought, but said only, "That sounds great."

"We have half an hour before your next tests. Would you like to explore the dome?"

"Can I?" I didn't have to feign my interest. The biodome was a new environment. After weeks in the sterile CDC halls, I needed that more than I could have guessed.

"I wouldn't have brought you here if I wasn't going to let you have a lit-tle time to roam," said Dr. Thomas. That damn paternal smile was back on his face. "Go ahead. Look around. You're completely secure here. No one will come in and trouble you." His smile slipped a bit, turning stern as he added, "But, Georgia, if you were to attempt to open any of the doors—"

"You wouldn't blame a girl for trying?" I asked.

Dr. Thomas's eyes narrowed, all pretense of a smile fading. "I most cer-tainly would."

"Understood." I offered a cool nod to the two guards who were still standing next to Dr. Thomas, and turned to walk deeper into the biodome.

I found the first wall less than twenty yards from where I'd started, mostly hidden behind a tall patch of something I assumed was probably immature corn. It looked like corn, anyway. I never spent that much time studying agriculture. The wall was white, and should have stuck out like a sore thumb in the primarily green biodome, but it didn't. Like the door we'd entered through, it was somehow part of its surroundings.

The dome wasn't a perfect circle, although it wasn't a square, either; after following the wall long enough to map the angles of two corners with my hands, I decided that it was most likely an octagon. This campus was even bigger than I'd initially assumed. I kept walking, enjoying the springy feel of the grass beneath my feet, and tried to figure out what else I might learn from the structure of the dome.

I crested a low hill and found myself facing a pine forest. It was small, no more than fifteen trees forming the edge, but it was enough of a sur-prise to stop me in my tracks for a moment. The shock was probably a good thing; it kept me from punching the air in sheer delight. We were in Seattle. The Seattle CDC was the only campus with an evergreen forest inside their biodome. I'd seen pictures.

As I stood contemplating the pines, I realized that my feet were cold. I looked down. My thick white socks—so perfect for roving the halls of the CDC—were less perfect for wandering around a grassy meadow. They were soaked to the ankles, with grass stains around the toes. There was no way Dr. Thomas would let me wear them back into the main building.

"Georgia?"

I stiffened, glancing back toward the sound of his voice. He wasn't in view; if he was coming after me, or sending his guards, he was still a little ways away. With only a few seconds to move, I didn't stop to think about what I was doing. I just bolted for the trees.

Shaun was always the one who put himself in mortal danger for kicks, but I still tried to stay in decent physical condition. It was the smart thing to do if I was going to keep following him into hazard zones, looking for the "perfect story" to slap up on his side of the site. I'd never been an athlete, but I'd been running ten-minute miles since I was fourteen, and that was enough to outrun any zombie that ever shambled into my path. I felt weirdly betrayed when I found myself gasping for breath, my heart hammering hard against my ribs as I slumped against a tree. All those hours of work, undone by one little death.

I yanked my socks off. The little gun fell to the grass. I scooped it up, lifting my top long enough to tuck the gun into my waistband, the muzzle digging painfully into my stomach. I pulled the drawstring on my pants a little tighter. The pajama top was loose enough that when I let it go, it fell to cover the weapon without a trace.

"Georgia?" Dr. Thomas's voice was closer this time; he was coming for me himself, rather than sending his flunkies to fish me out of the biodome. That was good. He'd be less attuned to the little details than a professional guard would have been—they would have noticed the high color in my cheeks and the slight unsteadiness of my legs as I stepped out of the cover of the tree line.

"Here," I said, proud of the way that I was barely gasping at all. My bare toes dug into the grass, tangling deep. I was going to need a serious shower when all this was over. "I'm sorry. Were you calling me?"

Dr. Thomas fixed me with a stern eye. "What did I say about no funny business?" he asked.

Cold arced down my spine. Someone must have seen me pull the gun out of my sock. *He knows,* I thought, desperately wondering if I could draw before he had a chance to call for his guards, and whether it would do me any good if I did. Even if I didn't shoot myself, they'd just decommission me, or whatever it is you call getting rid of a clone that you don't need anymore. They'd throw me out like yesterday's garbage—and all because of a pair of goddamn *socks*—

"That means you *come* when I call," said Dr. Thomas. "I'm willing to forgive it this time—we can call it youthful exuberance, and it doesn't need to go into my report of the day's activities. But that assumes you'll behave from now on. Can I trust you to behave, Georgia?"

"What?" Relief flooded over me, washing away the cold. I nodded so hard it felt like I was going to sprain something. "Yes, absolutely. I'm sorry, I didn't mean to ignore you, I was just…the grass, and then the *trees*, and…" I paused, making my voice very small before I said, "It reminded me of home, that's all."

If the CDC did their research on Berkeley, they knew we had more green space per capita than any other densely populated city in the state of California. Chalk it up to general perversity and being built around a university that resisted all attempts to render it fully secure. The idea of trees being something I would miss was believable if you didn't know me well enough to know that I'd been avoiding unnecessary exposure to the outside world for my entire life.

Dr. Thomas's expression softened. "I can understand that." His frown returned as he glanced down at my feet. "Georgia, what in the world happened to your socks?"

"They got wet, so I took them off." I held up my grass-stained socks. "At least we have plenty of bleach, right?"

To my surprise, Dr. Thomas actually chuckled. He seemed more human in that moment than he had since the first uneasy hours after I woke up in an unfamiliar bed. Too bad that wasn't going to make me change my mind about getting the hell out of here before they had me "decommissioned" and replaced me with something more tractable.

"We can get you new socks. Come on, now. We'll have just enough time to get you cleaned up before they expect you at the lab."

"All right, Dr. Thomas." I walked toward him, the grass damp beneath my feet. I was getting better at deceit. I didn't like it—I didn't think I would ever like it, and that was good, because the day I loved a lie was the day I stopped being even remotely Georgia Mason—but I was getting better. I was going to need those skills if I wanted to get out of the CDC still breathing, rather than going out in a biohazard container bound for the incinerator.

I took the deepest breaths I could as we left the biodome, trying to capture the smell of the green in my lungs. That was what freedom would smell like. And I was *going* to be free.

———————

Things I have done today that were *awesome*, whether or not I am currently a practicing Irwin: I shot a zombie bear in the head. Six times. Becks shot it four times, which I would gloat about, except she's the one who managed to shoot the damn thing straight through the eye, taking it down before it could, you know, maul and devour us. The denizens of the gas station came out when they heard the shooting, loaded, as the old colloquialism goes, for bear; I don't think they expected to actually *find* one.

Indy—the lady who runs the supply depot where we encountered the bear—said it was a grizzly. So hell, maybe we just killed the last grizzly in the world. I'd feel bad about that if it hadn't been *an infected zombie bear* that wanted to *eat my delicious flesh*.

Damn, that was fun.

**—From *Adaptive Immunities*,
the blog of Shaun Mason, July 26, 2041. Unpublished.**

Please tell me you know where they're going, and you didn't just lose track of our only known living human with a full immunity to Kellis-Amberlee amplification. *Please.* I don't want to be the one who has to come out there and kick your ass.

Seriously, Shannon, be careful. You're starting to get a little hard to follow, and that scares me. We both know who *didn't* build those bugs, but if you make yourself too big of a target, when the time comes, you're the one they're going to come for.

**—Taken from an e-mail sent by Dr. Joseph Shoji to Dr. Shannon
Abbey, July 26, 2041.**

Twelve

Berkeley was asleep. We pulled off Highway 13 onto the surface streets, using my still mostly accurate mental map of the area to guide us to the intersections and off-ramps that hadn't been outfitted with blood test units. I was only wrong once, and that one time, the line for the testing station was long enough for me to get into the back and climb under a counter, where I would be safely out of view. Our van's occupancy beacon was "broken," courtesy of Alaric and a socket wrench, and they're not yet legally required for a vehicle to be considered road safe. "Yet" is the operative word—I expect tricks like the one we pulled to be illegal within the next five years. God bless "yet."

Becks pulled up to the manned booth monitoring traffic as it moved from the highway onto surface streets. I heard the slap of her hand hitting the metal testing panel, and the disinterested voice of the nightshift security officer as he asked where she was heading. As a university town, Berkeley has never been in a position to crack down on traffic as much as, say, Orinda, where the city limits basically seal themselves as soon as the sun sets. In Berkeley, only the individual neighborhoods can go for that kind of expensive paranoia.

Becks's answer was muffled by the seat and the sounds of traffic coming in through her open window. Whatever she said must have passed muster, because she put the van back into drive and went rolling on after only about a minute and a half.

Don't even think about going up there until she says it's safe, said George. *This would be a stupid way to die.*

I couldn't answer without the all clear, and so I just glared into the darkness at the back of the van, trusting her to get the point. She did; her laughter filled my head, amusement tinged with a grim understanding of just how bleak our situation could easily become.

Finally, after what felt like an eternity, Becks called, "We should be out of range of the cameras. You can come out now."

"It's about time." I crawled out from under the counter and back into the front seat, not bothering with my seat belt. "I was starting to get a cramp back there."

"You would have gotten more than a cramp if one of those guards had seen you."

"I'm clean."

Becks slanted a disbelieving look at me. "Do you *honestly* think no one's going to be looking for you? After everything that's happened?"

"No." I shook my head. "I mean, we haven't committed any crimes—well, technically, we could probably be charged with breaking and entering at the Memphis CDC, since the Doc was legally dead when she let us in—but I know there are people watching for us."

"Watching for *you*," said Becks, almost gently. "You're the only remaining blogger from the Ryman campaign. You've got a level of credibility with people who aren't blog readers that the rest of us can only dream about—and here, you'll be recognized by just about anyone. Hometown boy makes good and then goes bad? You're the target, Shaun. Not me, not Alaric, and not even Mahir."

"You're a ray of sunshine, aren't you? Take the left on Derby."

"Forgive me if I'm not that excited about the idea of going to visit your parents."

"Adoptive parents," I said automatically.

Becks wasn't listening. That was probably a good thing. "I used to look up to them, you know? They were heroes. What your father did for his students—he should have received a medal for that."

"He agrees with you." I couldn't keep the sourness out of my voice. I wasn't trying very hard. Becks grew up with the Masons as celebrity faces for the news, but I grew up with them exploiting me—exploiting *George*—for the sake of ratings, and a kind of public approval so damn fickle it was almost unreal. And now here I was, creeping back to them under the cover of darkness, ready to beg for their help. Home sweet self-destructive emotionally abusive home.

"I didn't find out what they were like until I started working for Georgia. She talked about them more than you do. Which is sort of funny, since you talk about almost everything else so much more than she ever did."

"She loved them," I said defensively. I didn't know why I felt the need to defend George's love of the Masons, but I did. Maybe it was because I stopped loving them so long ago. Maybe it was because, awful as they were, she could never quite bring herself to do the same. "She didn't want them to be the people that they were."

"And you did?"

"What? No! No. I just…" I let the sentence drift off, watching Berkeley slide by outside the van window. I'd made this trip in the passenger seat so damn many times; any time we had to go out on location when the weather conditions made it unsafe for George to take the bike, or when parking was going to be at a premium. She insisted on driving after the sun was down, saying her retinal KA gave her an advantage over my puny, uninfected eyes. So I would sit in the passenger seat and watch Berkeley going by, tired, cranky, and utterly content with the world. Maybe it was nostalgia speaking, but I couldn't remember a single night trip home where I hadn't been happy to be where I was, riding in the van with Georgia, and both of us alive, and both of us together.

Finally, slowly, I said, "George knew who the Masons were—*what* the Masons were—as well as I did. But she wished they were different. I think she thought that if she could just bring home a big enough story, find a big enough truth, that maybe they'd get past Phillip—their son, the one who died—and finally start loving us."

"And you didn't think that?"

"They were never going to start loving us. That's why we had to love each other as much as we did."

"Oh."

Becks was quiet after that, and I was glad. I wanted to make this last little part of the trip in silence.

The GPS didn't take us down the streets I would have chosen—it was going by distance, not by a local's knowledge of road conditions and traffic lights—but that was good, too, in its way. I needed this trip to be a little different. I spent too much time living in the past, and I didn't need to encourage the part of me that would be happy to stay there forever. The businesses clustered around Shattuck and Ashby gave way to the outlying buildings of the U.C. Berkeley campus, and finally to the low, tight-packed shapes of the residential neighborhoods. Becks pulled up in front of a familiar house, the windows shuttered, the porch light dark.

"Now what?" she asked.

"This." I dug a hand into my pocket, pulling out the sensor disk I'd been carrying since we left Dr. Abbey's lab. It wasn't mine, ironically; my identity key to the Masons' house was lost when Oakland burned. This one had been Georgia's, and had been a part of her little black box—the only thing I'd taken the time to save before the bombs came down. I slipped the chain on over my neck, pressing the disk to my skin and flipping it into the "on" position. It beeped, twice, acknowledging that it had managed to locate a matching signal in the immediate vicinity.

A light above the Masons' garage door flashed on, blinking twice in response to the disk's location pulse. Without any further fanfare, the door began spooling smoothly upward.

"Go on in," I said, in response to Becks's surprised expression. "The house was programmed years ago to let this van inside with multiple passengers. It was an expensive enough upgrade that there's no way they've taken the time to have it pulled out of the security programming."

Unless they were really, really angry with you when you refused to give them my files, said George. *They could have done it out of spite.*

"'Could' doesn't mean 'would,'" I said.

Becks shot another glance my way, frowning, and started the engine again. "Please try not to talk to dead people while we're here? I don't want you getting shot because you look like you're getting the amplification crazies."

"Amplification doesn't make you talk to yourself."

"And you don't get better once you're infected. There's a first time for everything."

"Fair enough." The garage door slid closed again once we were inside. I unfastened my belt. "Come on. We'll need to pass security if we want to get into the house."

"I figured."

I hadn't expected the Masons to make any updates to the security system, and I hadn't been wrong: The two testing stations were still in place, each of them equipped with the standard wall plate for blood sampling and the more expensive display screens for verbal confirmation. Becks and I stepped into position. A red light clicked on above the door leading into the house.

"Please identify yourself," said the bland, computerized voice of the house system.

"Shaun Phillip Mason and guest," I said.

"Rebecca Atherton, guest," said Becks. Her words were almost precisely overlaid by Georgia's, as she said, *Georgia Carolyn Mason.*

The light above the door blinked several times as the house checked my voice against its records. I was allowed to bring guests home—had been since I was sixteen—but I hadn't done it very often. Part of me was even ludicrously afraid the house would somehow pick up on George's phantom voice and refuse to let us in until it had figured out how to test her for viral amplification.

The light blinked just long enough for me to get nervous before the house said, "Voice print and guest authorization confirmed. Please read the phrase on your display screen."

Words appeared on my screen. "Ride a cock horse to Banbury Cross to see a fine lady upon a white horse," I read. The words blinked out.

On the other side of the door, Becks recited, "Jack be nimble, Jack be quick, Jack jump over the candlestick." The light above the door began blinking again. She cast me a nervous glance, which I answered with an equally nervous smile. The feel of George's phantom fingers wrapping around my own didn't help as much as I might have hoped. Every time she touched me, it was just a reminder of how little time I had left before I wound up going utterly insane.

The light over the door changed from red to yellow.

"Please place your right hands on the testing pads," requested the house. I did as I was told, slapping my palm flat against the cool metal. It chilled half a second later, and something bit into my index finger, a brief sting followed almost instantly by the cool hiss of soothing foam. The light above the door began to flash, alternating red and yellow.

"Isn't this fun?" I asked, with forced levity.

Becks glared. She was still glaring when the light stopped flashing.

The door hissed open. "Welcome home, Shaun," said the house. "We hope you'll have a pleasant visit, Rebecca."

"Um, thanks," said Becks, looking to me for what she should do next. I shrugged, smiled, and stepped through the open door.

The kitchen hadn't changed since Georgia and I lived with the Masons. The floor was still covered in the same off-brown linoleum, and the walls were still papered in the same cheerful yellow floral print. Papers and clippings from the U.C. Berkeley student newspaper—printed on actual paper, although it was hemp, not wood pulp—covered the refrigerator. The urge to open it, grab a snack, and go up to my room was as strong as it was unexpected. Walking into that kitchen was like walking backward through time, into a part of my life where the biggest thing I had to worry about was whether the new T-shirt designs in my shop would sell well enough to justify their printing cost.

A part of my life where Georgia was alive, and not just a voice in my head and a ghostly hand on my arm.

"Shaun?" said Becks, voice barely louder than a whisper. "Are you okay?"

"I'm fine." I shook off the past, shoving it away from me as hard as I could. "Come on." I gestured for her to follow as I stepped out of the kitchen and into the front hallway, intending to wait in the living room until the Masons woke up and came downstairs for breakfast. It was a good plan. It was a plan intended to leave them off balance and catch them during the one time of day when they were as close to unarmed as possible.

It was a plan that died as soon as we turned the hall corner and found ourselves facing my adoptive mother, Stacy Mason. She was wearing a robe over sensible cotton pajamas, and holding a revolver. It was aimed straight at my chest. I stopped. Becks stopped. None of us said a word.

Correction: None of us said a word that anyone but me could hear. *Hi, Mom*, said George, her voice falling into the silence like a stone. I managed somehow not to flinch.

Finally, Mom lowered her pistol, saying calmly, "You must be hungry. Why don't you kids go back into the kitchen, and I'll see if I can't whip us up some pancakes or something?"

"That's okay, Mom," I said. "We didn't come here for breakfast."

"I know," she said, voice utterly calm—the voice that used to greet me when I came home late from school, or got another detention for fighting with the kids who picked on George because of her eyes. "I raised you better than that. At the same time, whatever you *did* come for can wait until we've all had a chance to sit down and eat like civilized people. All right?"

I know when I'm beat. "Okay, Mom." I hesitated before adding, "You know you can't upload any footage of us being here, right?"

"I invented the rules to this game, Shaun," said Mom. "Now go wash your hands."

"Yes, Mom," I said. Georgia echoed the words inaudibly, her voice half a beat out of synch with mine. "Come on, Becks."

Looking uncertain, Becks turned to follow me back to the kitchen. We had barely crossed the threshold when Mom called, "Oh, and Shaun?"

I tensed, not turning. "Yeah?"

"Welcome home."

Somehow, that didn't reduce the tension. "Thanks, Mom," I said, and kept walking.

Now that we were back in the kitchen, I could really look at it, rather than letting the overwhelming impression of coming home wash over me. Everything was old-fashioned to the point of parody, with frilled gingham curtains hiding the security mesh worked into the windows and fixtures originally installed sometime in the 1940s. It was all part of the homey atmosphere the Masons worked so hard to project—the homey atmosphere that had required, once upon a time, that they go shopping for adorable orphans to complement the rest of their décor. The worst part was the way I could see Becks buying into it, the tightness slipping from her shoulders and the lines around her mouth relaxing. Stacy and Michael Mason were heroes of the Rising. They were two of the best-loved faces of the media movements that came after it; between them, they *defined* what it was to be an Irwin, what it was to be a Newsie... what it was to be a blogger.

Maybe it's insane that a news movement that started as the chosen medium of politicos and techno-nerds and geeks of all stripes wound up with a college professor and a former dental hygienist as its primary poster children, but that's the thing about reality. It doesn't need to make sense. They were in the right places at the right times, they had the right level of heroic dedication and personal tragedy, and maybe most important, when their backs were against the wall—when their son was dead and the world was changed forever, and the things they'd been doing during the Rising to keep themselves from thinking about those two unchangeable facts weren't an option anymore—they decided to become stars in the highest-rated reality show anyone had ever seen. The news.

I dried my hands on the blue towel next to the kitchen sink before stepping aside to let Becks at the faucet. "Remember why we're here," I said, voice a little sharper than it needed to be. "This isn't a social call."

"I'm sorry. It's just..." Becks stuck her hands under the running water, using that small domestic activity to buy herself a few seconds. Finally, she said, "I thought she'd be taller. It's a cliché, I know, but I really did. I should know better—I've seen pictures of her next to you—but somehow, I still thought she'd be..." She stopped, and then finished, lamely, "Taller."

"I get that a lot." Along with requests for autographs, and occasional offers of money if I could somehow get my hands on naked pictures. My college journalism courses were hell. George had it a little better—I guess Irwins feel more entitled to demand the gory details, while Newsies just look for something they can hang you with.

"I wanted to be your mother when I grew up." Becks said it like it was somehow shameful, the sort of admission that could only be dragged out of her by a kitchen with yellow wallpaper and stupid curtains. Mom would have been proud of her environmental design. Hell, for all I knew, she already was. For all I knew, she was watching us from upstairs; they'd had this place bugged since before I could walk. "She was so... brave, and strong, and she always knew what she was doing. Not like me. I was just sleepwalking through the things my parents wanted me to do, until the day I finally got up the nerve to run."

We never did that, said George. Her voice echoed oddly, coming half from right beside me, half from the inside of my head. It was the house. I'd spent too much of my life in this house with her; she was haunting it as much as she was haunting me.

God, was that what it was like for the Masons after Phillip died? Did they see him every time they turned around, a bright-eyed little ghost that never refused to take a nap, never drew on the walls with his crayons, never screamed because he couldn't have another cookie? No wonder they adopted us. We weren't just another way of bringing in the ratings. We were a living attempt at exorcism.

"We never ran," I said softly.

Becks shot me a startled look that softened into understanding. We were raised by journalists; we grew up to be journalists. That wasn't the whole story, but it was enough to make a nice headline. We were raised by people who hurt everyone around them in their single-minded pursuit of the story. No one could look at the number of bodies in our wake and not believe that Georgia and I were two apples that didn't fall far from the transplanted tree.

"Shaun?" The voice was jovial and dry at the same time, the voice of every college professor who ever told a slightly off-color joke and laughed with his undergrads, proving he was "part of the gang" without giving up an inch of his authority. It was the voice of my childhood, the man I watched George beat herself to death trying to become.

Sometimes you *can* go home again. That's what hurts most of all. "Hi, Dad," I said, turning to face him.

Dad smiled as he studied my face, his calculating expression making him look so much like George that it hurt, even though the two of them weren't biologically related. "The prodigal son comes rolling home. And who is this charming young lady?" His smile turned more sincere as he aimed it at Becks, the consummate showman finding an audience he could charm. "Please tell me our son didn't bring you here thinking you were going someplace pleasant."

"Hi," said Becks, smiling glossily. I resisted the urge to groan. "I'm Rebecca Atherton. It's a pleasure to meet you, sir. I'm a real fan of your work."

"Rebecca Atherton, from After the End Times?" Dad glanced my way for a split second, like he was making sure I saw how intimately he knew our site. "The pleasure is mine. Your report on the events of Eakly,

Oklahoma, during the Ryman campaign was positively chilling. You have an eye for the news, Miss Atherton."

"Okay, you're laying it on a little thick," I said, unable to contain myself any longer. "Can you stop trying to spin Becks for thirty seconds and let us tell you why we're here?"

"Now, Shaun. Your mother was looking forward to having a nice family breakfast, just the four of us." Dad's smile faded. "I'm sure you wouldn't want to disappoint her."

"I gave up on trying not to disappoint her a *long* time ago." I glared at him.

He glared back. Something about that expression made him look as out-of-date as the kitchen, and somehow, between one second and the next, I started to *see* him, not just the man I remembered from my childhood. He was wearing pajama pants and a belted gray cotton robe, preserving the illusion of collegial dignity, but his already-thinning red Irish hair was almost gone, leaving an expanse of gleaming forehead in its wake. His eyes were tired behind the lenses of his glasses. I'd never really thought of him as tired before.

"Be that as it may, I'm assuming you wouldn't have come out of whatever hidey-hole you've been tucked away in without something you considered a very good reason, and that means you need us." Dad kept glaring as he spoke, choosing each word with exquisite care. That was something else he had in common with George. Both of them knew how to use words to wound. "If you want us to cooperate with whatever mad scheme has brought you back here, you will sit down, and you will eat breakfast with your parents like a civilized human being."

"Right." I shook my head. "And if you get some ratings out of the deal, well, that won't suck for you, will it?"

"Perhaps not," he allowed.

"Oh, good, we're all together." Mom appeared behind him, hair brushed, and a light layer of foundation on her cheeks. Not enough to show on camera—oh, no, never that—but enough to take fifteen years off her age. Her hair was the same silvery ash blonde it had always been.

How many times have you had to dye your hair in the last year? I wondered, and felt immediately bad about even harboring the thought. I didn't like the Masons. I didn't trust them. But at the end of the day, they were the only family I had left—and I *needed* them.

"Hands are clean," I said, holding them up for inspection. Becks mirrored the motion, letting me take the lead. I was so grateful I could have kissed her.

"Good. Now go set the table." Mom kissed Dad on the cheek—a glancing peck she normally reserved for public photo ops—and pushed past us into the kitchen. "Eggs and soy ham will be ready in ten minutes."

"Thanks, Mom," I said. I opened the nearest cabinet and took down four plates, passing them to Becks. Getting the glasses and silverware out of their respective places only took a few seconds more. "Come on, Becks."

"Coming," she said, and followed me out of the kitchen. Unsurprisingly, Dad tagged along behind her, looking studiously casual, but almost certainly making sure we didn't make a break for it before he'd had a chance to grill us on what, exactly, we had come for.

The lights were on in the empty dining room. I stopped in the doorway, a lump forming in my throat. The dining room table was clear. The dining room table was *never* clear, not even when someone was coming to interview one or more of us; it was a constant bone of contention between the two generations in the household, with Mom and Dad insisting the dining room was meant for eating, and George and I insisting it was a crime to let a perfectly good table go to waste for twenty hours of any given day. We fought over it at least once a month. We...

But that was the past. I shook it off, blinking away the tears that threatened to blur my vision, and felt Georgia's hand on my shoulder, steadying me.

The house is haunted, she said softly, *but so are you, and your haunting is stronger than theirs. You can do this.*

"Shaun?" asked Becks. "Are you okay?"

"Yeah," I said, answering them both with a single word. I stepped into the dining room and started putting glasses down on the table. "Sorry. Just memories."

"We have a lot of memories invested in this house—in this family," said Dad, moving around the table to keep us in view. "It's good to see you, son."

"Can we not?" This time, the tears were too close to blink away. I swiped my arm across my eyes in a quick, jerky motion. "Don't bullshit me, okay? Please. The last time we saw each other, you were threatening to take me to court over Georgia's will, and I'm pretty sure I told you to go fuck yourselves. So can we not play happy families for Becks's benefit? She knows better."

Dad's smile faded slowly. Finally, he said, "Maybe it's not only for her benefit. Did you consider that? Maybe we missed you."

"And maybe you're trying to get the best footage you can before I run out of here again," I said. Suddenly weary, I pulled out one of the dining room chairs and collapsed into it. "You missed me. Fine. I missed you, too. That doesn't change who we are."

"No, I suppose it doesn't." Dad turned to Becks, a seemingly genuine expression of apology on his face. "Would you like to wait in the kitchen while we have this conversation? I'm sure it's not very comfortable for you."

"I've come this far with your son. I think I'll stick with him a little longer." Becks took the seat next to mine, folding her hands in her lap as she directed a calm, level stare at my adoptive father.

He blinked, glancing between the two of us before clearly coming to the wrong conclusion. A smile crept back onto his face. "Ah. I see."

No, you don't, I wanted to scream. I didn't. Instead, I said, "We're here because we need your help. We didn't have any place else to go."

"That's the sort of thing a mother always loves to hear from her only living child," said Mom, stepping into the dining room. She was carrying a tray loaded down with quiche, slices of steaming artificial ham, and even a pile of waffles. It would have been more impressive if I hadn't known she'd pulled every bit of it out of the freezer. But it was food, and it was hot, and it smelled like my childhood—the parts of it that happened before I knew just what the score in our happy little family really was.

"At least I'm honest." I leaned over as soon as she put the tray on the table, driving my fork into the top waffle on the stack. She smiled indulgently, picking up the serving spoon and using it to deposit a slice of quiche on my plate. "Isn't that a virtue around here?"

"Sometimes. Rebecca? What can I get you?"

"It all looks fantastic, Ms. Mason. I'd like some of everything, if that isn't too much trouble."

"Nonsense. Why would I have cooked if I didn't want you to eat?" Mom made a flapping gesture with her free hand, indicating one of the empty seats. "Michael, sit down. Shaun's big pronouncement can wait until you have something in you."

"Yes, dear," he said, and sat. He winked at me, clearly trying to look conspiratorial, like we were the same because Mom was making us both eat. I ignored it, spearing a slice of "ham" with my fork rather than trying to come up with a less violent response. Anything I said would have ended with my screaming at someone—or maybe just screaming. The room, the hour, the false domesticity, it was rubbing at my nerves even more than I'd been afraid it would.

I may be a haunted house, but that doesn't mean I was emotionally equipped to sit in someone else's haunting, eating breakfast and pretending everything was normal.

It took about ten minutes to eat our breakfasts. While we ate, silence reigned, broken only by the clank of silverware against ceramic and the occasional sound of someone chewing a bit too loud. I kept catching glimpses of George. She was sitting in one of the otherwise empty seats, no plate in front of her, watching mournfully as the rest of us ate. She disappeared if I looked at her directly, and I was glad. If I'd been forced to sit in this house, with these people, looking at her ghost, I think I would have finally gone all the way insane.

At last, Dad pushed his plate away, patting his lips with his napkin, and turned a calm gaze on me. Becks was all but ignored; she'd had her opportunity to be a part of this little drama, to either side with the Masons or establish herself as a third party, and she'd chosen to stick with me. That meant she was basically a nonentity as far as he was concerned.

"Well, Shaun?" he asked. "To what do we owe the pleasure?"

"We need your help," I said again, not sure where else to start.

"With what, dear?" asked Mom, tilting her head inquisitively to the side. Light glinted off her diamond earring. My mother never slept in diamond earrings. That was a miniaturized camera. It had to be. She was recording us.

That wasn't unexpected. "Becks and I need to get to Florida without being stopped by the border patrols," I said, not bothering to sugarcoat the words. "I know you know people who can get you past the hazard lines. I need to know them, too."

"Why don't you go looking for your own contacts?" asked Dad. "You've never asked us to do your research for you before."

"Because there isn't time, and because any contacts I could find that easily wouldn't be as good as the ones you've been working on for years." I shrugged. "I'm smart enough to know a plan is only as good as the tools you use to carry it out."

"How were you planning to deal with the mosquitoes?" asked Mom. "Florida's a death sentence right now."

"Bug spray," said Becks. "Mosquito netting. The things they've been using to stay alive in regions with malaria problems for generations."

"Kellis-Amberlee is a bit nastier than malaria, young lady," said Dad.

"Guess that 'Miss Atherton' routine couldn't last, huh?" I took another slice of fake ham. "We have a plan for handling the bugs. What we don't have is a way to get to Florida without getting arrested."

"What you're asking for, Shaun...this isn't some little trinket. This is the name of a trusted ally, one who might never work with us again after we sell you his or her identity." Mom's eyes narrowed, that familiar calculating gleam lighting them from within. "What are you prepared to give us in exchange?"

"Georgia's files."

A momentary silence fell over the room, the Masons staring at me in startled surprise, Becks sitting by my side, and all of us waiting to see what would happen next. Then, finally, Dad began to smile. For the first time since we'd arrived, it actually looked sincere.

"Well, why didn't you say so? Let's go upstairs. You kids are going to need a map."

Dr. Abbey is edgy, which is making everyone in the lab edgy, which is making *me* edgy. I never realized how much space my coworkers occupied until they were gone. I keep expecting to find Mahir at one of the terminals, or have Maggie chase me out of the bathroom, or run into Shaun arguing with the air like he doesn't give a fuck who sees him being bat-shit crazy. It doesn't help that Dr. Abbey lost almost a third of her people in the security failure—and it doesn't make sense that the security failed. It's like the protocols all reset at the same time, and that sort of thing doesn't happen by mistake.

If someone here is letting the dead things out to play, then someone is feeding information back to whoever's driving this crazy train to hell. If someone here is against us, then the people responsible for all this know exactly where we are and what we're doing.

God, I'm scared.

**—From *The Kwong Way of Things*,
the blog of Alaric Kwong, July 27, 2041. Unpublished.**

Michael's gone to pick up Phillip from his school. My office has been shut down for the day, and I managed to get to the Andronico's before they closed the doors. We should have enough canned food to see us through the next week—maybe more than that, if it's necessary. We have a high fence. We have good doors. We're going to be fine.

Paul, Susan, Debbie: If any of you see this, please, leave me a comment; let me know that you're okay. I have my minivan, and I can come get you if I have to, but I need to know exactly where you are. Come on, guys. Just keep me posted.

It's not like this is the end of the world, right? :)

—From *Daily Thoughts*,
the blog of Stacy Mason, July 18, 2014.
Taken from the archives of The Wall.

Thirteen

The sound of alarms screaming in the hall outside my room slammed me from a sound sleep straight into adrenaline-laced consciousness. I was on my feet with my hands over my ears before I was aware I was awake, every muscle tight with the need to move, move, *move*. I didn't know whether I wanted to run away from the danger or toward it. In a more lucid moment, I would have embraced that confusion, because it was what my journalistic training told me I should be feeling—the need to get the story warring with the need to not die in the process.

Funny thing about dying, coming back from the dead, and finding out you're not actually the woman you think you are: Anything that goes the way it's supposed to becomes reassuring as hell.

The alarms were still going, making it hard to hold any single thought for more than a second. Curiosity and years of working the front-page news beat won out over the shreds of my common sense. I ran to the one-way mirror, uncovering my ears and cupping my hands around my eyes as I tried to squint through the opaque glass. All I could see were blurry outlines of people rushing past, none holding still long enough for me to get an idea of who they were.

None of them were turning toward my door. And the alarm was still going.

"Hey!" I shouted, stepping back from the mirror. "Monitor people! What's going on?" There was no response. A thin worm of fear began working its way through my guts, twisting and biting as it gnawed toward my center. I was alone in here. I had a little gun, but that wasn't going to be enough if things were going really wrong. If they didn't let me out . . . "Hey!"

A group ran by in the hall, making so much noise that I could actually *hear* them through the window and over the alarm, even if I couldn't quite make sense of what they were *doing*. Were they screaming? Singing? Laughing? Or—worst of all, and looking increasingly possible as the seconds slipped by with the alarm still screaming—were they moaning?

I shrank back from the mirror, putting another useless foot between me and the glass. If we were in an outbreak situation, a few feet weren't going to make a difference one way or the other. Either the infected would realize I was there, or they wouldn't. Either the people outside the building would decide it needed to be sterilized, or they wouldn't. Where I was standing wasn't going to do a damn thing to change the outcome.

I wonder if the clone lab is zombie-proof, I thought, almost nonsensically. A titter of laughter escaped from my lips, the sound bright and ice-pick sharp under the shriek of the alarm.

Somehow, that little sound was what I needed to snap me out of my nascent panic and back into the problem at hand. There was something going on outside the room; whatever it was, it wasn't a good thing. I wasn't unarmed, but I might as well have been, for all the good my little gun would do me if this *was* an outbreak. I was, however, observing Michael Mason's first rule of dealing with the living dead: I had enough bullets that they wouldn't take me alive.

Feeling suddenly calmer, I looked up toward the speaker and said, "This is Georgia Mason. I don't know what's going on outside my room, but I am uninfected. I repeat, I am uninfected. Please advise if there's anything I should be doing. In the meanwhile, I'm going to assume none of you people have time for me, and I'm going to go sit down."

I walked back to the bed, keeping my shoulders squared and my chin up. It would have been a lot easier without the alarm wailing in my ears. I was going to have one hell of a headache later, assuming we lived that long. Putting my hands back over my ears, I waited.

All sense of time dropped away, blurred into nothingness by the steady blare of the alarm. Occasional sounds drifted through the mirror—once there was a burst of machine-gun fire that lasted long enough to make the hairs on the back of my neck stand on end; shortly after that there was a piercing scream that rose, buzz saw–sharp, before tapering off and vanishing back into the din—but for the most part, it was just me and the alarm. Not the best company I'd ever kept.

The sudden cessation of the noise was almost shocking. I jerked upright, suddenly aware that I had managed to sink so deep into semi-meditation that I was almost dozing. Wide-eyed, I unfolded my legs and slid into a standing position, keeping my eyes fixed on the door. It didn't open. I took a cautious step forward. It didn't open.

"Well, isn't *that* just fantastic," I muttered.

The sound of the intercom clicking on sent a wave of relief washing through me, so powerful that my knees felt weak for a few seconds. "Hello, Georgia," said Dr. Thomas, in his customary mild tone. "How are you feeling?"

I stared at the wall for a long moment, mouth falling open. Finally, slowly, I said, "Did you just ask me how I was *feeling*? Seriously? What's going on? Is there an outbreak? Are we alone in the building?" A new thought struck me, horrifying in its reasonableness. "Am *I* alone in the building?" He could be using an outside connection to reach the intercom, giving me the opportunity to say good-bye before the sterilization of the facility began.

Dr. Thomas actually laughed. In that moment, any good feeling I might have held toward him died. "Oh, no, Georgia! I'm sorry, you were reacting so calmly, I thought you'd realized."

"You thought I'd realized? Realized *what*?" I balled my hands into fists, glaring at the intercom. It belatedly occurred to me that this could come off as inappropriately aggressive—by CDC standards, anyway; Shaun would have said I was displaying just the right amount of aggression—and I shoved my still-balled hands behind my back, trying to conceal them.

"This was a test. We wanted to see how you would respond to an extreme stress situation—especially one that was a close mirror to things you would have experienced"—Dr. Thomas paused for just a little too long before finishing the sentence—"before."

I kept staring at the intercom. I didn't say anything.

"Georgia?"

I didn't say anything.

More sharply this time: "Georgia?"

I didn't say anything.

Annoyed now, but with a thin ribbon of anxiety running under the words, like my silence was a sign that some unknowable bearing strain had finally been reached: "Georgia, please. Don't be childish."

"Don't be *childish*?" I echoed, my eyes growing even wider for half a heartbeat before narrowing, reducing my vision to a thin line. "Did you seriously just tell me not to be *childish*?"

"Now, Georgia—"

"You faked an outbreak to see how I would respond to stress, and now you're basically saying 'gotcha,' like that makes it all better! I *died* in an outbreak, you bastard! The fact that I'm not crying in a corner should be all it takes to prove that I'm not being *childish*. If anyone's being childish, it's *you*. You're the one playing asshole pranks and getting offended when your target doesn't find them funny."

The silence lasted several seconds before Dr. Thomas said, "I think you're being unreasonable."

"And I think you're being a dick. In fact, four out of five cloned journalists agree that you're behaving badly." I crossed my arms. "So did I pass?"

"What?"

"Did. I. Pass?" I repeated, enunciating each word until it was almost a sentence all by itself. "You said this was a test of how I would react under stress. Well? Did I pass? Am I a fully functional individual?"

Again, silence. Finally, sounding almost subdued, Dr. Thomas said, "We'll go over your test results tomorrow. One of the orderlies will be along shortly with your dinner, and to take you to use the facilities. Thank you for your cooperation."

"What cooperation? You blasted my ears out with your damn special effects and watched me like a bunch of sick voyeurs!" I realized I was yelling and took a deep breath, forcing myself to ramp it back. It wasn't easy. Very little seemed to be, these days.

There was no response. The intercom was already off.

I walked back to my bed, feeling the headache the alarm had summoned starting to construct itself, bit by bit, in the space between my ears. Dropping to the mattress, I let gravity pull me into a slump, catching my forehead on my hands before it could hit my knees. I stayed like that for I don't know how long—long enough for my wrists to start going numb—before I heard the door slide open. I lifted my head.

One of the familiar rotating guards was standing there with an orderly. George, from Dr. Shaw's team. I blinked.

"We're here to take you to the restroom," he said, giving no sign that we'd met before. "Your dinner will be waiting when we bring you back, along with painkillers for your head."

I frowned a little. "Do you have medical sensors in my mattress?"

He risked a smile. "No. We just have cameras that show us the way you're clutching your temples. If you would come with us...?"

Whatever game he was playing, he was probably playing it on Dr. Shaw's behalf, and while I still wasn't sure I trusted her, I trusted Gregory, and *he* trusted her. My relationships with the people around me were becoming increasingly conditional. Trust George because Dr. Shaw trusted him. Trust Dr. Shaw because Gregory trusted her.

Trust Gregory because he was the one who stood the best chance of getting me out of here without getting me killed. Again.

"Sure," I said, and stood.

There was another guard outside. He fell into step behind me, while the first guard took point, and George stayed to my right. We walked to the bathroom, stopping outside the door.

"How's your head?" asked George.

"It hurts," I replied. "How long was I in there?"

"About six hours."

That explained the way reality had seemed to stretch and blur into nothing but alarm bells and waiting. I scowled. "I'd better be getting a *lot* of painkillers," I said, even though there was no way I'd be taking them. The people who prepared my food could drug me at any time, and there was nothing I could do to stop them. That didn't mean I needed to make it easy.

"You'll be getting a medically safe dosage," said George, in what sounded like it was supposed to be a reassuring tone. "Now please, you have about twelve minutes before your dinner is ready. You don't need to rush, but you wouldn't want your soup getting cold."

The last time Gregory had come to remove me from my quarters, he'd done it at midnight. I nodded slightly, indicating that the message had been received—assuming it was a message at all, and wasn't just me fumbling for meaning where there wasn't any. "I'll be quick."

"We appreciate it."

The guards didn't accompany me into the bathroom. I still moved like they were there, watching me; it was the only way I knew to keep from getting annoyed by the knowledge that I was being watched by half a dozen hidden cameras. If Buffy had been here, she could have spotted them all by measuring minute inaccuracies in the grout, and disabled them with soap suds and mock-clumsiness. If one of us was going to come back from the dead, it should have been her. She could have treated it like just another story. She would have handled it better.

Then again, maybe not. The truth is allowed to be stranger than fiction, and the parts of this that weren't making sense yet might have been enough to send her over the edge. The only reason they weren't making me crazy was the fact that I had something to hold on to. Shaun was alive. Shaun was out there somewhere. And wherever he was, he needed me.

I undressed the way I always did, shoving my pants down my legs and peeling my socks off in the same gesture, concealing my little gun. It meant putting the same clothes back on when I was finished, carrying the clean pajamas they'd provided back to the room, and changing under the covers of my bed, but I'd been able to pass it off as a strange form of modesty... at least so far. I soaped up and rinsed down in record time, assisted by the fact that my bleach rinse only lasted for about fifteen seconds—a perfunctory nod to regulations, while acknowledging that I hadn't been near anything infectious since I was Frankensteined to life.

George and the guards were still waiting outside the bathroom when I emerged. "All clean," I announced, wiping my damp bangs back from my forehead. "Now, about those painkillers."

George nodded, motioning for the lead guard to take us back to my room. True to his word, my dinner tray was waiting when we arrived, tomato soup the color of watered-down blood and what looked like grilled cheese sandwiches. High-end hospital food. Tomato soup and cheese sandwiches seemed to surface at every other meal. I didn't mind as much as I might have. At least they were well prepared, which was more than I could say for many of the more ambitious things to come out of the kitchen.

Four small white pills were sitting on the tray, next to my glass of milk. "Thanks," I said, stepping through the doorway, into the room.

"Have a nice night, Miss Mason," said George. The door closed, cutting him from view.

I sat down at the table, palming the pills and dropping them into my lap as I mimed swallowing them. The room's white-on-white decorating scheme helped with that. Whoever was monitoring the security monitors currently airing *The Georgia Mason Show* would have to be paying extremely close attention to catch white pills being dropped onto the white legs of my pajamas, where I covered them with my white napkin.

My soup was hot, and had obviously been put on the table seconds before we returned to the room. That didn't fit George's twelve-minute estimate, so either he was wrong, or he really had been telling me to wait for midnight. That was fine. It wasn't like I had anything else to do.

An orderly came and took my empty dishes after I finished eating. The pills I'd managed not to take were safely tucked into the seam of my pillowcase by then. I smiled. He flinched. I smiled wider. If these people couldn't handle the results of their crazy science, they shouldn't be bringing back the dead. The orderly all but scurried from the room, and I started to feel a little bad. It wasn't his fault. None of this was. The orders that controlled my life came from way above his pay grade.

I paced around the room a few times, feigning my normal restlessness, before climbing back into bed. I'd been sleeping more and more, and all sense of time was going rapidly out the window. If the alarms were going off for six hours, and they'd been off for about an hour and half, that meant I'd been awake for less than eight hours. It felt like forever. I was exhausted.

Maybe they were putting something in my food after all.

The throbbing in my head kept me from falling into anything deeper than a light doze. It shattered when the door opened. I sat up, squinting.

"Hello?"

"We have sixteen minutes," said Gregory. He didn't leave the doorway. Maybe there was too much risk of him getting stuck in the room when the sixteen-minute security window closed. "I'm sorry. It was the best I could arrange on such short notice."

"Don't worry about it." I swung my feet around to the floor, wincing a little. "Did you bring any painkillers I can actually trust?"

"As a matter of fact, yes." Gregory dipped a hand into his pocket. "I even brought water."

"Thanks," I said. The word seemed to stick in my throat. Shaun was always the one who brought me painkillers when the light got to be too much and one of my migraines decided to start making its presence known. I missed him so much.

"We don't have long."

I paused in the process of getting up. Then I stood and walked toward him, holding out my hand for the pills. "What do you mean? Sixteen minutes, right?"

"We arranged the window when today's testing schedule went up on the intranet." Gregory sounded grimmer than I'd ever heard him. "Someone's going to get caught over this one. It won't be me, but whoever it is, they're going to be lucky if all they lose is their job."

A chill started in the pit of my stomach. "What are you saying?"

"They've started stress-testing you. That isn't good." He dropped two pills into my hand, producing a bottle of water from his other pocket. "Four subjects have made it this far. None of them got through the alarm sequence without permanent psychological damage. Georgia, I'm sorry. We didn't realize they were going to speed things up like this, but with your brother—" He stopped dead.

The silence that stretched between us was the loudest I had ever heard. I opened the bottle of water and tossed the pills into my mouth, washing them down without really registering the motion. It was something that had to be done, and so I was doing it; that was all. The silence continued, Gregory waiting to see how I would respond, my mind racing through all the possible ways that sentence could have ended.

None of them were good.

"With Shaun what?" I asked. Gregory didn't answer. "With Shaun *what*?" I repeated.

"Off the grid," said Gregory. He took the empty bottle from my hand.

"He and the rest of your old news site dropped off the radar following Tropical Storm Fiona."

He mentioned the storm like it was a big event. I frowned. "Were they in the area? Are they missing?"

"No. There have been a few sightings, all of them on the West Coast. The EIS has been planting sighting reports elsewhere in the country, but it's hard, with as little data as we have."

"So what, they're thinking they can tell me to find him, and I'll know where he's gone to ground?" I scoffed. "That's not going to happen."

"No. They're thinking they can finish running their tests on you, demonstrating to the investors just how stable a clone can be, and then they can decommission you in favor of a Georgia Mason who'll be willing to play the part they ask it to play."

The chill continued to uncurl, spreading to cover my entire body. "What part is that?"

"Bait." I couldn't see Gregory's expression with the light shining so brightly behind him. I didn't need to. His voice told me everything I needed to know. "They're going to put the new Georgia on the air, and they're going to use it to do the one thing they couldn't do on their own."

"They're going to use her to lure Shaun in," I finished, in a whisper.

"They'll use her to do more than that, if they possibly can. I'll be honest, Georgia, because this isn't a time for being anything else. Shaun's psychological profiles since your death have been…disturbing, to say the least."

"Disturbing how? Cutting up children and old ladies disturbing, or not showering anymore disturbing?"

"Talking to himself. Refusing to let go of the idea that you'll come back someday. That's part of what let the investors sell the idea that you would have multiple uses."

"But not me in specific."

"No," Gregory admitted.

I took a deep breath. The painkillers hadn't had time to work, but the chill was muffling the pain nicely, making everything seem a little more distant, and hence a little easier to deal with. "Well, all right. I guess that means it's time to get me the hell out of Dodge, doesn't it?"

"Yes, it does," said Gregory—and now he sounded sad, and deeply concerned. "There's just one problem."

I closed my eyes. "You still don't know how you're going to do that, do you?"

"No. We don't."

"Well." I opened my eyes, sighing once. "This is going to be fun."

BOOK III

Foundations

Given a choice between life and death, choose life. Given a choice between right and wrong, choose what's right. And given a choice between a terrible truth and a beautiful lie, choose the truth every time.

—GEORGIA MASON

Fuck it. Let's blow some shit up.

—SHAUN MASON

Every time I think my life can't get any weirder, it does. Today has included a missing Newsie from the Rising generation who just happens to be running a rest stop on the smuggler's route to Canada, rednecks with guns, listening to Shaun sing along with the radio (badly), and a zombie bear. Who knows what delights tomorrow will bring? And will tomorrow bring a shower with enough hot water to finish washing my hair?

Stay tuned for our next exciting update that I can't post because it might give our location away to some mysterious shadow conspiracy.

Fuck, this sucks.

—From *Charming Not Sincere*,
the blog of Rebecca Atherton, July 26, 2041. Unpublished.

———

IF YOU ARE READING THIS, DO NOT LEAVE YOUR ROOM. If you are already outside your room, find a secure location immediately. The following places on campus are currently secure: The library. The Life Sciences building. The student store. Durant Hall. The Optometry lab. The following places are confirmed compromised: The English and Literature building. The Bear's Den. The administrative offices.

THIS IS NOT A HOAX. THIS IS NOT A PRANK. This is Professor Michael Mason. We are in a state of emergency. If you are reading this, do not leave your room.

Stacy, darling, I'll be home as soon as I can.

—From *Breathing Biology*,
the blog of Michael Mason, July 18, 2014.
Taken from the archives of The Wall.

Fourteen

Dad's map was just that: a large piece of paper with roads and landmarks drawn on it. He spread it out on the dining room table, smirking a bit when he saw the disbelieving expressions Becks and I were wearing. "What?" he asked. "You've never seen a map before?"

"Not outside of a history book," I said. "Haven't you ever heard of GPS?"

"What isn't on a computer can't be hacked, oh foolish son of mine," said Dad. He was comfortably in professor mode now, that old "I am imparting wisdom to the young" twinkle in his eye. George used to love it when he'd get like this, like it was some secret language the two of them could share—the language of knowledge and the truth. Naturally, that meant I'd always hated it when he'd get like this, because he was lying to her. He was letting her believe he cared.

"Mom, make Dad stop acting like he knows everything," I said, without any real rancor.

"Michael, tell the kids what they need to know," said Mom. "And in exchange, Shaun will tell us what *we* need to know. Isn't that right, Shaun?"

"Yeah, Mom. That's right." *I'll tell you how to steal the last things in the world that belong to your adopted daughter, and you won't even think of yourselves as grave robbers.* The acid in the thought was almost shocking, even to me. I realized I was digging my nails into my palms again. I rested my hands on the edge of the table, forcing my fingers to uncurl. "So what are we looking at here?"

"The trouble is the distance. There's no single safe route from here into the Florida quarantine zone—maybe if you were aiming for something in the contaminated parts of Texas?" Dad glanced up, a canny glint appearing behind the amiable twinkle in his eyes. "You didn't mention exactly what you were trying to accomplish on this little road trip, come to think of it."

"True, and we're not going to mention it, so don't bother fishing," I said. The map covered the Southwestern United States, stopping shortly after it crossed into Texas. "Are you saying this is as far as you can get us?"

"I'm saying this is as far as we can get you before things become complicated," Dad replied. "You don't mind complicated, do you, Shaun?"

"I like to think it's a specialty of mine."

"Good." He beckoned me closer. I motioned for Becks to do the same. He began tapping highways and side roads, rattling off names, security levels, and known geographical quirks with a speed that was almost daunting. I was so busy trying not to lose track of what he was saying that I barely even noticed when Mom slipped out of the room. Dad pulled out another map, this one covering the space from Texas to Mississippi, and kept talking.

Shaun.

"What?" I asked, without thinking about it.

Dad glanced up, eyes narrowed. "What's that?"

"I think I'm confused, too," said Becks smoothly. "What do you mean about fuel shortages in Louisiana?"

Dad smiled at her and began talking again, saying something about fuel pipelines being compromised in the wake of Tropical Storm Fiona. I couldn't quite make out the details; George was talking too loudly for that. *You need to get Becks and get out of here. Abort the mission. Abort it* now. *There isn't time to argue.*

Maybe there wasn't time to argue, but there was time to scowl at the map, trying to wordlessly express my confusion to the voice inside my head.

It must have worked at least a little, because George groaned and said, *They're hiding something from you. You told them you had the files. They should have tried to make you hand them over before they told you anything, and they didn't. That means they think they can have their cake and eat it, too. You need to get* out *of here.*

I stiffened, hoping Dad was too focused on Becks to notice. George was right. We'd made this plan, which was, admittedly, a stupid, suicidal plan, expecting the Masons to be willing to make a trade. Normally, that would mean they wouldn't expect me to give them the files without proof of cooperation on their part. So where were those negotiations? Where was Dad insisting I give them a single file, just to show that I was serious? Hell, where was Mom? She should have been in the room, keeping an eye on us, making sure Dad didn't get too excited by the process of showing us how clever he was and show us a little bit too much. That was the most damning piece of the admittedly sketchy evidence: Mom should never have left the room.

"Who's paying you?" I asked conversationally, taking my hands away from the table. Becks cast a startled glance in my direction. I smiled reassuringly. "It's cool, Becks. They're just selling us up the river, and I was wondering who they were selling us to. That's all."

Dad paled. "I'm sure I have no idea what you're talking about. You've been on the run too long, son. It's starting to affect your thinking."

"Well, yeah. I know that part. I mean, it's driven me crazy and everything, which I know you know, since you've been looking for an excuse to have me declared mentally unfit and take my stuff since George died—great job mourning for her, by the way, really top-notch—but I don't think this is me being crazy. I think this is an unfortunate moment of me being sane, and when I'm sane, I have to admit that everyone in the world really *is* out to get us." I pulled George's .40 from my belt, bringing it up and aiming it at his head. "I'm only going to ask you one more time. Who's paying you?"

"No one's paying us, darling." Mom's voice came from behind me, calm and even cheerful, with the faintly manic edge that accompanied every mother-son outing we'd ever taken. The click of a safety being disengaged was basically just overkill. "It's simply that we don't think you should be running around besmirching our family name. Not after everything we've done to build the brand."

"Hi, Mom," I said, still aiming the .40 unwaveringly at Dad. He wasn't moving. I always knew he was a smart one. "Is this the part where you tell me to put my gun down?"

"No, this is the part where I save your ass," said Becks. The statement was accompanied by the sound of her revolvers being cocked. "Please believe me when I say that I respect your work greatly, Mrs. Mason, and I will blow your fucking head off if you don't stop aiming that gun at my boss right now."

Mom laughed. It was a joyful, tittering, purely artificial sound. "Oh, how cute. She's willing to step in and *save* you, darling. Such loyalty—and such a pretty girl, too. Is she sweet on you? So many of the pretty girls have been. Not that you ever paid them any attention. Not that your sainted sister, may she rest in peace, ever *let* you. Do you think things would have gone differently if she hadn't been so selfish?"

"Don't talk about George," I said, gritting my teeth to keep my calm from slipping away. "She moves, shoot her, Becks."

"With pleasure, Boss."

"It seems we have a standoff, son," said Dad, raising his hands. It felt almost unfair, letting him be the only one in the room without a gun. Good thing I've never been too hung up on playing fair. "So what now?"

"Now you stay where you are." I took a deep breath before asking, "What did you do, Mom? Who did you call?"

"No one a concerned citizen doesn't have the right to call," she replied, in the same happy, artificial tone. "You shouldn't have come here, Shaun. I'm glad you did—it was nice to see you—but you shouldn't have come." For a moment, I thought I heard genuine regret in her tone. As hard as I'd tried, I'd never quite been able to stop myself from loving the Masons. Maybe, difficult as it was to credit, they had the same problem.

Maybe they hadn't quite been able to keep themselves from loving us.

"The house logged our arrival, didn't it? And you let the information upload. You didn't have to. We're not residents, and no one saw us come. You could have scrubbed it, and no one would have ever known." That's what I'd been counting on when I suggested coming here. I knew what that security system could do. "Why didn't you?"

"Be reasonable, Shaun," said Dad. He shook his head, looking almost contrite. "People are saying you may have had something to do with what's happening right now in the Gulf. We can't even get passes to go into the restricted zones. Other journalists with similar credentials have managed to at least get around the edges, but we're being shut out. Bringing you to justice would counter that. It would show we weren't working with you."

"I'm sure the ratings wouldn't hurt, either," said Becks sourly. I risked a sympathetic glance her way. I'd been disillusioned by the Masons years ago. She was getting her disillusionment in one lump sum...and like anything that shows your heroes in an unpleasant light, it had to be bitter. So very bitter.

"No," Mom admitted. "It's been harder to keep the numbers up since we lost that family dynamic. We got a few spikes when things went bad in Oakland, and a few more when your names started coming up in conjunction with the tragedy, but nothing lasting. Nothing that would bring in the numbers remotely like an act of selfless heroism."

"So you're going to sacrifice us for ratings," I said.

"Now, son, it's not like that—" Dad began.

"Isn't it?" I lowered my gun, slowly turning to look at Mom. Feigning curiosity, I asked, "So if you're willing to trade one son for a better market share...what *really* happened to Phillip, Mom? Did he just *happen* to get in that dog's way, like the official story says? Or were you afraid your fifteen minutes of fame were already over, and just searching for anything that could make them last a little longer?"

Her eyes widened. There was a moment when I wasn't sure whether she was going to shoot me. Then she was striding across the space between us, Becks forgotten, gun dropping to her side. I could have ducked away from her hand. I didn't, and the sound of her palm hitting my cheek rang through the room like it was the loudest thing in the world. Becks stood frozen, staring. From the silence behind me, Dad was doing much the same.

Mom's eyes were filling with furious tears. "Don't you *ever*, *ever* say something like that to me," she snarled. The anger in her voice may have been the most honest emotion I'd ever seen from her. "You don't get to talk about him."

"Well, then, you don't get to talk about Georgia," I countered. "How is this different, Mom? I'm your son. You didn't give birth to me, but you raised me. You're the only mother I've ever had. And now you're selling my life—my *life*—because you want better ratings. How is this different from what happened to Phillip? Give me one good answer. Please. Just one."

She stared at me, seemingly unable to decide whether she should get furiously angry or break down and start to cry. Becks was still holding her pistols aimed at Mom's head, standing in an easy hip-shot stance that I knew she could hold for hours, if she needed to. I also knew she wasn't going to need to. Someone was going to break this standoff before much longer. I just hoped it would be someone in the room, rather than someone driving an official vehicle and commanding an urban cleanup squad.

"It was an accident," said Dad. I didn't turn. I didn't want to take my eyes off Mom. "Marigold wasn't supposed to be in our yard. Phillip was unlucky. This is different."

"Why? Because it's premeditated? Because you pulled me and George out of some state orphanage somewhere, and that gives you the right to decide how I'm going to die? Don't kid yourselves. If you keep us here, we're *going* to die. Someone's going to be careless, someone else is going to say we moved for a weapon, and we're going to be so much sterilized ash by lunchtime."

"You don't know that," said Mom. She seemed to be getting herself back under control. That probably wasn't good. "They may just take you in for questioning."

"The mosquitoes got loose while we were in the Memphis CDC, Ms. Mason." Becks's voice was as calm as it was unexpected. Mom's head whipped around to stare at her. "If it hadn't been for the storm—if it hadn't been for bad timing—they would have been confined to Cuba. They would never have reached the coast without the wind to help them."

"So?" demanded Mom.

"Stacy." Dad's voice was soft, thoughtful; the same sort of tone that George used to get when something occurred to her in the middle of the night. She'd wake me up and whisper in my ear in that soft, contemplative voice, telling me stories I only half heard, but that would be posted on our site within the week.

"What?" Mom turned back toward him, and consequentially, toward me.

"The weather maps *do* show that the mosquitoes originated in Cuba. They're on record as a mutation. Some sort of horrible trick of natural selection."

"You don't believe that, do you, Mr. Mason?" asked Becks. "Doesn't it seem a little pat? Twenty years of no insect vectors, and then one comes along at the right time to bury a news cycle no one wants to deal with? If it hadn't been for the storm, we'd be hearing a lot of different stories right now. The Cuban tragedy would be dominating the news for the next year, and no one would ever hear about a break-in at a CDC facility, or about the corruption leading to the death of Dr. Kelly Connolly, granddaughter of the man who broke the news about the Rising."

"But Tropical Storm Fiona had other ideas," I said, taking up her argument. "Whoever let those mosquitoes loose wasn't counting on a big ol' wind sweeping in and carrying their nasty little pets to American soil. So the cycle got buried, and so did a lot of innocent people. It was a mistake. It still did its job. You never heard about any of that, did you?"

"No." Dad stepped up behind me, and stepped around me, moving to stand beside Mom. Becks shifted her position, widening her stance as she adjusted to include him in her line of fire. "We never heard any of those things."

"So either I've gone entirely out of my mind—which isn't out of the question, I guess, since I talk to myself and everything; but if I'm crazy, I've managed to take my team with me—or someone is really out to get us. And whoever it is, they were willing to gamble with the Kellis-Amberlee virus in order to keep us out of the headlines." I took a breath. "Lots of kids died in Florida, Mom. Lots of little kids. And not because they ran into dogs that hadn't been chained up properly. Not because their parents did anything wrong. They got bit by mosquitoes, and it killed them, and it wasn't *fair*. Just like what happened to Phillip wasn't fair."

"I told you not to talk about him," she said. This time, the anger in her voice wasn't there, and the tears were beginning to overflow her lower lids, starting their slow tracks down her cheeks. She looked old, and tired, and like the woman I'd only ever seen in pictures taken before I was even born. She looked like someone who could have loved me.

"Please. We're trying to get to Florida because the family of one of our team members was there when the storm hit. His parents died. His little sister's still alive. We promised him we'd get her out."

Dad shook his head. "That's not going to happen, son."

What? demanded George.

"What?" I asked, half a heartbeat later.

"They've had our house under surveillance for weeks. Even if we'd wanted to hide your presence, we couldn't have done it for long. They'll be here any minute now." He turned to his wife, my adopted mother, the first of the world's true Irwins. "Stacy. It's up to you."

She hesitated. Then, finally, she nodded. Turning back to me, she said, "It's not like Phillip at all, Shaun, because we couldn't save him." She turned her gun around, offering it to me butt-first. "Make it look realistic, and get the hell out of here."

"Mom..."

"You have maybe three minutes. Four, if you're willing to leave the van and take mine instead—but you won't do that, will you?" A smile tugged at the corners of her mouth. "Michael, take Rebecca to the garage and get her set up with one of the portable jammers, will you?"

"Yes, dear," he said. Then he paused, looking back at me, and said, "I'm proud of you, son. We didn't do right by you or by your—by Georgia—but I'm proud of you, all the same. I think I have the right to that much."

"Yeah, Dad. You do."

"Thank you." He motioned for Becks to follow him. "Come along, young lady."

Becks glanced at me, eyes wide. I nodded, hoping the gesture would be reassuring, and not sure what I'd do if it wasn't. "It's okay, Becks," I said. "I'll be right there."

"Shaun..."

"Just go. I promise, I'll be *right* there."

Still looking uncertain, she followed him out of the room. Their footsteps drifted back down the hall; then the door connecting the kitchen to the garage slammed, and even that was gone. I returned my attention to my mother.

"You sure?" I asked.

"No." She laughed a little, still holding her gun out to me. "But hell, when have I been sure about anything? I think the last time I was absolutely *sure* of something was in July of 2014. I was sure that was going to be the summer when I finally learned how to swim."

"Mom…" I stopped, realizing I had no idea what else I could say to this woman. We were family and we were strangers. She was my mother and my teacher and the one person I had never been able to please, no matter how hard I tried or how much I played the clown. I took the gun from her hand. "What are you going to tell them?"

"That you realized we'd called the authorities, and ran." Her eyes were clear and calm. "Or maybe I won't tell them anything. The choice is yours."

It took me a moment to realize that she was saying I could shoot her: She was unarmed, and I had her gun. They wouldn't be able to use the ballistics to trace me, or to conclusively prove I'd pulled the trigger while she was still alive. I shook my head. "Tell them whatever you have to in order to get them off your back, and then find a way to get to Florida. Alaric's sister is named Alisa Kwong. She's in the Ferry Pass Refugee Center. Get her out."

"Then what?"

I stepped forward, leaning in to kiss her forehead the way she used to kiss mine when there was an appropriate photo opportunity. Until that moment, I hadn't really realized that I was taller than her now. "Do what you couldn't do for us, Mom," I said. "Love her. Until Alaric can come back for her, just love her."

She nodded. "I'll try," she said. "That's all that I can promise."

"That's fine." I smiled at her. She smiled back. She was still smiling when I slammed the gun into her temple. I wasn't trying to knock her out—the human head is thicker than most movies want you to believe, and knocking someone out without killing them is a precise science—just catch her off guard. I managed that. She staggered backward with a shout, the skin split and bleeding above her eye. That was going to be one hell of a shiner.

She didn't grab for the gun. She didn't swear at me. She just clapped a hand over the wound and pointed to the door, saying, "Go. We'll take care of things from here."

I went. As I ran through the kitchen, I threw Mom's gun into the sink. It was still half-full of soapy dishwater. The gun sank into the bubbles. I broke into a run.

Dad and Becks were in the garage with the door standing open. The sky was starting to lighten, hints of sunrise creeping up around the edges. "Come on," I said, gesturing for Becks to follow me. "Dad—"

"The scanner says they're eight blocks out. Miss Atherton has the jammer. Now *go*." He adjusted his glasses with one hand. His shoulder was bleeding copiously. There was no telling what Becks had used to make the wound. Mom's toolbox provided a wealth of possibilities.

He saw me looking and smiled. I smiled back and kept going, heading for the van. Becks ran behind me, a boxy object cradled under one arm that I recognized as one of Mom's highly prized, highly illegal jammers. If we were caught with it, we'd be looking at a nice long stay in prison... assuming we lived long enough to get there, which seemed less than likely. But Becks was laughing when we reached the van, adrenaline and exhaustion bubbling over, and I joined in, and we threw ourselves inside just as soon as we could get the locks to disengage.

I didn't even bother to fasten my seat belt before I started the engine and slammed my foot down on the gas. Becks put the jammer on the dashboard, connecting it to the stereo's USB power outlet before turning it on. A soft white-noise whine filled the cab, more psychological than anything else; it was there so we would know the equipment was working.

The sound of sirens was just beginning to split the Berkeley air when we turned the corner, gathering speed all the while, and we were gone.

———

You really can't go home again.

Sometimes, that's a good thing.

Sometimes, when you try, you find out that home isn't there anymore... but that it wasn't only in your head before. Home actually existed. Home wasn't just a dream.

Sometimes, that's the best thing of all.

**—From *Adaptive Immunities*,
the blog of Shaun Mason, July 28, 2041. Unpublished.**

———

Seattle is gray, damp, and far too proud of being surrounded on all sides by trees which never lose their leaves and hence, never stop providing cover for whatever might be lurking behind them. The natives are as friendly as any Americans, and tend to become extremely helpful when I produce my passport. "I'm an Indian citizen" carries a lot of weight here.

I'm worried about Maggie. We have yet to bribe our way in to see the Monkey, and she's not doing well with all this secrecy and illicit trafficking. I would have said Alaric was the weak link in our particular chain, with his sister as a possible hostage to his good behavior, but I am beginning to fear our dear Magdalene might be just as easily swayed with the promise of a return to her "real life"...

—From *Fish and Clips*,
the blog of Mahir Gowda, July 28, 2041. Unpublished.

Fifteen

I was left mostly to my own devices after the alarm. That was a good thing; my headache got steadily worse once Gregory's painkillers wore off. I wasn't willing to ask the orderlies for anything else, and I couldn't exactly ring for my buddy the EIS mole. So I spent most of what felt like a day in bed, huddled under the covers and trying to shove my head far enough beneath the pillow to block out the room's ambient light.

Eventually, I managed to go back to sleep. When I woke, my headache was gone. The isolation was another matter. Dr. Thomas didn't appear, and the orderlies who brought my meals were even more perfunctory than usual, like they were performing an unpleasant chore. I considered trying to talk to them, and dismissed it in favor of playing the good little clone, tractable, meek, and willing to be told where to sit, what to eat, and when to go to the bathroom. None of them appeared more than once, and I could see the guards waiting in the hall when the door slid open to allow the orderlies in or out.

That was enough to worry me. Were the guards there because they thought I might be smart enough to get wind of what was coming? Had some other clone of Georgia Mason seen the writing on the wall when her decommissioning approached, and tried to make a break for it? Or had Gregory slipped somehow—was our window not as secure as he thought it was, did he say the wrong thing, did he get *caught*? Were the guards there because the plan to bust me out, sketchy as it was, had been blown?

I realized the fear was irrational almost as soon as I finished figuring out what it was. I still had my gun. If Gregory had been caught, someone would have come to take my gun. As long as I was armed, I had to make myself assume that things were going as planned...whatever that plan turned out to actually be.

The next "day" inched by at a glacial pace. By the time dinner came, I was virtually climbing the walls. I forced myself to sit on the bed, holding as still as I could, and tried to focus on what I knew about the layout of the facility. I'd seen plenty of labs, but I didn't have a good idea of where they were relative to one another—the identical halls and rapid walk-throughs had seen to that. If I managed to get out of here, I'd be flying blind unless I had someone to escort me. All of which brought me back to Gregory, and the increasingly pressing question of where he was.

Another unfamiliar orderly brought my lunch, a truly uninspiring combination of cheese slices, soy spread, and sliced bread. "The catering has definitely gone downhill around here," I called after his retreating back. My stomach rumbled, making it clear that no matter how lousy the food looked, I was damn well going to eat it. I needed to keep my strength up.

The cheese was as bland as I'd expected. After the second bite, I started to doubt that it was even cheese, since it tasted more like a blend of soy and artificial flavorings. I wrinkled my nose and kept eating. Cheese meant protein, even if it didn't necessarily mean dairy, and protein was a good thing. That thought was almost enough to motivate me through the rest of the plate before I lost all interest, picked up the bread, and retreated with it to the bed. Who cared if I got a few crumbs in the sheets? It wasn't like there was anyone here to complain about them.

For some reason, that made me wonder if any of the Georgia Masons who came before me tried to seduce an orderly when they hit the last days of their captivity. The image was enough to make me snort with involuntary laughter. It wasn't just that I had no idea how to go about seducing somebody—seduction was never exactly required, given my particular set of circumstances. It was the idea of any of those stiff, buttoned-down orderlies trying to explain that dinner didn't come with a side order of clone sex.

Hell, maybe one of the other Georgias even made a play for Dr. Thomas. That would certainly explain why he was so careful to avoid physical contact, even now that we were well past the point of needing to worry about spontaneous amplification. Maybe he was afraid I'd rip my pajama top open and start trying to buy my freedom.

I was still snickering when the door slid open and a slim blonde woman in a lab coat stepped into my room. "Did I come at a bad time, Georgia?" asked Dr. Shaw. "I can come back later, if you would prefer."

I jumped to my feet, dropping my bread. "Dr. Shaw," I said. "I wasn't expecting you today." Or here. Or ever.

"There are times one must enjoy the privileges of surprise," she said.

"Have you finished your lunch? I do apologize for the blandness of the ingredients, but I was unable to come and brief you before your afternoon meal was delivered, and it was important that preparations begin immediately."

My shoulders tensed. I forced them to unlock. *Dr. Shaw is a friend*, I reminded myself. *She gave me the gun. She's not going to do anything to hurt me.* Not unless she had to, anyway. "Preparations?" I asked.

"Yes," she said, and smiled. She was gorgeous when she smiled. Not beautiful; gorgeous, like the cam-girl porn bloggers who make a living on looks and panty shots. Maybe that was the reason she didn't smile much. Save them up, and use them like weapons when she needed them. "I finally got approval for my deep-state sleep study. They would probably have dragged their feet on me longer, but Dr. Thomas has proposed a series of tests that will occupy all your time as of next week, and that gave me the leverage I needed to convince our superiors to let me have you until then." She paused, clearly expecting something from me.

"Um...yay?"

"Yes," she said, with an enthusiastic nod. "Very 'yay.' This is going to tell us so *much* about your mental state, Georgia. There are things to be discovered by examining your subconscious that, well...I won't bore you with details, but suffice to say that I expect us to both be very pleased with my results. Now, I am afraid you may be slightly inconvenienced by what has to be done..." She let the sentence trail off, again waiting for my reply.

This time, I was faster on my cue. "Inconvenienced how, exactly?"

"You'll be sleeping in my lab for the duration. I realize it's an invasion of your privacy, but it can't be avoided if we want to get good results."

I managed not to laugh at the notion of my possessing anything remotely resembling "privacy" in the room I'd been sleeping in. "I think I can handle it."

"Thank you," said Dr. Shaw. Her smile faded, replaced by her more familiar chilly professionalism. "Is there anything you'd like to bring with you?"

I blinked. I hadn't realized she meant we'd be leaving the room *now*. "No," I said, with complete honesty. My gun was tucked into the top of my left sock, and I'd long since finished reading the few books I'd been able to cajole Dr. Thomas into giving me. Nothing else here was mine. They could decant the next girl and put her in this room, and she'd never know I'd existed, just like I woke up not knowing there had been others here before me.

The thought was sobering. One way or another, I was never going to come back here. Either I'd get out, or I'd just be gone, and no one would miss me, or mourn for me, except for maybe Gregory. Maybe not even him. Assuming his cover hadn't been blown, he'd probably be busy trying to find out whether the new Georgia Mason was the one he could finally save.

"Good," said Dr. Shaw, breaking me out of the dark spiral of my own thoughts. "If there's nothing here you'd like to bring, then we're ready to begin."

"I didn't have anything else on my calendar for today," I said. Dr. Shaw started for the door. I followed, resisting the urge to look back at the room that was never mine, not really. It was a stopping point, and yet somehow, walking through the door with her felt very, very final.

Two of the technicians from our first round of tests were waiting for us in the hall, along with two guards I didn't recognize. I was getting used to that. I focused my attention on the technicians, smiling as earnestly as I could. "Kathleen. George. It's good to see you again."

"See?" crowed Kathleen, bouncing in place. The guards looked at her with visible discomfort but didn't move from their positions. "I told you the sleep studies would get approved!"

"I should never have doubted you," I said.

"You're looking...well," said George.

"I've had lots of rest," I said.

"Which is excellent for our purposes," said Dr. Shaw. "Now that we're all acquainted again, come along. We have much to do, and little time in which to do it." This said, she turned and strode down the hall, her heels punctuating each step with a gunshot-crisp crack. Kathleen and George fell into step behind her, and I trailed after them, with the guards following after me. Their presence kept me from getting too relaxed. This might be a step toward freedom, but I wasn't in the clear yet.

Dr. Shaw led us down the hall toward the lab where her first round of tests on me had been conducted, stopping at an unmarked door. "You are no longer required," she informed the guards, holding up her ID badge. "I assure you, the automated systems will make sure nothing untoward happens between here and our final destination."

"Our apologies, Dr. Shaw, but we have our orders," said the elder of the two guards, a tall, Hispanic man with a thin mustache covering his upper lip. He looked less nervous than his companion. Maybe that's why he got the unenviable job of telling Dr. Shaw he wasn't going to do what she wanted him to do. "We are to escort the subject to your lab and ensure that she's secured before we leave our posts."

"Bureaucracy will be the death of us all," muttered Dr. Shaw, with what looked like sincere annoyance. "Very well, then, if you must. But if either of you so much as breathes on something you shouldn't, the cost of decontamination will be coming out of your paychecks, and I *will* be speaking to your supervisors. Do I make myself clear?" Kathleen and George stepped up to flank us, presenting a united line. I was the only one not wearing a lab coat. For some reason, that struck me as funny.

The guards looked more uncomfortable than ever, but they stood their ground. I almost had to respect that. "Perfectly, ma'am," said the older guard. "We're just doing our jobs."

"Yes, well, I believe you've established *that*." She swiped her badge down the front of a magnetic scanner in the wall. The scanner beeped once. The door in front of us didn't budge; instead, a door on the other side of the hall swung open. The guards turned. Dr. Shaw looked smug. "Gentlemen, if you're so intent on managing my patient's welfare, you can lead the way."

I frowned at the expression on her face. Then I looked through the open door, and my frown struggled to become a smile.

The door opened in what appeared to be the side of a hall. A sign was posted on the wall visible through the opening—Caution: Active biohazard labs beyond this point. Contamination risk is set at Biosafety Level 3. Do not proceed without appropriate clearance. Beneath that, some joker had taped a printout reading "So come on in, and kiss your ass good-bye."

"Ma'am?" asked the older guard.

"I realize you've been working primarily in Level 1 and 2 areas, but my primary lab is maintained in the Level 3 wing." Dr. Shaw glanced to me as she spoke, giving me a brief but meaningful look that chased away any doubts I may have had about my fate. If I were still Dr. Thomas's pet subject, he would never have let me enter a Level 3 biohazard lab. He approved this. He was done with me.

All CDC properties start at Level 1, including the bathrooms and reception areas. No special training or equipment is needed to enter one. Level 1 biohazard facilities work with agents that don't harm healthy adult humans. Level 2 biohazard facilities work with things that *can* harm healthy adult humans, and will usually have some precautions in place to deal with contamination. It's only once you hit Level 3 that you start needing major protective gear. With the door standing open, I could hear the faint hiss of air being drawn into the hall, caught by the negative pressure filters. Airborne dangers could get in, but they would never make it out.

The guards stared at the sign. Dr. Shaw cleared her throat. "Gentlemen?"

The younger guard actually jumped. "Ma'am?" he asked.

"I realize you're simply trying to do your jobs, but I assure you, no amount of staring at the wall will get us to my lab. Can we proceed?"

"Just a moment." The older guard murmured something to his companion before raising a hand and tapping the skin behind his ear. "I'll be right back with you."

"Subdermal communications implant," I muttered. "Slick." Buffy would have loved to get her hands on one of those. With the way I went through the ear cuffs I used to contact my team, something subdermal would have—would have—

I touched the top edge of my left ear, where my ear cuff should have been. I hadn't even thought about it since waking up, and now that I remembered it, I felt naked without it. Somehow, I found that reassuring. It was one more piece of evidence that I was still me, even if I was someone else at the same time. For the first time, I felt myself feeling sorry for the Georgia Masons who had been cloned, studied, and killed before me. How many of them ever knew they weren't the woman they thought they were? How many of them touched their ears, feeling naked and wondering whether they'd get the chance to be properly clothed ever again?

I hoped none of them. If they hadn't been able to escape—and clearly, they hadn't, because I wouldn't have been here if they had—then there was no reason they should ever have needed to feel like this.

The guard finished his muffled conversation with whoever was on the other side of his connection and turned to face Dr. Shaw, tapping the skin behind his ear one more time as he did. "I apologize for any delays we have caused you," he said, stiffening to ramrod-straight attention. "My superior informs me that you have security of your own beyond this point, and that our services will not be required."

"Thank you for confirming that," said Dr. Shaw, with a smile that could have been used to chill water. "Now, if you gentlemen would please let us pass, I have a series of tests to begin."

"Of course." The older guard stayed where he was. The younger stepped out of Dr. Shaw's way as she advanced toward the door. He mumbled something that could have been "Ma'am," or could have been a short prayer of thanks. I didn't hear it clearly, and I didn't care. We were getting away from the guards. That was what really mattered here.

Kathleen entered first, followed by George, Dr. Shaw, and finally, me.

The door slid shut behind us as soon as my heel cleared the doorway. Dr. Shaw reached out and pulled the piece of paper off the bottom of the sign, folding it neatly and tucking it into the pocket of her lab coat.

"Never underestimate the power of a man's fear, Georgia," she said, sounding almost distracted, like part of her was no longer paying attention. "Level 3 labs are no more dangerous to the well prepared than eating at an Indian take-out. Yet somehow, just the name is enough to strike fear into the hearts of man, even though each and every one of us is a walking Level 4 biosafety lab in this brave new world we've created."

"Words have power," I said.

"True." She shook her head. "Well. This way, please." She began to walk briskly down the hall, heels cracking hard against the tile.

Kathleen and George exchanged a look. "Excuse me, Doctor?" called Kathleen.

"Yes? What is it?"

"Do you want us to come with you, or do you want us to initiate cleanup procedures in lab bay two? You're going to need it later tonight."

Dr. Shaw paused, head tilted at what was clearly a contemplative angle, even when viewed from behind. Finally, she nodded. "Yes; that sounds like the correct course of action. Georgia, come with me. We really *do* need to get started." She started walking again, not looking back. I hurried after her.

We passed through three more doors, each of which Dr. Shaw opened with a swipe of her key card. The second door also required a fingerprint check; the third was equipped with a retinal scanner. This was starting to look less like a Level 3 biosafety facility, and more like some sort of maximum security prison for the infected. The distant, steady hiss of the negative pressure filters just made that thought more difficult to shake off.

I was getting distinctly uneasy by the time we reached the fourth door. This one was flanked by blood test units that looked disarmingly like the ones we had in the garage back in the house in Berkeley. "You'll need to provide a sample for analysis," said Dr. Shaw. "It's just a technicality, at this point in the facility, but it came with the security system, and we couldn't disarm it without deactivating several other functions."

"What functions?" I asked, moving toward the testing unit on the left.

"All will be made clear shortly." She slapped her palm flat against the right-hand testing unit, cleared her throat, and said, "Identification, Danika Michelle Kimberley, authorization beta alpha zeta nine four nine two three. Designation, investigative physician. Affiliation, Epidemic Intelligence

Service." Her accent was suddenly British, softer than Mahir's, with a rolling edge that I'd heard only from bloggers who lived and broadcast near the Welsh border.

I stared at her. "What—?"

"You are accompanied," said a bland, pleasant male voice from a speaker set somewhere above the door. "Please identify your associate."

"This is Georgia Carolyn Mason, version 7c. Designation, electronic journalist, human clone, presently listed as deceased in the main network. Affiliation, Epidemic Intelligence Service." Dr. Shaw—Dr. Kimberley—sounded calm, and slightly bored, like she was reciting a shopping list. "Georgia, put your hand on the panel, if you would? I'd rather not be standing here when the security system decides we're a threat and floods the hall with formalin."

"Uh. No. That would be bad." I pressed my hand against the flat testing panel, feeling the brief sting as the needles bit into my palm. A cool blast of antiseptic foam was released through a slit in the metal, cooling the small wounds the needles had left behind, and the light above the door began to flash, red to yellow to green and back again. The light stabilized quickly on green, and the door unlocked with a click.

"Ah, good," said Dr. Kimberley. "Come along, Georgia." She pulled her hand away from the test panel and pushed the door open, revealing yet another standard-issue CDC lab.

Well. Standard issue except for the three technicians who were standing just inside with guns in their hands, aiming them at the door. I recognized the one in the middle as James, from Dr. Shaw's—Dr. Kimberley's—other lab. The others were new to me.

Dr. Kimberley sighed. "Oh, yay," she said, deadpan. "This is quite my favorite part. Is it Tuesday? It's Tuesday, isn't it?"

"Yes, Dr. Kimberley," confirmed the technician on the left, a curvy, medium-height girl with a riot of carroty-red curls barely confined by her headband.

"Brilliant. In that case..." Dr. Kimberley pointed to the girl. "Matriculate." She turned and pointed to James. "Alabaster." She turned again, pointing to the tall, dark-skinned man on the end. "Polyhedral."

All three technicians lowered their guns. "Glad to have you back, Dr. Kimberley," said James. "Did you encounter any trouble?"

"None that couldn't be handled." Dr. Kimberley turned to me, offering a small, almost apologetic smile. "I was able to depart with what we needed, and that's what matters. In the meanwhile... Georgia, I do apologize."

"What?" I blinked at her. Maybe it was everything I'd been through in the past few days, but I was suddenly afraid I'd trusted the wrong people. "What are you talking a—"

And then the syringe bit into the back of my arm, and the world, such as it was, fell away, leaving me in darkness.

Acquisition of the subject has been successful. We will begin analysis immediately. If Gregory is correct, and she is truly close enough to the original to be viable for our purposes, well...

I can only hope she'll find it in her heart to forgive us for what we must do. Expect further communication as soon as possible.

**—Taken from a message sent by Dr. Danika Kimberley,
July 31, 2041. Recipient unknown.**

Ms. Hyland is gone. All the chaperones are gone. It's just us kids now, and I don't know how much longer the food will last...us kids, and the soldiers outside. They don't let us out of the building, even during the day, even if we promise to wear lots and lots of bug spray. There isn't any hot water. Some of the soldiers are going away. I don't know what's going on. I just know that I'm scared. Hurry, Alaric. Please, hurry.

I don't know how much longer this can last. But I don't think it's going to be long enough, if you don't hurry.

My batteries are dying. I may not be able to write for much longer. Hurry.

**—Taken from an e-mail sent by Alisa Kwong to Alaric Kwong,
July 31, 2041.**

Sixteen

The drive from Berkeley to Seattle takes fourteen hours if you use major roads and avoid serious traffic. It takes twenty-three hours if you stick to back routes and frontage roads. We split the difference, risking our cover several times in order to eke out a few hundred miles on I-5 before returning to the shadows, and made it from city to city in just under nineteen hours.

We didn't stop in Shady Cove. Tempting as it was, there was too good a chance that we were being followed—and too good a chance that if we stopped there, we'd never leave again. Dr. Abbey tried to send us to the Florida hazard zone, and we failed. Fine. Barring another way to do the same thing, she'd probably insist we stay and start looking for a way to evacuate us all to someplace that was guaranteed to stay mosquito-free.

"I hear Alaska's nice this time of year," I muttered.

"What's that?" George looked up, blinking still-unfamiliar brown eyes at me in honest confusion.

"Just wondering where we could run when this is over. The mosquitoes are going to be pretty damn hard to kill."

"Maybe." She shrugged, returning to her study of the jamming unit. A lock of her hair—it was starting to need a trim—flopped forward, falling in front of one eye. I resisted the urge to lean over and brush it aside. Unless I was having a really crazy day, she'd just vanish if I tried to touch her, and I needed the company too much to have her leave again. Becks had been asleep in the back since we crossed the border into Washington. Without my hallucinatory sister, I would be totally alone, and I wasn't sure how much longer my own wakefulness would last.

"What do you mean, 'maybe'?" I asked.

"Like Dr. Abbey said, an insect vector for Kellis-Amberlee didn't just *happen*. They're probably the product of some lab like hers, full of scientists who think 'I wanted to see what would happen' is a perfectly valid justification for doing anything they want."

"Yeah, and?"

George looked up again, brushing the hair out of her eyes with a quick, economical wave of one hand. This time, she looked almost annoyed. "Shaun. You *know* this. There's nothing I can tell you that you don't already know. Why are you pretending you need me to say it?"

"Because I'm not pretending." I shrugged, trying to keep my attention focused on the road. I didn't want to get so wrapped up in arguing with her that I needed to pull over; not only would that potentially attract attention, but it would annoy the hell out of Becks if she woke up before we started moving again. "Maybe you can't tell me things I don't know, but I *need* you to be the one who says them. That lets me believe in them."

"You are a strange, sick little man, Shaun Mason." George sighed. "The mosquitoes were made. Man's creation, just like Kellis-Amberlee. If you were going to build killer bugs to spread the zombie plague, wouldn't you put in a little planned obsolescence?"

Despite the fact that George could only use words I knew the meaning of, I had to pause while I tried to remember what "obsolescence" meant. Sometimes it's annoying having hallucinations that make me feel dumb. "You mean they'd be built to break down?"

"Now you're thinking. I have to wonder whether the mosquitoes are fertile. If someone built them as a biological weapon, why would they have given them the capacity to breed? All that's going to do is increase the chances of them hurting the people you're trying to protect."

"So how did they wind up in Cuba?"

"Weapons test. Cuba did too well during the Rising. It was almost insulting to certain people. I'm sure they would have loved the opportunity to run a little fear-inducing trial on soil close enough to ours that they could look horrified and appalled when someone implied we might have had something to do with it."

"George..."

"I'm not being nihilistic, Shaun. I'm being *right*, and you know it."

"Yeah." I glanced out the window at the high concrete fence dividing the tiny back road we were on from the safe concrete river of I-5. "I just wish I'd stop reminding myself."

George was gone when I looked back. I shook my head, trying to clear the malaise brought on by her last statement, and turned the radio on, scanning channels until I found something with a catchy beat and simplistic lyrics. Then I switched to NPR.

National Public Radio is a dinosaur in the modern age of podcasts and Internet radio stations, but that's part of what makes it useful, because when you turn on NPR, you're getting the thoughts and opinions of the part of the population that has not yet moved into a purely virtual format. Things still move a little slower there. Not predigitally slow—I've read the history books, I know how long a single story used to dominate the cycle—but slow enough that you can learn a thing or two, if you're willing to listen.

Two experts were arguing about ways to save the Everglades. One wanted to send in CDC teams in full-on moon suits to rescue as many noninfected animals as possible, and then dump enough DDT into the water table to sterilize the ecosystem for a hundred years. "We can breed them in preserves and exhibits until we confirm that the Everglades are safe, and then return them to their original environment," was the gist of his argument, wedded to a firm belief that instinct would override generations of zoo-bound living and lead to an immediate, complete return to the wild as soon as the money ran out and somebody in accounting decided it was time to let the animals go.

The other expert claimed this would result not only in the permanent loss of a major piece of America's biological diversity, but render most of Florida uninhabitable whether we got rid of the mosquitoes or not, since pesticide would inevitably get into the human water supply. He was in favor of releasing thousands of insectivores into the impacted areas and letting them take care of things the natural way. And by "insectivores," he meant "bats." He wanted to gather as many bats as possible and dump them on the Everglades, where they could do their batty thing and eat all the mosquitoes. Because the people of Florida would, of course, be totally cool with this.

At no point did either of them mention the idea that the mosquitoes had been *made*, rather than being a natural worst-case scenario. All their solutions started from the premise that the mosquitoes just happened, much like the storm that brought them to our shores. Somehow, that only made me more certain that George was right. Somebody made these mosquitoes, and somebody was going to have a way to deal with them. They were just waiting for the time to be right, just like they'd waited for the time to be right before letting the bugs out of the box in the first place.

Becks climbed back into her seat right about the time the speakers got really involved in yelling at each other. Yawning and rumpling her hair with one hand, she squinted at the radio. "Do I wanna know?"

"I can't get a good wireless signal out here," I said. "So we're listening to the radio."

"Listening to the radio talk about *what*?"

"Bats."

Becks frowned, still clearly half asleep. "Bats?"

"Yeah. You know, flap flap, squeak squeak, works for Dracula? Bats. Because we need a vampire problem to go with our zombie problem." I opened the cooler we had wedged between the seats, pulling out a can of Coke. "Here. You look like you could use the caffeine."

"Oh, thank God. I thought I was going to have to deal with this without chemical assistance." Becks popped the tab before downing half the soda in one long slug. She didn't seem to realize what she was drinking until she lowered the can and blinked at the label. "Shaun...this is a Coke."

"I know."

"You gave me one of your Cokes."

"I know."

"Why did you...?"

"Because you needed it." I glanced her way, smiling just a little—just enough to show her I meant it. "If the Masons can let us go and agree to get Alisa out of Florida, I can be selfless enough to give you a can of Coke."

Becks's expression sobered. "Do you really think they'll go after her?"

"I do, yeah." The experts on NPR were still arguing. I leaned forward and turned the radio down. "I don't think they've changed completely. I mean, knowing Mom, she's probably already convinced herself I cheated by bringing up Phillip, and that she and Dad let us go out of the goodness of their hearts, not because it was the right thing to do. But rescuing a little girl from a refugee camp in an interdicted hazard zone? That's the kind of ratings you can't buy. It's just gravy that they have that whole martial law thing going on over there, which gives Dad an excuse to trot out a bunch of old chatter about personal responsibility and freedom of the press."

"So they're going to do it for the ratings." Becks's mouth twisted into a disapproving line. She took another large gulp of Coke, presumably to stop herself from saying anything she'd regret later.

It didn't matter. There was nothing she could say that I hadn't heard before. Some of it I had heard from George. Some of it I had said myself. "There are worse reasons, and the fact that they're always in the public eye means that if they get her back to Berkeley, they can't mistreat her. They can be themselves, which is bad enough, but Alisa's older than George and I were when they took us in. She'll be fine until Alaric can get there and take her away from them."

"You're willing to count on that?"

"I don't think we have much of a choice. We can't head for Florida. We'd never make it past the barricades. We need to get to the rest of the team and regroup."

"How long before we reach Seattle?"

"We're about twenty miles out. I figure I'll try calling Mahir right before we hit the city limits—if he picks up, we can go straight to where he is, and not need to keep the connection open."

"And if he doesn't?" Becks asked, taking a smaller sip of her soda.

"I have no idea. I'm sort of making all this up as I go along, you know."

You're doing an excellent job.

"Thank you," I said automatically, and winced.

Becks politely ignored my slip. "I know you are. I don't envy you the lead on this story."

"Hey, it's worked so far. What are you going to do when we meet the Monkey? You could be anyone. What's your new identity going to be?"

"I think I'll be an Internet journalist." She smiled. "I understand they don't need much in the way of training. Or brains. How about you?"

"I'm going to ask for anything that lets me disappear." I kept my eyes on the road. "This is going to end soon, Becks. It's gone too far to last much longer. Too many people have died. So if I get through this story alive...I just want to be left alone."

"You want to be alone with George," said Becks.

"Maybe."

"I don't...Shaun, I..." Becks paused, taking a breath. "You know I love you, right? As a friend. I may have loved you as something more once, but that's over now. You know that."

"I do."

"So it's as a friend, and as a colleague, that I ask...are you sure? You're not holding on that tightly as it is. Going off to be alone with the voices in your head—"

"It's not just voices anymore. I see her sometimes." That stopped her. I continued. "She was sitting in that seat not long before you woke up. We were talking. If I get deep enough into the conversation, if I forget long enough, sometimes I can even feel her. I'm *going* to wind up alone with the voices in my head. The only question is whether or not I get the rest of you hurt in the process. Mahir was Georgia's second. You're mine. You know how badly I could fuck everything up if I refused to let go. So let me plan to let go. It might help me hold on a little longer."

Becks sighed. "You're asking me to help you turn into a crazy hermit living in the mountains somewhere."

"Yeah. I am."

"As long as you realize it." She slumped in her seat, giving the jamming device a light smack with the heel of her hand. "How does this damn thing work, anyway?"

"You want the technical answer, or the honest answer?" I paused. "Actually, those are the same answer."

"Shoot."

"I have no fucking clue. Buffy was always real impressed with it, I know that; she wanted to build one for us, but other stuff kept getting in the way, and then we were working for a presidential hopeful, so it didn't seem like a good political move." And then she was dead, and she wasn't going to be building anything for anybody. Things would have gone so differently if she'd lived. She would have seen what was happening and turned on the conspiracy that had turned her against us, and all this might already be over. George might still be alive. And I might not be looking forward to going all the way insane.

"It was nice of the Masons to give it to us."

"Yeah, it was. I figure we'll kill it with a hammer as soon as it's served its purpose." Becks shot me a scandalized look. I shook my head. "You really think they don't have some sort of a tracking beacon in this thing? Buffy built alarms into the van security system that would have gone off if it were broadcasting—she had to reprogram them not to go off when Maggie got too close, since her parents have her rigged up with 'do not abduct' heiress crap. So I figure they're just waiting until we stop moving long enough that they can assume we're not in the vehicle anymore, and then they're going to start pinging our position."

Becks stared at me. "If they're planning to use the thing to track us, why did you let me take it?"

"Because it was the only thing that would get us out of Berkeley. Even if the Masons just called the local cops on us, they'd be turning on every tracking chip they could think of as soon as we ran. And I somehow doubt they just called the local cops—or called them at all."

"Why?"

"It took too long for them to get there. There's a police station less than eight blocks away. My parents were turning us in for the ratings, remember? They called the CDC. It's the only thing that makes sense." It explained both the delay in their arrival, and why the Masons listened when I said they were making a mistake. The CDC is still the government, and after what happened during the Ryman campaign, trusting them might not have come as easy as it once did.

"Right." Becks sighed and slumped in her seat. Then she leaned forward and turned the radio back up, signaling that she was done talking for the moment. I smiled a little, catching her meaning, and returned my focus to the road.

Things are almost over, murmured George.

"I know," I said, and kept driving.

The outskirts of Seattle loomed up with surprising speed; the relative obscurity of the roads we'd been taking meant that there was minimal traffic. I dug a burner ear cuff out of my pocket, snapping it on. A tap triggered the connection. "This is Shaun Mason activating security profile Pardy. Something's wrong with Brenda, we're out of Mister Pibb, and hunting season's here. Now let's go to Hollywood."

"Your taste in passwords is crap," commented Becks.

I made a shushing motion. Mahir picked up after two rings, asking, "Oh, thank God. Shaun? Is that you?"

"If it weren't, somebody would have just gotten really, really lucky trying to turn this thing on. Where are you guys?"

Mahir's voice turned instantly suspicious. "Why?"

"Because we've just reached Seattle, and we'd like to come join you. Especially if wherever you are has a bathroom. Is there a bathroom? Please tell me there's a bathroom. We've been driving for like, twenty hours, and I need to piss like you wouldn't believe."

"TMI, Shaun," said Becks.

"How did you get out of Berkeley?"

"Wait, what?" Now it was my turn to get suspicious. "What are you talking about?"

"Several local Berkeley bloggers posted yesterday morning about a surprise CDC hazard team drill being run in a residential neighborhood—and their target was your family home. The Masons have even posted about it. They said they were glad to cooperate with anything that might improve safety procedures and response times." He paused before adding, grimly, "We thought they might have turned you in."

I sighed. "They kind of did. They just changed their minds before things could go all the way horribly wrong. How did they look?"

"Your mum had a black eye—"

"Yeah, I gave her that."

"—and a broken arm. Your dad just had some taped-up fingers."

"What?" I demanded. "I didn't do *that*. Neither did Becks. The black eye was so it would be believable when they said we got away."

"Apparently, it wasn't believable enough for the CDC. Snap your transmitter to the GPS, I'll send you the address for our hotel. Wipe it as soon as you get here."

"Done. See you soon, Mahir."

"One hopes," he said.

I removed the cuff from my ear and handed it to Becks. "Here—connect this to the GPS. Mahir's going to send us directions on how to get to the hotel he and Maggie are staying at. Keep the jammer going. The Masons made the news."

"What?" Becks glanced at me in confusion as she connected the ear cuff to the GPS. The GPS unit beeped and began to display its "loading" screen.

"Mom has a broken arm. Dad has some broken fingers. Think they tripped and fell after we left the house?" I gripped the wheel harder than necessary, resisting the urge to slam my foot down on the gas and race my anger away. "The fucking CDC, Becks. My parents called the fucking CDC and said we'd be waiting for them, gift-wrapped and unsuspecting, and when we weren't there, the fucking CDC showed their disappointment."

"You can't be sure it was the CDC."

"That's what the blogs are saying. They're calling it a training exercise. As in, 'The CDC decided to train their employees on beating the crap out of my parents.'" My fingers clenched even tighter. "Those fuckers. They had no right."

"Ahead, turn left," said the GPS.

Do it, said George.

I turned left.

"This is insane," said Becks. "What the hell is going on here? What did we *do*?"

"Honestly? I don't know anymore." Something in my face must have told her to let it be. Becks shook her head, settling in her seat. After a moment's hesitation, she drew one of her pistols, resting it against her thigh below the window's sight line. If someone decided to use us for a "training exercise," they weren't going to find us as off guard as they might have liked.

The GPS led us through a maze of side streets to what looked like a relatively major road, one that led us away from downtown and toward the less densely populated residential areas. The buildings took on a dilapidated look as we crossed from one zone into the next... and then, abruptly, began to improve, until we were passing well-maintained mini-mansions surrounded by high fences instead of tenement apartment buildings. Some of them even had their own private gatehouses. The convenience stores and their kin were replaced by upscale grocery stores, fancy salons, and dry cleaners whose signs boasted zero-contact door-to-door service. There were no blood tests on the corners; instead, men on motorized scooters patrolled the sidewalks, running checks on anyone who wanted to get out of a vehicle.

More tellingly, as we drove deeper into the clearly wealthy part of town, people began appearing on the sidewalks. Some of them were walking small dogs, like Maggie's teacup bulldogs, or the more traditional pugs and Pomeranians. Others had cats on leashes. We even passed a couple with one of those bizarre tame Siberian foxes trotting at their heels, its bushy tail low and its triangular ears pricked forward as it scanned its surroundings for danger.

"This can't be right," said Becks, watching the fox slide out of view. "Check the directions."

"These are the directions Mahir gave me. Maybe they're hiding in someone's attic. I don't know. Wherever they are, they're going to be trying to stay unobtrusive."

"In two hundred yards, you have reached your destination," announced the GPS.

I looked forward. "Oh, fuck."

"You have *got* to be kidding," said Becks.

In front of us loomed the elegant, fenced-in shape of a luxury resort. It looked like it was large enough to host the entire Republican National Convention, assuming anything as gauche as politics were ever allowed to pass its pristine white gates. The guardhouse in front was staffed by four men, their concierge uniforms somehow managing to go perfectly with their assault rifles. Two of them moved out to the street, motioning for me to stop the van.

"There's no way we can reverse fast enough," said Becks. "They have to have cars."

"Or they'd just shoot the windows out." I set the brake. "It was nice knowing you."

"Same here."

The men took positions on either side of the van, one next to my window, one next to Becks's window. The one next to mine raised a white-gloved hand and knocked, deferentially.

Forcing a smile, I lowered the window. "Hi," I said. "What seems to be the problem?"

"No problem, Mr. Mason. We've been expecting you." The man produced a handheld blood-testing unit while I was still gaping at him. "If you would please allow me to verify your current medical state, I would be delighted to explain." On the other side of the van, his companion was making a virtually identical speech to Becks.

"Uh." I stared at him for a moment before focusing on the most disturbing part of that statement. "You've been expecting us?"

"Oh, yes. Miss Garcia contacted the front desk after you called." The man kept smiling. It was starting to make me nervous. "We're thrilled to have you joining us."

"Uh…huh." I took the testing unit, pressing my thumb down on the pressure plate. "Did she threaten your lives, by any chance? Tell you you'd never work in this town again? Cry?"

The man actually laughed. "Oh, no, nothing like that! She simply asked us to meet you at the gates, and to assure you that the Agora Resort is a completely confidential retreat for those who may be in need of more… confidence…in their security."

"Wait—did you say the Agora?" Becks leaned into my field of vision, her right hand still outstretched as she pressed her thumb to her own blood-test unit. "This is the Agora?"

"Yes, Miss Atherton." The man frowned, although his overall air of polite readiness to serve remained. "You've heard of us?"

"My mother stayed here once, when she was younger. She was a Feldman before she got married."

"Ah!" said the man, suddenly all smiles again. "Of the New Hampshire Feldmans?"

"Yes."

"It's a pleasure to have another member of the family with us. I hope we can live up to whatever fond memories she may have shared with you." He deftly plucked the test unit from my hand, holding it up to show the green light that had come on at the top. "You are, as expected, clean. Welcome to the Agora, Mr. Mason. I, and the rest of the concierge staff, am pleased to serve."

"Um, thanks?" I looked from Becks—who was being shown her own clean test unit—to the concierge, not bothering to conceal my confusion. "What happens now?"

"Now you enter. A valet will take your van"—he paused as my hands tightened on the wheel—"or not, as you prefer. Your party is waiting for you in the lobby." He stepped back. His partner did the same, and the gates in front of us swung slowly open.

Becks put a hand over mine. "It's okay," she said. "I've heard of this place."

"So?"

"So I wouldn't have if my mother hadn't stayed here. You need so many zeroes in your bank account to get in that there are *presidents* who never stayed here." Becks pulled her hand away. "They believe in discretion above pretty much all else. Now let's go."

"You're the boss." I started the engine.

Becks smirked. "I like the sound of that."

"Yeah, thought you might."

Getting past the valet without ceding the keys was easier than I'd expected. Every place I'd ever seen that was even remotely like this had been staffed by people who were so desperate for tips that they'd do anything to guarantee them—as long as "anything" didn't involve coming close enough to actually touch another human being. There's a commonly held belief that people who work in the hospitality industry are less paranoid about strangers than the rest of us. I'd almost been able to buy it, until I stayed in a few hotels and saw how careful the staff was to avoid touching the guests. It was almost funny, except for the part where it was so damn sad.

George theorized once that the people who worked in hospitality were even *more* afraid of other human beings than the average man on the street. "This way they never get attached to anyone," she'd said. "People come and go. They don't stay long enough to become anything but names on a ledger. There's no sense of loss when there's nothing to lose."

The Agora was disturbingly different. The valet's smile when I said I'd rather park myself seemed sincere, and the garage maintained for self-park vehicles was large, spacious, and well lit, with emergency doors located every fifteen feet along the walls. The bellhop who opened the hotel's main door for us was also smiling, and kept smiling even when it became apparent that our days on the road didn't leave us exactly minty fresh. And neither of them held out a hand for a tip.

"This is weird," I muttered to Becks, once I was sure we were far enough past the guy for my comment to go unheard.

"This is wealth," she replied, and slapped her palm flat on the test sensor that would open the airlock separating the outer ring of the hotel from the main lobby. I did the same. The doors swished open a second later, allowing us both to step through.

"Welcome, Mr. Mason. Welcome, Miss Atherton," said a polite female voice. "The Agora recommends that you make use of our lavish guest facilities. A hot bath has already been drawn in your rooms. We're glad that you're here." The door on the other side of the airlock slid open, and the main lobby was revealed for the first time.

Now that's just overkill, commented George.

"You took the words right out of my mouth," I said, and followed Becks out of the airlock.

The Agora lobby was decorated in shades of white and blue. It looked like the interior of the world's most expensive glacier. A piano was tucked away into one corner, half blocked from view by tall plants with broad green leaves and trumpet-shaped blue flowers. The sound of the unseen pianist's playing echoed through the room, soft enough not to be distracting, yet somehow unpredictable enough to make it clear that there was a live person at the keys. The front desk was set just to the side of a curved flight of stairs leading to the second floor.

Maggie and Mahir were standing near the center of the lobby, talking quietly. They looked around when the airlock door slid shut behind us. "Shaun! Becks!" exclaimed Maggie, the volume of her voice seeming inappropriate in this overly rarified atmosphere. "You made it!" She started toward us at a trot, Mahir following behind somewhat more slowly.

"Uh, yeah. We did," I said, transferring my staring to Maggie. "You look…"

"Like the heir to Garcia Pharmaceuticals," she said, and smiled. "You like?"

"Uh…"

Maggie was wearing a tailored blazer over a white lace shirt, no bra, and pants that could have been applied with a spray can. Maybe they were—they've been doing some incredible things with memory polymers in the last few years, and I know canned clothing was one of the things being worked on. Her normally curly, normally braided brown hair was both loose and straight, falling down her back like it had developed its own private gravity. Again, maybe it had. The ways of the obscenely rich are alien to me. Her makeup was elaborate enough that I was certain she hadn't done it herself.

At least she was still wearing sensible shoes, rather than teetering on a pair of impractically high heels. I've heard them called "fuck-me pumps" in some of the pre-Rising media. These days, we call them "get-you-killed heels." I think it's a little more appropriate.

"It's Shaun, Maggie, and you're a girl," said Becks, coming to my rescue. "He has no idea what the safe answer is, and so he's going to vapor lock until you change the subject. Hi. It's good to see you. You look wonderful." She stepped forward, sweeping the head of the After the End Times Fictionals into a hug, which Maggie gladly returned.

Mahir caught my eye and smirked. "Hallo, Mason."

"Hey, Mahir." I shook my head. "Looks like we've both been having an interesting time. I'll see your luxury hotel, and raise you one zombie bear."

"I can see that this is going to be a deeply enlightening evening." He put a hand on my arm. "I've been following the feeds about the Masons. Two of our juniors are covering it, due to the connection to our site's founders. How are you holding up?"

It took me a second to realize that by "our site's founders," he was referring to me and George. "Oh, okay, I guess. Totally out of my mind, but that's normal. Should we be hanging around down here?"

Maggie disengaged from Becks, glancing my way. "Our rooms are on the third floor. Did the Agora tell you about the baths?"

"That depends. When you ask 'did the Agora' tell us, do you mean—"

"The hotel."

"That's what I was afraid you were going to say. Yeah, it told us."

"Good." Maggie looped one arm through Becks's and one arm through mine, tugging us across the lobby toward the elevators. "Let's get you cleaned up and into something that doesn't smell like road funk, and then we can sit down for dinner and to plan our plan of attack for tomorrow."

"Road funk?" I asked.

"Plan of attack?" Becks asked.

Tomorrow? George asked.

"Your timing is impeccable, as always," said Mahir, moving to walk alongside the three of us. "Tomorrow morning we will finally be accomplishing our goal here in the city of Seattle."

"What do you mean?" asked Becks.

Maggie freed an arm long enough to push the elevator "call" button and leaned even closer, whispering conspiratorially, "We're here to meet the Monkey, remember?"

The elevator arrived with a loud *ding* and Maggie stepped inside, waving for the rest of us to follow. After exchanging a look with Becks, I did.

"I think I preferred the zombie bears," I muttered.

"That's just you, Mason," she said, and started laughing. Maggie and Mahir joined in. There was an edge of hysteria to the sound, like they were laughing to hold back the dark. I stood there, feeling the elevator gaining speed beneath us, and held my silence as we rose higher, and closer to the future.

I was never a "poor little rich girl." I had a lot of money, sure, but I also had parents who loved me, and who balanced the urge to give me everything I wanted with instilling me with a strong sense of personal responsibility. I never thought of my money as a burden. The only burden was the way it made people look at me. That was what I couldn't stand, and that's the reason I chose to go into the field I went into. I was good at being a Fictional. I was never that good at being a spoiled brat.

There are things money can't buy. People who love you, a job you're good at, a sense of personal respect...those are on the list.

**—From *Dandelion Mine*,
the blog of Magdalene Grace Garcia, July 31, 2041. Unpublished.**

Buffy was complaining today about how we need a new transmitter for the van, and we can't afford it right now. She wants us to ask the Masons for a loan. She doesn't seem to understand that having parents who are in the media business doesn't mean we can turn to them for every little thing we need. Sure, they'd probably give it to us, but we'd be giving up something a lot more valuable. We'd be giving up our independence. All it's going to take is one loan, and they'll have the leverage they need to start worming their way into our business. They want it. I *know* they want it.

And I am not going to let them have it.

**—From *Postcards from The Wall*,
the unpublished files of Georgia Mason,
originally posted on July 31, 2041.**

Seventeen

G eorgia."
The word was distorted enough to seem unimportant. I didn't
bother trying to respond. I was lying on something soft, it was pleasantly
dark, and if people wanted to talk to me, they could knock themselves out.
Nothing said I had to *answer*.

"She's unresponsive."

"I expected she might be. Let's assume she's awake, and put her back
under for now."

"Are you sure? The strain to her system—"

"We need to finish this."

A needle slid into my arm. The sensation was sharp enough to break
the haze, replacing soft darkness with sudden concern. I opened my eyes,
peering into a blur of light. There were figures there, wearing medical
scrubs, with clear plastic masks over their faces. That just made me more
concerned. What were they doing that might splash them with my bodily
fluids?

"Doctor—" The speaker sounded alarmed. Whatever I was supposed
to do, opening my eyes apparently wasn't on the list.

"I see her. Increase the midazolam drip—I want her *out* until we're
done." The taller of the two figures bent toward me. "Georgia? Can you
hear me?"

I made a sound. It was faint, somewhere between a gasp and a groan.

It was apparently enough. "Increase that dose *now*, Kathleen," snapped
Dr. Kimberley, her features becoming visible through the plastic as she
leaned closer. She raised one blue-gloved hand, brushing my hair away
from my face. "Don't try to move, Georgia. This will all be over soon."

That's what I was afraid of. The room was getting dark around the edges, hard lines turning into soft blurs as whatever they were pumping into me started taking effect. I tried to yell at her, to demand to know what she thought she was doing, but all that emerged was a faint squeak, like a hinge that needed to be oiled.

Dr. Kimberley smiled. "There you are, my dear. Just rest. It will all be over soon." Then she pulled her hand back, and once again, the world went away.

There was no sense of time in the darkness. But Shaun was there, somehow, and he held my hand, and we sat together in the black, and everything was fine, forever and ever and ever.

Or until his hand slipped out of mine, and the blackness began to fade, and I realized my temporary peace had been just another drug-induced lie. Fury flooded through me. How dare they keep playing with me this way? It wasn't right. It wasn't fair. It wasn't—

"Georgia."

Again, the word was blurred and warped by what felt like an immense distance. This time, I forced myself to strain toward it, struggling to open my eyes. Nothing happened. Frustrated, I tried to respond, and again, managed to make only the faintest squeak.

That seemed to be enough. "She's awake, Doctor. Not fully responsive, but recovering."

"Good." I heard the squeak of wheels rolling across a tile floor, followed by the soft compression of a body settling into a chair. "Georgia, this is Dr. Kimberley. I know you're confused, and you may not have an easy time moving, but if you can, please squeeze my hand."

Squeeze her hand? I wasn't even *touching* her hand. Furious, I managed to squeak again.

"Kathleen is getting something to make you feel better, but I need you to work with us. Please squeeze my hand." Her voice was measured, patient; the voice of a doctor who knew you wanted to trust her, because she was the hand that held the scalpel. "You've been under for about seven hours."

Under? Under *where?* I was becoming more aware of my body, which was lying flat on a padded surface. My head was somewhat higher than the rest of me, probably to help my breathing. I strained to focus, clenching my fingers in the process. They hit something yielding.

"Very good!" Dr. Kimberley sounded pleased. The something was pulled from my hand. "Kathleen, inject the solution into her IV line and pass me the stimulants. It's time for our Miss Mason to fully rejoin the living."

I squeaked in fury. If Shaun were here, these people would have been knocked on their asses so fast—

And then a familiar voice spoke, startling me out of my anger: "Is she all right?"

I froze, inasmuch as my current condition distinguished that from my efforts to move. Dr. Kimberley didn't appear to notice. "Yes, Mr. Vice President. The procedure was a success. Barring complications, I'm expecting her to make a full recovery."

"Good." A hand touched my forehead. I strained to open my eyes. "I'm so sorry you've had to go through all of this, George. Now do what you do best. Break this fucking thing wide open, and let the pieces fall."

I moaned. It was the best I could do.

Rick pulled his hand away. "They'll miss me if I stay gone any longer. Pass a message through my office if there are any complications. I want to know immediately. Do you understand?"

"Yes, sir," said Dr. Kimberley.

Sudden pain lanced through me, radiating out from a point somewhere near my heart. I couldn't speak, but I could scream, and scream I did, arching my back away from the mattress beneath me until it felt like I was making a perfect half circle.

"She's convulsing!" shouted Dr. Kimberley. "Trauma cart, *now!*"

Her voice began to slip away at the end, blurring into the general chaos as the dark reached out its tendrils and twined them around me once more. An alarm blared. I screamed again, so hard it felt like something tore inside my throat, and then the world fell away, leaving me to plunge into the black. There was no peace there this time, only pain, pain, *pain*.

Panicked voices in the dark, overlapping with each other: "—losing her, I don't know why, she's—" "—must have missed one—" "—check behind her collarbone—"

And then there was only the dark, so all-consuming it devoured even the pain, and the voices didn't matter anymore. And then there was, for a time, blessed nothing. Nothing at all.

"Georgia."

The third time my name called me out of the dark, it didn't have any blurred edges or comforting distance. It was near, immediate, and spoken with perfect clarity. I groaned, suddenly aware of my body as a part of my consciousness, and of my consciousness as something distinct from the dark.

"...what?" I whispered. Even that much motion triggered a hundred more realizations. I had a mouth; I could speak. My lips were dry, my throat was aching. That was the only pain, at least for the moment.

I was alive.

"How do you feel?" Dr. Kimberley sounded honestly concerned. I've spent enough of my life dealing with doctors to know when they're pretending to care, and she wasn't pretending. The edges of her words—still Welsh-accented; the masks, it seemed, were off for good—were soft and weary, like she hadn't slept for days.

"Water," I whispered.

"You're not dehydrated, but your throat will be dry. We've been feeding you via a tube for the past three days. It was removed about an hour ago. If you can open your eyes, I can give you some water. That's the bargain, I'm afraid. Responsiveness for water."

I opened my eyes. Light lanced into them like knives, and I quickly closed them again. There was a tap against the bridge of my nose as Dr. Kimberley settled something there.

"That will block the worst of it," she said. "I'm afraid we didn't have the equipment to keep reminding your retinas of light. They'll adjust if you give them a little time."

"What…where am I?" I opened my eyes again. This time, the disposable UV-blocker Dr. Kimberley had given me kept the worst of the light from reaching me. The doctor herself was standing in front of my bed, a glass of water in her hand.

"You're still in the Seattle CDC; we've been able to loop footage and falsify results to make it look like you're in my primary lab, but we haven't had any way to remove you from the premises. Not that we could have done so anyway, given the givens." She leaned forward, holding the glass to my lips and tilting it until I could take a few tiny, carefully measured sips. "Slowly, Georgia, slowly. You don't want to aspirate this."

I pulled my head back, coughing a little, and asked, "Why can't you just say 'don't breathe the water' like a normal person?"

"Because I'm a doctor, and they teach us never to use little words where big ones will do." Dr. Kimberley pulled the glass out of my reach. That made me focus on more of the room around us. It was packed with medical monitoring equipment, including an IV that was still anchored to my arm. I looked at it with disgust.

"What *is* all this?"

"It's what's been keeping you alive while we waited for the toxins to finish working their way out of your system." Dr. Kimberley put the glass down atop one of the machines before taking a seat in the chair next to my bed. "Gregory showed you your replacement, did he not?"

"Yes," I rasped.

"Then you'll have seen that they were tailoring her to their requirements. They did the same with you, my dear, although they left your mind basically alone—small mercies, and all of that. They needed you for display. The rest of you was free game."

"And that's why you drugged me?" I was too tired to sound as indignant as I felt. I still gave it my best shot.

"Yes." Dr. Kimberley nodded. "Have you ever heard of the sea wasp jellyfish? It's one of the many nasty surprises lurking in our world's oceans. This one comes from Australia, and has a sting capable of killing an adult human in minutes if untreated."

"So?" I whispered.

"The nice people responsible for making you wanted to be sure nothing akin to what is happening right now would succeed, and they implanted biological explosives at strategic points within your body. They were to burst, given the correct set of stimuli, releasing sea wasp venom into your bloodstream. The only circumstance under which death would not be instantaneous would be one in which the toxins were released while a full medical team was standing by, ready to counteract the poison."

The darkness was starting to make sense. I swallowed, trying to make my voice a little less unsteady as I said, "You could have warned me."

"No, I'm afraid we couldn't have. Some of the devices were set to trigger at specific key words that would inevitably have come up, if only because you'd have seen us dancing around them and demanded to know why." Dr. Kimberley patted my hand. She wasn't wearing gloves this time. Her skin was cool. "We removed eight venom packs from your intramuscular tissue, along with two trackers and a microchip identifying you as CDC property."

That managed to annoy me all over again. "You mean they *tagged* me? Like a dog?"

"It's not a bad comparison, sadly. If you ever made it out of this facility, they wanted to be able to track your movements, and to prove you were who—and what—they said you were. All that's been removed, and your incisions have mostly closed over. You should be fine after another day or two." A small frown crossed her face. "That doesn't leave us much time. I have custody of you for a week. We've already used up three days with your decontamination and recovery. We can move forward now that you're awake, but I'd hoped to have longer."

"What she isn't saying is that you nearly died three times," said Gregory. I looked toward his voice. He was standing in the doorway, a tray in his hands. "The first operation taxed your system enough that the remaining venom packs began to rupture. We got those out, only to find that we'd managed to miss one."

"And the third time?" I asked. It was hard not to smile, even with the things he was saying. I hadn't realized how much I needed to see a familiar, believably friendly face.

"Your heart just stopped. We still don't know why."

"But we did manage to get it started again; there's no reason to frighten the girl," said Dr. Kimberley sternly. "Now, Georgia, I'm sure that you must have questions—"

"Who are you, what are you doing, and how the fuck are you planning to get me out of here?" I pushed myself into as close to a sitting position as I could manage, using the pillows that had been supporting my head to support the rest of me instead.

Dr. Kimberley sighed. "And apparently, we'll be having question time now, rather than after you've put something solid in your stomach. I really am Dr. Kimberley; 'Shaw' was my mother's maiden name. My first name is Danika. I trained at Oxford, and then later with the Kauai Institute of Virology, under Dr. Joseph Shoji. I was recruited to the EIS six years ago. I've been undercover with the CDC for the past five years. I've been on the Shelley Project since it started. You're the first Georgia Mason to make it this far."

"The Shelley—oh, come *on*. They named the 'let's clone a reporter, it'll be fun' project after Mary Shelley? Couldn't they at least have gone with Herbert West or something?"

"I didn't get a vote," said Dr. Kimberley, looking faintly amused. "Gregory here is one of our best men."

"Dr. Gregory Lake, at your service," said Gregory. "I'm primarily a field epidemiologist, but I came here when Dr. Kimberley called for backup. I'm glad I did. The situation was more advanced than her reports led us to believe."

"It's not my fault they don't allow me access to the subjects until they reach the stage where the tests I'm supposedly here to run become necessary," said Dr. Kimberley, an edge of irritation in her voice. "Half the subjects went from lab to slab without darkening my door."

"Yeah, this is the sort of conversation that makes me feel really, really good about my prospects." I slumped against the pillows. "So what, you're the clone rescue squad?"

"Not quite." Dr. Kimberley leaned forward, resting her elbows on her knees. She looked at me gravely. "Georgia, we're here because we need your help."

I blinked at her, glancing at Gregory. He had the same solemn look on his face. The urge to laugh bubbled up inside my chest. "You need *my* help? I've been *dead* for the last... I'm not even sure. Not to mention the part where I'm not actually who I think I am, just close enough to her that I probably qualify as clinically insane. What can I possibly do to help you?"

Dr. Kimberley and Gregory exchanged a look. He cleared his throat and said, "Things have gotten worse since you died. Shaun Mason is currently unreachable, following a rather unpleasant incident at the Memphis CDC, in which he remains a person of interest. He—"

"Wait—Memphis? Is Dr. Wynne okay?" Dr. Joseph Wynne worked out of the Memphis office. He was one of the first CDC employees I'd ever met who seemed to genuinely care about people. Without him, we might have died in the desert between Oklahoma and Texas.

"Dr. Wynne was killed during the incident. It's still unclear what his role was—the CDC insists he was a martyr, but the EIS has reason to believe otherwise." Catching the stricken look on my face, Gregory continued reluctantly. "Dr. Kelly Connolly was also found dead in the Memphis CDC."

"Which was surprising when you considered that she'd been killed several weeks previously, in a robbery gone awry," interjected Dr. Kimberley. "Once we started analyzing video footage of your brother's team over the weeks leading up to the incident, we found a surprising number of shots including a blonde woman whose facial features mapped quite well with Dr. Connolly's. Perhaps she didn't die before that day in Memphis after all."

"What are you saying?" I asked.

Dr. Kimberley motioned for Gregory to bring the water over again. "I'm saying things are much worse than you knew at the time of your passing."

"That wasn't me," I said, almost sullenly. I'd just been drugged and cut open without my consent. I was feeling entitled to a little balkiness. Gregory held the glass of water up for me to sip, and I did, gratefully. The feel of the liquid coating the back of my throat may have been the sweetest thing I had ever experienced.

"No, you're right; it wasn't you," said Dr. Kimberley. "But it *was* you at the same time. You're a bit of a paradox, my dear girl, and possibly the only ace our side has left to play. We need you to be Georgia Mason, just as much as the other side needs for you not to be. We need you to think like her, we need you to act like her, and we need you to *be* her. We would never have made you. I like to think the EIS still has marginally more of a soul than that. Now that you exist, forgive us, but we *will* use you to our best advantage."

I coughed. Gregory pulled the glass away. "What do you think you're going to use me *for*? I won't betray Shaun for you."

"We never expected you would. Your loyalty is one of the things that makes you useless to Dr. Thomas and his ilk." Dr. Kimberley's lip drew back in a sneer. "That man's never understood the virtue of loyalty."

"Right." Moving my left arm felt like one of the hardest things I had ever done. Somehow, I managed, raising it to rest my hand against my forehead. "So you're the good guys. You're just going to find a way to set me free so I can run off and join Shaun, and we can blow this conspiracy open and go live happily ever after. Is that it?"

"I wouldn't have put it quite like that—" began Dr. Kimberley.

I looked to Gregory. "Is she stupid, or does she think I am? Because I know a line of bullshit when it's being fed to me."

"Florida has been declared a Level 1 hazard zone," he replied.

"W-what?" I managed, after that seeming non sequitur had been given a moment to sink in. "That's impossible."

"An insect vector for Kellis-Amberlee was swept over from Cuba by a tropical storm, and deposited along the length of the United States Gulf Coast. We've lost more than just Florida, but that's the only entire state to be designated Level 1. So far."

"Wait. Are you saying—"

"This isn't a natural mutation. These mosquitoes are three times the size of anything we've seen before—the perfect size for transmitting Kellis-Amberlee. Isn't it a little odd that they didn't appear until right after a major break-in at the CDC?" Gregory looked at me calmly. "The purpose of the EIS is tracking, containment, and eradication of infectious diseases. At this point, we consider the CDC a form of infectious disease. So yes, Georgia, we really are going to find a way to free you to find your team—what's left of them—and tell them what you know."

"It may not tilt the balance fully in our favor, but it will help," added Dr. Kimberley. "Your death was too well publicized, and you're too well made. There's no way you can be written off as a hoax once you get to the proper people. And if you can't find the proper people, we'd be happy to provide them."

I sighed. "Is this all just one big political ploy to seize control of the CDC?"

"Do you really care if it is?" asked Gregory.

Trying to think about this was starting to make my head hurt. I decided to try another approach. "Did I hear Rick? I remember waking up and hearing him here."

"You did," said Gregory. That was a surprise. I'd been half expecting them to lie. "He was able to sneak away to meet with us. I'm sorry you weren't awake during his visit."

"Vice President Cousins has been very concerned about you," added Dr. Kimberley. "He's the one who approached the EIS about infiltrating this project. He was able to get my security clearance improved—that's how we could pull off this little ruse in the first place."

"Not that it's going to do us any good if you don't recover fast enough for us to break you out of here," said Gregory. He turned to look at one of the monitors. "Your system is still stressed from all the excitement. You need to get some sleep."

"Sleep is the last thing I want," I objected. "I want to know what the hell is going on."

"And that's why you need to sleep." Gregory smiled a little, holding up an empty syringe. "I'm afraid you don't have all that much choice in the matter. I added a little something to your IV line. We'll see you in a few hours."

"What—?" My eyes widened. "You bastard."

"My parents were married."

"You could have...could have asked me..." My voice was already slowing down. I didn't know whether it was psychosomatic or just very well timed, but either way, I was *pissed*.

"You would have said no," said Dr. Kimberley, standing.

"Damn...right...I..." I lost my grasp on the sentence as the dark reached up to take me. This time it was softer, and less menacing. That didn't mean I had to like it, but when it became apparent that fighting wasn't going to do me any good, I let go and let it pull me under.

The fourth time I woke, no one was calling my name, and no one else was in the room; I was alone in my little half-folded hospital bed, with a yellow blanket pulled up around my shoulders. I was so used to CDC white that the color was almost shocking. I pushed myself into a sitting position with shaking arms, letting the blanket fall away. My white pajamas were gone, replaced by a set of pale blue surgical scrubs. More color. After so long in a world without it, even those little splashes were enough to make me feel disoriented.

After I was sure I was steady, I swung my feet around to the floor—my bare feet. A momentary panic lanced through me as I realized my gun was gone. I grabbed the bedrail, intending to stand, and paused as I saw the gun resting on the bedside table. I picked it up, hand shaking slightly, and relaxed as the weight of the gun confirmed that it was loaded. They hadn't left me defenseless after all. I tucked it into the waistband of my scrubs, checking twice to be sure the safety was on before I tightened my grasp on the bedrail, took a deep breath, and stood.

I didn't fall. That was a start. There was no immediate pain, although most of me was sore, and various parts of me ached in an irritated way that made me think of feeding tubes and catheters. Necessary evils, but not things I really wanted to dwell on.

There was a door on the far side of the room. I focused on it as I let go of the bedrail and started to shuffle forward, slowly at first, but with increasing speed as my confidence came back. The soreness actually began to fade a little as I stretched the muscles in my legs and back. Maybe most of it was from lying still too long.

I made it to the door without incident and grasped the knob, honestly expecting it to be locked. Instead, it turned easily, and I stepped out of my small recovery room into what looked like the central lab. Dr. Kimberley was there, reviewing test results with two of her technicians. All three of them turned toward the sound of my door opening.

For a moment, the four of us remained where we were, blinking at one another. Dr. Kimberley was the first to recover. "James?"

"On it, Doctor," said the technician, and stood, hurrying over to a small specimen refrigerator. He opened the door and produced a familiar red and white can, which he carried over and offered to me. "It's good to see you awake."

I took the Coke without a word, popping the tab and taking a long drink. The soda burned the soreness in my throat. All of them watched me. No one spoke.

I lowered the can.

"The first thing I will do—the *first* thing—is have myself checked for tracking devices," I said, directing my words at Dr. Kimberley. "If we find anything, I don't work with you people. I don't give you anything. You'll need to shoot me and start with another clone, and hope you can get away with it twice. Clear?"

"As crystal," she said, nodding. "We're playing fairly. Not because we're innately fair, but because at this point, it's in our best interests to do so...and it's the only thing left that distinguishes us from the other side."

"All right, then. How much time do we have?"

"Still three days. You were only out for a few hours this last time—long enough to let us do the last of the post-op cleanup work."

"Yeah, don't ever do that again. If you're going to knock me out, I need to know before it happens." I took another drink of Coke. "I need an Internet connection, shoes, and another soda."

Dr. Kimberley smiled. "I think all those things can be arranged."

"Good." My can was almost empty. I finished it before returning Dr. Kimberley's smile. "Let's have ourselves a revolution."

We've reached Seattle in one piece. It was a little touch-and-go for a while there, but now here we are, and Maggie has somehow managed to hide us by going the opposite of underground. Money. Is there anything it *can't* do?

We're about to leave to see the Monkey, the man who can supposedly make identities that fool anyone and everyone in the world. That makes this Maggie's last hurrah; when we're done here, she's heading back to Weed, back to her bulldogs and her grindhouse movies. I'm going to miss the shit out of her, but I'm also glad, in a way.

At least one of us is going to make it out of this shitstorm alive.

**—From *Adaptive Immunities*,
the blog of Shaun Mason, August 1, 2041. Unpublished.**

There are days when I wake up and realize I no longer know the man in my mirror. Who are you, with your graying temples and your two-hundred-dollar haircut? Who are you, in your fancy suit, with your vast political power that does you no good when it really matters? Who are you, with all those ghosts in your eyes?

Seriously, you asshole. Who the fuck are you, and why are you looking back at me whenever I look into my own eyes? What good will it be for a man if he gains the whole world, yet forfeits his own soul? It's on days like this that I really want to know.

I wish I could explain to them why I let this happen. I wish I could tell them what it was for. And I wish I thought, even for a second, that they were going to forgive me...

**—From the private journal of Vice President Richard Cousins,
August 1, 2041. Unpublished.**

Eighteen

The polite voice of the hotel roused me from my bed shortly before sunrise. I sat up, blinking in disorientation at the opulent room around me—it would have been a suite in any other hotel—before I remembered where I was, swore softly, and got moving.

My clothes were scattered near the bathroom door, under the panel with the light controls. I'd spent almost ten minutes the night before just playing with them, cranking them up to mimic natural sunlight for the seasonally depressed, shifting them into the UV spectrum for the sake of people with retinal Kellis-Amberlee. In the end, I'd gone to sleep with the black lights on and the white-noise generator turned to full. It was almost like being back in Berkeley, before everything changed.

I hadn't slept that well in a year. Being woken, even gently, felt like a betrayal.

There'd been no discussion of how we'd be getting to the Monkey's: We just assembled at the van, like all of us being together again was the way things were supposed to be. Mahir got into the front passenger seat, balancing his tablet on his knee. Maggie and Becks took the back, and in the rearview mirror I could see Becks sitting sentry, watching out the rear window for signs of pursuit.

"Where to?" I asked, as I buckled my seat belt.

"I've got the directions," said Mahir, and held up the tablet, showing me a black window with a blinking green cursor in the upper right corner.

I blinked. "What the fuck is that?"

"Our map." He lowered the tablet, swiping a finger across the bottom to make the keyboard appear. He typed the words "find Monkey" with quick, efficient taps before pressing the ENTER key. The cursor dropped to the next line.

Maggie was peering over the seat at us. I frowned at the tablet, which Mahir was watching with absolute focus. Minutes ticked by.

"Okay," I said finally. "This is officially stupid. In case you were wondering whether it had the 'Shaun thinks this is stupid' seal of approval, it does. Is there a plan B?"

"Yes." Mahir held up the tablet, showing it to me again. A second line of text had appeared beneath his, with the cursor blinking on a third line now.

EXIT GARAGE, it said.

"You've got to be fucking kidding me," I grumbled, and started the engine.

"It's based off a pre-Rising computer game," said Mahir. "So primitive it's invisible to most monitoring systems." He began typing. "At the end of the drive, wave to the guards and turn left. You'll come to an intersection with a 7-Eleven. When you get there, turn right."

"Fucking. Kidding. Me," I said.

At the base of the driveway, we all waved to the guards as we waited for the gate to open. They waved back, apparently accustomed to strange behavior from their eccentric, wealthy clientele.

"Are you sure this is necessary?" I asked, still waving.

"If the directions say to do it, we do it," said Maggie. "That's what everyone says. If you don't listen to the Monkey, he doesn't meet with you."

"Let's hope the directions don't tell us to shoot a man in Reno just to watch him die," I muttered, and pulled out onto the street.

The directions did not tell us to shoot a man in Reno just to watch him die. They did tell us to drive down dead alleys, only to turn around and go back the way we'd come; to drive in circles through residential neighborhoods, probably setting off dozens of security alerts; and to get on and off the freeway six times. It was incredibly annoying. At the same time, I had to admire the Monkey's style. None of the neighborhoods we drove through had gates or manned security booths. None of the freeway exits we used required blood tests. We might be driving like idiots, but we were driving like idiots without leaving a definite record of where we'd been, or why we'd been there.

We were crossing a bridge that actually floated on the surface of a lake—thankfully, the Monkey hadn't requested we do anything stupid, like drive into the lake; I would have refused, and then I might have had a mutiny on my hands—when Mahir looked up, eyes wide. "Shaun?"

"What?" I asked. "Are we being followed?"

"No. The directions…" He cleared his throat, looked at the screen, and read, "'Turn on your jamming unit. Tune it to channel eight, or these instructions will cease.' We don't have a jamming unit, do we?"

"Actually, funny story—hey, Becks!" I looked at the rearview mirror. She turned, the reflection of her eyes meeting mine. "Put the jammer's batteries back in and turn it on, will you? The text-based adventure wants us to get scrambled."

"On it, Boss," Becks called, and put down her gun.

I hadn't wanted us to kill the jammer in the Agora parking garage—no matter how upper-crust they were, there were bound to be *some* things that would upset them. We'd settled for checking it for obvious bugs and removing the battery pack before heading into the hotel. Now I was glad we'd taken that approach. If the Monkey knew we had the jammer, he would probably have been pissed if we'd killed it.

"This guy must think he's the goddamn Wizard of Oz," I muttered. "I don't like being spied on."

"We're off to see the Wizard," chanted Maggie, in a gleeful singsong voice.

"Before you start killing people with joyous abandon, you might like to know that the next batch of directions has arrived," said Mahir dryly. "Maggie, please don't antagonize him; he's had a hard week, and he's liable to bite."

"Spoilsport," said Maggie.

"Thank you," I said. "Where are we going?"

"At the end of the bridge, turn right," said Mahir.

There was no joking around after that. Whatever test we'd been taking, we'd apparently passed, because the directions sent us along a straight-forward series of increasingly smaller streets, until we were driving down a poorly maintained residential road in one of the oldest parts of Seattle. This was a million miles from the cultivated opulence of the Agora, or even from the reasonably well-maintained Berkeley streets where I grew up. This was a neighborhood where half the houses burned years ago and were never rebuilt, and where the remaining homes were surrounded by the kind of ludicrous fencing that was popular immediately after the Ris-ing, when people were frantically trying to protect themselves from the next attack.

"People still live in places like this?" asked Maggie. Her levity was gone. She stared out the window with wide eyes, looking baffled and horrified at the same time.

I shrugged. "Where else are they gonna go?" The question sounded rhetorical. It wasn't. There were patches like this in almost every city, tol-erated despite their sketchy adherence to the safety requirements, because there was nowhere else to put the people who lived in those slowly collapsing houses. Eventually, they'd all be condemned and razed to the ground. Until that day came, people would do what they always had. They would survive.

"Take the next driveway on the right," said Mahir. "To be more specific, it says 'Turn right at the serial killer van.'"

"You mean the big white one that looks like it was set on fire at some point?"

"One presumes."

"One right turn, coming up." I leaned on the wheel, sending us bumping down a driveway that was, if anything, even less well maintained than the street. It felt like my nuts were going to bounce all the way up to my shoulders. I gritted my teeth, clenching my hands on the wheel as I steered us to a stop in front of the one house on the cul-de-sac that looked like it might still be capable of sustaining life. "Now what?"

"Erm." Mahir looked up. "Now you and I are to put our hands on the dashboard, and Maggie and Rebecca are to put their hands behind their heads."

"What?" demanded Becks.

"That's what it says—oh, wait, there's another line. 'Do it, or else Foxy will shoot you until you are very, very, very, exceedingly dead.'" He frowned. "That sounds unpleasant."

"Yeah, and it'll hurt, too," said a chipper female voice. It sounded like it was coming from the speaker on Mahir's tablet. He and I exchanged an alarmed look. The tablet chirped, "Hi! Look in front of you!"

We all looked toward the windshield.

There was a short, slim woman standing in front of the van. The top of her head probably wouldn't have come higher than my shoulder. That didn't really matter. The assault rifle she was aiming at the windshield more than made up for any lack of size.

"Ah," said Mahir. "I believe we've found the right place."

"That, or we've found the local loony bin." I put my hands on the dashboard. "Everybody do what she says. We're going to go along with this for now."

"Good call!" chirped the tablet.

"Mason—" said Becks.

"Just chill, okay? They knew we were coming. Let's do things their way and see what happens."

One by one, the rest of my team did as we'd been told. Becks was the last to move, sullenly putting her gun down and lacing her fingers behind her head. She glared at me in the rearview mirror the entire time.

Once we were all in position, the girl with the gun half walked, half skipped over to the van, stopping next to the driver's-side door. She beamed through the glass, blue eyes wide and bright as a kid's on Christmas morning. Her hair destroyed any illusion of childishness, despite her size. Most kids have bleach-blond hair these days, a sign that their parents are properly respecting security protocols. Her hair was so red it was almost orange, and only the last six inches had been bleached, ending in about an inch of inky black, like the tipping on a fox's tail.

She tapped the barrel of her gun against the window, gesturing for me to open the door. I did so, moving slowly in case she decided to take offense at the fact that I was moving at all.

"Hi!" she said, once the door was open. She removed her right hand from the gun stock long enough to reach over and tap the skin behind her ear, presumably turning off the transmitter she'd been using to speak through Mahir's tablet. "I'm the Fox. Welcome to the Brainpan."

"Uh," I said slowly. "Nice to meet you?"

"Oh, that's probably not true," she said, still with the same manic good cheer. "Why don't you come inside? The Cat baked bread this morning, and I don't think it's poisoned or anything! Also, leave your guns in the car, or I'll not only kill you, I'll fuck up your corpses so bad that even DNA testing won't be able to figure out who you were." She flashed us one last, bright-toothed smile and started walking backward down the path to the porch. She kept her gun leveled on us all the way. Only when she reached the porch did she turn, bounding up the stairs and vanishing through the open door.

"Oh, great," said Becks, in a faint voice. "I was wondering how we were going to fill our daily quota of bat-shit crazy."

"Maybe we can make quota for the rest of the month." I unbuckled my belt and slid out of the van. Once I was clear, I removed the guns from my waistband, setting them on the seat. "Everybody drop your weapons and come on. We came to them. We may as well play by their rules."

"Yes, because allowing the crazy people to set the rules is absolutely always the way to ensure one's survival in a hostile situation." Mahir managed to sound almost amused, even though he scowled as he removed his own pistol from the holster beneath his arm.

"Thanks for the vote of confidence," I said amiably. He had the good grace to look abashed. I leaned back in through my open door and punched him in the arm. "Don't worry. The lunatics have been running the asylum around here for a long time. We'll fit right in."

Becks had to shed six guns before she got out of the van, and even then, I was reasonably sure she was holding back at least a couple of knives. Maggie didn't need to remove anything. That made me grimace a little.

She really isn't field ready at all, is she?

"No, she's really not," I murmured, and slammed the van door.

The four of us walked together down the broken concrete pathway leading to the Brainpan porch. As we got closer to the house, I started spotting the security enhancements and architectural tweaks hidden among the general disorder and decay. All of them were subtle, and from what I could see, all of them were designed to be effective. That meant they were recent. If they'd been done immediately post-Rising, when most of the improvements—such as they were—were being made to this neighborhood, they would have been flashy. These had no flash at all. They weren't here to show off how secure the house was. They were here to secure it.

"Look," I said, elbowing Becks in the side before nodding toward a camera mostly hidden beneath one of the shingles edging the roof.

She followed my gaze. "Not very well concealed."

"Yeah, but it's also a dummy. You know, for dummies." The Fox bounced back into the open doorframe, beaming at us. "If you think that's the only camera, you're a dummy, and I get to shoot you."

"That's an entirely reasonable and understandable mechanism for judging one's guests," said Mahir smoothly. "Might we come inside now?"

"Oh, sure. Just take off your shoes. The Cat gets a little crazy when you track mud on her floors." She disappeared back into the house.

Becks and I exchanged a look. "I'm not sure what's worse," she said. "The fact that she just implied someone else might be crazy, or the fact that everyone here has a name that starts with the word 'the.'"

"Just pretend they're all comic book villains and it starts to make sense." Maggie took off her sandals, swinging them casually from one hand as she climbed the porch steps and entered the house.

"I'm Batman," deadpanned Mahir, and followed her. Becks was half a step behind him, and I brought up the rear, looking back over my shoulder for signs of pursuit as I stepped inside. There were none. For better or for worse, we were alone with the people we had come to find.

I expected the door to swing shut itself as soon as I was over the threshold. Instead, it remained open until an aggravated female voice shouted, "Shut the damn *door*!" from somewhere at the end of the hall.

I shut the door.

It took a moment for me and Becks to undo the laces on our boots. Mahir and Maggie waited for us to finish, and we walked down the short entry hall to the living room together.

The house was constructed on one of the pre-Rising open-space models, with the living room, dining room, and kitchen essentially blending together to form one large space. There were multiple windows, which must have provided a lot of natural light before they were sealed up and boarded over. Now they were just plywood rectangles set into the walls, barely visible behind the banks of computer equipment and monitor screens. The place looked like a combination of a server farm and a college student's dorm room, with one big exception: It was scrupulously clean. There might be a futon on the floor, but there were no pizza boxes or take-out containers; there was clutter, but no trash. It managed to be sterile and lived-in at the same time.

"Bizarre," muttered Becks.

"*Awesome*," I countered.

"Expensive, so don't touch anything," said a voice. I turned toward the kitchen, where a brown-haired woman was standing, arms crossed, a stern expression on her face. She was wearing jeans and a tank top, and her hair was cropped short, leaving nothing for a zombie mob to grab hold of. She looked more like a normal human than the girl from the driveway, who was now sitting on the counter, drumming her heels against a cabinet. Somehow, that made her more difficult to trust. Nothing that looked normal in this place could possibly be what it seemed.

Mahir had turned along with the rest of us. He recovered quickly, stepping forward and offering his hand. "I'm Mahir Gowda. It's a pleasure to—"

"You're not here to meet me," said the brunette, in the same disapproving tone. "No one comes here to meet me. You're here for the Monkey. Well, he's not sure he wants to talk to you just yet. Who sent you?"

"No one sent us. We came—"

"Whoops! Wrong answer!" The Fox was suddenly holding a pistol in each hand. I hadn't even seen her draw. "Somebody told you who to look for, and somebody told you where to look. So who sent you?"

"Alaric Kwong. He said the Monkey was the best in the business," said Becks.

The brunette blinked. Then, to my surprise, she smiled, a little wistfully. "Alaric? Really? You're the people he's been working with?"

The four of us stared at her for a moment. Slowly, I nodded. "Yeah. He's part of my crew. I'm Shaun Mason, After the End Times."

"I know you," she said, smile fading as fast as it came. "I'm the Cat. You've met the Fox."

"'Met' is a word," I agreed. The Fox lowered her guns. "Do we pass the security check?"

"For the moment." The Cat turned, picking up a bread knife from the counter. "Why did Alaric send you?"

We could have tried for diplomacy. We could have tried for plausible deniability. In the end, that seemed like too damn much trouble, and I did what Georgia taught me to do: I went for the truth. "There's a good chance we're going to need to run for the border pretty soon, since the CDC is trying to kill us—"

"—we think," Becks interjected.

"Right, we think. Anyway, they probably released bioengineered death mosquitoes and accidentally wiped out the Gulf Coast trying to get us, so they're a little pissed right now. That means we need IDs the CDC won't be watching for."

"Why?" asked the little redhead, guilelessly.

I hesitated. I could give the answer we'd been giving everyone else—so we could get out, so we could run and escape and live—or I could tell the truth. I looked toward my team. Mahir was still watching the two women, the redhead drumming her heels, the brunette slicing obviously home-baked bread. Becks and Maggie were watching me, waiting to see what I would say. I took a breath.

"Mahir needs a new passport to get him into Canada, so he can get back to Europe alive. Becks needs an identity that can get her out of the country, wherever it is she wants to go. Alaric needs IDs for him, and for his sister, Alisa. We're going to get her out of Florida. Maggie—"

"Is paying for all this," said Maggie.

The Cat turned to me, knife still in her hand. Raising an eyebrow, she asked, "And what about you? What are you planning to get out of this deal?"

"Assuming this dude is as good as Alaric thinks he is, I'm going to get an ID that doesn't set off any alarms. I'm going to stay low until we finish finding the people who killed my sister. And then I'm going to walk right in their front doors and shoot them in their fucking faces."

"I like this one," said the Fox, giggling. "He's funny."

Maggie was staring at me, clearly aghast. Becks and Mahir, on the other hand, didn't even look surprised. Becks looked a little sad; Mahir just looked accepting, like he'd been waiting a long time for those words to leave my lips.

Seeing them like that made me feel slightly ashamed, and more determined than ever to set things right. I all but glared at the Cat. "So? Are those reasons good enough for you people, or do we need to find someone else to help us?"

"You're doing this out of a suicidal need for revenge, even though it may not change anything," said the Cat coolly.

"Yeah." I shrugged. "Pretty much."

You're an idiot, muttered George. I ignored her.

"Okay," said the Cat.

I blinked. "What?"

"I said okay. The Fox likes you, and I think you're a suicidal idiot with friends who will pay to let you kill yourself in an interesting fashion. She"— she gestured toward Maggie with her knife—"can give us obscene amounts of money without thinking about it, and the other two are nonoffensive enough not to matter. Besides, you work with someone that I owe a favor."

"Who?" I asked.

"Alaric Kwong." She smiled at our expressions. "He doesn't know I ended up here. Probably break his heart if you told him. I may as well pay him back by passing you through."

"A favor? For what?" asked Becks.

The Cat smirked. "I broke up with him when our Quest Realm guild was in the middle of a raid, and then I kept making him heal me without answering any of his whiny whispers about why, Jane, why would you break up with me, I looooooooove you. So we'll get you your IDs. Cost is fifty thousand each, up-front, before you leave here today...and a favor."

"A favor?" Becks frowned, suddenly suspicious. Given how on edge she'd been since we arrived, that wasn't much of a transition. "What kind of favor are we talking about here?"

"Nothing you'd lose any sleep over. We need you to break into the local CDC building and drop a little something off for us," said the Cat. She resumed slicing bread.

"Define 'a little something,'" I said. "We're not blowing anything up. That's their game, not ours."

"Nothing like that. Their main storage facility isn't online. We want access. So we have a pressure-point hotspot that we just need you to get into the proper place and switch on. Then you come back here and get your shiny new identities, and with them, the warm satisfaction of knowing we're going to screw the CDC over in some fun ways that you don't need to know anything about." She put her knife down, resting her hands on the counter as she looked at us calmly. "Do we have a deal?"

Looking into her calm, cold eyes, I realized the Fox wasn't the only crazy person living in this house. She was just the one who had the honesty to wear her crazy on her sleeve.

"Yeah," I said. "We have a deal."

...all attempts to culture a live infection in blood samples taken from Subject 139b have failed. More interesting, we induced amplification in a white-tailed deer, and injected it via dart with a serum derived from Subject 139b's blood. The deer showed signs of improvement before dying of massive cerebral hemorrhage. The necropsy was inconclusive. Unfortunately, I think we'll need to try this with a human subject before we can be sure of anything. My team is scouring the area for freshly infected individuals; thus far, we've had no luck.

No reports of mosquito-borne Kellis-Amberlee have come in from any of my sources in California, Arizona, or Nevada. It's possible that we may be able to dodge this bullet. I don't think so; we haven't dodged any of the ones that came before it. But I'm starting to believe that there may be an answer. All I need is a little more *time*.

—Taken from an e-mail sent by Dr. Shannon Abbey to Dr. Joseph Shoji at the Kauai Institute of Virology, August 1, 2041.

Well, that's that, then. We're all going to die.
    Charming.

—From *Fish and Clips*, the blog of Mahir Gowda, August 1, 2041. Unpublished.

Nineteen

Dr. Kimberley's technicians didn't have any street clothes in my size. They did manage to find me a pair of hard-soled slippers, which weren't quite the shoes I'd asked for, but were several thousand times better than the socks I'd been wearing since I woke up.

Better yet—best of all—they brought me a computer. A sleek, hard-shelled little laptop, which Gregory set in front of me with the top closed. I reached for it. He pulled it back. Only a few inches, but far enough to make it clear that I needed to listen before I was going to get my hands on the machine.

"You have a connection, and a guest log-in routed through one of the administrative offices," he said. "We can't spoof it forever, but we should be able to get you about twenty minutes without raising any red flags. Please don't run any open searches on phrases that might get the attention of our firewall."

"Like what?" I asked. "Governmental corruption? Conspiracy to defraud the American people? Cloning?"

"Yes," he said, without a trace of irony. "That's a good initial list of things to avoid. Don't log into any e-mail accounts with your name on them. Don't—"

"I promise I've used other people's networks before, and I've never managed to get anyone arrested when I wasn't trying to," I said, and reached for the laptop again. "We're all trying to trust each other here. For me, the last step to trusting you is seeing that I have a clear connection. For you, the last step to trusting me is seeing that I won't abuse it. So I guess we both start getting what we want when you let me have that computer, huh?"

Gregory chuckled and pushed the laptop toward me. "You're definitely feeling better if you're trying to use logic against me."

"That's me. Only rational when I'm not being cut open and dissected for the amusement of others." I took the laptop, breathing slowly through my nose to keep my hands from shaking as I opened it. The screen sprang to life, displaying a stark white background with the CDC logo in the center. I let my fingers rest against the keys, breathing unsteadily out. "Oh, wow."

"Maybe we only trust you because we don't have any other choice, but we *do* trust you, Georgia." Gregory touched my shoulder, causing me to look up. He smiled. "Let's try and earn it from each other."

I nodded. "I'll do my best," I said. And then I bent my head and started to type, and Gregory didn't matter anymore.

His warning about avoiding my e-mail was smart, if unnecessary: Anyone who's never worked professionally in Internet news would probably assume the first thing a journalist would do was go for their inbox. He was right, in a way. He was also wrong. All the public-facing e-mail addresses—the ones that fed into the customary webmail interfaces—were basically dummy accounts, feeding their contents into the true inboxes behind the After the End Times firewall system that Buffy had designed. The only time we ever needed to use those boxes directly was when we were somewhere that didn't allow for logging all the way into the system. Even if I only had twenty minutes, I had plenty of time to make it that far.

The first place I went was an online game site, the sort of thing that's been killing productivity in offices everywhere since the first computer was invented. Somehow, I wasn't surprised when the browser autofilled the URL after I'd entered only the first three letters. Not even the CDC is immune to the lure of brightly colored graphics and simplistic puzzles. The site presented a list of options, all with cute, easily marketed names and icons designed to catch the eye. I scrolled to the bottom.

"What are you doing?" asked Gregory.

"Not all computers have shell access these days, and any site that's obviously designed to be secure might as well have a big red label on it, flashing 'Oh, hey, look over here; people do things they don't want you to know about when they're over here,'" I said. The last icon on the list of games was a comparatively drab cartoon atom. I clicked on it. "So we have back doors, for those times when we need to get in, but don't have access to the normal equipment."

"And one of your back doors involves a game site?"

"Buffy designed their security." I smiled as the "loading" bar appeared on my browser. "Buffy designed a lot of people's security. She hid things all over the damn Internet."

"Well, I wish she were here," said Gregory.

"Yeah. So do I." The menu appeared, giving a list of options. I clicked a set of five that would have resulted in an unplayable game if I'd actually been trying to play, and hit START. The screen froze.

"Did it crash?" asked Gregory.

"Are you going to watch over my shoulder the whole time I'm online?"

"Yes. We're still in the 'earning trust' phase, remember?"

"Right. No, it didn't crash. This is what's supposed to happen." I tapped the space bar twice. "If I were a casual player who'd just chosen a bad set of options, this is where I'd reload and try again. Since I'm not, this is where we wait."

"Wait for what?"

"Wait for that." The browser flickered and vanished, replaced by blackness. A log-in window appeared, floating in the middle of the screen.

USER NAME? it prompted.

NANCY, I typed.

"Nancy?" asked Gregory.

"Remember how I said Buffy did our security programming? Well, Buffy was a pre-Rising media nut."

ADDRESS? prompted the window.

1428 ELM STREET.

There was a longer pause this time as the program controlling this particular back door checked my responses against the list. The pause wasn't necessary. It was one more trick programmed by our former professional paranoid. If I touched the keyboard before I was prompted, it would not only kick me out, it would lock this door until someone who was already inside the firewall decided it was safe to open it again.

Finally, the prompt asked, WHY DID YOU MOVE OUT?

Of the eight possible questions it could have asked, that was the one I'd been hoping for. I wasn't sure I remembered the answers to any of the others. I typed, BECAUSE A DEAD SERIAL KILLER WITH KNIVES FOR HANDS MURDERED MY BOYFRIEND.

The pause this time lasted less than a second. WELCOME, GEORGIA MASON appeared on the screen, and vanished, replaced by the After the End Times logo.

"That log-in won't work again for six months," I said, trying to make the comment sound casual. I probably failed, but it didn't matter as much as making sure I got my point across. "Buffy knew her business."

"Remind me—why wasn't she working for the CIA? Or better yet, for us?" Gregory dragged a chair over and sat down where he could watch my screen. Oddly, it made me feel more at ease, rather than making me feel spied on. There's almost always been someone watching over my shoulder while I worked. It was usually Shaun, but that didn't change the way Gregory's presence calmed me down.

"You guys didn't offer her enough opportunities for bad poetry, porn, or bad poetry about porn." I clicked the link that should have taken me to the staff directories. Instead of opening, it flashed a red "restricted" warning at me. "Crap."

Gregory frowned. "You're kidding, right?"

"About the poetry and porn? No. She was a genius. We all knew she'd been scouted by at least one of the alphabet soup agencies. I wouldn't be surprised to find out she'd been scouted by all of them." I glared at the screen. "I'm not kidding about this stupid firewall, either. They didn't close the loopholes into the system, but they locked down the staff directory. Who does that? Purge it all, or allow for the occasional spontaneous resurrection!"

"Most people who come back from the dead can't type, you know."

"Right now, I don't *care*. Let me try something else." I moved my mouse to the administrative panel for the forums. If anything was going to stop me, it would have done so on the first layer, when I accessed the full member list. Nothing pinged. "Oh, jeez. They let Dave do the purge, didn't they? He never finishes everything on the first go."

"David Novakowski?" asked Gregory, sounding suddenly hesitant.

I glanced toward him. "Yeah. Why?"

"I'm sorry to tell you this, but..."

Something in the way his voice trailed off told me what he didn't want to finish his sentence. My eyes widened. "Dave's *dead*? How the hell is Dave *dead*? He was the most careful Irwin I ever met!"

"There was an outbreak in the location of your team's new headquarters. It's unclear exactly why he did what he did, but he chose to remain behind after the quarantine sirens began ringing. He was still inside the building when it was sterilized."

"By 'sterilized,' do you by any chance mean 'carpet-bombed'?"

Gregory looked away.

Pressing my lips into a thin line, I looked back to the computer. The After the End Times forums were open in front of me like some sort of a miracle, with their threads and board titles looking so familiar that it was like I'd never left. It didn't matter that I didn't recognize even a quarter of them—that could happen when I spent a weekend in bed with a migraine and let Mahir take forum duty for me. What mattered was that they were *there*. I scrolled to the bottom of the screen, and closed my eyes for a moment from sheer relief.

The moderator's forum was listed. If there had been any changes to my profile following the purge of my core system access, the forum would have turned invisible, marking me as one more end user. I crossed my fingers, opened my eyes, moved the mouse to the appropriate icon, and clicked.

The forum opened without a pause. I started scrolling down, barely aware that I was crying. According to the admin script at the bottom of the page, only two users with mod privileges were currently online. One was me. The other was Alaric.

"What are you doing?" asked Gregory.

"Sending up a flare," I said. I opened a private message window and tapped out, ALARIC ARE YOU THERE? NEED TO CHAT ASAP, DO NOT HAVE MUCH TIME.

I hit enter.

"Georgia—"

"Just give it a second."

A message appeared in my inbox less than fifteen seconds later. HOW DID YOU GET THIS LOG-IN? THIS IS NOT FUNNY. LOG OFF RIGHT NOW OR I WILL CONTACT THE AUTHORITIES.

I grinned. "Oh, good. He's pissed."

"That's *good*?"

"Yeah, that's good. If he's pissed, he'll want to know who I am so he can have someone to be pissed *at*. That means he'll talk." I hit REPLY, typing, BUFFY GAVE ME THIS LOG-IN THE DAY WE WENT LIVE. ALARIC, IT'S ME. IF YOU DON'T BELIEVE ME, OPEN A CHAT. I CAN PROVE IT.

Gregory looked dubiously at my screen. "Let me guess. The goal here is to make him *really* mad."

"Kind of, yes. Alaric thinks better when he's mad—he doesn't second-guess himself nearly as much." I was speaking from a flawed model and I knew it: Not only had Alaric been alive while I wasn't, giving him time to adapt and change, but I was working off memories extracted from a dead woman's mind and implanted in my own. Even the way I thought about myself—half "me," half "her"—told me I couldn't trust my own judgment where the reactions of others were concerned. And that didn't matter, because my judgment was the only thing I had.

That was a depressing thought. I was trying not to dwell on it when a light blinked at the bottom of my window, signaling an incoming chat request.

"I don't want to sound like I'm rushing you, Georgia, but we can keep this window active for another ten minutes at best."

"That should be all I need." I opened the chat window. THANKS FOR TALKING TO ME, ALARIC. I APPRECIATE IT. HOW HAVE YOU BEEN?

The response was immediate, making me think it had been more than half typed before I said anything. YOU'D BETTER LOG OFF THIS SYSTEM RIGHT NOW AND NEVER COME BACK. YOU'RE JUST LUCKY MY BOSS ISN'T ONLINE, OR YOU'D BE SORRIER THAN YOU CAN IMAGINE.

DO YOU MEAN MAHIR OR SHAUN WHEN YOU SAY THAT? It was common knowledge that Mahir was my second; he was almost certainly also my replacement. I WOULD BE MORE AFRAID OF SHAUN, PERSONALLY. MAHIR MAY GET ALL PISSY AND BRITISH AT YOU, BUT HE DOESN'T HIT. IT'S ME, ALARIC. IT'S GEORGE. LICENSE AFB-075893, CLASS A-15. THE FIRST TIME WE MET IN PERSON, YOU BROUGHT ME A CAN OF COKE TO SHOW YOUR RESPECT, BUT YOUR HANDS WERE SHAKING SO HARD THAT IT EXPLODED EVERYWHERE WHEN I OPENED IT. SOME CAMERA JOCKEY FREAKED OUT, AND WE WOUND UP IN DECON FOR THREE HOURS. REMEMBER?

There was a longer pause before his answer appeared—at least in part, I was sure, because my reply wasn't what he was expecting. Finally, two words flashed on my screen: GEORGIA'S DEAD.

I took a deep breath. Then, more slowly than before, I tapped out my answer. ARE YOU REALLY GOING TO SIT THERE, POST-ZOMBIE APOCALYPSE, AND TELL ME THE DEAD NEVER COME BACK?

"Five minutes, Georgia."

"Hold on." I stared at the screen, willing Alaric to reply. Seconds ticked by, making me feel like my time had been wasted—maybe worse than wasted. If he thought I was an imposter, and told Shaun...

How?

I was so relieved I actually laughed as I typed, CLONING. THE CDC HAS BEEN A NAUGHTY, NAUGHTY GOVERNMENT ORGANIZATION. NEED TO GET A MESSAGE TO SHAUN. IS HE THERE? I regretted the question as soon as I sent it. If he still didn't believe me... Hurriedly, I typed, DON'T ANSWER THAT. IF YOU HAVE A WAY OF REACHING HIM, TELL HIM I AM BEING HELD AT THE SEATTLE CDC. I AM WORKING WITH THE EIS. I NEED AN IMMEDIATE EXTRACTION. I AM IN DANGER. PLEASE CONFIRM.

Again, seconds ticked by. I was still crying. I wiped my cheek viciously with one hand, watching the screen, praying to a higher power I didn't believe in for some sort of miracle. Alaric was a Newsie. Even if he didn't believe I was who I claimed to be, there was a chance he'd be interested enough in the idea of me to chase the story. If he did that, I might have a chance.

Finally: Why should I believe you?

"Oh, thank God, he's asking something easy," I muttered, and typed, Either I'm the real thing, a trap, or a great story. First option, you need to save me. Second option, you need to find out who's trying to trap you. Third option, you need to get your facts straight before you go public. Personally, I think I'm all of the above. In case that wasn't good enough, I added, Besides, if there's any chance I'm the real deal, and you don't go after it, Shaun will never forgive you.

Gregory's watch beeped. He looked at it and winced. "You need to log off *now*. IT has started scanning the wireless connections in this part of the building. Nothing indicates that this isn't random, but—"

"Better safe than sorry. I get that." Quickly, I typed, Got to go—security is looking our way. TELL SHAUN YOU HEARD FROM ME. He'll be so pissed he'll come to find the fake and bust me out instead. Please, Alaric. Believe me. I am begging you.

I hit ENTER and logged off. Gregory snatched the laptop as soon as I pulled my hands away from it. He flipped it over, ejecting the battery pack with a motion too smooth to be anything but practiced.

"I'll be right back," he said, and then he was striding out of the room, the battery in one hand, the laptop in the other. I stayed where I was, slumping ever lower in my seat, my eyes fixed on the space where the computer had been.

For just a moment, I'd been able to reach the outside world. I'd been able to tell someone what was happening—and whether he believed me or not, Alaric *listened*. He *knew*. I had put my hands on the keys, and even without the muscle memory of the body I was born in, they'd known what to do. Maybe I could still be Georgia Mason after all. As long as I could still tell the truth…

"Rise up while you can," I whispered. Then I slumped in my seat, put my head down on my arms, and sobbed until the tears ran out.

————————————

Mahir are you there?

Mahir I need you to reply RIGHT NOW. It's important or I wouldn't be trying to break radio silence.

Mahir, PLEASE. If you're ignoring these messages because you think I'm fighting with Dr. Abbey or something, PLEASE. I NEED TO TALK TO YOU. I can't talk to Becks or Shaun until I talk to you.

MAHIR GODDAMMIT YOU ANSWER ME RIGHT FUCKING NOW.

...fuck.

**—Internal chat log,
user AKwong to user MGowda, August 1, 2041.**

We have removed all tracking devices and self-destruct triggers from the subject, who continues to self-identify as "Georgia Mason." She was made aware of the realities of her situation by Dr. Lake before we reached this phase, and her psychological progress has been nothing but encouraging. I believe she will remain stable in the long term, providing we are able to secure her release. My team can keep her isolated for a few days more; Dr. Thomas and his lackeys are distracted with the final preparations to awaken her replacement.

This has crossed a line. This experiment has always been both disgusting and morally questionable, but for the first time, it has become obscene. She's a real person. She knows who she is, even if she is only that person because of us. She thinks, she feels, and she wants to go home.

How did we ever come to this?

**—Taken from a message sent by Dr. Danika Kimberley,
August 1, 2041. Recipient unknown.**

Twenty

We left the Brainpan and returned to the Agora. Breaking into the CDC in broad daylight would take a stupid plan and render it actively suicidal—not something I was in a hurry to do, all indications to the contrary aside. Besides, even if it had been full dark, I would have insisted on going back to the resort. There was no way we were going to take Maggie into the field with us. Not for something like this.

She was silent during the drive, almost shrinking in on herself as she listened to Becks and Mahir arguing about the best ways to bypass CDC security. She'd been a part of this team almost from the beginning, but that time was coming to an end, and we all knew it. When this was over, if she was still alive, she wouldn't be one of us anymore.

I parked the van in the Agora garage and twisted around to face her. "Maggie, I—"

It was too late. She was already out of the van and on her way to the airlock door. I froze where I was, not sure what I was supposed to do.

"Let her go."

For a moment, I thought the voice was Georgia's. Then I lifted my head and saw Becks looking at me.

"She's made her choice. That doesn't mean she feels good about herself. Let her go. We can talk to her when we get back."

If we get back, said George.

"Yeah," I said, answering them both, and unfastened my seat belt.

We didn't talk as we followed Maggie's path to the airlock. The lobby was empty when we arrived. Somehow, that wasn't much of a surprise. We didn't discuss our next move. We just split up, each of us heading for our own room to do whatever it was we had to do in order to feel like we were ready. If you can ever feel ready for something like this.

Becks and I hadn't had much time to get unpacked—or much with us to unpack—but there was enough that it took me about fifteen minutes to get everything together, double-checking the ammo in every gun and the straps on every holster. I even retied my boots. It never hurts to be over-prepared. Then I stopped, looking at the empty room, and closed my eyes.

"This is all I'm going to leave behind," I said aloud. "No apartment. No belongings. No family. Just a hotel room that won't remember me tomorrow."

"I'll remember you." Georgia's hand on my shoulder was gentle. I started to turn toward her. "Shhh. Don't open your eyes. Just come with me." She tugged me to the bed, pushing on my shoulder until I sat. "Now you're going to get some rest."

"George—"

"Don't argue. You don't do well on sleep dep. You never have. Now, go to sleep. You have hours to kill before the sun goes down."

She was right. I knew she was right, just like I knew she wasn't there; she was the part of my mind that gave a damn about keeping the rest of me alive. I still took an unimaginable amount of comfort from the feeling of her hand on my shoulder as I fell backward on the bed, eyes still closed, gear still on, and let myself drift off into sleep.

My dreams were full of screaming. I saw my team die half a dozen times, in half a dozen ways. Oddly, that helped, because every time I saw one of them get killed, I saw something else that wouldn't work for getting us into the building alive. We were going to need to be careful, and quick, and never hesitate.

The light in the room was dimmer when I finally opened my eyes. George was gone, but that didn't matter; she'd be back, and soon. She always came back.

I went to the bathroom, splashed some water on my face, and then began the final preparations to depart. I was loading my pockets with clips when a speaker hidden somewhere in the room chimed, and the voice of the Agora said, "Mr. Mason, I apologize for the interruption, but Mr. Gowda has been trying to reach you for the past fifteen minutes. I didn't want to wake you. Will you accept the call?"

"If I don't, he'll probably wind up coming down here to yell at me," I said, still working. "Hell, I'm surprised he hasn't already. I'll take it."

"Thank you." The Agora went silent, followed by another chime.

"Shaun?" It was Mahir this time, sounding worried. Business as usual, in other words.

"Hey, Mahir. What's up? Aren't you like, three doors down? This takes 'lazy' to a new level, don't you think? Then again, I just spent the whole day asleep, so who am I to talk?" I couldn't fit any more clips in my pockets. That was a bummer. I picked up my tablet, clipping it to my belt. There was one nice thing about this particular suicide mission: We'd downloaded floor plans for all the major CDC installations as part of our research weeks ago, right before we followed Kelly into the Memphis office and got her killed. Seattle was a major enough office that we had pretty good blueprints. It didn't show any secret tunnels, but it had the public areas. At least we wouldn't be lost while we were rushing off to our deaths.

There was a time when that thought would have made me uneasy, rather than reassuring me. It's amazing what has become comforting since the start of the Ryman campaign.

"Alaric tried to get in touch with me."

My head snapped up. No one respects radio silence like a Newsie. It's practically one of their sacred creeds, right alongside "protecting your sources" and "off the record." "Did he say why?"

"No, and that's why I'm concerned. The message he left was basically 'you know this matters, or I wouldn't be doing it,' over and over. I already tried dialing one of his burn phones."

"And?"

"There's no response. I've left a message and sent an e-mail to one of Dr. Abbey's encrypted addresses, but—"

"Do you want to stay here and keep trying to reach him while Becks and I go to the CDC?"

"What? No." Mahir actually sounded offended. "I didn't come this far to be left sitting on the stands when things are finally getting interesting. I do intend to return to my career once I'm no longer a wanted fugitive, and the more I can learn, the better my prospects will be."

"You're a natural-born snoop, Mahir," I said, and picked up my pack. "You ready to blow this taco stand?"

"Have you ever even *seen* a taco stand?"

"Sure. There was one right next to campus. Are you ready to *go*, Mahir?"

He sighed, attempts at levity dismissed in an instant. "Yes. Much as I'm afraid of what's to come, I rather do believe I am."

"Good. Meet me in the hall."

"Shall do." There was no dial tone, but something about shape of the silence filling the room told me that he'd hung up. I slung my pack over my shoulder and turned to head for the door. I didn't look back. There was nothing there to see.

Becks's room was between Mahir's and mine. I had barely finished knocking when her door swung open. "Yes, Mason?" she asked.

"You ready to go?"

"As ready as I'll ever be. I've been waiting on you." She was dressed almost exactly like I was: a charcoal-gray T-shirt, camouflage pants, combat boots, and way too many weapons to be on her way to a tea party. Her hair was slicked back in a tight, no-nonsense ponytail. This wasn't an expedition intended to be filmed and sold by the download. This was serious work.

She raised an eyebrow at my assessing look.

"Something wrong?"

"No. Just thinking how much it sucks that we can't post any of this."

Her grin was sudden, the flash of white teeth there and gone almost before it had fully registered. "Someday this story is going to make us legends."

"Only if it doesn't make us dead," I shot back, and then winced, waiting for Georgia to say something. She didn't. I wasn't sure whether that was a good sign or not.

Becks looked at me with concern. She'd clearly seen the wince, and was waiting to see what it was going to mean. "Boss?"

"I'm good. Come on." I turned to head for the elevator, waving for her to follow me. With barely a moment of hesitation, she did.

Mahir met us in the elevator lobby. "Are we ready?" he asked.

"That is a question for the sages, not for us, Mahir," I said. "But we're going either way, so what the fuck does it matter, right?"

He took that answer in stride. None of us said anything as we got into the elevator and rode down to the lobby. The concierge smiled at us politely, like journalists stormed through his hotel every day. I waved, and we walked on, to the van.

I had unlocked the doors and was about to get inside when Becks caught my elbow, saying urgently, "The jammer."

"...shit." If the Masons could use that thing to track us—still unproven, but still likely—then so could other people. The Monkey's people had known we had it. That made it a liability if we were going somewhere sensitive, like, say, the CDC. "Got a hammer?"

"I've got a better idea." She picked up the jammer, dropping her backpack on the passenger seat, and turned to walk back toward the hotel.

I blinked. "Mahir? You want to logic that one out for me?"

"The concierge is supposed to be the hotel's private on-call miracle worker," said Mahir, hoisting himself into one of the rear seats.

"Presumably, she's gone to ask him if he has access to an industrial-grade furnace of some sort."

"Rich people are weird," I said, and got into the van.

Becks returned about five minutes later, looking smugly pleased. She hopped into her seat, pushing her backpack to the floor, and slammed the door before announcing, "The staff of the Agora is more than happy to dismantle any unwanted professional equipment we may have, and can promise the utmost discretion in the destruction of the individual components."

"Is there anything money *can't* buy?" I asked.

Immortality, said George.

I grimaced and started the van.

The Seattle branch of the CDC wasn't technically in Seattle at all; it was across the lake, in Redmond. The facility was located on part of what used to be the main Microsoft campus, before the Rising demonstrated every possible flaw in their architecture. The CDC bought the site when the rebuilding of the area was getting underway; it was viewed as a major coup, since at the time, having a CDC installation nearby was seen almost as a magical talisman against further infection. That hasn't changed much in the last twenty years. People would rather live near the CDC than in areas with good schools or excellent hospitals. The CDC will keep the zombies away.

I chuckled as I drove, largely because laughter stood a chance of keeping me from screaming. Becks kept herself busy cleaning and double-checking her guns, while Mahir monitored the GPS. The only conversation consisted of directions, given quietly and with calm efficiency, like we were going to be graded on how fast we got there. The Cat's instructions included the location of a secure parking garage formerly connected to a grocery store. The store was long gone, but the garage remained, freestanding and abandoned. With the CDC so close, regular patrols checked the area for signs of zombie infestation. We'd be safe there, as long as the roof didn't collapse on us.

No one was in sight as we turned off the road and into a back alley that led to the old employee entrance to the parking garage. I parked in the darkest corner I could find, despite the fact that every instinct I had told me to avoid those shadows. Our headlights didn't catch any motion. I still signaled for the others to stay quiet as I turned off the engine. It ticked for a few seconds before stilling into silence.

Nothing moaned or shuffled in the darkness. We were alone. "Clear," I said.

"This place gives me the creeps," complained Becks. "Is there a reason we keep winding up in places that should have stayed in their horror movies?"

"I guess I just know how to show a girl a good time." I opened my door, sliding out of the van. My boots crunched on the broken glass and gravel covering the pavement.

"Then what are you showing me?" asked Mahir.

"I'm not sexist. I can show a guy a good time, too." I looked between them. "You all cool?"

"I'm cool," confirmed Becks.

"I haven't been 'cool' since arriving in this godforsaken hellhole you persist in claiming is a civilized nation. I am, however, ready to go violate a few more laws," said Mahir. "I believe at this point we're simply waiting on you."

I'm ready when you are, said George.

"I thought you were supposed to keep me out of trouble," I said, not caring that Becks and Mahir would hear me. We were long past the point where I could get any mileage out of pretending not to be crazy.

I gave up.

"Well, folks, even the girl who lives in my head says it's time to go, so we'd better get moving. According to the directions, we have a quarter-mile to go before we even hit the fence."

"Which means total silence and trying not to fall into any unexpected holes," said Becks dryly. "This *isn't* my first rodeo."

"No, but it's mine, so I appreciate the repetition," said Mahir. "Is the fence likely to be electrified?"

"Yes, but that's what these are for." I held up a pair of rubber clips. "They'll bridge the current and let us cut through the wire. We'll have to leave them behind when we run, but at least we'll be *able* to run."

Mahir eyed the bridgers. "Buffy's work?"

"Dave's." I smiled a little. "He'd love this shit."

"He'd already be halfway to the fence," said Becks.

"Whereas we still need to get moving," said Mahir. "Is there anything else I should know about the area?"

"Lots of blackberries, very little ground security according to the Cat's schematics; they don't patrol all that much. Once we're inside—"

"We run, we keep our heads down, and we pray."

"I do love it when you have a concrete plan, instead of making it up as you go along," said Becks dryly. She pulled a pistol from her belt. "Let's move."

The Seattle night seemed surprisingly bright after the darkness of the parking garage, the moon and the distant glow of streetlights providing more than sufficient light. Mahir lagged at first, but found a pace that kept him between me and Becks, all three of us tromping over the broken ground as quickly and quietly as we could.

The quarter-mile between the van and the CDC was mostly open fields. We hunched over as we crossed them, running low through the tall grass. No floodlights came on to mark our trails, and no alarms went off that we could hear. Arrogance was working in our favor once again—the CDC's, not ours. They'd been heroes since the Rising, and anyone who tried breaking into one of their installations wound up on trial for treason, if they were lucky. We'd always come in via legitimate entrances, whether we were supposed to be there or not. It had been so long since their external security was tested that they weren't prepared for a small group of people who really wanted to get inside.

The fence was only a few yards farther away than I expected; our map was accurate, if not precise. That was a good sign for the rest of the job. I tossed one of the bridging cords to Becks, jerking my chin toward the fence. She nodded, and we approached together, waving for Mahir to stay back. He didn't argue.

I told you he was a smart guy when I hired him, said George.

I held up one finger toward Becks. She nodded, holding up two fingers of her own. When we were both holding up three fingers, we leaned forward and snapped the bridging cords into place. A bright blue spark arced through them, and the air was suddenly filled with the hot, burning tang of ozone. Becks squeaked, and all the hair on my arms stood on end.

Slowly, I reached forward and wrapped my fingers through the links of fence between the cords. Nothing happened. Our bridge was successful; the current was no longer routing through this patch of fencing. I gestured for the others to come closer and pulled a pair of wire cutters out of my coat pocket.

It took only a minute, maybe less, for me to cut through the fence separating the Seattle CDC from the abandoned fields behind it. Then we were onto the manicured expanse of their lawn, running for the building, waiting for the sirens to start going off.

They never did.

I never thought of myself as a coward before all this. I actually thought I was kinda brave. Choosing to live in the middle of nowhere, where I could be attacked at any moment. But I was lying to myself. I was never brave at all.

I also wasn't nearly as stupid as the people I love tend to be. So I suppose that's something to reassure me as I wave from the window while they all march off to die. God, Buffy, why did you have to hire me? I could have worked for some other site. I would never have gone through any of this. And if you had to hire me—if God insisted—why did you have to go off and leave me to deal with all of it alone?

—From *Dandelion Mine*,
the blog of Magdalene Grace Garcia, August 1, 2041. Unpublished.

————

Hey, George. Check this out.

—From *Adaptive Immunities*,
the blog of Shaun Mason, August 1, 2041. Unpublished.

Twenty-one

Either Dr. Kimberley and her team were monitoring me or their timing was uncannily good, because no one came into the room until I was done crying. I was drying my tears on the sleeve of my shirt when two of the technicians stepped through the door, arguing with each other in low, urgent voices. Neither of them looked in my direction.

"Hi," I said, just in case they didn't know I was there.

"Hello, Miss Mason," said the female technician, waving. I still couldn't see her face, but I recognized her voice. Kathleen. "Is everything all right?"

"I don't know if I'd go that far, but things have been worse." I stood, the muscles in my calves protesting the movement. I'd been sitting still for too long. Everything had started to stiffen up. "Ow, damn." I bent double, kneading the muscle of my left calf with both hands.

That's probably why the first bullet missed me.

The shooter was using a silencer. There was a muted bang, too soft to be a proper gunshot, and the technician who entered with Kathleen staggered back, slamming into the wall. A red stain was already spreading across the chest of his formerly pristine white lab coat. He looked down at it before raising his head and looking at me, mouth forming a word he couldn't quite push all the way out into the world. It was George.

It took the sound of his body hitting the floor to make me start moving. In my experience, once a person goes down, they don't *stay* down for long, and when they get back up, they tend to be more interested in eating the flesh of the living than they are in finding out who shot them. I darted forward, grabbing Kathleen's wrist and yanking her away from the body.

"Come on!" I shouted.

"What?" She looked toward me, eyes wide and terrified. "George—"

"Is dead! Now, let's get out of here before he decides to wake up and make *us* dead, too! I've been dead; you wouldn't enjoy it!" I dragged her toward the door on the opposite side of the room, somehow managing to babble and shout at the same time.

The second shot was as quiet as the first. Kathleen suddenly collapsed, the dead weight of her body pulling her hand out of mine. I turned, looking back at her, and at the hole in the middle of her forehead like a third, unseeing eye. Unlike George, she wouldn't be rising. A shot to the head kills humans and zombies the same way: stone dead.

Suddenly aware of how exposed I was—and how *alone* I was—I drew my own gun and ran out of the room as fast as my legs would carry me. Gregory was in the hall outside, running toward the room that I was running away from.

"They're both dead!" I shouted. "What's going on?"

"We're blown!" He put on a burst of speed, closing the distance between us. He grabbed my wrist, turned, and ran back the way he'd come, hauling me the way I'd been hauling Kathleen right before she was shot.

Sick terror lanced through me as I struggled to keep up. "Is it my fault?"

"Not unless you called down a full security team while you were trying to get through to the outside world." Gregory didn't slow down. "Save your breath. I don't know how long we're going to need to run."

I didn't answer. I just ran. Terror had my body flooded with enough adrenaline that I wasn't in danger of falling down from a cramp in the immediate future. That was the good part. The bad part—aside from the unidentified shooter or shooters—was that I wasn't out of shape so much as I had never been *in* shape. My mind remembered hours of exercise, both in the gym and in the field. My body had less than two months of experience. Not the sort of thing that builds endurance. My lungs were already starting to burn, signaling worse things to come.

A door slammed open ahead of us, and Dr. Kimberley appeared, signaling frantically with one hand. The other hand was out of sight. "This way!" she hissed. Her normally perfect hair was in disarray, and there were spots of blood on the sleeve of her lab coat. Whether it was hers or someone else's, I couldn't tell.

Gregory changed angles, still hauling me along. She stepped to the side, letting us run past her into the narrow hall on the other side of the door. As soon as we were through, she stepped back and pulled her hand away from the sensor to the left of the doorframe. The door promptly slammed, the light above it switching from green to red.

"Report," she said briskly, turning toward the wall. She pried open what looked like a section of paneling to reveal a control panel. Not looking at us, she started typing.

"At least two shooters, at least three technicians down."

"Kathleen and George," I panted. I slumped against the wall, bracing my hands on my knees. There was blood on my slippers; Kathleen's blood. I kicked them off, shuddering. "They're both down."

"Dammit." Dr. Kimberley kept typing. "They've been with me for years—how many people do we still have in there?"

"Seven," said Gregory. I didn't like the resignation in his voice. "At this point, they're locked in with two armed hostiles and at least one risen infected. Sorry, Danika, but I think we have to call this mission compromised."

"And it was going so *well*," she said, with a note of mock peevishness. She stopped typing and pressed her palm against the control panel's testing pad. "Do we know how they made us?"

"James didn't report for his shift. Given the timing, we have to assume he was a mole, and had been waiting for the opportunity to report back. We've been too busy for the last several days for anyone to sneak away unnoticed."

"Remind me to punch myself in the mouth for agreeing to take anyone who didn't come with me from the Maryland lab," said Dr. Kimberley. She pulled her hand away from the test pad. "They haven't changed the biometrics yet. I'd move back if I were you."

Not being a fool, I straightened and took a step backward. Gregory and Dr. Kimberley did the same. A metal shield dropped from the ceiling between us and the door, slamming down with enough force that it was easy to picture anything caught between it and the floor getting smashed flat. "Decontamination procedures initiated," announced a calm, robotic voice. "Decontamination commencing in ten...nine..."

"Run!" shouted Gregory. He grabbed my hand and we were off again, racing down the hall. Dr. Kimberley pulled up next to us, her high-heeled shoes swinging from her left hand. That was smart of her. She would never have been able to keep up with them on.

An alarm blared, drowning out the calmly counting voice of the security system. I barely heard Gregory swearing. My heart skipped a beat as I saw the red lights clicking on all along the hall in front of us.

"Dammit, Danika! You triggered a full lab decon!"

"I did no such thing! Someone's playing silly buggers with the security protocols!" She sounded frantic. I didn't blame her. I wasn't sure what a full lab decon entailed, but I knew enough about CDC procedures to know it wouldn't be anything good.

Gregory snarled something I couldn't quite make out. It sounded profane, whatever it was. He let go of my hand, apparently trusting me to run on my own, and began removing his lab coat. He didn't slow down. I stumbled a little, but kept running, aided by Dr. Kimberley's hand on my back.

"Here!" Gregory turned, now running backward as he thrust the coat into my hands. "Danika! Give her your shoes!"

"Right!" Dr. Kimberley shoved her shoes at me. I took them without thinking about what I was doing. "If you make it out of here, get in touch with Dr. Joseph Shoji. He'll help."

"What are you talking about?" I demanded. "We're all getting out of here!"

Gregory smiled sadly. "No," he said. "We're not." Then he stopped running, grabbing my arm and jerking me to a halt as he pulled the ID card from his pocket. He swiped it over the sensor pad of the nearest door, which slid immediately open.

"Override," said Dr. Kimberley approvingly. "Nice one."

"I thought so," he said, and shoved me through the open door. Another of those metal shields slammed down a split second later, shutting them both from view. It was thick enough that it also cut off the sound of the alarms, leaving me in a sudden, almost shocking silence. I stared at the blank wall of steel in front of me for several precious seconds as I tried to process what had just happened.

There was a full decontamination cycle starting on the other side of that wall. And the only two people I knew were on my side were on the other side of it.

Okay, see the problem here? It's one of scale. That's all. It's like math. Evil math. Take five bloggers, split them into three groups, and scatter them along the West Coast of the United States. Impose a radio silence. Start the apocalypse. Now, if Blogger A starts trying to contact Blogger B, using a secure DSL connection from Lab X, how long before Blogger A has a full-blown nervous breakdown?

Just wondering.

**—From *The Kwong Way of Things*,
the blog of Alaric Kwong, August 1, 2041. Unpublished.**

RISE UP WHILE YOU CAN.

—Graffiti from inside the Florida disaster zone,
picture published under Creative Commons license.

Twenty-two

"This isn't right." Becks watched the door, pistol drawn. "There should be more security."

"Maybe there's something going on." I kept most of my attention on my phone. I had a scanner running, checking for security frequencies that might give away our location. "Mahir? How's it looking?"

"The booster should be online in a few more seconds." He was on his back on the floor, using magnetic clasps to affix the Cat's equipment to the bottom of a server rack. "I still feel odd about this whole thing. I think this is the first actual *crime* I've committed for you people."

"We'll put it on your résumé," Becks said dryly.

"And we're good." Mahir pushed himself away from the server rack and stood, dusting off his still-immaculate pants. "That should work until they find it. Which will be never if that woman is half as good as she believes herself to be."

"Let's say she's half as good as Buffy was, and assume that means she gets about a year." I lowered my phone. "There's still no security activity in this part of the building. We're either clean to evac, or they're setting up an ambush."

Becks snorted. "Let me guess what you're going to say next. 'There's only one way to find out.'"

"Sounds about right," I agreed. "Let's get out of here."

The light above the door turned yellow just as we started to move. "There has been a security breach," announced a calm female voice. "Please proceed to the nearest open lab and await instructions. There are currently no confirmed contaminants. Please proceed to the nearest open lab and await instructions. Remain calm. Please proceed to the nearest open lab..."

The three of us turned to look at each other.

"Okay," I asked. "Who touched the bad button?"

The door slid open. We stopped looking at each other in favor of looking at it.

"Is that good, bad, or horrible?" asked Mahir.

"Don't know, don't care," said Becks. "Let's move."

Finding the correct server room had put us deep enough in the building that we couldn't just bolt for the exit. I gestured for Becks to exit ahead of me. She nodded understanding, suddenly all business, and left the room with her pistol held at waist level. I motioned for Mahir to go after her, and I brought up the rear. It wasn't as cold a move as it might have seemed from the outside. Becks was well equipped to handle herself, Mahir needed the cover, and I...

I was the most expendable one here.

We made our way through the halls, ducking out of sight whenever we heard footsteps, and avoiding any room with a red light above it. Becks went around each corner first, signaling us to follow once she was sure the next hall was clear. I would remain behind just long enough to be sure we weren't being tailed. It was slow. It was nerve-racking. I would actually have preferred a zombie mob. At least you can shoot those.

We all wound up standing together at a T-junction, identical halls stretching out to the left and right. "I...I can't remember which way we turn here." Becks sounded horrified. "I don't know which way to go."

"You go that way." I pointed left. "I'll go the other way. If you find the exit, wait there; I'll catch up. If you don't, turn around."

"Shaun—"

"Still in charge," I said amiably, before turning and jogging down the right-side hall. They didn't follow me. They were smarter than that.

The hall was deserted. I kept going, looking for the outer wall. My attention was so tightly focused that I didn't hear the woman who was running barefoot down the next hall until she came whipping around the corner and ran straight into me.

I staggered backward, barely managing to keep my balance. She did much the same, ducking her head for a moment in the process—long enough for me to register that she was wearing doctor's scrubs and a lab coat, but no shoes or socks. Her hair was short-cropped and dark brown, where it wasn't bleached in streaky patches.

Then she looked up, and my heart stopped.

"George?" I whispered.

"Shaun?" Her voice was unsteady, like she wasn't sure how she was supposed to be using it. We stared at each other, neither of us seeming to be quite sure of what we were supposed to do next.

Then she grabbed my hand and shouted, "Run!"

—————————

"Impossible" is something that stopped having any staying power when the dead started to rise. Trust me on this one. I'm a scientist.

**—From the journal of Dr. Shannon Abbey,
date unknown.**

—————————

Every day I wake up thinking "We're all going to die today." Maybe it's weird, but I find that comforting. Every day, I wake up thinking "This is the day it ends, and we all get to rest."

That'll be nice.

**—From *Adaptive Immunities*,
the blog of Shaun Mason, August 1, 2041. Unpublished.**

GEORGIA: Twenty-three

I slipped the lab coat over my scrubs, dropping the shoes on the floor, where they landed with a clatter. I stepped into them, still moving on autopilot. There was no blood on me—it had all been on my slippers, and those were on the other side of the barrier. I was clean, and I was alone. If I was getting out of here, I was doing it under my own power. I took a deep breath, turned, and walked down the hall. It took all my self-control not to break into a run. Running would attract attention. I was one more person in scrubs and a lab coat, practically part of the landscape, and the last thing I wanted was to attract attention to myself.

Voices drifted down the hall ahead of me. Suddenly remembering my little gun, I dropped it into the lab coat pocket and kept walking. A group of unfamiliar technicians rounded the corner and walked right past me, barely seeming to register my presence. I really was invisible...until someone recognized me, anyway. That was going to happen sooner or later. I needed a plan, and "keep walking until you find the exit" wasn't going to cut it.

Rescue came from an unexpected source: the building's security system. "There has been a security breach," it announced. All down the hall, the lights changed color. Some turned red. Most turned yellow, followed by their associated doors sliding open. "Please proceed to the nearest open lab and await instructions. There are currently no confirmed contaminants. Please proceed to the nearest open lab and await instructions. Remain calm. Please proceed—"

I stopped listening in favor of turning and walking toward the nearest open door, trying to look like I knew what I was doing. The first lab contained three anxious-looking orderlies. They were murmuring amongst themselves with their backs to the door. I stepped out of view as fast as I could, starting for the next open lab. It looked oddly familiar—oddly, because so many of the labs looked exactly like every other CDC lab I'd ever seen. I stuck my head into the room, scanning for signs of movement. There were none.

But there was a heavy black curtain covering the back third of the room. A faint blue glow seeped around the edges, casting shadows on the floor and ceiling. "No way," I whispered, and stepped all the way into the room. The door slid shut behind me. I barely noticed.

Why would they unlock this lab? Wouldn't they be too worried about the sanctity of their big bad mad science project to let people get near the tank? Then again, everyone who'd seen me had to know I was a clone. Maybe this was a wing where no one who didn't have the appropriate security clearances would ever set foot. I walked across the room, pausing barely a foot from that dangling curtain. Did I really want to know?

Did I really have a choice? I reached out, grabbing hold of the nearest fold of fabric, and pulled the curtain aside.

Subject 8c floated peacefully in her tank, asleep and unaware. The window to 8b's room was open. She was lying on her bed, headphones clamped over her ears. They were finishing her conditioning, implanting the subliminal memories they hadn't been able to extract from the original Georgia's damaged brain—or maybe just implanting the memories they'd crafted to *replace* the ones they chose not to salvage. Rage crawled up the back of my throat, chasing away the last of my fear. This was my replacement. This was the reason I'd been slated for termination. Their controllable Georgia Mason.

"Fuck that," I muttered, and turned to survey the lab.

I'm not the technical genius Buffy was. I'm not even on a level with Alaric or Dave. I am, however, the girl who grew up with the world's first Irwin for a mother, and a suicidal idiot for a best friend and brother. You can't do that without learning a few things the Irwin's trade, including the art of improvising explosives. It's amazing how many of the things needed for a basic biology lab are capable of blowing up, if you're willing to try very, very hard, and don't much care about possibly losing a few fingers in the process.

No one came through the lab door as I mixed up my jars of unstable chemicals. That was a relief. I didn't want to shoot anyone. Not because I was concerned about their lives—I was getting ready to blow massive holes in the building; concern about a few gunshot wounds would have been silly—but because I didn't want to attract attention, and unlike our friend the sniper, I didn't have a silencer. Ripped-up rags provided the fuses I needed, and I found a box of old-fashioned sulfur matches in one of the supply cabinets. Some things will never stop being stocked, no matter how far science progresses.

When I was done, I had eight charges, none of which was going to be much good without a spark. I set two of them along the base of the tank and two more by the window of the room where 8b slept. I wanted to feel bad about what I was doing. I was taking their lives away from them, and they hadn't done anything wrong. Only it wasn't their life. It was mine, because I was the closest thing to Georgia Mason that they were ever going to get. Call me selfish, but if I was going to die, I was going to die knowing my replacement wasn't waiting in the wings.

I set the other four charges around the edges of the lab, where they would hopefully knock down a few walls and cause a little more chaos when they went off. Hell, it was worth trying, and it wasn't like I had that much left to lose.

"Here goes everything," I said, and lit the first match.

There's no guidebook to making fuses from the things you can scavenge out of a CDC lab. I had no idea how long they'd burn, or whether they'd burn at all; maybe my big boom would be nothing but a fizzle. I wasn't going to stick around to find out. After the third fuse was lit, I turned and sprinted for the door.

The locked door.

"Oh, *fuck*," I said. "This can't be happening. This *can't* be *happening*." I hit the door with the heel of my hand. "Let me out, you fucking machine!"

"Please clarify the nature of your request," said the security system.

"Uh…" I froze for several precious seconds before blurting, "The tank has been compromised. I need to get some sealant, now, or the experiment will be terminated."

"Please state the nature of the compromise."

"There's a break in one of the feeding tubes."

I was taking shots in the dark. There was a pause before the system said, "Please hurry. Movement is currently restricted due to security conditions." The door slid open.

I ran.

The halls were practically deserted. I paused long enough to kick off Dr. Kimberley's heels and kept running, heading for what I hoped would be one of the building's outer walls. I hit a corner and turned, hit another corner and turned again. The first of my explosives would be going off at any second. I had to run, or else—

I was so focused on running that I didn't look where I was going. I whipped around a corner and slammed straight into the man who was running in the opposite direction. We both staggered backward, my head going down as I tried to recover my equilibrium.

He spoke first. "George?"

"Shaun?" I stared at him. He stared back. I wasn't sure what I wanted to do first—scream, cry, or hug him until the world stopped spinning. I had to settle for the fourth option. Darting forward, I grabbed his hand and shouted, "Run!"

Thank God for habit. Shaun didn't hesitate. He followed my lead, letting me tow him down the hallway and around the nearest corner, where two more familiar faces were waiting.

Shaun pulled me to a stop, saying, "We need to get out of here."

Becks and Mahir stared at me in abject disbelief. They were clearly taking my appearance the way I'd expected Shaun to take it: with surprise, and no small amount of anger. A few seconds passed while none of us said anything. Then Becks reached for her gun.

"There isn't time to shoot me!" I said. I didn't let go of Shaun's hand. I didn't know what he was doing here or how he got in, but if I was going to die, I was going to do it holding on to him as tightly as I could. "This place is about to blow. Do you know the way out?"

"Why should we trust you?" she demanded.

Shaun's eyes widened. "Wait a second. You can *see* her?"

"Yes, Shaun, we can see her," said Mahir. He sounded more dazed than Becks, and less angry.

"I have no idea what that means, but if you don't trust me, we're all going to be dead before you can find out how I got here." I focused on Mahir. "Do you know the way *out?*"

Mahir looked at me for only a moment before making his decision. "This way," he said, and gestured for us to follow as he turned and stepped through an unmarked doorway. Shaun pulled me along with him, perfectly willing to accept my presence. Becks brought up the rear, and I knew without looking that she had a gun pointed at the back of my head. Shaun had trained her well.

The door led to a small storage room. A panel in the back wall was missing. I could see grass and the nighttime sky through the opening. Shaun pulled me along. I went without fighting.

We were almost outside when the explosions began.

―――――――――――――

This is not fucking possible. Do you hear me, world? THIS IS NOT POS-SIBLE. I don't care if she fools Shaun and Mahir and everyone else, she's not who she's claiming to be. This sort of thing doesn't happen in the real world, and if we were living in a science fiction novel, good would triumph over evil a whole lot more often than it does.

I am going to find out who she is. I am going to find out what she's doing here. And then I am going to take great satisfaction in blowing her smug little imposter head right off her fucking shoulders.

—From *Charming Not Sincere*,
the blog of Rebecca Atherton, August 2, 2041. Unpublished.

Genetic testing of the remains found in Lab 175-c confirms that they belonged to Georgia Mason. Perhaps if we had fewer Georgia Masons running around the premises, we could be sure our rogue killed herself in her efforts to escape. As we do not have any mechanism for confirming the identity of the deceased, and as the explosions caused too much damage to determine the number of Georgias to die in the ensuing fire, we must assume for the time being that Subject 7c is now loose.

Congratulations, ladies and gentlemen. We have successfully resurrected a woman with every reason to want us all dead. I hope you can feel good about this accomplishment. I certainly cannot. Please consider this my resignation. Further, please send someone to clean my lab, as I am about to get blood all over the walls.

Everything went so very wrong so very fast. I will not take the fall for this.

I hope you're happy.

—Taken from an e-mail sent by Dr. Matthew Thomas,
August 2, 2041.

SHAUN: Twenty-four

She ran back the way I'd come. I ran with her, trying to wrap my mind around how *solid* her fingers felt. They were warm and strong and *right*, and I didn't care if it meant I'd finally snapped. I had her back. Crazy or not, I had her back, and there was no way I was ever letting her go.

We caught up with Becks and Mahir less than a minute later. They turned and stared when they heard my footsteps. "We need to get out of here," I said, skidding to a stop. They kept staring, but not at me.

They were looking at George. Scowling, Becks reached for her gun.

"There isn't time to shoot me!" said George, not letting go of my hand. Thank God for that. "This place is about to blow. Do you know the way out?"

I opened my mouth to relay what she'd said, but Becks cut me off. Still staring straight at George, she demanded, "Why should we trust you?"

It felt like the bottom dropped out of the world. "Wait a second. You can *see* her?"

"Yes, Shaun," said Mahir, sounding like he wasn't sure quite what was going on, but was certain he didn't like it. "We can see her."

"I have no idea what that means, but if you don't trust me, we're all going to be dead before you can find out how I got here." George looked at Mahir as she spoke. "Do you know the way *out*?"

For a moment, I thought Mahir was going to refuse to answer. Then he nodded, gesturing for us to follow. "This way."

I pulled George with me as I followed Mahir through the nearest doorway, still not willing to let go of her hand. Becks was right behind us. I didn't look to see whether she had her gun out. I didn't want to know how I'd react if she did.

The panel we'd removed on our way in was still off to one side, leaving our exit clear. It looked like security hadn't been through yet, probably because of whatever breach had the lights going wacky. That was a small blessing. George didn't say anything as we climbed through the hole, but she looked like she was torn between laughter and screaming when she took her first breath of outside air.

Becks was just stepping through the opening when the explosions began.

And thus, in a single moment, did my life go from unbearably strange, but still tolerable, to actively impossible. I am willing to allow that, once one lives in a world where science can transform mosquitoes into the harbingers of the apocalypse, the rules of our forefathers have, perhaps, ceased to apply.

That doesn't mean that the dead should walk. Not unless they're zombies, anyway. It's simply impolite, and I don't think we should stand for it.

—From *Fish and Clips*,
the blog of Mahir Gowda, August 2, 2041. Unpublished.

Joey—

Not sure when I'll be able to reach you again. We've done it. She's loose. It wasn't quite like we'd planned—someone leaked what we were doing, and we lost half the techs—but it worked, and she's on the run. I'm going to be off the grid for a little while. Keep the lines open. God willing, Georgia Mason will be reaching out to you soon, and when she does, I want you to be ready to help her in any way that you can.

This may end soon. Pray to God it ends as well as it can.

—Taken from an e-mail sent by Dr. Danika Kimberley to
Dr. Joseph Shoji, August 2, 2041.

GEORGIA: Twenty-five

Shaun didn't let go of my hand once after he had it—not while we were climbing through the hole in the wall, and not when the explosions started. It was like I was the lifeline he'd been looking for. I wasn't going to object. I *knew* he was the lifeline I'd been looking for, and no matter how improbable his presence was, I wasn't going to let go of him until I absolutely had to.

Concussive booming sounds came from the building behind us as we ran. They followed a definite wave pattern, with a small crumping explosion followed by a cascade of louder, more enthusiastic booms. My little charges had managed to break through into something a lot more combustible—probably the formalin tanks. It's nice how many common chemicals are just looking for an excuse to explode.

We ran across a vast, manicured lawn, with evergreen trees standing between us and the fence. If there was a scheduled security sweep of the grounds, it had been canceled in favor of dealing with the explosions; no one stopped us or sounded any additional alarms as we fled.

"If this is anything like Portland, emergency services should start responding to the alarms any minute now!" shouted Shaun, glancing back over his shoulder at the others. "Extra confusion is good, but extra eyes won't be! Keep running!"

"Shaun—" began Becks.

"Talk later! Flee now!"

I didn't say anything. I was struggling just to keep up. No matter how much this body looked and felt like the one that I remembered, it wasn't, and it simply wasn't equipped for this sort of situation. Maybe it would be one day—assuming I survived that long—but right now, it was all I could do not to fall over and wait for someone to come along and shoot me.

Our path took us to a hole in the fence that looked like it was created by using a pair of magnetic current-bridging strips to reroute the electricity before cutting the wire. Mahir went through first, followed by Shaun, who kept my hand even while I was struggling not to snag my lab coat on the fence. Slowing down made me realize how much my lungs hurt, and how much my *feet* hurt. I didn't want to risk looking at them, but I was pretty sure they were bleeding.

This wasn't the time for first aid. We needed to get as far from the CDC as possible. I straightened, catching my breath as best as I could, and let Shaun pull me back into a run.

We got lucky; any zombies in the area had been attracted by the sound of sirens, and left us alone as we ran. We made it out of the grass and onto the broken sidewalk before my toes caught on the curb and I fell, gravity and momentum conspiring against me for one horrible moment. My hand was yanked free of Shaun's, but not fast enough for me to catch myself. The landing knocked the air out of me—what little air had been *left* in me—and I wound up prostrate and wheezing, trying to find the strength to get back up again.

"Are you okay?" asked Shaun. He sounded concerned, but calm. Too calm; scary calm, like he wasn't surprised to see me in the least.

I was still trying to get enough air to answer when the grass rustled, Becks and Mahir jogging up behind us. There was a click—the sound of a pistol safety being released.

"Move and you die," snarled Becks, tone leaving no room for argument. I froze, stopping everything but my efforts to breathe. "Now who the fuck are you, and what are you doing here?"

"She fell," said Shaun, sounding wounded. "Dude, what's your damage?"

"It's all right, Shaun," said Mahir, who sounded as calm as Becks was angry. "Let her deal with this. You just stay right there."

"What's my damage? What's my *damage*?" Becks laughed, a short, brittle sound that made the hair on the back of my neck stand on end. "I want to know what the hell game she thinks she's playing. That's all."

"I'm not playing a game, Becks," I said, voice muffled by the fact that I was talking into the pavement. "Can I get up before I try to explain myself?"

"Hold on," said Shaun. Now he just sounded perplexed. Not being able to see people's faces was starting to get to me. "I realize things were a little crazy in there before, so I was sort of willing to blow it off and all, but are you telling me you guys can actually *see* her?"

"What?" I said, lifting my head slightly. Becks didn't shoot me. That was something.

"We can both see her, Shaun," said Mahir wearily. He was panting from the run, although not as much as I was. "I don't know who this woman is, but she's no ghost, and no hallucination. We can see her perfectly well."

"And if she doesn't start talking soon, we can see her bleed," said Becks. She nudged my leg with her toe, snapping, "Well? Identify yourself."

"*Please* can I get up first?" I asked. "It'll be easier for us to understand each other if I'm not talking into the street."

There was a pause as some consultation I couldn't see took place behind me. Finally, Becks said, "Fine. Get up. But if you so much as twitch funny, you're going back down, for keeps. Understand?"

"I understand." I pushed myself to my hands and knees, wincing as gravel and chunks of pavement bit into my hands. It was worse when I actually stood, pressing my bloody feet down on the ground.

Shaun took a half step forward, reaching out to help me with my balance. Becks switched her aim to him.

"Don't," she said, very softly. "Don't make me."

He stepped back, putting his hands up. "Okay, Becks, don't worry. I'll stay right here."

"Thank you."

"Thank you all," I said. My hair was sticking to my forehead in sweaty, matted clumps, and the wind was cold on my cheeks. I hurt, I was possibly going to get shot in the next few seconds, and I'd never been so happy to be alive. I glanced at Shaun, reassuring myself that he was really there and really real, before looking back to Becks and Mahir. "I understand you're probably confused and upset right now. I was, too, when all this started. But I swear, it's me."

"There is no 'me,'" snarled Becks. Her eyes narrowed. "What the fuck kind of stunt is this? Plastic surgery? Natural lookalike so we wouldn't be able to find the scars?"

"Cloning and experimental memory-transfer techniques," I said. That was enough to stun Becks into a momentary silence.

Not Mahir. He drew his own gun, aiming it at my chest. "What's your name?"

"Georgia Carolyn Mason."

"What's your license number?"

"Alpha-foxtrot-bravo, one seven five eight nine three." I rattled off the number without hesitation, glad it wasn't one of the things stored in the fuzzy area of my memory. "I was issued my provisional B-class license on my sixteenth birthday. That license number was bravo-zulu-echo, one nine three two seven one. It was retired when I tested for my A-class license. I did that when I turned nineteen."

"What's my name?"

"Mahir Suresh Gowda. Your license was issued by the Indian consulate in London, so it's about ninety digits long and comes with diplomatic immunity and what are you *doing* here? Aren't you supposed to be on a different continent, objectively observing our problems?"

He snorted. "Well, my boss went and got herself killed, so it seemed I was needed on a more local level."

Becks recovered from her brief silence, asking, "If you're George, what's wrong with your eyes?"

I touched the skin below my left eye, grimacing. "Freaky, isn't it? Again, cloning. The scientists who grew me couldn't induce a specific reservoir condition. When they tried, they caused spontaneous amplification in the clones unlucky enough to be their test subjects. I guess it got pretty expensive, so they stopped trying before they got to me."

"Makes you a pretty lousy copy," said Becks coldly.

"I know." I dropped my hand back to my side. "I'm the show model, to prove that they can make a realistic copy of a person. I wasn't supposed to get out. The clone they were planning to send to you was surgically altered to look like she had retinal KA."

"The clone they *were* planning?" asked Mahir.

I smiled. I couldn't help myself. "She was in the lab where I planted the initial explosives. You wouldn't have wanted her anyway. She was programmed to betray you."

"And you weren't?" demanded Becks.

"If I have been, I don't know about it," I said.

"This is impossible," said Mahir.

"This is insane," said Becks.

"This wasn't my idea," I countered.

Shaun cleared his throat. "This is starting to make my head hurt, and that's probably not a good sign. Does somebody want to explain to me exactly how the CDC managed to bring George back from the dead?"

"They didn't," said Becks. "This woman is *not* Georgia."

"Yes, I am," I protested. "I know it's unbelievable, but it's true."

Mahir frowned. I knew that look. It was the look he got when something presented him with a really interesting problem to solve. "We'll not come to any conclusive decisions standing out here," he said. "Miss, if you'll allow us to search you for weapons—"

"And scan her for tracking devices," interjected Becks.

"Yes, of course. Search you for weapons and scan you for tracking devices, and if you come up clean, we can take you back to the hotel where we're currently quartered and try to sort this out."

I let out a breath I'd only been half aware of holding. "I have a gun in the pocket on the right-hand side of my lab coat. It's loaded, but the safety's on."

Becks stepped forward, sticking her hand into my pocket with more force than was strictly necessary. She pulled out my gun and stepped back, stowing it in her belt. I felt instantly less clothed. "Got anything else?"

"Not that I'm aware of. If there are tracking devices on me, I don't know they're there. They're probably subcutaneous." I shook my head. "The EIS would have removed any of those that they found, but that doesn't mean they found them all."

Becks sneered. "We'll just see. You picked the wrong team to try infiltrating, lady, and as soon as we find out who you really are, I'm going to kick the ever-loving crap out of you."

I smiled slightly, relief fading into a mellower look of generalized exhaustion. "See, that sort of thing, right there, is why I missed you guys so much." I glanced at Shaun. "Becks is with you, instead of working with the betas now? Good call."

"Becks is in charge of the Irwins," he said. Then he frowned. "Shouldn't you already know that, if they've sent you here to infiltrate us?" His tone was turning belligerent. He was starting to get angry. That was bad.

"They didn't send me, Shaun. I *escaped*," I said. "The one they wanted you to find would have a better cover story."

"This is all academic," said Mahir. "Whether or not she's really Georgia—"

"She's not," said Becks.

"—she's here, and we're going to have to contend with her, one way or another."

"At least we won't have any issues with the law if we need to shoot her." Shaun looked at me coldly. "She's already dead."

Seeing that look on his face hurt more than almost anything else in the world. "I'm not dead anymore, Shaun. I swear to you, it's me. Please believe me."

He suddenly lunged forward, grabbing my shoulders and turning me to fully face him. Becks started to moved toward us. Mahir grabbed her upper arm, stopping her. I barely noticed. I was too busy staring into the eyes of the man in front of me, the eyes I'd been waiting to see since the moment I woke up. They were looking at me with such *anger*. I'd seen that look on his face before, but never directed at me.

"Who are you?" he demanded, voice pitched low. The pain in it hurt almost as much as the anger in his eyes. My poor, poor Shaun...

"I'm Georgia," I whispered. "I'm not anyone else, and that means that I'm her."

He looked older, like he'd lived through more than just a year without me. His eyes searched my face, finally settling on my hairline. "Why haven't you dyed your hair?" he asked.

"The doctors responsible for my care didn't give me the opportunity. I would have, if they'd let me." I would have given myself retinal Kellis-Amberlee, just so I'd feel less like a stranger in my own skin. I would have done a lot of things.

"Can you prove to me that you are who you say you are?" He didn't let go of my shoulders. "Is there anything, *anything* you can do that will make me believe in you?"

He wanted to believe; I could see it in his eyes, a deep ache buried under the pain. That was why he couldn't let himself do it. There's no such thing as miracles, and when the dead rise, they don't look in your eyes and say their names. Maybe in some other world, but not this one.

I took a slow breath, casting another glance toward Becks and Mahir. Then I looked back to him and said, "There's only one thing we never wrote down. You know what it was."

"Do you?"

"I do, but, Shaun, I don't know if—"

"Prove it, right now, or I swear to you, I will shoot you myself."

"You have no idea how much I've missed you," I said, and leaned in and kissed him. His hands tightened on my shoulders, his whole body stiffening against mine as he realized what I was doing.

And then he started kissing me back.

That was the one thing we never wrote down—the one thing we *couldn't* write down, because no file or server is ever totally secure, and it would have gotten out. No one would have cared that we weren't biologically related, or that we'd gone in for genetic testing when we turned sixteen, just to be absolutely sure. No one would have cared that we didn't trust anyone else enough to let them be there while we slept. No. The media loves a scandal, and we'd been raised as siblings in the public eye. It would have destroyed our ratings, and then the Masons would have destroyed *us*, for blackening the family name.

There were a few people who'd guessed over the years. I'm pretty sure that Buffy knew. But we never, *never* wrote it down.

He squeezed my shoulders so hard it hurt. I didn't pull away, and after a few seconds, his hands relaxed and he pulled me to him, returning the kiss with a frightening hunger. I grabbed his elbows and pulled him closer still, until it felt like we were pressed so closely together that there was no room for anything to come between us. Not even death. We were home.

I didn't pull away until my lungs started burning. His hands dropped from my shoulders and he opened his eyes, staring at me. I stared back. Slowly, he reached out with one shaking hand and brushed my bangs away from my forehead.

"Georgia?" he whispered.

I nodded.

"How—?"

Mahir cleared his throat. "Unbelievable as I find all this—and believe me, I *do* find it unbelievable—this is, perhaps, not the best place to go into it. CDC security will find the hole we created sooner or later, and we've been standing here long enough that I feel it will be sooner. If everyone agrees, we should remove this reunion to a safer location."

"I still say we shoot her," said Becks.

I glanced at her, frowning. "Has she always been this bloodthirsty?"

Shaun kept staring at me. It was like there was nothing else in the world. Somehow, I understood the feeling. "I may have taught her a few things."

"If we're going to move, we should move," said Mahir. There was a core of cold efficiency in his voice that hadn't been there a moment before. "Shaun, you're unfit to lead the remainder of this mission. Becks, I outrank you. Georgia…" He faltered, realizing what he'd just said. "Miss, whoever you are, you are not currently a part of our structure. As that makes me the senior staff member here, I hereby command the rest of you to *move*."

I smiled at him. I couldn't help it. "Thanks, Mahir. I missed you, too."

Shaun grabbed my hand, starting to walk. I went with him, only wincing a little as my battered feet hit the ground. Mahir and Becks followed us, Becks never putting her pistol away. I didn't care. She wasn't going to shoot me now; not without getting the story of who I was and what I was doing with them. She was a Newsie for too long to throw away a lead like that once the heat of the moment had passed.

We didn't talk as we made our way across a decrepit parking lot to an even more neglected-looking garage. There was nothing we could say that wouldn't confuse matters further. Shaun and Becks produced flashlights from their pockets, clicking them on and using them to light the way into the darkness of the parking garage. I stopped when I saw what their beams had illuminated, a grin spreading, unbidden, across my face.

"You still have the van," I breathed. "I was afraid that after... well, after what happened, that the decontamination would have been too expensive." And that he wouldn't have wanted to keep it after he killed me in it.

"I had to replace all the upholstery, but I wasn't willing to lose the frame," said Shaun. "We spent too much time there for me to give it up that easily."

Tears welled up in my eyes. Becks took one look at my face before she snorted, snapped, "Let's get the fuck out of here," and went storming over to the van.

"She's not always like this," said Shaun.

"I've got a feeling she will be for the next few days," I said, and let him lead me to the van.

All four of us had to submit to a blood test before the locks would disengage. I held my breath until mine came back clean and the doors unlocked. Becks opened the back and pulled out what looked like a modified metal detector wand. "Spread," she ordered me.

I knew better than to argue with an Irwin who had that look on her face. I pulled away from Shaun, who let go of my hand with obvious reluctance, and assumed the position used by air travelers since the birth of the TSA. She ran the wand along my arms, legs, torso, and back, scowling a little more each time it failed to beep. Then she passed it to Mahir, who repeated the process. I had to admire their thoroughness, even though I knew that a false positive—or worse, an accurate one—would probably result in my getting shot in the head.

Finally, Mahir lowered the wand. "She's clean," he said. Becks scowled.

Shaun, on the other hand, grinned like he'd just been told that he was now uncontested king of the entire universe. He tossed Becks the keys. She caught them automatically. "You're driving," he informed her. "I'm riding in back with George."

She muttered something before getting into the driver's seat. I didn't need to hear it to know that it wasn't complimentary. I also didn't have the energy to worry about it just then. Shaun helped me into the back of the van, where he sat down on the floor, opening his arms to me. I climbed into them willingly, nestling myself as closely against him as anatomy and the space around us would allow, and closed my eyes.

I fell asleep listening to the sound of his heart beating. I have never slept that well in my life, and I may never sleep that well again.

BOOK IV

Reservoirs

Okay, that's it. No more Mister Nice, Heavily Armed, Really Pissed-Off Journalist.

—SHAUN MASON

The dangerous thing about truth is the way it changes depending on how you're looking at it. One man's gospel truth is another man's blasphemous lie. The dangerous thing about people is the way we'll try to kill anyone whose truth doesn't agree with ours. And the dangerous thing about me is that I've already died once, so what the fuck do I care?

—GEORGIA MASON

Miss me?

> —From *Images May Disturb You*,
> the blog of Georgia Mason, August 2, 2041. Shared internally only.

—

Yes.

> —From *Adaptive Immunities*,
> the blog of Shaun Mason, August 2, 2041. Shared internally only.

SHAUN: Twenty-six

The Agora guards were all smiles as they came out to meet us. "Welcome back to the Agora," said the one next to Becks's window, holding out a blood testing unit. "If you would be so kind—"

"We're going to need a fourth kit," I said, craning my neck to see the window from between the seats. George was still asleep, curled up against me with her fingers locked in the fabric of my shirt.

"Or we could just let them shoot her," said Becks sweetly.

Mahir put his hands up before I could say anything. "There will be no shooting of anyone who tests cleanly. Can we please get a fourth testing unit?"

"Of course, sir," said the guard, looking unflustered. Apparently, people drove up with battered, dirty women in CDC scrubs all the time.

"George." I shook her shoulder. She didn't respond. I shook her again, harder this time. "Georgia. Wake up."

"Problems, Mason?" asked Becks.

"Nothing I can't handle," I said. Leaning down until my mouth was only a few inches from George's ear, I said, "If you don't wake up *right now*, I'm going to get a bottle of water from the travel fridge. I will then pour it down your back. You won't enjoy it, and I won't care. Just in case you were wondering."

Her eyes opened. I had the time to think, almost academically, that my crazy was useful after all—all those hallucinations got me used to the idea of a Georgia without retinal KA, and now I actually had one. Then she smiled, and all thoughts went out the window except for holding on to her and never, ever letting go.

"You have no idea how much I've missed you threatening me awake." She untangled her fingers from my shirt and sat up, looking around the van. She stiffened when she saw the armed guards looking through the windows, patiently waiting for us to get our shit together. "Shaun? Where are we?"

"At our hotel. It's a long story. Can you sit up and let them run a blood test?" Seeing the look of alarm in her eyes, I added quickly, "This place has security that would have given Buffy, like, spontaneous orgasms for *days*. They're not going to share their results. They just want to know that we're all clean before they let us through the gates."

"If you say so," she said warily.

"Promise." I kissed her forehead before opening the van's side door. Another guard was waiting there, this one holding a testing unit in each hand. I gave him a smile. He didn't give it back. "My man! Is it time to prove that we're not planning to eat the other guests?"

"We have a strict policy of non-cannibalism here at the Agora," he replied, holding the tests toward us. His eyes flicked toward George's bloody feet, noticing and acknowledging them, but he didn't say a word. If we wanted to engage in dangerous behaviors, we could, as long as it didn't result in our bringing infection past their gates. It was an attitude I could definitely respect.

"We're good with that," I said, and leaned over to take one of the tests. George did the same with the other. "On three?"

A flicker of a smile crossed George's face. "On three," she agreed. "One."

"Two."

Neither of us said "three." Instead, we each reached out and placed our right index fingers on the test unit in the other's hand. The guard didn't say anything; again, if we wanted to be crazy, it wasn't his problem, as long as we were clean.

We didn't look at the lights. We just looked at each other. There were tears at the corners of George's eyes, and I wouldn't have been surprised to learn that she wasn't the only one. If she failed this, I wasn't going to shoot her again. I wasn't—

"Thank you, Mr. Mason, ma'am." The guard leaned forward, pulling the test units from our hands before either of us could react. I turned, and saw the green lights gleaming at the top of each small white box. He smiled genially. "We're pleased to have you back. Miss Garcia has been alerted to your arrival, and to the presence of your guest. One of our attendants will meet you at the door with slippers for the young lady. Please have a pleasant stay at the Agora."

"See? Cake." I turned to look toward the front. The windows were back up; Becks and Mahir had apparently passed their own tests while I was distracted.

"It's not going to last," said Becks. Her eyes met mine in the rearview mirror as she started the engine. "We just showed up with a woman who looks like she's been kidnapped from a lab, and is basically a walking hot zone right now, with those feet. This isn't cool."

"Maybe not, but what else was I supposed to do?"

"This discussion is not going to end well," said Mahir sharply. "We're going to go inside, meet with Maggie, and decide what happens next. No one gets the deciding vote. Am I understood?"

"It is *so* good to see you," said George. She got up onto her knees, half kneeling as she looked through the windshield at the hotel. Her eyes widened. "Where are we? Hill House?"

"Whatever walks here walks in the presence of a large, well-trained staff ready to attend to your every need," said Mahir. "As the gentleman said, welcome to the Agora. It's a resort of a kind, for people whose monthly allowance puts my annual income to shame."

"You let Maggie choose the hotel, didn't you?"

"Don't answer that," said Becks. "Until we know what's going on, we're not telling you anything more than we have to. I'm pretty sure this place is expensive enough that they'll dispose of a body for us if we ask them."

"The privileges of wealth." George sank back to the floor. She gave me an anxious look, and I took her hand, squeezing it. The solidity of her was still the most amazing thing I'd ever felt.

"It's going to be okay," I said.

"Maybe," she replied.

None of us said anything after that. Becks drove up the long driveway to the parking garage, where the valet waved us through the open gate, apparently remembering our preference for self-parking. Becks got out first. By the time I opened the van door, she was already there, pistol out, covering us.

"I think it says something deeply disturbing about me that I find this comforting," said George, wincing as her cut-up feet hit the cool cement of the garage floor.

"That's Becks. Always ready to offer a helping headshot." I restrained the urge to pick George up and get her feet away from the ground. I needed to let her walk on her own. She'd never forgive me if I didn't.

"I thought I learned from the best," said Becks. She stayed where she was, letting us step away from the vehicle. It was clear she intended to follow us to the door, rather than risking George getting the drop on her.

Oddly, it wasn't only George who found her paranoia comforting. Knowing there was someone behind me, ready to shoot if something started to go wrong, made me a lot more comfortable letting George take my hand, even though it would keep me from getting to a gun as fast as I might need to.

Mahir walked on my other side. He didn't say anything. He didn't need to. The worried, faintly disapproving look on his face said volumes.

True to the concierge's word, a man in the hotel uniform was waiting by the airlock with a pair of fluffy blue and gold slippers in one hand and a matching robe in the other. He held them out to us as we approached, saying, "The management is thrilled that you're here, but would prefer that you not distress the other guests."

"What?" I asked blankly.

Mahir cleared his throat and nodded toward George. I turned, looking at her.

There were stains on the sleeves of her once-white lab coat. Some were clearly chemical; others could have been blood. Some of the stains on the cuffs of her pants were definitely blood, as were the streaky smears on the tops of her feet. The fact that she was dressed like a medical professional would just make those little spots more terrifying for most people. We trust doctors because we have to. We never forget that they're the profession with the highest day-to-day risk of infection.

George looked down at herself, clearly coming to the same conclusion. "Thank you," she said, reaching out to take the robe and slippers. Putting them on made her look less disheveled, and oddly younger; the robe was at least three sizes too large, and hung on her like a shroud. She tied the robe around her waist, sleeves all but swallowing her hands, and flashed a quick, professional smile at the attendant. "It's great."

"Welcome to the Agora, miss. We hope you'll enjoy your stay." He bowed before turning and stepping into the airlock. I was pretty sure any charges associated with the robe and slippers would be appearing on our master bill, and would be hefty enough to make me choke. Good thing none of us were ever going to see the price tag for this place.

Once the attendant was clear of the airlock, George and I stepped inside. A little more of the tension went out of her shoulders as soon as we were past the first layer of glass, like even that thin barrier took us farther from her captivity. I couldn't reach her hands, swaddled as they were in layers of plush terry cloth, so I squeezed her shoulder instead.

The smile she flashed my way was a lot less professional. "You can keep doing that forever," she said quietly.

"Planning on it," I said. Then the door was sliding open in front of us, and we left the airlock together, letting it begin a new cycle as Becks and Mahir were processed through.

George looked around the Agora lobby with a cool, calculating curiosity, like she was assessing the whole place for acoustics, security, and exit routes—the three most important functions of any space as far as a journalist was concerned. Every move she made just convinced me a little more that she was who she said she was. I knew I wanted to believe her, which put me at a disadvantage, but...if she'd been off in anything but the superficialities of her appearance, I would have been the first to notice. So far, she was doing everything right. That meant she was either the real thing, or an unbelievably good fake.

Please be the real thing, I prayed, to no one in particular.

Only one of us can be real, replied the quiet voice of my inner Georgia.

I stiffened. She'd been quiet for so long that I'd almost started thinking of it as a transition. George dies, she moves into my head. George comes back to life, she moves out again. It was simple. Straightforward.

Impossible. You don't recover from going crazy just because the thing that made you that way is magically undone. If the human mind worked like that, we'd be a much saner species.

"Shaun?" George looked up at me, frowning. "You okay?"

For a horrible moment, I didn't know which of them I was supposed to respond to. Then Maggie stepped out of the elevator lobby, eyes wide. She was back in her normal clothes, a heavy cable-knit sweater over a long patchwork skirt, and her hair was braided into a semblance of control. She started toward us, her gaze never moving away from George's face.

"Shaun?" she said, when she was close enough to be heard without raising her voice. "What is this?"

"That's a complicated question," I said honestly. The airlock door slid open behind me, and footsteps marked Mahir and Becks falling into a flanking position, Mahir to my left, Becks to George's right.

"Hi, Maggie," said George.

Maggie stiffened. "She sounds like—"

"That's because she is," I said.

"Maybe," said Mahir.

"Probably not," said Becks.

"We should go upstairs," said Maggie, eyes still locked on George's face. "This sounds like the sort of thing that shouldn't be talked about in the lobby."

"That's probably a good idea," I agreed.

Maggie led us back to the elevator lobby, not looking to see whether we would follow. She knew we would. George freed her hand from the layers of terry cloth and reclaimed mine, sticking close to my side as we walked. I clung back just as fiercely. Becks and Mahir brought up the rear, and none of us said a damn thing, because there was nothing we *could* say. This was too big, and too impossible, and too important to crack open before we were secure.

"My room," said Maggie, once we'd reached the floor where the four of us—five of us, now—were staying. "It has the most space."

"Wait—more space than *my* room?" I asked. "How is that possible? You could call the room I'm staying in an apartment and not get busted for false advertising. I think there's someone living in the closet."

Maggie cracked a very small smile. "My father owns a share in the Agora. When I stay here, I get a specific room."

"Wealth hath its privileges," said Becks, with none of the faint disdain that so often colored her voice when she talked about money. Then again, she was normally talking about money in the context of her own family, and she didn't like them. Maggie's money must have been somehow less offensive by dint of not belonging to the Athertons.

"Yes," agreed Maggie, without irony. She led us all the way to the end of the hall, where a single door was set in a stretch of wall that could easily have played home to three doors leading into rooms the size of mine. Even that didn't prepare us for the size of the room on the other side.

Becks put it best: "Holy shit. That's not a bedroom, it's a ballroom."

"Also a living room, dining room, kitchen, and a bathroom with a private hot tub," agreed Maggie, holding the door open for the rest of us. "The hot tub seats eight, in case you wondered. According to my mother, I was conceived in a suite very much like this one, but thankfully, on a different floor. I'm pretty sure she told me that so I'd never have sex here, ever."

"Did it work?" I asked, curious despite myself.

She closed the door behind Mahir. "No. I brought Buffy here to celebrate when she first got the job working with the two of you. She wasn't the first, and she won't be the last."

"And we are now officially getting too much information," said Becks. "Thank you."

"No problem. Can I get anyone anything before we start going over exactly how we've managed to shatter the laws of nature today?"

George cleared her throat, looking a little embarrassed as she said, "I don't suppose you have any Coke on hand, do you?"

That was the best thing she could have said. Maggie blinked, looking briefly surprised. Then she smiled. "I do. Shaun? Same for you?"

"Coffee for me, actually," I said.

"Coffee? Really?" Maggie's surprise only lasted a few seconds. "Coffee and Coke, got it. Becks? Mahir?"

"Nothing for me," said Becks.

"Tea, please," said Mahir. "I have the feeling this is about to become one of those days wherein there is no such thing as too much tea."

"You're not alone there," said Maggie. "Go ahead and sit down. I'll be right back." She vanished through a door near the entrance, presumably heading into the kitchen to get the drinks.

George walked over and sat down on one of the room's two couches, burying her hands in the pockets of her robe. She slumped there, looking tired and frail. George was always smaller than me, but she'd never been skinny like this before. It was a little disturbing.

You're willing to accept that I might come back from the dead, but you're upset because I haven't been eating enough? What should I be eating, the flesh of the living?

"Be quiet," I said automatically.

George looked up. "Nobody said anything."

Shit. "Uh..."

"It's been difficult for all of us since Georgia passed," said Mahir, in a voice stiff enough to sound starched. He took the seat next to George, presumably so I couldn't. I could respect that, even as it annoyed me. She was, after all, claiming to be my dead sister, resurrected, and I had just demonstrated, openly, that I was crazy.

"Come on, asshole. Let's sit." Becks took my elbow and led me to the other couch, where she pushed me into a sitting position. She sat next to me, resting her pistol on her knee.

"You don't normally call me asshole without provocation," I noted.

"You don't normally act like one," she responded.

George looked between the two of us before turning to focus on Mahir. "I'm sorry about that," she said. "I mean, no one means to die, but... I'm so sorry." She hesitated before asking, "How much of this was our fault, Mahir? How many people died because we wouldn't stop telling the truth?"

Mahir's eyes widened. I think that was the moment when he started to let himself think that maybe believing her was an option. "I don't know," he said. "Quite a few, I'm afraid."

"Yeah." She sighed, glancing at Becks and me before returning her attention to Mahir. "Rick was at the CDC a few days ago."

"What?" Becks half stood. "You little bi—"

"Rebecca, sit *down*," snapped Mahir. It wasn't a request.

Becks sat.

George blinked, looking bemused. "Okay, does someone want to explain that?"

"We haven't been able to get through to Rick for a while," I said. "We're pretty worried, especially given everything that's been going on. If he was at the CDC, you're saying he knows what's going on and he just doesn't care. That's sort of a big deal."

"No." George shook her head, expression hardening into that old, familiar look of burning journalistic fervor. She wasn't a scared, bruised-up girl who might or might not be who she claimed to be. She was a reporter, and she had a story she needed to tell. "He's been helping the EIS. I think he was there because he *does* care, and something's been stopping him from getting to you."

"What are you talking about?" demanded Becks.

"She was about to politely offer to wait for me to come back before she explained," said Maggie, walking back into the room. She had a tray of drinks in her hands. It was embossed with the Agora logo, and looked like it was made of solid silver. Considering everything else around us, I would have been almost more surprised if it wasn't.

"Sorry, Maggie," said Becks, looking faintly abashed.

"It's okay." Maggie made her way around the room, starting with Mahir, who got a white ceramic mug and saucer. George got two cans of Coke, both cold enough to have drops of condensation on their sides. By the time Maggie reached me with my coffee, George already had the first of those cans open, and was taking a long, desperate drink.

Maggie leaned close as she handed me my coffee, cutting off my view of George. "If she isn't who she says she is, she can never leave this room," she murmured. "You understand that, don't you, Shaun?"

I nodded minutely. "I do."

"Good." She straightened again, walking over to an open chair and sitting with the tray, and her own cup of tea, in her lap. "So can I get the recaplet of what happened after you left here? I doubt we have time for the whole episode."

"We broke into the CDC through the back fence," I said. "We got inside just fine, managed to plant the bug and everything, but then we got turned around."

"You are in a maze of twisty little passages, all alike," said Mahir, and laughed for no apparent reason.

"Uh, yeah. Anyway, we split up. Becks and Mahir went one way, I went the other way. And then this lady comes running around a corner and slams into me, and it's, well..." I indicated George with my free hand. "Honestly, I didn't think she was really there until everyone else started saying they could see her, too."

"That's understandable," said Maggie, not unkindly.

"Yeah. So she says we have to get out fast, because the building is about to blow up. We get out fast. The building blows up. And then Becks starts threatening to shoot her in the head, we sort of negotiate a temporary peace, and we wind up back here, with you, having coffee." I took the first sip of my coffee and moaned. "Really fucking *good* coffee. What did you do, Maggie, sacrifice a bellboy to the coffee gods?"

"Not this time," she said, and sipped her tea before turning surprisingly sharp eyes on George. "What's your side of the story?"

George took a breath. "Do you want the long version or the short version?"

"Let's take the version somewhere in between. Mahir's never going to be satisfied with the short version, and Becks will probably start shooting people if you go for the long version."

"True," said Becks. "To be honest, I'm tempted to start shooting people right now."

"I missed you, too, Becks," said George. She took another drink of Coke for courage, and said, "I woke up about a month ago—maybe a little bit more; I don't really know, since they never let me have a calendar—in a CDC holding room. A man named Dr. Thomas said I'd been in recovery for a while, and that things were going to be better now. But my eyes were wrong, and my muscle tone was wrong, and the tattoo on the inside of my wrist was gone. I asked if I was a clone. He confirmed it."

Becks scoffed.

To her credit, George ignored her, and continued. "One of the orderlies, Gregory Lake, was actually an EIS doctor assigned to infiltrate the facility. He's one of the people who got me out. He told me I'd been created from a combination of electrical synapse recordings and implanted information. I'm supposed to be a ninety-seven percent match to the original Georgia Mason." She looked toward me. "I'm not her, and I am, all at the same time."

"So you're not really her, and we can shoot you now, right?" asked Becks.

Mahir shook his head, frowning. "No."

"What?" Becks gave him a wounded look. "Why not?"

"I've read some of the memory recovery studies. It arose from research aimed at assisting brain damage victims." His frown deepened. "We're nothing but electrical impulses stored in meat. If you can measure and codify those impulses, you can transcribe what a person remembers."

But I was dead, said George. *How could they measure my thoughts if I was dead?*

Whether I liked it or not, it was a good question. "George was dead," I said. "So how does that work?"

"Kellis-Amberlee keeps turning the electricity in the body *and* brain back on after the point of death," said Maggie. We all turned to look at her, even George. She shrugged. "Raised by pharmaceutical magnates, remember? Kellis-Amberlee really improved our understanding of the human brain, because it won't let the brain die. It turns back on again and again, trying to keep thinking. Only the virus starts getting in the way of those electrical impulses. It scrambles them. The body can't translate what the brain wants anymore, and so the virus just takes over."

"If the CDC's built a system for recovering the electrical impulses from an infected brain, cleaning out the static and then implanting them in a new mind, it's entirely feasible that they'd be able to accomplish what you're claiming." Mahir looked thoughtfully at George.

"I'm the closest match they ever made," said George. "That's why they decanted me. I was their show pony. I think they were planning to sell the tech that made me. Immortality for the highest bidder."

Every eye in the room went to Maggie. She blinked, and then slowly shook her head. "No way. My parents wouldn't do something like that, even if they could afford it."

"Are you sure?" I asked.

"Yes. I am." Her tone was firm, cutting off further discussion.

George bit her lip. "Anyway. I wasn't supposed to be here."

"You keep saying that, but how do we know you're not lying?" asked Becks. "Maybe you're telling the truth, only the ninety-seven percent Georgia died at the CDC, and you're the Judas."

"It's a possibility," George agreed. "I guess we'll just have to wait and see whether I'm consumed by the urge to betray you. Thus far, no urges."

"No one is betraying, or shooting, anyone right now," said Mahir firmly. "Please continue your story."

"Gregory said he wanted to get me out, but we'd need to find a way to do it. If we weren't careful, things could get ugly. He had another associate in the facility, working undercover with the CDC. She said her name was Dr. Shaw, but then after they managed to get me away from my handlers, she started calling herself Dr. Kimberley. She—"

"Dr. *Danika* Kimberley?" Mahir sat up a little straighter.

"Yeah." George blinked at him. "You know her?"

"She's an epidemic neurologist, specializing in infections that alter the behavior of the brain—including Kellis-Amberlee." He frowned, focusing on George. "Describe her."

"Tall, white-blonde hair, really blue eyes, looks sort of cold. She wore incredibly stupid shoes." Her face fell. "She gave them to me when she told me to run."

"And she had a Scottish accent?" asked Mahir.

George frowned. "Welsh, I think. She never told me where she was from."

Mahir nodded like she'd just passed some sort of test. "They got you away from your 'handlers.' Then what?"

"Then they drugged me and operated on me without my consent." Her lips thinned. "Guess the people who made me wanted to protect their investment. They had some lovely surprises implanted in my muscle tissue, designed to release neurotoxins when they decided they were done with me. I guess that seemed more humane than taking me behind the building and shooting me. Have I mentioned recently that I hate science?"

"You didn't need to," I snarled. The urge to go back to the CDC, find some survivors, and start punching them in the face was almost too strong to be denied.

Down, boy, said George.

"Oh, good. I hate science. That operation is probably why you couldn't find any trackers when you scanned me. The EIS doctors took those out, too."

"Or maybe the CDC always thought there was a chance the EIS would smuggle you out, and they wanted to be sure they couldn't get any useful information out of you," said Maggie quietly. Again, every eye in the room went to her. She reddened. "It makes more sense than 'and then we implanted really expensive biological bombs in somebody instead of using a bullet.' She was a booby trap. Just not for us."

"I wish that didn't make sense," muttered George.

My scowl deepened, while Mahir looked quietly relieved. Every word she said made her story a little bit more believable. That didn't make me happy about it.

Becks ignored my obvious unhappiness as she leaned forward and addressed George. "So where does Rick come into all this?"

"I was in recovery—still pretty drugged—when he came into the room. I couldn't open my eyes, but I heard his voice. He said..." She faltered, and took a long drink from her Coke before she continued. "He said he was sorry I'd had to go through all this. And he told me to do what I did best."

"What's that?" asked Mahir.

George looked at him. "He said to break this fucking thing wide open and let the pieces fall."

"Ah. And after that?"

"I told the EIS I'd only cooperate if they let me get online. So they got me a connection, and I managed to use one of the back doors into the secure server to talk to Alaric."

"Which one?" asked Becks.

"The Elm Street entrance."

Maggie laughed, once, sharply, and was silent.

George continued. "We were supposed to talk about evacuating me after that, but...something went wrong." She looked down at her soda. "Someone started shooting. I saw two of the orderlies go down. Gregory and Dr. Kimberley and I ran. They shoved me through a quarantine door as it was closing. I managed to get into an empty lab and set some charges. I mostly just wanted to create a distraction so I could try to sneak out in the chaos. Instead...well. That's where Shaun came in."

"I see." Mahir turned, looking toward me. "Well?" he asked.

"You know my vote," I said.

Becks scowled. "I don't like this."

"I didn't ask if you liked it. It's a horrible perversion of the laws of nature, we're doubtless to be struck down by the divine, should the divine ever bestir itself to remember that we're here. As we're still periodically having a zombie apocalypse, I doubt that's going to happen any time soon. Now what's your answer?"

Becks looked at George. Then she turned and looked at me. "I believe her," she said finally. "If she's not Georgia, she thinks she is. It's better that we keep her close."

I could have cheered. Instead, I looked toward Maggie, who smiled.

"This is the sort of thing that happens in comic books," she said. "I'm in."

"Thank you." Mahir turned back to George. "It's good to have you back. Disorienting and terrifying, and you'll forgive me if I don't rush to embrace you, but…good. Now, how would you feel about breaking this fucking thing wide open, to see where the pieces fall?"

George finished her first can of Coke and put it aside before opening the second. The carbonation hissed into the silence. Then she spoke: "What else am I supposed to do?"

━━━━━━━━

Shannon—

Danika was just in touch with me. Please provide the nearest safe meet-up point. I am en route to you. We need to talk. The endgame is beginning, and you're going to need all the assistance you can get if you're going to make it through this in one piece.

We all are.

**—Taken from an e-mail sent by Dr. Joseph Shoji to
Dr. Shannon Abbey, August 3, 2041.**

━━━━

They got her out. Kimberley and Lake…they got her out. She's alive, she's intact, she's clinically sane, and she's *out*.

Peter still doesn't know what I've done, or what I'm going to do. But history will remember him as a president worthy of the name, and not another in the long line of crooks and monsters to have held the position. He will be known for who he was, and for what he did, and for what he sacrificed. All of them will. If that means history must also remember me as a monster, well…

So be it.

**—From the private journal of Vice President Richard Cousins,
August 3, 2041. Unpublished.**

GEORGIA: Twenty-seven

After some discussion, we—meaning "Maggie and Mahir," who were the only ones still considered completely rational; the rest of us were treated as compromised, to one degree or another—decided the best course of action was to stay at the Agora long enough to recover, and then head out. Mahir also pointed out that we were better off keeping the van under cover for at least a few hours, in case it had been seen leaving the vicinity of the CDC. So we were staying put. I wasn't inclined to argue. The last few hours were starting to catch up with me, and I wanted nothing more than a dark corner I could curl up in until the urge to start shaking went away.

After a bit more discussion, Becks reluctantly agreed that I wasn't likely to go crazy and kill Shaun without setting off the hotel security system, which meant the two of us could do our recovery in the same hotel room. "The Agora takes the safety of its guests very seriously," Maggie assured her. "There are so few blood tests because the biometric monitoring system is so advanced. If either of them is in medical distress, the guards will be alerted within seconds."

"Nice place," I said, approvingly. "I didn't even know this was here."

"That's the point." Maggie smiled, still looking somewhat uncertain. "Is there anything I can have sent up to the room for you?"

I bit back my first answer, waiting a few seconds to be sure that it was what I wanted to say. Oh, well. In for a penny, in for a pound. "Can I get some clean clothes, a pair of sunglasses, and a bottle of the darkest brown hair color you can find?"

Most of the uncertainty went out of Maggie's smile. "We can do that," she agreed. "Shaun? Do you want to show Georgia to your room? I'll call the front desk and have things sent up." She gave me a measuring look. "I think the biometrics from the door will give us her size."

"Thank you," I said. There wasn't time to say much more—Shaun was making hasty farewells as he grabbed my hand and started hauling me toward the door. Mahir was still saying good-bye when the door slammed shut behind us, leaving us alone in the hall.

I expected Shaun to say something then. He didn't. He just kept pulling me along, walking briskly back toward the elevators. I glanced at his face and decided to give it a minute. He'd survived me being dead for over a year. I could survive him being silent for a little while. Still, my feet hurt, and even the soft carpet wasn't helping all that much. I was relieved when he finally pulled me to a stop in front of a door that looked like every other doorway in the hall.

There was a small green light just above the peephole. It blinked twice when he gripped the door handle. Then the door swung open, revealing a room that looked like the younger sibling of Maggie's room. I had to blink twice before I realized the dimness wasn't only because he had the curtains drawn; the overhead lights were set to UV. It was the kind of change that used to be second nature to both of us, making sure the lights in our hotel rooms wouldn't give me migraines that left me incapable of doing my job.

Shaun let me enter first. He pulled the door closed as he stepped inside and said roughly, "The bathroom's through there. You can change the lights if you want to. I don't mind."

"No. No, this is…this is good." There were no signs that he'd been in this room before, except for the curtains and the lights. I turned to face him. He was watching me, a deep, anxious hunger in his eyes. "I'm real, Shaun. I'm not going anywhere."

"What did you give me for my eighth birthday?"

"A black eye, because you said girls couldn't be Newsies."

"How did we meet Buffy?"

"Online job fair."

"Who was your first boyfriend?"

I had to smile at that. "You were. Also my second, and my third, and every other number you can think of. You can keep asking questions as long as you want, Shaun, but I'm only going to get ninety-seven percent of them right. It's up to you whether that makes me real or not."

"I missed you." He raised a hand, touching my cheek so gently that it made my heart hurt. I put my own hand over it, forcing his fingers flat against my skin. He sighed. "You *died*, George. I shot you, and you *died*."

"No. You shot Georgia Mason." He winced, but didn't pull his hand away. I forced myself to keep going. If I didn't say this now, when we were alone for the first time, I was never going to say it. And I had to say it. "You shot a woman whose DNA profile I share. I have ninety-seven percent of her memories. I remember growing up with you. I remember my first blog post. I even remember dying. I remember everything, right up until you pulled the trigger."

"George..."

"I remember thinking I was the luckiest woman in the world, because you were there to do it. But those memories aren't only mine. Do you understand?"

"You're Georgia enough for me," he said, finally pulling his hand away. "Neither of us is perfect anymore."

I nodded. Fine, then. If this was who I was going to be, then I was going to be her. "You saved me."

Shaun dipped his chin in what would have been a nod, if he'd raised his head again. Instead, he kept looking down at the floor, slow tears beginning to make their way down his cheeks. "I wanted to die with you."

"You didn't." I grabbed his hand again, squeezing his fingers. "You kept going. And now I'm back, and we get to finish this thing together."

He raised his head, looking at me anxiously. "What if you get hurt again?"

"We can't start living in 'what if,' Shaun. If we do that, I might as well have stayed dead." I smiled a little. "Is there a first-aid kit? I want to get some sealant on my feet."

"What? Oh!" He straightened, focus returning almost instantly as he realized he had something he could *do*, rather than standing around worrying until Mahir came back and said it was time to go. "This way."

He led me to the bathroom, where a search of the medicine cabinet yielded a first-aid kit that could have put some hospitals to shame. I sat on the edge of the bathtub while he wiped my feet off with a wet cloth, then sprayed them with a fast-drying layer of wound sealant. It would act as an artificial skin, porous enough to let my wounds heal, but thick enough to prevent infection. I'd used the stuff before, although never on quite such a large area. It's amazing how big the bottoms of your feet can seem when you've managed to run all the skin off of them.

He wrapped my feet in a layer of gauze once the sealant was dry, just in case. I didn't ask him to stop. I just watched him work, studying the tension in his shoulders and the new strands of gray at his temples, visible even through the bleached-out streaks of almost-blond. I saw the moment when that tension turned into decision, and was prepared when he straightened up, leaned forward, and kissed me.

There have been times when I wondered how people didn't put the pieces together. How many so-called siblings share hotel rooms after puberty, much less share bedrooms with a door connecting them? We never dated. We never went to school events with anyone but each other. We never did any of the normal social things, and yet people still assumed we were on the market, not that we'd been off the market before we even knew what the market was.

We were still in the bathroom ten minutes later when someone knocked on the front door. The voice of the hotel said politely, "Mr. Mason, your request from the front desk has arrived. Would you like to claim it now, or would you prefer that it be left for your convenience?"

Shaun pulled away from me, cheeks flushed. "Uh..." he said. Then, more coherently, he said, "I'll be right there. Thanks." He got up, leaving me sitting where I was as he walked out of the room. I'd expected being alone to make me nervous, but it did the opposite. For the first time since the CDC decided to bring me back, no one was watching me. I was genuinely free.

Low voices came from the hall, followed by the sound of the door closing. Shaun reappeared, a brown paper bundle in one hand and a bottle of hair dye in the other. "What do you want to do first?" he asked.

I smiled.

An hour later, I actually felt like myself again. My hair was damp and dark brown, sticking to my ears and forehead as it dried. The clothes Maggie requested were perfect, if two sizes smaller than I would normally have worn—black slacks, a white button-down shirt, and a black blazer with pockets for my audio recorder and notepad. I didn't have either of those at the moment, but just having the pockets made me feel better. Even the shoes fit. My eyes were the only things that didn't look right, and that was what the sunglasses were for. Once I put them on, I looked like I'd been sick for a while, but I didn't look like a clone.

I looked like Georgia Mason.

Shaun apparently thought so, too. When I put the sunglasses on, he stopped talking and just stared at me. Finally, in a quiet, reasonable tone, he said, "If it turns out that this is all some crazy, impossible hoax, and you're a fucking android or something, I'm going to kill us both."

"Cloning is crazy enough for me, so I'm good with that," I said. "Can we kill a bunch of other people first?"

"Yeah," said Shaun, and smiled. "We can."

"How much of this is our fault, Shaun? How much...how many questions did we ask that we should have left quiet? People are dying." I walked over to the bed, sitting down on the edge of the mattress. "Do we own this?"

Shaun barked a short, humorless laugh. "The people who started all this shit own it. We just made it happen a little faster. I think…enough of it is ours that we have to fix it if we can."

"We can."

"God, I hope so." He sat down next to me, taking my hands. "This is what you missed. Your post got out—you know that—and it changed a lot of things, and nothing, all at the same time. It's part of why Ryman got elected. You made it pretty clear he wasn't playing on Tate's team. It probably doesn't help that Tate went all bad movie villain when I cornered him."

My eyes widened. "When you what? Shaun—"

"Just listen, okay? See, after you…after I…I had to leave the van. Steve—you remember Steve, from Ryman's security detail? Big fucker, looked like he could stand in for the entire Brute Squad?"

"Please don't tell me Steve died," I said.

"No, he's fine. Still writes me sometimes, or did, before we had to go off the grid. See, Steve and I broke quarantine to get to Ryman…"

The story he told was crazy and impossible and enough to break my heart. I'd always known that Tate was bad, but Shaun was the one who confronted him, and got fed a line about restoring America to its roots through fear and control. Tate martyred himself. It might have worked, too, if he hadn't martyred me first.

Shaun buried me and tried to move on, but the world wouldn't let him; the world never does. Instead, he wound up neck deep in conspiracies and craziness. Dave died. Kelly Connolly died. Dr. Wynne turned out not to be an ally, but one more crazy man out to change the world into what he thought it should be. The longer Shaun talked, the more I realized that the only allies we had were the ones we shared a website with.

I only stopped him twice: once to ask about the reservoir conditions, and once to make him repeat, several times, that he'd been bitten and hadn't amplified. Crazy as it might sound, that was the part I had the most trouble believing. The additional details on the insect vector for Kellis-Amberlee just left me cold. Maybe mankind was going to lose the war against the living dead after all—and this time, it might not be because someone dropped a vial.

Eventually, Shaun stopped talking. Then he reached up and removed my sunglasses, putting them beside me on the bed. "We could run," he said. "You and me. Head for Canada, or something. The others could finish this without us. You know they would."

"And we'd never forgive ourselves," I said. "We finish this. And if we survive, somehow, through some miracle…then we run. You and me, and anywhere they won't find us."

"It's a date." He leaned back, reaching for the phone.

I blinked. "What are you doing?"

"Calling room service. I don't want you to blow away if there's a stiff wind."

I laughed and hit him without thinking about it. That brought a totally sincere smile to his face before he turned away to deal with placing our order. Less than fifteen minutes later, two massive bowls of chicken cacciatore were delivered to our door, along with a six-pack of Coke and a piece of tiramisu the size of my head. My stomach growled when I saw the food, and I realized that I was genuinely hungry for the first time in a long time.

The only thing I wanted more than food was access to the Internet, which Shaun provided as soon as our dinner was just memory and crumbs. My laptop wasn't at the Agora—why would it be?—so he let me borrow his, both of us stretching out on the bed with our backs to the headboard, my shoulder pressing into his chest as I began doing the most important thing I could possibly do.

I began catching up on the news.

Working as a professional journalist meant years of learning to absorb as much information as possible in as short a time as possible, since failure to stay on top of current events could easily result in posting a story that had no relevance at all. I was always a little slower than most of my contemporaries, because I was always so damn careful to check and double-check my facts before I put my name behind them. Oh, I had my op-ed blogs—*Just the Wind* when I was a teenager on a provisional license, and *Images May Disturb You* once I was old enough to go full-time—but those were thoughts. Opinions. Ideas. It was the articles I put on the main site that really mattered, and those were the things that needed me to do my research.

Using After the End Times as my start point, I pulled up the archives, going all the way back to the day after I died. Shaun's posts from that period were a jumbled mess; half the time, I wasn't even certain they were written in English. Mahir and Alaric did most of the real reporting, following the rest of the Ryman campaign with a clinical detachment that told me everything I needed to know about the depth of their grief. Shaun wasn't the only one who'd been hurting. And the headlines rolled on.

Ryman elected in a landslide vote, stuns voters by choosing Richard Cousins as his replacement vice president! The Democratic candidate, Susan Kilburn, is so devastated by her loss that she takes her own life! Ryman takes the White House!

Shaun Mason goes quietly crazy, while his staff scramble to cover up the cracks in his facade. Maggie Garcia moves into Buffy's place, and does a good job, especially considering the circumstances. Shaun cedes his position to Rebecca Atherton, letting her run the Irwins while he runs deeper into the damaged recesses of his own psyche. Mahir continues shaping the site into a force for the truth, doing as much as he can to stand against the tide of ignorance and corruption.

CDC researcher Kelly Connolly is shot in a robbery gone wrong! Downtown Oakland is sterilized following an outbreak, resulting in the tragic death of thousands, including reporter David Novakowski! An insect vector for the Kellis-Amberlee virus appears along the Gulf Coast, killing millions more! The members of the After the End Times core team are wanted in conjunction with potential bioterrorism, and should be reported if seen! Ryman grieves for his wounded nation!

The CDC decides to raise the dead. Someone tells a whole lot of lies, and someone else makes sure the world will believe them.

Everything goes wrong.

The effort of filtering the headlines for the truth hidden beneath them—the truth hidden between the lines, in the places where it was less likely to be seen—left my head pounding. I slumped backward, letting my head rest against Shaun's shoulder.

"I couldn't have done it," I said, closing my eyes.

"Done what?"

"What you did. Kept things going. I wouldn't have—*couldn't* have—done it. I would have fallen apart."

"I *did* fall apart," he noted, in a tone that was almost comically reasonable. "I went nuts. I've been talking to you since Sacramento, and you've been talking back."

"I thought it might be something like that. You never did do 'alone' very well."

"Neither did you."

"That's why I would have killed myself by now."

Silence fell, and stretched out for almost a minute before Shaun said, "Well, then, I guess it's a good thing I'm the one who got out of Sacramento, huh? Which is kind of funny if you stop to think about it."

I put the laptop aside on the bed and pushed myself up, twisting around to look at him. "What are you talking about?"

"Dr. Wynne died because Kelly—the Doc, that's what I called her while she was with us—stabbed him with a scalpel while he was in the middle of a big-time bad-guy soliloquy. I mean, I don't know if there's an Evil Fucker 101 class that they all take, but between him and Tate, I'm about ready to slap the next person who wants to tell me about his evil plan." Shaun's eyes were haunted. "The Doc was a good person. Maybe the only good person left in the CDC. I don't know. I never had time to find out."

I thought of Gregory and Dr. Kimberley, both of whom had chosen the EIS over the CDC. "Maybe you're right," I admitted.

"Anyway, before Dr. Wynne died, he as good as said that whoever shot you wasn't *aiming* for you. The needle was supposed to be mine." He brushed my hair away from my cheek. "You were supposed to shoot me, not the other way around. Then Tate would give you his big bad guy speech, and you'd think it was over, because you believed in black and white."

My stomach felt like a solid ball of pain. "They knew how to beat us."

"Yeah. But the cold equations fucked them up, because the math doesn't care. They subtracted the wrong half of the equation, and I've been kicking them in the ass ever since. For you." He looked at me earnestly. "I was doing it all for you."

I sighed, folding my hand over his before I scooted closer. "I know."

Some time later—once the laptop had been put back on its charger, and the "do not disturb" light had been lit on the door—we slept, both sprawled on top of the covers. Shaun kept one arm around me as we drifted off, clinging like he was afraid I'd vanish before he woke up. I've never been the world's cuddliest person, and that didn't seem to be one of the things that dying and coming back had changed, but for once, I didn't mind. Anything that kept me from waking up and thinking I was back in CDC custody was okay by me.

We'd been asleep for a few hours when a gentle chiming noise filled the room, followed by the voice of the Agora saying, "I do hope you've enjoyed your rest. Miss Garcia would like to remind you that you have an appointment that cannot be rescheduled."

"Huh?" I sat up, wiping the sleep from my eyes with one hand and fumbling for my sunglasses with the other. It's amazing how quickly habits reassert themselves, even when they're not really needed anymore.

"She means it's time to go see the Monkey." Shaun leaned over to grab his shirt off the floor before sitting up.

"The who?"

"I'll explain on the way. Come on."

Having just the one set of clothes made getting dressed to go substantially easier than it used to be. Not that I ever spent that much time thinking about what to wear, but when you own ten identical pairs of black pants, you sometimes have to spend a few minutes figuring out which ones are clean. We were both ready in half the time it would have taken before I died. Shaun led the way to the door, where he paused, looking back at me.

"I was tired of being a haunted house," he said. "Thank you for coming home." Then he stepped out into the hall, not leaving any space for my response. Maybe that didn't matter. Maybe this was one of those things that didn't need to be responded to. I followed him out of the room. The door swung shut behind me, the locks engaging with a muted "click."

Mahir, Maggie, and Becks were already in the lobby, standing near the entrance to the airlock. Mahir paled when he saw me, looking for all the world like he'd just seen a ghost. In a weird way, I guess he technically had.

"Everything fit?" asked Maggie, as we walked into conversational distance.

"Like a dream," I said. "Even the shoes are perfect. Thank you. You have no idea how good it feels to be *dressed* again. They wouldn't even let me have a bra while I was under observation."

Maggie shuddered at the thought of that indignity. Becks kept eyeing me, expression not giving away what she might be thinking about the whole situation.

"We were thinking you might not feel completely clothed just yet," said Mahir, shaking off his shock. He dipped a hand into his pocket, pulling it out with the fingers curled around some small object. "If you would be so kind?"

Blinking blankly at him, I held out my hand. He dropped an ear cuff into it.

It was a small thing, barely weighing a quarter of an ounce, but it felt like the heaviest, most valuable thing in the entire world. I raised my free hand to my mouth, suddenly doubly glad for the familiar screen of my sunglasses. They would keep everyone else from seeing the tears in my eyes.

"Oh, God, Mahir, thank you." I blinked the tears away as firmly as I could. More rose to take their place. "Thank you so much."

"It only has three numbers in its address book," said Becks, tone still tight with suspicion. "Tap it once for Shaun, twice for Mahir, and three times for me. *Don't* try to reprogram it. There's a safety lock on the controls. You mess with the directory, the whole thing will short out, and we'll know."

"I wouldn't dream of it," I said. "Seriously, thank you all. You have no idea how much this means to me."

Maggie smiled. "I think I might have a bit of a clue."

I smiled back before reaching up and delicately affixing the ear cuff to the shallow outside curve of my ear. It pinched the skin in a way I remembered from high school, back when I started wearing the portable contact devices on a regular basis. I'd have raw spots and blisters for at least a week while I got used to it. And I didn't really give a damn.

"If we're all prepared to wander gaily off to our dooms, we should really get moving," said Mahir, tearing his eyes away from my face. "I'm sure our gracious hosts would prefer the doom not find us early."

"You are always such the little ray of golden sunshine, Mahir, you know that?" Shaun grinned. "Let's roll."

Joey—

What the fuck do you mean, "Danika was just in touch with you"? Danika hasn't been in touch with anybody in *years*. She's still on crazy safari in the crazy jungle, looking for the crazy magical herbal cure to the walking dead. Seriously, that woman is so much crazy crammed into a small space that she's practically a crazy singularity. Have you been sticking your dick in the crazy singularity? Because that's how you catch the really *good* social diseases.

My coordinates are attached. They're good for another four days. Then I'm cutting bait and we're getting ourselves to higher ground. The floods are coming, my friend. Try to disengage from the crazy long enough to get the fuck out of their way.

—Taken from an e-mail sent by Dr. Shannon Abbey to Dr. Joseph Shoji, August 3, 2041.

I'm not sure which is worse: the fact that Shaun was willing to accept this woman as his dead sister, or the fact that I'm beginning to believe it might be true.

Georgia Mason had a certain way of reacting to things—a kinesthetic language, rather than a verbal one. It wasn't the sort of thing you could fake without years of practice. If this woman is an imposter, she hasn't had years...and she moves like Georgia. She has all the little ticks and twitches down cold. When she came out of that elevator dressed, with those sunglasses on ... I was ready to call her Georgia and ask what we were going to do next. And that's not a good thing.

If she's the real deal, then awesome, the laws of science have been twisted even further away from what they were intended to be. Bully for the laws of science. And if she's not the real deal ...

If she's not the real deal, I'm pretty sure she's going to get us all killed.

—From *Charming Not Sincere*,
the blog of Rebecca Atherton, August 3, 2041. Unpublished.

SHAUN: Twenty-eight

There was no handy text-based adventure game to guide us back to the Brainpan, which meant I had to drive, since I was the one who'd driven us there the first time. I didn't appreciate being separated from George. I've never been clingy—codependent, sure, according to every psychologist I've ever talked to, but not *clingy*. That didn't mean I appreciated having her out of arm's reach now that she was alive again.

The need to have her where I could touch her would fade, given time. I was sure of it. Or at least I hoped I was sure of it, and not just lying to myself.

You've had a lot of practice lying to yourself, commented Georgia. She didn't sound angry. Just resigned.

"Quiet," I mumbled.

Maggie, who was sitting in the passenger seat, gave me a sidelong look but didn't say anything. I appreciated that. I had absolutely no idea what I would have said in return.

In the back of the van, Mahir and Becks—mostly Mahir—were quizzing George, trying to feel out the limits of what she knew. She fielded most of their questions without hesitation. I stopped breathing a little bit every time they asked her something and she didn't answer right away, waiting for the sound of Becks taking the safety off her gun, but George recovered every time. If there were questions she wasn't going to get right, they weren't the kind of questions the two of them would think to ask.

I didn't care what answers were hidden in the three percent of herself she'd lost by dying and coming back to life again. She'd already given me all the answers I needed.

Maggie surreptitiously hit the button to seal the doors as we drove through the neighborhood leading to the Brainpan. Her worried glances out the window confirmed the reason why. Even after visiting and surviving once, the decay of the buildings disturbed her.

"It'll be okay, Maggie," I said. "I doubt anyone lives here except the crazy people we're on our way to visit. And sure, they may decide to shoot us and store our bodies in the freezer or something, but at least that's a normal thing, right?"

She muttered something in sour-sounding Spanish before saying, "It was never normal before I started traveling with you."

"See? It's like I always say. Travel is broadening."

Maggie showed me a finger.

I clucked my tongue. "Really? You're going to flip me off? I mean, jeez, Maggie. In the last twenty-four hours, I've broken into the CDC—"

"Again," called Becks from the backseat. "Don't forget Portland."

"—okay, point, broken into the CDC *again*, which, PS, kind of blew up while I was still there, seen my sister come back from the dead, and had a *lot* of coffee. It's going to take more than a middle finger to upset me."

Maggie raised both hands, backs to me, and showed me two fingers.

I nodded agreeably. "Much better. Hey, look! There's the serial killer van!" It seemed a little odd to use a burned-out pre-Rising van as a landmark, but it made a certain amount of sense. In a neighborhood as decrepit as this one, you couldn't exactly use paint colors or house numbers to navigate, and saying "turn at the house that looks like it was painted to blend in with viscera" would probably inspire even less confidence than "turn at the serial killer van."

"Goodie," said Maggie.

"You don't *sound* excited."

"That's because I would rather be home, with my dogs, writing porn," she said.

I glanced over at her. "Soon you will be."

She didn't have anything to say to that.

The van bumped and jounced down the driveway to the Brainpan. I parked outside the garage and killed the engine, waiting.

George poked her head up between the seats. "Is there a reason we're just sitting here?"

"Yes."

"And that reason would be...?"

"The house is full of crazy people who would love an excuse to shoot us in one or more of our extremities—probably more—so we're going to wait in the car until they tell us we're allowed to go inside." Said aloud, it sounded even more ridiculous than it really was. That wasn't enough to make me move.

"Crazy people like that one?" asked George, pointing toward my window.

I turned.

The Fox was perched in one of the half-dead trees still clinging to the soil around the edges of the yard. She'd somehow managed to become almost unnoticeable, despite her tricolored hair and rainbow leg warmers. She raised one hand in a jaunty wave when she saw us looking her way. Then she jumped easily down to the cracked dirt of what used to be lawn, sauntering toward the van.

I had the driver's-side window rolled down by the time she reached us. My hands were resting on the dashboard, clearly visible.

"Hi!" she said, peering past me to George. There was a large gun in her hands. I was reasonably sure it hadn't been there when she jumped out of the tree, and I knew I hadn't seen her draw it. My conviction that this woman was not just crazy, but very, very dangerous, grew. "What's your name? You weren't here before."

Georgia looked at her coolly. The sunglasses helped. She was better at maintaining a neutral expression when her eyes couldn't give her away. "Georgia Mason, journalist. You are?"

"Me?" The Fox blinked at her, then cocked her head. "I'm Foxy. I used to be called Elaine, and everything was boring, and I was sad all the time. But things are better now. I wouldn't ask that question again, if I were you."

George frowned. "No? Why not?"

"Oh, because if you ask it where the Cat can hear you, she'll tell me I should shoot you in the head a couple of times to teach you not to pry. And then I'll probably do it, because she makes the best cookies, and I don't like remembering that I used to be someone who was sad." The Fox said this as if it were entirely reasonable. In her scrambled little head, it probably was.

I broke in before George could say anything else. "Foxy, we've finished the errand we agreed to do. Can we come inside and talk about what happens next?"

"Oh, sure." The Fox smiled, taking two short hop-steps back from the van. "Come on in. I bet the Cat's going to be thrilled to see you!"

Behind me, I heard Becks mutter, "Only if she's got a really good idea for ways to skin people alive."

"You heard the lady, gang," I said, hoping the Fox hadn't heard that. If she had, it didn't seem to have bothered her. She was rocking back on her heels and looking at the sky, with the gun still in her hands and pointing at the car. I was pretty sure her crazy wasn't an act, but her clueless definitely was. "Let's get ourselves inside."

"Don't forget to leave your weapons, or I get to shoot you all," said Foxy blithely. "I'll start with the shouty girl. She probably needs shooting more than all the rest of you combined."

"I do believe she likes you, Rebecca," said Mahir.

"Shut up," snarled Becks, and began disarming.

The Fox turned and wandered toward the house, apparently dismissing us. George, meanwhile, grabbed my shoulder and demanded, "Are we *actually* going to get out of this van without any weapons?"

"That would be the plan." I removed both guns from the waist of my jeans, putting them on the dashboard. George gasped a little. I paused, really *looking* at the guns for the first time in a long time. "Oh. I guess this one's yours, isn't it?"

"She can get it back *after* we finish dealing with the happy neighborhood psychopath brigade, okay?" said Becks, dropping three clips of ammo onto the floor. "Right now, I want to get in, get what we came for, and get the hell out of here. Seattle is not a good place for us to be anymore."

"Tell me something I don't know." I opened the van door. Still looking unsure about the whole thing, George followed Mahir out the side door. Maggie walked around the van to meet us, and the four of waited as patiently as we could for Becks to finish disarming.

"What are you carrying, an armory?" I called.

"I'm prepared," she shot back, and slid out of the van. Part of the reason it had taken her so long was revealed; she had already unlaced her combat boots, making them easier to remove. Seeing the understanding in my expression, she smirked. "See? Prepared. You should try it some time, Mason. You might discover that you like it."

Mahir snorted. "And swine may soar. Now come along."

"Yes, sir," said Becks, in a lilting, half-mocking tone. She was still chuckling as we walked toward the house.

I dropped back, letting Mahir and Maggie lead George as I asked Becks quietly, "You okay? You're all...chipper...all of a sudden."

She shook her head. "I'm not, really. I feel like I've been put through seven kinds of emotional wringers in the last year, and I can't even begin to imagine how you feel right now. Thing is? It's not going to change, and it's not going to stop, and it's not going to go away. The dead are coming back to life, and this time, they want to give us a piece of their minds instead of taking a piece of ours away." Becks nodded toward George, who was walking up the porch steps. "The more I talk to her, the more I think she's for real. That's terrifying. That's my whole life, falling down, because my parents are the kind of old money that funds politicians who fund places like the CDC, and now the CDC is bringing back the dead, *again*. So no, I'm not okay. I just don't have the energy left to be miserable about it all the damn time."

"So you're in a good mood because it's easier?"

"Yeah." Becks gripped the crumbling remains of the banister, holding it as she started going up the stairs. "You went crazy because it was easier. So what's so bad about deciding to stop scowling for the same reason?"

I didn't have a good answer. I shrugged and followed her into the house. The others were waiting for us there.

Once we had all removed our shoes, we proceeded into the living room. George hung back to walk beside me, our hands not quite touching. Her presence was almost reassuring enough to make up for the fact that none of us were armed.

The Cat was sitting on one of the room's two couches, feet up on the coffee table and a tablet braced against her knees. The Fox was nowhere to be seen. I honestly couldn't have said whether or not that was a good thing.

"You know, I did *not* think we would be seeing you again," said the Cat, not looking up from her tablet. Her fingers skated across the screen with the grace of an artist, making connections in some pattern I couldn't see. "If there'd been a bet, I would have lost."

"We're here for our IDs," said Becks. "We did our part."

"Oh, I know. I knew as soon as the bug started transmitting. They've been naughty, naughty boys and girls there at the CDC. They're going to be very sorry when they get the bill for this. Killing people, cloning people, arranging outbreaks...it would have been so much cheaper if they'd settled their debts in a civilized manner."

I went cold. Grabbing blindly for George's hand, I asked, "What do you mean, 'the bill'?"

The Cat looked up. For a moment, the smug, almost alien look on her face told me exactly where her nickname had come from. "We're free operatives, Mr. Mason. You can't blame me for taking my money where I can get it."

"It was you." Mahir's voice was tinged with a dawning horror. I turned to look at him. He was staring at her, the white showing all the way around his irises. "One thing always seemed a little off to me when I reviewed the tapes we managed to recover from Oakland. Dr. Connelly was traveling on one of *your* ID cards. She should have been safe. She should have been untraceable. So how is it the CDC tracked her less than two hours after she arrived? And why did they lose track of her after that first ID was consigned to the fires?"

"I don't know," said the Cat. "Why don't you tell me? You're the journalists. You're supposed to be the *smart* ones."

"Wait." Becks turned toward Mahir. I didn't like the edge on her voice. "Are you telling me this woman got Dave killed?"

"If you answer that question, you don't get your new identities. Think about that." The Cat looked back down at her tablet, seemingly unconcerned. "You came here because you wanted a free pass out of your lives. You committed an act of treason because you were willing to do whatever it took to get that free pass into your hands. Are you going to let something that happened in the past come between you and getting what you paid for?"

"I guess that depends on whether getting what we paid for is going to get an airstrike called down on our heads," I said.

Then a small, perplexed voice spoke from the stairs: "Kitty, what did you do?" I looked toward it. The Fox was descending from the second floor. The look on her face was almost childlike in its confusion, like whatever was going on was so far outside her experience that it verged on impossible. "Did you do another bad thing? You know what Monkey said he'd do if you did another bad thing. You remember what he did to Wolf."

"Go back upstairs, Foxy," said the Cat calmly. "Watch a movie in your room. I'll bring cookies later."

The Fox frowned. "You're not answering my question."

"That's because I don't have to answer to you."

"No, but you do have to answer to me." We all turned toward the new voice, Becks reaching for a gun she didn't have. Her hand hovered in the air next to her hip for a moment, and then dropped back to her side.

The man who had emerged from the short hallway behind the kitchen looked at us mildly, like he had groups of strangers appear in his living room every day. Then again, maybe he did, considering his line of work.

"Mr. Monkey, I presume?" I said.

"No, no, Mr. Monkey was my father." His voice was vague enough that I couldn't tell if he was joking or not. "You must be the journalists."

"Yes, we are," said Mahir. "Are you the gentleman in charge of this establishment?"

"Not sure anybody really runs the Brainpan, but I guess it's down to me." A certain sharpness came into his eyes as he surveyed our motley group, belying his earlier vagueness. "Now what am I going to do with you?"

The Monkey was average-looking to the point of being forgettable almost while I was still looking at him. Caucasian male, average height, average weight, features that were neither ugly nor attractive, brown hair with bleach streaks, just like every other man on the planet who cared more about functionality than vanity. No one's that forgettable without working at it. We were probably looking at the result of years of careful refinement, possibly including some plastic surgery. This was a man who never wanted to stand out in a crowd. He could disappear into the background before you even realized he was there. In its own way, he was as terrifying as the Fox. At least there, you'd probably see the crazy coming.

Or not, said my inner George. *Remember the front yard.*

I bit back my response to her and smiled at the Monkey instead. "You're going to give us our fake IDs, whip up another one for my sister here, and send us on our merry way?"

"Monkey!" The Fox shoved her way through our group, all but flinging herself into the arms of the unassuming man. "Kitty did a bad thing, she *did*, she didn't say she did, but she didn't say she didn't, either, and that means she did!"

"I did *not* follow that," said Becks.

"The Cat killed Dave," said Maggie. There was a low menace in her tone. I didn't like it. I knew how the rest of us would act if we decided this would be a good time to lose our shit. Maggie...I had no idea. I'd never seen her really flip out. Suddenly that seemed like a genuine possibility.

"Who?" asked the Monkey. He stroked the Fox's head with one hand as he looked at us, waiting for an answer. She snuggled into his arms, posture half that of a lover, half that of a pet. "I don't remember anyone by that name."

"He wasn't one of your clients," Maggie practically spat. Mahir put a hand on her shoulder, preemptively restraining her. She ignored him, eyes locked on the Monkey. "You made a new identity for a woman from the CDC. Kelly Connolly."

"You used the name 'Mary Preston,'" interjected Becks.

"Ah!" The Monkey smiled. He wasn't forgettable when he did that. For a moment, his face pulled itself into a configuration that was handsome enough to explain how he was able to shack up with two attractive, if psychologically damaged, women who did his bidding without complaint. "That was a tricky piece of work. I don't usually do that much image replacement for a simple death-and-rebirth routine, you know? It was a challenge. I like challenges."

I spoke before I had a chance to think better of it, saying, "Yeah, well, that challenge came with a tracker that led the CDC right to her, and hence, right to us. They bombed the whole block. It destroyed our offices and killed one of our staffers."

The Monkey's smile faded, replaced by a frown. "That's not possible. I don't place trackers in my IDs. It would damage my reputation among my primary clientele, and I've spent quite some time building it up."

"The reputation, or the clientele?" asked George.

"Both." The Monkey squinted at her. "Aren't you supposed to be dead? I remember your face from the news feeds—and from the CDC records I've been reading all morning. Fascinating stuff."

"I got better," she said.

"We're losing the thread here," I said, wanting to divert the Monkey's attention from George. Somehow, he struck me as the kind of guy who'd love to take her apart, just to be sure she was a clone and not a cyborg or something. "We planted the bug at the CDC for you. We want our papers."

"You killed Dave," said Maggie, not budging from her core point.

I was starting to feel like there were at least three conversations going on, and I wasn't directing any of them. "Can we all settle down for a minute? Please? It's getting sort of hard to figure out what's going on here."

"No, it's pretty simple," said the Monkey mildly. "You exchanged currency and services for a set of false identities that could potentially get you out of whatever trouble you've managed to get into—which I have to say, is extremely impressive trouble, especially given where you started. You don't trust me or my girls, but you didn't have anywhere else that you could go for this sort of service. I understand that. I've worked hard to keep down the competition."

The Fox pulled her face away from his chest long enough to look over her shoulder and inform us solemnly, "That's part of my job."

"I'm sure it is," I said. "You look like you do it very well."

She offered a hesitant smile, and then turned to nestle back against the Monkey. He stroked her hair and said, "Now, you're also having a crisis of…call it faith…because you've decided I was somehow responsible for the death of your friend. I assure you, it's not the case. Not unless he was trying to establish himself as one of my competitors."

"He was a journalist," said Becks quietly.

"So he wasn't trying to set himself up as the competition. Huh." The Monkey looked toward where the Cat still sat calmly, fingers skating over the surface of her tablet. "Cat? Does what these people are saying have any merit?"

"Mmm-hmm," she replied. She didn't raise her head. She might as well have been responding to a question about whether she wanted soup for dinner.

The Monkey frowned, a flicker of irritation crossing his face. He pushed the Fox gently away from him. "Look at me while I'm speaking to you."

The Cat still didn't look up.

"*Look* at me." The Monkey's annoyance was entirely unmasked now. He didn't look forgettable at all. "Jane. Put it down, look at me, and tell me what you did."

"That's not my name." The Cat finally took her eyes off the screen. Her lips were pressed into a thin, hard line as she raised her head and glared at him. "My name is *Cat*."

"Your name is scared little girl who couldn't deal with all the boys who only wanted you for your body, but wished you'd put your brain in a jar so that they could fuck you and be smarter than you at the same time. Your name is 'I took you in when you said you wanted out.' Your name is 'you came to me.' I *own* you. Now what. Did you. Do?"

Carefully, like she was in no hurry at all, the Cat put her tablet aside. She stood and strolled over to us, stopping barely out of the Monkey's reach. "You took the man from the CDC's money. You said you'd build him the perfect disappearing girl—one who'd never set off any red flags or raise any alarms. And then you went into your damn workshop, like you always do, and you left me alone with Princess Crazy-Cakes here"—she gestured toward the Fox—"to entertain your client until he got bored and went away. He didn't get bored. He knew how you worked. He was waiting for you to leave."

"What?" The Monkey glanced at the Fox. "Why didn't you tell me about this?"

She sniffled. "Kitty told me to go outside and play with the crows. We found a dead squirrel. I set it on fire."

"Kids these days," said Becks dryly.

The Monkey ignored her. His attention swung back to the Cat. "What did you do?"

"He offered me a hundred thousand dollars to plant a tracker in her state ID. You know how easy it is to bug those things. Just swap out the RFID chip for one that broadcasts what *you* want it to broadcast, and you're in business."

"You're supposed to refer all business decisions to me," he said in a low, dangerous voice.

"You would have said no."

"Yes, I would. That isn't how we do business."

"Maybe it isn't how you do business, Monkey, but times are changing, and you're not changing with them. There are a lot of people out there offering services we aren't. We need to stay competitive."

"And that means going behind my back and getting half of downtown Oakland bombed?"

The Cat shrugged. "They only took out half."

The Fox paused, a thought almost visibly struggling across her face. "Is this why you told me I should put things in their shoes?" she asked.

"Hold up there," I said. "Whose shoes? What things?"

"Don't freak out," said the Cat. "They were tracking devices for the CDC to follow, so they'd be able to take out the horrible bastards who broke into their facility. They must have been too busy to come after you until you'd ditched the shoes. You got lucky."

"That, or we were staying at the Agora," said Maggie. "Best security screening technology on this side of the state. No matter how much those trackers were broadcasting, they wouldn't have gotten through the shields."

"I haven't changed my shoes," said Becks slowly. She looked at me. "Have you?"

"No."

The Cat stared at us. Then she pointed at the door and started shouting, "Out! Get the fuck out of here! You have to leave!"

"What's going on?" asked the Fox.

For a moment, I felt almost bad for her. Sure, she was crazy and homicidal, and probably the most dangerous person in the room, but she was also the one who had the least responsibility for her own actions. She needed to be taken care of, and the people she'd chosen to do that had used her as a weapon. That wasn't her fault.

And it wasn't my problem. "Kitty did a bad thing," I informed her. Looking back to the Cat, I said, "Well? Turn them off already."

The Cat licked her lips, eyes darting from me to the Monkey as she said, "I can't."

There was a moment when it felt like the world stood still, all of us considering the meaning of her words. Then Becks shouted, with all the authority of an Irwin in a field situation, "The van! Get to the van, get armed, and get Maggie out of the line of fire!"

"*Just* Maggie?" I asked.

She smiled thinly. "Georgia Mason always knew how to defend herself." Then she was off and running, heading for the front door. The rest of us followed her. George didn't complain as she ran, even though it must have been painful—the dressings on her feet were designed to deal with light walking, not a full-out sprint. She just gritted her teeth and kept going.

We left our shoes where they were. If they were bugged, they were more of a liability than a little barefoot running.

I could hear the Cat and the Monkey yelling at each other when we hit the front door, although I couldn't tell what they were saying. I wasn't aware that the Fox was following us until she took hold of my hand and asked, "Is this going to be *very* bad?"

Mahir and Becks were trying to pry the door open. The security system had clearly engaged once we were all inside, and it just as clearly didn't want to let go again. I exchanged a glance with George before looking back to the Fox. "Well..."

The sudden shriek of alarms stopped me from needing to figure out the rest of that sentence. Metal sheets slammed down over all the windows, and red lights came on at the tops of the walls, flashing almost fast enough to qualify as strobes. The Fox yelped, yanking her hand out of mine. As she clamped her hands over her ears, I saw that she was holding a nasty-looking sniper's pistol. At least she came prepared.

Becks kicked the door viciously before turning and jogging the few steps back over to me. "I'm going to go punch our host in the face until he lets us out of here," she said.

"Punch the woman instead; she seems to deserve it more," said Mahir. He walked back to where I was standing. "We're proper trapped now. Probably all going to die here. I'd say it was nice knowing you, but as you've effectively ruined my life, it almost certainly hasn't been."

"What he said," said Maggie.

"Aren't you sweet?" George was frowning at the door, looking thoughtful. "Hey, George? You planning something, there?"

"A place like this...Mahir, remember when we did the report on the clone organ farmers? The ones who were so used to getting raided that they almost treated it as a reason not to bother washing the windows?"

"Yes!" Mahir's eyes lit up. "They knew they'd be caught in a death trap if they ever let themselves be taken unaware—"

"—and so they never set up a headquarters without at least three escape routes." She turned to the Fox. "How do we get out? All our weapons are outside."

The Fox brightened, lowering her hands. "I have weapons!"

"We know you do, but we need *our* weapons. Please. How do we get out of here?"

"Oh." The Fox thought for a moment. Finally, she said, "This way," and trotted back toward the living room. Lacking anything better to do, we followed.

As we rounded the corner, we were greeted with the fascinating sight of Becks slamming the Cat rhythmically into the wall while the Monkey looked calmly on. "You're a feisty one," he said. "Do you have a boy-friend?"

The Cat wailed. Becks slammed her into a wall again.

"Last guy I was interested in turned out to be an incestuous necro-philiac," she said. "So no, not currently dating, and definitely not doing any more shopping in the 'sociopath' category. Now tell her to open the doors."

"She can't do that," said the Monkey. The Fox trotted past him without pausing; he turned to watch her go. "Foxy? What are you doing?"

"Opening the garage!" she called back cheerfully, before pulling a pic-ture off the wall to reveal the control panel it had been concealing. She slapped her palm against it, and the light above the nearest door went from red to green.

A look of horror spread across the Monkey's face as he realized what she was doing. He lunged for her, one hand stretched out to grab her shoulder. "No! Don't! That's not—"

It was too late. The door swung open, revealing a garage packed with servers and computer terminals, and a garage door that was slowly rolling upward. As it rose, it exposed the men who were standing in the driveway between us and the van, their rifles trained on the house. They were all wearing hazmat suits, with rebreathers covering their mouths and noses.

"Oh," said the Fox. "Oopsie." Then she slammed the door.

The gunfire started a split second later.

Oh, don't worry. You don't need to tell *Alaric* what's going on. You don't need to tell *Alaric* who was in our system claiming to be Georgia Mason, or why the Seattle CDC is on CNN, in flames, or whether you're all still alive. *Alaric* likes sitting around with his thumb up his ass, waiting to find out whether he's got a bunch of funerals to not attend, since he's still under house arrest with the paranoid mad scientist brigade.

Assholes.

—From *The Kwong Way of Things*,
the blog of Alaric Kwong, August 3, 2041. Unpublished.

Upon reflection, I must note that I have, in fact, had better days.

—From *Fish and Clips*,
the blog of Mahir Gowda, August 3, 2041. Unpublished.

GEORGIA: Twenty-nine

None of this made any sense, and none of Shaun's explanations had done anything to help the situation. Not that it mattered. As soon as people started shooting, I stopped needing to understand and started needing to react. I ducked, grabbing Maggie's hand—she was the one with the least field experience, at least as far as I remembered—and dragging her around the corner into the living room. They'd need to shoot through more walls to get to us here.

"Shaun!" I shouted, hoping I'd be heard over the gunfire. "Get the hell out of there!"

"The wall's holding for now!" Shaun shouted back. Mahir rounded the corner, taking up a position on the other side of Maggie. He flashed me a wan smile.

My hand went to my waist, habit telling me that when I was dressed, I was also armed. There was nothing there but my belt. "Dammit, Shaun! If you don't have a secret escape plan, you need to make the crazy people give us guns!"

The woman they called the Cat shouted, "We don't let strangers go armed in this house!"

"Sort of a special circumstance, don't you think?" I demanded.

There was an answering burst of gunfire from the hall, followed by the sound of the door slamming. Someone who actually *had* a weapon must have opened the door, taken a shot at our attackers, and closed the door again. "I think everybody should have *lots* of guns!" said the cheerful, faintly lunatic voice of the little redhead. "Monkey, can we? Can we please give everybody guns?"

"Yes, Monkey, please?" asked Shaun. He backed into view, not joining our cluster against the wall, but getting farther away from the door to the garage. "We promise not to shoot up any more of your shit than is strictly necessary."

"Fascinating as diplomacy is, perhaps *during a firefight* is not the time?" Mahir sounded frantic, like he was the only one taking things seriously.

Shaun gave him a startled look. "Dude, chill. We're fine until they shoot through the door."

"Then we're fine for another ninety seconds," said the Monkey. "Foxy, give them guns."

"Yay!" The redhead ran to the other side of the living room. She opened what I'd taken for a coat closet, exposing enough weaponry to out-fit a good-sized tabloid. Shaun whistled.

"Okay, I'm in love," he said.

"Fickle, fickle heart." I started for the open closet, the others following. This whole situation seemed faintly unreal. We were trapped in a decrepit-looking private home while a small army tried to shoot their way in. The fact that they hadn't already succeeded told me this place had some pretty good armor plating under the peeling paint. The people who lived here were concerned, but not panicked. That made it a little too easy to be casual about things, like there was no way we could get hurt.

We could get hurt. I'd already died once. That sort of thing tends to teach you that no one is invincible.

"Here!" The Fox handed me a revolver, and gave Shaun a semiautomatic handgun. She kept passing out guns, grinning like a kid on Christmas morning. "We're going to shoot them reeeeeeal good, so it's important everybody be ready to look their best!"

Shaun and I exchanged a look, his expression making it clear that he understood what was going on about as well as I did—which was to say, not at all. Somehow, that didn't make me feel any better.

The Monkey and the Cat joined us at the closet, both of them taking weapons of their own. The Cat glared at us the whole time, like this was somehow our fault.

"This is what's going to happen now." The Fox was suddenly calm, like having a group of armed men firing on her house was what it took to bring out her saner side. "We're going to go out the back door. We're going to circle around the side of the house. And then we're going to shoot those fuckers until they stop squirming. Any questions? No? Good. Follow me."

"I'm not sure which is worse," muttered Shaun. "The fact that we're following the crazy girl, or the fact that she sounds so damn happy about it."

"I'm going to go with 'the fact that we don't have a choice,'" said Becks. "Maggie, you're in the middle."

"Yes, I am," said Maggie, putting herself behind Becks and Shaun, and in front of me and Mahir. We followed the Fox, with the Cat and the Monkey bringing up the rear. I had the distinct feeling we were being used as human shields. Not that it mattered. There were men with guns outside, and as long as the Cat and the Monkey weren't shooting us in the back, I didn't care where they walked. I already knew we couldn't count on them.

We reached the Fox as she was prying the last sheets of plywood off the back door. Shaun stepped in and helped her finish, revealing a pre-Rising sliding glass door that had been boarded over for good reason.

"This place was a death trap," I muttered.

Mahir shot me a half-amused glance. "Was?" he asked.

It felt odd to be laughing during a firefight. Then again, if you can't laugh when you're about to die, when can you? The sound of gunfire covered any noises we might make, at least until we left the house.

The back porch had been reinforced at some point, more structural improvement concealed by a veil of cosmetic decay. The seemingly rotten wooden steps had no give to them at all. The Fox slunk through the knee-high grass as quietly as her namesake. I tried to emulate her, failing utterly as the gravel beneath the grass bit into my already injured feet. The best I could manage was not making any more noise than was absolutely necessary as I followed the rest of the group to the corner.

Once we were there, the Fox turned, smiled at the rest of us, sketched a curtsey clumsy enough to seem entirely sincere, and bolted back the way we'd come.

The Monkey realized what she was doing before the rest of us did—he knew her better than anyone, except for maybe the Cat, who had already locked her free hand around his elbow. He tried to run after the Fox as she pelted up the porch steps and back into the house. The Cat held him back.

"No," she hissed. "Do that, and this was for nothing."

He turned to look at her, a cold anger burning in her eyes. "Don't think I'll forgive you."

The Cat didn't say anything.

The sound of gunshots from the front of the house suddenly took on a new, more frantic timbre, accompanied by the distant but recognizable sound of the Fox's laughter. At least someone was having a good day. Shaun looked back to me.

"There's no plan B," he said.

I nodded. "I know."

There was no one left for us to run to, and nowhere to run except the van. That meant we had to take the opportunity the Fox had created for us, no matter how insane that opportunity seemed. Shaun looked to Becks, making a complex gesture with one hand. She nodded, picking up on his unspoken command. I felt a flush of jealousy. Just how close had they gotten while I was dead, anyway?

I forced the feeling away. It was none of my business, and even if it was, this wasn't the time. The Fox was still laughing, but it had a pained edge to it, like she was running out of steam. It was now or never. Being occasionally suicidal, but not stupid, we chose now.

It wasn't until we were running around to the front of the house that I realized the Cat was no longer with us. The Monkey was running alongside Mahir, but his...whatever she was...was gone. The Fox was still shooting from the kitchen window, keeping the majority of the team in the driveway occupied through sheer dint of being impossible to ignore. Either her aim was incredibly good or she was using armor-piercing bullets; five of them were already down, leaving another nine standing. Part of me was pleased to see that they'd considered a bunch of journalists enough of a threat to send fourteen armed CDC guards to take us down. The rest of me wished they'd been willing to settle for a sternly worded cease-and desist-letter.

Journalism must have been very different before people resolved so many of their conflicts with bullets.

The men from the CDC were so busy shooting at the house that we made it halfway to the van before they noticed us. Three more of them went down in the interim. I was starting to think we might make it when the Fox screamed, a gasping, quickly cut-off sound, and the gunfire from the house stopped. The Monkey froze, face going white. Then he screamed and rushed toward the driveway, opening fire as he ran.

The guards who were still standing turned toward the sound of gunfire. "Oh, sh—" began Shaun, and then they were firing on us, and there was no time left for conversation.

Maggie and Mahir hit the ground, leaving Becks, Shaun, and I to return fire. Fortunately for us, the guards were distracted by the Monkey's suicide charge; he took down two of the six remaining men before going down in a hail of blood and bullets. That left four standing, all with more firepower and better armor than we had. Our next step didn't need to be discussed. We stopped firing, raising hands and weapons toward the sky. If we were lucky, they'd want prisoners they could question even more than they'd want bodies they could bury.

Luck was with us. The man at the front of their ragged little formation signaled for the others to stop firing. He held out one hand, palm facing us, and then gestured toward the ground, indicating that we should put our guns down. We knelt to do as we were told. It might have ended there, except for one crucial detail:

The Fox hadn't been trying for headshots.

My hand was still on my borrowed revolver when the first of the downed guards lurched to his feet and grabbed for the still-living man beside him. His chosen victim screamed and started firing wildly. His commander shouted for him to stand down, but it was too late; panic had already set in. Four men suddenly finding themselves surrounded by nine potential zombies weren't going to listen to orders anymore.

Grabbing my gun from the ground, I ran full-tilt for the van, trusting the others to follow me and praying the zombies would be so busy going for the accessible prey that they'd let us by.

There were no bullet holes in the van. That was something. Becks and I reached it first, ducking behind the bulk of it while she fired at the guards and I fumbled with the door. The blood test cycle to open it had never seemed so long. Mahir reached us as I was waiting for the door to finish processing, leaving only Shaun and Maggie in the open—and Maggie was still on the ground, not moving.

"Oh, fuck," I breathed. The lock disengaged. I jerked the door open, motioning for the others to climb in. Mahir promptly clambered over the driver's seat and into the back, bypassing the blood test.

Becks shook her head, digging a set of keys out of her pocket and tossing them to me. "I'll cover you! Now hurry!"

"On it." I slammed the door, shoved the keys into the ignition, and started the engine, hitting the gas hard enough to send Mahir sprawling. Becks waited until she was clear and then opened fire on the guards, living and dead alike.

Driving was another thing I didn't have the muscle memory for anymore, even if I intellectually understood the process. I barely managed to skid to a stop in front of Shaun and Maggie, the tires digging deep divots in the lawn. Mahir opened the side door and hopped out, helping Shaun lift Maggie inside. The entire front of her blouse was bloody.

"Is she breathing?" Mahir demanded.

"Yes," said Shaun. "First-aid kit, *now*." He slammed the door. "George, get Becks."

Becks had taken cover behind a half-fallen pine tree that listed at a severe angle across one side of the tiny courtyard. She was firing at the two guards who remained standing, but their attention was more focused on their formerly dead compatriots, who were still attempting to take them down. I pulled up next to her and she grabbed the passenger-side door, waiting impatiently for the lock to release.

"Oh, God, there's so much blood," moaned Mahir. I didn't let myself look. I needed to focus on getting us out of here alive.

The door opened. Becks climbed inside. I looked back toward the house and saw the Fox waving weakly from the window, blood running down the side of her face. She had what looked like a remote control in one hand. Becks looked that way, and her eyes widened.

"Oh, fuck," she breathed. "Georgia, *drive*."

I hit the gas.

We were all the way to the end of the driveway when the house exploded.

The edge of the explosion caught us, hot wind buffeting the van. The frame was weighted to make it harder to tip us over, but even so, it was a struggle to maintain control of the steering wheel. In the back, Maggie screamed. That was almost encouraging. If she was screaming like that, they hadn't managed to puncture a lung, and with two Irwins playing field medic, she might be able to hold on long enough to get us—

I had no living clue where we were going, and no one else was available to take the wheel. "Where am I going?" I demanded.

"Take us back to the Agora!" shouted Shaun. "Just tell the GPS to retrace the last route we took. It can guide you from—aw, fuck, Becks, keep the pressure on, will you?"

Wincing, I turned on the GPS, tapping the screen twice to make it show me the way back to the Agora. A red light came on above the rear-view mirror as the GPS began scrolling the names of streets. "Shaun, I'm getting a contamination warning up here."

"That's because Maggie's bleeding all over the fucking van!"

"Still showing clean here," said Mahir. His voice was tight, verging on panicked. "Becks, how's her breathing?"

I took a deep breath and tightened my hands on the wheel, trying to focus on the road. Maggie was shot, not bitten. Her blood would be a problem, especially if she ran out of it completely, but as long as no one else had open wounds on their hands…or on their legs…or anywhere else…

We were fucked. We were thoroughly and completely fucked, and all we had to show for it was a bunch of corpses and a house that wasn't even there anymore.

As if he had read my mind, Shaun called, with manic cheerfulness, "Don't stress out about it, George. Things could be worse!"

"*How?*" demanded Becks.

"We could still be wearing shoes full of homing devices!"

For the first time since she'd been shot, Maggie spoke: "I am going to...kill you...*myself*, Shaun Mason." Her voice was weak, but it was there. If she was talking, she couldn't be too far gone.

Shaun laughed unsteadily. "You do that, Maggie. You get up and kick my ass just as soon as you feel like you can manage it."

She mumbled something in disjointed Spanish, voice losing strength with every word.

"This would be a good time to drive a little faster, Georgia," said Mahir. His tone was utterly calm. I recognized that for the danger sign it really was. Mahir only sounded that serene when he was on the verge of panic, or getting ready to pounce on some fact that every other reporter to look at a story had somehow managed to miss. That detachment was the way he handled the things that otherwise couldn't be handled at all.

I pressed my foot down on the gas, envying that cool veil of calm. It was all I could do not to start hyperventilating as we blew through downtown Seattle, slowing down only when the lights forced me or I had to take a turn. I doubt I could have done it under pre-Rising speed limits, back when they worried more about pedestrian safety than they did about getting people from point A to point B as quickly as humanly possible. I was still running the very edge of "safe driving" when the GPS signaled for me to slow down; we were approaching our destination.

We were approaching our destination in a vehicle that was essentially a traveling biohazard zone. "Guys?" I asked. "Now what am I supposed to do?"

Maggie mumbled something. It must have made more sense to the people around her, because Mahir spoke a moment later, saying, "When we reach the gate, roll down your window but do not attempt to put any part of your body outside the car. Tell them Maggie is injured—use her full name—and that we need immediate medical assistance. The Agora has protocols that will take it from there."

"Do those protocols include a full tank of formalin with our names on it?" asked Shaun. Nobody answered him. He sighed. "Yeah, I figured as much."

The Agora gatehouse was in front of us. I slowed, finally stopping the van as the guards approached. The urge to slam my foot down on the gas and go racing off to anywhere else was overwhelming...and pointless. Driving away wouldn't make things any better.

I rolled down my window when the first guard reached the van, careful to stay well away from the opening. "We have an injured hotel guest," I said. "She was shot."

The guard's expression of polite helpfulness didn't falter. "Would you like the address of the nearest hospital with field decontamination capacity?" he asked.

"I'm sorry, I said that wrong. Magdalene Grace Garcia is in the back of this van, and she has been shot. We need immediate medical assistance." I hesitated before adding, "Please."

The effect Maggie's name had on the man was nothing short of electric. His expression flickered from politely helpful to shocked to narrow-eyed efficiency in a matter of seconds. "Drive through the front gate and follow the lighted indicators next to the road," he said. "Do not attempt to leave your vehicle. A medical team will meet you at your destination." Almost as an afterthought, he said, "Please roll up your window."

"Thank you," I said. He stepped away, and I rolled the window up before putting my foot back on the gas. The gate opened as we rolled forward, and bright blue lights began flicking on next to the driveway, indicating our route.

The lights followed the obvious path to the Agora for about a hundred yards before branching off, leading us down a groundkeeper's road that had been cunningly surrounded by bushes and flowering shrubs, making it almost unnoticeable if you didn't know it was there—or weren't following a bunch of bright blue lights. I kept driving, inching our speed up as high as I dared. The road led us around the back of the Agora to a separate parking garage with plastic sheeting hanging over the entrance.

I took a breath and drove on through.

The garage was brightly lit, and already swarming with people in white EMT moon suits, their hands covered by plastic gloves and their faces by clear masks. I managed to kill the engine before they started knocking on the van's side door, but only barely. The door slid open, and suddenly the van was rocking as EMTs poured through the opening.

Someone knocked on my window, making me jump. I turned to see another of the EMTs looking through the glass at me. I lowered the window. "Ma'am, please leave your vehicle and prepare for decontamination," he said, voice muffled by his mask.

A chill wormed down my spine. The idea of going through decontamination—of going through *any* medical procedure, no matter how standard—was suddenly terrifying.

The others were climbing out of the van. Mahir and Becks were already in front of the van, being led along by more EMTs. I knew Shaun would wait for me as long as he could, unwilling to let me out of his sight if he didn't have to. That was what it took to spur me into motion. I didn't want Shaun getting sedated because I wasn't willing to get out of my seat.

One of the EMTs grasped my upper arm firmly as soon as my feet hit the asphalt, not waiting for me to shut the door before he began pulling me toward the building. I didn't resist, but I didn't help him, either, letting my feet drag as I looked frantically around for Shaun. He was being led toward the building by another of the EMTs. He broke loose as soon as he saw me, ignoring the way his EMT was shouting as he ran in my direction.

"Shaun!"

He stopped in front of me. There was blood on the front of his shirt, but his hands were clean. Either he'd been wearing gloves, or he'd some-how managed to avoid touching Maggie. Given what I'd heard from the back, that seemed unlikely. He'd played it smart. For once. "Are you okay? Are you hurt? Things were so hectic back there, I didn't have time to—"

"I'm fine, but I think you're scaring the locals."

"What?" Shaun looked over his shoulder, seeming to notice the EMTs for the first time. They were all holding pistols now, and those pistols were aimed in our direction. Smiling cockily, Shaun waved. I doubt any of them saw the hollow fear behind his eyes. I doubt anyone but me would even have realized it was there. "Hey, fellas. Sorry to frighten you like that. I just have a thing about being separated from my sister. Makes me sort of impulsive."

"Makes you sort of *insane*," I corrected, without thinking. Then I winced. "Shaun..."

"No, that's pretty much true." Four more EMTs walked by us, carrying a stretcher between them. A clear plastic sheet covered it, Maggie visible underneath. A respirator was covering her face. I just hoped that meant that she was still breathing, and that she still stood a chance of recovery.

"Sir, ma'am, you need to come with me now." I glanced toward the EMT holding my arm. He looked at us sternly through his mask. "I under-stand your concern, but we need to clear and sterilize this area."

Shaun's eyes widened. "Our van—"

"Will be returned to you once it has been decontaminated. Now please, sir, you both need to come with me."

Shaun and I exchanged a look. Then we nodded, almost in unison. "All right," I said. "Let's go and get decontaminated."

The EMT led us out of the garage and into the building. Metal jets emerged from the ceiling as we stepped into the airlock, beginning to spray a thin mist down over the area. The smell of it managed to sneak through the closing doors, tickling my nose with the characteristic burning scent of formalin. I shuddered. Nothing organic was going to survive that dousing.

"We're going to need to replace the rug again," commented Shaun.

I glanced at him, startled, before starting to laugh under my breath. I couldn't help it. He looked so sincere, and so annoyed, like replacing the rug was the worst thing that had happened to us in a while. Shaun blinked, his own surprised expression mirroring mine. Then he started laughing with me.

We were both still laughing when the EMT led us out of the airlock and into the Agora Medical Center. My laughter died almost instantly, replaced by a feeling of choking suffocation. White walls. White ceiling. White floor. The EMTs looked suddenly hostile behind their plastic masks, like they had been sent by the CDC to take me back.

"George?" Shaun's voice was distant. "You okay?"

"Not really," I replied. I turned to the startled EMT who had led us inside. "Do you have a room with some color in it? I have a thing about white." It made me want to curl up in a corner and cry. A phobia of medical establishments. That was a fun new personality trait.

Working at the Agora had apparently prepared the man for strange requests from people above his pay grade—which we, traveling with Maggie, technically were. "Right this way, miss," he said, and turned to lead us away from the rest of the action. I felt a brief pang of regret over letting us be separated from the others, but quashed it. The EMT assigned to work with me and Shaun wasn't one of the ones who was needed to help Maggie, or he wouldn't have been with us in the first place. Me having a panic attack over the white, white walls wasn't going to do anything to help anyone.

The EMT led us to a smaller room where the walls were painted a cheery yellow and the chairs were upholstered in an equally cheery blue. We didn't need to be told that this was the children's holding area. The testing panels on the walls and the double-reinforced glass on the observation window cut into the room's rear wall made that perfectly clear.

Oddly, the window made me feel better, rather than setting my nerves even further on edge. It was honest glass, letting the observed see the observers without any subterfuge. If it had been a mirror, I think I would have lost my shit.

"If you're feeling better now, ma'am, sir, I would very much appreciate it if you'd let me begin the testing process."

Shaun and I exchanged a look, and I jumped a little as the blood on his shirt fully registered. Maggie wasn't dead when she was bleeding on him. That didn't mean her blood couldn't potentially carry a hot viral load.

"Please," I said.

"Sure," said Shaun, sounding oddly unconcerned. I frowned at him. He mouthed the word "later," and gave me what may have been intended as a reassuring smile.

I was not reassured.

The EMT produced two small blood test units, using them to take samples from our index fingers. No lights came on to document the filtration process. Instead, he sealed the kits in plastic bags marked "biohazard," nodded as politely as a bellhop who'd been doing nothing more hazardous than delivering our luggage, and left the room. The door closed behind him with a click and a beep that clearly indicated that we had been locked in.

Shaun looked at me. "You okay?"

"No." I shook my head. "Is Maggie going to be okay?"

"I don't know." Shaun folded his arms, looking at the closed door. "I guess we'll find out soon enough."

"Yeah. I guess we will." We stood there in silence, waiting for the door to open; waiting for someone to come and tell us how many of us were going to walk away alive.

———————————

When Maggie went down ... fuck.

Maggie was one of the first people Buffy hired after we said "sure, we want a viable Fiction section." She's never been anything but awesome. She took us in when we had nowhere else to go; she took care of us when we would have been frankly fucked without her. She's been our rock. If Mahir is the soul of this news team—and I'm not an idiot, I know that when George died, the mantle went to him, and that's cool, because I never wanted it in the first place—then Maggie is the heart. And when she went down today, the only thing I could think was "Thank God it was her. Thank God it wasn't George. I don't think I could survive that happening again."

George being back is a miracle, and it's also what's going to mean this all ends bad, because I'm not thinking straight anymore. I lived without her once. I can't do it again.

Fuck.

**—From *Adaptive Immunities*,
the blog of Shaun Mason, August 4, 2041. Unpublished.**

Madre de Dios... Mother Mary, hold me closely; Mother Mary, love me best. Mother Mary, treat me sweetly. Mother Mary, let me rest.

I have never hurt this much in my life. Morphine is supposed to make the hurting stop, but instead, it shunts the pain to the side, like a houseguest you never intended to keep. It isn't in your face, but it's there, using the last of the milk, leaving wet towels on the bathroom floor...

This hurts. I am alive. The two balance each other, I suppose.

This was supposed to be Buffy's revolution. It was never supposed to be mine.

**—From *Dandelion Mine*,
the blog of Magdalene Grace Garcia, August 4, 2041. Unpublished.**

SHAUN: Thirty

I don't know how long they left us in that room. Long enough that George was pale and freaking out a little by the time they came back, even though she was trying pretty damn hard to hide it. I watched her anxiously, not sure what I was supposed to do. She'd never had a problem with hospitals before. Then again, I guess being brought back from the dead and used as a CDC lab rat would fuck up just about anybody.

The delay may have put George's nerves on edge, but it helped settle mine. When those bullets started flying...there was a time when that would have elated me. With George in the field, all it did was make me sick to my stomach. She could have been hit. I could have lost her again. *Again.* And I couldn't even grab her and hold on until I stopped feeling sick, because there was blood on my shirt. If it was hot, even touching her could kill her. I should never have grabbed her hand. I should have stayed away from her and observed proper quarantine procedures. And I *couldn't.*

It was sort of ironic. I couldn't catch the live form of Kellis-Amberlee because I'd managed to catch the immunity from her, and now that she was back where she belonged, she didn't have that same protection. Even when I was safe, she wasn't.

"I hate the world sometimes," I muttered.

"What?" George stopped staring at the wall, turning to look at me instead. She removed her sunglasses, rubbing her left eye with the heel of her hand. "Do you think we'll find out what's happening soon?"

"I hope so." I sighed. "All that for nothing. We didn't get the damn IDs."

"Didn't those people send you to the CDC?"

"Yeah, they did."

"So it wasn't for nothing." George shrugged, trying—and failing—to look nonchalant as she said, "It got you me."

I was still trying to find a response for that when the door opened and the EMT who had escorted us inside stepped through. He was wearing clean scrubs, and the plastic face mask was gone. We both turned to face him, waiting for his verdict.

"We apologize for any inconvenience the delay may have caused. Miss Garcia required immediate attention," he said. "If you'd come with me, I'd be happy to take you to your party."

"Does that mean we're cool?" I asked.

The EMT nodded. "Yes, Mr. Mason. You're both in fine health. Your internal viral loads are well within normal safety perimeters. Now if you would please come with me?"

"Right." George looked faintly ill. "Back to the white rooms."

"Hey." She looked my way. I smiled at her. "I'm here. It's all different now."

"Yeah." George returned my smile before turning to the EMT. "Lead the way."

We followed him back to the hall where we had first entered. The sound and motion that had been my only real impression of the place was all gone now, replaced by cool, sterile peacefulness. If it hadn't been for the airlock looking out on the garage, I would never have realized it was the same hall. George kept her eyes locked straight ahead, looking like she was going to be sick at any moment. I just hoped no one would see her and take that for a sign of spontaneous amplification. Another fire drill was the last thing that we needed at the moment.

She relaxed a little when we passed through a sliding door and into a hall where the walls were painted a pale cream yellow. Interesting. It was just the white that bothered her. I made a mental note to punch the next CDC employee I saw in the face.

"Mr. Mason, Miss Mason, at this point, I do need to ask that you proceed through these doors," the EMT indicated two doors in the wall to our right, one marked "Men," the other marked "Women." "There will be clean clothes available for you to wear while yours are being sterilized."

I glanced at George. "You going to be okay with this?"

She laughed unsteadily. "If I can't handle a basic sterilization cycle, I may as well give up and go back to the . . . go back to the place where you found me right now. I'll be fine."

"Okay." I risked reaching out and squeezing her hand before stepping through the appropriate door.

The room on the other side was small and square, and—to my relief—tiled in industrial gray. I could have kissed whoever was responsible for that particular decorating choice. As long as the women's side was decorated the same way, George might not flip out. As expected, there were no windows, and a large drain was set in the middle of the floor. The door I'd arrived through was behind me. Another was on the wall directly in front of me.

"Hello, Shaun," said the pleasant voice of the Agora. "Welcome back."

"Thanks," I said, hauling my shirt off over my head. "Where do you want me to put my clothes?"

A hatch slid open in one wall. I hadn't even been able to see the outline of it in the tile. "Please place your clothes in the opening to your left. I promise they will not be damaged in any way by the cleaning process. We are only interested in your comfort and well-being."

"Great." I finished stripping before shoving my clothes, shoes and all, through the hatch. I held up my pistol. "What do you want done with the weapons?"

"Please place them in the same location. They will be separated out before the cleansing process begins."

"Right." I wasn't happy with that answer. I didn't see another way. Automated sterilization systems can get mean when they feel like protocol is being violated, and no matter how nice the Agora was programmed to be, refusing to give up my weapons would qualify as violating protocol. I placed them in the opening with everything else, barely pulling my hand back before the hatch slammed closed again.

"Thank you for your cooperation, Shaun," said the Agora. "Please move to the center of the room and close your eyes. Sterilization will commence once you are in the correct position."

"On it," I said. I moved to position myself directly over the drain, closed my eyes, and tilted my face toward the ceiling. The water turned on a second later, raining down on me from what felt like half a dozen differently angled jets. I didn't open my eyes to find out.

Sterilization follows the same basic protocols no matter where you are or how high class a place pretends to be. First they boil you, then they bleach you, then they boil you again. If the powers that be could get away with dipping us all in lye, they'd probably do it, just to be able to say that one more layer of "safety" had been slapped on. The Agora was nicer about it than it technically had to be; the hot water lasted almost thirty seconds, followed by eight seconds of bleach, and then a citrus-scented foam that oozed down from more jets in the ceiling. Sterilization *and* a shower.

Twice, the Agora instructed me to change positions or turn, letting the bleach, hot water, and cleansing foam cover every part of me. The hot water jets were repeated three times; the bleach was only repeated once. Guess I was dirtier than I was potentially diseased.

Finally, the water turned off, and the Agora said, "Thank you for your cooperation."

"Didn't you say that, like, five minutes ago?" I opened my eyes. The door in front of me was open, revealing an antechamber that looked like the locker room of a really upscale gym.

"My range of programmed responses is wide, but sometimes, repetition is inevitable," said the Agora patiently. "If you would like to register a complaint—"

"That's okay," I said, cutting the hotel off midsentence. "Thanks for the scrub. Do I get pants in the next room?"

"Yes, Shaun," said the Agora.

"Awesome," I said, and proceeded on. The "pants" were drawstring cotton, purple with the Agora logo over the hip, like they were advertising a high school pep team. The bathrobe that went with them was a few shades darker, with the same logo. I pulled everything on, checked to be sure the ties were tight, and stepped out the door in the far wall.

George was waiting in the hall, tugging anxiously at the sleeves of her own bathrobe. Her feet were bare, the legs of her sweatpants pooling over their tops, and her sunglasses were gone. Without a medical condition to make them mandatory, she could have them confiscated at every sterilization checkpoint we encountered. Another EMT was standing nearby, using that weird gift that some people in service industries seem to possess, and basically blending into the furniture.

I ignored her, focusing on George. "Hey," I said. "All clean?"

"All clean." She sighed, giving up on tugging her sleeves into place. "Do you think that after we see how Maggie's doing, we can get me a can of Coke?"

"We can get you a *gallon* of Coke," I said.

"Good." She looked to the EMT. "Where to now?"

"This way," said the EMT. She started down the hallway and we followed, only lagging by a few steps. The hall ended at a pair of sliding glass doors, which opened to reveal a small but well-appointed hospital waiting room. There was even an admissions desk, with a woman sitting behind it, tapping away at her computer.

"The Masons are here for Miss Garcia," called the EMT, as she led us past the desk. The other woman nodded, looking up with a smile. Her fingers kept moving the whole time, and her eyes snapped quickly back to the screen.

"Do you get many medical emergencies here?" asked George.

"The Agora is proud to provide hospital services to our guests, both past and present," said the EMT. "We have patients most days, seeing our private doctors. It offers a guarantee of privacy and discretion that is unfortunately not present in many more public hospitals."

"Better care for rich people, right?" I said. "Figures."

George didn't say anything. She just looked thoughtfully around as we followed the EMT past a row of unlabeled doors, finally pausing at one that looked like all the others.

"A moment, please," said the EMT, and pushed the door open, vanishing inside. Only a few seconds passed before she pushed the door open again, this time holding it to let us through. "Miss Garcia will see you now."

"Awesome," I said, and stepped past her into the room. I stopped dead just past the threshold, too stunned to speak.

George ducked in behind me. After a few startled seconds, she said, "Remind me to come here the next time I decide to get hurt."

"You and me both," I said.

The halls of the Agora's medical center might look like the ones you'd find at any other upscale hospital, but the patient rooms were something completely different, at least if Maggie's was anything to go by. The walls were painted a warm amber, and there was actual carpet on the floor—easy-clean industrial carpet, sure, but a world of luxury away from normal hospital tile. The only medical equipment in sight was a flat-screen display that flickered periodically between images, apparently doing the work of multiple monitors.

Maggie was lying in the middle of a comfortable-looking bed with a wine red comforter and more pillows than anyone needs, sick or not. She was too pale, especially for her. An IV was connected to her left arm, and there were sensor patches on her collarbones, but apart from that, she could have been taking a nap. Mahir was sitting to one side of the bed; Becks was standing near the wall. They both turned to look at us.

There was a moment of awkward silence before Mahir said, "If Maggie were awake and mobile, this is doubtless the point where she would leap to her feet, announce how worried she'd been, and run to embrace you. Please forgive me if I choose to take all that as written, and move straight to asking what the bloody hell we're meant to do now."

I nodded. "Forgiven. How is she?"

"The bullet went clean through. That's about the only good thing I can say about it." Becks didn't look at Maggie as she spoke. She didn't really look at us, either; her gaze was fixed on the wall, preventing anything

uncomfortable, like eye contact. "Several of her internal organs were damaged, and her liver was nicked. She lost a lot of blood."

"But she didn't amplify," I said.

"No. She's going to be fine. They're transfusing her with scrubbed
plasma and filtering as much of the viral load out of her bloodstream as
they can, but she never started to amplify."

"What Rebecca isn't saying is that Maggie came very, very close to
crossing that line, and she can't be moved." Mahir dropped his head into
his hands, voice muffled as he said, "She can't be moved, and you can't stay
here. This is a disaster."

"No, it's not," I said. For a moment—just a moment—I wished the
George who only existed in my head would speak up and tell me what to
say. Then I glanced to the George who was standing beside me, alive and
breathing and as lost as the rest of us, and the moment passed. "Maggie
can't be moved, but she'll be safe here. The Agora would never let anything happen to her, and she wasn't involved with the actual break-in at the
CDC, so it's not like she can be accused of anything more criminal than
letting herself get shot."

"Harboring fugitives," said Becks.

"Criminal negligence—she should never have left the van," said Mahir.

"Being a journalist," said George. The rest of us turned to her, startled.
She shook her head, expression grim. "I read as much of the last year's site
archive as I could before we left to get shot at. Whoever's running this
game, they don't like journalists, and they're not discriminating between
the branches. To them, a blogger's a blogger."

"She's right," whispered Maggie.

Mahir raised his head. Becks whipped around to face the bed. Maggie's
eyes were still closed, but there was a tension in her that hadn't been there
when we entered the room, a tension that spoke of consciousness.

"You know...they're targeting the bloggers," whispered Maggie. Every
word seemed heavy, like it was being dragged out of her. "Martial law in
Florida. Arrests all over the country. They're...hiding something."

"Hey. Hey. Don't try to talk, honey. You need to save your strength."
Becks moved to crouch down next to Mahir. Looking at the three of them,
I felt suddenly left out, like they had formed a unit I wasn't meant to be
part of. Then George touched my elbow with one hand, the sort of quick,
subtle contact that had always been the limit we allowed ourselves in public, and I realized they'd formed their unit because they understood—
probably before I did—that they were never really going to be a part of
mine.

I was always going to be a haunted house. The only difference was that now my ghost wore flesh and held me when I needed her. Somehow, that made it better...but it didn't stop the realization from hurting.

"No. Need to talk." Maggie struggled to open her eyes, managing a single blink before they closed again. "Shaun, you have to...you have to take Georgia and go. Go back to Dr. Abbey. She'll know another way to hide you."

"What about you?" I asked.

The ghost of a smile flitted across her face. "I am going to lie here until I can feel my toes. And then I'll ask the concierge to call my parents so I can tell them that the CDC is being naughty."

Mahir actually laughed. "Well, that'll certainly complicate things in our favor."

"You have to stay with her," said Becks.

"What?" Mahir twisted to face her, eyes narrowing. "I don't believe I heard you correctly."

"I'm staying out of this," I murmured to George. She nodded, not saying anything.

"One of us has to stay here and make sure Maggie keeps breathing until her parents get here—and that if she stops, there's someone ready to tell them the real story." Becks grimaced. "Sorry, Maggie."

"It's okay," Maggie said, another ghostly smile crossing her face. "Medical family, remember? I don't kid myself about things like this." The smile faded, replaced by a grimace. "Could've done without getting shot, though."

"And I'm volunteered to remain behind precisely why?" Mahir demanded.

"Shaun's crazy, Georgia's a clone, and I'm prepared to shoot them both if they so much as look at me funny. Whereas you have virtually no field experience, and have never shot someone you care about."

"I've had field experience," said Mahir.

"Was any of it voluntary?" asked George.

He grimaced. "No," he admitted. "But I don't care one bit for being the one who gets sidelined. It seems that's always what you lot do right before you kick off the endgame. Remember Sacramento?"

"Bet I remember it better than you do," said George quietly.

Mahir grimaced again. "I'm sorry. But you take my point."

"Yeah," I said. "You lived. You're staying here, Mahir, and Becks is coming with us. You'll like Dr. Abbey, George. She's probably clinically insane, but she's good people, and that's harder to come by than sanity these days."

Maggie made a thin choking sound that made us all freeze, until we realized she was trying to laugh. "You people," she whispered finally. "You still think any of this is a choice. Get out of here. Get in your van, and get out of here, and finish it. Do you hear me? *Finish it*." This time, she managed to force her eyes open for almost five whole seconds, glaring at us. "Finish it, or I swear, I will die, and come back, and *haunt* you."

"I've had enough of being haunted," I said. "We'll finish it. But only because you asked so nicely, Maggie."

"I can live with that," she said, eyes drifting closed again. "Now go 'way. I want to sleep. Can't do that with all you reporters here staring at me."

Mahir stood, pausing long enough to glare at me before he stalked out of the room. Becks walked back to Maggie, bending to kiss her on the forehead. Then she followed Mahir, leaving me and George alone with Maggie.

"Let's go," I said.

"Wait," whispered Maggie.

We froze.

"Tell her to come here."

I glanced at George, who stared back at me, eyes wide and somehow helpless. I nodded. She sighed, nodding back, and walked over to Maggie.

"I'm here."

"Closer."

George leaned down until her ear was next to Maggie's mouth. Maggie whispered something, expression as urgent as her voice was weak. George hesitated before replying, "I understand. And yes. I promise."

"Good," said Maggie, loud enough for me to hear. "Now go."

George walked away from the bed, looking unsettled. She didn't pause before leaving the room. I followed her, grabbing her arm before she could head for the admissions desk, where Mahir and Becks were speaking with the EMT.

"Hey," I said. "What did she say to you?"

George turned to face me, her eyes meeting mine with a directness that her sunglasses had always prevented before. "She said that if I'm even a little bit Georgia Mason, I'll kill myself before I'll let the CDC use me to hurt you more than they already have. And I agreed.

"I *think* I'm mostly me, Shaun. I really do. But I know that mostly isn't entirely. If there's any chance I'm less myself than I think I am—if I feel even the slightest bit like I might be slipping—I will take myself out of the picture." Her smile was humorless. "I won't be the one who stops you from avenging me."

There was nothing I could say to that.

We think we have an idea where she's been, if not where she's going. There was an explosion in one of the supposedly deserted neighborhoods; police found evidence of a massive amount of computer equipment there. It's possible she and her friends were trying to buy themselves new identities when something went wrong. How things went wrong, I don't know. We thought we'd removed all the tracking devices from her body. If we didn't...

If we didn't, you may have to prepare yourself for the idea that all of this was for nothing. There's nothing we can do now but wait and see what happens next.

—Taken from a message sent by Dr. Gregory Lake to Vice President Richard Cousins, August 5, 2041.

Alaric took less than kindly to the message that Maggie had been injured and I was remaining behind to tend her while the others returned to the lab. I didn't mention Georgia. There's complicating matters, and then there's blowing up Parliament just so you can make a few adjustments to the seating chart. He'll find out soon enough.

Please God we all get out of this alive. Please God Maggie gets better. I want to go home. I want to see my wife again.

I want this all to be over.

**—From *Fish and Clips*,
the blog of Mahir Gowda, August 5, 2041. Unpublished.**

GEORGIA: Thirty-one

We left the Agora shortly after sunset, when the cleanup crew declared the van road-serviceable and unlikely to infect and kill us all. Shaun took the wheel, since Becks wasn't willing to let me drive. She said it was because I didn't have a license; from the way she refused to meet my eyes while she was saying it, I suspected it was more an issue of her not quite trusting me yet. I couldn't blame her. If I'd been in her position, and someone I'd already buried had come back...yeah. It was a miracle any of them trusted me at all. A miracle, or the kind of madness that was going to get us all killed.

With no real idea where we were going, and nothing I could do to help, I contented myself with pulling up the site archive on the local server and reading as we drove down the length of Washington State and into Oregon. This was a slower, more careful read than my earlier looting for information; I could take the time to really absorb what I was looking at, rather than just clicking the next report as quickly as possible. There was even a link to the site's financials. I was somehow unsurprised to see that Shaun had maintained ownership of my files, and was using them to finance a large percentage of the site's overhead. I was one of the higher-profile journalist deaths since the Rising. That made me fascinating, and made my previously unpublished op-ed pieces lucrative, even when they'd been written to parallel events that happened years before. That's the human race. Always willing to slow down and look at the train wreck.

Becks kept watch from the passenger seat while Shaun drove. The route he chose involved a disturbing number of frontage roads and narrow trails that were basically glorified footpaths. He drove them like they were familiar, and after everything that he and the others had been through since I died, they probably were. I stopped reading and leaned back in my seat, closing my eyes for just a moment, missing the familiar ache I used to get whenever I forced myself to look at a brightly lit computer screen for too long. I never thought I'd miss having retinal KA, but now it was just one more thing about my life that I was never going to get back.

This was my fault. I was the one who pressured Shaun into agreeing to follow the Ryman campaign, and together we'd strong-armed Buffy into going along with us. If I'd just been willing to work my way up through the ranks the way everyone else did, taking it one step at a time instead of rocketing straight to the top—

Then someone else would have died in my place, and in Buffy's place, and someone else's brother would be the one making this drive. This was all going to happen eventually. The only thing that made us special was the thing that has distinguished one journalist from another since the first reporter found a way to distinguish gossip from the real headline story: We were the ones on the scene when everything went down. We weren't better. We weren't worse. We were just the ones standing in the blast radius.

Everything that happened from there was inevitable.

That didn't absolve us of blame—there's always blame when the wrong stories get told and the wrong secrets get out—but even if we weren't innocent now, we were then. We really believed in what we were doing. It wasn't our fault that we were wrong.

I drifted off reading Alaric's analysis of the political situation after Ryman's election—situation normal, all fucked up, with some interesting developments in the regulation of larger mammals and a few changes to the rules for determining hazard zones, but nothing earth-shaking—and woke to see the first rays of false dawn painting the edge of the sky in shades of pollution pink and caution tape gold. Becks was driving. Shaun was asleep in the passenger seat, his head lolling back and his mouth hanging slightly open. He looked exhausted.

Becks must have heard me stirring. She glanced at the rearview mirror, her reflected eyes meeting mine, and raised one eyebrow. That was all she needed to do; the message couldn't have been easier to understand if she'd posted it on the front page of our news site.

I nodded. I understood, and I wasn't going to hurt him. Not if I had any choice in the matter.

My mouth felt like the ass-end of a Tuesday morning. I cleared my throat and asked, "Where are we?"

"Oregon. We're almost there."

"There where?"

"Shady Cove."

I paused, trying to convince myself I'd heard wrong. It didn't work. Finally, I demanded, "*What?*"

Shaun didn't flinch. Becks replied, "Shady Cove, Oregon. Our friend Dr. Abbey has a lab there. Right now, anyway. She'll probably move it soon. Possibly after she demands that we let her dissect you."

"In Shady Cove."

"Yes."

"But there's nothing *in* Shady Cove." Shady Cove, Oregon, was on the list of cities abandoned after the Rising, when the economic cost of rebuilding was determined too great to balance out the benefits. We'd take it back someday, when the great march of progress demanded we leave the dead with no country of their own. Until then, Shady Cove would stand empty, just like Santa Cruz, California, and Truth or Consequences, New Mexico, and Warsaw, Indiana, and a hundred other towns and cities around the world.

"That's why she has her lab there," said Becks curtly, before leaning over and snapping the radio on. Further conversation was rendered moot by the sound of a pre-Rising pop star informing us, loudly and with enthusiasm, that she was a rock star.

Shaun jerked upright, eyes open, hand going to the pistol at his belt. "Wha—"

"Settle, Mason. We can't all be as polite as the wakeup call at Maggie's fancy-ass hotel," said Becks, turning the radio down again now that its purpose had been achieved. "We're almost there. I need you on watch."

"Right." Shaun ground the heels of his hands against his eyes, wiping the sleep away. This time he finished the process of drawing the pistol from his belt, flicking off the safety. Once he was done, he twisted in his seat, shooting his old, familiar, who-gives-a-fuck? grin in my direction. "Sleep well?"

"Like a rock," I said. I almost said "like the dead," but realized he might not take that well. Like it or not, Shaun was going to be a little sensitive about that sort of thing for a while. Possibly forever.

"Good, because the good Doc's going to be real interested in talking to you." Shaun twisted back around to face forward, watching the darkened forest roll by outside his window. "She's a little hard to explain if you haven't met her. Hell, nobody explained her to me."

"I read the files."

"There's reading the files, and then there's the reality of a mentally disturbed Canadian woman throwing a live octopus at your chest so you can tell her whether exposure to Kellis-Amberlee has changed its reflex speed.

Which, in case you wondered, doesn't happen. An octopus infected with Kellis-Amberlee is still fast, smart, and incredibly easy to piss off." Shaun shuddered. "All those suckers..."

"Wait. Octopuses aren't mammals."

Becks smiled coolly at me in the rearview mirror. "And that's why Dr. Abbey is difficult to explain to anyone who hasn't met her."

I sighed. "I'm not going to like this, am I?"

"Probably not," said Becks, and turned off the narrow dirt road we'd been traveling down, onto another, narrower, dirtier road. This one seemed more like a deer trail with delusions of grandeur than an actual thoroughfare, and the van shuddered and jumped with every bump and pothole. Shaun whooped a little, causing Becks to shoot him a wide-eyed look. He grinned unrepentantly back. I got the feeling that there hadn't been much whooping while I was away.

The dirt trail—I refused to dignify it with anything that sounded more maintained—emptied us onto a road that was just as decrepit, but had obviously been better, once upon a time. Chunks of broken pavement jutted up where the roots of the encroaching trees had managed to break through the surface. Becks swerved around them with practiced ease, and actually sped up, cruising through the dark like she'd driven this route a hundred times before. Judging by the calm way Shaun was watching the trees, she had.

The road ended at a large parking lot in front of a large, glass-fronted building that was probably originally some sort of government building or visitor's center. "Forestry center," said Shaun, before I could ask. "Welcome to Shady Cove."

"...thanks." I shifted in my seat, putting my laptop to the side. "Is someone going to come out and meet us?"

"No, but you should probably count on lots and lots of people with guns waiting for us inside." Shaun shot me another manic grin. "Dr. Abbey knows how to greet visitors."

"With terror and intimidation?" I asked.

"Something like that," Becks agreed. She slowed down but kept driving, steering us into a covered parking garage attached to the back of the building. There were only a few vehicles already parked there, including—

I sat up straighter. "My bike!"

Shaun's grin softened, becoming sadder and more sincere. "You didn't think I'd leave it behind, did you?"

I didn't answer him. I couldn't speak around the lump in my throat. As soon as Becks parked the van I opened the door and climbed out, heading for my bike in what I hoped looked like a reasonably nonchalant manner. Not that it made a damn bit of difference either way. There was nothing—absolutely nothing, including the sudden appearance of a shambler from the shadows, which thankfully didn't happen—that could have kept me away from my bike in that moment. I actually hugged the handlebars, I was so damn glad to see it.

Shaun and Becks followed, pausing long enough to get their duffel bags from the car. They stopped about eight feet away. Out of the corner of my eye, I saw Becks elbow Shaun in the side, mouthing the words, "Ask her."

He looked at her uncertainly before he cleared his throat and said, "Uh, George? Did you want to start the engine? Make sure I've been doing regular maintenance and all that good shit?"

"That depends." I stopped hugging the handlebars, straightening as I turned to face them. "Do you actually want me to check the condition of the engine, or do you want me to run my fingerprints against the ones in the bike's database?"

"The second one," admitted Shaun.

"Right. Did you engage the biometrics when you locked the bike?" He nodded. I sighed. "Fine," I said, and stuck out my right thumb, holding it up for both of them to see, before pressing it down on the pressure sensor at the center of the bike's dash. A blue light promptly came on above the speedometer. I held my breath, and kept holding it until the light turned green before shutting off entirely. "Biometrics disengaged," I announced. "Happy now?"

Shaun turned to Becks, grinning as he said, "Extremely. Told you she could do it."

Becks nodded slowly. "Okay. You got one right. Come on. Dr. Abbey knows we're here by now." She started walking toward the nearest door, not waiting for the two of us.

I took a deep breath before heading over to join Shaun. Maybe he'd been sure that I could trigger the bike's biometric lock, but I hadn't been. Identical twins don't have the same fingerprints. Why would clones?

Answer: because at least in my case, the clone was intended to pass for the original in every way possible, and that meant that if my fingerprints could be matched to my old body, they would be. I was just glad they'd taken the trouble with this body, given that it was never intended to see the outside of a lab.

Thinking about that too much made me feel nauseous. I shuddered and sped up a little, matching my steps to Shaun's. Becks was already at the door, her palm pressed against a blood test panel. The light above it turned green, and she opened the door, stepping inside. She waved before slamming it in our faces. I moved into position next, slapping my hand down on the panel. The light cycled and the door unlocked, letting me inside.

"Be right there," said Shaun.

I smiled at him and closed the door. "You know, for a black-ops virology lab, this place has pretty straightforward security," I said, turning to face the room.

"No, we don't," said the short, curvy woman standing next to Becks. She was wearing a lab coat, blue jeans, and a bright orange T-shirt, all of which paled a bit when taken together with the hunting rifle she had pointed at my chest. "We just take slightly different steps to enforce it."

I froze.

The door opened behind me. "Hey, Dr. Abbey," said Shaun.

"Hello, Shaun," said the woman. She had a faint Canadian accent. "Who's your friend?"

"Oh, right, you never met George, did you?" Shaun closed the door and moved to stand next to me. "Georgia Mason, meet Dr. Shannon Abbey, mad scientist. Dr. Abbey, meet Georgia Mason, living dead girl."

"He must be feeling better if he can make bad Rob Zombie jokes," said Becks.

"Feeling better doesn't mean sane, stable, or thinking clearly," said Dr. Abbey. Her eyes swept across my face, assessing me. "What do *you* think your name is, girlie?"

"Georgia Mason," I replied, relieved that she'd asked a question whose answer I already knew. "I'm a ninety-seven percent cognate to the original. Don't quiz me on my fifth birthday party and I'll be fine."

She raised an eyebrow. "You sure you should be telling me that?"

"I'm sure that if you're going to shoot me, you'll do it regardless of what I say now, and if you're going to study me, you're not going to shoot me regardless of what I say now, so I may as well be honest with you." I smiled despite the tension. "I like being honest."

"You brought me a mouthy clone," said Dr. Abbey, looking toward Shaun. "And here it's not even my birthday."

He shrugged. "I try to be thoughtful. How's it hanging, Doc?"

"Well, let's see. You went to get me mosquitoes. You didn't bring me any mosquitoes. Instead, you bring me a clone of your dead sister. So I'd say it's hanging pretty damn poorly right now." Dr. Abbey sighed, lowering her rifle. "Thank God you're not the only people I have to work with. Come on. There's someone here that I want you to meet."

She turned, starting to walk away. I followed, and got my first real look at her facility. I stopped, staring.

I'm not sure what I expected from an off-the-grid virology lab run by a woman with the fashion sense of a traffic cone. I certainly didn't expect a fully equipped, if somewhat quixotically designed, research facility. Racks of medical equipment, computers, and lab animals were everywhere I looked. The place seemed slightly understaffed for its size, but that was probably a function of its underground nature—it wasn't like they could advertise for staff on the local message boards. "Mad Scientist seeks Minions. Must be detail-oriented, well educated, and unconcerned by the idea of being charged with terrorism if caught." Just no.

As she walked, Dr. Abbey asked, "How's Maggie?"

"Gut-shot and cranky, but the doctors say she'll live," said Shaun. "Is there any news about Alisa?"

"You haven't been looking at the non–world shattering news feeds recently, have you?" Dr. Abbey paused to hang her rifle from a hook on the wall and said, "Alisa Kwong was removed from the Ferry Pass Refugee Center two days ago when well-known Internet journalists Stacy and Michael Mason made an eloquent plea for custody of the tragically orphaned girl. They ran their reports from just outside the interdicted zone, making it impossible to shut them down without causing a massive Internet shitstorm. So the feds gave them the kid. Alisa's been e-mailing Alaric constantly. He can't tell her where we are, but being able to communicate with her without worrying about the mosquitoes getting into the facility where she's being held is doing them both a world of good. We'll worry about getting her back when it's safe."

Her words were clearly directed at Shaun, who nodded, a serious expression on his face. It was still a little weird, seeing him look so grave about something that wasn't related to risking his neck or getting a good ratings share. His priorities had shifted while I was gone.

He shot me a look, a smile curving up one corner of his mouth. Well. Not all his priorities.

"This is impressive," I said. "Did you set this all up yourself?"

"Golly-gee, Miss Clone, no! The government used to set up surprise scientific research facilities all over the country, just so they'd be around for people to stumble into when they were needed. If you break a few jars, you'll probably find guns and bonus lives inside." Dr. Abbey's smile was closer to a snarl, leaving her teeth half bared. "We're here for your amusement."

I raised an eyebrow. "You could have just said 'yes.'"

"And miss the opportunity to see what you'd do if I called you stupid?" Dr. Abbey's smile faded. She grabbed a small testing unit off one of the shelves, lobbing it at me. I caught it. She nodded slightly, apparently taking a mental note of my reflexes. "Go ahead and get yourself another clean blood result while we're all standing here. I want a portable sample."

"Doesn't Shaun get one?" I asked, concerned. The unit was heavier than I expected, with no visible lights on the top.

Dr. Abbey actually laughed. "You mean he didn't tell you? The lucky boy's immune."

"Probably due to extended exposure to someone with a reservoir condition, which brings us back to you, Georgia." The man who walked up behind her was clearly of Asian descent, even if his accent was pure Hawaiian. He was wearing knee-length khaki shorts and sandals, which wouldn't do a damn thing to save him if we had to run. He had a round face, and a kind expression that put my teeth instantly on edge. I was quickly learning that no one who looked at me kindly was planning to do anything I'd enjoy. Call it the natural paranoia born of dying and coming back to life again.

Shaun's hand clamped down on my shoulder. "Dude," he said, voice radiating suspicion, "who the fuck are you?"

The stranger's smile didn't waver. "I'm Dr. Joseph Shoji. You must be Shaun. You know, I don't think this could have been engineered to go any better if we'd tried. I really had no idea how we were going to get the two of you into the same place, and then you go and manage to perform a rescue op—"

The rest of the word was cut off as Shaun let go of my shoulder, pushing me back a step, and lunged for Dr. Shoji. Becks and Dr. Abbey watched impassively as Shaun's momentum drove the two men backward, stopping only when Dr. Shoji's shoulders slammed into the nearest wall. I made a startled noise that was shamefully close to a squeak.

"You CDC asshole!" snarled Shaun.

"He's not with the CDC," said Dr. Abbey. Shaun didn't seem to hear her.

"Bets on the crazy boy," said Becks.

"Joey's pretty mean when you get him riled," countered Dr. Abbey.

I stared at them. "What are you two *doing*? Make them stop!"

"Sweetcheeks, there's only ever been one person who could make that boy do anything he didn't want to do, and she's ashes in the wind." Dr. Abbey's gaze was assessing. "You're close, but you're not sure you're good enough, are you? Now take that blood test."

"You're insane," I said, and started to move toward Shaun and Dr. Shoji.

"Isn't that what the 'mad scientist' after my name is meant to imply?" asked Dr. Abbey. Then she sighed. "Look. You can go along with what I'm asking, which isn't much when you stop and think about it. Or you can try to intervene in Shaun's attempt to throttle the life from my colleague—way not to fight back there, Joey—and I can have one of my interns shoot you where you stand. Pick one."

Cheeks burning, I muttered, "I am getting damn sick of scientists," and popped the lid off the testing unit. I slammed my thumb down on the panel inside, feeling the needles bite into my skin.

Dr. Abbey nodded. "Good. You can follow directions. That's going to be important." She placed two fingers in her mouth and whistled. On cue, an impossible terror came lumbering down the hall, jowls flapping, eyes glowing with menace.

I couldn't help myself. I screamed. It was a high, piercing sound, and I was ashamed of it as soon as it left my throat. It had the unexpectedly positive effect of stopping the terror in its tracks. The huge black dog cocked its head, looking at me. Shaun also stopped trying to strangle Dr. Shoji, twisting around to regard me with alarm.

"George? What's wrong?"

Mutely, I pointed to the dog.

"Oh." Shaun blinked, releasing Dr. Shoji's throat. The Hawaiian virologist took a hasty step away from him. "That's just Joe. He won't hurt you."

"He will if I tell him to," said Dr. Abbey, leaning over to pluck the test unit from my hand. She didn't bother with a biohazard bag. She just snapped the lid closed and tucked the whole thing into the pocket of her lab coat. "Joe, guard."

The dog sat, gaze remaining on me. Something in its posture told me it wouldn't regard ripping my throat out as the high point of its day, but it would do it all the same if Dr. Abbey gave the order. The idea of moving seemed suddenly ludicrous, like it was the sort of thing only crazy people did.

"You're a bit high-strung, aren't you?" asked Dr. Shoji, rubbing his throat and giving Shaun a sidelong look. "Have you considered the benefits of marijuana? Or at least reducing your caffeine intake?"

"Don't push it, Joey; he's had a long day," said Dr. Abbey.

"He just tried to strangle me."

"Yes, but he failed, which means we're still playing nice."

"Don't you touch my sister," snarled Shaun, seeming to remember that Dr. Shoji was there.

I sighed, reaching out to grab Shaun's elbow. "He's not one of the doctors from Portland. It's okay."

"I heard screaming—is everything okay out here?" Alaric emerged from one of the side rooms, showing an admirable lack of self-preservation—it takes a reporter, after all, to run *toward* the sound of screaming. Reporters and crazy people, they were the only ones who would be moving in a situation like this. So which one was I going to be?

"The dog startled me," I said, turning to face him. I tried a smile. It felt foreign, like it wasn't quite designed to fit my face. "Hey, Alaric. Long time no see."

Alaric stopped dead, blood draining from his face. Then, with no more ceremony than that, his eyes rolled back in his head and he hit the floor in a heap. The five of us stared at him. Even Joe the giant fucking dog turned his head to study the prone blogger for a moment before returning to the serious business of staring at me.

"Dude really needs to toughen up," said Shaun.

Becks sighed. "Or maybe we need to stop doing twelve impossible things every day. Are we all done waving our crazy flags around and proclaiming ourselves the Kings of Crazytown? Because I want to know what the new guy is doing here, and I want you to do whatever you need to do to prove that she"—she jerked a thumb toward me—"is close enough to legit that we can let Shaun keep her. I think he'll cry if we don't."

Shaun glared at her. Becks ignored him.

"If I may?" Dr. Shoji looked from Shaun to Dr. Abbey, and finally to me. "As I was saying, I work with the Kauai Institute of Virology. I've been consulting with their Kellis-Amberlee research division for the past seven years, which is fairly impressive, considering they think I'm on loan from the CDC."

I paused before saying slowly, "But you don't work for the CDC, do you?"

"No. I believe you've already met some of my associates, Drs. Kimberley and Lake? They spoke very highly of you, even before they were sure you'd be able to make it out of the facility. They certainly thought you were the most promising subject—forgive me for using that word; it's an ugly word, but it's the only one I have—to arise from Project Shelley. We were all rooting for you from the start." He was smiling again. It was such a *kind* smile. What was my life going to be like if I didn't trust people who looked kind?

Probably a lot like it was before, when I didn't trust anyone who wasn't on my team. "You're with the EIS."

"What?" said Becks.

"What?" said Shaun.

"That was quicker than I expected," said Dr. Abbey. She gestured toward Alaric, who was still lying on the hallway floor. "One of you, get him up. I don't want an intern coming along and shooting him before he can wake up and tell them he's not dead."

"Giant dog," I said.

She sighed. "Fine. Joe, *down*." The dog abandoned its watchful position, lumbering back to its feet and trotting to stand next to Dr. Abbey, tail wagging wildly. She placed a hand atop its head. "Happy?"

"Not really, but I'm not seeing much of an alternative here." I stepped closer to Shaun, still watching the dog warily. "Why is it *here*?"

"Joe is, like, a super-long story, and I'm a little more interested in the story that makes you meet Mr. Hawaii here and jump straight to him being with the EIS," said Shaun. "Does that mean he's working for the people who were holding you captive?"

"No," said Dr. Shoji. "It means I'm working with the people who helped her escape, and it means I'm here to make sure you get her where she needs to be—where you both need to be. The man who funded most of Project Shelley needs you. This is what he was hoping for all along."

"Who?" demanded Becks.

I didn't need to ask. A quiet certainty was growing in the pit of my stomach. Maybe it had been since Dr. Shoji showed up, and I realized that everything—*everything*—was connected, whether we wanted it to be or not. There was no running away from the past. Alive or dead, it was going to catch up with us in the end.

Alaric groaned, starting to stir. I looked at Dr. Shoji and said calmly, "Rick. He paid to bring me back, didn't he?"

"Yes," said Dr. Shoji. "And now he needs your help."

I sighed. "Right. Let's peel Alaric off the floor and get him up to speed, guys. I think we're heading for Washington D.C."

———

Oh, of course. Georgia isn't dead. Or, well, she was dead, but now she's not, because the CDC is running an underground cloning lab, and the best thing they could think of to clone was a dead journalist who was a pain in their asses when she was alive the first time. And ninety-seven percent memory transfer? That isn't science fiction, that's science lying-through-your-teeth. Either she's not as perfect as she thinks, or there have been a lot of scientific advances that no one's bothered to share with the rest of us.

And then I think... Kellis-Amberlee in mosquitoes. Someone killing all the people with reservoir conditions. Dr. Wynne trying to kill half the team. That Australian scientist. All that census data. All the things that don't add up, that never added up, that have been not adding up since before... well, since before Dr. Matras hijacked his daughter's blog and told the world the dead were walking. All the things that never added up at all. And I think. Well.

Maybe this isn't so impossible after all. And that scares the pants off me.

Thank God Alisa's safe with the Masons. And if that's a sentence that I can write without irony, maybe nothing is impossible anymore.

**—From *The Kwong Way of Things*,
the blog of Alaric Kwong, August 6, 2041. Unpublished.**

———

Dear Alaric.

The people I am with, the Masons, say I should send this e-mail and tell you I promise I won't e-mail again for a while, because I won't be able to check mail and I don't want you to feel bad when you send messages that aren't answered. I can check e-mail again when we get back to Berkeley, but we aren't there yet.

Mr. Mason is nice, but he stares into space sometimes, and it scares me a little. Ms. Mason isn't so nice, I don't think, but she's trying hard, and I know that should count. Anyway, they said you sent them, and I should go with them, and they had pictures of those people you work with, the cute guy and the dead girl, and so I figured it would be okay. Please don't be angry. I needed to get out of there before the mosquitoes got in, and I was so scared, and you said you'd send someone.

Thank you for sending the Masons. I'll see you soon. I love you.

**—Taken from an e-mail sent by Alisa Kwong to Alaric Kwong,
August 6, 2041.**

SHAUN: Thirty-two

The engines of the Kauai Institute's private jet hummed smoothly, just loud enough that we could be confident that we were still on the plane and not, I don't know, sitting in a really funky modular living room. It didn't help that we were practically alone on the plane. Becks and Alaric were sitting on one side, reading through the files Dr. Abbey had loaded onto their phones before we left. Dr. Shoji was at the front of the plane, monitoring the autopilot and giving us a little privacy in the last few hours before we landed. That left me and George, and she'd been asleep for the better part of an hour, head pillowed on her arm, mouth relaxed from its normal hard line to something softer and more vulnerable. I kept glancing over to make sure she was still there, but I couldn't look at her for more than a few seconds when she was like that. It felt like I was stealing something. George was never that vulnerable, not even for me.

According to the little trip monitor at the front of the cabin, we were approximately two hours outside of Washington D.C., where presumably, Dr. Shoji would find a way of getting us out of the private airfield we were aiming for without anyone getting shot in the head. If you had to fly, there were worse ways than hopping from one private airfield to another in a fully outfitted corporate jet. Of course, there were better ones, too. Ones that didn't mean we were going in essentially blind, on the word of a man who just happened to know the people responsible for cloning my sister.

I pinched the bridge of my nose and groaned. "Things were a lot simpler when all I had to worry about was what I was going to poke with a stick today," I muttered.

George didn't stir.

Becks looked up, waving a hand until she caught my attention. Then she beckoned me to their side of the plane. I shrugged and stood, picking up my half-empty cup of in-flight coffee before walking over to join them. The coffee was lukewarm. I didn't care. Just being able to drink it without feeling guilty made it the best cup of coffee in the world.

"What do we know?" I asked, plopping down next to Becks. She wasn't wearing her seat belt. Alaric was. That, right there, tells you most of what you need to know about both of them.

"The clone tech they used for…" Alaric cast an uneasy glance toward George, seeming to lose the thread of the sentence.

When several seconds ticked by without him continuing, I nudged him with my foot. Just a nudge, but he jumped like I'd kicked him. I sighed. "The clone tech they used to bring Georgia back," I prompted. "What do we know?"

"They force-grew her body with a lot of chemicals, a lot of hormones, a lot of radiation, and a lot of luck," said Alaric slowly. "It only worked because they didn't need to worry about getting a clone with cancer. She probably *was* cancerous by the time they finished maturing her, and they just let the Marburg Amberlee part of Kellis-Amberlee do the mop-up when she was exposed to the virus."

"She mentioned that she wasn't the only one," said Becks. "What I'm pretty sure she doesn't know is that she wasn't even one of ten."

I raised an eyebrow. "No?"

"Try more like one out of ten *thousand*, if you're starting from the zygote level and then moving up to full-on vat-grown humans. Most of them never made it out of their petri dishes. The ones that did…I don't understand half this science, except to understand that I don't like it. It was technically ethical, or would have been, if they hadn't been growing bodies with functioning brains, but the fact that the CDC can do this at all disturbs me." Becks shook her head. "I mean, what next? The military starts force-cloning soldiers?"

"Only if they feel like paying five million dollars for every functional model," said Alaric. "That's the cost of the cloning—the starting cost. It doesn't include the cost of the subliminal conditioning, the synapse programming—"

"Which is how she can actually *remember* things, like dying," chimed in Becks.

Alaric gave her a look that was half glare, half fond exasperation. "I would have gotten to that," he said. "But yes. The synapse programming is why she *remembers* things. And then there was the physical therapy to keep her muscles developing, the immunizations, the process of getting her to maturity...you're looking at thirty or forty million dollars of medical technology. Easy."

There was a pause while we turned to look at George. She shifted in her sleep, one foot kicking out a few inches before it was pulled back to nestle against the opposite ankle. I turned back to the others.

"Well, I hope they don't think they're getting her back," I said. "What else can you get out of those files?"

You want to know if I'm going to die again. Georgia-in-my-head was talking less and less the longer there was a living, breathing George for me to hold on to, but that didn't mean she was gone. It just meant my crazy was biding its time, waiting to strike when I was least prepared. You don't go that far past the borders of Crazytown and come waltzing out unscathed.

The worst part of it was that she—the dead girl's voice in my head—was right, because she was always right. I wanted to know if George was going to die. There was no way I could survive that twice.

Becks looked at me levelly. "She's stable, Shaun. Those doctors from the EIS took out the CDC fail-safes, and they couldn't actually build a human body that would self-destruct without help. The science isn't that good."

"Yet," said Alaric. He shook his head. "I believe in her now, Shaun. I mean, she's right when she says she's an imperfect copy—the Kellis-Amberlee kept turning her brain's basic functions back on, but there was a little bit more tissue loss every time. That doesn't mean she's not who she says she is. She never had the chance to become anybody else."

"God." Becks shuddered. "Headshots just became a hell of a lot more important to me."

I frowned, finishing off my lukewarm coffee before I asked, "Why?"

"Because Miss Atherton has just realized one of the things the CDC would prefer the population not be aware of." Dr. Shoji took the seat next to Alaric. "I hope you don't mind my joining you. When I realized you were finally getting around to discussing the science, I thought you might like the opportunity to question someone who used to be involved with it."

My eyes narrowed. "You mean—"

"No, no." He put his hands up, motioning for me to stay calm. "I left that part of my life behind a long time ago. There were some ethical lines I couldn't bring myself to cross, and at that point...I was still suited to work in the private sector—hence my work with the Kauai Institute—but I could no longer stomach the CDC."

"The cross-infection trials Kelly mentioned," said Alaric.

It took me a moment to realize what he was talking about. When we first got to Dr. Abbey's lab—what felt like a million years ago—we'd still been traveling with Kelly Connolly. In an effort to show us that the CDC wasn't all rainbows and roses, Dr. Abbey asked her about some cross-infection trials using prisoners who "volunteered" to be injected with multiple strains of KA. All of them died.

"Yes," said Dr. Shoji. "Those men and women died horribly, and they didn't have to. That was when I realized it had to end. I stopped working on things that we didn't need to do—and forgive me, Shaun, but finding a new way of bringing back the dead wasn't something that needed to be a priority. We'd already done that. It didn't work out well."

"It's cool," I said.

Slowly, Becks said, "Kellis-Amberlee 'raises the dead' by turning the body's electrical impulses back on. It's like a viral defibrillator that just keeps on working, and working, and working, until there's nothing left to work with. If they got a clean brain scan off of Georgia after you shot her, that means her brain was turned on at the time. They took their scans off a living brain."

Dr. Shoji nodded. "Yes," he agreed. "That's how the technology works. It was originally intended to be a treatment for Alzheimer's, a way of calling back memories that were still present, but had become...clouded, let's say. Misplaced somehow. Once we realized that it could be used on the victims of Kellis-Amberlee, there was hope that we'd be able to bring them back to themselves—that memory recall could be used as a form of treatment, that, combined with antivirals and proper therapy, they could be cured."

"So why didn't it work?" I asked.

"The virus didn't give up that easily. Nothing we did resulted in anything but agitation in the subjects. Some researchers, myself included, were concerned that we might actually cause the infected to become self-aware. People with rabies are aware that they've done horrible things. They simply can't prevent themselves from doing them. No one wanted that with Kellis-Amberlee, and so the project was suspended."

"Why didn't you publish?" asked Becks.

"For the same reason the government is shooting everybody with a reservoir condition," said Alaric. "If they let it get out that people are still thinking, no one's going to pull the trigger. And then there won't be anyone left to do the curing, because we'll all be zombies."

I frowned. "I'm not following."

"They're saying that once someone is infected, the virus takes over, but they're still in there." The engines might be soft, but they were loud enough that I hadn't heard George walking up until she spoke. I turned to see her standing beside me, hair still rumpled from sleep, sunglasses in her hand. She looked at Dr. Shoji and asked, "Do zombies think?"

"No," he said. "The virus does their thinking for them, thank God, because Alaric is right. If people stop shooting because they're afraid of committing murder, we're all going to die. But there's a chance—not a huge chance, but a chance—that zombies dream."

George nodded, leaning against the seat next to me. "That's what I thought you were going to say. How long before we land?"

"We have about an hour before we begin our initial descent into Washington D.C.," said Dr. Shoji. "How are you feeling?"

"Exhausted. I need a Coke."

I was never going to get tired of hearing those words. "I'll get you one," I said, standing. "I needed to get another coffee anyway."

She slid into my seat, flashing me a quick, grateful smile. Then she leaned forward, posture making it clear that she was asking Dr. Shoji a question. Probably more things about zombies thinking. Whatever it was, they would fill me in later.

I walked to the self-serve kitchenette at the back of the plane, pulling a can of Coke from the refrigerator unit before pouring myself a cup of blessedly hot coffee. There were wrapped cheese and turkey sandwiches in one of the cold drawers over the coffee machine. I took down three of those—one for me, one for George, and one for the first person who asked where their sandwich was. We needed to keep our strength up if we were going to go take on the United States government. Which was, by the way, insane.

You should know, said George.

I didn't reply. It felt weird, trying to reject that little inner voice when it was the only thing that had kept me even halfway functional in the months following the real Georgia's death, but I couldn't have them both, and given the choice, I'd take the George I could share with other people. That made her real. I needed real. I needed real to anchor me to the world, because otherwise I was going to slip right over the edge.

Going all the way crazy seemed a lot less appealing now than it had a few weeks ago. I used to view a total break with reality as a sort of psychological permission to spend the rest of my life—however long or short it happened to be—with George, and maybe even be happy. Having a living, breathing woman with her face made me admit that it wouldn't make me happy. The George in my head wasn't the real thing. Neither was the clone, if you wanted to get technical, but I've never been a technical guy.

I needed Georgia in my life. I chose the one who was sitting in the cabin, waiting for her Coke.

Alaric had come around surprisingly quickly, after he finished yelling at us for not keeping him updated while we were in Seattle. Typical Newsie; he was less upset about the CDC raising the dead than he was about us not sending him regular reports. He'd spent about half an hour quizzing George on everything he could think of while Becks and I were getting us packed to go. She must have passed, because when he was done, he'd looked at me, said, "It's her," and started listening to her like she'd never died in the first place. If only it was going to be that easy for everyone.

"What did I miss?" I asked, walking back over to the group. George stuck her hand out as soon as I was close enough. I passed her the Coke and a sandwich, and was rewarded with a brief smile. She was wearing her sunglasses again, even though she didn't technically need them. We were all frankly more comfortable that way.

"Dr. Shoji was explaining the landing plan," said Becks. "We're going to set down at the Montgomery County Airpark in Maryland, and drive from there."

"The airport has been owned by the EIS since shortly after the Rising," said Dr. Shoji. "We've managed to resist all CDC efforts to buy it from us, and since we're still officially on the books as a functional organization, they haven't been able to simply take it. There's a ground crew waiting, and they've promised to have a vehicle ready."

"How are we going to get off the property?" asked Becks. "I don't suppose you're running a completely unsecured airfield less than fifty miles from the nation's capitol."

"We're good, but we're not that good," said Dr. Shoji. "You'll take a blood test when you deplane, and another when you exit the airport. Both will be performed on EIS equipment, and logged in our mainframe. If the CDC is tracking you by blood test results, they won't get anything from us. We stopped sharing all our data a long time ago."

"Isn't that illegal?" asked Alaric.

"Isn't human cloning illegal?" asked George. She opened her Coke and took a long drink before adding, "The CDC isn't playing by the rules anymore. Why should anyone else?"

"What a wonderful world we've made for ourselves." Alaric scowled, slumping in his seat. "I'm getting sick and tired of everybody double crossing everybody else. Can't something be straightforward?"

I raised my hand. "I'm just here to hit stuff."

Becks glared. The anger in her eyes was impossible to miss, no matter how hard I might try to pretend it wasn't there. "Don't you dare, Shaun Mason. You may have been here to hit stuff once, but things have changed since then, so don't you dare. You don't get to go back to pretending you're an idiot just because you have Georgia here to hide behind, you got me? I won't *let* you. Even if you try, I won't *let* you."

A moment of awkward silence followed her proclamation, each of us trying not to look at Dr. Shoji, who had just witnessed something that felt intensely personal, at least to me. That wasn't something that should have been shared with anyone outside our weird little semi-family.

Dr. Shoji clearly knew that. He stood, clearing his throat as he jerked his chin toward the sandwiches in my hand. "That's a good idea. You should all eat before we land. I don't know how much opportunity we're going to have to stop once we hit the ground. We can't risk any of you taking CDC-operated blood tests before we get to where we're going." That said, he turned and walked away, heading back toward the cockpit. In a matter of seconds, the four of us were alone again.

We looked at each other. Finally, Becks took a slow breath, and said, "Shaun, I'm sorry. I shouldn't have said—"

"It's okay." I shook my head. "It's true. I spent a lot of time letting George do the thinking for both of us, because I could get away with it. I've been doing all the thinking for a year now. I don't think I can stop. But that doesn't mean I want to do anything at this point beyond smashing things and shooting people and making sure this ends. You get me? This is going to end."

"No matter what?" asked Alaric, almost defiantly.

I turned to look at him. Out of all of us, he was the one who still had something to lose. His little sister was with the Masons. If he died, she'd wind up staying with them. There were too many orphans in the world to take one away from an apparently loving family. They'd probably be more careful with her than they were with us, but that didn't make them good parents, and that didn't make them good for her. Not in the long term.

"If you need to get out at any point, you get out," I said. "But aside from that? For me and George? Yeah, no matter what. If this doesn't end here, they're never going to stop coming for us. So it ends, or we end, and either way, I won't blame you for running."

"Thank you," said Alaric quietly.

"So what are we doing?" asked Becks. "What's the plan? Does *anybody* have a plan? Or did we just get on a plane with this guy and cross the country because, hey, at this point it was the only stupid thing we hadn't done?"

"Rick was involved with the program that had me cloned," said George.

"Dr. Shoji is taking us to Rick. Rick wouldn't have done this if he didn't think it was absolutely necessary."

"Wow, you mean people *don't* arrange to have their dead friends brought back at huge financial and ethical cost just because they miss them?" asked Alaric dryly.

There was a pause, all four of us looking at each other wide-eyed. Then we all burst out laughing. Becks leaned forward, resting her elbows on her knees as she shook with laughter. Alaric sank back in his seat. George leaned sideways, her shoulder pressing into my hip, and tried to cover her mouth with the hand that wasn't holding her soda.

Becks was the first to get herself back under control. Straightening up, she wiped her eyes and grinned at Alaric. "Glad to see you're feeling up to being an asshole again, Kwong," she said.

Alaric half saluted. "Just doing my part for Assholes Anonymous of America."

"Somebody has to," I said. I sat down in Dr. Shoji's abandoned seat, tossing the last turkey sandwich to Alaric before taking a sip of my still-warm coffee. "So basically, we're going to hit the ground running."

"Do we ever do anything else?" asked Becks.

"No," said George.

I toasted her with my coffee. "And thank God for that."

Becks laughed again as she stood and made her way back to the kitchenette. Alaric started unwrapping his sandwich. I smiled one more time at George before unwrapping my own sandwich and taking a large bite. We needed to keep our strength up. I had the distinct feeling that not only would we be hitting the ground running, we were probably never going to slow down again. Our lives—all our lives—had been measured in calms between storms for a very long time. Even when we were dead, in George's case. Well, this was the last calm, and I was going to enjoy it while it lasted.

—————

I've always lived my life—

No. That's a lie.

Georgia Carolyn Mason, b. 2016, in the final year of the Rising, d. 2040, during the Ryman campaign, always lived her life by one simple commandment: Tell the truth. Whenever possible, whatever it requires, tell the truth. This blog was for opinions and personal thoughts, because those, too, are a part of the truth. No one is truly objective, no matter how hard we try, and unless people knew where her biases were, they couldn't know when to read around them. Georgia Mason lived to tell the truth. Georgia Mason died to tell the truth. It's not her fault some people couldn't leave well enough alone.

I am not Georgia Mason. I am not anyone else. I am a chimera, built of science and stolen DNA and a dead woman's memories. I am an impossibility. These are my biases. These are the things you need to know, because otherwise, you won't be able to read around them. I am not her.

But my name is Georgia Mason.

And I am here to tell you the truth.

**—From *Living Dead Girl*,
the blog of Georgia Mason II, August 10, 2041. Unpublished.**

Listen to the clone girl. She's got some pretty good ideas, and oh, right, if you so much as look at her funny, I'll blow your fucking face off. We clear? Good.

**—From *Hail to the King*,
the blog of Shaun Mason, August 10, 2041. Unpublished.**

GEORGIA: Thirty-three

Despite Becks's dire predictions, no one shot us out of the sky. The computerized voice of the autopilot came on over the intercom as the plane touched down on the main runway of the Montgomery County Airpark, saying, "Welcome to Montgomery County, Maryland, where the local time is nine fifty-seven P.M. Thank you for flying with the Epidemic Intelligence Service. Please remain seated while the sterilization crew secures the plane. Any attempts to get up and move about the cabin will result in the immediate activation of security measure Alpha-16."

"Meaning what?" asked Shaun.

"Meaning the plane fills with knockout gas and we stay unconscious until somebody comes along and shoots us full of the counteragent," said Alaric. We all turned to stare at him. He shrugged. "While some people were taking naps and fucking around with their guns, I was reading the security information card. Well. Security information booklet. They take security seriously around here."

"They *are* the EIS," said Becks.

"Which has meant basically jack shit for the last twenty years," said Shaun.

"They saved me," I said. "They can secure us as much as they want."

That killed the discussion. We looked at each other, then toward the front of the plane. There was still no sign of Dr. Shoji.

"You know, if he was planning to double-cross us, this would be the best time to do it," said Shaun.

"If he was planning to double-cross us, wouldn't he have just crashed the plane somewhere over Iowa?" asked Alaric.

"Not if he wanted to live," said Becks. "And not if he wanted to dissect us. I mean, Shaun's immune, Georgia's a clone..."

"And I'm an asshole," said Alaric helpfully.

Everyone laughed nervously. There was a soft "thump" as the plane stopped rolling down the runway, followed by the sound of clamps affixing to the wheels and windows. This was one plane that wouldn't be flying anywhere until it was certified infection free. Blue antibacterial foam began cascading down the windows, blocking our view of the airfield.

"The foam they use to sterilize planes costs eight dollars a gallon," said Alaric. "It takes approximately two thousand gallons to sterilize a plane this size."

Becks gave him a sidelong look. "Why do you know these things? What inspires you to learn them?"

"It impresses the ladies," said Alaric. They both laughed. Shaun didn't. I turned to look toward the front of the plane, and waited.

The blue foam slowed from a torrent to drips and drabs, finally stopping altogether. A steady stream of bleach followed it, washing away both the remains of the foam and any biological agents foolish enough to think that hitching a ride on an EIS plane was a good idea.

"Overkill much?" muttered Shaun. I surreptitiously reached over and squeezed his knee.

Alaric must have heard him, because he held up the security information booklet and said, "If they had any reason to believe we'd flown through or over an active outbreak, they'd be rinsing the whole plane down with formalin. Twice. And we'd be praying the plane was properly sealed, since otherwise, we'd probably melt."

"It's just our way of saying 'thank you for flying EIS Air,'" said Dr. Shoji, shrugging on a lab coat as he emerged from the cockpit. His black T-shirt and shorts were gone, replaced by khaki pants and a loudly patterned Hawaiian shirt covered with purple and yellow flowers. I raised an eyebrow. He shrugged. "It's camouflage. I'm supposed to be the visiting director of the Kauai Institute of Virology—which is technically true, even if I'm not here on the business of the Institute—and this is what they expect. I'd wear shorts if I thought I could get away with it, but the CDC dress code forbids exposed legs. Something about caustic chemicals." He waved a hand, clearly unconcerned.

"Why are you up and moving about the cabin?" asked Shaun. "Not in the mood to get gassed because you had a cramp, thanks."

"Ah—sorry." Dr. Shoji produced a small remote from his pocket and pressed a button.

The "fasten seat belts" sign turned off, and the voice of the autopilot said, "We have finished external decontamination. Please rise and collect all personal belongings. An EIS representative will be waiting on the jet bridge to confirm your current medical condition and offer any assistance that may be required. Once again, thank you for flying with EIS Air. We appreciate that you have many choices in government-owned health services, and would like you to know that the EIS has always been dedicated to the preservation of the public health, above and beyond all other goals."

"Wow. Even the private planes have to say that shit," said Shaun.

Alaric stood, snagging his laptop bag from the overhead compartment as he asked, "By 'offer any assistance,' do they mean bandages or bullets?"

"I don't know." I stood, stretching, before retrieving my jacket from the overhead bin. I shrugged it on, checking to be sure my holster was covered. I probably wasn't legally allowed to carry a concealed weapon—my field license almost certainly expired after I died—but I wasn't going to tell unless someone asked me. "It probably depends on your test results."

"You are a ray of sunshine and I don't know how we got by without you," said Becks.

I nodded sympathetically. "I'm sure it was hard. But it's all right. I'm here now." Inwardly, I was ecstatic. She was acknowledging me in the present tense. She was admitting that, real Georgia or not, I was the one they had. And it felt wonderful.

"If you're done squabbling with each other, please follow me," said Dr. Shoji. He walked back to the plane door, where he opened the control panel next to the lock and pressed a button. There was a hiss as the hydraulics released, and the door slid open, revealing an airlock. I closed my eyes, shuddering.

We were going into an EIS facility. An endless succession of white halls and people dressed in medical attire rose behind my eyes. I pushed them aside. It wasn't like I had a choice. If I wanted to develop fun new phobias, however justified, I was going to deal with them. However I had to.

Shaun's hand was a welcome weight on my shoulder. "Hey," he said. "It's cool."

I opened my eyes and forced a smile, glad that my sunglasses kept him from seeing my eyes. He knew how scared I was if anyone did—I was still enough of the woman I'd been programmed to be to react in ways he recognized—but that didn't mean I needed to shove it in his face. "Cool," I echoed, and followed him into the airlock.

I was expecting to find men in cleanroom suits waiting for us with blood tests in one hand and guns in the other, ready to shoot if our results were anything other than perfect. It was a little odd that the EIS had a manned jet bridge, rather than using one of the safer, more convenient automated systems, but it was possible they hadn't wanted to attract the attention a major renovation would draw. They were trying to keep the CDC from taking them seriously, and being the kind of small, unassuming organization that still needs to process incoming passengers by hand would help with that.

I wasn't expecting to find a smiling woman with ice-blonde hair loose around her shoulders, wearing a lab coat over a blue tank top and jeans. She smiled when she saw us, the expression lighting up her face in a way that would have seemed impossible when I thought her name was Dr. Shaw and she was dancing to the CDC's tune.

"Hello, Georgia," said Dr. Kimberley. She looked to the rest of the group, assessing them each in turn. "Who are your friends?"

"Dr. Kimberley." I had the sudden urge to hug her—another point of deviation, as my memories were quick to inform me. I stiffened instead, rejecting the alien urge. "You made it out of the building."

"I did, barely; we were able to delay the cleansing sequence long enough to get into one of the incinerator shafts, and climb from there to the roof," she said. "Gregory is safe as well. We're both hopelessly compromised, but we'll find a way around that. We always do."

"Such is the life of the epidemiological spy," I said. I half turned to the others, gesturing to each in turn as I said, "Rebecca Atherton, Shaun Mason, and Alaric Kwong. The staff of After the End Times. This is Dr. Danika Kimberley. She saved my life."

"I'd say she was exaggerating, but she's not," said Dr. Kimberley. She looked toward Dr. Shoji, who was hanging back, waiting for us to finish. "Were there any issues?"

"None. Our flight plan was approved without a hitch. No mechanical troubles, and the plane was swept for transmitters before we left and three times during flight. We're clean."

"Thank God for that," she said fervently. She rummaged through the bag she had slung over one shoulder, producing five slim-bodied testing kits with the words EIS OFFICIAL USE ONLY stenciled on their sides. She handed one to each of us and said, "We use these for internal testing, which means they don't upload to any servers but our own. If any of you come up positive, you'll be isolated for six hours before we make a final determination."

Becks paused in the act of opening her test kit. "What does that mean?" she asked.

"It means that if you have any chance of recovering from the Kellis-Amberlee amplification process, you'll have started to show signs by the end of that time. If you haven't shown any signs, we can either decommission you or retain you for further testing. We'd prefer to keep you, of course—undamaged live subjects are difficult to come by—but the choice would be yours, providing you made it before you finished amplifying."

"You should absolutely be on the Maryland tourism board," said Becks, and slipped her thumb into the kit.

There was a moment of quiet as everyone waited for confirmation that we were still among the legally living. Shaun watched the ceiling rather than watching the lights blinking on the test kits. Each set of lights blinked at its own tempo, analyzing the blood sample the kit had taken, looking for signs of seroconversion. One by one, they settled on a steady green. Clean. All of us were clean.

I elbowed Shaun in the side. "It's good," I said. "You can come down now."

"Huh?" He looked down, eyes fixing on the green-lit test kit in his hand. "Oh." He cast a quick sideways glance at my kit and visibly relaxed, some of the tension going out of his jaw.

Dr. Kimberley plucked the kit from his hand, sticking it into a small biohazard bag, which she then made disappear into the bag on her shoulder. The other kits went into a separate, larger biohazard bag, which she pushed into a chute in the side of the jet bridge. Then she smiled, not quite as brightly as when we first deplaned, and said, "Well. I suppose we'd best be moving along. Follow me."

She turned and walked away. I was almost disappointed to see that she was wearing sensible sneakers instead of the impractical heels she'd sported at the Seattle CDC. The heels must have been one more part of her cover as Dr. Shaw, and sneakers would be a lot easier to run in if there was an outbreak. Still, it was odd to hear her walking without the gunshot clatter of her shoes hitting the floor.

The jet bridge let out on a small pre-Rising room painted a merciful shade of yellow-beige. I'd never considered beige the color of mercy before, but anything was better than that dreaded medicinal white. Chairs lined the windowed walls, presumably to give passengers a view of the airfield. There was no one there, and the air smelled like disinfectant and dust. We might have been the only things alive in the entire building.

Alaric was the last into the room. The door closed behind him, locks engaging with a loud beep. Dr. Shoji moved to the front of the group, waving for the rest of us to follow. "Come along," he said. "The decontamination fumes can cause severe irritation if you stand too close."

"And of course a door that actually sealed would look too much like competence," muttered Alaric, and started walking faster.

Dr. Kimberley stepped back so that she was walking on my right. Shaun cast a suspicious look her way. She ignored it. "How do you feel?" she asked. "Any unusual pain or strange sensations in your hands or feet?"

"Hold on," said Shaun. There was a tightly controlled note in his voice that I recognized as dawning alarm. "What are you asking her that for?"

"It's okay, Shaun." I put a hand on his arm as we walked, trying to soothe him. Looking back to Dr. Kimberley, I said, "I'm tired a lot. I ache. Everything feels pretty much normal."

"You're achy because you're getting proper exercise, rather than the illusion of it," she said, nodding. "That will fade as your body comes into alignment with your idea of what it's capable of. I'd like to do a full physical, which there simply isn't time for, but if that's all you're experiencing that seems out of the ordinary, I'd say that you're entirely fine. Better than fine, really. You're alive."

"And she's going to stay that way," said Shaun.

Dr. Kimberley flashed a rueful smile his way. It was odd seeing her this emotive. Adjusting to her accent had been easier. "Let's hope you're the prophet in this scenario, rather than anyone with a more dire view of what's to come."

The hall ended at a pair of old-fashioned swinging doors. I frowned, studying them, but couldn't see anything that looked even remotely like modern security upgrades. They were just doors, unsecured, with no scanners or test units installed beside them. We stopped in a ragged line, all of us looking at those doors—all of us looking for the catch. There had to be a catch.

There was always a catch.

Dr. Shoji didn't seem to notice our dismay, and neither did Dr. Kimberley. They kept on walking, pushing those unsecured doors open to reveal an underground parking garage, and the big black SUV that was waiting at the curb.

There's a certain shape of car that just screams "I belong to a private security force." They're always big and black and solid-looking, with run-flat tires and bulletproof glass in the windows. And then there are the cars that belong to the Secret Service. The differences are subtle, but you can see them if you know what to look for. Wireless relay webbing built into the rear window, for those times when cell service is compromised. Thin copper lines through the rest of the glass, ready to be turned on and cut off *all* service, cellular or otherwise. The glass in a Secret Service car isn't just bulletproof, it's damn near indestructible. A group of Irwins who modeled themselves after a pre-Rising TV show called *MythBusters* managed to get hold of a decommissioned Secret Service vehicle a few years ago. They set off six grenades inside the main cabin. The explosions didn't even scratch the glass.

I once asked a member of Senator Ryman's security crew whether the Secret Service had a sign on the wall somewhere counting off the number of years since a sitting president had been eaten on their watch. He laughed, but he didn't look happy about it. I think I was right.

"I miss Steve," I said quietly, looking at the car.

"Me, too," said Shaun.

The passenger-side door of the SUV opened, and a big blond mountain of a man unfolded himself, straightening until his head and shoulders were higher than the car's roof. "It's good to be remembered," he said. "Shaun. Georgia."

Shaun's mouth fell open as a grin spread across his face. "Steve, my *man*! What the fuck are you doing here?"

"I could ask you the same thing. Last time I saw you, you were in no condition to be causing this much trouble." Steve turned his face toward me, expression unreadable behind his government-issue sunglasses. I hate it when people use my own tricks on me. "You, on the other hand, were in an urn. Because it was your funeral." His tone telegraphed what his expression didn't: He was deeply uncomfortable about my presence.

I shrugged. "Sorry. I guess I was just too stubborn to stay dead for long."

"Mad science," said Alaric. "What *can't* it do?"

Shaun shook his head, snapping out of his delight over Steve's appearance. "Sorry, man, I got distracted. Steve, this is Alaric Kwong, one of the site Newsies, and this is Rebecca Atherton, one of our Irwins."

"Call me Becks," said Becks. "Everyone else does."

"It's a pleasure to meet you," rumbled Steve. "If you'd all get in the car, please? I have instructions regarding your destination."

"I'm afraid this is where we leave you," said Dr. Shoji. "I'll see you again, but I can't arrive with you. That would be suspicious."

"And I'm on house arrest," said Dr. Kimberley. She smiled at Steve. "I couldn't even have come this far if we hadn't been sure of who was going to be coming to collect you."

"Always glad to help, Dr. Kimberley," said Steve. He opened the rear passenger door. "We need to get moving. The security changes at midnight, and it will be best if we're past the checkpoints before that happens."

"Where are we going?" asked Becks.

Steve didn't answer. He just folded his arms, and waited.

"Come on," I said, and started for the car. Working with Steve during the Ryman campaign taught me a lot of things about professional security. Chief among them was that once Steve made up his mind about something, that was the way things were going to go. He'd explain where we were going on the way.

Becks and Shaun followed me. Alaric stayed where he was, looking unsure. I waited until the others were in the car before turning on my heel and crossing back to him.

"What's wrong?"

"This seems a bit…convenient, don't you think?"

I surprised us both by laughing, a single, sharp expression of both amusement and regret. "This has all been 'convenient,' Alaric. They've been herding us since Seattle. Maybe before, I don't know. I wasn't with you to see the signs. At this point, what's one more leap of faith between friends?"

"Seems like it might be a long fucking way to the bottom," he said.

"So what?" I shrugged. "If we're going to fall, let's do it with style. Now come on. That's an order."

He blinked, and then smiled. "You're not my boss anymore, you know."

"Alaric Kwong, I will *always* be your boss. Now get in the damn car."

I followed Alaric to the SUV. He climbed in ahead of me, and I paused to wave to Dr. Shoji and Dr. Kimberley before getting in. Steve closed the door as soon as I was inside, and the locks engaged automatically. There were no handles inside. We wouldn't be getting out unless someone decided to *let* us out. Becks and Alaric had gravitated to the far back, leaving Shaun and me closer to the partition that separated us from the driver's cabin.

"Isn't this cozy?" said Becks. "If they fill this thing with gas and kill us before we know what's happening, I swear, the first thing my reanimated corpse eats will be your face, Mason."

"I'm pretty sure I could kick your ass even if we were all dead," said Shaun.

Becks shrugged. "You won't reanimate. It won't be a contest."

The two of them continued teasing each other, using sharp comments and verbal barbs as a way to keep calm. Irwins. They all have a few basic personality traits in common, and one of them is a strong dislike for being pinned in small spaces that they don't control. That sort of thing is a death trap most of the time, and Shaun and Becks were both well trained enough to know it. I ignored the bickering as much as I could, squinting at the black glass divider between us and the front of the car.

If I had still had retinal Kellis-Amberlee, I would have been able to see through that glass and tell who was driving the car. I would have had at least a little more information to use in determining whether or not we were being driven to our deaths. If you'd asked me before I died whether I liked my eyes, I would have looked at you like you were insane. Now that I was someone different, I missed their familiar limits and capabilities. Maybe it was just a matter of firsthand experience—Georgia Mason had it, and I didn't. Regardless of what it was, or wasn't, I kept squinting at the glass, wishing I could see what was on the other side.

I was still squinting at the glass when it slid smoothly downward, revealing the shoulders of Steve and our driver. Shaun and Becks immediately stopped sniping at each other, straightening. My shoulders locked, going so tense that it hurt. Shaun grabbed my hand where it was resting against the seat, squeezing until my fingers hurt worse than my shoulders did.

Steve twisted to look at us. "We're almost there," he said. There was an odd tightness in his voice, like he wanted to say something, but knew he couldn't get away with it. That tightness hadn't been there before, when we were at the EIS—when we weren't in the car.

Lowering my sunglasses enough to let him see where I was looking, I glanced toward the window. He shook his head. I tried again, this time slanting my gaze toward the dome covering the overhead light. Steve nodded marginally. We were bugged. I looked to Shaun, and saw him nodding, too. Everyone who'd come with me was a trained journalist. They all knew what that exchange had meant.

"Going to tell us where 'there' is, big guy, or do we get to try and guess?" Listening to Shaun trying to pretend that he was still the careless thrill seeker who'd signed up to follow the Ryman campaign was almost painful. That man was dead. As dead as the real Georgia Mason.

We were both pretending. We were just doing it in different ways.

"You'll know it when you see it," said Steve. "There are a few ground rules I need you to understand. I advise listening closely. Anyone violating the terms will be shot. Your bodies will never be found."

"Wow. That's…direct," said Becks. "What are they?"

"First, you will not broadcast or record anything that happens after leaving this car."

Yeah, right. "Will there be an EMP shield up to prevent it?"

"Yes, for broadcast, but we're trusting you on the recording." He smirked a little. "I managed to convince my superiors that you didn't need to be searched for recording devices, mostly by showing them the list of what we never managed to take off you when we were on the campaign trail. I suppose they don't want to be here taking your transmitters off until dawn."

"Got it, no recording," said Shaun. "What else?"

"Second, you will not in any way initiate physical contact with anyone who does not initiate physical contact with you."

"Shake a hand, get shot?" asked Alaric. When Steve nodded, he looked faintly ill. "This gets better and better with every day that passes."

From the look that crossed Steve's face, Alaric had no idea just how bad things had gotten. I filed the expression away for later. Whatever was happening here, Steve didn't like it. That could be useful.

"Third, you will ask questions only when given permission to do so."

We all stared at him. Telling a carload of reporters not to ask questions was like telling a volcano not to erupt; not only was it pointless, it was likely to end with someone getting hurt. Steve sighed heavily.

"These rules weren't my idea. I know better. Then again, you coming here wasn't my idea." He shook his head. "This is going to end badly. Please try to postpone that as long as possible." Steve pulled back, and the divider slid upward again, blocking the cabin from view.

"I want to punch someone," said Shaun conversationally.

"Do it with the hand that's currently crushing my fingers," I suggested. "You're endangering my ability to type."

Shaun let go of my hand, grimacing. "Sorry."

"Don't be sorry. Just be ready for whatever's coming."

"He didn't say anything about weapons," said Becks. "Bets that they're going to take our weapons away?"

"No bet," said Alaric. "These pig-fucking sons of diseased dock workers aren't going to let us out of this car armed."

I raised an eyebrow. "You're really enjoying the possibilities of the English language today, aren't you?"

"Just wait," said Becks. "When he gets really worked up, he swears in Cantonese. It's like listening to a macaw having a seizure."

Alaric glared at her. She grinned at him. And the car stopped moving.

All levity fled, the four of us assuming wary positions that made our earlier tension look like nothing. Shaun put one hand on my shoulder; the other, I knew, would be going to his gun. We'd started out among friends. Now we had no idea where we were.

The car door swung open, revealing the bulky shape of Steve. He stepped aside, letting us see the man who was standing behind him.

"Hello, Georgia," said Rick, smiling as he offered me his hands. "I know we've never actually met before, but I have to tell you...it's been a long time."

***

The concierge just came to tell me my parents have landed at the Seattle/Tacoma International Airport, and will be at the Agora in less than an hour. I look like hell. My hair doesn't even bear thinking about. But oh I am so glad they're coming.

Mahir and I have discussed what to tell them, and we've settled on the only thing they're likely to accept: the truth. He's pointed out (a few too many times) that they're in medtech, they have contracts with the CDC, and they could be on the wrong side. I can't find a way to explain that I don't care. If they're on the wrong side now, they'll change when they find out what happened—what that bad, bad side was willing to do to me.

I have hidden the truth from them for too long. It's time I started living up to the mission statement that Georgia Mason chose when she founded After the End Times. It's time for me to start telling the truth.

But ah, it hurts.

—From *Dandelion Mine*,
the blog of Magdalene Grace Garcia, August 6, 2041. Unpublished.

***

The lab is very quiet.
I'm not sure that I like it anymore.
I miss you, Joe.

—From the private files of Dr. Shannon Abbey,
August 6, 2041. Unpublished.

SHAUN: Thirty-four

Rick had more gray in his hair than I remembered. It would make him look distinguished in the right circumstances. At the moment, it just made him look old. He was wearing a tailored suit that probably cost as much as three rescue missions into the Florida hazard zone, and his shoes were shiny and tight. He'd never be able to run from a zombie mob in those shoes.

Then again, he wouldn't have to—not with two Steve-sized Secret Servicemen flanking him, each of them wearing their firearms openly on their belts.

"Rick?" George got out of the car. Her movements were jerky, like she wasn't sure what she was supposed to do. She grabbed the edge of the door as she stood. "What are you—?"

The question was cut off as the Vice President of the United States— our former colleague and one of the only bloggers to survive the Ryman campaign—swept her into a hug. She made a squeaking noise, clearly startled, and her arms stayed down, but she didn't pull away. For George, that was practically a passionate embrace.

Becks shoved against my hip. "Hey, Mason. Move out of the damn way."

"What?" I tore my eyes away from Rick and George. I hadn't realized I was moving, but I apparently had; I was standing, blocking Alaric and Becks from getting out of the car. I stepped to the side. "Oh. Sorry about that."

"Sure you are." Becks stood, moving far enough to the side for Alaric to squeeze out, and eyed Rick suspiciously. "So that's Richard Cousins, boy reporter."

"Pretty sure we're supposed to call him 'Mr. Vice President' now, but yeah, that's him." Becks was already with the After the End times when Rick joined us, but they'd only met once, at Georgia's funeral. Rick had just been asked to stand with Ryman. He'd been in shock, and so had the rest of us.

Becks looked at him critically, finally saying, "I could take him."

"And I could take you," said Steve. "Let's not get into a pissing contest. We both know who'd come out the winner, so there's no point."

"Sometimes the contest *is* the point," said Becks piously.

Rick pushed George out to arm's length, eyes avidly scanning her face. That was going to keep him distracted for a few more seconds at least. The fact that George hadn't pulled away from him yet meant she wanted us to be studying something else—namely, our surroundings.

I turned to look around, not bothering to be subtle about it. Let Alaric and Becks be subtle; I'd play the happy buffoon, a role I've been practicing since I was a kid. People underestimate you if they think your only interests in life involve poking zombies with sticks and getting that perfect camera angle.

We were in an underground garage. There was a row of SUVs identical to the one that drove us from the airfield parked nearby, presumably waiting to be needed. The lights were smooth and clear, and the doors weren't just gated; they were sealed with metal sheeting that looked almost like blast protection. This place was locked down tighter than a bank vault.

Oh. Crap. Feeling like an idiot, I turned to Steve and said, "I've never been to the White House before. Do you think we'll get some of those cool souvenir key chains before we leave? I've wanted one of those ever since I saw a video of this one dude from Newfoundland using his to pop a zombie's eye out."

Spreading it a little thick, don't you think? asked Georgia.

I forced myself to ignore it and keep on smiling. Crazy doesn't go away overnight. Especially not crazy you've watered and tended yourself. But wow was this not the time to have an incident.

"I don't think this is a souvenir key chain kind of visit, but man, it's good to see you," said Rick. I turned to see him walking toward me, leaving George behind. He kept talking as he stuck out his right hand, clearly expecting me to shake it. "There were a few points where you went quiet, and I was afraid—let's just say I've had reasons to be worried about your welfare."

"Really?" I took his hand, squeezing his fingers until that big politician's smile he'd acquired somewhere started to look strained. "Because it seems to me that if you knew we were having problems, you could maybe have answered your fucking e-mail and helped us."

"No. I couldn't have." His smile died as he pulled his hand away. "And just so you're aware, if it were up to me, I would have stuck a bow on her and delivered her to your doorstep on your birthday. I never wanted things to be this way."

Dr. Wynne. Buffy. Rick. How many of the people we considered allies were never allies at all? "But they are," I said.

Rick sighed. "True enough." He turned, starting toward the sealed blast doors behind him. His Secret Servicemen continued facing forward, watching us with what I could only describe as suspicion. They were waiting for one of us to do something.

Instead, we just stood there. Finally, Alaric asked, "Are we supposed to go with you?"

"What? Oh. Yes." Rick waved for us to follow him. "Right this way."

"Blood tests...?" asked Becks.

"We don't bother with the security theater here," said Steve. There was a deep disdain in his voice—less, I thought, for the lack of security in this garage, and more for the idea that the security everywhere else in the world was flawed.

And it *was* flawed. I used to believe in that level of security, in blood tests every ten minutes and checking your reflexes and response rates constantly. Even as an Irwin, I swore by following the rules. And then I met Dr. Abbey, who maintained the absolute minimum where security was concerned, and I learned that half the tests we take on a daily basis are useless. If you haven't been exposed or gone outside, what's the point of sticking another needle in your finger? Those tests didn't tell us anything we didn't already know...but they reinforced the idea that we had to be afraid, always, that our humanity was fleeting, maintained only by a constant web of government oversight.

Rick tapped out a code on the keypad by the blast doors and they slid open, revealing a hall that could have belonged in any government building I've ever seen. I'm not sure what it is that identifies their hallways, but there's something in the inevitable combination of beige, white, and green that just screams "seat of power." Mind, the Presidential Seal etched on the sliding glass doors that had been concealed behind the blast doors didn't hurt.

"You know, my mother always dreamed I'd wind up here someday," said Becks. "Pretty sure she wanted me to be First Lady, not a semi-hostage journalist on the run from a global conspiracy, but hey. At least I'm in the White House."

I laughed and started for the doors. They slid open at our approach, and, once again, there was no blood test required to get inside.

"Getting into the White House through any of the public entrances requires six blood tests and a retinal scan," said Rick as we walked. "If you're unable to successfully complete a retinal scan for any reason, you have to submit to whatever further testing security deems necessary. Refusal to be tested will result in your being removed from the premises."

"And shot," said George. "Correct?"

Rick looked uncomfortable. "It generally doesn't come to that."

"Mm-hmm." She had stepped through the doors a few feet ahead of me. She stopped there, waiting until we could walk on side by side. "What are we doing here, Rick?"

"You're here because…it was time for you to be brought up to speed." He kept walking, trusting the rest of us to follow. I'm sure the presence of three enormous Secret Service agents had nothing to do with his degree of confidence.

No, really.

The four of us stuck close together as we walked along the hall, George and me in the lead, right behind Rick, with Becks and Alaric behind us. Steve and the two unnamed agents brought up the rear. The driver of our SUV stayed in the vehicle when we went inside. Presumably, he or she had been left in order to park the car. This was all very well organized. I stepped a little closer to George, whose face was set in the grim mask that meant she was as uncomfortable as I was. That was good. I didn't want to be the only one who knew we were walking into a trap.

We stopped at an apparently blank wall midway down the hall. Rick gave the rest of us an apologetic look as he said, "This is where we have to take your weapons away. I'm sorry. It's just that we're about to go into some very secure areas, and I don't have the clearance to authorize you to go armed."

"You're the Vice President of the United States," said George. "If you don't have the clearance, who does?"

He didn't say anything. He just looked at her.

"Right." George sighed and removed the gun from her belt. Steve stepped up with a large plastic bin; she put the gun inside.

That was the cue for the rest of us to begin shedding our weapons. Alaric and George were clean in a matter of minutes. Becks and I took longer. The bin in Steve's hands was dangerously full by the time we finished.

"Can we get a claim check for those?" asked Alaric.

Steve snorted, expression darkly amused. "Unlikely."

"Just checking," said Alaric, unruffled.

"Thank you," said Rick. He pressed his hand against the wall. A light came on behind his palm, and the wall turned transparent—a trick I'd only seen once before, in the Portland offices of the CDC. There was an elevator on the other side.

Alaric whistled. "Where can I get me one of those?"

"First, get a six-billion-dollar security budget. After that, I'll put you in touch with the DOD," said Rick. The transparent patch of wall slid to the side as the elevator doors swished open, revealing a surprisingly industrial-looking metal box. This elevator could have been located in any dock or warehouse in the world, and yet here it was, in the White House. Rick beckoned us forward again. "After you."

"If this is a trap, someone's getting a very stern talking to," I said blithely, and stepped into the elevator. George was barely half a step behind me.

Of the three Secret Service agents, only Steve got into the elevator with us, leaving the other two behind after handing one of them the bin containing our weapons. The doors swished shut again as soon as Steve was through, and Rick opened a metal panel on the wall, revealing, for the first time since our arrival, a blood testing array. It had eight distinct panels, one for each of us, with two to spare.

"I thought you didn't do security theater," said George.

"This is just a precaution. We're going into a highly secured area," said Rick. "We all have to test clean before the elevator will move."

"Oh, great," said Alaric. "I wanted to hang out in a death trap today."

Becks elbowed him in the side as she pressed her thumb against the first testing square. The white plastic turned red behind her finger, remaining that color for a count of five before turning green. Rick did the same with the next square, cycling it from white to red to green. Then he stepped back, looking at the rest of us.

"You're up," he said.

None of us were infected. The elevator chimed softly and began sliding downward, moving with a smooth efficiency that bordered on unnerving. I realized that the four of us were standing clustered together on one side of the elevator, leaving Rick and Steve on the other. Steve was watching the wall. Rick was watching us, a deep longing in his eyes.

Talk to him, said Georgia.

I glanced toward the George beside me, wincing a little when I realized she hadn't spoken. Still, it was good advice. I took a half step forward, focusing on Rick, and asked, "Rick, dude—what the fuck happened to you?"

"Do you remember how your sister used to say the truth was the most important thing in the world? That if we all knew the truth, we'd be able to live our lives more freely and with fewer troubles?" The elevator was slowing down. "It's funny, because she always seemed to forget that a truth you don't understand is more dangerous than a lie. Robert Stalnaker told the truth when he said Dr. Kellis was creating a cure for the common cold, and look where that's gotten us."

Robert Stalnaker was the muckraker—sorry, "investigative reporter"—whose articles on the infant Kellis cure resulted in its being released into the atmosphere, which led in turn to the creation of Kellis-Amberlee. If he hadn't decided to "tell the truth," we might not be in the pickle we're in now. No one knows what happened to Stalnaker during the Rising. Whatever it was, I hope it hurt.

"Robert Stalnaker made up a story to sell papers," said George. "And by the way, I'm right here. I can *hear* you."

The elevator stopped. Rick turned to her, looking faintly abashed, and said, "I know. I just... I saw you made, Georgia. I can't quite wrap my head around the idea of you knowing everything you knew, well... before."

"I don't, because I'm not the same girl," said George coldly. "You of all people should know that. You can't really raise the dead."

"Great. Even the clone master has issues with Miss Undead America 2041," said Becks. "This is really the guy who paid to have you resurrected, Georgia? Because so far, not impressed."

It was nice to see that my team's "us against the world" mentality extended to George. "So what is it you're saying here, Rick?" I asked. "Are you saying we're here to learn how to lie?"

"No," he said. Rick pressed his hand against the panel next to the elevator door. It slid open, revealing the featureless gray hall beyond. "You're here to learn why *we* have to lie, and why we can't let you run around telling the truth without consequences. It's time you learned the truth about Kellis-Amberlee." He looked back over his shoulder at us, and his expression was haggard, like he'd personally witnessed the end of the world. "I am so, so sorry."

Then he stepped out of the elevator, leaving the five of us—my team, plus Steve—behind. I looked at the others. "Did that creep anybody else out, just a little bit? Or was it just me who was getting the weird 'and then they found out he was dead all along' vibe?"

"This isn't good," said Becks.

"No, and it isn't getting any less creepy while we stand in this elevator arguing about it." George stepped briskly out to the hallway, where she stopped, turned, and looked at the rest of us. "Well? Are you coming, or am I going to go get the scoop of the century by myself?"

"I don't know about you guys, but I'm not letting the dead girl make me look like a wimp," declared Becks, and shoved her way past Alaric to exit the elevator. She stopped next to George, folding her arms. "Okay, three dudes hiding in the elevator while two girls are hanging out in the scary hall? You are now officially wimps. In case you were wondering."

"We can't have that." I put a hand on Alaric's shoulder, propelling him along with me as I stepped out of the elevator to join them. Steve was close behind me. The elevator doors slid shut as soon as he was clear, and the light above them blinked off.

Someone to my left began applauding slowly. I whipped around, hand going for a gun that wasn't there, and found myself looking into the face of a man I hadn't seen in the flesh for over a year—not since George's funeral, which he made by the skin of his teeth. The others turned with me, some of them reaching for weapons they didn't have, others just staring.

It was George who managed to find her equilibrium enough to break the silence first. I guess after coming back from the dead, nothing else is going to seem like a big enough deal to knock you off balance for long.

"Hello, Mr. President," she said.

President Peter Ryman smiled. "Hello, Georgia."

Maggie's parents have arrived, or so I'm told—I haven't been allowed to see her since their plane landed, and for all I know, they've come, bundled her into their private jet, and gone, leaving me to settle an utterly astronomical bill. I do hope they take physical labor in exchange. Washing dishes should have us paid off in, oh, three or four hundred years. Give or take a decade or two. Nan will shout when she finds out I've become an indentured servant in America. Probably say it serves me right for being so damn stubborn, going off and leaving her alone.

Dr. Abbey sent an e-mail last night, saying the others were leaving her lab on another mission. She wouldn't say where, and my mail to her has started bouncing. Either she's blocked me, or she's changed addresses. Either way, we're cut off for the nonce, because none of my colleagues are answering their e-mail. And I alone am left to tell thee...

Damn. I thought I was done being the one who stayed behind to write the story down. Bloody journalists.

May they all come home safely.

**—From *Fish and Clips*,
the blog of Mahir Gowda, August 6, 2041. Unpublished.**

Michael and Alisa are at the gift shop near the front gate, getting her some clean T-shirts. We've been at Cliff's Amusement Park in New Mexico for two days now, and we're all starting to run out of clothes. It should be safe to head back to Berkeley soon. Right now, it's a media circus, and the only way we can avoid it is by acting like everything is normal. Alisa's been a good sport about things, thank God. It probably helps that after Florida, *nothing* looks dangerous to her.

She's a good kid. Even after everything she's been through, she's a good kid. Shaun and Georgia...they were good kids, too. Even after everything we put them through, they somehow managed to grow up to be good people. I don't know how that happened. I guess that makes sense, because I never really knew *them*. I never wanted to. I suppose that makes me a hypocrite, because now that they're grown and gone—gone for good, in Georgia's case—I'm proud of them.

I wish I'd been a better mother when I had the chance.

**—From *Stacy's Survival Strategies*,
the blog of Stacy Mason, August 6, 2041. Unpublished.**

GEORGIA: Thirty-five

President Ryman was flanked by three Secret Servicemen of his own, along with a man I didn't recognize, but whose CDC-issue lab coat immediately made my heart start beating faster. I managed to hold my ground only by reminding myself that Georgia Mason—the original—would never show fear in the face of a man who wasn't holding a gun to her head, and maybe not even then. If I was going to deal with these people, I had to do it the way she would have done it. Nothing else was going to work.

"You don't seem surprised to see me," I said, tilting my chin up just enough to be sure my sunglasses would entirely block my eyes. I didn't want him thinking of me as a science project. I wanted him thinking of me as *Georgia*, and Georgia's eyes didn't look like mine.

"That's because I'm not," he said. He looked tired. None of his Secret Servicemen were familiar—the only familiar face I'd seen among the guards was Steve, and Steve would probably have a job until everyone who'd been on the campaign was dead and gone. There's something to be said for loyalty like his.

Shaun took a step forward, planting himself beside me, and all but glared at President Ryman. "You mean you knew about this cloning shit, too, and you didn't tell me? Don't you people think that sending me a note might have been a good idea?"

"No, they didn't," I said, as calmly as I could. It was surprisingly easy. Losing my temper wouldn't do any good, and I was starting to become accustomed to the idea that everyone in the world—except Shaun—was going to betray me. "I was never supposed to leave the lab."

Rick moved to join President Ryman. He met my eyes as he turned to face the rest of us. President Ryman . . . didn't. He looked away instead, and the set of his jaw said everything he wasn't saying out loud.

"You bastard," whispered Shaun. He started to take a step forward. I grabbed his elbow, stopping him.

"The last thing we need today is for you to assault the president," I said quietly. "Take a deep breath, and let it go."

"He was going to let them kill you."

"He let them make me in the first place. Let's call that part a wash, and see where he takes it from there." I kept watching President Ryman's face. He kept not meeting my eyes. "Why are we here, Mr. President? You never had to let us make it this far."

"Yes, I did." His head snapped around. For a moment, I saw the man I knew behind the beaten shadows in his eyes. He looked angry. Not with us—with the world. "I owed you this."

"Did you owe us this before or after you let your people call an air strike on Oakland?" asked Becks. "David Novakowski stayed behind when those bombs came down. He was an Irwin. A good one. He wasn't involved in your campaign because he was in Alaska at the time, but he would have liked you." Her tone was calm and challenging at the same time, daring him to give an answer she didn't approve of.

"The air strike on Oakland was called in response to an outbreak, and did not involve the president," said the man from the CDC. I managed not to cringe at the sound of his voice. "Consider your words before you make accusations."

"It was a pretty convenient outbreak, considering one of your people had just shown up, running for her life," snapped Shaun. "Don't try to bullshit us, okay? We all know we're not leaving this building alive. So there's no point in fucking with our heads."

"Shaun." President Ryman actually sounded offended. "Please don't make assumptions. You're absolutely going to leave here alive. At a certain point, it became inevitable that we'd bring you here to fully explain the situation."

"Does that point have anything to do with us having secure footage of a living clone of Georgia Mason running around Seattle?" asked Alaric. "I ask purely out of academic curiosity, you understand. I know you're going to lie through your teeth."

President Ryman sighed. "You don't trust me anymore, do you?"

"Have you given us a reason to?" I asked.

"You're alive, Georgia. I'd think that might be enough to buy me a little patience."

"You were planning to have me killed and replaced with a more tractable version. I think that explains a little crankiness."

The man from the CDC cleared his throat. "It doesn't matter who's angry with whom. You are here to have the true nature of the Kellis-Amberlee infection explained. With that in mind, I believe it's time we make you understand why you have been remiss in your lines of inquiry."

"Ever notice how people like to use five-dollar words when they know they're wrong?" asked Becks, of no one in particular.

President Ryman shook his head. "Arguing is getting us nowhere. This way." He gestured down the hall before starting to walk. His Secret Servicemen promptly moved to get behind us, making it clear that we'd be herded along if we didn't come on our own.

We went.

The hallway led to a room with walls covered by crystal display screens. Two of them were already showing the structure of the Kellis-Amberlee virus. Another showed an outline of a generic human body. Ryman walked to the large table at the center of the room and stopped, clearly unhappy, as he turned to the man from the CDC.

"I believe that, at this point, I must remind you that national security depends on your silence," said the man from the CDC. "Nothing said here can leave this room."

"Uh, *reporters*," said Becks. "Or did you forget?"

"Even reporters have things they care about," he said, with chilling calm. "Perhaps you feel immortal. Perhaps you consider martyrdom something to aspire to—a thrilling entry for your much-lauded 'Wall.' But you have a family, don't you? Rebecca Atherton, of the Westchester Athertons. Your youngest sister was married this past summer. Katherine. A very pretty girl. It's a pity they live in such a remote area."

Becks's eyes widened before narrowing into angry slits, filled with a murderous rage. "Don't you even—" she began.

"And you, Mr. Kwong. *Your* sister is your only remaining family. She's currently in the custody of Stacy and Michael Mason—not people renowned for their ability to keep children alive, when you stop to think about it."

For possibly the first time in my life, original or artificial, the urge to defend the Masons rose inside me. "You've made your point," I snapped. "We'll keep our mouths shut. Now do you want to explain what the hell is so important that you need to tell us your evil plan before you have us all shot?"

"It's not an evil plan, Georgia; it's the truth." With those words, President Ryman went from sounding weary to sounding utterly heartbroken. "You've become too associated with this whole situation, and that means we need you. You're the ones who tell the truth, and the ones who fell off the radar when things turned bad. People will believe you."

"Even when we're lying to them?"

His silence was all the answer I needed.

"Please sit," said the man from the CDC.

Grudgingly, I sat. The others did the same. Only the man from the CDC remained standing.

"The first thing you need to understand is that the KA virus, being manmade, bonds tightly to anything it encounters," he began, in the sort of easy, lecturing tone that all doctors seem to learn in medical school. Ignoring the tension in the room, he produced a remote from his pocket and pointed it at the nearest screen. The Kellis-Amberlee model displayed there began to rotate. "This tendency created the hybridized virus to begin with. And it is what has complicated our cure for the infection."

Shaun frowned. "Complicated your *search* for a cure?"

"No," said the man from the CDC calmly. "Complicated our cure." The model was suddenly surrounded by smaller, semi-spherical images that looked something like slides I'd seen of pre-Rising flu virus. They began attacking the larger KA virus, surrounding it before engulfing it entirely. "We've managed to create several treatments that work remarkably well, destroying the Kellis-Amberlee infection in nine out of ten afflicted."

We all stared at him, even Steve. It was Alaric who found his voice first, asking slowly, "Then why haven't you released it?"

"The Kellis-Amberlee virus has become so entwined with our immune systems that killing it kills them as well. Without a functioning immune system, the cured become targets for every opportunistic infection that comes along. None of our subjects have lasted long." The image on the screen reset itself, returning to the single Kellis-Amberlee virus, floating serene and undisturbed. "To put it in simpler terms: Kill the virus, kill the population."

"So why don't you just *tell* people that?" demanded Shaun. "We're not idiots!"

"Try telling Alexander Kellis that people aren't idiots," suggested the man from the CDC. "We cannot say 'there will never be a cure.' People need hope. The hope that someday, Kellis-Amberlee will be banished, and we will be free to resume the lives that we remember."

"Why?" asked Alaric. He shook his head slowly. "We can live with the virus. The reservoir conditions are proof of that. We can find a new status quo."

"One where anyone could become a zombie, anytime, and you don't dare shoot them because they might—*might*—recover their senses? This nation barely recovered from the Rising when the lines were clear and infection meant death. I doubt we could hold together as a people if we were told that recovery was an option." I was starting to hate the absolute calm of the man from the CDC's delivery. He continued to watch us coolly. "A cure may be impossible, but a solution *will* be found. A strain of the virus that doesn't generate anomalous reservoir conditions will be discovered, and will be used to standardize the tragically incurable condition that now informs our society. No one will ever need to know that a cure is not possible. No one will ever need to give up hope."

"No one except for all the people who would have recovered if you'd just failed to shoot them in the head," said Shaun. The bitterness in his voice was strong enough to worry me. I put a hand on his arm, praying that would be enough to keep him from doing anything stupid. "The ones who would have *gotten better*."

"Sacrifices must be made," said the man from the CDC.

Something in his tone provided the last piece I needed to fully understand what he was saying. "You want to infect the entire world with the same strain of the virus," I said slowly.

"Yes."

"You're going to need a better distribution method if you're planning to accomplish that. You can't be sure of everyone getting exposed the natural way."

For the first time, he looked uncomfortable. Alaric, meanwhile, was staring at him, mouth actually falling slightly open in shock.

Finally, Alaric said, in a hushed tone, "You built the mosquitoes?"

"'Built' is a strong word—" began Rick.

"They were never intended to reach the American mainland," said President Ryman.

I had heard that man speak with conviction a hundred times on the campaign trail; I had heard him make promises he damn well intended to keep. I had never heard him deliver a party line with that little sincerity. He wasn't lying. He might as well have been. "What happened?" I asked. "Was there a leak?"

"No," said Shaun, before anyone else could speak. "They let them go. They wanted to bury the news cycle, keep what happened in Memphis from getting out. Isn't that right?"

"The storm was an unexpected complication," said the man from the CDC. "The carrier mosquitoes were never intended to make it out of Cuba."

I was busy holding Shaun's arm, keeping him from doing anything we might regret later. I didn't think to grab Alaric. Neither did Becks. Before any of us had a chance to react, the normally nonviolent Newsie was launching himself at the man from the CDC, locking his hands around the taller man's throat and slamming him into the wall. The crystal display screen shook dangerously, but didn't fall.

"YOUR COMPLICATION KILLED MY PARENTS!" shouted Alaric, slamming the man from the CDC against the wall again. No one moved to pull them apart. "THEY WERE IN FLORIDA! YOU KILLED MY FAMILY TO BURY A NEWS CYCLE, BECAUSE YOU COULDN'T READ A FUCKING WEATHER REPORT!"

The man from the CDC made a strained choking noise, clawing helplessly at Alaric's hands. Still, no one moved to pull them apart.

Finally, wearily, President Ryman said, "It would make everyone's job easier if you would stop trying to actually *kill* him. I understand that you're angry. This isn't helping."

Becks glared at him as she stepped forward, putting her hands on Alaric's shoulders. He slumped, fingers still locked around the doctor's throat. "Let him go, Alaric," she said quietly. "It's time to let him go."

"They killed my parents," Alaric mumbled.

"They killed a lot of people. They even killed Georgia. But strangling this man won't bring them back, and he hasn't finished telling us everything he knows. Now let him go. It's time to let him talk. You can kill him later."

Reluctantly, Alaric let go. The doctor staggered away from him, coughing, one hand coming up to clutch at his throat like he was going to finish the job of strangling himself. Pointing at Alaric, he demanded, "Restrain that man!"

"Begging your pardon, sir, but no," said Steve. "I serve at the pleasure of the president, not at the whim of the CDC."

The man from the CDC glared daggers at him. President Ryman ignored him, turning to us. "The mosquitoes are a modified form of the species that carries yellow fever," he said. "They're purely artificial. They can't reproduce, and they can't survive in temperatures below a certain level. The loss of American life has been tragic. It will end when winter comes."

"They can't reproduce?" said Shaun incredulously. "That's your big solution? They won't fuck? Did none of you people ever see *Jurassic Park*?"

"It may take us years to clean out the zombie mobs left by the outbreak, but I assure you, the mosquitoes will not be a factor for long," said

President Ryman. He met my eyes for an instant, and I almost recoiled from the pain lurking in his face. He was the president. He was the man at the head of this conspiracy—somehow, he'd gone from being Tate's patsy to the man in the position Tate once aspired to. And he looked like he was being tortured.

"Tell that to my parents," said Alaric. He sagged against Becks, glaring daggers at anyone who made the mistake of looking his way. If he'd been armed, I think more than one person would have been in danger of dying.

Still clutching his throat, the man from the CDC said, "Regardless, you were brought here for a purpose. You will do as you're told, or you will not leave here alive."

"What purpose would that be?" I asked warily.

"You have a certain reputation for honesty," said the man from the CDC. "You will begin reporting the news as we present it, rather than reporting it as you see fit. By adding your voices to ours, we can hopefully control some of the more unpleasant rumors to have arisen since the events surrounding the most recent presidential election."

It was my turn to stare at him. Finally, I said, "You want me to *lie* for you."

"Oh, no," said the man from the CDC. "You know, I'm disappointed. I really thought you'd be smarter. I suppose the cloning process wasn't as reliable as we had hoped."

"No," said Shaun. He pulled his arm free of my hand. "You're already out of the game as far they're concerned. You said it yourself. The George I got was supposed to be the brainwashed agreeable one who thought they had the best damn ideas ever."

"Then why?" I asked.

President Ryman sighed. "Shaun, I'm sorry."

"No, you're not." Shaun glanced at me. The look on his face was enough to make me wish I'd never come back from the dead. "They brought you back so they'd have something they could use to make me do what they told me to do. They brought you back for leverage, so they could make *me* lie for them. You always told the truth, George. But I made people believe it."

"Oh." My voice was barely a whisper. It hurt to even force myself to speak that loudly. "Well, then it's over. We won't do it."

"Again, I thought you'd be smarter."

I turned to the man from the CDC. He was shaking his head, and holding what looked like a fountain pen in his hand. Shaun went rigid, barely seeming to breathe.

"You'll do what we tell you to do. If you choose not to, well. We'll have to find ourselves some replacement reporters, because you are all going to die."

Because we chose to tell the truth
(The cool of age, the rage of youth)
And stand against the lies of old
(The whispers soft, the tales untold)
We find ourselves the walking dead
(The loves unkept, the words unsaid)
And in the crypt of all we've known
(The broken blade, the breaking stone)
We know that we were in the right
(The coming dawn, the ending night).
So here is when we stop the lies.
The time is come. We have to Rise.

—From *Dandelion Mine*,
the blog of Magdalene Grace Garcia, August 7, 2041.

The problem with people who have power is that they start thinking more about what it takes to keep that power than they do about what's right or wrong or just plain a bad idea. Here's a tip for you: If you're ever in a position to be making calls on right and wrong that can impact an entire nation, run your decisions past a six-year-old. If they look at you in horror and tell you you're getting coal in your stocking for the rest of your life, you should probably reconsider your course of action. Unless you want to be remembered as a monster, in which case, knock yourself out.

—From *Charming Not Sincere*,
the blog of Rebecca Atherton, August 7, 2041.

SHAUN: Thirty-six

The pen in the doctor's hand—so much like the one Dr. Wynne used to kill Kelly in the Memphis CDC, what felt like the better part of a lifetime ago—was enough to make me go cold. I was immune to Kellis-Amberlee. None of the others could say the same. Especially not George, who made me immune, but didn't confer the same immunity on her own clone.

Do you think you could survive losing me again? asked her voice, sweet and low and somehow poisonous. She'd never taken that tone with me before. But why shouldn't she turn on me? I was replacing her, and doing my best to shove her away.

What kind of world were we living in, where the people we trusted to keep us healthy were the ones keeping us sick, and a man couldn't even depend on his own insanity?

I raised my hands defensively and said, "There's no reason for us to do anything crazy. Let's just settle down, okay?" Out of the corner of my eye I could see Becks restraining Alaric, keeping him from moving toward the now-deadly doctor. He wasn't with us in Memphis. We'd told him what happened, but he didn't really understand.

"It's a pen," said George.

It took me a second to realize that it was the live George who was speaking, not the increasingly malicious voice inside my head. I glanced her way, giving a quick, tight shake of my head. "We're all going to stay calm," I said, hoping she'd decide to listen. "Okay?"

George frowned before nodding slowly. "Okay." She put her own hands up, mirroring my defensive position. "I'm sorry. I spoke too hastily. We'll consider your proposal."

"Why don't I believe you?" asked the doctor. He glared at President Ryman. "I knew this was a terrible plan from the start. We should have arranged for an outbreak in their hometown as soon as the campaign was over. Wynne was soft on them, the old fool. Leaving them alone was his idea, not mine."

"That sounds less like 'soft on us' and more like sensible resource management," said Becks, pulling the doctor's attention back to her. I winced, but didn't try to stop her. She was keeping him from focusing on any one person. That was valuable. I just hoped it wouldn't get her shot.

"Put down the pen," said Steve. His tone was clipped, indicating that he, too, knew exactly what it was.

"No, I don't think so," said the doctor. "The agreement was simple: I would allow the president to bring his little covey of pet journalists here, and try to sway them to the side of reason. If it failed, they would be mine to dispose of. As I expected, it has failed."

"Who says she speaks for the rest of us?" The words sounded alien even as they left my mouth. *George, please, forgive me*, I thought. "I mean, come on, man. It was nice of you to let the science dudes grow me a replacement, but you could have just sent a card. She's a *clone*. She's not a real person. She doesn't get to be the one who gets the real people dead."

The man from the CDC paused, an uncertain look crossing his face.

I decided to press what little advantage I had. "I'm not going to pretend we're happy about this bullshit. I mean, dude, you killed Alaric's parents. That's pretty crappy, and it doesn't make us feel like playing nice. But that doesn't mean she speaks for the rest of us. You know she's not a perfect copy of my sister. You built a broken Georgia. Maybe you could've done a better job if she hadn't managed to get away from you—that happens a lot, doesn't it? Clones, mosquitoes, reporters. You've been running the country for like twenty years. Shouldn't you be better at this by now?"

"That's quite enough, son," said President Ryman. Turning to the man from the CDC, he said, "Put the pen down. They're willing to listen to what we have to say. Isn't that what we brought them here for? To sway them to the right way of thinking?"

I could see George out of the corner of my eye. She had her face turned toward me, jaw slack in the way that told me she was staring behind the dark lenses of her sunglasses. I was briefly, terribly grateful she'd chosen to keep wearing them. I wouldn't have been able to keep smiling if I'd been able to see her eyes.

She believes every word you're saying, whispered my internal George, sounding pleased and disappointed at the same time, like she couldn't decide which was better. *I bet she's said those same things to herself every day since she woke up. Not good enough. Not Georgia enough. Not real. And now you've confirmed it. Think she'll ever forgive you?*

That seemed like a less pressing question at the moment than whether I was ever going to be able to forgive myself. We had to survive before I could find out one way or the other.

George sniffled before saying, in a small voice, "If I'm not going to be a part of this decision, can I please go lie down? My head hurts. I don't understand what's going on." She sounded utterly pathetic. I had to bite back a sigh of relief.

Georgia's migraines were the one thing that ever got the Masons to let her out of public appearances when we were kids. Her eyes meant that sometimes, migraines just happened, and the best thing for her to do was lie in a nice dark place and wait for them to go away. I used to wonder why the Masons never noticed that she always seemed to have a migraine when we were supposed to go to the government orphanage where she was adopted—lucky her, she was found within driving distance of Berkeley. The Masons had to go all the way to Southern California to get me.

As far as I knew, she never once visited that orphanage. And if she was claiming a migraine now, she was faking it. She was playing along.

Slowly, the man from the CDC said, "If he feels we built him a, as he says, 'broken George,' he won't mind if I shoot her right now. We can always make him a better one."

I froze, every nerve I had screaming two contradictory commands— *save her, save her, don't let her die again* warring with *no, you can't, you'll all die if you try, and you can choose that for you, but you can't choose it for Becks and Alaric.* I had to let him pull the trigger. I couldn't let him. As soon as he started to tense his fingers I'd jump for him, and whatever came after that would be anybody's guess. I knew that, even as the sanest part of me was telling me it was the worst thing I could possibly do. Becks and Alaric knew it, too. They glanced my way, uncertainty in their eyes. I was the boss. I was the one they counted on to keep them safe. And that wasn't going to stop me from getting them both killed.

Rescue came from an unexpected quarter. Steve cleared his throat before saying, with professional calm, "If your hand so much as twitches, sir, I *will* be forced to shoot you. Intentionally beginning an outbreak in the presence of the president is considered an act of treason. Intent to commit an act of treason authorizes me to take whatever steps are necessary to prevent that act from being carried out."

"Now," said President Ryman again. "Your point is made. He didn't stop you. They'll listen to us. Put the pen *down*."

"Fine." Looking disgusted, the man from the CDC slid the pen back into the pocket of his lab coat. "You say the clone has no part in your decision making process. Prove it. Agree to distribute the news on our behalf."

"Please, can I go lie down?" whispered George.

I knew she was faking. The pain in her voice was still enough to make me want to put my arms around her and never let go, men from the CDC and Secret Service agents and government conspiracies be damned.

"You treat all your science projects this badly?" asked Becks.

"Of course not," said President Ryman. "Rick, take her somewhere. Calm her down, give her a glass of water, whatever it takes to settle her. We'll decide what's to be done with her when we finish sorting things out here."

"Yes, Mr. President," said Rick. He moved quickly, taking George's elbow before I could formulate a protest. "Come with me. I'll see if we can't find you something to make you feel a little better." If it had been anyone other than Rick, I would have stepped in. I wouldn't have had a choice. But it was Rick, and he used to be one of us, and so I didn't say anything. Steve followed after him, a hulking, defensive presence. He'd keep her safe if Rick couldn't.

George sniffled and let herself be led away. She didn't look back at me. Not once.

See? whispered the George in my mind. *She believed every word you said.*

"Shut up," I muttered, and grimaced, waiting to see what effect that would have on the already questionably stable nameless doctor from the CDC.

He didn't appear to have heard me. Instead, he watched as Rick led George away, waiting until they were out of sight before turning back to me. "My apologies if I seemed somewhat aggressive before," he said finally. "Had things gone as originally planned, this is the point where we would be presenting her to you—not this clone, perhaps, but one that was not, as you put it, 'defective.' She would be a gift, given in good faith, to show you that working with us is the right thing to do."

I wanted to tell him that if he'd reached the point where giving other people away like party favors was "the right thing to do," he was too crazy for me to want to work with him—and I know from crazy. I wanted to tell him they shouldn't have worked so hard to make a person when they cloned my sister, because an empty shell and excuses about brain damage would have been an awful lot easier for them to control. I didn't say any of those things. I guess I never went all the way crazy after all.

Instead, I did what I do best, and went on the attack. "If you wanted us to get this far, why did your men try to kill us in Seattle?" I asked. "I mean, not exactly 'hi, let's be besties' behavior, you know?"

"That was an unfortunate misunderstanding," said the doctor.

"A surprising number of your misunderstandings involve bullets and body counts," said Alaric. He was glowering. If I were the man from the CDC, I would've been considering a fatal accident for Alaric as a simple matter of self-preservation.

"There are automated security protocols that go into effect whenever we have reason to suspect industrial espionage—and it does happen, especially in a place like the CDC. Our discoveries are often quite lucrative. The theft of subject 7c was enough to activate those protocols."

"Subject 7c?" I asked blankly.

"Georgia," said Becks.

Once again, I weighed the merits of punching someone, and regretfully decided I couldn't afford the fallout. "Do those automated security protocols usually include pre-bugging our shoes? Because your dudes only found us by following the bugs we already had on us."

The doctor looked uncomfortable. "It is sometimes necessary to protect our investments through extra-legal channels. We had an...agreement... with certain elements of the local underground that, were they approached about an infiltration of our facility, they would ensure we could apprehend those responsible."

"And by doing it after a crime was committed, you avoided getting in trouble for working with the 'local underground,'" said Alaric, with grudging respect. "Slick. Stupid, but slick. Why bother screwing around? Why not just stop them from getting inside in the first place?"

For once, I had the answer the Newsie didn't. "Because a few break-ins keep everybody believing the CDC is at risk, and we never look too hard at the budget for security upgrades and growing new people in big tanks. All of which loops us back around to the thing we're not talking about here. *Why* did you clone Georgia? There are way cheaper ways to convince us that you're the good guys. And yeah, I know, I said 'leverage' earlier, and I meant it, only again, way cheaper ways to do it. You could have threatened my parents, my team..."

"But we couldn't get to your team if we couldn't get to you, and we knew that was a risk as far back as the campaign trail," said the doctor calmly. President Ryman looked away. "She wasn't the only one we were prepared to resurrect, although her death meant she was the best candidate. We were able to extract her brain almost immediately, and get to work while the Kellis-Amberlee virus was still working in her system. It's a fascinating behavior, considering how little of the brain the virus actually requires—" He must have seen the storm warnings in our faces, because he changed topics in the middle of the stream, saying, "She was to be leverage, as you've indicated, but she was also going to help us be sure you were getting the information we needed you to have."

"Manipulate the old media during the Rising, manipulate the new media to keep the world from finding out how much of this you engineered," said Becks. "How did you get the rest of the world to go along with it?"

"I'm not Tate," said the doctor acidly. "I don't need to convince you that I'm in the right. I'm here to present you with a choice. Work for us. Help us to shape the next twenty years. Or never leave this building again. It's up to you."

I looked at Becks and Alaric. They looked back at me. None of us said anything. I don't think any of us knew what to say.

Finally, Alaric asked, "You promise the mosquitoes are going to die on their own?"

"You have my word as a scientist."

I somehow managed not to snort.

Alaric continued. "And none of us are being charged with any crimes?"

"The reverse. Once we've worked things out to our mutual satisfaction, we'll announce that you've been added to the list of bloggers with White House press access. The only reason you weren't added before was out of respect for your loss." The doctor smiled. The expression seemed alien on his face. "I think you'll find that we can be very reasonable when you follow the rules and behave like rational people."

"And George?" I asked.

"You can keep her, if you can keep her in line and out of sight."

"My sister?" asked Alaric.

"Will be returned to your custody as soon as possible. She was fortunate to escape Florida."

Becks didn't say anything. Her family was more likely to be supporting the CDC than at risk from their actions.

"Well?" asked the doctor.

I opened my mouth, not quite sure what was going to come out of it.

"We'll do it," I said.

"Good," said the doctor. "I hoped you'd see sense. Welcome to the CDC."

You know what? Fuck it. Just fuck it. The Rising didn't manage to wipe out the human race, it just made us turn into even bigger assholes than we were before. Hear that, mad science? You failed. You were supposed to kill us all, and instead you turned us into monsters.

Fuck it.

**—From *Adaptive Immunities*,
the blog of Shaun Mason, August 7, 2041. Unpublished.**

Testing. This is a test post to check formatting and be sure the files are uploading correctly. Test test test.

Is this thing on?

**—From *Living Dead Girl*,
the blog of Georgia Mason II, August 7, 2041. Unpublished.**

GEORGIA: Thirty-seven

S teve was a constant, silent presence behind us as Rick steered me down the hall. It was weirdly like being back on the campaign trail, only I wasn't carrying a gun, Rick wasn't carrying a cat, and I was no longer sure who the good guys were.

On second thought, it was nothing at all like being back on the campaign trail.

The hall ended at a door that looked like real oak. Rick let go of me to press his palm flat against the testing panel next to the door. A small red light clicked on above it, oscillating rapidly between red and green before settling on green. It remained lit for less than five seconds. Then it clicked off, and the door clicked open.

"I'm going to be waiting for you on the other side," said Rick. "Do you trust Steve?"

It was an interesting question. If Ryman was no longer one of the good guys, I wasn't sure I trusted anyone. But of the people I didn't trust, Steve was one of the ones I distrusted the least. "We'll be fine," I said.

"I'll see you in a moment," said Rick, and opened the door. Part of me wondered what kind of awesome security procedures they'd have in place to prevent people from following each other through—always a risk, no matter how much the people who design the airlock systems try to keep it from happening. Some airlocks will gas you if you try to go through without getting a blood test. Somehow I doubted they'd use something that crude on a door that might be opened by the President of the United States. The rest of me understood that playing with the security system was something too stupid for Shaun to do, and that meant it was absolutely too dumb for me.

The door closed behind Rick, the little red light making another brief appearance before shutting itself politely off. "Cute," I said, stepping forward to press my hand against the testing plate. Needles bit into the skin at the point where each of my fingers joined my palm. That was an unusual spot for a test array. I took a small, startled breath, finally pulling away as the light turned green and clicked off. "That's my cue."

"I'll be right through," said Steve. He smiled encouragingly when I looked back at him, and I held that image firmly in my mind as I stepped through the door to whatever was waiting on the other side. Steve wouldn't have smiled while he sent me to my death. I might be a clone, and Ryman might be corrupt, but some things about a person's essential nature never change.

The door opened on a narrow hallway that looked like it was constructed hundreds of years before the Rising and never substantially redecorated. Rick was waiting. A relieved smile spread across his face when he saw me. "I was afraid you wouldn't come."

"What, you thought I'd go back to the nice man in the lab coat who was about to have me recycled?" I dropped the pretense of having a migraine, straightening and looking at him flatly. "You could have warned me what we were walking into."

"No. I couldn't have." The door swung open as Steve joined us in the hall. Rick switched his attention from me to Steve, asking, "Anyone following us?"

"Not that I saw," rumbled Steve. I raised an eyebrow. He explained, "This is one of the tunnels built during the Cold War, in case we needed to evacuate the capital. They probably wouldn't have been any use in a nuclear strike—a nuke's a pretty damn big deal—but there's one thing they do manage, quite nicely."

I nodded slowly, catching his meaning. "We're underground. No wireless transmission."

"We sweep this hall hourly for bugs. For the moment, we're in the clear." Steve looked past me to Rick. "You can proceed, Mr. Vice President."

"Thank you, Steve." Rick sighed, beginning to walk. "It really is good to see you."

"Most people just send flowers. Raising the dead is a little extreme." I matched my steps to his, watching him as we walked. "What's going on, Rick? What's *really* going on?"

"I meant it when I said that, if it had been up to me, I would have simply handed you over to Shaun as soon as you woke up enough to know yourself." A muscle in Rick's jaw twitched as he continued. "I will go to my grave knowing that I have been responsible for your death more than twenty times. Each time one of the clones of the original Georgia Mason was decanted I told myself, 'That's it. No more. If she's not real, we find another way.' But each time, I couldn't think of another way, and we needed you. *I* needed you."

"Why?"

"Same reason those people back there were hoping you'd play nicely with the other children—people associate your face with the truth. If you tell them a lie they want to believe, they won't question it."

"And the government can keep on killing people like me. People like your *wife*. God, Rick, is that really what you want?"

"No. That's what *they* want." Rick stopped at an unsecured door, pushing it open. Gregory was sitting at a terminal on the other side, with Dr. Shoji looking over his shoulder. I couldn't even be surprised. Rick kept talking: "I want you to tell the world the truth. I want you to blow it all to hell. People believe you. People believe *in* you, because of the way you died. They'll believe the truth even if they don't want to, as long as they're hearing it from you."

"I don't understand," I said.

"Hello, Georgia," said Gregory, looking up from the screen. "It's good to see you again."

"It was touch and go for a while there, but I pulled through," I said. "How about you?"

"Minor burns, concussion, and I won't be working with the CDC again anytime soon. That's all right. I was tired of them anyway."

"Good." I turned to Rick. "Now please. *Explain*. A huge global conspiracy has ruined my life—hell, has *ended* my life, and then started it over again, leaving me with probably the worst identity issues I could imagine—and they did it for what? So you could clone me and use me to sell ice to the Eskimos?"

"A huge global conspiracy has ruined your life. If it helps, they also killed my wife." Rick's smile faded like it had never been there at all. "I took Lisa's death for a suicide, because that's what they told me it was. I found out differently only when I saw her file. They did it because of what you saw back in that room—there is no cure for Kellis-Amberlee. There's never going to be a cure. There's just going to be a war with the virus, one we can't win, but can only adapt to. We can only survive it. And that's not acceptable to some people."

"So they're doing *this* instead?"

"It didn't start out like this, Georgia. It started out with good intentions—God, such good intentions. They thought they were taking steps to protect the country. In the end, no one noticed when protection turned into imprisonment, or when 'for the good of the people' turned into 'for the good of the people in power.' It was all baby steps, all the way."

"Aren't the worst things usually that way?" I asked. "So why's Ryman on their side now? Wasn't he supposed to be the good guy? The one we could depend on?"

Rick didn't say anything. He just looked at me, waiting. He didn't have to wait long.

"Emily," I whispered. "Emily Ryman has retinal KA."

"Which makes her an excellent candidate for an 'accidental' death if he stops playing along—and you're not their first clone. Just the first one that really replicates the person you were based on. If you'd been alive for the last year, you would have noticed that Emily rarely speaks in public. She just stands and smiles. Does that sound like the Emily Ryman you know?"

I stared at him in mute horror. Rick continued: "They replaced her the night after the inauguration, and now she and the children are hostages against the president's good behavior. He's in the same position you are. He's a perfect figurehead, because even people who believe all politicians are corrupt remember his association with you on the campaign trail—and they remember what happened to Rebecca Ryman. They believe in him, even if they don't realize it." Rick laughed a little, bitterly. "I think this may have been the plan all along. Tate was never going to wind up in power. Ryman was too good a puppet to pass up."

"I think I hate the human race," I said.

"There's the Georgia Mason we all know and love," said Steve. "Now the question is, what are we going to do about it?"

I paused. "You mean I'm standing in a room with the Vice President of the United States, a member of the Secret Service, and two renegade EIS scientists, and you expect the clone to make the decisions? See, this is why this country is in trouble all the damn time. The people running it are crazy."

"We just want to know if you'll help," said Dr. Shoji.

"And by help, you mean . . . ?"

"Will you do what you did in Sacramento?"

What I did in Sacramento was reveal Tate's dirty dealing and the fact that someone had been bankrolling him—but we never suspected the CDC, and so mostly, what I did was make sure Ryman got into power.

That, and die. I knew they were asking me to tell the truth again, to tell it for them this time, but I couldn't help remembering the way it felt to know that I was coming to an end. It wasn't my memory, just a snapshot stolen from the virus-riddled mind of a dead woman, but that didn't make it feel any less real. I *died* in Sacramento. If I did what they wanted me to do, I could very well die again.

And if I was going to be the kind of person who valued her life more than she valued the truth, I wasn't going to be Georgia Mason at all. Unless I wanted to find someone else I was willing to be, this was what I was made for.

"We have to get Emily—the *real* Emily—away from the CDC, and get the kids out of here," I said slowly. "They're going to be civilians in a position to confirm my story. If I start posting while they're still hostages, they won't make it out of here alive."

Steve cracked his knuckles. "Don't worry about them. The First Lady still has friends in the Secret Service. We can extract the kids at any time."

"Dr. Shaw is organizing a team to extract the First Lady from the CDC installation where she's being held, and move her to a secure EIS facility near here," said Dr. Shoji.

"The EIS has been a busy little secret government organization." I looked levelly at Dr. Shoji. "If I do this, I need to know that we're not replacing one bad deal with another. What are your plans?"

"I don't speak for the EIS as a whole, and I can't see the future," he said. "But for the past ten years at least, we've been bleeding off the best recruits the CDC gets. We've been getting the members of your generation, the ones who want a solution that doesn't always involve a bullet. I think that corruption is a risk for every organization. Even ours. But we're going to be very busy for quite some time, just cleaning up the mess that's been made for us. If the EIS is going to go the way of the CDC, it probably won't be within my lifetime."

"Whereas the CDC is a bad deal right now," I said. "That's fair. But you realize that if I do this, if I get involved, and you ever, *ever* start to cross the line—"

"I can't promise what the future will be. All I can do is promise that the EIS will try to make sure we have one."

I nodded. "Fine. Steve, get the kids out of here. Dr. Shoji, do whatever you need to do to get them to safety, and make sure Dr. Shaw takes care of Emily. Does anybody here have a gun I can borrow? The Secret Service confiscated all of ours."

Rick blinked. "I was expecting you to ask for an Internet connection."

"Oh, I'm going to need one of those, too, once we get everybody back together, but first, we have a job that requires weapons." Steve unsnapped his sidearm and passed it to me. I accepted it before smiling coolly at Rick. "We need to go and kidnap the president."

"And here my mother said a job in medicine would be dangerous," said Gregory.

Rick didn't say anything. But slowly, with an expression of almost painful relief, he nodded.

I regret to inform you that we have lied to you. Last year, when most of the site went "camping," we were in actuality running for our lives, being pursued by no less an adversary than the Centers for Disease Control. Our flight began when Dr. Kelly Connolly, believed dead following a break-in at the Memphis CDC, arrived at our Oakland offices and asked for our help. The destruction of Oakland followed soon after. In the interests of concealing our location and activities, we were forced to present a cover story to the world. For this, on the behalf of the Factual News Division, I apologize.

We are not lying now. Please download and read the attached documents, which encompass everything leading up to our departure from Oakland. If they do not load, please visit one of our mirror sites. Continue trying. This is important. These are things you need to know.

We are telling you the truth.

—From *Fish and Clips,*
the blog of Mahir Gowda, August 7, 2041.

The mosquitoes that swept from Cuba to the American Gulf Coast, resulting in the death of millions, did not arise naturally. They were genetically engineered by scientists in the employ of the CDC. Please download and review the attached documents for further details, including a full description of the life cycle of the modified yellow fever mosquito.

We are telling you the truth.

That will not bring my parents back to life.

—From *The Kwong Way of Things*,
the blog of Alaric Kwong, August 7, 2041.

SHAUN: Thirty-eight

The man from the CDC kept on talking; to be honest, I had pretty much stopped listening. Alaric and Becks were paying attention and periodically asking questions that seemed at least vaguely connected to the things coming out of his mouth, so I figured no one would notice—or care—if I checked out for a little bit. As long as I didn't start to drool, they'd probably figure I was just being a big, dumb Irwin and letting the smart people talk. That's the useful thing about being a figurehead. Nobody cares if you're an idiot, as long as you're a useful one.

They're never going to give her back to you, murmured Georgia. There was a faint echoing quality to her words, and I knew that if I turned my head she'd be there, watching me, waiting for me to admit that she was right. That scared me almost more than the things she was saying. I used to welcome the hallucinations, viewing them as the only way I could see her anymore. Now...I knew I wasn't going to go un-crazy as fast as I went crazy. But the idea of being left alone with a voice in my head and the occasional delusional vision was suddenly terrifying. I got her back. Why the hell wasn't the world going to let me keep her?

You don't need to worry about their little replacement. The world will let you keep me, she said. *Just you and me, forever. That's what you said you wanted, isn't it? You volunteered to be a haunted house.*

"Shut up," I muttered, trying to keep my voice low enough that no one else would notice.

It didn't work. "What was that?" asked the doctor, attention swinging back around to me.

Uh-oh. "Uh..." I began.

"He talks to himself," said Becks, matter-of-factly. "I'm actually impressed that this is the first time he's done it. Just ignore him and keep telling us why immune response in babies is enough to cause reservoir conditions, but not enough to avoid spontaneous amplification when they cross the sixty-pound threshold."

"He *talks* to himself?" The doctor frowned at me like I had suddenly become an exciting new medical mystery. I wondered how he'd feel if he knew I was immune to the Kellis-Amberlee virus. He'd probably start asking whether he could dissect me—assuming he cared about asking. George had already proven that people were now a matter of crunch all you want, we'll make more. Maybe he already had Shaun II baking in one of their cloning tanks, ready for his triumphant decanting.

Fuck. That.

"Turns out being forced to shoot the one person in the world you thought would outlive you in the head sort of fucks with your sense of reality," I said coldly. "I mean, my choices were a nice, mellow psychotic break with talking to myself and the occasional voice in my head, or climbing the nearest cell tower and playing sniper until somebody came and gunned me down. I figured option A would be better for my long-term health, if not my sanity."

"And you still listen to him? You still do what he says?" asked the doctor, his attention swinging back to Becks and Alaric.

Alaric shrugged. "Sure. He's the boss."

"Fascinating." The man from the CDC shook his head as he turned toward President Ryman. "You see the power of trust? Once you believe a person won't mislead you, you keep believing it, even after you realize they've gone insane. This plan may actually work."

"Or maybe not," said George. "It's a little bit of a coin toss right now, if you ask me."

The doctor whipped around, eyes widening. "What are you doing?"

His reaction made me realize she was really here, rather than speaking into the dark inside my head. I turned to see George standing in the doorway, an unfamiliar gun in her hands. She had it aimed squarely at the doctor's chest. Rick was behind her, expression grim, standing next to a man I didn't recognize. Steve was nowhere to be seen.

"If you so much as twitch, I swear, I will shoot you," said George.

The doctor ignored her, reaching for his pocket. The sound of the safety clicking off was very loud. He froze. "You're making a mistake," he said.

"Maybe your mistake was focusing so hard on my replacement that you forgot to give me an off switch," replied George.

"No, they gave you one," said the stranger. "We just took it out before they had the chance to use it."

"Oh, right," said George. "Silly me. I always forget about the excruciatingly painful nonelective surgeries."

The doctor's eyes got even wider, if that was possible. "Dr. Lake?" he demanded, looking toward the unfamiliar man.

The stranger smiled, the expression bordering on a snarl. "I resign," he said.

"So this is mutiny." The man from the CDC slanted his eyes toward President Ryman and his remaining agents. "This is *treason*."

None of the Secret Servicemen were reaching for their guns, and the look on President Ryman's face wasn't shock or outrage—it was relief, like this was what he'd been waiting for all along. "You'd know about that, wouldn't you?" he asked. I'd never heard him sound so bitter. "Treason? That's something you at the CDC have been experts on for quite a while."

The man from the CDC's eyes widened in exaggerated shock. "I don't understand what you're implying, Mr. President."

"Emily's safe," said George. "The EIS has her. Steve's getting the kids out of the building. They can't hold your family over you anymore."

"Do you think it's that simple?" asked the man from the CDC. "We've had a long time to get to where we are today. You're making a large mistake. People have died for less."

"People have died for nothing," George shot back. "And no, I don't think it's that simple. But I do think you made one major tactical error when you invited us here."

The man from the CDC sneered. "What's that?"

"We're the ones that people listen to...and we're the ones who learned about backups from Georgette Meissonier." George smiled. "Anybody here who doesn't have six cameras running, raise your hand."

Not a single member of my team raised their hand. Becks grinned. Alaric smirked.

And the man from the CDC, perhaps realizing that he was finished, moved. Jamming his hand into his pocket, he pulled out the pen he'd been holding before, aiming it at the president. The Secret Servicemen shouted something, grabbing Ryman's shoulders. Not fast enough. There was no way they'd be able to get him clear fast enough. I didn't think. I just jumped, putting myself between the man from the CDC and President Ryman half a second before I heard the sound of Georgia's gun going off.

The man from the CDC froze, looking slowly down at the spreading red patch in the middle of his chest. The pen dropped from his hand and he fell, crumpling to the floor. The last sound he made was a hollow thud when his head hit the tile. It was almost comic, in a weird way.

No one was laughing. They were all staring at me. Becks had a hand covering her mouth, and Alaric looked like he was about to be sick. Only Georgia didn't look distraught; mostly, she looked confused. Lowering her gun, she asked, "What is that?"

I looked at the needle sticking out of my chest, anchored in the flesh a few inches to the right of my sternum. It hurt a little, now that I was thinking about it. It would probably hurt more once the adrenaline washed out of my system.

"Oh," I said, my words almost drowned out by the sound of one of the Secret Servicemen emptying his gun into the man from the CDC's head. "That's a problem."

You know what's awesome? Assholes who do all their research, and have all the pieces of the puzzle, and can't be bothered with anything that doesn't fit the picture they've decided they're putting together. You know. Idiots. The kind of stupid you can manage to achieve only by being really, really smart, because only really, really smart people can reach adulthood without having any goddamn *common sense*.

Seriously. Thank you, smart people, for being absolute idiots. I appreciate it.

—From *Adaptive Immunities*,
the blog of Shaun Mason, August 7, 2041. Unpublished.

Kill me once, shame on you.
Kill me twice, shame on me.
Kill my brother? Oh, it's on. And you are *not* going to enjoy it.

—From *Living Dead Girl*,
the blog of Georgia Mason II, August 7, 2041. Unpublished.

GEORGIA: Thirty-nine

Everyone stared at the needle sticking out of Shaun's chest, their expressions showing varying degrees of shock and horror. I put the safety back on my borrowed gun and slowly lowered it, shoving it into the waistband of my pants.

No one said anything. One of the Secret Service agents pulled President Ryman back, putting more distance between him and Shaun. I tried to force myself to swallow. I remembered being hit by a similar needle in Sacramento, although mine had been attached to a syringe. "Shaun?" I said, very softly.

"The CDC weaponized Kellis-Amberlee a while ago," said Shaun. He grimaced as he pulled the needle out of his chest. "Okay, fucking ow. Could we go with a slightly less ouch-worthy doomsday weapon next time? Not that I don't appreciate it failing to, you know, puncture my lung or something, but that stings."

"Put the needle down and step away from the president," said one of the Secret Service agents. His gun was in his hand, and from his tone, he meant business.

"Shaun..." said President Ryman.

"Oh, right. You guys didn't get the memo, did you? See, part of why they're so into killing the people with the reservoir conditions—like, you know, George, or your wife, or Rick's wife, who probably didn't kill herself, and isn't that a bitch?—part of why they're so into that is because of whatchamacallit—"

"Antibody transference," said Alaric. He relaxed as he spoke, some of the tension going out of his shoulders.

"Yeah, that. Turns out the reservoir conditions are sort of like, the middle step in us learning how to live with our cuddly virus buddies. People with reservoir conditions get better because they're making antibodies. And then people who spend a lot of time with those people get something even better." Shaun grinned at me. "We get to be immune."

"What?" said President Ryman.

"What?" said Gregory.

"Can I get a biohazard bag over here?" said Shaun. He grimaced again. "And maybe some gauze or something? This *really* stings."

"This is impossible," said one of the Secret Service agents. He leveled his handgun on Shaun. "Sir, we need to get you out of here."

"No," said President Ryman. We all turned to look at him, even Shaun, who still looked perfectly lucid. Conversion takes time, but he should have been showing some of the outward signs of infection after being shot with that large a dose of virus.

"Sir?" said the Secret Service agent.

"I said no. We brought these people here because we were looking for a Hail Mary. If they're going to give us one, we're not going to turn our backs on them." President Ryman's gaze settled on Gregory. "I'm sorry, son. I didn't catch your name."

"Dr. Gregory Lake, sir. EIS." Gregory produced a testing kit from his lab coat pocket, tossing it to Shaun. "If I may be so bold, this might help keep these nice gentlemen from shooting you before we can get out of here."

"Practical *and* prepared. That's what I like to see in a public servant." President Ryman turned to Shaun. "Shaun…"

"I know, I know. Prove that this isn't just preamplification crazy." Shaun sighed as he popped the lid off his testing kit. "You know, George, if you'd just listened when I said I wanted to skip the presidential campaign and petition to go to Yellowstone instead, none of this would have happened." He stuck his thumb into the opening.

I managed to smile. It wasn't easy. "But imagine all the fun we'd have missed. Meeting Rick, that town hall in Eakly…"

"Burying Buffy. Burying *you*. I would have been okay with missing the fun." The lights on his test unit seemed to be confused. They were flashing, returning to yellow over and over again. Finally, the green light stopped flickering, and the red and yellow began to oscillate, like the unit was trying to make up its mind. The Secret Servicemen drew their guns.

I could see what came next as clearly as if it had already happened. Blood on the floor; Shaun falling, and no handy CDC madmen to bring him back to me. "Stop!" I shouted, putting both my hands up in front of me. "It hasn't stopped yet!"

It *hadn't* stopped. The light was still flashing between red and yellow—and as I watched, the green came back into the rotation. The flash began holding there, a little bit longer each time. "Fascinating," murmured Gregory.

"You can't dissect him," I said.

"No, but can we have some blood? Say, a gallon? For starters?"

"We'll see." The light wasn't flashing red at all anymore; instead, it was flickering between yellow and green. Then the yellow cut out entirely, and it was just green, uninfected, *safe*. I let out a slow breath, only then feeling the terror that had been burning in my veins the whole time. Shaun was safe. Shaun was going to be okay.

Shaun was holding up the green-lit test unit with an expression of vague amusement on his face as he asked, "Well? Does that clear me? Or do I need to do a little dance, too?"

"A little dance is never amiss," said Alaric, straight-faced.

I started to move toward Shaun. Gregory grabbed my shoulder, stopping me. "Don't."

"What?" asked Shaun and I, in unison.

Gregory shook his head, not letting go. "He may be immune, but you're not. If the virus on his clothing is live, it could cause you to amplify."

"This gets better and better." Becks glared at the body of man from the CDC. "I should have taken the headshot."

"Maybe next time," said Shaun.

"In the meantime, Mr. President, your wife and children are safe," said Rick. "We can get out of here. We can find a way to make this right."

"It's going to be a little harder than we thought."

The sound of Steve's voice was a surprise. We turned to see him standing in the door, with plaster on the shoulders of his formerly immaculate black suit and the bin holding our equipment in his arms.

"Steve?" said Shaun.

"The building is surrounded," said Steve. He moved to put the bin on the table. "I took the liberty of retrieving your weapons. We may be shooting our way out."

"Surrounded?" asked Becks, as she moved to rummage through the bin. "By what, political protestors?"

"No," said Steve. "Zombies."

"It's always zombies," complained Shaun. No one laughed. He frowned. "Tough crowd."

"What is it about you two and massive outbreaks?" asked Steve. "We were outbreak-free until you got here."

"Just lucky, I guess," I said. "Where's everyone else?"

"With Dr. Shoji. I doubled back when I saw the moaners on the lawn."

At least something was going right. The Secret Service agents with President Ryman looked stunned, although whether it was at the zombies or our flippancy, I couldn't have said. They weren't with us on the campaign trail. They didn't understand that this was how we coped.

"Can't we get out through the tunnels?" asked Rick.

"Only if you enjoy being zombie-chow," said Steve.

"The CDC is nothing if not efficient." Shaun took his gun from Becks, careful not to touch her hand. "Is there any route out of here that doesn't get us eaten?"

"We go through the parking garage to the covered motorway," said Steve. "We may still get eaten, but we'll have a better shot at getting out alive."

President Ryman was starting to look distinctly unhappy. Poor guy. Leader of the free world—and unwilling tool of an international conspiracy—one minute, potential zombie-food the next. "How did this happen?" he demanded.

"Our extraction of your wife may have trigged some alarms," said Gregory. "Between that and the situation here...the CDC is taking steps to resolve the matter. Congratulations. We are all expendable."

"Cheer up, everybody," said Shaun, and grinned—the grin of a manic Irwin getting ready to shove his way into danger. "This is going to be *great* for ratings. Let's go."

We went.

—————

The past thirty years bear a startling resemblance to the Greek myth of Pandora when looked at clearly, in the light. A box that should not have been opened; a plague of pains and pestilences loosed upon the world; and, at the end, hope. Hope that we refused, for many years, to allow ourselves to look upon with unshadowed eyes. What were we afraid of? Were we afraid hope would prove another phantom, slipping through our hands like mist? Were we afraid something worse was hidden in its wake?

I think not. I think we were, quite simply, afraid to admit to hope because admitting to hope would mean admitting the world had changed forever. There is no return to the world we knew before the Rising. That world is dead. But as the Rising itself took such great pains to teach us...

Even after death, life still goes on.

—From *Pandora's Box: The Rising Reimagined*,
authored by Mahir Gowda, August 10, 2041.

———

Look, Ma! I'm abducting the president! Aren't you proud of your baby girl now?

—From *Charming Not Sincere*,
the blog of Rebecca Atherton, August 7, 2041. Unpublished.

SHAUN: Forty

We fell into a ragged formation with President Ryman at the center. Alaric was almost as well protected; he'd never passed his field certifications, and none of us was particularly enthused by the idea of him firing a gun in an enclosed space. The next ring was made up of Secret Servicemen—all of them except Steve, who was on the outer ring with me, Gregory, and the rest of my team...including Rick, who'd taken a pistol from one of the agents and was walking next to Becks. None of them objected to the vice president endangering himself. Either they were giving up, or they figured they'd be lucky if they managed to get any of us out alive, much less both of the elected officials.

"You people still know how to throw a party," he said nervously.

"Practice. Alaric!" I didn't turn to face him; my attention remained on the hall ahead of us. Steve was on point, since he was the one who actually knew the way, but I wasn't going to let him hit the first wave—if there was a first wave—alone. "How are you doing with bouncing a signal out of this loony bin?"

"I'm still trying to get a clean connection!"

"Well, keep trying. We need to get this footage to Mahir *before* we get ripped to pieces by the living dead."

"You're always such an optimist," muttered George.

I slanted a grin her way. "Like I said. Practice."

"Is that also where you learned to be such an asshole?"

"Yup. How'm I doing?"

"Good."

The halls were eerily silent. That would have been a good thing—moaning usually means you're about to become a snack food—but we didn't know whether or not the zombies were inside. Eventually, even the nervous banter stopped. The only sounds were breathing, footsteps, and the occasional soft beep as Alaric tried and failed to make a connection with the outside world. I wanted to be comforted by the fact that George and I were walking into danger together, but I couldn't manage it. I kept thinking about how fragile she was, how breakable…how easily killed. She might have gotten better the first time, but now? In a new body, with a new immune system that never learned to coexist with the virus? She'd die, and this time, the CDC wouldn't be standing by to miraculously resurrect her. She'd stay gone.

"Fuck," I muttered.

No one said anything. At a time like this, me talking to myself was the least of our worries.

Steve led us to a T-junction and paused. "We can't take the elevator back up to the public garage; we're going to need to use the private vehicle pool. It's the only way to be sure we haven't been compromised."

"It's too quiet," said Rick.

George grimaced. "Why do people say that? Wouldn't it be quicker to just ask if that noise was the wind?"

Something moaned down the corridor to our right. I sighed. "That wasn't the wind."

"No, it wasn't," said Steve tightly.

"But how—" began Alaric.

"Questions later, running now," said Becks.

We ran.

The Secret Servicemen fell back until they were running behind the rest of us, moving at that strange twisted half jog men use when they want to cover the ground behind them as they run. Becks and Rick moved to flank the noncombatants—Alaric was still frantically slapping his PDA, trying to get a solid connection even as we were fleeing for our lives—while George and I took the front, running close on Steve's heels.

The moaning behind us continued, now getting louder. The zombies were fresh; they had to be, if they were gaining on us that fast. "I hate the fucking CDC," I snarled.

"Save your breath!" George advised.

We ran.

The hall seemed like it might be endless, right up until the moment where we turned a corner, and it ended, terminating in a set of clear glass doors leading into an airlock. There was a red light on above the door.

"It's gone into security lockdown," shouted Steve. "We're going to have to check out clean one at a time."

One of the Secret Servicemen moved through the group to slap his palm against the testing panel. The other agents were close behind him, dragging a protesting President Ryman in their wake. His safety was their job; ours wasn't. And the moaning was getting louder.

The light turned green. The first agent took his hand off the testing panel and stepped through the now-open door, letting the airlock cycle around him as he stepped out into the parking garage. Nothing attacked him immediately. He turned back to the rest of us, signaling for the second agent to send the president through.

"Got it!" said Alaric, his delight sounding almost obscene, considering the circumstances. The rest of us stared at him. He held up his PDA. "Upload established. I'm transmitting."

"Finally," breathed George, a certain tension slipping out of her shoulders. "Get those files up as fast as you can."

"Working on it."

"Even death doesn't change your priorities, does it?" asked Rick, tiredly amused.

"Not really, no," said George. She grinned at him, gun still aimed toward the unseen zombies.

I could have kissed her. It would probably have been a good thing, since we were all about to be zombie-chow. Instead, I adjusted my position, calling over my shoulder, "A little speed in the carpool lane would be appreciated, guys. We've got incoming, and I didn't bring enough limbs to share with everybody."

"The system's cycling as fast as it can," said Steve reproachfully.

"Don't really give a fuck how fast the system is cycling. Just don't want to get eaten by zombies right after uncovering a mass conspiracy to deceive the American public. Seems a little anticlimactic, you know what I mean? Like getting empty boxes on Christmas morning."

"You got empty boxes?" asked Becks. "Lucky bastard. I always got *dresses*."

Alaric glanced up. "Dresses?"

"*Frilly* dresses," she said with disgust. "*Lacy* frilly dresses."

"Are all journalists insane, or did I just hit the mother lode?" asked Gregory.

"Yes," said Rick and George, in unison.

We were still laughing—the anxious laughter of people who know they're about to die horribly—when the first zombies came around the corner, and laughter ceased to be an option.

At least the sight of the zombies answered the question of where they came from. They were wearing White House ID badges, dressed in respectable suits and sensible shoes. Someone must have triggered an outbreak inside the building, opened the right doors, and let the feeding frenzy commence. Anyone who hadn't been caught by the initial infection would have been taken out by the first wave of actual infected.

I'll give my companions this: No one screamed. Instead, everyone but Alaric and Gregory braced themselves and opened fire, giving the people at the airlock time to cycle through. Alaric moved to put himself behind Becks and out of the line of fire, attention still focused primarily on the device in his hands.

"Forty percent uploaded!" he called.

"Not enough," muttered George, and fired. Her shot went wild. With a wordless sound of frustration, she shifted the gun to her left hand and used her right to pull off her sunglasses and throw them aside. She resumed her stance and fired again. This time, she didn't miss.

"Mr. Vice President!" Steve's voice was anxious. "Sir, you need to go through the lock!"

Rick didn't move.

"Go on, Rick," I said, firing twice more into the seemingly endless tide of zombies. "Get out of here. Go be important. If we don't get out, somebody who understands the news is going to need to interpret what Alaric's putting online."

Rick still didn't move. He fired again; another zombie went down.

"Go on, Rick," said George. "Mahir gets left behind, and you leave when we need someone to make it off the battlefield. That's how this story goes." She never looked at him. She just kept shooting.

Rick shot her a stricken look, and he went, turning and retreating toward the airlock. I stepped a little closer to her, closing a bit more of the distance between us, and kept shooting. We were all falling back now, just a little bit, just a few steps. There are people who'll tell you the worst place to be in an outbreak is a narrow tunnel with a limited number of exits. They're probably right. But a narrow tunnel with a limited number of exits is also the *best* place to be in an outbreak, because the zombies can only come at you so fast.

The airlock hissed. Rick was through. "Dr. Lake!" called Steve. "Come on!"

Gregory didn't need to be told twice. He turned and ran, vanishing from my range of sight. My clip clicked on empty. I ejected it and slapped a new one into place, twisting the stock until I felt the clip snap home. George repeated the process two bullets later. By then, I was firing again, covering the hole she made. We still worked together well, even if neither of us was really the person we used to be. Even if neither of us was ever going to be that person—those people—again.

"If this is crazy, I don't care," I said, and fired. Another zombie went down. We were losing ground fast now, and still they kept coming.

"Neither do I," said George, and kept firing.

"Alaric!" shouted Steve.

"Coming!" Alaric started forward, and froze, eyes widening as he looked at the screen of his little device. "There's no signal there. I almost lost the connection."

"Alaric, just go!" snapped George.

"I can't! I have to get these files up before somebody hits us with an EMP screen!"

Becks took two long steps backward, firing all the while, and snatched the device from his hand. "I can manage an upload as well as you can," she snarled. "Now *go*."

Alaric stared at her. "Becks—"

"*Go!*"

He turned and fled. The zombies were still closing. There were five of us left now. Me, George, Becks, one of the Secret Service agents—I still didn't know his name—and Steve, who was urging Alaric through the air-lock as quickly as he could.

"You see the failure inherent in this model, don't you?" asked George. She fired; a zombie went down. They were closing in.

"What are you talking about?"

Becks groaned, the sound similar to a zombie's moan only in that it held no actual words. No zombie could have sounded that aggravated. "You can't shoot while you're going through the airlock. That means someone has to watch your back. One person to stand guard, one person leaving. Until eventually…"

"There's only one person left," I said, feeling suddenly numb. A zombie lurched forward. I put a bullet through its skull. It fell. "Fuck."

"It always comes down to the cold equations," said George.

"*Fuck!*" I fired again. This time, I missed.

"Next!" shouted Steve.

"Go," said Becks, nodding to George. "Both of you, go. You need to get out of here."

"We're not leaving you."

"You're not leaving him, either." The last of the Secret Service agents was running for the airlock. "You're not going to leave her, and she's not going to leave you. We can't ask your big friend to stay behind, not when he may be the most muscle we have left. That leaves me. Now get out of here." Becks held up Alaric's PDA with the hand that wasn't holding her gun. "We're at ninety percent. I'll make sure the news is waiting for you when you hit the surface."

"Rebecca—"

Becks shot me a venomous glance. "I don't have her nose for news. I don't have your total lack of regard for my own safety. What I have is a family that doesn't want me, and a job that I know how to do. And that job says I stand here and let you get out, because you're the ones who can do the best job telling this story. Now *go!*"

"Shaun, come on." George took a step backward, still firing.

"I don't want to do this," I said quietly.

So don't, said George, in the space behind my eyes. Her voice was soft, cajoling. She would never ask me to do something I didn't want to do. She would never try to convince me to leave a teammate behind.

She would let me die here, and take everything we'd fought and bled for with me.

"*Shaun!* Go!" shouted Becks. She shoved the PDA into her pocket, and called, "Hey, big guy! How sturdy are those doors?"

"Sturdy enough," rumbled Steve. "Georgia, come on."

"Coming." She kept shooting as she backed away, until she had to turn and press her hand against the test unit, and shooting ceased to be an option.

"Good." Becks dug her hand into a different pocket, producing a small round object that I recognized, after a few seconds, as a concussion grenade. "Then I'm taking no prisoners."

"You had a grenade in your *pocket*?" I asked, unsure whether to be impressed or horrified.

"Dr. Abbey gave it to me. She swore it was stable."

"Dr. Abbey isn't stable!"

"Doesn't matter now." Becks grinned, still firing. Gunpowder streaked her cheeks and forehead, mixed with sweat and cleaned in narrow tracks by the tears I wasn't sure she was aware of shedding. "Get out of here, Mason. We had a good time, didn't we? It wasn't all bad."

The zombies were getting closer all the time. I kept firing. "We had a great time. You were amazing. You *are* amazing."

"Same to you, Mason. Now go."

"Shaun!" shouted Steve.

I took a deep breath, fired twice more into the throng, and ran.

Steve and Becks covered me while the airlock cycled. By the time I was through, there was a distance of barely ten feet between the leading wave of zombies—slowed by bullets, sickness, and the bodies of their own fallen—and the airlock door. Steve was the next one through, Becks covering him by herself. She fired faster than I would have thought possible, and almost every shot was a good one. Still, she was outnumbered, and the zombies were nearly on top of her when Steve stepped out into the parking garage with the rest of us.

Becks stopped firing. She turned to face the glass, a smile on her face, zombies looming up hard and fast behind her. We couldn't hear them moaning anymore, or the sound her gun made when it hit the ground. She raised her free hand in a perfect pageant wave, seemingly oblivious to the hands reaching out to grab her hair. Then she went over backward, vanishing into the teeming river of infected flesh.

The blast came a few seconds later. There was no sound, only a sudden red rain as the detonation destroyed everything it came in contact with. There was nothing of Becks in that redness—there was everything of Becks in that redness—and so I let George pull me away from the flames that were beginning to consume the hall, leading me toward the motorcade idling in the middle of the parking garage. Alaric was standing next to the lead car. He was crying, silently but steadily, his eyes fixed on the flames now starting to show through the streaks of blood on the glass. The hall was burning. Depending on how many alarms had been disabled before the zombies were released, the whole building might go with it.

I put a hand on Alaric's shoulder. "She got the news out," I said.

He nodded. "I know."

"Good."

There was nothing else that anyone could say. We climbed into the waiting cars, pulled the doors shut, and drove away into the darkness.

━━━━━━━━━━

This is where I'm supposed to say something mealymouthed and meaningless, like "we regret" or "we are sorry to say." That's what you do at a time like this. But the thing is, there was never anything meaningless about Becks. She was one of the most calculated people I ever knew—and I don't mean that in a bad way. She always knew her angles; she always knew where the light was. I guess in another world, she was probably Miss America or something, one of those women who lived and died by the light. But we didn't live in that world, and so she grew up to be something else.

Something better.

Rebecca Atherton was a reporter before she was anything else. She was a crack shot with any ranged weapon you've ever heard of, and a few you probably haven't. She was honest and she was faithful and she was strong and she helped me kill a zombie bear.

She's also dead. So this is where I say we'd better live up to her sacrifice, because there's nothing in the world that can ever replace her. Good night, Becks.

You told the truth.

> **—From *Adaptive Immunities*,
> the blog of Shaun Mason, August 8, 2041.**

GEORGIA: Forty-one

True to Steve's word, the zombies came surging in as soon as the parking garage doors were open. Their grasping hands and gaping jaws were no match for an armored presidential motorcade. We mowed them down in droves, their viscera splattering the windshield until Steve activated the wipers and cleaned the gore away. It was surreal, like driving into a bloody red rain. The barrier between the front and back of the car remained down the whole time, which was a mixed blessing. We could see what was going on...but being able to see meant, in some way, that we couldn't look away.

Alaric, Shaun, and I had been hustled into the same car, along with Steve and Rick. President Ryman, the rest of the Secret Service agents, and Gregory were in the other car. Presumably, Gregory was giving directions to the nearest EIS safehouse. Maybe, if we were lucky, we'd even make it there in one piece.

I wasn't feeling lucky.

My phone rang shortly after we were clear of the parking garage and its signal-suppressing architecture. I clipped my ear cuff on and tapped it, saying tightly, "Georgia. Go."

"Did you just blow up the bloody White House?" demanded Mahir, loudly enough that everyone in the back of the car turned and looked at me.

"Yeah, Mahir. We kind of did. Although technically, that's not entirely true. Becks kind of did."

There was a pause as he thought through that statement. Then, slowly, he asked, "Georgia, did Becks...?"

"Shaun was her immediate superior, so I believe he'll be making the official announcement, but I am sorry to say that, as of August 7, 2041, Rebecca Atherton's name has been added to The Wall."

Mahir breathed out slowly. Several seconds passed in silence before he said, "Maggie is doing better. She's taken to swearing at the nurses."

"I'm sure everyone will be glad to hear that."

"Georgia...?"

"Yes?"

"Did you kill the president?"

I glanced toward the red-streaked windshield. We were through the last line of zombies, and I could see President Ryman's car ahead of ours. The whole back window was blocked out by blood and chunks of flesh. Decontamination of our vehicles was going to be a massive undertaking.

"No," I said. "We just kidnapped him a little. Technically, I suppose he kidnapped himself. I guess that's one for the courts."

There was a long pause before Mahir said, "I'm suddenly glad to have remained in Seattle."

"It's conveniently close to the Canadian border, in case you need to make a run for it. Mahir, I need you to gather all the betas and moderators we have—wake people up if you need to—and get them online. We're about to have a massive fire drill."

"What's that?"

"Hang on." I turned to Alaric. "Where did you upload those files?"

"They were set to upload to my private folder. Mahir has the administrative password." Alaric's voice was dull, like all the life had been leeched out of it. He didn't lift his head.

I relayed this to Mahir, adding, "I need you to download, listen, and sort through the data. Get as many of the Newsies on it as you can; start cutting the data into coherent chunks, minimal editing, no two files the same size or length. We're going to need to get them out without making them easy to suppress. Do not post anything until you receive my next transmission. I need you to match my information."

Shaun shook his head. "Times like this, I wish Buffy were here."

I put a hand over his, waiting for Mahir's response. It came quickly: "Georgia...what is this?"

"This is the end. This is the last story." I sighed and closed my eyes, leaning until my head hit Shaun's shoulder. I was suddenly tired. So tired. "This is where we tell the truth and get the fuck out of the way while the experts figure out what they're supposed to do with it."

"I'll download the files," said Mahir. He took a breath. "After I tell Maggie about Becks, that is. I have to tell her."

"I know."

"Godspeed, Georgia Mason."

"Same to you, Mahir. Same to you." I tapped my ear cuff without opening my eyes, cutting off the connection. "When this is over, I want to find a new profession. Something with fewer zombies."

"I could get behind that," said Shaun, pushing me gently away. I opened my eyes, giving him a startled look. He indicated his shirt, where a spot of blood marked the needle's entry point. "Still potentially hot. Sorry, but I'm not losing you again. Not over *laundry*."

The statement was so ridiculous that I actually smiled before sobering again. "We all checked out clean when we went through the airlock."

"Yup. I remain immune. Thanks for that. I mean, really. It sort of explains how I got out of so many close calls—and here I'd been attributing my survival to sheer awesomeness on my part—but I'm okay with that if it means I'm going to survive." Shaun looked toward Alaric. "You okay? Not hurt?"

"She's gone," Alaric whispered, voice barely audible above the sound of the engine. "Becks is gone. She was there, and now she's just gone."

I exchanged a look with Shaun before saying, carefully, "I know. I'm sorry."

"Will she come back? You came back. Will she?"

We exchanged another look. This time, it was Rick who spoke, before Shaun or I could say anything. "I'm sorry, Alaric. What we did with Georgia was unethical, and it would have been impossible if Shaun's shot hadn't left her brain essentially intact. We might have been able to replicate her body, but we would never have been able to re-create her mind."

"I'm sorry," I said again.

Alaric sighed—a shaky, shuddering sound—and said, "I knew you were going to say that. I just needed to hear it." He lifted his head, regarding us with tear-filled eyes. "This wasn't worth it."

"It never is," said Shaun.

We rode in silence after that, blindly following the lead car down twisting back roads and half-hidden residential streets. The motorcade wasn't running its lights, but it was still equipped with the transmitters that changed the lights in our favor and allowed us to dodge the random blood tests on certain streets. It was possible the CDC could also use those transmitters to track us. I put the thought out of my mind as firmly as I could. If we were being followed, there was nothing we could do about it. We were out of places to go.

It felt like we'd been driving for an hour or more when we made a sharp left onto a private driveway. We had gone barely ten yards when a steel gate slid shut behind us, and blue guiding lights clicked on along the sides of the road.

"Wherever it is we're going, I think we're just about there," I said.

"Think they'll have cookies?" asked Shaun.

"I think they're more likely to have full-immersion bleach tanks," said Alaric darkly.

"Your optimism is duly noted," said Steve. He cocked his head, apparently listening to something on his own earpiece, before adding, "Welcome to the EIS."

"So that's a 'yes' on both the cookies and the bleach," I said.

We followed President Ryman's car into a low parking garage that was better lit than the one we'd left. It was also substantially fuller. Dr. Shoji and Dr. Kimberley were standing in front of the doors to the main building, flanked on either side by orderlies with tranquilizer rifles. It said something about the past week that I found the sight extremely reassuring.

The car stopped, and one by one, we climbed out, squinting under the bright fluorescent lights. Shaun stood just out of reach, both of us turning to look toward our welcoming committee. Once everyone was out of both cars, Dr. Shoji stepped forward and said, "According to the news, there has been a terrorist attack on the White House, and both President Ryman and Vice President Cousins are missing, feared dead."

"Where is my wife?" asked President Ryman.

"The clone died in the attack. The original is inside," said Dr. Shoji. "She and the children are safe, and have been waiting for you. What do you intend to do?"

President Ryman paused before turning to me and smiling that faintly off-kilter smile I'd seen so many times on the campaign trail—the one that promised he'd do his best to change the world, if only we'd be patient with him while he figured out exactly how to do it. "I think it's time I gave a little State of the Union interview. If Miss Mason would be so kind?"

I nodded. "It would be my honor, sir."

"Great," said Shaun, clapping his hands together. "Let's go through decon, get in there, and change the world. And then? Cookies."

"Cookies," agreed Rick.

I started toward the door. Alaric grabbed my arm before I took my second step, stopping me. I turned, blinking at him.

"Was it worth it?" he asked.

"God, I hope so," I said.

He let me go, and as a group—reunited at last, for whatever good it was going to do us—we walked into the building.

RED FLAG DISTRIBUTION RED FLAG DISTRIBUTION RED FLAG
DISTRIBUTION
CREATIVE COMMONS LICENSE ALERT LEVEL ALPHA
SPREAD TO ALL NEWS SITES IMMEDIATELY
REPOST FREELY REPOST FREELY REPOST FREELY
FEED IS LIVE
TRANSCRIPTION FOLLOWS

[IMAGE: A woman who appears to be Georgia Mason (ref. The Wall, 6/20/40) stands in front of a podium bearing the logo of the Epidemic Intelligence Service.]

WOMAN: My name is Georgia Mason. My name is Subject 7c. I died on June twentieth, 2040, during the Ryman for President campaign. I was resurrected earlier this year by the CDC, using illegal and unethical human cloning technology. If you are viewing this video or reading a transcription on a download-enabled site, you can verify my DNA structure by downloading the file labeled "G. Mason genetic profile."
[DOWNLOAD FILE HERE.]

GEORGIA: I am here because the CDC wanted a more effective mechanism for lying to you, and believed I would provide a viable control for my brother, Shaun Mason, as well as serving a potential role as a mouthpiece for their version of the truth. I am here because I was not allowed to rest.

[IMAGE: The camera swings around to show Shaun Mason (ref. "After the End Times") holding a whiteboard on which the date 8/7/41 has been written.]

SHAUN: Listen to the dead girl. She's telling you what you need to hear.

[IMAGE: The camera returns to Georgia.]

GEORGIA: Before I died, I told you all that someone was trying to keep you afraid. Someone was trying to keep you from realizing that you were being controlled through unnecessary security and exaggerated fear. I begged you to rise. I begged you to stop them. Unfortunately, words are cheap, even today, and actions are expensive. I did not change the world by dying. All I did was die.

But you still have the opportunity to change things—and that opportunity is greater and more immediate than any of us could have known. Kellis-Amberlee is not the scourge we have been led to treat it as. It is a living thing, and like any living thing, it seeks to evolve, to find a balance with its hosts. Kellis-Amberlee has been trying to adapt to us, and we have been trying to adapt to it. But our government, believing that it has the right to decide for everyone, has not allowed that adaptation. They have been killing those individuals who represented our best chance of finding peace with this disease. For more information, download the file labeled "reservoir condition fatality rates."
[DOWNLOAD FILE HERE.]

GEORGIA: You may already be hearing reports that we are terrorists. That we have destroyed a part of the nation's capital, and either killed or kidnapped the president. These reports are untrue. One of our reporters, Rebecca Atherton, was killed in the process of rescuing the president from those same individuals who had me brought back from the grave—those same individuals who had me killed in the first place.

[IMAGE: At this point in the video recording, a five-second clip of Rebecca Atherton, filmed a year previous, plays. She is wearing khaki, her hair is loose, and she is shooting a zombie with a paintball gun. Each paintball appears to be filled with acid. She is laughing. Her face goes to still frame, and the image returns to Georgia.]

GEORGIA: And why did they kill me? Why did they arrange a set of circumstances that resulted in Rebecca's death, and the death of countless others? Because there are things they didn't want you to know. This is one of them: The virus is changing. I repeat, the virus is changing. But there are people who wanted to control those changes, no matter how many lives it cost. They believed that only by keeping us afraid could they keep us under control. But we have had time to learn and grow since the Rising. We are smarter now. We have adapted.

There are things we cannot tell you, because there are answers we do not have. But we have more information than we did, and please believe me when I say the information that is left unshared is only that which must be studied further before it is safe to reveal. The EIS will be working with the government to codify that information. In time, you will know everything.

The CDC's motivation for resurrecting me, as opposed to any of the others they could have chosen, was simple: They thought you would listen to me. They thought you would accept my words as truth. Let's prove them right. Believe me. Believe the contents of these files...and believe your president.

[IMAGE: President Peter Ryman walks into the frame, followed by Vice President Richard Cousins. Georgia Mason moves to the side, and President Ryman takes her place. Vice President Cousins stands to his other side.]

PRESIDENT RYMAN: I am speaking now, not only to the citizens of the United States of America, but to the citizens of the planet Earth. Because Kellis-Amberlee is a global issue, not a national one, and the conspiracy in which I have been engaged over this past year is thus also global in its scope. Ladies and gentlemen, I am here to tell you that I have been held against my will, with my family as hostages to ensure my cooperation. The individuals responsible for this have a simple goal in mind: to continue to forward their control of the American public through manipulation of the Kellis-Amberlee virus.

I regret to state that, during my time in office, I have approved immoral, unethical, and illegal scientific experimentation, resulting in the murder of both American and international citizens. I have signed papers approving the weaponization of Kellis-Amberlee. I was present when the decision was made to release a modified strain of mosquito capable of carrying the Kellis-Amberlee virus into the sovereign nation of Cuba. The fact that I did these things under duress does not absolve me, or ameliorate the nature of my actions. I have betrayed my country. I have dishonored my office. I have betrayed myself.

Read the files accompanying this report. Read the comprehensive articles I am sure these and other reporters will shortly present to you. Realize that you have been betrayed. Realize that you have been misled. And heed the words of a very wise woman, who spoke from a place of genuine need when she addressed you a year ago. My name is Peter Ryman, and I am begging you.

Rise up while you can.

DOWNLOAD ALL ATTACHMENTS? Y/N
TERMINATE LIVE FEED
RED FLAG DISTRIBUTION RED FLAG DISTRIBUTION
RED FLAG DISTRIBUTION
REPOST FREELY
RISE UP WHILE YOU CAN

CODA:

Living for You

Rise up while you can.

—Georgia Mason

It's the oldest story in the world. Boy loves girl. Boy loses girl. Boy gets girl back thanks to the unethical behavior of megalomaniacal mad scientists who never met a corpse they wouldn't try to resurrect. Anyone coming within a hundred yards of my happy ending had better pray that they're immune to bullets.

—Shaun Mason

We did the best we could with what we had, and when what we had wasn't enough, we found ways to make it work. We told the truth, even when it hurt us, even when it killed us, even when it set the wolves at our doors. I can't speak for the dead. But I think the living will agree that anything we did, we did because we felt we had to. History will judge us. The future will decide whether what we did was right, or wrong, or without meaning. In the here and now...

This is as close as we could get to an ending. The world goes on. Zombies or no zombies, political conspiracy or no political conspiracy, the world goes on.

I think I like it that way.

—From *Living Dead Girl*,
the blog of Georgia Mason II, May 17, 2042.

Who wants to see me wrestle a zombie moose?

—From *Hail to the King*,
the blog of Shaun Mason, May 17, 2042.

MAHIR: Forty-two

The phone rang at half-three in the morning, waking both Nan and Sanjukta from a sound sleep. Nandini glared as she levered herself from the bed and left the room, following our infant daughter's wailing. I swore, rolling over and grabbing my cell off the bedside table, bringing it to my ear before I was done sitting up.

"This had best be bloody important, or I'm letting my wife give you what-for," I snarled.

"Mr. Gowda, this is Christopher Rogers, from the All-Night News. I apologize if I woke you—I thought I had calculated the time difference between London and San Francisco correctly."

Smug bastard. I could hear it in his voice, the vague self-congratulatory tone of a reporter who thinks he's put his subject off balance. "How did you get this number?"

"Mr. Gowda, I have a few questions, if you don't—"

"I bloody well *do* mind. This is an unlisted number, and I know what you're calling about. You want to know where the Masons are, don't you?"

Silence greeted my question. That was a sufficient answer in and of itself.

"When will you people learn to *listen*? I don't know where the Masons are. No one knows where the Masons are. They disappeared after the management of the CDC was given over to the EIS. Last anyone saw of either of them, they were in an unmarked car heading God-knows-where."

That wasn't entirely true. The last time I saw them was on the border between the United States and Canada, when Steve handed them the keys to their own van, which was waiting for them on the Canadian side. They mailed back all the bugs the CIA had planted a week later, and they were gone.

It was true enough. Every version of their disappearance ended the same way, after all: and they were gone.

"Mr. Gowda, your site is still syndicating blogs provided by both Masons. We find it difficult to credit your continued insistence that you do not know their whereabouts."

"You little nit. They're using relays put in place by Georgette Meissonier. So far as I know, your FBI has been trying to unsnarl that woman's mad coding since before she died. What makes you think I could do it from here? I'm a reporter, not a computer technician."

Nandini came back into the room, Sanjukta held against her chest. She cast a glare at me, demanding, "Who is it?"

"Another reporter. I'm getting rid of him."

"Let me."

"Not sure he deserves that yet, dear." I turned my attention back to the phone. "My wife is about to take the phone off me. You'd best hang up, and never call this number again, or I'll have you cited for harassment. Surprisingly, your government takes quite an interest in my complaints."

Emily Ryman had taken her place beside her husband while pictures of her clone, killed during the attack on the White House, were shown to the world. President Ryman was found guilty of betraying the public trust. He was not found guilty of treason. He had been coerced, he had been afraid for the lives of his family, and he had been uncovering a treasonous group within his own government. He barely escaped being hailed as a hero.

Shaun and Georgia's reports had a great deal to do with that, and President Ryman's gratitude to the Masons had transferred to the site when they vanished. Having the President of the United States indebted to me had proven very useful in some situations—such as this one.

"Mr. Gowda, please. The people have a right to know."

"The people know everything they have a right to know, Mr. Rodgers. I'll be hanging up now." They didn't know there was no cure. Someday they would—someday we'd take back India, and a great deal more of the world beside—but not yet. The world wasn't ready. Too many shots would go unfired, and too many more would die in the blind hope that their loved ones would be among the saved. Recovering from the first Rising took us twenty years. It might take twenty more to reach the point where we could recover from the second one.

"Mr. Gowda—"

I hung up on his protests and stood, dropping the phone onto the bed. "I'm sorry about that. Let me take her. You get some rest."

"I hate that those people call here," she complained, placing Sanjukta gently in my hands.

I drew my infant daughter close, smiling down at her sleepy face, her dark eyes almost closed. Looking up, I said, "I hate it as well. They'll stop eventually."

Nandini snorted her disbelief and climbed back into the bed, rolling over to face the wall. Her breathing leveled out in minutes, telling me that she had drifted back to sleep.

Sanjukta was less obliging. I left the bedroom, walking slow circles around the living room as I waited for her eyes to close. "Would you like to hear a story, my love? It's about some very brave people and the way they tried to change the world."

I wasn't lying to that reporter when I told him I didn't know where Shaun and Georgia—the second Georgia—were. They sent their posts and articles via blind relay. They sent their very rare postcards much the same way. So far as I knew, they were somewhere in the vast empty reaches of Canada, making a life for themselves. Maybe they had come back into the United States to rejoin Dr. Abbey—a few of her letters had led me to believe she might have seen them, at least briefly—but I doubted those would ever be more than visits. The Masons had lived and died in the public eye. Now, finally, they were free of it, and they were living for themselves, rather than living for anyone else. I wasn't going to be the one to take that away from them.

Especially not now. They were clever to vanish when they did, while the world was still reeling from their final revelations. Things exploded not long after. The new director of the CDC, Dr. Gregory Lake, publicly redirected their research into reservoir conditions and possible vaccination paths, while privately redirecting it into spontaneous remission and transmittable immunity. Oversight committees were called, and arrests were made through all levels of several governments. The world slowly began to change as the people began, finally, to rise.

Maggie recovered, and remained with the site. Her parents even assisted in funding replacements for the equipment we'd lost, both to disaster, and when the Masons insisted on reclaiming their van. Alaric and Alisa moved in with her; Alaric and Maggie will be getting married in the spring, mirroring the ceremony into several virtual worlds for the sake of those of us who have had quite enough of the United States for now, thank you very much.

Alaric took over the Newsies; one of our more promising betas—another George, amusingly enough, although he goes by "Geo" to prevent confusion—took over the Irwins; and I? I took over the entire operation, with Maggie as my second. We work well together. Maybe it's not as flashy and exciting as it was during the Mason era, but it does well enough by us.

We changed the world. That's all the news can hope to do, I suppose.

The last postcard I had from the Masons came not a week before that reporter's early-morning call. It summed up the whole situation rather neatly:

"Still having a wonderful time. Still glad you're not here.

All our love—G&S."

Sanjukta sighed, drifting back into sleep. I kissed her on the forehead as I turned to carry her back to her own room, where I settled her down on the mattress of her crib. She fussed, but didn't wake.

I drew the blanket over her and backed out of the room, pausing in the doorway to whisper, "They may not have lived happily ever after. But they lived happily long enough."

And then I turned, and I went back to bed.

Acknowledgments

Well: here we are. The story of the Masons is finally told, and it wouldn't have been possible without the assistance of an amazing assortment of people. As before, they ranged from medical professionals who worked with both humans and animals to gun experts and epidemiologists. *Blackout* has been an incredible adventure to both research and write, and I am grateful to everyone who has contributed to its creation.

Michelle Dockrey once again lent her incredible eye for blocking to the action scenes and logistics to my work, improving the book beyond all measure in the process. Brooke Lunderville consulted on medical standards and processes, while Kate Secor not only edited, she tolerated endless dinners where I talked about horrible viral outbreaks over dessert.

The entire *Deadline* Machete Squad returned for this book, and I remain honored by their willingness to work with me to make sure it comes out mostly right. Priscilla Spenser and Lauren Shulz joined the Squad for the first time with this book, and did incredible work. Many thanks to them all, and to the endlessly patient, endlessly tolerant, absolutely wonderful staff of Borderlands Books, who have put up with more from me than any one bookstore should.

Most of all, on this volume, I must thank DongWon Song, my editor, and Diana Fox, my agent. Both of them put in hours upon hours improving and refining the text. They are truly amazing people to work with. (Not to discount all the other amazing people at Orbit, both US and UK. A special thank-you must go to Lauren Panepinto for her amazing cover design. I am seriously amazed by the work she does.)

Finally, and once again, acknowledgment for forbearance goes to Amy McNally, Shawn Connolly, and Cat Valente, who put up with an amazing amount of "talking it out" as I tried to make the book make sense;

to my agent, Diana Fox, who remains my favorite superhero; to the cats, for not eating me when I got too wrapped up in work to feed them; and to Tara O'Shea and Chris Mangum, the incredible technical team behind www.MiraGrant.com. This book might have been written without them. It would not have been the same.

Both the CDC and EIS are real organizations, although I have taken many liberties with their structure and operations. To learn more about the history of the EIS, check out *Inside the Outbreaks: The Elite Medical Detectives of the Epidemic Intelligence Service*, by Mark Pendergrast. (Thanks to Bill McGeachin for supplying my copy of this wonderful book.)

Rise up while you can.

extras

orbit

meet the author

Bestselling author Mira Grant lives in Washington, sleeps with a machete under her bed, and highly suggests you do the same. Mira Grant is the pseudonym of Hugo, Nebula, and Alex Award–winning author Seanan McGuire.

if you enjoyed
THE RISING

look out for

INTO THE
DROWNING DEEP

by

Mira Grant

The ocean is home to many myths.

Some are deadly.

Seven years ago the Atargatis *set off on a voyage to the Mariana Trench to film a mockumentary bringing to life ancient sea creatures of legend. It was lost at sea with all hands. Some have called it a hoax; others have called it a tragedy.*

Now a new crew has been assembled. But this time they're not out to entertain. Some seek to validate their life's work. Some seek the greatest hunt of all. Some seek the truth. But for the ambitious young scientist Victoria Stewart, this is a voyage to uncover the fate of the sister she lost.

Whatever the truth may be, it will only be found below the waves.

But the secrets of the deep come with a price.

Founded by James Golden in 1972, Imagine Entertainment was intended to "restore the fun" to the entertainment industry. Golden—an aspiring media mogul who felt movies and television had become "too serious"—proceeded to make his name producing a string of B-grade horror movies, latter-day grindhouse films, and remarkably ambitious science fiction epics. Called the King of Schlock by his detractors and Monster Midas by his fans, there was no question the name Golden carried substantial weight by 1993, when he announced the establishment of the Imagine Network.

Originally envisioned as a home for Golden's prodigious backlist, many dismissed the Imagine Network as the final vanity project of an aging man, noting that the Sci-Fi Channel, launched the previous year, had a larger and more robust stable of original programs. Still, the Imagine Network endured and, by 2008, was providing a reasonable return on Golden's investment.

The first Imagine "mockumentary" was conceived and scripted by the Imagine Network's then president, Benjamin Yant. *Loch Ness: A Historical Review* brought in high ratings, renewed advertiser interest, and strong DVD sales, sparking a wave of similar programming. *The Search for the Chupacabra* aired in 2009, followed by *Expedition Yeti* in 2010, *The Last Dinosaur* in 2012, and *Unicorn Road* in 2014. It seemed the public's thirst for cryptozoological fiction thinly veiled as fact was insatiable.

Then came 2015. The filming of *Lovely Ladies of the Sea: The True Story of the Mariana Mermaids* should have been routine. Imagine filled a ship with scientists, actors, and camera crews, and sent it out into the Pacific Ocean.

Communications were lost on May 17. The ship was found six weeks later, adrift and abandoned.

No bodies have ever been recovered.

—From *Monster Midas: An Unauthorized
Biography of James Golden*, by Alexis Bowman,
originally published 2018

extras

People like to pretend that what happened to the *Atargatis* was a normal maritime disaster: the people on board got too wrapped up in filming their little "mockumentary" and forgot to steer the damn thing. They ran afoul of a storm, or pirates, or some other totally mundane threat, and they all died, and it was very sad, but it's no reason to be scared of the ocean, or start wondering what else might be out there. The *Atargatis* was what they call an "isolated incident," the recovered footage was and is a hoax, and there's nothing to worry about.

Those people never explain how the camera crews on the *Atargatis* did their special effects in real time: no amount of prosthetic work in the world could turn a human being into one of the creatures seen swarming the ship during the most violent of the leaked footage.

Those people never explain why, if what happened was weather related, not a single scrap of data supporting that theory has ever been released by either Imagine or the National Weather Service. The loss of the *Atargatis* was a public relations nightmare for the company: if Imagine had a way of reducing their liability, they would certainly have offered it by now.

Those people never explain a lot of things.

The *Atargatis* sailed off the map, into a section of the sea that should have been labeled "Here be monsters." What happened to them there may never be perfectly understood, but this much seems to be clear: the footage was not faked.

Mermaids are real.

> —Taken from a forum post made at
> CryptidChase.net by user BioNerd,
> originally posted March 2020

Monterey, California: June 26, 2015

The sky was a deep and perfect blue, as long as Victoria—Vicky to her parents, Vic to her friends, Tory to herself, when she was thinking about the future, where she'd be a scientist and her sister Anne would be her official biographer, documenting all her amazing discoveries for the world to admire—kept her eyes above the horizon. Any lower and the smoke from the wildfires that had ravaged California all summer would appear, tinting the air a poisonous-looking gray. Skies weren't supposed to look like that. Skies were supposed to be wide and blue and welcoming, like a mirror of the wild and waiting sea.

Tory had been born in the Monterey City Hospital. According to her parents, her first smile had been directed not at her mother, but at the Pacific Ocean. She had learned to swim in safe municipal pools by the age of eighteen months, and been in the ocean—closely supervised—by the time she was three, reveling in the taste of salt water on her lips and the sting of the sea spray in her eyes.

(She'd been grabbed by a riptide when she was seven, yanked away from her parents and pushed twenty yards from shore in the time it took to blink. She didn't remember the incident when she was awake, but it surfaced often in her dreams: the suddenly hostile water reaching up to grab her and drag her down. Most children would have hated the ocean after something like that, letting well-earned fear keep their feet on the shore. Not Tory. The riptide had just been doing what it was made to do; she was the one who'd been in the wrong place. She had to learn to be in a better place when the next riptide came along.)

Her big sister, Anne, had watched Tory's maritime adventures from the safety of the shore, slathered in SPF 120 and clutching her latest stack of gossip magazines. They'd been so different, even then. It would have been easy for them to detest each other, to let the gap in their ages and interests become a chasm. Anne had seven years on her baby sister. She could have walked away. Instead, somehow, they'd come out of their barely shared childhood as the best of friends. They had the same parents; they had the same wheat-blonde hair, although Anne's had started darkening toward brown by the time she turned seventeen, prompting an endless succession of experimental dye jobs and highlighting processes. They both sunburned fast, and freckled even faster. They even had the same eyes, dark blue, like the waters of the Monterey Bay.

That was where the similarities ended. Tory was going to be a marine biologist, was doing a summer internship at the Monterey Bay Aquarium and starting at UC Santa Cruz in the fall on a full scholarship. Anne was a special interest reporter—read "talking head for geek news"—and well on her way to a solid career as a professional media personality.

The last time they'd seen each other in person had been three days prior to the launch of the SS *Atargatis*, a research vessel heading to the Mariana Trench to look for mermaids.

"We're not going to find them," Anne had admitted, sitting on the porch next to Tory and throwing bits of bread to the seagulls thronging the yard. "Mermaids don't exist. Everyone at Imagine knows it. But it's a chance for the scientists they've hired to do real research on someone else's dime, and it's a great opportunity for me personally."

"You really want to be the face of the cryptid mockumentary?" Tory had asked.

Anne had answered with a shrug. "I want to be the face of *something*. This is as good a place to start as any. I just wish you could come with us. We could use some more camera-ready scientists."

"Give me ten years and I'll come on the anniversary tour." Tory had grinned, impish, and leaned over to tug on a lock of her sister's sunset-red hair. It was a dye job, but it was a good one, years and miles and a lot of money away from the Clairol specials Anne used to do in the downstairs bathroom. "I'll make you look old."

"By then, I'll be so established that they'll let me," Anne had said, and they'd laughed, and the rest of the afternoon had passed the way the good ones always did: too fast to be fair.

Anne had promised to send Tory a video every day. She'd kept that promise from the time the ship launched, sending clips of her smiling face under an endless ocean sky, with scientists and crewmen laboring in the background.

The last clip had come on May seventeenth. In it, Anne had looked...harried, unsettled, like she no longer knew quite what to make of things. Tory had watched the short video so many times she could recite it from memory. That didn't stop her from sitting down on the porch—so empty now, without Anne beside her—and pressing "play" again.

Anne's face flickered into life on the screen, hair tousled by the wind, eyes haunted. "Tory," she said, voice tight. "Okay, I...I'm scared. I don't know what it is I saw, and I don't know how it's possible, but it's real, Tory, it's really real. It's really out there. You'll understand when you see the footage. Maybe you can...maybe you can be the one who figures it out. I love you. I love Mom and Dad. I...I hope I'll be home soon." She put her hand over her eyes. She had always done that, ever since she was a little girl, when she didn't want anyone to see her crying.

"Turn off the camera, Kevin," she said, and Tory whispered the words along with her. "I'm done."

The video ended.

Six weeks had passed since that video's arrival. There hadn't been another.

Tory had tried to find out what had happened—what could have upset her sister so much, what could have made her stop sending her videos—but she'd gotten nowhere. Contacting Imagine led to a maze of phone trees and receptionists who became less helpful the moment she told them why she was calling. Every day, she sent another wave of e-mails, looking for information. Every day, she got nothing back.

She was starting to think nothing was all she was ever going to get again.

She was sitting on the porch six weeks and three days later, about to press "play" one more time, when the sound of footsteps caught her attention. She turned. Her mother was in the doorway, white faced and shaking, tears streaking her cheeks.

Tory felt the world turn to ashes around her, like the smoke staining the sky had finally won dominion over all. She staggered to her feet, unable to bear the thought of sitting when she heard the words her mother didn't yet have the breath to say. Her laptop crashed to the steps, unheeded, unimportant. Nothing was important anymore.

Katherine Stewart put her arms around her surviving daughter and held fast, like she was an anchor, like she could somehow, through her sheer unwillingness to let go, keep this child from the sea.

Footage recovered from the *Atargatis* mission, aired for the board of the Imagine Network, July 1, 2015

The camera swings as the cameraman runs. The deck of the *Atargatis* lurches in the frame, slick with a grayish mucosal substance. Splashes of shockingly red blood mark the slime. There has been no time for it to dry. There has been no time for anything. The cameraman is out of breath. He stumbles, dropping to one knee. As he does, the camera tilts downward. For a few brief seconds, we are treated to a glimpse of the creature climbing, hand over hand, up the side of the *Atargatis*.

The face is more simian than human, with a flat "nose" defined by two long slits for nostrils, and a surprisingly sensual mouth brimming with needled teeth. It is a horror of the deep, gray skinned and feminine in the broadest sense of the term, an impression lent by the delicate structure of its bones and the tilt of its wide, liquid eyes. When it blinks, a nictitating membrane precedes the eyelid. It has "hair" of a sort—a writhing mass of glittering, filament-thin strands that cast their bioluminescent light on the hull.

It has no legs. Its lower body is the muscular curl of an eel's tail, tapering to tattered looking but highly functional fins. This is a creature constructed along brutally efficient lines, designed to survive, whatever the cost. Nature abhors a form that cannot be repeated. Perhaps that's why the creature has hands, thumbs moving in opposable counterpoint to its three long, slim fingers. The webbing extends to the second knuckle; the fingers extend past that, with four joints in place of the human two. They must be incredibly flexible, those fingers, no matter how fragile they seem.

The creature hisses, showing bloody teeth. Then, in a perfectly human, perfectly chilling voice, it says, "Come *on*, Kevin, don't you have the shot yet?" It is the voice of Anne Stewart, Imagine Entertainment news personality. Anne herself is nowhere to be seen. But there is so much blood...

extras

The cameraman staggers to his feet and runs. His camera captures everything in fragmentary pieces as he flees, taking snapshots of an apocalypse. There is a man who has been unzipped from crotch to throat, organs falling onto the deck in a heap; three of the creatures are clustered around the resulting mess, their faces buried in the offal, eating. There is a woman whose arms have been ripped from her shoulders, whose eyes stare into nothingness, glazed over and cold; two more of the creatures are dragging her toward the rail. The cameraman runs. There is a splash behind him. The creatures have returned to the sea with their prey.

Some of the faces of the dead are familiar: employees of Imagine, camera operators, makeup technicians, all sent out to sea with the *Atargatis* in order to record a documentary on the reality of mermaids. They weren't supposed to find anything. Mermaids aren't real. Other faces are new to the silent executives who watch the film play back, their mouths set into thin lines and their eyes betraying nothing of their feelings on the matter. A dark-haired woman beats a mermaid with an oar. A man runs for the rail, only to be attacked by three of the creatures, which move surprisingly swiftly out of the water, propelled by their powerful tails.

Around the boat, the sea is getting lighter, like the sun is rising from below. The camera continues to roll. The cameraman continues to run.

A thin-fingered hand slaps across the lens, and the video stops. The screaming takes longer to end, but in time, it does.

Everything ends.

Western Pacific Ocean, east of the Mariana Islands: September 3, 2018

The yacht drifted on the endless blue, flags fluttering from its mast and engine purring like a kitten, the man at the helm making small adjustments to their position as he worked to keep them exactly where they were. On any other vessel, he would have been considered the captain. On any other vessel, he wouldn't have been subject to the whims of a reality television personality and his bevy of hand-selected bikini models, all of whom had been chosen more for their appearance than for their ability to handle being on a yacht in the middle of nowhere. They weren't just miles from shore; they were *days* from shore, so far out that if something went wrong, no one would be in a position to rescue them.

That was what Daniel Butcher had been aiming for. The married star of three reality cooking shows just wanted to "escape" and "unwind," far from the prying eyes of the paparazzi and their long-range telephoto lenses. He had the resources to take his entourage to the ends of the earth, and enough of a passion for fresh-caught seafood that this was his idea of paradise. He had the waves. He had the sun. He had a wide array of beautiful women happy to tell him how smart and handsome and witty he was, without his even needing to prompt them.

"Dinner's at sunset, ladies," Daniel called, checking the lines hanging off the side. This far from the commercial fishing lanes, they should be drifting in fertile waters. He'd even gone to the trouble of buying data on the known dead zones manifesting in the west Pacific, just to be sure he wasn't being steered away from where the fish were. Wouldn't that be a kick in the teeth? Pay tens of thousands of dollars to rent a top-of-the-line yacht, stock it, crew it, sail it away from civilization for three days straight, and wind up someplace where nothing was biting. But no. They'd eat well tonight.

(The actual gutting and cleaning of the fish would be left to his sous-chefs, two of whom had been brought on this voyage for just that reason. Daniel Butcher believed in roughing it, but he was still a star, and stars didn't get fish guts on their hands unless there was a camera rolling to capture the rugged masculinity of the moment.)

The bikini models giggled and preened, their oiled skins shining in the tropical sun. This was the life. This was the way things were *meant* to be: just him, and the sea, and people who actually appreciated his brilliance.

He didn't notice that they stopped preening as soon as he walked past them, or that some of them directed looks of frank disgust at his retreating back. He stopped to check one of the lines. A pretty black-haired girl in a green bikini withdrew a camera the size of a flash drive from under the skimpy fabric covering one breast and snapped a quick series of pictures, making sure her shots included as many of the other women as possible.

The redhead next to her gave her a quizzical look before asking, voice low, "Wife?"

The black-haired girl's fingers tightened on her camera. "Yes."

"Network," said the redhead. "I set my cameras when we came aboard."

"Nice," said the first girl. She tucked the camera back into her bikini before offering her hand. "Elena."

"Suzanne."

"We looking at cancellation, or...?"

"Not yet." Suzanne turned a predatory eye on Daniel, who had stopped again, this time to flirt with two *actual* bikini models. "The network's concerned about reports of debauchery. They wanted someone to come on this trip and see how accurate they were. They hired me."

"How did they know Daniel would pick you?"

"How did his wife know Daniel would pick you?"

"You saw the man behind the wheel when we boarded?" Elena nodded toward the cabin. Sunlight glinted off the windows, making it impossible to see inside. "He's my brother. Technically I'm along because I wanted the ride, not because Daniel wanted access to my sea chest."

"Clever," said Suzanne approvingly. "We're not going to make problems for each other, are we?"

"Why should we?" Elena's smile was quick and predatory, a shark cutting through calm waters. "We're both getting paid. Your pictures don't change mine. And the man's an ass. Let's take him down from every angle at once."

Suzanne laughed. So did Elena. They were still laughing when there was a commotion from the side of the boat, a splash and a scream and the sound of bodies rushing toward the rail. Their heads snapped around, Elena half-rising from her deck chair before she realized what had happened.

Daniel was gone.

"Oh my God," she said, in a tone of fascinated horror. "The narcissistic bastard knocked himself overboard."

"Come on." Suzanne grabbed her hand, dragging her toward the chaos. "I want pictures of this, and all my cameras are *on* the boat."

There was no sign of Daniel when the pair reached the side. The sea was calm, giving no indication that it had just swallowed a man. Bikini models leaned over the rail, shouting and cursing, eyes scanning the horizon. Elena felt her stomach sink. She'd grown up in the Mariana Islands, been born and raised on Guam, and she'd heard stories about this stretch of ocean.

How could I have been fool enough to take this job? she thought, turning to the cabin. *Only fools sail where so many have been lost.* She waved her arms frantically, hoping he would see her even though she couldn't see him. They needed to turn around. They needed to get out of here.

Elena didn't consider herself a superstitious person, but she would have had to be living under a rock not to have heard people whispering about what happened around the Mariana Trench when the sun was bright and the waters were still, when the fish had moved on and the things in the deeps grew hungry. There had been that mess a few years back, with a research vessel and the television network that showed all the *Star Trek* reruns. How she'd laughed at the thought of their being foolish enough to sail there, in the open waters where the bad things were.

She wasn't laughing now.

She wasn't laughing when the screams started behind her, high and shrill and terrified, or when she felt the touch of a hand—oddly long and spindly, covered in a cool, clammy film, like aloe gel was smeared across the skin—on the back of her ankle. Elena stopped waving her arms. She closed her eyes. If she couldn't see it, it wouldn't be real. That was the way the world worked, wasn't it?

Her scream, when it came, was short and sharp and quickly ended. The boat began to move, her brother finally throwing it into gear, but it was too little, too late; his own scream soon joined the fading chorus.

The yacht rented by Daniel Butcher for his private entertainment was found three days later, drifting some eight hundred miles from its chartered destination. No survivors were ever found.

Neither were the bodies.

orbit

Follow us:

 /orbitbooksUS

 /orbitbooks

 /orbitbooks

Join our mailing list
to receive alerts on our
latest releases and deals.

orbitbooks.net

Enter our monthly
giveaway for the chance
to win some epic prizes.

orbitloot.com